OF KINGS

JAMES THACKARA

THE OVERLOOK PRESS
WOODSTOCK & NEW YORK

First published in the United States in 1999 by
The Overlook Press, Peter Mayer Publishers, Inc.
Lewis Hollow Road
Woodstock, New York 12498

Library of Congress Cataloging-in-Publication Data

Thackara, James.
The book of kings / James Thackara.
p.   cm.
1. France—History—German occupation, 1940-1945—Fiction.
2. World War, 1939-2045—France—Paris—Fiction.
3. France—History—1914-1940—Fiction.   I. Fiction
PS3570.H28B66   1999   813'.54—dc21   98-47732

Book design and type formatting by Bernard Schleifer
Manufactured in Canada
3 5 7 9 8 6 4 2
ISBN 0-87951-923-1

This is for you, D.

CONTENTS

CONTENTS

Their sin is written with a pen of iron, and with the point of a diamond: it is graven upon the table of their heart, and upon the horns of your altars. . . . O my mountain in the field, I will give thy substance and all thy treasures to the spoil, and thy high places for sin, throughout all thy borders. And thou, even thyself, shalt discontinue from thine heritage that I gave thee; and I will cause thee to serve thine enemies in the land which thou knowest not: for ye have kindled a fire in mine anger, which shall burn forever.

—JEREMIAH 17:1, 3-4

PROLOGUE

IN SWITZERLAND, TEN THOUSAND FEET ABOVE THE SNOWFIELDS, FORESTS and pale-green valleys, stands the massif of interconnecting peaks known as the Berner Oberland.

At its high point—sheer and elephant-gray amid a blinding sun and pillars of cloud—rise three famous summits: the Eiger, the Mönch, and the Jungfrau. Though climbers of all beliefs test themselves on the Eiger's vertical face, and though the Virgin has been tunneled to the roots of her hair by a cog-wheel train, still only antelopes and a few men know the Oberland. So bare and uninhibited are the forces of nature here that none but lichens, mice, and ravens can long abide these heights, and no disgrace in the cities of man could alter them. As for the glaciers in their booming silence—their ancient waters crushing stone and splitting cliffs—they are like European memory itself, feeding the civilizations bordering here, whose influence extends to the extremities of the earth. And the hard men who venture on these giant snow plains are as dull and rudimentary as the lichen and the crow. They have shrunk to the mere dimensions of their bodies. Their ruddy faces are as opaque as stone, and in the towns they appear dumb.

Far below, in the hazy bosom of the green land, lie the villages and farms of man, as welcoming as a perennial Eden. Yet the souls in these villages are not at peace.

PART ONE

THE MIST

1

ON A CLEAR JUNE MORNING LATE IN THE 1960S, A CONVERTIBLE BLUE TWO-seater started quickly southeast from Calais down files of poplars, long rising and falling over the great gray-green and yellow squared carpets of farmland. Before St. Omer, where the wheat and barley was high, began the *cimetières des soldats*—first for Canadians, then one for the French, an English one, then a *visions de guerre* with two lifesize, uniformed puppets. The thin-legged American at the wheel, who was called Jim, raised his voice.

"You can't get away from it!"

"My invitation will come any day," his companion called back, the wind blowing his hair. "Albert Sunda will present himself at the court of the czar, the salon of George Sand!"

All the horizon ahead was a hazy cloud wall of sun-topped cumulus. As they drove east, the daylight weakened, and presently James Penn and Albert Sunda were in a dense fog.

In fact, this fog covered Europe without a gap. Outside the ministries of the Quai d'Orsay and the gray Kredit-Banks of the Bahnhofstrasse, from valley farms in the Adige and the bright-lit cafes of Valencia, men were staring up with a vague and guilty unease. At two o'clock, somewhere between Rheims and the river Meuse, the young men stopped for lunch at a *relais* crowded with truckers watching world football. Then they raised the top and they were traveling again, in a drizzling rain now, and scudding fog. After he had driven for over an hour in second gear, Jim realized they were on the wrong road.

"We won't reach the mountains tonight." He made a face. "Clermont, four kilometers," Albert read. "We're in the Argonne."

"The Argonne Forest?"

Yes, the Great War . . . the trenches."

"Hitler's war was the big one." Jim murmured the name that had killed his father.

Even as Albert had spoken, the *cimetières des soldats* had begun again. Little green signs floated through the cloudy glow of the headlamps. But so near now to the silent mysterious fields, Jim was feeling strange emotions: dread, intense curiosity, and somehow embarrassment. A lonely grief rose from his stomach and tightened in his throat. A *cimetière anglais* came toward them, then a French and an Indian one facing across the road. And then the first German cemetery, on a farm corner by a rusted water pump.

"Why are we stopping?" Albert looked at Jim's absorbed profile. "Oh, God. Well, go ahead if it won't take long."

"Good. We wouldn't make your chalet tonight anyway."

Jim engaged gear and twisted the wheel. The blue sign swept left in the fog and vanished. On it, in white, were the words GRAND CIMETIÈRE DE VERDUN.

2

STOPPED ON THE ROAD TO SWITZERLAND, JAMES PENN AND ALBERT Sunda turned up the slowly winding drive. The fog overhead brightened with a strange yellow light.

"A great-uncle is buried here, I believe," Albert said.

"Isn't this sort of grave unmarked?"

"Not a general's. He was a general."

Outside, it looked cold. The heater whirred and made grating noises. Now the asphalt narrowed to the track of the wheels. Whining in low gear, the small car swam up into the fleeing cloud, mists sucking past without sound or wind.

"What a dreadful place," Albert said.

"I *am* impressed. What a stage."

Then Jim looked into the woods, and there were the trenches. The fog was moving and rolling among the trees, and beneath them the grass-grown, dew-silvered earth rose heaving again and again, like swells made by the current of fleeing mist. After a mile came the first vanishing track, marked by a white card with a stenciled serial number. Then, in ponderous silence, an opaque billow of fog tumbled up off an invisible slope, choking the road. Jim braked, the motor stalled. Lit by an amber sourceless light, a wide space was opening ahead to the gravel summit of the hill. He got out, looked down to the right, then back at the hill. And for an instant he thought he heard the awful keening of a hundred million women's souls, a tremendous organ rumble of throats rolling up, pulsing, echoing, then withdrawing across the world.

The smoking skies were silent. Nothing moved. There was no one.

"Are you all right?"

"A headache," Jim said, dropping his hands. "Too much fog."

Their shoes crunched along a border of wet grass. Falling away below was an emerald amphitheater the size of a town, with ceaseless files of small bare white crosses, arranged in dizzying symmetries, that rose and descended until they seemed to merge in a chalk whiteness. Jim stopped alone on the gravel and stared, and these crosses were like a hundred thousand hands reaching through the grass, begging for their lost lives. I guess this is it, he thought. I guess this is it, forever and truly it.

"Now look at that!" Albert called.

On the summit, rooted unremitting against a sky blackened by smoke from horizon to horizon, was a huge, unwindowed granite mausoleum. From the shoulders, where the wings met, towered a bayonet, bearing high into the last light the faint elongated outline of a cross. It was the cruelest, most hopeless thing Jim had ever seen. Suddenly he felt his eyes watering.

"A temple for no god," he said.

"Nonsense, just the tombstone for a dead century. *Absit omen.*"

"*Absit omen,*" Jim whispered.

A prickling rain had begun to fall. The cloud had already swallowed the curve of the forest far below. Jim looked again at the crosses, then up at the monument's great spire.

"Think what this means—what has happened," he said.

Albert turned to him with an expression of pity.

"*What* has happened? All of it is finished and gone. You see, no one comes here."

The steep grass was wet. It skidded under Jim's thin soles. There was a last glow in the west. The still-high sun emerged briefly between the blackening tide of fog and the mattressed overcast. Albert's shadow was bent over, one knee on a long stone slab. Jim leaned by the headstone set in the grass bank. "Theodore Barthold von Sunda zu Saale," he read out. "*Maréchal dans la Grande Armée?*"

"Yes," Albert laughed bitterly. "And my grandfather was on the Kaiser's side. He was a hero of the Somme. Then in the last war my father, a deserter on the Russian front!"

With great delicacy he brushed the grass clippings off the stone.

"All right," he said then, and rose to his feet. "Enough of this. We're going now."

3

WHAT IF IT IS SO? JIM PENN THOUGHT SOME HOURS LATER ON THE ROAD after Neufchâteau, as he stared into the headlight beams. Albert was driving, and they were well into Resistance country now. What if all bodies *are* buried and all things forgotten? What if there can be no improvement, if destiny is ruled by material laws, and love is only a decoration necessary to organize conscience?

Jim thought of his own father, who had died at the Bulge. Major Penn's body had never been found, so probably he did not even have one of the little white crosses. Switching the map light on, he slipped a two-month-old newspaper clipping from his wallet and unfolded the headline: JUSTIN LOTHAIRE IS DEAD. Jim held the clipping steady, reading through again the famous man's rise from a North African slum to the height of his powers and the years of genius, when "Lothaire became a legend, which in turn was the symbol of an age." Jim experienced freshly the incorruptibility of the past. Finally he read about the automobile accident in which Lothaire had died in eastern France. Then he folded the clipping and turned off the map light. Albert had not spoken for two hours.

"He was very great, I think. In what he lived and wrote," Jim said, "he had no equal."

"There's a crossing ahead. Which road do we want?"

"I know a manor house in the Loue valley," Jim said. "Take the Ornans road."

"Is that nearer than Besançon?"

"A little nearer," Jim lied. He was all at once very hungry and excited to be on a French road, headed for the old stone manor on the Loue. Forty minutes passed. They were through sleeping Ornans and on to the straight, climbing Carbonne road. This was the road in the newspaper piece, the road of Lothaire's wreck. Jim sat forward in the passenger seat, his whole being concentrated beyond the hissing windows. White-banded trees flicked by in the headlights. I am rolling near the death of Justin Lothaire, he thought.

Suddenly they were crossing the church square in Carbonne, and the road and its secret lay somewhere behind. Pushing back with a sigh, Jim looked ahead at the storm gathering above the car lights. Its coming was announced with flickered tongues of lightning.

"Look what you've brought down on us."

"Just water and electrons," Jim said. "Turn down there."

As Albert twisted the car steeply into the river gorge, bushes began threshing wildly in the lights. Then hail drummed deafeningly on the canvas roof and rattled on the paintwork. But a minute or two later they came to Mouthier and wound up a narrow village alley. In walled vineyards that overlooked the river stood a stone *manoir*.

"Monsieur Penn!" said the red-haired *patronne*, looking up from the register. "And where is madame?"

"To be honest, madame, we have separated."

"God pardon us, what times we are in!"

4

"TELL ME SOMETHING OF THE JURA," JIM WAS SAYING TO THE *PATRONNE* ten minutes later in the bright dining room. "During the war were there not resistance fighters here?"

"Oh, yes, the valley was famous. There are scenic caves one kilometer from here where the Germans burned forty *maquisards*."

"Didn't we see enough today?" Albert said when the woman had left them. "Anyway, she would have been a *collabo*."

"Some things are worthy of memory."

"You're so happy about these horrors. Really, you're being a ghoul," Albert said. "You know, you often remind me of Father's stories of Justin. That is" he added, "when Father deigned to visit us."

Jim's head swam. Abruptly he was unaware of the *patronne* and of the soup she was setting before him.

"What do you mean? Your father knew Justin Lothaire?"

"Surely, James, your own father . . . I mean, you knew they were at the Sorbonne together in the Thirties, my father, Lothaire, and your father? They shared an apartment. There was a fourth, Godard, I think, a philosopher. . . ."

The simple dining room with its whispering families had dissolved in a mist as all of Jim turned inward. Lothaire, David Sunda, and his own father living together?

"You really didn't know?" Albert said, watching him.

Jim was humbled and very moved. "If only I had. . . . "

"Parents avoid those subjects, James. Father hardly spoke to us of that time." Albert paused. "He didn't tell us much. Of course, I got some of it from Hélène." Albert called his mother Hélène. "You knew that Rickie, Jo, and I were born in the thick of it: Russia, then Germany, then France."

"Isn't your father on his boat right now?" Jim said.

"Oh, no, you had twenty years to find out. No, tomorrow night we will be in the mountains."

"He must be at Trieste or in Venice. We could reach him on the radio," Jim pressed. "Would he come in?"

"He might," Albert said coldly.

"But, Bertie, would he talk about that time? Is there some reason he wouldn't?"

"All right, he might talk." Albert swallowed the last of his soup, washing it down with wine. Why should he pursue a man who had abandoned his wife and the von Sundas' position in Europe, to float about on some old scow like the raft of the Medusa? Albert and David Sunda had not met for years.

Outside, while the two travelers argued the question of where they would spend the next days, the storm was clearing. The black sky glowed with the iridescent outlines of moving clouds, and the moon slipped out behind wisps of misty gauze.

Now the moon falls from clear skies to glitter on the Adriatic. Above Verdun it hides among thin clouds, throwing a weak light on the great and terrible mausoleum. And in that moonlight, all round the spire of a cathedral without a god, spread the graves of the forgotten dead. Their ranks are nameless and sleepless, and their weeping for their own lost families is choked in mud. All along the empty roads across the dark face of the world crowds a restless, groaning shuffle of rags, bones, hair, and sinew—monstrous tramping mobs, overflowing the highways and shouldering past the locked rooms of their sleeping sons. And this ghastly horde, fleeing through the faint gray light of eternity, is the murdered multitude of the refugee dead.

LEGEND

1

OFF THE COAST OF PESCARA, AT A POINT MIDWAY BETWEEN YUGOSLAVIA and Italy, a schooner-rigged trawler was lurching and banging her bows in the last of a westerly gale.

Belowdecks in a teak-paneled chart recess between the library shelves sat a slight well-proportioned gentleman of sixty, his arms flung over a confusion of charts, compasses, and surveyors' maps. Across the cabin a small globe trailed a tape of stock prices. The man's eyes were shut, his lean cheeks and somewhat bitter mouth were set in meditation. The passage door rattled twice.

"I've known you for thirty years," the man murmured, without stirring.

As he spoke, a thickset Slav came in, sliding the panel shut behind him. The man under the chart light had been dreaming of his lost children.

"Yes?" Baron Sunda opened his eyes.

"The drillers. . . ." Otto Horvath faltered. "A message came."

"Still no water? That was two thousand feet."

For some seconds the library rose and plunged, the teak bulkheads filtering the gurgled sea-and-rigging sounds from the heavy thud of the bows. In silence, both men saw before them the epic sterility of the Australian desert, which had been purchased through some absurdly human negotiation. A deal, Baron Sunda knew well, in which the soil belonging to all life is sold back for purposes of lonely exhaustion to a very few of those to whom it had immemorially belonged, but who, because they have paid for it, no longer respect it. Thus a land not owned but owning, enslaving and breaking.

"Tell them to sink another bore, then go to bed."

After Horvath's step receded in the passage, the man in the chart alcove turned his concentration back to his wife and children. When had they stopped loving him? Perhaps after his years in South America, when David had rebuilt the Sunda fortune lost in the war? They had changed so—or was it he? Yet who was left now to judge David Sunda, he thought, and a powerful pride surged in him. The sufferings of his lifetime, terrible relics sealed in the altar of his modern security, bore him up on a great, chaotic flood tide. And suddenly David Sunda's closed eyes filled with tears—for those beloved farmlands and mountains, for those towns with names like chords in a perfect and everlasting symphony written by a once-virtuous race of Europeans. For all these and this, the heritage, only God knew what David Sunda had given. Before him now rose the beautiful, condemning faces of the wife and children he had not seen for ten years. Joanna, as she had come to sing him rhymes long before she appeared half naked on the covers of fashion magazines. Albert, with his morbid air of civility; and Alaric—willful, innocent, intolerant Rickie, his firstborn, unlike anything the family had produced in three centuries. *You will die before you see your children again*, David thought. He groaned out loud, clutching the table as the mast next to him creaked and the old hull rolled sickeningly. The door rattled once more.

Otto had pulled on his short-sleeved white shirt but forgotten his tie. "Again, Pescara radio. In the storm they were out of range. The names were not clear. A *Berto* . . . and *Penna*? I think so. Someone in Pescara wishes us to go in."

After a long silence, David trusted himself to speak. "It's not out of the way. We can take on diesel and water."

When Otto had left him, David flattened his palms down on the table. Then, with a sudden, almost tender motion, he swept the charts onto the bench cushions, rose, and crossed the cabin. *How could this be?* he thought, lighting a cigar.

He began pacing up and down the steeply pitching library, pulling timidly at the cigar. Abruptly, he paused, then took two steps to a cabinet by the dogged porthole. The only mirror on the schooner was mounted inside. Sliding the panel, David looked at the wasted face. Giving a little moan of anger and anxiety, he ran his fingers three times over his thin hair. Then he went to his empty cabin and locked himself in.

2

JIM AND ALBERT CROSSED INTO ITALY THE NEXT DAY THROUGH THE GRAND-Saint-Bernard. As they left the freezing summit guard post, the sky to the south cleared. Soon they were swinging down through terraced stone vineyards just turning green, past farms like formations of granite and slate. At Aosta, the foster brothers made a silent lunch of *fettucine al pesto* and *coniglio,* then folded down the canvas car top. Catching the autostrada, they set out very fast through the lushly poplared corn and wheat fields of Piedmont to Milan, and from there southeast, flanking the limpid *campagna* of cypress and hilltop monasteries to meet the Adriatic at Rimini. Below Ancona, in the shade of the Abruzzi, the old coast road straightened and slowed, always tending south. And as the Mediterranean night edged its tender shadows, Jim raced the car down a long file of poplars, and suddenly the black harbor lay out below.

In the business rush of Pescara, with all the cars united in a stubborn bray, they finally came to the waterfront hotel. Jim was glad to escape Albert's depressed face and go looking for the radio office, while his friend found a garage.

At nightfall the hot wind died. From the blackness of the Adriatic came a heavy heat. It was necessary to leave the windows open, and the male shouting and pop music in the port kept Albert awake until after two. Lying still on the next bed, Jim let the ripe smells and sounds of Italy enter him. And listening to the sea in the night, he thought, *Let him come, please let him come.*

In the morning the harbor was empty. It was already glaring hot, and everyone was at work. Jim and Albert took breakfast alone by a shady window. The young waiter approached.

"Signor Sunda?"

"Yes?"

Albert pushed his shirtsleeves off his thick forearms and took the green slip without looking up. He unfolded it, read it once, and returned to his newspaper. He held the cable across to Jim.

PESRADIO 09:05 12 JUNE, said the irregular type glued onto a telegraphic blank. DOCK AT PESCARA WEDNESDAY. DAVID.

A triumphant laughter had begun and Jim could not look at Albert's face. He thought of the old man putting into Pescara to take them off to sea. And just for one dangerous instant, there was a revenge in it against all the towns where James Penn had ever suffered and been outcast. Then there was only gratitude, and this drab modern dining room in the middle of nowhere was suddenly familiar and fated.

3

"ALBERT, COME AND LOOK!"

"Well, I hope you're happy."

Outside the hotel window the early morning was a pool of gold, the fishing smacks like sunspots. The air was rinsed very pure. A blue and yellow trawler listed steadily by, clearing the jetty light, its spars glistening with dew. Stern to at the outermost elbow of the breakwater was a broad but graceful sailing boat with three tenders lashed on her deck. The dock lines trailed in the blinding reflections, her unequal masts a higher world against the sea outside. Someone was hosing the deck with fresh water. Two figures, one in white trousers, appeared from behind the big tender. They paused, then the second moved away alone.

Ten minutes later Jim and Albert were being rowed stern first out over the oily green. And thirty strokes ahead, like the walls of some siege fort, were the black bows and towering masts.

"A humble little scow," Jim said.

Albert looked at him as if he were a stranger. "Remember, I'll speak to him alone."

They were passing under the bows, gliding near the heavy-stretched anchor chain, and it was as if Jim had never come near property so totally owned. Overhead there were shouts. Rope pulleys squeaked and a ladder banged the hull. As Jim stepped over, the great decks were streaming fresh water.

"James Penn," he said, holding out his hand to a bald Turkish-looking sailor. The man quickly frowned, then met the gangling American's grin. He held out his free hand.

"I am Nikos."

Albert Sunda went up a ladder that he had never climbed, knowing and dreading what would be on deck. Suddenly weighed down by memory and shame, he stepped onto the wet teak. And as he did, he glimpsed the brown girl lying asleep on the foredeck hatch. Turning quickly, he saw familiar short-cropped hair, white skin, and a short-sleeved office shirt.

"Hello, Otto," Albert said. "You haven't changed."

"What should I be?" the older man laughed, his accent as thick as ever. "How long do you stay?"

"I have no idea. This is James Penn."

"Oh, yes, I remember."

Jim shook hands with a strained smile. Along the deckhouse the salt had been hosed off; the varnish looked hot. They passed below, and Otto rolled back the last passage door. At the threshold Albert took Jim's arm.

"Remember, just say hello."

"That suits me fine!" For as he bent after Albert into this low cabin, the American felt stricken by the story waiting inside. The only light fell from an alcove on the left across a table covered in papers. Jim hung back, recognizing through his intense emotion the short strong-legged figure rising to his feet: the attractive head, the fine skin close to the bone, the sad oriental droop of the eyes.

"Well, my boy," said a slightly hoarse, musical voice. "This is a remarkable surprise."

"Hello, Father."

"And you, James?"

"It's fine to be here, sir." Jim held the subtle fingers. Freeing his hand, the old man reached both shirtsleeved arms in the dark. He tugged, and in the flood of sunshine Jim saw the labyrinth of fine wrinkles on David Sunda's face, the thin gray hair brushed back over sun spots.

"So, before anything else," David said softly, in his too perfect accent. He made a gesture toward the bookcases and the sea beyond. "I have taken off some weeks for Abi. We are sailing through the islands to Cyprus, then on to

Tel Aviv. I hope that both of you will come at least part of the way. The car can be dealt with. . . . But no need to answer now." David finished quickly, after a glance at his son.

What an invitation! Jim almost shouted. Then, noticing Otto backing discreetly toward the passage, Jim became confused. Muttering an incoherent excuse, he moved to the open door.

"James, lunch will be at eleven-thirty." David stood in the pillar of sun, looking after him. "I am delighted you are with us."

4

IN THE STERNMOST CABIN, JIM PENN UNDOGGED THE PORTHOLE, SHUT THE DOOR, and climbed onto the bunk. He lay back under a watercolor of the Jardin du Luxembourg.

Where now are the urgent questions you felt at Verdun? he asked himself, listening to the great hull massed around him. *Where are the children burned alive by firestorms? Where are the gangster tycoons and the hideous nations who sold their love of God to their destroyers? Where is Justin Lothaire?* But as he stretched very still on the bunk, the splendid unrealism clung to him as if just seeing David Sunda's face had told him all he needed to know. Brilliant water reflections snaked and trembled like giant protozoans over the cabin. Jim listened to the soft rustle of Pescara and the pulse of fishing engines carried on the harbor morning.

Suddenly he was trying to remember something and rushed upward out of sleep. Jim was in a silent cabin, sitting barefoot on the bunk. He blinked at his watch. The hands pointed to 11:45. He was fifteen minutes late to his first lunch.

A green-striped awning had been bent over the boom and strung to the shrouds. As Jim climbed into the heat he heard arguing and a woman's voice. He walked toward a table set in the shade of the sunken wheel deck. A silence fell, and Otto turned. Across the elaborate setting, Albert wiped his tensed upper lip.

"We decided to let you sleep," said the young woman next to him, trying to smile.

"This is Abi . . . Abigail."

Jim muttered guiltily, then sat in the canvas chair beside her, not daring to meet any eyes. He could only guess—though presently he would know—that seconds before there had been a scene of breathtaking ugliness. That the girl next to Jim, in a red sarong, with freckles, wavy black hair, and eyes as hard brown as hazel nuts, was David Sunda's mistress. That Albert had just insulted his father publicly for abandoning his mother, the Bavarian estate, and the family's life in New York, to live on a yacht with a Polish cutthroat and a lover the age of his own children. He had only come, Albert had said, to satisfy Jim

Penn's interest in the family history. Now Albert and the girl were red-faced, Otto's eyes glittered unpleasantly, and their host wore a grave, wooden smile.

"Well, after the war came Brazil," the old gentleman began. "Then a period in America. But instead of coming back to Europe . . . instead of Europe, I bought the *Marta*. Her first owner, an Alexandrian Greek, sold her to me in Malta. You knew Socrati, Albert," David added, not looking at his son.

"I remember him," Albert whispered.

Around the luncheon table, they waited for their host to resume his story. But the baron's cold blue eyes had narrowed as if he had seen something in the remote distance at a point above the breakwater where the hazy sky came to the scarcely darker blue of the Adriatic. As if he were looking back down corridors of sealed memories and history, back across the unwritten virulence of the Amazon forest, the gray tank-tracked wastes of the frozen Ukraine and the godless Silesian *Lager*, back to the halls of the family estate, Oberlinden, filled with music and light.

"You recall?" Otto lightly slapped the table. "In those days, you flew off to do business every port we came to."

"The first two years, I did three cruises," David continued. "The first took six weeks, following Ulysses to Sicily and back to Ithaca. That same year, after the hurricane season, we went from the Canaries to San Salvador. Then in the spring we followed the explorers right around the world. That took ten months."

"And where were we then, Papa?" But Albert's bitter words vanished in a drumming crash. Around the table of cheese and figs the smiling faces glanced up. A hot gust had spilled from the breakwater, and the awning had lifted soundlessly, then fallen with a sharp, rumbling report. They saw the two stern lines rise from the green water, straighten to the rings on the breakwater, and wring out a shower of drops.

"Pescara is no place to stay anchored." David drew himself up, with a ruthlessness that broke the communion of lunch. "Oliver?"

"Mr. Sunda, sir?"

"Tell Nikos we'll put out in twenty minutes. Take down the table and awning. And James?"

The baron stood over them under the flapping green tent. The girl had lifted her brown arms to unfasten the clips holding her hair. Seated beside her, Jim felt a cold shaft go from his head to his stomach.

"Yes, sir?"

The old man smiled vaguely down at him. "Albert tells me you are looking into . . . the wartime. If you like, we might perhaps talk about it. Come for tea tomorrow in my study."

"Tomorrow? Oh, yes, that would be excellent," Jim said.

Albert pushed back his chair and walked past the upturned boats to the pulpit over the bow netting. He tugged the cigarettes from his jacket pocket and stared grimly at the modern waterfront, thinking of his mother—alone now—at the piano in their Manhattan living room, of her charm and courage. The sun poured down with a sickly fever. And as his eye followed a cyclist under the harbor trees, Albert felt an almost unbearable loneliness and grief.

The auxiliary rumbled consolingly. Albert was still at the pulpit, dropping unlit matches by the anchor chain as the schooner cast off from the breakwater.

Jim watched the sails being set from behind the wheel, though not so close that the old man might speak to him. Across ninety feet of deckhouse, spars, crewmen, swinging lines, and rattling winches, Albert's disapproving figure on the bow looked very small. He saw the great sails fall over the deck, rustling like voluminous skirts, then drift up free on the swaying gaffs. The winches slowed and the two great booms rose from the padded crutches, moving resolutely over the rails toward the rusted coaster. Now there was only a remote rattle of the windlass and a whisper of the heavy wheel as David wound it to the stops.

Behind him, Jim Penn lifted his face to the shady summits of sail as the breeze hollowed a current, tightening the wrinkled dacron. For several seconds the broad, shaded decks were without movement as two jibs streamed up the forestays. Then Jim felt rather than heard an almost female sigh of life pass down the masts, creaking into the massive decks to the deep-sunk mystery of the keel, binding cloth, wood, and steel in a single motive. And standing in the midst of so much privilege, Jim looked back without shame at the crew lining the rail of the Yugoslav coaster and at the groups stopped along the docks to watch with modern envy and ancient wonder this universal sailing. Just then, as the *Marta* swung on the wind, hardening toward the harbor mouth, the white tower of sails yielded mildly, stiffened, and flooded with the full brilliance of the sun. A minute later they rounded the end stone. They were at sea.

5

NEXT MORNING, WHEN JAMES PENN AWOKE, THERE WAS NO COASTLINE. TEN minutes after breakfast, he was searching a forward sail locker for rain gear when scarcely familiar voices came to him through the overhead hatch.

Albert was whispering. "Papa, I swear I am not hiding anything!"

"Your brother always went with you."

"There was so much between us!"

"Do you mean your sister, Joanna? What do you mean?"

"Much more. I could never tell it all."

"But think . . . imagine!" The old man's voice rose sharply. "Even my agents cannot find him. Albert, did the boy hate me so much?"

There were muffled steps. James Penn lay holding his breath, rigid on a cushion of sails. He had just heard, for the first time in his life, a father's love for his son. The old man had begun muttering.

"Where is my son? When did he renounce the life I gave him?" The baron's weight shuffled massively on the beams just above Jim's head. "Can he know the price I paid for that life?"

"You never told us, Papa," Albert's voice suddenly cried. "You would always go away."

"Is it possible, under these skies, that he will never come back?" The deep old voice groaned, then it broke. "'Rickie, my son, my first son!'"

Beneath David Sunda's feet, doubled on a mound of sail bags, he who needed to find justice in the world listened for his name and wept with anger.

6

THAT AFTERNOON AT THE TEA HOUR EVERYONE BUT THE OLD BARON WAS ON deck. No one commented when James Penn left Albert with Abigail between two tenders and moved aft under the great sails, solid-lit as Japanese lanterns. The baron turned with his slow gentle smile as the tall American stooped in under the library beams.

"Thank you sir."

"So, would you like milk in your tea?"

"Yes, thank you."

The chart alcove was perfectly quiet. The only sign of the cabin's motion was the intermittent tortured creak of a bulkhead. As the pleasant silence over the silver tea service lengthened out and tensed, the morning's secret anger with this man left Jim. The fever he had brought from the cemetery of Verdun cooled. In their place he experienced an almost holy concentration on the person just two arm's lengths across the cleared table. Jim saw then the high-domed forehead, the hooked nose and sad-sunken, scarred-looking cheeks. He saw small ears close to the skull, fine temples, and leathery skin on the strong neck. And as the baron carefully rested the teacup and smiled with veiled penetration, Jim thought of the beautiful afternoon on deck with Albert and the girl, and he would have given his soul to be up there.

"Tell me, Jim. Has Albert not changed?"

"He was always morbid." Jim felt relieved by this small talk.

"He seems more sullen than morbid."

"Maybe it's not an age for temperaments like Albert's."

"No!"

Jim and the ship's cat both flinched as the sun spotted old hand shot among the tea service, under the animal's ginger belly. Jim felt the mass of the schooner run through a swell. There was a faraway shudder and a sound like heavy bolts being overtightened.

"One is not often asked to speak of that time." David Sunda glanced across the table with faint alarm. "What is it you would like to know?"

Jim felt his face burn; a shaft of monstrous excitement went through him. "Tell me about the Russian war and the German generals," he said. "And about how you met Hitler and joined the plot on his life. And what was Berlin like, having a French wife?" He leaned on the table, gesturing with his hands, oblivious to the reddening, alarmed face now out of the light against the alcove paneling. "Tell me what it was like to come in sight of the Kremlin roofs and then desert the German army. And how must it have been to walk all the way out of the Ukrainian snows, then be mistaken for a partisan and thrown in a labor camp. Tell me about Justin Lothaire. . . ."

Jim's voice died with a faint wheeze. In the absolute hush, the two men sat staring at each other. They both clearly heard the overtightened bolt tighten one further *crack*. After what felt like a very long time, the baron audibly let out his breath. He leaned forward, taking the teapot in both wrinkled hands. As the old gentleman's face came harshly under the yellow light, Jim saw that it was a deep red. Veins stood out on the fine, high brows with a glitter of perspiration. The corners of David's thin mouth were tugged down in an incredible hardness, the eyes narrowed to rifle slits. Then all at once the face relaxed in a vague, old man's defeat.

"My boy, your cup is empty."

James Penn blushed—from his belly to the crown of his scalp. "Please. Thank you, sir."

The baron rose from the chart table. Motioning with a stiff smile to the neat triangles of buttered bread, the old man crossed on his still springy legs to the facing bookshelves. Jim saw the groomed nape of the old neck. A thick book had appeared under David's arm. He lifted down a leather box the size of a bookend. As he watched this frowning gentleman return to him out of the shadows, Jim experienced an almost abject affection. Setting the heavy volume on the table, David opened the cover. Then the wrinkled hands freed the brass hooks on the leather box. Jim stared at the ink inscription on the title page and swallowed. The book was Cervantes.

"It is the one expensive thing that I ever saw Justin purchase."

"He gave it to you?" Jim slid his fingers along the tiny, barely legible black letters.

"There was still a community then," David said slowly. "Before this political hatred."

"He gave it to you after the war?" Jim translated the French handwriting in his head. *For my great friend and benefactor, from the Knight of the Mournful Countenance.*

"No, when we were students on the rue de Fleurus," David said with grim dignity.

"Near the Jardin du Luxembourg?"

"Overlooking it. By the Hotel Perrève, *numéro un*." David smiled at the young American's excitement. "Justin, your father, Duncan, and Johannes Godard, and I."

"Where is Godard now?"

"He is also dead—but look." David had opened the leather box. Inside was a heavy pewter ring with angular inscriptions half worn away. He balanced it on his palm. Then, resting the ring lightly on the open title page, he lit a small cigar.

"It looks very old," Jim said.

"It is said that this buckle belonged to a Sunda ancestor, Arminius. In the year fifteen, when Christ was still teaching in the temple, Arminius led the rising of German tribes against the Roman eagle."

"Truly!" said James Penn, who in his life had seen relics in famous museums, though never beside the living heir.

David stretched out his wrists on the chart table. Through the open skylight came a faint summer-muted cry, then on deck a questioning shout from Nikos. Seeing this boy's absolutely sincere interest in him, David knew he was not afraid to hear Hélène's and Justin's names spoken aloud or to admit that his children had banished him. In his great excitement David Sunda was remembering his life: each thing, the immense and the humble. Each with its sensations and smells, just as it had happened.

"Tremendous!" The young American shook his head and looked up into the old gentleman's face. Albert's father was watching him, one brow raised, the drooping eyes no longer offended. This heavy buckle had been in the field with Roman legions, but the moist eyes just across the chart table—the baron seemed fifteen years older than his sixty years—had witnessed the most monstrous invasion in all history.

The old man filled the evening sun with a billow of blue smoke, looking as if he would laugh. Instead, he rose with dignity from the chart table, paced to the end shelves, and turned. His face was dark with emotion.

7

"I FIRST SAW LOTHAIRE IN THE SWISS ALPS ON CHRISTMAS EVE OF 1931. IT WAS my first year at the Sorbonne. Anti-Semitic riots had closed Warsaw University, and I was traveling to Gstaad with my Polish cousin Anya. The family Daimler broke down in Lausanne, so we took the mountain train to Saanen. And there in the compartment, facing us, was Justin Lothaire."

His back to the schooner's library, half obscured beyond the column of light, the baron hesitated. Hearing his own first words, and how they were his story, David had abruptly remembered tragedy.

"Justin had on a raincoat, with sandals and heavy socks," he continued gruffly. "Probably I took him for a Spanish waiter at the hotels. I noticed that he kept looking curiously at Anya. Confident, you understand, absolutely proud. He had such a poet's face, a quality of the desert, which he passed on to his daughter. Anyway, we would never have spoken if it had not been Justin's first sight of deep snow. He was completely astonished—imagine! The frosted windows, a long clattering tunnel, then blinding fields of unmarked powder. Ha! It was the discovery of a new element. During that hour Justin was so excited he would have talked to anyone. He was traveling through Europe on his own. He had selected Gstaad from those posters in the Gare de Genève of girls holding skis. At the time, Justin was a scholarship student from Algiers. He had arrived in Paris early for the winter term at the Sorbonne. For all his suspicion, Justin had no inkling of Swiss prices. By the time we came to Château-d'Oex, we had been through Nietzsche, Kant, Cervantes, and Euripides. By the time we left Saanen, Justin was a guest of the family. By the time we came to Gstaad, we were friends for life.

"At the time I was something of a snob. But instead of being annoyed by this fellow staring at Anya, I was more uneasy—as if he undermined us, my God! And Justin had quite a gift for anger. There he was, a half-breed from some Algiers slum. But that great sensibility made him our equal at least. Looking back, it seems a freak that such a meeting lasted even five minutes."

"Or ever took place," Jim said.

"Yes, who could imagine it today?" There was a silence. "Of course, Justin was unfamiliar with the subtleties of great wealth. All was fresh; things had their integrity. Existence for me had not yet been sliced in goods and evils. And my family was not ostentatious. But it was not that. It was that our bond as students forgave everything. I was interested in him, I was open. Who knows, perhaps I was the first person in Europe his own age he'd ever spoken to. We had read the same writers and would be attending the same lectures. I was fixed in that fanciful mind as his idea of a Sorbonne student. It never surprised him in those long discussions that we agreed on the obscurest points. But I, at least, never made the mistake of considering Justin Lothaire to be like anyone else."

After a long pause, David went on in a new voice. "During the next ten days the three of us were generously, carelessly, and tenderly happy. But underneath was that temper, withheld but weighing everything, and some primitive anger at any man with a beautiful woman—both, ready to crackle out on the world any moment and restore justice. Below the family chalet there was a *grand hôtel*. One of the staff was a lean young Basque, who sprayed the ice rink three times a night so that the children could pirouette and fall about. Justin noticed this Basque. Later I saw them drinking together in the local *Stubli*. Then a skiing episode came close to spoiling things."

"Justin knew how to ski?" Jim inquired and he watched Baron Sunda nod.

"The skiing he picked up in the way of children, with the same fanaticism he felt for his enlightenment at the Sorbonne." The baron paced slowly forward under the blazing skylight. "That day my brother Friedrich arrived from Berlin. We took Justin to the top of the longest run. He was tremendously eager. Then, on the trail down the next valley, we became separated.

"Imagine!" David stood over the young American with an urgency to be understood. "In that wrong ravine Justin turns, the skis do not. He falls in headfirst. Under his head the snow is unbroken and deep. You can imagine— the snow is alien; he is aware for the first time of its white, feathery weight. He begins fighting his way down across the fields, floundering and tumbling in. Perhaps he remembers the lace shop in Algiers, his dead father's rebel friends, his mother's hopes for him. Justin has betrayed them. He is wild to throw off these foolish rich people's skis, to end this humiliation. Or Justin longs to submit, and that is worst of all.

"I waited for him by the station, perhaps twenty minutes. I was grateful when our guest slid out on the *piste*. I did not understand then the stiff, careful way he walked toward me, the look on his face." David paused heavily. "He must have seen how much I was his friend. But something happened to Justin on the mountain that afternoon." Then, as if he had felt the heroic mood among his richly paneled shelves sink to embarrassing intimacy, the old gentleman laughed with indifference.

"I'll bet you were a good skier," Jim offered.

"No, no." David laughed again. "Friedrich was the skier."

"But did Lothaire really have a daughter?"

"She lives in Paris. You would like to meet her?"

"Meet Lothaire's daughter? Yes, of course!"

"It is easily arranged."

"Thanks very much, sir."

"Oh, no, my boy," David said, in a soft, controlled voice. He held out his hand. "It is I who am grateful."

So it began. And soon the schooner's masts had towered over the ancient olives in many bays along the coast, and on to Ithaca, Crete, and Jerusalem. And each morning before breakfast, in raw and delicate words never heard on deck—as if the older man could only utter them to the bland sunburnt face of perfect trust and the younger could only listen without witnesses—Baron Sunda told the legend of his time.

By the island of Ithaca, Jim knew he could do nothing graceless enough to be put ashore. By Santorini, David Sunda had told too much to give the story up.

THE FRIENDS

1

"IN PARIS, ON THE RUE DE FLEURUS," ALBERT'S FATHER BEGAN THE SECOND day, afloat in a lagoon at Corfu, "each of us had his own room. That must have been 1932 . . . *1932!*

"Our corner balcony faced across the iron fence of the Luxembourg gardens, over a pond. The parquet salon had six tall windows. There was no extra money, so the furniture was seedy, though your father made an effort. Johannes Godard spent the most time in his room. It had all the display of that egocentric nature—an oak desk, a harpsichord, reproductions of Renaissance masters, one of those yellow globes on a boxwood stand. And, yes, I remember now, Tischbein's portrait of Goethe. But Godard was darkly private, and everyone came to me. Anyway, the prize student always kept his room overheated."

"And Lothaire?" Jim leaned closer.

"Furniture did not mean much to Justin. His room was drab and bare, without even curtains. Still, in some way it was elegant, even the cigarette ends on the floor."

"And yours?"

"My room? Like this—" Haggard in the latticed sun that fell from the skylight, the old face turned to the bookshelves—"And this, I recently realized, is like my father's study at Oberlinden, the family property in Bavaria. But listen, my boy."

"I couldn't not listen, sir."

"When I try to think about that time, knowing what was to happen to us all . . . "

"Everyone being dead?"

". . . and the way we died," David went on, "I cannot grasp how we were friends. I think we scarcely knew your father. But at the time our motives seemed indistinguishable. In fact, we were exceptionally close. We reveled in being *similar*, we celebrated it! We were happy. I remember, in particular, a scene in a crowded restaurant—yes, Polidor!"

2

THE LEASE WAS SIGNED THE SECOND WEEK OF JANUARY.

That evening it rained. Huddling home through the place de l'Odéon, David Sunda had stopped for a bottle of champagne. When he turned in at the carriage gate, he noticed Johannes Godard's tall figure pushing past the crowd outside the *boucherie*. Catching sight of David, the usually scowling Godard smiled with childlike enthusiasm.

The philosopher had spent the last hours playing trios with his new friends, a logic professor and his wife. As he left the rue d'Assas, the music still rang in his mind. The human contact, however, had irritated Godard, and as always sensing that people could see this in his eyes, his manner was groveling and impatient.

When he caught sight of his countryman on the cobbles outside Number 1, Johann was released. He knew that David could fathom him. And Johann had never met anyone with so old a name. It gave life a permanence, like ideas. Both sensations were novel.

"David!" Godard's breath sputtered white in the dusk. "I took the long way home. You see, the street names are victories by Bonaparte. This city will make men of us. And is this the lease—it's really ours? I will study the thinkers living in a palace?"

"Scarcely a palace. But it's ours."

Side by side they looked up at their windows.

"*Sunda, du bist ein Zauberer!* Do the others know?"

Wheeling together, the two students raced past the concierge's door and galloped up the low-ceilinged sweep of staircase. They halted outside a worm-eaten doorway, laughing and panting. David turned the handle, and they squeaked along a passage into the salon.

Four collapsed sofas stood beyond a chandelier that dimly lit the center of the big room. Sideways in one of them sat a stocky, sandy-haired foreign student in a tweed jacket, listening to a dark young man with bony features. The American sat uncomfortably, fingertips pressed together, his face already flushed with drink. The Algerian paced back and forth, with a floating, athlete's stride, and puffed clouds of acrid smoke. Their discussion had gone on for days. Though the argument never seemed to advance, it was making the two close.

"But Justy!" Duncan Penn burst out. "You haven't lived with it. Our system is more Henry Ford than Henry Thoreau. In selfish isolation, so much prosperity is ruinous."

"That cannot be." Justin Lothaire's somber face turned from a balcony window. Catching sight of the fresh arrivals, he paused among the sofas.

"Sunda, tell them!" Godard was smiling broadly.

His eyebrows raised, Justin measured Godard's grin, then David's modest smile. He heard the American.

"You dog, did you manage it? Glasses, gentlemen?"

As Penn hurried off to the kitchen, David freed the bottle's wire mesh.

"Do you mean the lease?" Justin frowned. He had never tasted champagne.

"It is ours. With options for five years."

They stood in the square of sofas under the high ceiling. Outside, the branches in the Luxembourg gardens shone with a clear yellow light. The four glasses hissed.

"Damn," Duncan said, looking at each of their faces. "Damn!"

And it was, to them all, like the dawn of some new wisdom. Beyond those rooms were the famous boulevards and, beyond those, France, with her galleries of cultivated men and her ancient faiths, and the war-wizened societies of petulant despots and crumbling empire. And beyond all those lay half-savage Russia. But at this moment—for Lothaire, whose father had died in the Sahara; for Godard, whose father had been gassed at the Somme; for Sunda, whose uncle had fallen fighting for the French; and even for Penn, whose father had cast the first tank armor—there was a perfect certainty that none among them would bear onward so much horror. David von Sunda raised his glass.

"That the performance live up to the setting," said Johann.

"That the actors," Duncan added, "learn more than their lines."

In the silence their glasses softly clicked.

"That we learn nothing that cannot be forgotten." David held the bottle for each of the three men.

"And forget nothing that cannot be relearned."

"Precisely, Johann!" Justin put in steadily. "That we neither succeed nor fail but continue to love life."

"That we marry women of grace," David said.

"Moral women," corrected Duncan.

"Passionate women," Johannes added.

"Intelligent women," Justin said, with such gravity that the others turned to meet his gaze. "Yes, and that we are listened to when just, and serve no dictators."

"Serve dictators?" Duncan laughed incredulously. "Impossible . . . never!" And they were like new conscripts in an army of enlightenment, gazing on a world of limitless possibilities.

A warmer light was coming from the street. Outside, they all heard the echo of a throng, then came singing and a chant. The balconies along the Jardin du Luxembourg were already filled. As the four friends stepped out, a good-natured mob rippled toward them behind a row of grim organizers in ragged coats and shoes that turned up at the toes. The moving feet made a sound like rain. The new Popular Front placards—À BAS MAURRAS, DEMOCRACY OF THE LEFT, WAGES NOT WORDS—waved among the flow of hats.

A small dog ran in front, barking hysterically as the first protesters passed under the windows.

A voice had shouted Justin's name. Against the balcony railing, Johann turned to him.

"Who are they? What are those books?"

"*Le Capital*," Justin said, searching the sea of berets below. A dark, ragged head was turned to their balcony, smiling broadly. "Lothaire . . . Lothaire," the face mouthed, and Justin recognized Eli Hebron. Justin had only recently met him at a student rally, though Eli's father ran a Hebrew press in Algeria. The little man's eyes took in the group holding glasses. "Come down, join in!" voices in the crowd shouted, as Eli's upturned face was carried on across the rue de Fleurus.

"David, throw down the wine!" Justin said. His grin was both affectionate and sad.

"The champagne?"

"Go on, David. Throw it down, *vite!*"

David stretched far over the balcony. Holding the half empty bottle by the neck, he swung it gently. Some rows behind Hebron's receding face, a dozen coat arms flapped up. The bottle disappeared in the current of heads. There were more shouts. Someone called, "Long live Léon Blum!" and the lean faces lifted in the revolutionary anthem. The sentimental, triumphant chant rose into the evening above the gold-tipped roofs of Paris. And to the Fleurusians standing on the balcony it was incredible that already so much had happened and that there was so much to discover. The four stood until the last stragglers had disappeared down the rue Guynemer. Then they moved back inside to prepare for Polidor.

3

POLIDOR WAS A STUDENT RESTAURANT KNOWN TO DAVID SUNDA IN A SIDESTREET very near the Théâtre de l'Odéon, with thin white columns and sawdust on the floor. Half an hour later, the friends were inching through the smoke between the thundering communal tables. The fat, downy-cheeked *patronne* made a great fuss and pushed the notable-looking group toward a long table against the wall.

"*Là-bas, mes beaux garçons, mes anges;* sit down, eat a good dinner!" she shouted, with the discernment of old women for young men. But the four were too drunk on the wealth of their erudition to notice the faces that were turning to them. At raised tables to the rear, a drinking party of student doctors was already close to oblivion. The plates had not been cleared. Duncan placed a fish skeleton under his nose, and Johannes leaned in front of him.

"Poseidon? . . . Thersites? . . . Bacchus?" he shouted.

"Oh, please! So what are you?"

"This one is Achilles." Justin placed his arm tenderly over Johann's neck. "But I will vouch for him."

And already—as if to confirm their love for one another that night and its power to make things happen—David had pointed out two redheaded girls escorted by an English journalist and two Americans. The party of five was heading toward their table.

"Justin, the Englishman, Wilfred Rouve, with the silk scarf around his neck, is a sort of encyclopedist and wit. He will try to provoke you," David said.

"I am ready." Justin smiled as the taller American, called Bowden, bent by David's ear. No one had risen when the two redheads sat down.

"You see, *barone mio*?" Bowden ignored Justin. "I told you the food here was cheap. Let's hope no one turns up from the legation."

"Oh, it's splendidly cheap, old man," cut in the Englishman. "It depends on whether you like organs."

"Tripes are a specialty?" Justin offered, and he heard the Englishman roar with laughter.

"Of course Bowden likes organs, Rouve!" observed the second American, named Neuville, speaking English with a French accent. "But he will be sacked if he is seen out with two tarts."

The party around Justin Lothaire had grown to eight. But with all his strength, his face stinging red, he was trying to call back the spell of earlier that evening. Had this obviously intelligent Englishman, with a stupid laugh, reduced him, Justin, to idiocy? And his friend Sunda, a baron? Unable to follow another word of the amused conversation at their table, he stared around the room of arguing students. Cheap? Was this not the finest place Justin had seen in Paris? His eyes met David's.

"Titles are obsolete, my friend. I gave up mine when I was twelve."

Justin grinned with a sudden vivid happiness. "It is your burden, my friend."

So, their first minutes at Polidor, Justin's reflex of instinctive hatred for the cynicism of the English journalist, Rouve, and the decadence of Neuville was already past. It felt like failure, for studying in Paris commanded a scholarship student to understand his presence among so much freedom and enlightenment.

Through the next hour Justin ate in silence. Even with his full concentration he could not match the careless humor among these five men who knew so much and ridiculed it all. Only Johannes and the two girls did not join in. As for the others—David Sunda and Rouve, Robert Neuville (who was at the Beaux-Arts), and the other American, Bowden—they seemed as intimate with affairs in the ministries of Europe as with their own lives. Justin felt enthralled and humiliated, and as if he were among enemies who must not overwhelm him. Already he was able to follow the talk of the declining dollar, and how this had forced Bowden and his fellow aides to move into humble quarters and to frequent cheap restaurants. Now there was a debate on whether the Great

War had spoiled the social life in Europe, then a scathing rundown on friends and associates, which Justin absorbed to the last detail.

In the evening's second hour, their group was joined at the table by two slim young women named von Siebenberg. They were in floppy slacks, which for diplomats' daughters was apparently considered wild. By now Justin's thoughts had drifted from *le tout Paris* and the Quartier Latin. All he could see of the group crowded around him—who found that the food was cheap, that this chilly blonde Monica was wild, and who did not question a gloomy *pied-noir*—was a haze like narcosis, though Justin had not touched his wine. Yet he was not unhappy, for he had sensed tonight in David's manner that he would never lose David's friendship.

Presently, Bowden, who worked in his country's embassy, gave a tug of the cuffs and without altering his bored tone launched into a rumor going the rounds that Yagoda's agent maintained a furnace in the basement of the Soviet embassy to dispose of their enemies. Before Justin could take in the fact of such an accusation, or Rouve's withering denial, the chatter turned to Ivy League clubs. Through a torrent of snobbery, cruelty, and trivia, conducted in a manner that glittered over the surface of things, he heard himself laugh along with views he did not believe in, and at things he held sacred.

It was a relief when at last Justin detected his own voice, conversing with the redhead pressed against his right shoulder. These two girls with their feather boas were not like the others. They ordered, ate hungrily, and leaned across his lap to exchange phrases. Seeing their pocked cheeks, Justin felt giddy.

"I am from Algiers."

"I was in Zurich once," said the one called Maline.

"In Zurich?"

"Because of my dreams. To see Dr. Lindt from Salzburg."

Justin met the girl's suspicious stare; the remark meant nothing to her. She had said it automatically.

"That is very interesting, Maline."

"You know him?" Suddenly alarmed at this *pied-noir*'s confident tone, the girl was reassured by his sad eyes. "In fact, Lindt was very interested in me. I was sent to him by Father Duroc."

"You mean, your father?"

"A priest in Carbonne, it is my village." The girl fingered her glass. "My father was a *colon* from Tunis. He died, and I went to work in Besançon. There I had dreams. Duroc sent me to Zurich."

"Dreams?"

"Oh, stupid things." Maline bent near to light her cigarette from Justin's. "I am very big. Beetles come out of my hands. My parents are an emperor and a virgin. . . . Beyond, it is dark but nobody goes away. He liked that one."

The indifference was back like a film on the girl's light-blue eyes. She leaned over in front of Justin. "Julie, what did you have for dessert?"

The chants and singing from the rear of the restaurant had risen to a new pitch, and the table subsided into silence. Justin met the eyes of Duncan, then Johann. For the first time, Rouve's and Neuville's faces were half serious.

"Speaking of organs," observed the Englishman. "I wouldn't put mine in the hands of these louts!"

Justin had turned on his seat. Above the packed tables and crowd standing along the center aisle, he could see chairs rise and fall in the young doctors' chamber. Polidor's *patronne* stood in the connecting steps with her hands in her hair. Through the main room fear spread like a gas.

"Now, now," Rouve called, "*les médecins, vous oubliez votre* Hippocratic oath. Damn Frogs!"

"That will not stop them," commented Neuville, his soft features ashen.

"Terrible, this is terrible!" Johannes stared around the tables of flushed, eager faces. For though he was the tallest person in the restaurant, the philosopher never fathomed the reality of physical violence. He had even managed to ignore the ugly mood in Paris and its labor riots, whose motive was collective and therefore unserious. Across the table's litter of dishes and empty bottles, Justin observed his unhappy face. At the fellow's side, the chilly beauty Monica von Siebenberg looked excited for the first time that evening. David had risen from his place between the sisters, and was unbuttoning his jacket.

"Gentlemen, we should intervene!"

"Won't that make it worse?" Duncan had restrained their friend by a sleeve, but the jacket came loose in his hands.

Justin was on his feet between the backs of chairs. He pushed along the crowded tables, overcoming his feeling about Rouve as the two of them met Sunda at the end. They were grinning with nerves and pride. As the three pushed up the aisle, attention focused on them.

"My little room!" wailed the *patronne*. "My kitchen!"

As Justin went ahead up the steps into the heaving crowd of students, one of the sweating shirtbacks turned. Seeing him, the boy—he had a black mustache and red hair—gave a roar, as if this *bicot* had been his oldest enemy. Somewhere above the belt, Justin felt a hard blow. He was stretched flat on the sawdust. More falling bodies crushed him down. And then, looking up, Justin saw a familiar blue shirt. It was David Sunda. At once the pressure on his chest and legs slackened and Justin struggled to wrench himself to his feet. A murderous rage clamped his chest. He searched for the mustached redhead.

But now the bloodied doctors were crowded cheering round the remaining tables. Stepping carefully across their tops was David. In his arms was the thin, scared old cook who had fed them. Justin's nose was tickling, the nauseous passion had gone as it had come. And staring up at his friend's amused smile, Justin thought, *There is something astonishing about this Sunda.*

Outside Polidor the Paris night had cleared. The wintry chill was gone. No one was hurt, though Rouve's velvet jacket had horsehair torn from one shoulder. As they were driven home through the bright boulevards in Robert Neuville's big American convertible, the Fleurusians were boisterous and heroic. First they dropped the Siebenberg sisters by a gate in one of the tree-lined alleys off the avenue Foch. Then Rouve and Bowden disappeared into the place Vendôme beside the two redheads, who did not wish anyone good night. Duncan was still bent forward in the back seat arguing with Johann for Monica Siebenberg's grace over her sister's wit as the Buick raced up the empty rue Bonaparte. Behind them in the night sky, Sacré-Coeur was like a tiny acropolis.

"You are very quiet, Justin," David said to the shadow in the back seat. "Did you know that one of the redheads was analyzed by Lindt in Zurich?"

"Really—and did you know they were tarts?" Sunda laughed. "Now that Siebenberg beauty is fascinating, though she would not be right for you. Wait, I'll tell you what!" David was suddenly excited. "You must meet Hélène!"

The corner shadow replied with a gesture. Justin Lothaire had not found the courage yet to deal with taxi drivers, and tonight was only the second ride of his life in an automobile. Civilization is a very curious thing, Justin reflected, meaning by this, the car's slippery seats, and Bowden's careless knowledge of power, the style of the dinner and of these boulevards, Monica's attraction, and his share of the rent for the rue de Fleurus, which he had no idea how he would pay. Even Neuville's constant air of boredom with his own wealth had lost its power to hypnotize Justin.

He shut his eyes in the winter wind. Then, reopening them to the star-misted sky above the Jardin du Luxembourg, Justin wondered what Hélène would be like. And thinking then of the simple roof in the Algiers medina where he had always slept under the desert sky, Justin felt an angry, excruciating homesickness.

4

JOHANNES GODARD SAT IN THE MELANCHOLY YELLOW LIGHT OF THE BEDROOM, his eyes on the Tischbein reproduction. Tonight his mind would not focus on Goethe's harmonious stance, nor on the green pastures visible through the window in the portrait. His skin was burning and his thoughts swam. That afternoon, as he played Brahms, Johann's soul had been pure and hungry for God. He had known then that incorruptible love of truth which lifted him above the daily life of the streets. After the music, Johann had enjoyed the ceremony binding his student friends. But the Fleurusians' dinner at Polidor spoiled it: in particular, the staggering beauty of the German sisters, and the familiar way the rest treated them—as if the two were no different from ordinary girls. And then the brawling of the young doctors! Still, must one not sometimes wrestle with Satan?

He lifted his mother's letter from the desk. As he touched the square white envelope, a warmth went through Johann. He smelled again the scent of wood smoke on snowy Bavarian nights.

Wildisches-Gladbach
9 January 1932

My dear Son,
    Times are hard even in our little village. My only consolation is that my son, the last Godard, has reached the highest summit of learning.
    My old head is full of our new dictator. For that is what the Austrian agitator undeniably will be. He publishes his intention to be Emperor of Europe and Russia and eliminate the Jews! Impossible, even insane, as it would have sounded just three years ago, there are now one million in his party! Though only three people here listen to me—all very old—the burden of Germany's destiny is fully upon me. I go to our little chapel, and in my prayers I hear terrible warnings.
    Truly, God has been forgotten by so many of the German people, and they clamor for a king in his place. God's prophecy comes to me just as it did Samuel. "He will take your sons, and appoint them for himself, and some shall run before his chariots. He will appoint him captains over thousands, and will set them to make his instruments of war, and instruments of his chariots. He will take the tenth of your seed, and of your vineyards, and give them to his officers." And to that, Hannes, our brave Germans answer: "So now we also may be like all the nations, and our king may go out before us, and fight our battles." And do you remember what God tells Samuel? Then make them the king they ask for.
    All this is madness. I am not ashamed to be German—I am ashamed to be a Christian! I cannot even say God help us all, since God has washed his hands of the matter. . . .

    In his Paris room, Johannes Godard was smiling. The tone of his mother's letters gave him a tender amusement. Like most devoted sons, Johann respected his mother's affections without feeling any necessity to listen to her words, especially on tedious political matters beneath the mental register of an heir to Kant. With a sigh, he turned out the light.
    That night on the rue de Fleurus, only David did not feel lonely. Tossing his well-tailored clothes in a heap, he slipped on his maroon silk dressing gown, brushed his fine black hair, and fell back on his bed, propped under the wall light with a pad of stationery.
    My dear Luz his hand scribbled. Luz was the exceptionally attractive daughter of an impoverished Austro-Hungarian diplomat, Anton von Holti. David and the girl were secretly engaged. *Is it possible you were not here tonight, my love? That you are in Budapest? If only you could have seen the evening we just had! First, I must tell you about my new friends!*

The moment these words to Luz were written down, her reality intensi-fied—especially his sense of the girl as an Ophelia. Did that make David a Hamlet? Instantly, his feelings for her were not enough and vanished. To complete such an evening would take much more than Luz.

Twisting off his bed, David paced up and down past the framed pho-tographs on the bookshelf. The first was of his mother and father in their ball dress, medals, and sashes; the second, of the white baroque façade of Oberlinden. You could not see his parents' intricate cultivation, nor that the ball was in the Palazzo Farnese, just after the war. And at once David recalled his years of oppressive safety in the ancestral mansion, and how he had arranged this Paris life and escaped here. Was it not he who had discovered these three exceptional persons and staged their evening? It moved David that they had drawn closer, and that he had won the trust of someone like Justin. How fateful that the doctors had brawled in Polidor and that his friend had seen the cook rescued.

But just as Luz had fallen behind, the evening itself was falling behind. Even these events were not enough.

David stood under the dark ceiling, outside the circle of the lamp. Past these walls, beyond the cobbles of the rue de Fleurus, lay awake the city of dreams. And beyond France lay continents of forests and mountain ranges uncharted by the imagination, the sleepy farms of a thousand wisely ignorant peasant cultures. Amid all this human wealth, rising from the dawn mists, swarmed the capitals of great nations, ruled by beings like himself, beings whom David Sunda had the power to charm and gather behind him.

Presently, feeling giddy and vaguely oppressed, he went to bed.

5

JUSTIN LOTHAIRE'S TEACHER AT THE ALGIERS *LYCÉE* HAD BEEN A MODESTLY known writer called Michel Lavil. When Lavil's pupil sailed for Marseille, he had carried a sealed envelope addressed to Marcel Doré. Doré was France's one living master.

In Algiers, the letter had seemed to Justin a natural step within the priest-hood of learning. But now he came to feel the power and cynicism of the European capital, as he discovered the quality of his three friends' education and finally dared to walk in his humble clothes through the garden of the Palais-Royal, frowning above the statues at the tall windows atop the arcades—in whose cafés France's revolution had been plotted—wondering which was the apartment of an immortal genius, the specter of rejection rose before him, and Justin's mind clouded over.

Yet the imagined possibilities continued to fly often through his aggra-vated pride. What if the letter succeeded? Justin would meet the finest thinker of his time, be introduced onto a stage where he might create for himself the role of prophet—a prophet sprung from North African soil. At once the nightmare would return. Would not a genius living within the massive architecture of a palace ignore such a letter? Who was Justin? . . . Who was Michel Lavil? Searching his provincial youth, Justin would scratch for a single moment of grandeur that might redeem him. But there was only a humiliating nonentity. And from the moment his pitiful envelope was committed to the post and no reply came, that nonentity would stretch ahead with the seal of his damnation upon it. At the thought of such an insult, above all to his old teacher, a hatred burned in Justin so harsh that his jaw clenched until it ached.

This struggle continued for two months after the dinner at Polidor. Then one evening, while thinking about something quite different, Justin scribbled a brief note. He put it into an envelope with Michel Lavil's letter and mailed it to an address at the Palais-Royal.

When he reflected on why this had come so easily, Justin was rich in theories. But the true reason was the gray-green jacket. This tweed had been Sunda's, yet it was not too short for Justin. His friend had contrived to present it by first lending it, then disparaging it when it was returned. Justin came to view the jacket as redeemed by him. This jacket would save Justin. Then, feeling confused and frightened by such ambition, he would again try to give the discard back. Still, Justin was feeling almost calm when a white card dropped through the door a week later. It was an appointment to call on Marcel Doré at six o'clock on a Friday evening in March.

Instantly, Justin's memory of his first torture fell away. With it, forever, went the seal of nonentity that Doré might have handed down. During the next weeks, Justin's anger burned again imagining the mortal errors and absurdities he might commit. Despising himself, he reread Doré's two masterworks in search of clues and wondered why the books did not move him as they once had.

On the appointed Friday, feeling faint, Justin crossed the river. He followed a wide street near the Comédie-Française to a door marked number 39. Inside, he went up three well-polished staircases. Breathing heavily, he stood facing an unmarked door for some time, struggling to be free of his passions. And at that moment, Justin Lothaire's entire being longed for a future in his cousin Ahmet's bicycle shop.

Yet at six o'clock when Justin returned to the landing, lifted his brown hand, and heard a bell ring deep in the invisible chambers, he felt that the worst was behind. Justin heard footsteps: *the footsteps of Marcel Doré?* The door opened.

"Come in, Lothaire, come in."

Perspiring on the dark landing, Justin blinked at the obscure shadow framed in the sunset. He could just see two eyes observe him mildly. Justin grinned back, despite his jacket, loathing himself so much that he could not move.

"Step in, young fellow. The coffee will be cold."

"Thank you." Justin's voice thundered in his ears. Could someone so human, someone who lived and breathed, carry the name Marcel Doré?

Justin was led, as if blind, into a broad sunny salon. Four worn sofas faced one another in a square. On the walls hung portraits on silk of stiffly seated mandarin dowagers. Where the rich ginger sunlight fell on the silk, the delicate outlines seemed to dissolve. Justin's host paused in the door to the next room. Marcel Doré had a Roman nose and bony cheeks.

"You know, nothing at all is expected of you here."

6

FOR SOME MINUTES JUSTIN STOOD, LOOKING DOWN ON THE INNER GARDENS, offended and confused. Was Doré testing him? A strange resignation was creeping over Justin. He began to imagine the famous Europeans who had been in this room—and in this society of great wisdom, Justin tasted for the first time what it was to be free. The portraits gazing down from the wall seemed almost familiar. His mind cleared with the flight of lofty subjects. Hugo, Voltaire, and Balzac were presences here.

"Well, then!" Doré had come back into the room, bearing a small tray. They sat down on facing sofas. The writer busied himself, seeming not to notice that long silence, and again Justin experienced stirrings of hostility.

"How is Michel Lavil?" the old man inquired. "You know, he is a fine man, though as an artist he has lived too close to the desert. Do you intend to make that mistake?" Doré was suddenly watching Justin's face with such sympathy that he could only wonder what the old man wanted to hear. "You must build and build, with never a moment's rest. If you stop, all is lost. Look" —Doré waved at the walls, the sunset in the windows, the gloomy facades of the Palais-Royal—"aesthetics, a rich unashamed life of austerity. But do you expect to marry?"

Doré's quaint tones rustled mysteriously among the ancient silks, and Justin felt overwhelmed and grateful. Yet as he recognized the superior spirit whose distant light had once guided Justin's solitude, the mood of opposition stirred in him. "I have not considered marriage," he said.

"Be very careful—in marriage you risk your ear for the truth. Have you not heard people who have come to grief in their marriages? They speak of humor without laughter. They speak of tragedy and do not weep."

Justin could not help laughing at such perfection. Doré answered with an infinitely gentle chuckle, and again Justin felt anger stir. There was something degrading in such certainty. The old man seemed to be seeing things in him that Justin could not. The sensation was intolerable.

"Why do you need this palace?" he asked, and felt sick at the edge in his own voice.

"If I live here"—Doré gazed around the pleasant room—"some corrupt man will not use it for his ambitions. Taking these things for granted reminds me what has true value. Also, because such architecture has power over others, I must work harder to justify my right. Finally, Justin, one is not afraid of life."

The last words were spoken with an air of studied patience that irritated his listener even more.

"I suppose you believe in God?" Justin said, and his heart sank, for his inadequacy had never struck so clear a note. Was Justin an instrument unsuited to play great music? Yet Doré was considering the question with the utmost respect.

"God, my dear fellow?" he reflected. "God is the same in all religions, even communism. He is the single missing principle. Yes, I believe there is a single missing principle. But harmony comes from nature—that is a principle which is not missing."

As this strange old man under one of the Chinese ancestors answered his question, Justin felt his heart sicken. Had his last defense just fallen? What had he been defending? Doré was sipping his coffee, it seemed, as if watching to see what Justin would do next. Questions flooded up. What did the writer live for, what had he seen? How much more did he know than ordinary men? Marcel Doré had sunk down until his childish eyes were scarcely above his knees.

"Do you feel a need to know everything?"

Justin took out a cigarette. "Everything, Monsieur Doré? Who knows everything?"

"Yes, to have complete mastery?" Doré insisted kindly. "Why such impatience? Why is it so painful to wait?"

Justin had no answer to this question, which probed at some deep, unanesthetized area of his sanity. Still, he heard his voice answer the Frenchman. "Because I am desperate. . . . I have nothing!" And through this breach in Justin's pride surged up the whole shameful, indigestible bitterness of his life. He felt himself close upon the most abject confessions.

"No, wait!" came Doré's soft, beautiful voice. "Don't say what you will not forget having said."

Justin looked up, and at that instant he had understood. He and Marcel Doré might actually become friends.

"Listen to me, Justin. I will tell you what you would like to hear. You must forget being perfect now. Have you never heard of time? One day you will achieve whatever you wish. But do not forget how to live. It is not enough to lament with the damned in the streets. It is your work to save them with beauty."

Their laughter rang through the room. Justin's despair had awoken Doré to say things he only said to himself on paper.

"So why not tell me now about your golden Mediterranean youth," he went on. "Then you will meet my sister Anna, and I will show you our attic. Many excellent men have worked there. When you are out of finances, you may stay as you wish. Now go on, tell me. I would like to hear."

Twenty minutes later, Justin was still crouched forward on the sofa telling Marcel Doré the story of his life, something Justin had never done before. He had lost hold of his anger. This old sage and he were bound now by the astonishing promise of the atelier. But as Justin spoke, it was not like his life at all, with its insoluble cruelty and desolation. Instead, it seemed almost rare, a glorious exploit made acutely fascinating because it led out of damnation to this room, which they both knew was the summit of the civilized mind. It was no longer the story of despair but of salvation.

Justin did not notice when the sunset fell behind the facing roofs, nor when the chandelier was lit. Nor how the tray had vanished from the low ebony table. But at a certain hour, Justin's story came to an end.

"And thus you worked your way out of the casbah. Yet tell me now, Justin. Was the desert not sublime, and even preferable to this?"

"It was inarticulate!" Justin said bitterly, and a fresh terror of that life overwhelmed him.

"You were awoken by . . . understanding? Ideas made you discontented?"

"Intelligence gave me hope."

"And without this hope, could you not have stayed and discovered happiness?"

"You think I should not have come?"

"We are immensely grateful—but *should* we be?" The old man smiled, holding up one finger. "You saw before you in your dream the vision of a tremendous enlightenment. What *you* have accomplished your whole class could accomplish. All that is needed is a prophet capable of complete and uncompromising love. Am I not right? And with a morality as unselfish as yours, you demand that it be you who leads the flock out of Egypt. There is no choice. Not for you, not for the flock. The capacity for spiritual life you discovered in yourself is a law which cannot be the accidental property of a self-recognized few. Only utopia for all men would excuse such personal pride."

"I know . . . I know." Justin's face twisted with concentration. "That has been the principle of dictators and generals."

"Perhaps, but think of wars like the last one. Think of a species willing to commit any crime. What if this were the condition of the human masses? What if, as you perfect yourself, you find that common men are not saved with you?"

"They will be!" Justin said. "They wish to be saved."

"Let us hope. But if they do not? If your qualities do not arouse the general populace to erect a new Athens? If you are forced to a decision between accompanying the people into darkness or cultivating your own enlightenment for its own sake? What would be your choice?"

"Darkness!" Justin said with feeling. The moment it was out, they both heard the contradiction, and an embarrassment came between them. Had not the whole gist of Justin's story been the flight from ignorance?

Suddenly he felt that the meeting was over, and he was afraid. Obscurity was waiting for Justin Lothaire outside Doré's windows. And with a horrible shock he recalled the last hours and knew what had happened, and he thought, This strange old man knows everything I think and feel as no one in Paris or the desert ever did—not even Lavil! And thinking of the sweetness of this old man's soul, a wave of the most chaste and grateful love rose in Justin's throat. He fought to master his voice. His face was very grave.

"Thank you, Monsieur Doré," he said. "You honor me."

These were the first words of respect that Justin had ever spoken, and they felt good.

"It is a small thing." The Frenchman rose feebly from his sofa. He bent to switch on the table lamp. "I confess Lavil has not done badly with his protégé. Visit me next week."

"Like today?" Justin said, in a suffocated voice.

"Thursday, for coffee," replied the little man softly. It was as if Justin were no longer there.

Justin Lothaire never described his meeting with Doré to the Fleurusians. But from that early spring, there could be seen about him a mysterious certainty, almost like holiness. Gradually he stopped being seen in the gray-green jacket.

7

EASTER WEEKEND HAD COME, AND DAVID SUNDA'S STUDENT CIRCLE WAS INVITED to dinner at the Le Trèves'. Pierre Le Trève, who owned oil wells in Arabia, had studied at Heidelberg with David's father before the war, and David was like a son to the family.

Neuville promised Johannes that he would drive the Fleurusians. A friendship had sprung up between Johannes and Robert, and as they crossed Paris the philosopher was in a mood to laugh at the ironies of this American, in whose life sleek mistresses came and went without a trace of seriousness. Especially tonight, after several hours playing Brahms sonatas, tormented by melancholy glances of his new partner, Helga. Just as with Gretchen, at home in his mountain village, Johann had not discovered the way to respond.

The Le Trèves lived near the Étoile, in one of those baroque mansions Bonaparte had presented to his marshals. Only as the car turned in through its iron gates did the five students break off their humorous advice at Johannes's expense.

Presently, after climbing a staircase of pink marble, they were welcomed into an ornate drawing room among fifteen people of both generations.

Justin and Duncan quickly fled to the fire, cheerfully snapping and gusting under a mantel clock. But now David Sunda's friends were being introduced. Turning from the clock and its two reclining gold nymphs, Justin held the hand of a red-faced old gentleman with an oblivious smile. Someone spoke the name of the German ambassador, von Siebenberg. Arriving beside a powdered grandmother seated by the hearth, Justin felt himself pulled down by the wrist onto a tapestry bench, close to the burning logs.

"A *pied-noir*—thank God!" The ancient woman jerked Justin's hand. "There are altogether too many Germans and English here tonight. So tell me about yourself. Your country is dear to me. There is Arab blood?" Her deep, vinegary voice rang out. "And your mother's lace concern—tell me where, Justin. By that mosque above the casbah? No? Then which?"

Grandmère Le Trève had reached that insatiable old age, in which curiosity is as unfiltered as a child's. In five minutes, despite her victim's sober smile and stubborn evasions, she had—with that talent of old peasant women for beating mules down steep trails—teased secrets out of Justin that even his close friends did not know. In ten minutes he was disarmed, his kidneys throbbing from the heat, feeling not unpleasantly violated.

"Look, oh, look—he's smoking!" sang a shrill, merry voice.

Justin felt a tug at his tweed jacket. A smell came to him of singed wool. As he stumbled to his feet, a short, black-haired girl skipped in front of Justin with a peal of laughter. She began to tug at his buttons. Even before he remembered why, Justin knew that this jacket must not come off.

"Come along! Quick, quick!"

Giggling now, the girl drew him by his jacket until they came to the entrance table. On the marble stool a basin of floating roses.

Scooping the flowers onto the floor, the girl pulled the tail of Justin's jacket until it went in the water. Looking up then at this grave young man with his jacket draped in the bowl, she clasped both hands over her mouth. In the glitter of crystal and brasswork, their glances crossed. The girl's smile faltered and she danced away.

Justin took out a cigarette, feeling annoyed, yet somehow in human contact now with this threatening place. Through the next hour he imitated the others: that is, he moved about carrying a glass of Pernod. Yet despite his habit of absorbing all impressions, tonight he noticed only the girl—who must be the Hélène whom David had mentioned, the old woman's granddaughter. What was there about her? Justin wondered, and he felt a deadly relief that no one had seen his ancient striped braces. The Frenchman surrounded by young people close by Justin must be the girl's father, a handsome man in his mid-fifties, in a burgundy jacket.

At that moment, Monsieur Le Trève stood at the fireplace between

Johannes and Monica von Siebenberg, listening to a speech aimed at him with consummate flattery by Neuville, on the splendor of oil.

"I am afraid Robert is right, but of course, there is uncertainty over our Syrian fields at Mosul."

Nearby, on a sofa dwarfed by a tapestry of knights in battle, Justin noticed David seated with Hélène's hands in his. The two were smiling and David seemed to be flirting with her, as older men tease young girls.

"I do," Hélène protested, in a voice choked by excitement. "I do have secrets!"

"No, you don't. I know everything. Nothing is hidden from me."

"Tonight I have a deep, deep secret."

Assuming a hurt expression and holding out his arms, David said, "But I love you anyway." Then he laughed.

"No!" Hélène snapped, pretending not to forgive him. "You belong to Luz now."

What a strange face she has, thought Duncan, standing next to Justin and near enough to smile too. With her large nose, overfull lips, and insufficient chin, the girl would not be called pretty. Yet she was so very frank, so taut with feeling. Duncan watched her huge eyes, somehow sad and laughing and already sprayed with wrinkles. And then all at once Duncan was struck by a resemblance—was it to Lothaire? Unmistakably, alone among all her family, Hélène did look like Justin.

The dinner bell had rung, and the guests moved into a room lit by candles. Duncan found himself seated next to Monica von Siebenberg, dressed in a lilac sheath with her face like an exquisite invitation to love. At once the American's mind drained of things that he might say. Instead, he observed Le Trève at the table's head, tenderly helping his wife to avoid catching her dress on her chair.

For, unmistakably, after twenty-five years of marriage, the Le Trèves were still in love. Pierre Le Trève was still the thin, gracious veteran of industrial battle, in which the strong took the day. Eunice Le Trève, with her generous figure, waved reddish hair, expensively dull clothes, and her rather shrill and aggressive triviality, seemed a typical French *haute bourgeoise*. Yet behind its conventional bigotry, the household was oddly shy and lonely in its closeness. Its harmonies and disharmonies could still torment both parents and children—even Hélène's stupidly handsome brother, Jean-Marc, whose conservatism protected him from most strong emotions. In the Le Trève home, unusual among Paris's great families, there were always new faces, along with a few foreigners and others of indeterminate origin.

Duncan was not the only Fleurusian distracted from the conversation along the candle-lit table. Halfway down stood two enormous urns of fruit. This fruit was so unnaturally large and ideally colored that Johannes was about to reach out and give a pear an exploratory prod when Hélène seized a plum and sank her teeth in it. The red juice spilled down her chin.

"My God, Hélène!" Madame Le Trève burst out.

"Eunice," Le Trève called, his manners verging on pomposity, "our daughter can take her dessert now and watch us eat the surprise later on."

"Surprise, Papa?" Hélène stopped eating the plum. "What is it?"

"But you have had your dessert already. You could not be interested in *bananes flambées.*"

"Papa!" Hélène cried miserably, though quite pleased to be the center of attention. "*Maman,* it's *my* dessert, my favorite dessert! Oh, look!"

There was general comment as two soufflés were carried in through the pantry door. *This girl does not look as young as she behaves,* Johannes was thinking. Feeling vaguely suspicious of her, the philosopher was surprised to hear himself laugh at Hélène's chatter more loudly than the rest. He noticed the way that Sunda was blushing, and his own face stung with jealousy at what seemed to be between them.

David's reaction, however, had a meaning the others could not have known. For already, at twenty, his successes were becoming a habit that threatened to turn all women into one. When Hélène bit into the plum, she had left his imagination forever. Seeing her now still at his side, laughing and trusting him, David turned quickly to Justin. But his friend was listening to Siebenberg, now conversing with Johannes.

"You ask the connection between this Blum and our own upstart?"

Siebenberg paused heavily, resting his fork. The older man hesitated so long that Johannes might have wondered if the man had guessed his ignorance of politics. But as the diplomat ate the lovingly prepared soufflé without noticing it, he was reflecting that Monica and Linda had to travel abroad to meet the most promising of their own countrymen. It did not occur to him that in Berlin his own snobbery would have kept a provincial prodigy like Godard from ever meeting his daughters.

"Well, one banner said BETTER HITLER THAN BLUM," the ambassador continued, and a draft seemed to pass among the six guests now listening to him, as if he had opened a cabinet where meat is kept frozen. "Both men are Socialists." The old man emphasized each word patronizingly. "Both are men of 'the people,' committed to uplifting the poor. But it seems, as always happens, that each will be forced by reality—how should I say it?—to modify his ideals."

From across the table, Justin had heard Siebenberg's note of uncertainty. Since the collapse of Weimar, the old fellow must have had a terror of progressive ideas. That fear was hardening the remains of his natural humanity.

"But can you really say that?" Justin cut in. "Léon Blum is a good and gentle man, while . . ." As Justin stared at the expectant faces, he abruptly thought of himself as the others had seen him, with his jacket in a flower bowl. "Why do you say, 'as always happens'? Must everyone sell his soul?"

The moment Justin said the words before this company seated among the crystal and candles, he lost his sense of their meaning. Pride stirred in him.

"You are perfectly correct." David relieved the ominous silence. "'As always happens' is only the language of diplomacy."

"The best men in history leave most of themselves behind," said Duncan from the far end of the table.

"Only the ones with nothing to leave become dictators," David concluded, gazing benevolently around their attentive faces.

"Are there really a million Nazis?" Johann joined in, and at that moment Hélène's voice was heard.

"You are all so bored and cynical! Only Monsieur Lothaire cares about what he is saying."

With this, and like someone who knows that she is the true lady of the house, Hélène rose and left the room. And somehow she was so appealing that the guests only felt entertained.

Justin might have made a scene over the suppression of his argument—which was unacceptable only in being true—but at the sound of the girl's voice he immediately forgot his anger. How had she remembered his name?

Moments later the guests heard the ballroom piano echo under the great ceiling—playing rich with insult to pompous dinners at which people did not care about what they said. Yet around the table everyone smiled and listened, and Le Trève shrugged with his usual indulgence.

"Will your daughter give us a recital?" Godard asked him.

"She will be delighted to!" Madame Le Trève called from the other end of the table, and Johann looked embarrassed.

Will she? Justin thought, still hearing the sound of his name and the piano rooms away. *Oh, no, she won't.*

Soon after, when the party moved upstairs to a music room with huge salmon curtains, Hélène was gone from the piano. Her brother, Jean-Marc, went looking for her in the servants' quarters. The political argument raged on among the men. Duncan found himself seated on a sofa with an uncomfortably low back, struggling to endure a long speech by Madame Le Trève on spas, superstitious cures, and the secret requirements of the "system." Her melodious but hectoring voice seemed to warn that neither he nor anyone else must draw her husband's attention to the fact that her conversation might be stupid.

Presently Jean-Marc returned to the guests, leading his sister. But she was no longer the Hélène bursting to overthrow adult hypocrisy and awaken true passions.

"Don't hesitate, Hélène. The show must go on," Neuville teased her.

Hélène stood in the doorway where her brother had left her, not seeming to hear. Her shoulders were drawn in, her face was set.

"Hélène," Johannes called softly. "Could you play something for us, please?"

"Oh, *do* play something for us, Hélène!" cried Linda von Siebenberg, who was unable to say anything that did not sound vaguely spiteful.

Jean-Marc drew the piano stool from behind the curtains, and to encouraging remarks from the older generation, his sister arranged herself on it. For a moment, Hélène examined their faces with a look almost of pain, then her eyes paused.

Only Johann followed that glance. Justin stood with a frown by the last curtain, lighting a cigarette. Instantly Johann's jealousy flew from David to the Algerian.

"Good!" Hélène said impatiently. She searched among the music folders. Then, knitting her strong, thin fingers, she began.

Next to her father, Johann folded his arms. *Beauty will save the world*, he thought, and a shiver passed through him.

"Ah," Madame Le Trève commented audibly as the opening notes were played. "Beethoven," she added, as if thereby not required to perform the piece herself.

At those first sounds, everyone in the room felt the moment to be his. Only Johannes was disappointed. The Moonlight Sonata, which every little girl learned to play and everybody knew? Yet he was listening. There was something strange in the familiar chords.

And as he listened, it was as if Johann had never heard the Moonlight Sonata before. It seemed almost an illusion that those childish hands were finding such emotions. It was as if, until this moment, he had had no justifiable reason to be here, but that now all was clear. Everything had led to this.

Justin stood stiffly at Pierre Le Trève's elbow. The adventures of his evening among these artificial people, who somehow could not help talking down to him, had become for him an exhausting effort to be polite. Now, across ten paces, he could watch Hélène Le Trève's face and listen to the gathering weight of the music. He felt himself soften. And as he did, the unimaginable rooms, in which lace was the poorest material, softened to insignificance beside this girl and the chords that came from the piano. Once more—as at Doré's—Justin felt the struggle of his life spoken for, and a tolerance warmed through his veins like wine. This family and its elegant evening were not only a corruption but also in some way deeply true.

Under the piano's raised lid, Hélène's face was almost haggard with absorption. No one in the room moved. Unnoticed by the others, Justin smiled. His imagination had just flown back down the unfathomable chain of accidents that united this stupefying scene with the bare lace shop where a mother had begged her son to be grateful for the rich. Then his attention returned to this rapt silence in the drawing room of a marshal's palace. Even softened by the music, the force of Justin's independence was stronger than the narrow life of these people. He felt himself alone, alone as this strange girl in the blue dress with the pleated skirt, who was capable of such art. Watching her arms and shoulders, and before he could stop himself, he thought, *You have never met her equal, and only you can see it.* A sharp pain shot through his chest. And when he thought again of the penniless struggle waiting ahead and of justice and the building of a great literature, half the darkness had gone from it. He could no longer imagine that struggle without this person beside him.

The music suddenly broke off with a loud bang.

"That is enough!" Hélène folded away the music. Ignoring the outburst of admiration, she smiled grimly at everyone but Justin. "We will miss the midnight mass."

8

AS SOON AS THE SMOKE, FRAGRANCES, AND RUMOR OF SOCIETY VOICES HAD vanished from the house—which Hélène loved when its rooms were empty and she could roll on the carpets with Gnome, the family Labrador—she ran up the three staircases to her bedroom on the top floor. Slipping on her dressing gown, she sat in front of her dressing-table mirror. It was the hour when goddesses received their lovers, anointed their breasts, set free their hair. Alone with that deep mystery, Hélène touched her cheek, the wave of black hair on her wide brow. Her too-conscious eyes stared sadly back.

She sprawled on one elbow and began a letter to Luz Holti. Soon her agitated script overwhelmed the page, circling the border and trailing arrows.

Dearest Luz,

I cannot wait until Easter morning, this morning, to write! Even if I did just write you on Thursday. Only hours ago I met—no, let me begin at the beginning.

You know the state I have been in, Luz. I have worried—truly frightened—Papa. Enough, tonight all that is finished. Maman gave an Easter dinner, and your David came with his "discoveries," who share the new apartment. How it must confuse the Faculté to have these four under one roof! Reading this letter in your house in Cetneki, Luz, you cannot know what they are like! The American, Duncan, is tense and dignified, like a great gentleman from some primitive tribe who does not understand what is going on around him. And Johannes! Well, he is far too handsome and has three different scholarships, but his eyes are cold. Being with him is like being dwarfed beside his physique while his head looks round above the clouds.

But Luz, Luz—tonight I lost the world! In its place I love one man! His name is Justin Lothaire, and he is from North Africa. Luz, when I say that name I am alarmed! This man—how am I to think of him as a student?—will never notice me! He looked down on all of us. No, I think we troubled him. I put his burning jacket out in a vase, he hid his old braces from us—no, I will explain some other time. If I only had your beauty, Luz, even if I do know what a burden it has been to you! But let me tell you—if this man Justin is to be nothing in my life, then I will die an incomplete old woman. Don't ask me how this is possible. It just is! I worship his authority, his ambition to be great. You can see that on his face! I even worship his desert. I would live with the mosquitoes on the Congo River if he asked me. But none of these miracles will happen. I am alone at this altar, and do not dare look back. I am twenty, I am powerless! Pity me, my sweet friend.

Your
Leni

9

ANOTHER TWO MONTHS PASSED IN THE FLEURUSIANS' FIRST PARIS SPRING, AND they were confronted by the Sorbonne examinations. One morning Justin sat with Duncan outside the corner cafe behind the Théâtre de l'Odéon. He had worked as a waiter at these tables, and it satisfied something in him to bring the others here.

It was a sunny June morning and exams were almost over. The residents of the rue de Fleurus had generated a dozen papers on various abstruse themes. Several hundred books had been mastered, and even Johannes now tolerated Justin's sense that they were in a race toward a firm hold over the world and its problems. Before him lay a pile of newspapers and the remains of their breakfast. In America, the candidate, Roosevelt, was traveling to the Democratic Convention; Field Marshal von Hindenburg's government in Germany might share power with Adolf Hitler. Now, very alertly, Justin was reading about a new wave of Soviet collectivizations in that tenth year of the communist state. On the next chair, Duncan stirred.

"I've been thinking—about Maline."

Justin collapsed the world news and met the glance of a passing blonde in ankle-strap high heels. Side by side, the friends gazed across the street through the fence of the Luxembourg gardens. Duncan luxuriously tilted his metal chair.

"Now why do they always look at you?" he said.

"Because they know what I think. And now, about Maline?"

"You give this lady your time, Justy. Would you ever marry her?"

"What if we were from the same mold?" Justin said, holding his coffee in both palms.

"What about the Trève girl?"

"So even you are in love with her. Listen, when you wish for the truth you go to books, I go to Maline."

"To reassure yourself—like Dr. Lindt."

Justin smiled, then nodded his dark curly head. "Hélène is a surprising character. But that is David's life. I'm not what she wants. What *does* a girl like that want?"

"Justin, why waste time with Maline? See Hélène once. Find out what she wants."

"Le Trève would not let me in his palace off my leash."

"Trève's not such a bad type. There isn't anything to be proud about."

"No. You take Hélène out!"

"Oh, you'd expect her to fall for Godard. But David says it's you."

The two students paid. They continued lazily on under the heavy tree branches, Justin feeling a little giddy after Duncan's words. To anyone else Maline's basement, smelling of cats and pasted with pictures of models cut from magazines, would seem unnecessarily miserable. Whatever Justin said, the Le Trève girl had given his thoughts no peace. Could she really be interested in someone like him? He had not come all this way for such questions. Justin thought of Doré's invitation to a prize-giving in two days' time.

"Bring one of your muses," the old man had told him. "Be careful, I will judge you on your taste."

Justin's heart was beating violently. Excusing himself, he returned quickly along the Luxembourg gardens. Upstairs in the empty apartment the balcony stood open. David's address book was in the salon. Le Trève—it was a Passy number.

"Good morning, is Hélène at home?" Justin felt drowned by his own voice.

"Yes . . . hello?"

"You probably won't remember me." In the student kitchen, he bowed his head.

"Is it Justin?" Her voice laughed musically.

Almost before Justin recognized the gentle frankness which made it Hélène, he felt the strain in her silence. Yet she accepted the invitation at once. That was only because it was to a gathering of writers, he told himself. Again, as with Doré himself, as soon as Justin's gamble met with success, it felt so natural he forgot the warning taste of defeat.

10

ON THE APPOINTED EVENING, JUSTIN WAS WAITING FOR HÉLÈNE IN THE GREAT hall of the Le Trève mansion.

She came down to meet him in low shoes and the same blue dress with the pleats. Her black hair was held back by two combs from her high forehead, out of her gray eyes, which seemed about to laugh and cry at the same moment. But this French girl's way with him was cooler and more polite than in my memory of her he would have thought possible. Barely conversing, they took the train to Palais-Royal. By the time they got there, Hélène's politeness had turned tragic.

"Aha, Justin!" Doré answered the door himself, smiling puckishly in his sagging gray pullover. "So, your young lady?"

Trailing the old sage into the inner salon, Justin saw the change in the girl. Her somber chill had vanished. At his side was the generous, excited being he remembered—a spirit as full as the voice of dreams in a child's bed-time story.

"You are Marcel Doré," Hélène said softly. She sent Justin a questioning look as the old man took her hand. And in her subdued respect it was clear that this young woman held literature in reverence above all earthly things and had a special intimacy with Doré's writings, but that she would not embarrass the old man's modesty by treating him other than in an ordinary and casual way.

With a surprised grin at Justin and a little bow, Doré acknowledged her tact. "I hope the ceremony will not bore you," he said. "At least, *à trois,* we can have a pleasant dinner beforehand."

Hélène laughed warmly without looking at Justin, and his earlier anger turned to depression. She was not an unworthy distraction, after all. The old man had seen her quality at once.

But it was too late. Through dinner—at a favorite bistro with a fine Breton menu—the injustice stayed between Justin and Hélène, a flaw in the elements. Though Justin was outwardly calm, he grieved inwardly at the trust from which he had excluded himself. Doré now began questioning Hélène on her knowledge of his books. And she answered without affectation, even criticiz-ing certain subtleties of tone and structure, but always with charm. The old man was delighted, once even thumping the table with his fist. But whenever Justin added something, or their gaze met, Hélène dropped her large eyes.

Some time after nine they rose from the table. And waving down a taxi, Justin's first, they recrossed the river by the Pont Neuf. The gathering, Doré explained, was at Gregor Lambert's *salon-gauchiste* in the Marais, in honor of the little-known winner of an influential prize. The three were soon entering the damp courtyard in one of the quarter's old *hôtels.*

Though the faces in the casually crowded room upstairs might belong to the most celebrated thinkers of his time, to witness their welcome of Doré and their curiosity about his young friends only deepened Justin's sick feeling. For months he had kept his pride secure, but he could not help being in love with Hélène now, so sure was he of her moral depth.

Presently, they sat side by side with wineglasses against the rear wall, fac-ing the door to a winter garden. A series of excited, painfully self-important introductions was being made. Rosa Lambert paced the carpets, smoothing her short gray hair and speaking with an American accent.

"You all know Jean-François d'Issipe's writing," her warm voice said, "but you will hear more today. Jean-François, I have made sure there are no publishers here"—there was laughter—"or other businessmen. So you can say your worst. Afterwards, Nina will ask you for contributions for our comrades in Barcelona. These are exciting days for Spain. Yes, but even with the Jesuits broken and the amnesty, even with Catalonia free and seven thousand new schools, it is not enough! Comrades, this is only the beginning! So I thank you in advance. And to our esteemed Marcel Doré, my thanks that you could come!"

Justin and Hélène sat soberly on their sofa, with the old writer between them. Beside what was taking place in Justin during these first thirty minutes, the activities in the room seemed hopelessly dull. He was so conscious of Hélène's fingers and knees, motionless beyond Doré's, that all arguments and faces dissolved before him—even the meaning of this woman's speech and the fact that at last Justin had come to the heart of the revolution.

A slight, fastidiously dressed pedagogue of thirty walked to the far lectern, improvised from a tea table and a stack of encyclopedias. For the first time, Justin was aware of abstract paintings, African statues, and potted trees. This fellow's book had hypnotized Justin two years before in Algiers with, as the critics observed, its "precise and merciless recitation of human futility." D'Issipe's wall-eyes, which seeming to focus on nothing at all, gave the impression of privileged absorption. With a slack smile and a soft lisp, he began to read.

Justin's arm, stretched behind Doré, was touching Hélène's raincoat. Did she already know of his state? Straining to hold his hand still on her collar, Justin could not doubt that she did. At the thought that she might be taking pity on what appeared to be an advance, a fury rose in him. Drawing his arm away, he instantly felt the bliss of renunciation. But his freedom was brief.

The reader standing before the glass wall had paused. Justin felt the eyes of fifty men and women focus on him; no (to his deep relief)—on Doré. The old man sat very still. Was d'Issipe going to read from Doré's work? It was at this moment that Justin saw how far he had come from a lace shop on the rue Mahbu. How was a mere student to enter into this vanguard of intellectuals over whom he had no conceivable influence? At this ultimate irony, the last independence drained from Justin's already weakened soul.

Clearing his throat, d'Issipe read from the chapter in Doré's *Voyage* where the lovers meet at the Gare du Nord after three years of anguished separation. The familiar words calmed Justin, but next to him on the sofa Doré was drawn and pale. His freckled fingers rolled the creases of his trousers. At the lectern, d'Issipe seemed to find that the words he was reading into the expectant hush moved him as his own had not. And those same words were coming back to their author—terribly definite and polished by readers' eyes, to the exact limit that his ruined generation had lived and felt them. Then the words receded from the old man as boyhood summers recede, and it was over.

There was clapping, and a young Vietnamese whom he might one day know well said something to the man at Justin's side. As if remembering he was not alone, Doré abruptly held up his hands, with a smile that seemed to say, Ah, my children, that was long ago! Glancing at Hélène, Justin saw her fold away a handkerchief.

Then, with a suddenness that made him flinch, Rosa Lambert paced between the hanging bulbs, rowing her arms and swinging her lace shawl. The talk returned to the world movement. And at last, even as he sensed Doré's aloofness and the distracted way that Hélène was staring at the bronze nude of a kneeling sprite, Justin Lothaire heard the talk, which once the desert wind had whispered to him, of discipline, cells, the oppressed multitudes, and revolutions already well under way. Sooner, much sooner than he had dreamed, people like this girl's father would be extinct. These intent faces along the walls would be the *chefs*. Now, for minutes on end, the old man and the girl vanished from Justin's concentration, freeing him from his vulnerability. He soared on the purest moral ether, tasting the day when the trusting multitudes would be led out of bondage, when this new world elite—a genius aristocracy in rags, wise and incorruptible—would seize power. Justin was not afraid of an absolute state. Only the state could do for the human conscience what millennia of prophecies and emperors' tombs had failed to do. What could it matter if Justin never wrote a masterpiece or ever saw Doré and Hélène again? This was a faith worth dying for, maybe even killing for.

The Lambert gathering drifted apart well after midnight. Outside was the breathless, humid night. As soon as the gate banged shut and he was alone again with the old man and the girl, Justin lost his strength. The vague grief was back. Hélène sat between them on the taxi seat, with Justin turned sideways to see Doré's face.

"The evening was a triumph for you, Monsieur Marcel," Hélène said, the moment the taxi had started.

"It is hard to hear oneself read out loud."

"Oh, no," Hélène cried softly. "What the other man read was not art at all. It was mechanical and easy. Your scene in *Voyage* had such emotional courage."

"You think so, my children?" Doré turned his wrinkled face to the spring breeze coming through the open window. When the taxi stopped on the rue Saint-Honoré, the old man did not let them get out. He paid the driver enough to finish the trip.

"Take good care of this young person," Doré said, looking closely into Justin's turbulent face. "There are not many like her in Paris." And holding Hélène's shoulders, Doré gave her a fatherly kiss on each cheek: slowly, to emphasize his great honor.

11

"JUSTIN, HE IS SUCH A WONDERFUL MAN," HÉLÈNE SAID, LOOKING BACK AS THE little figure in the overcoat and homburg vanished into a blackened arcade. Hearing the warmth in the girl's voice, Justin experienced a sudden violent jealousy.

"Yes, Doré is the best of the old school," he said.

Hélène looked at him in the shadows. Justin's intelligent face, the face she loved, was set and hostile.

The moment Justin had spoken he felt a shock of remorse, and a charmless silence deepened between them.

When the taxi was two minutes from the Le Trève house, Doré's money ran out. Forgetting his few francs, Justin let them climb down and walk. The empty streets around the Arc de Triomphe were nearly black. He could not see Hélène, but he heard the firm rhythm of her steps at his side. Twice Hélène bumped against him, and neither said a word. The abyss was back between them, so stark and terrible that the hard edges of Justin's mind kept dissolving.

They turned past a walled garden that spilled its bushes, then a corner, then another, neither conscious of leading. Fed on this unnatural silence, their emotion had swelled to a violent passion for some sweet contact—a word, a brushing of hands—but both now felt a physical fear of further speech. And as the ruthless pride, the adult passion, tightened between them, their silence had no way out. Then they turned a shuttered corner past a locked kiosk. They were in Hélène's street. Justin thought he heard Hélène laugh faintly then, and a wild, profane hope flew up. In ten steps, they were near the Le Trèves' pebbled drive, still not having said a word. She despised him for being no different from the other two billion people on earth, Justin told himself. And remembering his mother's poor lace shop, he felt a savage hatred of this lavishly protected child.

Beside him, Hélène felt faint, stars moved before her eyes. Still keeping bravely at the arm of the sullen Algerian—he whose bleak pride she feared but could not help trusting—Hélène thought, What could someone like this want with a plain, ignorant girl like me?

The Paris night stinging their cheeks, sick with disappointment, Justin and Hélène came to the gate lamp. Neither wondered any longer whether so excruciating an emotion might be anything but mutual loathing. As they paused in the circle of light, their only concern was to manage their separation with tact.

"So?" Justin set his jaw.

"Thank you, Justin," said Hélène haughtily. "To have met Marcel Doré was remarkable."

"He is a good man."

"A very good man," Hélène repeated, feeling tears in her eyes and no longer sure what she was saying.

"So . . . goodbye."

"Good night!" Hélène said, turning so quickly that her thick hair swung out from her head.

Justin turned from the gate without pausing to see if Hélène reached the front door. Winding quickly away through the sleeping streets, hating her now, Justin felt released, alone with the passion of his people and the nameless struggles of all men. And remembering the trusting poor of the medina, Justin felt the old prophecy of the desert, and how he had been chosen, and the sweetness of life and of universal love.

But as he came out on the floodlit boulevards of the Étoile, he thought again of Hélène and how she had rejected him. And at once, the wonder and prophecy went out of things, and even the rue de Fleurus was not a home. For the first time in his life, Justin hailed a taxi.

"Les Halles," he called into it.

12

SOON THE COBBLED STREETS NARROWED AND WERE UNLIT. IN THE HEADLIGHTS A pack of cats streamed under a parked cart. Presently Justin was conscious of Maline's basement's being very near. He was back in the obscure streets of the poor. Remembering the scrap of paper he had scribbled with names at the Lamberts', Justin read them in the taxi light: W. Brandt, H. C. Minh, d'Issipe, Malraux. He recognized only the last two and could have matched just one to a face, but they were his brothers.

"Stop—stop here!" Justin jumped out, almost laughing. At a grated *tabac,* he turned down a side street, then down a cul-de-sac with a passage at the end.

Through it, at number 3, the basement handrail was wet and cold. Justin's knuckles made a metallic rattle, he waited for the floor inside to squeak. But without a sound the door opened. Maline stood before Justin in her pink pom-pom gown, looking hard, coarse, and carrot-haired. A smell came past her—cats and cheap perfume.

"Come in, then."

"You open without asking?" he said.

"The swine?" Maline turned away without smiling. "Could the swine still surprise Maline?"

Justin closed the metal door. He stared at the cutout models smiling on the wallpaper. To this woman all men were swine. A dim reddish lamp swung over the unmade bed. Maline's jaw, her long neck, and the animal suspicion in her pale eyes were terrible—yet pitiful and wise. Justin would be safe here.

Maline was looking at him with quiet interest. She had just sensed who he was. Dropping the pink robe, she moved close to him.

"Stay tonight. I will give you something."

Justin heard the dim gratitude in her voice, and he experienced a sharp pity and desire. His throat tightened. Resting his hands on the slight, hot shoulders, he bent to kiss Maline's bony cheek.

"I remember," she said, "I remember now."

"I have seen you many times," Justin said, without accusation.

Afterwards, after the loneliness, Justin lay very still while the prostitute slept. She lay with her cheek on her hands, against the hollow of his arm. Sometimes she twitched, like a puppy in its dreams. By the weak light that Maline never put out at night, Justin looked at the mildewed wallpaper of roses, the smiling cutouts in primary colors, the neatly laid out makeup table and two papier-mâché dolls under the Lido poster. He thought about the way her hands had touched him, with a humiliating precision learned through a thousand men. In the depths, love was harder, but Justin Lothaire could be happy anywhere.

Without warning he wondered, was the Le Trève girl asleep at that moment in the palace by the Étoile? And again he began to disintegrate.

Hating her, Justin fought to hold his love for this sleeping woman, who had been ruined by an evil he would never submit to. But did he really love Maline? Sweating with the struggle, Justin remained still. He thought back. After their lovemaking, the woman had shown Justin her garden. It was two meters square and smelled of snails and mildew. Walls with ivy made a chute to the open sky.

"Look, Justin," Maline had pointed up. The slot of night was a faint blue in the surrounding black of the houses.

"That's Gemini—the twins. It's brighter in the desert," Justin said, her back a moist weight against his skin.

"In the desert?" said Maline. "But Justin, you can't see those stars in your desert."

"Ssh, of course—only far brighter. Right now, in the Atlas, a Berber observing the night watch looks at those very stars."

"Oh," came her soft voice.

"Maline, are there many tomorrow?"

"Who? Oh, two during midday."

"Could you . . . ?"

"I can send them to Micheline."

"I would like it," Justin had said then, feeling an almost unbearable holiness. And had that not been love?

The morning after the second day, feeling purified and free, he rode the breezy platform of a bus to the Luxembourg. His final examination was on the French Revolution. That required no preparation. Still, when he saw Johann and Duncan looking down at him from the corner balcony, Justin felt alarm for his studies.

Somehow, though, he was received as a hero. David had passed on Hélène's description of her exalted evening with Marcel Doré. But Justin's defeat that night, and the two days of torment in Maline's basement had shaken him. He felt only the immense relief that no one would ever know of his ordeal.

A week later, having obtained a full summer's work at the cafe, Justin was left alone in the rue de Fleurus. And it was at this time that, with Eli Hebron, Justin Lothaire founded the magazine *Justice*.

13

BY LATE SEPTEMBER, THE FRIENDS WERE BACK IN FRANCE AFTER QUITE DIFFERENT summers. Johannes had been in his mountain village, reading Luther and Hegel, and on climbing trips among the summer pastures to pick wildflowers with the farmer's deaf-mute daughter, who had worshiped him since childhood. And finally, with his mother's urging, Gretchen and he were betrothed.

One day north by train, at Oberlinden, the Sunda family estate, David had been received home as a grown man. That summer there were never fewer than fifteen for dinner at the huge oak table, and there had been many witty, exhilarating arguments for and against the untested phenomenon of a Fascist party, which had tripled, and then again doubled its power in the Senate. There had even been a freakish incident over an old family retainer whom it had been necessary to sack after he marched about in uniform shooting the trainer's poodles for being French.

In Paris, the first three issues of *Justice* had sold well on the street. Justin had formed a new circle of engagé friends. He was even able to rent a one-room office from Lambert.

For Duncan, the summer was sacrificed on Long Island glamour, which flourished despite the Depression. A Penn was invited to every bootleg party, and Duncan had had to endure the ribbing over his European clothes and accent, the monotonous sight of ball gowns in midnight swimming pools, and the contrast between the drinking camaraderie of college swells and his Fleurusians. It had ended squalidly with a Smith girl, in the bilge of a drifting catboat, and Duncan sailed back on the *France*, reaching the rue de Fleurus with a thrill of intellectual awakening.

But the mood of their group had altered. Through those rainy weeks, Duncan and David grew closer. In the comings and goings from the rue de Fleurus, the American detected in the immaculate European's ever greater generosity the vague perfume of his secret life with the unapproachable Monica von Siebenberg. A curious bond had formed too between Johannes and Justin, which marked the first time their philosopher had respected a thinker who was not already dead. As the days grew short, the Fleurusians' alliance darkened.

One evening in early December the students were invited to join the Le Trèves in their box at the Opéra for a performance of the Verdi *Requiem*. David had returned with the news at five.

"Lothaire left two days ago!" Johann called to them.

"Do you know where he is, Hans?" Duncan rose from his armchair. At the mention of Hélène, he had felt his blood quicken.

"Of course we know," David said, looking outside at the storm.

"Yes, and we can hear the *Requiem* without him."

Johannes had come in threateningly, dressed in the narrow-waisted suit the others teased him about. A half hour later, still sparring, the three arrived under an umbrella on the Le Trèves' doorstep. David pulled the bell and turned to his friends with sudden solemnity.

"Well, now. Who will sit next to Hélène at—?"

The daughter of the house had just drawn back the door, and David broke off.

Hélène looked from one to another. "Where is Justin?" Before anyone could answer, she turned to David with a laugh to bestow an authoritative embrace on him.

"We lost him," Duncan mumbled, as she kissed him next.

"So he wouldn't come?" Hélène gave them a careless glance, and then her face twisted. She turned away as a panting Labrador came from the study, followed by her parents. The older Le Trèves were dressed with stuffy elegance for the Opéra.

"Three men are not enough for me." Hélène faced them all, once again in impish humor.

"Hélène!" cried her mother, as Gnome sniffed each of them and trotted off with his mistress.

The three students followed, exchanging glances. Unmistakably, Hélène had changed. Though she had lost none of her contempt for uninspired adult ways, her manner seemed to say, All right, but if I *must* live beside you as a woman, at least let it be rare, vivid, and exceptional!

" Hélène, truly!" Madame Le Trève's rouged face turned to her husband. But Le Trève did not wish to be serious tonight either, and he joined in the guests' laughter.

"That's enough, little one," he commented, with formal benevolence, resting his hand on Hélène's head.

And for a moment his affectionate smile seemed to them all, as they stood shyly in the hallway, to single out a moment of great beauty in their lives, to take along with his family's happiness enclosed and protected from the troubles of mankind—these three brilliant skeptics and the unreliable passion of his daughter. Appearing not to notice the fourth Fleurusian's absence, Le Trève rested his watery brown eyes on David.

"And so, welcome, gentlemen! I think this will be a first-rate evening. Toscanini is conducting."

From that moment in the hall, and as the party rode through Paris in the family's black automobile and climbed through the elegant crowd to the box on the second tier, the Le Trèves' warmth and excitement seemed to cloak the world's ills in a haze of well-being. The only realities were the audience, as it filled the stalls and boxes; the tuning of violins and oboes; the urgent whispers of Duncan and Johann about the seat next to Hélène; and the expectant warble from the floor below of many voices, awaiting the arrival of the conductor and of another, higher sound. The highest art of all—music.

14

AS USUAL, PIERRE LE TRÈVE TOOK THE END CHAIR BESIDE HÉLÈNE.

But behind his formal charm—now leaning out to wave a manicured hand or exchange smiling shrugs with equally soigné personages in boxes overhead and below—was a dread that never ceased to draw at Le Trève's amiable spirits. Among polite society, and in the boardrooms of the Faubourg, the Le Trève enterprise might still be considered a solid venture. Yet the weekly expense of supporting a domestic establishment that made possible an evening like this was at the limit and still growing.

Even before the war, times had been changing, though so imperceptibly that Le Trève had first become aware of it almost subliminally. Already, as he left the École Normale—in fact, at the exact time that he took over the chairmanship from his dying father—Pierre Le Trève had begun to detect around him a tidal drift in the business ethics of associates his father had always perceived as honorable and true. Le Trève was suddenly aware of a certain precariousness in the family's position.

For centuries before Robespierre, the Le Trèves had made the "accommodations" necessary to keep their rank in society. But as he took his place at the ancient walnut desk, Pierre Le Trève had not been prepared for either the destructiveness of the new technologies under his control or the ferocity of his competitors. Even now, years later, Le Trève was without the unprincipled art needed to appease Pan-Arab nationalists over his oilfields. At the same time the monarchists and socialists in the Assembly, in the name of democracy, continued to shift tax structures and the terms of worker relations like a carpet under his feet. Having to face the spectacle of highly cultivated men like himself unable to inspire an increasingly sullen rabble, whose abilities he did not trust, Le Trève had asked himself whether the era for further accommodations was at an end. It was not that he had failed to grasp the ideals of socialism, or the disgraces of colonial rule, or the justification for paying his own employees out of his profits. But Le Trève could imagine none of those things in a Europe without the enlightened family happiness of such an evening as tonight. He knew very well his exceptional intellect and moral nature. What then, if *he* were unable to find a way through the question?

Yet behind these intricacies, the reality of impending disaster was simple. At this very hour, Le Trève was still in thrall to his father's mask of rectitude. He had failed to lower his principles, while around him in the Faubourg were enterprises run by men who had succeeded and whose businesses grew by bounds.

Pierre Le Trève was not used to the sensation of stupidity as he groped more urgently for a solution. At the same time, he was as powerless to humble the family's style of living as to prevent this ominous state of affairs from continuing. So it had been particularly alarming to discover in his only son a hatred of democracy and Jews, as well as a smug confidence in military theory, and then to see Jean-Marc enroll as a cadet at Saint-Cyr. These last months, Le Trève had caught himself considering the question of Hélène's marriage and wondering whether David von Sunda might not have the ideal credentials to take over the family's future. Ten years earlier, when the Germans had madly inflated their economy and defaulted on their war indemnity, and France had invaded the Ruhr, the Sundas had redeemed their land mortgages and grown hugely richer. And David's elder brother, Friedrich, would be managing the Sunda interests.

Just now through the opera house the chaotic din of tuning instruments reached a peak, then fell away. Le Trève rested a hand on the red plush balustrade. He gazed to the level overhead, where his cousin Couve de Gendron was entertaining the Socialist prime minister Léon Blum, and for some reason thought about the subscription being paid for those boxes, and a gloom settled over the evening. No, surely that was unthinkable! He leaned back in his chair. Glancing over his shoulder at David's attractive face, Pierre Le Trève smiled his unfailingly benevolent, self-satisfied smile.

"My boy, would you sit here by Hélène?"

As David exchanged seats with Hélène's father, a thundering applause began.

Hélène was pressed to the balustrade, her whole being focused on the stage far below. A little bony man with a mustache hurried among the violins and jumped onto the conductor's stand. He bowed twice, and a hush fell over the orchestra. The audience suppressed its rustlings. Hélène sank back and gazed at the massive chandelier and the rococo dome from which it hung on a long chain. She sighed, closed her eyes, then opened them and exchanged a searching smile with David. No, she thought, he cannot understand either. No one understands but me and the composer and the musicians. And Hélène experienced a sharp envy of the artists and a need to be free of the pedestrian souls in her box, even of Johannes.

Hearing the silence stretch tight, and then the first ominous plaintive woodwinds, Hélène felt her soul rise in her throat with a willingness that was almost violent. When she looked up, the chandelier lights were spinning drunkenly. It was a piece by the Russian, Stravinsky, to do with the pagan sacrifice of a chosen virgin. The music had all the mysterious intensity that Hélène had always known was in life, which merged with the note of her pulse and with the rhythm of her breathing.

From the corner of his eye, David watched Hélène's profile and bare shoulders. He saw her beautiful skin, her generous bosom, like her mother's, and her sensitive hands knotted devoutly on her knees. Observing the secret expression that tightened around the girl's lips and eyelids at each new mood, he found that the orchestra's disturbing thunder made perfect sense to him, and he felt strangely moved. The music had ended. Everyone round them was clapping and staring curiously at their neighbors. But Hélène stayed perfectly still, only after a long while opening her eyes with a joyful little smile. The rustle of intermission resumed.

"Rubbish! Complete rubbish!" Eunice Le Trève's piercing voice rose in triumph. "How can they ask civilized people to pay money to sit through such nonsense?"

Duncan and David laughed with her husband, as they rose from their chairs to stare at the crowded boxes. Madame Le Trève stayed seated.

"Oh, *Maman*," Hélène said. "*Maman*, it was wonderful—so wonderful."

Noticing her daughter's patient frown, Madame Le Trève had forgotten her own fear and resentment. She was thinking of the girl's odd temperament: how it was in some way excessive and must make Hélène unhappy. With a twinge of tender anxiety, Eunice Le Trève folded her program and rose.

He would understand, Hélène thought, as she was left seated alone. To Justin, who was like the music, it would have been perfectly simple and clear—and in that certainty Hélène felt taken out of herself. Remembering their terrible evening together with Doré, she experienced a merciless pain. A drabness came over the Opéra and its crowds.

The rest of the program was taken by Verdi's *Requiem*. This was vigorously and comprehensively conducted, and Hélène's mother exchanged satisfied glances with Johann and Duncan. Then, very soon, came a tragic moment when David's absorption with Hélène's tragic face was broken by the thundering chords that opened the *Dies Irae*, like the footfalls of an impatient God, followed upon by a strident ascent, then a dizzying descent—leaving Hélène sick and helpless with her own fall—in preparation for the great drumbeats summoning all humanity to the Last Judgment.

When David looked again, the chair next to him was empty. Glancing round, he saw Hélène's bare shoulders disappear behind the curtains.

In the dark at the rear of the box she had stretched out full length on the floor!

From their places, the three Fleurusians exchanged grins and shrugs with Hélène's horrified mother, who had clutched her husband's knee. Because

Hélène could not be seen from the other boxes, it was less embarrassing for Le Trève just to smile.

Hélène was left to lie very still on the carpet until the *Requiem*'s tumultuous finale. During the ovation, she got up and stood with her fingers resting on the back of her father's chair, refusing to meet anyone's eyes.

What she had done was too shocking for Hélène's parents even to mention. Soon Duncan and Johann were escorting Madame Le Trève down across the packed landings. Hélène followed austerely behind her bantering father and David. As they made their way out under the invisible night sky, David found himself falling into step with the plain little girl it had always been such fun to tease, helping her on with her lamb's-wool coat, even lifting her over a puddle by the car so that Hélène's feet would not get wet.

By the time they were back home at dinner—facing each other over the candles and talkative with hunger and the exhilaration of the music—the episode in the opera box, like so much else that evening, had been forgotten.

15

THROUGH THE AUTUMN AND WINTER, JUSTIN HAD NOT, AS THE FLEURUSIANS assumed, spent his missing nights in Les Halles. On the first day of spring the friends were shocked by the news that Eli Hebron had been arrested in a Front Populaire riot. The riddle of Justin's nights was solved three weeks later, when Eli was released from Fresnes in time to help close the tenth issue of *Justice*, and it was necessary for Justin to move back onto his mattress of news sheets. At ten that morning he was alone at last with Eli and with Eli's ordeal.

"Were they harsh with you, Eli?"

"In Fresnes? I am more at home in La Santé."

"Come for a *croque* at Saint-Sulpice. I have a franc."

"One franc? What will you eat?"

"Me? I am patronized by the rich." Justin smiled grimly, remembering the emotion of an evening he wished never to repeat. He rose to his feet as Eli pulled on his jacket.

"A baguette would have been quicker," his friend remarked fifteen minutes later in the place Saint-Sulpice, sitting opposite the sunless façade of the church. They stared at the empty tables around them, both thinking of *Justice*'s dangerous headline concerning the Duce's links with the French secret police. At that moment the story was radiating out through the boulevards of Paris.

"Isn't it strange, what we are doing?" Justin said.

"It is like a miracle."

"Perhaps a miracle that will be closed down."

They looked out on the empty square as the unfriendly waiter brought Eli's plate with a coffee.

"You could tell me about Fresnes," Justin said. "It will make you eat more slowly."

"Ah, the poor wretches!" sang Eli, and he bit without hurry into the hot oily cheese. "As for the condemned—it must be said I made no converts. The revolution will not come there. The victims are even more destroyed than their guards. It was my faith that was shaken."

"You, Eli?"

"Listen," Eli said softly. "In Fresnes there was an old Jew from Kirov. He said that last year in Russia his family was clubbed to death in front of him. He said he saw many, many shot to death in the streets. He escaped to France. Now he is locked up. Do you know, we laughed very much, Justin."

"Yes, we should worry about such stories."

"They say Bukharin may fall." Eli spoke soberly, passing Justin the last of the *croque-monsieur*. "And you yourself know what our little Turk, this Joseph Stalin, is doing to the peasants. These things hurt me very much, Justin. Sometimes one doubts the Comintern."

Justin watched the pigeons circle the bell tower. "There are sure to be mistakes. In a new consciousness there will be sacrifice."

Hebron licked his fingers and sighed deeply. "Are not sacrifices a superstition?" he said.

"And is there a choice? Would you turn back?" Justin said, as the waiter approached among the tables. "Before there was only the barbarism of privilege. Now we have an instrument."

"*Les messieurs voudraient . . . ?*" The waiter stood sideways, tapping his feet. They were two very poor, dark-skinned, unshaven young men at an isolated table. Justin held out his last coins. The man counted them and withdrew. Eli was still concentrating on their last words.

"What you said is powerful in its simplicity!" Eli whispered. "Justin, I envy such simplicity."

"I think we are still hungry." Justin scraped back his chair. "Come home, and I'll boil us some potatoes and cabbage."

"So the rich will patronize me too?" Eli laughed as they walked slowly across the square under the stone saints.

16

ON THAT SAME MORNING IN MID-MARCH, HÉLÈNE WAS LEANING ON HER WINDOW ledge high above the garden. Her hair fell forward as she stretched to touch the willow's uppermost twig. Its rows of buds were like baby's teeth.

Yesterday she had been twenty-one. Across the sunny room her reflection in the mirror was mournfully intelligent—if only it were that of a stupid doll! Hélène thought of her friend Luz, in Budapest. If she were that stupid doll, Hélène might have accepted the invitation to Longchamps—or even to the debutante garden party at Fontainebleau. Instead, she was left alone with her Schubert.

Picking up a slipper, she threw it at the piano. By Hélène's ear there was a sound, a riffle of playing cards. Near her right arm were two sparrows. As she held still, they twisted their heads, then leapt together, plummeting down a whole story before opening their wings and fluttering up into a branch of the willow. Instantly sorry about the piano, Hélène jumped up, crossed to it, and sat down.

But her hands stayed in her lap. My God, she thought, what a responsibility life is! Must I live it as others do? What I have fought in solitude to save was for him. Yesterday I became an adult. Today I will go and speak to him frankly.

Hélène rose and stared at the door. Beyond it were the voices who said no to life. But when she thought of Justin Lothaire, Hélène so longed for his company that tears of shame came to her eyes. She chose her threadiest school dress and an old shoulder bag.

Gnome was dozing at the top of the stairs. He thumped his tail and lifted his head. "Poor Gnome," Hélène hugged the thick blond neck. "Poor old beast."

"Hélène, is that you?"

Hélène called down through the banister. "Yes, *Maman*."

On the landing below, Madame Le Trève blocked her daughter's way, her eyes full of warning. "Hélène! Where do you think you are going? Your father will not—"

"Oh, *Maman*," said Hélène softly.

"Don't speak to me in that innocent tone!" Her mother's voice was shrill, her powdery cheeks quivered. "You think I don't know what you are doing to your father?"

Hélène stood frozen, her eyes filling with compassion.

"You think only of yourself, you are so selfish!" Madame Le Trève's voice rose in the horrible silence, for like all possessive parents, she would attack her child even for the virtues she had given it. "I always tell your father he shows you too much love. You are so full of yourself!"

Just then, standing paralyzed face-to-face with her mother, Hélène experienced a strange relief. How ruthlessly her mother's mouth twisted, how coarse her imagination! Words of outrage Hélène had never conceived rose to her lips. She hung her head meekly.

"I am sorry, *Maman*." Her voice was gathering strength. "I do not want any more parties. I do not care to dream in my room with life shut outside. I do not want to be watched from cracks in doors. I do not wish to meet excellent people I never see again!" And hearing the suffering in her own voice, tears streamed down Hélène's cheeks—tears not of shame or anger but of gratitude. She scarcely heard Gnome barking against her braced legs. "I want to be a person, *Maman!*" And again she hung her head, half expecting her mother's blows.

But there was only Gnome, thrusting his cold wet nose. Hélène lifted her head and saw her mother's tired old eyes fill with tears as she turned away. *What have I done?* Hélène thought, and her soul ached to go and comfort her mother. Just then, to her left, a door slammed. The girl jerked at the sound. What was she doing here, what was it she wanted? Gnome waited on the top step. When he saw his mistress staring back, the dog turned and plunged down the stairs, thick tail waving eagerly.

Hélène took one step down, then another. Surely this was a dream. Now the silk walls opened out on the hall far below. The spring sun fell over her. She could hear Gnome's claws click on the marble. She threw a timid glance back to the landing where the scene had taken place. Then she went quickly down the carpeted stairs. As she let herself out of the entrance, Gnome understood he was not going. He began to bark. And hearing his bark all the way down the sunny drive, Hélène took deep breaths.

It was not until she gave the taxi driver the address she had never been to—*numéro un, rue de Fleurus*—that Hélène remembered she had only ten francs in her bag! To her this seemed a microscopic sum of money. If she were to eat, she would not be getting home that evening. Despite herself, Hélène felt relieved. But what would the bearded prophets of the *rive gauche* think of such weakness? How did they live, how did they get by?

Ahead, through the taxi's windshield, she saw a crowd of bicyclists wheel together onto the Pont de la Concorde. A clear-eyed young man in poor clothes went past her open window, flourishing a newspaper. *"Justice?"* The voice was cut off. And glancing over the heads and feather hats of the hurrying pedestrians, Hélène suddenly knew how little she understood of her father's business empire.

She looked at the back of the driver's head. It was wide and balding, and his face was hidden. Is life hard? she wanted to ask the man. How does privilege seem to you? What are my sufferings beside yours? "Is it far?" Hélène said aloud. Eyes appeared in the suspended mirror, sympathetic eyes.

"Not far now, mademoiselle."

Five minutes later, she was standing by the Luxembourg fence with her tapestry bag. She looked up at a first floor corner balcony. The modestly elegant young woman in the gray skirt did not notice the passing men who stared at her. Her knowledge that, up there, she might face Justin again had appeared on Hélène's face as a flush of alertness, and no one could have avoided seeing this. But the first shock of freedom had taken away her courage.

17

FIFTEEN MINUTES BEFORE, JUSTIN LOTHAIRE HAD RETURNED TO THE RUE DE Fleurus with Eli, in search of the potatoes and cabbage. The French academician Alexis Millerand, who was the head of Johann's faculty, had earlier turned up with his friend Peter Zabrovsky, the Polish anthropologist, to drop off a letter to Johann sent care of Millerand's office. The envelope was embossed EMBASSY OF GERMANY.

These two were not the only distinguished professors who called at the rue de Fleurus. Among university circles it was rumored that there was "importance" in this apartment by the Jardin du Luxembourg. The notion appealed to that figment in every educated man who has dreamed of a Socratic studio, where the subtlest thinkers can debate advanced ideas in relaxed and cynical comfort over Chablis and Brazilian coffee. But as Justin steered Eli along the narrow corridor to the kitchen, the droning voices from the salon beyond were not important.

"Is that you, Lothaire?" David called. "Come and meet Professor Zabrovsky."

"One minute!" Justin called back. Eli had shrugged and ducked into the kitchen. "The potatoes and cabbages are in the bin by the sink," Justin whispered after him. And swinging his leather jacket over his shoulder, the Algerian walked on into the salon.

Their jackets off, the professors sat with David, Duncan, and Johann on the two facing sofas. Giving each a little smile, Justin squeezed the guests' upheld hands. How unwashed and exhausted he felt after three nights spent on newsprint. Struggling to concentrate on these well-fed gentlemen now smiling at him with interest, he exchanged a few polite words, then excused himself.

Eli was slicing cabbage and potatoes into a bubbling pot. Justin heard the ring of the doorbell, then a familiar voice. Noticing his face, Eli grinned and stepped to the passage door. Just then Duncan went past, leading Hélène Le Trève. Neither looked into the kitchen.

"Now that, *compañero*, is a woman!" Going back to his stew, Eli turned down the gas.

After a pause, Justin followed Eli down the passage. In that instant, the proud defenses of an entire year had dissolved. A helpless curiosity came over him. He walked back into the sitting room.

Everyone had risen from the sofas as Duncan introduced Hélène and then, with some confusion, Eli Hebron. The young woman flushed as she sat down between Millerand and Johannes. Justin leaned stiffly on the mantelpiece under the big mirror. Hélène could see him over the back of the Pole's shining cranium. He lit a cigarette and tried not to look at her.

The young woman was having a similar effect on the entire room. Listening with a thoughtful smile to what each person said, she sat submissively in their midst without appearing to hear. Her gray blue eyes circled with an odd warmth from face to face but did not glance up at Justin. Sometimes her fingers smoothed her flannel skirt, sometimes they rose to lift a wisp of hair behind an ear. And because all present felt her emotion without any idea where it was focused, the student salon seemed suddenly radiant with spring sun.

The discussion grew tense, then heated. The question had arisen: What is politics? Surprisingly, not one of them seemed to know. The two professors seemed unashamed to talk seriously in front of students. The more the subject was examined, the less clear it became.

"In Poland we have *always* known what politics was," Zabrovsky said, giving a princely laugh. "On our west border we have Ludendorff's 'East-politics,' a unified Germany of Machiavellians; to the east, the Czar Stalin's dictatorship of the people. And yet, has it not always been so? You see, my children?" The anthropologist smiled over at Hélène. "Politics is simply the lies necessary for crushing your enemy. Don't you agree, Johann?"

With a glance toward Justin, Godard jumped to his feet. "I agree, Herr Professor," he said. "We know very little about order. It is an ignorance amounting to lies. Though why must we see things through the lens of history? When I look back, I see only the few truly brave men who brought light and beauty into the world. The rest were innocent farmers, shopkeepers, and a few aristocrats. A minority of these were enlightened patrons—but the majority kept armies for murder and thievery. These are bad habits man cannot overcome with more armies. Politics itself is a bad habit! Is it not as dangerous to put one's hopes in politics as in history? That is why the Great War was no blow to me, except in the few artists it took from us."

Johann had taken a pace or two, his sunken eyes no longer focused on this sunlit drawing room. In the corner behind him, Eli Hebron sat motionless. Peering at Hélène, Johann softened.

"My hero stands far above politics," he went on emotionally. "He is frightened neither by his critics nor the fresh bad habits of each age. He has the full God-given powers of imagination and passion. But his mind is the master of his base animal nature. In this beautiful being the most powerful forces in nature would be under such harmonious control that simply to be in his presence would be more intoxicating than to stand before any emperor. Think, my friends—a Euripides, a Beethoven, or a Goethe."

Johann had paused beside Justin under the mirror. Arms crossed, he tried to meet their encircling eyes.

"But, Hans," Penn said, waving his empty coffee cup. "Isn't that a sort of feudalism?"

Confused by Duncan's words, then irritated, Johann met his professor's encouraging smile. "*Ach,* these Yankees and their precious equality. What would a world of three billion kings be like, hmm? Will these kings plow your fields and run your trains?"

"We Americans built the damn things, Hans."

The young German ignored the ripple of laughter. He faced Justin. "*Et toi* . . . what do you think?"

At the mantelpiece, the unshaven young man of the streets started, then frowned. "Well, Johann, why not three billion well-fed workers?"

Justin had barely heard a thing up to Godard's last words. He had been thinking that this girl now seated at the far end of the carpet had not once looked at him. In the same instant that he became aware of Johann, Justin felt her eyes fix on him. The blood rose to his head. He took one last puff of a short cigarette end.

"Of course politics may be lies," he began softly. "But after the trenches and the colonial experience? Is it enough to trust in aristocrats? Why not a system of law that all men can believe in? Not of property owned by selfish fools, but a system to which all men willingly sacrifice their personal freedom to share in the struggles of their brethren. Haven't we come further from lies than ever before? Beside the hundreds of millions, what are a few selfish poets, rotten emperors of industry, thinly disguised gangster politicians?"

Justin broke off at the sound of his own name. Had *she* called him? He had not noticed David leave the room. Face stinging, he straightened up off the marble, frowning at the source of the voice.

"A priest is asking for you." David grinned.

"A priest?" Justin said.

"Aha! A deus ex machina," joked Millerand.

Hearing in his friends' laughter that his words had surprised and moved them, Justin laughed too. It was an acute relief that the voice had not been Hélène's, for it gave him the excuse not to look at her. As Justin left the room, Eli sent him a pleased grin.

In the coat passage, Justin glimpsed a black cassock. A fat, black-goateed priest stood waiting, his arms behind his back. The man attempted a smile but did not lower his pinkish eyes.

"Father Jean-Baptiste Duroc," said a soft, controlled voice. "You are Lothaire?"

"I am Lothaire."

"A girl you know well, who is dying of an operation, asks for you."

Justin felt his stomach start down. He asked quickly, "Does she have no chance?"

The healing words of humanism he had spoken among the high priests of civilization had already receded. A negative wind was blowing. Justin felt an angry shame at where they were standing, and his mind flew back to a poor basement in Les Halles pasted with smiling models.

Eli Hebron came from the kitchen as Justin tugged on his leather jacket. "I will leave too," he whispered.

And minutes after Hélène had heard Justin called away by a Father of the Church, she too left the rue de Fleurus.

18

ACROSS PARIS, AS THEY TRAVELED IN SEPARATE DIRECTIONS—HÉLÈNE ALONE IN a taxi, Justin on the priest's motorbike—the afternoon had hazed over.

Hélène's large eyes were not seeing the familiar cafés and sidewalks through the window that blew her hair. How could Justin have left! He must have known, she thought, and she could not help feeling that desperate hope again. Hélène remembered the hot rush of her love—now seeming scarcely focused on him at all but instead suffusing the smoky salon and the world outside with the inextinguishable beauty of all living things. And feeling again the way her own inspired charm had transformed the people and talk around her to gold, Hélène's heart sank. Of course he knew. How could he not have known?

Beyond the Louvre, the motorbike had to wait in a flock of bicyclists while four columns of infantry came off the bridge. Justin waited behind the priest like a criminal being taken to face his crime, listening in a daze to the swinging slap and creak in the afternoon hush. The soldiers were his age.

"These would not stop an army, the poor things!" Duroc called.

"Royalists," Justin agreed, shakily lighting a cigarette.

In the rue de Lingerie, an ambulance was just reversing out. The driver glanced at the unshaven student jumping off the priest's motorbike.

Justin nearly fell down the iron stairs. The priest followed. In the daylight, through the open door, Maline's basement was sordidly real. A girl's body lay utterly still on the bed. Pacing the narrow space around it, a tall thin man in a baggy suit clicked a stethoscope with rubber-gloved hands.

"Hello." A penetrating voice addressed them. "I thought Lothaire might be you. We met at Lambert's last year with Doré."

"Yes, of course . . ." Justin whispered. But he was bending near Maline's matted carrot hair. The pasted magazine models kept smiling as the three of them stood grimly over the low bed.

"Mademoiselle will live, but she must not practice, not for at least a month—to avoid infection, you understand? A shame, such a healthy organism. The women in the *quartier* will be rubbing their hands by now, the hideous crones. Yes, I morphined her. Here is my telephone number if she decides on more bleeding."

Justin felt a rush of humble gratitude for the life motionless on the bed, one that he was bound to. How jarringly remote were the expert gestures and the murmuring of this fat priest and the radical doctor. (Justin vaguely remembered the man now—also a writer of novels on poor folk.)

At last the metal door banged shut. Justin stood alone under the low ceiling. With a groan of furious pity he sank to his knees. For the first moment since he had seen the Le Trève girl pass the kitchen all the brooding moral pride left Justin's face. He leaned closer. Maline's wash-blue eyes, with bruised circles under them, had been fixed steadily on his since he came in. Her cheeks were pallid, the roots of her hair dark.

"*Sûre . . . ne viendras pas.*" The bloodless lips were moving.

"I would not come?" said Justin, remembering the elegant rooms on the rue de Fleurus. He remembered his privileged friends, the sunny balconies, and the expensive clothes and books. And remembering the spoiled rich man's daughter he had chased, Justin knew that he almost had *not* come.

"Will you stay?" The face on the pillow was hardened with fear.

Yes, he would be staying. He was himself again: Justin Lothaire of the lace shop on the rue Mahbu, in the cruel city of salt.

And pressing his face on the cheap quilt, under which the girl was lying very still, Justin began to weep deep, wrenching sobs.

19

HIS FRIENDS WOULD NEVER KNOW WHAT THE PRIEST WANTED WITH JUSTIN, NOR where he had spent the next four days.

Late on the following Wednesday, in a confident mood inspired by their own limitless promise, the others sat up talking in their drawing room, as they often did during that early spring of 1933. First, to compete with Justin, they invented adventures with loose women. They discussed the trench battles of the Great War, little of which, it was apparent, their families had talked about. The Fleurusians spoke of the death by fear, which must pass with that generation. They, at least, were talking about it. And because they were, no such fear would come to them.

At some point that night, the discussion turned to David's metaphysics prize. Metaphysics was a subject no longer taken seriously by philosophers, and fortunately for their friendship Johann had submitted none of his own work. In fact, David's blandly nihilistic essay, "Idleness," had been written only to tease Johann about the grimly pedantic Hegel, with his déclassé worship of mass power and history. It began with a defense of the Russian character Oblomov, whose single function in life was to lie in bed. But this parody had then struck off more urgently into a second and quite original argument on leisure. Yet even after winning the prize, David would confide only to Duncan his gathering discomfort with the intellectual life of cities.

"Therefore, all that is beautiful in life," went one curious passage, "lies in celebrating, among as many persons as possible, that which is contemplative and free—in other words, that which is idle: the honorable idleness of art, which replaces youth with another simplicity; the idleness of love and the chaste idleness of Plato's friendships; the idleness of motherhood, of farmer's between crops, and of schooldays." Such idleness, David's argument seemed to run, proved Time the friend of living things. But when this idleness of growth fails, Time becomes each man's enemy. Then men flee into collective idleness—the industrial city or the army. In terror, man tries to stop Time with his mind, employing mineral inventions to pursue growth outside the human dimension. Vast, tormented crowds build technological cities of death in which they dream of camping and hunting as of luxuries. They have forgotten that in this original idleness there was a fertility in which Time grew everything they needed. For when Idleness grew infertile, cities divided into armies of a greed and minerality beyond all imagining.

At midnight the hall door slammed. Justin came straight in across the murky salon. The electricity had failed. He advanced into the weak candlelight and began pacing around the backs of the sofas, seeming not to listen. When Johann left the story he had been telling, they called to Justin with such sincere affection that he came near. Sitting among them suspiciously, he lit a cigarette.

"So all the world prospers," Justin said.

"It has only been four days," David said, with a shrug.

Justin received a glass from David's hand. Suddenly he looked haunted. As he leaned into the circle of light, Duncan and Johann stared at this hostile stranger's face, come among them out of the night. David held the flagon past the candle, and their friend automatically raised the crystal in his lean hand.

At that moment, Justin Lothaire could feel the bitter concentration tighten on his face, and the holiness leave him. Yet all the loathing he had turned on these comfortable rooms and his student friends during the nights while Maline's fingernails peeled the smiling magazine models from the wall and she sobbed in his arms, sweating until she was dehydrated—all Justin's burden of injustices and undiluted revolt—found nothing in this room that hate could feed on. "Dardanella" was scratching its nasal melody on the Victrola.

"To the devil, my friends." Justin's glittering eyes traveled round their faces. "To the very devil!"

At the last word the chandelier flickered weakly above them like distant lightning. The high ceilings and four young men sprawled on the sofas were lit up, and the treetops beyond the balconies were sealed out by reflections. Amid their calls and clapping, David rose to his feet, staggered, and pinched the candle out.

"Gentlemen, even the Trojans slept."

"But did the gods?" Johann towered over them with a sort of aggressive modesty.

Lothaire had reached up and caught Godard's wrist in a firm grip. "Johann," he said, "have another glass . . . did your embassy visit ever take place?"

As Duncan and David left the room, the chandelier flickered off again. Johann stood obediently as Justin relit the candle, slowly shook out the match, and poured more wine.

"Oh, that was not so special," Johann said.

"All the same, I would like to hear."

Yet tonight the German embassy did not interest Johannes Godard any more than did the tiresome argument in the daily papers over the burning, some weeks before, of the Reichstag in Berlin. For some reason, Fascists were being accused of blaming the incident on Communists, all to polarize European feelings against radical movements. To Johann, such crude goings-on only distracted from the subtle fascination of his own life. He was prepared to trust a civilization made up of people more or less like himself, or who wished to be. But this Reichstag wrangling was so futile and charmless! Could anything on earth be worth all this absurd shouting—and merely over a piece of such ugly architecture?

20

JOHANNES FELL INTO THE SHADOWS OF THE FACING SOFA. HE SPOKE IN A LOW voice, embarrassed by Justin's concentration and groping for any detail that might interest his friend.

It seemed that the philosopher had dressed formally and gone that morning to a boulevard connecting the Champs-Élysées with the commercial Faubourg. At first Johann had assumed that the legation summons must follow on his conversation at the Le Trèves' with either the ambassador or one of his daughters. Wondering if they imagined him wealthy, Johann had felt a vague guilt.

But when his taxi bounced up under the rustling trees between the gendarmes at numbers 13-15, when he saw the efficient bustle inside and heard the melodious, cooing voices of his countrymen, Johann had experienced a sudden light-headed anxiety. Up a carpeted staircase, an old Saxon secretary in a brown suit and glasses led Johann through an empty waiting room.

"This way, please, Herr Godard." The eyes behind the lenses examined him.

And for some reason, Johann had blushed, bowed, and kissed the old lady's hand before he continued through the tall doorway. The sensation intensified of being there under false pretenses, though he could hardly turn back out of the hushed office, with its reflections from the fountain outside. On the wall ahead hung the portrait of a scowling Bismarck. And rising from behind the desk was a much shorter, leaner old gentleman than Johann remembered.

"You are Herr Godard?" The man came forward without a sound, staring appreciatively at Johann's manly jaw.

"Yes, your Excellency." Both men bowed twice stiffly. Feeling his hand wrung once, Johann sank into the deep red armchair. Can it be he does not know me? Johann thought, grinning nervously at the ambassador's small bloodshot eyes, from which the red skin hung in folds, as if from two pegs. Then why had he been invited?

But even stranger was the change in von Siebenberg over the past year. In place of the weary Old World raconteur who had stood by the Le Trèves' fireplace was a dangerously charming German official who stared back at Johann with scarcely disguised impatience.

"We met at Monsieur Le Trève's," Johann continued obsequiously. Whatever von Siebenberg thought the handsome Bavarian scholar with the overbearing manner had just said, he waved it generously aside.

"We have received a message," the ambassador continued. "It is from a deputy of the Berlin Chancellery. You see—two names are mentioned next to your own." The unfolded memorandum that lay on the ambassador's desk had been pushed toward Johann. An acute oppression was descending on his soul. Was his Fatherland accusing him of something?

"Shall we come to the point?" Von Siebenberg interrupted himself with heavy formality. "Times are changing, you understand?"

Johann inclined his head and smiled to disguise his dread of a crime that he might well have committed. *Time . . . changing?* Johann's mind hurried on. How did time change? But this thread of consciousness became lost in the watery sprites that danced on the walls around the splendidly tailored shoulders that faced him.

"A new ministry is being formed," Ambassador von Siebenberg went on. "A ministry for propaganda and education. A very few of our *most* outstanding young scholars will be granted roles in this important event. And you, Herr Godard, are first among thirty names. After all, your father and your grandfather—"

Johann was bent forward in the armchair with idiotic relief, almost forgiveness. "Yes, I never met them!" he cried. "My father was the first soldier on French soil during the World War." In fact, all the Godard men for five generations had died in military actions. For Johann, however, such violent events held no more terror than what the ambassador had just offered him.

"May I answer, then, that you are interested?"

"Oh, no, please don't!" Johann politely waved his hand, "I could not possibly, your Excellency. Philosophers have no business in politics."

The ambassador sank back in his big chair until his elbows brought his fingertips before his eyes. Though it was clear that this guileless student had little grasp of what politics was, that he had spoken on impulse, his comment struck the old aristocrat as an arrogant and tactless insult.

"Oh? And you are quite certain of this attitude? You will *not* be asked again."

"Quite certain, your Excellency!" So it was to be just another tribute to his exceptional qualities. "However, please do convey my gratitude to the deputy."

Hearing such levity from someone so young—a student, who should be

cowed by a room where the earth's most powerful statesmen came and went—
the ambassador blinked several times. "Very well, then. . . ." Von Siebenberg
slowly and gracefully prepared his fountain pen. Unscrewing it and pressing a
ribboned pince-nez into the flesh surrounding his eyes, the ambassador made a
firm mark on the memorandum. Across the table, Johann could just see the
inverted black eagle and, to the left, a file code and the notation, *cc: J. Goebbels.*

Von Siebenberg had leaned back, erect in the high-backed chair. He stared
at Johann with profound coldness as the sprites leapt and trembled around him.

"Well, that is all, Herr Godard. You may leave."

At the time, the ambassador's absolute disgust at Johann's decision had
shocked and hurt the young philosopher. Instantly, Johann had felt an excruciating remorse. Vague, glorious visions rose of himself enthroned and adored
in crowded galleries of European enlightenment. Had he just been face to face
with his historical moment? Even tonight as he described the meeting to Justin
among their comfortable sofas, Johann's voice broke with emotion.

"But Hans, you were superb!" Justin's earlier hostility had turned to boyish excitement. Ignoring the hour and Johann's unhappy face, he walked up
and down the Turkish carpet smoking. "You understand? *Please thank the
deputy for me*—ha! Hans, I could not have dreamt such wit."

"It was only polite." Johann shrugged, thinking how Justin was just a
provincial scholarship student like himself. "You think it was the right thing?"

"Don't you know? It was instinct." Justin gazed at him with respect.
"Look in today's *Justice* before they ban it, Hans. The special camp these
people are opening in Munich."

"What does it matter?" Johann stood pitifully still, feeling even more
upset to be weighed before the mob.

"You are a good fellow, Johann," Justin said. "I love you for this."

Presently the two put out the candle and went to their bedrooms. The great
salon of sweet student memories was left in silence, its walls and ceiling lit
only by the streetlamp from among the branches, throwing speckles of light
that softly swayed and revolved as in the planetarium of a relative universe.

But tonight Johannes Godard had heard again God's prophecy to Samuel—
just as in his mother's letter—that his nation would choose a king. And that
when they had, and they cried again for God, he would not hear them.

21

OUTSIDE BERLIN, ON THE TWENTY-FIRST OF THAT MONTH, ANOTHER TRIUMPH WAS
being celebrated. Throngs of Germans, with a sprinkling of tourists and press,
had been arriving since sunrise outside the old Garrison Church in Potsdam.
Buried among this building's foundations, in a bronze and marble crypt, lay
the husk of the Prussian composer-tyrant Frederick—that same Frederick who

once had shouted to his fellow Germans as they fled the battlefield, "Fools, do you want to live forever?" But today was a brilliantly sunny spring day. The hidden corpse and whatever soul remained to Friedrich der Grosse had long since parted. The guildhalls, crowded colonnades, and gilt statues of the historic old town were hung with streamers, blood-red swastika banners and the red, black, and white flags of the old Germany.

Waiting inside the church were two strangely different sorts of German, strange even for the race of Hegel, which cherishes the antithetical play of yin and yang. Behind the Kaiser's empty pew sat the crown prince, and spread deep behind the latter a sumptuous throng of nobles, ministers and military commanders, led by Field Marshal von Mackensen. Most of these elderly gentlemen, nodding to one another or dozing, were dressed in the embroidered and bemedaled costumes of Germany's ghost legions and dream fleets, the true ones having been stripped from them by the French at Versailles. Down the center aisles, facing these morally defeated upholders of knightly honor, stood files of handsome, slavish young men in brown shirts: the new storm troopers. And in the center section sat their brown-shirted deputies. These browns had obtained their right to be present through fourteen years of "people's" street violence, in which each week sometimes several hundred Jews and Communists had been killed, thus finally murdering the middle ground and—with the death of Gustav Stresemann —German democracy itself.

This, however, was quite to the satisfaction of everyone present. Most of those nodding and murmuring aristocrats knew each other intimately, while the troopers had no need at all to persuade, let alone to know, each other. They had only to wear brown shirts. Naturally, no Social Democrat in the Senate had been invited. For what was presently to follow was a mystical rite, beyond the understanding of liberals and designed to revitalize the undemocratic husk in the crypt.

The Frankenstinian aspect of the proceedings was soon confirmed. At precisely the appointed hour, a rustle of excitement spread through the church and the congregation rose to its feet. The heavy doors swung ponderously in.

Down the long table, framed in blinding sunlight, two men appeared. They stood with a space between them, left empty, like the royal chair—though even at his desk the Kaiser was said to have preferred a saddle. The mustached old gentleman in the spiked helmet was of such enormous stature, his festoon of medals so wonderfully heavy, that the meadows of gray material and ranks of gold buttons necessary to make decent his person could not kindly be asked to fit. Propped on a gold-handled cane, this martial pillar stood, glowering dully towards the altar. The commonplace little man fidgeting solemnly beside him was bare-headed and dressed formally in a morning coat. His straight brown hair was greased, schoolboy-like, to one side, and his moustache cut to fit in a fashionably common square under his nose. This much younger personage was no less imposing than the old general. Though like a harbor tug beside an oceangoing clipper, his force seemed of an opposite nature, dependent on uncouth vitality and the absence of any majestic or graceful feature. Those near the door could see the womanly flushes and faint smug smiles that tugged at this otherwise elusive expression.

The band played a march outside and speakers crackled a *Festspiel* recording of the "Siegfried Idyll" across the roofs of Potsdam. Then everything fell silent. An even deeper silence descended. The two men started awkwardly forward: the soldier, due to his antiquity (the old man had first entered the same church in 1866, next to Bismarck himself); the politician because he was always so. The soldier was Field Marshal von Hindenburg. The politician, an Austrian, was the new Chancellor of Germany. The ceremony was the opening of the Senate for a Third Reich.

Among the nobles at one end of the fourth row, dressed in his father's splendid uniform of the prewar guards, Baron Friedrich Barthold von Sunda waited eagerly. He was placed beside a bespectacled admiral who knew Friedrich's father well, as indeed did everyone.

"Imagine the new deputies taking their Reichstag seats in those hideous brown shirts," the admiral whispered.

Friedrich agreed, though the affront to tradition still seemed to him refreshing. He stretched discreetly to see Hindenburg and Hitler as they passed. Unlike many of his friends, Friedrich had never seen this new chancellor who had already so affected his life. Now, pushing up on his toes as Hindenburg paused above the heads to salute the crown prince with his marshal's baton, Friedrich felt exhilaration and dread. His father's uniform pulled tightly under his arms. He was conscious of perspiring copiously and of the spring heat penetrating the cool in the vaulted church.

From his throne among knolls of red and white flowers, the famous old marshal—old as German Unity itself—laboriously read his short speech, set in words simple and luminous yet devoid of deeper emotion.

"May the ancient spirit of this celebrated shrine infuse the generation of today."

22

DURING THE THREE YEARS SINCE HE HAD TURNED TWENTY-FOUR, FRIEDRICH VON Sunda had been called to the side of his father in the struggle to save the family farmlands and securities, and the three hundred tenants, from the moral and financial ruin to which Germany's cities had been condemned by the unions and the war debt. At the time that his younger brother, David, was excelling at monastery school, Friedrich had assumed these duties with obedience and enthusiasm. Along with the old baron's loyal banker, Ellic Levin, who grasped better than any Sunda the intricacies of their finance, Friedrich had shouldered, like Atlas, the ancient family's future—and, with it, the specter of disgrace. His soul

had been wracked on the deadly mathematics of survival. Every week, sometimes every day, friends and neighbors went bankrupt. Nothing was certain, no
measure mastered one day might not have to be remade the next. Friedrich had
entered the campaign at Oberlinden in full retreat. Shock followed shock, one
unforeseeable reverse following another . . . so Friedrich's good-natured detachment had been broken away. What in 1929 had seemed a troublesome setback to
the family's recovery became a walking nightmare—the flailing against an
undammable tide of loss, compounded by a depression of the value attached to
people and things. What virtue in the European soul could resist such darkness?
How was a young Sunda simply to abandon the traditions of family, honor, and
ceremonial comportment? He had no place below among the rabble. Friedrich's
robust health was ruined. He scarcely slept. Some nights, as he lay awake to
remember what he had once assumed to be his life dreams of marriage, well-bred
children, and serenity—Friedrich felt he might go mad. Gradually he became
aware that the right side of his face was slightly paralyzed.

And then one man had risen among them, a man unafraid to boast again
of Bismarck's great unifications, gather the splinters of Austro-Hungary, and
speak of Ludendorff's glorious ambition to harvest the wealth of Russia.
Who but that man could have guessed what powers might be harnessed in the
single-minded organization of the industrial state, or have called back the
sickened mountain spirits of a proud and noble Germany? After the punishments of the last year, Friedrich now knew he could never live without those
truths. He knew that this one man was prepared to make any sacrifices to gain
them—even daring to resort, as Friedrich never would, to crime and murder.
Could such a being, his genius shrouded in godlike mists of terror and blood,
have been a postcard artist in a Vienna slum, a mere corporal in the World
War? It seemed scarcely possible.

These thoughts were seething drunkenly in Friedrich's head as without
warning the huge congregation of nobles, ministers, brown-shirted deputies
(Friedrich recognized Himmler's spectacles), and uniformed marshals clattered to their feet. A hymn was sung.

In his pew young Sunda swayed with faintness, wondering by what magic
it had all led to this. As he joined in with the others, not hearing his own voice,
Friedrich's eyes filled with grateful tears. But his full concentration—his
entire being, like everyone's in the church—was directed, pure as falling light,
toward this man now hidden by the pulpit save for two jutting legs in striped
trousers.

The hymn was ending. A stillness fell over the congregation. From the brilliant afternoon outside they heard a restless murmur. Occasional shouts floated
in from the crowd in the church square. Friedrich saw the two legs stir under the
pulpit.

The small dark man stepped out. He gave a stiff bow toward the banks of
flowers, though the old marshal's disapproving frown had softened on the

verge of sleep. At once Friedrich's passions—all his education and the breeding of a thousand years, all his despair, hope, and youthful willingness—focused on the flesh and blood standing fifteen paces away. Only Friedrich could appreciate this man. The young Sunda gazed through a golden smoke at the low wide forehead, the straight brows, the staring eyes.

Hitler's speech was somewhat longer than Field Marshal von Hindenburg's. The new chancellor's voice rose, shrill and unmusical, to bound among the shadowy Gothic vaults. The speaker made a visible effort to subdue it, speaking with elaborate yet somehow unctuous gentility.

"So, by a unique upheaval," continued the voice, thus explaining the years of street violence, "in these last weeks our national honor has been restored. And thanks to your understanding, Herr General Field Marshal, the union between the symbols of the Old Greatness and the New Strength has been celebrated. We pay you homage. A protective Providence places you above the new power of our nation."

Across the ranks of uplifted heads, there was an awesome silence. Friedrich Sunda's scalp tightened. Balancing a little forward for a better view of the thick-whiskered *Landgraf* in front, he examined the little politician over the fifteen paces that separated them. At that moment when Friedrich would gladly have offered up his life in devotion, the low-browed stare of the man standing by the lectern had met his. And in that same instant, where so many had succumbed, young Baron Sunda detected an imperfection in his faith. *Can it be that to* him *all of this means something quite unlike what it means to me?* Friedrich thought. But if it was not the same for them both, then what could it all mean, this Teutonic chivalry, this grand spectacle, and the crowd that waited faithfully outside? Then asking himself just what this might mean to the politician with the emotionless eyes, now standing in plain view of the whole church, Friedrich was suddenly afraid. He became aware, over his braided right shoulder, of Hitler's deputies, brown-shirted as Boy Scouts.

The speaker on the altar steps could not resist concluding his words with a tremulous flourish, then glowering down at the three faces in the front row of deputies—one gaunt and deathly, the next dashingly plump, the third somewhat pig-faced. These three, Goebbels, Göring and Röhm, were in reality a narcissistic, crippled, fallen writer; a sly drug-addicted bon vivant; and a sadistic army pederast. They glowered encouragingly back at him from among the shoulder-strapped National Socialists.

Chest-deep in the sea of heads, Hitler solemnly folded his speech. Turning his back to the congregation, he slowly descended the steps into the crypt.

In the stone vault the cool candle-lit air smelled of tallow. A blue velvet cushion was set at the foot of Frederick's tomb. Kneeling on it, Hitler bent the shaven back of his head in meditation. Waiting for him outside the tomb were the most illustrious names in Germany. The body of the man bowed on the cushion felt drained by perverse excitement. *Oh, fools! Were they not fools?*

Fools, yes—that at least was true. For at this hour, all Europe stood within two days of a Law for the Removal of the People's Distress, which this unctuously charming man, as he knelt among the candles, already knew he would force through by senate vote, with a speech of blood and iron and a squad of Blackshirts. And with which, by decree, the devout and duty-ridden German people, whose duchies had once spawned Bach, Kant, and Goethe, would free from all restraint a monster of diseased ambitions. To the imposter dreaming by Frederick's sarcophagus, his well-bred congregation waiting overhead were fools because they placed their trust in him, a man who had nothing to share with them and who never would; a being who feared no god, who was without the limits of moral judgment, and who had openly championed so many impossibly evil causes that the only truth left to him was the power of race. A man, Hitler, whose soul had crawled into this supreme vault out of the human ordure of the trenches. And precisely because the refined strangers in the church above felt the warmest trust in themselves to exploit such a person as he, Hitler knew they were fools.

Alone among the stone inscriptions, the man was wiping his bony brow. Now he rested the handkerchief on Frederick's bronze plaque, beside the folded speech. He peered at the hands on his watch. His mind writhed on behind flexing temples, rehearsing yet again the new Europe on which he would lay his will. This was no natural reign of plants and animals, or of men and ancient cultures too subtle and delicate ever to be understood by one man. No, and again no. This was a huge empty canvas, with himself and Goebbels alone at the foot of it with tubs of paint. So Hitler thought, bending closer to examine the gold Hohenzollern cartouche. Waves of hatred went through him, and perspiration streamed down his swollen temples. Hitler gripped the marble sarcophagus with both outstretched arms. Yes! He would crush everything foreign or modern. He would bend history back by brute force. He would erase Germany's fifteen years of humiliation, along with its slavish culture of pity. He, Hitler, would redraw the lost heroic age. There were no limits to what he would do!

Hitler stayed for one more minute, kneeling in the crypt, alone with Frederick's corpse and the specter of his flight from his own origins. For of one thing he was perfectly certain. He would never be going back down *there!* No, and again no—never again! And that was all that mattered. So Hitler reflected, for his was a ruined life so steeped in the opium of greatness that he would degrade all human virtue before he could admit that he was without it.

Then, with his impeccable sense of timing, the chancellor of the new Reich rose unsteadily. The candle flames danced round him. He passed a comb through his hair, which fell in a straight lock over his brow. Five minutes after he had disappeared, the absolutely hushed church witnessed the black hair, glowering eyes, and little square mustache rise again up the crypt steps—cleansed of Germany's last fifteen years. On his bench in the fourth row, Friedrich stretched to watch Hitler cross briskly to von Hindenburg. The politician bowed deeply over the wrinkled old hand, but without the gesture having a particularly moving effect. Now he was helping the field marshal to his feet. Somehow the old man seemed scarcely to know the person he was leaning on.

Observing from the ranks of nobles, Friedrich felt for some reason embarrassed by this spectacle. He saw Hindenburg take one unsteady step down from the altar. Turning his back and moving like someone far away in a dream, the old soldier gradually disappeared with his historic memories down into the crypt. Now in the light from the stained-glass windows, only the top of his gray head was visible. Then it too was gone.

Outside in the spring afternoon, the Brownshirt band brayed a military tattoo. Several dozen cannon shook the innocent blue sky with an echo that rolled like thunder. Through the streets of Potsdam and Berlin, Nazi bill posters were already pasting up images of Hindenburg and Hitler's unsmiling faces, side by side. On a parade ground close by, two battalions of Röhm's *Sturmabteilung* began to march. A vast frenzied roar, like the first rumble of a breaking dam, burst from the sea of heads packed in the square.

Inside the church, overcome by a loneliness he scarcely understood, young Friedrich von Sunda was the only one among the nobility who remained before the altar. Staring with his asymmetrical gaze up at the body bleeding on the crucifix, Friedrich crossed himself twice.

God's prophecy to Samuel was fulfilled: "Hearken unto their voice, and make them a king. For they have rejected me, that I should not reign over them. And ye shall cry out in that day because of your king which ye shall have chosen you; and the Lord will not hear you in that day."

That night in Berlin, ten thousand grim young troops of the *Schutzstaffeln* formed an immense procession of torches that flowed like an endless river under the Brandenburg Gate. And at the Opera House, Furtwängler conducted a performance, considered brilliant, of Wagner's *Meistersinger.*

JUSTIN

1

ALONG THE AFRICAN COAST TO THE WEST OF HERODIA, PERFUMED Alexandria, and Constantine—at a point where the paleolithic skin of the Sahara softens into vineyards before eluding an infernal sun in the water of the Mare Nostrum—stands Algiers the White.

On the cracked classroom wall, inside a gray *lycée* building screened by the Palais de Justice from the casbah and the sea, the Holy Day calendar indicated 2 May 1924. Over the two dozen heads called by Spanish, Italian, and French names, there was only the humming of flies. A familiar boys' crisis was taking place between ideas and the desert heat.

"Justin! Justin Lothaire!"

At the rear window sat a dark youth with lean cheeks and large abstracted eyes. The boy was awakening from a daydream, for he had recognized the name and the tone used by strangers when they wanted control of him. But he was unafraid.

"Yes, *mon père?*"

"Come forward, please. Face the class."

A sudden anger iced in the boy's veins. No one in the class turned, but Justin felt the current of excitement among the hidden faces. Outside in the friendly world he could hear palm fronds scratch the shutters.

"Yes, *mon père*," Justin repeated to gain time, still tearing himself from his dream. This dream had somehow begun with the sensation of his skin when the class was allowed to take off their shirts during football. *He had been walking the sands at Troy after the attempt to set afire the Greek ships. The sun was high and glittered feverishly on the Scamander. A cloud of flies buzzed among the dead, their postures now fixed and vacant as the fallen rubble of once-sacred temples. Justin stood to watch Agamemnon pass, arm in arm with Ajax of Telamon. Recognizing Justin's high, obedient heart, the Greek king had paused—*

"Lothaire. Lo-*thaire!*"

The boy rose from his desk. He walked slowly up the classroom aisle. When he turned, forty-six eyes sought his with a delicious dread and triumph.

"Lothaire? This is your first essay," the priest began. "It is a shameful beginning. Now please explain to the class what you mean when you answer that '*l'esprit classique* is the love between goatherds and their goats'!"

Justin felt a profound alarm. Was such a sacred truth being spoken aloud in this company? He closed his ears, not to hear the profane laughter. Father Xavier's words were followed by a silence like that of curiosity. For some seconds, Justin did not grasp how this could be. Then he saw: none of them, not even this priest, had understood! It was the most natural thing on earth, yet they had not seen it. The most joyful pagan act, but they thought he meant sentimental love. Justin alone must have seen it. Or was he simply wrong?

"Pardon, *mon père*, I misunderstood," Justin lied.

"Lothaire?" Father Xavier's voice softened into his unpleasant smile. "Pull down your trousers. Now bend over. No, further. Touch your toes, my boy . . . touch, touch."

When it ended, the *lycée* bell was ringing. They were free for the afternoon. Justin went to the acrid hall closet with the letters w.c. on it and wept bitterly for his mother. It all had to do with her. Had it not been she—her flesh—exposed and beaten before the class? But now it was the lunch hour, and Justin's imagination rushed out into Algiers, teeming with the golden sap of his resplendent dream.

Justin took the stairs two at a time. He dived into the blazing siesta heat. Michaud was waiting in the corner arcade down the shady steps with the flour merchant Ordóñez's sons.

"Slumbird . . . goats and goatherds! *Espèce d'ordure! Bicot!*"

Justin skidded on his knees. Fists battered him in small intimate jolts—punishing him, his mother's flesh, wishing to hurt it, wishing to reach in and wound his soul. Now he was up, panting. Murderous tears wobbling in his eyes, he kicked back, kicking at their pale, well-fed, unjust bodies. Michaud slipped and fell backward in the alley. Swinging between the walls, Justin kicked at his face. Punish! Punish the rich merchant flesh!

Then Justin had torn free, weeping with the shame of it. He ran with his satchel past the pastis bar, out across the blinding square where women knitted under the trees. In a minute he was at the little arch into the casbah. He slid under the belly of a donkey staggering with bloody sheepskins and raced into the spice bazaar. Up between the burlap sacks bulging with colored seeds and powders—pungent stench, holy snow-white awnings overhead that stirred and rippled, bellying shadily as sails. Justin fell into a walk. Arab faces grinned and softly called his name. *Justin . . . Justin!* Warm, dark eyes recognized him above hurrying white haiks. Poverty closed kindly around him. He submitted to being freshly alive.

In the pale green shop, Madame Lothaire was mending lace by the wireless set. She had on a darned black dress with padded shoulders. Two combs caught back her brown hair.

"Justin, you scuffed your shoes," the woman said, in her mournful, self-pitying tone.

"What is for lunch?" Justin asked, stooping inside. "And this?"

"It is Madame Michaud's magnificent lace. We shall have to eat noodles."

The scarred tables stood against the coal stove. As he worked around to his chair a shadow fell on Justin's soul. It was the same Michaud who had waited for him after school. Now Justin would eat boiled noodles, in case the Michauds' tablecloth should be stained by the fumes of normal cooking.

Jeanne Lothaire glanced disapprovingly at her son's stained sleeve. "Imagine, Madame Michaud came all the way to my shop herself. I will pray for her; one must be thankful for the rich. Without them, what would become of us poor?"

Justin stared out of the door at the passersby in the rue Mahbu. The woman was ruining his victory over Michaud. He had won back their honor, and she was giving it up! Justin heard his mother's submission and fear every day, and he was helpless against her defeat. Now even the open doorway made him sick.

Justin rose to shut the glass door. The dishonorable noodles were on the table. He concentrated so as not to give himself up. "*Maman*, the scuffed shoes. There was a fight. I kicked Michel Michaud in the head." But instead of triumph he experienced a terror of this staring woman, of her fear and defeat.

His mother's mouth twitched spitefully. "Justin! Oh, Justin, how could you? Michel is such a good boy."

His shoulder almost touching this lace that divided their room in two, Justin crouched over the bowl of *pâtes*.

"You are a ruffian, Justin!" The voice went on, gathering strength out of bitterness. "Simple-minded and brutal like your father! And your essay for Father Xavier?"

"It failed." Justin hung his head. And just then striking the lowest depth of its shame, his soul flashed with outrage. Justin pushed his fork down in the bowl so that the *pâtes* squished up between the prongs.

"Justin!" Jeanne Lothaire's voice warbled with disgust.

"I'll be back by night when the magnificent Michaud lace is put away." Justin had stood, but his legs were weak with terror.

"Justin, you make my life so hard. Where are you going?"

There it was, the note of need that set him free! A hot gust of love and compassion blew through Justin. He bent by the tablecloth and kissed his mother's warm cheek, feeling the down and smelling the familiar scent of lye and jasmine. The noon sun, cool and lazy, came through the gauze curtains into the lace shop. "I am sorry, *Maman*, you know I try." Justin nearly wept with the joy of the confession, even as he knew that she would use it against him. Yet for that second they were tenderly bound in anxiety over his father's wild, undominated Arab blood.

Then Justin stood at the bead curtain, his bare toes crooked on the step. He was ravenous with hunger. Then he was running.

2

JUSTIN RAN DOWN THE STONE ALLEYS, TAKING THEM SURELY. HE WALKED INTO the empty builder's lot. There in a patch of shady rubble was the foreman, Omar. His three fiercely shy Berber workmen squatted round an iron pot. Omar's white teeth flashed as he beckoned to the panting boy. A shrill burst of laughter came from the group.

"So, little camel!" Omar's thin lips grinned tenderly. "The little camel looks hungry. Go stack those bricks."

For three long minutes in the furnace sun, Justin's small brown hands labored over a dozen heavy red bricks that had slipped from the pile. Then, drenched and gasping, he sat down next to Omar. Justin did not meet the eyes of the hawk-faced Kabyles.

"The little camel is a great thinker; he goes to the *lycée,*" Omar said impressively. Justin was trying not to gulp the stew of red beans and lamb fat, nearly singing out at the way the wine from the dusty bottle burned his throat. I will find Abu, he secretly exulted. Then we will go to La Source.

When the tin plate was empty the boy thanked Omar. Then he climbed high into the heart of casbah, looking for his best friend Abu Grinda, the horse breeder's son. Gliding splay-toed over the camel dung, sheep's blood, and charcoal, Justin twisted up the balconied narrow chasms, sometimes crushed against the walls by passing mules. Each door or shop, carved into a single chalk-white stone, poured forth the shouts, the bartering cries, and the good strong reek of roasting kebabs, crushed citrus, cumin and pistachio, saffron and sage.

After the beans, Justin's legs were strong again and knew the way. He paused in the shade by a small mosque, distractedly balancing on one foot at the mosaic fountain. Cupping the water from the cold underground, he gazed over the heads of the smaller boys, watching a frightened-looking German follow a bearded guide down the alley. Trotting now on the level, he passed a mound of stacked, peering chickens bound like kindling, dodged a whipping from a donkeyman, and skipped into the Mosquée Ketchaoua. Justin concentrated to look the correct age.

The tiled courtyard was hushed and shady, with low mosaic colonnades and arches. The central fountain splashed and fell, making zephyrs of cool. Bony figures curled or squatted in the shade. Justin squatted against a column the way the men did and watched the water, cleansing his soul. It was wonderful and mysterious here.

Suddenly his hand was gripped. "Abu," Justin whispered, and a pang swelled in his throat. It was good to have Abu's clear eyes beside him, the strong open smile. It was good the way their bare feet were like the men's: brown on top, calloused dusty-white on the bottom. "La Source?" Abu laughed, their backs side by side against the column. He sniffed a cluster of jasmine, squinting with his ironic eyes along the colonnades, then across the fountain. Abu had never lost a fight.

It took the friends just thirty minutes to reach the artesian springs, in a grove of blue-gum trees behind the city generators. They had cut over the platform that divides the leather dyer's vats, where Justin slipped on some fat and would have bathed in blood-red dye had they not been holding hands.

The others were already there. Little one-eyed Mahmut had even stolen two watermelons. They clustered laughing and shouting on the shady bank over the dark pool. And like them Justin stripped off his blue shorts and his shirt to stand before their eyes, as on the day he was born, with the roasting desert breeze overhead that rustled the sabered gum leaves and caressed his naked soul.

"Yee-hah! Yee-hah!" Justin shouted, high-hearted, full-souled, and victorious. And he threw himself kicking over the cold waters, the ichor tearing back his limbs and neck, tickling and rumbling in his ears.

Later the band lay, giggling, spent, and prickling, like wet fish among the eucalyptus nuts. And they split the watermelons, and showered one another with the blood of the watermelons, and spat the flat black seeds from the tips of their tongues.

3

THE *LYCÉE* CLOSED FOR THE HOLIDAYS. AND WITH IT THE WORDS AS YET WITHOUT meanings—heavy as stones on the tender flesh of the boy's inner tongue—*torment, joy, moral, paradise.* Now Justin could devote himself to the riches of Mediterranean summer. Soon there would be the great fast of Ramadan, and the resonant groan of the desert faithful and the nasal cant of the criers would fill the streets of Algiers with the Prophet's invisible spell. And as the nights fell, there would come the braziers and couscous of *iftar*, the evening meal, and the ravening of the starved worshipers.

Two weeks had passed since the afternoon at La Source. In the faint light before dawn, Justin lay sweating in his iron cot on the roof of the lace shop, watching the steel-blue herald of the mother sun consume the stars one after the other. Each morning, while whole peoples slept, the continents were created anew. It was more than the human imagination could conceive, more than once in a lifetime. Yet it happened every day, twenty-five thousand times in one life. Justin felt oppressed and exhausted by such wealth, and he squirmed on top of his sheets. But the minutes would not pass. And if they did not, his mother might wake before he could leave. Old Grinda would not wait.

Justin must be on the six o'clock coastal bus. He had Abu's directions, who himself had been almost to Oran to visit a sufi holy-man. Justin had just considered the entire earth, but he had never before gone so far from the rue Mahbu. He had never been on a bus or bought a ticket. He was terrified, and he struggled to be brave. Then it was dawn.

More stealthily than ever before, Justin fumbled to put on his shorts, his shirt and sandals. Grinda's farm was all that was fine and glorious in the world. When Justin thought of Abu and his family he felt such poverty that his pride was crushed. Stealing across the wet roof, he stepped onto the kitchen ladder. His heart leapt.

"Justin? Go and comb your hair!"

His mother was below, peering up with the coffeepot in her hand. Afraid of losing him, she had risen early. Abruptly the glory was gone, and Justin knew he had been contemplating a serious crime. He climbed down to the kitchen table.

"Yes, *Maman.*"

You must look proper when people are generous. Otherwise they will regret it."

When finally Justin could flee down through the empty alleys, the ancient wool merchant who never slept had spread his wares. Still trembling with the terror of life, Justin held on to his anger and ran all the way.

Outside the post office stood a huge green autobus.

Under the arcade, a crowd of emaciated Arabs were shouting around its door. Justin stood between the columns. He would never find out how to pay. He should turn back. The fat, white-shirted *pied-noir* driver had come out of the *Poste*. He looked round and saw Justin standing apart. The man shrugged and Justin walked to the bus, his eyes lowered. Remembering, he held out his coin. With a laugh the fat man gave it back and lifted the boy into the bus. Justin sat backwards before the crowd of expressionless faces. Under him the motor whined, and there was a violent shaking. The arcades and *Poste* began to pivot and rush. A searing blast of air hit Justin's ankle and he clutched two shining silver handles.

For a while Justin could not tell if he was monstrously happy or was going to be sick. Then presently, looking out of the window, he saw a grove of eucalyptus. Justin sprang to the window.

"La Source, La Source!" he shouted, and on the seats of the bus the charred, hooded priesthood of the desert burst out laughing. From that moment, Justin lost his terror and knew that this was an adventure. And every once in a while he jumped to the open windows to cry out at some camels or at a cluster of bedouin tents like giant bats crouched on distant yellow wastes.

Later, the bus stopped by a giant stone, and Justin climbed down. With some encouraging chatter the door banged shut, and the swaying windows of the bus grew smaller and smaller. There was nothing on the lifeless plain until a far purple fringe of mountains. Turning, Justin saw a straight track, distinct from the raw earth only in being polished harder. In the hushed yellow immensity, hearing a faint singing, he divined a tiny whiteness receding on the asphalt, down which the autobus had ceased to exist. Then it too was gone.

And then Justin experienced the heat. He had felt it bang shut like an oven on first climbing out of the bus, but only now did he really know it. Justin's feet went quickly down the clay road through a constant drone of wasps. It seemed a long time, and a long way of scuffing sandals over the scalding dirt. Justin did not know how this road would end and could not feel if anyone had needed to go down it in the last thousand years. There was just Abu's word. In this immovable heat and emptiness, the memory of Abu and their alley maze was as unfathomable as the thought of chilled lemonade. Justin trotted on through the dust, for if he stopped there would be nothing.

First he glimpsed a frame tower and windmill, then a rusted roof. There, ending the road, was a farm—a low building clustered haphazardly with corrals and enormous racks of timber. As Justin drew near, two mangy yellow pariahs raced snarling at him, leapt, and were spun onto their backs by chains so long he could not see where they began. Standing rooted, he recognized the battered gray truck he had seen in town.

Then Justin caught sight of Grinda in the far corral, swinging a yearling on a long halter. Walking forward, the boy saw the big lathered body swing away from the man, who easily anchored it to a stake in the billowing dust. Abu and his half-sister Melanie were bent on the shady fence against the water tank. Justin stopped when he saw her. The far-off red hair tossed, and she saw him. A blue-shirted arm waved as Abu jumped down and came toward Justin with his easy grace.

In the corral Père Grinda tossed the coiled lanyard to an Arab in khaki. Hooves banged violently, so close to Justin that he flinched.

4

ABU CAME UP TO THE BARN LIKE A PRINCE WELCOMING AN ESTEEMED GUEST TO his father's pavilion. Justin was shaken to see these people setting aside important matters for him. Grinda fell in with them, stubby in his open shirt, boots, and breeches. He beat dust off his legs with a riding crop and frowned at Justin.

"Good, Justin! We will go to Sidi Idriz for the fair. Do you agree?"

A splendid reek of hay, sweat, and horse droppings enveloped Justin. Loving this family so fiercely, he did not trust his ears. Was it not clear that to be near them he would eat with the dogs? To have a preference was impossible luxury. Melanie was approaching.

"You see, Abu?" Grinda shouted. "What did I say, heh? But first some beer!" He left them by the barn.

"Hello, Justin." Melanie shielded her eyes, taunting him.

At the sight of her, a powerful discomfort and curiosity attacked Justin. He smiled, but the muscles in his face made a frown. She walked to the farmhouse ahead of them, and Justin tried not to see her ankles.

Shortly they were climbing into Grinda's truck. Abu pushed Justin over the tailboard into the bed. Melanie climbed in front with the horse breaker.

"You see?" Abu grinned angrily. "Papa takes the sister everywhere like a wife."

Justin paid no attention and fell laughing on the mound of oat sacks. He went on giggling as the truck rattled back up the dirt road, trailing dust like a curly beard. But in his heart he disapproved of Abu's words. For Justin felt the splendor of Grinda's French and Arab wives and his mixed children. How quick and easy was this road, traveled with the family it belonged to! The truck on empty asphalt whirred and jolted for one hour straight inland, then made a sharp turn, and went on for a second hour up a steady grade. Justin did not think of the hours. He was so insignificant and knew so little, and the Grindas were so sure and in command of the world. Justin slept, then woke and wrestled with Abu. They stood and fell back on the sacks, shouting jokes about the priests at the *lycée* that left them weeping with laughter. Then they slept again.

When Justin woke, the truck was inching into a shouting mass of Arabs along the side of a square. Had they come to the holy town of Sidi Idriz? Justin balanced on the cab next to Abu, wishing it were not. But it was, and with a sinking dread he knew the journey on oat sacks to distant lands was over.

The great square of Sidi Idriz was so wonderful that Justin quickly forgot. The *marché* was ringed by flat white houses. Here and there in the stands were performers crowded in by throngs of hypnotized merchants, shepherds, and open-mouthed camel drivers. There were comedians, and *kef* storytellers, and tumblers from Tunis, who bounced and bounded ceaselessly, always laughing and calling. Quick Sudanese dancers jigged, whirled, and spun their pompoms to a thundering, cracking row of drums. Justin and Abu moved through the crowd after Melanie. Clinging to Grinda's moist shirtsleeves, the boys stared at the red Berber costumes covered with bells and gasped at the smells from the tables of kebab and couscous.

"No, please! Let's stay, let's stay!" Justin shouted, pulling back Grinda and Abu.

They had stopped by some magicians from the Rif mountains, then turned away. Justin could not take his eyes off them.

The two magicians faced each other, seated at the opposite ends of a purple rug and smoking water pipes. The crowd around them stood five deep. But the magicians were involved in themselves, as if they were alone, and unlike the others of the bazaar they did not ask for money. The two had greasy, shoulder-length hair and beards and wore clean white robes. Even when not chanting, they watched each other's swarthy faces with gentle musing smiles, as if in secret communion. Arranged on the rug between them was a pattern of green bottles with oranges balanced on top and clusters of pink carnations sprouting from the oranges. Between the bottles strutted a dozen white doves, bowing, chuckling, fanning their tails, and pushing out round breasts until their heads seemed carried on their backs.

Now one of the magicians shut his strange eyes. He gave a piercing shriek as if to someone inside him. Instantly, the doves rose in the desert sky, circled above the crowd, veered in unison, and settled on the first magician's out-stretched water pipe. They began climbing and turning over his greasy head and shoulders. "*Yuuu-mi, yu-mi-yu-mi-yu-mi-yumi!*" shrieked the second magician. The man was holding up a small fur pouch. He knotted his hand and began very carefully drawing something out in furtive tugs, clamping the mouth tight around his fingers with the other hand. "*Yuuu-mi, yu-mi-yu-mi-yu-mi-yumi!*" the magician shrieked again, as if enduring the pain of labor.

Pressing round the rug with the crowd, Justin held his breath. Now he could see: something terrible and mysterious was coming out. Something wet, brown, and hairy—A tiny paw? But at once the magician pushed it back, and returned to chanting. The white dove swelled, bowed, and turned. Justin felt his scalp prickle. "*Yuuu-mi, yu-mi-yu-mi-yu-mi-yumi!*" the far magician shrieked again and swayed on his crossed legs. His eyes fluttered open, smil-ing straight at Justin. "*Yuu-mi-yumi!*" And again the pouch swung over the pink carnations. Gradually, tug by tug, the wet furriness reappeared. The magician's fingers plucked the sack and spread it, as if arranging a bouquet. Now an awesome, wet, indefinable, furry fold glistened from the mouth of the pouch. Justin was breathing hard. This time he would see. "Ooh!" Justin groaned with the crowd, and again the threatening pouch slipped away unex-plained. The first magician gave a shriek. The white doves beat up and again, circled, and veered.

And instantly Justin knew. They were settling on him! A rustling hot wind beat his hair. He stood rooted, too terrified to move. Melanie's hand let go of his; the crowd sighed back. In the sudden silence, Justin felt tiny claws prick-ing his shoulders and scalp. Still he stood frozen. Somewhere in the flaming noon sun there was another shout. With myriad tiny thrusts, a whirl of white-ness beat around him. Then Justin was set free.

"Justin, Justin!" Melanie called in a shaken voice. She was clutching his left hand, Abu held his right. For a while, Justin did not notice either of them walk beside him—nor Grinda ahead, with a very tall Arab in black robes. The Arab led them out of the clamoring, spice-and-lamb-smelling throngs of the bazaar, up steep passages. Justin was ravaged and limp. And, when at last they stopped by a procession outside the mosque and he saw through a low arch the glare of the white marble terrace, his soul was prepared and he lusted to be at one with the passionate children at their hour.

Da-da-boom! Da-da-boom! Da-da-boom, da-da-boom, da da-boom!

Giant drums, heavier than any Justin had ever heard, thundered around them. Six fiercely laughing Berbers in red wool jackets and huge hats with dangling bells spun and jumped in unison, waving long muskets. They moved in through the arch, followed by a straggle of white-*jalaba*-ed fathers shouldering small boys. The children huddled, wide-eyed, and too terrified to cry in the din and press.

Justin gazed entranced after the waves of anxious Arabs and tiny clinging boys, and he was sick with his new passion and the lust to be among them. The drums had stopped. In the silence a small voice screamed, muskets clicked, sandals scratched and shuffled. Then again the great drums cracked and thundered out. The procession went on, passing into the mosque. Now, regularly, single screams shrilled out.

On the cobbles outside, Justin stood weak-kneed and panting, held between Abu and Melanie. What were they doing—what were the sons going through? Now the drums stepped up to an unbroken roar, half drowning the piercing, small, animal cries. The Berbers burst out, still grinning, eyes soaked and glittering. Then the drummers, followed by a rush of fathers still guiltily clutching their now stained and wild-eyed sons. Boys screaming again and again with outraged trust and injury, pounding small fists.

As that terrible, panicked wailing bled out of the mosque and streamed past where Justin stood in the crowd, the sweating Berbers discharged their muskets. *Crack-crack, crack-crack!* Then, taken up by a shrill female keening, the din rose, mournful, disturbing, inexpressible. *Crack-crack, crack-crack!* The crowd surged forward.

Next to Grinda, the tall black-eyed Arab had turned. Cavernous eyes met Justin's. The man, weathered, pitted, animal-toothed and faintly smiling, the boy mortified and enraptured. And as their eyes met, Justin's heart was crushed, severing the past and refusing a future. White doves had possessed him; the magician's pouch; drums cracking and thundering; the shrieks; the tribal fathers and sons in each other's arms—yet Justin's wildness was still unspoken for by any father. Tearing from Abu and Melanie, Justin ran from the Arab's stare—and, running, fled into black robes and fell sprawling on dust and manure. Alien hands clamped his arms, a harsh laugh exploded behind his head. He felt himself rush up gasping and sick against the cool blue sky—then strangely, miraculously, settle lightly on his feet facing Grinda.

"Too much for you, eh, Justin?" Grinda laughed, and Justin would have died with shame. But Grinda rumpled his hair. Justin's heart lifted; he knew that he was one of them. Struggling angrily with grateful tears, he ran after Abu and Melanie.

Grinda drove them back to the coast to be near the beaches during the worst of the heat. Justin lay with Abu on the oat sacks, half asleep with the sky between his lashes. The heat was near the limit of consciousness. The truck was alone on the road. Under the few trees big enough to throw a solid shade, drovers and sheep were clustered, motionless on the empty yellow plain. As Grinda's family rattled on, it began to cool.

In the late afternoon, the gray truck halted on the track to a bay flanked by a bare mountain: Tipasa! Abu and Justin raced down the wide beach and swam, while Melanie spread chorizo, cheese, wine, and bread on a great marble shelf. Soon the friends ran up through the cactus and flopped panting on the hot stone. Justin's happiness was like wild honey. In his hunger this place was Eden—forever perfect and unchanged, belonging to the horse-breaker and his children.

"Tipasa was a city," Grinda suddenly said, waving at the irregular rubble of stones. "This was the temple. All of it built by the Greeks."

The Greeks? Justin rose with his cup of wine. The Greeks? These stones and broken columns belonged to the classics? Abruptly, Grinda and his children began to shrink on the great altar stone, while round them strode far taller and more noble figures. For until this hour, it had not been necessary to think that the Greeks were real. Justin turned to the beach. Of course, a Greek city! And heroes' blood spilled in the sand, the fallen dead drying in the sun! The skegs of the Greek fleet cleaving the wet sand, and Agamemnon's thick calves!

Later he wandered alone down the beach. The breeze-whipped wavelets lapped at his feet, and the hot wind blew through his stiff black hair.

That night, Justin went again on the roof beneath the constellations, and his salty body lay on the palm of the medina in offering to the heavens. He heard the criers as they sounded through the new electric speakers. And he was filled with wonder and sadness at the great lust and hunger in his soul, which no one had known.

5

SINCE THE WHITE DOVES AND THE CIRCUMCISION AT SIDI IDRIZ, SINCE THE SACRED afternoon with Grinda and his children at Tipasa, the Greek ships and heroes were with Justin Lothaire constantly. Even when he was not thinking of them, they ran in his blood and drugged his senses. And in the absence of a single person in the world to speak to about such things, the boy grew pale and tragic. Must every fresh drop of his wisdom be spilled out wordless upon the parched earth, minutes later to be forgotten and so lost forever in a continual succession of crimes against Justin's days? His mother's soft, cloying confidence that her son was as hopeless and insignificant as she was seemed, to Justin not mother love but cruelty. Yet how much he loved and pitied her! As often as he could he would escape to stalk through the elegant white French quarter, until he exchanged glances with some young girl and could return with an aching heart to his rooftop.

That same autumn, a lay teacher came to the *lycée* to teach literature. Monsieur Lavil, a Parisian of thirty-four, took Justin's class. In this class, Justin had the lowest standing. The new teacher was grave, with bushy brows, and it frightened Justin to be held after class on the occasion of his first book critique. As he came near the familiar desk and he saw the Frenchman's faint smile, Justin's body sickened with its memory of past beatings.

"Lothaire?" Cool melancholy eyes examined Justin from his hair to his sandals.

"Yes, sir."

"How old are you?"

"Eleven and a half, sir."

"Really? How astonishing."

Justin recognized the final defeat his mother had foreseen. He longed wildly to turn to the windows and the desert sun.

"Justin, I think you will have an extra hour once a week, plus extra work."

Justin thought he would cry out. He could live through a beating. But to lose a precious hour with Abu was more than he could bear. Imagining the others splashing in La Source while he sat with this tyrant in a breathless classroom, Justin's heart sank.

"Why?" he said, between his teeth.

"Why? Because you are not an ordinary pupil." The Frenchman took off his glasses and smiled, his eyes abruptly larger and kinder. "You have a grasp of language. You seem wiser and more acute than all but a few of the much older boys."

Justin's mouth fell open. Could he trust his ears? Trying to, he experienced an altogether different pain, as of a limb first moved after an old and accepted injury.

"In fact, Justin . . . "

But Justin already knew what a thing it was to have such a teacher, and he fought down a vengeful schoolboy voice saying, *Exploit this kindness.*

" . . . you may drop one ordinary lesson in place of our intensive hour."

"Thank you, Monsieur Lavil," he whispered. And in his gratitude, an impulse came to Justin to warn Monsieur Lavil—to tell the truth—that the work on his critique had been easy and obvious. "Thank you," he repeated.

That afternoon Justin did not make the long climb to La Source but wandered in the Jardins Marengo. He sat on a bench under a palm, concentrating. What did all this mean? Though easy and obvious, the book critique he had written on a lined card glowed in Justin's thoughts like the talisman of a new priesthood. The words had been in his soul. Justin had taken them out and set them on the card—from which they had leapt into the Frenchman's head and been praised. It was like having his soul caressed. Justin felt less alone than he had ever felt. And he had a strange thought. *What if Melanie were to see the card?* Jumping up, Justin leapt the bench and rolled ecstatically on the grass.

But at dusk, when Justin stood outside the lace shop's bead curtain, he was seized with pity and dread. He could see his mother's broad round shoulders bent over the ironing board, the print dress hanging over the scarcely female back and waist, her plump white arm passing back and forth, the vigorous, professional twist of the iron meaning that this was a particularly valuable lace. Coming upon her there, Justin knew that his mother would not see. Only Monsieur Lavil could see and, naturally, Grinda's children.

"Oh, Justin, it's you!" Justin gave his mother a mysterious look, but she made no sign. "Could you take these curtains up the street to number seventeen?"

"Who is that?" Justin said.

"The public library."

He stood there, hesitating to ask her again. Was this too a dream? A library on the rue Mahbu? Snatching the neatly wrapped package, Justin ducked out of the little house. He wove between the market trays through the sunset of rose sails, automatically leaping Amal's shoeshine box. Number 20 . . . there it was, number 17. But number 17 was the picture-frame, radio, and absinthe shop. Justin stood there anxiously, staring up. Number 17 would not move to another wall. Arranged in the window were empty frames and painted photos of popular singers gazing at the sky. The violins and nasal sighs of an Egyptian crooner groaned from the murky shop through a cloud of angularly spinning flies. Justin stepped back, confused.

To one side, included in the blue shop front, was a cramped staircase. The passage reeked of urine. The stairs creaked and doubled back to the upper landing.

On the floor of a corridor lit by a grated window, an old Arab in a skullcap and two loiterers looked up from a game of dice. Justin tried the door on the right. He stepped into a bright, narrow room. There was a table with some wooden chairs, and shelves on two walls. The window looked out over the awnings and roofs. You could see the sea! A glorious sun fell on to the table. The Arab was in the door, watching him. Justin unwrapped the curtains and began hanging them.

Above the vibrating rumble of music under his soles, he heard the clicking of dice. Heart pounding, the heroes of Troy swarming like flies, Justin reached up and lifted out a thick book with a green cover. *Les Voyages de Gulliver.* Justin felt so unworthy that he just sat there before it. Then finally, wiping his palm on his shorts, he turned the first page. And inside him, the things Justin loved—the sun and the desert night, Grinda and his children, Tipasa, and magic doves—stirred with a strange passion. It was as if Justin had stowed away, and now the voyage had begun.

Abu knew, and soon the others in the cool of the eucalyptus at La Source knew. Presently Grinda and his daughter, and perhaps even the black-robed Arab, came to know. Jeanne Lothaire's neighbors on the rue Mahbu seemed to know, and they discussed it. And there were school reports, so that even Justin's mother in her lace shop finally heard. So, among those who would never change, came tidings of a new Justin.

Only Justin did not know, for whom this passion for books came so truly and simply that it seemed to have been there from the beginning. Now, seeing little of his friends, Justin was sure that people knew less of him than even before. And that all of them, La Source, Grinda and his children, and the life of the rue Mahbu, in the end would be there to go back to.

6

THE HOUR WITH MONSIEUR LAVIL TOOK PLACE BY THE FOUNTAIN IN THE teacher's patio, where a Berber girl—the first Justin had seen with her face uncovered—brought them sweet mint tea. Naturally, Justin was in love with her and with Monsieur Lavil, especially when the Frenchman spoke about the lives of writers.

At first Justin read starting at the end of each library shelf, imagining that great works resided, as people did, in neighborhoods. Then Monsieur Lavil taught him to sift out those books that were unworthy from those of essence. And so his pupil's soul, which like some primitive lamp produced a hot flame on any fuel, grew refined and fed on more distilled spirits. When Monsieur Lavil leaned against the jasmine-hung tiles and spoke of the Greek thinkers as if they were no less living than he, Justin's heart beat with terror. But once these Greeks were summoned near enough and spoke to Justin through Monsieur Lavil's mouth, Justin could hear their arguments and he argued back.

Hassan was the keeper of the Mahbu Public Library. The Arab was grudgingly satisfied to have the room appear used other than as a storage place for his private trade in hashish. And so, even when Lavil lent his pupil books, Justin brought them here to read. As no one else ever entered, it was to be the boy's private study. Justin even found courage to push the table against the window, where he could look across the familiar roofs of the casbah to the lighthouse and jetty, and the great bay beyond. Sometimes as the pupil read out the last light of dusk and a deep-hued sunset burned on the west faces of the medina, he would lift his grave eyes from the book. And an ache of love for the romance of that hour would twist in his heart, and tears come to his eyes, and Justin would feel dread that he might ever forget such happiness.

That spring, when he was just twelve, Justin Lothaire made a discovery that shook his conception of the world. Until then, the books in the Mahbu Library had seemed as final, undeniable, and remote from him—rooted, scarcely marked by human intention—as the great stones of Tipasa. Justin knew literature as the fossil remains of giant minds. And then one stifling twilight, as he sat with *Don Quixote* lying open before him, Justin understood. He straightened, alert, the desert heat lifting from him. He thought, *Once there was nothing. The world was as vacant as the desert road to Grinda's farm. Then out of that vacancy a few men dug, transported, surveyed, and built a higher city of wisdom.* And at the realization that neither Tipasa nor these books had been heaved up perfect and whole, Justin felt overwhelmed. For what must these men have been? As if in answer, he seemed to see the *quartiers* of Algiers swarm round him, all dull and petty-minded, insatiably nibbling and incapable even of recognizing the grandeur of their inheritance. They were like idiot chickens, ignorant of the flight that once was theirs. While above them, towering out of sight, were the few men for whom Justin had recently learned a word: the word *superior.*

In the dusk, the souk greeted Justin with its usual romance of the senses: jasmine, desert violins, mysterious throngs, and the gentle gravitational force of desire. But it could not satisfy his outrage, for where were the just and lofty men? Justin reached his teacher's house in five minutes, drenched in sweat and indignation.

The girl Shalla let Justin in at once. He found Monsieur Lavil at the patio table, dressed in a white linen suit. Two older men were with him, one like a hard little merchant, the other tall and sad. Justin stopped under the arch, heart racing. "Good evening, Justin," Lavil called to him. "Gentlemen, this is the son of Ben Kacem, my most promising pupil."

Justin did not hear their names, introduced among the shadows in that calm, polite voice that mingled with the faint splash of the fountain. What was this? He *had* no father.

"I'm sorry, sir," he blurted, shuffling his feet. "I will come later."

"Speak, Justin." The boy heard the friendly smile in his teacher's voice. "Say what you came to say."

"Monsieur Lavil, today I understood what you meant by genius." At the patio table, the three men exchanged looks and turned expectantly. They seemed not to see Justin's stained shirt and blackened skin or his bare dung-covered feet. Was there something in the world he could say that they might not have heard? Then he saw the small, tough Frenchman smile ironically.

"Go on, my boy," the old gentleman said, examining him.

"Sir," Justin began weakly, "I traveled to Tipasa a year ago, to the fallen city. Only I did not ask how the stones came there. It was the same with the books at our library." He faltered, in pain at the memory. "It was like fruit appearing without fruit trees." This image helped, and Justin was suddenly excited. He raced on. "It was as if the stones of Tipasa and the books had— well, had always been there. But it was not that way. I was wrong. The stones had to be transported to fulfill the prophecy of a city—not a filthy encampment but a beautiful city." Now Justin was so excited that his emotion and the words of books ran together. "And the books were not always so formed and immortal and above question as . . . as nature. Before the books and the stones there was emptiness, there was nothing. Think"—Justin threw up his hands, lowering his voice before the emotion—"think of the men they must have been. We have inherited their stones and their words, but where are there such men today?"

Abruptly Justin thought where he was and broke off. Now back in the twilit patio, with the fountain lapping and the three men's stares fixed on him, he felt suddenly lost and emptied.

"Machiavelli too has expressed such a preference for princes," observed the stubby Frenchman.

"Michel, you teach your pupils well," cut in the sad one, and slapped his knee.

"No." Their host reflected, twisting his teacup on its saucer. "It is Justin who teaches me."

"Now listen, young man. That was very wise, very poetic!" The harsh little sage sent Justin a reluctant smile. "But who can agree that the ancients were as superior as you seem to think? Look at our cities and courts, our scientific knowledge, our institutions of learning."

"No, you mustn't compare them!" Justin waved his arms, wild ideas afflicting his mind. "What are our teachers if their knowledge has died? Or our politicians if they serve a corrupted history? Do not compare us, today, to the simple man who first saw God or who could make nature into art." Justin looked round their faces in terror, but not without noticing the short one's sarcasm turn to amazement. His companion was smiling with gentle pleasure.

"Well, Justin, you are not an ordinary young man. You might yet grow up to be one of these . . . these giants of our time, *ces génies.*"

The sad Frenchman's words for some reason sickened Justin. He hurried to stop bothering Monsieur Lavil and his guests and to extinguish in the desert night the fever of his concentration. The teacher unlocked the door for him.

"Justin, Tipasa is a short drive; I visit it often. We might go there for our classes."

* * *

Justin was deeply relieved to reach the rue Mahbu, where no one saw anything unusual in him. He was actually moved to see an expensive lace hanging over the sink and to find that dinner would be boiled rice and cold sausage. Yet far down in that fertile region of Justin, which thirsted for justice along with the suffering multitude among whom a boy without a father had no place, that night's image of what was happening in him lodged, took root, and grew.

Nearing the great fast of Ramadan, Justin read deeply in the Old Testament and Koran. "Observe the night watch!" The prophet's words had flamed in the dusk.

On the first dusk of fasting, he stood with Grinda, Abu, and Melanie in the Carré Mosquée, waiting for the sun to go down, releasing the faithful to *iftar.*

Here and there in the crowd were his French schoolmates. Yet in all Algiers there was not one like him, Justin thought. And he shuddered, feeling his strangeness pour into the hungry throng, flowing into Grinda's children and the uplifted faces of the children of Allah.

High on the minarets of the Grand Mosque, the criers began their call to prayer. Below, a sea of robed backs stooped low toward Mecca, like waves driven by a universal gale. A sudden hot wind, close and deliberate as the blast from a kiln, blew the mimosa above their heads, and Justin's heart was faint.

"Abu, why could not these have been my people?"

"But their blood is in you." Abu gave Justin a frightened look. "Who would they be to deny one like you?"

OBERLINDEN

1

I T WAS SUMMER AGAIN, AND THE STUDENT CIRCLE OF THE RUE DE FLEURUS divided up. Only Justin was left in Paris.

After Frankfurt, David changed trains twice before winding up through the murky Franken Wald, the nape of old Europe, which extends unbroken into Czechoslovakia. And there on the sunny platform at Neustadt was Gustav in his plus-fours, his freckled face watching the coach windows glide past.

"Welcome home, sir!" Gustav bowed his bare head.

"None of that, Gustav." David reddened, embracing the stiff old man.

The sun was not yet low when the polished maroon Daimler turned in between the gate lodges. During the summer, a canopied aisle of limes hid the building until the top of the hill.

Holding the windshield, David stood up in the warm breeze under the canopy of leaves. "Gustav, isn't it beautiful?"

"The finest estate in Bavaria, sir."

First they saw the stable yard, then the upper windows of the east wing. The Daimler circled the base of an ancient oak as broad as the roadbed, and suddenly the long white façade of Oberlinden opened out.

Below the front steps stood a black saloon car with two steamer trunks lashed to its roof. As David jumped down in the hot silence of dust and insects, the old baron emerged through the tall doors dressed in his breeches and knee boots. Behind him was Ellic Levin. Today their family friend's usually mobile features were set. David noticed Levin's wife and two sons waiting in the car.

"Aha, David!" But before David could reply, his father exploded: "God in heaven, *you*, Levin! Now my own son will imagine some disgrace. I never thought this business was serious—not now, not ever! Tell me, why are you leaving, what have we done?"

Taking out a fresh handkerchief with a strange patience, Levin observed the baron's suffering. The banker removed his hat and gently dabbed his bald temples. His sad eyes passed in faint apology over David's face. "You understand? These people, the times."

"A few episodes, Ellic, and in Berlin! But you are one of us."

Levin settled his hat back on. A faint derision tugged the corner of his mouth. "And my children? Better a pretty little house in Küsnacht, by the lake."

"My God!" von Sunda shouted. "You had this planned. Very well, then, go, go!"

Abruptly recovering his dignity, and appearing to forget the Levin family, his newly returned son, and a frightened servant's face in the window, David's father turned away. In the doorway he started back and sprang down the steps to where Levin stood by his car, neatly folding his jacket.

"Yes, you must go, Ellic," the baron resumed, in a voice suddenly gruff and tired. He gripped the banker's shoulders. "Don't stop before Konstanz. You will telephone here at once if you need assistance. And from your Swiss lake, a letter each week. Not one less!"

David was hanging back, for he had never heard his father address anyone outside their closest family by the familiar *du*. And without fathoming a word of this disturbing scene—or that what he had just heard was the opening chord of Europe's guilt—the young man felt that something profound had happened.

When they had watched the car disappear down the colonnade of limes, the baron put his arm over his son's shoulders. Almost as if nothing had just happened, the two Sundas paced into the great hall of Oberlinden and were at once knee deep in barking setters, Labradors, and beagles.

"Welcome home!" the baron said, with his startling charm. "You'll stay the summer . . . yes? Excellent. Your brother's out somewhere. Your sister has been waiting to see you—your mother too, but these days she naps in the evening. Oh, the man was right enough. But how am I responsible? Anyway, we will discuss that at dinner." And without waiting to hear what David might say, the old baron shut his office door, leaving behind a pleasant odor of leather, perspiration, and hay.

At once David had begun the long walk through the ground-floor corridors, pantries, and workrooms, greeting everyone, without the slightest discomfort before retainers who shyly welcomed him with tears and respectful handshakes. First, thin, schoolmasterly Heinrich, the cook; then the mustached Grimmel brothers, who were carpenters; then Hanna, the spinster seamstress, too bashful to speak; and finally balding, red-faced Gerta, David's old governess, knitting meekly in her tapestry chair. Passing through into the stable yard, David greeted twenty more of these hard-working, devoted souls who had always belonged to the great family that was Oberlinden, and so never doubted who they were or that they were superior to the people in the villages below.

But it was a relief when at last David was upstairs in his corner room, overlooking the plum orchard. A manservant had already unpacked his suitcases and vanished with the dirty linen. Just as he was glancing lovingly around the room, the door reopened without a knock.

"Karin!"

In a rush, a black-haired young woman had flung her arms round David's neck. Then, stepping back, her brilliant blue eyes examined him.

Karin von Sunda was nineteen and nearly her brother's height. She had a wavy-haired, long-necked boy's looks. And as with many very shy beauties, her eccentric nature had given her a reputation for wildness and loose morals that she disdained to defend herself against. She was already dressed for dinner, in high heels and a black silk dress with gauze shoulders. Leaning forward with a frown, Karin kissed her brother on the mouth.

"Welcome home, *parisien*," she said, then burst into laughter.

"So how is the future bride?"

Karin blushed and pushed past him, Her kiss had tasted smoky. Turning, she said. "Don't you see I am in black?" Brother and sister were so conscious of each other's moods that they spoke only in little teasing jokes. "What a lady I will make, what a Countess Esterhazy! Ah, *grenouille!*" Karin cried huskily, using her brother's earliest pet name. She threw herself into the depths of his window chair, legs draped over the arm. "Froggie, he is such a bore!"

"You could never marry a bore." Tossing his jacket on the bedspread, David came forward a few steps to the splendid view, standing by his sister's uplifted face. "Then come to South America with me."

"South America?" Karin gave a little pained cry. "Oh, David you don't understand." She sprang up and began circling the furniture, nervously lighting a cigarette. "Papa told me I should accept Richard's proposal. Richard wants to bring the Esterhazy millions to support our cylinder business in Stuttgart. Friedrich says if he doesn't we will have to liquefy . . . no, liquidate." She threw up her hands. "Even this house will be in danger!"

David motioned his sister to him. Karin sat obediently in his lap.

"Surely they are not serious," David said. "Papa is simply being overly prudent. It is his *strengverboten* education. Anyway, Richard is not a bad fellow, even if no genius."

"No, *no!*" Karin had twisted to face him. "That ghastly snobbery, the 'as it were' each second sentence—and missing every joke! Besides, he has bony legs and pasty skin."

"But, my dear," David said. "He plays polo so marvelously, *as it were.*" And squashed together in the armchair, brother and sister laughed their teasing laugh.

Suddenly slipping from her brother's knee, Karin knelt on the Afghan carpet with her chin on David's arm. "Froggie, it's great to have you here! Is it true that in Paris you have friends who are revolutionaries and philosophers? That you live in the university quarter, and go to restaurants and nightclubs? Do you stay up all night with loose women?"

David stroked his sister's head with his free hand. "Now who is jealous? I promise to tell you all about it. But let me take my bath or I shall be late for dinner."

"Do you remember, we used to take all our baths together. Well, I'd rather take my bath with you than with Richard—or Ronald Colman."

"We are too old for that now," David said.

"We shall see," Karin teased, "we shall see." But she was blushing.

"And close the door. Quickly, or Mother will smell the smoke!"

Five minutes later David was afloat in his beloved lion's-paw bath, with its gold taps and view of the evening sky. He heard a door slamming and the distant voices of servants preparing after a long summer's day for the dinner hour at Oberlinden, and it seemed fantastic that he was home.

2

IF THE DOMAIN OF THE VON SUNDAS WAS UNDER THREAT, DAVID SAW NO SIGN OF it that night.

There were a dozen guests staying at Oberlinden, and at nine o'clock a party of twenty-two dressed in evening suits and satin gowns surged laughing and chattering along a gallery of ancestral portraits into the dining room. Tonight, all present felt too exalted by the occasion to flag for a moment, either in their repartee or in their fascination with anyone in the magnetic field of the family's prestige. And the least hampered by common scruples, and therefore the most charming, were Natalia and Dimitri Obolensky—the last from among the titled assassins of Rasputin. Having lost their wealth in the revolution, the Obolenskys existed now as full-time guests. In such company, the least witty—being too unnerved by these gossiping aristocrats to assert himself—was an American diplomat named Freeman, on his way back to Moscow with his wife after stopping in London with the elder Rouves. And here also was the towering figure of the family friend, Furtwängler, who had come from Berlin with a student trio and would play Brahms after dinner. Across the table from David, Karin and their spoiled cousin Katie were flirting mercilessly with the embarrassed cellist and deliberately ignoring Georg Hasslein, the new director of Geiger A.G., who cared nothing for music but who was already famous for cornering numerous German industries.

At the end chair, on David's right, sat his still beautiful Venetian mother, her black hair drawn into a thick chignon. She was describing her religious retreat to Obolensky, lifting her chin and speaking with a lisp. Up at the table's head sat the baron, as usual nodding and shaking his lean gray head, as if hearing all discussions without joining any one. What has happened to Freddy's face? David mused, returning his brother's crooked smile. As if reading the thought, Friedrich's expression hardened, and he looked away.

For some reason that evening, the men did not wait for the women to leave the table to discuss serious issues. The pleasant chatter between dinner partners soon gave way to a general discussion.

"But your chancellor talks about nothing but peace," they all heard Freeman say in a bland drawl, addressing Friedrich, Hasslein, and Furtwängler.

"The man is superbly clever!" Obolensky joined in, far down the table. "Your Hitler will taunt and challenge the world with this word 'peace' until the world doubts its own senses!"

"Yes," Friedrich said. "And then our Führer will lead us from the disarmament conference."

"Too early to count on that!" Hasslein stirred, twitching his short mustache as he cleaned his spectacles on a napkin. "Though that would be a windfall for Geiger."

At the far end of the table, the baron had impatiently pushed back his chair. "Neither Geiger nor Oberlinden requires violence to survive!" he called down to them, and even to Hasslein this truth seemed momentarily certain. The argument between Katie, Karin, and the musicians about Munich and Vienna cafés fell silent. The whole company had turned to their host.

"Hasslein, do you know how we kept running when the mark went to pieces?" the baron continued. "We simply abandoned the currency and set up a local bartering economy based on agricultural values." He never tired of taunting his city associates with that success, as if he saw in it some ultimate redemption.

Six servants, three of them young women wearing little caps like white paper birds, moved with fearful concentration behind the chairs, carrying crystal bowls of sorbet and profiteroles. Across the young people's half of the table, Karin gave a theatrical yawn, pushed her hair back with the heel of her hand, and fixed David with an expression of wanton boredom. Cousin Katie sent him a derisive, beady-eyed look which seemed to say, I know I have power over all men; you have the misfortune to be a man; therefore I have power over you. As usual, David felt vaguely mortified, and his face reddened. He grinned drowsily at Karin, and she became confused.

After the profiteroles, the baroness led out the women. Releasing satisfied sighs, the men leaned back in their chairs, lit cigars, and prepared for serious matters with all the assurance of powerful men that any issues and events they discussed were their personal affair.

3

"WELL, PAPA"—FRIEDRICH OPENED THE DISCUSSION, STARING ROUND AT THE expectant faces—"I may have begun as a disciple, but I have some doubts about our new chancellor's upbringing."

As he watched his brother through the candelabra's crystal branches, David thought, *Freddy is such a fool*, and his stomach tightened with shame. Was he himself also getting old?

"It is an epoch of contagious ideas," Obolensky cut in, still seeking openings for his trump dinner story of himself in the Petersburg stairwell, waiting for the poisoned Rasputin to drop dead. "The cities of Europe are full of them."

"This book burning at the Opera last month was an embarrassing excess," Furtwängler said, broaching a dangerous theme. "But I am all for these regenerative storms. The morale in the orchestra has never run higher. Is that not so, Arturo?"

"Absolutely, maestro, tremendous vitality!" the Italian cellist blurted, and a tense anticipation spread down the table.

Hasslein, who cared little for the sentiments of artists and was thinking of the guaranteed sale of cylinders for tank diesels to a regenerate army, cleared his throat.

"Perhaps." The American diplomat turned engagingly to his host. "But the drift in Europe seems against it. It is like *The Cherry Orchard*. We would like to control historical change but we cannot."

"To resuscitate the old order may be more dangerous than to adapt," David agreed, the idea somehow having sprung from his throat on the charm of the hour here among his father's famous guests.

"My English friends say the dismantling of their empire is a certainty in the nearest future," Freeman put in, smiling at Hasslein, whom he knew of through the financing by an American bank of certain weapons cartels. "In Moscow they say there will be no more empires. The Comintern is training the revolutionary elite of a dozen countries."

"Perhaps our Hitler has no empires in mind," Friedrich said innocently, tilting back his chair with an unpleasant laugh.

"What need to talk of empires?" said Hasslein. "We have this *canaille* destroying Europe. Who will discipline them?"

"Perhaps they believe they are Europe's saviors," David commented, and instantly he felt his face burning. Instead of sounding obvious, at this table the words were both subversive and foolish.

"Germany could still achieve Bruck's thousand-year empire," Hasslein resumed, as if David had not spoken. "But it may be the last chance to purge these traitors."

The baron's sunburnt face creased indulgently. "At best they are misguided. I find much to agree with in the words of a Spaniard I am reading—have you heard of Ortega y Gasset? He claims that the common man will not admit that all the facilities of civilization continue to require the support of what he calls 'certain difficult human virtues.' And that the least failure of these would cause the rapid disappearance of the whole magnificent edifice."

"Exactly!" Hasslein burst out, filling his lungs as if Ortega's certain difficult virtues could be held in them like smoke. "Which is why unpleasant methods are justified—to remind the common man."

But could the facilities of civilization not to be made more just? David reflected, sitting with his eyes lowered. And just how magnificent was the edifice? But he said nothing.

"I could not agree with that," Furtwängler said with tactful dispassion. "The people doing your reminding are the coarsest rabble of all."

"Thugs, to be frank." Friedrich looked questioningly round the table.

"Quite so," said Obolensky, adjusting his cigarette holder and forgetting Rasputin. "This use of thugs makes for uncivilized civilization."

"Of course the Greeks and Romans, the Spanish and English all employed force," Friedrich elaborated, reflecting that the Nazis were most popular in the universities.

"Right, Freddy. Force is a *reality!*" observed the architect of weapons cartels, emphasizing his words heavily.

"Surely, sir, they employed force," the American said, retreating further behind his careful mask, "but not to burn books and torment Jews."

"Microscopically insignificant." Hasslein held up both plump hands. "That is no more than the exuberance produced by wearing uniforms. Have you seen the poverty in our cities, in Budapest, Vienna, and Prague? This is the age of mass states. From now on we need a Mussolini, a Hitler—or we will have a Lenin."

"Yes! Any assumption that the legal code can be exercised without force—" observed Baron Sunda, who had risen to pace behind Friedrich and Hasslein. "That is in itself a form of decadence."

For the next twenty minutes, David sat half listening, his thoughtful smile averted from these vastly powerful patricians, thrusting and parrying with sheathed swords. And what then was the common man? Surely Justin Lothaire was the common man. What difficult virtues did Justin lack?

David looked up, and met his father's eyes. The baron stood behind Friedrich, holding the back of the chair, splendid in his red and black shoulder sash. The worldly faces flanking the table were watching David. His brother's sagging grin was fixed on him.

"What career after my Paris *diplôme*?" David repeated his father's words, trying to grasp the mood down the table. What responsibility did he have for a Germany which had world ambitions and which his father knew was rearming? "Well, in fact, I am attracted to the offer from an old friend, for a post at the League of Nations in Geneva."

"An excellent decision!" Freeman said with automatic approval.

"League of Nations!" Obolensky exclaimed. But he could think of nothing sarcastic to add.

"A waste of time," observed Hasslein.

The baron, who had been grimly examining his son, smiled weakly, frowned, and bowed his head. "I think we will need you here, my boy." Then, with a sudden engaging gesture at the Italian cellist, he turned to his guests.

"Gentlemen, now it's time for Brahms!"

4

DAVID WAS THE FIRST DOWN NEXT MORNING IN THE SILENT BREAKFAST ROOM BY the baroness's rose garden. The house was utterly still, but the sideboard was arranged with all sizes of cups and plates, wild honey, *Pfannkuchen,* and even scrambled eggs for the Freemans. David listened to the peace through the great building, and he could not recall a single thing that had been said the night before. He remembered only his mother's dark tone as she described a cripple crawling up the steps at her retreat and his father's words: *We will need you here.* David hurried to finish his coffee.

In two minutes, without meeting a soul, he was down in the gun room. His English gun boots were just as he had left them. Climbing out of the coal ramp and kicking the doors shut, David followed the stable wall, shivering a little in the shade of the main building.

And now, on this clear blue morning of late June 1933—a morning taut with bees, birdsong, and the ring of distant bells—David Sunda walked the soil of his ancestors. Avoiding the secret bowers of childhood and the south woods, where years ago he had found a French pilot, he took the ridge path to the gazebo on Templar's Hill. From this hill, Sundas had ridden to the Second Crusade. Thick fields fell away on either side. The horizon opened, echoing with silence under a bland sky. Far to his left, at the border of a barley field, three men waved to him. The gamekeeper, Willi, with two tenants. David's heart filled.

We will need you here. His father's iron voice of duty came to him again. David dropped his arm and walked on. Yes, that time was near, and he thought he would be ready. Yet what had he done to himself in Paris? What was its charm, and what for? Was he to degrade the rest of his years among scholar bohemians or chasing women?

David had reached the great oak on Templar's Hill. Facing back, he sat against it with a cigar and gazed across the sloping fields to the main mansard roof, hidden among the limes. What did Oberlinden embody, other than lavish meals, costumes, and pretentious conversation? Everyone seemed to grasp what such an existence meant except David. Each time he though of obeying the baron and renouncing his life in Paris to perpetuate this estate and the Sunda name, David experienced a sensation of dread and a blind passion to see this monument shaken to its roots, burned to embers, and erased.

He followed the grassy banks of the Saale walking under the ivied ruin of the castle and past Oberlinden's oldest elm, which every spring was somehow festooned with leaves as tender and green as any sapling's. Gradually his turbulence subsided in the rhythm of his strong legs. This was the way David made all his decisions—abruptly and firmly, though only when forced. He paused to toss a worm into the smooth-slipping river. Yes, it was time to bring the Fleurusians here. Also, David would marry Luz. She loved him enough for both of them. And how could it be a scandal if he took the League of Nations post? He was not ready for Oberlinden. But these plans would be respectable enough to calm his father.

5

THE BARON TOOK HIS USUAL RIDE AMONG THE WESTERN FARMS AND WAS BACK AT the house for lunch. He jumped down off his lathered chestnut, in a fury at what he had just seen on Templar's Hill. Ignoring a yelp of pain from the golden retriever, the baron sat on a shaded bench against the stable wall and held up his boot.

"Take the heel, the heel," he groaned. "You, Götz. Come here, if you please. Do you know Krauss fed his mares early grass? Do you know they sowed dead seed on the small pasture? Eh? And whose idea was it to pile that manure by the water trough?"

The foreman stood before the baron with two of his farmers, glowering at a nail on the cobbles. It had never occurred to Götz to return Baron von Sunda's usually affectionate manner, not even when he had saved his master's life at Ypres. But now it shook him to the core to be cast down from the old man's good graces. Götz stooped to pick up the nail.

"All right, old girl," Sunda murmured, in a voice abruptly kind and tired, bending to thump the frightened retriever. "Come, children, come."

Götz had been deciding to risk an excuse. But, as he lifted his eyes and took a step, the baron blocked his way to let the dogs pass. Striding after them through the stable, the master banged the storeroom door. Halfway up the main stairs, he encountered his wife, whispering to three giggling blond servant girls with vases. The baroness swung her beige skirt to avoid the saliva from the dogs.

"Have you seen David, *amore?*" she asked. "We have barely exchanged a word since he came home."

But the baron gave her a look of such revulsion concerning their son that his wife involuntarily reached for the railing.

"Um!" Sunda grunted, so that one of the girls gave a little cry. The dogs panted devotedly after him, the retriever pressing his legs. He would soon be alone in his study. And at the thought of the dark, masculine library with its walls of books and family relics, his mood softened.

But when the baron stepped through the door, his elder son was seated at the window, bent over some documents. The moment he saw his father, Friedrich began to speak.

"Father, there is a way of shipping that prize bull straight from Aberdeen."

The baron paced around his big desk. He noticed Friedrich flinch at his glance, the twitch of that sagging eye. "Not now," he said. "Please leave me alone, you and your Hasslein."

Friedrich icily and unhurriedly left the room. The moment the door closed on the boy, his father was sorry. I will call him back, the old man thought, knowing that he would not. Were his son here before him, he would not have been able to control an urge to criticize the young man's character. And what would have been the point? Character was not taught. Wisdom and judgment were not imposed.

Downstairs in the great hall, the old man could hear David's voice calling to his brother. The baron's thoughts leapt back to Templar's Hill. The damned fool. It was the fault of the boy's mother. Aesthetic raptures, the inner world! The boy lived on dreams. And suddenly von Sunda lost his anger, and with it his sense of clear purpose. With so much to be done, and David in every way the abler of the two, what could be the matter with him? League of Nations, indeed. What of Thomas Mann's spirit, to carry in one's heart the dream of preserving an ancient name, an old family, and adding to it more honor and luster? That took imagination. The man brooding at the desk thought of David as, with Götz, Willi, and a farmhand, he had caught the boy *meditating* on Templar's Hill. His shame at that moment came back now so vividly that the baron's cheeks burned and his stomach heaved. For all his hopes lay in his younger son.

Sitting stiffly upright at his big desk, Sunda had fallen asleep, the insensible transition of old age, which sleeps so lightly and lives so heavily that the two are as one. He woke, sat forward, and frowned. The dogs stretched and waved their tails. "*Komm, Kinder,* you don't see my wrinkles and gray hair, do you?" The dogs crowded around the baron's morocco chair, curling their tongues. He had always despised people who preferred animals to human beings.

Could today be the first time in his life that Baron Sunda had lost his temper before the entire household? He remembered Götz's stricken face. Götz, who at his side had seen ten thousand men writhing in mud, maggots, and a sea of feces and had saved him. And his poor wife. Had he even felt satisfied to see Friedrich humiliated—his own son? What indispensable virtues did Barthold von Sunda possess that these people who trusted him should be degraded in his honor?

But again he remembered his son on the hill of oaks. And he knew that never must Baron Sunda lay down his authority. Or was it too late?

He dropped heavily onto the corner sofa beside the walnut cabinet where important documents were kept. His wrinkled hands tugged the bottom drawer. The glass panels rattled, Arminius's buckle rocked on its velvet mount. The baron shook open a set of ten-year-old plans of Oberlinden, blueprints for reducing architect Fischer von Erlach's overconfident palace by a third. On what whim had he commissioned work to truncate the building?

And why abandon it? But there it was: plans to cut away the unused royal wing, along with a cavernous space from the entrance hall.

They must go ahead with the plans at once. Tomorrow. And the baron did not pause to think back to the time in his distant boyhood, under Bismarck, when his family's magnificent hall and its wide-circling staircase—seeming to sweep up to heaven—had awoken in him the noblest pride of all.

WILD MAN

1

BENT OVER HIS DESKTOP IN THE ALGIERS CLASSROOM, JUSTIN LOTHAIRE scowled steadily at his initials, three years old and fossilized in varnish. Quaking at his coming laughter, Justin still could not forget his teacher's exasperation. Irony hovered with the cloud of flies over the twenty-five boys' heads.

"Sbaglio, will you read to the class this line from Spinoza?" Monsieur Lavil said now in a menacing voice. "The class will explain what it means!"

There was a silence; then a boy's toneless voice began. "'The love of God is man's highest happiness and the final end of all human actions.'"

Reaching him by his window, the pious words tickled Justin's soul as a supremely beautiful plume created by God might tickle the ball of a saint's foot. He knew they were true—he knew that happiness well! Had Justin not loved God by La Source or on the roof at night under the stars? Or with Grinda at Tipasa? But he also knew these sensual boys' minds. Laughter lunged again for Justin's vocal chords. His chest contracted, and he bit his tongue, struggling to douse this evil laughter with the hatred he had felt before class as Michel Michaud boasted of setting a cat loose with a needle through its testicles. Yet somehow, as Michaud's tragic cat fled a second time through Justin's imagination, it was absurdly funny.

All in a rush, Justin knew he would choke to death if he did not laugh out loud in Monsieur Lavil's literature class. In the next row one of Michaud's gang, carefully gauging his condition, made a face at him. Gasping for breath, suddenly Justin reared in his desk.

"Ha! ha! ha!"

"Is that you, Lothaire—a second time?" Hearing Monsieur Lavil's disbelief trained on him, as on a distant stranger, Justin's heart sank. "Please leave this classroom at once!"

Twenty-four boys' faces twisted to watch. Justin pushed together his poor blue *cahiers* and somehow stood. He passed the teacher's table without daring to lift his eyes. Fumbling with the knob, Justin stepped out into the vacant corridor. The instant he was alone the laughter vanished.

The boulevards and the Marché de la Lyre were empty. In all Algiers, only Justin Lothaire was not at work. He stood in the square's blinding sun, thinking hard. What was there out in the glaring streets? Then Justin remembered Tipasa and the black bicycle that his cousin Ahmet would sell him so he could get there. And in just one hour there was the siesta job at the French tennis club.

Exulting now, Justin ran at a loose and lazy pace through the cool galleries full of shopping women, on into the casbah. Soon he was in the dusty lot of the bicycle bazaar. Outside the one-room shops hung dozens of bicycle skeletons, wobbly bike intestines with orange patches and mudguards glittering and rusted. Ahmet's was a wheel shop. Justin's cousin was adjusting spokes with small deft twists of a key: pausing, spinning the wheel, then again adjusting.

And there leaning against the wall was Justin's bicycle. Ahmet looked up, his long teeth bared. Metal fillings showed through his mustache.

"So, cousin, how much?" Ahmet laughed at Justin.

Justin flushed, toying with the pouch under the bicycle seat. Ahmet's teeth worried Justin about his bicycle. "Three francs," he said. "Tomorrow."

"So?" The wheel buzzed, then abruptly stopped.

Justin lingered for some time, toying with the pouch and watching Ahmet to see if the teeth would appear again.

"Ahmet?" he finally asked tenderly. "My bicycle isn't a stolen one, is it?"

Justin ducked, taking the door in a single jump. Behind in the shop, the spoke-key ring rang three times on the wall and floor before Ahmet could put his foot on it.

2

ABU WAS ALREADY AT THE FRENCH CLUB, WHICH STOOD IN A PINE COPSE ALONG the sea.

"Look who we chase balls for today," he said, grinning.

Across the third court, under a honeysuckle arbor, two girls in long white skirts were uncovering their tennis rackets. The blonde girl with the thin brown ankles was Nana Michaud. At the sound of her fluting chatter his heart leapt and fluttered. He had seen this girl twice, but Nana Michaud belonged to Justin for all the nights he had writhed with the idea of her on his roof under the stars. He had even thought of taking her to Tipasa.

Presently the air was full of the intermittent *pock . . . pock* of tennis balls. Crouched against the fence, Justin was soon drenched in sweat. *Pock . . . pock . . . pock.* Justin had hated the Michauds so passionately, alone in his world of the rue Mahbu, that he had come to love them. His habit of hating them had brought the Michauds close to his heart, so close that he must forgive them. Through Nana he could purify himself of this dishonorable hatred. If he could save her from them, they would all be redeemed—and so would Justin, whom the Michauds dishonored along with themselves.

The two French girls came to the end of a set. They paused to talk on the shady bench under the honeysuckle. Justin's heart began to pound. The last ball had rolled into the gully below their white shoes. Justin blinked and started across the court.

Nana was leaning back, tossing her blonde hair from side to side. She sat cooling, with her skirt drawn up from her calves. It was then that Nana glanced at Justin and caught his gaze fixed on her. Reaching the gully, Justin crouched nimbly for the tennis ball. There was a concerted silence between the two girls.

"Nana?" he began. "After your game, would you come with me to . . . ?" Justin faltered at the astonished irritation in her blue eyes.

"What?" the girl snapped. "How do you know my name? What do you mean speaking like that? Give me that ball, *sale bicot.*"

Justin lung's filled sharply; he would throw the ball in her face! But as he thought this, he saw Nana draw back, cringing. Justin dropped the ball. As slowly and erectly as he could, he walked away across the court.

"Come on, Abu. We will go to the sea."

"What happened?" Abu had jumped up to meet him. And glimpsing his friend's face, Justin knew Abu could never have loved Nana Michaud. "What did she say? What about the money?"

"Abu, let's go," Justin said, and he was shaking with hatred.

3

LEAVING THE STADIUM, THE TWO BOYS FOLLOWED THE ESPLANADE TO THE WESTERN beach where the American warship was anchored.

By the time the friends jumped from the concrete sea wall and ran down the scorching beach, Justin felt better. Nana Michaud was a shrew, a witch, a bad seed like all the Michauds. But he had loved her and known her beauty. He was victorious. Nana had lost. The soft hot sand under Justin's soles cooled and hardened. The first spuming sweep of salt waves tore at their ankles, slowing their brown legs in thrashings of warm brine.

Ahead of him, Abu plunged first and rose shouting, white shorts billowing in the translucent hump of a wave. And there, a kilometer beyond them, looming on the horizon of the wave—huge, gray-skinned, and impervious as a machine of fate—was the impossible warship bearing the airplanes Abu had promised. Justin had never seen so much metal gathered together. Treading water, he was suddenly afraid and very excited, and the Michauds slipped from his mind.

Past the waves, Justin did a crawl to catch up. "Why isn't it in the port?" he called, spluttering and gasping.

"Perhaps it's too gigantic," Abu panted back.

The green sea was oily calm, and resting on its surface like watermelons, their heads got smaller and smaller, and the warship got bigger and bigger. The closer they swam, the more tiny and scared Justin felt. It was much farther than they thought, and as they came nearer it seemed less like a vessel built by man to lap upon the waves, and more like a gray city-topped piling driven into the heart of the sea. Justin could see no ends to it. Figures were moving high on its deck, so far above the water that they were like the tiniest ants. And there were clusters of planes with the double wings of dragonflies. Justin felt weak and smaller than he had ever felt before.

"Abu, don't go closer." Justin was treading water.

"Your bicycle," Abu said, laughing fearlessly. "We'll get your bicycle."

Yes, the bicycle, so that Justin could cycle to Tipasa. But how foolishly small the bicycle and Tipasa seemed here in the deep water by the warship. Now the lip of the vast decks moved far up against the sky, closing out the blinding sun. Under the surface, where the sea lapped ineffectually at this iron-gray wall, the warship's great power sank into the shadowy unknown.

"Abu, are there sharks this far out?" But Abu had paused, treading the dark water. Suddenly he was waving his arms and plunging up and down. And in the water around him Justin felt a passing to and fro of cruel companion shadows of the great machine. He longed to swim for his life. But when he saw Abu's courage, Justin kicked after him still farther beneath the ledge of the aircraft deck. Floating on his back with his toes in front of him, Justin looked up to where Abu had waved. A small group of figures was gathered, looking down at them. Strangely, it seemed, one figure seemed to be waving too.

"Who are they . . . are they like us?" Justin's tiny squeak rose above the droning hum that came from what looked like a gate and drawbridge in the swelling gray wall.

"Watch out! Here they come," Abu shouted, and in front of Justin's face there was a small splash. Abu's heels kicked where his head had been, and for ten seconds Justin was alone under the great city of steel. Then Abu's face shot out, grinning proudly. In his hand he held up a glittering silver coin.

"A dollar, a dollar!"

Abu laughed and spat, and Justin laughed too. He had never heard the word, but he knew at once that a dollar was as mysterious and powerful as silver rain let fall by gods on Olympus. Now Justin was excited too.

There was a splash on his left, and he willingly dived under the surface. The humming was louder. Blood rushed to his head. He kicked and kicked upside-down after the blurred, wobbling disc. But the metal had a headstart and Justin's fingers did not reach it for two or three meters. Then, for one second, holding the coin in his hand, his sight went down past the glitter. And Justin saw below him, and as far around as he could see, the awesome black shadow, blacker even than the heavens he saw from his bed on the roof of the medina, and without the friendly moon and stars. A blind terror came over him. Kicking, he thrashed clawing back to the brilliant green, gasping and choking on salt water. He saw Abu's face, full of love and expectation, and the lonely terror vanished.

"Another dollar, another dollar," Abu sang out.

The two friends dived and dived, eight, eleven, fourteen times, until the pockets of Justin's shorts were full and pulled heavily. Then they paused, and Abu lunged and waved encouragement. But the beings far above them had gone back into their strange city of steel. Justin felt exhausted and sick, and Abu had to carry his shorts half of the long swim to the beach.

But as the blinding shore came near, the more the minutes by the vast ship seemed to Justin a rare and fantastic adventure and the more his chest thumped at what their friendship had accomplished.

Finally Justin and Abu rode through the waves, flopping in the warm shallows. They staggered up and fell triumphantly on the hard sand. Abu emptied the pouch. There were eagles on the coins, but they were not dollars.

"Twenty-five cents," Justin said.

"Twelve silver coins!" Abu's narrow brown chest heaved, the dry sand sticking to it. "It's still three dollars."

Justin rolled onto his back and looked out at the gray steel island in the serene blue of Algiers Bay. Justin knew the ship, and it belonged to him now as to none of those on the crowded beach. He longed to tell them how close he had been and of the alien beings who had peered down. To dispense his new riches like fish and wine. Then Justin remembered his bicycle and the road to Tipasa.

"Abu," he cried. "You are the bravest one I know."

Abu laughed, sprinkling the coins over the sand. "It was you who caught the most," he said. "Justin, let's go to La Source."

"Yes," Justin shouted, kicking his heels on the sand. "Yes!"

In the cold, dangerous immensity of what they had gone through, he had forgotten the water hole. Now Justin breathed again the scent of the clear warm water and the safety of its breezes beneath the gum trees. And he was delirious with wonder that life should have this further perfection to add to a glorious adventure.

"Yes," Justin shouted. "Yes, that's perfect. Isn't life amazing, amazing, *amazing?*"

And Justin kicked up his heels and threw handfuls of sand, so that it fell all around them in the searing heat.

4

HIS BLACK BICYCLE WAS THE ONLY THING JUSTIN LOTHAIRE OWNED BESIDES THE clothes he wore, and he loved it as he loved life.

When at first dawn he climbed off his bed and down the ladder, there was his bicycle. And after school there it would be in the bicycle shed, tangled amongst the shiny new bikes of the French boys. Yet his bicycle had a being of its own. When Abu rode it Justin was sure that it still beckoned to him, and he was jealous. He knew each of its patches of rust, its dents, its misalignments. And toward these deficiencies, Justin felt a stubborn pride that no expensive bicycle would have merited. On the road to Tipasa he would notice the chain, which had mysteriously stopped vibrating only the day before. And imagining the chain breaking, its ends hanging lifeless, Justin would nearly cry out with anxiety until he and his bicycle were safely home.

He had dreamt of riding on his own to the Greek ruins at Tipasa. He had paid Ahmet with the money from the tennis club and the Yankee warship and was free to go anytime he liked. But it was not the same. It was as if the gods of Tipasa were jealous gods and knew of Justin's low, common passion. When he came with his bicycle, all the suspicious dealings and restlessness of the city came with him, and the Greeks held their silence. Wherever he hid it, he and the gods of Tipasa knew it was there. Even when Justin removed his clothes and went pure and naked among the ruins, the gods turned away. For Justin this was terrible. He grew ashamed, and felt the loneliness of his passion and its price.

Eleven days went by. Riding home in the evening heat, Justin stopped by the roadside fruit-juice bar to spend his few sous. In the sultry shade of a eucalyptus the usual group of Arabs stood gossiping on cobbles made of countless bottle caps crushed into the soft asphalt. Justin returned slowly to the grove, gulping the cup of orange juice.

And then, for just a moment, consciousness drained out of him. Justin's bicycle was *gone*.

Without betraying his catastrophe to the watchful Arabs, Justin continued, choking with shock, along the road to town. A half hour later, he turned up the towering alleyways into the whiteness of the rue Mahbu. Through the groaning desert violins from the absinthe and picture-frame shop, down under the window of the library, where his books waited on the window table, Justin's feet found the goodness of the familiar bumps and the slippery incline by the baker's underground ovens. He felt so free and like himself again that he burst out singing: "*Yu-mi, yu-mi, yumi.*" And he swore bitterly. Ashes to ashes, thievery unto thievery, never will I own a thing again.

In the shop's obscurity, behind a hanging tablecloth, Madame Lothaire was standing with her arms lifted, her thin fingers twisted in the web of a burgundy stain. Justin felt a sickening pain. He frowned and hung his head.

"Where is your bicycle?"

Justin did not answer, for he knew this tablecloth. It was from the Michauds, who had many dinners at which guests spilled expensive wines. His mother's fingers had stopped. In the dark behind the lace, her pale eyes were gathering self-righteous malice.

"Justin! The bicycle?"

Though Justin had earned the money for it, his bicycle was property. And property brought it into his mother's sphere.

He passed around the lace, remembering not to touch it with his oily hands and angry that he remembered. Justin sat at the kitchen table. It sickened him that someone like his mother could have known all along about the town's heartlessness. Out there in this city of people willing to wound someone like him was his bicycle. At the thought of its rusted mudguards, now somewhere unknown to his love and among strangers, Justin's eyes narrowed with angry tears.

"I lost it, *Maman* . . . it is gone." His soul convulsed with shame and relief at the lie. For this way, life was innocent, and Justin could go on.

"You mean it was stolen." His mother's voice shook with rage and sanctimony.

"No!" Justin snapped, fiercely standing up for life. "I lost it."

In the following nights, Justin's bicycle spirited through sad, tender, sometimes vengeful dreams. When school was out, he grimly searched the shops, bicycle bazaars, and squares of Algiers. Once, on the Boulevard Bonaparte, a rusty black bicycle rattled by with a certain familiar tone. Justin's heart leapt into this throat, and he felt faint with regret long after he saw it was not his bicycle.

The fourth day after the catastrophe was a Sunday. Feeling a fateful optimism, he set out for the bicycle bazaar. He turned up the steep incline of the rue Rosette and was stopped short. Balanced over Justin, filling the street and blue sky, the pitch-black robes seemed taller than ever and the sunken lawless eyes darker and more ironic. Muffled by the wrappings, a laugh rang out. Then, without apparent volition, the wrappings fell away, and Justin saw again the charred hawklike face and hooked animal teeth that he remembered from among the drums, the shrieking, and guns of Sidi Idriz.

As once before, and forgetting the bicycle forever, Justin turned and ran. Yet fleeing he collided with the black robes, tripped, and was caught up by powerful hands that shook with laughter.

"Ha, boy, Ben Kacem! You know me. I am Ibn Moushmun."

Justin was suddenly calm. "I know you," he answered. "You are Ibn Moushmun."

"I knew your father," sang the melodious voice, a voice free and iron-willed such as Justin had never before heard. His heart leapt, but he did not let it show. He circled past the tall fellah up the steep street until their eyes were on the same level.

"Yes?" the boy said.

"We will fish for tuna next Saturday?"

"Yes?" Justin said again, never having heard of an Arab fishing.

"Bring yourself before light. Four o'clock on the Quai d'Agadir." The black eyes were grave.

"How do you know my father?" Justin began.

But flipping the cloth round his head with a sharp laugh, Ibn Moushmun turned away. Justin watched him stride down the rue Rosette. His black robe billowed briefly in the white crowd of the Sunday promenade, then vanished. To Justin it was as if this rough, pleasant-voiced sorcerer of the desert had spoken intimately of knowing God.

5

JUSTIN RAN ALL THE ELEVEN TURNINGS TO HIS TEACHER'S HOUSE. MONSIEUR Lavil would explain Ibn Moushmun and his prophecy of the fish. Shalla swung back the studded door. There were yellow blossoms in her hair. Seeing him, she bit her lip.

"Oh, it's you. Please come help me with Monsieur." The girl had never said so much, and without dropping her black eyes.

With a shock, Justin felt his teacher's secret life opening to him. But he was not ready to see the Frenchman sprawled under the acacia, queerly asleep in a canvas chair. Two fancy bottles stood by the splashing fountain.

"Monsieur Lavil! Monsieur Lavil!" Justin cried.

The Frenchman's face hung slack as an old cabbage.

"He is drunk and the principal is coming. I made a cold bath," the girl said.

"Drunk?" Justin looked down at the wet open mouth, which had recited the words of Socrates. "He is the finest man in Algiers. It is impossible!"

But Lavil was thoroughly drunk. After checking that the neighbors' shutters were fastened, Justin and the girl dragged him inside to the old sitting bath. By the time that Justin and Shalla, now silently weeping with shame, had undressed Lavil and put him in it, the strong adult emotions of Justin's day had hardened to confidence. He still knew and loved his teacher better than ever, but not as before.

Finally a voice began grumbling in French. Shalla reappeared from behind the bath partition. She was looking even more unhappy.

"Thank you, Justin." The girl held the bronze door for him, lifting her eyes and attempting to smile.

6

JUSTIN WOKE SHIVERING WITH THE NIGHT DEW ON HIS BLANKET. IT WAS NOT YET first light. He knew at once that it was the earliest hour he had ever risen to. Then he remembered and twisted off the mattress on to the damp, cold tile, his toes on the lip of the ledge. Wavering up from the port far below but sounding close in the dark came the only sound, the resonant *kunk, kunk, kunk* of a trawler's engine.

Close by in the murk, the stork nesting on the cooper's chimney flapped its wings twice. Then, as if another and greater white stork had shifted on the human nest, a ghost of pale light crept into the world. Now Justin could see the harbor, its surface still unbroken. At the thought of Ibn Moushmun, Justin's stomach tightened with dread and ecstasy. The great bay was still dark. What would the tuna be like? Could Ibn Moushmun, robed desert goblin of Sidi Idriz, call up the great fish from this mild lake? Maybe they were out there right now!

Not even pausing to scribble a note, Justin jumped to the roof below. He dropped into the rue Mahbu and ran down the empty black alleys. Without stopping for breath, without seeing a soul, he reached the cargo yard. All Algiers was asleep. He ran down the railway line for a hundred meters, then cut behind the warehouse onto the docks. In the obscurity of the *môle de pêche*, Justin stopped, suddenly frightened. If only Abu were here. What if Justin never returned to the casbah, to his mother, or to Monsieur Lavil's patio to discuss the great writers?

Out on the water, shadows of trawlers floated in a line. Nothing stirred. Justin's heart leapt with relief and disappointment. Then up the Quai d'Agadir came a heavy *kunk, kunk, kunk*. A dark superstructure was moving towards Justin, silhouetted against the blood-red sky. Below his feet the water lapped. Justin stood paralyzed at the end of the warehouse fence. *Kunk, kunk, kunk.* The heavy strokes thudded underwater, then were loud. Justin turned to run, but his feet stayed where they were. The filthy, unpainted specter emerged, listing over him. He saw a vessel with a long deck, low wheelhouse, stunted spars, and six boats piled on the stern. Three sullen crewmen were picking over a stack of nets.

"Justin? Jump, jump!" Ibn Moushmun paced dangerously toward him, balancing along the gunwale, then swinging on a taut cable. His black robe flapped in the harbor's windless hush.

"Jump, little rebel, jump!"

Then suddenly Justin obeyed, and he leapt. Clutching a cable, his fingers tore loose. Instantly, strong hands caught and lifted him. Justin skidded on the oily, slanting decks. The quai where he had been standing alone was gone.

"Good! You did well to come!" Ibn Moushmun laughed.

Justin went to the stern rail by the lashed boats. One after another, the handsome blue, yellow, and green French trawlers glided by and were gone. The Jetée Nord wheeled round, closing on the Môle à Charbon, and slipped by. For a long time Justin pressed against the old scow's shaking transom, watching the city he loved, pink and still now. He could even see his roof and the tiny window of the Mahbu Library at the crown of the casbah.

Algiers grew smaller and smaller, then whiter against the greenish coast-line. The steady breeze of their passage rumpled Justin's thick black hair with the clammy vapors of brine. The tar- and grease-smeared deck under the boy's feet juddered roughly, and a heavy, translucent blue swell moved smoothly with them.

The sun was up. Algiers and the coast of Africa were swallowed in haze. The morning warmed Justin, and, feeling better, he moved near the three crewmen. Justin watched them mending nets. In these nets, they would capture the great beasts of the deep. But now the nets and the men were pleasant and still.

Suddenly Justin laughed out loud. He had just thought of his mother mending her lace.

"So, the little friend likes our boat."

Justin turned. In a work shirt, Ibn Moushmun looked more like the crew. Never before had Justin seen anyone built so powerfully.

"Ibn Moushmun," Justin cried. "how big will they be?"

"The smallest"—the animal teeth flashed—"will not be as small as you!"

"Oh," Justin breathed.

"We have seen none this year. But this week they are in pilgrimage from Greece." Ibn Moushmun's sunken eyes focused away to the west. "The ones of the schools are no more than eighty kilos, but a solitary bull is sometimes five hundred. They never stop growing. Soon there is not enough food in the schools."

"Will we see the old bulls?"

"Never," said Ibn Moushmun, looking away. "Hey!"

The three Arabs on the deck looked round.

"The tower."

A short Arab with wide shoulders rose from the net. He climbed to the bridge. From there he swung up the frame tower until he was standing on the platform high over their heads. Then a hatch banged open, and nine more Arabs emerged from the hold onto the deck. One of them had on a jacket like Michel Lavil's. But Justin had forgotten to be afraid. He was praying as hard as he could that today would be the day.

And today *was* the day, though not for many long, hot hours. Then the boats were being pushed over. They strung out behind, with the net passing over boat to boat. Finally, when the trawler had been rolling for hours in a glass-smooth swell, an eager cry came from the tower. With the others, Justin slid to the rail. He stared and stared. The only thing in the distance of blue sky and sea was a whirling confetti of white birds. Now for several seconds the old trawler stood up straight, changing course. Then again it was leaning far over, with the birds somewhere ahead.

"Go up front!" Ibn Moushmun was perspiring heavily.

When it came, Justin was by himself in the bow, leaning out watching the birds circle ahead. He saw a large burst of spray on the water. Then a second. And then for five hundred meters round the first splash, Justin saw myriad bulges rushing the surface. The boat heeled again. They were angling ahead of the school. Justin stared and stared, eyes aching to penetrate the mysterious ocean, where undecipherable forms turned and rolled. Wills and strange passions not like men or the four-leggeds but *life*—violent, silver, and projectile. Fish, Justin thought, the great fish!

A black tail lolled in the air, as perfect, warlike, and beautiful as an arrow's quill. A flank glinted under the surface, waving a pointed pectoral fin. Justin's small hands held the railing tight. His teeth ground with adoration of their living, of their free, mute bathing in the supreme element.

Under Justin's feet, the trawler's deck shook. Justin stretched to see around the wheelhouse. The second crew had dropped astern, the net between the boats tracing the arc of the trawler's wake.

"Run, fish, run!" Justin screamed to them.

One of the pole boats fell astern, pitching in the trawler's wash. The two Arabs in it were rowing four-handed to circle the hemisphere of net. The scow's engines died away. In the vast sea silence, the fish were suddenly very close. The breeze fell away, and the sun crushed down on the decks. Fifty meters away, the two pairs of Arabs in the boats lunged and swayed. The boats crept, tightening against the immense strain of the net. Justin watched the agitated sea stretching on all sides, far outside the sphinctering oval of cork markers. The invisible society of life seemed to accept the boats of men, but still Justin did not see the fish.

On the fantail, holding tight to the mast cable, Justin balanced next to Ibn Moushmun. No one spoke across the smooth desert of water, the bare-backed men toiling in the heat as Justin had never seen Arabs toil. The circle of markers closed, and the pole boats were made fast. And still whatever mysterious captive life the net contained did not revolt.

Around the circle there were signals. In the pole boats tow ropes were being hand-over-handed. Justin guessed that far down the skirts of the net were closing. *Then he saw them!*

A cheer went up from the circled boats. The deck under Justin's feet began to shake: *kunk, kunk, kunk.* His stomach quaked as the trawler swung around and pivoted out over the deep gulf in the net. The engine ceased and was silent. The big decks swung close alongside the pole boats. Staring into the inner sea of the net until his eyes ached, Justin could see nothing. In the net was only a sapphire-blue emptiness. They got out, he thought and felt happy for the great silvery fish. But also hurt, as if they had spurned him.

Justin staggered backwards on the fantail. Not where he was looking but straight below his feet in the deep blue outside the net, he had seen a giant, leisurely, silver glimmer. And in that moment it was like the abysmal shadow under the warship when they had dived for the silver coins.

"How many?" Ibn Moushmun scarcely raised his voice in the calm. Like the man in the jacket, he seemed to take no part in the fishing.

"Many, very many!" called back the men in the pole boats, giggling as they heaved a wet coil up over the deck to the big winch. The drum began to grind, and there was much hysterical cursing back and forth to the trawler. Shouts flew among the six boats across the calm blue estuary of the net. The circle began imperceptibly to tighten.

"Very many!" Justin repeated, and he jumped back to the gunwale and caught the cable.

7

THE NARROWING GULF SEEMED EMPTIER AND A DEEPER BLUE THAN EVER. THE SIX boats were sinking in the water, steep-heeling with the drag of the net. In each boat, long gaffs and wood-shafted harpoons were coming out, brandished above the sweating backs of the fishermen.

The sea, stretching out to the horizons, was abruptly empty of life. Above their heads the birds screamed and circled the net. The ring of boats was so close now that there were only two lengths between them. The bilge of each boat was piled with netting. Then in the second boat from the trawler a man jumped fiercely onto the prow, balancing a harpoon above his head. The line on it looped from the trawler's rail. The rope was wound along the shaft, and the muscle and sinew of the man's uplifted arm coiled and bunched. For thirty seconds, during which the screaming of the birds was the only sound, the harpooner, Justin, Ibn Moushmun, and all of them stared down the milky ribbons of sunlight. Then without warning the sweating muscles jerked, the arm drove on. The harpoon went down without a splash, line sizzling.

Instantly, a shouting rose from the boats, gaffs and harpoons rose and fell. On the trawler, three men swung together on the harpoon line. And it was then that Justin saw the fish. At the glassy center of the net the sea boiled white. A silver glittering being, larger than a man and far stronger, half leapt and fell back violently, pumping and skidding, the harpoon pivoting above it. A rose-red flame ribboned from the fish's flank, staining the sea.

"Shadahah!" Justin screamed with the others. "Shadahah, shadahah!"

On the fish's second lunge, it was flanked by two others equally large. Close to Justin the three men fell and were dragged halfway to the ramp.

"Weaklings!" Ibn Moushmun roared. "Pull, pull!"

The white-capped water inside the net was streaked, then clouded red. The great fish thrashed in all directions, flinging geysers of spray high into the whirling cloud of birds. One and then another was pulled onto the boats. Two more fish thumped up the ramp, the brilliant, black-scythed tails thwacking the wooden deck. Eyes expressionless, jaws and gills panting, they slammed down, skidding over the deck on their blood and slime, and the captain gaffed them down the storage chute onto the ice. Justin saw the welts where the hooks punctured the delicate metallic skin, he smelled the mysterious odor of sea, blood, and fish. Out among the boats, the fishermen's brown backs rose and fell to hack the great silver beings that raced among the bleeding waves.

Justin leaned out. Below, in the boat banging the trawler's hull, a tuna was twisting in a stack of nets. The short bearded Arab left the gunwales. He began to beat the fish with a thick truncheon. Justin saw the bone crack, the black expressionless eye pushed in like a button. Now the glorious silver creature lay slowly back, awaiting the blows. The truncheon rose and fell on the crushed skull, and the fish stiffened and arched, terrible and helpless and yearning for life, the beautiful tail fluttering in the sun, the crushed eye moving, trying to see.

"Oh, God," mumbled Justin. "Oh, God!"

Over all their heads there was only the fierce, avenging sun. Here below, where Justin could not look, still came the thuds and thrashing of the great fish. But something deep in the churning gulf of the net went on rousing the wildness in him, and he looked. And at that moment they all heard the single, sharp, frightened cry. It rose over the screaming birds and the captain's threats, over the thrashing water and the thundering of heavy bodies on the wooden deck. Suddenly Ibn Moushmun and the captain were at Justin's side, staring out over the net to the little figure waving and pointing down from his half-sunk boat.

"What? What is it?" the captain roared out.

"He said a monster." Ibn Moushmun's long teeth were brown in the sun.

"A monster? What monster?" A silence had fallen over the trawler, the circle of boats. Three gray-green shapes cut back and forth in the churning gulf.

"Look," Justin called, pointing. "There!" And abruptly the surface was calm, as if all the fish were huddled at the bottom of the net. Even the birds were silent. They hovered, peering as if waiting to see what would happen.

Now the shadow grew distinct towards the far side of the circle. A twisted shaft of rusted steel lifted from the water, then, lying across it, a lesser, straight but equally rusted one that appeared fixed, as if firmly rooted in some floating hulk. As the crews stood watching, drenched in the breathless heat, the mass began to glide along the borders of the net until a scarred black bulge emerged looking as wide and long as one of the boats and crusted white with barnacles. Circling, the monster angled toward them.

Justin held the cable tight and leaned far over, though he was so scared he could scarcely breathe. Now somehow they would all be saved from what they had been doing to the fish.

"A great shark," someone called in French.

"No, a whale!"

"A bull from the great ocean," Ibn Moushmun observed.

The captain waved his arms. "The net! That net cost thousands."

But the captain gave no command, and the silence deepened. All around the net the crews looked on. Clinging with wild excitement to the cable, Justin remembered the mercilessly beaten head of the beautiful fish. And suddenly he loved this great gliding bulk as he loved his life.

Now the thing was turning towards them. The giant came abreast of the trawler. And in the clear blue sea without a trace of blood, they saw the huge curved pectorals, and jagged spine with the stiff crescent of a tail fanning gently behind. The ebony platter-eye stared opaquely, deep below the surface. As the monster completed its circle, the silent birds gliding above suddenly streamed to it, squealing and plunging onto the water in ludicrous panic.

Then the giant seemed to awaken. Veering towards the closest boat, the fish advanced with sudden force into the net. With a shriek of terror, the bald red-faced crewman stabbed with a harpoon at the broad back. The point bent off, and he sprawled on the gunwale half under water. The net wrenched tight on the near rail. The hull drove sideways. A wave broke over the struggling man as his boat violently swamped and righted. With a loud twanging, the net tore loose.

Still the men standing with Justin seemed incapable of movement or command, only waiting in stupefied submission.

"There!" Justin burst out. Where he pointed, the shimmering of the smaller fish deep in the net was blotted out by a huge speeding shadow.

The giant struck the net under the left pole boat. The straining lines all swung together, pointing out to sea. The bow jerked clear under, and the Arab scrambling for the stern flew heels up into the water. For two seconds, the steep-buried hull dragged out to sea. Then, with a crash of thwarts and cleats and the popping of nets underwater, the boat was free. It floated slowly up, the two men scrambling back head first over the gunwales. But in its rush the giant had become tangled in the torn net. The lines began to wrench, savagely dragging the remaining boats. And as if by a signal, the living shoal of fish rose. And they rushed on the shredded net, boiling, churning in plain view of the trawler's deck, battering the planks of the swamped boat. Then, abruptly, the net relaxed, and Justin groaned. The remaining boats were floating up. The great fish was gone. There was a desolate silence on the deck around him.

"The devil! The devil has ruined my nets!" the captain was screaming. "The devil has ruined my boats!"

"Praise Allah!" One of the old men raised a palm to his forehead. "Praise Allah!"

"Praise him! Praise him!" several voices called, and they laughed as Justin had seen the children of the desert laugh in the presence of blood. And Ibn Moushmun laughed with them.

8

IT TOOK WELL INTO THAT AFTERNOON TO HAUL UP THE WRECKAGE AND GATHER and untangle the shreds of netting.

Now it was truly hot, a hotness like anvil heat. Along the trawler's decks, the captain and the men cursed and blamed one another for the loss of half the school. Finally, there was angry shouting between Ibn Moushmun and the babbling captain—not about the net but about a certain launch. Justin felt sick and longed to be far away from this graceless talk. He carried onto the wheelhouse roof the goat cheese, bread, and orange that Ibn Moushmun had given him. He climbed the ladder to the lookout.

Long after the sea birds had flocked westward after the school and the trawler far below had begun its monotonous *kunk-kunk-kunk . . . kunk-kunk-kunk,* and the wake like a vanishing white tongue projected and lengthened astern on the deep blue carpet, Justin went over the great moments. For minutes in the hot wind, he sat still with a mouthful of cheese until it dissolved, dreaming of the way the twisted harpoons had gently swayed on that solitary hulk, like some wreckage on the naked mount of Calvary. Of the way the opaque eye had gazed upon them. And finally of the breaking up of man's sly and arrogant machine and the obedient churning exodus of the captive flock.

He woke to a quick-moving dot that his eyes had been trailing for some minutes. A fast power launch was coming from where the fish had disappeared, trailing a white tail ten times its length. Only then did Justin notice. They were not traveling south toward home but straight west into the blinding sun. He could see Ibn Moushmun with the man in the jacket like Monsieur Lavil's. They were at the bow rail, staring out. The rest of the crew were hidden from sight.

In a minute or two the blue launch closed with them, swung out behind the trawler's thin wake, and drew alongside. After the fish, there was not room in Justin for this launch. The three men on it were dark but not Arab. On the wheelhouse roof Justin slipped down on his stomach. His head was directly above what was taking place on deck.

The Arab in the linen jacket was talking to the three new men. He stared from face to face. Then hands were being shaken. The Arab climbed awkwardly down to the launch and stood at the stern, staring out to the east. Ibn Moushmun and the three new men swung down after him. Twelve crates the size of children's coffins were passed onto the trawler's deck. The four men grunted and blasphemed as they worked. Finally the crates were all on deck.

Minutes later, the sun swung around to a new horizon. Justin's heart leapt with relief, seeing the launch break away. He was bearing his adventure home. Soon he would sit with Abu by the splashing fountain of the mosque and tell all of it. But as he imagined the telling, all at once he felt that something was wrong. The coming of the fish was very clear and glorious. Justin kicked the platform angrily. It was the crates down on deck. And why had Grinda's Arab put on his *djellaba*? Why had his friend immediately pried open one of the boxes and not let anyone else see in?

Justin dropped off the roof on to a heap of netting and ran up the deck. Ibn Moushmun was hammering down the last nail in the crate. As he straightened, Justin saw his strange look.

"Ibn Moushmun, what are those boxes?"

Justin stepped back from the criticism that shot from the Arab's shaded black eyes. Then he saw a triumphant smile that was open and amused.

"If I told you, would you never tell it?"

This was harsh. The story would be damaged if Justin could not tell Abu the whole of it.

"Never," he whispered.

"Until you die?"

"Until I am dead, Ibn Moushmun."

"I believe you, Justin."

It was as if they were old and close friends. Some familiar spirit Justin knew well had come into Ibn Moushmun, and he was moved. The shaded, uncharitable eyes stared hard into his.

"The boxes are from Cartagena. Ammunition for Abd-el-Krim. This was your father's affair too. He died on such a day."

"But," Justin said, and he could not go on. It was as if the Arab had hit him. Grief and hurt swelled in Justin's chest, where the pride had been. He turned from the sunken eyes.

Justin climbed up to the lookout. He wedged his bare heels, fixed his eyes in the glittering distances, and did not look down until the white ledges of Algiers emerged again from the haze. Alone, high over the water, Justin could think. He hated what Ibn Moushmun had told him. He felt foolish and heavy with the terror of Abd-el-Krim and the hundred-year war against the Spanish and French, and at not having known that his father was in it. Now he was bound to this frightening Arab with the guns. Such power instantly changed Justin's feeling about all French—even the Michauds. It poisoned his freedom to love everyone in humanity.

Justin balanced on the narrow platform in the salty hot wind, concentrating hard on the fish from the great sea beyond the pillars of Hercules. The lonely old bull had shown Justin things you could not learn from men's ugly affairs. By loving the fish as hard as he could and despising Ibn Moushmun's words to him, Justin was able to push the heavy evil crates back in the distance, with things of little beauty or meaning. And his heart filled with the great mystery of the fish.

9

JUSTIN NEVER SAW THE BLACK TRAWLER WITH THE WATCH TOWER AGAIN. NOR did he ever go out after the great fish. And it was a long time before Ibn Moushmun would come sometimes to the Mahbu Library, and they would stroll among the cafés he frequented by the Place du Gouvernement, which one day in Justin's life would be called the Place des Martyrs.

But from the day of the fish, there was something new and immense in being Justin Lothaire. He continued to go to school and to have seminars with Monsieur Lavil and adventures with Abu. But there was a great meditation in Justin, leading back to the market at Sidi Idriz, which no one knew how to speak to. To be with anyone very long filled him with impotence and grief, as if he were betraying some noble dream and could not get back to it.

It was at this time that Justin became conscious that in his class he was thought of as strange. But to make the simple gestures that his schoolmasters required to prove he was one of them would also be a betrayal. And as soon as Justin gave up being like the others he began to see how even less French he was than he had imagined. Strangest of all was his deepening sense that these French had not always lived on this land. That it must have been people like Nana and Michel and Monsieur Michaud who had caused his father's death.

One suffocating summer dusk two months later, after a triumphant debate on Platonic love by the fountain in Monsieur Lavil's garden, Justin went to the mosque. Abu was living there now to study the Koran. His friend appeared through an arcade in rough wool robes, and he pretended to walk past Justin. Then they sat in one of the arches, giggling.

"I'm sacred now," Abu said. "You must speak to me with reverence."

"We have always been sacred, you and I," Justin muttered, as always when with Abu hearing his own ideas for the first time.

"It is so. But what is this mood? Does the bull scent a cow?" Abu stared round the courtyard at the bearded men praying and meditating in the hushed shadows, and Justin convulsed with soundless laughter.

"Abu?" Justin was deeply serious now. Abu saw his face and was serious too. "Is it not time I saw Melanie?" Justin was instantly sorry. A look of hurt pride showed at the scarred corner of Abu's mouth.

"Are we not friends?" Abu said. "You the prophet, I the faithful?"

Justin chose not to accept the bond in this, for in some ways he would never be all Arab. "As a priest, you will call up the most ancient spirits," he said. "But have we not often talked of the women who will help us?" Justin paused. "Would we not be truly brothers?" he said.

Abu was sitting on the courtyard step at his friend's feet. Feeling Justin's evasion, Abu's eyes narrowed with a glint of sensitivity and bitterness. He was about to add something, to remind Justin of La Source, Sidi Idriz, or the silver coins. Instead he rose abruptly and walked away, vanishing into the hive of low white arcades. Justin waited, needing such a curse to be lifted.

After a few minutes, Abu returned. He sat against the column beside Justin. Abu's nostrils were flared and his lips pressed tight. "Melanie will be fine," he said. "She has always loved you."

Justin's pulse quickened at the sweetness of this promise in so young a girl. He bowed his forehead on his knees.

"But she will take no interest in your brain," Abu said.

"My brain is not special. It asks for nothing."

"I'll take you tomorrow—before dinner."

Next evening he and Justin were on the Oran bus. As they reached the *Poste,* the bus had been so full of shouting Berbers that the French driver was forced to kick the door shut and climb in the front window. Justin and Abu rode high on the roof. Can these be my people? Justin asked himself, staring out over the yellow plains dotted with black bat's-wing tents. Since he had known he was going to Melanie, Justin no longer cared what went on around him. Noticing Abu's brooding reproach from the corner of his eye, Justin thought, He is right. There can be nothing else for me now. This is as it should be and cannot be helped. A calm certainty settled over the world. And all the vague, sickly torments of the last interminable summer months were forgotten as completely as imperfect friends.

Justin's thoughts raced ahead down the Oran road. Then along the track of polished mud and wasps to the horse farm, where she—red-haired, dark-skinned, with thick strong legs that always moved teasing before him—was daughter, sister, and mother. No incident or image had slipped his memory. Justin had adored Melanie and watched her grow for him, knowing that she knew his life as he knew hers. So there was nothing to be told. They looked out on the same world. Now Grinda and Abu would be his father and his brother, and Justin would let them love her through him. Yet still no words had passed between himself and this girl, and Justin's pride did not consider their submission to each other in finer detail.

10

JUSTIN AND ABU REACHED GRINDA'S FARM DURING THE SUMMER'S LONG DUSK.

This was the hour when the sun, long before its true setting, seems to splash into the molten pool of the earth. At that hour the sand, burnt clay, and even the green prickly pear dissolved in a color as of great fires. As the two friends' sandals approached the doorless house a harsh singing came to them. A Berber, Justin thought, and it was a good omen.

"Yerba!"

Abu ran through the circle of the chained pariah. The dog leapt and was jerked on its back, choking and yapping. An older woman faced them in the entrance with a haughty laugh. She had a Berber lace shawl over her yellow hair.

Justin hung outside the little kitchen, shy of so many others. Grinda looked strange under the hanging garlic, and, with his hair brushed back, more French. Behind him, Jeanne, the youngest, was braced in the passage. Without looking, Justin knew that Melanie was in the dark by the petrol icebox. When he saw Justin, the horse breaker gave a shout.

"What does this mean? Eh, *toi*, Justin, without a book?"

"Father!" Abu frowned. But Justin let himself be drawn into the kitchen.

"Yerba, he is like a priest who carries a cross," Grinda went on. "When Justin feels the devil is in you, he fends you off. Ha!"

The Berber woman, standing at the far end of the table, was smiling at Justin. She had a square jaw and was very handsome. Justin could see that there was nothing Yerba feared and nothing she did not know.

"Perhaps this young man has other things in mind," the woman said, and in her harsh voice there was still singing. Justin felt his face sweat. Keeping the table in front of him, he held the cold bottle of beer that Grinda had given him. He could not look at Melanie. Yerba had stamped her foot twice under the table. She waved her arm as if warning them not to miss her words out of embarrassment.

The Berber song was quick and cruel with the enigma of the desert. Much of it was without words, and sometimes Justin barely understood. Yerba paced along the wall, pausing to act the words. Her voice was as angry as if she were the girl of the song.

> "Beloved, how long then shall I wait? Forever!
> My hair is long.
> The sun is low and burns my eyes.
> My father promises we will never meet again.
> My father does not see the fine steel
> I cherish at my breast.
> My love, you will not be taken!"

Yerba suddenly laughed, dismissing the song and her expression. "Come, Melanie, dance!"

Again the woman sang, clapping, Then Justin blinked at the dark corner, and there was Melanie. She wore an embroidered black dress that Justin had never seen. As she came forward to the kitchen table, she was under the spell of Yerba and Yerba's song. Justin watched her, and Melanie did not look back. She stepped under the low ceiling into the red light. Justin had not known that she danced. Was it possible that such beauty and accomplishment could enter his life?

In the doorway, two steps from Justin, Melanie began. Through the dance Grinda's daughter hid her face, rising and falling lightly on her toes in the lament of the older woman's song. Her arms sometimes bent over her head to make strange signs, her eyes seeming to look out timidly on the dance, as if it knew something she did not. Standing close to her, rigid against Grinda's shotguns, Justin thought of Melanie in trousers, smeared with dust and wild-tempered. But this evening Melanie was more subtle and mysterious than he could have conceived.

Suddenly Justin was afraid. What if she was not to be his?

"Good," Abu said when she paused. *"Bon, ma petite soeur, bien fait!"*

"My good daughter!" Grinda said. "Now Yerba has cooking to do. Go with Justin. He can take the gray."

The dappled stallion? Justin had never seen anyone but the horse breaker on the big gray. Beside him he glimpsed the girl's eyes. All at once, he feared being alone with her, feeling as he did. As soon as Melanie left the kitchen, the others became busy round the big table.

The sun was not yet down as Justin waited for her at the corral gate. The dusk smelled sweetly of straw, dust, and manure. Justin watched Abu's sister walk down to him. Her long hair was twisted behind her head. From the stable came a crashing *bang, bang, bang.*

"The gray wants to run," Melanie said, in a strange soft voice.

Inside the cool barn they saddled the horses in silence. Riding Grinda's pure Arabs, here beside the mystery of the horse breaker and his children, Justin had always felt his ignorance of how this farm came to be. Now, pulling up onto the big English gray, he knew what it must be to be master of Grinda's farm. And then, abruptly, Justin felt his own father close by. Was Grinda one of *them* too?

Melanie's mare broke into a trot on the glaring road. The desert shapes were darkly indistinct as they went towards the heat's great navel of red. Following Melanie, Justin saw her straight back and the slightly rakish set of her legs. She made a silhouette against the crimson earth and horizon of black hills. Her behind and the back of her legs were like Abu's or Justin's, but different, and he was sick with her. Justin kicked up the big gray. The horse broke into a light, rolling canter. As he drew even, Justin heard the other saddle pause in its quick squeaking. The mare fell in as they passed out between the three oleanders onto the dust plain, accompanied by a smell of heat, alkali, and horse. Justin's stomach was taut with loneliness. Must he tell her that he loved her? Something in Justin that loved only Greek goddesses and great fish was not quite sure that this oath would be true forever.

"Keep clear of the mares!" Melanie called. She gestured out to a small herd by a water hole. Now they were laughing together, laughing at the rhythmic squeak of saddles and the stupidity of the stallion. Both horses surged faster. In front of Justin the two gray ears pricked, then lay back. The gray was shouldering her mare to the right. They began to gallop. Justin braced against the reins. He pulled back and lurched forward on the horse's neck.

"Pull in . . . turn him, Justin!" Melanie laughed.

"The devil, I am trying!"

Justin braced back. He waved across the horse's right eye. The lathered neck was like a bent bow, the mouth had lost all sense of pain. Justin pulled and yanked back, bracing stiff-legged. The girl struggled beside him, the mare keeping pace in the shadows. The herd was two hundred meters ahead on the flat. The gray stretched its neck. The mane fluttered against Justin's cheek. Twisting back, Justin saw the mare just behind, the girl still fighting the reins. The herd circled away, cantering steadily now. The darkening ground was uneven, broken by opaque depressions. Turning again, Justin saw Grinda's daughter lurch in the shadows. Then she fell, and his life came up in his throat.

Before the girl struck the ground, Justin had jumped. There was a jolt, a shock on his hip, and a centrifugal tumble tore his arms. His mouth filled with dirt.

"Melanie!" Justin stood up and ran. He fell and was running again. "Melanie! Melanie!"

Justin found the little body lying still on its back. It was already night. He was on his knees shaking with fear. Hearing a movement, Justin gave a cry.

"Melanie," he swore. "Melanie, I love you."

"Yes, Justin," said Melanie's voice. And seizing his hand before Justin knew what she was doing, the girl kissed it. Past her head, silhouetted against the cooling pink sky, the herd tightened in a circle and stood still. Then, holding her, Justin Lothaire saw the head of Grinda's gray against the blue horizon.

In the sky was not a cloud or a star. There was a perfect silence.

THE VÁR

1

IN THE DAYS WHEN JUSTIN SAT AT THE BROW OF THE DESERT READING Europe's great writers for the first time, Karin Sunda, Hélène Le Trève, Luz von Holti, and the Siebenbergs had been together at the Villa Donatello, a finishing school in Florence. Now grown women, the only one of the girlfriends with either financial difficulties or a career was Luz.

Count von Holti had served stylishly in the Budapest delegation to the court of Franz Josef, ruler of Austro-Hungary since 1848. After the emperor's death and the disintegration of the empire in 1918, von Holti's character was laid bare. With the guile of Metternich, he became adviser to the opposed Leninist regime of Béla Kun—until this succumbed in turn to the fragile republic of Admiral Horthy. Yet the formerly spoiled and despotic chevalier's one sincere, if covert, enthusiasm during those painful times was for the racist agitator, Gyula Gömbös.

More dedicated than ever to outward appearance, Luz's father clung to a post for some years more as Horthy's ambassador to the Vatican. In 1929, however, a financial scandal among his circle over the League of Nations loans finally ruined the graceful *bon vivant*'s reputation, his fortune, and his health. Von Holti retired from his mansion in Budapest's walled citadel, the Várnegyed, to a modest nineteenth-century brick house on Cetneki Utca, where the family's meager existence was augmented by his wife's earnings as an opera singer's coach. Their doctor son, a spiritless and cynical fellow, contributed little. The last extravagance of the chevalier, once a famous figure of the Danube ballrooms, had been Luz's years at the Villa Donatello. Immediately afterward, the girl's astonishing beauty, sulky but touching, won her a place in Hungary's national theater.

Holti lived to regret his daughter's refined schooling. Her protected nature seemed impervious to the family's straits, and her blowsily attractive mother appeared content to sit about between singing lessons in Chinese gowns, her long red hair loose, flowing tendrils of Magyar charm. The peeling rooms were in permanent disarray. Much of the splendid furniture the family had saved was under sheets. The surrounding rose garden was nearly impenetrable, the untended bushes grown as tall as a man's head.

For a while, von Holti nurtured in society a precious connection with the exiled Count Károlyi—as if Hungary must soon realize that it could not hope to proceed without Holti's civilized presence. But Károlyi did not return, and Count Holti's unacknowledged favorite, the Jew-baiting Gyula Gömbös, became a premier too embarrassing even for Anton Holti. It was just as if he had died. His devotion to the refined gesture, to flattery, and to worldly etiquette vanished from the chevalier's heart. The ever-handsome, fiercely snobbish Hapsburg intriguer had once been a generous and thoughtful friend . . . but, like Job, what did his virtues avail him, confined to a banished household? His wife and daughter's cheerful acceptance mocked so grand a tragedy. Holti swore to make them recognize their position. He had no success with Luz until he heard that David Sunda was to visit Budapest that December for his sister's marriage, and like a bolt the invitation had come from the Esterhazys themselves to the wedding in the Vár.

Luz's father knew nothing of his daughter's secret engagement, though letters came regularly from Paris. He thus set out, without delay, to enlighten the girl on how a union with David Sunda would mean the redemption of the Holtis' influence.

At last Luz reacted, though not in the way the expert intriguer had intended. She began to ask herself whether she was good enough to marry David Sunda. Perhaps she was simply selling herself to him. Nothing in Luz's background gave her the strength to resolve such a question. Her one clear instinct was to guide the one she adored, blindfolded, through her father's snares. By December, Luz had become remote toward her friends, was having bad dreams, and sometimes whispered to herself.

2

BECAUSE THE LE TRÈVES HAD NOT RETURNED FROM PERSIA, HÉLÈNE MADE THE train journey to Hungary with family friends from London. David had been held up one day through an error in a train schedule and so found himself on the same wagon-lit, due to arrive the night before the wedding. Justin accompanied David to the Gare de l'Est, but Hélène did not see him.

In the morning, they passed through Vienna. There was ice on the overcast landscape now and David felt confused to be meeting Luz again and anxious at facing his parents. More than any rebellious episode in the past, David knew that arriving late for his sister's wedding would be taken by his father as a calculated insult to the choice of bridegroom. His mother would be thinking about David's influence over his sister. Already, he had been cabled that he might be left out of the church preparations. At least he had made sure that Luz's parents were invited.

Hélène sat facing him by his window. She smiled at David's sober face and spoke softly. "No, David, no. Karin will be far too busy to notice, and your parents will forgive you. Luz hasn't seen you for a whole year. Surely you should make things clear to her. Wasn't your mind made up last summer? Why not suggest a wedding date?"

David stared out toward the Danube as he relit his cigar. Beyond the water, a bleak mist hung over the Velký plain. Czechoslovakia. Could Friedrich be correct, that war with Russia was inevitable?

"What a mistake to have told you," he said gloomily. "Isn't one wedding bad enough? I wonder how well you remember Karin—perhaps I could have rescued her. Now I am too late."

"That isn't your fault," Hélène cried sympathetically. "Karin is a grown woman."

Hélène was unperturbed by David's air of surliness and condescension. She understood better than he did the powerful spell cast by family ceremony. She sat forward, hands clasped on her knee.

"David, how little you know of women's feelings," she said. Have mercy on poor Luz, or you will kill her."

"Ingenues die of great emotion only in Italian opera.

"I'm sure you don't mean that, David Sunda!" Hélène turned red, falling helplessly into her childhood manner with him.

At last, the rail lines multiplied outside the sleeping carriage. Now porters were coasting by the open window. The long train clanked repeatedly under a great dome circling with pigeons; the peaceful interlude of travel was at an end. And leaning out into the cold, David's eye found at once, coming through the excited crowd, a very beautiful young woman in a dark dress, her arms folded under her nutria coat.

"Hélène . . . look!"

"Yes, she's seen you. David, isn't this wonderful."

Then Hélène was in the passage ahead of him, springing down onto the platform. Instead of going up to them as the two women embraced, David hung back to direct the porters to Hélène's compartment.

"My dear Luz." Hélène held Luz's tremulous smile at arm's length. And seeing their separate disappointments, they kissed again in a cluster of coats and scarves. "Luz, you are just the same."

"Your last letter, Leni . . ." murmured Luz, her face even more flushed and remote. Then she could no longer help turning to David, and her gaze met his. She held out her hand, her green eyes glittering.

David bent over the hand, which was burning hot. Am I kissing the hand of my future wife? he wondered, feeling a more immediate agitation. He had ceased hearing either the crowd or the welcoming band playing Lehár.

"Father has invited you both to dinner," Luz said, and before David could reply, she took Hélène's arm with a careless flourish. Luz was acting now, and her voice had regained its full musical note. "It's all been arranged, David. You'll see your parents at midnight."

He turned pale. "But Luz, I must go to Karin at once!"

"Oh, that's quite impossible. Everyone's at a banquet on Lake Balaton. Your mother said to tell you you're forgiven . . . that your wedding duty is to take care of Hélène and ourselves."

As they hurried to keep up with their luggage, the thought came to David: *This woman has stopped loving me.* It was as if he had just seen Luz von Holti for the first time.

Despite Christmas being near, the Budapest streets and buildings, the faces outside their taxi windows, had an unloved, drably respectable look. David tried to absorb himself in the present question of Luz. Hélène was huddled between them, holding her beautiful friend's arm tightly and laughing her frank laugh. She began to ask about the ceremony to come.

In the mansions of the Vár, several hundred guests were readying themselves for the alliance of two famous families. Luz answered her friend's questions with still more careless warmth, never looking at David. When Hélène touched briefly on her theater career, a feverish excitement David had not seen before came into Luz's eyes. What has changed? David wondered, summoning his usual indulgent smile, as he tried to remember his fiancée's last letter to him.

The taxi stopped in a short tree-lined street. The Holtis' front hedge was freshly clipped.

Presently, with easy Hungarian tears and more embraces, they were ushered into a bright low-ceilinged salon dominated by a grand piano and a huge sofa bed. Signed photographs of opera stars lined the hall and stairway. Count Holti hurried to meet them, arms outstretched, smiling the ingratiating smile he had once reserved for senior ministers. Through the pantry came the heady odors of roasting pork, cheese, and stewing cherries.

And to David, her family's extravagant welcome seemed to make Luz even more aloof and therefore even more fascinating.

3

THAT NIGHT AT DINNER ANY DESPAIR THERE MIGHT BE IN THE HUNGARIAN CAPITAL seemed forgotten, even by Anton Holti. There was an exuberant abandon at the huge table by the piano, and David felt envious of how easily Hélène joined in with it. This mood, seeming in some way directed toward him, gathered to a kind of romantic frenzy, with Madame Holti laughing and crying at the same time, while her physicist cousin Leo delighted Hélène by singing gypsy love songs to her.

Even in his distress at being kept separated from Karin, David noticed that not once had he caught his fiancée's eye. Suddenly he, who had always tactfully accepted the enthusiasm of Europe's most courted young women, felt the chilling emotion of a man rejected by the one he loved. His certainty of this was now so intense and degrading that he began to feel acute hostility to the stunning woman seated under her father's crossed sabers. As a servant carried in a silver coffeepot, some of the table were discussing the macabre images used by the latest German painters. With a frozen indulgence to hide his sense of inner disarray, David sat apart, smiling at Luz's golden skin and chestnut hair.

Yes, she is more ravishing than ever, he reflected . . . and she is involved with someone else. The girl had a grace that men loved automatically. Yet somehow Luz's spirit had shrunk inside its outline. And this inner shrinking gave her presence a tragic quality. Before, Luz had reflected David's sense of himself. Now her indifference merged with his deepening remorse at his sister's fate and the sense of foreboding as he remembered their father's words at Oberlinden: *we will need you here.* Watching her, oblivious of the cries and laughter around them, David noticed that Luz's old childish self-importance only returned when she spoke of the theater.

"I like Chekhov's idea, Uncle Leo," she said, smiling and raising one eyebrow with instinctive effect. "His holiest of holies was the human body."

For a moment, then, her gaze fell kindly on David, whose expectant face no longer was that of the much-loved ideal she had worshiped but of an honorable stranger in her father's trap, with herself the bait.

"Maybe so, Luz. However!" Loosening his tie in the heat from the fireplace, Leo spoke his poor German in gasps and pants, yet with the absolute confidence peculiar to scientists. All the while he wiggled his bushy eyebrows comically. "However, knowledge changes artistic values. How can the human body be holy after Darwin? This is what the Expressionists have seen."

Uncle Leo was quite drunk, and everyone was amused without understanding a word.

"And now I will tell you something that Chekhov could not have imagined . . . that will change values more than everything else together. Physics colleagues of mine are at play with forces that any day could bring us close to the power in the sun!"

"But Leo," Countess Holti teased him, leaning under the stained-glass lamp, "how will you get there?"

"Uncle Leo will be fired from a cannon," mumbled Luz's brother Stefan, waking from a trance and tipping his cigarette holder.

"The diplomatic trick, of course," interceded Count Holti in his drawing-room baritone, not having forgotten the serious object of the evening, " would be to entice the sun down to earth."

Which was enough to spill more laughter from the Holtis' pink faces, appearing to David at that painful moment to be suspended round the table like overripe fruits.

"Down to earth is not *strictly* correct . . ." Uncle Leo began.

But tonight Count Holti was feeling sufficiently impressed by recent successes of the otherwise repellent Gömbös—not to mention the Hungarian premier's Fascist cronies in Vienna, Berlin, and Warsaw—to cut short his wife's Jewish second cousin. After all, could you not see that Leo was an alien? The intoxicated party rose and moved amiably to the far end of the room, where Countess Holti began her anecdotes of the lessons she gave to a hugely fat and famous Swedish soprano. To David, the rather debauched Hungarian gaiety had come to seem like some exquisite punishment thought up by his parents, and he lingered as the table emptied. Rising languorously, Luz came around it and sat beside him. David felt her fingers touch his hand. Hélène's reassuring laughter seemed very far away.

"Hello, my David," Luz said to him tenderly.

"Hello, Luz . . . am I your David?"

"It's better if I say goodbye to you tonight. Please, you mustn't tell Papa."

"Oh?" David felt himself reel. "So, you are saying goodbye?"

He was thinking of the years across which he had held monopoly on Luz, without making his feelings public. David's earlier hostility was turning to panic.

"Some principals of the theater are catching the morning train to Paris. I'm sorry to leave Leni alone with my parents. Will you look after her, David?"

"And Karin's wedding, Luz?" David managed to say. "Have you seen her yet? Surely she wants us all there?"

"I will be dismissed from the company if I don't go with them. Karin will have Freddy, yourself, and Hélène. I saw her this afternoon in the Vár with her bridesmaids, adjusting the dress. You know, it is so extraordinary to be married like that—fantastic, really. David, she did seem a little strange, but isn't marriage strange?"

"You would be dismissed?" he heard himself repeat bitterly.

"I need the job, David," Luz said, with another questioning glance.

David looked at the wisps of hair round Luz's temples, at her full lips, and at the feverish pity he had never seen before in her eyes. Possibly everyone knows who my rival is, he thought, and David felt his dignity harden against the spell of this actress. Luz blinked, seeming close to tears.

"I have the lead in *Orpheus* at the Théâtre de l'Odéon," she said.

"The lead? Congratulations, Luz," David said, and rocking back his chair, he heard his own hollow laugh.

To Luz Holti, dreaming wildly that the one complete hope in her life might yet tell her not to go, David's laugh sounded indifferent. She felt a sudden terror and the need to escape her suffering.

"The Odéon is quite near the rue de Fleurus," he went on. "Do you remember? I'll write to my friend Justin that you are coming."

On the chair beside him, Luz swayed, the blood draining from her cheeks. In the unreal glow of the Holti salon overlooking the frozen rose thickets, no one had noticed, not even Hélène.

"Thank you, David," Luz said quickly. And with a little laugh, her black-velvet figure and bare arms poised momentarily with theatrical grace. "Should we go and sit with the others?"

No one at Count von Holti's dinner that evening knew that they were at the last festivity the dashing chevalier would ever give. Nor that, through Uncle Leo, they were among the first to hear of subatomic calculations already under way that would seize from nature destructive powers beyond any prophecy in the Book of Revelation.

4

THROUGH THAT NIGHT, A LIGHT SNOW FELL ON THE BYZANTINE DOMES AND ARCHES of the Vár. A few hours before dawn—in his huge bed with silk sheets in a palace neighboring the Esterhazys'—one member of the bride's entourage still lay awake, considering whether he might yet ask Hélène to speak to Luz.

Then it was Karin Sunda's wedding morning. A new fire was lit when David, already in his tailcoat, walked back into the Holtis' empty sitting room. He felt at once the change in himself. His father's pleasantly ironic acceptance of his apologies the night before had restored his strength and in Karin's rather mad high spirits there had been little sense of anything terrible about to happen.

Yet David was too late to see Luz. She had just left for the station, and presently he heard Count Holti's shouts overhead and her mother weeping. David scarcely followed Hélène's quiet words as she sat next to him in a sweater and trousers.

"All this will seem insignificant afterward. You and I must concentrate on Karin's beautiful wedding . . . you look so handsome and well-rested." Hélène teased him softly.

David smiled crookedly. "Surely she knew I would be here? She said nothing of leaving so early."

"She told me to give you her love."

"That?" David looked at her. "And what explanation did she give you?"

With a perplexed frown, Hélène rose and stood at the window. There was a white glare from the snow outside.

"I'm not sure, David. I simply don't know." She sat down again beside him and looked into his tired eyes.

Even Hélène must never know what he was feeling. David stared away from her kind face toward the Holtis' now snow laden rose-hedges. In the fresh powder, separate sets of taxi tracks curved in, zigzagged, then went straight back out.

"Well. And if she didn't even explain this to you, Hélène—her best friend? I suppose it's quite a success to have a lead role in Paris."

"Poor Luz!" Hélène made a pained gesture with her fingers. "I know she'll come to regret this."

"Anyway, I suggested she should meet Justin."

Despite himself, David felt that Hélène's words had lightened the pain in his chest. He didn't notice her sudden gravity, the way she hung her head and fell silent. Then they were joined, with somewhat shamed good manners, by Luz's parents. The count seemed so touchingly humbled that David felt at once there was no one he would rather accompany to his sister's wedding. As they had been brought up to do, he and Hélène suppressed their mood and joined in the wedding gossip. They must arrive early for Karin's sake. He sat alone to collect himself, smoking a cigar and looking out over the fresh snow while the others prepared.

Upstairs in Luz's room, Hélène was gazing at herself soberly in the mirror. Justin, she thought, Justin and Luz. Numbly, she put on her stockings and slip and then her long beige silk dress. And what of David? Then she placed the black fur hat over her chignon and round forehead. Finally, feeling shaken and very dignified, Hélène pulled on her coat and kid gloves.

The wedding guests were in the Holti salon, waiting nervously. As Hélène came down, Holti—his medals clinking on his court uniform—was apologizing graciously for Luz's rudeness to the bride. How many of David's family, he inquired, would be present in the front pews?

The Esterhazy marriage was to take place in a medieval church in the Vár. By ten-thirty, a dozen automobiles already blocked the square outside, over which drifted a cold sun among threatening clouds. A crowd of curious uninvited townsfolk waited in the snow to either side, staring and trying to attach names to the ladies and gentlemen as they trudged in. Prince Colonna's familiar bald head appeared, and a mustached Bourbon-Parme. A family of Thurm und Taxis was in the car behind David's, and he glimpsed Anne-Catherine d'Estainville as she moved into the church with the Comte de Paris and Count Széchenyi.

Inside the Gothic doors, there was much bowing over outstretched hands. David caught sight of his brother, standing by the central aisle with Michael Bismarck, two of the Keswicks, and Zigi Zamoyska. Friedrich waved with a little grin and, handing some programs to a footman, he came forward. They formed a group under the organ balcony.

"You disappeared again—strangely, our father chooses not to notice. But can this be Hélène?" Friedrich bent playfully over her gloved hand and clicked his heels.

David answered stiffly, "An urgent matter needed settling. Anyway, Karin seemed blissfully taken up . . . when will she be here?"

"Was the urgent matter settled?"

"Yes," David said.

"Our sister? She is like Joan of Arc going to the stake." Seeing his brother's face, Friedrich laughed. He bent to whisper, "Mother was convinced that if you and Karin were allowed one second alone, she might leave the poor fellow at the altar. . . . You should probably speak to Mother now."

For some moments more, David stood with Hélène and his brother, watching the elegant groups come through the doors. He felt too overcome with love and pity for his sister to move.

"Let's find Mama," he finally said. "Freddy, I'll meet you on the steps before eleven."

"We can at least enjoy the wedding," his brother said. "We won't see many more like it."

"What has happened to Friedrich?" Hélène whispered, hugging David's arm. But as they inched into the crowded aisle, she tried to set aside her distressing impression. "There, in the front row isn't that your mother? Oh, look at the candles and the flowers!" Hélène said softly in his ear as they moved slowly forward. "David, somehow despite everything, this is so lovely. . . . " But she did not finish.

Presently, Hélène was seated among the bride's family along the second row. David left hurriedly to meet Karin, and Hélène leaned forward to exchange encouraging whispers with his mother, so impressively innocent. Then, forgetting her elegance, Hélène perched on the edge of the bench, not to miss the slightest detail of the ceremony in which her eccentric roommate of Florence was to give her life, her happiness, to a man.

Hearing a rumble that set her heart fluttering, Hélène rose to her feet for the procession. But as the organ burst forth, and through the rows of heads she saw Karin—a cloud of chiffon advancing on her father's arm, flanked by David and Friedrich—Hélène felt nothing. Her innermost being was concentrated on Luz in Paris, and on the moment when for the first time Luz would see Justin Lothaire. Feeling an instinct verging on fear, Hélène stared reproachfully at the three men escorting the bride . . . then, turning to the altar, at the bridegroom's stupid decadent face. How vacant Karin looked, how lusterless and pale.

A time came when the kneeling couple were saying their vows, the groom's voice flat and nasal. David's sister replied in soft, uncertain Hungarian. Before the hushed cathedral, with all her family's eyes fixed on her, the bride reached for her train. As she rose, Hélène saw Karin's stricken face turn toward them, as if without sight.

The mighty organ pipes rumbled. Music flooded the cathedral, the congregation peered and smiled. And passing through them, the bridal pair disappeared from the church.

5

FROM THAT HOUR, THE WEDDING BELONGED TO THE GUESTS, TO BE CELEBRATED
and devoured. The throng dispersed into Budapest through a dense blizzard
to meet again in an ornate Hapsburg palace on the Danube. There, among
tables piled so high with delicacies that the pleasure lay in not being able to
consume them all, the frivolous chatter, drinking, and eating went on through
the afternoon.

After what had befallen Karin and himself on the very same day, and with
Luz out of reach in Paris and alone with Justin, David felt wearied and
depressed to be among this crowd of spoiled young aristocrats and was
relieved to discover an old acquaintance of his German schooldays, Adam von
Trott. Trott was on Christmas vacation from Oxford, where he had gone to
read politics and economics. They found that they had much in common and
soon had made plans to travel together to the ball arranged for that evening.

By nightfall the blizzard had stopped. At eight o'clock, David and Trott
went to Cetneki for Hélène in a sleigh with three black horses driven by a
Tatar in a ragged sheepskin.

The night was moonless, with only the glow of floating snow. In the
sleigh, the three huddled in their ball dress under a heavy bearskin.

"I'm so tired and excited," said Hélène. "And this night is a complete
dream!" The sleigh lurched on its runners, hissing after the horses' heavy
bodies.

David settled back under the hairy animal-smelling rug. The sky was
clearing. Responding to Hélène's mood, he scented the cold breeze and looked
up at the stars, infinite and tiny over the dark roofs of Budapest—and, beyond
Hungary, over the roofs of Berlin, Paris, Moscow, and the other capitals of
civilization. Suddenly David was conscious that all the blows and cruelties of
the last twenty-four hours were subsiding. A peaceful sense came to him, of
fate's workings and of the grandeur of life seeming to stretch out, fresh and
unbroken, like the snow-coated boulevard ahead. As the horses broke into a
canter, he leaned across Hélène.

"Adam, about what you were saying at lunch . . ."

"About your brother, or the future?"

"My God, no more relatives!" Hélène broke in. "Let it be the future."

Trott gave a quick little laugh. "Yes, it's dangerous to wake a sleepwalker.
Which of us will wake old Germany and tell her she is being kidnapped by
a gang of brigands and astrologers dressed as police? Yet many people keep
trying."

"There's sleep in all our eyes," David said.

Trott was momentarily grim. "Perhaps Germany won't wake at all.
Perhaps we will be asked to banish God."

"*Comincia la commedia!*" David laughed to hear an acquaintance from his own background put into words what he had felt to be so painfully wrong at Oberlinden. He and Trott could easily become friends.

"Rather than serve these vile persons, I plan to try for a post in Peking. What about you, Sunda?"

"World travel exerts the strongest attraction!" declared David, half seriously. And falling back on the leather seat, the three kicked up the bearskin, drunk with the release of the night, the freedom of their minds, and their conviction that they were equal to whatever changes might come.

"What a pair of shabby romantics!" Hélène taunted, and it was clear that she considered the two of them the only interesting men at the wedding.

Three boulevards freshly coated with snow converged at a stone wall below the dark gables and domes of the Vár. The driver skidded the sleigh in the deep fluff, the runners crashed deafeningly on the bare cobbles under the archway, and they swung steeply uphill behind the laboring horses along an alley of carriage entrances.

Presently, the three walked across a frozen courtyard, passing into an entrance hall hung deep with mink, chinchilla, bear, wolf, and seal coats. They went through the reception line of Esterhazys and Sundas—from which only David was missing—the women with sashes and hair piled high in waves and curls, the men bending over a procession of perfumed hands. Baroness von Sunda's steady smile softened as she kissed Hélène's cheek, then the cheek of the prodigal. She straightened David's crooked tie with faint displeasure, ignoring his abstracted face. David tried to meet Karin's dazed eyes, withstood her husband's conceited scrutiny, squeezed Friedrich's arm, and for the only time in his life saw his father welcome him with an embarrassed, grateful smile.

Then he passed into a tapestried ballroom, shimmering with candles, ribbons, and glass spheres. There was a din of excited voices and the husky groan of a New York jazz band. And as David paused by the swaying dancers, and saw again the young women's bare shoulders and familiar, exhilarated faces, they meant nothing to him. There was only one person he wished to be with.

"Would you dance with me?" he heard himself say.

"Yes, David," a voice answered gravely, over the soft ripple of saxophones. "Of course I would." He felt a warm hand in his and a taut supple back against his palm. The young woman came lightly, fittingly, against him.

Unable any more to see one another, David and Hélène began to dance.

6

JUSTIN LOTHAIRE SPENT CHRISTMAS IN PARIS. IT WAS UNUSUALLY COLD, AND THE snow stayed on the grass in the Luxembourg. He divided his days between the empty rooms on the rue de Fleurus and the office of *Justice*. His life and work were only here. Duncan might be somewhere across the Atlantic, Johannes with his mother in the snow of the Bavarian Alps, and David with Hélène Le Trève at a wedding in Budapest. But their lives were not his, and he did not risk thinking about them. It was a relief to be alone, naked before his books. Outside the salon window hung the gray northern winter, a cold that drove him deep into himself, far beneath the surface of his body.

Only months before and just a few hundred kilometers to the east, books had been burned—by edict—in city squares throughout Germany. To Justin, such an act was the darkest enigma. Books had brought him to Europe; now Europe was destroying its books. Yet nothing in the crowded, bright-windowed *quartier* streets that Justin loved seemed changed. To be on vacation from Paris would have been unthinkable.

On New Year's morning, Justin set aside Machiavelli on state violence and walked through the empty streets to Saint-Sulpice.

It was too cold to notice the beautiful weather. In the little carriage yard of *Justice,* there was ice on the cobbles.

The office door was ajar. Through the glass he could see a stranger with Eli Hebron. Neither man spoke as Justin stepped in. He held his hands with theirs over the coal grate. The stranger wore a heavy sweater. His oversize flannels were skillfully patched. The man's accusingly intelligent eyes were sunk in a waxy face, his hair shaved so close to his skull that you could not see its color. His eyes fixed on Justin.

"Max, this is Justin." Eli turned to Justin, "Polonsky is a mathematician."

Justin noticed Eli's luminous smile. The visitor might still be young, though he looked worn.

"Go ahead," Justin said quietly.

"A week ago Max escaped from internment in Munich."

"Thursday night," the man corrected, his voice sounding unnatural.

Abruptly, the room was dense with physical fear. Justin felt his head swim. Thursday night—in Fascist hands? On Thursday he had been at the Old Masters exhibition. On Thursday, David had mailed him a postcard from Budapest. Justin looked up and met the man's eyes with a faint smile. This was the first victim to come to them. To sit in this office.

The stranger's face relaxed, looking older. He frowned into the powdery coals. Galleys of type stood on the table. There was the medicinal smell of printer's ink.

"They have started the serious roundup." The man spoke so softly that Justin and Eli held their breath to hear. "I saw men hang with their wrists behind their back, long after their shoulders dislocated: Jews, revolutionaries, artists. Anyone with opinions."

Justin breathed deeply. "Eli, I've left my pen."

"Here, Justin, take mine."

The visitor remained all morning in the cramped office of *Justice.* It was

the first day of 1934. In Chicago and San Francisco, legal champagne celebrations were still in full swing. But here in Paris, in this cold printing shed
among empty streets, Justin and Eli sat for the first time speaking to a victim,
their young men's voices soft and grave, hearing, as if from a broken bell, the
dull clank of arrests and beatings. *Jews, revolutionaries, artists—anyone with
opinions.* Abruptly the new Europe had appeared between these peeling walls,
beside the glowing brazier. It came like a premonition of the silent drawing
away of peoples, as before a tidal wave. A Europe of mass migrations, of
exiles and refugees, of pocket states called camps, with lengthening borders
of barbed wire inside which innocence was tortured to death.

At midday, Justin stood with Eli at the window of *Justice,* watching the
shaven-haired man outside delicately open a torn umbrella.

"Where will he stay?" Justin's melancholy eyes followed the nondescript
figure out of the courtyard.

"With a friend," Eli said. "Justin, what do you think?"

Justin took out a cigarette. "I think that we in this room have loved the
truth. We have tried to prepare ourselves for it. And now the truth has come
to us."

Presently, when he left *Justice,* the Paris crowds were back as usual along
Saint-Germain. It was as if the sacred disaster of the visitor's words had been
left locked in the drab little office. And remembering that David Sunda's
Hungarian actress was opening tonight at the Odéon, Justin felt a quite normal
rush of curiosity.

7

YET THE LONG COMMUNION OVER THE COALS AT *JUSTICE* LEFT A WOUND. IT WAS
somehow a relief when the evening came and it was time to circle the Odéon
and enter the theater crowd. On the posters was printed the name *Orphée.*
Justin looked through the ticket grate.

"Is there one for Lothaire?"

"Will the center of row D suit monsieur?"

"Suit me?" When had Justin Lothaire sat anywhere but the cheapest upper
tier?

The cream-colored foyer was packed. Avoiding two critics who might
recognize him from the Lamberts', Justin drifted among the splendidly
dressed French. In the European night an immense brutality was awake,
against which clothes, connections, and money had no defense, and in three
days *Justice* would put words to it in the Paris boulevards. Passing into the
theater, he found his place in the fourth row.

Tonight's pre-Christian tragedy was acted in modern dress. Justin sat forward and tried to concentrate, but he could not fathom the stilted language of

the actors moving above the darkened audience. The drama of the refugee played through his thoughts in that morning's whispering voice.

At the backdrop, the heroine appeared. She was a full-bodied young woman in a flowered dress, with thick reddish hair. She came forward, feet bare, her large eyes blinking with a curious wonder and pathos. Through the theater passed a faint sigh.

Crossing his arms, Justin leaned back, suddenly conscious of the uplifted faces motionless around him. In the taut silence, Eurydice spoke her first lines. With a defensive glance at the balcony lights, she moved a little, then spoke with an absorption so naive, eccentric, and flowing that she seemed to have no need of acting at all. A freshness billowed over the darkened stalls like dew out of a clear night sky.

From the moment he saw Luz Holti, the morning at *Justice* went from his thoughts. Justin's breath came steadily and the audience, with its disturbing clothes and perfumes, receded. When presently the German actor playing Orpheus bent over her, an absurdly violent jealousy stirred in Justin.

The intermission came. Justin went outside to the artists' door, as Luz had instructed him in her note. But instead of the dressing room, he was shown to a stage wing and leaned among the pulleys. Twenty minutes later in the dark, watching Eurydice wander in the underworld, he was thinking, Could this be Luz, Hélène's best friend? Never before had he imagined such beauty could exist in flesh. He felt confused by a sensation of limitless freedom. Now Eurydice was being led by Orpheus up from among the damned. Orpheus glanced back at her.

As Justin watched, the actress turned and floated back over the stage through the faint blue shades. Her exotic green eyes were fixed on his face. Justin flinched at the sudden thundering of applause. As Eurydice reached his darkened space between the wing curtains, the lights flooded on. The curtain must have fallen. She came in past Justin with a spicy smell of makeup and perspiration. She was a head shorter than him.

"Luz?" Justin said firmly. Now behind the curtains there was a whispering scurry of theater people, everyone smiling at Eurydice. She faced him.

8

"*VOUS ÊTES JUSTIN?*" THE WOMAN SAID, IN A HIGH, THIN VOICE, HER HANDS tugging at the gold braid in her hair.

Exhausted, elated, and raw from the play's final moments, Luz had two seconds to smile up at the austere young man frowning in the blaze of lights. In that instant she felt disappointed. Then, with a warm stab of pain, she remembered. This was the "Greek" Hélène had fallen in love with, the person David admired above himself. Smiling again, she turned and walked back onstage.

Luz felt herself drowning in the renewed thunder of these hundreds of clapping strangers. She lifted her arms, and flowers struck her shoulders, dress, and hair. Turning, then, she glided back through the curtains.

"I kept forgetting the French." Luz laughed.

"The French will not forget you!" Justin said, and for a moment deep embarrassment came over them.

"Do you have to change?"

"It will take ten minutes."

"I'll wait for you then."

"I think there's a space in the artists' passage."

For fifteen minutes, Justin paced, stopped, then paced. Again and again, the phrases he and the actress had spoken to each other returned like a fabled dream, sweet and significant as no words he had read or heard before. He tried to make his hands strike a match.

"Justin, shall we go?" said a voice. Just one step from him under a passage light, her green eyes looking steadily into his, stood a young woman in a nutria coat. Feeling his pride drain out of him, Justin took Luz's bag and held the door.

"We can have dinner at Polidor—it's nearby."

They crossed the Place de l'Odéon in a strained silence. But Justin remembered the stage, and Eurydice's passion, and how this was Hélène's closest friend.

Inside Polidor's misted windows the deep room was jammed. Through the thin white columns, faces stared at the gloomy poet and his fabulous girl. Luz avoided their eyes, looking uncomfortable and disturbed. The kitchen had stopped serving. Seeing Justin's face, the *patronne* laughed and took them to a table anyway.

"We often come here with David," he said to Luz.

"Really?" Luz looked around the noisy room with some interest. Pushing her coat off her shoulders, she stared at Justin's face. For five long seconds he had his first lucid picture of her—of the fine Magyar cheekbones, the face so rich in subtle angles and suggestions that the eye could not rest on any single feature. Over this mature architecture hovered an unmistakable childish sulk. And somewhere in those exotic eyes, Justin detected a simplicity as poignant as sacred music.

"Your French onstage was remarkable," he said.

"You don't sound like a native either."

"I'm from Algiers."

"My father once worked in Paris, years ago." She looked away.

"Mine was killed by the French—" Justin said to her, as they were interrupted by the *patronne*.

He could not tell if Luz had heard. Marooned in a din of voices and dishes, they had to lean near the wall to understand each other. But when Justin saw shyness among the subtle play of emotions, and when Luz's eyes again met his with perfect trust, he felt a sudden need to weep, or to sing at the top of his lungs.

As for Luz, the strange person before her seemed to convey the first sincere conviction she had ever known.

Their plates arrived, to be paid for with his last five francs. Justin heard himself begin telling her about the desert and the souks and Grinda's horse farm, about his scholarship and how he and David had met in Switzerland, about Marcel Doré, and about *Justice*. When the hypnotic face only gazed mildly back, Justin began to boast as he had never boasted in his life. The strange idea grew in him that this angel had somehow been sent to him for some purpose, and he murmured to her movingly of the new infamy of barbed-wire frontiers, of the present dictator in Italy where she had once been in school, and of the revolution that was coming everywhere. He was offering Luz all he had. What could it matter that this exotic Hungarian, now abstractedly eating a hot tarte Tatin, did not show emotion or even say very much?

And so on New Year's Day of 1934, in perfect innocence of one another, they fell in love. *Orpheus* ran at the Théâter de l'Odéon for another week. And the day after they met, Justin for the first time took his small wage from the cashbox in the office of *Justice*.

9

IN THE BAVARIAN MOUNTAIN VILLAGE OF WILDISCHES-GLADBACH, JOHANNES Godard spent the first two cloudless days of January walking in the forest paths with his mother's beau, who he knew as Uncle Franz. Like all men whose closest friends are women, Franz Kind tended to an appetite for spiritual conjecture, so the talk was on metaphysics.

During their last walk, before returning to his mother's ham and noodles, Johannes had paused with Uncle Franz at a bend on a gloomy cow track. Both felt at peace after a near delirious debate during which Johannes had compared the ecstasies of the prophets, by analogy with the medievalist brothers Grimm, to certain researches of the Gottingen astrophysicists—bringing all this home neatly to highlight the opposed Christian and Hegelian conceptions of historical power.

The river below them splashed over ice-capped boulders, on into the gorge. Through the passage the river made in the trees, the darkened snow ridges looked cold against the evening sky. Taking off his spectacles, the older man chuckled.

"You see, Johannes? Flecks of conversation, frozen to my lenses."

"Are they not like Hegel's city"—Johannes's eyes glowered triumphantly— "the collective mind with its body clothed and focused by architecture?"

Uncle Franz laughed, shook his head, and sighed deeply. "My boy, Kohler in Berlin is an excellent friend. What if I wrote to him on your behalf?"

"Do you know Professor Kohler?" For many years Johannes had been aware of Uncle Franz's influence with the philosopher. Now all his devouring intellectual ambition was abruptly transformed into a childlike, almost fawning modesty. Berlin University . . . to follow Paris? It was his greatest hope. At that Olympian moment both men were aware that Johannes considered the offer a matter of destiny, something beyond coincidence, surprise, or even gratitude. What in Christendom was more appropriate or deserved?

"Wait until Mother hears!" Johannes burst out, turning them slowly back down the path.

"Of course, I can only do what I am able," Uncle Franz added, though it was clear to them both that this too was modesty. This quiet citizen of Basel was one of Europe's most renowned thinkers.

Next morning the genial doctor was back on the train crossing the picturesque Oberbayern snowfields to Munich, there to perform a less comfortable task. Tomorrow he would deliver to a symposium of medical men interested in clinical psychoanalysis an address entitled, "Stress Within Mythology: The Present Nordic Crisis." Was it not, after all, the most aggravated issues that were most worthy of examination? Still, Uncle Franz had had to steel himself not to omit the word "present."

The following day, nearly a hundred of Germany's most distinguished doctors, neurologists, and analysts were crowded into the darkened amphitheater of the medical academy, when Johannes's benefactor appeared far below on the rostrum. Through a host of monocles, Doktor Kind was observed to nod, arrange his papers, then smile up at his colleagues. Some of those close enough for him to see them nodded and smiled back shyly at their famous friend. A reverent hush spread through the audience, the gravity common to the innermost sanctums of German research.

Uncle Franz's address did not last the customary hour. His objective was to analyze the basis for racial hatred in the contrasting personae of the Germans and the Jews. Within minutes his voice—quite naked in the terrified hush around him—was praising the Jewish kings of scripture for their accommodation of human weakness. Then he described the German heroes as less fertile spiritually, more recent and childish, with a Christianity grafted onto the living trunks of forest demons.

"The blond beast is lurking in his cave"—Uncle Franz hesitated, aware of tumbling monocles—"waiting to break loose. My dear colleagues, the German people are on the verge of serious mental disorder. Of an epidemic of schizophrenia that could lead to mass hysteria."

Then, clutching the lectern for support and ignoring the gasps and agitation spreading overhead, Uncle Franz informed his colleagues that the new minister Goebbels had invited the great Doktor Kind to give his chancellor a medical examination. The Doktor had declined.

"The only way you will get rid of Hitler, my dear friends, is to induce him to commit suicide by invading Russia," concluded Uncle Franz, peering up through the rows of shocked faces. For some reason the amphitheater lights had come on.

"Doktor Kind! Doktor Kind!"

Red cheeks addressed him, mustaches twitched. Old men's voices protested, faint and anguished. From their eight chairs behind the rostrum, the faculty elders had gathered around Uncle Franz. His attempt to speak about anti-Semitism was over. From the benches of embarrassed middle-aged men, of whom many were Jews, arose a disturbed buzzing, as neighbors fell into angry argument.

"Doktor Kind," one voice hissed repeatedly, "this is *racism.*"

Tasteless . . . preposterous . . . inflammatory . . . superstitious! other voices were calling out. Then the sudden uproar subsided. Everyone turned back to the speaker among the group onstage.

Behind the lectern Doktor Kind now stood alone, crushing a ball of English tobacco into his pipe bowl. Somehow overcoming his sensation of grief and horror, Uncle Franz gazed up with a martyr's gentle irony at the hushed ranks of his colleagues. On their intelligent, reasonable faces he saw clearly the wounded pride—and an unmistakable trace of fear.

"All right, gentlemen," he said, in a strange voice. "I will say no more. But only for the time being . . . for the time being."

THE WATER TOWER

1

OR THE BOY JUSTIN LOTHAIRE, IN THE WINTER OF HIS FIRST PASSION, THE Mediterranean shore was as lonely as a great beauty without love.

Not for many months had there been word from France. Then, early one Saturday in April, there was. Justin lurched up from the table and stood at the bead curtain. In the alley, a drenching rain tore and splattered, making a river over the stones that bore away the odors of saffron and wool. Justin turned to face the lace shop and his mother's accusation, the letter unfolded on the table between them.

"But, Justin! Are you ungrateful even for this?"

"Grateful?" Justin blurted. "I know how you need to be grateful to everyone. However, no, I am not grateful, and I would like to have some time to think about it."

Not daring to discuss the disturbing letter another second, Justin wheeled and jumped out into the rue Mahbu. Immediately his shirt stuck to him, tugging at his arms.

Justin paced through the market until the sun came out and golden steam poured through the alleyways. And as he walked, his whole soul rose in revolt against Professor Lavil. Paris, the Sorbonne—what did Justin require a French education for? Had he not created himself out of the dung, leather, and spice of the casbah without these French? Were they now laying claim to what *he* had created? The worst of it was that the idea of such an education satisfied Justin deeply, basely. For this he despised himself.

University could save him from the memory of Father Xavier's whippings. It could save him from being fatherless among the French and raise him above the brutality of Ibn Moushmun and his crate of guns. Worst of all, a university was freedom from the Michauds—from Madame Michaud's lace tablecloth and from Nana, who had disdained his worship of her beauty. When he tasted this last revenge, Justin's soul panted with a satisfaction so powerful and profound it frightened him. Instantly, his imagination broke loose. Justin saw himself rise to reign in fame and brilliance over the capital of the French and over all the Michauds forever.

Then what if he did not? What if he gave up this one fateful opportunity for justice so that the world went on just as it was now? At the thought of this, Justin's soul convulsed. It was almost as if Monsieur Lavil had book-trained him to crawl, and, looking down, Justin now found he was on a narrow catwalk over a bottomless gorge. Only if he submitted to this dishonorable crawling might he reach the other side.

Lost in this debate, Justin found himself entering the Café de Thebes, where young Neapolitans and Arabs vaguely known to Justin boasted and shouted to one another. At the back, four old men sat stiffly behind glasses of mint tea. But before Justin could sit, he remembered the day it had been before the scholarship arrived in the post.

On the wall tiled with tiny mirrors the clock said ten-thirty. Melanie Grinda was in Algiers! At this very moment she would be under a mimosa tree at the Café Mosquée.

2

JUSTIN REACHED THE CARRÉ MOSQUÉE TEN MINUTES LATER. MELANIE WAS AT A table facing the great minaret.

Grinda's daughter had on a new yellow dress, cut lower than those of the town girls. She kept her eyes aloof from the crowd of young men at the tables. Meeting her look—haughty, devout, and utterly true—Justin felt unsteady.

"You came with the rain." Melanie watched his face.

"I am very late. In the post this morning . . ." Frowning at his palms, Justin thought of the avenging hatred of his ambition. A desolation closed over him. "Listen, Melanie, the Sorbonne has granted a scholarship."

"The university in Paris. So, you will be able to go?" Her eyes feasted on Justin, unwilling to miss the flicker of an eyelid.

"The scholarship is nothing. It is a trick, an artifice." He saw that the last word brought a look of respect to Melanie's face. "It means nothing to me."

In the shade, their eyes were close. She must see the treachery in him, Justin thought, forgetting his love for the Greeks and the great artists.

"Sir?" a voice repeated.

"Two coffees," Justin said.

The short waiter knew his name. Melanie had made the man polite.

"Black or white, sir?"

"Dark brown," Justin said, and Melanie and the waiter laughed together. "You know, with just a *soupçon* of milk."

"A *soupçon*," the girl sang huskily, and the waiter seemed almost reluctant to go for the order. Then Melanie looked into his face, and Justin knew that Grinda's daughter had not understood their danger.

"Sir, your dark-brown coffees—with *soupçons* of milk."

The blue-glass cups were filled to the brim but not overflowing. Melanie gave the waiter a dazed smile, and he seemed to dance as he walked away.

"Justin, I brought your nougat."

"Melanie, your gift! I forgot it."

Justin looked past her round the murmuring tables. When he thought of this whole day that they had together a panic tightened his jaw. What were they going to do in all those hours? For a moment Justin saw himself at sunset, alone with his books in the Public Library, and he felt sick with remorse. Life had come to him. Now he must live.

As they left the café the waiter waved to them. And presently Justin discovered himself taking Grinda's wild daughter to all the secret places he knew best. In his library room over the rue Mahbu she was excited by the view of the sea and immediately seemed to know the corner shelf where Justin kept his chosen books. When they went out past the kef dealer, sitting as usual in the passage, Justin to his surprise saw the old Arab smile. Finally, his heart breaking at the peril all these simple things were now in, *from Justin,* he hid Melanie in the alley above the lace shop while he went to buy her a little felt camel. When he returned she gazed above the billowing awnings.

"Is that your roof, where you lie under the stars?"

"Very soon I will take you to see," Justin swore, and Melanie gripped his hand. Bent now against the stones of the alley wall, Justin kissed the corner of her mouth. It made no satisfying sound, but they both knew that it was a kiss. By now his whole being was intoxicated with the sublime smells of neat's-foot oil, soap, and hay and with her warmth.

From that moment the day was different. And from the moment he smelled Melanie's smell, Justin knew there was much more of her to know, and he wondered that Melanie could have such treasure without speaking of it.

Late that evening, the terrible hour drew near when the *poste* bus must carry Melanie away. He felt melancholy as they looked at the carpets and tin crucifixes in the shop windows. Melanie sat on a weather-stained boom at the boatyard, and Justin told her the story of the great fish—all except for Ibn Moushmun's crates. When Justin finished, he and Melanie went and sat on the Môle de Pêche, where they looked over the oily calm and listened to the evening crowd. He had adored her for so long, yet before this they had never been alone together for a day. They were flushed with the sun and tired and rich with all the emotions of those hours. How could they separate after coming close?

"Melanie?"

"Yes, Justin."

"I want to be alone with you. Not like at the farm or today but truly alone."

"Yes," she said. "I too would like us to be alone."

Next to her, dangling his shoes over the water, Justin's heart tightened. A mad speculation rose in his throat. Melanie twisted against him and threw another snail's shell into the water. The shells left little clouds of sand where they fell in.

"There is an empty water tower in the trees behind La Source," Justin said.

"Could we get into it?" Melanie asked, in a weak voice.

"Do you mean you would?" he whispered.

"Yes. I think so." She blushed with pleasure and alarm. "Next Saturday . . . perhaps."

In their last half hour, a great seriousness came between them. Justin and Melanie paced arm in arm, turning and turning up alleyways. They paused in the throng by La Marine to buy ices. A Neapolitan drunk was propped in the recessed doors of the Cabaret Ouedi. Melanie's hand tightened on Justin's. The drunk was absorbed with something on the pavement—a paper cup, spinning with the dust in an eddy of wind. The beggar glanced over his shoulder, then stared away as if not wishing to be observed. Again he looked away, but his head jerked back and his reddened eyes followed the rolling cup.

"The cup hurts him, because he thinks it is like him," Melanie said softly.

Lying awake on the roof that night, long after the *poste* bus had carried Grinda's daughter away, Justin wondered at the perfection of what Melanie had said about the beggar and the paper cup. How easily the idea had come to her, while he with his books had to work at understanding the simplest things.

3

ON SUNDAY MORNING JUSTIN WOKE WITH THE IMPRESSION OF MELANIE'S LOVE and her promise of the water tower. Escaping the lace shop and mass, he went down to the Jetée Nord to watch Ibn Moushmun at work.

"*Salud,* little rebel."

"It is beautiful, Ibn Moushmun."

A boat stood on blocks sunk in the tiny beach. The sand was cool in the shade of the hull. For an hour the dark, pitted face spoke to Justin from inside through a gap in the planks. Ibn Moushmun spoke about Arab workers being superior to all others for their virtue of never being drunk, while the French took the wages and the land. Justin had heard this futile talk before and it soothed him. A true devil would not repeat himself.

The construction was at the satisfying stage when the keel and ribs are laid and enough planks have been warped on so that a fleshy form moves into the wood, making it unmistakably a boat.

"Could I make such a boat?" said Justin, who for the last hour had been thinking how he would earn the money to live with Melanie.

"You do not learn by reading books. *Alors, viens,* it is the hour for tea."

Soon they were pacing into the alleys of La Marine. Justin's satisfaction had already flown ahead to the five-table café of men between the fish markets. He barely avoided a gathering of Arabs round a gray donkey, which was swaying like a rack of bones between two wicker baskets of mussels.

"Ibn Moushmun, Look!" The animal had bald patches on its wizened gray coat. It lurched and staggered, and the long, furry ears flopped back on its neck. A handsome Sudanese gendarme stepped past, his teeth flashing.

"Too poor to buy a colt?" someone shouted, and the donkey's master—an ill-tempered Kabyle in a soiled robe and head cloth—appeared round his animal, waving a cane. Seeming afraid to look at anyone, he rushed back and forth, brandishing the stick and then pausing to beat his donkey. But the animal only coughed hoarsely and hung its head. At this, the man renewed his blows, jabbing the stick under the donkey's tail and kicking its stomach. As the animal's hind quarters gradually sank, then lolled to one side, the mussels crashed down, clattering over the cobbles. The driver stared round him wild-eyed at the growing crowd, as if he expected some awesome judgment. Then, seeming to lose all touch with what he was doing there, the man began to club the donkey's eyes and mouth, as if to make it vanish and thus end his notoriety. Red blood appeared on the brilliant gray cobbles. The donkey's head slowly fell, until its muzzle came to rest. Then it rolled sideways, so that only the splayed front legs were upright.

"Ibn Moushmun, the animal is dying!" Justin said.

"*Inshallah*. And he is not your donkey, little rebel."

The black *cachabia* beside Justin rustled with indulgent laughter. Just then the donkey's front legs folded.

"Ibn Moushmun, do something!"

Under the suddenly oppressive sun, Justin's mind clouded. When Michaud had tortured the cat and told Justin about it, Justin had laughed and stayed on the earth. When the helpless fish were blinded, Justin had stayed on the earth. Was Justin Lothaire going to stay on earth again, now, in love with Melanie, while this thing was being done? Suddenly he seemed to feel the eyes of the crowd. Shoulders buffeted him, his knees weakened.

On the street in front of him the donkey lay still. Only its flanks heaved, swaying the top basket. At that moment the driver's stick flew apart on the donkey's skull, and he began to kick the beast's narrow spine.

"Boy—boy!"

Justin felt a powerful hand grip his arm. He struggled free. And suddenly it was easy, all of it easy and strange. The lamb of God lay at Justin's feet. And bending over it was shameless Evil, awaiting Justice. In Justin's dream, things moved so slowly and with such clear direction that he could measure the snarling, upturned face and feel the perfect bulk of his own fist as he pushed forward.

His feet skidded. Uniformed black sleeves clamped him from behind. Justin wrenched and kicked foolishly, and against the sky Ibn Moushmun's face was serious and alert. The driver had sprawled on the baskets and was getting up. Then he was loose in front of Justin with the broken stick, his nose crushed and darkened. Now I will kill him! Justin thought. But the broken stick whooshed and stung Justin's neck, and all three bodies fell. Justin was fighting free, and there were more gendarmes.

Tearing himself loose, he ran after Ibn Moushmun. Only this time, instead of running into the Arab, Justin was running hard alongside him. Their quick-running feet made the same sound. They did not slow until they were in the casbah and had reached Abu's mosque.

Justin's friend was not in the courtyard, but the fountain was. Justin kneeled by the running water and bathed his neck.

"Ibn Moushmun," he panted, barely controlling the shake in his voice, "you are an animal."

"*Et toi, Ben Kacem*?" Ibn Moushmun laughed terribly. "*Tu es chrétien!*"

The next afternoon after literature, Justin went up to Monsieur Lavil's desk and told him that the letter had arrived. As the teacher grasped Justin's arms, an expression of deep affection came into his eyes. He glanced at Justin's bandaged neck, his humble face.

"It is your fate. Now come with me for a *pastis*."

"But this scholarship, Justin . . . you will accept it?" Monsieur Lavil inquired presently, as they walked under the palms on the rue Bonaparte. In the cool arcades the young Frenchwomen passed, their legs swinging fresh and elegant below colorful summer dresses.

"Go to Paris?" Justin answered. "Yes, but it's only the beginning."

4

DAY AFTER DAY, HOUR AFTER HOUR, AND STILL NO MESSAGE CAME FROM THE horse breaker's farm. By Friday at dusk, Justin felt so moved to despair that he could not speak to his mother without shouting at her for not being Melanie.

Leaving his books, Justin moved his mattress back onto the roof. For hours he sat cross-legged, staring westward over the darkening terraces toward Oran. How did I ask such a thing? Justin kept questioning himself. How and why? Only now, lying rigidly awake on his ledge, glaring up at the stars, did Justin hear an old friend. The little throat raised its song over the constant din of the alleys. It trilled, rose, found the note again, and faltered into silence. Then it took up the note again, fluttering over it, then sank into a deep moan so full and trembling that it merged with silence.

The nay, he thought. And listening to it, Justin was asleep before he had even stopped smiling.

Knowing that Grinda's daughter would not come, still he went next morning to the *poste*.

The bus was late. When finally it came it was so packed that Justin could not see in the windows. Then the engine died, and drums and chanting were heard inside. No one could get out until the front door was sprung from outside. Justin skipped back as six boy musicians jumped down into the arcade and spun wildly without dropping the rhythm. On the bus steps above them stood Melanie.

As she climbed unsteadily down and walked to Justin the musicians took up *"Jabalia."* which means mountain girl. Then suddenly the dancers had surrounded her, half naked in colored shirts and sashes, green, purple, and carmine paint glistening on their cheeks. As Justin took Melanie's hand, the flute and drumming picked up. The musicians came after, as the dancers twisted and spun around them. Like some violent procession of Dionysus, the group passed loudly under the arch and up into the Arab town. With a coy, satiric flourish, the leader flashed his teeth and bowed low to Melanie and Justin, never dropping his ironic blue-edged eyes. Then the dancers paced away down an alley towards the great market, striding in a thunderous roll of drums.

Justin and Melanie walked without a word the two blocks to the Café Mosquée. Their shady table was free. He guessed that Melanie had nothing on under her yellow dress.

"Café au lait—deux," Justin said, so that the waiter had to bend to hear him. Then, touching the bark of the mimosa tree, he said, "Melanie, do you remember the water tower?"

"Remember?" she answered in a strange, light voice, and she laughed.

"It is possible for you then?"

Justin leaned close, taking her hand between his. Melanie tugged it free with a second small wild laugh. Then she seized Justin's right hand, holding it as if it were his soul.

"Yes, I asked Yerba. Today it is safe."

"Is this . . . is it the first?" Justin frowned, his ears burning. Along the promenade the French husbands were staring at them.

Melanie nodded. "There was never anyone else."

"No one knows about the place, not even your brother. I found it by accident," Justin said. He watched as the girl sent a strange, agitated glance round the busy café, the windy square, the glaring white mosque. And minutes later they went, free and young, to begin a new world.

A *chergui* was blowing hot from the Sahara. After the long climb through town, Justin brought her to a eucalyptus grove thick with oleander. Boys' voices carried to them from La Source on the dusty wind. The grove was empty and still except for the rustling drone of wasps.

"Do you see, Melanie—there?"

The old tower rose from the oleanders. The tank above them was painted a long-since faded red. Up the side of the triangular frame was a rusty ladder.

They stopped on a soft bed of yellowed leaves and bark. In the reek of euca-lyptus among the trees Justin stood, heart beating. She leaned gently back on him, and he felt her against his legs. He smelled her smell of perspiration, washed hair, and garlic. A suffocating heat closed around them. They owned nothing else. This was the kingdom of heaven.

"It is lovely," Melanie whispered, and Justin felt as proud as if she had liked an old friend.

The rungs of the ladder were rusted thin. Justin climbed first into the oblivious heat. In the quick scrape of the girl's shoes below him, Justin heard their conspiracy. Climbing into the trees it got hotter, and the thrashing fronds struck their faces, hiding the rim of the tank, but as they reached the top the late-morning sky blazed down on them. Justin stepped over, pausing to listen and look down through the branches. Melanie's strained eyes followed him, as if hypnotized. Then she was above him, and he saw the length of her brown legs. She stepped down and rested in his arms.

They stood in the bottom of the tank, where the sun half fell, their heads below the waterline. Under their feet was a soft mat of leaves. It was strange and lawless here. The circle of sky above them was neither the cold Christian sky nor the more placid sky of the Aegean. It was the merciless desert sky of Berber shepherds.

Her eyes were drugged with feeling. "Ah, Justin, I like it here. I could stay forever." She had loosened the yellow dress.

"Melanie," Justin repeated. It was all he could say.

"Hurry, Justin. Oh, hurry."

5

IT WAS STRANGE AT DUSK TO SIT AGAIN IN THE NOISE OF THE CARRÉ MOSQUÉE. IT seemed that he and the least-tamed beauty in Algiers had just come from some place of sacred passions that these people knew nothing of. Justin could not help staring at Melanie. And when he did, Melanie could not look at Justin or speak.

Then quite abruptly they were in the crowded arcade at the Oran bus, and the driver was collecting tickets. Melanie fixed her eyes on Justin's, and he saw her afraid and confused.

"Next Saturday, Melanie, will you come?"

"Yes, Justin. Will it be like today?"

"Like today . . . only much more," Justin promised, holding the hands that knew him. He did not kiss her because of the noisy crowd pushing around them in the darkened arcade.

But when he saw Melanie's face in a murky window of the bus full of crude men, Justin's heart broke that he had not. Despite the Arab faces laughing in the next windows he ran beside the bus as far as the Esplanade.

6

A MONTH LATER JUSTIN LOTHAIRE SENT A LETTER TO THE UNIVERSITY OF PARIS, declining the scholarship.

From that hour Monsieur's Lavil's face hardened whenever he saw Justin. The glorious debates by the fountain in his friend's patio abruptly ended. Now Melanie caught the bus into Algiers regularly: on Sabbaths, as his mother called them. But Justin never took Melanie to the lace shop. And he was afraid now of Grinda—and of Abu, who would soon be joining the new puritanical Ulema. Without asking himself why, Justin avoided the small mosque where Abu was studying. On Sabbaths he and Melanie vanished together in a profane glory where no one else could follow.

On the Easter Friday of his seventeenth year, Justin set out to walk alone in the rose garden of the Jardin d'Essaie. How could he be as tormented and alone as before now that he was in love? How could his feeling for Melanie change, and with no way to control it? Why did their partings tire him so, as if each time he loved her he had to relift a heavier weight?

Pausing on the garden path, Justin looked up to watch the swallows twirl and dip high in the warm tangerine sunset. He noticed that when two swallows came together to mate or to fight they immediately fell from the soaring flock, fluttering awkwardly. When their mating was done, and just before the swallows reached the ground, they separated and raced up the sky. This excited Justin. Nature did not intend them to give themselves utterly, but only to make their nests. When I have Melanie beside me, Justin thought, and I am teaching at the *lycée* to feed our children, then we will be in love and happy all the time, and we will soar together.

And so there in the French gardens it came to Justin that he could marry Melanie. That this was all he had ever wanted, and that with one act all the anger and dissatisfaction of his life could come to an end. Tomorrow Melanie would travel in from the desert, and he would speak to her of families.

When Justin returned home the windows of the lace shop were dark. In the depths, he could see candles burning at the cardboard Virgin.

Justin nearly fell over his mother. Jeanne was a huddled mound kneeling on the carpet, her forehead pressed to the stone floor. A gurgling voice droned in the weak light.

"Mary, Mother of God, have compassion on thy wretched children."

At once Justin knew that something terrible had happened. His mother sat back, lifting her face to the kitchen ceiling. She knotted her thick fingers to her breast. The yellow candles glinted on her swollen cheeks.

"*Maman, maman*, what has happened? What is it?"

"Our Father, who art in Heaven—"

"Don't call to him, *Maman*," Justin hissed, sinking onto one knee beside her. "Tell me . . . tell me!" He squeezed his mother's plump shoulders, feeling revulsion and pity. But when she turned her eyes, Justin's fear turned to terror.

"Tell me!" he said.

"The Michauds' tablecloth."

"You sent it back yesterday, *Maman*."

"Madame Michaud says it is torn. That I ruined it—after all these years!"

"That is impossible!" Justin cried. "I took it back myself."

"She told Madame Lasalle and Madame Courtenay!" wept the broken face. "This morning, Madame Cambon sent her cook for the doilies. I hadn't even begun them yet."

Kneeling with her on the carpet, Justin opened his mouth but no words would come. Was it not what he had always prophesied for his mother's gratitude to the Michauds? Yet it was no help to have foreseen it. His mother was being ruined, and her son humiliated with her. And nowhere in this world was there a father to keep them from sinking without a sou among the lowest rabble of Arabs.

"I will speak to them," he whispered. "They cannot be serious."

"They said—" The old woman choked.

"Out with it, speak!" Justin shook her.

"Madame Michaud said . . . I was not to send my obnoxious son with excuses."

Justin had exploded to his feet. An uncontrollable vibration spread from his knees to his stomach. When he spoke again, his voice was strangely deep.

"Well, then, and what did you say?"

"That I was sorry you were like that," she muttered self-pityingly. "That it was difficult to raise you without a father."

In the dark above her, the lace cleaner's son half lifted his hand to his face. The he let it fall and leaned against the damp wall. Justin thought of his life in this little shop in a slum, dreaming of gods, kings, geniuses, and love. A strange new lust of uncompromising rebellion churned deep and strong in his soul. In the violence of this anger, a peculiar peace came over him. Then from deep in Justin arose a quick, sharp, uncontrollable laughter that he scarcely recognized. It rang sharply off the low dark walls. The candles jumped around the blue, pink, and gold Virgin.

"Justin, how can you laugh? Put that down."

"Who is it?"

Justin's mother had climbed to her feet. "Obey your mother at once! Put that photo back!"

"Maman, why do you hide it?"

On the candlelit ledge beside the Virgin, Justin had noticed a yellowed portrait in a black frame: a dark face with a familiar high forehead and a mustache.

"It is my father, isn't it?"

His mother was trying to prise the frame out of his fingers. Justin held it up high. Walking through to the bulb that hung in the next room, he stared into the grave, intelligent eyes of her secret portrait. Though the photograph was filmed by time, and though he had never seen the face before, Justin instantly knew this man as he knew himself. Abruptly he lowered the frame to his mother's hand.

Without a word, he plunged out through the bead curtain into the noisy street.

Through the minutes that followed, Justin did not think of Jeanne Lothaire, who had hidden his father from him for seventeen years. He felt nothing for Melanie Grinda. She now belonged to a time when Justin had dreamt of being at peace with the world. From this hour, he would be on bad terms with everyone. I prefer it this way, Justin thought to himself as the evening crowd carried him down among the French. The photograph stared back at him—still alive and possessed of the knowledge that Justin had sensed in Grinda and Ibn Moushmun. A sharp Arab pride flickered in Justin's soul, and his eyes shot hate at each approaching face.

Only then did Justin remember the Paris scholarship. He seemed to catch sight of it receding from him, and with it the promise of a greatness from which Justin Lothaire might have towered over all Algeria, protecting the simple and poor from the vileness of the rich.

Coming out on Bab-el-Oued, Justin began to run. If he could only fly over the rooftops to Monsieur Lavil's villa! Now as he ran Justin seemed to hear the drums of Sidi Idriz rumbling after him and the keening of all the invisible downcast of the casbah.

On the great stairs Justin fell. He skidded on the heels of his hands, then was up again. Seconds later he pounded on Lavil's door.

7

WHEN JUSTIN LEFT THE VILLA AN HOUR LATER, IT HAD BEEN SETTLED. MONSIEUR Lavil would write to a friend in Paris, asking that Lothaire's refusal be ignored. Seeing his teacher's forgiveness, Justin experienced a humble gratitude.

Then he hurried to a café in La Marine where he might find Ibn Moushmun. The night boulevards were exotic with strolling colons. Presently, when Justin stepped through a second bead curtain into the back room, Grinda's Arab was there, sitting with a dozen grave strangers over a game of canasta. Only he was in a *djellaba*.

"So, it is the little Christian!" called Ibn Moushmun in his rasping voice.

Several at the table turned to examine Justin. Seeing their hard faces, Justin experienced his old fear, but tonight the memory satisfied him. Ibn Moushmun and his world would have to fear Justin Lothaire, who from this hour was on bad terms with everyone. Consequently, Justin felt quite friendly toward them.

He waited for Ibn Moushmun in the dark under the palms.

"So, Lothaire, what is there to say?"

"I am going to be a student in Paris. I will learn to think how the French think."

"So." Ibn Moushmun whistled between his teeth.

Justin look at his hands in the café light. "When it is done," he said, "I will come looking for you. We will go to the Atlas, to Krim's people."

"Ha!" Grinda's Arab slapped his chest, and his hooked teeth glistened. "Justin, you are the son of your father."

Justin bent his head, feeling an emotion so childish and profound that his ears burned and his eyes clouded over.

As he climbed the alley stairs back to the rue Mahbu, Justin thought about what his mother would say when he told her that he would live his life as a writer.

Madame Courtenay's servant had brought a pair of curtains, but Justin refused to kneel with his mother before the cardboard Virgin and give thanks. The ledge next to the Virgin where the photograph had been was empty.

That night Justin lay awake until the shop was silent. Then he felt under his cot for a book Monsieur Lavil had lent him. With great caution he stole out into the wet alley. The night lay ahead. Tomorrow was Easter, and the Public Library would be closed. Justin had never used his forged key before. He locked himself upstairs and lit the small paraffin lamp. Arranging the heavy book, he opened to the first page and read:

> The wealth of societies in which the capitalist method of production prevails takes the form of an immense accumulation of commodities.

And so, hour after hour, at a dim table above darkened roofs, the contents of this book—written in England by a German Jew married to an aristocrat—entered Justin's imagination, where only the Greeks, Grinda's children, and the Michauds had trod. As the Arabs and French of Algiers slept, a bold prophecy, once delivered to snowbound industrial masses, passed into his heart.

After an hour, the tissues of Justin's mind were aching from the unnatural shock. All that was passionately free in him heaved back from these iron bands that entangled his life in an economic class. Weakling, he cursed himself, open your mind. What if this should be the key to a better world?

Under the weak flame, as he turned the pages, certain of the abstractions were beginning to seem familiar. "The only wealth a worker has is the labor he can provide—only if the capitalist needs it," and, "The capitalist appropriates the vast majority of the workers' profit, simply for the favor of having manipulated them."

Justin thought of his mother, asleep in their little shop. He thought of Madame Michaud, who did his mother the favor of letting her clean the wine stains from tablecloths. He thought of the impoverished fellahin, now crowd-ing into shantytowns, and of the French landowners. Above all he thought of Ibn Moushmun, of his father, and of the guns.

Justin awoke to the early dawn and slowly shut the book. The paraffin lamp went out with a hiss. For ten hours Justin had not drunk or eaten, and his head was splitting. He would never open Monsieur Lavil's book again. But Justin was moved, for he had felt the work's power and its closeness to his own life, and to a shame that he had once thought only he could know.

All that day he walked through Algiers, though never in the same street twice. Finally he shouldered slowly back through his beloved market, where no one but Justin had communion with the prophet called Marx. Then it was the sacred hour of dusk, and the air of the spring evening carried the smell of roasting meat, nougat, and spice. For a moment Justin clearly heard a nay. Then it was drowned by the simplified groaning of a popular singer.

Now when he thought of Melanie, and even of being a writer, it was not all. Justin Lothaire belonged to a world movement.

8

NEXT SATURDAY AT THE *POSTE,* JUSTIN WAS WAITING AS USUAL IN THE ARCADE crowd. But today the sight of the blue-and-white bus nosing out of a narrow street did not make him smile foolishly with happiness. Melanie jumped lightly from the bus, swinging her rope bag. Her hair was brushed back and coiled like a woman's. Walking to him under the arcade, her nostrils flared and her mouth hardened.

"Justin, *never* look at me like that," she said.

Justin turned from this young Frenchwoman to hide a surge of irritation. "How did I look at you?" he said, walking slightly ahead of her.

"As these men look at street girls," Melanie said softly, so that no one under the echoing arcades would hear.

Justin felt shocked that she had seen into him and could disapprove of what she saw.

"Everything has changed. Come to the roses."

"And La Source? The water tower?" Melanie asked.

"We must talk," Justin said.

They rode the harbor tram, passing the Gare de l'Agha and the Hôpital Mustapha, and jumped down from the rear platform at the iron gates of the Jardin d'Essaie. Justin led Melanie to a bench.

"I am accepting the scholarship. I am going to Paris," Justin said, and he felt the violent twitch of her hands. "It is for us. When it is done, I will return."

"Justin, do not do it!" Melanie cried out, her voice very alone among the sunny paths. "Why is it so important?"

"Justice, the truth. There is so much more than *this*." Justin stood in front her, arm raised. "There are books, Melanie, and great men, artists, histories, philosophies. . . . Here I am worse than the soles on Michaud's—"

"No," she interrupted, her voice confused as always when Justin spoke of books. "It is stupid to talk of such people."

Justin had stopped pacing to break the thorns off a rose. His fingers fumbling, he pushed the stem into the hair over Melanie's ear. Seeing her devout passion for him, he felt drugged.

"I will come back," he said. "I will be a writer, and people will say, 'Look what this boy from the souk has done.' Then these Michauds and all the dull bourgeois who love nothing in this world, and act as if they created it themselves, will be forced to hear the truth."

"You can insult the Michauds without going to Paris, you can write without going to Paris. If you must go to Paris, let it be because you want to learn."

"Oh, it is knowledge I am after—the power to turn man into a respectable species. Then I will be free."

"And it will be the same with us?" she said.

"My father was a Kabyle and I am a Kabyle," Justin swore, their hot faces very close.

"Justin, will you teach me all you learn?"

Justin smiled triumphantly. He bent to kiss Melanie's bare shoulder. Her skin smelled of garlic, horse and jasmine.

"I will, I swear it—everything."

"No, Justin, there is only one thing in life." Melanie held up the cup of her hands. "It is what we have."

"We will have it." Justin took her hands. "But first I must learn So wait, Melanie—you will see the world turn to hear what I say. Would that not be yours?"

Melanie had twisted toward him on the bench. And when he saw the wild dreams in her eyes, Justin was afraid of his words. The words of an urchin from a slum.

"If that could be!" she was saying. "And when you are the greatest Algerian, will you remember Abu and Melanie then?"

"How could I not remember?"

Remember? They were his life. How could his life be forgotten, any more than roads could be bent or trees simply vanish? It had never crossed Justin's mind.

Presently, he walked with Melanie hand in hand along the leaf-matted waters of La Source, at that hour foaming with the naked brown bodies of small boys. Their secret eucalyptus grove closed round them, hot and dry and dusty. The iron rungs rang against their soles.

"Sssh!" Justin warned. But the wooden floor was unchanged. Their old blanket was partly coated with a new falling of leaves.

Justin and Melanie had never made love so poignantly as then. Never had their skins been so moist and sweet on their bed of leaves. Never was the body that was the nave of Melanie's spirit so beautiful to Justin, never her dark eyes so helpless with the mystic passion he could go back and back to forever. Everything would be possible. Everything was good.

9

THE PUPIL KNEW EVERY BEND IN THE FIFTY KILOMETERS TO TIPASA.

Justin sat in the hot gale beside his teacher, staring through the windshield. Had he often covered such distances on a bicycle—and tomorrow would he begin the longest journey of his life? Justin got up to stand with his head out of the car roof. And, squinting into the wind, there by the road far ahead was the monolith. Justin dropped back in his seat.

"Would you like to meet Grinda?" he said.

"The father of the girl? Is there not enough to discuss?"

"The horse breeder is your equal."

"So?" Lavil sent Justin a grin. "You tempt me."

They were turning off the road. Why had Justin never thought of this? Today his two teachers would meet like Enkidu and Gilgamesh: the horse breaker and the philosopher.

"On such a road he is wise to ride horses," shouted Lavil, holding onto the wheel.

"Stop, Michel! Stop!" Justin suddenly shouted, hands braced on the dashboard.

A cloud of alkali dust and smoke rolled past them, skirting the burnt clay. What would Lavil think of a farmer like Grinda?

"What is it?"

Justin had jumped down from the running board. Lavil walked round to him. A kilometer below the rise they could see the windmill, stable, and corral of Grinda's farm. By the timber were yellow spots—the dogs on their invisible chains, panting in the red dust.

"Look . . . Grinda!" Justin was pointing to a little figure in the corral.

Grinda had jumped on a black yearling, the animal's head pinned by Amet. Abruptly, Justin's stomach tightened with grief and love.

"I cannot see so far"—Monsieur Lavil was wiping his spectacles on his shirt tail—"The lenses do not keep up with my blindness."

"Grinda is in the corral with a stallion," Justin said, taking a step. Down among the fences, smoking with dust, the horse had just bolted. It plunged, yawing and jolting Melanie's father. The sound of Amet's shouts rose faintly on the clear desert morning. The black snaking body spun three times under Grinda, lost its balance, and crashed in a white ball of dust in which only a straw hat was visible. Then Grinda reappeared, hatless. With a studied motion, catching the horse by the head, he twisted and threw it kicking back down in the dust.

"*Jésus*," Justin muttered. And for a moment he longed to run from the side of this alien philosopher and fly down to the old man in the corral, the father of his earliest friend and of his first love.

"Come then, Monsieur Lavil, we should go," Justin said, quickly turning back.

"Yes, there really is not time," Lavil agreed.

They got back into the car. And soon the Chenoua, the massed mountain on the west jaw of Tipasa Bay, rose violet-colored above the coast plain. Instantly, the Greeks were with them.

There was no one at the excavation when they climbed down. Justin made his way up the temple steps.

"*Maître!*" he called. "If Socrates could see! Two millennia, and we are just the same, the philosopher and the disciple."

"Metempsychosis, Lothaire." Lavil climbed after him with a grin. They set out their lunch. Then the teacher crouched against the base of a column and took out his pipe. "But pay attention," he went on, when they had listened to the ancient silence. "It is time for me to tell you how you will live your life in Paris. What you will learn, how you will cultivate your scholar's reputation and your intellect."

Stretched on the steps, the disciple shivered and looked out to sea. He thought again of Grinda's farm, where there were no books and no reputation.

The teacher had emptied his cup. He pointed his pipe out over the bay. "First we swim. The two kilometers to that point will give us appetites."

Monsieur Lavil rose with Justin and, leaving their clothes in the temple, they went down to the water.

It took more than an hour, swimming rhythmically in the cold winter sea. Justin did the gliding sidestroke he had seen in a film of pearl divers. With his breaststroke, Monsieur Lavil fell behind and Justin had to slow his motion. And this slow swimming, despite Lavil's strength, somehow worried Justin for literature. Abu, Melanie, and Grinda all swam faster. Finally, they crossed back over the bay.

Skins stinging, they sprawled for some minutes on the sand. Then, in the temple, they ate. Justin had never heard Monsieur Lavil speak of Paris before. It was almost as if Paris were not a mythical place but a city you lived in, like Algiers.

"Here, Justin, I brought you a map. You can keep it."

The moment the map was spread before him on the marble by the smoked fish, Justin forgot his misgivings. It showed streets, parks, and quais and in that respect was like Algiers. Yet here in the North African sun were the famous names, proving indeed that Paris was the city of Balzac and Stendhal: Faubourg

Saint-Honoré, Tuileries, even the Étoile, where the body of Victor Hugo had lain in state. Not just the poetic tropes, but actual finite streets and squares.

"This is wonderful, beautiful, impossible!" Justin cried out, forgetting Grinda and the lace shop. And such gratitude rose in Justin's throat that he found it necessary to rise and pace along the fallen colonnade.

"Where did you think I was sending you?" Monsieur Lavil laughed as Justin sat down. "To the catacombs?"

Smoothing back his salt-matted hair, Justin leaned against the column, one knee drawn up so he could look over the map . . . his map.

"Here, these are for you." Monsieur Lavil held out his hand. Justin took from him two envelopes of a blinding whiteness. One was a letter to the Paris office of the French Communist Party.

"And this address, Palais-Royal?"

"Well, Justin, you have read all Doré's work," he said.

"The author?" Justin was suddenly dizzy. "Is he still living?"

Then Justin understood.

"You *know* him, Monsieur Lavil?"

"In my *Quartier latin* days"—Lavil smiled—"he was very kind. I'm sure he will be kind to you too."

Justin laid the precious letter carefully on the map, his fingers trembling. He had just been presented with the greatest capital in Europe and a pass to meet its finest writer. This was a wealth greater than the villas and tennis clubs of the Michauds, and for some long minutes Justin sat limp and amazed.

"One day," Lavil said, "a certain Lothaire will return to Algiers as its foremost thinker. You and I know what is going on in Spain. One day it will come to the Saharan colonies—your day, Justin—and Algiers will be free."

They lay in the sun on the temple steps looking over the bay, and the Frenchman's words floated pleasantly out in the afternoon hush. If the revolution was so near, Justin mused, who could stop it anyway? Or why? What would be lost if the old princes and industrialists, who sent poor people to war, vanished once and for all? Nothing would be missed. Justin shut his eyes and bit into the goat cheese.

"It is said that poets have no business in politics."

Lavil stretched in the pale sun, considering this with an idealist's gravity. "Yes, we will have to find a new poet," he said. "An individualist who doesn't mind being like everyone else."

The pupil's gaze moved from a solitary fisherman setting his net under the Chenoua. A white schooner was anchoring off the beach, its owners sitting on deck with their lunch. These might even be the Michauds. The Apollonian noon was suddenly feverish. In the temple the cicadas had stopped singing. Justin listened more closely to Lavil.

"In Paris you will have room to expand," the Frenchman went on. "University is like military service. One is thrown in with all types from all places. But you will stand out, and that will give you strength in your judgment. It will amaze you how stagnant and provincial things are here."

"I love it here. These are my people."

Lavil laughed. "Algiers will always be here."

In the temple ruin their last talk went on with the dedication of the bumblebees visiting the thistles that grew in the sand. But the truth was that this conversation already seemed to Justin limited and unsatisfying. He scarcely felt surprised to hear his teacher say that these ruins—which Justin had always accepted to be Greek—had been built by Romans. The presence of the yacht beyond the breaking waves stirred his imagination, while these lessons only traveled in circles. From the moment Justin saw the map an intuition of Paris had begun. If in life anything was powerful and noble and true besides Grinda and his children, Ibn Moushmun, and the desert sky, Justin would find it in Paris. It was as if Justin's soul needed to stretch and take on dimension. So as evening fell on Tipasa, he had only half heard his teacher's final advice. Though Justin would not have understood it anyway, and the Frenchman did not truly grasp it himself.

"Listen carefully," Monsieur Lavil had said. "Out there will be false dreams along with great dreams. I hope, Justin, that you will learn to tell the dreams that are true from truths that are only dreams."

10

WHEN THE NIGHT OF THE SAILING CAME, JUSTIN LOTHAIRE STOOD WITH HIS mother on the steamer's bottom deck, crushed close by the children of Allah. Above the Grand Quai and Agha hovered Algiers the White, dimly pearly and mysterious. The keening of a Muslim wake came to Justin like sea-birds through the dark. The city was a fortress from which his soul had sprung, and drawn wisdom, and now he would leave it behind. Justin felt empty and sick.

Against the ship's rail Jeanne pressed near her son, holding his hand in both hers. Tonight, Justin was happy to have her warmth against him, even if she wore a lace shawl. Her fear made his mother tense and childishly devout, and Justin saw that she had been beautiful once.

"Justin, the deck is moving under my feet," she said.

Justin opened his mouth, but his voice sounded faraway and unfamiliar. Someone was elbowing him.

"It's all right, *Maman*." He squeezed her fingers. "You must get down there in two minutes."

"Justin. Oh, my boy."

"Mother, I wish I could stay with you."

Justin's heart leapt with a wild hope. His mother could free him from this. She had only to forbid his going.

"I love the rue Mahbu," he said.

"Oh, no, Justin! Your name was in the newspaper. Now you must go."

Abruptly Justin was alone, crushed on the wooden rail by lunging shoulders. His eyes followed his mother's white shawl down the gangway, past the porters, between white-uniformed French officers. He saw her jostled by a tall Arab. She lurched, without a French officer's taking her arm. Did they not know that the little woman in the flowered dress was his mother? Justin clenched his jaw against angry tears.

The quai was moving beneath them. "*Maman, Maman!*" Justin shouted. He waved down to the tiny uplifted face behind the darkened barrier. She could not see him. Tugging loose from the crowd at the rail, Justin ran behind the wall of struggling backs to a mound of ropes.

"*Maman, Maman!*" He leaned far out, waving. The steamer had gathered way, and his mother was coming level again. Around the motionless figure at the white barricade, the crowd waved and threw paper streamers across the widening space

"*Maman!*" Justin shouted, and his soul wept that she did not see him and that they had no paper streamers to throw at each other. Justin's throat made a small explosive sound and he waved again. Then his mother saw him, and she began to wave with the others.

At that moment Justin Lothaire recognized the Frenchman in the overcoat, waving among the red faces just behind her. It was Monsieur Lavil, whom she had never met. Justin stood motionless with his arm upraised. He looked over the harbor among the dark ledges of the souk, and he heard the sweet clamor and excitement of the night. His home, his alleys . . . his land. Tomorrow he would not hear the voice of the lemonade man or the shrill cries of glorious small boys under the eucalyptus by the waters of La Source. He thought of the sacred places, and how tomorrow they would not have Justin to love and give them their meaning, and he experienced an excruciating pain. The steamer had glided back. Its bows came to the end of the quai, and a black abyss of water opened under him. Justin wiped his sleeve across his eyes. Yes, there was a familiar gray truck parked over the dark pilings.

"Melanie!" Justin shouted. "Melanie—here, here!"

Justin gestured. But neither the girl nor the solid Frenchman in riding breeches stirred where they stood, a little apart from the final lamppost.

"I promise!" Justin shouted to her across the slowly tearing paper streamers. "I promise!" But the tiny figure made no sign.

Later he went below to his cabin. The seven fellahin he shared it with lay asleep. Justin had imagined the hallowed bed on which he would make the journey to the capital of the world. This curtained bunk smelled of unknown bodies. Hugging his mother's old suitcase in the dark, Justin vowed not to entrust the dreams he was bearing to these strangers. He lay alert in the blackness of his bunk, his skin bristling with dread.

"Eh, toi, mon garçon. Tu dors?" It was the insinuating lisp of the thin-mustached Paris Arab on the berth overhead.

Justin gripped the oily sideboards, his jaw clenched with disgust and fury until he thought the bunk might creak. Finally he heard the regular, selfless breathing of sleep. Throwing off the suffocating blanket, he lay wide awake. It was early in 1931. Already the grief over Melanie was receding. Justin's thoughts turned to the struggle ahead and to the prophets of a new humanity. For without knowing how, he knew that he would stand among them. And that when Justin had the terrible power of the truth in his grasp and the best thinkers of his time around him, the greed and cruelty of small minds would vanish. But quite soon he slept like the others. And in his deep sleep his hands found the gray blanket, rank with nameless bodies, and he drew it round his neck.

BONDS

1

THREE YEARS HAD PASSED SINCE JUSTIN'S FIRST NIGHT ON THE MARSEILLE steamer. A second dictator, Hitler, had joined Mussolini on France's frontier. In Paris, Justin Lothaire was a familiar figure of the *Quartier Latin*, the editor of *Justice*, and a protégé of Marcel Doré.

But in that January of 1934, after the Hungarian actress Luz Holti left the city of Justin's exile, it was as if nothing had changed. Along the wide paths of the Jardin du Luxembourg dunes of leaves rustled underfoot, mixed with the blue leaflets of the Fascist riots, and pinafored schoolchildren hurried home through shadows scented by wood fires and roasting chestnuts. In the barest room at number 1, rue de Fleurus, the desk lamp glowed above some papers. Next to a suitcase that was never unpacked Justin lay stretched on his bed, feeling deeply shaken. Had he truly just read Melanie Grinda's letter without emotion?

Yet tonight there were the Paris streets, where he might be known yet never have a place. For the first time then, Justin Lothaire blasphemously compared Grinda's daughter with the angel who had been sent to him— Hélène's best friend. When he beheld Melanie's simplicity and her unworldly manner, Justin was afraid for their innocence together, and he felt no love.

Lunging to his feet, Justin went through to the salon. He stood at the blackened windows, his heart fluttering as when the magician's white doves had settled on a boy in the great market at Sidi Idriz.

"It is not impossible," Justin said out loud, the sound unnatural in the silence. "You might marry her."

Sitting then at the Fleurusians' long table, Justin found a pad of stationery. He felt a sudden calm, almost a happiness. How effortless to write to Luz Holti of love, far easier than to Melanie.

By ten o'clock Justin had scribbled six sheets of confessions and madness, and he went out to mail them. When he came back, Justin threw himself on to a sofa. It was done. He was free of the abyss. He had won back his strength. Exhausted by his struggle with the European night, he fell instantly asleep.

But in fact the matter had been settled many days earlier, on the stage of the Odéon—at the moment Justin first saw Luz come toward him, barefoot and in a simple dress.

2

LUZ HOLTI RETURNED TO PARIS IN LATE FEBRUARY, WITH TWO OLDER ACTORS IN the Budapest theater. Every night Justin Lothaire would be standing at the stage entrance when she came out.

By now, *Justice* was able to pay him more for his current articles about Barcelona under the leader Largo Caballero. Justin could take Luz to cheap couscous parlors, to the Rotonde, and once even to the Boeuf sur le Toit. And over these tables, and along the paths of the Bois de Boulogne, he spoke of his dreams in the desert. Justin spoke as he had never dared to with Hélène, and the breadth of his rebel vision alarmed even him. Yet it bound him to this woman. And Luz would listen, looking back at Justin with gentle, disturbed eyes, her submission suggesting some infinite knowledge of him. Often they spoke of the stage, Justin with the devotion of a novice, and Luz reacting with an actress's vain intuition. Justin had no experience of a society in which beauty and enlightenment were not the invention of genius, and he respected Luz's aura of grace without qualifying it. On their second Sunday, at dusk by the Tuileries pond, Justin caught Luz's generous figure in the curve of his arm and drew close the scarcely real face. Was it this mouth that had shared the breath of Euripides and Racine? And Justin kissed Luz then, with all the sensuality of long ago in an Algiers water tower.

Qui est-ce? . . . Qui est-ce? he penciled the next day in a notebook, during an editorial meeting at *Justice*. For when Justin and Luz were apart, he remembered their constraint. There was an irrelevance of gesture and thought in this Hungarian that constantly irritated him and seemed to contradict the generosity of her figure. Luz was so willing. How was it that he never met with the slightest resistance? No matter how intensely Justin advanced, his instincts never encountered a distinct will, but only diffuse impressions, like the smoke of hurriedly doused campfires. Was this love? He had never asked the question with Melanie. The two women were so different that Justin could not feel his guilt. When he thought of Melanie's words—*When you come back, will you still be Justin Lothaire?*—he did not know why they had once hurt him so. And of Hélène, Justin did not dare to think at all. Each night after a performance, when Luz's exotic, gentle, almost humble face lifted to his under the stage door light, Justin felt the wildest certainty that she would be at his side in the struggle ahead. Still, after their first two weeks, he had not taken Luz to the rue de Fleurus.

Then one day, as he left a lecture on "Slavic Autocracy and the

Superfluous Man," Justin was halted in the vestibule by David Sunda. "David! So you are back?" Justin embraced his friend with nervous enthusiasm.

"Dreaming of your republic in Spain? Come to the Maggots."

"You know that Luz is in Paris?"

As they came out a light rain was falling. David stopped in the wet pavement. "Do you remember what I told you? Luz owes me nothing. I only heard from Hèléne that she was here."

Justin stood frowning, confused by his emotions. What if Luz saw Hélène and he were discussed? The situation was being made to go faster than Justin could follow. They walked together for some minutes in a silence tense with questions. As they emerged in the Place Saint-Germain, Justin stopped in front of his friend.

"David, what if I were to move out? What if I asked Luz to marry me?"

"So it's that!" David laughed. "Well, it would have little to do with me . . . but *marriage?*"

"To me it is just as strange. I cannot say no to her." Justin had gone pale.

"And the young lady in Algiers?" David was suddenly thoughtful. "I thought you had the hardest head, Justin."

As they sat down at a corner table Sunda slipped out a tin of cigars and lit one. Among the bohemia in this bright room (the rightists met next door at the Café Flore), his formal suit, which David never unbuttoned when seated, gave him an aura of detachment.

"Listen, Justin," he began. "You should know what I know. There is not much that I have not been told about your circle at *Justice*. I must tell you about your future with Luz . . . oh, a genuine actress, and exceptionally attractive. However, there is a wounded soul. Holti's cruelty . . . the mother's drinking . . . other problems of the family. Luz is without the moral resource you will need. There is not enough endurance between you, Justin."

"You almost married her! Can her family be worse than mine?"

"Yes, I must have decided against the idea." David stared away wearily. "How long it took me."

"But that is why. You have been fed on too many women's love. You are crushed by the slightest frailty."

David's laugh was good-natured. He made a sign to the waiter. "All right, Justin. You present yourself as someone who is starving."

"I do not present myself," Justin said.

"A figure of speech. You are a soul so hungry that you could be fed on any food. And when you cease to starve—how will Solomon judge Luz? I would not like to see it."

"How will my hunger end?" Justin said quietly. "From my first breath, I have been hungry. I will never be your Solomon. If there can be almost no woman that you love, then I can love any woman. All women."

David stared at Justin incredulously.

"My God, surely you do not believe that? Don't you know life's most elementary lesson? One day you will stop growing. Then you must have, fully developed, a cultivation of what is best in your life. Without this perfectibility you will never be free. You will go in circles."

"My marriage will not be for connoisseurs. Or I will not marry."

"You will marry, Justin, because you fear solitude, and yours is so vast." David took hold of his friend's shoulder. "No, wait . . . so do I. Yet I fear spiritual squalor even more. We are both starving, but I would rather be hungry than mistaken—"

"—and die of a mediocre marriage?" Justin smiled with grim pleasure. "I can see that. But as my soul could never be satisfied, better to strive inside a marriage."

"But, Justin, that too. What if your blessed hunger depended, actually grew, *sprang,* from the nonentity of your casbah? What if marriage anesthetized you?"

Justin leaned his head back against the cold window.

David gazed at him, and both their faces were grave.

"*Merci,*" Justin murmured. "I am giving that thought."

"Let us put it another way." David proceeded urbanely. "What is a person without his powers? If he is very wise, a man may be married without losing his freedom. But if he is too sudden—*snip.* It is gone."

David concluded with such mock innocence that Justin could not help smiling.

"And so, my friend, at least promise me this. That you will ease—ease ever so slowly—into this marriage."

"Like the very snail of destiny."

3

ON LUZ'S LAST NIGHT THE HUNGARIAN CULTURAL ATTACHÉ TOOK THE ACTORS TO dinner at the Grand Vefour, within view of Doré's windows. For this Justin borrowed a suit from David, who had not been invited. Despite his promise of caution, Justin's sense of Luz suggested that this might be his last opening to propose. In such a setting she would be less shocked by the insane prospect of his life.

At the long table that night, Luz wore a beige sheath with squared shoulders. And as the minutes passed, even when the conversation touched again on the evil rumors Justin had argued over that very morning with Eli Hebron of alliances between London and Berlin, on the one hand, and Paris and Moscow on the other—he was conscious only of an ethereal happiness he felt with each glance Luz gave him.

Well after midnight, when the boisterous party streamed out of the Palais-

Royal, the rain had turned to snow. Justin abandoned his plan of showing her the bridges from which he had first seen Paris. Instead, they sat alone in a dark corner of Luz's hotel lounge on the rue Jacob.

"Why are you so remote tonight?" she asked at once, her unusually chilly tone quavering sweetly. "Say something to me—tomorrow I will be gone. What if we never meet again?"

"Am I remote, Luz . . . to feel this?"

Poised at the edge of their sofa, he flushed. All through dinner Justin had been sinking deeper and deeper into the powerful illusion that surrounded Luz—of her white skin, the wide brow and traces of stage passion; above all, of the troubled promise in her green eyes. From where they sat, the bald top of the concierge's head was just visible. The hotel was perfectly silent, and they spoke in lowered voices.

"Marry me, Luz."

Justin was trying to look into this woman's face. But Luz drew back. He bent to hide his eyes from her, kissing the inside of her wrist.

"Luz, be my wife . . . marry me," he said. "You are beyond any dream I have dreamt. Tonight I am no one at all. For you, I could make myself any man's equal."

He crushed Luz against him, feeling her unattainable beauty so close now. "Shall we, then?" he heard a voice reply coolly. And glancing up Justin saw, for just an instant, the mad light of humiliation in those eyes. And not until that embrace had he felt the full bleak tragedy of Luz's soul. Justin was moved and frightened, as if he had just met her for the first time.

Next morning, when she was already gone, David Sunda appeared late in the sunny kitchen at the rue de Fleurus. He was in his Chinese robe. It was Sunday, and Johannes, who had joined a choir, was off rehearsing an oratorio. In a state of apprehension Justin sat waiting over his coffee by the window, observing Duncan finish a second plate of bacon and eggs.

"What is this?" David lifted an envelope off the ice cabinet.

"It must be a great event—look, special delivery," the American said without turning. "Say, I thought that you'd given up being a baron."

"I have." David frowned. "It is my father's conception of a joke—ah, yes, a family reunion. I suppose I shall have to go."

Pulling back a chair, he sat beside Duncan. The American soon gathered the cereal boxes and shut them in a cupboard before shuffling out of the kitchen with his *Herald-Tribune*.

"Well Justin, how was the actors' dinner?" David said benevolently, when they were alone.

"No one must know before you."

"Oh, yes? What is that?" David smiled at Justin's impassioned face without appearing able to see him.

"Last night—" Justin began, and abruptly he felt his face burn with a curious shame. "Last night, Luz agreed to marry me."

For thirty seconds David stared at Justin as though he had just said something completely deranged. Then his expression softened with sad and tender irony. Rising, he came round the table and took Justin's shoulders.

"You are the most magnificent of gamblers. I do love you both."

4

AND SO JUSTIN TOO CAUGHT THE NIGHT TRAIN TO BUDAPEST TO BE PRESENT AT a marriage. Only this time the ceremony was his own.

That evening, the three Fleurusians took him to dinner at Lipp. Later they accompanied him to the station. Justin carried his few good clothes in a suitcase borrowed from Duncan and enough savings for two weeks. He also had two third-class tickets to Barcelona—paid for by *Justice*—to report on the hunger strikes and on the gains of the popular movement.

It was a relief, though, when the train at last coasted east through darkened Paris suburbs. Justin felt oppressed by the sudden wealth of kind people who gave him things, took care of him, and seemed even to admire him. They could make him grateful, and gratitude, he knew, was a perversion of the lonely prophecy that had chosen Justin Lothaire to rise out of an Arab slum and give his rebellion independence. Yet as he gazed out of the train at the moon coolly afloat over the farms of Champagne, Justin experienced a gratitude as vivid as any his mother had felt for the Michaud lace.

When he woke it was morning, and the flat countryside was racing under a gray sky. There were eight hours more to Budapest. Justin was unable to read or to eat lunch, his hands were perspiring, and in the light of day this frivolous journey was clearly a mistake. Where did it belong in an adventure as urgent as Justin's life?

Far too soon, the compartment was rattling over a maze of junctions on the outskirts of Pest. They had come to the ruins of Austria-Hungary. Would he be expected to meet her family at once? Justin wondered, and reflected that he had no idea how to behave. The train had entered the station. Almost blind with dread, Justin pushed along the passage and swung down. Why should he not simply collect her and leave tonight?

Luz stood facing the platform near the crowded gate. Their gazes met, and Justin came to a halt. His anger vanished. Was such a being here for him?

As if she had detected the fantastic conviction on Justin's face, Luz ran forward. Without a word, her mouth spread small, fervid kisses all over his cheeks. As they fell in with the passengers from the Paris train, Justin saw how quickly her spontaneity died. It was a chilly March afternoon.

"I told Father that I should come alone," Luz said. "Was that right, Justin?"

"If you knew how right." Carrying his own bag, Justin passed beside her along a noisy arcade. "Luz, what have they heard about me?" he said.

"It only matters what I think, and tomorrow we will be married." She looked at Justin a little wildly. "Only be careful with Papa, won't you?"

He remembered that Holti was a highly cultivated diplomat, an egotist who felt some unnamed guilt about his daughter's life. But when they had climbed to the veranda and entered the drawing room of the family house—a villa far more elegant than Luz had described—a dashing gray haired gentleman came vigorously to meet him.

"Bienvenu!" he burst out, as if Justin were an old friend. "It is so wonderful to meet my future son-in-law."

A half-dozen people were pressing round him. Justin stood paralyzed among them, his right hand folded tenderly in Anton Holti's, his face smiling and scowling at the same time . . . *and then Justin Lothaire felt this thing: a family*. A substance seemed to close round him, hot and penetrating, a substance of smiling cheeks and eyes, congealing to love him.

Now he was sitting on the edge of an enormous brocade sofa. Justin talked and grinned back at Luz's parents, and surprisingly droll anecdotes about the trip poured from his mouth. They accepted him; he thought, they actually did like him. And the Justin of the Algiers lace shop broke out into a laughter that the Holtis might have found perturbing. Yet they did not appear to. In this unforeseen success a hopelessly corrupted Europe was suddenly lit up with family love.

Through that evening, Justin drank a good deal of some sweet white wine, which could add little to his intoxication. He did not mention North Africa. How much was known of him, how much might they accept? Luz's expression when he glanced at her—of some secret peace—encouraged him in everything.

But later, when Justin was alone in a guest room overlooking her garden, and the voices of his new family were still audible through the walls, his heart sickened. What would their judgment be? Justin could remember only the way he had held forth out of gratitude, inventing the best of himself. How vain it must have sounded. What if they pitied him?

In the morning when Justin went down to breakfast Luz had already left, to be at a cousin's until the wedding. When he saw the Holtis' welcoming smiles, Justin's anger vanished and he fell into silence. If only he might last until noon, he thought, and he sank still deeper into the enveloping family warmth. Even when he caught Luz's father watching him with gathering impatience, Justin had no idea why. He only became more humble and shy.

Their brief wedding in a neighborhood church came and went, an ordeal so strange that Justin did not even dare to ask how he had arrived on his knees before an altar. Finally there was an hour when the enigmatic face beside him—until then hidden behind lace—lifted to Justin's with an expression of utter forgiveness, and he understood that Luz was his wife. At that moment Justin almost wished for her that he could be a husband. He felt angered for them both and sick with relief.

After three more hours, he was with Luz back on a train at Budapest station. In his exhaustion, Justin appeared to have made a mistake. When their luggage descended from one of the barouches hired by his new father-in-law, Justin had neglected to take charge of his new wife's bags. The ambassador was forced to return for them with a porter.

As Holti reappeared in the wagon-lit passage, his effetely charming mask was pink with fury. The wedding couple were in a rush of relatives and porters outside their compartment door. Are these my family? Justin was still, wondering, and he could only smile round at their faces.

"I seem to know very little about you, Justin." Holti was pressed forward with Luz between them. "My daughter has obviously lied."

"Not here, please, Anton." Elizabeth Holti turned to her son-in-law with a laugh. Her eyes were mild and kind, but her husband was distinctly frightening.

"You are a conceited, ill-bred, and obnoxious young man!" Holti stammered, his passion intensifying. "You will never be welcome under my roof, even if you *are* Baron Sunda's friend."

Baron Sunda's friend, Justin repeated to himself, backed against the double berth. In that one moment the sea of his new family had begun to withdraw. His father-in-law's great pleasure in him had been strange-from the beginning. Now the diplomat was shouting at Justin.

"And do not come again—even if Luz begs you!"

"I wouldn't think of it!" Justin said in English, speaking as this man's equal.

"Communist!" Holti whispered, with well-composed contempt. "I hope you are happy now, Luz."

Moments later, the remainder of the wedding party reappeared under the compartment window. Count Holti and his son could be seen, striding urgently into the main gallery. Several more terrible minutes went by. Justin stood beside Luz in the open window. Finally the train jolted, then reversed, starting along the crowded platform.

"Goodbye, my Lupic!" Madame Holti reached up, clinging to her daughter's fingers. "You are a good boy, Justin. Take care of my child, I beg you!" Mascara was running from her once-beautiful eyes.

"Oh, Mother!" Luz cried out.

"Don't fear, Madame Holti," Justin called to her. "She is my child now too."

Then the train was gathering speed out under the cloudy sky, and they sank down, facing each other. Justin felt himself overwhelmed by anger and shame.

What did you tell him? Have you hidden something?"

Luz's tears made her feverish pride even more poignant. "Of course not, of course not," she whispered. "You do not know him. Why did you have to be rude?"

For some time Justin sat stunned by her words. What was this strange girl doing to the first hour in their life—for were they not liberated? Was Luz not his wife, a grace Justin had scarcely dared dream of in the Mahbu public Library? He could almost feel the lurking injustice of the firmament lighten round him. Here in one compartment were the tremendous force of his life's prophecy and this young woman who would be the constant judge of the years lying ahead.

"Luz, my wife, my beloved, all that is insignificant now—you and I are *free!* On Saturday night, in Barcelona, you will join a movement of millions more important than ourselves. Later there will be children. From today, all that we touch will be as independent as any two lives ever dreamt of."

He stood at the compartment window, smiling faintly out over a bitterly poor sector of his wife's town. Yes, all this must change, and Luz would be there when Justin found the words to do it. Nor would he forget, any more than she, the ugly scene in Budapest station. For it was not until the old diplomat accused him that he had known. Never in his life would Justin Lothaire be truly a Communist.

Ibn Moushmun was right, Justin thought to himself. You are simply a Christian, like everyone else.

5

THAT NIGHT IN THE BUDAPEST-PARIS TRAIN, IN A COMPARTMENT SMELLING OF hot metal, Justin made love to Luz. Once, after Vienna, in the faint glow of the window, they sat naked and watched the slow moonlit gorges and peaks of the Tyrol. Outside their train, the Socialist papers were banned and Parliament dissolved. The Catholic Dollfuss was dictator of these mountains. Yet seeing Luz—even amid such ugliness—Justin gratefully lifted his young bride to the berth and loved her like a young sensualist of the Algiers beaches.

In Paris, the Lothaires changed to third-class benches. From now on there would be little money. They reached Barcelona late on Easter Saturday and rode straight to a colonnaded square in Barceloneta, just off Las Ramblas, the great boulevard of cafés leading to the port.

Señor and Señora Lothaire? There were two letters, one from Eli and one from someone called Figueroa. Justin was too exhausted to open them, and Luz followed him without a word to their little room. They rolled into each other's arms on a lumpy mattress and were quickly asleep.

Figueroa's letter said that he would come for them the next day at three o'clock. At eleven the Lothaires got up and walked to some sidewalk tables in the port where they fed each other prawns. Justin could not help smiling at Luz's oblivious face, which hour by hour appeared to him more childish.

"Justin, who is Figueroa? Where are we going?"

"To meet some people in the Popular Front," Justin said.

"Today is Easter," Luz said. "Should we not go to the cathedral?"

"This is serious work, Luz. I could take you to evening mass."

"It will be fun not to go at all." Luz laughed, shading her eyes. "When Father said you were a Communist, Justin, he was not right. Was he?"

"No, Luz. But, like them, I am for the poor."

"And I am for you."

Señor Figueroa was a gaunt, bearded, extremely polite schoolteacher. He was sitting in a chair under their arcade when the Lothaires returned. He seemed disappointed.

"You must be a fine writer for *Justice* to send someone so young." Figueroa turned to Luz. "And this charming señorita?"

"I started *Justice*—and this is my wife."

At once Figueroa was friendlier, though his eyes went on weighing and measuring. "Then I am honored. You know that in Spanish *luz* means light."

Justin smiled. "It is also the place where Jacob saw his ladder."

"Neither meaning does you justice, Señora. Now come with me. I must tell you that yesterday in Barcelona the Socialist Youth riot had some martyrs."

"Justin, I am afraid," said Luz in a small voice, as they walked with Figueroa to a side-car motorcycle.

The meeting took place some kilometers outside Barcelona in the hills of Esplugas in a bare agricultural lecture room. More than sixty informally dressed Spaniards, and also many foreigners, heatedly discussed what was happening in Austria. For the Popular Front here was still young and vulnerable. The miracles that had been gained under Largo Caballero—the reforms of tax and land, and the many thousands of new schools—might be utterly swept under in a similar coup from the Right.

"Bomb General Mola first!" someone shouted. He was hissed down by a grimly disciplined group that stood along the windows.

These were the Communists. Justin recognized one of them, Cortada, by his turned-down ears. The sensitive-looking Nin of the pure-left POUM stood nearby. There was great intensity of feeling on all the faces. No one smiled, but their eyes were very bright. Many of the younger ones stared innocently at Justin's wife.

Luz shrank against his arm. Between scribbling notes inside the cover of *Les Conquérants,* Justin examined the faces round them trying to work out factions. The agents of the Union General looked respectable. The Communists were overrepresented. Justin's eyes paused on a figure propped in a window at the front of the audience, a man of about thirty-five with graying hair cropped flat and a thick neck. Through the discussion about whether the army was united enough for a coup the man's narrow face was set in a homely, imperturbable smile. Justin could not stop looking at him. He nudged Luz

At sunset the gathering broke up into noisy groups. Figueroa stayed behind the speaker's table, talking to Nin, the man from the window, and a third, a humorless-looking man with light-blue eyes. As Justin led Luz forward by the hand, Nin moved on with a smile, and the third man watched her approach. Figueroa turned to them as they came up.

"So Lothaire," he said quickly. "Here are two other visitors."

"Orlov," said the good-looking humorless one. As he moved away, the homely short-haired man got up. His glance rested on Justin, then on Luz.

"Colonel Tiolchak," said Figueroa, still in French, "this is Justin Lothaire from the Paris paper *Justice*. Madame is a Hungarian actress."

"*Enchanté!*" the Russian said, his guttural voice accenting the polite word so that they all laughed. "*Enchanté*, comrade. You too find Spain interesting?"

Tiolchak's amused smile passed slowly from Luz to Justin and back to Luz. Then Justin heard her say some words that he did not understand. The Russian's smile widened. He bowed slightly and replied with great slowness, mouthing each syllable. Then he laughed an indulgent laugh and turned to Justin.

"And what do you think of the danger here? Will Spain follow Italy, Germany, and Austria?"

Justin was experiencing that sudden agitation and urge to argue he always felt when he met a strong personality.

"Yes, there is a danger in restraint. Though think of the risk in uniting the Right."

"I myself hope they will unite." Tiolchak smiled his imperturbable smile. "You are a good fellow to have on our side. Yet you are not a Marxist?"

"All my life I have felt Marx's horror of class oppression," Justin said quickly. "However, his economic solutions seem to be too incomplete to make a universal system."

"If this comrade is interfering, colonel . . . ?" Figueroa had edged between them. The dark auditorium was nearly empty.

"No, no!" Tiolchak stopped him. "Never distract a young man who is thinking subtle thoughts. . . . You do not believe in the genius of the people?" The Russian was watching Justin thoughtfully. "You cannot feel entire continents awakening from a monstrous enslavement?"

"I can feel Marx's belief that he is awakening from an anesthesia of the general will," Justin said. "Who among us today is satisfied to pin his hope for justice on God? Yet is it realistic to pin every last hope on the state—even on this republic?"

"Is it not better," Tiolchak said, testing him, "to choose our leaders from among our own ranks?"

"Yes, if once they are leaders they can still be questioned. Have the people not known enough of such bondage? In Paris we hear strange stories from Moscow."

Seeming not to hear, the Russian nodded to Figueroa and Luz. Then he gripped Justin's arm in his stubby hand, and they walked to the darkening windows. Outside, on the yellow mud engineers had cut from the hillside, a flock of sparrows picked for seeds. Justin could feel the remaining group's attention fix on Tiolchak. The other Russian was back with Figueroa and Luz. Her face was sober.

"Better not in front of Orlov."

Tiolchak swept the dead flies off the windowsill and began to roll up his shirtsleeves.

"But do you not think," he went on, "it's time that we trusted ourselves? Marx trusted himself, and look how far we have come."

"I have heard that peasants have died in the collectivization," Justin began, and he felt giddy, uttering words of violence.

"You would put us back in the hands of the czars?" Tiolchak smiled. "You see, the present methods of our leaders are only a setback."

Justin spoke quickly now. "Yes, Marx was a great man. But in a state evolved out of Marxism is there still play for the restraint of moral men? What of those who are merely outraged for their people—are they not the enemies of the state?"

Tiolchak lit a cigarette. The humor had gone from his eyes. They leaned on the window ledge, smoking. Across the darkened plain below, the roofs of Barcelona clustered to the sea.

"Do we need great men?" The Russian raised his eyebrows.

"If compassion is to be state policy"—Justin was trembling a little—"it is through the outbursts of honest men that society evolves. Marx saw all this clearly. But neither Marx not anyone else has thought of a state which actually frees the genius of the people from the cruelties of power. On the contrary, the new dictatorship strips the people even of the right to their lives. It gives all the people genius by honoring no genius. No, colonel, to me the ideas of the genius of the people and the moral character of single men are incomplete without each another."

"Now I understand—you are an anarchist," Tiolchak said with a grin. "But when there is no ground between the dictators of the rich and the dictators of the poor, what then?"

"I am with the many against the few," Justin said quietly.

"Then you are a Republican." The Russian's steady gaze suddenly softened; his eyes twinkled. And Justin thought, *Whether you agree or not, this is a man you might follow into hell.*

"I know we will meet again, Lothaire," Tiolchak said. "Perhaps you will be my guest in Russia. When we do meet, I will tell you what I have lived through for the future of communism. It is a useful story."

Their humor together rang out spontaneously, and Justin felt his cheeks burn with pleasure. He walked with Tiolchak in silence, back to Luz and Figueroa. Orlov had slipped away.

Outside the building, the twilight was hot. Beside Figueroa's motorcycle, Justin bent to smell the freshness of Luz's hair. He wanted a sign of the new world he had given her. The debate with the Russian had left him with strange impressions of vast inhuman forces and of his having stood fully exposed in his beliefs. Yet what position had he argued beyond the limits of the law? Would Lavil have followed him, or Grinda, or Ibn Moushmun? As they stood on the steep roadway in the fragrant Catalan dusk, Luz's dazed smile seemed to tell Justin that nothing had changed.

"The short Russian was very interested in you," she said. "Isn't life strange, Justin? I have never met such intense and intelligent men."

"So, you even speak Russian. What did Tiolchak say?"

"I said he too was a long way from home. Then he said that we were here for the same reason. I told him I did not understand a word, but that you were my husband now. Did I say something wrong?"

"No, Lupic, I think he liked us," Justin said.

Was it possible, at that hour, that Luz still had not understood? It was then that Justin remembered, almost with longing, the Spanish bullfights which Ibn Moushmun had spoken of and Lavil had despised.

6

THE LOTHAIRES HAD MONEY FOR ONE WEEK BEFORE RETURNING TO THE PARIS atelier that had been lent by Doré. He walked with Luz all over Barcelona, attending churches for their architecture, and museums, and keeping away from journalists. These were the first careless days of Justin's life, and they dulled the realism of the world. By the Sunday after Easter, Justin was ready to take his new wife to La Monumental, which was as garish outside as a Moroccan palace.

From the moment inside the arena that Justin Lothaire held the brightly illustrated tickets and sat crushed against Luz on their concrete bench, he had smelled again the wine- and blood-soaked sands of Agamemnon's beach.

"Justin, look at the little bird."

The men inside the barrier below shouted back and forth and pointed. At the center of the ring a tiny spot began to hop. The wagon sprinkling the sand circled nearer, and the murmuring in the crowd grew. The men behind the *barrera* seemed to argue. Finally, one of the police, almost a boy, stepped into the ring, his shiny black hat in one hand. His boots left dry tracks on the wet sand. Stooping, the boy spread out a handkerchief, put the sparrow on it, lowered the bird and cloth into his hat and hurried back to the *barrera*. Far up in the stands there was some clapping, and the first bull raced out on the sand. And thinking then of the magicians at Sidi Idriz, Justin could not look at the woman beside him.

7

HÉLÈNE FIRST HEARD ABOUT LUZ'S MARRIAGE TO JUSTIN LOTHAIRE DURING A tea dance at the Carlton in Saint-Moritz.

The Le Trèves had brought their daughter here in the first week of February, the high season for winter sports, when the hotels flatter the better sort by raising their prices. The tea dances took place in a low-ceilinged salon scented with pipe smoke and were attended by a mixture of Austrian archdukes, Swiss bankers, and Argentinian *estancieros* amid a strictly family atmosphere.

Madame Le Tréve had urged her daughter to accept the *invitations* of certain handsome young men she described as gigolos, who came up frequently to their table to ask Hélène, with great delicacy, to dance. Through her boredom, Hélène understood that these attentions were to do with her not being pretty, and she would find some excuse to refuse. She felt released on the third afternoon when they ran into David Sunda's brother.

Friedrich had just set aside his officer training for a tour in the diplomatic corps and seemed in irrepressible high spirits—at least the more animated side of his face. The young baron made Hélène laugh constantly with a mixture of relief and genuine delight at his cynical humor. Friedrich was also an expert skier and a good dancer, and Hélène loved to waltz.

"No, Freddy! what did you say?" She had stopped him in the middle of a tango. "Come and sit with me at once."

She tugged his hand until they were at a small table, hidden from her family by the dancers. Friedrich's amusement when he saw Hélène's agitation made his bad eye weep.

"Of course. Luz was a friend of yours too." Friedrich nodded, tapping a cigarette. "Yes, indeed, it is only too true. *Hélas,* a seductress has been crossed off the menu of exceptionally marriageable morsels."

Hélène stared at him. For ten seconds, an emotion so painful swelled in her breast that she thought she might cry out. How had Luz not mentioned such an event in her last letter? For when in her intense vision Hélène imagined the two people she loved side by side, the bond seemed dull and wrong. The orchestra had begun a sentimental waltz from *Fledermaus,* and across the smoky room there were rapturous ohs and ahs. Hélène gave a deep sigh and rose.

"Friedrich, I want to dance," she called over the music, her voice harsh and unsteady. "But how droll to hear a poisonous old baron like yourself talk of someone like our Algerian."

Friedrich bowed crisply, then took Hélène in his arms.

"Oh, I met the young intellectual last spring in Paris. You know, his radicalism is finished already. He's a sort of *chef* now. I suspect he is unaware of it himself."

"A *chef!*" Hélène laughed a little wildly as she swung with her partner under the bow of a smiling violinist. "Yes, that is it exactly. A chief without a tribe."

8

ON THE FIFTEENTH OF FEBRUARY, HÉLÈNE RETURNED TO PARIS WITH HER mother, and a new phase in her life began. She became very serious. And for the first time Hélène thought continually about marriage. But she kept this secret from her parents and, as usual, frustrated her mother's plots to have her meet promising escorts. By the suitors with whom she was presented, she knew that her mother was judging her in gradations of outward charm and social position.

In fact, Hélène exerted a strong attraction. But she lacked glamour, without which conventional men do not consider a woman worthy in their competition for a feminine prize. When she thought of this competition among her circle and of the few shallow, ambitious, and dull-witted males who had tried to pay her court, Hélène trembled with disgust and humiliation. Could such a cruel display lead to a marriage of love?

Locked with Gnome in her room under the gables, Hélène would examine herself in the mirror—imagine her brother, Jean-Marc, being given the face of an angel! And without bitterness, she would laugh out loud at such a perfect irony. *Beauty!* Beauty sung by classical poets. Beauty singled out, inflated, vanquishing all, and bringing down slavery on those without it. Beauty filmed, beauty sculpted . . . beauty hailed, attacked, and soiled. Beauty always the heroine, always revered.

She was absorbed in such reflections when at Easter David Sunda stopped through Paris from the south, on his way home to Oberlinden, and was invited to dinner. Hélène first saw David taking off his coat in the great marble hall as she came down the stairs. Noticing at once how drawn his face was, for some reason she was pleased.

"Aha, little Leni." David laughed, his old playful manner instantly back. And, as always, he spread his arms like a good-natured bear.

"No, no!" Drawing back, Hélène held out her hand, and their eyes met. Deep in the privacy of David's glance she felt something soften. And suddenly Hélène could feel her soul becoming charming. Her limbs and face and every cell in Hélène's body—all suddenly charming and beautiful.

"*Bon soir, Hélène.*" David took Hélène's hand and bent to kiss her . . . once on each cheek.

"I'm glad you came, David," she said. "Papa is waiting in the library. I will see you at dinner."

Reaching the first landing in silence, Hélène continued up the next. Gnome ran ahead, waving his blond tail almost to the carpet with embarrassment and excitement. And Hélène felt David's eyes on her back and knew her walk could not help being beautiful.

When presently she came down to the dining room, spinach soup was being served. At the Le Trèves, spinach soup was for special occasions. Hélène ignored her mother's glances and the heated discussion between her father and their guest, across the candles and clinking china. Without looking even at her old grandmother, Hélène slipped onto her chair and became absorbed with her soup.

"But after all, David, what can be new in this?" Le Trève settled back with pleasure. "There have always been jealous extremists. These have simply expanded their constituency. The leftists cannot seem to accept that some people like to possess things, to work harder and live better."

"Is that all?" David commented, with an embarrassed smile to appease Madame Le Trève. "In Spain they say the poor are mad with hunger, the rich with fear."

"What of civilization then?" Le Trève gazed at him with fatherly indulgence.

"There . . . well, must there not be moral progress? We cannot judge souls by their bank accounts. On the other hand, those who eat well, who live with great architecture, in educated society, cultivate the highest sense of life's preciousness. They above all can keep mankind out of darkness."

"What David means," Hélène quietly broke in, "is that a civilization of free men will never be sustained if its leading figures are not also its moralists."

"Yes, that is it precisely." David turned to her across the huge bowl of waxed fruit.

Seated very straight, Hélène felt her face burning. Again, alien words had risen to her lips—and David had accepted them, as from a close and trusted ally. What is happening to me? she thought. Lifting her large, gentle gray eyes, Hélène concentrated among the shadows beyond the candles, and her eyes found David's. He smiled, then frowned and looked down thoughtfully.

They did not say another word to each other during the rest of dinner. But from that hour Hélène knew that God had given her a power to charm this old friend deeply.

When David left at midnight, Hélène went alone with him to the front door. Just then the ornate Empire clock on the marble table under the mirror began to chime. Neither of them spoke, and the pure, fragile peals were to

Hélène like drops of sound, tiny arrows that pierced both their hearts. Confused by their emotion, Gnome started barking at the clock and snapped his jaws in the air. The twelfth chime pealed. A silence spread upward through the darkened hall.

"I'm sorry that you have to leave Paris so soon," Hélène said. She looked steadily into David's face.

"I will be back in two weeks."

And among the familiar tones Hélène heard a tense note she had never heard before in a man's voice. David's lips brushed lightly on hers, and he was gone. For two minutes Hélène stood in the dark, trembling uncontrollably. The she sat on the hard tapestry chair. Soundless, convulsive sobs shook her.

"Two weeks?" she whispered. "Two weeks?" And when she thought of how things had gone for her with Justin Lothaire, she was terrified.

7

TWO WEEKS BEFORE HIS VISIT TO THE LE TRÈVES', DAVID SUNDA HAD PACKED his bag and traveled south to certain beautiful settings where he had once been happy. Back in Paris to register for his examinations, David's depression continued. The day after his dinner at Hélène's he was on the night train to Frankfurt.

In Bavaria the heavy rains had stopped. At noon the provincial train made a two-minute halt at Neustadt. David noticed, even here, the unusual number of aggressive posters. But as he swung his suitcase to the platform he was enveloped in the tender mists of Catholic Germany. A stocky figure was coming toward him in a gray jacket, riding boots, and a new mustache.

"Gustav!" he cried, and they embraced.

"Master David, sir." Gustav held David's hand in a powerful grip.

Soon the Sundas' Daimler was twisting through the roe forest. And feeling then the first well-being in months, David leaned back on the front seat, ready to laugh at the always lively gossip of Oberlinden.

"But tell me, Master David, did you hear in France that this Hitler has ordered a military call-up?"

Gustav spat out over the walnut door panel. He glanced nervously at David.

"These are curious times. They have seized the radio; the air is filled with strong words. You will see—"

Gustav was forced to brake the heavy car. The wheels bumped onto a grass field. The forest road had emerged in the long descent to the plain of the Saale, and as they came into the sun the way ahead was blocked. A clattering roar drowned their voices. David rose from his seat and held the windshield.

"What is that? What is going on?"

"Tanks!"

Withdrawing down the farm road ahead were what looked like tractors hung with boiler plates. As the Daimler coasted behind the last tank, a second, advancing, column reached them. The gray-jacketed officer atop the first passing tank turret looked down with interest at the young gentleman in the open car. As their eyes met, the fellow smiled happily and waved to David. The gesture left him nauseated. How did this blond youth riding on an ugly steel tumbrel dare to wave at David Sunda? Yet before he could think—perhaps out of some well-bred reflex of politeness, or because they were young Germans—together David's left shoulder tightened. He was waving back.

"The grays hate the browns," Gustav shouted to him. "But there are more browns, the *Schweinerei*."

David shrugged and grinned. These faceless feuds that fascinated Justin—the very existence of such machines—only depressed him further. But the officer in the following tank had seen, and he waved too. David was compelled to reply . . . and to the third and the fourth. . . .

He counted twenty-four of the clattering monsters. Finally the scarred left lane was open, and Gustav pulled out. They began to overtake the brown-shirt column along the road ahead. Sinking down in his seat, David faced Gustav until they were past the last tank. He had waved at all the tank men—and by the last it had seemed easy. It was a lesson to remember.

"Sir, what do you think of them?" Gustav called, glancing twice at his silent passenger.

"I hope the Nibelungs do not expect to conscript me." David grinned cynically.

A moment later, the Daimler had wheeled through the familiar gates, rattled over a cattle grid, and David was safe on the soil of his ancestors. They swept up the hill and circled the huge lawns. Under the white façade of Oberlinden, he counted seven cars. On two of them fluttered little red *Hakenkreuz* flags. David managed to reach his room in the east wing without being noticed. The instant he threw himself half dressed onto the canopied bed and sank his face into the cool pillow, he fell into the drugged, dreamless sleep of his boyhood.

When he woke it was dusk. David lay still in his room, listening to the ripple of voices from the great drawing room. Recalling that there had been fear on Gustav's face, he felt vaguely uneasy. Downstairs too he would find Katie: Cousin Katie, for whom he had always felt a sort of base passion—even once bared his heart to her, though her conceit and cruelty disgusted him. Even Katie's mother was alarmed by the girl's memory for malicious gossip, whether or not it was true. If only Hélène Le Trève were here. And suddenly David found himself missing painfully Hélène's resonant passions and her wise laugh.

David got up and showered. Minutes later, he paced down the hushed corridor of portraits. As he went down the great staircase, David for some reason laughed out loud. He caught sight of an impressive figure watching him from below.

"What is this—has Paris made you soft in the head?"

"Father, no . . . no, sir!" he faltered before his father's intolerant gaze. Recovering his poise, David kissed the old baron on both cheeks. "I am truly saddened about Grandfather Friedrich, Father—and for you. He was ill so long."

To his surprise, the old man took out a handkerchief, turned his back squarely on the guests in the drawing room, and blew his nose twice. David noticed the black ribbon on his breast.

"Don't worry, my boy. Well, it is inevitable enough. We were never close."

Taking his son's arm, the baron steered him gently into the room beyond as the guests turned to meet them. Between introductions, his father went on.

"I suppose you have heard about the Wehrmacht's call-up? So, come, I will introduce you to our friend the general. Guderian is inventing a new tank army. Better if you are on his staff than rolling about in the trenches."

In the shock of that moment's realization—*could he too be called up?*— David stared round the gilt and white walls, barely aware of his introduction to this heavily decorated officer with the sandy hair and intelligent eyes. His gaze had fallen on someone conversing close by in the shadow of the book alcove. As he stepped over, the slim woman in the black velvet gown turned to him. Her wide-set brown eyes met his with anxiety and love.

"My dear, when did you arrive? You didn't visit me."

"Hello, *Maman*," David murmured, as he bent to kiss his mother's soft cheek. "How well you look."

8

"MY DEAR HEINZ, I WOULD LIKE YOU TO MEET MY YOUNGER SON," THE OLD baron was saying just next to them, in the tone he reserved for those occasions which he considered of sufficient dignity.

The general observed David closely. "Aha! At last I meet the famous scholar, spoken of by some as the hope of Germany."

"They cannot know me well."

Releasing David's hand, Guderian acknowledged the younger man's modesty with a polite nod. "Well, perhaps I, at least, will come to know you better. Your father tells me that in June you leave the Sorbonne with many honors. You speak French, English, Italian, and Russian and have given some promising months to officer training. Your knowledge of European history and politics is excellent, and you have shown unusual courage. I understand you piloted a French aircraft."

Standing obediently between his parents, David smiled at his father with some surprise. He and the general, however, continued with pleasantries familiar to both, by which they were able to establish the exact base of each other's personalities without exposing private beliefs or offending points of sensitivity. One such belief, which David did not reveal to his father or to their guest, had been strengthened that afternoon on the drive from the station. It was that he, David Sunda, had no part to play in any modern army, certainly not one employing tanks.

This veiled debate was interrupted at precisely eight o'clock when Gustav's son, Oberlinden's second cook, hurried red-faced among the company in his white tunic, ringing a small crystal bell. Doors opened, revealing massive Russian malachite urns. The forty or so family and friends passed with a waving of plumes and their usual vain laughter into the famous dining room, where both Frederick of Prussia and Bonaparte had once banqueted.

David hung back in the doorway to greet his brother, then his sister—how Karin had changed! His once spirited sister now drew her cheek away with a matronly chill, as if vaguely repulsed. He felt almost relieved when she went to her seat at a far table. The brothers were left standing side by side.

"What's to be done?" Friedrich commented, slipping his arm through David's and drawing him out of the bright doorway. "Our sister is a prude. But let me teach you some statecraft of the day—which I know you consider beneath you." The profiled half of Friedrich's face was grinning at him.

"Teach me then," David said, joining his brother's mock conspiracy without looking into the cold eyes.

"Look carefully! No, to the right, by Willy—and do not be obvious. Yes, those two old stags, Franz Papen and Walter Brauchitsch."

Willy was a suit of ancestral armor with a bullet hole in the breastplate, behind which David and Friedrich had hidden during boyhood games. Conversing next to it now was a horse-faced old aristocrat with a grating voice and cantankerous manner. A bird-necked officer with vacant, innocent eyes listened intently.

"Those two"—suddenly agitated, Friedrich turned his back on them so that David could see over his shoulder—"are the last men of our blood to dream of damming the little chancellor's passion. Do not underestimate that Austrian as I did: he is our history's Paracelsus. Those two are his patrician eunuchs. Can you imagine, Papen dreams he will share the chancellorship, and Brauchitsch believes that he commands the army. Eat well, laugh, and be gay. We will be proud to be Nazis."

Wiping his face with a handkerchief, Friedrich squeezed David's shoulder and slipped away in the sudden hush of the grace. David was left staring over the bowed faces at the two old men.

The main company of twenty-four was presided over by Baron von Sunda and his *principessa*. David found his place near Guderian at a table for ten

headed by Karin and young Esterhazy. Immediately noticing his double helping of *palmiers,* David glanced through the faces and met his mother's eyes.
But why had she put Cousin Katie between the general and himself?

These goings-on at Oberlinden seemed suddenly alien and unnatural.
Beyond Katie, Guderian's sleekly pomaded head nodded toward David. What
was the general thinking? What *could* the thoughts be of a man who was
engaged in building a legion of tanks? Was there not already violence in the
streets of Europe? What was tonight's glittering celebration?

9

SUDDENLY DAVID EXPERIENCED THE SENSATION OF BEING BALANCED ON HIS CHAIR
over some vast throng.

"General?" he said, taking his fork.

"Please, you must call me Heinz."

"Thank you. Heinz, I hoped you might throw some light on these military
goings-on. It is said that we have more than fifty divisions. Is that not a
violation of our covenant to the League?"

The older man's smile hardened, as if he might be forced, in this exalted
household, to lose a skirmish in military discretion.

"The League of Nations could mean a diaspora of the German race," he
said quietly. "Must we live by such a *Diktat?* However, by no means did all
the Führer's generals agree; I for one did not. Who in Europe wishes for war?
What enemies do we have? The policy is essentially economic."

Guderian smiled at David politely, and between them Katie began to squirm.

"May I call you Heinz too?"

"Such an honor might make me reckless." Guderian laughed, still looking
at David.

"Oh, you don't have to pay attention to David," Katie observed. "No one
in our family takes him seriously."

At her side, the accuracy of his cousin's insult had driven the breath from
David's lungs. He heard Guderian.

"I take your cousin *most* seriously. I was about to suggest a place on my
staff."

"That is a very attractive offer," David said, with all the grace he could
summon, "especially so from a person they say is behind the country's
strength in armor."

"Oh, many others saw the necessity." Holding the Iron Cross that dangled
from his neck, Guderian examined the two fillets of poached sole being
arranged on his plate.

"It seems to me tragic, though," David heard himself continue, "that such
an approach should be necessary. A return to armor, after four centuries, seems

a blow to humanist ideals . . . dignity, honor. War has been, at least occasionally, a moral and civilizing force. Might not such machines become the instrument of faceless scientific slaughter?"

Guderian had listened to young Sunda as he chewed the delicate white flesh. Now the officer settled back with the distant expression of an astronomer possessed by a fruitful conception.

"David, that is a noble view, but consider. If in the sixteenth century when firearms came into use, motors had existed to drive armor heavy enough to resist the new projectiles—would armor ever have disappeared? If we had had tanks to overrun the trench defenses in France, imagine the millions who might have been spared monstrosities like Passchendaele. My young friend, in the strategy of war there is no success without movement. And mankind has never known a power of surface movement like the tank—"

The ugly phrases were interrupted by cries as a roast boar entered the hall on the shoulders of four red-faced cooks.

As David raised his wineglass with the rest, he grasped from the general's lingering tone that this grown man believed mankind to be perpetually at war. What if David were the only one not impassioned by improvements in the instruments of murder?

Not until he had smoked a cigar in his father's library and finally escaped upstairs was David Sunda able to face these impressions of organized violence. Safe in the familiar darkness, he sat quite still in his armchair for an hour or more, his teeming thoughts resisting the country stillness. Did this household not embody all that humanity had been guided by for centuries? And had tonight's confidences not come to David because he belonged to the military class? Was he not doubly a traitor—to his family and to his life on the rue de Fleurus? It was at this point that the moral thread was lost and humanity appeared doomed by its rotted morals, its degeneracy, and its violence. Now imagining the Berlin Senate as it was gutted by flames, David was plunged in deeper solitude.

I will join no army, unless my family and the soil of my fathers are overrun. The words had seemed to float in from the fields below. His joints relaxed. David felt his soul rise gratefully.

"Hélène," he said aloud. And again David wondered at the moment in a Paris hallway when he first saw that the willful child he had teased was now a mature woman who could be loved . . . loved like the others David had made love to, yet not at all like any other. "Hélène." He repeated her name, as if for approval, to the surrounding objects of his childhood. And quite unexpectedly, the strangest idea came to him.

Jumping up, he switched on the light. Had he just imagined himself rushing Hélène out of her parents' house and away from Europe, to hoard her on some new continent?

And standing there blinking at his old room, David saw Hélène's sensitive face before him. Fool, that reproachful face seemed to be saying. How could you have taken so long to recognize that we were always intended for each other?

10

In the brilliant spring morning, the evil spirits of the banquet had gone. David was down early in the breakfast room, and Gerta herself brought in his eggs.

"Welcome home, Master David."

"You look well, Gerta. How is the boy?"

"Thank you, sir. My boy will never be like other boys—but he seems very happy."

Gerta's son had been born an idiot, and David's old governess had come to him for help with a sanatorium.

"Will you come to visit us in the pantry at teatime?"

"For heaven's sake, of course I will." He laughed.

David finished his coffee and left the room before his father came down. For the first time in eight years he took the path leading from the plum orchard down toward the bottomland where, not so long ago, he had flown the plane.

Thirty minutes later, David was stretched on the grass outside its barn with a stalk in his teeth. The meadow moved with him under the gentle blue sky, as wild thoughts of Hélène, marriage, Oberlinden, and the.preciousness of life drifted through his head. Of course, there would be Grandmother Le Trève, who detested Germans. And it was then that David remembered: Was not the last Saturday of the month the one on which his father and Friedrich habitually met the tenant farmers at the local guildhall? Why had he always refused to go? But the answer—that David could not bear to doubt that the local people loved his family—was too shameful even to seek words for. Instead, he glanced at his watch and jumped to his feet.

In his casual dress the young baron back from Paris received only a few suspicious stares as he approached the crowd of men under the guildhall's low arcade. Ignoring three young Brownshirts, strutting by in their hard boots with hats cocked back, David shouldered his way among the farmers. He glanced at faces he vaguely recognized, faces as trusting and honest as the fields the men plowed and the beasts they tended. He eavesdropped openly on their ponderous talk—as if to be in love could make even a Sunda invisible and invulnerable.

"The low pasture's better . . . good water pan . . . fences need mending . . . soil overworked. Best well in these parts . . . Schuster will get it, *Wie denkst du davon?*"

A farmer with excellent pastures had died without an heir. Everyone was here, scrubbed and clean, for the usually acrimonious event of settling the new tenancy. Today, with Hélène's eyes on him, such ritual seemed to David indescribably precious and exciting.

The clock high above the cobbles began to strike ten, and the packed arcade echoed with voices. David heard a motorcar.

"*Der Baron* . . . the young master!" called out several voices.

Above the press of heads, David glimpsed his father coming among the crowd, followed by his much taller brother. The old man wore his baggy suede beret, the emblem of the guild master. Several of the young men stretched their necks for a better view. Then the farmers were pressing through the doorway and up a wide staircase.

Soon the crowd was gathered in a dark paneled room. Six elders sat with Friedrich and the old baron at a raised semicircular table. On the wall above their heads, flanking a family escutcheon—the wheat sheaf, sword, and buckle of Arminius—hung a Bavarian banner. David found a place behind a wooden pillar. On the far wall, Kastner, the butcher, was on his feet, demanding that future meetings hang the *Hakenkreuz* flag and begin with the Horst Wessel song. There was embarrassed laughter and some clapping. Then David heard his father's voice thanking the butcher. With a significant frown at the faces surrounding him, the man took his seat, and the old baron called for first business first. The meeting began.

David remained for another hour, completely absorbed. This was the world into which Friedrich and his father had long since given up inviting David. Yet here Friedrich was expert, judicious, and commanding. David listened to his brother's rather flat, nasal voice recite work schedules and address men in the crowd by name. He saw the way—without affection, and sometimes with audible dissatisfaction—the farmers seemed to understand perfectly, and consider significant, the obscurest detail Friedrich mentioned and to answer him with a lively respect. Far from being insufferably tedious, as David had always assumed, all this seemed to him to have a truth and grandeur he could not have dreamt of.

"So, you think we could find a better price in Munich?" Friedrich called to a fellow behind David with shrewd blue eyes and a scarf round his brown neck.

"No, sir, I tried," the man called back. "They are suspicious of you northerners."

Laughter rippled among the crowded pews, and David smiled too, even if it was at the expense of his family. He sniffed the atmosphere. Here amid the harshness of the seasons, these simple farmers, without claim to fame or history, were in agreement to tend—with an expertise and assurance akin to genius—the overwhelming fact of their successful survival. It was a wonder of the species. And at the height of this self-respecting tribe were David's father and his brother, Friedrich.

11

IN A DAZE DAVID CLIMBED HOME THROUGH THE SPRING HEAT, UP ONE OF Gustav's deer tracks. In the mansion the halls were cool and dark. David was starting up the pantry stairs when he heard the piano. He went to the door of the rose-garden study.

His mother was at the Bechstein, playing an autumnal piece David remembered from his boyhood. He had never felt able to interrupt before she had finished—and not until this moment had he thought what this day might mean to her. On the wall above his mother's absorbed face, David now noticed with vague distress, was a new painting by a Swiss surrealist. The *principessa* patronized living artists, as a duty of her class as well as a pleasure. Several— especially the Russian émigrés—corresponded obsequiously with letters beginning, "My dear Maria."

"Well, where have you been?" she said, suddenly turning to him. Her face softened almost childishly.

"I had to see the old places. I also sat with the farmers at the guildhall for Father's meeting."

"It is a shame that sons cannot see their fathers as young men." David's mother watched him thoughtfully as he rose. "Barthold was like you once— imagine how it has hurt him to discipline you over similar qualities."

"Oh, that is finished." David laughed as he approached her round the piano. "I can understand Papa and Friedrich. After all, I have my own secrets," he said.

A momentary confusion passed over his mother's features.

"No, not that—" he said quickly, "not Guderian's offer." All of David was trembling at what his mother was about to hear.

"Then tell me, my dear . . ."

"Mother, I"—coming forward from the window, David took his mother's cool hands—"I intend to ask Hélène Le Trève if she will marry me."

For ten seconds in the silent study, mother and son stared at each other. The fragile hands in their ruffles had jerked sharply. But then abruptly David understood. That if it were with Hélène—and among the women of his class perhaps only with Hélène—his marriage could not help seeming to his mother a vessel of great truth and completeness. Without warning, the *principessa* tried to smile, and tears filled her eyes.

"Mother?" The hands in his had loosened. His mother took a handkerchief from her sleeve.

"It is perfect, David," she said softly. "It is quite beautiful really."

From the hour that David found the strength to face the *principessa* and had sworn her to secrecy, there seemed no further reason to stay on at Oberlinden. Still, he mastered the impulse to make any departure that might further wound his earliest ally.

Then one evening David knew his stay had been long enough. Three days early, he took leave of Oberlinden along with its round of house parties and expeditions. He was able to catch the Frankfurt express at Bamberg.

Passing through the glorious spring scenery, David wondered if it had not been too long. Would it not be justice, after his dissipations in the past, if Hélène had meanwhile met someone else? So, during the last hours of his freedom, David's entire being prepared itself to be given to Hélène—that is, to the person he imagined she was. In anxious detail, he reviewed the moment ahead. It must be between three and four o'clock, before her parents returned. His imagination traveled ahead to the way Hélène's face would look at the altar, and the tears he would shed by her bed when she bore their children.

On the afternoon that David reached the empty rooms over the rue de Fleurus, it rained heavily. Justin was at a trade union conference in London, Johann was in Berlin, and Duncan had begun the return voyage from New York.

Next morning, the sky over the Jardin du Luxembourg was blue, and the lake busy with governesses and perambulators. David experienced then a sensation almost of physical safety. Why had his mother not asked where he and Hélène would live? And for the first time, David Sunda wondered if he would ever return to Oberlinden.

12

AT TEN O'CLOCK HE TELEPHONED THE LE TRÈVE HOUSE. WITHOUT ASKING whether anyone was at home, he left a message with Bertrand to tell Mademoiselle Hélène that Monsieur David would call at four and that he hoped she would be there. After paying a fruitless call at the Siebenbergs', then visiting his law professor, he paused at the Café Flore to read through a *Herald*. As he crossed the street to lunch at the Brasserie Lipp, he noted the few clouds apprehensively. But the fine spring weather held, and after his lunch, at three o'clock, dressed in a freshly pressed suit, David set out on foot.

An hour later, he was at the Le Trèves'. The heavy door swung back and Bertrand stood before him. She must have gone out, David thought.

"Good day, Bertrand," he said coolly. "Is Mademoiselle Hélène in?" Feeling all at once sick and defeated, David almost turned away.

"Yes, monsieur," Bertrand said, stepping back. "I think mademoiselle is upstairs. Shall I say you are here?"

"Yes . . . thank you, Bertrand," David added, taking three steps through into the marble hall.

She was in. David's heart had begun to beat in his ears. How oddly normal everything looked. How incredible that the whole Le Trève household was not conscious of the tremendously important matter that David Sunda had come on, and which would influence all their lives. How was it that Bertrand was so sleepy? How was it that this hall clock went on ticking as usual? Their indifference astonished him.

David had never before asked to see Hélène alone. It made him feel vaguely guilty. He waited under the chandelier. He waited almost fifteen minutes, and then he heard the click of Gnome's claws on the topmost landing.

The young Frenchwoman coming slowly down the stairs was in a blue sweater and skirt, which showed off her slim ankles. She had a silk scarf round her throat, and her dark hair was caught up loosely behind her head. This woman was far more attractive than David had remembered. Her movements as she stepped down to him were so firm and independent, the expression on her face so serious, that David began to feel distinctly sordid and beneath her. Confused by such a welcome, as they met on the middle landing, David bent and made a show of patting the Labrador and muttering endearments. When he straightened, Hélène's bearing had become even colder. There were red patches on her cheeks.

"Hélène." David leaned to kiss her cheek.

"Well, it's teatime," Hélène said, starting back to the stairs. "Would you like some tea?"

"Yes, that would be nice. And Hélène?"

"Yes?" Hélène turned to him, and they stopped.

"Can we take it in the garden?"

"Isn't it too chilly?"

"No," David said, almost proudly. "It is quite warm out."

"All right then, we'll have it in the garden."

Hélène went down to a door under the staircase that led to the kitchen. David watched her move out of sight.

She had left him alone in the library. He pushed open the doors behind the salmon curtains and went out on the steps.

As soon as his foot touched this silent gravel path in the heart of Paris, David's spirits lifted again. It was all just as he had conceived it: the high walls cloaked in ivy, the oval lily pond with its little patinaed Mercury beckoning at the center. He paced forward out of the shadow of the house and crossed to the corner under the willow, where a white iron table and chairs stood. Half turning, he breathed the moldy air seasoned by the sun's warmth. The moment was close upon him now. Behind these ranks of windows above the hydrangeas was the young woman who would be the mother of his children, but to whom David had never spoken of love.

13

A METAL DOOR RATTLED. UNDER THE WILLOW, DAVID TURNED, HÉLÈNE WAS holding the side door for a maid carrying a silver tray.

"*Bonjour, Joselita,*" David said, as the two women approached. The maid blushed. Without answering, she fussed deftly over the table.

When Joselita had hurried back out of the garden, they were alone. David sat in the chair next to Hélène. The sun fell in speckles through the willow branches. Hélène began to pour the tea. David did not comment on the speed of the tray's appearance or on the sudden absence of the Labrador.

"English cakes?" He lifted the warm napkin covering the wicker basket.

"Scones," Hélène corrected, without looking up. "Don't you like them?"

"Can't you remember how much?" he said.

At the iron table under the willow, and through the fragrant old garden, there was a long, unnatural silence. David watched Hélène's hands move steadily from the teapot to the sugar spoon to the basket. He was conscious that the subject most obvious and ripe for them was the sudden astonishing marriage of Justin and Luz. But about this there was something so terrible that David could not bring himself to speak of it. Abruptly, he was aware that Hélène had made no mention of it either. The spoon for the crystal jam dish clinked on David's plate. Her hand was trembling.

"*Bon!*" Hélène sat back with her cup. "So it was you who brought this absurdly fine weather?"

"Oberlinden was beautiful," David said. "Though you know, Hélène, weather travels from west to east."

"Oh? I see," she breathed, but this note of helplessness vanished immediately. "Well, so tell me about the Easter banquet of the Sundas. It must have been impressive."

"The most significant I can remember. But there were . . . I had other things on my mind."

"What could that be? Do you mean you have a secret?"

From over the high walls of the silent garden came the murmur of the capital. Alone together under the budding willow, facing the silver tray flecked with sunlight, their voices were at the same time strangely heavy and light. At the word *secret,* Hélène sat forward, took a scone from the warmer, and began to spread butter on it with great concentration. Watching her, for some moments David could not remember what Hélène meant by *secret.* Then, with a rush of tender feeling, there came to him a happy evening three years earlier, an evening when he had sat on one of the Le Trève sofas, teasing a wild-eyed, giggling child.

Hélène handed him the scone without meeting his eyes.

"A secret?" David replied. "Oh, I am rich in secrets."

Hélène looked up triumphantly. "I have secrets too, David. I have more secrets than you do."

Hélène sank back, and their laughter rang across the garden.

Taking the little linen napkin from his saucer, David gently wiped a drop of jam from the angle of her lips. Instantly, Hélène seemed to vanish before him. She did not meet his eyes. David saw again the aloofness of a young French aristocrat.

"I think no one must have more secrets than you do, Hélène," he said quietly.

"Tell me what your secret is."

Hélène's voice was so soft, pained, and tender that David leaned closer. She glanced up, and her expression told him that all this was intolerable. Did he not love her? Was he not about to tell the things closest to his soul?

"My secret at Oberlinden," David began, "was to think about family and marriage. I was quite inspired." David smiled faintly. And then other words were there close round and he had only to pronounce them, weighing each one to give his emotion its perfect meaning. "I thought of all my empty fantasies. Then I thought of love"—David had set down the cup to free his expressive hands—"of the trust a man and a woman can build in each other. How only a woman's passion knows what a man might be—how she can exist wholly only in his pride. I thought, Hélène, how this reverence is the very essence of love."

David paused. Hélène's sun-freckled face was even more drawn and melancholy. Her look seemed to beg David not to torture her with beautiful sentiments.

"I have never been happier, Hélène," he went on, his voice resonant. "And when it came to me how really very difficult all this was—well, at that moment life seemed wildly worth living."

In his excitement, David suddenly found Hélène's left hand resting in his, as if it had fallen there from the tree. Her fingers were burning hot, her face was cold. She drew away, but seemed powerless to take back her hand. David closed it in his.

"Since I last saw you, Hélène, I have been a good man."

"Are you not always a good man, David?" Hélène began in an agitated voice, and then her intelligent eyes darkened with tears.

"I needed to struggle with a spirit superior to mine in every way," David went on, looking away from her face.

"But I am not . . ." Hélène shook her head. A faint, frightened flush was spreading from the corners of her mouth.

"Could you not have seen? No, don't stop me." David laughed. "You were everywhere with me, a continuous music never twice the same. At Easter I felt so many evil spirits—so degrading, when it is one's own people. But even detesting one's time, a thousand memories of you filled those strange hours, like whispering angels. I have never been more ready for anything in my life than I am now for you. Beside such a passion for happiness, I can almost see a future. . . ."

They were leaning close in their chairs, the air was suddenly damp and sharp. Still staring into his eyes, Hélène finally took her fingers from his lips.

"Is this crying?" David whispered. He gently lifted Hélène's chin with his finger.

"Because I love you," she said. "Because I am so proud."

He would always remember Hélène as she was at that moment, in the Paris dusk, with the fountain bubbling in the shadows. He would remember the animal warmth of the mysterious young body, stiff with tension on the chair edge, and the character in Hélène's cold, restrained words. But at her faint note of eagerness, David felt a sharp disappointment and loss.

"Hélène?" He hurried on, bowing his head with self-loathing and pressing her hot little hand to his cheek. "Will you marry me?" And then David felt for the first time the touch of a strange hand on his head.

"And will you always love me?" her voice whispered. Her hand tightened in his with surprising strength.

"Look." She laughed. "*Grandmaman* has been watching."

David rose quickly and looked up at the salon balcony.

In the last light, Grandmother Le Trève was outside taking flowers off the bushes with quick rude yanks.

"Will we tell her?"

"Not yet." Hélène squeezed his fingers.

"*Et alors,*" a voice came down, "*c'est Monsieur le Baron von Sunda?*"

"It is," David called up, and his voice too was strange to him. How dark the Le Trève garden was. He felt dazed by his sudden affection for this insolent old Frenchwoman now peering down at them from the balcony—dazed and moved by what had just taken placed in his life. Had everything changed forever, while all round them everything was the same, manifesting itself with the same light, the same voices and smells?

"Hélène," the coarse old voice complained, "what do you mean sitting there all alone? Come up here at once, both of you."

"At once, *Grandmaman,*" Hélène called back, in a voice ringing with a thousand emotions.

Under the porch lantern, hidden from above, Hélène stopped very close to David, gazing gravely into his face. All of it is strange to me too, her eyes said. But look how we are, then tell me how this could be wrong.

"I do love you," he whispered to her, and they kissed for the first time.

"You are crying too," she whispered against his ear.

14

THE ENGAGEMENT OF BARON VON SUNDA TO HÉLÈNE LE TRÈVE WAS ANNOUNCED
in Paris in early July 1934, and all David's family—even Cousin Katie—
traveled from Germany to celebrate the event.

So it was that the old baron missed by one hour his school friend von
Papen's urgent telephone call from Berlin. At a lakeside *Kurhal* near the
Austrian border, that bandy-legged pig-faced little S.A. brute Röhm (whose
passion for happiness had little to with faith or the future) had been arrested
by Hitler himself *in flagrante* with Röhm's own personal soldiers, then flown
to Berlin and driven with his cronies Gregor Strasser and General Schleicher
to Göring's villa on the Leipzigerplatz. There, with the encouragement of the
unfortunately quite useful Himmler, von Papen himself had added their names
to those of sixty other Brownshirt leaders on a writ of execution without trial.
Marx's class war, exiled to England and then smuggled to Russia, had come
home to Germany.

So the immense Brownshirt rabble, who in the last fourteen years had
ecstatically carried Hitler to power; who, only mildly rebuked by Papen,
generally out of sight of polite society and only now fully surfaced in the
awareness of Friedrich and Justin, had enjoyed the village burnings, tattoos,
mock battles, songfests, and torch rallies of 300,000 at Nuremberg; who had
gleefully burned books, gutted synagogues, and cracked the skulls of Jews and
Communists (in other words, those for whom peace now meant only loneliness, obscurity, and failure) was at a stroke decapitated. In the hour of
Germany's moral disgrace, the law would be in the more respectable hands of
the Blackshirts, with the Junkers—the honorable class—safe in their country
houses. Across a thousand God-fearing German villages and towns, things
would go on almost as usual.

THE PILOT

1

"ALL GREAT ARCHITECTURE," THE FAMILY TUTOR HAD OFTEN TOLD DAVID, "has its foundations in time." And, in fact, the Bavarian estate of the Sundas had not been the first structure to command this lovely site in the Franken forest, overlooking Templar's Hill and the river Saale, at the very epicenter of old Europe.

In 801, the Teutonic emperor Charlemagne chose to build here a bastion fortress for his holy empire, then loosely embracing Europe from the Pyrenees to the Elbe, from the Baltic to the Po. Later, the grassy knolls had felt the hooves of the Templars, the Teutonic knights, and returning Crusaders—and one of these was a Baron Sunda. The fortress was strengthened in 1102 and made into a castle by Richard, Earl of Cornwall, in 1260. In 1400, the wells were resunk and a monastery added, but the defensive structures were destroyed during the religious wars that followed. In the seventeenth century, the barons von Sunda zu Saale became rich, and, in 1685 (the birth year of the musician Bach), the architect Fischer von Erlach was commissioned to build on the site a small country palace. The result, christened Oberlinden, is considered among the noblest manifestations of Europe's architecture.

The three-story main edifice is white, with a slate mansard roof and long wings prettily rounded at the corners. Inside, the halls are of elaborately inlaid Pentelic marble, and scores of paintings by Renaissance masters line the walls in three tiers, with the largest canvases uppermost and the smallest below; there are trompe-l'oeil designs and engraved mirrors set in cabinetwork; immense Gobelin and Brussels tapestries cover entire walls, including a *Triumph of Fame,* which shows a virtuous Fame blasting the fates out of their chariots and raising the dead.

This wealth of art is united by a maze of passages, stairs, and corridors, all vaulted and many-columned. But the most overwhelming feature remains the great hall staircase, poised on the shoulders of naked Titans.

In sum, Oberlinden is a baroque and heroic structure—the reflection of an absolute power that knows its meaning—yet it is comfortably lived in, with laughter that is unrestrained, worn carpets, and the present baron's dogs freely tracking mud through its halls. After so many centuries, the manner of the lives within these walls is of an elaborate kindness and charm, unshamed by the common sufferings below. Entrusted with so much beauty, is it surprising that such beings are indifferent, if not actively suspicious, of all changes— especially so recent an embellishment as German democracy? Through Oberlinden's labyrinth of rooms, the Sundas have enacted generations of feuds, loves, deaths and births, failures, perversions and intrigues, cowardices and heroisms, follies and triumphs—that is, they have lived despotically. And Oberlinden, an oak among mushrooms, has remained as fertile and happy as any of the farm huts standing in the shadow that its buildings throw across the land. Indeed, for as long as anyone can remember, the family names among the surrounding farms and villages have also been more or less the same.

It was in 1751 that a visit by Frederick II, accompanied by Voltaire, ushered in Oberlinden's golden age. Over the German principalities there descended that blessed century of peace roughly demarcated by the birth and death of Goethe. The Sunda mansion became the site of gay and brilliant celebrations and international intrigue. Goethe himself came to recite the first part of *Faust,* and Mozart conducted his "Jupiter" Symphony in the upstairs ballroom. Emmanuel Kant paid a rare visit, as did Byron, Schubert, and Bonaparte with three divisions of his men. A less reasoning age was ushered in by Wagner, who neglected to fulfill a Sunda commission for three lieder. Here Bismarck expounded German unification, Turgenev stopped through in 1862 with news of the serfs' emancipation, and General Sherman arrived ten years later with descriptions of Shiloh and the burning of Atlanta. The kaiser was at Oberlinden on a shoot in the victorious May of 1918, only months before the Reichswehr's crushing reversal on the Western Front. Then history moved on. The great halls and sunny aisles were left as always, silent and changeless. And through all this, while less brilliant families advanced to prominence and disintegrated, the Sundas married new blood and wealth. And somehow sons were produced, unyielding as those who came before.

And so when in 1924—that winter of beer-hall putsches—the younger son of baron Barthold von Sunda zu Saale and his Venetian *principessa* was suspended from a strict monastery school for insubordination, the shock was felt through all the family, even to the remotest cousins in Shanghai, Alexandria and San Francisco.

But the Sundas were never at a loss for what to do.

2

Just one week later, the educator and disciplinarian Ernst Hagedorn arrived from Heidelberg, bowing from his full-dress tails to his sandy mustache and not in the least taken aback by the nude Titans. For was Oberlinden not in another enchanted Ingelheim, where the blood flowed to Charlemagne and his paladins? Was he not here to reforge out of this intelligent young rebel a link worthy to carry the honor of one of Germany's fabled names?

And yet, strange to say, that very name—far from inflaming the boy's aristocratic pride—seemed to produce a diminishing effect. On his first day, the aging bachelor was shocked to observe that Oberlinden's gallery of ancestral portraits, which gave him a sensation of being on Olympus, was to this suffering princeling more like the tunnel of symbols in an Egyptian tomb for guiding the already dead into the underworld.

The lessons took place in the baron's gloomy library. The entire household had instructions to avoid the landing outside. Seated in a chair between walls of books, the boy could not see out over the fields. And here, Hagedorn—heightened by the occasion to that pitch of conviction which in priests and politicians may pass for eloquence—set out to instill in his pupil the lofty destiny of German *Kultur*. In such a destiny Hagedorn believed absolutely. On the fifth morning, when Master David inquired in a small voice about the kaiser's ruin and the humiliations of Weimar, the great disciplinarian had a Platonic solution.

"Os-cil-la-tion," the long face hissed between thin lips. "Oscillation and weakness!"

"What is oscillation, Herr Professor?" David suppressed an involuntary smirk, mingled with the yawn of someone dying of cold.

"There must be no oscillation," Hagedorn was saying. "Affairs must be managed consistently. Once oscillation is permitted, matters will go from one extreme to the other more and more each time."

"But is not human nature—aah-aah—basically contradictory?" David's dying yawn had escaped.

The educator sat rigid in his morning coat, his face turning the color of liver. When he saw this attractive young Sunda—who grasped any idea with easy indifference, who was athletic and obviously not frivolous—remain unmoved by his noble role, the tutor experienced a deep anxiety. Hagedorn clenched his fist above the table. But in the same instant the tutor recalled the young ruffian of the Munich street rising, the young Hitler, now appropriately jailed in a mock medieval castle called Landesberg, and he lowered his hand.

David was sitting framed between the complete works of Goethe and Schiller, his head tilted politely to one side, eyes fixed on the brow of this hired Moses. His gaze veered to the clock on his father's desk. Half the lesson to go. Hagedorn had sprung to his feet. Presently he returned through the shafts of sun, bearing a studded antique volume. If anything crushed David's spirits more than the rows of family portraits it was this Sunda genealogy, boasting more than one thousand entries back to 1337. His own name was entered last, in Gothic script. Now, watching his tutor's hairless hands caress the leather, the boy felt disgust and anger. A single malicious impulse could cloud David's soul; how was he to bear five hundred years of evil Sunda memories? If the book stayed shut, today's lesson would end in a draw.

Hagedorn cleared his throat. "Well, now, my boy."

"Please, Herr Professor. Can we do Arminius?"

The educator smiled triumphantly, for he had caught the note of enthusiasm. The blood of the Sundas had stirred!

Without a word, Hagedorn went for the leather box, which stood on a separate shelf. By tradition, the relic it contained was taken to have belonged to the first-century chieftain Arminius and to be proof of descent. But for the boy the buckle's meaning lay among the half-naked men of the forests, men like the first Christians who overthrew Rome. Before his tutor could re-command their table, David had reached across and twisted the brass lock. The box's three panels fell open.

"Tell me"—the young baron was staring into his cupped hands—"tell me how Arminius won Varus's eagle." The color was back in his cheeks. "Tell me about the Romans' short swords and how Arminius trapped them in a swamp and destroyed a whole legion!"

And thus the captured Roman eagle carried educator and pupil to the end of the lesson. A half hour remained until lunch. Karin would be in the stables. David trailed the formal coattails out into the corridor. Then he escaped ahead, racing down the stairs over the hidden Titians and across the hall, which smelled of roast pork, then of fish. The doors were open.

"David, *tesoro!* Come and meet someone."

David was halted on the porch as his mother came toward him across the drive, leading two laughing, fur-coated women and a gentleman in a top hat. For a moment the boy thought he would be sick. The row of headlamps flashed in the chilly noon like Hagedorn's spectacles, and behind the cars were the subdued and manicured gardens and lawn. The only untamed things were Karin and the stables.

David skipped backward through the doors. His legs carried him quickly along the scullery passage, then down to the gun room. Three minutes later, the boy was in his shooting jacket, crossing the stable yard.

3

THE STALLS WERE SHUT, ALL BUT THE SIXTH. DAVID STEPPED INSIDE AND PULLED the iron ring until the door closed. The chestnut buttocks of the Arab gelding stamped away. A humid sweetness filled David's lungs.

"Careful, you'll worry him," said a voice.

Karin's white-bloused figure straightened next to him, holding a sponge. Light fell from the small barred window. David could see his sister's long neck and teasing eyes. Leaning her forehead against his chin, she put a hand behind his head.

"How was it, what did they do to you?"

"Am I really so worthless and such a criminal?"

Karin frowned, her mouth small and sensitive with sympathy. A tutor was the most dreaded punishment.

"Poor David, poor David," she said. "Is he excruciating?"

"Much worse. Worse than any of them at Ettal."

"At least you won't be made to run barefoot in the snow at dawn," Karin said. "But how is it?"

"Like being sealed in a glacier."

"In a glacier," she repeated, and shivered.

"Why should I be driven to learn all that? What else can I be but what I am already?"

"You are the favorite, not Friedrich." His sister laughed and David's heart jumped. The horse's belly nudged them gently against the hanging tackle.

"They would prefer me broken," he said simply. And seeing in his mind all the incomprehensible farms, grown men, and German factories that supported and depended on the Sunda estate, David felt an urge to sin perversely. Standing with his sister on the straw and droppings, images moved before him.

"Because you are brilliant," she whispered. "You frighten them."

"If I could be like you," David said. At the thought of it—the luxury of being Karin, who was freer than any boy, and of just living—everything round them felt sweeter. In the yard outside, two grooms were telling jokes. Pushing David away, Karin knitted her fingers behind her head and swung her elbows.

"Your head looks just out of an eggshell," he whispered.

Karin shook her wet curls and looked at David. "Stay with me, darling grenouille. I must sponge Selim; no one else knows how."

Selim's English saddle hung on the corner rail. Climbing up from the straw, David settled on it.

"It was a long hard ride, wasn't it, Selim?" Karin chanted softly, "Selim, Selim," and Selim lowered his head suspiciously, pretending to mouth the hay. He eyed the being in tweeds balanced on his saddle. "Over to Templar's Hill, Selim," the young woman sang, bending to sponge under the twitching legs. "Then we galloped into the forest, Selim, didn't we? We jumped two fences, then we were alone to run in the paddocks—Selim, Selim, Selim."

"Karin! You are forbidden to jump alone." David gave an admiring laugh. His sister could break any rules.

"Forbidden?" Karin dropped the sponge in the bucket. Her boots rustled, and she swung slowly on David's left knee, back and forth. "Last night," she whispered, "I slept without anything on."

"Karin, what if you were caught? What was it like?"

"Nice." She gave an embarrassed peal of laughter. "Now it's lunch."

David's heart sank. He was not ready for the formality of the main house, with its guests and servants. "Don't say it yet." David gently held Karin's wrists. "I don't want it to end."

"Then we must make a plan."

David stared at her. Had he not disgraced himself enough? David felt Karin's hands turn eagerly in his.

"We will be expected to stay the first hour of Mother's ball. I will wear my white silk gown."

"And then? Go ahead."

"Beforehand, *grenouille,* we will bathe together, remember?" Karin hid her face against his shoulder.

"Sieglinde."

"And Sigmund," she said.

David had slipped down beside his sister on the deep straw. For a moment her voice made him feel strange and afraid. Then, he remembered the great tables of pompous Junkers and sly diplomats, and the sin of a brother and sister splashing together in his huge bath seemed only an infinitesimal breaking of rules.

"All right," David said. "Come through the linen closet at six-thirty— only don't be caught."

"How can I be caught, darling?" Karin kissed her brother's cheek, then ran her hand across the flat of Selim's neck. "I am a girl."

But several mornings later the spirited young baroness left Oberlinden for her convent, where she was near the top of her class. In the old baron's study, the terror of Hagedorn's inquisition resumed.

After two more weeks of this, Maria Sunda noticed that her usually energetic boy was looking gaunt. David seemed listless and avoided his parents' eyes over dinner. Was this teacher being too successful?

4

SPRING RETURNED TO OBERLINDEN. BUT IN THE ELDER SUNDAS' ROOM, AT THE southernmost end of the main wing, the strained atmosphere only deepened.

At the time of her parents' deaths, that winter on the Grand Canal, Maria Sunda had moved to a small bed in the neighboring boudoir. Because such devoutness and melancholy were sincere, they only added to her charm. But ever since Barto's return with Gustav from the deep trenches of Passchendaele, there had been an element of dread in Maria's relations with her much older husband. This angst affected both Sundas, making even the most ordinary feelings hard to discuss. Neither cared to be seen by the other to offer more than duty required; without stooping to argument, husband and wife fell into a bitter graciousness. Not once in the last three months had either alluded to the baroness's new sleeping regime, though to analyze such painful implications in silence exhausted both of them.

Maria was the first to speak. She chose the last Monday afternoon in March, when her husband invariably answered their private correspondence. Quietly opening the door to what had been their bedroom, Maria immediately noticed the empty vases, and she blushed with compassion. Then she thought, It is I coming to him, and her small expressive mouth hardened, for duty did not require this.

"Barto?" she called, to the absorbed figure between the tall windows. As the woman approached him round the bed, cloaked in all her dignity, the baron swiveled sharply to face her. His wife was forty, and even with tightly coiled hair and in a severe flannel suit her quattrocento beauty was at it's full ripeness.

"My dear?" Forcing a faint uneven smile, the baron held up a letter. "I was thinking of that curious fellow over in Landsberg. . . ."

Sensing their formality, husband and wife felt then what was between them and the damage it had done. In the ensuing silence, the woman moved past him and stared out through the rain over the bare plum branches.

Maria von Sunda had suddenly remembered a convent girl in Venice long before the war, and the grave German gentleman who had courted her one summer. "The only product of Heidelberg," her father had been forced to admit, "without scars on his face." She remembered how—through the hot dusks as they glided down endless canals in her mother's gondola—this powerful man had been tongue-tied in her presence. How, late at night, they had sometimes stolen half an hour to sit together on the moonlit marble of the palazzo's landing, too confused to speak or embrace, and how this man's hands had first felt taking off Maria's shoes to cool her feet in the Grand Canal. Well, that music student and her possessed lover were gone forever now. In their place were the haughtily civilized Baron and Baroness von Sunda, responsible for a household with social, diplomatic, and financial connections all over Europe. Yet, incredibly, though she feared none of these duties, Maria von Sunda trembled now at the politeness of the man seated behind her. Somehow it was even worse than his famous bad temper, which no one—not Hindenburg himself—dared oppose face-to-face.

"I must talk to you about David," she began, with an edge of pride in a power that would have crushed a woman not raised to it since birth.

"I see," her husband answered.

"Barto, to come to the point"—Maria faced her husband—"I am not convinced by this man Hagedorn."

"So? What has Hagedorn done?"

"Watch your son, my dear. Hagedorn is breaking his spirit."

The baron began pacing up and down the patchwork of carpets without looking at the woman frozen beside their bed.

"David's behavior," he said, glancing at his wife each time he turned, "is a constant anxiety—even a threat—to me, to this family's future."

"Barto! It is the sign of an original nature."

"If it were not, I would pity the boy. As it is, he will have to be disciplined."

"This is barbarism!" She stamped her foot.

"It is civilization; barbarism is waiting in the wings." They were silent,
facing across the waist-high mattress on which David had been conceived.
"Maria, please sit down there," the baron said.

For several seconds, the woman remained defiantly by the bed column, all
her motherhood resisting any submission to brutality. Dropping her arm,
Maria walked to the loveseat in the window and arranged her hands in her lap.
She gazed evenly at her husband.

"Well, now. . . ." His voice trailed away.

"Barto, Friedrich is diligent."

"Diligent, yes. But Freddy lacks flair. And just think, Maria." In the gray
light, her husband squinted over the forest. His cheeks were veined from the
Flanders frost. "I was one of four sons, father had five brothers, grandfather
was one of fourteen—yet I am the only living Sunda of the line! If there is
another war and Friedrich falls, do we leave Oberlinden in the hands of a
poet? My dear, we have no latitude for gambles.

"What do you want from David?"

"What a Sunda should take for granted: a respectable school record, so
that he can continue to Berlin or Heidelberg and acquire a mastery in history
and law."

"And if"—Maria hesitated, looking fragile among the big rain-spotted
windows—"if he satisfied your first wish, then would Oxford or the Sorbonne
do as well?"

Inclining his head, the baron risked a playful note. *"Tu sais,* Maria, we
Sundas have never been *chauvins."*

"Very well." His wife rose, appearing not to notice his smile. "Then I will
speak to the boy. No, it is better that I deal with Hagedorn. The man is a
bully, Barto."

Uncertain quite what it was they had apparently agreed to, Baron Sunda
accompanied his wife out of their rooms.

Pausing in their open door, his wife gazed up into his eyes. "Thank you,
Barto."

"Maria . . . ?" the baron called after her.

His wife turned to him with an air of pleasant obedience, utterly devoid
of any invitation to intimacy.

"Nothing," he said. "I will be down at six."

Baroness von Sunda continued along the silent corridor. Then, ignoring
the new Bohemian chambermaid and walking more quickly, she turned down
an oak-paneled passage that led to the upper pews of the family chapel.
Once inside, she sat in the gloom, breathed in the perfume of wax and mildew,

and peered towards the Carolingian crucifix below on the stone altar.

The afternoon passed. She no longer thought of a barefoot music student and her lover on enchanted Venetian nights so long ago. The instant she had heard his guttural note of invitation at the bedroom door, Maria had known she would never go back to *that*. No, never again. Sitting here now thinking of it, as of some once-splendid feast long since gone rotten, a little shiver of terror and humiliation shot up her spine. In fact, her denial had begun in the hour her parents died, leaving Maria as the eldest of the Pisani—the blood of doges, and of a pope, who was in turn the servant of Saint Peter the fisherman of Galilee and of Christ's apostles. David was her son too.

Quickly kneeling, the baroness pushed a strand of hair out of her eyes. As she clasped her hands, there rushed up in her breast a vivid compassion for all those in the spiritual sea lying far out beyond this estate, all longing for redemption. For old Europe, now wounded and sick, and Russia in its barbarism. For all the hosts of the blind, seeking the path of true light to lead them to salvation. Then, with sudden passion—just as in her girlhood at the convent—Maria wished that she might find in herself that goodness, might *be* that light.

"My Lord!" she said aloud. "Have I done the right thing?" By this Maria von Sunda meant her intercession with her son's father and her denial of venal pleasures. Yet far more than these, she meant all that she had made of her life and—her decision from now on to live only in the eyes of God.

But, after all, there was something dark and a little mad in so much devotion, which left her feeling giddy and distracted. When presently the baroness went downstairs to the busy kitchen and stumbled into five little blond maids hysterically giggling, she had to catch herself before she too burst into childish giggles.

5

THE WEATHER OVER THE SAALE TURNED WARM AND SUNNY. BUT ON THAT MONDAY morning there was only the terror of Hagedorn, in his stiff collar and impeccable cutaway, whose cold glittering eyes drilled deeper and deeper into the boy's most secret love of life. David knew now that he could not hold out much longer. Several times close to tears, he lifted his eyes to stare at the open doorway.

Then the library door swung shut. Along the shelves advanced a stocky brown-bearded stranger in a green sweater and silk scarf. Flushed and frowning, the man set three books on the desk, and David's chest contracted with shame. Had even Hagedorn given up on him?

"You are David?"

"Baron David Barthold von Sunda zu Saale, Herr Professor."

"Hochchild, Georg," said the stranger. And hovering there over David, suddenly a shy friendly smile tugged at the man's face. "Allow me to teach you a thing or two."

"And Hagedorn?"

"You will not see him again. . . . Now we will concentrate on mathematics." The new tutor sat down and fumbled with some tortoiseshell spectacles. "You will find the subject easy. So easy, in fact, that we will have time left for a field trip. Pardon me, are you unwell?"

The boy, cornered against the bookcase, had shut his eyes. He was trembling. Tears of gratitude and disbelief rose hotly under his cheeks. He had not been condemned. Someone at Oberlinden still loved him.

"Speak, boy. What is the matter?"

Across the table, laughter began in David's throat. "A field trip?" he asked. "Today?"

"Why not today? But first let us settle this simple algebra." As he prodded open the leaded window, the tutor's beard, soft and pointed as a paintbrush, gestured this way and that. Quite suddenly, David was sure that this strange person was to be his first friend among adults.

Georg was a naturalist and the first Hochchild in the three generations since 1848 to return from America to study at Göttingen. He was to conclude his doctorate with a study of breeding rituals among *Cervus elaphas*: that is, the Sunda stags.

The same morning, David began to work for the first time since he could remember—Georg must *never* be dismissed. To educator Hagedorn, knowledge had been the instrument of power. But wherever this new tutor's enthusiasm went, his pupil was aware of fear drawing back, his own fear and the world's. That very afternoon the tutor kept his promise, and they went together into the thickest forest.

Yet David had not failed to sense in Georg a hidden anger. These Franken forests were not the same for the naturalist as they had been for the barons Sunda. Georg knew the Latin for every animal, plant, and insect, and to hear the beautiful names spoken made the forests as alive to David as cities. He found that it was easy to think like a stag, or honeybee, or fox, but that you did not mention this. Instead, they talked about the Wild West, the naturalist swinging his gnarled stick and glancing at David with a sort of questioning alertness, as if he had not seen into his pupil's heart. And in his passion to reassure Georg that there was nothing there but love, the boy discovered a talent he had never even imagined. At the age of twelve, David was a sharp-witted, even eloquent conversationalist.

Meanwhile, as the tutor and his young idolater tracked for weeks along the secret trails of the great Oberlinden shoot, to map the red deer's calving sites and dueling grounds, Georg Hochchild sang on about America, the soft brown beard trembling this way and that. And a vivid impression came to

David. There existed a land of rigorous and happy folk, ranging limitlessly free across an immensity of wilderness. A vastness where all that civilization required was accomplished in a state of perfect tolerance. As the naturalist talked, this place seemed so near that the boy could almost reach it. For hours, he would forget who he was, and walk beside the Pilgrim fathers on soil without a past.

When summer came, he went to try out his new talent on Fritz, the chief cook. Then, racing upstairs, the boy tried it on Gerta and Gustav. Finally— forgetting that children were seen and not heard—David tried it at Oberlinden's banquet table. And strange to say, the prodigal's discourse on vast mountain ranges and deserts, on overland stage lines, wise chieftains, and lumberjacks with the hearts of children, delighted everyone. Even the old baron listened with amusement. Then after dinner the tutor gave them all his alert, questioning look, brought out his violin, and stood under *The Triumph of Fame* to play Brahms with David's mother.

Yet more than America, it was the naturalist whom David loved. And somehow it was necessary to show Georg the most beautiful thing he possessed. One morning when the tutor entered the library, there on the baron's desk was a handsome leather case.

"What is this . . . for me?" Georg said softly.

Bending mysteriously to unfasten two thongs, David felt inside for the delicate walnut throat. He carefully drew out the gun, his father's present on David's tenth birthday. It was a 6.5mm Mannlicher with a revolving magazine. His heart beating with emotion, the boy balanced the suggestive weight on both palms.

David was not prepared for his idol's reaction. The tutor had halted with their books and did not come nearer. His face flushed momentarily, then turned white. The friendly eyes, which had always searched into David, were hardened now on his chest. The boy felt himself looked into, as he had only been looked into during his darkest hours with Hagedorn.

When Georg broke the dizzying silence, David did not recognize his voice. "Yours? A beauty. Do you shoot well?"

"Papa says I am the best shot in our family."

The tutor had rested the books on the desk. He took the hunting gun out of his pupil's hands, and the boy's throat tightened with grief. Until that moment, David had felt toward the rifle as toward a thing free and pure that knew no fear, a single all-including motive, an absolute. David had been moved by the Mannlicher's balance and lashing kick. He had loved the thundering crack that split the air, rolling through the forest, and the smell of burnt powder misting in the breach as the hot cartridge spun out. All this was in the tutor's hands.

On his feet beside the bookcases, the tutor abruptly balanced David's rifle before his chest, clicked the bolt free, and sighted the gun on the ancient window. The gesture was like a gun dog coming to point. Each sharp motion was a lash across David's affection.

"Humans are shot with far cheaper guns," the tutor observed. "Excellent, fresh oil in the barrel."

"I will not hunt until I am thirteen," David blurted. "This summer"—he chattered on desperately—"General von Hindenburg will come for the Oberlinden shoot."

"Ah, yes, the sport of princes. I will be forced to finish up rather sooner than I had wished."

The naturalist clicked home the rifle's action. Without further interest, he set the Mannlicher down. When Georg looked up again at David, there was no curiosity in his eyes.

"Yes, we must work harder at our studies"—he tapped his teeth with a pencil—"and I myself on the field work."

The boy sat in silence behind the desk. Finally he got up and slid the rifle back into its sheath. Flushing feverishly, he tied the thongs and carried the gun to the end cabinet.

Then David waited, head hanging, by the shelf that contained the genealogy and Arminius's buckle. He did not have to ask. When Georg went into the afternoon, down the secret stag trails to the depths of the forest, David would not be taken.

6

IT WAS THE TIME OF THE HINDENBURG SHOOT. THROUGH CLOUDLESS LATE-summer days, along the corridors of guest rooms there was a swarming of activity. Shutters swung open, floors were mopped and polished. Several highly polished automobiles bearing Spanish, English, or Italian markings already occupied the gravel under Fischer von Erlach's blindingly white façades. Then, on the last day, the skies turned an obstinate smoke-gray. A cold moist wind blew out of the east.

Only one among the Sunda family failed to notice the change in the weather. The tutor, Georg Hochchild, had departed with his research case and violin at the beginning of the week. His pupil would be readmitted to Ettal that autumn. David and the naturalist had shaken hands stiffly at the base of the staircase. They had made tiny figures beside the crouching Titans, and David had seen that his greatest friend's thoughts had already flown back to the life beyond Oberlinden. Then that free spirit was gone without a trace, leaving the boy to wonder at Georg's verdict on him. He felt the naturalists's displeasure as he had never his father's or Hagedorn's. The excitement of his family and their household over Hindenburg's arrival drowned out David's former rapture over the Pilgrim wilderness. Not even his mother seemed to notice his sober face or trembling lips.

That night David lay awake under his canopy, while the downstairs windows blazed over the lawns, and he suffered again through each word and gesture of the terrible months in his father's library. He concentrated, until in the end both tutors' disgust with their pupil became hopelessly confused, canceling each other, and he was left without even the right to his natural impulses. What might David Sunda do next? Would there be some final disgrace?

Next morning, Friedrich and Karin were back from their summer trips. By noon a large number of distinguished guests had arrived. Very quickly the infectious fussing of snobbery became intolerable.

In the brilliant entrance hall, David stood near the servants to see his parents welcome von Hindenburg's party out of a roaring downpour. Beneath the chandelier waited formal files of apparently bored noblemen in stiff collars and gaiters, their hair clipped short at the back and sides, and vain women in slim suits, feather hats, and boas. Now the field marshal himself came nodding up the outside steps, his huge face and mustaches, which meandered like rivers down and up his shining cheeks, appearing much as they would to David's brother nine years later in Potsdam.

"*Willkommen, Herr Feldmarschall*"—David's father was bowing with his customary charm among the snapping umbrellas—this is a splendid occasion for Oberlinden."

"I have often been here at your father's invitation," the old man muttered gruffly, bending over Baron von Sunda. "It is a pleasure now to accept the invitation of his son."

For a moment, towering over his nobles, Hindenburg seemed the equal of the crouching Titans. In the spaces between the armor and tapestries, there were muffled clickings of medals, twitchings of feathers, and sudden theatrical smiles, accompanied by little pouncing bows like those of fighting cocks. Peeking out from behind Gerta and Gustav—who was in his gamekeeper's jacket—David saw the Chief of Staff of the Great War, an unvanquished hero of the old Germany, lurch heavily across the marble hall on the arms of his groveling father and mother. And quite suddenly, without knowing why, the boy experienced a wave of the most violent terror.

Presently David took his lunch in the kitchen. Then David escaped on foot down a rear path to the village.

7

OBERLINDEN WAS A CLUSTER OF HOUSES, SPRINKLED ON A FORESTED BANK OF THE Saale, built in the style beloved of the brothers Grimm. Under the steep, gabled roofs were low doorways which only children could stand in, and at the village center a colonnaded guildhall flanked by a few cosy shops. Here life was lived without note, other than the gossip from the great house or the rumor that some lonely spinster might possess the evil eye.

The boy had taken Gustav's track down across the open pastures, the rain sluicing off his umbrella. He had just reached Pfann's sweetshop atop the river wall when lightning crashed and the downpour redoubled.

David was so glad to have left behind his icy impression of the strange puppets who were occupying his home—his parents among them—that he did not notice the two farmers' wives who trailed him into the shop or the confectioner's sudden tenseness. The boy could just make out Pfann's bony rabbit's face, nearly out of sight behind the counter. Collapsing his umbrella, David smiled and breathed in the perfumed, sugary air.

"*Ach, so! Es ist der junge Baron*," Pfann rasped, from behind his thick lenses. "An excellent surprise."

"Don't call me that, Herr Pfann," David said politely, rocking slowly on his toes. He peered inside the glass cabinet of chocolates. The rain on the shop roof was like a thunderous applause. For some moments Pfann agitatedly wiggled his waxed mustache, almost as if he *were* a rabbit. The two women were whispering.

"No, no, sir," broke in Pfann. "The chocolates are last week's. The marzipan is fresh this morning. I call that one Caspian Confection," he said, glancing from the women to the marzipan sturgeon to the boy's face.

David's suddenly naughty eyes met the sweetmaker's on a level just above the trays, which was possible in Pfann's case because the confectioner had received an Iron Cross, first class, at Lens in exchange for his right arm and both legs.

"*Friss* . . . eat it!" The discharged corporal nodded obsequiously, using the verb employed for animals.

"Could I, Herr Pfann?" David reached under the glass.

Across the counter, Pfann was closely watching the boy nibble the Caspian Confection. "Is it true, my young gentleman? Is Field Marshal Hindenburg—*der Alte* himself—a guest up above?"

Through the sweetshop there was absolute stillness. At once David became conscious of the two women's eyes, and his heart leapt again with dread. The rain spattered the little windows, roared distantly on the green river, and dripped in the fireplace.

"I saw him, Herr Pfann," David admitted. "He is not nearly as nice as you are." Surely the confectioner had not sacrificed his legs in honor of his parents' weekend guest. The field marshal did not even know Pfann existed. And tomorrow the bored giant with the meandering mustaches would shoot stags, *Georg's* stags, and both the stags and Oberlinden's guests would fall at Hindenburg's feet—neither of which the field marshal had given for his country.

"Don't say such things, Master David," Pfann said, swaying behind the counter on his special stool. "*Der Alte* is a very great German."

"You are the real hero, Herr Pfann!" David cried, for these people's worship of his parents' ceremonies was making him feel even lonelier.

Now Schmidt the cobbler entered the shop, just as one of the women was hurrying out of the door. As he peered at Pfann, instead of feeling admiration, David suddenly began to feel exasperated by the little cripple's tremendous excitement.

"My dear little youth." The rabbit face below the chocolates cleared its throat with tender sentiment. "You cannot imagine what *der Alte* was to us at Lens. The very day I was hit, sir, we had been shelled underground for two weeks. Up above, it had rained for a month, harder than this. *Diese schlechte Nacht*—yes, that attack, when grown men wept and went mad in the mud."

David was leaning politely on the counter, but he scarcely heard. At a respectful distance, Schmidt and the woman listened with their mouths open. Pfann's sticky voice rose and fell. In the dim light, the sweetshop seemed to melt into a perfumed dream.

"Yes, and then, my young baron, I looked above us under the trees. There, on the high road, stood the field marshal himself, with his staff in their spiked helmets. I could see at once that it was him—and Mackensen too. Well, they came down to us in that muddy lake, right through the barrage. *Der Alte* said not one word, just looked. And oh, there was not one of us alive who did not shed tears and call to him! That night when I was hit—and much later, in the hospital train—I thought, It was worth it, Pfann, to have seen that."

The sweetshop was absolutely still. The windows were brightening; the rushing sound was only the river. And trying to imagine what, if anything, Hindenburg had been thinking in that last hour when Corporal Pfann had been a man with legs, David could bear to hear no more of this.

Quickly escaping the shop, he started back up. The rain had left the forest cobwebbed in mists, and the beaten grass was soft under David's boots. It was as if he had no parents. Stumbling up the ghostly hillside, David glimpsed Gustav far below, on his way with some of the men to inspect the shooting blinds. The boy stood for some time with his umbrella, staring after them and feeling an aching homesickness for Georg and for the naturalist's free and gentle Americans, somewhere out beyond the Franken forest.

When David entered the great hallway and found himself alone with the Titans, never before had he felt so small. Self-satisfied laughter issued in bursts from the entrances to both salons. He bolted all the way up the sweep of stairs and down the long corridor to his room, where he locked the door, turned on the light, and sat at his desk.

David had to force himself to copy the letter three times in neat, measured script. But then it was done.

Gnädige Herr Feldmarschall,

Please pardon me for disturbing your visit, Excellency. But I have been thinking very hard about the need to be called baron. I will never be a baron for heartfelt reasons. And who but Your Excellency can permit it to end? I hope very much that this will be suitable.

Your obedient servant,
David Sunda

Because the words *your obedient servant* had concluded all Grandfather Sunda's letters to Bismarck, and because of David's formal script, he felt less terrified and shameful when five minutes later he nearly collided with three generals on the guests' landing. He went on down the wing and stopped outside the last door. Making certain that he was alone—and holding his breath—he stepped into a cavernous bathroom. After pausing to listen for Hindenburg's manservant, he pushed into the special guest suite.

For ten horrible seconds, David stood staring at the field marshal's uniform, which completely engulfed a clothes stand. Then, quickly resting the envelope on the nearest table ledge, he leapt back out of the door.

8

LATER THE BOY COULD NOT REMEMBER THE FLIGHT TO HIS ROOM BUT ONLY THE pounding of his heart. When the dinner bell passed underneath him and dwindled among the salons, David was upstairs in the dark.

Yet presently David was descending behind his parents' guests round the great staircase into the bright halls of white-tied gentlemen and crop-haired ladies in clinging lace, with their cigarette stems and sashes. Over the sea of heads, he glimpsed Friedrich and Karin beckoning by the suit of armor. Then voices surrounded David and he felt their adult mastery, mysterious with roasts, candle wax, perfumes, and tobacco. He sat through the first course beside his mother at the center table. David could just hear an old Roman *duchessa*—like a death's head, with a mustache and monocle—ridiculing President Wilson to her neighbor Pacelli, the papal nuncio, for harping on the old idea of a League of Nations.

"*Caro mio,*" she cried with satisfaction, "nothing serious is ever settled peacefully." Which somehow immediately turned into a discussion of the almond blossoms at Agrigento.

"But you must promise, *duchessa,* to send me a branch every week," exclaimed the aquiline cardinal.

At the center of this symphonic gossip in many languages David twice felt his father's face turn his way, each time with an approving smile. Now surely it would happen. But still it did not, and minute by minute David's terror was dissolving as the candlelit faces seethed with vitality. He heard his name.

"I'll come and tuck you in later." David's mother was bent close to him with a smile that dimpled her upper lip.

It will come *then!* David thought, and he fled stumbling up the stairs—all one hundred and three of them. Yet thirty minutes later he lay with his arms crushed to his sides as the sheets were tugged tight.

"Good night, my dear," his mother's voice whispered into David's ear. "And *merci*, you are being so good about Ettal."

The boy felt then, on his eyes, an unbearably tender kiss. They filled with tears.

David had always slept a drugged sleep in his four-poster bed, on sheets as velvety as his own skin. But tonight he lay rigid, listening through the open windows to violins playing a Strauss waltz. Only he, the heir of the Sundas, was conscious of the thing he had done, *the one unthinkable crime.* For suddenly the dark landscape belonging to Georg appeared threatening and bestial. He saw his parents' lives and the life of Oberlinden—its arts, statesmen, and farmers, and everything they knew—rejected by future generations, humiliated and condemned, never to be again. And feeling then the existence of an immense intelligence outside his own, David's heart beat violently. Fallen masonry and treasures whirled round his head. Yet he did not dare to go for the letter. What if it were not there?

When David woke, the daylight round his curtains was a colorless gray. His first thought was that they would come for him as soon as possible. He rose and prepared himself. Behind every door, as the boy made his way down the gallery of ancestors, there were voices. He saw the butler Giles's sober face appear ahead, and he thought, This will be it.

"The Baron your father is waiting for you in the billiard room, sir."

Scarcely seeing where he put his feet, David turned down the pantry staircase. The door was shut. It was only when he stepped through it, and saw his father waiting in his hunting jacket and breeches, that David remembered. Today was the Oberlinden shoot. But even this awoke no revolt.

His father had spread a leather sheet at one end of the billiard table. Without looking up, he made a sign for his son to keep his distance. As the baron slowly laid out three rifles, David waited, separated from his father by a green expanse of felt. Shivering feverishly, he stared past the three suspended disk lamps at the Mannlicher in his father's hands, then up at his old friends the rhino, the bison, and the snow leopard. They too had stood before this juggernaut.

"And so," the baron said. "What shall we do with you now?"

Before his father's scrutiny, David dropped his eyes. Far down the immense table, the baron worked the rifle bolt.

"Fortunately, the old man's secretary opened your message and brought it directly. A good joke, he called it. Joke?"

Hearing a terrible laugh ring out, David lifted his eyes. "Father—"

"Imagine," the baron continued, emptying a box of cartridges onto the leather and stirring them with his fingers. "A child of mine disgracing the eight-hundred-year title to a great name to the most admired man in Germany—and under my own roof. Well, aren't you the mad young sap? And do you think that every Sunda who brought us to this epoch would not have liked the freedom to indulge himself? They were disciplined. Who are you to be different? To think that I dismissed poor Hagedorn."

The baron had rested the gun delicately on the billiard table. He leaned his two fists on the cushion.

"I am sorry, Papa." David raised his voice. "I will be good."

"Good? *Good?*" A shiver of pain seemed to draw down the corners of the older man's mouth. "Listen to me, my boy," he went on, without affection. "Listen carefully, as I expect the lesson to be learned. Yes, you will be good. But this is only the least of it. You will go to Ettal. You will be Baron von Sunda. And there is no experience on this earth short of death that will alter the fact."

As he swayed under the far lamp, shadows fell over the baron's sunken eyes.

"These are strange times—for me too. But there are no times to which family and honor cannot be adapted. So you will be a Sunda and a man. And if you are unwilling to be the best of both, do not soil the rest of us with stupid gestures. Simply make your life a short one."

Seeing his son's pallid face and hearing his own voice, the older man straightened from the table.

"You will be good," the baron concluded vaguely, and he began pushing the shells into the loops of his cartridge belt with little preoccupied jerks. "And you will not be at the shoot today. In fact, you will go to your room and not leave it again until Paul—the field marshal—has left for Berlin. You yourself will stay the rest of the summer in Venice with your mother, until it is time to go back to Ettal. Now, my boy, leave my sight. I do not wish to hear or see anything of you until Tuesday."

David waited, breathing hard. He had been punished, it was over. Venice—a summer with his mother in Venice? He turned away from the figure standing with a rifle under his arm.

"No!" the voice rang through the big room. "First kiss my cheek."

As soon as David was free he fled up the pantry steps two at a time. For, terrible to say, instead of feeling shamed and broken by the strength of his father's will, he had just experienced an outpouring of love for all things—the way they were, and just because they were. He and his father had been face-to-face.

So David's first revolt was absorbed by the household. Yet it was from the time of the Hindenburg shoot that he referred to himself simply as David Sunda.

9

AT ETTAL, DAVID SUNDA LEARNED HOW TO DISGUISE HIS TRUEST FEELINGS. Soon he was second in his class, had discovered a certain grace in athletics, and was much in demand among the boys. Though never forgetting the authority of his name, David remained aloof, and he never overcame his disgust for the bravado of the shower room. This independence gave young Sunda's unclassical looks a tense austerity that made even enemies remember him. After this silent struggle to defend his soul, the returns to Oberlinden came like sleepy interludes.

The world, too, was struggling to save its soul. It was a year of depression following the collapse of the American exchanges and the spectacle of people leaping from bridges—not, as in Rome, for their lovers but for money. And here on the Continent, Baron von Sunda's "Bohemian revolutionary" (released from Landsberg Castle after only one year) was, without shame, betraying the workers of his own workers' party to the industrial elite. "Through natural selection," the fellow now claimed, "these tycoons have proven themselves interested in more than bread and circuses." Even in Russia, that sultan of people's revolutions Joseph Stalin was setting his secret armies on his own peasants.

Aloof from this historical *commedia* of metaphysics, ideology, and "scientific" opportunism—that is, from the hysteria of obscure egos close to inconceivable power—Oberlinden was host to windless, hazy weeks of ripening fields and fattening calves. David was a well-built young aristocrat with a beard to shave, who had traveled all over Europe and to New York and Cairo. His suits were from London, his shirts from the Faubourg Saint-Honoré, and his shoes from the Via Condotti. He was taller now than the baron, and almost as tall as his somewhat gaunt brother. It was increasingly noted in the servants' quarters that Master David seemed preoccupied with cross-country riding, even perhaps with some secret romance.

The feud between the baron and his son was long since healed. The scene in the billiard room had faded from memory. But David had not forgotten Georg Hochchild, or the puritan romance of his four months with the naturalist. Following his return from Ettal that Christmas, he was reminded vividly of their field trips.

One afternoon just after the family festivities round a huge *Tannenbaum* decked with candles, Gustav found David bent over the newspapers in the baron's study. David turned to the gamekeeper with an impatient laugh.

"Look, Gustav, how this arrogant Nazi flies back and forth over Germany!"

"Master David?" Gustav looked toward the passage door. The gamekeeper seemed especially to enjoy his confidences with the young master. "There is something interesting to be seen—before the others rise."

Like his friend Pfann, Gustav had been wounded below the waist, and it was said that this was why he had only the one dull-witted son.

"All right, then, Gustav. Tomorrow morning at six?"

"Done, sir. We'll take the horses to exercise them."

"*Komm, Gustav, was ist's?*" But the older man only shrugged and slipped out of the study.

At six o'clock precisely David crouched up the gun-room ramp, pulling his fur hunting coat round him. This morning the frost was as heavy as snow. In the stable yard, as Gustav handed David the horse's reins, puffs of condensation exploded under his mustache.

There was a first lightening of dawn off to their right as they cantered along the drive. Side by side, the riders passed between barns steaming with hay and manure, where the cows would spend the winter. They bounced stiffly on the cold saddles, the air too bitter for either to look up at the fading stars. Then they took a cart track that bent west along the shoot across furrowed paddocks, then north again on the plateau above the village. Thirty minutes passed, and more barns. The first sun on their backs had crept over the plowings. Ahead now lay a valley of granite with tangled forests and uncultivated fields where not even the naturalist had taken him.

"I tracked the blood of your father's stag"—Gustav's shoulders turned—"from up there."

"Papa's eyes are weakening," David called back. They had halted the steaming horses nose to tail on a steep, forested slope. The gamekeeper swung his arm toward the narrow gorge, then up to the fringe of spruce tips that was the farthest limit of the shoot. This was still the Sunda estate, but never had David felt farther from home. Then, just as the horses began to shiver, Gustav started down into the gorge.

Coming to the forest flat, they walked. There was enough light now to see their way and to stoop under branches. Gustav crossed a deep brook, and the trees thinned.

The two riders emerged on a very long, straight field of short frozen grass that lay parallel to the granite ridge. Across the clearing, in the trees, was a red barn of gapped timbers, where hay was stored. They cantered the horses over to it. Kicking his feet from the stirrups, David jumped down.

10

"OVER HERE, MASTER DAVID! THERE IT IS, DO YOU SEE?" GUSTAV CALLED TO HIM.

Twenty paces behind David was a ditch of scrub spruce, then the forest recommenced. Where the white frost stopped among the trunks, David saw a dozen stakes supporting a platform: a deer-feeding station. Poor simple-minded Gustav, he thought. Feeling a bitter disappointment and the desolation of this forgotten place, he trudged forward. He would make a polite show of interest. At the center of the stakes was a rusted hub, balancing two scythes. Stepping around to Gustav's side, David rested his gloved hands on the roof. It gave slightly, like a drumhead. He could see a large cylinder stretching beyond, painted with a colored target.

Taking a sharp inward breath, David dropped his hands and stumbled back. He looked for Gustav, who was watching him in solemn expectation. Then, turning back, David saw a second platform below. The contraption lay still, unmistakably of wood and painted fabric, yet as strange with divinity as the body of something once alive.

"My God, Gustav!"

"Never mind, sir. He's been there quite a while."

David gripped the short cowl strut. Placing his boot carefully, he stepped through the wings to the bamboo rim of the cockpit. Inside it sat a rotted leather suit and helmet. There were still shreds on the skull.

"He had brown hair," Gustav said. "He must have tried to hide the machine."

"Then climbed back in and died?" David attempted an ironic smile. "Gustav, he was French, yet somehow he was all the way here in Bavaria."

"I will bury monsieur. What did Gustav tell you, sir?"

David did not reply. He was drugged with emotion. He scarcely noticed that Gustav had not understood. Death and flight? This dead being and his glorious machine had seen the inconceivable heights, then died—while David had never in his life seen a dead man or known flight. Taking slow, unsteady backward steps, his gaze ran exulting along the fuselage to the gun, the cowling bulges, the wings.

"It is not the body," David said. "It is because I intend to fly."

"David, sir! You would kill yourself. Your father will not hear of it."

"The wheels perhaps, that wing. But the frame is unbroken," David said. "Naturally I will give you a letter. The responsibility will be mine. At least until the repairs are complete you will not tell Papa."

Now Gustav was examining the machine as if his soul depended on its being a hopeless wreck. Instead, it was mysteriously intact. The trees overhead made a thick canopy. "The motor is rusted solid. Look at this undercarriage."

"The machine shop could make it run in a week," David answered, suddenly calm. It was daylight now. They should be starting home for breakfast. The cobalt sky made the gorge below seem even colder.

"David, sir . . . Herr Baron!" the gamekeeper objected, forgetting David's rule. He trudged back through the branches. "To work on the engine of a warplane? The Versailles Convention strictly forbids it. No German warplanes in these skies!"

"All the better!" David was now experiencing a terror that he might convince himself. "To the world the thing is French," he went on, the arguments crowding in, "and the gun can be removed. You were an army mechanic. If the machine came all the way to Oberlinden, it can fly again." He took the game-keeper's green lapels and tugged playfully, but David's face was concentrated. "Admit it, Gustav. Would it not be splendid? I am quite serious. I wish to have your word that you will keep this secret."

"All right, sir," Gustav said grimly, after ten seconds of silence. "But only for the repairs."

"Then we must show respect for our visitor."

"Leave that to me, sir. The ground here is not frozen."

"He may have a name," David persisted. "I will read something for him. But Gustav?"

"I swear it." The man shrugged. "Better if nobody knows."

The moment Gustav gave his oath under the spruce branches, David turned to the Frenchman. The Spad lay just as it must surely have fallen—an enemy—from the German skies. The leather helmet still stuck out from the cockpit. And in the full winter light the machine was more grimly real than anything David Sunda had ever seen.

11

THE SAME AFTERNOON, GUSTAV HAD RETURNED TO THE VALLEY AND PULLED OUT the flying suit with its contents, which included two squirrels' nests but no papers. Glancing over his shoulder and muttering prayers, the gamekeeper dug a short, deep grave at the edge of the field.

The following day the ground was frozen. After breakfast Gustav and David made the much longer journey in a wagon. Banging loose the cowl bolts and mountings, then freeing the propeller, they winched the motor onto the wagon bed. Later, using automobile jacks, they raised the machine's nose until it could be lashed to the wagon bed for the team to haul into the open.

"We must take out the seat," David said.

"Why? It is not broken."

David passed slowly around the wingtips to the cockpit, lifted out the stained wood, and carried it to the fresh mound. Opening his mother's missal, he read in Latin the Mass for the Dead. The pilot's seat would make it a grave.

They reached the machine shop at dusk. By the last light, David and Gustav winched the engine into a greenhouse, which had last been used for an experiment with Egyptian wheat. Back in the stable yard, the two men shook hands. They could hear the rumble of cars arriving for New Year's dinner.

"I will have the wheels welded by spring, Master David."

"Good fellow!" David called softly. "Also have a look at the engine. And, Gustav—is this not a beautiful adventure?"

"It is, Master David. We must be cautious, extremely cautious."

That semester, back in the stone cloisters of Ettal, the young Baron von Sunda, who once had suffered feverishly through his science courses, became the tireless student of physics and geometry. He posted an inquiry to the Club Aeronautique Française and soon received manuals on the techniques of piloting and navigation. Not long after, a package of plans and specifications for the Spad armed pursuit airplane arrived at the monastery. These David pored over, and absorbed, with more poetic feeling than he had ever experienced in reading Shakespeare or Goethe. In the long curtainless hall, with its thirty sleeping pupils, where once as a boy he had stayed awake in terror of initiations and seductions, David now lay dreaming of a field of grass, a reddish barn, and a delicate winged sculpture poised at that very hour in darkness, awaiting his return.

On the night that the young baron came home, he finally escaped alone on his horse. Gustav had rewelded and bolted on the axle struts.

Showing then a sudden passion for hunting, they spent hours away in the barn, tediously sawing out and replacing rotted wing ribs. The squirrels had eaten holes in the fabric of the lower wing and fuselage. Together David and Gustav learned to stretch on sheets of wet linen, which dried drum hard and then were lacquered to become an airtight skin. Still, the engine magneto must be renewed, and it pained David to see his lovely aircraft standing there with an empty cowl.

Back at Ettal, David seemed to have forgotten literature and music altogether. Then, as if by providence, he found out that the class lout, Schnelling—in company with the school's two most predatory young Prussians—had been stealing to a valley airfield to train in gliders. By late May, David had four times been catapulted, and then landed with the instructor's hands off the controls. In the nights he lay awake, imagining the final bolting on of the propeller. And in sleep his fingers and toes would move the controls beneath the sheets, as he floated up again and again from the grassy fields into the soft mystical element to play among the clouds, shrinking forever the meadows and farms of Oberlinden.

At last summer came, and with the long days the patching was soon complete. By the end of August, David could sit in the cockpit with the barn doors thrown open to the grassy field, and rehearse maneuvers from the manuals with the stick and throttle.

There came a day when he found a note from Gustav. A magneto had been located. The engine was now in an abandoned farmhouse by the shoot, mounted on the timbers of a seventeenth-century winepress.

This was the week before the first of a quick succession of German elections. Oberlinden was a place to stop off between the Berlin and Munich campaigns. Heinrich Bruning, who had recently dissolved the Senate; Papen; the British press lord Max Beaverbrook; Joseph Kennedy, now American ambassador to England; the politician Julius Curtius; and several other eminences passed through, talking of the industrialists Krupp and Thyssen and how they had made Hitler rich. In the cities, Nazi and Red Front gangs were fighting along streets papered in gaudily threatening posters and paved with election handbills. David, however, was not reading newspapers. In the grip of a single ruling passion, he took note only of the polished limousines replacing one another on the front drive. Through the Sunda household, it was commented that David was maturing at last. The young baron seemed deeply absorbed and, like someone in love, he laughed with guilty solemnity when spoken to. The eccentric motions of his hand at the dinner table were noticed and interpreted: to the baron this was the locking of rifle bolts, to Maria the conducting of an orchestra. But the truth was hidden under the table, where David's feet and left hand were coordinating rudder and throttle.

On the day of Gustav's note, David stood at last in the mud beside the huge winepress. He watched Gustav pull through the stiff ash blades: again, then again, using both hands. Each time, David toggled the magneto. On the seventh try, the heavy wood lurched, waved flimsily, then spun out of sight—a *crack*, the belch of half-burned fuel from one cylinder, then a popping, shuddering, droning roar. Hopping clear, Gustav gestured triumphantly, and his hat vanished, spiraling up under the rafters in a cloud of hay and dust.

Suddenly David felt his knees double. He was fumbling for the magneto switch. The great blades flickered into sight and stiffened. The barn walls were still.

"Master David! What is it, sir?"

David shook his head without looking at Gustav. For at that first deafening thunder of the wine drum, he had felt the engine's power, the weight of its block and blades, and its violence. In that instant David had seen his own body hurtling through the firmament—the fantasy of sticks and linen in the grip of shattering forces—and the magic had gone out of him.

"But, Gustav . . . what if I crash?"

David looked up, struggling to stand. Gustav's freckled face stared at him, a flush rising to his cheeks. He has done this only out of blind belief! David thought, and somehow he grinned at the gamekeeper's alarmed face. Were there no limits to what this man would follow him into? If so, the risks in turning back were greater than his own danger.

"I meant, Gustav, what a waste of your splendid work!" he observed with a laugh and went to pick up the hat. "Wonderful, but we must run the machine a solid two hours. When can we mount it?"

"Would Saturday morning do, sir?" Gustav said, and the gamekeeper grinned broadly.

12

BUT THE DREAM, *FLIGHT,* WAS GONE. THAT NIGHT AT OBERLINDEN THERE WERE no visitors. Friedrich and Karin were home from Nairobi with stacks of wild-animal photographs from their safaris to the Ngorongoro crater and Kilimanjaro. David had never felt more humbled or tender toward his family or toward life.

He continued nevertheless to be absent for entire afternoons, unnoticed amid the election intrigues. Fatigued by all this democratic concern for the popular will, Friedrich had asked Gustav to drive him to an interview in Berlin for a diplomatic post. Alone now in the remote barn, David rehearsed for the trial by drilling his reflexes in the airplane's worst tricks: ground loops, stalls, sideslips, spins, cutouts. And with such doubts, the last of the Spad's sweetness drained away. David saw flight in its awful detail. He loved the machine still, but he feared and hated more the way the great wingtips stirred in the darkness that smelled of hay and mice as he swung on the top wing. The way the control surfaces moved and squeaked. And his body—the pampered body that had lain awake nights in his canopied bed—knew then the heat of metal, the frailty of glued wood, the cruelty of tree branches, the hardness of uneven turf. Above his feet, like Achilles's shield, was the bulk of the engine whose song would crash upon the valley's hush.

A few days later, Friedrich was back from Berlin. Next morning David taxied the Spad.

For hours he jolted the biplane from one end of the field to the other, stick to stomach, pumping the throttle grip, as Gustav had counseled, to unfoul the plugs. Then David tried wheeling in full circles. The engine spluttered and backfired, sometimes stalling, and Gustav would run over the grass to swing the blades. When circling became easy, David spent two days accelerating in bursts, until he felt the skid lift, the controls harden, and the machine come light on the undercarriage.

On his sixth day, and third tank of fuel, David felt a half-crazed release. "So you want to go?" he shouted, and he kept on until the jolting ground lightened away, the grass ahead racing through the swarm of the propeller, and David held the machine balanced horizontal on the floating of the wings. "One . . . two . . . three." He pulled the throttle, the machine began to sink back to the turf—crashing down hard, then bouncing twice, and lunging violently right and left almost into a loop. They came to rest. Gustav was running from the barn.

"Tomorrow you will fly," David swore into the silence. And hanging in this cradle of wing struts and wires, he tore off his goggles and shut his aching eyes.

It was the day of the general election, and by teatime in the music room

Barthold von Sunda had the results from Berlin. That evening Oberlinden was once again still. At dinner, the impeccably white-jacketed baron sat sideways, his monocle dangling, as if at such a moment the sight of fine cuisine was insulting. Karin, Friedrich, and the baroness took all this in high spirits. Seated across from them, David seemed not to listen.

"The second party of the Reichstag, Maria," the baron was saying. "One hundred out of six hundred seats, and the English send us their compliments! Did Levin tell you? Last week, two of these fat brown-shirted senators chased him over the Marschallbrücke. Yes, of course the poor fellow ran. Are these really what—Karin, stop that! I will not have you laughing at such a disgrace. I would renounce a democracy of this kind." The baron stared at Friedrich. "But then I would be in their league. 'Democracy must be defeated with the weapons of democracy' the very words of Hitler. By all means, let us give him our last vote!"

Even in this outburst, the head of the family had not failed to manage a certain inspiration. Through the candles the Sundas exchanged affectionate laughter.

"You are very quiet, David," Friedrich observed. "Are you suffering for democracy?"

Everyone at the table had turned to the younger son. David's sunburnt face stared round him at the pale, smiling faces.

"Well, Papa," he began, "I have been meaning . . . I have a presentation to make, a reparation." From around the table there were oohs and aahs. "But you must come to the abandoned farm on the west of the shoot."

The baron examined his son's face with thoughtful benevolence. On this particular evening, finding Oberlinden to be in a comic Europe fought over by impudent thugs and sorcerers, he was touched by the boy's gravity. "Well, of course I will. Would eleven tomorrow morning suit you?"

"Eleven?" David licked his lips. "No, twelve."

Glancing round at their curious faces, he nodded grimly. From then on, David Sunda was a prisoner of that hour.

13

IF, AS PASCAL MAINTAINED, THERE CAN BE NO GROWTH WITHOUT RESPONSIBILITY, that night David grew with the violence of a universe coming into existence.

After dinner, feeling that the family's frivolity might make him ill, he had excused himself from the gossip on the garden porch. There were fireflies and not a breath of air. His bedroom was hot, and he lay feverishly awake, cursing the obedience and the obsession that had put his fate in the power of such an idea. Somewhere deep in him there was also a fervid longing to live. Somehow, many hours later, David remembered God and he fell into an exhausted sleep.

At first light, David was in the stable yard. Both horses were already saddled. It was to be a clear, crisp, windless dawn.

The gamekeeper greeted the young baron with nervous festivity. The boy looked dashing in his boots and belted leather-jacket. Gustav tipped his hunting hat.

"Bright and early, eh? Have you told your father, sir?"

Twelve o'clock," David said. "They will be at the farm."

"What a shock you will give him."

"Yes." David hesitated, one foot in the stirrup. "Yes, I suppose I will."

This morning they took the naturalist's shortcut through the heart of the shoot, a track even Gustav did not know, and they were at the secret field by nine. David had never seen the gamekeeper in such high spirits. Gustav twice burst into song as they pushed the Spad through the doors and out under the open sky. The fabric was cold to the touch. Even in the shadow of the valley ridge, the emerald green they had painted over the Escadrille markings was reassuring and gay.

By the time they had warmed the engine and then topped the tanks, it was nearly dawn. David belted his jacket tight around him. He pulled on the leather motorcycle hat and looped the goggles over it. Gustav was mopping spilled fuel off the wing.

"I trust they will see me from below," David said, and he laughed somewhat shrilly.

The first sun was on the gold-painted cowling. Behind the barn along the forest, dew twinkled in the grass. David looked up at the dark stone ridge of the shoot. he looked at the narrow field, swallowed at each end by the trees. Then he looked at the varnished struts, the emerald fabric and gold wheels, the symmetrical blades, and the headrest in the shade of the higher wing—and it was unbearably ugly.

"This is impossible!" David burst out. "I am going now."

The gamekeeper jumped aside as David stumbled along the wings. Balancing on the pilot's step, David felt one of Gustav's hands under his arm, the other tugging his jacket. Gripping the bare gun mount, he swung over the hoop and lowered himself into the cockpit. Above his head was the towering sky. David looked forward through the low struts. With a concentrated effort, he started breathing again. The machine shook with the other man's weight, and David pulled down the goggles. Gustav was laughing, but his eyes were moist. Hands tugged at the harness and squeezed David's shoulders. In a dream, David noticed that Gustav was shouting.

"Good, sir, good. You'll show them, by God and heaven. You're the finest Sunda who ever lived, sir."

"I'll do my best, thank you, Gustav. Let's get on with it."

The gamekeeper walked over the grass out around the wings. In front of the Spad now, he spun his hat toward the barn.

David nodded, and a spasm of futility shook him. Gustav had reached up and was pulling through the blade. The engine caught on the second pull, and David's heart jumped up in his throat. He saw Gustav skip clear and blipped the throttle. The airframe started forward. David stood against the right rudder bar, holding the stick to his stomach.

It seemed to take a terribly short time before they came to the trees at the end of the field. David worked the machine's nose around through the sun. The fairway of untouched dew stretched ahead. He could see Gustav waving, standing well out on the field. David slowed the engine, still blipping it. He struck his forehead with his gloved fist. Eyes on the horizon . . . keep your balance . . . no sudden movements . . . let the evil thing fly itself!

David pushed the throttle knob. The propeller swarmed—a deafening roar—and the machine surged clumsily. Three-quarters throttle, now full. The seat lifted him, and straight ahead through a gold haze spread the full length of the field. The heavy machine rushed forward, hardening into a murderous ungoverned life of its own.

Almost level with the standing figure, the shuddering ground smoothed. The trees and now Gustav moved past. Abruptly, the silver turf racing under the wing slowed. Am I flying? David thought, and another wave of defeat swept him. Do anything, make this end!

The trees fell from the vacant blue sky. The pilot's hands and feet were all moving at the same time. The engine broke off, then raced, the giant ridges lurched and swept up. David braced against the sickening sensation. Opening his eyes, he saw the granite rim of the shoot standing on its end between the wings, as if history had torn it from the earth and flung it cartwheeling.

"The horizon!" Shouting with terror, David braced the stick and throttled back. And as if by magic, the granite giant vanished from between the struts. Rocking before his tears was a fixed green patchwork that spread out to a hot yellow horizon. Germany wallowed before his eyes, like pool water on a battered ocean liner. Sobbing now, David took his hands off the controls, and the rocking stopped. Then he tilted his chin over the side, and his stomach emptied itself.

David's first consciousness was of a mechanical scream, the gulf below, and the jolting. He retarded the throttle and focused on the horizon, now framed in the struts. Gradually his senses resolved. Twisting his head out into the gale, David saw red roofs, a river bend, three forests, and a dozen fields he had never seen before. But in place of his fear was a bitter concentration. The seat came up under him, and the world turned slowly at the end of the wing. When the sun was behind him, David lifted the wings level. He peeled back his glove. The watch hands pointed to eleven forty. First he must find the field.

The machine was low over the forest mat. Seeing the shadow of his head on the instruments and the chasm of blue above, David shouted wildly, not hearing this any more than he was aware of his bitten tongue, the blood and vomit in his nose, or of the violent jerks of the hand holding the stick centered. And there ahead through the swarm of the propeller, standing naked above the Franken forest—huge and golden as some Parthenon or Taj Mahal in the morning sun—were the white façades and gray roofs of Oberlinden, commanding the landscape far into the haze.

The wings and singing wires slipped toward the great oak on Templar's Hill, the green paddocks rising and falling. Tiny figures were running from the rose garden. It was then, with the massed architecture almost in the propeller, that the pilot had his first detached thought. *To the devil with this dumb machine and unnatural flying!* He was in a dangerous state of mind. He scarcely cared whether his father saw him. You *still have to land it.* And before he could recognize the maroon car stopped on the road ahead, David pulled back.

Up And up in the deep blue the Spad climbed, the engine laboring. Sometimes David banked the machine round until—looking straight down over his shoulder—he saw Oberlinden again, dwarfed far below. Up and up he went, oblivious of the minutes and of the immensity of Germany stretching out, harmless, flat, and tranquil, to Bohemia. The propeller was throwing sun cobwebs on to the scratched windshield. David noticed ice crystals spreading over the isinglass. Then he saw the blueness of his hands. His teeth were chattering. It was the summit of creation. David pushed the stick, the cowling dropped, and they started sickeningly down.

It took several wide, descending circles round Oberlinden before he made out the shoot. Beyond it was a tiny strip of green, where Gustav must be waiting.

On the first approach the Spad was still well over the treetops as it came level with the barn. David throttled up and started round again. This time the wings floated him along half the field without settling. Control had been facile in the abstract heights. Down close to his soil, the terror was back. The machine was in the grip of forces—patience, patience. David was shaking with exhaustion. His head, ears, and eyes throbbed. Land it, or the nobility of the thing is lost! Lining up, he began a third approach low over the trees.

This time the Spad's undercarriage slapped the last treetops. David cut off the throttle. The green wings floated, wobbling and yawning above the hurrying grass. And David heard the silence, like the echo of an eternal peace. But he forced himself to hold steady, the blades flickering—hold. The machine trembled delicately and struck with a thud, lurching and jolting with sudden rude speed. Then, with trees rising all along the top wing, the biplane made a half turn. The world rocked to a stop.

David Sunda did not wait to hear the depths of the noon hush. Tearing loose the harness, he twisted out over the cockpit hoop.

He fell hard on one shoulder in the deep grass. Getting to his feet, he stumbled away from Gustav's excited cries, away from the green-and-gold warplane. Passing into the trees, he leaned his forehead against a trunk. When he had finished being sick, David went on until he reached a bank of moss. And falling into it on his face, gradually the ugly chaos of the world was still. A holy silence spread over all things.

14

BY THE TIME DAVID HAD BATHED AGAIN IN THE LION'S-PAW TUB AND JOINED HIS mother and sister for tea, and Friedrich had come with a strange expression to say that their father wanted David in the library, Gustav had been to the tenant farms, then down to the village inn, and told old Pfann.

"I always knew it," the gamekeeper kept repeating with an excitement that no one had seen in him for twelve years And Gustav would tell again how the dead Frenchman and the pursuit plane had been there all along on the baron's land. How it was young Master David who had been the pilot that morning over Oberlinden and how afterward he had found the boy lying quite unperturbed on a moss bank, staring at the sky.

"*Verrückt, verrückt,*" the men had said, looking at each other and shaking their heads. And as if they had not seen the flight with their own eyes, three groups of farmers had tractored that afternoon to the secluded valley and stood in the barn with their hats off, staring in silence at the Spad in its fresh green-and-gold Sunda colors. There had not been such a mystical feeling at Oberlinden since the return from the Crusades.

The baron was not in the library. David stood by his old desk, watching the shadows lengthen in his mother's rose garden.

From that moment on the forest moss, David knew nothing more of Gustav or the others. He knew only that he had been quite mad, that somehow he was still living, and that nothing seemed as it ever had before. David could not keep the foolish smile off his face, and at tea, seeing his mother and sister's gentleness, he had to hide grateful tears. Now, feeling the guilt of such derangement, David longed to see his father. How strange, had there really been years of bad feeling between them? Hearing the library door, he turned quickly with a deep flush and tried to speak.

"You asked for me, Father?"

The old man fastened the door without replying and came slowly through the library. David was shocked by his grim face.

The baron hesitated by one of the tall morocco chairs as if he might sit. Then, with a glance, he motioned his son into it. When the boy was seated, the old man picked up two books—David recognized these, a philosophy of war and a narrative of Bonaparte's Russian campaign—and walked slowly to the window. The silence between them deepened.

"Tell me, did you have a parachute?"

"A parachute?" David repeated and bowed his head. Then he met his father's steady eyes.

"Had the engine failed . . ."

"I believe, Father, that I did not think of it."

"I see," said the baron, very politely.

For some reason they both looked towards the eagle clock, ticking loudly on the desk.

"It is all so unnecessary," the old man began again. Dropping his arms, he paced the breadth of the window. "None of this need be."

"Father," David said, his face stinging with shame, gratitude, and dread.

"Acting with no thought of others. Is this civilization?"

"Father, are you unwell?"

The baron had halted, his head bowed as if the last words had taken away his breath. Presently he straightened, holding one book in each hand.

"I am fine," he said.

David's confusion deepened. Was the baron not enraged with him? Did he speak like this to Friedrich? Suddenly David remembered the hundred Nazis in the Reichstag and his father's cynical humor over dinner.

"All history in two books." The baron put the books together. "To the devout Russian count, in an invaded country, the forces of society are beyond the control even of tyrants; while, for this Prussian autocrat, the civilized order can be secured through the scientific denial of love, hatred, and charity. My boy, there was a time when I *venerated* our philosopher of war, Carl von Clausewitz."

I know, Father."

"But now, perhaps I too am an invaded nation. After what I saw in the war—and I was an officer like Clausewitz—there is something obscene in the way the noble fellow speaks of slaughter, with his superior detachment, his contempt for peace, his unhealthy absence of hatred. My boy, I don't know what Pfann told you (yes, I knew of your talks), but tonight I will tell you myself. In the field there is only hatred and incomprehension. In 1914 we were excused, for no one could have imagined. But this time? How have we failed in order to choose these people who never stop boasting of their violence and are encouraged in our courts? Or is it that after a thousand years of Sunda hands on the tiller I cannot surrender to outsiders."

The baron had gestured. Then, as if afraid his son might risk an answer, he turned away. Unlocking a cabinet, the old man took out Arminius's buckle.

"Look, presently this continent will be unconscious. Prague, Berlin, Warsaw, Paris, Rome, Vienna—how intimately I have known and loved them all. I must tell you, my boy, that yesterday we took the fatal step. And yet look how peacefully old Europe seems to sleep. Soon, in the lifetime of my sons, the reckoning will come. Millions of these who sleep will be torn limb from limb, and a million others know it this very night; yes, and the courts could stop it on Monday, and it would never be. We could rein it in next week, or in the spring. Every day that goes by we could turn back, and Europe would be saved. But even the philosopher-kings are sleepwalking. And what redemption will there be *then* to remember that on this civilized evening none of it needed to be?"

David had no idea how long they had been in the library. But as the window gradually darkened, he was hearing his father for the first time. And hearing that majesty—which David had only guessed at and always hated—fall silent, and the click of the buckle going back into the cabinet, he began to weep. The table lamp had been switched on, but he felt no shame.

"Did I say something?" the baron murmured, and David laughed a little.

"Yes, Father—something. I am so glad to be still alive."

"You intend to fly again?"

"Only if you wish it," David said.

"What I wish . . . " The baron paused, twisting a cigar over a match flame. "I think I may reconsider the question of university. After all, your brother Friedrich is already such a good German. Perhaps your idea of Paris would not be so bad for all concerned."

"Father, I was not sure that you knew." David had gone pale. "Thank you . . . thank you. You will not regret it. And thank you for all you said."

But the old man across the desk only nodded gravely. He did not look up again. Their meeting was over.

THEBANS

1

TWO PARIS WINTERS HAD GONE BY SINCE THE MARRIAGES OF LUZ AND Hélène. The European peace was unraveling.

    This was 1938, and civilization could no longer be contemplated without considering Hitler. For it was Hitler—perverting beyond even Stalin the methods of Lenin—who had occupied the scarcely imaginable vacuum generated by mass culture and the new science. Three years before, employing aircraft, Italian Fascists had dropped bombs on Abyssinian tribesmen. Not long after, the biplane-ace Göring's splendid new *Fliegerkorps* had reinforced General Franco to drive the elected government of Spain out of Madrid . . . and the Comintern had rallied to the stricken Republic, so extending Yagoda's purges to the Mediterranean. As a lawless din rose over the ancient capitals of civilization, the tragicomic peace movement convened in Belgium to celebrate a sacrament of nonviolence. This very spring, uniformed anti-Semites had occupied Austria unopposed. Now there was trouble over the two million Germans in Bohemia.

    For the disciplined few at *Justice* it was not only clear, but satisfactorily predictable, where all this would lead. The Curia knew; Churchill and a minority in Parliament knew; and no one knew better or expressed it more frankly than Hitler himself. And because even Hitler was sometimes appalled by his own unnatural acts—but had been resurrected from the trenches and later from a Vienna slum for just such a role, and knew that it was expected of him—the Führer flew into rages whenever he was challenged. He was like some starved and brutalized watchdog, chained to history, who barks hysterically at any approach of pity. Yet on the surface of this moral compost, life remained as romantic and absorbing as ever, and nowhere more so than in France.

    It was during this time that invitations were sent out by the Le Trèves for a ball to celebrate the New Year. And in New York, Berlin, and Paris, all four Fleurusians had known at once that they would accept.

2

AFTER HER MARRIAGE TO JUSTIN LOTHAIRE AND THE MOVE TO FRANCE, LUZ DID
not work in the theater. Her first success at the Odéon had only made auditions
more treacherous. Faced with her foreign judges, Luz reminded herself that
she had been brought up to feel contempt for professional women, as a virgin
might look down on divorcees. Her French was adequate, and her Magyar
accent bewitching, but the histrionics of the Comédie Française were beyond
her. It could scarcely be called an artistic failure.

In the end, though, Luz had lowered her standards. Only then, during the
preparation for a detective film—and confounded by the requirement that
emotion be expressed in fragments—had she realized that she was dangerously depressed. She must have six months off.

When Luz remembered now the theaters she had tried out in, and the
French faces as they grew cynical over her, she relived the nightmare of
the loans scandal and Count Holti's ever-deepening disgrace. On top of this
she was exiled in Paris, where her first love was the husband of her best friend
. . . who in turn kept in close contact with the other Fleurusians and all their
circle across Europe. Luz had only Justin, and a great deal of time free.

On the weekend after Christmas, Hélène came for Luz at the Palais-
Royal. They were to help prepare the family salons for the ball—*a bal masqué*
without the silly masks, Madame Le Trève had called it. So as not to interrupt
Justin's work, which in some way fed her, Luz was waiting downstairs when
Hélène turned into the rue de Valois.

As she climbed into the sports car, Luz saw her friend's good spirits and
momentarily dreaded the afternoon ahead. They embraced, and Hélène examined her. Luz nestled down inside her coat. The fur muff, at least, was new.

"Let me see your hands."

"They are just the same, Leni." She held them out.

"Oh, Luz. With fingers like yours, why chew the nails?"

Luz turned away, feeling a vague panic at the importance this
Frenchwoman now had for her.

"Heavens—dear Luz!" Glimpsing the eerie trace of torment in her
friend's eyes, Hélène had suddenly recalled a bitter morning in Budapest when
Luz Holti had rejected David and left for Paris. She added softly, "You are the
most fascinating person in Paris, married to someone remarkable."

"I'm happy if I fascinate you. Ah, Leni, is there the slightest possibility
that you may move to Mexico? You mentioned something. . . ."

"So you heard me? Yes, we may temporarily join the cultural exodus. But
we would have to stay with friends. Mexico would be a first stop." Hélène
laughed bravely as they accelerated along the Tuileries. "David needs time off

from his tortures in still being German. These depressing military rumblings may not go on much longer. Anyway, we'll quickly be back. Luz, you would tell me if something was wrong? If there was anything I could do?"

But even her own affectionate cry had sounded false to Luz, and she said nothing. David and Hélène's briefest absence from Paris would be devastating. A few minutes later she was upstairs with Hélène, trying to abandon herself to the excitement of a great house preparing for a splendid event. How could a Le Trève ever need to stay with friends?

The two women found Hélène's mother in the ballroom, pacing among her maids. The girls were perched at the tops of ladders among festoons of ribbon and balloons. A dozen balloons burst with a sharp report. Throwing up her hands, Madame Le Trève came toward them.

"At last, *chérie*. Why, Luz, you too! Excellent, I need to sit down."

With their heads still among the balloons, the maids giggled until they wept. And hearing a woman with a life like Madame Le Trève's complain of being tired, Luz began to laugh too. It was so pleasant to be laughing again that she could not stop until they were seated together in the sunny tea alcove above the garden.

"So tell me, my dear, how are you?" the older woman began. "How did you spend Christmas? Alone with Justin! My God, have you not met his family yet? What a shame we were away at *sports d'hiver.*"

Luz laughed again, this time a little sadly. As so often since their marriages, she sensed, in Hélène's slightly guarded scrutiny, something that made her uncertain how to reply. Was this the fault of a certain awkwardness Luz now felt among such people? Elegant society might be another role for which she was now out of practice.

"Don't say such silly things, *Maman!*" Hélène was teasing her mother; again she glanced at Luz.

"You are hard on me, Hélène," cried Madame Le Trève. "However, there is one thing you cannot stop me from saying. I am so glad, Luz, that you have given up that degrading business of the theater. It was beneath you. Now that you are established at the Palais-Royal, it is time that you reentered society. In what dress will you come to the ball?"

"She has *not* given up acting. Do you understand, *Maman?*"

"Never mind, Leni," Luz heard herself say. "I'm quite happy, too, that it's over."

The three of them gossiped on for some time about costumes and family affairs. But Luz noticed the way that Hélène's easy eloquence turned from any mention of their husbands. Nor could she help reacting gratefully to Madame Le Trève's motherly wisdom, whether or not it bore any relation to the woman's own life with Monsieur Le Trève.

At dusk, when Hélène kissed her goodbye on the Le Trèves' front steps,

Luz was feeling exhilarated by her Paris life for the first time in months. Yet to have revisited this mansion was somehow a further admission. As she walked home through the crowds down the Champs-Élysées, Luz was staggered by the cynical words she had been prepared to listen to and say in exchange for a few hours among the beau monde. She reflected on the not altogether comfortable tension that seemed to bind her to Hélène. And now a quite unforeseen idea came to her.

Could there once have been something between her best friend and Justin? Yet like so much else during that long afternoon, this was too undermining to be contemplated. Remembering then the bare rooms ahead and the powerful will she lived beside, suddenly Luz felt almost impatient.

Despite his warnings about money, she caught a taxi. Knitting her fingers inside the muff, Luz allowed novel images to flit through her mind. Justin might have no family or position, might be half savage—could there not also be a hearth and the smell of good things baking? Luz could almost imagine her husband seated with a pipe in her mother's tapestry chair, reading to their children. It was time for them to speak of children.

She paid the driver his rather large fare, went quickly up the stairs, and crossed Doré's landing. She climbed to the attic door. The silence was broken by the clink of her keys. But already, Luz felt herself shaken by familiar specters: that of a rock blasted by merciless elements, and of a naked madman who sprang up at all hours of the night to rage over his domain. She fumbled with the lock, turned the knob, and stepped inside.

3

THE ATELIER HAD A SLOPED CEILING, BROKEN BY THE ONE SKYLIGHT AND TWO windows that looked over the interior gardens. A trapeze bar, on which Doré claimed a famous mime had once exercised, hung from the ridge beam on guy wires.

As Luz entered the bar was in motion, throwing a pendulum shadow on the wall of German and Spanish posters. Justin sat in the far armchair, with his papers on his lap. He did not stir as Luz went over the rugs and knelt against his leg. The pages rustled. Fingers touched the nape of her neck.

"Justin?" she began.

"What is this, Luz?" Justin's free hand held the fox muff, crushing the soft fur. "Did you buy it?"

"Yes."

"For how much?"

"Fifty francs. Is that too much?"

"Fifty francs—fifty?"

A harsh voice had broken over her. Looking up into her husband's face,

Luz thought she saw a limitless hatred. Then it was mastered and he rose, half knocking the muff from her hands.

"Ah, Luz!" Justin stood over her, gripping his forehead. "Think, how many might depend on this work. Do you not trust what I told you about our lives and what has happened to us—a lace shop?"

For a moment she thought she saw tears in Justin's eyes. He drew her up into his chair as the words fell on her, words not sensual with her power over him but confirming her worst premonitions. And most unthinkable of all were the words *lace shop*—the den of a slum rat. If only Justin would not ask her to believe in that! He was walking to her out of the dusk. Now he was bent by her knees, in the lamplight was a face filled with an astounding gentleness. Seeing his nobility, in place of desire Luz felt pure fear.

"Justin, you mustn't tire me so."

"This isn't easy for you."

"Perhaps I should go back to Budapest."

"No! We've begun to win."

"Who is we, Justin, what have we won?" Luz said desperately.

She sank back in the armchair—at that moment seeing the hold she had over him, yet no trace of the visionary Pan who had been David von Sunda's most respected friend. She thought, *If he says the wrong thing to me now, I will leave him.*

"Never let me drive you away." Justin touched her.

"Not if you're like this."

"I prefer you off the stage, Luz. There is so much to be done."

"You must mean your book." She smiled at Justin for the first time, feeling that she had not answered him, her smile was cynical.

"Luz, work at *Justice*."

"I will never, never do that, Justin. Father would not speak to me."

"What are you saying, is there anything else?"

Luz was shaken by her failure. "Justin, give me a child."

She watched him pace into the atelier's deepest shadows. The hands that had touched her were in his pockets like the denial of hope. She did not dare to mention her premonition about David's trip. Now Justin was back, standing over her, thoughtful and gloomy.

"Not yet," he said. "When we are strong enough."

"Oh, Justin, you will never think that." Luz hung her head. "At least take me to Hélène's."

"Europe is already a masked ball to which everyone will go."

"I'd like us to be there together."

"If it makes you happy," he said.

In that instant, Justin barely heard Luz's depression. It was not that as usual she had misunderstood him, or that this was like so many accidents across three years without peace. Nor was it that tonight she had at last spoken of children—as if any new state could be lasting, while each week events seemed to overtake all things permanent. These realities had been about to overwhelm him again, when Justin had been saved.

For simply by his words, *If it makes you happy*, he had become certain to see Hélène once again.

4

SOULS MAY BE MAD WHILE A STATE IS SANE. AT OTHER TIMES, THE STATE IS MAD and it is individuals who are sane. When a man can no longer live by his reason—that is, when a soul is going mad—he will seek to reassure others that all is normal and well. It is at this point that his madness becomes apparent. And it is the same when a State goes mad.

In November, weeks before the Fleurusians were to meet again in Paris, a young Jew named Herschel Grynszpan had entered the German embassy, several blocks from the Le Trèves, and shot a diplomat called Ernst von Rath.

Justin Lothaire had heard the news only two hours later, when Eli Hebron arrived at *Justice* from the offices of the Communist party. David Sunda heard it that same night from the German ambassador, Erich von Siebenberg—the intended victim. Duncan Penn noticed the story next morning in the *Herald* over breakfast at his Gramercy Park townhouse.

In official reply to this single act, Hitler ordered National Socialists all over Germany to break Jewish windows. It was exactly fifteen years since Hitler's first cowardly scuffle in the Munich streets. Now, on this one night—9 November 1938—two hundred synagogues were burned and twenty thousand Jews were arrested, seventy of them to be executed at a new prison called Buchenwald. So it was that in Berlin, as he took his stroll at dawn, Professor Godard—lost in meditation on Hegel's concept of will—paused with an embarrassed crowd on the Lutzowstrasse to watch smoke drift from the neighborhood synagogue. A quarter million German Jews had already heard of it. And very soon the five million Jews in Poland, Czechoslovakia, Austria, France, and Italy heard it too. During that night, all Jewish possessions, including Jewish lives, were bereft of the slightest security in German courts.

In the six weeks after *Kristallnacht*, an unmistakable awareness rushed like an escaping wind through homes and cafés across Europe. A grotesque disproportion was affecting the reactions of German law, a gathering internal pressure of senseless and unlimited spite. And everywhere the need intensified to be reassured that all was normal and well—a need not so easily satisfied as that within the *Front Populaire* over the distant whispers from Russia of another state madness.

In a trance, as before some impending loss, the guests outdid themselves to prepare for the capital's most celebrated *bal travesti*. Perhaps alone among them, as Justin came in that evening he could not avoid mention of the attempt on von Siebenberg's life.

"But did you ever meet this young Jew?" Luz turned on him at last, her dress already spread on the kitchen table. "I only feel glad that it was not Linda's father he shot."

"That boy gave Europe its truest hour."

"Justin, don't ever do such a thing for me!"

Justin flushed, for the Jew's story was his own.

"There are those who will."

"Such people must be cruel." Luz gathered up the costume, an eerie glitter in her eyes. "Justin, you won't talk like this at Hélène's . . . in front of Erich Siebenberg? Look, I'll show you why your wife might make you conspicuous tonight. Do you like the costume?"

"You wish to humble me, Luz?"

"And you will be taken for an ancient deity in your black robe."

"There are no gods, Luz."

But Justin could not take his eyes off the angel standing before him.

5

By NINE-THIRTY ON THE LAST NIGHT OF 1938, THE LE TRÈVES' MANSION, NEXT to the Étoile, was blocked with cars.

As the costumes and conceited faces crowded in the Le Trèves' doorway no one noticed the Berber or his slave girl now unfolding from a nutria coat. Abruptly, Justin and Luz were in a deafening crush under the darkened chandelier. Someone was calling to them.

"Who is this, a Franciscan . . . ah, and Luz?"

"Fool, not a monk! He is a bedouin."

"A Kabyle of the Mahgreb," Justin said, but he could not help laughing as he turned to meet David and Hélène.

Only ten minutes before, he had been with Luz in a taxi on the rue de Rivoli, trying to remember these people he felt such happiness to be seeing again. Would he trust them as much—could he tear them from his heart when sides were drawn? Or was Justin Lothaire, at twenty-five, secretly hungry to be received on the Olympus of Europe's arrogant rich? Yet what could it matter when all this was about to be swept under by history? As amused Attilas and silver winged ladies turned to stare at Luz, Justin had been conscious of only one being. And just then he again heard Hélène's voice saying, "Fool, he is a bedouin!"

"And you are Brunnhilde," Luz guessed, embracing Hélène nervously at the bottom of the huge stairway.

As their husbands clasped arms, the aged butler Jean stood by protectively with a tray of champagne glasses. All four were trying to make themselves heard as they joined the throng on the wide stairs.

"Are Godard and Penn here?" Justin repeated.

"Who is not here?" Luz said. She had ignored David's first greeting to her since Budapest.

David turned to Justin. "Duncan is having a sincere discussion with my father-in-law."

"I thought the theme was native dress," Justin said.

"It is. I confess, the pilot's suit is French."

"*Bon*, David and Justin"—Hélène joined in—"look who I see!"

Waiting for them at the head of the main stairs was Johannes, absurd in a flop hat and jerkin. His face twisted into an aggressive grin.

David laughed. "Well, now, is this Luther?"

"Perhaps the Grand Inquisitor'" said Justin.

Johannes appeared to be hurt. Then he caught sight of the slave girl.

"David, and Justin! And this must be Luz." Johann bent to kiss her hand, and on both his face and Luz's was the same staring intoxication.

"You are Goethe, I am quite sure!" Hélène teased him, and her eyes met Justin's. Yes, I know, said her look. In this foolish game of who is who, only you have revealed yourself.

6

AS THE REUNITED FLEURUSIANS MOVED INTO THE BALLROOM IN SEARCH OF Duncan, Luz paused at the marble balustrade to watch a Robespierre and some last guests arrive below and climb towards her. For when she had felt again the effect that she could have not only on a Berlin philosopher but on the cream of Paris society, the long burden of misery had lifted from Luz's bare shoulders. Turning with a radiant smile, her head poised like an idol's, she went looking for David.

And David was the first person Luz saw, talking to someone in a Confederate uniform. At the sight of him, tears came to her eyes. Noticing Justin by the fireplace between Hélène and Pierre Le Trève, Luz changed course. With a tremulous smile at the older man, she pushed in beside Hélène. Her friend seemed agitated.

"Look at her, Papa, admit it!" Hélène gripped Luz's hand. "But there is Johann."

"And what of *Grandmère* Le Trève tonight?" Justin held Le Trève's attention, his face in the firelight sober with emotion. He no longer had to ask himself about Siebenberg's presence, or to engage his student friends over the events that were overtaking them. Nor did he need to ask why Hélène's brother was not there. Jean-Marc's regiment had been mobilized to reinforce the Maginot Line. Yet tonight this fact seemed mantled in fateful significance. Justin found himself feeling saddened by the alteration in this formerly strong-minded French magnate. Just now the man was at a complete loss.

"*Grandmère* Le Trève?" Justin repeated.

"Ah, yes, my boy, of course. Well, the reality is this. After my daughter married a German, Grandmother Le Trève swore not to set foot in the house again."

"I am sorry. I'd looked forward to seeing her." Justin smiled at Le Trève's story. And at that moment he could detect in himself not a flicker of hostility to this embodiment of a class he had despised.

After the shock of Luz's rude welcome, David steered Duncan well out of her sight.

Sidestepping the swoop of a pair of dancers talking boisterously, the friends had moved into the buffet line accompanied by Johannes.

From their first sight of each other David had known that he admired his Fleurusians as much as he had ever done in their student years. But though it was not yet ten o'clock there was an unrestraint in their conversation, and an immodesty in the milling costumes, which would have been unthinkable two years before. This was true also of his friends—and most alarmingly so of his wife and Luz. It was as if none of them had married, or taken up their grave responsibilities, but were still trapped in some endless celebration of hopes and delusions.

Then, without the slightest warning, David Sunda found himself face to face with Justin's wife—not the gentle, enigmatic Luz he had last seen on the night she broke their engagement but a ravishing half-naked Salammbo he scarcely knew.

"So you don't speak to me even now." she said, pressing close.

"You didn't speak to me in Budapest?"

"And why should I have?"

"Why should you have? Why *should* you?" David repeated, staggered by such a misunderstanding.

"After all these years and—" Luz began.

But just then Johannes approached them in his flop hat. He glanced from one face to the other.

"So, has Justin given his publisher the book?" David managed to say.

"Publisher?" Luz stared into his face. "Justin has no publisher yet."

"That is typical of our friend," Johannes joined in with concern. "He is such a rebel, so unrealistic."

"Justin unrealistic?" David said. "He simply doesn't play the game."

Johannes had noted Luz's agitation as she glanced from David to the swaying shadows in the ballroom. This actress was one of his circle now, yet more bewitching than any of the singers he never dared to address in the artists' canteen of the Berlin Opera.

"Luz, if you are not hungry yet"—Johann's cheeks were burning red—
"will you dance with me?"

Luz had turned her back on David. She began to laugh.

"Warum nicht, Herr Goethe? I love it . . . oh, I love all of it."

7

THROUGH THE TWO DIMLY LIT FLOORS OF THE MANSION, THE LE TRÈVE BALL HAD
entered the last hour before midnight. And it was now—for the first time in
five years—that Hélène found herself alone with Justin Lothaire.

They had been drinking steadily. Later, after the buffet, Hélène had
observed his sudden gravity as Wilfred Rouve arrived, wearing a kilt and an
uncut leopard-skin cape. At this last hour of the old year, it seemed quite natural when she and Justin came together on the tapestry bench by the fireplace.
In her absurd costume with its tin breastplate, trying calmly to meet his gaze,
Hélène heard herself ask about his work.

Justin stared back in a sort of rage at her lips as she spoke, at her fingers
gesturing in the close shadows, then up at her forehead. And feeling upon her
the impenetrable obscurity of those sad eyes, Hélène did not think of Luz's
complaints of this man's cruelty, or how until tonight she had always been at
her worst before him.

"Is much of your time spent on *Justice?"* Hélène continued, too grateful
that they were speaking to mention that she had read every issue. Justin helped
her unbuckle the armor.

"Yes," he replied, no longer knowing what he said. "We have a lot to print."

"Will you tell me? What is the truth? No one seems to know."

Leaning away from him, Hélène tried to smile. Justin was aware then of
a strained softness round this woman's mouth, and how somehow in another
life they had become married to other people. Why did neither of them have
children?

"Johann and Duncan know very well, Hélène—your husband too."

"Tell me. You must tell me, Justin," Hélène said, as on this same bench
she had once begged David for his secret.

"No one tonight needs to be told," Justin said.

"Tell me!" she said passionately.

Justin felt Hélène's hands seize his braced arm, and for some seconds a
wave of drunkenness beat in his head. The ballroom's lights and bizarre costumes swayed with strange beauty in the French night.

"Very well, Hélène." Justin adjusted his weight, so that the young
woman's bare shoulder was against his wool robe. To hide the grief pressing
in his throat, he stared blindly at the balloons clustered above the dancers'
heads.

"The ancien régime, all this tonight—"

"*Tout ce qui est beau,*" Hélène cried sadly, and Justin heard in her words that she knew already.

"Of all these, Hélène, there is not one who will save them from their danger." Justin went on, speaking to her now the words of *Les Thébans,* which no one had heard or read, and Luz had never asked to be told. And as he spoke of the historical abyss that waited just ahead, he and Hélène were as close as if they were in each other's arms.

Presently, when Justin finished—when it was almost midnight—the jazz band took a rest. As the dance floor cleared, several of the elder guests noticed with disapproval Pierre Le Trève's very *décolletée* daughter on the corner bench, her head bent as if in confession with a black-robed young man who was not her husband.

"When will it come?" she was asking him. For the civilized world that her father had taught Hélène to believe in, all that she knew and loved, now lay broken to pieces at her feet.

"It was clear in Madrid—but it began long before," Justin answered, feeling lightheaded at Hélène's intelligence. "It is being prepared in Germany and in Russia."

"And the people who are doing such things? What will happen to them?"

"There are some here tonight. What would you do with them?"

"They must be stopped!" Hélène cried.

Justin paused before this woman's relentless vision. He almost regretted then the loveless words that he had spoken here. A saxophone was playing a gentle swaying ballad. As the dancers' faces milled close to their bench, Justin felt the madness of his wish for them both that night. Turning, he found Hélène watching him with steady compassion. After the extinction of entire peoples he had described, what could their own feelings amount to?

"Enough of this. This is not the place."

"Are you leaving? You won't stay for the New Year? Luz will be upset if you don't." Hélène had almost said *poor Luz.* "She has waited so long for tonight, Justin—see how happy she is." Hélène went on agitatedly, still needing to keep him by her side. "Will you speak to David? I think we should remain in Europe."

Justin had risen, scarcely seeing her face. "There is nothing David can do. His family are sick on the slavery of a thousand years." he spoke almost with hatred, as if trying to awaken from a dream.

"Come and dance with me, Justin."

"I have never danced, not like this. Not even with Luz."

"It is nothing," Hélène said to him in the richest tones Justin had ever heard. "Please, Justin. I want to be dancing when midnight comes."

Then Justin saw Hélène, waiting now among the dancers. They came together, and her fingers tickled behind his neck. Her hair smelled of jasmine and smoke. Hélène disguised the motion of her body as she drew him against her in the silky rhythm.

"*Tu sais,* Justin, I have believed the things you say . . . all of them, always."

But Justin's answer was drowned in the thunder of bursting balloons. All around, laughing couples jumped to tear the clusters. A few American and English guests struck up "Auld Lang Syne."

In the din, Justin and Hélène stood half separated. Elegant couples were stooping to kiss. The blood rushed to Justin's head.

But all across the ballroom during those first seconds of 1939—as Pierre Le Trève passed through, wearing the gray beard of the old year—it was only Justin and Hélène who stood face to face without embracing, their bodies aching with the realization that this would not come to them. That they could not stop it, but would not join in.

8

THE BALLOON CLUSTERS IN THE SALON WERE BEGINNING THE SAG ABOVE THE dancers' heads as David discovered his father-in-law downstairs with a group of his older guests in the library. He closed the door behind him.

The ambassador to Berlin, François-Poncet, and General Weygand—the Robespierre Luz had seen on the stairway—were among them. Both men were boyhood friends of Pierre Le Trève and of Barthold von Sunda. Erich Siebenberg was there too, as well as a French defense minister in deerskin breeches and a high-collared jacket.

"Clemenceau put it this way," said the minister, appearing between the curtains like a body in an upright coffin. "*Alors, Dieu nous* a *donné les dix commandements*—and gentlemen, we broke them. Now Wilson has given us his seven points. We shall see."

Around the dim writing table, the stately figures holding glasses and cigars laughed with relief at so exclusive a cynicism.

"Yes, and we have certainly seen," agreed Le Trève, tossing his false beard onto Hélène's piano. "Any who observe the League's covenant become the automatic fools of the first rogue who comes along. *Cette marionette aux moustaches noirs* is annexing an empire without firing a shot. Gentlemen, we are back in the nineteenth century."

Von Siebenberg—who had remained ambassador to France under "the Master," as Hitler now called himself, and who answered to Ribbentrop— lifted his red face with its sagging eyelids and shrugged noncommittally. Since discovering at dinner that Le Trève had invited both of them, he and François-Poncet had been avoiding each other. Now, shut among intimates in their host's library, they were politely alert.

Next to David the door rattled, and Wilfred Rouve side-stepped in. "Wouldn't have missed this for anything," he whispered.

"I am not so sure." David smiled gloomily, conscious of the German ambassador. On the staircase ten minutes earlier, Siebenberg had inexplicably invited David to visit him at the embassy on Sunday morning.

"No, that is true," Weygand cut in from the piano. "The first advantage goes to the one who breaks the rules."

Von Siebenberg's French friends fell silent, being careful not to embarrass him.

"Progress," the German growled, coughing out cigar smoke. "Mass production, electronics, speed, size. Progress is the cause of it all. Thus power is concentrated."

"True," Le Trève observed sympathetically. "But has not technology strengthened the defensive position, Maxime?"

"When the enemy within does not block its use," snapped Weygand, whom the radical government had retired as Chief of the *Grande Armée* in favor of Gamelin. It was Weygand who had engineered Jean-Marc Le Trève's commission in an elite infantry division.

François-Poncet had been sitting, his legs crossed, under the bookshelves, where he would not have to look at Siebenberg. "God has not kept up with progress," he muttered. "It is the plaything of the masses."

"You wish to stop progress, André?" the minister inquired. "To put knowledge on a permanent diet? Have you experienced a voluntary diet?"

"Yes, and I was miserable." Von Siebenberg laughed with sudden indulgence. "But what has Europe become that is worth defending?" he went on. "Hitler is quite correct about communism."

"That is not the first question," Le Trève cut in from his new position by the far bookshelves, where Weygand and the two ambassadors would be safely in front of him.

"The first question, Pierre?" Weygand fixed a frown on their host. "Is not the survival of Christianity the first question?"

In the brief silence, they could hear the American band playing a German tango.

"But what can Christian democracies do with a fanatic—forgive me, Erich." Le Trève paused, bowing to von Siebenberg, who nodded and smiled wearily. "Hitler has at least saved Germany from these Communists. The rest of Europe is an overripe Roquefort."

Weygand's laugh was appreciative. "I agree. I have even heard a rumor that the Russians here in Paris have an oven in the embassy basement that they use to dispose of their enemies' corpses."

"And their own best people, I should say," snapped the minister.

"Good Lord, I have never heard that one," Rouve whispered.

It occurred painfully to David then that Wilfred had followed him to the

library. He remembered a comment of his wife's that the Englishman must
be in love.

"And what of the English?" François-Poncet changed the subject with an
exhalation of cigar smoke, peering at them loftily. "Why have the English not
taken a position?"

By now everyone in the room was aware that their tact with Erich von
Siebenberg—after all, the victim of the original assassination attempt—was
depriving them of any advantage to be gained by discussing Hitler's most outrageous act to date, *Kristallnacht*. On the other hand, what were the Jews to
them? Since an embarrassing rumor had it that Britain's Berlin ambassador,
Neville Henderson, was sympathetic to a German invasion of Russia, no one
answered the question.

"It is all this espionage which is turning Europe into a rotten cheese,"
broke in the French minister, and he slapped aside a curtain to reveal nothing
but blackened windowpanes. "There are a dozen spies behind every curtain.
You cannot say a thing without being overheard . . . and no one can be trusted,"
he added, without looking at either von Siebenberg or David, the two Germans
present. Privately, the minister suspected Berlin of intercepting every coded
message that his office had exchanged with the Czechs during that winter's
war of nerves between Hitler and Prague.

"Infamous, I quite agree." François-Poncet shook his elegant head.

"Depressing, ungentlemanly, and dishonorable," offered von Siebenberg,
who that very morning had personally handled the decoded version of a
French Defense Ministry message. This was a guarantee to the Czechs—even
after Munich, still allied to Russia and militarily equal to Germany—assuring
them of France's continued allegiance.

To David the mood among these old men seemed subtly to have changed.
Gone was the moral question being asked in all Europe about what must be
done, and done immediately, to protect precious freedoms from a criminal in
supreme authority who was prepared, without shame, to break every rule of
human decency. Could Europe survive another war? Suddenly everyone in the
library was aware that they were all lying.

On the piano bench, General Weygand shrugged impatiently. A blue cirrus of
smoke hung under the low chandelier, as if undecided whether to rise or to sink.

"And David, you're very silent," Le Trève said benevolently. "You have
strong sentiments. What do you propose?" In fact, at that moment Le Trève
was thinking less of any possible answers than of how his German son-in-law
might soften his old friend Siebenberg's embarrassment.

Standing against the door, acutely conscious of Rouve's scrutiny, David
Sunda felt the old man's eyes turn on him.

Was this rustling silence now his responsibility? In what way was he considered to be German? Was one of his own countrymen planning to stir mass
hysteria and trample down the cities of Europe?

"What I propose?" David began. "I would start off . . . it is a question of not being afraid of this one man." But hearing the insult in what had seemed a fundamental truth, David's meaning vanished in confusion.

"True, Hitler is only a man," Le Trève reflected.

"But have you ever met that man?" Von Siebenberg began to cough.

"Many times," said the French diplomat. "He is a talented performer."

"Tell us, then—what is he like?" General Weygand stirred forward. The minister of encoded messages took three steps out of his curtained bay. And on all their faces was an expression of men on a diet beholding a grand banquet.

9

SOON AFTER ONE O'CLOCK, THE GATHERING IN THE DOWNSTAIRS LIBRARY BROKE up in a mood of self-satisfaction at so much inside knowledge of the crisis in Europe. And somehow this prestige was only enhanced by the realization that all of them were too steeped in intrigue, cynicism, and lies even to broach the dimension of moral solutions.

Zipping his flying suit, David excused himself from a somewhat flushed Rouve and escaped into the garden. He walked slowly down the path, past the frozen pool with its silent Mercury, where he had proposed to Hélène. The ballroom curtains made faint rose slits in the mass of the palace, darker now even than the Paris night.

And suddenly David Sunda could not remember the frivolous costumes, or personalities, or the things he had heard said inside just minutes before. There was only Luz as she had come to reproach him, looking tonight as she had never looked before. No, not even when David had seduced her in her father's suite at the Adlon Hotel in the belief that she would be his wife. Was it possible that the fault had been his own? And remembering as if it were yesterday Luz's thick hair and vulnerability, and Justin's claim to them now, David angrily flung away the remains of Le Trève's cigar.

10

AFTER THE UNPRECEDENTED SUCCESS OF THE LE TRÈVES' *BAL TRAVESTI*, THERE suddenly seemed nothing further to look forward to. Europe's deformity lay naked to view. Tempers grew short. On the rue de Fleurus the Sundas took breakfast as they had since their marriage, looking over the Luxembourg gardens.

"Ah, my poor friend. You should see yourself!"

"Hélène, this must stop," David said softly, unable to hide his hunted look. Was it not this afternoon that the friends they most cared for would meet again in these rooms, perhaps even for the last time?

But Hélène, who had taken her marriage vows as a sacrament before God, could not stop. Two days after the ball and her first serious scene with her husband in her parents' driveway, she found herself still fighting him.

Since that night, she had accused David of everything . . . everything, that is, except his single great transgression. This she could not find the words to say out loud. Somehow, under her parents' roof, had not the man entrusted with Hélène's soul revealed himself as bewitched by a woman who had rejected him? And that woman had been Luz, her most cherished friend. All the questions that Hélène had never asked about her right to inspire passion were now answered. The world was under the influence of hidden forces that could make strangers of even herself and David. Yet she and this cultivated and honorable man remained bound together.

"Do you never keep your vows?" She somehow managed a bright smile for the maid Sylvie, who had moved with Hélène to her new home and now lived in Justin's old room. "What of your promise to Bernard at the League, or even to Friedrich? I cannot understand what you are doing here. My God, you can't even keep to a diet. You say you despise journalism and you read three papers. I don't believe a single word you say."

"So, am I such a hypocrite?" Across from her, David sank back with the stiffness of a cornered animal.

"*Bon,*" Hélène said in a tone which challenged her husband to deny that they were at war. "If you won't tell me where you are going, at least think of your friends. They will all be here at noon."

"Then, if you must know," David said, "I am visiting the embassy."

"Your embassy—on a Sunday?"

"*Monsieur l'ambassadeur* suggested it," David added with insulting carelessness.

"Do you know why?"

"Johannes was summoned once like this," David said with a shrug. Abruptly rising, he took his overcoat from the sofa. "I should be back before twelve."

David had been far more shaken that his wife knew by her renewal, just this morning, of the disharmony that had engulfed his marriage since his former mistress's revelation at the ball. Now the summons by Hitler's ambassador—bringing closer still the dilemma of David's moral identity in his Paris exile—seemed like a test that he might lack the good character to pass with dignity. David scarcely noticed the ten minutes it took in Hélène's sports car to reach the lifeless facade of the German legation. As he climbed out, two gendarmes turned and slowly converged.

"*Ja?*" a protruding head called from a side door, eyeing the caller up and down. "Ach, *Baron von Sunda? You* may come in. Heil Hitler! Come in, come in. *Entschuldigen*—your hair is so long." The wiry Third Secretary shrugged in apology for a world of Jewish assassins.

Presently they were upstairs, clicking down the complaining parquet floors of overheated white corridors.

David sat down in a sunny window bay and idly picked up a toy water globe. Inside it the delicate snow whirled up and raged round a tiny steeple. Remembering the Third Secretary's smirking, accelerated efficiency, the likes of which David had never seen in his country's diplomats, he suddenly thought of the famous experiment with the frog in hot water. The water is so imperceptibly heated that the frog neglects to jump out and is boiled alive.

"Sunda, my dear fellow," said a voice behind him. "Please come in."

11

THE GERMAN AMBASSADOR MOVED TO A CHAIR PLACED EQUIDISTANT BETWEEN two flags, each the rich vibrant red of unclotted blood. Feeling even more desperate, David sank into the facing armchair. The only subject he felt ready to discuss this morning was Hélène's metamorphosis from the friend of his youth into a vindictive wife.

The alteration in Hélène was slight, however, beside the change in Erich Siebenberg. In place of the florid drawing-room diplomat of two nights ago, with his shuffle and his sagging eyes, sat an alert agent of total suspicion, exuding an unnatural feminine vitality. Their brief moment of mutual horror vanished in a burst of embarrassed urbanity.

"So, you have heard from Friedrich?"

"Yes, yes." Von Siebenberg grunted at this mention of another bearer of the most ancient German blood—one without troublesome leftist friends. His jaw and lips began to quiver with agitation. "You knew that your brother has been made First Secretary in Rome? He will live at the embassy residence. Have you seen the Villa Wolkonsky? Splendid, especially so after last summer. Apparently our man kept fleeing home from the heat. The Führer needed him there, so he built a splendid pleasure pool in the garden—"

"Can it be true," David suddenly recalled, "that Mussolini has destroyed a Renaissance quarter and built a highway over two Roman forums, to clear his view of the Coliseum?"

"Naturally you know that your brother answers directly to von Ribbentrop now?" Siebenberg continued, as if David had not said a word.

"My worthy brother is a great dilettante and cynic." David waved his fingers. "State affairs amuse him."

"It is more than amusement, I assure you of that, my boy! On Tuesday, Ribbentrop and our leader will meet that Pole, Beck—then we shall see how amusing."

David felt his cheeks burning. He had pulled himself up straight in the armchair, struggling to keep his eyes level with the diplomat's. The ferocity of the phrases and the gentle intimacy of their delivery had driven out clear thought.

"Hallo, Max? . . . Yes, could you bring us two cups of coffee?" The ambassador rehooked the earphone. "Poor Max, that Jew shot his best friend."

"If you will excuse me," David continued, "in fact, it is my impression that the German race is planning . . . that we will soon be at war with almost everyone." David sat braced for the old gentleman's shock and indignation. He was not prepared for the face beaming sentimentally across the huge desk blotter.

"My dear fellow, do not leave out Spain and Italy," the man confided in a musical wheeze. "But you are quite likely right—sooner or later."

When the Third Secretary reappeared carrying an English coffee service, the Reich's ambassador and the young baron appeared engaged in the play of graces between Germans of a similar class.

"No need for violence yet," von Siebenberg resumed in a whisper, having begun to enjoy this attractively healthy young emissary from ten centuries of Sundas. "Our Fatherland now has a master at the controls. After Munich, how crude war would seem. I would not be surprised if the rest of Czechoslovakia were ours by spring—though of course you never heard it said in this legation."

David smiled down at his cup. To talk of war at the Closerie des Lilas had tasted bitter, just, and vaguely exhilarating. To breathe it here—so near the throttles of power—made him feel deranged. David felt himself getting nowhere. What was the old man saying?

" . . . and in their hearts most civilized persons will support us. Europe is a fickle horse and must be firmly ridden. We were thrown once, and the horse ran off before we could remount and regain our nerve. This fellow has changed all that. Today's army could not be stopped. A million Hitler *Jugend* have been trained. Europe is back in the paddock. The runaway is humbled and docile. . . ."

Gradually David Sunda was becoming aware that this old family friend was quite unmistakably speaking of a warrior empire to equal ancient Rome. With a compulsive motion, David's feet twisted under him. But instead of exploding in argument, he quietly poured himself another cup—half coffee, half milk.

"The man agreed with me. We must prepare a few exemplary young nobles to occupy the most responsible posts, not just these Hitler youth, these Schirach romantics. This could be settled, in your case, before Ribbentrop leaves this morning. You knew he was in Paris for the Friendship Pact."

To hide the depth of his depression, David stared at the portrait on the wall of a glowering scoutmaster. He laughed loudly and flushed. "I'm afraid that if you knew me better . . . I am so badly suited." He held up his palms, leaving the coffee balanced in his lap. For a moment, before a wave of suffocating futility rolled over him, David had seen himself in the councils of Europe, dispensing wisdom and becoming indispensable. No, he must have some months at the greatest possible distance from Europe, his family and their interests. He must think his position through.

"Naturally, I shall have to consider this with Hélène," David managed to conclude. The spilled coffee in his saucer kept the cup from rattling audibly.

Five minutes later, the audience ended with more family pleasantries. Baron Sunda was shown outside by "poor Max." It was almost twelve-thirty. In the wintry air he could feel his trousers soaked with perspiration. He had not yet turned down the ambassador's offer!

Feeling distinctly nauseated, David hurried a hundred meters under the bare trees, almost running, before he remembered that Hélène's car was parked in the other direction.

It was not until David turned into the rue de Fleurus that he saw what was about to happen. For there could be no doubt now of the intentions that Godard had so utterly failed to detect in their countrymen. And once David had publicly denied the sovereignty of his motherland, there would be nothing left to him but Hélène's goodwill. How had so many disasters overtaken a life of duty in a single week? At that moment David was overcome by an almost unbearable love for the fine and original natures waiting upstairs, whom he might never see again.

He remained for some minutes parked under the balcony, until he had subdued his passions. Gradually, he became aware of being watched from the carriage arch. And looking up, David saw the most glorious soul of all.

12

AS DAVID LED JUSTIN LOTHAIRE FOR THE LAST TIME DOWN THE FAMILIAR passage, their wives were already with Penn and Godard.

In the doorway Justin paused. Apart from Hélène's grand piano, nothing had been added. With tender gravity he looked at the typewriter, at the books stacked behind the worn sofas, and at the Moroccan carpets with tears hidden in the designs. Justin looked at this room where so much had begun, and he saw that these accomplished people belonged now to the world. Duncan came forward—unmistakably, with the bounteous air of a corporate executive. He was followed by Hélène.

"Well, David?" She laughed carelessly, but without looking at Justin. "Tell us now what you were doing."

Duncan's voice broke a little, for they had not spoken soberly until this hour. "David. Were you in that legation where they shoot each other."

David shook his hand. "Yes, Siebenberg survived to recruit me—even here. I am to be a good son."

"You are spoken for. You belong to us!" Johannes protested.

With a glance round their faces—here once again—David went to the park windows. Among the Fleurusians, only Luz had never seen them in this setting. She was watching David now, draped on a sofa as if stricken by some childlike shame after her success at Hélène's ball. Just now, Luz had no further power to disturb him. He experienced an almost magic sensation of safety.

"Germany has made its decision," he said.

"Then we must make ours," observed Duncan.

Johannes came forward. "How could the most enlightened of peoples pursue such mediocrity!" he exploded. "It is incomprehensible."

Still frozen in the entrance after the mention of the German embassy, Justin spoke at last. "David is correct, though evidence is still necessary to convince most people."

"Austria, the Sudetenland—these provocations are systematic." David almost whispered, as if he had falsely praised life and now life had failed them.

Johannes began to pace in front of the windows. "This degrading and boring talk of invasions is not for us—not this afternoon."

Justin rose again to circle this well-loved room. He lit a cigarette and examined their interesting faces, which already bore the marks of strain. Yet to someone on his lonely road, all this was just as it had seemed when a student first came out of the desert. As distinctly formed as each of them appeared to Justin, at this moment they were still a group.

"I think the bunch of you would be better off in New York. When you come over, simply stay on at my house."

They all thanked Duncan with embarrassed affection, knowing that their friend had spent the last two days in a room at the Ritz with a guest from Hélène's ball. That this young woman from Richmond, whom he had last seen on a prep school date ten years earlier, was called Eustacia Wick. They even knew that Miss Wick had proposed to Duncan.

"While humanity sinks into the depths, must Europe go to a wedding that you thought up two days ago?" Johannes said. And seeing then the comedy of sexual envy and apology on their philosopher's face, they all struggled with laughter.

For half a minute no one could speak. Then, as if in his absence Johann had at last grasped the secret of his egotism, he continued the joke at his own expense. "Yes, I *knew* you would be fascinated to hear about the superb minds on my faculty; I am worshiped by them. And when Doktor Godard is not with his students, he spends his hours at the opera house. Oh, my friends, there is nothing on this earth like these Wagnerian sopranos!"

Yet somehow it was not until late afternoon, when the Fleurusians had only ten minutes left, that David Sunda found himself standing at peace beside Justin. With their backs to the Luxembourg gardens they watched Johannes on a sofa between Luz and Hélène, trying to amuse both women. Finally David spoke.

"I didn't know how it might feel, to have this taken from us."

"I knew," Justin said. "Since the day I discovered my father, I knew."

"That with so much civilization, there could be this loss of reason?"

"Since the time of my father."

"You never spoke of him."

"I never met him," Justin said.

"Perhaps I could help you," David said.

"In the morning, stop at *Justice*. Tell us about your famous embassy."

"The source will be recognized," David said, after a pause.

"It can be disguised."

David's eyes met Justin's. You see? the Algerian's melancholy gaze seemed to say. Do you see now? At the same instant the two men smiled.

"And tomorrow you'll tell me about your father?"

"Yes, tomorrow I will," Justin said, turning back to the others. And seeing Hélène sit at the piano, he looked at her as he had never dared look at her before.

No, he would not know until long after this hour if he could give her up. For now, Justin must believe that there would be another chance.

13

THE NEXT DAY, DUNCAN SAILED FOR NEW YORK AND JOHANN CAUGHT THE Berlin Express. Then, in February, Luz's fears were confirmed when David and Hélène hurriedly set sail for Veracruz on the first leg of their three-month trip.

Into the spring and summer of 1939, as the people of Czechoslovakia handed over their industries and armaments to Hitler's uniformed cutpurses, without a defending shot from Poland or France, Justin worked on his book. But neither *Les Thebans* nor Luz could hold him. He spent days now in the dingy courtyard off the rue de Mézière. Stranger and stranger knowledge came trickling in daily, commanding the moral scientist in Justin for a solution.

On the day that Madrid fell to Franco, a Ukrainian army defector walked into *Justice*. They heard, then, a fantastic tale: that four hundred genuine signatures of Stalin himself graced a similar number of Yezhov's death lists. Almost to the last apostle, the original Workers' Revolutionary Party had been denounced—the evidence delivered by a Nazi, General Skoblin, Yezhov's messenger from Himmler at his castle at Wewelsburg. This time, Eli Hebron and two Communist printers stood listening in silence. But with Europe's strongest army in the hands of astrologers and murderers, what time was left to disprove such names and fables? Now, in the splendidly cloudless days of late August, Hitler legalized the killing of the crippled and insane. German radio commenced broadcasting in Polish, French, and Ukrainian.

On the twenty-third of the month, Hitler gave up trying to make a satellite of Poland. And, in a sacrament of cynicism, Ribbentrop and the chieftains of the Soviet revolution joined their signatures in a pact to rend the Poles. For one week, Eli Hebron was not seen at *Justice*. When he appeared, he told them he had returned his party card to the French Communist leader, Thorez.

Each day the handful of professional *intrigueurs*—Ribbentrop, Henderson, Lipski, Ciano, Molotov—continued simply to catch their trains back and forth. At each stop from London to Berlin to Warsaw to Moscow, state control was further massed and tightened. Yet in the shop arcades of the Palais-Royal and the crowded cafés of the Quartier—as in towns all across Europe—every family, each individual soul, seemed even more self-importantly dedicated to its own petty affairs. And Justin Lothaire would leave the rue de Mézière and move in the crowds—once again a *bicot* of the desert—through the heart and stomach of Paris, among the sleepwalking multitude.

It hurt him now to see the children at play in the streets. For to Justin, these scurrying State ministers were like the first uprooted trees adrift on a flood tide. Instinctively he prepared himself, sinking his roots even deeper among common folk. Surely it must be that if he called down on himself the full focus and purity of the truth, a million geniuses would awaken to redirect the course of the events. Of that he was quite certain.

That August, Justin wrote two or three of his finest editorials each week. And the words had never come more easily.

14

JUSTIN FELT NO SURPRISE WHEN THERE WAS NEWS OF GERMAN TANK COLUMNS ON two Polish borders. Among Poland's thirty infantry and cavalry divisions, not one was armored. He did not join the crowds in the street to hear the absurd French ultimatums to Hitler.

On his way to *Justice* that September day, Justin was overrun by newsboys with fresh headlines. Paris and London had been at war with Berlin since eleven o'clock. Justin experienced then such a terror of what was in the little office ahead that he had to stop in the place Saint-Sulpice for a cognac.

A woman he had worked for here brought two drinks.

"You have heard, Marcelline? We are at war."

"It's no joke, Justin. Marcel will be called up." Marcelline leaned on his table.

"Better that it is now. The Boche have only a few divisions facing us."

Justin instantly regretted having spoken. For twenty minutes he could not stop fat Marcelline from talking about it. They drank a second cognac together, sitting in the sun at the white iron table.

For three weeks the Polish lancers did meet the enemy tanks and dive-bombers among the harvesting villages and somber baroque cities. Then the Russians were on their rear. The cities fell—Poznan, Krakow, Lodz, Bialystok—and the smell of burned flesh and ashes rose above the ruins. Soon, in the newsreels of the world, Hitler paraded in Warsaw, and the two armies of autocracy met uneasily at Brest on the river Bug. During those three weeks, *Justice* tripled its circulation in the streets of Paris.

It was Justin's heroic period. He had never been deeper in love—or more an exile. With Hélène in Mexico, Justin loved his wife. But Luz missed going to the Le Trève's, so Justin took her twice a week to the Lamberts' salon, where the Lothaires were known among radical thinkers, journalists and government ministers. The salon's talk was always argument, over Hitler, Stalin, and the revolution, and twice his wife had scenes with Justin there.

As always Justin loved the Paris bridges, the print sellers' cabinets along the quais, and the lamb gravy and millet taste of the couscous in the *quartier arabe*. But none of these was enough. It was the time for Justin's publication.

During the last four months it took to finish the book, the French and English did no more than drop leaflets. Meanwhile Stalin's army overran Finland, while Soviet proletarians and Nazi racists did an obscene trade in machinery and grain. Now Jews coming in from Poland appeared regularly at *Justice*. Then one winter morning, *Les Thebans* was a neatly tied package on the kitchen table. Justin had no doubts about the power of his truth. Even a Hitler would wither before such a manuscript, like a witch before a cross. Did not the parable lay bare the wheels that drove the fascist psyche—how Dionysus came to town, with all his criminal panoply of carnal delights and magic? And how noble Thebes lost its happiness and its love for the law when the city beheld the mass debauch of its women? *This* was the very promiscuity of violence.

"Have you asked Doré to write to the publisher for you?" Luz asked Justin that morning.

He did not answer. There could not have been a doubt in his wife's tone—under this roof! In the gray winter light, Luz looked pale and unwell. Sitting before her in his unpressed suit with his hair brushed, Justin fought the anger of the lace shop, where there had been no latitude for doubt.

Minutes later he was downstairs, hurrying over the wet cobbles, the package held tightly under his arm.

There was a smell of rain on that day, as Justin Lothaire cut through the courtyard of the Louvre and crossed the Pont des Arts. Paris was at work. Some soldiers in blue went past but no other men. As he turned up the rue de Seine, Justin felt upon him the eyes of a million simple folk, and he the most obscure among them. How would they be, the highest priests in the place where sacred prophesies were enshrined: Éditions Saint-Phael? Was it not the name imprinted on the mildewed books of the geniuses in the Mahbu Public Library? Then, as if he had been blown there, Justin noticed that he was on the rue Bonaparte.

Justin walked slowly up the street, counting the blue numbers. Éditions Saint-Phael was through a carriage entrance. There were windows at the end of the courtyard. The cobbles were not worn, and he stumbled. As he stepped inside the curtained door, he saw an empty desk and a gaunt, goateed older man sitting with both his hands under it. Instantly Justin felt a love and terror of this being and this room, where legends had passed through.

"Oui, monsieur?"

"Is Monsieur Saint-Phael in his office?"

"You may speak to me."

The eyes of the mute multitude who trusted Justin were upon them.

Justin said the beautiful words. "I have a manuscript."

"On the second shelf."

"I can wait until Monsieur Saint-Phael is free."

"Monsieur Saint-Phael will not be free this morning."

"He will wish to speak to me himself," said Justin, in the absolute silence. Under his arm he held the truth that would free a dying civilization.

The steady eyes behind the man's lenses moved from Justin's glaring face to his jacket and down to his sandals. "And your name?"

"Tell Monsieur Saint-Phael that Justin Lothaire is here."

"Justin . . . ?"

"Justin Lothaire," Justin repeated.

The man locked the desk and left him. The room was white and very bright. In a minute the man came back, sat down and unlocked the desk.

"Monsieur Saint-Phael is not free. Write your address on the cover. Permit us to contact you."

Justin's face was burning. He was terrified by what it might mean not to trust someone who sat permanently at this desk, in these rooms. Justin set down the package. Yet if he wrote down the address of France's most famous writer, might it not corrupt the power of the truth? Justin wrote only his name and lifted the package to the crowded second shelf. He would come back in two weeks.

15

FOR FOURTEEN DAYS JUSTIN LOTHAIRE LIVED AT *JUSTICE*. HE BURNED COAL AND slept on newspapers under the printing table, something he had not done since the early days when Justice was only an idea. Now there were thirty journalists contributing and eight working full time. With *Les Thébans* at Éditions

Saint-Phael, something in Justin Lothaire had come to rest, a thing that he had brought a long, long way. His hope made him vulnerable. But at Justice they were all comradely in youth and idealism and strong coffee, and it kept the peace to have Justin there all day.

The offices were still two connected rooms set in a carriage yard, with their lower windowpanes painted white. Yet these untidy rooms were known across Europe, and refugees from Prague, Warsaw, Vienna, Munich, Milan, and Barcelona would sooner or later stop by the rue de Mézière. And there were the ones from Moscow and Leningrad, who caused the arguments. Often these refugees came after dark. Quiet, angry, haunted men in borrowed clothes, who brought word fragments from an unrestorable mural of fear and persecution. Among them were two kinds, the humorous and the mad. Many brought the names and whereabouts of hundreds still locked and forgotten inside, names that Justin and Eli kept in fireproof canisters behind the toilet wall. *Justice* had become the center of an underground.

For Justin the days were charmed, and his friends treated him as if he could make no mistakes. Besides the invisible net of lonely rebels and the more disciplined ex-Communists, there was Justin's manuscript. By now his words must have been read. The desk owl would have been reprimanded for not taking Justin's address. They would be preparing to contact him. A desert prophecy, which had been Justin's truth, might soon be the truth of multitudes. This consciousness blasted the wastes of his mind and froze its beaches. A half-caste, who on a casbah rooftop had dreamt words to break the spell of tyrants, was becoming his own dream of salvation.

The seventeenth of January 1940 came and went. Hitler did not invade through Belgium. There was no French and English attack through Norway and the Low Countries. The two weeks that the editor at Saint-Phael had given Justin were up. That night he left *Justice* and went home to Luz in the Palais-Royal.

The next morning, as Justin again made the walk over the Pont des Arts, his soul was humble and ready, and very pure.

16

THE FRONT ROOM AT ÉDITIONS SAINT-PHAEL WAS EMPTY. SO WAS THE SECOND wall shelf on the right.

Justin took off his soaking raincoat. In a trance, he moved past the desk. Somewhere down this narrow corridor of offices was the child of his soul, the naked words. He had never brought his shame to a place where it was so exposed. It was the judgment hour.

The fifth door on the left was stenciled C. L. SAINT-PHAEL. Justin knocked softly. Taking the handle, he pushed the heavy door. The office was empty.

Stepping in, Justin sank into an armchair that faced the famous publisher's desk. Outside in the garden was an elm, grown with ivy to the uppermost branches. The leaves flickered, shedding the rain. Justin forced himself to breathe.

"Good day."

The office light had gone on, and Justin turned.

In the open door was the man from the front room. His long face was hardening, his gray hair stood up like grass. "*Quoi donc?* This is not for you." He kept down his voice.

"I am here for Monsieur Saint-Phael," Justin said.

"But what do you mean?" The man advanced in unnatural jerks on the young ruffian seated like a lord in the single armchair. "What can this mean? You came into Monsieur Saint-Phael's office?"

"I wish to speak with Monsieur Saint-Phael," Justin said.

"You will not speak to Monsieur Saint-Phael," the man said.

Their arguing voices broke off. Was it true? Justin felt his head begin to spin with horror. The man circled him to the window, unmistakably debating with himself how to throw out this Algerian madman. Justin felt the office floor quake under his chair. Abruptly he was aware of the wild gamble of his life. There could be no turning back.

"Then you and I will speak about my manuscript," Justin said.

At these words, almost whispered in the crushing silence, the struggle ended. "Your manuscript is not acceptable," the man said carefully.

Justin opened his mouth. He was trying to speak. The silence deepened. What was he doing here? To these offices had come the manuscripts of Balzac, which an Algiers slum urchin had worshiped in the loneliness of the Mahbu Library. It was no longer clear whether it was this man with the goatee or Balzac himself who was rejecting *Les Thébans*. Justin licked his lips, sensing the complex problem. It was blasphemy to doubt either Saint-Phael or Balzac. Opening his mouth again. Justin could remember neither who he was, nor his book, nor Luz, nor anything else he was doing. His knees had begun to twitch, his throat felt sore. Rejected. This was what it was to be rejected.

"I will discuss it with Monsieur Saint-Phael," Justin panted.

"Monsieur Saint-Phael will not be in today," the man repeated, with the emphasis of someone hammering back a stubborn plank.

Do not cripple the promise of our people, Justin begged wordlessly. The jaw muscles under his high temples stood out. He spoke aloud.

"Is there no opinion . . . ?"

"*Ah, oui. You* wish to hear it?"

The man stooped out of sight. Then a familiar package stood between them on Saint-Phael's desk.

"I have a strong stomach," Justin boasted, caught up now in his own destruction.

"It is confidential. I do not know if I should." the man smirked.

Justin had risen menacingly. He could see three lines on the paper that was unfolded in the man's hands.

The man read the words. "'Pompous, quasireligious allegory of sex and revolution. A Russian prince in Greece . . . or a Greek in Russia. No matter which, no one would read it.'"

Justin laughed bitterly, unable to see anything round him. His felt on the desk for his parcel. "Éditions Saint-Phael are influenced by idiots?" he said.

"This idiot is a teacher at the École Normale."

Would this man leave no fragment of Justin's soul intact? "In the idiot's career, he will not forget the day he wrote those words," he answered.

"I hope that will reassure you. Now please leave."

Moments later, Justin was stumbling in a fever across the cobbled carriageway. It was drizzling, and he held the package under his raincoat. Without looking, he crossed the rue du Bac and hurried into the alleys. He was disintegrating. He stopped in the middle of the rue de Buci, and the driver of a market cart cursed him. No one paid attention as Justin stood staring at a rack of skinned rabbits.

He was not strong enough to go back to *Justice*. He started toward the river; Luz would be waiting. Then he stopped again. He had suddenly understood with a chill how afraid his wife was. She would panic seeing him like this, and they would sink together in her madness. *Rejected, you are rejected.* The words made Justin start down some other street, like a supplicant soul beaten back into hell. He turned another corner, then another, terrified of the words that sliced through his head. You are not on good form, he thought, without noticing where he was going. Certainly you are not on good form. But his mind churned mercilessly on.

17

ALL THAT DAY, HIS HEAD SWIMMING WITH DIVINE FEVER, JUSTIN LOTHAIRE hurried the streets of Paris as he had not since the days when he was no more than a friendless immigrant—only now without hope, and sane only in the ache of the parcel held under his arm like a dead baby.

Fight it, Justin cursed, many hours later as his legs once more carried him past Éditions Saint-Phael. Do not give this doubt the time to take root. But whenever he started to win, and to notice with warmth some street that he recognized, the words came back, *You are rejected,* and the terrible images rushed up, like the blaze of a fire that would consume all love and beauty and enlightenment.

At eight o'clock a heavy rain drove Justin to the Palais-Royal. He slowly climbed the steep staircase. Before he could use the key, the attic door opened.

Luz stood before him in a long dress, her hair glittering and her eyes innocent. She stared at her soaking-wet husband and the package under his raincoat.

"Hurry, Justin, take off the coat. Where have you been?"

Under the entrance lamp Justin was looking at her strangely. Through a stupor, he let himself be pulled into the dark atelier. Did she not see the smoke from the terror that was burning his pride?

"What is it?" Justin said.

"Wait until I tell you." Luz was tugging at his buttons. "Stand still, let me undress you. There is time for a bath. My water is not dirty."

"Luz . . ." Justin clutched the sink under the mirror, for the end of the world was upon them. But he was already half stripped, the hair pasted on his white temples.

"Justin?" Luz stood back nervously. "I don't care what you told me, I have spoken to Marcel. He asked us down to dinner at eight-thirty."

Justin held the package in his hands. Stepping heavily out of his wet trousers, he stood with his head bent over it.

"And Justin, Claude Saint-Phael will be there too."

Only Justin's lips moved. "No, it cannot be."

"Yes, it is so!" Luz cried. "Tell me, Justin, am I forgiven now?"

"Forgiven . . . forgiven?" he repeated, looking from the package to Luz's frightened face.

With a twisted smile, Justin stared through the familiar atelier. But already there was only a pleasant physical exhaustion as after heavy exercise. His laughter was a little wild.

"And is the water still hot?"

"Yes, it is perfectly hot." Luz's laugh broke off at Justin's glance, the look of a saint or revolutionist. "I've just got out."

18

TEN MINUTES LATER THEY WERE DOWNSTAIRS, SITTING IN MARCEL DORÉ'S drawing room with Claude Saint-Phael. In her satin sheath, Luz was flushed with charm. But the Justin Lothaire who sat among them on the window bench framed by the inner windows of the Palais-Royal was a Justin none of them knew.

The publisher of prophets was a prettily handsome man of fifty with crinkled gray hair. He spoke to Doré from the sofa with the substantial wit of someone rich in famous-friends, occasionally making gallant comments to the superb young woman next to him. But when the young man silhouet-ted against the Paris night—he whom the old master had described as the one authentic visionary of the new generation—simply examined Saint-Phael with thoughtful indifference, the publisher became interested. Twice he referred to a certain manuscript that Lothaire had recently completed. Yet instead of jumping at the chance which thousands of young poets would have pawned their souls for, this *pied-noir* only narrowed his melancholy eyes. Gravely, so that they had to breathe with care to hear him, Lothaire began speaking of a journal called *Justice* and of the captive peoples of the French Sahara. In a modest, even tone that made his wife look at him nervously, then stare at her crossed legs, Justin went on like a man whose opinion is urgently required.

The conversation turned to the war now surely to come and whether Europe could survive this pestilence of Fascists. When Saint-Phael's eyes shone with anger, Justin spoke of the refugees from Germany and Poland and of the few faithful simple folk of the towns and farms who would never consent to a criminal occupation, or to live without trust or in fear. Of how their rebellion, not books, would keep pure the air they all breathed.

Later, over the splendid dinner, the elegant publisher smiled across the plates at the passion on the young writer's face, wanting this holiness to be on his side. But each time Saint-Phael brought up the manuscript, the subject would change. After the third attempt, he began to feel bored and uncomfortable. Soon after dinner he excused himself.

The meeting at Doré's dinner party left Justin too with a depressing sense of failure. For somehow that long, rebellious speech—there in the finely scented rooms where he and the old man had spent such beautiful hours—had let in something deathly and harsh.

19

Not long after Justin's evening with Claude Saint-Phael, Luz complained of sensations in her abdomen. He was to be a father.

She caught the train to Budapest to be with her parents. Justin gave the manuscript of *Les Thébans* to Eli Hebron and began to forget it.

Once Luz had gone, Justin worked round the clock at *Justice*. He no longer thought of himself as a writer. Since Poland, the Communist Party had been banned and Eli had secretly rejoined. Somehow *Justice* had not been closed. Justin knew now that he could never gamble his conscience on a system convinced of its own infallibility, yet he did not join in the general outrage over the sabotage in aircraft and tank factories. For days at *Justice*, Justin did not smile. He felt himself disintegrating into bitterness and politics.

In Paris it was spring. The sharpness had gone from the sunny April days, and the office door was left open. Early one morning before anyone had arrived, Eli stuck in his head.

Justin folded away his draft of a new article, and they padlocked the courtyard door. As they hurried down the freshly hosed pavements, Eli was polite and cold. Had someone died, Justin wondered? They walked to Saint-Germain des Prés without speaking. At the corner table of the Café Flore, under an umbrella, some red-faced boy soldiers were calling in mulish voices to the woman behind the counter. "They are like schoolboys," Eli said.

"Schoolboys who learn nothing."

Eli hesitated. Then, shading his eyes, he put an opened letter on the table. "Éditions Nestor?" Justin glanced at Eli. He read on.

My dear Elisha,
What a great thing you have done for Nestor. There is far too much in it even to begin saying what our feelings are. As for Lothaire himself, he must certainly be the first Algerian to have written a Euro—

Bent forward over the shaded table, Justin read the letter through, oblivious of the soldiers and the waiter who took their order. Then, shutting his eyes, the folded letter in both hands, he sank back in the sunshine. For in place of a wild, sweet glory, Justin felt himself sucked down in corrosions of suffering. After two minutes he gave Eli a haunted smile.

"You are my friend," Justin said softly.

Eli shrugged, and together they were very proud and embarrassed.

"Who ever doubted you were this master?"

"Master, Eli? That person no longer exists."

"I see him beside me. He's the spirit of our time."

"That person of books and vanity no longer exists," Justin said, with tears hot in his eyes. "I trusted him in the hands of these vermin. They rejected him. Now they reward him."

Justin paused and began again. "The soul of our time is an egoist like the *Übermensch,* he returns from atrocious rapes and tortures in as high spirits as from a student's prank. Nietzsche was right about the age, Eli. Posterity will look back with envy and reverence on this parade of grotesque wars and upheavals."

"Nietzsche went mad," Eli said.

"I must leave Europe, Eli," he said suddenly.

Eli sat straight, steadying his cup on the table. "*Leave?* Your name is hope from Warsaw to Barcelona—and here too. All of them will soon be Fascist. Leave *now*? No, Justin."

Justin laughed bitterly. "To my father and his father and my grandfather's grandfather, France was tyranny . . . always. As England is tyranny to Africa and India—as all Europe has been to China, Russia, and the Americas. It is the culture of Europe that is Fascist and a religion. Do not believe in it."

"There is already resistance, " Eli said. "There will be revolution."

"Let Europe destroy itself, Eli. I have heard from the desert. I have heard from Abd-el-Krim."

Justin and Eli stared at each other among the sunny tables on a Paris boulevard. Justin's last words had left a silence filled with the defeat of true things, even of their friendship. But Eli was too political to hear Justin's soul.

In this silence, his sober smile sought to tell his friend how a *sale bicot* wished to lie again on the sands of Tipasa, where the heliotrope grows, and to listen to the hiss of the Mediterranean. How he wished to see again the white sails over the rue Mahbu and smell the pungence of Abdullah's spice sacks—even to hear his mother say Hail Marys to the cardboard Virgin—and how he wished to go again with bare feet in the dung of the alleyways and to stand at Ramadan with the simple folk at the hour of dusk when the pine air is thick and roseate.

Now on this Paris morning, Justin said to Eli, "Yes, the French have made Krim a prisoner on Reunion. But I am not yet a prisoner, and his people—my people—have sent for me."

"Isn't the power and its refinement here?"

"The struggle there, Eli, is for the soil of my fathers."

"When will you return?"

Justin said finally, "If there is this war, if the resistance comes. If ever they should need me, if there is no one else, then I'll come."

20

IN THE SPRING OF 1940, TEN DAYS AFTER THE CONVERSATION WITH ELI—AS Hitler's mystic racists overran Denmark and Norway unopposed—Justin Lothaire was on the Algiers steamer. For the wise man dreads to have a single person see in him moral powers he may not possess.

Now over Europe there came a term of glorious days. From the Baltic to arid Sicily, from the meadows of Galway to the vineyards of Georgia, windless skies were deep with fluttering wings and the shrill of birdsong. Village steeples seemed to sway against a parade of cottony clouds—clouds as white as the forests were green, as the wheat was yellow or the cows were brown or black. A supernal grace hung over living things. The death rattles of the few who had the poor taste to expire at such a time were drowned in a droning, twittering symphony of the seasonal succession. In the goat pens of Corinth and the dairy yards of Gloucestershire, along the wooded banks of Lake Balaton, in the neat pastures of Saxony and the dry sage hills of Chianti, Provence, and Valencia, pods spilled showers of seeds, calves and colts fell in damp heaps, lambs bleated, rabbit eyes stared, and overladen honeybees rolled angrily in the clover.

Only along the swarming French border, embrasures and giant fixed guns of the Maginot Line stretched scenically under a single sky from Flanders to the Alps, and all across Germany, now a bourgeois Valhalla of grinding machines and macadam Autobahns, there was a different and restless passion afoot.

SEDAN

1

"AS LONG AS MANKIND SHALL CONTINUE TO BESTOW MORE LIBERAL PRAISE on their destroyers than on their benefactors," Gibbon wrote, "the thirst for military glory will ever be the vice of the most exalted characters."

Through the early hours of 10 May 1940, alone in his blacked-out rooms at the Sonnenhof, a two-story *Gasthaus* on the road behind the Rhineland village of Bitburg near the Luxembourg border, the von Sundas' friend Guderian had been sleeping uneasily. At three o'clock, the handsome gentleman was wide awake. He stared up at the ceiling. For several moments, the sensation lingered of something desperately sweet. Was it his father's house along the Vistula on the morning of a hunt? The bitterly cold attic at Karlsruhe Academy?

And suddenly Heinz Guderian was tasting again the beauty and preciousness of his life, and of all lives. He felt for the bedside lamp. Pulling the chain, Guderian found himself in a simple room, blinking at the altar of roses the manageress had made on his dresser. Only then did he remembered the previous night at the tables downstairs. At once, Guderian's consciousness was flooded with images of his waiting staff, the three tank divisions lining the dark roads ahead, and the far larger hordes of French waiting for them beyond the Ardennes forest.

At this hour, mankind was still asleep. By nightfall, the nations of the world would know that the Wehrmacht had invaded France. And here at the heart of such a truth, the sensation was so vast, so mysterious, so potent that for several seconds, stretched rigid in his bed, the aging soldier was barely able to breathe.

But this moment of humility instantly passed. Almost against his will, General Guderian was flooded by the intoxication of duty, strategy, self-discipline—even *Kadavergehörsam*, the old corpse-friendliness—on which he prided himself above all earthly pleasures. There could be no turning back, now, and therefore no responsibility. From the courtyard below his windows, out over the rolling wheat fields of the Eifel, was spread the murderously aggressive German tank army that Guderian had exercised in Poland. The most powerful instrument of force on earth was in his hands. Only this time the enemy would have tanks as well.

In another ten minutes his orderly would call him to breakfast. Guderian could hear carefully modulated voices downstairs. Rising, he went to the window and looked up at the stars. The night air was warm. He moved without a sound to the plain wooden wardrobe. Inside it hung the neatly pressed uniform from Gunen Brothers in Berlin. Guderian's fingers pulled the gray trousers on over his garters and underclothes. He drew on the finely tailored jacket.

Once dressed, General Guderian lingered over his glistening boots, his hair pomade, and his various eagle pins, crosses and ribboned insignia. The very walls around him, this *Gasthaus,* would presently belong to destiny. Finally, in perfect innocence, the general rehearsed his mustached face in the little mirror above the sink—the face, scarred by the French at Aisne, of a respectable Prussian of fifty-two. Its features alternated easily from severe preoccupation to exuberant smiles.

As the tank leader completed his toilette, his absorbed movements grew slower and more ponderous. The first shameful consciousness of his own life was pleasantly replaced by intricate mental maps of *Sichelschnitt,* with phase-of-battle markings, vectors on penetration of armor, logistics, their tactics and countertactics. All of this must be set off now against the realm of his men's strength, which together would create the character of the campaign. And what if the French blew the Ardennes passes? How quickly would their tank battalions engage him?

Just then the profound hush throughout command quarters was broken by the sound of approaching boots.

Drawing up his tightly tailored shoulders, General Guderian took ten confident steps through to the low-ceilinged staff room, where the curtains had been drawn across the open windows.

2

THE DOOR SWUNG OPEN, THE BREAKFAST TROLLEY APPEARED IN THE BRIGHT passage with Niemann behind it. Reaching the large vase of carnations under an antler chandelier, the sergeant straightened, snapped his heels, and saluted with such violence that his hair bounced.

"Generals Kirchner, Veiel, and Schaal, sir!" he cried, and his glance toward his commander seemed to say, We all know that you are an immortal, and we are willing to share in and die for your glory.

"Keep those wheels well oiled, *Feldwebel,*" Guderian commented, with a fatherly smile, pointing to a caster on the trolley. This was an allusion to his position as Hitler's prophet of tanks and was intended to say, That is all right, young man, I have glory enough to share with you too.

Clasping his hands behind his back, Guderian frowned past Niemann's clean good looks. The young fellow set the other places. From the passage came the sound of more boots and familiar voices.

"Good morning, gentlemen." Standing around the carnations, Guderian and his sunburnt division commanders saluted with the sober shyness peculiar to career officers. "*À table, messieurs*," Guderian added, with an excellent accent, grinning at each officer in turn.

The three younger men laughed, taking their places with a clumping of boots. Out of uniform, these three would have been nondescript. Here in the Sonnenhof their faces were animated and unsoiled by guilt. Their lean souls gleamed through their cold eyes like foils glimpsed in the polite depths of an antiques shop. This morning, their leader would depend heavily on these men for the success of the pivotal wager against France. And for this Guderian was prepared to love them as long as they were alive.

"So, and were the beds satisfactory? We have some traveling to do today." As Guderian took in their faces, he was seeing the divisional supply columns on a dozen roads stretching from Bitburg all the way to the Rhine.

"I'm sure the beds were better at Finkenstein," Kirchner said, over the rim of his coffeecup, and the others laughed explosively—laughing because they were with Germany's most celebrated field commander at the dawn of the homeland's "one last fight" against its ancient rival, and because they had overcome all metaphysical fear. Theirs was the historic business between armies.

"Well, we certainly shall not have time for a hunt but we can look out for chateaux," Guderian said, with an indulgent smile.

Finkenstein was the palace on the Vistula of a Count Dohna-Finkenstein. There, during that autumn's conquest of Poland, Guderian had slept in the same bed as Napoleon once used on his Prussian campaign. Emerging from the desolate Tuchola heath, the Frenchman had been heard to cry, "*Enfin un château.*" Although the count had not been at home to receive Guderian, a hunt was nevertheless arranged, and the tank commander had shot a fine three-point stag.

"Niemann," Guderian called, to the group of aides listening in the passage door. "Pour General Schaal more coffee. These croissants are excellent."

Sampling looted delicacies would soon be a daily routine. Setting down his cup with a deep sigh, the general bent over the flowers. The black cross dangled under his neck.

But Guderian's lingering sense of confusion before his aides went deeper than the sudden thought of his son, at that hour on alert in the 3rd Division. Once those honorable young Germans now waiting at attention put on the pale-gray uniforms, their acts became Guderian's responsibility, for him to decide and justify. So great was the relief he had just glimpsed on their faces, in surrendering their souls to a supreme authority, that he knew each would eagerly commit any crime before questioning Guderian's virtue. Yet what of that even higher authority? Something cold, dark, and vile had stirred in his breast.

Straightening, Guderian gave the three composed faces an impersonal frown, to reestablish the tyranny of his rank and their privilege in the society of a landed gentleman. The chandelier threw a gold dome over the table. Hovering with the others in the doorway, Sergeant Niemann suppressed tears of worship. To the generals round the cherry-smeared plates and empty cups came the sound of sharp voices and starting engines and the perfumes of leather, gun oil, and fresh uniforms.

"Gentlemen," Guderian began, in a voice inaudible beyond the table, "I think you know my views of this campaign. I can rely on you not to falter. The enemies of success will be as much in army headquarters as across the border. Our commanders will be alarmed by the speed of our advance. They will attempt to halt us. However, we are heavily outnumbered, and if we break our pace there can be no success. General Rundstedt and the Führer himself are in authority, but they will be far from the field of action.

"I emphasize that you must let nothing slow you. You must resist the temptation to regroup constantly. Prepare your men to go without sleep for forty-eight hours. Do not be afraid to take risks. The mothers and wives of our men will have no cause to blame us—the tank is a lifesaving weapon." Guderian solemnly raised his finger. "Gentlemen, today is the tenth of May. On the twelfth, I will expect all your divisions to be on the north heights of the Meuse. We will begin our crossing at ten A.M. on the thirteenth." He concluded with a wolfish glance at his listeners.

"And when we have broken through?" General Veiel inquired, looking at Kirchner and Schaal.

"You have no orders for after the breakthrough." Guderian rose impressively under the antler chandelier. "After the breakthrough, gentlemen, we will be free to move at the maximum speed to our objective: the English Channel. *Feldwebel!*"

Niemann leapt forward, bearing Guderian's field coat. The young man's face flushed with adoration as his general stooped briskly into it, then caught his peaked hat under his arm. The three division commanders had jumped to their feet as if to affirm the aggressiveness with which their crews would assault the enemy.

"My good men, good luck and bon voyage." Guderian grinned at them.

The four officers clicked their heels and saluted low, so as not to strike the chandelier. Then Guderian swept out into the passage, closely followed by Niemann, who was clutching the ledger of charts and papers.

The Sonnenhof was fully alert. As the tank leader paced along the humming passage, down the wooden staircase and into the front beer parlor, faces peered into his. Uniformed arms jerked out at him. And in this rite of dutiful submission Guderian felt his army's love, like the love of children for the authority of an iron-handed parent. He tightened his back and his stride became even more springy.

A little crowd had formed. *"Danke, Herr General"* . . . *"breakdown in the Tenth Corps"* . . . *"rations for nine days."* The tank leader nodded without comment. The Sonnenhof's oak door was swinging back. He could see his convertible Mercedes idling by the roadside with its lights off. Behind it, glowing against the dark farmlands, was the armored command truck whose radios would keep Guderian in constant touch with his tank leaders and each one of his group's two hundred light and medium tanks.

Stepping outside, Guderian again glanced with satisfaction at the stars. He stood tugging on his pigskin gloves. The predawn chill stung the hairs in his nose. The idling engines were muffled. Visible along the flat eastern horizon was a faint iridescence.

Yes, the miracle had come: a great campaign in his lifetime. It would be the first full-scale tank assault on an equal adversary in the long history of warfare. This was Guderian's hour, the moment when the destiny of Europe would balance on his historic idea. Guderian had devoted all the years since a ball at Oberlinden to this idea, when the Sundas and their guests had first heard him speak of it.

"General?" the *Feldwebel* blurted out. "I must tell you, sir, that I consider you the Bonaparte of Germany. I am proud to serve you."

Guderian gestured to the shadow beside him with a broad smile. Then he set his hat on his head and tugged the peak. The single-engine whine and concussion of Messerschmitts had begun overhead, coming one after another.

"Quick, get in!" he shouted.

The field car roared; a dozen arms flicked erect in the dim headlights. A cheer went up from the grinning faces. The machines accelerated forward under the courtyard tree, then onto the straight road, climbing west towards Bitburg.

The three divisions under Guderian's command—a tenth of the 2200 tanks committed to the attacks on France and, to the north, on Belgium under von Reichenau—were drawn up in blocks along the Sûre between the castle towns of Vianden and Echternach. Fifty more divisions were massed behind them. Von Leeb, whose regiment had cleared up Hitler's street mob in 1923, was now a decoy facing the Maginot Line on Guderian's left.

Ten minutes after the command column had left the Sonnenhof, its dimmed lights began catching the ghostly silhouettes of half-tracks, 88mm cannon and support vehicles. Soon, lining the road end to end, were the treads and driving wheels of tanks.

Through the cold wind in his field car, Guderian could hear a persistent cheering, and he felt a sudden contempt for the insignificant citizenry of the towns. As if in reply, groups of farmers were now visible beside the flickering trees—Germans who until that night had known nothing of an invasion through their farmlands and grasped little of its brilliant organization and who, instead of gaping with disbelief at this horde of madmen in iron tumbrels, could be seen grinning and waving and apparently wishing in some way to be involved.

At 5:25 A.M., one after another and then in hundreds together, the guttural thunder of unmuffled diesels rose on the dawn air over the farm fields and lanes.

Five minutes later, at the forested Luxembourg frontier, the tank leader sprang out of his field car. He walked between two lieutenants through the first pink light to the striped gate beside the border hut.

At once, the lead tank rocked forward with a grinding bellow, jerked round to its course, and accelerated, splintering the gate and leaving even-spaced welts on the asphalt—the spore of a new era. Tiny as a snail without a shell beside the fifteen-ton tank, Guderian flourished his hat to the *Panzerführer* perched atop the turret. The machine rocked again and redoubled its speed, billowing swan wings of ground fog from its armor.

Over the Ardennes forests the skies were lightening. It was another day. The *drôle de guerre* was over.

3

NOW, AT THE INVASION HOUR, AS GUDERIAN STOOD WITH HIS HANDS CLASPED behind his back at the broken gate as the snorting tanks gave way first to half-tracks and then a mass of mantislike .88s, his pride was set free.

Catching the rail on the radio truck, he swung up between the busy operators and banged on the driver's cab. The brakes loosened, and they rolled forward out of Germany.

The tank leader looked back only once. Then he concentrated ahead on the ground fog. His mind emptied of everything but technical formulas embracing all eventualities, from a crushing victory over the enemy to an unforeseen efficiency among the excellent French antitank artillery, to a bloody rout of his own men—even to his own death. Since Guderian had been cultivating a mastery of such possibilities for organized violence all his adult years, what to someone who had attained a sacramental consciousness of his own life, and of all life, might have seemed an unthinkably bestial view of the weeks ahead stirred in the tank leader no special moral feeling, alarm, or horror—only a pride in his power to crush men's lives. This, and only this, is what is meant by the word "military."

But what if their aircraft catch our tanks in the gorges before we reach open ground? Guderian thought, braced against a roof stanchion in the truck. And twisting around he looked up between the racing shadows of trees, where the stars were being overtaken by a dawn light from Russia.

A thousand-year empire was within the German grasp. Ahead through the Ardennes forest lay the great beauty of Europe, awaiting her destroyers.

4

To the north, the Belgians' impregnable Eben Emael fortress was quickly taken by glider troops, landed at the invasion hour on its huge roof. France's grand strategy of rigid defenses was already disrupted.

Through the thick Ardennes forest, Guderian's flak guns had kept pace, lacerating the few enemy flyers to penetrate Göring's fighter screen. It was not until two mornings later—when the three divisions had advanced exuberantly under clear skies through the scenic forest gorges, crossed the French frontier well to the west of the fixed long-range cannon on the Maginot Line, and were approaching the heavily defended Meuse valley at Sedan—that the Germans experienced their first serious attack from the air. At his headquarters in the Hotel Panorama, General Guderian himself was nearly struck down by the tumbling head of a stuffed boar.

During that afternoon of 12 May, as the antagonists emerged on their ancestral battlegrounds, it had become necessary for Guderian to fly back to Command Headquarters to see General von Kleist. Kleist had already once tried to halt the tanks for fear of a counterattack by French horse cavalry. During Guderian's return flight into a splendid sunset, the pilot of his little Storch missed the landing strip and flew over the Meuse valley. For the next two minutes, Germany's most effective field commander found himself banking in and out of smoke columns—like giant seaweed slowly growing from the bombed French positions and villages—shouting at his pilot and as alarmed as the many thousands of men amid the horror he was generating below.

Unfortunately for mankind, this second act of God had no more success than the boar's head. The tank leader was shortly back on the ground, among his welcoming staff. Guderian had brought back with him hard-won new orders. In view of their astounding progress, and despite the equipment jams behind them along the Ardennes roads, all three tank divisions were to attack across the Meuse at four o'clock the following afternoon. This did not leave the tank leader time to draw up detailed assault plans. But so unmerciful is the bureaucracy of modern warfare that it was only necessary to change a few details for him to reuse the plans from that winter's maneuvers at Koblenz— all of which Guderian found "agreeably quick and simple."

5

ALL THAT NIGHT GENERAL GUDERIAN LAY AWAKE AT HIS NEW QUARTERS IN A farmhouse. He was imagining the rout if the French were to surprise his exposed infantry positions. But in the morning his own artillery had come up. The enemy apparently considered that it had still a month to reply.

On the east flank of the marshy river salient where the 1st Division's attack was focused, the charming town of Sedan and its famous *château fort* were to be the first major French spoils swallowed. Along the fertile valley eight kilometers to the west and east, the 2nd and 10th Divisions would force two more bridgeheads across the river.

At noon on the twelfth, General Guderian was shocked to hear that Erwin Rommel—a tank man in his corps for only three months—was the first to cross the Meuse, 60 kilometers north at Dinant, with the 7th Division.

At three that afternoon, Guderian and General Schaal were still on the river's steep north flanks, bouncing in a field car along an exposed ridge toward a forest knoll on the heights above Saint-Menge. The position commanded a view of the winding treeless flats of the Meuse and of the beleaguered French positions. Since breakfast, the German artillery preparation had been building up. At noon the planes had arrived. For the last three hours, waves of dive-bombers in wings of forty had been falling unopposed on the French artillery positions across the river. The hot afternoon spaces were busy with the persistent *punk, punk* of long-range guns. Sometimes enemy shells worked their way over and fell with a crash in the cornfields where the tanks waited, each time stirring clouds of insects and starting up a slow column of gray-green smoke.

From this ridge above the Meuse, the fields fell away steeply on both sides. In the trees ahead, twelve 105mm howitzers kept up a withering fire on the invisible river positions. As Guderian's open car moved slowly towards their knoll, the four officers accompanying him held down their binoculars and maintained their shouted discussions. Even here, the thunder of the bombs falling below pressurized their ears. Just then an incoming round rattled the car with stones from the slope to their right. Yet no one present thought it strange that this shell had been fired moments before, by men like themselves, with the hope of taking their lives from them.

Where the cart track joined the forest, Guderian and Schaal climbed down and continued on foot. Under the canopy, a hush fell over several gun crews crouched in the cool shadows. Each blackened face hungrily followed the *Panzerführer*'s movements as he made his way down with his staff to the dugout under the forwardmost trees.

Below them, for kilometers in both directions, stretched the river valley and the defenders' positions. The general trained his periscope down across

the light-green slopes of young corn at the outermost villas of Sedan, bordering the near bank of the Meuse. He saw with satisfaction that the entire enemy
side of the valley floor was marbled in black and white smoke. Beyond and to
the left, the French command positions atop La Marfée seemed to float in the
clear air. And above all this, rising and falling like sea fowl against the cloudless blue, were Göring's Stukas. It was one minute to four. The hour had come
for the homeland's revenge.

Harsh voices screamed commands. Engines roared, and there was the pur-
poseful clatter of heavy breeches being worked. And suddenly across the
German heights and the French river positions below, many thousands of men
were conscious that the pummeling of their ears had stopped. In the command
dugout Guderian lowered his binoculars, glanced at his watch, and looked up
at the sun moving behind a single fleecy cloud.

"Now," he said, his voice strangely polite in the immense silence.

In the truck behind them there was a whistling and chatter as radio silence
was broken. Several kilometers to the north, some long-range field cannon
had thumped, instantly drowned by the crash of all sixty pieces in the
advanced positions. Clouds of dust rose through the forest branches.

Now an ugly whining of insects again filled the sky. Four more glinting
waves of Heinkels and dive-bombers began crossing the afternoon sun, their
shadows rushing down the fields and vanishing on the smoking valley floor.
Were there no enemy aircraft? It was beyond belief. Then the earth began to
shudder. Through the dugout periscope, Guderian could see branches falling
along the line of river poplars. Now thousands of infantry appeared in long
flanks, moving into the wheat. Ahead glided the tanks, their cannon recoiling
as they clattered over a rise and started down toward the river, with turrets
traversed leftward across the villa roofs to the far bank at Floing. At the edge
of the trees, the commander could not help hopping on one foot.

"Magnificent!" he cried, though his voice could scarcely have been heard.

From the unstirring flat fields across the river rose a dense black wall of
smoke, tangling slowly in the deep blue sky. The French artillery had still not
found his range.

Within the hour, General Guderian and his staff were driven down to the
central sector through the village of Saint-Menge. For the first time since
dawn, the river's quick-slipping surface was perfectly smooth.

The road behind the waterfront villas was already swarming with jubilant
infantry and bridge engineers. Guderian followed a stark-naked technician
through a rose garden and down onto a grass peninsula. Climbing nimbly into
an assault boat, he balanced one boot on the gunwale. As they skimmed
through the hunting swallows over the smooth water, he gazed knowingly at
the smoking French bunker ahead.

Left behind on the gravel river bank, *Feldwebel* Niemann framed
Guderian in his camera, silhouetted against a towering wall of smoke.

6

ALL THE NIGHT OF 13 MAY 1940, AND THROUGH THE FOLLOWING DAY, THE German armored infantry divisions and their supply and artillery columns streamed across the valley bottom, through the French advance positions. Continuing up the winding farm gorges beyond, General Guderian's three tank divisions pierced the already surrounded and disintegrating French infantry lines. As darkness fell there were still no French tanks, only horses.

All that night the earth of the Mazarin forest trembled, the horizons of Champagne flickered and flashed. And gradually, over the hordes of both armies, there came into being two realities as simple and distinct as the gray and blue uniforms—the realities of German invincibility and of an inevitable French retreat.

At first light, General Guderian awoke from a short deep sleep. He ate a good breakfast, then motored forward through a sunny spring shower to see what had taken place.

During the night, the 2nd Division tanks and infantry—as possessed by their frantic aggression as the French were by the Germans' power to drive them back—had fought past the World War cemeteries of La Marfée and up the nine kilometers of winding farm roads to the village of Chemery. A dozen tanks were lined up in the square, being photographed by a *Life* magazine journalist who had fallen behind the fleeing French. Guderian commented to him, pleasantly enough, that the unabated dive-bomber attacks had kept down the enemy machine gunners and that his own casualties were light. The American only gaped at him. Guderian's satisfaction would have been complete had an embarrassing scene not taken place just below them.

As the doors of the command trucks flew open under the village elm, everyone had noticed a girl in a torn dress standing by a ruined barn. The soiled thing in her arms seemed to be a legless body. Guderian's staff began hurriedly spreading maps on a dry picnic bench. But having seen the uniform of a Nazi general, the young mother was limping up the square. Her twisted face was streaked with mud. Her eyes had fixed on Guderian with stupid disbelief. The American photographer made no resistance when *Feldwebel* Niemann snatched his raised camera.

Once the girl had been hurried away, the officers resumed their conference in the shade of the elm. The tank leader at once immersed himself in tactics designed to meet the first heavy French armor, which had been detected approaching on the road from Stonne. He would exploit the enemy tanks' lack of radio communication.

As the tanks—followed by the *Panzerführer* of the 19th Corps and his staff—roared out of the square at Chemery on the Stonne road, three wings of German dive-bombers swarmed out of the big squall cloud and pillars of smoke and were seen to break formation overhead. Rolling their yellow bellies, they fell slowly with Valkyrian sirens toward a platoon of the corps's 1st Rifle Regiment, which was just overtaking the command column from Wadelincourt. Thirty seconds later, the square was littered with smoking German uniforms, collapsed masonry, twisted vehicles, and objects less easily identified. Pausing on the road outside town, the tank leader took note that the casualties were heavy.

7

YET DESPITE THE CHAOS OF BATTLE, IN WHICH GENERAL OBJECTIVES ARE CLOUDED by terror, hatred, and the obsession of myriad souls with the lonely detail of survival, General Guderian's frenzied forcing home of the initial tank trauma—his "historic idea"—worked to his advantage, as it was also doing that day for his colleagues Rundstedt and Bock in their thrusts into Belgium and Holland.

Although the village of Stonne changed hands several times during the second day, the French 3rd Motorized Division succeeded in convincing neither themselves nor their German tormentors that the defenders had either the fanatical efficiency or the murderous will to break Guderian's advance. A similar impotence could be heard in the tone of an intercepted radio message from General Gamelin at Vincennes to the several Allied fronts: "This torrent of German tanks must be stopped!"

During his fourth morning since the Meuse crossings, the 19th Corps commander watched from a captured culvert beside a slightly elevated forest at Montcornet as his 1st and 2nd Brigades engaged the first French armored attack. The tank leader's professional vanity led him to imagine this to be young Colonel de Gaulle's 4th Division with a brigade of Algerian spahis.

After Stonne, the terrain was opening out. Under the camouflage nets of the crowded command center, Guderian overlooked an impressionist landscape of distant plains, farms, and copses. The wheat fields before him had been tracked down here and there by the advancing tanks. The drone of motors beat against the vast spaces. His machines were moving in wedge formation, gliding through the thickening wheat. The infantry flanked out behind, pausing singly to fire their cannon towards the turrets that dotted the horizon. The sneezing whine of incendiary bullets bounding off armor and the hollow *clank* of armor-piercing shells came dully through the summerlike heat. There seemed to be no enemy artillery whatever. Sometimes a solitary French or English aircraft fled across the dark blue overhead, while above the enemy plain the unopposed German dive-bombers wheeled, fell, and rose again like giant bats drunk with success.

The facing retinues of tanks closed upon each other. At a range of under a thousand meters, oily black clouds puffed up here and there. In the dark inside each machine, the tank leader knew, were braced the naked sweating bodies of his men, half crazed in a kind of ecstasy among the jolting controls, hot breeches, and shell magazines. Through their observation slits they would be seeing the threatening targets, just visible over the distant hedgerows.

Now these targets were being chased by Guderian's inspired crews. One after another the disorganized enemy tanks were hit, some of the crews spilling out and scurrying to cover through the wheat behind flanking tanks. The French attack was faltering, and presently it had stopped. The remaining enemy tanks could be seen gliding away past the motionless hulks in which their comrades' flesh was splitting and sizzling.

Two hours later, under a showery afternoon sky, Guderian's staff was able to count two dozen blown-out enemy R-25s and D-2s. No one counted the soft and vulnerable contents, and the armor muffled the shrieks.

8

THE FOLLOWING NIGHT AT GENERAL GUDERIAN'S HEADQUARTERS IN A WOODED château at Sapogne, on the south bank of the Meuse, a telephone conversation took place that left little doubt as to who controlled the principal German assault.

The telephone had interrupted an officers' banquet of spitted boar to celebrate the surrender of Holland. In London, the pacifist Prime Minister Chamberlain had been replaced by Winston Churchill. Along the boisterous table, Colonel Balck and the elegant General Veiel of the Vienna Division—whose assault engineers had taken heavy casualties on the Meuse but who now had broken west to Donchery—rose repeatedly to toast Friederick the Great, the Führer, but above all Guderian. They were launched upon a comparison between their own recent days and the campaigns of Caesar, Napoleon, and Sherman—all of which they knew in detail—when a field telephone was carried to the table. From the very highest command an order had just arrived to halt the tank thrust into France. The speed of the advance had exposed an inviting left flank to the wily enemy generals.

Rising in front of his staff and flourishing his napkin, Guderian began angrily to denounce the order, first to General Zeitzler and then to Kleist, whom Guderian telephoned himself, arguing—in much the same style as he waged war—by inflexible counter-attack. Were the French not in rout? Even over the weak connection, Guderian could hear that Kleist was shaken. The order must have filtered down from an even higher authority. The Führer was still bewitched by the reverses of 1914 and 1918 and the French counterattack on the Marne. For an hour, Guderian argued insubordinately. He struggled with the invisible supreme will. Finally, at midnight, the tank leader won a twenty-four-hour reprieve.

And so the hunger of one man for his place in the rolls of history—to be won by a single technical innovation at the risk of no matter how much untold suffering—overcame even Hitler's will. In that hour, Guderian had warded off any early frustration of the first imperial conquests in the age of advanced technology.

Guderian's breakthrough came the next morning 16 May. At dawn, he rode his radio truck through a fresh shower past Vendresse, then to Omont. The *Fliegerkorps* had reaped the brilliant skies. Under the shimmering poplars, the straight country road streamed freely with troop-laden tanks and support equipment of the 1st, 2nd, and 6th Divisions. The day was a pastorale of misery and death. Twisted French machines, riddled farmhouses, and stiff-legged horse carcasses lined the march.

The tank leader finally found his infantry commander Balck stalking the main street of Bouvellement. The town had experienced the last fierce defensive stand of De Lattre's elite 152nd Regiment. The victorious Balck climbed up into the truck, and they drew up before the brick town hail. Guderian lingered among his radio operators. Bouvellement was in flames. Large quantities of flowerpots were scattered in the streets. The scaffolding for a village fair hung in charred shreds. Every wall was splattered with bullet holes.

The road, stretching far out beyond the town, was flanked by two vast waiting mobs of muddy, bareheaded poilus and spahis, along with a few gog-gled tank men. Unshaven faces turned to stare curiously as a Nazi comman-der's half-track drew in to the town hall. The enemy stood with their hands pushed into their long coats. No one looked up when a plane raced overhead. The sky was German now. Among the thousands of faces some were crazed, some sullen. Others along the packed lines guiltily shuffled their feet and joked to their German guards. Just below the tank leader and the crackling radio sets, an old peasant held a yellow dog, which was licking his beard. A boy with a bandaged hand wept bitterly.

There must be ten thousand, Guderian observed to himself. Then he noticed the silence over the surrounding countryside.

"What do we do with the *Grande Armée*?" Colonel Balck called from the town hall steps. Balck was a thick-necked enthusiast for the soldier's life who never failed to let it be known when he deserved decorating.

All down the long, crowded main street of Bouvellement there was not a movement. A moist breeze stirred the potted flowers strewn on the cobbles. Balanced against the truck's overhead frame, the Nazi conqueror gazed with princely benevolence over the sea of French faces. The air was tense with the brotherhood of the living. Mist rose from the road, pungent with mud, hay, manure, and blood.

"Tell them they fought like men," Guderian called back, the words noble to his ears. "Tell them to go home."

At once the prisoners' guards were shouting his words all along the road ahead. A vast murmur rose from the sea of heads.

General Guderian swung down to the road. Three of his staff fell in behind Balck. They continued along the street between the grinning guards and mute crowds. The tank leader scarcely took in Balck's colorful portrait of himself capturing Bouvellement almost single-handed, illustrated with thrusts of his walking stick. Nor how Balck's genial face was distinct from these great crowds of disarmed Frenchmen in bearing no trace of revulsion, narcissism, perversity, or guilt—or of any other weakness that betrayed the monstrous act they had all just shared in. Good fellow, Guderian thought, giving the dented armor of one of his Czech-made tanks a thoughtful caress.

The crashing roar of a sightseeing Heinkel faded quickly to a distinct drone. A silence hung over the shop grating and signs advertising Pernod. Among the grim rabble and the scarred gray tanks waiting to have roads assigned them, the only sound was the rumble of burning houses. Throngs of swarthy faces—the extinguished pride of France—watched as Guderian, Kirchner, Balck, and their staffs walked without fear along the narrow human passage.

As their boots splashed through a black puddle where bodies had been piled, the tank leader's heart thundered in his ears. Sniffing the mood of this main street of Bouvellement, Guderian halted with glittering eyes. The officers made an expectant group, their faces now mild with satisfaction.

"We have done it, gentlemen. We are through."

Excited voices joined in on all sides. General Guderian turned among their erect arms. Again he took in the smoking house fronts and crowds of what had been the enemy. Bonaparte could not have felt more than this, he was suddenly thinking. There was no one now to stop their rolling all the way to the Channel coast.

9

BY THAT NIGHT, THE DIVISIONS UNDER GENERAL GUDERIAN'S COMMAND WERE advancing seventy-five kilometers to the west of Sedan. The machinery rolled on into the tranquil sunset, overtaking lines of fugitives with their belongings piled onto carts and surrendering soldiers struck dumb by the sight of Nazi tanks so deep in France.

Early next morning at a grass airfield by Soize, a Wehrmacht reconnaissance plane bounced down. From inside, the stuffy person of General von Kleist, in his beloved leather coat, unfolded itself. The visor of his peaked hat was drawn down to his nose. Guderian was waiting on the border of the landing strip.

The two tight-collared generals walked stiffly to meet each other, the tank leader advancing quickly over the short wet grass. There were repeated Heil Hitlers and heel clickings.

"General Guderian," Kleist began, in the rude, sneering tone he had used over the telephone and which so oddly resembled Hitler's own. "What do you mean by disobeying our Führer's order to stop your advance after twenty-four hours?"

Some minutes later, Kleist and Guderian at last paused to draw breath. They stood alone under the cloudless dawn skies of Picardy, observed at twenty paces by whispering groups of officers.

"General von Kleist," said Guderian, visibly shaking with frustrated ambition. "I wish to be relieved of my command."

"Yes, but . . . all right, then!" Kleist stamped his boot. "In that case, consider yourself relieved."

But even before the tank leader had left the airfield, von Rundstedt himself had dispatched General List to settle the argument. List arrived after lunch. General Guderian's resignation could not be accepted. The new order to advance would be rewritten to read, *Reconnaissance in force.*

Six hours after this attempt to contain his will Guderian had field wires laid to his advance headquarters so that his own superiors could find out nothing by monitoring his radios.

By nine o'clock, earlier that same morning of the seventeenth, the tank columns had already resumed movement. The routed French armies would be allowed no time to regroup. Pausing only to sweep aside an unsupported raid by twenty-four French tanks at Montcornet—this time de Gaulle's—Guderian followed his spearhead divisions west. (The Frenchman would later claim Montcornet as a major action.) The tank leader's staff cars and radio truck raced at full speed down roads cleared of refugees by the corps' motorcycle troops—roads leading to Normandy and the English Channel. Presently the open vehicles began overtaking the tanks of the 2nd Division, which were already cruising towards Saint-Quentin.

It was a cloudless evening. The warm wind in the back of Guderian's car was fragrant with grass, and the wheat fields rippled silver and green. White butterflies floated back and forth over the country road. The young German ruffians lounging in pleasant exhaustion on the tank mudguards showed their muscles and sang lazily. The colonnade of poplars sprinkled the crowded road with shade. Ahead, under the canopy of leaves, a file of gray infantry filled Guderian's windshield.

Several transports were unloading outside a village. Men climbed off the road between the trees as the car of this high-command general inched between them and the tanks. In the back seat, Guderian grinned out at the strangely animated faces.

"Good going, sir." "Look there, *das ist der Mensch selbst.*" "Look, it's him." "Yes, fast Heinz!"

The words were being shouted down the flanks ahead of the staff cars. They swelled to a chant, then a toneless roar.

"Schnell Heinz! Schnell Heinz! Schnell Heinz!"

In the front seat next to Guderian's driver, the blond young *Feldwebel* who had replaced Niemann after his head was blown to shreds at Stonne, twisted round and smiled worshipfully. "You have a new name, general."

"I will live up to my new name," his hero called back warmly. And taking of his hat, Guderian tossed it over the heads of the troops lining the road. There was a deafening shout, and Guderian turned on the back seat with fatherly good humor to see his men scramble. Far behind, a stubby soldier with spectacles and a long nose appeared waving the officer's hat.

"Fast Heinz! Fast Heinz! Fast Heinz!" his men chanted in the dappled shade of the French poplars. As the cars accelerated and his tanks became a blur, Guderian lifted his arm in the warm wind and he waved.

And in those same minutes, on the porch of his Felsen-nest beyond the Ardennes and Bitburg, Hitler was weeping for joy. With his invincible army streaming below under these gliding waves of aircraft, how sublime was such an evening!

10

AMONG THE THOUSANDS OF FRENCH PRISONERS WHO SAW NAZI GENERAL Guderian in the main street of Bouvellement on 16 May was Hélène von Sunda's brother, Jean-Marc.

Lieutenant Colonel Le Trève had been commissioned into General Baudet's 71st Division of Huntziger's 2d Army, under the overall command of General Georges, two years before Hélène had left Paris with David. And there in the army Jean-Marc had discovered his great talent.

Young Le Trève had been promoted quickly, not without the help of his father's friend, General Weygand. During the time that Weygand was away in Syria, at the very hour when, in the nearby Élysée Palace, Prime Minister Daladier was composing his last letter to Hitler—"If French and German blood is now to be spilled as it was twenty-five years ago, then each of our two peoples will fight confident of its own victory; but whatever the result, Destruction and Barbarism will be the victors"—Jean-Marc had been forced to leave a splendid ball at the Hotel Crillon and rejoin his division at Vouziers. General Gransard had ordered the 71st on a forced march to the Meuse valley at Sedan to take up a position between the 55th Division and the 3rd North African. Substantial movements of German armor had been detected beyond the Ardennes forest, though it was not considered essential to be in place before 12 May.

In the last eight months, after the Nazi rout of Poland and the Anglo-French declaration of war, Jean-Marc had studied a number of books on the new theories of tank warfare including Guderian's, the Englishman Liddell Hart's, and Colonel de Gaulle's recent memorandum on the German tank threat. Now as Lieutenant Colonel Le Trève's regiment approached the lines of defense, his impatience grew agitated to the point of panic.

It was as if Jean-Marc's magnificent *Grande Armée,* the victors of the Marne, had been preparing for a war that would not take place.

In the cultivated Le Trève household, Jean-Marc had always seemed the coldest and least human. Life in the army had come as a revelation. From the day he put on his uniform, the burden of his inadequacies had been lifted. The young Parisians among whom Jean-Marc now found himself came from all backgrounds, most far less privileged than his own. And as if by some miracle, the same neutral good manners and heavy wit that had made his towering figure a discomfort for the Le Trèves gave Jean-Marc huge popularity in the ranks of the 71st Division. It was even said by the men of his regiment that Le Trève was no snob. Jean-Marc discovered a talent for drinking and artful obscenity. Wherever his wavy black hair, square jaw, and bemused smile were seen, the toughest poilus gathered like sheep round a goat. And out of Jean-Marc's gratitude there arose a passion for these cynical veterans of the Paris slums who guarded the glorious *frontières* of France.

The final dawn march on 11 May, the six kilometers past General Baudet's headquarters at Rancourt down to his sector at Sedan, should have permitted Lieutenant Colonel Le Trève to enjoy the most reliable satisfaction of army life—that of touring beautiful scenery without any cares and at someone else's expense. But rumors of the Boche's having on the previous dawn used some secret weapon to take Eben Emael, Europe's most powerful fortification, had confused the already exhausted men. Privately, Jean-Marc was far more shocked by the vaguer rumors of armored columns already halfway through the Ardennes and by the absence of aircraft.

Where were their own excellent Somua tanks? How could General Huntziger be so euphoric about the Maginot defenses 80 kilometers to the east? Sometimes Lieutenant Colonel Le Trève would nervously dismount and walk with his silent men down the farm ravines. Their file was just discernible now in the first blue light of dawn.

"Pull together! Pull together!" Jean-Marc called, noting the way stragglers quickly caught up at the sound of his voice. In a half hour they would be visible from the air. His racing thoughts returned to the vast landscape of the French defenses, which he had no difficulty grasping to the last detail or imagining in total disarray. Then his thoughts took another tack.

Jean-Marc Le Trève, once of *le tout Paris*, had come to love these farm villages of the Haute Champagne with their well-tended rustic stone houses, their tiny windows richly hung in lace curtains hiding family heirlooms and cool walnut floors. He loved the old steeples pointing up among the clouds, and the occasional chateaux, with their courtyards and panting dogs and shady tin-roofed haystacks. *La terre, la terre de France, la Patrie,* he thought to himself. Only the evening before, small girls with bare brown legs had giggled at the marching column and peeked at them shyly through cottage fences. Having heard the rustling, slapping tread of the regiment's approach, farmers had come running through the last light to grin enviously at the swaggering young men's blue uniforms. A freckled young milkmaid standing at her gate had smiled at Jean-Marc and held up a chicken and a kicking white rabbit. And smelling the garlic and frying sausages, Jean-Marc had loved it all and known it would always be so.

But this dawn the descending terrain was dead. No one came out. You could feel it in the air.

11

LIEUTENANT COLONEL LE TRÈVE'S REGIMENT WAS THE FIRST IN THE 71ST DIVISION to resume its position on the Meuse. The geraniums on his double bunker needed watering and the carpet had to be shaken out.

Jean-Marc spent the first light on 12 May with his tired sappers on the valley's flat river approaches near Wadelincourt, repairing trenches and artillery dugouts. At just after five they heard the first faint drone of motors from the facing heights above Sedan: tanks.

Jumping onto a sidecar motorcycle, Jean-Marc raced back to the elevated 155mm batteries in the forest behind, as they opened fire across the great valley spaces toward invisible Bouillon. Then he wound up to Gransard's headquarters on the spectacular heights of La Marfee. Then back down to his regiment's line of bunkers on the river marshes, blinding with dew in the first sun.

When Le Trève got back to Wadelincourt, the 155mm field guns were inexplicably being sent to the rear.

After the men's release from their long march, a jaded unreality seemed to hang over the concrete turrets and earthworks, like props for some war of the worlds. And there was something absurd in the aspect of these thousands of adult males in metal hats and baggy trousers, firing giant field guns into the clear blue sky, releasing balloons, and still digging over on the drowsy far banks.

As that long day wore on, the Flying Pencils—Dorniers—came more frequently. By evening, the valley floor was shivering continually underfoot, and cavalry from the front lines was pouring back through the streets of Sedan. Very quickly they heard that the Germans were in town. Soon La Marfée was shrouded in bomb smoke.

In his river bunker, Lieutenant Colonel Le Trève did not sleep that night. In the downpour of bombs the communication wires kept being severed. From the moment he had seen the 155s being sent away Jean-Marc's agitated impatience was back.

He rose with a splitting headache and a craving for orders. At ten that morning, the thirteenth, Jean-Marc and Marchant, the regiment's intelligence officer and two reliable poilus—Louis and tough little Lacoutte—were mining the shady road up to Thélonne. Le Trève had given this order himself. On the farm pasture below the Wadelincourt road, they could see the second detail frantically searching bomb craters for more telephone wires. The high-pitched droning of the Dorniers and the shock of bombs had become constant. They had to keep their heads down and shout.

"It's time," Jean-Marc shouted, waving to the others. "Go back on the river."

"Merde alors . . . ooh-la, look at that." Louis was pointing up, eyes shaded. "One of ours at last."

The *poilus* of their unit had mounted their bicycles and begun to coast down through the fresh mines. All along the trees that lined the contested river, immense stalks of smoke were slowly blooming into the sky. Behind them, high over La Marfée, Jean-Marc could see a minute silver glitter, then three more, closing fast. The four aircraft slipped behind the branches and then reappeared, black and much closer. Stopped on the road, everyone heard the remote whine, then tiny guns through the booming flak.

Kak-kak, kak-kak, kak-kak went the summer-muted rattle above the empty fields. *Kak-kak, kak-kak, kak-kak.*

Far up, the round-winged Frenchman suddenly towed a twisting gray ribbon northward. A tiny white parachute appeared.

Lacoutte whistled. "He's dropped his handkerchief."

"It makes you sick." Marchant lifted one fist. "Oh, the *salauds!*"

Marchant's voice was lost as a wing of Junkers dipped into the valley, dropping in low from the Sedan heights. As the officers ran for the two motor-cycles, everyone saw the parachute collapse.

Down by the forward flak battery at the Wadelincourt road, Lieutenant Colonel Le Trève's detachment was blocked by an overturned transport. The crossing was not yet under fire. In the pause as the men rocked the truck over the grass bank, Jean-Marc crouched to look forward over the river fields to Sedan and up to the enemy hills. The booming flak gun sent waves over the grass. Flicking his cigarette, Jean-Marc saw three slow-moving V's drift down from the northeast. As they slanted in low over the river, the first machine pulled away. It performed a sharp diving turn, followed by a second.

"It's a flying circus," Lacoutte shouted, his arm pointing up. The valley sky swarmed with racing black dots like bees.

The twenty poilus on the cleared road hesitated, holding their bicycles. They stood exposed, watching six of the planes lower back over the treetops. Somewhere a second flak battery joined in—*punk, punk, punk*—and as the square-wingers went overhead they rolled again, then came straight down.

"Look!"—Louis's deep voice—"what on earth . . . ?"

From the two silenced flak batteries came frantic voices. Head still aching, Jean-Marc crouched by the garden wall. There was something familiar about these falling wings. Then for just one instant he remembered a newsreel of Spain long ago on the Champs-Élysées.

"Stukas! Get off the road!" he shouted. He walked round the truck toward the frozen men. "Off the road! Off the road!"

The first enemy machine was a thousand meters over their heads, standing on its ugly nose—falling wide-winged, shrieking, immense, on their helplessness. As the men tumbled head first into the ditch, holding their ears, the flak gunners went flat on their stomachs. The valley skies and earth sang with a prehistoric scream . . . then *wunk, wunk.* A flash. Hot gravel stung Jean-Marc's neck. The ground, the trees, rose on their edge and lurched to throw him off.

"Mary-mother-of-God!" Lieutenant Colonel Le Trève wept, digging his forehead into the dirt. "Mary-mother-of-God!" Terror blossomed in his heart.

Then they were struggling out of the ditch, powdered with dry mud. Jean-Marc was on his feet in the stinking Nazi smoke. He stumbled toward the road. Others fell in with him. The smoke was thinning, and he saw Marchant and Lacoutte. Blood ran from their noses and ears.

As the men grouped by the motorcycles above the battery, the flak gunners were on their feet loading the guns. The detachment started to jeer them. Jean-Marc pulled out his revolver. He was shouting.

"Shut up, *imbéciles.* This is the army of France."

"Commandant, give us orders. Are we here to be pounded?"

"We are Communists," Louis explained to Jean-Marc, when he had climbed back into the sidecar. "The French army is irrelevant. If you were a Communist you wouldn't worry."

Lieutenant Colonel Le Trève's detachment came under dive-bomber attack four more times before it could reach the command bunker. By then they were pounded half senseless. The deluge of flying metal had grown so heavy that to cover the last 700 meters had taken ninety minutes, most of it spent clutching the ground.

Battle had not yet been engaged. The enemy tanks were still invisible on the facing heights.

12

AT ONE O'CLOCK IN THE PACKED BUNKER, LIEUTENANT COLONEL LE TRÈVE AT last made contact with division headquarters. Through his remaining ear he heard that the English were withholding air cover.

The bombing and shelling intensified. Through the bunker's lateral slits the observers could see mountains of smoke all down the valley positions. The landscape of fields, poplars, riverbanks, farmhouses, and flanking bunkers was without movement. The army of France was pinned under concrete. One by one, the lines to the rear were being cut.

There was a grim crowd in the main chamber. A young machine-gunner screamed monotonously in the back tunnel, holding his ears.

"The arrogant bastards!" Marchant cursed steadily over the radio operator, then he faced them all.

At that moment the radio crossed General Huntziger's beacon. The bunker listened as an academic voice drawled that there had been some little fracas at Dinant. Thirty seconds later, they picked up a shrill voice babbling in German. Rommel's tanks were across the Meuse.

Crushed with the others round Marchant, Le Trève looked up and saw Colonel Lalande. Their eyes met, and in that moment Jean-Marc knew that things were going very badly indeed.

Here they come . . . look there . . . look! several voices called at once.

And then they heard a magical stillness.

Crowding with the others to a slit, Jean-Marc squinted out across the stretch of water and through the trees. A thousand meters above the far flat, tanks had appeared, rocking and plunging out of the forest paths. The trees moved with enemy troops.

Jean-Marc noticed then the silence from his flak bunkers to the east and west. Had they been abandoned? In that instant, an incomprehensible, droning thunder exploded all around them—shocking, shocking, sending men reeling across the chamber. The gunners were firing now. Dust rose from the carpets. Lacoutte and three other men struggled to tie down a second screaming machine gunner, who flailed about at every blow.

One unthinkable hour inched by. A first few dead Germans could be seen across the river. Even at flat trajectory, shells from the bunker's three antitank guns were bouncing off the Nazi armor. With difficulty, several fanatical attempts by German shock troops to rush rubber dingies down to the water had been driven back. Just now four tanks were tracking freely up and down the open fields, their cannon traversed to fire at the bunker's six embrasures. Inside the concrete chamber, a few men could still hear the two 88s join in from the trees five hundred meters beyond. At once the smoke in the bunker filled with splinters and cordite. There was a shock.

Glancing over his shoulder, Lieutenant Colonel Le Trève made out a half-naked artillery officer rolling on the carpet with a sliver the length of a bayonet stuck from one eye. Someone was already back at the gun. Was their position fighting alone?

Jean-Marc and his colonel were crouched together over the glowing gun barrel. Lalande's face was very white and moist. He kept licking his lips.

"Lieutenant Marchant." Lalande rose unsteadily to his full height. "Get me Central."

The gunners stopped work as the colonel of artillery turned from them. Even the four wounded men in the tunnel watched as the group gathered over the radio table.

"Hello? Colonel Lalande . . . what! Baudet has lost contact, *withdrawn* . . . *and Gransard?* Yes, reference 1530. . . . we are under close attack by tanks. Yes, close; we are surrounded. Request permission to break out. . . ."

Le Trève had become so fascinated by the colonel's licking of lips and his cool voice that at first he did not notice the men's eyes on him. Then abruptly he heard the lie: *surrounded?* The tanks were not even across the river. It was so enormous, so terrible, that for several seconds Jean-Marc only felt himself choking. Then, as if in a dream, he was fumbling for his revolver.

But in that instant's paralysis the remaining thirty men had bolted for the rear tunnel, trampling over the bodies. As they threw the metal door open, Le Trève saw a blinding meadow of smoking wild flowers. Then he was alone in the thundering chamber with Marchant, Lacoutte, and the dying. Lalande was not among them. Jean-Marc waved the two men to the embrasures.

One assault dinghy was almost across the water. The Germans' four paddles rose and dug frantically. Before Lacoutte could traverse the machine-gun, the shock troops were under the near bank.

A minute later, four helmets appeared in the grass sixty meters away. Lacoutte squeezed off three bursts. With hypnotic cold blood one German ducked up, balancing a *Panzerfaust*. The first charge came straight in through the embrasure.

13

AND SO IT WAS THAT AT DAWN ON THE FIFTEENTH, LIEUTENANT COLONEL LE Trève found himself alive, though a much older man now, falling back into the Meuse valley along a mountain road of bramble hedges. He still had with him Marchant, Lacoutte, thirty infantrymen from the disintegrated river bunkers of the 2d Army, and a horse-drawn 25mm flak gun.

General Huntziger was calling this a pivot, but everyone had seen the 71st Division panic and run like a mob, filling the roads, and Le Trève knew that it had begun with Lalande. Jean-Marc had been ready to stop the man, but that moment in his life was lost forever.

In the night he had halted two French officers, deserters, with their shoulder bars torn off, and Lacoutte had executed them. Today as the sun rose again over France, Jean-Marc was no longer even trying to understand. After the Nazi bazooka had blown the bunker's rear wall, he remembered nothing.

An hour later, on the level road, Marchant was having difficulty keeping up. Le Trève was on a bicycle, cycling grimly ahead through a widening crowd of villagers and carts. Marchant had stopped cursing the Germans.

"*Ces cons, Baudet et Huntziger!*" he shouted after Jean-Marc. "We could have held them. Now we cannot even fall back!"

"The tanks can be cut off!" The lieutenant colonel stopped, balancing his bicycle. "Lacoutte—those two there!"

A pair of poilus was cycling ahead under the trees, rifles swinging.

"They're running, the filthy Reds!" Marchant snapped his breech bolt without conviction.

"Let them go!" Jean-Marc held him. They felt the hot sun burning on their necks.

In the villages, life was falling apart. A stream of women, children, and old men pushed along the road, droning with rumors.

They're halfway to Paris . . . they fire on ambulances . . . the Americans have declared war . . . the fifth column has betrayed us . . . the Boche are using gas . . . spies . . . sabotage . . . gas, gas!

Women began shrieking. Halted again, Jean-Marc spun around. He squinted back over the helmets of his grim soldiers. In the dawn glare was something black, stationary over the sun. Underfoot the cobbles had given way to hard mud.

"Clear the road!" Jean-Marc screamed. Crouching, he blew his whistle.

Kak-kak, kak-kak, kak-kak, the guns began. And along the lane ahead— as if a comb had passed down the middle—the shrieking crowd parted. Abandoning their possessions, they emptied frantically down the grassy road-side to hide under the poplar trees.

Jean-Marc saw bullet gouts come stuttering along the bare road, somehow passing a blond child left screaming in the wreckage. One wagon lurched and sank forward as the horse collapsed in its traces. A single Messerschmitt thundered close over the treetops, then an even noisier brace of bombers. The bombs hit instantly in quick, shuddering strides, neatly straddling the two crowded road banks.

As the five aircraft engines planes narrowed away in the country hush, cries arose from under the poplars on both sides of the lane.

Jean-Marc and Marchant were quickly back on the road. A bomb had struck very close. Marchant's gravel-pocked face streamed fresh blood. Swaying unsteadily in the sun, he pulled out his revolver. In the cool under the trees an old farmer sat on the grass. He was looking down at himself, his griz- zled jaw straining open. There was nothing below his belt. Shaking all over, Marchant aimed the revolver.

There was a *crack,* and the others began pushing the caisson.

"Oh, the bastards, the efficient bastards!" Marchant shouted. He shook his revolver at the rich blue morning sky. "You see? Not one crater on their precious road!"

Peddling together hard for another two kilometers through the choking dust, the unit came to a bridge between two orchards. The bridge arch gave a good view back over two long fields of wheat and a straight kilometer of road. The corn would be behind them. The forests bordering the wheat would keep the Germans on the road.

Lieutenant Colonel Le Trève gave Marchant instructions to mine the bridge. In five minutes the flak gun appeared among the unending stream of people. Jean-Marc directed the crew off the road behind a large mound of manure. The mob on the road streamed steadily past, their carts piled high, showing no interest in the sweat-soaked poilus toiling around the bridge. Six cavalry officers clattered across on jerky horses, the braid and epaulettes glittering forgotten on their muddied uniforms.

"Comrades, finish that mine!" Marchant shouted down from the wall. "The road is clearing."

The last vehicle to escape over the bridge was a rusted tractor driven by a scared-looking boy. An old woman and a pregnant girl in straw hats sat facing on opposite mudguards. As it coasted down, its engine fluttered and died.

Resting a tank mine on the stone parapet, young François, a mechanic from Neuilly, ran to the stalled machine. He smiled shyly at the girl and began tugging at the distributor. Slowly pacing the spine of the bridge, Le Trève looked down at them without a word. It seemed incredible to him now that he had never held his sister Hélène in his arms. Suddenly there were tears in his eyes.

Then, just as the men below were arming the four mines, a twenty-ton mobile cannon appeared from the distant forest and approached along the road. When it reached their bridge, they all held up their helmets and cheered. The machine rocked snortingly backwards over the bridge, crumbling one of the parapets. It came to a halt by Le Trève. The front hatch lifted. Three heads appeared.

"General Georges has collapsed!" a handsome blond captain with a head bandage shouted cheerfully down to Jean-Marc over the rumbling motor. "Belgium and Holland are falling—our airforce is finished. Halt here? Impossible. We must proceed to Bouvellement. Those are the orders."

"*Espèce de deputé!*" Marchant cursed him, and the three heads disappeared.

"There are no orders, you swine—you son of a whore!" Jean-Marc's shouts were drowned by the big diesel. And now tears of pity came to his eyes, until he thought he would choke.

Lieutenant Colonel Le Trève stood with his men on the bridge and watched the mobile cannon grow small between the cornfields. Then they faced round to the fields and the smoking horizon of Sedan. To the forest where the Germans would come. Without a word, they completed the mining.

14

AFTER THE RATTLING THRONGS OF REFUGEES, THE SILENCE BY THE ORCHARDS deepened. Crouched along the bridge wall and a dry gulley, the soldiers watched a hare lope out on the east road. No one moved. Standing near the gun crew behind the manure, their lieutenant colonel lit a cigarette.

And just then, as he inhaled the hot tobacco smoke, Jean-Marc Le Trève experienced his own death. Within the hour these men and he would all be lying here dead, while that hare, these farms and refugees, his mother and Hélène, and the generals and cowards in Paris would live on into future years. There would be no *him*. A dark wind of evil blew toward him over the green corn. This space, this air he was breathing, were the enemy's now.

Turning away with an ugly expression, Jean-Marc paced the bridge. He scraped the machine-gun tripod on the stones. The growl of what must be tank engines came clearly now from the line of forest, then the *punk, punk* of field guns. He and Marchant watched three waves of Junkers pass over for the rear.

"And our tanks?" Marchant croaked. "And our orders? *Ah, les crétins.*"

"The stinking vermin will have to kill me to get past."

Over the landscape the morning silence was drawn taut. The birds had stopped twittering among the apple blossoms. Along the gully, the men fidgeted without looking at each other. There were footsteps. Hearing Lacoutte's voice, Jean-Marc glanced round at the ugly little poilu. The clown's face twisted in the sun. Some of the others were on their feet.

"*C'est fini, camarade.*" Lacoutte shrugged, closed one eye, and blew smoke past his cigarette. "They've all gone . . . our generals are buffoons. Lalande is still running. There's only us. I salute you, commandant, but to be heroes for one bridge? It's a farce."

"Go back, Lacoutte. You want a court-martial *à pistolet?*" Terror had seized Jean-Marc. Hatred throbbed between his temples.

Quick, down! voices called at them. Everyone had seen the Germans at the same moment. In the lead was a hive of bicycle shock troops.

"Distance?" shouted the flak gunner, Rousseau.

Lacoutte lay on the manure beside the gun carriage, sneezing.

"One thousand . . . but wait." Jean-Marc poked up the periscope. "I count eight light tanks plus eighty-eights."

Marchant was crouched behind him on the grass, wiring six grenades to fire the mines. Their eyes met.

"Can our gun blow them?"

"If not we'll meet in heaven," Jean-Marc said.

"With pleasure," Marchant had been saying. Then something suckingly violent and furnace-hot happened on the grass where they had crowded. And that was the last thing Lieutenant Colonel Le Trève heard for what seemed like a very long time.

He seemed to have been thinking about it and remembering it nostalgically for a lifetime. Then he was looking at his blood-soaked trousers curled on the grass, and it had only been seconds. Marchant was twisted on his front beside Jean-Marc. His hair bubbled blood. No, it was the remains of Marchant's face.

A tearing shock had come from near the big gun. It lay fifteen paces away on the manure, canted forward on its barrel, surrounded by little sacks of blue cloth. Here and there in the sun several others struggled up or lay moaning and whimpering. Jean-Marc balanced on his legs and retched with sobs.

"Oh, God, look at us!" he screamed, getting tangled in his coat. "Oh, God! Oh, shit."

There on the grass next to Marchant's hand were the clustered grenades. In one motion, Jean-Marc clutched the thong and rolled as he threw them. A muffled shock came from the embankment. Again he stood and stared around him in the grip of an animal passion.

Jean-Marc walked unevenly onto the road. The German turrets were still sailing forward through the cornfields, barrels trained like a firing squad. They had reached the farmhouse. One .88 had stopped to find the bridge's range.

Wheeling, he saw three of his men on their feet. One of them was Lacoutte. Throwing his rifle on the manure, Lacoutte began jumping on it in a frenzy.

"Lacoutte, I order you!" Tears and blood spluttered in Jean-Marc's mouth. He watched the poilu strut impudently towards the cornfield gate, almost jigging like a clown in his huge coat. The lieutenant colonel held up his revolver. Shaking with terror, he aimed. The little man's shoulders were hidden in the flapping coat.

Lacoutte tripped and fell on his face. His boots flopped in the air.

"Come with me," Le Trève croaked, without seeing who was there. In eight more steps he had crouched at the base of the stone parapet.

Ten meters away, the first Nazi tank was clattering cautiously onto the crevasse the French mines had blown in the bridge. Above the turret a blond head peered over, right, then left.

Jean-Marc pushed himself upright. As the machine rocked past, the hard clean face stared down at him with disgust. Then, seeing the blood-fouled Frenchman raise a pistol, the German ducked his head. Jean-Marc emptied his revolver at the dented turret, the bullets slap-whining off across the apple trees and summer meadows, across the villages of Champagne with their pretty steeples and the well-loved farmhouses of France.

When the cylinder had emptied, Jean-Marc's arm fell to his side. He stood in the warm sun with two others, who were sobbing like children, scarcely watching as six more of the tanks rocked over the broken bridge. The Germans ignored them, gearing up and gliding off down the Bouvellement road, followed by the fast-pedaling swarm of shock troops.

In five more minutes this road, with its bridge and torn bodies and apple trees, was perfectly still. A peace came over the glorious pastures—not that peace when treaties are being signed, but the peace when the soul of a people is dying.

Lieutenant Colonel Le Trève and the little bridge at Omont were already ten kilometers behind the German lines.

15

BY THE MORNING ON WHICH JEAN-MARC SAW GENERAL GUDERIAN IN THE MAIN street of Bouvellement, the roads between Laon and Cambrai had become throttled with fleeing French soldiers. Abandoning his smug self-confidence, the French commander in chief at last telephoned Daladier in Paris.

There were no more reserves. France was facing the destruction of the *Grande Armée*. And the order for that day, issued by General Gamelin to his suffering men, was "Conquer or die."

But the French capital was already in panic. Next evening, Winston Churchill, fresh to this arena of war, flew into Paris and was driven straight to the Quai d'Orsay. He had been sitting for some time in Daladier's gloomy office with Gamelin and Premier Reynaud, waiting for someone to assume responsibility for the course that events were taking, when he became aware through the open window of files being burned in the ministry gardens.

That night, one week after Guderian had set out from the Sonnenhof and almost as if there were still a French army, Reynaud secretly cabled Maxime Weygand in Damascus. With a display of passionate dedication he had not shown in the Le Trèves' library on the night of the New Year's Eve ball, the general at once began his return to succeed Gamelin as commander of the army of France. An airplane bore the spirit of Foch toward Tunis but was forced back at Benghazi. After having refueled at Mersa Matruh, Weygand finally crash-landed at Le Bourget, two precious days after his summons. The Supreme Commander of the *Grande Armée* crawled from a turret, proceeded to his new headquarters, and performed a hundred-meter sprint for his aides. Then the general retired to his bed.

The next day Weygand set out in search of his army and his allies. Flying through enemy air attacks, he pursued General Billotte to Bethune, then on to Calais, finally overtaking his colleague with King Leopold at Ypres. One hour before the Englishman Lord Gort could join them, Weygand set out again, riding a torpedo boat from Dunkirk to Dover and then continuing to Cherbourg. He reached his headquarters in Paris on 22 May.

It was already two days since Guderian had broken the last enemy formations.

16

THE NUMBER OF SOLDIERS INVOLVED IN THE DESPERATE DAYS AND NIGHTS AMONG the farm roads and villages of Champagne and Normandy—followed like a school of fish by the flock of plunging Stukas—was a small percentage of the five and a half million German, French, English, Dutch, and Belgian attackers and defenders. But during that week, the blind imaginations of tens of millions among a hundred races, who had never seen Sedan, turned toward this zone of violent death at the heart of civilization with a sort of reverent dread, as one might involuntarily stare into the swamp where a mass murderer is said to have buried his victims.

As the French army disintegrated, its new commander in chief first canceled General Gamelin's plan, then resumed it three days later—thus failing to combine at Arras with Gort's two battalions breaking south out of Belgium. (That gesture nevertheless had almost halted Hitler's war machine.) Guderian's columns turned west with jubilant efficiency, pausing in their healthy outdoor life to take snapshots of famous monuments.

Only two weeks after Sedan, the Allied Expeditionary Force formed huge snaking lines on the broad tidal beaches of Dunkirk, to be evacuated on a flotilla of pleasure boats and river craft. Astoundingly, the encircling Germans were allowing them to go. It was a last gesture of uncertainty from the Führer to an empire he had revered as the racial model for his own. Leopold, king of the Belgians—who had fought bravely and been repaid with a devastation of their cities that gave a new meaning to war—surrendered on the evacuation's second day.

On 14 June, one month after Sedan, the peak-hatted Nazi officers and their grinning camera-strapped soldiers entered Paris. As if this were Unter den Linden, they wound past the Napoleonic palaces of the Étoile and through the Arc de Triomphe, goose-marched the length of the Champs-Élysées to the Palais-Royal, and settled down to enjoy their voluptuous prize. Through Paris, terror spread like a gas. But the desolate hotels, brasseries, and strip clubs of Montmartre and the *Quartier* were soon crowded again.

That same night on the Lyons and Marseille roads seven million citizens riding carts, trucks, and bicycles swept south with their belongings, accompanied by a rabble of what once had been the victorious Army of the Marne. It was only then, having mesmerized the world with this exhibition of historical mastery, that Hitler himself appeared in a closing scene.

17

SINCE DAWN ON 22 JUNE, IN A FOREST CLEARING AT COMPIÈGNE TO THE NORTH of Paris, two dozen Wehrmacht engineers with hammering drills had been breaking up the walls of a concrete stable. Presently, from this proud little museum of the Great War a blue-and-gold wagon-lit was winched out under a hot sky already ominous with clouds.

At the center of the clearing stood a flat granite monument with the inscription: *Here on the eleventh of November 1918 succumbed the criminal pride of the German race—defeated by the free people it sought to enslave.*

By the border of trees, an excited crowd from the world press was herded by black-uniformed guards. The quality of their excitement was strange, for there was no good reason that these men should be here. Their reason was history. In this railway carriage Marshal Foch and General Weygand had dictated terms of surrender to the envoys of Kaiser Wilhelm. Shortly after, the kaiser himself had been forced to sign the peace at Versailles in the Hall of Mirrors, where his grandfather had long ago proclaimed himself emperor. The surrounding trees had already been cleared of any local folk, children or stray dogs, who could not grasp and therefore might diminish so glorious a moment.

In mid-afternoon, there was an agitated passing to and fro of Nazi aides. Then, with a drone of motorcycles, a black Mercedes, trailed by four others, rushed up the forest aisle. The cars pulled into the clearing, a line of doors flew open, and Adolph Hitler stepped down.

He was surrounded at once by Ribbentrop, Hess, Keitel, and the towering Wehrmacht chief, von Brauchitsch. They were quickly joined by Admiral Raeder, the submarine wizard, and Marshal Göring, whose pilots had pounded Lieutenant Colonel Le Trève at Sedan. The group looked hot and humorless. But to the press, watching through binoculars, they were beautiful with power. Attention was fixed on the figure wearing a black suit and schoolboy haircut. In a village pastor the man's rigidity would have provoked laughter. But in Germany's Führer, it was distinctly fascinating.

None of the Nazi chiefs turned as three more cars joined the file. General Huntziger, the commander of the routed 2d Army, was climbing down, followed by his staff. The French officers looked bewildered and drawn after a sleepless night under escort from Tours.

Hitler lingered in the sun, glowering about him; then he paced to the monument. With a glance toward his one aristocrat, von Brauchitsch, Hitler stretched to see the bronze inscription. Had his Wehrmacht chief not sworn that the German army was unready? And had he, Hitler, not insisted that the French were soft with good living and would crack after the first blow?

A humid breeze scented with rain ruffled the Nazi flags over the railway car. Under the thick trees the speckled shade was invitingly cool. With a step back, Hitler wheeled and paced slowly through the clearing. He had made the moment his. He was untouchable. And though this person's manner suggested profound contempt not only for his French victims, as well as for all Communists and Jews, but also for the little jury of journalists, for his own officers and countrymen, even for the trees and grass and this lovely afternoon—in short, for all creatures and things but himself—those present still followed each gesture with shameless respect. As they watched, their destroyer paused by the forest a little apart from his generals. In the afternoon silence, a hundred eyes saw him gaze slowly round the scene.

Just then the Führer's body was shaken by a spasm. His hands jerked behind his hips, his narrow shoulders pulled at his buttons, and his feet jumped

apart in the gravel. Turning from the summer clearing and clusters of uniforms, Hitler moved solemnly to the wagon-lit steps, trailed by his generals.
He reappeared inside the fourth window and could be seen taking the end seat,
the one in which Marshal Foch had sat. Only then were the French motioned
to enter the sleeper.

Fifteen minutes later, Hitler climbed down. From under the trees a
Wehrmacht band struck up an anthem. Hitler strutted alone across the
clearing without looking up. Then, climbing into his car, he raced off on a little holiday to see the marvelous subterranean fortresses of the Maginot Line.

To the world's politicians, the performance seemed over. The German
power machine had overrun France in a month. Hitler was a master of history.
Yet in truth it was only the beginning.

At dusk two evenings later at Nuremberg, a quarter of a million brown-
shirted Nazis gathered in the Zeppelin Wiese. A vast orchestra began playing
Beethoven. As the sun fell, kettle lights flicked upward, great shafts that joined
among the stars like the vaults of Saint Peter's. In the bowl of light, twenty-
one thousand banners waved like processional candles over horizons of sweating faces drunk with vanity. Infantry formations freshly arrived from the battle front, marched in perfect drill up and around the stadium.

For another hour, the tribal ecstasy mounted. Thousands of newly arrived
pilgrims were bearing torches up the narrow medieval streets of Nuremberg.
Brigades of Labor Youth marched through the parade, naked to the waist, carrying shovels and kicking their toes in unison into the air.

Then a hush fell like obedience over the stadium. Torches blossomed
great flames. A quarter of a million Teutonic faces lifted, smiling like babes.
In the distance, like ants atop a pulpit built for God, the same troupe from the
wagon-lit at Compiègne could be seen moving along the crest under banners
that billowed like sails of blood. At the sight of the human speck at the
center, the embodiment of Herod, Caesar, and Genghis Khan—their Führer—
delirium seized the women in the legions below. There was a swooning and
shrieking, eyes rolled, and here and there older women fell into surrounding
arms. Now a second hush fell over the sea of heads. Giant amplifiers hummed
with power, tensing the night sky. Then a familiar harsh, demanding voice was
heard, breathing intimately in every ear, down to the very least.

"The Fatherland has done everything possible to assure world peace." The
sacred voice breathed again, then gathered force. "Only brainless dwarves fail
to grasp that Germany has been the breakwater against a Communist flood
which would have drowned all Europe and its culture!"

The voice fell away. A monstrous weeping roar of submission rose from
the blazing stadium into the starry night.

And yet, in Hitler's own capital, there was one famous young philosopher
who did not fully take note of Germany's crushing assault on France until a
month after the devastating scenes at Sedan.

THE PEDAGOGUE

1

I N THE FOUR SPRINGS SINCE JOHANNES GODARD LEFT PARIS HE HAD COME far enough to afford his first apartment. It was above a corner shop on the fashionable Friedrichstrasse, only a twenty minute walk from the Reichstag.

In these two rooms, with their stained-glass lamps and curved balcony, the philosopher's powers of reason had never burned so brightly. Inside the balcony windows stood his clavichord, with a framed photograph on it of Johann's handsome parents seated long ago in a mountain meadow. Here also were his oboes and flute, a yellowed Latin globe with monsters in its seas, and Grandfather Otto's brass telescope. By moving the instrument onto the balcony, Johann could just see the treetops of the Tiergarten, and he could also glimpse the Quadriga—the bare-breasted charioteer atop the Brandenburg Gate.

In Johann's mind the huge arch made his new study seem a miniature of the Le Trève mansion by the Arc de Triomphe. The trees suggested his pastoral childhood and the Quadriga his ascent to classicism. And this in turn reminded Doktor Godard, blushing at the telescope, of Mephistopheles' remark that the Nordic mind is never quite at ease with Greek nudes.

Frau Godard's letters arrived three times each week in Doktor J. Godard's letter box as faithfully as they had in the rue de Fleurus. Though they made no further biblical allusions to the German people's choosing a king, his mother's letters conveyed the same devout anxiety for humankind and the worship of her son as its savior. And Johann answered his mother with equal loyalty and his same condescending trust in her opinion of him. For was her faith not echoed in the amphitheaters and staff rooms at the Institute? Was it not confirmed in the way his older colleagues—even Heidegger at Freiburg— indulged him? Even the folk at the grocer's and the cheese shop now bowed and addressed him as Herr Doktor.

But respectability only intensified the embarrassing light that had burned in Johann since birth: an overwhelming light that must penetrate the mind's darkest corners and the mysteries of human fate, so that Doktor Godard might weave—from the pre-Socratics to the latest Einsteinian theory—beautiful patterns to reveal the seams where he might build his life's work—alienation, nihilism, the death of God. It was a brilliance that sometimes shamed Johann and at the same time made him long for some equal with whom he might experience it. Such passions would keep Johann locked for days in his study with the curtains drawn, almost as if in the hope that he might extinguish them forever. And so Doktor Godard settled down to study himself—the *Dasein*— and to cultivate his curious radiance for the betterment of mankind.

It was a glorious life, poor in outward events. After four years in Berlin, Johann did not have a single close friend. Then that autumn, without warning, he had two of them—both his students, and several years his juniors. That they were also among the university's most eccentric, outstanding, and aloof personalities seemed natural, even appropriate. The Swiss Peter Sachse was a worshiper of Nietzsche, while the other, the Argentine Francisco Larreta, imitated the French sentimentalist Proust down to the subtlest mannerism. Even the rich young men's appearances were conspicuously bizarre. Sachse, who had glittering eyes, shaved the back and sides of his head and sported a mustache; while Larreta's huge face, with its watery eyes and flounce of hair, topped an immaculately dressed physique of distressing frailty. But the grotesque affectations that isolated these two young men from the staff and students only reassured Doktor Godard.

In return, his two acolytes seemed to understand everything about Johann's strange, intense life, and they moved in and out of his cloistered rooms as if this sanctuary were their own. In fact, Sachse and Larreta were utterly opposed in temperament, but Johann easily kept them on friendly terms. One prejudice they all shared was a contempt for current affairs. On this they were pure to the point of perversion.

2

THE MOST MOMENTOUS DAY IN DOKTOR GODARD'S LIFE—PERHAPS ITS ONLY one—had begun in the company of his new friends. As the three had walked in an unfrequented corner of the Tiergarten forest, happily ridiculing university figures they never dared speak to, Sachse had come upon what seemed a new monument. This turned out to be the same statue of Bismarck that had previously commanded the park's proudest site.

"My God, can it be the Great Unifier, Germany's most legitimate noble?" Peter said.

"Even states become jealous," said Johann. "Our Nazis are not unlike Ramses on the Nile."

"Ramses only scratched his name on old monuments," Francisco remarked. "These people are redecorating our souls."

"*Macht macht dumm!*" Peter said with contempt.

"We have been insulted."

But somehow so crude a disrespect for Bismarck, whose dignity all three had taken too much for granted even to consider, plunged them into depression.

"Nothing is sacred before their stupidity," Johann said. "Come along, it's time for tea."

As they turned into the fashionable crowd a gang of Brownshirts came parading swastikas up the Schubertgasse. The three friends stepped into a bookshop. It was possible to get a beating if you did not salute.

Kurfürstendamm was too far to walk, so Doktor Godard took his protégés to the tearoom under the Potsdamerhof. A condescending waiter led the effete young men to a center table, from which they stared nervously round at the women in turbans and veils, the bored foreign correspondents, the ministers and staff officers—all of them talking, nodding, and smiling with the exaggerated politeness of people who are part of what is going on.

"Politics and war blah-blah," Peter mocked them. "Money blah-blah, power blah-blah, newspapers blah-blah"

"Excellent subjects," Johann said, widening his eyes. "Which one shall we choose?"

On a stage across from the pastry counter, a little string orchestra was playing *Wienerblut* airs. Huddled together, with their elbows very close, the three pantomimed respectable nods. Then they burst out laughing. Johann averted his eyes from the stare of a black-uniformed *Oberführer* at a nearby table of men. Like some ghost of Doktor Godard's father, the officer had a monocle and dueling scars, and Johann was uncomfortably reminded of what a German ideal he himself looked.

Sachse and Larreta had resumed their light mockery of his morning lecture.

"I will tell you a secret," Johann said, "I am writing a little book called *The Black Prophets*. It will expose the three atheist heresies of our time: Marx's materialist god, Freud's god of sex, and Nietzsche's race god of amorality. Freud and Nietzsche abandon the Jewish deity for cults perverted from Greek myths. But Marx is the most dangerous. His biblical inspiration drains the strength out of the Christian spirit."

"Ah, yes," Sachse broke in. "But without acknowledging the reality of spirit!"

"All three heresies reflect the crisis of Christian love." Doktor Godard glowered over his tea. But he was already thinking of a moment ahead when he would escape to his philosopher's study.

"*¡Caramba!* You will be the Saint Augustine of Berlin."

"He will be thrown off the faculty," Sachse said, with admiration, "even if he did take the Nazi oath."

"Thank you, thank you!" Johann laughed. "I was saved by Christ's words—'Agree with thine adversary quickly, lest he deliver thee to the judges and thou be cast in prison.'"

Just then Johann's smile turned from his students to the table of the monocled officer. The four men had all turned. The Oberführer was staring at Johann with an unmistakable leer. The blood drained from Doktor Godard's head, and he was conscious only of jaded Berlin faces, the suffocating babble, and a woman's velvety singing. Had the officer heard every word? Why would he smirk if he had not? But why would he smirk if he had?

Fleeing the Potsdamerhof thirty seconds later, the friends strolled behind a lamplighter as he moved from streetlamp to streetlamp. Soon after, Doktor Godard muttered a nervous good night and started quickly homeward.

But it was not for another half hour that he could forget the officer's humorless, leering face or the sensation of a threat hanging over his most sacred beliefs—as if Johann himself were the next idol which might topple in the park.

3

JOHANN TOOK NO NOTICE WHERE HE PACED THROUGH THE BOULEVARDS OF THE Berlin night, until he looked up and saw the mountainous facades of Unter den Linden. A figure hurrying under the opposite streetlamp veered in his direction.

"Willst du, Sami, willst du?"

Godard turned toward the slim shadow. Then with a lunge he hurried the other way, walking as fast as he could without daring to look back. Could she be one of *those*? Could one of *those* have spoken to him? A moment later, he was upstairs, with the studio door bolted behind him. He stood breathing hard in the faint glow from the landing.

Johann felt for the lights and there, quite suddenly, were the ordinary humble things that he had always loved and felt loved by. He laughed aloud. Outside in the night sky were Ursa Major and all the other dragon shapes, fixed for all time. His evening stretched out before him in perfect freedom, across the greatest works of the human soul, to the childlike hour of rest. Johann drank in the sweetness of the silence. All round, the Berlin of pompous marches, possessed rulers, ornate balls—and of the alarming, frightened poor—was also harmonious and childishly at peace. Yet something was special, for tonight Doktor Godard would begin his third reading of Kant's *Critique of Pure Reason*.

Johann's papers lay neatly on the cherry-wood desk, as if arranged by a ghost. Resting his fingertips on the lacquered globe, he allowed his eyes to travel over the wall of bookshelves—over the sublime opera, as it were, of all human vision and discovery: Latin, Sanskrit, and Hebrew tracts, and the great religious and heroic myths from which they are inseparable; Chinese sages and European scientists; the German Idealists; the tragedians of Greece and England; the Tang poets; the master writers of Europe and even a few from the Americas. And just as Johann knew the precise position of any book on the shelves, so could his mind focus back along a work's many evolutions to experience man's single but intricately faceted understanding of himself down thirty centuries. He knew now how well he saw these things. It was his humble gift to God.

Johann glanced at the clock hands. It was seven thirty. Slowly, lovingly, he lifted down the *Critique* and rested the book's weight, feeling upon him the eyes of antiquity and of posterity. Then, with a passionate sigh, Johann sank into his father's armchair. He turned the first page.

But the moment that Johann's eyes took in the Gothic letters of the title page, something quite unforeseen occurred. Instead of his usual childlike awe before this greatest of works, Johannes Godard was gripped by a spasm of impatience.

As if to protect Kant from such blasphemy, he snapped the precious book shut. Sinking deep into the chair, he ran his eyes over the library shelves. Locke's *Treatise*? *The Poetics*? Again he could see no work he had not read and, worse, not one he wanted to reexplore. Read the *Critique*? Why should he, for the third time? Was he not still a young man and the evening just begun?

Already, though, the sacred music was escaping from the philosopher's study. The wardrobe of painted angels, the globe, and lovingly laid out texts and correspondence—suddenly all these had a sad, pitiful look.

Johann stepped out onto his balcony. The glow of the streets below was no longer civilization. It was Germany.

The mammoth Graf Zeppelin was floating with a silent motion through the night, lit underneath by the lights of the eastern city. For some reason Johann thought then of the last Olympics: the exhilaration of the people in the cafés, dance halls, and gardens; the endless varieties of uniforms and pageants; and the fragments of symphonies and operas blared through loudspeakers. What could such ecstasies of German pride mean compared with his noble task? Why did these things Johann wanted no part of have the power to torture him in his vigil?

Far below, in the weak gaslight by the boarded storefront that had been Rosenberg's *Apotheke*, paced a girl in a pheasant hat. And somehow he was sure the girl was pretty and thinking of love. The ticket, he thought. Was it for tonight?

Going quickly to his mantelpiece, Johann held up the card. Tuesday, at seven-thirty, for *Die Meistersinger*. But who had sent it? If he hurried he might still make the second act.

4

IN A FIT OF ANXIETY NOT TO MISS THE PRELUDE, JOHANN ALMOST RAN UP THE
Staatsoper steps under the floodlit red banners and in past the black-uniformed
guards.

The intermission was ending. Johann froze between the stalls curtains
and blinked at the bare-armed society women rustling with jewelry and
sequins and the fat gentlemen with pomaded hair.

A black-gowned usher had carried Johann's ticket far down the aisle. The
philosopher waded out into the sea of heads. As he took his place, a dreamy
blonde with her hair parted like a boy's smiled at his perspiring face, and
a sun-burnt, monocled officer thrust a program into his hand. There was a
massive rumbling and explosion of shouts. Rising again as the house lights
fell, Johann turned with the others to the rear.

The center box of the grand tier was draped with a red flag. Three officials in uniform with shoulder belts were taking their seats. The middle one,
who had an unusually large square face, had just waved his open hands with
a sort of fatherly pride. Around Johann there was a ripple of sympathetic
laughter. Now the audience resumed their places. After some trills from the
orchestra, the curtains parted to reveal an artificially bright afternoon outside
what Johann knew to be the workshop of Hans Sachs in Nuremberg, the city
of mastersingers.

Through the next hour, though Johann found the music as sonorous as
ever, the performers seemed to him as clumsy as leaden marionettes.
Somehow the action did not mime the nobility of the music, and the stamping
audience and common fellows in the imperial box made a further gulf to separate Johann from glorious Nuremberg.

When the curtain fell, he left the stalls amidst the delirious ovation to
avoid any conversation. He was looking for a corner in the tightly packed
vestibule when his gaze encountered a familiar pair of eyes among a group
of officials. Was it really Ambassador von Siebenberg of Johann's Paris
days? He had only to go forward and he would meet the German Führer. In
the shock of that temptation, Johann fastened his cape and escaped into the
Berlin night.

As he emerged alone, he was overwhelmed by a longing for his
fellow beings that was so acute he almost cried out. Johann could face
neither his studio nor Act Three. He would go around, as he had so often
in the past, to the musicians' canteen. Bowing to Frick, the stage door
guard and father of his best logic student, he started down the underground passages. He stepped into the canteen just as the first costumed
marionettes from the second act came in. The sight of their intelligent,
painted faces and the sound of their relaxed chatter turned Johann's

head, and he could not help his timidity as he carried a sausage and *Pfannkuchen* to a corner table behind a pillar.

At once a bony hand gripped Johann's shoulder. A man in a brown ski sweater was looking down at him, his free arm wrapped round the pillar. Godard stared at the domed forehead, the down-turning lips, and the eyes, veiled by a feminine delicacy.

"My God, Joachim, is it you?"

"Herder, from Wildisches-Gladbach, Herr Doktor Godard," the man replied, in a high-pitched voice.

"Joachim, Joachim. . . . So, it was your ticket!" Johann squeezed the back of his old schoolmate's neck.

"No!" Herder laughed shrilly. "Well, in a sense you did hope for it, did you not, Hans? Does the famous Doktor Godard approve of our little show? Did you see the great man? And you noticed that I put you beside General von Reichenau?

"Thank you, Joachim. But who is he, the monocle?" Johann asked.

The tables around were filling with grease-smeared citizens of old Nuremberg.

"*Heh, du, Herr Doktor Dummkopf!* Have you not heard? Last month in Poland your monocle was the first across the Vistula. He swam it absolutely naked. As for myself, I answer to the stage manager," Herder went on, gaining confidence, but as if still not quite certain that this exalted thinker was listening to him. "I work on the *Ring* at Bayreuth. Winters I employ my powers here among the Brandenburgs."

Joachim Herder lit a cigarette and pushed it into a holder.

"And your Paris years—was it the rue de Fleurus? Are you surprised, Johann? We followed your career very closely."

And so, over the next forty minutes, long after the canteen emptied for the final act of *Meistersinger*, Doktor Godard described to his nervous but attentive companion the highpoints of his metaphysical adventures: Paris and his encounters first with Doktor Kind, then the exiled Einstein in London, and recently Heidegger. Such spoils must be shared between old friends.

When the philosopher finally fell silent, his friend was twisted on the bench, examining Johann's face. Herder had still not said a word. Johann was embarrassed.

"And you, Joachim. You know all these people here?"

Herder laughed impatiently. "And many more. You understand, these artists are only the flutes and pipes in history's organ. I even know the master architect in the grand tier, who invented the overall design. Do you still follow me, Herr Doktor?"

"Naturally," Johann said, and he smiled faintly.

Herder said suddenly, "Your loyalty to reason disappoints me."

"I'm not loyal to reason, Joachim, but to light."

"To glitter too." Herder suddenly knitted his fingers and laughed explosively. "So why not come upstairs? I have a thousand tricks hidden in the wings. Alchemists, astrologers, other fascinating people."

"No, no, really." Johann had taken Joachim's arm. "I live such a—"

"Simple life, did you mean? While you explore your universal passions, the fruits of the earth go unplucked. Ha-ha! I fear your philosophy is a Mecca built of withered leaves."

"Clearly, you've not known the joys of contemplation," Johann replied.

"I hope, Herr Doktor, that this snobbery does not dismiss my right to thought," the stage manager observed.

A hair-netted old waitress scurried to their side and began sponging their table. Herder laughed indulgently. Overhead in the silent opera house there was a muffled shout, followed by a heavy thundering of feet.

"But you're quite right," Joachim said carelessly. "I have not known that joy of yours. So, have we time? I will tell you."

5

"DURING YOUR BEAUTIFUL PARIS YEARS, HANSEL, WE WERE IN MUNICH. THE Munich of the godforsaken."

"We?" Johann asked.

"The old guard: the faithful, the insulted, the ignored," Herder said gruffly.

"Ah, yes." Godard felt that gnawing in the stomach which the sight of uniforms produced in him.

"In that period, when I could, I lived in boardinghouses, or with gypsies, or off old women. And the jobs I took? Do you know what jobs need doing in the city? To maintain the joys of contemplation?"

Herder leaned across the table.

"For nine months, until the pigment came out of my skin, I cleaned Munich's sewer grates. Then I worked under the Lutheran hospital, stuffing human joints and organs into the furnace. One morning the police came and dragged me out of bed. They needed a sacrifice after all those unsolved murdered Reds. What a joke! I was locked up for a month without being charged." Joachim licked his lips. He was whispering now. "Later, I made a tiny sum allowing old pederasts—but I see that you are squeamish. And did all that make a Communist revolutionary out of me? No, my dear fellow. It was a job I needed, not brotherhood. Those were the best years. For the other five, I starved. And then Providence intervened. Two square meals a day and clean sheets. All I had to do . . . Jews . . . to the hilt of the castrator's knife—"

From overhead, more thundering had drowned Joachim's incomprehensible words. The doorway began to swarm with musicians carrying instrument cases.

Joachim turned back to his childhood friend's twisted face.

"Couldn't you have gone home?" Johann asked.

"Go home? You do not run from such a thing as the city. The city is our future. There was no going home then—as, now in Berlin, I could never go back to Munich. And as you, my dear Hans, will never go back to Paris or home."

"Ah, my friend!" Johann had seized Joachim's hand, scarcely noticing the applause in the canteen as the luridly handsome Walter entered in his wig of blond curls. "It's a terrible story—terrible, vile, unspeakable. But to have been in such a monstrous abyss and then to be delivered. You're saved, Joachim. You'll have the sweetest fruits of life again."

"Ha-ha, and are there not sweet fruits right here?"

"Yes, yes, my dear friend." Johann took a handkerchief from his coat and blew his nose. "Tell me more about your new life."

"Oh, my little Doktor, your Herder could certainly show you Berlin."

"I would bet on that!" Johann laughed.

Joachim watched him. "I might dirty the altars of learning."

"If learning were such a child, then ignorance would be father to every last man. No, truly, Joachim, our coming together is so splendid. You must show me your city."

"All right, then." Joachim glanced nervously around but kept up his careless tone. "I'll guide your intellect from the depths of Alexanderplatz to the most powerful society in the Tiergarten. There is no place where your head will not be known."

"No, no," Johann burst out, "not pleasure and society but the truth of existence. Show me real life, Joachim, even perhaps help me find a wife."

"A muse to reign over a mind like yours? Then you must see us at Bayreuth this summer. Those are my terms."

"The Wagner vaudeville? Is that all?"

"It's only ten-thirty. Why not begin tonight?"

"Not tonight. I must get back to work."

"Those books again."

They pushed out of the stage door, through a knot of opera fanatics waiting to glimpse their heroes. Outside the front entrance, a file of guards had lined the way to some waiting cars. As Johann and Joachim entered the throng the three uniformed officials from the imperial box emerged, accompanied by two women with incongruously simple haircuts. There was a racing of motorcycle engines. The three Mercedes limousines made wide U-turns, then headed west into the lights of Berlin.

And so it was that Joachim Herder's ticket to *Die Meistersinger* gave Johann his first close view of the being his old schoolmate called their savior.

6

THAT SPRING OF 1940, DOKTOR GODARD DELIVERED HIS TWO MOST CELEBRATED lectures at the Institute: "Being: Christian and Pagan" and "Atheists and Idealists." As usual, he rose early and went to bed early; played weekly in chamber trios with a physicist and a female classicist, to whom he rarely spoke; and, like Kant, lived through his day so methodically that a clock could be set by his movements. For what greater good could there be than to live in the highest Christian perfection of a single soul at the pure musical heights of moral knowledge? But since his encounter with Joachim in the canteen of the Staatsoper, Doktor Godard felt a change taking place in the air around him. It was almost as if he were shedding his isolation.

The change began on the night Joachim took him to the White Felix, an absinthe club below Kurfurstendamm which stank of sweat and talc. There in the cynical society of boxers, loose women, and gamblers—and two days later at a cabaret table of Joachim's bizarre friends, whose professions were unclear and who slanged each other with such quick intricacy that Johann could not follow a word and kept blushing foolishly—Doktor Godard had found himself aroused by the metropolis around him. It came as a revelation to feel the sincerity of crime and of people who must know all the secrets of Eros and of violent death.

Perhaps this was no more than the charm of a visceral impression, but in the trance of his studio apartment Johann was sometimes interrupted in his historic reading of the *Critique of Pure Reason* by a consciousness of his childhood friend Herder, somewhere out among the mysterious forces that ruled modern Berlin. At such moments, Johann felt himself disturbingly close to falling in love with life. The sweet meditation over his books, which swallowed the hours like sleep, would disperse. No amount of the philosopher's concentration would restore the base things of the world to their humble places in nature. Sometimes they eluded his powers and went whirling in his imagination like a waking dream, so that he must visit a nearby church to pray. But usually a brisk walk was enough to restore his chastity. And yet to Doktor Godard's colleagues in the Institute, their handsome young philosopher had never seemed to show a more Olympian absorption in Classical enlightenment or a more exemplary indifference to the ominous goings-on in what the loudspeakers called German History. Perhaps it was the strain of having to guard his mind against the idolatrous new power state, but Johann had felt distinctly relaxed by his two evenings among the members of the Thule at their villa by the Tiergarten.

For—as with the pleasure Doktor Godard had taken in the secret knowledge of Eros and violence during his night adventures with Joachim—the fun here depended on his not being personally involved.

7

THE THULE WAS MUCH LIKE SCORES OF SECRET SOCIETIES THAT SPRING UP
among troubled traditionalists in times of religious decline. So it had been
for Rasputin in the last hours of the czar; for the Golden Dawn in England,
frequented by the Irishman William Yeats; and for the Austrian Edelweiss
and German Ahnenerbe. So too for innumerable astrologers, theosophists, and
freemasons—whose pleasure depends on a craving for social commitment,
even a paradise on earth, and on having time free.

On his first visit, Doktor Godard had managed to show no more than a
polite interest in the neoclassical mansion, scented with sandalwood incense
and overlooking the Tiergarten. He had admired the collection of archaeology
and tribal art, the fine bronze and wooden Buddhas, and the Tantric wheels of
life. Here, at least, the idols were not treated like poor Bismarck's statue in the
park outside. Furthermore, among the sixty elegant initiates whom Joachim
Herder identified to the philosopher, there were four Tibetan monks, some
famous musicians, an ex-general, and a fellow philosopher from Munich
University named Haushofer. Godard's Berlin colleague, the unorthodox biologist Jakob Stodel, was also present.

In the Thule's drawing room, Johann had felt at once a pleasant mystical
intensity colored by a certain sensualism. That evening, the solemn discussion
concerned some bearded prophet of eternal fire and ice called Horbiger. It
seemed that this prophet had recently died after passing his message to the
redeemer, though it was not clear to Doktor Godard what this message was.
Still, not wishing to hurt anyone's feelings, he listened politely to the talk of
great floods, secret powers, astrological signs, and superior beings from lost
civilizations. Such a civilization, Johann gradually pieced together, had been
destroyed in the Gobi Desert forty centuries earlier. The god Thor was among
the survivors, and the German race were its descendants. The planet was an
enclosed hollow sphere, and a race of giants had once inhabited its interior
skies. But the titanic powers of those gods—here Johann had with difficulty
suppressed a grin—were not a lost secret. They were in the possession of this
very society, the elect who were destined to rule the earth again when the
Redeemer returned. Since Herr Doktor Godard was the purest of Aryans, he
too could join the Thule and so rule the world. Why should the brilliant
Godard spend his life blind and struggling in an age of materialists,
Communists, and common men?

Sitting at that moment with Herder under a bronze Buddha, Johann had
felt embarrassment for these refined men and women who knew so much yet
would believe anything. With a faint smile and a wave of his fingers, Doktor
Godard had politely declined Haushofer's invitation. Still, it had been difficult
to keep the aggressive grin off his lips when these desperate dreamers turned

to stare at him with pity—as if it were Johann who had just made a tragic decision. But Doktor Godard knew who his redeemer was and had felt pleased by the gentle certainty of his answer.

"No, thank you. I am quite certain."

Still, Johann could not help feeling vaguely bewitched by the elegance and grandiose nostalgia of his new friends at the Thule, not to mention the excellent curries. His strictly organized morality enjoyed these liberating dips into the irrational. It was like stripping the costume of reason and taking a swim in Nature. Until now, he had paid little attention to the tedious flags and symbols of the new politics. Suddenly he became aware that Berlin was decked in magic signs out of deep antiquity.

But Doktor Godard's third experience of the Thule was different.

8

DESPITE THE DISTRACTIONS OF A GREAT CAPITAL, GODARD COMPLETED HIS THIRD reading of Kant's *Critique of Pure Reason* by late spring. And from this, Johann's fertile mind had taken its greatest leap forward. He had glimpsed a new approach to the theory of memory that would extend Kant's perception of God to inhabit the mysterious sliding matrix between individual memory and the collective cultural memory. The revelation had come with a burst of light and the conviction of his power, at the age of twenty-eight, to hold civilization together in a harmony of God and Reason.

During those weeks Doktor Godard was almost delirious with inspiration, and also sometimes with regret that he had no one but Peter and Francisco to share the adventure with. No less frustrating were Herder's efforts, as he put it, to spread Johann's genius high and low in Berlin.

On a suffocatingly hot evening in early May, he went to join his old schoolmate outside the mansion where the Thule met.

Across from the front gate, soldiers were piling sandbags around a large gun. Johann stood with some bystanders, watching Joachim question an officer while the soldiers called back and forth self-importantly, once even breaking into song. Catching sight of Johann, his gaunt friend came through a cloud of bees and zigzagging butterflies.

"That is one of our splendid antiaircraft eighty-eights," he said. "It can be used against tanks as well."

"Tanks in Berlin, Joachim?"

In the garden drive were six spotless limousines and a yellow two-seater flying a swastika on its mudguard. Five handsome young giants with bulging jaws and submachine guns were on guard along the porch.

"*Schmeissers,*" Herder confided happily. Then, noticing Johann's face, he stopped his friend on the steps.

"Curious things amuse you," Johann burst out. "You know of course that your acquaintances inside are merely entertaining themselves. Is it not time you kept your promise?"

"Ssh! You wish to see me in trouble?" Herder lifted his hat to mop his naked head, and at once Johann remembered the man's miserable story and felt ashamed. Why spoil such an evening?

"Patience, you will have your beautiful woman. And the Thule is no entertainment, Herr Doktor. Its members simply admit their deepest passions. Just look at their health."

"But what is it they want then?"

"Want?" Herder threw up his hands. "Ha-ha. They have got it. Tonight you will see."

9

THEY PASSED DOWN A DARK CORRIDOR. THROUGH THE LAST DOOR WAS A gallery of idols. Seated among the placid Buddhas and grimacing fetishes riddled with nails, the society had already begun its meeting. Haushofer was speaking. As Johann found a chair under a familiar Tibetan silk *Mahakala*—the protector of science, with a blood-filled skull cup and severed heads round its waist—Jakob Stodel gave him a familiar nod. Doktor Godard had the strange sensation of being an established member even after he had declined. His eye rested on the solemn faces along the opposite wall.

Against the curtains in a slit of rose light sat an astoundingly beautiful red-haired woman, her head thrown back, listening with a dreamy smile. At her side was a plump fellow in a tight-fitting black uniform. Behind them stood a bony-faced man with a distracted expression, and next to him Doktor Hirt, with his connoisseur's frown. To recognize these three here—two of them the high state officials Himmler and Hess—disturbed the society's pleasant flavor of amateur adventure. In its place, as echoed by the cannon in the street, was the blunt immediacy of power.

Without listening to Haushofer's fervid murmur, Johann's thoughts flew ahead. What did responsible state bureaucrats have to do with these fanciful astrologers, or with their talk of Superior Ones? Suddenly he was thinking passionately of his study and his well-loved books. He glanced back at the group. Yes, the stunning redhead had frankly met his eyes with her dreamy gaze.

Doktor Godard faced blindly toward the source of the droning voice. From the moment his eyes met that heavy-lidded smile, the physical reality of the officials dwindled. Why not stay a while longer? Beyond the villa's walls, every word, symbol, and system could be known. But here inside was a childlike realm of fairy tales and magic.

A girl with black ringlets sat blindfolded at the speaker's table. Sometimes she scribbled a note on a slip of paper. After each writing, Haushofer would read the message to the gallery with a haunted voice. "In the second gyre, the lamb devours the flesh of the lion," "The Great Ones cannot sleep for the clinking of gold," and so forth.

Johann looked round him discreetly. Even Herder was listening with breathless fascination. The redhead had shut her hypnotic eyes. The four Tibetan monks sat expressionless in their saffron robes, as if they could wait happily until the end of time.

"The interpretation of the sixth message sent by the Fathers of Eternal Fire and Ice," Haushofer was saying in a gentle scholarly tone, "refers to the second of the two Himalayan cities built by the Great Ones long ago. Not Agartha, Shangri-La of the good and meditative, but Schamballah. In Schamballah, my fellow initiates, Violence and Power are enthroned, from whence they command the elements and the lumpen masses. To protect and nourish the powers the Fathers have given us, human sacrifice is demanded. From the researches of the Ahnenerbe into racial heritage, we know the meaning of the sixth cryptogram. 'The Great Ones cannot sleep for the clinking of gold' tells us that it is the Jews who offend. And it is they whom the Black Order among us must sacrifice."

Seconds later, a buzz of excited voices broke out. The initiates were adjourning for another curry buffet.

Doktor Godard did not stir. He had fallen into a trance. Haushofer's mention of the two cities—of Meditation and of Power—had been a shock. Johann had actually caught himself listening, not with the vague pleasure of taking a swim in the irrational but with the hypnosis that only the truth can induce. Black orders, Jews, sacrifices? What of Rosenberg's shop outside his studio, Joachim's huge gun, the city of Violence and Power? Yes, and did he not hate the Jews? Johann stood up unsteadily, his pulse pounding in his ears. Where had that thought come from? His light—he must protect his light! He looked for Herder.

His friend was across the room, next to the redhead. With a series of little bows, he broke off talking to Himmler and came toward Johann through the press of murmuring initiates.

"I think I will not remain for dinner," Johann said.

Joachim's grin hardened mockingly. "Come, come, my friend. The adventure has only just begun."

"In that case I will go on my own," Johann offered, anxious not to hurt Herder's feelings.

"What? No!" Joachim hissed, taking Johann by the arm and nervously searching his friend's face. "That would not make the right impression."

"The right impression?" Johann repeated. "Are we in a diplomat's salon?"

All at once, he and Joachim were pacing quickly through the ground floor, out of the Thule's overpowering atmosphere, out past the armed guards, out into the summery Berlin twilight. In the driveway, Doktor Godard took a deep breath. From the Tiergarten came the sound of birdsong and children's voices.

"Don't let me spoil your evening, Joachim. Go back in."

"But, Hans, you *will* be coming again?" Under the gateway Herder had gripped his wrist. "You're not dropping our bargain?"

Johann squeezed the meager arm. "The pilgrimage to Bayreuth? No. But tell me, who was the redhead?"

"Ha, ha!" Herder cried without hiding his excitement. "This villa belongs to her. She is Heidrun Dolin, the soprano. You'll meet her at Bayreuth."

"Dolin!" Johann cried, and suddenly he blushed. "Do you mean you know her?"

"Aha! My friend, are you already in love?" Clutching Johann's hand in both his, Herder shook it vigorously. "Yes, yes, it is my business to know everyone."

Doktor Godard strolled home through the playing children in the last orange light. And he was so grateful to be himself again, to have protected the instrument of his light from whatever had attacked it in the Thule's roomful of idols, that he began at once to erase the whole episode from his mind.

Yet it took him most of his walk home before another impression subsided—the sensation of having been heightened to the stature of a giant.

10

THE SENSATION OF GIANTHOOD MIGHT HAVE BEEN LESS COMFORTABLE THAT evening, had it been mentioned to Johann that the fellow in the tight uniform had power over the judges in half the courts in Europe and controlled an army of secret police obliged to carry testaments as to their Teutonic blood, or that his colleague Jakob Stodel believed in the subjection of mankind by scientific means, or that the polite Doktor Hirt had in his laboratory a personal collection of Jewish skeletons obtained from a model prison camp near Munich.

Back in his rooms, the philosopher bathed and put on his dressing gown, ready to anoint himself for the immense, purifying flight of original thought. All that lingered now was the feverish charm awoken by the Thule. Taking off the dressing gown, he went to his cramped bedroom.

Until the last week, Doktor Godard had owned no mirrors. As with all who are monks by temperament, he was inclined to resist any interest in his material self. But after he began taking out Herder's racing skiff from the rowing club, he had had forced on him the knowledge of his physical strength. Now, in the solitude of the philosopher's studio, where there could be no guilt, Johann had indulged his curiosity to the extent of replacing his cupboard mirror. Was the reflected flesh not the one soil that Johann had brought to Berlin from among the cows and the meadows of wild flowers? It was a sort of proof.

Yet tonight, when Johann saw again the childlike silence of his flesh, the feverish disturbance of the German capital subsided. He was alone, quite alone, except for the curious eyes in the mirror. Yes, it was the same look that Heidrun Dolin had given him that evening. The singer must have flesh too, as he did.

With an ashamed laugh, Johann slipped on his dressing gown. He felt humble and simple-hearted again. To prove it, he threw open the balcony doors to the rumble of the city and swiveled his telescope to the west. The circle in the eyepiece just enclosed the floodlit charioteer on the Brandenburg Gate. The giant figure still caught the last gold light. Across the roofs of Berlin, the huge statue was alone as Johann was.

Yes, he thought with satisfaction, her naked breasts are as embarrassing as ever.

SAINT JOHN PASSION

1

SINCE THE BEGINNING OF TIME, A BEAM OF NORTHERN LIGHT HAS PIERCED the ice of certain temperate glaciers and glittered yellow beneath the green wavelets of the Rhine. Its energy rises as a humble mist from the hot soil of mountain pastures and drifts over the forests, glowing with the ghosts of all things that ever lived. Ripening in a given eon, the candescence leaps down without a sign to merge with the being of earthly creatures caught among its reflections. And feeling this love, those so struck are possessed by a thirst to seek out the light and love it in return.

For several months in the spring of 1914 there was a quickening in the firmament. A flash of light, more powerful than ever before, escaped and shot down upon the earth. The glaciers glinted back like diamonds. In the muddy beds of great rivers, nuggets of gold glowed like the eyes of snakes.

At a mountain village on the German border with Switzerland and Austria, a handsome young woman soon to bear a child was at breakfast with her mother. As the daughter lifted her spoon, an unspeakable brilliance struck the silver and leapt into her soul. She knew nothing of this. But two weeks later the young woman received word that on that very morning, both her husband and her father had died in a great battle of the earth-wide war. Soon after, Elsa Godard felt an odd stirring deep in her spirit, which she took to be the first movement of her child.

From that moment, a strange and not altogether pleasant hunger came over the widow to have the child before her and to love it. Before Elsa Godard even saw the boy, she called him Johannes.

2

JOHANN'S FAMILY HAD OWNED THE LARGEST HOUSE IN WILDISCHES-GLADBACH since 1430, the year a Godard walked over the Alpine passes to Rome to ask the pope's permission to build a village church.

The Godard chalet was built of timbers as broad as Johann's shoulders.

Vines of flowers and grapes embraced its three balconies. In each room there was a huge fireplace. Yet the ceilings—painted with strange animals and angels—were so low that from the age of twelve Johann had to stoop and was ever after somewhat round-shouldered. Following Stefan Godard's death, much of the family furniture had been sold. In the room where Johann kept his musical instruments there was no furniture at all.

In the summer before he began to prepare for university, young Godard worked in the forest above the vineyards with the farmers of his village to cut up spruce and fir and chain the logs to workhorses. At first Johann had liked the work and did it well. But over the weeks their heavy humor, the boring talk of depression prices and national pride, and the monotony of the work so weighed on Johann's spirits that he could scarcely join in their talk. In this green and lovely valley was there nothing to release him from the light that glowed in him?

In Wildisches-Gladbach, excitement grew as Easter finally came near. Everyone knew that young Godard would be the only soloist from the village to sing in the *Saint John Passion,* and the ancient beams of their house rang half the day and night with his rich clear baritone.

The night before the *Passion,* Johann was so ready that he could not sleep. He lay in his attic by the open window under the snow-laden eaves, the thick comforter drawn up under his chin, and he thought of the man he would become tomorrow, born surely on the immense, placid tide of Bach's faith. He thought of Christ's youthful vigor and conviction, and of the Baptist's instantly recognizing such perfect faith, saying, "And comest thou to me?" Then, lying very still, Johann thought of the dove descending and the voice of God calling among the clouds. "This is my beloved son, in whom I am well pleased." To be so loved as this by a father! And for that love to suffer as Christ suffered! Johann twisted in his bed with the splendor of the idea and with his own willingness once again to hang naked on a cross for the love of such a father.

At ten o'clock the next night, Johann ate lightly, refusing to speak. In his chorister's gown he walked alone up over the fresh snow, skirting the icy path, already filled with climbing townsfolk, their hair piously smoothed down. He stole through the gravestones to the rear door. And then he heard only the one violin inside, repeating over and over a phase from the great opening tide.

Climbing on to the scaffold, Johann saw Pastor Manlius with Fricker, the young conductor from Freiburg. Minutes passed, and someone sat down next to him and said something. Then he heard the quick pacing of a man's feet. With a rush of giddiness Johann stood up, and the choir rumbled behind him. Fricker's face was bright red, and his eyes glittered. Thrusting back his hair, the conductor lifted his arms. Then abruptly the nave was plunged in candlelight.

3

ONE HOUR HAD PASSED. THE JEWS HAD CRIED OUT FOR THEIR SAVIOR'S BLOOD. Christ was nailed on the cross under an angry sky, ringed by the cruel and mocking faces of the crowd.

Now, for the first time since he had taken his place, Johann lowered his gaze to the uplifted faces before him. In the sixth row, as in a dream, Johann found his schoolmate Joachim's dark quizzical stare. In the pew behind was his mother's austere face, softened by her pride in him. And at the rear of the organ balcony, he saw Gretchen—whom Johann still had never dared to kiss, or seen in a skirt—seated beside her father. They would have left the high pastures before lunch. Gretchen's face was radiant, though her poor ears could not hear. Johann returned his gaze to the organ pipes as the outraged tenor of the Evangelist at his side cried out, "And the temple veil was rent, the earth quaked. Stones split, and the graves of saints flew open!"

The Evangelist's voice died away, and there was complete silence under the great rafters. The candles flickered on the stone walls. Christ was dead. Johann's face stung. He felt weightless. He turned and stepped down from the stage behind the round-faced Evangelist. In front of them, the female soloists stood facing the church. Johann sank down, feeling exhausted and sick. There was very little room, and the legs of the contralto were pressed between his knees. Next came her aria calling for tears to drench away their grief.

The eyes of the young woman standing over Johann rested on his face. Johann's heart leapt as she raised the music on her slender fingers. He stared at her soft Oriental eyes, strange with knowledge. As the flutes began, the girl looked down, then slowly up, smiling vaguely into the candlelight. Then her lips parted with a tiny intake of breath, and the perfect words floated into the silent church on a voice so pure, so sweet, that it pierced Johann's spirit almost without passing through his senses.

" . . . zerflies . . . sen, mein Herze . . ."

Johann held his breath, afraid for this girl as he had never feared for himself. Was someone else feeling what he did in the music?

When the aria was over, the soloist took her place on Johann's right side. Through the last movement's final surge of desolate and noble resignation, Johann sat rigid, feeling the warm life in the singer's shoulder. Had she recognized him? the pressure of Johann's arm inquired. Would they live together forever in this sublime beauty, beyond reach of ordinary mortals? And the steady sensation of the singer's shoulder replied, *You are beloved to me—my life is meaningless without you.*

Quite suddenly, they were engulfed by a rumbling of boots. Above them Fricker had turned on the podium and was smiling down at the soloists. Johann remained seated as the church began to empty. The slight figure at his side had not moved either, her shoulder still pressing his arm. The blood rushed to Johann's head, and he felt almost sick with her willingness and the desire to seize and kiss her. He sat beside the strange girl for a full minute, blinded by passions and doubts, until he felt that he might cry out with pain.

Then, with quick simplicity, the young woman rose and moved off. Johann was instantly conscious of his mother and Gretchen standing behind him. Johann jumped up, suffocated by self-loathing, and pushed after the soloist.

Outside, snow was falling. Shadows milled under the stone portico, but the singer was waiting alone by the cemetery arch. Johann stopped at the edge of the crowd, a host of morbid ideas seething in his imagination. They could be engaged in a year. He would move his studies to Freiburg so she could continue her work at the Conservatory. But wait—they still had not spoken! Miraculously, the slender figure in the black suede coat and fox ruff still stood apart.

Just as Johann started into the open, a shadow stepped out. With astonishing bravery, another man penetrated the sacred air around her.

Johann heard the familiar tones of his schoolmate's voice. He cannot know her as I do, Johann thought. She would never speak to him. But the mysterious face six paces from Johann was looking up into Joachim's eyes. A smile transformed her features. Then Johann heard her voice, the ethereal voice of the *Johannes Passion*. And suddenly he hated her. And he hated Joachim. Their friendly manner together was obscene.

The Evangelist and a girl with blonde curls had joined the couple under the arch. They both shook hands with Joachim. The four moved off through the thickly settling snow, and Johann stumbled helplessly after them. The little group paused by the cemetery, then moved loudly on down the steep road, and Johann followed, feeling too weightless and pure with the *Passion* to be seen. Surely at any moment she would grow sick of the ordinary beings around her and return to the higher world that only she and Johann knew of.

The couples had reached the Post Café. The sound of a polka poured into the street. The four burst out laughing again, and the door banged shut. Johann waited for her under the low roof of a barn, behind a row of icicles suspended from the eaves to the snow. He began to shiver violently.

Thirty minutes later, Johann was driven out into the deepening drifts. He fled back up the church road toward the Godard house. A few groups of muffled villagers from the *Passion* were still hurrying down in the darkness. But any idea of stopping to hear their praise was humiliating.

That Easter of 1929, young Godard had lain awake into the small hours. And each time he thought of the contralto's eyes gazing down into his soul and the way the scarcely human wisdom of her voice had pierced the church, his chest would burn and he would bury his face and weep.

4

THE TRAIN TO BAYREUTH AND THE *WAGNERFESTSPIEL* LEFT FROM THE SPLENDID
Anhalter Bahnhof and took most of the day.

Doktor Godard of the Berlin philosophy faculty made the trip in the
cloudless July of 1940. Johann did not regret the long hours on the train, for
in many ways these were special weeks. He could not help being glad that
Paris was no longer cut off. Now his world was reunited and Paris inside it
again. Some of the victorious soldiers were even on this train with him.
Yesterday he had completed the first outline for a *Tractus Memorium*. He was
a most eligible young bachelor, traveling by invitation to a famous festival
where he would be introduced to the red-haired singer from the Thule. Johann
could not help thinking now of the mysterious little contralto he had fallen in
love with long ago in the mountains on the night he had sung Christ in the
Johannes Passion.

The handsome old officer puffing a pipe on the facing bench seemed to
have caught the young professor's mood. He kept politely nodding and asked
Johann questions in a kind, fatherly way. On the train there were also new
tanks, which the colonel was delivering to Austria.

The old man waved his pipe stem. "After Salzburg, all is possible. The
Balkans, Greece."

"I wonder, could you tell me—what is the situation?"

"Ah . . . the situation," the colonel said with academic interest. He medi-
tated on this question concerning the captive population of all Europe with
tender precision. "The situation is very quiet, very sensible."

They laughed softly as a field shot by where women were reaping early
corn. The old and the young man fell silent to watch a terrified herd of mares
and foals race away in a stampede to the distant fence. Yes, Johann thought,
this was how he wanted to hear of his country's war. He felt himself being
freed from the disturbing impressions of Berlin. During the rest of the trip, he
feasted on the panorama of fertile farms and chaste villages—the Holy Europe
of Goethe's Weimar and Dante's Florence.

On the station platform, Johann forgot to look for the colonel's tanks. He
took a taxi straight to the old Anker Hotel, where he was welcomed by the
manager—"This is an honor for our little hotel, Herr Doktor"—and found an
envelope from Joachim. Inside was a ticket for *Tristan and Isolde* and a backstage pass for the dinner intermission.

That night Johann slept the deep, drugged sleep of a child. Early next
morning, he put on his cream summer suit and hurried out to see the famous
old theater town.

5

THE FESTIVAL HOUSE, BUILT AT BAYREUTH BY KING LUDWIG FOR RICHARD
Wagner, stood among gardens on a low hill. The building was surrounded
by a promenade overlooked at one end by a balcony from which the master
had appeared to his flock. In the gardens, there were many statues but no
fountains. After two hours, Johann had seen all of it, the Wagner house and
whatever else was to be found in town, and he had reached that stage of
obsessed boredom that is inseparable from the experience of Wagner and
of sexual desire. Pacing the streets, he noticed the blood-red flags, bunting,
and banners that bore the words NEVER CAPITULATE. What was the redhead
doing at this moment? Johann paused before a bank window displaying
daguerreotypes of horned goddesses and bull-like Titans in bird feathers and
gold. There was also a portrait of the composer genius, with his broad forehead, drowsy eyes, and small intolerant mouth. Yes, that face carries the
meaning of greatness, Johann reflected. It was for a meeting like tonight's that
he had denied himself all others; only this was worthy of him. So thought
Johannes Godard, who had never yet conversed with the women at the counter
of his Berlin cheese shop.

At three o'clock that afternoon, Doktor Godard put on his evening
clothes. He walked up to the great brick *Gymnasium* on the hill. As he
milled in the hot sun among ladies and gentlemen who appeared dazed by
their own wealth, Johann felt somewhat possessed. Had not Wagner
himself, Brahms, Nietzsche, and Baudelaire walked this same ground? In
the audience were Europe's crème de la crème. But only Doktor Godard
was to meet Isolde.

Perhaps it was this which biased Johann's judgment of the opera. At any
rate he did not—as on recent occasions—feel bored, embarrassed, or degraded
by the first act. This time the scene was a boat at sea off Cornwall. As the
philosopher shifted positions in his cramped wooden seat, the morbid music
poured into his depths. His happiness was flooded by a delirium of sleep and
death. Still, Johann made the effort to recognize the redhead, concentrating on
the robed Celtic queen—from whom floated a rich voice of aphrodisia—until
his eyes ached and he forgot to breathe. And the mature power of his light,
which he had until that hour focused only in his study, was turned on the soul
and flesh of a beautiful woman.

Johann sank back. The house lights were on. The moment of their
meeting was upon him. Rousing himself, the chosen one got to his feet. As
he moved out of a side door and circled the *Festspielhaus,* the rumbling
within broke over him. He felt then his solitude, each motion, all creation,
unbearably new.

At the stage door, an assistant took the pass from Johann's hand and

pointed to a busy staircase. Johann climbed the three flights and paused for
some seconds outside a door stenciled H. DOLIN, waiting for the strength in his
legs to return. The newness of all things had intensified to a blinding saturation. People hurrying by glanced at him.

"Yes, come in," called a voice. "Come in—*avanti.*"

Suppressing an impulse to fly from this glare, Johann opened the door.
Instantly there came to him a familiar spicy odor. Another door opened to a
dusky room beyond. Coming quickly to meet him was a small, strongly built
woman in a cream gown. Her damp hair was red.

6

"IS IT DOKTOR GODARD?" THE WOMAN SAID, PLACING HER SMALL HAND IN HIS.
She examined his face with a sort of gravity. "Herder told me you might visit.
Enchanté, monsieur."

Not seeming to notice the philosopher's flushed face and stricken smile or
to think an introduction of herself necessary, Heidrun Dolin guided him to a
chair. Johann sat awkwardly in the corner formed by a window and the long
dressing table. Now the famous singer was locking the passage door.

In a fever, Johann watched her sit at the mirror. Running her thumbs over
her eyelids, Dolin wiped the perspiration from her temples, staring into her
eyes under the rows of naked bulbs. She began brushing her copper hair in
neat waves, her bare arms lifting her bosom. Johann had never seen a woman's
toilette or been so close to anyone with these looks, and it came as a miracle
of intimacy. Examining her tense, mobile face, he thought that she might be
slightly older. He was beginning to feel oddly at ease.

"Your closing scene, Madame Dolin," Johann began, swallowing at the
firm masculine sound of his own voice. "It was sublime, truly. When you take
this potion of life and Tristan and Isolde look at each other, then recoil, it is so
simple yet so full of meaning."

Heidrun gave Johann an amazed glance. Had he grasped such a fine
point? She stared into the mirror.

"Ah, yes, doctor, the love potion . . . the intoxication," the singer repeated,
and her blood-red lips made a shape like seagull wings. "They say that not one
in a hundred Isoldes can do that scene."

"But you have done it!" Johann burst out, with an unforeseen recklessness, and the light rose again in his head to blind him.

"*Sehr, schön,*" Dolin acknowledged in a purring voice. She had flushed
at the compliment. "And now—may I call you Johann?—I must think a little
about our next act. Isolde is blind with love. She will call her lover Tristan to
her by putting out the castle torch, *Sehen Sie, Johannes?*"

The soprano had propped one elbow on the table and was looking into

Johann's face. With a toss of her hair, she rose and stepped to the window. She let fall the bamboo blind and turned.

"You see," she said, "I must be ready for the night, eager to worship the darkness, ready for this mystery, this annihilation."

Sitting down at her makeup table, the woman looked gravely at Johann. A light knock came from the door.

"Forgive me," she said. "That must sound simpleminded to a philosopher. Truly, doctor, I think you are the best-looking man I have ever seen. Come in, Heddi."

Heidrun went to open the passage door. A young girl with coiled yellow plaits entered with a tea tray. Johann felt himself being examined as no shop-girl or any other being had ever examined him before. The prima donna and her maid fussed over the Sacher torte and ice cream that Dolin always ate between acts.

This intoxicating woman's interest in his appearance left the same sensation of embarrassed degradation that Johann had felt before his new mirror on the Friedrichstrasse. But her little ceremony of helpless surprise lingered as a sort of beauty, which mingled in his simple soul with the woman's face and rich voice—a beauty that could only be good. Beholding Heidrun's gestures, her moments of distracted indecision, Johann's unnatural light—all he had ever fought to protect—flooded round her. And he knew, though scarcely even aware of it, that he was already letting this woman into his innermost trust. Here, with Heidrun Dolin, all things felt easy. This woman could conduct him into the secret world of Eros and violence that Doktor Godard had detected in the eyes of Joachim's nightclub friends. And the journey would be as easy and free as in the philosopher's study, where there could be no guilt.

Johann's face smiled into Heidrun's. Her gaze lowered to the tea splashing into his cup. He was unconscious of Heddi's having closed the door or, as Heidrun relocked it, of her seeming to have forgotten Act Two.

"As a village boy, I sang the *Christus* in the *Johannes Passion*."

But Johann only half heard himself as he described the alpine village from which he and Joachim came. His heart had already escaped on the current of his unnatural light, flying to meet the maturity and sadness of the world and to visit for the last time the beloved places of his youth.

The long dinner intermission had trickled away. The singer was back at her dressing table. When Heidrun murmured to the Isolde reflected in the mirror, the handsome young philosopher answered, almost whispering. She turned to him.

"Doctor, tell me, are my eyebrows straight?"

Johann nodded gravely before her eyes, for by now this heroic brow was as sacred to him as his innocence and the Delphic oracle combined. He had already conceived their long evening ahead. Seizing on it, Johann alluded to a Hungarian restaurant he had noticed in the town.

"Thank you." Heidrun threw him a smile. "Yes, I agree, rice is preferable to potatoes. But maize is best of all. I ate only maize as a girl in Manaus. Truly, Doktor Godard. You didn't know I was from Brazil?"

Johann visibly recoiled. This glorious Wagnerian soprano not a European? In some sense she was an impostor. But it had been Heidrun's indifference as she spoke of her childhood that jarred their perfect happiness. Johann hurried to defend both of them.

"Naturally I knew that." He laughed his aggressive laugh. "But you see, Heidrun, we have only ten minutes. We must make a rendezvous for the evening. Would you prefer to join me for dinner at the Anker?"

"Oh, I could not do that."

"But why not?" he whispered urgently.

A heavy pulse thundered in Doktor Godard's head. Now the woman sitting at the table was lifting the braided gold wig from its rack and lowering it over her hair. Have you just exposed your whole life to her? Johann was thinking. Given her all of it?

"I thought you knew, doctor. Surely Joachim told you I must leave for France tonight. Our handsome soldiers are in Paris. On Friday, the Führer will be at the Opéra to hear me sing *Parsifal*. And for the next month I will be traveling. And so, *mein Herr Doktor*, I must concentrate on Isolde's next scene. My lover Tristan is with the hunters in the forest, waiting for his signal. Isolde must not fear the darkness. She must find the courage to extinguish the castle torch and welcome Night."

In that moment, Dolin was ravishing. But waves of almost physical pain swept through the dashing scholar at this intrusion of fables and names.

There had been a loud knock. Heidrun rose regally, and the admirer bent over her dressing table jumped up. Feeling too sick to speak, he helped her on with a heavy black-and-gold cape.

"Has this not been pleasant?" The singer held up her hand. "I would have enjoyed our dinner together. But listen." She turned again in the doorway. "I will send a stagehand to guide you. The best place for the *Liebestod* is in the loft."

"Thank you." Johann forced the words out. His red face stooped over the singer's hand. Four men were waiting in the corridor.

"I will be at the Georges Cinq the first week in September. Might you be in Paris? But now watch carefully my *Liebestod*."

Johann bowed a third time, abject with relief that their immense creation had just been saved.

"I am sure, Madame Dolin," Johann said, "that not one in a hundred Isoldes can perform that either."

"Ein nettes Kompliment."

With a charming smile at Doktor Godard, Heidrun turned into the passage ahead of her retainers.

7

THAT NIGHT ON THE MUNICH-BERLIN EXPRESS, WITH THE COMPARTMENT BLINDS drawn, the philosopher could not remember the stage manager who had guided him, or the crowded passages of the *Festspielhaus,* or even the details of the great soprano's face and manner.

Nevertheless a sensation came away with Johann of the catwalk high above the scenery, of the musicians radiant below in their pit, and his aggravated emotion when he had seen Heidrun alone on stage by her lover's body. He could hear still the delirious power of the words she had sung: ". . . In the great wave of the earth's breathing, to drown, to sink unconscious, supreme bliss." Then Wagner's music gathered its exhaustion to fling itself into one last thundering annihilation, into which Heidrun's voice sank, mellow and spent, far below where Johann was suspended among the stage rigging. And grasping that he could not see her for another month, Johann had felt suddenly angry and alarmed that he was to meet Joachim that evening. In this morbid state, he had decided to cancel tomorrow's *Parsifal* and return immediately to Berlin.

Yet as the hours clicked by, and Bayreuth fell far behind, the brutal impression left by Heidrun Dolin had softened to poetry. The philosopher's light revived—*her* light now—and he began to tell the strangers in the train compartment about his momentous afternoon. Johann's three grim companions, in spectacles and raincoats, did not even lower their newspapers in reply to his friendly comments.

By the time the Berlin Express entered the darkened suburbs of Tempelhof, Heidrun had been transformed into a silent, gentle Gretchen and Johann was experiencing a blinding love for her. He did not regret having left Herder and his festival behind. As he carried his suitcase—absolutely alone—up the Friedrichstrasse, even this return seemed romantic to him.

Waiting in the entry with his mother's usual letter was one from a colleague, the theologian Ackermann. Johann threw open the study curtains to the first pure dawn light. Though he had not slept all night, he felt overwhelmingly awake.

Johann had always considered the theologian somewhat eccentric. The letter concerned rumors and scholarly intrigues involving a certain Munich professor along with two students and a Pastor von Bettelschwingh. The aforementioned group had accused the central government of planning some purge of retarded children. Johann's gaze fell to the last paragraph. "In view of Herr Doktor Godard's connections in high government circles—"

Johann reeled to his feet, his brain throbbing. He pressed his hands to his temples. What high government circles? Purge of children! Was Ackermann not reputed to be a man of reason? At least one thing was sure. If such monstrous things were happening in Germany on a morning like this, Ackermann would not dare to put them on paper. The poor fellow must be mad.

In a sort of suffering clairvoyance, he ripped up the letter, threw the shreds into the toilet, and pulled the chain. Then he opened the balcony door and went out to lean on the wet railing.

Over the city scarcely a sound could be heard. Johann breathed in deeply and smiled to himself. It was going to be a hot day. There was nothing now to keep him from this nirvana. Filled to overflowing with the miracle of life, Doktor Godard slowly turned. There above the silent rooftops was the stone charioteer on the Brandenburg Gate.

Berlin, with its pageants, rippling swastikas and bombings, was a city of violence and power decked in magical signs. And in the morning's fresh rose light, the great bare breasts seemed made of flesh and blood.

8

PIERRE LE TRÈVE HAD NEVER ADMIRED HIS SON. BUT AFTER THE ORDEAL OF Hitler's crushing assault on Sedan, Jean-Marc's embittered letters from the front, and his wife's nervous collapse, Le Trève could not help loving the boy.

By 1 July 1940—as crowds of Parisians standing in the great squares of their city were informed by loudspeaker—France's dismal Third Republic had given way in the still unoccupied southern zone to the government of the popular *Maréchal* Pétain and his minister, Pierre Laval, an old business acquaintance of Le Trève's. The *Grande Armée* was to make no heroic stand in North Africa. All that mattered, Petain reassured the men of France, was food and women. In Paris, groups of battle-hardened German and Austrian heroes with cameras now toured the boulevards. Across this capital there was a nine o'clock curfew, and a giant red swastika flag could be seen rippling at the tip of the Eiffel Tower.

At the time of Johannes Godard's letter to the Le Trèves, asking if he could stay with them for the first week in September—Grandmère Le Trève had already moved to her sister's house in Neuilly "where there were no Germans under the roof"—Minister Laval had required Le Trève's immediate presence at the Quai d'Orsay. Like many rich and aging opportunists who attach their ambitions to radical political change, Laval had, through the National Front years, made the classic move through his ministries from the left to the far right. Pierre Le Trève went to their meeting with extreme discomfort.

Laval did not keep him waiting. Le Trève was conducted into elegant chambers piled with thousands of recently unsealed corporate ledgers. He received the unattractive little fellow's embrace and stood staring round the airless offices. He had always prepared in detail for even the most insignificant of meetings. Yet for this confrontation, which he knew very well might settle the future for his family, Le Trève had prepared nothing at all, not even a handy ammunition of noble ironies.

Le Trève's audience lasted thirty minutes. In the gloom under the window there was an alert German stenographer. As he spoke, the minister examined Le Trève's refined, impassive face with the ease of someone convinced of his own generosity.

"Consider our offer, and consider with care—you control the most extensive French petroleum refineries and oil reserves. My dear Pierre, I will be open and to the point. *Entre les vieux loups*, eh? Europe—yourself, eh—is part of the German Empire. You know of Abetz, here in Paris? . . . of course, through your von Siebenberg. Perhaps the wages we discussed for you did not seem to be a first-rate coup. But . . . the *alternatives* . . .? Think too of the wells on British lands; as with Cyrenaica, we would eventually be recapturing them for you. This is the wave of the future, Pierre. This genius will inevitably be master of the world."

"You refer to Churchill?"

Laval's face—like an old boot, Le Trève thought—smiled across the desk indulgently.

"I said *genius!*" You will see Hitler from Vladivostok to Los Angeles. I will give you just five minutes to save yourself from these Communist-infested inhibitions, *ce liberalisme épuisé. . . .*"

They sat facing each other without the slightest movement. The steady snicking of the stenographer continued, then stopped. In the profound hush, Pierre Le Trève felt two pairs of eyes on his elegant person. He tried to overcome a wave of giddiness. How could this fool expect him to decide such a question in five minutes . . . or five decades? Le Trève's thoughts spun on. He already knew of the plentiful and apparently painless betrayals, not to say grovelings, among his social circle. Could it matter what uses Le Trève oil was put to? Any hesitation in joining in would compromise all the many Le Trèves and thousands of his employees.

Quite suddenly, and just because it offended Le Trève's sense of honor even to be sitting here and deliberating so complete a degradation, he felt himself rising to his feet.

Le Trève had never before been so unpleasantly aware of his physical height above an office floor.

"What you offer is not a solution. It is an invitation to crime."

9

BUT ALREADY THE NEXT MORNING, WHEN PIERRE LE TRÈVE FOUND THREE VERY polite Saarbrucken engineers at his head offices on the Faubourg—sorting through his personal papers—his first smug sense of rectitude, face-to-face with Laval, had turned to uneasy guilt. How had he jeopardized his family and his employees?

The answer came that afternoon in a telephone call from the ministry. Company wages were to be reduced and controlling stock in Le Trève Industries shifted. Even the family's private gasoline would be rationed.

Le Trève's social background had not equipped him for lonely moral stands. Through the next days he felt disoriented and discovered patches of gray hair on his temples. Nor was the Le Trève household a happy place. His beloved daughter was cut off now in Mexico, and her brother had grown secretive and surly after his three-month internment at Laon. There would be coal and food shortages soon. Worst of all, most of Le Trève's lifelong friends—the most austere of Catholics—were associating with Vichy. He noticed them trying to hide their discomfort in his presence and he pitied them.

So the arrival of an affectionate letter from Hélène's prodigious friend Johannes Godard; now a doctor of philosophy in Berlin—brought back sensations of happier times. Here was a detached, distinguished intellectual with whom Le Trève could discuss the future of Europe. Never mind that among his daughter's circle the fellow had sometimes seemed awkward and arrogant. Had Hélène not always defended young Godard?

And that week there was a second piece of good news. Even after the saturation bombings of Britain's metropolises, the English had somehow denied the Prussian war machine a coastal invasion. There was still a western front. Good. Tomorrow Le Trève would travel with his son to Toulon and address their workers. They, at least, would understand him.

10

AS THE FIRST SEPTEMBER EVENINGS CAME TO PARIS, THE LE TRÈVE CHAUFFEUR drove to fetch the young philosopher from the Gare de l'Est. An hour later, as the visitor sprang from the car into the late-summer heat, Le Trève came eagerly down the steps to meet him.

"Welcome, my boy," Le Trève said. "Or must we now call you Doktor Godard?"

"Yes, no well—thank you," his guest muttered, apparently experiencing a somewhat tactless fit of delight.

Le Trève trailed the tense, athletic figure into the hall. How little recent events seemed to have affected the brilliant fellow's self-involvement. A little more savoir-faire, Le Trève thought, but childlike as ever. Only the boy's spectacles were new. Under the great staircase, Godard was gazing around the Napoleonic mansion, as if understanding that at last he had Hélène's family to himself.

"I'm afraid it will be quiet for you here," Le Trève said, as they climbed the stairs after Bertrand. "You have come to lecture?"

"Quiet?" Johann paused on the landing. "Oh, no. You see, Monsieur Le Trève, I am in Paris to see Heidrun Dolin. I am in love."

They continued into the sunny grand salon, with its familiar balcony overlooking the garden. For several seconds Hélène's father—who that summer had seen the disgrace and enslavement of his country, who only days before had confronted Pierre Laval and made a lonely decision that might ruin the lives of thousands (at Toulon, the company's technicians had been uneasy that the *patron* was risking their jobs), and whose own household was facing an indefinite period of hardships—stood smiling into the young philosopher's expectant face, completely unable to remember who Heidrun Dolin was.

"Ah, you mean the opera diva?" Le Trève burst out. "Well, congratulations, my dear fellow."

Johann interrupted him with a happy cry. "Hélène's piano! Does anyone play it?"

They went to the garden windows. Sitting eagerly on the bench, Johann rubbed his hands and brooded. Then with a deep sigh he played several somber chords, and the sunlit silence of the salon rippled again with a current noble and tender.

Schubert's B flat major, Le Trève thought, motioning to his wife in the doorway. This young scholar played the piece better than Hélène had ever done. And suddenly, Le Trève was quite sure that anyone who could express such emotion must have felt deeply the tragedy of Europe in these last few months.

Jean-Marc had stubbornly remained in Toulon to settle with the union *chefs* the question of the invisible Nazi presence. So on Johann's first evening in Paris, the garden table under the willow tree had been laid for only three. And with Madame Le Trève fluttering good-naturedly between her husband and their guest, Le Trève's first sensation of something unnatural vanished. Johann was soon telling them with boyish optimism of his new career, as if presenting it for their approval. With complete openness, he spoke of faculty colleagues, his little studio, and recent philosophical works. No mention was made of Hélène or of their absent friends.

Through the simple dinner of soup and *côtes de porc,* Johann's initial shyness gradually turned to aggressive self-confidence. He seemed less and less aware of his hosts' responses to him.

Doktor Godard had already telephoned the Hotel Georges Cinq. Madame Dolin was indeed expected that night. This more than made up for the two Jewish colleagues whom he had tried to contact, only to find that they had made hurried departures for America. It was growing dark in the Le Trève garden when Johann's conversation turned to his romantic meeting with Heidrun at Bayreuth and his coming to Paris.

Presently the two men were left alone with their cigars.

"Yes, Johannes, these are difficult days for us," Le Trève murmured. The words were painful to speak aloud.

"Do you think so?" Johann said with polite distraction, remembering his ignorance of the city beyond these walls. "Paris seems much the same as I remember it."

"It is on the surface," Le Trève said, with a hint of emotion. "In fact, Johann, I should be most interested to hear your opinions . . . as a detached thinker."

"Yes, of course, of course." Johannes replied, with nervous embarrassment. He propped his sun-tanned temple on two fingers, the cigar coal glowing by his ear.

"For the first time, I believe Europe is doomed," Le Trève went on. "These wars will leave her mortally sick."

"That is an old debate," Johann replied easily. "Europe could be evolving—"

"No. The tone has gone flat. Somewhere honor has slipped overboard." Le Trève's voice grew firm, though he had scarcely spoken to this young German before tonight. "Only two figures still dominate Europe—Churchill and Hitler. Both understand that civilization could be ruined by the Communists. But while Hitler would rather turn his conquest into a dominion rather than submit, Churchill considers a Europe without civilized decency not worth saving. Do you see?"

In the light of the one candle, the young professor nodded eagerly, seeming not at all affected by the grave turn in the conversation.

"Yes, but there is nothing curious about Hitler's forbearance towards England," Johann said. "England also has an empire. Wagner worshipped Shakespeare. England and Germany share a mystical soul," he said, thinking of the Druidic Celts and of the pagan Germanic counterpart, now reactivated by the Thule Society.

"*Tiens!* That's most interesting." Le Trève reflected, feeling somewhat exhilarated but not quite sure how the young philosopher had shifted them from the mortal blows of the last months onto a mystical plane.

Almost immediately the discussion drifted back to literature, music, and Heidrun Dolin.

"My boy," Le Trève said then, somehow unable to let go of this vital fellow, "why not ask your Heidrun to stay here . . . as a friend of the family. She could have Hélène's room."

"Truly?" Johann laughed. "You cannot be serious. May I? But that is beautiful."

Later, as Le Trève lay in bed without listening to his plump wife as she slipped on her negligee, he thought of Hélène's piano. Yes, it was pleasing that there would once again be youthful romance in the old mansion. The young man certainly had a pleasant gift for lifting weary ambiguities to a passionate singlemindedness. The vivid impression that Doktor Godard had made on him—of a great and civilized European freely in command of every faculty— had come upstairs with Le Trève. But there was still that first sense of something unnatural in the scholar's good spirits. As when a person has been drinking . . . or worse.

The moment Doktor Godard had said good night to both Le Trèves and escaped to the top floor, to the silence of his little room with its canopied bed, the "great European" was possessed by thoughts of Heidrun.

Heidrun *here*, in the Le Trèves' house? Was not Hélène's room on this floor? And suddenly Johann's blessed student days in this house were close about him—this warm, generous French household where he had been happy and had sensitively worshiped little Hélène without once making a sign of it. Tonight, Johannes Godard, the lonely village boy, had been treated by these people as a son. At least he would sleep under this roof, safe from the modern city.

But as he stood half dressed at the open window, listening to the hush of Paris streets under curfew, Johann sensed an imperfection in his taste of paradise, as of something obtained under false pretenses.

11

THE NEXT MORNING WAS THE FIRST ON WHICH PIERRE LE TRÈVE'S SERVICES WERE not required at the Faubourg offices of Le Trève Industries.

Scarcely aware of any change in the mood of the house, the philosopher took late breakfast on the sunny terrace with both of Hélène's parents. A little after ten o'clock, feeling quite the student prince in his new linen suit, Johannes Godard once again set foot into Paris. In the long month since he had stood on his Berlin balcony, it was the first time Johann had felt at peace with his feelings for Heidrun.

The crystal and cream lobby of the Georges Cinq was bustling with stiff Wehrmacht generals. At the concierge's desk, among the sheaf of messages in Madame Dolin's box, there was one for Doktor Godard: *Johannes, there will be a ticket at the Opéra. H.D.* At the sight of Heidrun's rather large handwriting, Johann wheeled and passed out into the beloved streets of his student days. With her note in his jacket—the singer's only sign to him since her invitation at Bayreuth—Johann felt himself lift from the pavement and walk upon a river of light.

That evening at the opera, because of the curfew, the opening curtain was early. The first act of *Lohengrin* dealt with the early Saxon Emperor Henry I—of whom one of the attendees, the Thule's Himmler, imagined himself to be the reincarnation—who in the tenth century had rescued the

Christian church and led the hesitant Brabantines on conquests. But somehow Doktor Godard's thoughts kept wandering to a sweet memory of Hélène Le Trève stretched on the floor of the Le Trève opera box. Then the fire curtain came down. Shortly after, the philosopher found himself jostling backstage among the shouting cast.

Heidrun was in a dressing room with her naked back to a circle of mirrors, smiling dreamily among baskets of red and white roses. The singer's eyes met Johann's.

"Aha, Doktor Godard!" Heidrun called to him. "Hänslein, come in. I present to you Prince Malatesta and our new Field Marshal Walther von Reichenau."

Doktor Godard had stepped in under the low ceiling. Hot, strong little fingers gripped his hand, taking away Johann's power of speech. The philosopher stiffly returned the urbane bows of Count Ciano's emissary and of the monocled officer Johann remembered from his first evening at the Berlin Opera. In the older men's competitive charm there was no trace of seriousness. Heidrun smiled curiously into Johann's tense face and released his hand.

But as the minutes fled by, borne upon Heidrun's bewitching laughter, Doktor Godard's fellow admirers made no sign of leaving them alone. Johann had brought this beautiful woman the supreme traditions of the mind. His gift hung on her consent.

"I must speak to you. The Le Trèves have invited you to stay."

"Who? Impossible, the hotel is wonderful."

"But, Heidrun—Johann's face was red as it appeared in all her mirrors—"a great French family welcomes you like parents to sleep in the palace of a Napoleonic marshal."

"You hear, gentlemen? A Napoleonic palace." Heidrun laughed triumphantly. "Herr Doktor, you are also a conjurer—*ein Zauberer. Und warum nicht?* Arrange it then, my dear Johann. Will you? Yes, come for me after the finale."

The dressing room was feverishly hot. The prima donna had risen among her admirers. Before their blasé smiles, her exotic face uplifted, Heidrun kissed Johann on the mouth. The hand behind his neck seemed to tremble.

And so it was that Doktor Godard—the youngest doctor of philosophy in the history of the Berlin Faculty—first kissed a woman. After that he went unsteadily to telephone the Le Trèves. Then he rang the hotel to send across Madame Dolin's affairs, including two cats. Later, as the *grands boulevards* of Paris emptied of French, the intricate heir to Kant found himself riding beside the famous beauty up the Champs-Élysées in the rear compartment of a Daimler. Heidrun watched Johann's face from among her furs. In the darkness, her high cheekbones seeming to draw up her lips in a feline smile. But so intense now was Doktor Godard's light that even the sensation of his own starched cuffs, elegant suit, and shirt collar seemed remote.

Johann was scarcely aware of the Le Trèves welcoming the handsome young couple in the dark hallway, with the amusing story of how the two cats delivered by the Georges Cinq had immediately chased Gnome into the scullery. The old people soon withdrew so that Johann and Heidrun might have dinner by candlelight on the garden terrace.

Perfectly alone at last, Johann was only mildly conscious of Heidrun herself as he began to speak, to the eyes he loved, of what he had never dared to tell even his best students: the most inscrutable riddle of human meaning from his *Tractus*.

Heidrun cut him off simply. "Their daughter's room. Is it near yours?"

An hour came when the Le Trève home was darkened and still. On the top floor, Doktor Godard hesitated outside Hélène's room. His untouched skin was bare under his gown as it had only been in his study, where there could be no guilt. Johann was still free. The godly Europe of Bach still spread out round him, but the night was growing dense. Raising his arm, Johann gave a light knock. The bedroom door swung inward. He passed through, and the door closed. And in the candlelight inside Hélène's room, Johann saw the body of the bare-breasted charioteer.

Now the timeless landscape of snow lakes, farms, and wildflower meadows heaved round Doktor Godard and took on the deformed shapes of delirium. Flames burst from his light and, one by one, smoke rose from the spirit shrines of men. Strange mountains emerged tipped with blood, plains of white undulating mud, stinking chasms, with bridges that tightened and leapt, dark tunnels, dangerous with internal gales and cataracts. Across all this unchristened land, Johann's sacred light was dashed, scattered and dispersed to sprinkle down upon an unslakable desolation reigned over by the cannibal eyes of that impersonal god who needs no name. And upon this dark and lawless dust, Johann flung himself and groveled with delight, until all civilization was consumed.

"*Du bist ein Güter*," Heidrun whispered to Doktor Godard then in Hélène's candlelit bedroom. "A good, good man."

CLAVICULA SALOMONIS

1

A T THE UNIVERSITY OF BERLIN THE NEW, REDUCED CLASS OF 1940 WAS enrolled. Already dim were that summer's victory marches through the Brandenburg Gate and the ceremonies at the Staatsoper. In his little studio over the Friedrichstrasse, Doktor Godard's distinguished labors resumed.

Only now the sun that fell across the philosopher's desk conveyed less warmth, and Grandfather Otto's telescope had been moved from its view of the stone charioteer. For instead of returning from Paris with the glorious fires of his adventure, Johann was aware at once that Heidrun must have taken them with her to Madrid. Even when he looked out on the city, Berlin seemed depressingly drab and coarse. The thought of Herder's nightclub friends disgusted Johann now. And it was the same with his urgent revisions of the treatise on memory. Somehow the work was not inspiring.

But most distracting was the sensation of something crude, untrue, and somehow degrading having been ushered among the Le Trèves—the household of Hélène and David's student circle, where Johann had known his greatest happiness.

Through the autumn, Doktor Godard was so dedicated to being saved from these evil impressions that it was remarked by his colleagues that they had never seen him so kind, so disciplined, or so self-effacing. Johann's resurrection even gave him the detachment to disdain his neighbors' nightly flights to the basement shelter. He would lie relaxed in his bed, triumphing over the effect on his sleep of the crashing thuds—the advance and retreat of the flak batteries as they tracked the British bombers through the Berlin night, with their inanely wagging search beams. "Like the legs of the cockroach in Kafka's *Metamorphosis*," the philosopher would joke to Peter and Francisco. But to hide the secret of his own metamorphosis from his devoted students was more difficult than hiding it from himself.

Yes, Joachim had kept his promise. Past the door of Hélène Le Trève's bedroom, Johann had experienced life—more of life than he had imagined existed. A feast, a desolation, of which the heir to Kant felt more ignorant than the most impoverished fool in the street below. Its pagan fires had left him weary of clarity and light. In his most sacred concentration on the symbols of the holy paternity and virgin bride, Johann would find himself half mad to hear again the sweet delirium of Heidrun's laughter.

Thus began Doktor Godard's series of short lecture tours to the universities of Paris, Rome, Warsaw, and Vienna—all of them now cities of Violence and Power, hung with magic symbols. And by a curious chance those visits coincided with four productions of Wagner's *Ring of the Nibelungs.*

2

THESE WERE THE MONTHS OF THE EUROPEAN EMPEROR'S RESTLESS TRAVELS BY private train in his first effort to discipline the Fascist allies' grip on the new territories. It was an empire that now ranged from the North Atlantic coast and the Mediterranean to the immense border of the Russias.

Doktor Godard glimpsed the Führer's train twice, at Innsbruck and outside Frankfurt. But the philosopher still allowed no newspaper near him, and despite the vague thrill of sighting the black express splashed with red insignia, he only hardened his contempt for the unfailing ugliness of earthly goings on. The more Johann saw of his time, the more unworthy it seemed of his light. The circuses of politicians were so utterly transient. Meanwhile, his passion for Heidrun only grew.

Upon his return to Paris for *Rheingold,* Johann somehow found himself afraid to tell the Le Trèves he was back in the city. It scarcely seemed to matter; Heidrun's operas were the centers of high society in the capitals of the new Europe. To see Heidrun, Doktor Godard too must be seen. And as the escort of Dolin, Johann was introduced to the officials of the day: dozens of cynically energetic *principi, condes,* and *ducs* under the management of party agents, who crowed of their cultural superiority and of their right to defend it at any cost. For her—the woman he loved—Johann politely forgave their illiteracy, hiding the fact from himself that Heidrun gave him no choice. Doktor Godard even displayed enjoyment when he was shown the ruins of the Colosseum by Prince Malatesta and later swam with the bath-capped young Italians in the pool of the new Italian Forum.

In Warsaw—at the banquet of Silesian boar for the cast of *Siegfried* given in Pilsudski's Belvedere Palace by the new governor of Poland, an effete lawyer named Hans Frank—Johann's sense of some imperfection intensified.

Like all incurably weak people, Governor Frank seemed ill at ease with his own power. Despite the effect on him of Dolin's spells, the man's recital of Chopin for his fifty guests had been vapid, contrasting unpleasantly with the French furniture, the suspended lamps and the Venetian *Triumph of Venus* on the ceiling. This governor of Poland had also crowed about

German culture, and talked of painting over the naked Venus with a arbor of wisteria. Then, to Doktor Godard's alarm, Frank had begun criticizing the empire's police chief. This was that same narrow-shouldered Himmler whom Johann remembered from the Thule séances. For some reason, the governor then insisted that Dolin and the doctor should accompany him to see for themselves—naturally from locked cars—the tragic starvation in the Jewish quarter.

With considerable agitation, the philosopher had declined. Only then, for the one and only time, did Johann hear Heidrun beg for his support. Next morning the governor collected them from the hotel.

At the first instant that Doktor Godard beheld the red brick gate to a forbidden city, which their host had built on the Marszalkowska, he had shouted to the driver to turn back. Even Heidrun's fascination with everything powerful and Teutonic had faltered in the face of Johann's violent emotion.

But the delight that Doktor Godard took in his first love, who sweetly sang Schubert *lieder* to him in their bed at night, had survived even the rearing up of that high brick gate, with its black-uniformed guards and barking dogs. Ten days later, with feelings of painful remorse, Johannes Godard was again on the night train to Vienna to hear Heidrun sing Gutrune in *Götterdämmerung*. Why should the woman he love be punished for her professional life? Was it really so unlike life at the Le Trèves?

3

IT WAS THE TIME OF HITLER'S FIRST CONFRONTATION WITH VYACHESLAV MOLOTOV, veteran of the purges and foreign minister of all communism to the shores of the Pacific.

On 12 November the Soviet minister traveled by railway from Stalin's Kremlin, crossing Poland to the throne of fascism over tracks lined unbrokenly with German soldiers from the Russian border to Berlin.

Presently, in the Berlin chancellery, seated with his most cherished enemy across a bare desk under a giant portrait of his scowling self, Adolf Hitler began as usual. That is, by placing the fate of Europe and mankind on the level of medieval fables, with himself as the mystic hero.

"We, the two most powerful leaders in history"—Hitler raised both fists from his desk—"must divide up this bankrupt Pax Britannica of half a billion human souls."

"Yes, on every side," the Russian snapped back, quoting the very Trotsky whom Stalin's own agents had murdered two months before, "that slug humanitarianism leaves its slimy trail, obscuring intelligence and atrophying emotion."

"I believe we owe that wisdom to a former colleague of yours," Hitler replied limply. For the first time since his days in a poor Vienna lodging house, he had in his presence a man unmoved by the glory of his will. Momentarily stripped naked by the hammering series of questions that followed—on Germany's practical intentions in Finland, the Balkans, and so forth—the Führer quickly rose and adjourned their conference so that he might regather the evidence of his splendor.

That evening, Hitler issued his field marshals the confirmation that Germany would invade Russia, the "breeding ground of Jewish culture," whose 161,000,000 citizens had just dared to ignore his magnificence.

4

AT ALMOST THE SAME HOUR, IN VIENNA, DOKTOR GODARD ARRIVED AT THE Sacher Hotel and checked in his bag and lecture case. Then he hurried out and purchased a large basket of lilies. As if skating on mercury, Johann reached the stage door of the blazing Staatsoper minutes before Act One of *Götterdämmerung*. On the night train from Berlin, he had decided he would marry Heidrun.

"Yes, Herr Doktor, Dolin left one ticket," the pink-cheeked manager said, in a voice that could be heard down the crowded passage. "It was for an Italian gentleman."

"No, no," Johann whispered. "Quite impossible, she and I spoke only yesterday."

"Look, the envelope: Count Malatesta. And there is not even standing room." The fellow was almost shouting.

Johannes paced out and thoughtfully circled the empty Opera Square. He was breathing a little quickly. No one must see Doktor Godard helpless in love. Johann knew that this liaison had become the most clearly visible thing about him. Calmly enough, his mind sorted back to their three days in Poland, to his insults about the officials Heidrun knew. Johann, who owed so much to the noblest spirits, had plunged his radiant light deeply in the wrong. Yes, he must marry her. His mind tilted dangerously.

Back inside the stage entrance of the Vienna Staatsoper, two young Nibelungs were smiling curiously at Doktor Godard, who had no ticket to see the woman he loved. She has not forgiven me, Johann thought, and he was suffused by a rich wave of self-pity. She has simply decided to forget me. Johann felt tragic with the beauty of his passion. That novel idea then plunged toward madness. She had lost interest in him!

Seconds later, the Berlin philosopher was moving with his bundle of flowers very quickly through the foggy streets of the Austrian capital. His highly trained concentration had torn loose. That charlatan Malatesta! No interest in him? Turning guiltily into one unknown Gasse after another, Johannes Godard was stopped three times by the Austrian secret police, showed his documents, and was forced to exchange repeated Hitler salutes. His head spun with images of leather jack boots, the Führer's black train splashed with mystic symbols, and Himmler at Heidrun's villa. Images flickered by of the irritable young *fascisti* posturing in the Roman baths and Heidrun's conceited raptures in the Hotel Georges Cinq over everything German, of the Warsaw governor's pompous, fragile face talking of "cultural superiority." Of a high red brick wall, the gate of a forbidden city.

No, it was impossible! Johann awoke from this hallucination standing on a blacked-out bridge of statues over what must be the Danube. Such thoughts would destroy his light—for he could only love her. And remembering that beautiful dream of complete trust, Johann saw a tender light fall again over the ivory domes and roofs of Vienna.

Doktor Godard was saved. But as he found his way back to the hotel, it was hard not to think of *Götterdämmerung* playing on without him. Johann had never loved Wagner until that hour.

5

WHEN DOKTOR GODARD REACHED THE SACHER HOTEL'S SECOND FLOOR, HE easily impressed the chambermaid into unlocking Dolin's suite. The philosopher would be expected at the Academy at ten the next morning. He was still sitting in the dark at two o'clock, when he heard the wooden floor squeak outside. The lock clicked, and the most stunning beauty in the world came in.

"Johannes?" The singer closed the door and tossed her bundle of roses on the loveseat.

"Were you in voice?" Johann spoke with a husky tenderness.

But at the breaking note in her young philosopher's tone, a displeased look crossed Heidrun's face. Without taking off her silver-wolf furs, she went to the balcony windows. Doktor Godard rose stiffly, feeling sick with awe at the grandeur of his submission. Heidrun's gaze seemed to understand him— only in a different way from the one in which Johann understood himself. His arms and legs were quivering.

"Heidrun, is there a need for us to be proud?"

"You might have considered that in Warsaw," Heidrun answered, by the darkened windows. "How long have you been here?"

"But last night! Heidi, where are you going, what can this rotten fellow Malatesta mean to you?" Words were not enough. Johann needed to hold his love against him, to smother his trembling jealousy.

Still in the fur, the woman circled away as if from a savage animal. "Where I go is not your business."

Heidrun's hurt and pride made Johann adore her even more. But the note of boredom with him, and with his strict morality, was unmistakable.

He halted, blinking under the crystal chandelier.

"You musn't go," he said, and staggered like a man in a strong wind. "I will kill him."

"You are a fool, Johannes." Heidrun faced him from the balcony windows. She clutched the door handle.

The glaring walls had begun to spin, and Doktor Godard thought he might faint. Her stunning words had been spoken by the very being he had allowed closest to his phenomenal sources of light, of truth. The great glaciers cracked and thundered in his mind, and a violent hatred tore free for all that this conceited woman represented. Yet he must not damage their love, not ever!

The philosopher had advanced on Heidrun. They stood frozen face to face, staring at Johann's hands. He had stopped just short of Heidrun's brown neck.

"You could never do it," the woman hissed. "You could not even kill yourself."

The curtains flanking the doors were covered in huge pink roses. With a muffled animal sound, Doktor Godard began banging his head against them. His skull made dull wooden thuds. His legs weakened under him.

"That's not enough"—he could hear Heidrun's laughter—"no, not nearly enough."

She never loved you! a voice was shrieking as Johann tore open the balcony door. Outside was a wintry moonlight chill. Johann's whole body was shaking violently. He was scarcely aware of the voices and dressing gowns on the neighboring balconies.

"Then jump, you fool, jump!" a voice behind him shouted, and Johann steadied himself, gripping the cold iron railing. There was one way to forget what this woman had done. He felt himself climb over.

And that was the last thing Doktor Godard knew, until he woke in the first warm sun with a crushing headache. The woman he loved was smiling childishly, asleep on the lace-trimmed sheets beside him. He could remember none of last night's passions, the things that had been said, or the degrading spectacle of the past months. He felt only a sweet and tender relief. There were still two hours until Johann's lecture. Afterward, he had six days with her.

6

AS DOKTOR GODARD'S TRAIN DREW INTO BERLIN'S "GATEWAY TO THE BLUE Horizon" late on the following Sunday night and he walked home through a drizzle, the air-raid sirens were wailing with an eeriness like giant wolves. A group of arguing Russians hurried past from the direction of the Reichstag.

Johann's neighbors were whispering on his staircase. The philosopher pushed his wet suitcase through the studio door, then he stiffened. Someone was there. A gaunt, bald figure in a cotton dressing-gown very much like his own was watching him from the desk.

"*Ach so*! The hero is back."

"Joachim." Johann smiled. "My dressing gown, Joachim? And Father's pipe too?"

"Yes." Herder laughed. "Your students will miss my impersonation of a learned man."

"What viruses have you been spreading to virgin minds?" Johann inquired uneasily. He hung his coat with the dry side against the wall.

"I argued for the futility of learning and gave you as the example." Joachim rolled his *r*'s with mock pretentiousness. "But didn't you overdo your little escape? The Berlin press. Why, your balcony scene with Dolin makes the war seem passé."

Herder's black pupils were fixed, leering, on Doktor Godard's handsome face. The room was suffocatingly close.

"The newspapers?" Johann's breath came quickly.

"True! Ha-ha, I'd wager your emotions are more famous now that your mind will ever be."

Herder jumped up and paced through the study, puffing blue smoke. There was a crackling of guns from the western suburbs.

"Still"—the man gestured—"I admire your generosity to Malatesta. For me, Hansel, there are limits to what is owed a political ally. But look, here is more news to test your genius on."

Pausing at the balcony doors, Herder pulled the blackout curtains. Then he nudged a letter toward Johann under the lamp. Through the smoke, Johann blinked at the signature—*His Respectability, Chancellor Kohler*—and read on.

Would Herr Doktor J. Godard kindly submit himself for examination by an Extraordinary Tribunal of Five on the twentieth of November. . . .

Slumped under his lamp, Johann lifted stinging eyes to the portrait of his young parents.

"If you are sacked, old friend!"—Joachim was sympathetic—"the Propaganda Ministry will have you at twice the salary. And even higher powers are interested in the celebrated Doktor Godard of *Principiae Rationis*." Doktor Godard had risen instantly at the last words. Staggering slightly, Johann took three steps to the low cabinet with its framed photograph.

The mountainside, on that long lost afternoon before Johann's birth, climbed in hummocks past the boulder on which his parents were seated in their leather shorts. Behind them towered two sheer granite peaks, like gates to the bulging lip of an ancient glacier. Yes, nature had lost none of its beauty. But a new depraved generation walked the earth, and now Doktor Godard belonged to it. In the awful hush of his Berlin studio, there was only the steady drone of approaching bombers.

The philosopher turned dangerously, with the same contorted face Heidrun had recently seen in Vienna.

"The pipe, Joachim, at once!" he said, very softly. "Get out of my dressing gown, out of my study. I erase you."

Joachim lingered confidently to light a cigarette. "Friendship is an over-rated institution. But when you need me—and you certainly will—I can be reached as usual at the Kroll Opera canteen."

7

WELL BEFORE THE APPOINTED HOUR OF HIS APPEARANCE BEFORE THE TRIBUNAL, Johann put on his morning coat and adjusted his spectacles.

He found Francisco and Peter, also in formal dress, waiting downstairs among the blowing leaves. The three set out, turning along Under den Linden in the morning sun, past the netted batteries by the Staatsoper and some gardeners filling in two green-edged craters. As on their afternoon not eleven months ago, Doktor Godard's acolytes affected a contempt for all this— even the smoking rubble of a church. Still, an embarrassment hung over the proceedings.

"This gossip is grotesque." Peter Sachse laughed in disgust. "They will not dismiss the finest logician in Germany over a romantic quarrel."

"You should have gone years ago with the others," Francisco said, waving his cane as they started down the facing promenade.

Such arrogant words frightened the philosopher now, and when he shook his students' hands under the university gates, his smile faltered. Johann could barely wait to lie at the feet of his aged colleagues, who were not men of special vision but who had always shown a loyal interest in him.

Inside the library stacks, the curtainless windows had been piled with sandbags. The voices arguing behind the end door were silenced by Johann's quick knock.

"Come in. Enter, Herr Doktor Godard," called a familiar voice from the Kaiser Wilhelm Institute.

With a forced smile, Johann walked in. The silent faces were turned to his from tables piled with books. Kohler's, impish and freckled, and shaggy old Marquardt's. Then Ackermann's, looking sunken-eyed and tense. (Johann had never answered his letter.) Bukovic the linguist, and Schlemmer the Enlightenment historian. Doktor Godard bowed to each in turn. He was the only one dressed formally.

"Please lock the door, doctor. These days one is never sure," Kohler added. His smile vanished.

"Oh?" Johann bowed. "Of course—at once, at once."

Taking the desk set a little apart, he inhaled the library air, exalted by the fragrance of bindings and ink, the incense of honor, contemplation, and truth. Doktor Godard was safe at last.

"Well, Herr Doktor," Bukovic began, without sitting down. "This is an odd sort of notoriety for a philosopher."

An hour crept by. Johann had begun to feel more and more uncomfortable. If there were so many arguments in defense of his singular intellect, if the noble tradition Doktor Godard represented was so clearly the victim in a conspiracy of evil forces, why had these just elders not yet forgiven him? After all the departures and the Nazis' foolish replacements, the six scholars were among the last of the decent old regime. Then an absolutely horrifying idea came to the philosopher. What if they considered Johann's, too, a Nazi appointment? He thought again of Ackermann's letter. And for the second time that morning, Doktor Godard feared the simplicity of his light.

"We are not an Inquisition or a constitutional court," His Respectability Kohler was saying fifteen minutes later. "As for etiquette, this incident is only newspaper hearsay. The Berlin Faculty has suffered sufficient losses of freedom as it is."

"But we must not be left open to further humiliations," Ackermann repeated, stroking his narrow jaw. The Lutheran was very ugly and had never married.

"Doktor Godard?" broke in Marquardt, who had been examining Johann from the filing cabinets. "May I ask you one sensitive question?"

"Of course, Herr Professor Marquardt," Johann burst out, happy to take part in his judgment.

"Then allow me to ask you this. Do you love the truth?"

"We must live by such beauty . . . what little we know of it," Johann said.

"And as a classical philosopher who has mastered many fields," said His Respectability Kohler, taking up this theme, "could it be said that you have an encyclopedic knowledge of the truth?"

For some reason flushing with shame, Johann glowered down at his tabletop.

Now at last Schlemmer spoke, in a voice that seemed to vibrate in his mustache. "Yes, Doktor, is it not also you who frequents secret astrological societies which erect unprovable cosmologies? And who then, abandoning your duties, follows all over Europe a half-educated older woman of notorious character, if I may say so? And all of this—and scenes, Herr Doktor, scenes— in full public view? Is not this, too, the truth? The other truth? What consequences for students bred before such an altar to the supreme logos?"

The half circle of old heads surrounding Doktor Godard and his crushed and bleeding life nodded. All except little Bukovic, who had been staring thoughtfully at Johann's lowered profile.

"For heaven's sake, Kohler, the man is in love."

"And haven't we all of us, too, been in love?" Ackermann gazed solemnly around at their faces.

The tribunal was entering its third hour. The five academics no longer looked at Doktor Godard. Their hands were nervously gathering their papers in front of them. Johann awaited whatever these good men thought best. But at that instant it occurred to him—what if they had already passed judgment?

As if at a signal, all five professors rose. Doktor Godard remained erect at his desk, until he was quite alone in the room. And even then, he left the library through the basement to avoid facing Sachse and Larreta.

Doktor Godard stumbled, with his tailcoat flapping, towards the hunting forest. It was the hour of his canceled lecture. No, he repeated to himself, this need not affect his work. A flock of sparrows tumbled past like so many brown leaves. Suddenly Doktor Godard felt such terror at the loss of his students and his reputation that his heart took flight to the last earthly resting place for his unnatural light—to a certain warm, soft body. Had it not all been done for her?

In thirty minutes, Doktor Godard had arrived, breathing hard, by the sand-bagged doorway of the Adlon Hotel. He searched the clientele of Romanian, Italian, and Turkish diplomats, Werhmacht generals, and agitated correspondents. With some bystanders, Johann gaped shamelessly into the back seat of a black and yellow limousine. A stunning beauty with mink boas accelerated past at the shoulder of a mustached gentleman—Malatesta and Heidrun!

Bent over, Johann ran alongside the car, oblivious of the staring passers-by. The elegant couple inside scarcely turned.

Then they were gone, and he was pacing quickly along the windy boulevard. Doktor Godard no longer had to beat his head against a wall. Searing images tore his mind like bomb splinters. How could so brilliant a day seem so dark? He glanced in horror at the poor, doomed Berlin faces grimacing inside the café windows. Ahead of Johann on the pavement, other faces seemed to quiver in the dull light.

Yes, Johann had been at the summit of the mind, but he had fallen. The high pastures, where the celebrated Doktor Godard had made his historic reading of Kant's *Critique,* had emptied of him and he of them. Johann was no better now than the thieves and loose women he knew from Herder's clubs. And without his position, how could Johann win Heidrun and have his light back?

Why then should Joachim and the ministry not support his research? Johann thought in a wave of panic, still banging his skull against Heidrun's wall. Was not all this Herder's doing?

From a telephone behind the pastry shelves at Kränzler's, Doktor Godard dialed the ministry number.

"Ha-ha," crackled Joachim's voice, almost at once. "As it happens I am visiting the Wannsee this very afternoon. I'll pick you up in forty minutes."

By the time the philosopher caught sight from the corner kiosk of a blood-red cabriolet wheeling into Unter den Linden, the crushing fear had vanished. The glaciers of knowledge again felt secure in their unnatural light. Just one hour after seeing Heidrun outside the Adlon, Doktor Godard was sitting behind Joachim in a well-polished launch on the Wannsee, running the choppy milk-green water.

8

THE BOAT'S FOREDECK POINTED TO A WOODED ISLAND AT THE CENTER OF THE lake. Once again, Johann was being conducted by Joachim Herder. Only this time it was in broad daylight, and Doktor Godard had no choice.

Under a cold sun, the mist of spray over the sequined waves obscured the shoreline. As Doktor Godard trailed his fingers in the rushing ice water, it seemed a lifetime since he had gone to be judged by the learned men and reeled pitifully through feverish crowds. Now the launch's white-suited sailor commenced a slow curve toward a low pier and two waiting figures. Joachim's face was a black pool among the glittering reflections.

"Joseph will appreciate an educated man . . . he himself was at Heidelberg," Joachim called to him, and for once Johann could detect no sarcasm in his boyhood friend. "Truly this man knows how to make blood boil, to keep a dozen capitals steamed up at one time, and bring masses into the streets with a phrase or two!"

Doktor Godard smiled across the watery spaces, admiring the lake villas. "And the burning of books?" he called back.

"That? He did not mean it. Joseph writes books himself."

Joachim was stretched, his face red, far out over two hissing swans. Clasping a log, he drew the launch slowly against the jetty. He called familiarly to a round-shouldered fellow who had already climbed down with his hands in his pockets. The long face with the dangling cigarette glanced nervously at Doktor Godard and nodded without a word. His companion, still on the pier, was a scarred, bull-necked officer.

"That is Fritsche, our voice on radio," Herder confided, as he led the philosopher up the steep lawn toward a white villa.

Johann's surprise deepened, for Joachim's spite had now utterly gone. In its place was a fawning interest in every detail of the surrounding scene.

"The other fellow was *Gruppenführer* Dietrich, who purified us of the SA perverts."

"Oh?" Johann noticed someone angling through a maze of flower beds to meet them. The man was of Joachim's exact stature, though with an irregularity in his stride.

"Gentlemen, you must forgive me!" cried a musical voice. "It is urgent that I go ashore. We can talk on the boat. My utmost respects, Herr Doktor

Godard." The minister held the philosopher's hand with an animated grin, while Joachim shrugged and bowed with satisfaction. "I read your *Idols of Decline* with very much interest."

Five minutes after their arrival, Goebbels's power launch was running them back. As they crossed the Wannsee into the haze, the three men conversed in low tones. On the windless bows, Fritsche and Dietrich faced ahead like twin figureheads of lies and force, apparently having nothing to say to each other. Reclining on the transom cushions between Godard and Herder, Goebbels crossed his weak leg away from Joachim as if he found him distasteful.

"Herder has informed me of your troubles with the university, Herr Doktor." Doctor Goebbels's face showed deep and sincere concern. "Great minds are often great cowards," he continued, neglecting to add that it was he who had terrorized Germany's distinguished faculties. "I must tell you frankly, my mother thought I would be a priest. *Ja aber*, what I discovered early about your universities is that there are no universals. No universals, you see, *liebe Herr Doktor*, but the reality of power. The modern state is a cathedral of appearances. The mass is the body and must be made blindly to follow the head . . . even when it is none of their business."

"Yes, Fangak"—Herder meant van Gogh—"retells nature, Virgil a legendary battle. Our Joseph tells the building of the German power state—"

"—while it is happening." Goebbels propped himself on the stern deck, which was sunk deep in the launch's wake. He had twisted confidentially away from Herder.

Noticing this, and feeling the freedom generated by all great earthly prestige, Johann experienced a certain pleasure at being respected over his old comrade, who had so often humiliated him.

"Now Germany has swallowed France," Goebbels went on. "Tomorrow we will swallow England, Africa, and America and convert Russia. They will dissolve willingly in our superior culture. Though first I must put them to sleep with a potion of words. Join me, Godard, we are on the side of civilization."

"All I require, Herr Doktor," Johann said, "is a modest state commission so that I may complete my work."

At the lakeside the figure of a photographer could be seen on the pier, holding up a big press camera. Several cars waited under the trees.

"Yes, yes, naturally," Goebbels said, cocking his bony head and apparently unable to calm the rush of his own wisdom. "Well, and in this new truth, my young friend, we can create not only the future but the past. We can bring heroes into being, and make them disappear again—*anyone*. We have the power of truth, dear doctor. Imagine the potential for your own great intellect, so far unexplained and unexploited."

The three men from the launch's stern now made a close group on the grass landing, observed by dozens of waiting staff. The minister held Johann's lapels playfully. The excited photographer busily snapped his shutter. Several engines had started up.

"We could send you our documents weekly, Herr Doktor." Goebbels's cold eyes passed inquiringly over the younger man's reddened face. "By trial and error we will move toward an absolute world policy, *verstehen Sie*? So, Herr Professor—this has been exceptional, extremely fateful. You must meet my wife, eh. We will have a *Bier Abend*. Look, Herder. Is this not a good heroic head, despite the costume of the English don? Do you know Reinhard Heydrich? And Herder, why not take Doktor Godard to see the boss?"

9

THE AUTUMN AFTERNOON BY THE WANNSEE HAD CHILLED. THE BOYHOOD FRIENDS unfolded the car top for the drive back into Berlin.

"Did you hear, Hänslein? Take you to see the Führer!" Herder swung the large steering wheel, and the machine raced ferociously on to the butter-smooth new autobahn. Joachim kept glancing, as if he had never seen him before, at the philosopher reclining on the next seat. "I will arrange that at once. And you must absolutely accept the invitation to Joseph's home. Everyone goes there."

But Doktor Godard was feeling the drowsy tenderness toward life of someone who has done what everyone expects of him. He stared into the virgin depths of the forest through a blur of tossing boughs. All Johann remembered now of this endless day was the nirvana he had experienced in Goebbels's launch, rocked on the hazy expanse of the Wannsee. He had secured the freedom of his life's work.

This time, as Doktor Godard passed into the Adlon lobby, he saw a crowd of ladies and gentlemen turn to the main staircase, politely clapping. Descending the stairs with a faint, languorous smile, Heidrun came toward him.

Only then did Johannes Godard—late of Berlin University—experience a power he had never felt before and scarcely understood. Folding his spectacles, the philosopher crossed under the chandelier and took the woman's hand. It was like his first sight of her at Bayreuth, at the moment when Tristan and Isolde take the love potion and recognize each other.

Within moments they sat down side by side at the singer's reserved dining table, with its crystal and silver and its Polish waiters. Half blind with his own light, so that he scarcely heard Heidrun's teasing interest in his new role beside Europe's most powerful minister, Doktor Godard begged the beautiful woman to marry him.

"Heidrun, I could not live without you," he said. "Will you be my wife?"

And—oh, miracle!—there came from Heidrun's full lips, in that strange and marvelous voice: "Of course I will, my dear boy, if you will live with me on the Tiergarten. There is even an empty study."

So on that same night, Doktor Godard and Heidrun Dolin had exchanged the most sacred vows. But before a Catholic church could be found for Heidrun to marry in, or an answer came from Wildisches-Gladbach to Johann's long letter telling his mother of his engagement and greatly increased wages, Doktor Godard's new position required an overnight journey to Salzburg to meet "the boss." Only five minutes after Herder collected Johann for their dawn drive to Tempelhof airfield, a postman had dropped a small envelope into Herr Doktor J. Godard's box—a box Johann would never open again.

My only son [the letter read],
How am I to begin? I have spent the last two days on my knees beside Pastor Manlius. But even he does not understand. My child, my child—what have you done? How can it be, I asked? To be the one good, honest philosopher, famous in all Europe. Your mother was so full of pride that you did not run away to America like all the cowards. Now, by a single act, to cast such things away. And I, Johannes, who brought you up to fear God and obey the law— I ask you, what have you promised them—they who kidnap men of the church and let retarded children die, who fill the pure air of Creation with a smoke of lies? Yes, Johannes. It is not said, but everyone knows it. And is it this you salute?
I prayed, Johannes. Please let it be that he is stupid. Let it be that I have brought an idiot into the world, who is not responsible for his pranks. Yes, Hansel, they call you a genius. Pray God, let you be a stumbling cretin—no, I cannot say the words. Johann, Johann, do you marry before I have met the young girl? What kind of girl must this Catholic be, your mother asks you. My son, I become sick, sick. I can find no more words—I cannot even read these. I must send such words out of your father's house before they offend God and the angels. But it is not too late. As she writes them, dear child, your mother still loves you. I would love you as a ruined, penniless, crucified woodcutter. But if you do not take back this monstrous decision at once, I must curse you, Hannes, and your father's fathers will curse you. Do you remember? And ye shall cry out on that day because of the king ye shall have chosen you. And the Lord will not hear you on that day. For God's sake, Johannes, send me the news that you have found your senses. I barely remember my own name.

I am your mother.

But Doktor Godard was already in flight—closer to home than his mother knew—to the east of their village on the Alpine frontier.

At noon, just a week after the university tribunal had convened, Johann sat bundled with Joachim Herder in the back seat of an open car. They were winding fast behind motorcycle guards, up the passes that lead from Salzburg through Berchtesgaden. Soon, as the road entered a river gorge, it tightened to one lane between naked, streaming granite walls that generated a living cold—as if here human will had cut deeper and deeper, with an ever sharper chisel, into the ever-varied surface of the eternal mother.

10

"WE ARE NEARLY THERE." HERDER WAVED HIS GLOVED HAND.

"It is terrifying." Doktor Godard searched high above them for the sky, in a sort of trance, his voice lost in the echoing rumble of engines.

Through the time that separated his proposal from his first airplane flight, Johann had been constantly with Heidrun Dolin. Now back on the ground, Doktor Godard's flesh, his entire soul, was irradiated and humming with the force of those hours, shameless as the beasts and sprites on the ceiling of the Le Trèves' dining room. Two days become as one unending feast of earthly love, until the gentle, acutely shy Doktor Godard—at this moment wrapped in a brown tweed coat and trying not to laugh as each Death's Head sentinel they passed snapped violently to attention—felt all-powerful in the ravishment of things. The road and the machines they parked among, the bronze doors and the tunnel that "the boss" had had drilled into the mountain—all these now seemed to Johann the possible signs of a noble and fantastic greatness.

"Yes, papers, please, gentlemen," murmured hard-faced men in black leather coats. "Heil Hitler . . . an excellent day on top. Thank you, *alles in Ordnung.* You have forty minutes."

In a stone grotto by the lift there was more heel-clicking, slapping of black leather, and waving of the stubby, shoulder-strapped guns. But the newly seduced Doktor Godard scarcely noticed the things that once had shocked him outside the Thule. As he and Herder rose in the lift, Johann's ears began to hurt again.

"All things to all men," Herder whispered into one of them. "The reach of his will—" The lift was flooded with almost unbearable sunshine.

The boyhood friends removed their coats in a circular pine and glass pavilion. Three civilians were waiting to ride down, and Herder self-importantly introduced them.

"Rosenberg, Sauckel, and Frick, Herr Doktor Godard. Johann, the *Alte Kämpfer* have been together as long as you and I have."

The three older men exchanged curious, intimate nods with the notorious philosopher, then hurried into the lift.

Emphatic voices were coming from behind a center island of pine columns and cabinets. As he trailed Herder round the windows—even the labrador bumping Johann's legs was the color of pine—naked gray crags encircled them in the glaring blue, like points of a giant's crown. Snow-dusted forests fell far below, the valleys invisible under a quilt of clouds. And just then, turning from this spectacle, beloved to all Germans, Doktor Godard saw his new benefactor.

Hitler had been watching them as he leaned with both uniformed arms on a huge table at the center of the pavilion. A tall, distinguished field marshal advanced past Johann, his jaw clenched over his tight collar. Joachim seemed to wilt—this was the Wehrmacht commander in chief. Completely fearless, and drunk with Heidrun, Doktor Godard went forward to meet the scowling, fatherly figure.

"It is you, Herder." Their host straightened to meet them, apparently still absorbed with the last visitor. "And this is Germany's most accomplished young scholar."

"How do you do—a great honor," Doktor Godard burst out, quite forgetting to address the man by the customary *mein Führer*. In the muffled silence, standing between Joachim and Hitler, Johann felt his face almost in flames.

The table was a giant relief map of all Europe, Russia, and North Africa. The concentrating blue eyes of the undistinguished-looking fellow with the schoolboy forelock were fixed oddly on Johann's smiling face. The man remained so for two seconds with his arms crossed, one finger bent under his nose.

At his first close view of the young philosopher's trusting and happy expression, Hitler's aggravated thoughts of Germany's mechanized armies spread thin over Europe, of inefficient collaborators, stubborn Bolsheviks, and of his future revenges on Molotov and those vermin the Jews—that is, thoughts of a world he hated and which hated him—had momentarily broken off. He experienced a confusion of forgotten and not altogether unpleasant impressions of the freedom and the sweetness of life. Above all, of someone utterly unafraid in Hitler's presence, yet who had no power over him.

For a moment Hitler's unhealthy face brightened with a surrendering warmth. At once remembering his hatred of all scholars, the Führer turned from these impressions of unnatural light to his white plaster model of civilization.

"Heavens, is the Reich already so large?" Herder was saying.

"Good, gentlemen." Their host's toneless voice interrupted. "In a moment we will sit down together for some excellent Indian tea and Sacher torte. You are familiar with the Sacher Hotel in Vienna, Doktor Godard? Yes, you have come at a glorious moment. Listen, they say I have not ended the war. I will tell you why."

Joachim and Johann bent obediently over the glistening table as their host gestured between them. Apart from the vigorous rustle of the man's sleeve and scratching of a worshipful stenographer, there was not a sound in the pavilion. The plaster continents swam before the philosopher's eyes. Could his new patron, the leader of the German people, already know of the balcony scene in

Vienna? Johann wondered, steadying his weight on the coast of Portugal.

It was the first time during that entire week that Doktor Godard had thought of Heidrun's suite at the Sacher, or of her nightmarish taunts. Now, suddenly manifesting a sleek, wolfish satisfaction, the master of the pavilion moved along the plaster coastline with energetic stealth.

"Look, Herr Doktor Godard," he cried. "Soon our soldiers will drink with the peasants of Corinth. Is that not civilization? Is that not Providence, *hein*? Our empire grows with geographic inevitability to command the entire Eurasian land mass. Here, the besieged English bullock eats its mess. While today—look, all along here and here—the Bolsheviks proclaim their friendship. Ha. But there are unpredictable forces at work."

For some ten minutes, as Doktor Godard kept close to Herder and avoided Hitler's fevered glances, the harsh voice beside them gained strength— boasting to the frozen peaks of unpredictable forces as if he could see them before him.

Then the older man halted, his eyes again fixed on Doktor Godard across the little red flags of western Europe, this time with the impersonal intimacy of a cook measuring a fresh stag for the first slice. Herder slowly circled the map.

"So now, Doktor Godard, our tea and cakes, and I will ask your distinguished opinion on lofty subjects." Their host's round cheeks flushed pink. "Like Bonaparte, I too am something of a philosopher—*nicht wahr*, Herder?"

"*Ganz so, mein Führer*," Joachim burst out over Siberia, bowing to them both and apparently having difficulty breathing at this altitude. "If I may say so, bringing a new world into existence."

11

HITLER SAT DOWN FACING THE BOYHOOD FRIENDS, WHO HAD MOVED TO A WINDOW sofa with their backs to the mountain abysses. A plump blond secretary brought tea and rich-looking chocolate cakes. At the sight of these, Johann suddenly felt physically ill—Sacher torte.

He took off his spectacles and wiped perspiration from his forehead. In this pavilion, the few poor ideas that once had impassioned a scholar in his study seemed no more than coins to throw in a fountain. Johann had become conscious, even through the romance of that day, of Hitler's passion for police and guns, and of his having armies here and there about Europe. As Johann began to speak, he experienced a sudden crushing pressure on his head.

The older man leaned back with his legs crossed, examining the red-faced young philosopher slumped under the panorama of mountains. Doktor Godard was at that moment delivering, in a halting, disjointed manner, the visionary speech he had prepared about Gibbon, the rise of Rome from austere martial law, and the failure of the British empire to allow local cultures to earn their sovereignty. Then he began to elaborate a mandarin system for Germany's new empire. In a half century or so, Johann offered weakly, a tolerance of the arts and the global cultivation of ethical standards might be aspired to. His voice failed.

It was true that the man seated across from him had not been able to avoid a violent twitch. *Book fools*, the master of Europe was thinking. This boy had been listening to lullabies while *he* was being gassed. While *he* had been rejected and starving in a Vienna slum, this pedagogue was flattered and fed. Had he, Hitler, not had all such ideas before himself?

"Half a century be damned, doctor!" shouted the Führer, his pleasant jowls expanding upward toward his temples, the lipless mouth now an oval. "There will be no cultivating of a single rose"—a harsh voice rang through the pavilion—"until the bankers and Bolsheviks who thought they could degrade the German race are begging at my feet!"

Quite abruptly, Hitler's cheeks swelled again into a gloating pink roundness. Not a head among the pavilion's desks looked up.

"Now, my dear doctor, let us be truly subtle," Johann's new boss went on thoughtfully. "I have made these unpardonable Bolsheviks allies of the Fatherland. How—how, doctor—might I explain to our *Volk* an invasion of Russia?"

"Well . . . Bonaparte's alliances? The Crusades?" Doktor Godard offered with a tragic shrug, suppressing an urge to weep at the ruin of his week-long bliss, for which he had paid so terribly. Johann was pitifully conscious of Joachim twitching nervously, in the sun to his right, fawning on every word that was spoken.

Hitler glanced at his watch, then bent forward to offer another slice of the partly melted cake, balanced on a silver knife. There were no hairs on his white, wrinkled hand.

"Never mind, Godard." The Fuhrer again was examining the young philosopher's face. "You can tell me next week in Berlin. Yes, look! This serving knife belonged to Frederick of Prussia. But now tell us, why has your friend von Sunda gone to Mexico?"

Johann's heart leapt. And as he sank back on the sofa there came to him a sensation of Hélène's vulnerability, of the drawing together of the continents, and of the extinction of all human feeling. Had Johann somehow brought her into the orbit of this politician, who had just crushed Doktor Godard's glorious happiness with a single phrase?

"I wrote to Baron von Sunda last month," he heard himself say, sitting uncomfortably with the untouched chocolate cake on his lap. "I suggested that he come back and help Germany build its golden age."

"A golden age . . . a golden age," Hitler repeated, slapping his plump thigh.

Without warning, he rose. In utter indifference to both Herder's pitiful worship and Doktor Godard's deepening distress, the master of the pavilion conducted the young men around the panorama of mountain peaks and abysses. "I am delighted when degenerate artists and jealous petty aristocrats run from me," Hitler muttered heavily, as they returned before the electric doors. "But the barons von Sunda are a different matter. Does not Churchill have his lords and ladies round him?"

Noticing a familiar figure behind the opening doors, the Führer instantly forgot Johann and Joachim.

"Und so, Hermann, was noch auf Manchester?"

As they turned back to the pavilion, Doktor Godard had a final fantastic impression of a jovial old woman in a powder-blue uniform standing with the emperor of civilization's hand in both hers. Was this not Göring of the hunting estates and wild balls—only much fatter than when Johann last saw him on the steps of the Berlin Opera? Then the doors whined shut on this apparition framed against the rich blue of the advancing night, pierced here and there by pink granite peaks.

Neither of the friends spoke during the long ride down through the gorges into a drizzly charcoal dusk. But for Doktor Godard the reality of that last hour was already wearing off, and withdrawing with it was the specter of the Sacher Hotel. Now he remembered almost with satisfaction the few words he had left, for all time, in the pavilion of power and violence—like a fresco on wet plaster. Removing his spectacles, scarcely listening as Joachim regained speech after Berchtesgaden with a litany of the boss's godlike powers, Johannes Godard was overcome by a passion to be far from Olympian ideas and once again with the woman he loved.

And so in a mountain terminus above the clouds—in the month of November 1940—the soul of the last solitary endeavor bred in the tradition of Kant and Bach was sold into the service of Adolf Hitler, tyrant over a hundred million human beings.

THE PROPHETS

1

O N THE HOT SEPTEMBER EVENING THAT JUSTIN LOTHAIRE ESCAPED VICHY France, as the overcrowded Algiers steamer listed between the Marseille breakwaters and rumbled across the guns of a light cruiser decked in giant swastikas, he saw Europe through different eyes.

With a silent group under the stern awning, Justin watched the Provençal coast widen out and begin to recede—still innocent of the time when its young men would be chased down its streets and shipped north to the factories of the *Herrenvolk*. Across the deck, the frightened children of the desert—the field workers, porters, and pouf-pouf vendors—were already rolling up in their blankets. Having seen the bitter intelligence of his face, they left Justin the favored stern locker, though without knowing that this quiet man was wanted by German state security and that his name was in every Vichy police station. Presently an old Kabyle detected Justin's resemblance to Ben Kacem and gave him wine and bread.

Night brought sleep to the steamer's passage. A universe away from Johannes Godard and his studio, Justin Lothaire sat wide awake against the stern netting. For the questions came with him. Why had the Comintern allowed Chiang Kai-shek to crush the Communists who took Shanghai? And Barcelona—Justin knew now, beyond any doubt, his friend Figueroa's end. The Moscow-backed Socialists had shouldered aside the very workers who had fought in rags with rusty weapons to win the opening days for the Republic. And what of Stalin's murder of all the folk musicians in Russia? Had that too been necessary? The godless arrogance of the question alone made Justin shudder.

At sunrise, the fellahin found him seated against the net as before. No one spoke to this man, for they had seen his education and knew that thought did not tire his belief.

During that Sunday, two Capronis twice came over low, reappearing with quick purpose out of the immense crawling oblivion of water. Finally, in the oven-hot dusk, the blue haze of the African littoral rose from the sea and closed over the horizon. As the Algiers breakwaters slipped toward them, the steamer steered slowly around a steel tower that protruded from the sea. The tears of an old French shoe salesman at his side told Justin that this was the ruin of France's navy, which the English had taken care to scuttle three months before.

Two gendarmes were at the head of the gangway. Someone had been arrested, but a dozen shouting fellahin crowded round Justin. The Vichy official glanced at his filthy forged papers without touching them. At last the stone quay was underfoot. Justin tried not to run.

Then he was winding up from the harbor, every turn a place of memory. Looking left and right for familiar faces, Justin walked in his tire-tread sandals through the crowded arcades of the *grands boulevards*, carrying his scarred camel bag.

As he passed under the thick arch of the Porte Said, the perfumes of jasmine, mint, and roasting lamb closed upon him. A husky voice carried by violins groaned from a radio shop. His throat tightening, Justin walked in a trance up through the pink sails of the spice market.

2

FINALLY HE WAS IN THE RUE MAHBU, AT THE DOOR OF THE LACE SHOP. HANGING across the front room in the weak light was a tablecloth. Through the lace, Justin could see a drab Frenchwoman in a flowered dress.

She put down her iron. "What do you want?"

Justin stood swaying. This was his mother. The woman's life was on her face. He set down the suitcase.

Jeanne Lothaire had paused halfway to the parted bead curtain. Stooped forward, her head tilting, she looked seriously at this man's high forehead, his strong, sloping shoulders.

"Justin? You, Justin, my son?"

Outside the shop was the constant rippling shout of the medina. Justin heard her voice, and there was a sharp pain in his chest.

"Yes, *Maman . . . Maman*," he said thickly, releasing the beads.

The woman came closer. And then Justin was holding her soft body in his arms. For had he not come to save her too?

"God have mercy," the old woman whispered. "God have mercy, it is my son."

An almost intolerable anguish and bitterness seized Justin. "Yes, *Maman*—yes, I'm home."

They had never before seen each other's feelings. But as if Justin Lothaire had not traveled beyond these bare white walls, the discovery quickly passed. Presently they were again eating boiled lamb and noodles by a paraffin lamp and speaking without pleasure or humor after long silences. Justin stared past his mother's shoulder.

"Have I seen this tablecloth before?"

"It is the Michauds'," his mother said. She looked at him. "Justin, don't you have a wife?"

"She is in Budapest, *Maman*." His voice shook. "*Maman,* I wish to see the photo of my father—tonight."

"Is it true the French newspapers talk of you? *Cela te profite?*"

Had he not sent his mother money? "Like Papa," Justin said, "I am against them there. Also, I have written a book."

"What will you do here? Police have been to the shop."

"Is it not enough that I am back, *Maman?*"

They stared at each other. The old clock beside the cardboard Virgin clicked loudly.

"It is all the same," she said. "It is just the same."

That night, Justin slept again on the roof of the casbah. The shouting and the glow of the bazaar rose around the pillow where he had once lain his head. And he heard, as long ago, the sweetly innocent song of the *nay-hosseiny,* calling its mate. But he could think only of his mother's terrible words: *just the same.* He felt the great loneliness and desolation of all things.

From tonight on, Justin Lothaire's dream of justice belonged to mankind.

3

AT DAWN, JUSTIN PUT ON HIS FRENCH SHIRT AND TROUSERS AND HE WENT TO THE little honey-combed mosque at the top of the casbah.

Leaving his sandals, he waited against a column in the inner cloister and listened to the drone of the morning prayer. When he looked up, Abu Grinda was kneeling in cream robes at the fountain to wash the hands of an ancient beggar. Abu had a beard now. For some minutes, Justin watched the delicate motion of his friend's fingers as they rinsed the withered claws. Then at last the familiar black eyes lifted, and Abu stared at him.

Justin walked forward until they were face-to-face. Without a word, the childhood friends embraced.

"I didn't believe it when they said you would come," Abu whispered into Justin's ear.

"Believe it, my friend, my brother," Justin said.

"Justin, it's dangerous for you here."

"Yes, but for now let us sit. I have a world to tell you."

So again, as when they had been small and the earth immense, Justin and Abu Grinda sat shoulder to shoulder against the base of a tiled arch. And their naked feet, which had trampled the blood of watermelons, warmed in the heat of the desert sun. It was then that Justin heard the impossible. Melanie Grinda had married Michel Michaud.

"It was after we heard that you had married a beautiful Hungarian actress," Abu went on, in a whisper. "Know it, my brother—Melanie waited for you. Michel? He has changed, Justin. He left his family completely and works breaking horses with *père* Grinda at the farm. He asks often after your career. I think that for him your life has been a kind of heroism."

Justin was staring into the courtyard's whirling reflections. He felt Abu's increased religion. . . an ethereal mildness of temper, which Justin did not recognize him in. A hero to Michel Michaud? Justin smiled, remembering the *lycée* beatings.

"Fate works its way through," he said, and his voice broke. "And Melanie—she's happy?"

"She is happy, Justin." Abu looked away. "But she hasn't forgotten that she has been happier.

"My friend, where are your steps going now?" he said presently. "Might the way of the Prophet not open to you? Come and keep the night watch with me."

Justin looked away from Melanie's brother and from the pattering fountain. He had forgotten the raw intensity that he had last felt at Sidi Idriz. Yet hearing the confirmation of his own power, Justin could feel his friend falling behind in the decay of Islam.

"A way has opened to me, Abu," Justin said. "But it's not the one of temples, academies, or tradition."

"In your walk, Justin, I see an Arab. In your eyes, someone possessed. In your voice, an enigma that men will follow."

"If men follow me," Justin said, "then I see before my eyes where I will take them. Justice and truth are cruel mysteries."

After promising Abu he would return at dusk to keep the night watch, Justin pulled on his sandals and went quickly down into the French quarter.

He followed the old path from La Source to the table under the mimosa where he had first waited for Melanie. And as he inflicted upon himself that walk through the sacred places, Justin saw—in a fat storekeeper scolding an Arab assistant and in a group of lawyers at the rear of a bar—the bewildered shadows of his schoolmates. Once they had been brash young heroes of the Mediterranean beaches. Now a new rabble of oblivious young men had forced them into this boredom of the elders' table.

But wrestling with these hardest truths, Justin found in the human movement that lay ahead the strength to despise his own tragedy. After a glass of sweet mint tea in the Carré Mosquée, he went quickly through the heat toward the arranged meeting place. Soon he was shouldering his way between fish stalls. He turned under an arch into the thunder of an arcade—and before he could stop, Justin ran hard against some black robes. In the din of the market many eyes were upon him.

"So, little poet! They said you had returned," cried a familiar voice in the odorous shadows. Hooked yellow teeth flashed; whiteless eyes, sunk in a skull weathered as an old saddle, glittered over Justin's clothes.

"Ibn Moushmun?" Justin whispered. "You were slow to find me, *fellagha*. Your tent may smell sweet but does not teach the enemy ways."

"The enemy ways are the ways of women." Ibn Moushmun completed the code words. "Lothaire, you skin is fat with French foods."

Justin laughed out loud. Turning, arm in arm, they wound slowly toward the Place des Martyrs and crossed the square into the dust-blown heat.

"So, Ibn Moushmun, you are forced to keep your promise."

"Abish asked after the famously enlightened son of Kacem only last week." Ibn Moushmun grinned. "Come, I'll buy us lemonade and talk to you of the mountains."

4

THAT NEXT DAY, AS THE MOON WAS WAXING, JUSTIN LOTHAIRE RODE THE ROOF of a train west along the cost to Oran.

From there they took the *poste* bus inland onto the desert plateau, finally coming to Aïn-Sefra, near the frontier with Morocco.

Justin now wore a black djellaba. On the front seats had been three legionnaires, who sang with great coarseness and did not notice the silence through the bus. Justin and Ibn Moushmun rode at the back without speaking, until they reached the bedouin tents at the edge of the bazaar at Aïn-Sefra. There they spoke French heatedly, on crowded benches set under the market awnings, trading stories and devouring roast lamb and millet that later loosened Justin's stomach. Or perhaps he was sickened by Ibn Moushmun's admiration for the speed and violence of the war in Europe. Nor did Justin like this man's curiosity about Luz. Gradually his hopes focused on Abd-el-Krim— exiled fourteen years now on Réunion—the voice of the revolt and a great *caïd*. Was Krim, like Justin, to return? At Bou Krelala they would find news of the guerrillas.

It was not until they were resting on the third afternoon that Justin found the desert in himself.

"Keep down, little brother! Lie patiently."

They were stretched on a gravel bed beneath a stunted orange tree. With their chins on their hands, they watched a column of mounted legionnaires wind down a riverbed a thousand meters away, trailed by a faintly grunting armored car.

"The year of Krim's surrender your father and I lay at this very place," said Ibn Moushmun. "He slew four of the jackals . . . there."

The sunken eyes indicated a yellow island of boulders, past which the column was filing. Justin's father alive so recently, and with the Moroccans? Suddenly this wasteland seemed to Justin Lothaire as intimate as his own flesh. He was charmed even by this *beled* of the orange tree where they lay, reduced to the scratchings of the humblest creature by so harsh an immensity.

All that day and into the next, they went up steadily through his father's land. And then in the late afternoon, crossing a black desolation too jagged for the airplanes to reconnoiter, after Ibn Moushmun had four times missed the way, the mules carried them between to sheer boulders and Justin saw sheep. All round them under the granite walls were tents. A throng of dogs, shouting children, and tribesmen with carbines followed the two mules through the camp. On raised ground, shadowed by a rock overhang, stood a black tent with red tassels.

A dozen guerrilla leaders feasting in its wide shade, watched the two visitors jump down. Justin's sandals sank ankle deep in burning sand, and a cloud of flies flew against his mouth. Down the rows of faces he met one expressionless stare; a small, red-bearded man in a white linen suit, whose glance had an almost feminine penetration. This man had known the cruelties of Francisco Franco and fought the French generals of Sedan. He had known Justin's father well. The chatter of the throng behind trickled to silence.

"Justin, or is it Kacem?" Allah Abish spoke slowly, in a musical baritone. "Welcome among our people."

"Would that they were mine," Justin said, and he saw several of Abish's company smile.

"So they shall be, God willing. So they shall be." Abish bowed a little, extending his arm.

Letting go the mule's halter, Justin stepped to the back of the tent. Under the haircloth it was cooler. He heard the names of the other men recited.

"So, Justin Lothaire, come sit here beside me," Abish said in good French, resuming his place on the carpet beside a bronze *jidda* of millet and lamb, swimming in fat. "No, there, where I can watch your face. You're like your father, a little heavier perhaps with knowledge. But let us have silence. By bread and salt is peace established."

Justin sat cross-legged at an angle to Abish, feeling acutely ill. A cloud of flies rose in the tent and streamed in the heavy air. Looking out from this shade into the blinding heat, he could scarcely conceive the distant rooms of *Justice*, where this journey had begun.

"My knowledge," Justin answered in Arabic, "is a weight that I can neither eat nor drink. I would give it to anyone who asked for it. For wisdom one comes to one's father's people."

"Listen, all of you!" Abish wiped his lips delicately and rested a hand on Justin's shoulder. "The son of my dead friend is welcome. Listen to him with care. If we face north, we see only the desert of the fellahin. But this great writer looks north, and he fathoms the philosophy of deputies and the science of their engines."

Counting Abish and Ibn Moushmun, more than twenty seated men watched Justin's face. He rested his fingers on the edge of the *jidda*. With the last of his strength, Justin quoted Abd-el-Krim.

"Brothers, the Great Powers are sharpening their knives. It is our turn next. So respect their machines, but never honor them. Despite all the colon's noise and fire, the French and their German masters are now greater slaves even than we. For here there is still the freedom of our father's fathers to be won."

"Eat, Justin." Abish laughed and released Justin's arm. "There is time and more time for such words."

And soon Justin Lothaire learned a strange thing. For it was the horse-breaker Grinda who had always supplied the munitions of the FLN guerrillas.

5

IN THE WINTER OF 1941, AT THE TIME OF HER MISCARRIAGE, LUZ ONCE AGAIN lived in her family's house in Budapest.

One morning, an unsigned love letter fell through the door. The packet had been addressed and counter-addressed. Inside, written with a new devotion, were her husband's last words from Algiers, alluding to a deeper exile in the Sahara. Somehow Luz was forced then to notice what was happening to a world in which it had once been enough to be Luz Holti and at the center of a romantic life.

Luz had found that her childhood friends would not risk being seen with her among their old social circle. Luz was the notorious Holti girl, an actress, and now one who had married—and been abandoned by—a half-caste Algerian troublemaker. Luz told herself that such friends were not worth suffering over. But, after all, they were the only friends she had. So the seasonal balls of her youth came and went, and younger girls were invited to them.

Having observed the alien Bolsheviks only barely overcome Finland, and then witnessed the Nazi humiliation of the French, Hungary and Romania had elected to be satellites to Hitler. In Budapest, the glamour of the chestnut-haired actress in Cetneki Utca quickly become famous among the German officers billeted in households about the town. These young men could not be discouraged from passing on Luz's name, accepting Count Holti's frequent invitations or sending flowers. Nor could Luz any longer avoid seeing them through her husband's eyes. Still, to protect both Justin and her parents, she was afraid to call attention to herself by snubbing her suitors. For a time, she settled on a stuffy old *Generalmajor* as her opera companion.

But she no longer felt comfortable leaving her parents' house, especially so after the sudden return to America of kindly Uncle Leo. It seemed to Luz unimaginable that someone so gentle and harmless as her uncle could be in danger from any living being. Whenever, on an evening at home, Luz thought of her uncle's plump, laughing face and his childish need to play, she would lower her needlepoint. Her expression would grow almost ugly with concentration. Since her retirement from the stage, Luz had painfully missed the bouquets and the tributes of lovesick young man. But there was something in these swaggering Germans that made their enthusiasm seem shameful to Luz, and somehow threatening. Could these be David and Johann's countrymen? The officers' persistence dangerously clouded her memory of Justin. Week by week, Luz was sinking again into depression. She thought often of Hélène in Mexico, leading a quiet life in a valley called Oaxaca, waiting for the Sundas' baby.

What could David's secret work be, for which he had set aside his League of Nations advisorship? Even Hélène seemed not to know. Luz could not avoid a happy feeling that in this there was a sign to her. How much easier to attach her hopes for Europe's resurrection to so uncorrupted a nobility as David's, rather than to believe in the deepening obscurity of her half-Arab husband, now adrift with the grains of sand across a great desert.

PART TWO

From the blood of the slain, from the fat of the mighty, the bow of Jonathan turned not back, and the sword of Saul returned not empty.

—2 SAMUEL 1:22

CLOISTER

1

WHEN DAVID AND HÉLÈNE HAD GONE, GERMANY'S COLONIAL HORDE rolled forth, spreading like sand in an arena across the struggling peoples of Europe. As the Sundas sailed west, the ultimate sacrilege was under way—an overthrow of Christendom. Still this was not yet called war.

Now on a black, fragrant Zapotec night in 1940, one winter and two summers since the Sundas had reached safety among the volcanos of Mexico's southern Sierra, David smoked the last of his cigars, sitting on upper balcony of their walled garden, without any idea where his wife might be, though it was tonight that they must speak. The coming hiatus would not have escaped Hélène. She must know what he would say.

Amid the day's interminable siesta—marooned in this colonial villa that alone in Oaxaca had survived the earthquake of 1931—Baron Sunda fought to subdue doubts that would destroy him if he and Hélène remained. Strange thoughts hurried through his head. For centuries had the Sundas not traveled through civilization, seeming always to reach property that was their own? Were there not palaces in Venice, Alexandria, and Ceylon, even a houseboat in Kashmir? His great-grand-father had penetrated the Sepik River in New Guinea. Yet everything depended on Oberlinden. And now as if Hitler had understood this long before David, there were the Nazi decrees of 1933. Any renegade from the homeland who criticized his leader's actions or refused an order to return faced the confiscation of his property.

Abruptly feverish with guilt before his family, David rose. He groped down the balcony railing. The laughter of the Zapotec girls in the kitchen had long since given way to a din of frogs and cicadas. Hélène had never been out so late. In his suspicions, David was bewitched by the ghosts of other exiles: of Bonaparte, and Leon Trotsky, who had executed the Czar's children and escaped to Mexico, only to be butchered in turn this very autumn. By his silence, did David carry the guilt of crime being enacted nine thousand miles away?

Emerging in the starlight below, he circled on a path round the garden, kept green by a seemingly inexhaustible artesian well. His lifelong sense of authority had left him. As in the experiment of the frog that a student had once reflected on in Erich von Siebenberg's Paris legation, David had waited while the water imperceptibly heated. Now in voluntary exile, his honor was to be boiled alive. With what innocence such evil had crept up—the lease expiring to the rue de Fleurus; his mother's old suitor Evaristo Montoya mentioning an empty provincial villa in Mexico; the unforeseen League of Nations assignment from Bernard Piers. David had been asked to submit legal notes for a time after Hitler, justifying a revival of the Protocols on disarmament. How Noah-like the task had seemed, how superior to the *Nazi Bunds* now recruiting almost everywhere.

But on this moonlit night, as David paced in anguish through the perfume of night-blooming creepers, this simple journey abroad suggested an irredeemable lapse of judgment. He had underestimated how terrible Hitler might be and how long he might survive. David and Hélène were very nearly out of funds. It had already been difficult in Paris to receive currency out of Germany. When they first set eyes on this Moorish garden, Hitler was entering Prague and the League was disgraced. Very soon the remissions from Bernard had broken off. Nor had Hélène—strangely happy working among her new socialist friends from the provincial intelligentsia—asked to be paid for her piano and French lessons to the schoolchildren. By the time David had located social contacts from Milan and Hamburg, living off one another in Cuernavaca, he could not afford to pay the rent on another house. They must endure their worsening marriage in this primitive setting.

Even then, David had not brought himself to abandon his work after their first autumn, when the radio broadcast news that Poland was being overrun. His and Hélène's families were once again in opposing ranks. Finally, this spring, the *Grand Armée* had been humiliated at the hands of a tank commander named Heinz Guderian. On an evening when the Le Trèves' cable had arrived, saying that Jean-Marc was safe, Hélène had seen her husband's icy suffering as he described Heinz Guderian dining at his father's table.

But David's final disgrace had been in his own eyes. It had come in his third draft for the League—an appendix on arbitrating conflicts between the world's theocracies. Here Baron Sunda had discovered himself, like some Dead Sea mystic, setting down ideas for an amalgamated world religion, a composite God!

At the memory, David struggled out of the hammock suspended by the gate and continued down the dark pathway. If they did not leave Mexico at once, they might be forced to beg from Hélène's friends—or worst of all, from the suitor she seemed so enthralled by: a slovenly, radical local muralist called Henri Aguilera, and his motherless daughter.

It was almost four o'clock! Faint with the claustrophobia of impending disintegration, David circled the lotus pool and returned. He sank on a bench facing the iron gate. Yes, tomorrow, he must reread his correspondence. Had there been in it not one plausible trace of a plan to collapse Hitler's regime? Had his brother Friedrich's hero reduced them all to these stupid intrigues? Thinking of Adam von Trott, recalled to Berlin without finding foreign support for a German resistance, he felt a need to be at his friends side. And only then did David submit his full concentration to the question of his position inside a Nazi empire.

What was he to make of his parents' urgent summons? There was Guderian's renewed offer also to be fathomed. If any of the Fleurusians were compromised by their association with *Justice*, one among them would not now be some sort of minister-philosopher in Berlin. Or might there be a veiled command in Johann's story of a Teutonic revival, in which it was David's duty to play a role? After Johann's own invitation to their Paris embassy, had his friends not applauded his disgust for a less sinister collaboration? The sense behind such riddles waited halfway across the earth. Here in this humble town, David lacked the dignity even of the *campesinos* in their cornfields.

Outside the border of bamboo, something stirred. A figure was gliding toward the gate! Rising with new conviction, David almost ran to meet her.

2

"HÉLÈNE. MY GOD! WERE YOU AT THE STUDIO ALL THIS TIME?"

"You're still up," she said. " It's terribly late."

They stood under Montoya's fig tree, David not letting go her tensed little hand. He tried to see Hélène's face. Hearing her coldness, measured somehow against his accusation, David saw his wife in a more sinister light than on the evening long ago in the Le Trève garden when he had been unable to speak, discovering his love for her. What evil spirit had come between them in this impoverished paradise? Had he shown contempt for the affection in which Hélène was held by her teachers and social workers—people Justin would have admired?

"Please," David whispered to her. "Sit with me for ten minutes."

Hélène was confused by his mood. "Something has happened in Paris."

"No, no . . . ah, Hélène! How have we become so unhappy in this place?"

Hélène drew back from him, and David followed her to the hammock. Already, what he must say appeared in a kinder light. Was it necessary to speak to his wife of money?

"It was your idea to stay here in this valley," she said quietly, "I refuse to feel guilt . . . not for the friends I have made here, not for Zoe's birthday. You are never excluded."

Pressed against his wife in the netting, David mastered his hatred for Hélène's irresponsible artist in his de-consecrated church splashed with hotly-painted peasantry. "Have I made things so difficult for you?" he said.

"I have never met people so unselfish. Papa's last letter was right—nowhere have I been happier."

Ignoring their strained murmurs, the cicadas had resumed singing. The delicate starlight fell on Hélène so tenderly that David could scarcely bring himself to go on. They slowly rocked the hammock with their toes.

"Hélène, I have made a decision."

"I will not go with you to Cuernavaca. Those lotus-eating socialites, surrounded by such poverty . . . brrr!"

The hammock had stopped its moving, the chorus of cicadas was still. At his wife's words, David felt overcome by a ruthless hunger for conversation among the highly cultivated. To preserve his powers, he must keep this woman at his side. Thinking of the surrounding town and its insignificant people, David shuddered.

"I'm afraid it's a long journey," he said.

"David, I'm tired. It will be light soon."

"On Unter den Linden it is midday."

"Then you must say it, without help from me."

"This year in Oaxaca is lost. We must go back."

"At *once*?" she cried. "What has happened?"

"I think now we should never have come. Strange as it may seem, I can't protect you here," David told her.

"In Oaxaca . . . protect me from whom? What of back *there*?"

"Why, the family name . . . our interests in Germany. So far, I have not spoken publicly against the regime."

"But you would, wouldn't you?" she said

"In silence there is room for maneuver," David answered. "As a Sunda you will have some immunity."

"David, I know you haven't been treated warmly here. They're a little frightened of you, nothing else."

Surprisingly then, David felt his arm seized with a generous affection that he had almost forgotten in this brilliant woman. Tears came to his eyes. "You think I am taking you away from your artist?" he asked gently.

"Then it must be the letters from Adam."

"I expect to see him." David felt the hammock cords jerk as she rose, and he whispered, "Hélène, tell me now, why have you starved me so?"

Standing over David in the darkness, seeming not to have heard, she continued in compassionate tones. "My love, what I first admired in you, even when we were children . . . was your independence from German vanity, and also from your family."

"Yes, I'm innocent of their crimes," he groaned. "Now I must assume their guilt."

"David," she whispered, taking his bowed head between her fingers, and a familiar impression came to him of his wife's sensitive light-gray eyes, her deeply tanned skin and summer dress. What had he accused her of? "David, my dear, have you truly given up—after such dedication? I know no person of greater courage, but this is the most difficult thing you have had to do. Also, it's just in time, you will see what I mean." Hélène continued. "Believe me, there's no one here, not even Henri, who has not been conscious of this last noble effort—my husband's vigil for the League. David, if they were in this garden, they would applaud you . . . and now you'll have a reason to accept being happy here. You see, I'm almost certainly pregnant."

"What? . . . What are you telling . . . ?" Again, he was trying to see her face. "How can this be?"

"Yes, just that one time. Have you forgotten?"

"Just that one time . . . just that once?" David repeated, searching himself for deeper emotions and thinking instead of his rival. At that moment they both knew David suspected his pregnant wife—she for whom he had given up Luz—of betraying him. "Then Hélène, more than ever we must go back. I won't leave you behind . . . unless I could put you in Duncan's hands."

"A pregnant woman? With our friend in a divorce court?"

"The Atlantic is infested with submarines and mines. I'll have to take you across Russia. . . ."

David concentrated. Then, to dispel the dread of those words, he lurched to his feet. No longer conscious of the hour, he and Hélène started around the garden with its constant note of trickling water.

"In fact, we should leave at once, although I'm afraid we have responsibilities. Fifteen months have slipped away."

"Oh, my poor Sunda," she cried then, "you will die of being civilized."

3

IT HAD BEEN NECESSARY, HOWEVER, TO WAIT UNTIL JANUARY, WHEN A CHILEAN ship bound for Yokohama put in at Tehuantepec. Hélène had four months with her schoolchildren.

The morning after the meeting in the garden, Baron Sunda abandoned his work on the disarmament protocol, and the labyrinths of the absolute state further enmeshed him. His soul very quickly forsook their peaceful cloister, hardening itself to enter a Europe in which enlightenment was being roasted on a pyre of murdered innocents. Even in the brilliant sun of Mexico, things grew dark.

After Adam's return to Berlin, there was no further word from him. In the nights, Göring's air enthusiasts filled England's towns with gales of ashes. Very soon, Italian tanks reunited Fascism with Plato's Sparta. David consigned his trunk of papers to New York and gave himself over to an ugliness without end.

Music accompanied the Sundas on their voyage homeward across the Pacific. Aboard the *Aconcagua*, they ate at the captain's table, and a small lusty orchestra played sambas and tangos until dawn, as if to celebrate a world living at the very limits. On the cabin radio, Hélène picked up operas by Mozart and Puccini, and after a stop in Mazatlán she practiced preludes in the empty lounge. At San Francisco this gave way, as stars slowly spun on the dance-floor ceiling, to a swing band playing Glenn Miller. The *Aconcagua* had taken on only passengers— a number of them discreetly unsociable Japanese—and David explained to Hélène the new American restriction on any trade with Shinto militarists.

Then the ship passed out under the colossus of the Golden Gate and assumed a course west after the setting sun. They were already six weeks behind schedule in David's plan for them. Ahead lay continents that swarmed with armed death. Hélène no longer awoke sick in the morning, but in the face of her husband's bleak absorption she disguised her premonitions. After Honolulu, the Flying Clippers disappeared and it was too cold to swim. The Sundas sat wrapped in blankets on deck chairs, reading and exchanging books as they finished them. Hélène withdrew further into silence. By day, the Pacific horizons were blandly empty. In the nights, the ship's radio sifted Elgar marches from Hong Kong, Slavonic ballads, and Japanese court music. And there was something else.

For the Sun Emperor's advisers, in the years following Hitler's activities in Spain, had marched the Shinto soldiers on a three-thousand-kilometer trek from Manchuria, across China, toward Siam. Somewhere east of the *Aconcagua,* at Nanking, they had just slaughtered a quarter of a million children, women, and men. In the South Pacific, invisible Japanese, English, and American warships sniffed each other's positions and feinted among the archipelagos of paradise. The music now was continually trampled and volleyed by twittering codes and propaganda in a dozen languages—all races struggling for ownership of the truth with the same strident confidence.

After the great harbor of battleships at Yokohama, the Pacific's gray winter swell slackened. It grew colder still. As the island of sacred gardens, starvation, and samurai street gangs fell behind, David and Hélène bundled to the ship's rails with the remaining travelers to watch an iceberg glide by, its green ice as firmly rooted as an island among the waves. Now David was rereading Sun-Tzu, and Hélène, Sappho and Catullus, and they did not exchange them. After Yokohama there was dinner music by a string orchestra of Turks, Chinese, and Lithuanians, playing music-hall airs. The company at the captain's table was a Yale University veteran of the Lincoln Brigade, a Japanese diplomat, and a Swedish munitions dealer. Their wives all liked Hélène.

And then one morning, she and David awoke in the whaling port of Vladivostok, under an amphitheater of onion domes. Moscow was nine days away. They took leave of their new acquaintances and went down the *Aconcagua*'s gangway for the last time.

It was April. Hélène was eight months pregnant, and the Trans-Siberian Express had no berths available for a week. At the local hospital, the doctor shrugged. Perhaps madame should not travel. Hélène insisted with a little laugh that they would continue at least to Moscow, where her brother-in-law might look after them. Hearing that they were Germans, everyone at the Hotel Metropol was gloomily polite. Hélène could not help feeling threatened by the downtrodden cleaning women who sometimes walked in when she was in the bathtub to comment on the height and firmness of the foreign sister's swollen belly and breasts. They shook their heads at Hélène's otherwise undernourished figure.

After so many delays, David's earlier mastery over the racial guilt that had bloomed in his heart was leaving him. He grew morbidly preoccupied with the equally silent misery that he saw on these citizens' faces as he trudged to and fro through the mounds of thawing snow and mud. Once David waited almost a day at the post office for a reply to repeated cables announcing Hélène's condition and addressed to Hitler's embassy in Moscow. He was relieved to have these hours without the evidence before him of the mortal struggle she now faced. The pity and foreboding that he felt at the sight of this Frenchwoman's swollen body—and over the sense that it somehow conveyed to him of an almost alien conception—had merged with the fear and sadness of these people, with Siberia's indifferent skies and its deadened horizons, a sadness terrible, crushing, inexpressible, but one that assuaged the lingering failure of his long absence.

On the fifth day in Vladivostok, something curious took place. Long columns of oversized tanks began to arrive through the main street. Shortly after, as Baron Sunda paced on his circuit—from the Metropol, to the post, to the railway offices—he sensed an abrupt, unanimous chill. It was as if someone somewhere had given a tap marked WARMTH TO GERMANS a twist. David did not mention the impression to his wife, and he was still able to obtain what he needed if he exerted a glacial firmness. He had grown lucidly familiar, though, with a cold face that he took to be a police spy.

In the last day before their train was to leave, the skies were clear. David sat for many hours with Hélène at an empty tea pavilion, playing gin in silence or watching the gray Pacific swell. Sometimes he would stare at her averted face and reflect on the embrace that had brought them to this abyss. He wondered then at another embrace—of a vast, political ignorance that stretched ahead to the Atlantic. What were Hélène's passionate obsessions, or his own now quite different ones—or even the deaths of themselves or their child—beside the barbarism that these Communist throngs continued to endure? David could not find in the blank resignation of a single passerby an answer to what it was the Russians lived by, or what they imagined he might live for.

At last it was five-thirty on the day of their release. As laden as Hélène, David struggled behind her with all their bags along a wall of wooden carriages. The gold plaque on one of these read MOSCOW. His wife turned to him, her face flushed with gratitude. It was too late to repeat what he had just overheard from an Italian traveler. The journey might take as long as two weeks.

"*Chéri,* you took such good care of us," she said without irony.

"In a few days we will be home. Up you go!"

He and his pregnant wife were to have a soft-bunk compartment. While David made three trips down the passage with the luggage, he examined their companions for the ordeal ahead. Near the platform door stood a samovar tended by the carriage's sly *provodnik*, with his Stalin mustache. There was a blond party agent, in his mid-twenties, with a turned-up nose, who paced up and down, flaunting his unbuttoned uniform. A grizzled peasant with a beard and wearing a quilted jacket had commandeered the end of the passage with a pack and his cluster of rifles. There were what might be two Tartar schoolteachers, facing four Red Army officers, one of these a woman; two American missionaries ("This trip used to take a year," the older one was saying) shared a compartment with a massive woman wrapped in shawls. She winked at David and gave a deep laugh. Outside there was high-pitched confusion. Doors banged, and the carriages clanked forward.

In the Sundas' compartment, the temperature rose. David found that the ice-coated window was bolted shut. As he moved again along the carriage, his way was blocked by a well-dressed, scholarly gentleman. Already, this fellow's stare had troubled David. The man had an intelligent face without the slightest trace of human warmth. He nodded, smiling faintly, and in the momentary sunshine David saw a profusion of centimeter-long scars on both his cheeks.

"You are English . . . no, German." The Russian's voice was surprisingly soft and musical.

"In fact, yes, German."

David made a movement to pass. The man seemed not to notice. Their shoulders brushed.

"I am Russian—Ilyushin," he said. "I would enjoy talking to Westerners."

"Please excuse me. Perhaps later on."

The train was already climbing through barren snowfields. A winding road accompanied them with more of the big tanks on it—maneuvers. David turned away. When he returned to their compartment, the old woman with the shawls and coarse hands sat stroking his wife's slender fingers. Hélène's cheeks were drained. Beads of perspiration lined her upper lip.

David almost shouted. "Tell me! What is it?"

His wife rolled her head and stared out through a clear patch in the frosted window. Plowed terraces were dotted with green under a colorless sky.

"That it is hard to imagine there was ever Paris or Oberlinden. Did we really have that life in Mexico?"

"God, not here." David felt momentarily sickened by the thought of Oaxaca. "Is it coming now?"

"Of course not. I thought I might have had a little contraction. It is simply that I am so tired."

And then, it seemed to him astoundingly, Hélène rested her head on his lapel. Holding her awkwardly, he looked around. The opposite cushions were empty. It was for some reason terrifying to have been taken for a romantic couple by these harsh, impersonal Russians. Not far to the north must be Magadan and the slave labor camps. David no longer wished Hélène and himself to be birds of paradise, caught in the slow gears of history.

He, on whom their three lives utterly depended, was at the limit of his strength. Yet that night, to everyone in their carriage, the pregnant woman's husband appeared calm and assured.

4

BY THE NEXT MORNING DAVID HAD BEEN TOLD THAT A NEW STATE DIRECTIVE prohibited the express from stopping at any of the larger Siberian towns— Chita, Irkutsk, and Krasnoyarsk—where there were good hospitals.

For almost that entire day, he managed to avoid Ilyushin, only visiting the samovar or the toilet immediately after his tormentor. In the Russian's familiarity there was something repulsive, perhaps something that could even detect a German traitor. Or perhaps it was David's sense that the man had a shred of degraded refinement about him, as an abandoned house pet will trail a pack of dogs. Or was there something evil about Ilyushin and the fact that— in the Russia of Stalin, and now of Beria—this man was not afraid to be seen talking to a foreigner?

Then, on the second afternoon, when David had almost forgotten the man's name, the scarred expressionless face was suddenly thrust close in front of his. David and the Russian stood outside the Sundas' compartment, clinging to the handrails.

"You Westerners are depressed by our country," the man said genially, as if resuming a past discussion. "But for us Russians there is nothing else . . . nothing but this."

"No, really. It is very picturesque here," answered David in desperation. The warm odor of rotted gums blew round his face. He had the sensation that others in the passage were observing this scene and that he and Hélène were about to lose their privacy. "If you will excuse me."

Yet the Russian remained, lurching back and forth in the passage. "I am going to visit the hospitals in Moscow," he went on. "All these citizens go to Moscow. Only Valery is getting off." He lifted his chin toward the little peasant with the shaggy beard, now dozing against his guns in the *provodnik*'s corner.

Can this person be a doctor? David wondered, and he felt his detachment weaken further. "Perhaps you could tell me, who are these people?"

It was as if David had just sworn friendship for life, so eagerly did the Russian hurry to make himself intimate.

"At the window is an American missionary from Manchuria. These are technicians from Kazan, and that handsome young man in the uniform is Volkovo, also a captain in our NKVD. Interesting case—he is an experiment from an orphanage. And the babushka?" The doctor's stare rested on the old woman in the next compartment, who was adding figures on an abacus. "Anna Mihailovna. She is the head of peasants on a Smolensk collective. Valery is a wolf hunter. He will be getting down after Novosibirsk."

At some point David was able to free himself and weave back to his seat. The iced window had blackened, the compartment lamp shed a dim light. Hélène was asleep on her side, her face pushed against the pillow, lips slightly parted.

David sat smoking a cigar and watched a strand of his wife's hair jerk below her mattress with the violent motion of the train. He did not listen to the muffled singing from a party down the corridor or the rustle of the blizzard against the frosted glass. He was thinking of a sensitive, capricious child long ago, playing with her dog in the eternal safety of the Le Trève garden.

5

THE THREATENING DAYS AND NIGHTS CREPT BY. HOURLY THE TRANS-SIBERIAN Express carried the Sundas deeper across inscrutable wastes toward the uncertainty ahead. And as if Hélène were simply perplexed that the being inside her no longer kicked, she kept up an exuberant discussion of each exotic happening outside the train window: a band of Mongolians on gaily blanketed dromedaries; the spring fair in a village clearing; naked boys on a tethered board, aquaplaning on the swift current of a river. No interesting face, no new race or costume, passed uncommented upon. For Hélène had seen behind her husband's careless gravity. So urgent had become this second charade between them—the artifice now coming from Hélène—that when the train coasted through Novosibirsk on the sixth day, neither of them made any mention that the journey could still be abandoned before Moscow. And indeed, Moscow felt so near that it seemed cruelly unjust when, that same night, Hélène's contractions began.

"*Chéri!* Will it happen now?" she asked. "I am so, so sorry."

"Don't be silly. Why talk like that."

David had awakened in the dark compartment to the sound of a woman's soft moans. Now, under the nightlight, he was kneeling beside her. Hélène sat on the edge of the lower berth in her gown, her arms trembling on his shoulders. All around them, beyond the overheated compartment walls, the Trans-Siberian Express shuddered, jerked, and shook. The rest of the carriage was asleep.

"David, I am very truly sick—" The words broke off in a stifled animal shriek. She gripped the frame of the berth.

"My God, Hélène!" David muttered. "Not here. Not now."

"I'm so, so sorry," she said. "Am I horribly noisy? I wanted everything to go on for years and years."

"Why talk like that, Hélène? You are not going to die!" David heard their voices drowned in the drumming thunder of this medieval continent, the sleeping train.

"I have loved life, even Mother. Yes, I even loved *Maman*."

"No!" David seized her shoulders as if sentenced by Hélène's delirious certainty. "

"Maybe God will protect me . . . it kicked!" Hélène stared at David's face. She started laughing, then again began to pant. Instantly she was silenced by another swift wave. "Oh, God, at least he is alive," she whispered when it was over, without seeing the tears on her husband's cheeks.

The laboring woman's eyes focused far away, no longer seeing David or the compartment but something far more immediate. She moaned, and at that sound—a long whining dirgelike groan unlike any David Sunda had ever heard from a human being—his scalp bristled. As his wife rolled clumsily against the bolster, David lurched up. With a fear, almost a hatred, of her power to make him love her now, he turned and wrenched at the compartment door.

Outside, the dim passage was empty. Two forms lay curled by the samovar. The dripping windows glowed in the moonlight.

"Ilyushin!" David shouted at the row of compartment doors, everything in him still needing to pretend that they were not here, still two thousand kilometers from Moscow, that the Hélène he had always known was not giving birth in this train, on a railway line to Stalin and Hitler. "Damn you, Ilyushin!" And where there had been the insinuating, evil-smelling face he knew as Ilyushin, David now conceived a benevolent eccentric on whom he would happily confer the most secret aspect of his wife's body.

"Ilyushin . . . Ilyushin!"

David's second shout had woken the entire sleeping car. A bald army officer poked his head out, saw the German dressed in silk pajamas stamp his foot, then hurriedly withdrew. There were angry curses behind the neighboring door. Was it possible that none of these people would help them? A massive form with legs like tree stumps had loomed in the dim passage. It swayed towards him, and David recognized the peasant of the shawls, now with a thin braid hanging over her shoulder. The huge woman seemed neither curious nor perturbed. She pushed into the compartment, with a glance at him that all women reserve for the begetters of all motherhood. Three compartments away, Ilyushin's scowling face appeared briefly. Seeing who it was, the man vanished. He reemerged in a torn gray dressing-gown, carrying a bag, and entered their compartment.

Still braced in the dim passage, David tried not to hear the sound coming from the doorway. Something dark and primeval was pressing down on him. The sound was intensely intimate but excluded him completely. She—*it*—was calling to him. He heard his name, followed by a pitiful, insistent groan. Passing his hand over his eyes, David stepped back inside. He stared round the dim compartment.

His wife lay panting on the lower berth, with both knees bent up. The lace-trimmed nightgown was rolled up under her breasts, her navel stretched on a mound of skin. Mihailovna sat firmly by the pregnant woman's hip. Ilyushin was bent over the sheets between Hélène's feet, his wrist between her shaking legs. At his first glance, David saw that she was allowing this, that she was in the grip of an instrument of torture, and that none of these strangers seemed moved by the senseless suffering of the beloved person on the sheets. He experienced a wave of humiliation and despair. They were going to help.

The last contraction released the trembling body on the berth. Hélène's chalk-white face, tangled with wet strands of black hair, lay so still David thought she had died.

"Hélène," he called to her. Pressed against the jolting berth, David reached his fingers toward lips as bleached as the pillow. The lips parted, then stirred in a faint smile.

"Yes, yes," Ilyushin commented. He shouted something in Russian to the faces crowded in the passage.

"David? My love?"

"Hélène." David bent near and tears fell on her cheek. "Don't be afraid, this man is a doctor."

"You won't leave me alone? Stay by me."

"Always," he said. Lifting her hand, he pressed it to his lips.

But already Hélène was drawing away, preparing again for another round of pain. Her breast rose and fell. A drop of perspiration slipped down her temple, gathered other drops, and gained momentum. The berth, the whole compartment, shook violently. The lights flickered, and the train whistle gave a long hoot in the dark night.

Hélène's gaze moved slowly past David, first to Ilyushin and then to the old peasant, whose huge hand rested on her thigh. In that look, which David scarcely recognized, was a trust and love and indifference to her nakedness in front of them. Hélène's eyes met Mihailovna's and stayed fixed on her broad face. The cruel alien noise began again—deeper and even less articulate than before—then the panting. David stretched across the berth and held his wife's rigid, shaking body. Her head rolled on his shoulder, and David saw his watch. It was only one o'clock.

What if she dies? he thought.

And suddenly death was close upon David Sunda. It was this thing that his wife was struggling with! Now, for the first time in death's company, no longer the abstract death of demented police states, David felt himself slipping toward that absence of will which is without pain because it is without hope, almost as if all thought has been no more than a dream of immortality. There was no immortality tonight in this hot, humid compartment deep in Russia. But everything around the barbaric, straining flesh that had once been little Hélène Le Trève was intense and humanly clear with mortal ceremony. And David thought, *If she dies, then I will die.*

6

SOON THE MINUTES WAITING BESIDE HÉLÈNE IN THIS SHAKING COMPARTMENT deepened, became familiar, and lengthened into hours. David saw but did not see Ilyushin timing the contractions, setting out syringes on a towel, and threading a short hooked needle. David saw but did not see, when someone folded away the upper berth, that Hélène's exhausted, struggling face was fully visible between her naked legs to the coarse faces in the compartment door, which also seemed to know better than he the meaning of a woman in labor. He heard but did not hear Ilyushin's laconic commands and the way a pail of steaming water arrived from the samovar. He heard how Volkovo, the boy officer, was sent to use his authority to search the train for a nursing mother and returned, grinning cynically. Once in his fevered imagination David had risen to beat away the stupid gaping faces. But his own arms and legs and his breathing chest stayed bent beside his wife. He only knew that the waters had not yet broken. Her contractions were steadily weaker.

Some time before dawn—as the doctor snored against the bulkhead, as Mihailovna sat between them, humming and mournfully sponging Hélène's stomach and legs, and as the remaining faces in the passage outside were laughing and cursing softly over a card game—the wet, exhausted head against David Sunda's arm gave a low, urgent, horrible shriek, caught back at the end in terror.

"Oh, God! I'm bleeding, I'm bleeding!"

Hélène had risen on her elbows but sank back. Her eyes widened at David with a look mute, reproachful, and pleading, as if for some explanation of so much cruelty. Tearing himself from that look, David stared round wildly and saw Mihailovna's grinning face. Ilyushin was bent over Hélène's legs, passing a towel between them.

"Good. At last she broke, eh?" he said.

"Oh, *chéri*," Hélène whispered in David's ear. "*chéri, tu sais—il arrive.*"

"Good, my love. I'm here," David said, and he could not control the sobs that wrenched his chest. The strange heads were back in the doorway, solemnly curious. Mihailovna cursed and slammed the compartment panel. It sprang open again. Ilyushin leaned forward and showed his long rotted teeth in a yawn. Suddenly David felt his shoulder gripped powerfully.

"Look, you see? There it is!" Ilyushin was drawing David forward across his wife's legs. Between them, David saw something blotted and pink-rimmed with black like the mouth of a large fish. Hélène shrieked; her body was shaking violently. "Look! You see?" Ilyushin repeated. Hooking the fingers of both hands inside her, he was spreading the flesh. And David half saw, buried deep in the fish's throat, what looked like a huge egg matted with black feathers.

Faces were crowded in the compartment door, the head visible to them all. Hélène screamed piercingly; her body rocked and lunged. Catching her shoulders, David saw the look of surprise in her eyes, which seemed to say, Why is this happening to me?

Will it never end? he thought.

"Push! Push!" Ilyushin shouted behind him. And despite Hélène's violation before these people, a wild hope leapt in David's heart. Tears started down his cheeks.

"I can't anymore! I can't!"

"Good . . . good!" the doctor said then, softly. "Is there no leather?"

A moment later, Volkovo's arm came over Mihailovna's shoulders. Now panting again, Hélène set her teeth in the leather of a gun holster. Could the worst still be ahead? David hid his eyes in his hand until the dizziness passed. He wiped his face on the sheet.

Under the night sky the express must be approaching a mountain pass. The rail bed grew still worse. The bunk on which Hélène lay back, haggard and bloodless, began to lurch violently from end to end. She screamed as Ilyushin was nearly thrown to the floor.

"I want to die, please let me die!" Her face contorted. A look of passionate hatred came into Hélène's bruised eyes.

"Valery! Valery!" Ilyushin called in a sharp nasal voice, waving a pair of hooked scissors.

At the compartment door, the bearded hunter grinned imperturbably down at them. The doctor said something very quickly, then repeated it. With a shrug, the little Tartar reached over the door arch. An electric bell rang. For five long seconds, the train trembled and shook. Then the brakes under the compartment began to scream. There were several more violent jerks, the last throwing Mihailovna to the floor.

The train had completely stopped. Out in the passage everyone was shouting at once, except Valery. The wolf hunter had gone back to the samovar. They could hear him kicking open the carriage door with his boot.

"For her there would be trouble," Ilyushin said, bent over Hélène, both his shoulders working at something. "The hunter is permitted to get down; that is permitted." And next to David, Hélène suddenly gave three desperate shrieks and fell back.

Abruptly the crowded compartment was steady and hushed. On the berth, Hélène's wet face lay peacefully to one side. Her breast rose and fell in catching sighs. Now David heard another small voice in the compartment. In the corridor outside, the shouting ceased. The door rattled and banged shut. And then as if wishing to be heard across the continent, the new voice wailed with an astonished and tragic reproach. David stretched over the head buried in the obscurity of the bulkhead. There were emotional whisperings. Glancing around, David saw but did not see Ilyushin's hand rise with pliers, pulling a long thread.

"*Hélène! Hélène, tu entends?* Let me hear your voice." David slurred the words.

Hélène's lips were moving in the shadows. Her words were unclear. "A boy?" she repeated.

But David could not take his eyes from this woman, from his wife, from her white tortured face.

"A boy," Ilyushin's soft, satisfied voice said behind David.

"Ilyushin . . ." David grasped the Russian's arm but could not speak.

"Alaric," Hélène breathed faintly, without opening her eyes. "Alaric." And as if she had only been waiting for that word to release her from her task, Hélène slipped into a deep sleep.

Outside the train, brakes groaned heavily. The Trans-Siberian carriages rolled slowly forward up the frozen tracks. In the compartment, David bent over the berth and began to sob.

7

IT WAS NOT UNTIL THE TRAIN HAD CROSSED THE URALS AND WAS CLICKING toward Gorky and Moscow, and his son was four days old, that David Sunda began to grasp what his wife had just undergone.

The skies were turning sunny and dry, and the ice had disappeared from the compartment window. David could stare away from Hélène over the tremendous blinding horizons of snow and search for the urgency of this journey home as he waited for her to find her strength. For next to such a trauma— and finding them linked forever by a child—it no longer had the slightest significance to David why he had returned or what he might accomplish in Berlin.

For the last time, without shame, he remembered the vision that had kept him in Oaxaca; of a globe covered in drops that continually expand and contract, each culture separated from its neighbors by a delicate membrane. Whenever this globe was shaken, drops would rupture and form larger, clouded drops. Finally, all the drops would have burst and mankind would be as one drop, clouded with all souls, legends, and moral laws. This in turn would be purified, until it was so rich and clear that any soul, anywhere, could learn and be filled by it.

As Moscow came near, the canasta parties resumed. Ilyushin once again grew repulsive with whatever rottenness lurked in his conscience. Volkovo dangerously paraded his blond hair and moist red lips, playing pranks and showing off to attract the German gentleman's attention. The two army officers stopped by less and less often. Even Anna Mihailovna now cared for the baby grudgingly and had stopped singing to him. The intense fraternity of that night seemed to live on only in David. And just as the last of Hélène's girlhood charm had vanished in the barbarity of his son's birth, David's senses, his entire being, gently craved that communal drama. Yet to his shock, as he stared into the Mihailovna's wicker basket at the tiny wrinkled face and shifting blue eyes, David found himself thinking of Luz—alone, abandoned, and childless, somewhere ahead in Fascist Hungary.

On Alaric Sunda's fifth morning, the express stood for two hours in the old station of Gorky. Across the platform, a heavy rain stained the sides of the waiting eastbound train. Stretching his legs among the crowd, David paused to tip his hat and offer a few words in French to a well-dressed family of Warsaw refugees his own age. They were traveling not to Stalin's new city for Jews but on to Peking and Shanghai. He could not prevent himself from speaking of the birth of his baby, Alaric. However, as they heard the old German name, the people's burst of happiness for him broke off. Sobered by this painful riddle, David Sunda climbed back into the carriage.

When he knocked on the compartment door and stepped in, he saw at once that Hélène had recovered. David's heart sank, for what was now between them had come too late. A formal distance must be resumed. It was unthinkable that someone of his wife's wayward tendencies—which after Mexico he could no longer deny—should ever know his intense feelings toward her. For at their worst hour, David had loved and also hated Hélène in ways having nothing do to with the drawing rooms in which they had been brought up—ways to which Baron Sunda was no longer free to succumb.

As Hélène's eyes cleared, her husband was holding her hand. Without appearing to notice the suffering in his smile, she looked first out of the window at the river under a misty rain, then into the basket. She laughed.

"Heavens, my breasts! Where are we, *chéri?*"

"That was Gorky. We reach Moscow this afternoon," David said. He had just brought them across half the planet.

Hélène was gazing down at the tiny pink body. It was this that she had carried alive in her belly all the way from Mexico, these vague upward-staring eyes in which a first spark of curiosity had just stirred. The baby appeared to examine each feature of its mother's face. Then it waved its feet in the air, its lower lip protruded.

"Give him to me. Lock the door," Hélène said. "My God, I am bursting. Look, the bed is soaked!"

David closed the compartment door. In the basket was the soft living bundle. He felt it lift free between his hands. The paneled compartment was cosy with the misty fields outside. Could all this be going on as before, after what had happened to them and to the world?

"Which will he have first?" His wife held the now screaming bundle across her lap. She glanced up at its father immodestly.

David felt himself blush. "Well," he said, "the left seems slightly more mature."

They laughed together, and David Sunda's heart ached. Not knowing what to say, he sat on the berth watching the tiny perfect fingers press the soft skin of his wife's breast, then assume the instinctive kneading motion. *This is my son*, he thought suddenly. And that mysterious word seemed to rise up through his chest and sing through the train end out over this strange land, greater than fear or death. *This is Alaric—this is my son!*

8

IT WAS IN SUCH A STATE OF MIND THAT THE RETURNING BARON VON SUNDA STOOD that afternoon at the compartment window and watched legions of giant factory stacks sail through a sky filled with towering thunderheads: the Third Rome.

Soon the express coasted for the last time along a station platform, under a forest canopy of girders and sunlit red banners. Hélène leaned out of the unbolted window. Georgians, Slavs, Tartars, and Gypsies stared up at the well-dressed Europeans gliding past in the compartment windows.

"Will Friedrich come for us?"

"If he doesn't, it could be troublesome," David said, and he recalled the rumors of purges by a legion of secret police.

In the passage outside, the intimate companions of their long journey pushed and called. Their familiar faces belonged to strangers once again. Stretching, David could see neither the peasant woman nor Ilyushin.

Below the carriage steps, he paused for a group of soldiers and a strong hand fell on his shoulder. Hélène had turned, and a sudden desperate smile lit her face.

"Freddy!" she called in a weak voice. "Dear Freddy!"

Two paces away, among the flowing mob—framed by the monumental head of Lenin on a field of red—was David's brother, every bit the European diplomat with his suit and cane. Even the slack side of Friedrich's smile seemed to add to his eccentric charm. Waiting behind him were an embassy aide and a stiff young Russian in civilian dress.

The brothers embraced with an unaccustomed warmth. Superciliously affectionate, Friedrich turned to Hélène.

"Now what is this about a pregnancy, Hélène? You do not seem—"

Frowning, Friedrich removed one suede glove. He bent over the basket, and David was amazed to see his brother's eyes moisten.

"Surely not on the train?" he burst out. "Was there a doctor?"

Halted in the rough current of peasants, David was searching far down the long platform. For an instant, he had the impression that he had seen Ilyushin's limp figure shuffle into an archway under the face of Stalin.

"This is Alaric. Are you taking us straight to your dacha?" Hélène was chattering a little wildly. "Isn't that what they're called?"

Friedrich looked at David's strained face, blew his nose thoughtfully into a silk handkerchief, and resumed his careless manner.

"*Liebe Kinder*, the romantic journey is not yet over." He started Hélène down the platform. "Your train leaves in two hours. Father wishes you to meet him in Berlin, not necessarily with Hélène."

"Most necessarily with Hélène!" she objected.

"We have enough time for lunch in the station restaurant," Friedrich continued. "So I can explain. You knew that with our allies, the Balkan monarchs, we just overran Greece . . . you see? Now, follow me. Yes, let me carry my nephew. No, no, I will explain."

"Look at this crowd." Friedrich went on in English, speaking in a frivolous tone. "It is not usually like this here. If you had arrived twenty minutes ago, you would have seen Joseph—yes, himself! The boss came to see off the Japanese minister, Matsuoka. This is quite unusual, quite significant. Hélène, you must give me your German passport. Klaus will take it to the consul and have the child's name stamped inside."

As David followed his brother through a billow of metal— scented vapor, he understood that "Joseph" was the Soviet dictator and that Friedrich's Russian companion was noting all they said. Their bodyguard paced behind Klaus's luggage wagon, somewhat ahead of the three Sundas. They crossed a wooden bridge over more tracks. The Russian turned after the aide into a blue-tiled gallery, and for a moment they were out of hearing. Friedrich made a display of halting Hélène to play with the child in the basket, further widening the distance between them and the Russian. He burst out laughing in his airiest tone.

"Listen carefully, you two!" he said. "We—Germany, Hitler, you understand—are about to invade Russia. No, listen! You absolutely must"—Friedrich laughed playfully, to cover the look on David and Hélène's faces— "get out of the country at once! That is a very dangerous state secret. Now laugh, laugh!"

David noticed the chilly young NKVD man start toward them from the restaurant doors. David laughed gaily, and Hélène joined in, despite her flush of panic.

Presently Friedrich's aide left them, carrying Hélène's passport, and she sat between the brothers at a small table in the gallery restaurant. Their guard sat farther along the bench with a glass of beer. The clientele were men in threadbare overcoats, smoking. The bar girls watched Hélène as she stared round the tables.

"*Ils ne s'amusent pas*," she said.

Friedrich laughed cynically. "Perhaps they are ready to be set free."

In David's first shock outside in the station gallery, he had seen before him the thousands of German machines coming like a wall over the gloomy plains. Now the Sundas would have to continue south through Georgia, into Turkey, and from there perhaps embark for Trieste, Vienna, and Berlin. Attack Russia? What would this rampant demagogue think of next? Or was the ambitious power state—which David had spurned since his boyhood and which somehow he must now bring to a reckoning—about to become less controllable than at any time before?

Thus the two hours in Kazan Station passed quickly, their monstrous awareness masked by family gossip. Later, the Sundas could not remember what they had eaten. But at a certain moment as they rose from the table, David became aware of his brother watching their two faces, amused and melancholy, his chin on the gold cane knob.

9

IT WAS 26 APRIL 1941. IN THE DAYS SINCE DAVID AND HÉLÈNE HAD REACHED Vladivostok, Yugoslavia had fallen and the British been driven out of Greece. There had been no point in asking Friedrich the date on which Germany would attack the Soviet Union. It could cost them their lives to know.

The Sundas' Ukrainian express, heading south past Tula through the young wheat fields into the Don basin, and on to the Caucasus, took two more days to reach Rostov. In his wicker basket, little Alaric shrieked all night, and the food David bought on station platforms was the usual beer, kasha, and undefinable meatballs in cumin sauce. Their fellow travelers were soldiers and also Cossacks, whose sheepskins when soaked with rain gave off a suffocating animal smell. And whenever the baby allowed his parents to sleep, the guards came. The passports in David's jacket were black with fingerprints.

All through those hours of their nightmare, and now as their third and even slower Black Sea connection from Krasnodar to Tbilisi clicked along empty beaches—a Côte d'Azur of medieval castle towns, where they saw wild boar playing along the waves—the images moved before Baron Sunda's tired mind of the immense corridors of nature they had crossed and of the big tanks he had seen in the streets of Vladivostok. Despite himself, he felt humbled by the grandioseness of Hitler's plans to open a second front against such a giant.

The Sundas' fourth train, from Tbilisi to Leninakan, ran through the night. The baby let them sleep from two o'clock until five. When David awoke, their compartment was empty and another of their suitcases had disappeared.

At first light, a heavily armed border guard in breeches and high boots woke the foreigners, firmly and with satisfaction. After much gesturing, they understood that the train was not permitted over the Turkish frontier to Kars. They must walk across. Half a day behind his brother's itinerary, David climbed down the carriage steps after Hélène, carrying the baby's basket. Their remaining pieces of luggage were handed down. The train reversed.

They were alone with the guard on the hot stones in a silent pine gorge. Too tired to sit down, David and Hélène stood between the rails. They watched the rusty carriages withdraw like a worm into the pines. Slinging his machine-gun and pushing his cap to the back of his head, the guard started off along the diverging rail line. The wooden sleepers wound off to the right between narrow granite bluffs. Birds twittered, and there was a scent of thyme and sage.

The guard had disappeared behind some rocks. Covering the basket, David lifted the two heavy bags, and they started along the tracks. Had this fellow expected them to follow or not? One could not tell. There were vine-yards now, and the spring morning was turning hot. After twenty minutes the Russian reappeared, stumbling far ahead of them. Then they saw that he had stopped in a shady ravine and sat watching David and Hélène come panting between the tracks, up and down over each sleeper. When the absurd foreign-ers reached him and had sat on their suitcases, the man stood up and saluted. Then without a word he started back in the direction from which they had just come.

"*Alors*," Hélène said brightly. "I suppose I might charm the bandit chief."

David grinned. "Some of the emirs are handsome fellows." It was cold, seated in this ravine. Where were they to go now? Rising, he continued on along the blind curve. Hélène went ahead of him. The baby was crying again. And then quite suddenly at the sight of Mihailovna's basket in Hélène's arms a crushing grief pierced David's chest. With a groan he dropped the suitcases and clenched his fists to his temples. Making a desperate gesture, he looked back.

"David, don't leave us here alone!" Hélène called hoarsely. But her hus-band was already running back into the sunshine, back along the curving rail bed, after the Russian guard. The man was out of sight. The striking of David's soles on the wooden sleepers made a lonely echo off the stone walls. At that moment, the terror of not finding the evil-looking guard seemed to David the most powerful emotion he had known. *How was it possible, how could I have forgotten?* He cursed himself as he ran on. For, seeing the wicker basket, David's numbed imagination had all at once recalled a Trans-Siberian Railway compartment on the night of Hélène's labor. He recalled the doctor Ilyushin, Mihailovna, the faces in the door, then the train stopping, and his son's first cry. And remembering the mysterious continent and the sad, throng-ing Russian cities, David had seen himself as he was this very hour—stealing like a thief from among his child's saviors, carrying a monumental secret with mortal power over millions of their fellow beings.

Running steadily along the curve, David had covered the half kilometer back through the ravine. His view of the rail bed opened out. He stood gasping in the glaring sun. The tracks ahead were empty, and the vineyards on both sides. He had lost his hat.

"*Soldat!*" David shouted, trembling with the immensity of the moment. "*Sol-dat!*"

In the serene and majestic morning, with the snow peaks in the distance, his voice struck a delirious note. No answer came. The silent skies stretched out like absolution. Only then did he remember Hélène, waiting alone with their child on the tracks. A horrible confusion gripped him. Would the guard believe him? Would the Soviets believe the guard? David wheeled round and round, staggering over the rails. Then he was running just as feverishly back into the gorge. Hélène would be naked in a ditch, with Turks on top of her and their baby dashed against a tree. Worse, they might not be there at all.

Ahead of him now was a dark spot in the glaring yellow. Hélène was seated as he had left her on the little pile of suitcases. With her chin on her hands, she watched her husband come stumbling up. She watched his swollen face sadly, for it was the most insane thing that she had seen anyone do. Or was it something even more terrible? Had he run away?

"I wanted to warn them," David said, between panting groans.

He picked up the suitcases. Hélène rose. Lifting the basket and their medical bag, she struggled after him along the shaded ravine. Her breasts must hurt her, David was thinking. But what difference when in a few minutes we shall all be dead or worse? Slowly, one step up, one step down, they were emerging from cool shade into the heat. A breeze scented with mint and pine came to them.

"Oh, David, David," Hélène called to him softly.

She was halted, hugging the basket to her breast. Hearing defeat in his wife's voice, David looked ahead of them. Fifty meters farther along, in a ditch by the rail bed, was a sandbagged machine-gun. Six or seven shirtless, unshaven soldiers were sprawling in the sun. And again David Sunda thought of the Russian guard and what he must do.

"My dear, don't hesitate," he said. "Remember what we are."

David had put down the suitcases, as someone who saw porters in sight. Drawing himself up, he walked forward into the hot sun. One soldier had slowly risen with his machine-gun. David heard excited voices, and a tall fat man in a shantung suit stumbled toward them on the tracks. His cranium glared almost blindingly in the sun.

"Do commissars wear silk suits?" David glanced up for what he thought was the last time at the sky and the muted forests.

"David, he is a Turk."

Now the man was on the tracks twenty paces away. He had a blond moustache and spectacles. His precise, metallic accents vied with the fresh shrieks
coming from the basket.

"*Sie sind der Baron und die Baronin von Sunda zu Saale?*" crackled a
spritely, familiar-sounding voice. "*Ihr Excellenz, gnädige Baronin—grüsslich
Wilkommen*. May I present myself? Hans Auerbach, Reich Consul of
Erzurum. You were expected at midnight. I thought we had lost you."

10

TWO WEEKS LATER, AS THE LAST BRITISH TROOPS EVACUATED CRETE UNDER
heavy bombardment, the Sundas sailed from Istanbul to Greece and from
there on to Trieste.

By then, their longing to breathe again the luminous air of civilized
Europe had grown into a passion. It was strange to stroll once more along the
waterfront of Piraeus, past the fish tavernas where David had long ago danced
and broken glasses during a student summer among the islands. Now there
were weathered Wehrmacht troops patrolling everywhere, and the Greeks
were tense.

On 20 June, the steamer reached Trieste, and with the last of their money
David bought tickets for them on the next train to Berlin. There was little that
could be found out from Oberlinden, and his wife had fiercely opposed any
exclusion from the decisions ahead. Only at sunset, in their clean well-
polished wagon-lit compartment halted alongside the flower-decked Salzburg
Bahnhof, when Baron Sunda leaned out the window to buy a Munich paper,
did he read that on this very dawn Nazi Germany had launched against Soviet
Russia the greatest invasion of all time.

Through their last terrible months, Hélène had not once shown bitterness
toward him or even argued. Yet the only sense David had that they had ever
been together at Oaxaca was in the evidence of the baby, who slept through
the day and was awake all night.

It was not until they crossed the German border and were approaching
Munich that at last Alaric von Sunda waited for dark and then fell into a
deep sleep.

THE ABSOLUTE IDEA

1

I T WAS SUMMER 1941, AND FROM HELVETIC GLACIERS, SILENT AS THE TONGUES of snow giants, ice waters poured down ancient beds. They leapt and roared and became broad rivers: the Rhône, the Danube, and the Rhine. Yet not even the most peaceful farmlands were proof for the natural flow against chemical change or strange new poisons as they entered at its source among the peaks.

Perhaps it was the world's submission that gave the Sundas' homecoming to the monuments and green boulevards of Unter den Linden its flavor of sweetness and dread. The Americas, Africa, and Russia, and also Asia, lay in the shadow of Europe, and all Europe lay in the shadow of the German dictator in his chancellery. After David's obscure defeat in Mexico and the ordeal of Russia, the first taste of so much authority came as a spell cast over his reason.

2

SIX DAYS EARLIER, FRIEDRICH SUNDA HAD QUIETLY FLOWN IN FROM MOSCOW on Ambassador Schulenberg's airplane. Hearing during a brief call to Gustav that the prodigal had reached Trieste, Friedrich reserved rooms for his brother at the Adlon Hotel before he left for East Prussia. On the afternoon that David and the new mother arrived with their baby under the dome of Berlin's Anhalter Bahnhof, the elder Sundas were making the drive from Oberlinden. They would reach the hotel in time for an evening reunion.

In the face of all this forgiveness of him, and after his years in exile, David's homecoming was concentrated to a kind of enchantment. He had wished for this so long. It seemed impossible that he might not have a lifetime to appreciate it. David could not remember tonight why he had frightened his parents with the war plane or why he had gone to study in Paris or left the running of family affairs to his eccentric brother. What had he accomplished to defy a tradition that awoke in him such powerful feelings?

The discomfort of that question—the very one that his father had once asked—distracted David's sense of the ugly questions that could be answered only in Berlin, as the hour approached when his parents would arrive. He could scarcely fathom his wife's aura of mourning as they took their first baths among rooms filled with silks and crystal. At seven-thirty they put on newly pressed evening clothes and rang for the hotel nurse. It was necessary for Hélène to knot her husband's tie, and David took note that she had grown still more lean.

"You are very excited," Hélène observed, in a sad, timid voice.

"It's incredible how much I remember from our trip here when I was fourteen."

"Don't forget, David—even tonight. All this should seem as forbidding to you as it does to me."

He had not seen Hélène in her beige gown since her parents' ball in Paris, when his marriage had seemed all that David had left. Now France was a German colony. She had nothing but himself—and, of course, her place as a Sunda. Just now, even this did not awaken the correct emotion.

"Forgive me, Leni. It's difficult to reject such old sensations. I must have time. Father will know everything that is happening here."

"Ah, Sunda!" she cried bitterly. "This Prussian air is working on your blood." But there was no time to consider her husband's sudden vitality. On the table decked with roses, the telephone was ringing. His parents were in the hotel.

3

TONIGHT WAS THE SECOND IN GERMANY'S INVASION OF RUSSIA. IT WAS IMPOSSIBLE not to know this as she and David were lowered like precious birds in the brasswork elevator past several landings, to emerge in the busy foyer. A restless group of correspondents had gathered by the tobacco kiosk.

"There they are," whispered Hélène, and for a moment she could not walk forward.

The truth that their journey might have ended as finally as it had for David's mother, Maria Pisani—here, a few streets from Hitler—came to Hélène now with a crippling shock. Was she shortly to hear the explanation for what was happening to her? From under a palm tree, Barthold Sunda had risen to meet them. He embraced his son without a word. Hypnotized, Hélène observed her husband as he bent with tenderness to kiss his mother's cheek. The two old people's faces betrayed only kindness.

"Hélène, my dear." Barthold turned to her as if not daring to believe in their safe arrival after such a journey. "You have brought us back our son."

"We have brought you back a grandson," Hélène somehow replied. Faced with these unhurried good manners, she could not smile as her father-in-law's thin lips brushed her forehead.

"We will view our grandson after supper. All this emotion is too much for an old man . . . But how well Hélène speaks German. Motherhood suits you, my dear."

A few moments later, the elder baron was making his usual impressive entrance into the Adlon dining room, with little bows and greetings to a dozen different tables. Twice he stopped by more important guests, one of them the towering ex-minister, Franz Papen—now reduced to ambassador in Ankara. The Judas of German democracy waved to David familiarly, and Hélène saw the man whom she had respected all her youth bow in return. Four waiters hovered near the centermost column to help the Sundas with their chairs and draw napkins across their laps.

"It's a disgrace," the baron commented when they had opened their menus. "And even sandbags in the cloakroom!"

"Yet so much seems just as it was." David glanced from the menu's forgotten poetry of dishes. His gaze lingered on a number of bureaucrats and their tasteless women.

"Nouveau scum and spies!" his father snapped. "You have been away from us, my boy."

"Not tonight, Barthold," David's mother cautioned him. "We have not seen our remarkable daughter since . . . ?"

"Since the wedding at Notre Dame," Hélène offered, and she experienced an excruciating homesickness. Cruelest of all was the short distance that now separated her from her own mother and father.

"I am amazed," Barthold continued more gently, when the waiters had withdrawn. "When you reached Moscow, why did Friedrich not suggest a rest in the legation?"

"What! Can it be that *you* have not been told?" David stared with profound astonishment at the old man propped against a huge column— the famous nobleman who had been christened by Bismarck, friend to Hindenburg and King George—who could be found at the center of every intrigue in half a dozen European cabinets. David's father was turning red, his deep-set eyes watered. He gazed back at his son with an anxiety that sent a chill down David's backbone. Why then had they been invited to Berlin?

"So now that delinquent will betray even Stalin!"

"He has done that already." Hélène reentered the suddenly serious conversation. "Yesterday—at dawn."

"Of course . . . and so, the second front?" The old man tried to laugh, but the piercing coldness was missing from his glance. "A campaign in Russia? Europe will be ruined by it. Yes, yes, I should have guessed! Yesterday one of the Poles asked to stay on, 'even if Russia loses.' I thought the man was mad. Imagine!"

David sank back in his chair. "Poles at Oberlinden? Forced labor?" At once he regretted his tone. His father's face had fallen as if David had slapped him. "No, Father, I did not mean—"

"I know, my boy." The old man shrugged. "It is the poor devils in the factories who are suffering. Their Führer mopped up unemployment with his war industries. Now the war kills off the workers, and he fills their place with foreigners. At least ours petitioned us to stay. You will see for yourself."

"*Ours*, Papa?"

An ugly silence had overcome their table, filled with things that could not be spoken aloud. There was no time for David to reflect that he had always been correct about his family; already tonight he had expected his father to place him at the heart of a movement to collapse the regime. For three seconds, David imagined himself continuing with Hélène to Paris. But had they not just come round the earth?

"Papa," he continued quietly, "it may be some time yet before I can go home."

"Of course." A weary shadow passed over the old man's cheeks. The sun-spotted hands picked at his uneaten terrine. "Maria, we must tell the boy why we have come."

"My dear Hélène, you cannot keep a baby in Berlin if the bombings become serious."

David's mother had addressed her daughter-in-law quite as if she had not noticed the two men return to their old struggle or the young Frenchwoman's distressed pallor. She had spoken almost as if she considered the huge violence being done at that very hour somewhere to the east no more than a crude distraction.

"David, my dear, you have been called up by the General Staff. This time your father was powerless to do better."

The two couples waited in silence while the waiters surrounded them, bearing the reunion roast. His cheeks burning, David looked neither at his father nor at his wife's ashen face.

When they were left alone, the old man bent near. "My boy, they will ask to see you at their offices here. Still, I have channels in Berlin to explore. Whatever you may think of me, I did not live through the last war in order to lose a son in Russia.

"David, are you unwell?"

"Did you hear your father?"

"David?"

"For heaven's sake, child. We wish to stand by you."

David Sunda sat with his head bowed and waited for the mist to clear from his mind. He did not hear the Adlon's stringed orchestra of old men as he aged before his own eyes—the way that only a good man may age, when he has underestimated the array of evil. Before David had even slept in Berlin, these people had identified him. He had been stripped of a lifetime's discretion.

"Barthold, surely this can be dealt with."

David had drawn himself up with icy dignity. "I will deal with it. Tell me, has there been word of Adam Trott?"

His father looked at him. "Why, yes, he has contacted us three times this month."

Only then did David turn to Hélène. And in the suffering of that glance, they both understood that he could no longer ask to be forgiven.

Eventually the two generations rose together from dinner, their faces flushed with so many fateful events and remembered disharmonies. David was able to slip outside through the hotel's revolving doors. He found Gustav in the dim chauffeurs' room, lost in the late Berlin newspapers. His old ally gave David an anxious embrace and made leading allusions to "the crazy times." Minutes later, upstairs by the crib, David saw his son's tiny hand close round the old baron's wiggling forefinger. He heard his mother ask about "that filthy old thing" resting on a chest of drawers—Mihailovna's wicker basket. Then he was alone with Hélène in Hitler's capital.

David Sunda's exile from his family, which had begun in Paris ten years before, was over. It had ended for him at the summit of power, more alone than he had ever felt at Oberlinden.

4

YET IT WAS PLEASANT STILL TO SIP *APFELSAFT* AT SIDEWALK CAFÉS UNDER THE summer lindens as little orchestras played *Weinerblut* for shy maidens in gray suits, while David's father kept his promise and his mother made the rounds with a nurse, showing off their new grandchild to various friends and relatives.

His schedule, however—forced on David by his bland welcome next morning at General Staff headquarters—left him little time to satisfy Hélène's urgent wish for a single sign as to how so harsh a return might lead to worthy action.

Alarm now overcame her at every glimpse of these deceiving boulevards (somehow so like Paris) and of their self-righteous crowds. She felt a longing to move south at once to the pastoral setting she recalled from David's photographs of Oberlinden. In Europe's new capital of magic and violence, Hélène detected the sensation of her old self only once: at a private concert of *Ein Heidenleben* and the Ninth Symphony. In the vivid emotion, hearing such music once again, she had almost forgotten that she was the one Frenchwoman at a reception for the conductor, a friend of David's family. After this shock, Hélène felt as a constant wound that her parents now knew she was in Germany. She could not return to them with her German baby, and they might be compromised by her slightest indiscretion.

During the same hours, as he scented the Prussian air for traces of his purpose, David experienced a subtle shrinkage in the value that he attached to his
life, and therefore to all lives. He was far too easily undermined by the ampli-
fied voices of his countrymen telling him what to think, and by the equally
impertinent posters: FÜHRER, WE THANK YOU! and NATIONAL SOCIALIST ORDER
OR BOLSHEVIK CHAOS! On a Siberian train, David had felt close to an immense
and humble force of human love. Here in this seductive police metropolis, the
daily cruelty of the German race's giant invasion, involving many millions of
human beings across a three-thousand-kilometer front, was hidden from view.
It was as if at its summit the conscience of Christianity had ruptured and was
melting away.

As for David's hunger to play a role, which had brought him halfway
across the planet, he had only Trott—now a lawyer—and Johannes Godard
left to speak to. And each said quite opposite things.

On a Friday fragrant with breezes from a rain-drenched countryside,
David hurried to meet the one person who would have links in any active
opposition. When at last he recognized a handsome figure approaching him,
David had paced by the Spree Canal for half an hour. In the sunshine the
friends gravely shook hands.

"Welcome home to the Third Reich. It has taken me eight letters"

David smiled. "I seem already to be disarmed."

"Yes, I heard. That may prove just the thing."

"And you?"

"A different case. Whatever has happened, it is of utmost importance that
you are here."

"How, *how*, have things reached this stage?" David burst out.

"Now there is a story."

After these few words, he and Trott treated each other with humorous
sympathy, like two patients in a ward. Upstairs in the Law Union, where for
some reason Trott had chosen to meet, was a cool oak-vaulted hall, hung with
stuffed elk heads, arbolets, and carved escutcheons. Soon they were in wall
pews at the deepest corner.

"May I suggest the venison and *Preiselbeeren*?" Adam said, with a somewhat American enthusiasm. One of the lawyer's ancestors had been a
Supreme Court judge. These two half-Germans had last spoken during a
sleigh ride across Budapest.

"Thank you, I have seen the new German's appetite. I could not bear to
look at another menu."

"Is Hélène well? And what of your brother Friedrich?" Trott went on with
an elaborate carelessness. "Is he still grateful to our Führer for the miracle of
the Nordic Renaissance? Usually, one would have to be attentive for wires."

Adam Trott pretended to feel under their tablecloth, as if for gumdrops
left by children.

"So we are alone here?" David smiled sadly toward the pews crowded with arrogant faces. These old men were the pillars of German law, and today was the fifth in the invasion of Russia. His friend's smile had imperceptibly frozen, as with a change of inner climate.

"Yes, see them for yourself!" Trott observed. "Every last one has put his name to antidemocratic legislation. Sunda, you wish to be told what happened here? The reality, for you too, will be like a dream that comes only occasionally during our national sleepwalking. Simply to utter one truth among these cowards is an act of violent revolution. For that privilege, you have come home to us.

"At this hour, our fat little brethren in Paris are destroying the artworks that you loved." David's friend had begun to speak in a monotone, with an almost tender grin. "Many, I think even thousands, of our priests have begun to perish in the penal system. Perhaps you have heard of the slave labor policy? The brutalities to our Jews? We have millions in our territories—if only Nansen were alive! And, my God, those foreign idiots at Évian, washing their hands of refugees. As for our generals in Russia, they have been told to liquidate all commissars without the slightest regard to the Hague Convention. All this to demonstrate the superiority of German culture. Believe me, our superiority will not be forgotten—not for three thousand years! It will eclipse Goethe and Brahms, as Pontius Pilate eclipsed Virgil. And yet all *le programme d'un seul homme.*"

David was finally able to reply. "I need to understand, Adam, how such things are accepted." At the mention of slave labor, tears of rage had come to his eyes—and of shame for his skepticism toward Justin and his circle at *Justice.* For David knew now that he had never quite believed their prophecy of an ultimate crime, to be committed by civilization itself.

"Heavens, man, look around you! These are happy men. In a winter of lies," Trott continued, when he had composed his face in a careless smile, "hail is mistaken for rain and lightning goes unnoticed. Our finest spirits have praised this inquisition. Artists commit suicide if Hitler dislikes their work. I see that I have spoiled your lunch. As I told you, we are so disgraced that nobody abroad can even stomach our dissenters."

"I should have returned long before," David whispered.

"It would have been no different. We are the very few. Though don't misunderstand. More than a dozen significant persons are aware that I have met you."

"Surely this cannot be allowed to continue," David said, clinging as if for redemption to his friend's cynical words. "Why has the man not simply been eliminated? This hydra has only one head."

Suddenly Trott stared ruthlessly into his eyes, David's eyes. "Are you suggesting, baron, the assassination of Germany's elected head of state?"

The blood rushed to David's head.

"You see?" Adam laughed, and he squeezed his stricken friend's arm. "Do you think that you are gifted with criminal genius? Death is not a simple matter. However, listen, our cabinet are excellent and highly placed people, the kind never to be popularly elected. Only one vote will be cast for us— by God or by the Devil. And do not imagine that we are noble heroes. All periods, virtuous or dark, have their traitors; jackals and gazelle carry fleas equally. Napoleon, Alexander, Pericles, Augustus, Genghis Khan, Ivan the Terrible—all of them had willing enemies. In the end, the Russians forgave Ivan, and perhaps many will forgive Stalin. What if one century of chaos-free enlightenment followed a Fascist Reich? Who would fault our tyrant then for a few Poles, priests, and Jews in the beginning?"

The lawyer examined his lunch companion with desolate tenderness. He waved away David's look of shock. "Despite such questions several German constitutional societies are being prepared—Christians who conceive of a European federation that will include Russia. We have found no support abroad. I offered them a chance to snuff a bonfire with a pail of water. Later, they will not stop it by setting half the world on fire. Here you will be called upon. I am often asked, What will Sunda do? What does he think? You are one of our natural leaders."

"I have only to be asked." David bent his head, feeling crushed by the things that were being said. Under these lofty beams there would be high-court prosecutors.

Trott inhaled the bouquet of his wine. "Do not imagine either that we are a secret around the capital. Sometimes Adolf's contempt for us turns to anger. Old Witzleben has just been relieved of his command in the West—though only as an example. From him we were aware of Guderian's interest in you. We have prepared for your entrance to the Army.

"Yes, David," Adam went on, as if to lighten the burden of the oaths that were being administered, "our plottings are not only ignoble, they are impotent. Honor does not even fetch a ransom. Truth has lost its fertility, et cetera, ad nauseam. But listen carefully. If you do end up in an army group center, you might look up my reliable friend Fabian Schlabrendorff, the lawyer . . . and also his friend Claus. And there are others. Please take time to consider. Simply reply, yes—or, equally, no."

So saying, the graceful lawyer burped discreetly. He smiled and nodded to three neighboring judges who had turned before they noticed who it was.

"You are a peasant, Adam." David could not help laughing, and again tears rose to his eyes.

"For these," Trott murmured, "it was my comment on our legitimacy. But for you it is a high Chinese compliment."

5

DAVID LEFT HIS BENEFACTOR ON THE SHADY STEPS OF THE FOREIGN OFFICE. This afternoon there would be no army briefing. He turned his steps toward Greif & Greif, his family's firm of lawyers on the Spreebrücke, directly over the river.

But instead of spending that afternoon settling his confused affairs— above all, the technicalities surrounding his updated commissioning papers— David was forced to excuse himself from the three stuffy old men. These were his first hours alone without Hélène in six months. The rich food that he had eaten only because he was oblivious to it had brought on a liverish feeling. Furthermore, a Baron Sunda had that day conspired to commit high treason.

What if an invisible penal maze of torturers truly existed? In what circles was David's name being circulated, and what was required of him? When he tried to conceive of himself murdering Hitler—somehow David imagined it to be easy—he felt revolted by the act's crudeness. Around him, the Berlin streets seemed to drum with indifference to their fate and to their newly resurrected baron.

A painful hour went by. He had paused by a pond on which he had once sailed a toy boat, when he noticed a crowd forming round him. Venusberg music crackled from loudspeakers on a nearby rooftop, then was replaced by a male voice. In a gloating singsong, the voice began to recite alien names: Slonim, Rovno, Vilnius, Bialystok, Pinsk. During the electrical pauses that followed each Russian city, the whisper of the Berlin afternoon was height- ened to a giddy freshness. David peered round him at the childlike faces as they listened in the sunshine, people who needed to be happy and proud at any price. With all his heart, David wished he might escape the dwindling hours left to him and join in that innocent hope. Perhaps tonight Johann might still offer a less incomprehensibly evil view of Nazi motives.

Hélène had been offered the family establishment for as long as she insisted on remaining with David in the capital. From here they were a ten-minute walk from the cream-white villa on the Tiergarten where Doktor Godard lived with his new wife. The Fleurusians would meet alone the next day.

This was fortunate, as the reunion that night was dominated by the new- comer to their circle. Heidrun had arranged for them to have the center box at the Opera for an unscheduled performance of *Meistersinger*. Dinner in a cellar lined with photographs of opera stars began at ten o'clock and did not end until long after the few British bombers had approached Berlin and been turned back. After the preoccupations of that day, David responded willingly to the redhead's theatrical high spirits.

It had been Hélène—feeling intimidated at the sight of her husband and this frivolous singer showing off to each other, and having sensed the torment in their old friend—who had talked with Johannes all evening about the changes in his life.

6

AT THREE-THIRTY THE FOLLOWING AFTERNOON, WHEN THE STREET BELL RANG, Baron Sunda had still not put his signature on the commissioning documents. By tonight a decision must be taken. Stepping outside, he leaned over the balcony. The remains of a single mysteriously fallen aircraft had already been removed from the church grounds opposite. Johannes reappeared from the cemetery gate.

Downstairs a few moments later the close friend of David's Paris days hurried forward with his old aggressiveness. As they came face-to-face in the sunshine, David glimpsed the misery that Hélène had observed.

"How do you like her?" Johannes slapped the fender of his car, an ivory-colored sports Mercedes. "I am becoming rich—get in for a run. This is Plato." He stroked an agitated Labrador.

Then they were off. Having little interest in what sights they might see, David was content to cool his increasingly fevered thoughts in the rush of wind and the swing of the car down vaguely familiar Berlin streets. He wondered if he played a part in his friend's curiously abject tone. Now Johann was pointing out bomb craters as if they were dueling scars. They slowed for a parade of brown-shirted boys.

"Safe from our women at last! So, how is the noblest of Germans?"

"I thought your patron was Europe's new nobility," David said gently, and again the ivory car accelerated with great violence. On the folding seat, Plato raised his nose so that the wind lifted the jowls from his teeth and his ears fluttered above his head. What if this once trusted friend, who had wished for David's return, already knew of the meeting with Trott? This aimless circling must not continue. There were immense questions to be settled by tonight.

"Yes, at the opera, did you hear?" Johann shouted to him, his profile at that moment distinctly eccentric. "When Hans Sachs sang his famous song— how we must keep alive the ancient roots of the Nordic people, so that if the mother church should falter Germany will stay strong? This is what has happened. It is why in ten years Hitler has possessed civilization! The gods in Valhalla have rebelled!"

David Sunda nodded sympathetically in the hot gale as he watched the cafés and night spots of the Kurfürstendamm flicker past. Would democratic fraternities forever fall to the first race that reclaimed its primitive ego? Holding his straw hat, he turned to the prodigy of reason concentrated behind the steering wheel. The short back-and-sides haircut did not suit Johann.

"What did you think of Heidrun?" Johann went on, as if under compulsion to be the first with a point of view. "She is not the sort of person someone like myself should be married to. Don't you think I'm right?"

David hesitated. How strange that his friend did not notice, as they flew along the boulevards, the attention they were attracting. Strange how the faces stared at them without surprise. What if the celebrated Doktor Godard spent his days cruising the sports car around Berlin, unable to find a way out?

"What do you mean? She is a beautiful, talented woman. You are like fabled lovers."

"Really? Do you think so? That makes me happy."

Never having seen the sensitive scholar so in need of wisdom and affection, David was equally amazed by the ecstasy that now seized him. The sports car began slowly to circle the heavy columns of the Brandenburg Gate, with its billowing blood-red banners. Johann had swiveled to stare up at the bare-breasted charioteer.

"It is a beautiful thing to be of the same splendid blood. Who else could have achieved all this but the race of Hegel and Beethoven? Can you not hear our people sing from the towns and villages—just like the choral movement? *Dah-dah . . . dah-dah . . . dah-dah . . . dah-dah.*"

David smiled back at his friend's tortured face with a mixture of encouragement and grief. Where this afternoon was the touchingly shy Johann of their Paris days, the simple-hearted Johann who had been awed by the slightest affection he received? Had they both utterly lost their way? Ten minutes later, the sports car drew up in a side street by the Bristol Hotel. Through the sudden heat they heard a faint subterranean sound of dance music.

"At last, are we to have tea? Johann, we must talk!"

"Tea, yes, but not only that." Johann's face was red from his singing. "I hinted to you that the supreme power has many times expressed an interest in meeting you. As it happens, the man flew in this morning for a little conference of his armaments chiefs. You will have no other chance."

"Surely, Hitler is not here in Berlin?"

David had turned sideways on the scorching leather seat. There were uniforms under the hotel's porte-cochère. A wave of terror hit him. He struggled to summon his conversation with Adam, to remember a single guiding principle.

"Let me find some shade for Plato. The music makes him hysterical," Johann called from the well-stained lamppost to which he was tying the Labrador. "What with Russia, Hitler is not in town for more than a few hours. Tonight he will go back to East Prussia. And do not mention the business of Hess going mad."

Baron Sunda had steadied himself. "To be perfectly honest, Johann, I don't understand what purpose a meeting can serve. Anyway, I have already eaten quite enough."

"Do you not like *Sahnetorte*, good conversation, and pretty women? Then come along and don't be a snob."

David paused with his hand on the door. For a moment the meaning of that coy and scathing manner was not clear. Then he understood. His old friend had simply not believed that David Sunda might sincerely be indifferent to meeting the conqueror of Europe. David experienced a sudden hot sting of contempt.

The Bristol Hotel had been erected on the site of an underground distillery. At the far end, as they emerged into the huge basement, was a two-story wooden oval decorated with grape clusters. It was the head of an antique vat. Along the upper balcony the tables had been cleared.

In the smoke downstairs a string orchestra was playing the usual Lehar and *Wienerblut* waltzes to an elegant middle-aged crowd. Baron Sunda was led behind Doktor Godard along the balcony to a round table. Back by the street entrance, several tall officers had appeared. A group of animated older men with some women approached quickly along the low arches, unseen by the crowd on the floor below.

7

DAVID AT ONCE RECOGNIZED ONE OF THE GROUP AS HITLER. HIS FIRST impression was of someone his own height, a smug plebian of a type that he had never liked.

As the new arrivals gathered at the table, the politician, who was standing five steps away in a soldier's coat, noticed the philosopher and his guest. With disconcerting warmth the man's eyebrows rose, and David Sunda heard again the gloating tones that over the loudspeakers had recited conquered Russian cities. He felt his legs go weak, and his right palm rose defensively in a salute that he had never made before. There were introductions, and David—hearing himself introduced as Baron David Barthold von Sunda zu Saale—shook and kissed several hands with considerable charm. No one took much notice of him.

When the armaments chiefs were seated, waiters began to serve what looked like a *Gemüseplatte*. Hitler took a chair directly opposite Johann, facing the hall below.

And soon, like someone flailing in a strong current, David was entertaining these people with scenes from his return across Russia. He had quickly distinguished Doktor Todt from Hjalmar Schacht. And there was Goebbels, now engrossed with Johannes. David was about to mention the giant tanks he had seen in Siberia when he became conscious of a rumpled person seated on his right, gazing down over the rail. The hairless face turned to him.

"Baron Sunda?" inquired a cloying voice. "I was interested to hear from Doktor Godard that you would join us."

"Professor Stodel?" David tried to concentrate. "Of the experiments with proteins and heredity?"

"You are well informed. And I was fascinated by your article on systems of global power."

"I was unaware that Swiss journals were available here," David said, trying to remember his argument at the time.

"Ha-ha! You underestimate the prestige of science in the modern state."

Their exchange continued, despite a Wehrmacht officer who had just approached the table and bent next to Hitler's ear. David felt momentarily calmed by the childlike self-confidence of the scientist, a person rewarded since youth for the pure contemplation of theory and natural law. The musicians below were playing "The Gold and Silver Waltz."

"No, I liked that particularly." Stodel reclined on the balustrade with his chin on his hand. "Your argument pushed the idea of legitimate rule to its furthest position; you mark the exact point of the crisis? Ah, but imagine our capacity to master populations through the study of what moves the collective will. Today a thousand dying Christs are insignificant beside the instinct of billions. We can sift and erase entire nations of undesirables, electrify the skies with our commands."

More officers had come and gone through the low arches. In David's head the turbulence intensified.

"What we must do is to recruit the enlightened minds from among our own peoples."

"And liquidate the rest," David offered, once again borne on the powerful current of these peoples' unnatural confidence.

"Exactly so." Stodel concluded with a sad smile. But before David could register alarm, he overheard more fragments from the politician now on his feet beyond the table of tea plates.

"*Meine liebe Kamaraden*, the Bolshevik army that we captured only this morning is one half million in number!"

Above the table's crescent of turned heads, Hitler spoke on, his fingers raised. His eyes had rested on David with an intimate smile.

"Come, dear baron. Come."

Faintly hearing those words, David freed himself with automatic good manners. As he straightened, Hitler grasped his arm and drew him toward an elk's head under a low vault on which pink-breasted nymphs danced around a satyr. David's companion's thin lips were in motion. The blue eyes and deeply furrowed brow were exactly on a level with his own, their noses almost touching. David was conscious of the faces below, lifting to him, of vast crowds in the boulevards of his beloved Paris and across the capitals of east Europe and the ruined cities of Russia—all eyes everywhere lifting to witness him standing here on this balcony. The older man's stare hardened. An icy unnatural vigor seemed to gouge deep into David's being. Angrily shaking off the impression, he covered his confusion with a smile. The spectral temptation had passed between them like two seconds in snow water. The whistling had stopped. David's head was clear.

"Baron Sunda," Hitler began, tilting his huge face and pushing his thumbs into his belt, "we have heard much of your reputation and of your ancient blood." David hung his head, knowing that a display of gratitude was called for. "Classical Europe was threatened," the mouth just in front of his went on in guttural tones, a drop of Hitler's saliva hitting David's chin. "The peasants and commissars loomed over the greatness of the old Teutonic orders. But soon, Herr Baron, we will have the most splendid victory ever seen. Young men of your enlightenment will be the poet knights of our great empire."

"What will you build in the new territories, my Führer?" David inquired, feeling curiously at peace. He wished only to escape this good humor that sought to bend and string him like a bow.

"There is no need whatever to be polite about such people." His companion snorted with rich mirth, pinching his nostrils. "The question is, how will we dominate? Who must be removed?"

"Removed?" David's felt an intensifying need to be away from these words having no meaning other than reality.

"Yes, Baron, purified!"

Something was happening on the floor below. Visible through the balcony rail, people were on their feet.

"These Russian peasant towns are like tree stumps on what will be our richest German pastures. Like stumps they must be uprooted. Moscow, and its bullet-headed masses, I will simply remove. Leningrad I will flood to make a lake. Excuse me, Baron." Releasing David's arm, Hitler stooped under the arch. He who would turn St. Petersburg into a lake leaned on the balustrade in full view of the room below.

Already David had turned and started through the arches along the empty tables. Behind him, and below, the romantic charm of the tea dance was broken by undignified shouts, from which arose a chant.

Victory! . . . Victory! . . . Victory! . . . Hail! . . . Hail!

The oak balcony quaked under David's feet. He walked quickly, feeling eyes on his neck and afraid to look back. In the entrance, the guards saluted with mechanical violence. Then the doors closed, muffling the political noise inside.

When Doktor Godard caught up with him, David was seated on a shady fender, breathing in the evening air. He stroked Plato's head.

"What is this? My friend, are you mad!" Johann's eyes were sunk into a skull on which the muscles stood out like roping. "Think of the insult. It could even be dangerous. Do you imagine that your family name will protect you?"

"Don't be hysterical, Johann. Tell them I had food poisoning."

"I consider this—" Johann began in an ugly voice, drawing back his fist.

"The end of our friendship?" David sadly met his friend's eyes, but he was twitching uncontrollably. "It would be unwise to choose between us. Whether they succeed or fail, these people will destroy everything you know."

"It is the opposite!" Johann shouted. "Germany is to live again!"

It was not for ten minutes after he had watched his friend disappear forever from his life through the hotel's revolving door that David's limbs ceased to shake. He was still perched on Johann's ivory sports car. A youth club of laughing cyclists in white skirts whirred past the hotel entrance. Abruptly he was aware of a guard from the Mercedes watching him attentively. He had stroked the dog rather a long time.

Thirty minutes later, as David Sunda stepped out of the evening heat into the Adlon Hotel, he still felt nauseated—the nausea that comes from losing one of the assumptions on which a view of life is based. Yet at the moment that his fate had come to him, nose-to-nose with the merely human face of evil, David had been for the first time at peace.

Now in the Adlon foyer, groups of restless correspondents stood about as usual, chatting about advances to the east. No one paid attention to him. The old baron's surprised tones over the hotel phone sounded grateful to hear from his son. He would be downstairs in ten minutes.

Trott was still at his offices. As Adam's also quite normal voice came on the telephone, David overcame a wave of dread.

"I was thinking about you. So have you seen for yourself?"

"I just met the fellow. He is rather common—and I was almost arrested for fondling a Labrador!" Their laughter together was a terrible sound. "Should we continue this evening?"

A long silence followed David's rush of conversation. He had spoken to Adam with great warmth, as if needing to ease the wound left by Johannes.

"It would be my privilege," came the reply.

Only when he sat under the corner palm tree in the salon and stared at the chandelier, like a hovering mountain of ice, did David remember his words to Trott about murdering Hitler. And grasping then that Hitler was the very flesh and blood to whom he had one hour ago been speaking—that he had been free to attempt the thing *then* and might at this very minute be in the hands of the state police—David was so shaken that he walked to the men's cloakroom and rinsed his face with cold water.

8

OVER THE MECCA OF BERLIN, THE CLEAR BLUE SKIES HAD COME TO STAY. AFTER the days of shock on having first been told that they had invaded the Soviet Union, an unnatural vitality came over the German people. At last all the stakes were laid. The most exalted game, the blind game of legend, was in play.

And even as they slept in the same bed, tragedy took root between David and Hélène. She now appeared to him poignantly free of the disgraces that had deformed his life beyond recognition. What need was there for her to be poisoned by the responsibilities that were twisting his heart? Were they not already lost to each other?

Several mornings later, as his wife slept, David went out in the shopping district. At the second tailor who catered to officers there were someone's canceled uniforms, with boots that fitted perfectly.This mask was the last simplification left open to him. The boots, uniforms, and long coat were folded in a cardboard box. David carried the box home and locked it in the hall cupboard. As his father had arranged by a single telephone call from Guderian to the OKW head of personnel—and as agreed with Trott—tomorrow Lieutenant von Sunda would report for the last time to Zossen. Today was for Hélène. They both understood how much there was that she had not been told about David's day-long absences. She knew only that he had seen Trott.

The one-legged carriage driver was happy to have clients for the day. Waving a pipe, he bantered about how a bomb had cleared pasture for his sorrel. The spoked rubber wheels ran softly over the cobbles through a forest to the Wannsee.

Later, they ate freshly caught trout on benches by the turquoise water and David began to speak of what their already painful relations might now mean to Hélène. As she listened in silence, he took off his jacket and rowed her slowly along the lakefront gardens. A string of cygnets was bobbing outside an empty boathouse. Inside, chains hung down to the water.

"Look at the tiny swans," she said at last. "Will the pike chase them?"

"Not if they stay by the shore."

"You see? They are like little ducks."

"Hélène, if only you would go to Paris, to your parents. It could be arranged."

She laughed carelessly. "I cannot go because Grandmother has sworn never to allow my German baby in the house. No, I will go to your mother— I will be there when you are done. What do I care now where I am in the world?"

You are my little swan, David had wished to say. But he was too sickened by how much more Hélène had yet to hear and how much more she might have to face. Most excruciating of all was what David was not free to tell her, which she might never know.

Then it was evening, and the carriage took them back into Berlin. They halted on the corner by Kräntzler's. Taking off his slouch hat, the old driver bent down to kiss Hélène's forehead.

"We must be the first couple he has driven in weeks," she said.

David could not answer her. While he ordered champagne, his wife gazed round the busy gallery. There were many young women in feathered hats.

"What more is there?" Hélène slipped her hands under the marble table-top. "I have followed you all that journey here. Or are we still in Oaxaca? Have you made another decision without me?"

"Then I will tell you, Hélène," he began softly. "By Friday night I may be in Brest-Litovsk."

"Brest-Litovsk?" She repeated the unfamiliar name deep in her throat. Her cheeks turned red. "Russia . . . *again*?"

"Yes, Russia," he whispered. "It is settled. Over the weekend I am to join Guderian's tank group."

"*Tank group*! I didn't expect *this*," she said. "Why not another army? Why any army at all?"

"They would take me for a spy," David went on with a shrug, when the waitress had left the table. "Even Johann might; you must be prepared even for that. All armies are vicious, Hélène. It is their job. I am no more German than I am anything else."

"Then don't go, David!" She placed her hands on his open palm. "We will slip into Switzerland."

"Hélène," he said. "Oh, Leni."

"David . . . what about kindness and children, what about right and wrong? Also love. What about love?"

"You are cruel, Hélène," he said quietly, as he measured champagne into each glass. "All Europe is totalitarian. The things you mention have no existence. Love is treason."

"And in your army?" She seized David's hands as if they were his escaping soul. But she had accepted it—what nothing in Hélène could be prepared for—that it was for this war that they had come back. At once the process of Baron Sunda's hardening resumed.

"I cannot live like Justin, as a renegade," David said, speaking more tenderly than he had spoken in his life. "The only institution left on this continent where honorable men still hold any authority is the German army."

"It's Adam, isn't it?" Hélène was frightened. "He has done this to you. What does your father say?"

"Father is happy that I am with my country."

"And Adam?"

"He is happy that I will try and bring it down."

"Bring it down? You have gone mad!" she whispered.

How well, in this crowded room, his wife masked their argument with casual humor. David felt himself losing his fear for Hélène's vulnerability, which until this hour had kept the final decision uncast.

"You wish it to stand?" he whispered. "One hundred thousand priests and freethinkers like Justin, and all sorts of others, are already in prison—enough to make a city."

"Do you think you will save them?" Hélène said, wildly, and her eyes filled with tears of pity. "You and your honorable soldiers? You don't even have a uniform."

"I found two this morning, Leni," David confessed.

For some minutes in their cubicle he and Hélène examined each other in silence.

"Then tonight is our last night," she said finally. For even here, as her marriage consumed her, Hélène needed to believe in its ultimate fertility. "If that is so, *mon coeur*, can we go home? I want to be with you. I don't want to waste any of you. Can you understand that?"

"Yes," David said. "We still have one night left. It will be a long, long night."

"The longest night that has ever been known. And now shall we leave here? I don't want any of these people even looking at us."

EMPIRE

1

I N BARON SUNDA'S ABSENCE, A FORMER CORPORAL AND STREET ARTIST HAD
gone about the business of his empire—that is, of exporting coarse
bureaucrats by violence and importing contraband and slave labor. In
somewhat more than a year, Hitler's dominion had expanded over territory
equal to that of the Caesars. By 1941 he could reduce his activities in the west
merely to night-bombing the island throne of the English, who after nine
centuries had as yet submitted to no one. In the east, enraged by his friend
Mussolini's insufficiently brutal campaign, Hitler had himself overrun the
Yugoslavian tribes in just three weeks of April and now was goading
Churchill's army out of Greece.

Then, at a quarter past four on the morning of 22 June—as the train that
bore the sleeping Sundas back to Berlin climbed into the Tyrol—three and one
half million adult (and not so adult) German, Austrian, Italian, Hungarian,
Spanish, and Romanian men swarmed across Russia's three-thousand-
kilometer European frontier. As at Sedan, under fierce air cover, these hordes
diverged in three immense armies on to the far vaster desolation of the
steppes: General von Leeb advancing toward Leningrad in the north;
Rundstedt south toward Kiev; and, at the head of von Bock's Army Group
Center, Guderian's tanks, rolling up the Smolensk road toward Moscow, seat
of all the Russias.

As they experienced for the first time the violence manufactured by this
most efficient assault in the earth's history, there immediately spread through
the three million men of Marshals Voroshilov, Budenny, and Timoshenko
(whose 24,000 tanks outnumbered the invader's by three to one) that confusion and paralysis which is the mind's submission when it is forced to contemplate its own extinction.

On that fine summer morning, these two great tides of complete strangers
broke against each other. And they were like a wave breaking through all
along a dike—or like gangs of ignorant boys scrapping over a fence on which
to scrawl obscenities, for whom it is not enough to capture sections of fence
but their chiefs must erase and rewrite the obscenities as well. So it was that

ideological gangs of SS followed behind the German army to erase and rewrite the minds of fresh captives with Fascist obscenities. At the same time, falling back behind the terrorized Russian divisions, squads of NKVD still fresh from the great purges held flagging defenders at gunpoint or executed anyone capable of dissent in towns shortly to fall captive.

From that dawn, along the dusty roads, in the marshes and the drab wooden towns from Riga to Odessa, under the horizonless windy skies of Minsk, Orel, Smolensk, Vitebsk, Bryansk, and a thousand provincial towns, quite ordinary, devout, and law-abiding people considered it their pride and duty to commit crimes so pitiless and on such a scale that no constitution, no Vatican or courts—not even, it would seem, God himself—could ever again confidently pass judgment or punish or restore the reign of conscience and human decency.

Across sixteen hundred kilometers of peasant farms, mothers, children and old men lifted their eyes helplessly to the smoking expanses of the western horizon. A mute and pitiful animal terror and human prayer rose up—as when in a lonely forest one hears the cry of a predatory beast—until the dusty summer winds seemed to be filled with voices, and the leaves rattled in the trees.

2

So it was at Zossen airfield late one morning in the summer of 1941 that David and Hélène left one another.

Unable to look back, he crossed the grass and climbed into a transport already crowded with uniformed men. It had taken him only days to meet the dictator of Europe, plot his fall, and join history's most ruthless army. Now Baron Sunda would travel where there is no speaking of it, into the wide, darkening horizons of death.

Alone at the fence, Hélène stood for a long time with her eyes shaded to the east. Soon the machine that carried her childhood friend had become a black dot low on the skyline, trailed by two glittering specks. Then she could not see it anymore.

Three of the staff officers who made that jolting flight with Lieutenant von Sunda—Flicke, von Niel, and Alberich—continued with him in a second trimotor for the short evening flight to Brest. David had with him a briefcase filled with manuals and with the excellent Russian maps of the Smolensk area. The officers faced each other in tense pairs, belted to the fuselage. Major Alberich, traveling to inspect a captured Soviet KV, was a wizened, quick-tempered tank specialist whose only human interest was in lives justified by the performance of their function units. Beside him sat Adjutant Flicke, who was athletic and good-looking. Visible to them all was the boy's longing for heroic suffering—to experience and inflict great pain and die in battle before his commander's eyes. Just now, Flicke was pea-green with airsickness.

David exchanged smiles with his neighbor, General von Niel. Manhood was the general's passion, and he automatically loved any man he met simply for sharing it with him. He tolerated no inhibitions in manliness. On David's left, strapped rigid to the jolting panel, was an icily aloof liaison officer with dueling scars. After two friendly fighter aircraft appeared under their wings, von Niel unbelted to peer at the dimming landscape below.

They were approaching the theater of war. In the early dusk, the transport's low windows commanded a fine view of the Polish countryside. Tonight, for some reason, these typical army types did not bore David. Was it because now he was an adult among his people or because of his link with circles that were morally immune? Or was it simply that since the crusades Sundas had gone like this to war? David had begun to grasp Hitler's interest in him.

Von Niel was apparently feeling on the most intimate terms with Lieutenant Sunda's uniform and he took no notice of its wearer's agitation. It was an effort for David not to think of Hélène, alone at Zossen, or the question of whether this very Junker had flown with the Condor squadrons to bomb Spanish peasants. He concentrated on the great unknown animal suffering of Russia, ahead in the deepening night. This David was to see alone.

"We had it easier at Sedan," the general shouted, looking into David's eyes. "You remember . . . out-of-date tactics? But these Reds are no pacifist *poulets*, not at all *poulets*. This will be some little squabble. You saw Sedan, eh?"

"I was out of Europe," David shouted back. "Are they predicting that Moscow will collapse?"

The older man looked at him. David's voice had sounded small and lonely in his own ears. From now on, only the party line. As he gazed far below without hearing his companion's voice, the green-piled forest mat ended in a ragged line. A paler green patchwork of farmlands began, stained with cloud shadows. David made out an unbroken progression of little black beetles stretching east into the murk: support convoys. A sensation came to him, grown familiar since he had first tried on this uniform: a grief and heightening of the senses peculiar to images associated with violent death. Now, among so many uniforms, his own had lost its power.

"They say we surprised them!" von Niel was shouting. "How could we have surprised them? If, as they say, Joe was really going to attack, eh? And we cannot keep surprising the commissars all nine hundred kilometers to Moscow!" The old Saxon laughed good-naturedly, showing a double scar that dented his forehead. "Whether we rush them strong enough—*ja?*—and whether we can pincer out a few million of their fellows. We must clean them out by August, that is all."

David looked down. A large blunt hand was holding out a pack of cigarettes. He took one with a polite nod and felt the force of fraternity draw at his heart. Through several seconds of panic and shame, David could not remember the reason for his presence here.

At his shoulder, von Niel fell silent, and David instantly missed the human contact. The roar of motors closed around the flanks of hard faces. Almost at once the buckles along the shadowy pink compartment jingled violently. The floor tilted, and they began a steep droning descent. Flicke was being sick into a canvas sack.

In its desolation, David's spirit struggled to grasp what lay ahead and on either side for hundreds of kilometers. Tightening the shoulder harness, he concentrated his reason on the tactics by which their field marshals were to bite away whole armies. He fought to rehearse Lee's campaigns—a theme during the term of staff training that his father had extracted in exchange for Paris. Instead, there rose before him the faces beside whom David had experienced his own son's birth. Where were Ilyushin and Mihailovna and the tough, pleasant soldiers at this hour?

3

THE CAPTURED AIRFIELD AT BREST-LITOVSK, ON THE EAST BANK OF THE RIVER Bug, was swarming with David's countrymen. A long file of spotted-gray fighters stood noses up in the last light, waiting to be refueled. As he jumped to the hard grass, the evening air carried the sound of happy shouts and the thrilling scent of cordite and black powder. It was a German factory. Along the perimeter lay squadrons of twisted Russian fighters.

David paused at the gate to let through a swaggering crowd of airmen in leather jackets. A hook-nosed driver advanced from an open field car to meet the new arrivals.

"*Oberst* von Geyer . . . Lieutenant von Sunda?" the man shouted. "Adler, sirs, Army Group Two."

David's traveling companion with the dueling scars glanced at him curiously. Flicke strutted forward, though his face was still pale.

"General Guderian," the driver boasted, "is already two hundred and fifty kilometers from here, with the Eighteenth Division! You will overtake him tomorrow at Minsk."

"Minsk?" broke in von Niel, who had joined the group by the field car. "That is halfway to Smolensk."

"Yes, and Smolensk is two-thirds of the way to Moscow," observed Colonel von Geyer with a faint sneer. His horse face turned back to the sunset and the pillar of black smoke rising from the city's famous fortress. Clearly audible now was the *punk, punk* of artillery.

General von Niel bowed stiffly to David and his companions. "Why not be my guests at the artillery barrage? I can guarantee that you will see the fortress fall before the sun goes down."

In two staff cars, the party rushed quickly through boarded-up back streets. The gun positions were behind the Brest Hotel and overlooked the rooftops of the captured town. But Baron Sunda was not seen to enjoy the evening's entertainment—that is, observing the deafening barrage of the picturesque fortress walls at a range of 1,100 meters by the .88s on the rail embankment. What sort of men were fighting to the death to hold a position already almost three hundred kilometers behind enemy lines? What sort of men had given them such orders?

The Hanoverian battery commander, Egbert, was as delighted as a music conductor to show off for his guests behind the embankment wall. Egbert was in love with the satisfying breech locks and optics on his cannon. He was enraptured by the suffocated crash of the powder and the drumming of each shell through the chasm of evening air and the inevitable dusty blow on the murky ramparts.

Finally Egbert put six shells consecutively through a breach at the top of the wall.

"Hurrah!" shouted his agile young gunners. "Hurrah!"

4

BY THE FOLLOWING MORNING, WHEN LIEUTENANT SUNDA LEFT BREST ON THE Minsk road, the fortress had surrendered. The beautiful weather had passed on. It was as if he had been at war all his life. Soon David began to see large numbers of Russian soldiers. Most of these were alive.

A dirt road stretched over the untended green fields, decorated only by telephone poles and lined with the convoys that David had heard grinding past all through the night. The three pairs of telephone wires rose and dipped over the heads of scattered peasants, who stared at the officers without emotion.

Oberst von Geyer had emerged from the Brest Hotel in a clean uniform and greeted his colleagues energetically. He had been seated ever since with his bootlegs crossed in the manner of someone prepared to enjoy a spectacle. But after five hours, during which their car had bounced at violent speeds through the billows of dust from the endless convoys—turning neither right nor left, and with nothing to see but German men hurrying into the drab and motionless immensity—the horse face leaned toward David with disgust.

"Ugh, what poverty. What ugliness, what primitive swine."

"It is certainly not the Tyrol," David said.

"We must hope their soldiers are not hard like their land," the driver, Kurt, shouted back to them. "The Ivans take no pleasure in life!"

"It is like going back to the dark ages." Von Geyer grimaced. "But, my God, our corps are beautifully efficient."

Across the seat, David nodded gravely. More and more smoke was visible along the horizon ahead. Was all this minutely orchestrated misery and destruction the work of that confident Prussian gentleman whom he remembered so well from a banquet at Oberlinden? David could remember his own idealistic words on that evening long ago.

The field car had just now entered a devastation of cratered streets and charred cabins. This would be Baranovichi. A wall of black smoke towered over the parked armor and the groups of oil-stained tank drivers. Some weeping peasant women momentarily filled the road, and David turned to see behind a nest of sandbags. There was a mountainous heap of what appeared to be rags and white melons.

He faced forward quickly, unable to control the heave of his lungs. Neither Flicke, Geyer, nor the driver took any notice. It was as if his colleagues too were keeping a secret that David must join in. Feeling the unbearable grief that lay around them, David was drawn to the other men despite himself.

They took late lunch in a crowded mess hall at Stolbtsy, and Baron Sunda noticed again how the other officers quickly formed groups around him. Then they climbed back into the car and continued east, and the colonel grew animated with technical comments on the detail of the German movement. Sometimes they passed a blown-out tank or a long column of stocky Russian soldiers—their faces either curious or sullen—straggling below the road, trailed by an armored car. Then followed more sad expanses and burned log villages. As they entered their tenth hour on that terrible road, now approaching the front at Minsk, the impression intensified of the alienness of the land and the closeness of the enemy. To David, everything seemed to confirm that the Soviet regime faced an early collapse and that his own circle might quickly go into motion. Yet what if they were held here for months while this rout continued?

It was late afternoon when they reached the devastated capital of Belorussia. The sky was now almost black. As they parked in the cathedral square with its two-story yellow houses, David caught sight of several half-tracks parked along a front porch. A motorcycle regiment was jeering six tank men in shorts as they struggled, like nurses trying to dress an immense child, to stretch a tread onto the driving wheels of a short-barrel tank. The driver, Kurt, ran back to their car in an agitated state.

"General Guderian has been fired upon by tanks!"

"Presumably he is well?" von Geyer retorted.

David narrowed his eyes against the flying grit and stamped his boots to drive out the trembling of his legs. Appalled and moved, he listened to his mother tongue as it was shouted back and forth in the square of this Russian city.

A group of German officers had appeared on the porch, led by a coldly handsome general with a mustache and cheerful step. The man saluted an officer who was even shorter than himself, with a laconic face and drooping nose. David recognized Hoth, known to his men as the "poison dwarf." Noticing the three officers by the field car, the first general came towards them.

Brushing his sleeves, von Geyer stiffened. Adjutant Flicke's arm shot up, his entire body seeming to arch. With a welcoming smile, the famous tank leader stepped past them, gripped David's hand, and drew him aside. Watched hungrily by thirty men, they stood alone under one of the oaks by some motorcycles.

"My dear boy." Guderian spoke softly, and his foxy eyes crinkled. "I am overjoyed that you've come so quickly. Eight years, is it? You look cold—ah, but you'll get used to things. Look, that is Hermann Hoth. Tell me, how is your father? I was so glad to hear from him. And did they teach you the mysteries of our maps? Yes, they are truly ghastly."

From the instant that David had seen Guderian's well-bred, detached person, the depression of the last days lifted. Even the sickening images of the long drive to the front vanished magically. In the company of this man, he would see the Russian peoples freed from Stalin. Then together they would return and save Berlin and, finally, all Europe.

General Guderian blew his nose, laughed, and gestured. Beyond the smoke-blown onion domes, there was a view of tossing yellow wheat.

"Out there are half a million Russians," Guderian said, pointing. "From there to there, between Hoth's Third Group and ours behind. Imagine, my dear fellow. We have joined columns. They are like fish in a net. Even so, they fight like madmen. Their leaders send their men against us without battle orders. A nasty business, to say nothing of our tank pistons. Dust everywhere, we are in Texas. If this continues, in three weeks we will be in Moscow."

David's heart leapt at the words. For the first time since putting on his uniform he spoke with complete sincerity.

"And then, sir? What will come then?"

His father's old friend looked into David's face with an expression that seemed to say, As a young nobleman whom I respect, you may ask. But do not expect an answer.

"We will discuss that at dinner, dear boy. My new headquarters is at the Radziwill Castle, in Nesvizh. The villagers will give us a thanksgiving celebration tonight for their liberation. And so, welcome. I will anticipate many fine talks."

The tank leader drew David aside as a truck convoy started past. Then, apparently forgetting him, Guderian took five brisk steps into the current of diesel smoke. Over the grinding of gears and the distant thud of the guns, a chanting could be heard.

"Fast Heinz! Fast Heinz! Fast Heinz!" the men cried.

The little Prussian laughed and waved his hand. At once twenty arms were stretched down the flank to touch it. For a moment, in the dust spun up by the tires, Guderian appeared to be wading in a cloud.

It had begun to rain heavily. But all along the column, the sight of their commander filled the men with the belief that theirs was beyond all doubt the

406 J A M E S   T H A C K A R A

one great cause. That the soil of Eurasia was being cleansed by the blood they spilled and that this German who led them was as great, and as inevitable, as any Alexander, Caesar, or Bonaparte.

And this belief was more precious to them than their own lives or than any other thing on earth. Across the great fields of burning Russian wheat, the rain was turning to a downpour.

5

SO BEGAN FOR DAVID EVENTS THAT HE COULD NOT HAVE FORESEEN, AS THEIR like had never been seen before.

On 28 June, Guderian and Hoth's tank columns met at Minsk, three hundred kilometers from Brest. They found the city partly ruined, on orders of Stalin. Despite attempts to break out with cavalry charges and then by armored train, a third of a million men from Marshal Timoshenko's armies were thus "freed" and became the property of the Nazi bureaucracy for eastern policy. The wide Dnieper was bridged on 10 July; in one pocket three Russian divisions were found to have shot their NKVD handlers and surrendered. Two days later, Lieutenant Sunda was with Guderian at Smolensk, when three hundred thousand more Russians were encircled, disarmed, and left behind to starve in barbed-wire encampments. Through August, the campaign bore David south, like a man swept upon a mighty torrent as it breaks its dikes, someone who has flung himself in after an innocent child and who himself at once begins to drown. On and on he was carried, across five hundred kilometers of rainy swamps and thick fir forests. In late September, he was with the tank columns as Guderian combined with von Kleist and a further two-thirds of a million soldiers of Budenny's 5th Army were enslaved on the soil of their fathers.

As October came, still with a little contact from the conspirators, David Sunda was back with Guderian's staff on the Smolensk road—beloved of the balladiers and down which Stendhal had passed with Napoleon's *Grande Armée*—now only two hundred kilometers from Moscow, when another six hundred thousand Russian sons and fathers were disarmed, eventually to be slaughtered or starved.

The roads, the rail lines, and the telegraph wires that connected the provinces of Belorussia had been destroyed by Kesselring's bombers. In a hundred regions, the underlying social membrane, barely healed from the Civil War, was disrupted and torn. The few pitifully urgent messages to reach the Kremlin found no one who would dare to believe them. So, week after week in wave after wave, whole populations of young Russians marched blindly on to be torn by German fire or to fall back on the guns of police squads. The Moscow-to-Leningrad railway was cut. The mighty Volga had been bridged.

Through the weeks of summer, the warlords over massed souls had listened to that terrible urgent whispering. At last, in the hour of humanity's disaster, Churchill declared his support to Stalin. Immediately Stalin, who was Hitler's betrayed ally, dispatched to England a list of Russia's needs. Thenceforth, the three were allied: Churchill, who had subtle shrewdness but lacked production; Roosevelt, who had production but lacked public opinion; and Stalin, who had butchered thirty million of his more gifted countrymen but now wished them to save what was left of his state. And when the English reply came, as the whispering grew louder in all their ears, to say that none of the Russian needs could be supplied, Stalin's reply was "no regrets and no reproaches." It was said that when Churchill was told those words, he wept.

With Guderian at Vyaszma, David Sunda had it before his own eyes—the moral ruin of his people.

The bulk of Russia's western army had been devastated. In October, at Borodino, even the fresh Siberian divisions equipped with the powerful tanks that David had seen in Vladivostok failed to cripple the advance. The road to Moscow lay open. It was known that the Russian generals Konev, Yeremenko, Zhukov, and Vassilevsky—all of them old Romanov soldiers—had paid the dictator grim visits in the Kremlin. The preserved corpse of Lenin was being shipped to safety in its glass case. The industrial boulevards of the eastern suburbs were blocked with a chaos of carts, horses, and trucks bearing panicked refugees. In the mud of Moscow's Ykhna approaches, thousands of the city's women had begun to dig giant tank trenches.

Yet since August the Russian defense had seemed mysteriously to harden. There were delays, and these delays originated from a single mind in which Siegfried's "hi-ho!"'s and the flutes of the Rhine maidens had dimmed to silence. Then, on the morning of 6 October, the first wet flakes of snow settled on the gold domes of Saint Basil's cathedral.

6

AS THE NAZI FLOOD BORE DAVID ON, ONE DAY OF HIS HIDDEN DROWNING FOLLOWED the next in the curious outdoor life of men at war. No longer did he deny to himself that his new associates on Guderian's staff might be exhilarated to pit themselves against the enemy's will or be fascinated by the sight of any destruction or terror that they could cause. Yet because the late arrival's effectiveness had been quickly accepted among his fellow officers, there was now a distinguished conspirator against Hitler on the 2d Army staff during the Moscow offensive.

At the same time, it was necessary to care for these men and to work beside them to the peak of his powers. In this way, a Fleurusian witnessed the spectacle of captive armies and burning cities and was at the feast of life and death in the company of military men whose conversation was often of Tacitus, or Rimsky-Korsakov, or of literary manners.

General Guderian's first enthusiasm for Lieutenant Sunda at Minsk now seemed to have been based on no more than a great name. At the vaguest suggestion from his aide that an hour for mortal decisions might soon come, his father's old friend briskly changed the subject. David might have discovered Guderian's inflexibility as a premonition of his own derangement. He might, after such warnings, have condemned himself as an idiot had there not been before him the atrocious sufferings that each dawn brought the people of the Russian countryside. And before any strategy could be pursued, David heard rumors that he did not know how to accept.

Only days before at the town of Borisov, deep behind Guderian's own lines, there had been a festival of police to honor Himmler's quarter of a million blackshirts. To test their limitless powers—so the rumor went—a drunken anti-Semite gang had herded together seven thousand unarmed men, women and children, forced them to dig a forest trench and then, naked, to climb into it in order to be shot.

That Baron Sunda no longer had difficulty attaching reality to such intelligence—so much more evil than anything that Adam Trott had shocked him with—suggested that somewhere David had accepted his inevitable degradation in the ranks of soldiery. After a first long night, struggling for the sense of his life, he had experienced a most exalted gratitude to hear that there had been violent scenes at Center Army headquarters. Could it be credited that Field Marshal—Bock that master of *Kadavergehorsam*—had been approached by the chief of staff, General Tresckow, to make a decisive move against Hitler? In Berlin, David had been directed by a voice over a telephone to await just such an episode. Yet what kind of conspirators were these—to have allowed Bock to flee the conference room?

With detached cynicism, David's first ally, the uniformed lawyer Fabian Schlabrendorff, had described precisely the detail of these events. He at last managed to see Trott's friend in the art-nouveau smoking lounge of a Smolensk mansion.

Seated in a threadbare armchair, David heard that Bock's own two aides were counted among the conspirators.

"Dear fellow, you must learn to wait," Schlabrendorff had advised.

David had watched Schlabrendorff remove his spectacles, which did nothing to diminish the polished innocence of his gaze. Learn to wait? Had he not waited all his years in Paris and Mexico? Now they were to wait, not hours but day after day *here*—with what was taking place behind the lines and their own daily task of destruction! It was from their second meeting, after he had withdrawn to be sick, that Baron Sunda had first suspected an ominous truth. Might it be that he lacked not the obtuseness of these cultivated templars, but their far subtler moral masks? The one accurate measure of the German citizenry's passion for obedience was the catalogue of monstrosities David had heard Trott describe in a Berlin guild, crowded with corrupt judges.

What if behind the conspirators' masks of piety lurked no more than the design on a comfortable place in history? Such a crime could be atoned for not even by martyrdom, only by a decisive act. For the first time, then, David saw in a different light his minutes, sublimely alone and free, at Hitler's side.

Yet the terrible hours and days, like the invasion of Russia itself, persisted in advancing. Through the fateful summer, as Baron Sunda came to know well the miserable rain-sodden roads from Smolensk to Kiev and practiced his Italian, Spanish, and French on men from every country and class in Europe, one by one the conspirators materialized. There was Oster in intelligence; the ex-Leipzig Mayor Goerdeler, emissary from the conspiracy's leader, Ludwig Beck—who had smuggled himself to the front, spreading news of an underground of German bishops. Eventually David had encountered the dryly scathing Henning von Tresckow and, on his staff, someone with a recklessness like his own, the very "Claus" whom Trott had recommended. Then at last—from this ferociously ambitious military man who despised Hitler for his unworthiness—David heard the word "mutiny," spoken without shame or qualification. And as if finally to deprive his soul of all means of escape, David was introduced to an SS *Einsatzgruppen* commander called Nebe. Here was a man who could swear as a witness to the undeniable truth not only of the Borisov massacre but of one five times larger in September near Kiev, during the very week that Lieutenant Sunda had been with Guderian in the Ukrainian capital!

Very quickly, David became addicted to meeting his new friend Claus for discussions of a literary cast. Like two librarians in some insane *bibliothèque*, they traced a hundred shelf-filings by which a bomb might find its way to the chair on which even the devil must rest. David described to Stauffenberg his own deranged behavior with the Russian guard on the Turkish railway and his later meeting with Hitler. Each time one passed over an opportunity to take moral action, one soon faced the decision again under worse circumstances. Like a good student of von Bock, the death preacher, David was preparing to leave his life. He remained at Guderian's side and awaited a sign.

What alone sustained David's reason across that time was a love, which bloomed like something sacred, for this land of their sins. The very poverty and simplicity, the plainness of the people, their gloom and their naive inefficiency—for which the other officers despised the Slavs—awoke in him the most profound emotion. It was as if the German army had invaded some vast monastery, preoccupied since long before their coming with the cells and punishments of Calvary.

By then, in Smolensk, David Sunda had experienced a different shock.

7

THE REMNANTS OF THE SOVIET 24TH AND 28TH ARMIES WERE BOMBED OUT of Roslavl on 8 August, and tanks of the 16th Army under Rokossovsky were forming for a counterattack. On the same afternoon, Lieutenant Sunda had hurried Guderian's staff maps forward to the cool library of an estate to the south of Smolensk, which had been Napoleon's headquarters in 1812. Two hours later he was almost shot.

Though David had not slept for several days, he had saved the break in his duties to answer his wife's recent letters. He and Hélène had never once corresponded before, and David had been taken aback by the almost masculine intellect at work in her writing—every bit as strong as any mind on Guderian's staff.

But almost at once, that afternoon, he was invited on a tour of the old city. David had discovered that Guderian would accept some influencing, though only if Baron Sunda showed no hesitation in the pursuit of his favor. A curious, unspoken contest had sprung up between them. For the first time, David found that he was not unwilling to humble himself to someone he did not completely trust—a man whom David had imagined himself prepared even to command at gunpoint. Still, Guderian's "history drives" were excruciating affairs. Among the surly, competitive officers, David could not hope to escape the eyes of the citizenry—most particularly of the Russian women, who sometimes came out of doorways to present his conceited colleagues with flowers and black bread.

Today, as the tank leader's motorcycle guard snaked ahead into the cathedral square, David saw the few dozen old men, women and girls melt away down side streets. The heavily armed soldiers spread out, eyeing the housefronts.

Nevertheless, it was a hot August afternoon. Craving a few moments' peace, David stood bare-headed, looking up at the cathedral's ornate but naive saints. At that moment he felt almost free of angst and close to the hundreds of invisible eyes among the surrounding house fronts. There was even a fantastic touch of the Maryinsky theater about the building. Through the low doors, chandeliers hung from chains that rose into hazy vaults. The air was rich with tallow. David joined the other officers, who were staring into a chapel at a life-sized nativity scene. Something about the wooden figures was strange.

"An atheist museum!" someone burst out, seized with terror.

David gaped through the iron bars. In the chapel, six muzhiks were tethered to a plow driven by a hook-nosed landlord in a top hat. The second display was of a peasant girl at a loom, with a red-faced burgher clasping her bare neck. In the last, a foxlike Christ was taking money from three diseased beggars. The group of officers avoided each other's eyes. It was the first time that David had seen the commander of the 2d Tank Group shaken.

"Satanism!" Guderian shouted. "Please have this filthy spectacle destroyed at once."

8

NO ONE FOUND ANYTHING TO SAY WHEN THE CARS DROVE EAST TOWARD THE front to inspect a giant tractor factory. Behind them the sun was setting between two distant cumuli, and not a soul was in sight as Guderian's party crunched in a speechless depression along the base of a gravel hill above a small rust-colored lake.

"I believe this is the first Alp we have seen in six weeks," said the general, glancing up at the mound of gravel.

"The Matterhorn," David remarked flatly. Laughing off the mood, they wound left around the slope.

Four muddied officers appeared, coming quickly toward them. The groups halted ten paces apart, staring at each other's jackets—one set gray, one brown with red stars. In front was a bony officer with intelligent brown eyes, then two yellow-haired peasant boys and a Tartar with nearly black skin.

In a spasm of embarrassment, they all moved at once.

"*Achtung*, Reds—arrest them!" the tank leader cried shrilly, and the three young Russians threw down their guns.

In the evil silence, under a deep-blue Smolensk sky, General Guderian and the enemy officer worked to unsnap their holster flaps. During that infinitesimal portion of a second, David was vividly conscious of the sparrows chirping near the lake and of a distant murmur of insects and water. Their belts were squeaking. David had reached down. He unslid his catch and felt the heavy automatic swing loose in his hand. He held it up and there was a *crack*, then another so violent that his knees jerked.

In front of them, the Russian officer's piercing brown eyes were fixed reproachfully on David's face. Abruptly sitting down on the path, the man held his damaged wrist. They both stared stupidly at what David had done; then the Russian's long face darkened red. He doubled at the waist and rolled clumsily sideways.

David stepped forward. Across the quarry, there were excited German shouts. The three Russians had turned back and were standing with their hands well above their heads. David's knee sank into the sand beside the officer. The fallen man's shoulder was thin and felt familiar and alive. David's stomach had begun to heave. Surely this could not be, how had all this happened? The one shot had only splintered the bone of the right wrist, but the fellow was quite dead.

Becoming aware of Guderian's excited voice, David looked up. He was breathing hard. He could not understand what the general was saying. It was almost nightfall. Now David was on his feet over the man he had just shot.

"A good thing if we could scare more of them to death," Guderian said. "We'll question the others. How did they get here?"

Then somehow their party was marching stiffly back—and himself among them—toward the cars, the three Russians going ahead. The general's hand fell firmly on David's shoulder.

"Thank you, dear fellow," he said. "Nerves of steel, a Sunda to the core."

9

THROUGHOUT THE DRIVE BACK TO THEIR NEW HEADQUARTERS, DAVID STARED west toward the darkened horizons of the *Einsatzgruppen*. Dully now, he thought of his withering honor in a movement that had yet to act and of how he had just killed a man and saved the life of the general at his side, who was systematically destroying Russian lives. The driver snapped on the high beams; these were German roads now. The eyes of fleeing refugees glittered along the roadsides ahead. Guderian leaned against David.

"This will mean a citation for bravery. How do you feel?"

"Confused . . . confused," David repeated, scarcely believing his ears.

"I must say, it is unusual to see the enemy so close. They imagined that Rokossovsky had already driven us back, the scoundrels!"

David nodded. He scarcely heard von Geyer, Liebenstein and Guderian as they politely talked over the news that the Finns had joined General von Leeb's advance on Leningrad and that heavy casualties had been inflicted by General Vlasov's artillery on the Yelnya salient. A grieving rage had begun in the pit of David's stomach. He must be alone at once.

In the headquarters foyer, a dozen kulaks were waiting with plates of roasted meat. When the peasants welcomed Guderian's party with obsequious smiles, David's knees began to shake and he excused himself. He had remembered Egi, who wanted always to be his friend. A moment later, David pulled the library door shut.

Stretched out on the chaise-longue, the Roman staff surgeon rubbed his eyes. Then he shaded them.

"So, *Barone*, what ails you?"

"I just saw a man, a Russian, shot."

"Well, why are we here? What is a muzhik?" Del Bianco rose to his feet. His expression turned grave, as if he had never seen David before.

"It was me—I did it. I did it, Egi."

The images from the factory had weakened to an unreal haze. The surgeon's humiliating reaction came as a second shock—the thing was true enough! The scene was to be David's forever. Again he saw clearly the Russian's startled, reproachful face, and he thought, *If it were not for the persistence of my own life, that other life would still exist.*

"Just to kill one Russian—and you did not even torture him?" Suddenly Egi was angry. "One bloody soldier?" He struck David's arm. "You are a hypocrite. You know how it has been at Yelnya, for fifty hours? If I become drowsy, then three die in their filth. If I sneeze, an artery ruptures. My God, smashed bodies like stacked wood, agony like sawdust. Hypocrite, I killed a hundred and I never noticed the color of their uniforms! And some of them I saved, the very ones I saw with my own eyes slice women's breasts and strangle children!"

Beneath their murky ceiling, David bent over the maps. The surgeon followed, still speaking into his ear.

"Now swear to me this one thing. That no one will be allowed to shoot you, even a person who recites Pushkin."

"I promise, *dottore.*"

"On this you will drink three vodkas. Then you will shave and wash your disgusting body, and you will sleep until dawn."

"It sounds wonderful," David whispered, his eyes averted.

"But wait." Egi had clasped his arm around David's neck. "This shooting. The general was with you?"

"Just at my side."

Del Bianco glanced toward the busy position room. "No, listen! I have seen you hover around the man. Do not tell me, I do not wish to know. But think. If it is influence you people want, this man you have saved owes you more than a medal, eh."

His cheeks twitching, David gripped Egi's arm. "Yes, I will make him feel this death."

"Make him feel it. Now, let us drink—I have had enough of feeling."

10

DURING THE SIX-WEEK ADVANCE FROM SMOLENSK TO THE GREAT ENCIRCLEMENTS at Kiev, Baron Sunda was to detect many signs that Guderian held him in special trust. At each moment, David would trust himself less.

In the autumn, he might again see Fabian Schlabrendorff with the half-Russian Strick-Strickfeldt in their smoking lounge at Smolensk. Similar contacts were forming all along the front. But David had been forced to understand that no plan would be set in motion until the Communist state was dealt a decisive blow or until their own side suffered a crisis. By then, he knew, his moral strength would be dissipated.

Already in these August days the mind at the *Wolfschänze* had developed new deformities. Having uneasily checked the momentous tank thrusts of the opening weeks, Hitler now seemed to glimpse in his overstretched eastern positions a ghost of the siege war that he had known in the kaiser's army. To drive out this hallucination, another flight of genius was called for. And Hitler was in a mood to gamble everything, though most everything was not his to gamble.

On the 21 August 1941, with Leningrad under siege and Moscow only just out of reach, Hitler composed a new directive to his eastern field marshals. The center and southern tank armies, read the neatly typed memorandum, must pivot south, across the Ukraine's rich harvest land, to Rostov and thence to Stalingrad. From there, rolling on across the Crimea and the Caucasus, they were to secure the oilfields at Baku. Baku was fifteen hundred kilometers away.

And this decision by Hitler came to be deemed the turning point—the moment at which the German conquest of the eastern continent ceased to be a possibility.

Many years later, when David would search for answers about what had become of himself and all those around him, of the lands they had desecrated and towns they had crushed, no such clear answer would come to him. The historian Liddell Hart would blame the lack of drive treads that might have allowed the German supply trucks to negotiate the mud roads; the Marxist, Ingersoll, would claim Stalin foresaw that the weight of Soviet production and revolutionary youth must eventually overcome even German efficiency; Field Marshal von Bock cursed the blind stubbornness of a peasant people; David's friend Schlabrendorff would finally blame his circle of assassins who had deferred action while debating how to help the citizenry overthrow their commissars; the American utopian Werth would depict Arcadian Red Army officers picknicking on tablecloths by recaptured Russian villages; while the anti-Communist Strick-Strickfeldt bore witness to a Russian populous only waiting to overthrow Stalin—even when Guderian himself had quoted old czarists as saying that the Russian citizenry had long since come to terms with communism; the Fascist Malaparte, craven with guilt, would portray a noble peasantry wishing to be freed, whether their torturers were agents of Beria or Himmler. For the Pope, Pacelli, the struggle was a holy one between Christendom and atheist barbarians, while for Marxist revolutionaries the struggle was a parable of impoverished masses rising against a rich and corrupt Europe.

Yet for David Sunda, the news of the decision on 21 August to press for Baku had seemed no more significant or comprehensible than that of a change of course for a ship about to be swept backward on an irresistible current.

As ponderously as a bear awoken from the inwardness of hibernation by the sharp teeth of a small but fierce mountain cat, the many nations stretched a continent away to the Sea of Japan began now to rouse their strength. And as they locked and relocked in violent advances that spoiled villages, crops, and human lives, the two Great Lies wore thin, and the truth showed through. It was a simple truth: that the Russian people were tired of having their country spoiled, their sons killed, and their daughters raped, and that these conceited Teutonic warriors were quite ordinary men who did not belong there.

September would come, and the rains would turn the Ukrainian roads to canals of mud into which machines would sink, with their engines burning futilely. By then, the young men of Germany would have had their feast of looted food and forced girls, of life and death—their weathering of famous tragedy. There would be no more than this.

From among the millions, across two scarred continents, there arose a myriad intricate truth. In two thousand towns and hamlets—beneath a rain of bombs and shrapnel, in houses where arms and legs were being cut off and people driven mad—a generation of children came to sweet consciousness of their immortal earth.

The children ran in the rolling fields of the late summer harvest. Uniformly beautiful as kittens, they whispered of calamities, played forbidden games, and sang of the mysterious behavior of their soldier heroes. Even in games of war, the children felt only the deliciousness of fear and instantly forgot the undertone of death. And sometimes, in the midst of their summer impressions, they would awaken in dispensary beds, wrapped in bandages. But even these episodes were forgotten. For they knew that they would never lose their freedom, worrying as adults did.

11

AFTER THE STALLED PUSH TOWARD VYASZMA, BEYOND THE CENTRAL SMOLENSK front, General Guderian's tank groups had left the Moscow road to skirmish with Timoshenko's four disintegrating armies down dust-choked lanes. In early August, well before the rains, General Zhukov had arrived from the defense of Leningrad to take command of the reserve armies lying between Smolensk and Moscow.

On Guderian's staff, at the fulcrum of moral catastrophe, Baron Sunda became possessed with his struggle for redemption. As he did, he could not avoid the intensifying ugliness between himself and von Geyer, which had followed on Lieutenant Sunda's decorated act at Smolensk. He had heard by now of the self-portraits that the *Oberst* was said to carry, posed in uniform, his eyebrows penciled. As it turned out, they also both knew that in his cadet days Geyer had been rejected by David's cousin Katie.

One suffocating mid-August dawn on a farm track near Yelnya, as the tanks awaited an attack on Vlasov's units, David heard unfamiliar sounds.

Behind the command column across the canal, he could see a horse plunge beside a log cabin. Turning from the tensed officers around Guderian, he paced over a burnt field onto a mud bridge. Approaching the cabin's empty doorway, David saw the straw roof collapsed inside.

In the sun at the far wall, roped half naked to a chair, was a redheaded soldier. Across the boy's entire shoulder was a bruise. David had also glimpsed the *Oberst,* seated on a chair with a note pad on his knee. Flicke was about to do something to the boy's other shoulder with pliers and a smoking nail. Somewhere a camera clicked, and Baron Sunda's legs stepped forward jerkily.

"Stop this, Geyer!" he panted, incredulous. "Stop at once or answer to me personally!"

"Shall we choose weapons, Sunda?" The *Oberst* turned with his cigarette held near his lips. "I myself prefer the nails these Bolsheviks pounded into the Whites."

Rising, von Geyer took the pliers and hammer from Flicke. He waved the nail under the soldier's dripping chin and bared teeth. High in the open skies above their heads, a first tumbling shell from Vlasov's .76s groaned past. The pug-nosed Russian said something, and all his muscles tensed. His eyes had fixed on David's face.

"Coward," the *Oberst* said, without looking up." Last week with Reichenau I shot children."

"Stop this or you will regret it the rest of your days!" David was almost screaming.

"Lieutenant von Sunda!"

Recognizing the voice, David spun round. He and these grotesque beings were crowded in the sun between the log walls. The tank leader glanced at their faces.

"You are speaking to a superior. *Oberst,* you are a Wehrmacht officer. Quickly . . . explain!"

"A commissar, sir!" Von Geyer's grin further narrowed his temples. He held out the note pad. "And you have here the strategy for the Yelnya counteroffensive."

"I see. You will at once take this case to our medic. Lieutenant, come with me."

Yet when David marched back with acute anticipation at the side of his · father's friend, Guderian merely gave David a perplexed shrug and climbed onto the radio truck. Five minutes later they were in action.

It would be some days before David again spoke easily to anyone at Guderian's headquarters. A lonely terror of the *Oberst* had seized him. Or was this a fear that after the Smolensk quarry Baron Sunda had no right to hate even this man? Then hatred came. It grew in him quickly, and it was so crippling to his judgment and his self-possession—being now in part a hatred of himself—that David's soul wearied trying to overcome it. Twice during those nights, he woke, his teeth still gritted after a dream in which he was hammering hot spikes into von Geyer's shoulders.

There had been no opportunity for David to inform either Claus or Schlabrendorff before the tank leader suddenly left Smolensk for Poland on 23 August to see the Führer. Lieutenant Sunda's special liaison duties to Hungary and Germany began at once, miraculous orders that had come not through Guderian but from Hitler's own headquarters at Lötzen. David had almost broken down, at the thought of Luz perhaps still in Cetneki Utca. Through Luz there would be word of Justin Lothaire. In the vividness of that insane dream, David had not paused to wonder what effect his person might now have on such people. For their names had come to him bearing the smell and taste of his lost happiness.

It was in that last hour, that the feelings between Lieutenant Sunda and the *Oberst* broke out in front of Guderian's entire staff.

12

UNLIKE NAPOLEON, WHO HAD DEPENDED IN THE FIELD ON MOUNTED MESSENGERS for contact with his armies, General Guderian was able to keep order among his commanders by radio and observe their positions from the air. So complete a tactical model allowed even less space in Guderian's imagination for what might be taking place in the souls of his men as they killed or were killed in plain sight of him. For the terror of death, Plato reminds us, is invisible to the eye.

On the pallid, windy day that he would fly to face Hitler, the tank leader spent the morning with his embattled 10th Division in the critical Yelnya crescent, facing Vlasov's 20th Army.

So it was that David Sunda found himself on the command half-track beside Generals Schaal and Liebenstein and also the *Oberst*—as Guderian led a column of twenty tanks along the perimeter of no-man's-land. And suddenly they were lost. No infantry was in sight. Nothing moved.

"*Panzerführer! Panzerführer!*" The radio crackled shrilly. "*Zwanzig mehr Drei-viere . . . bei Desna Wald, zwei acht zwei!*"

The staggered line of tanks was halted, with motors idling, between two reedy bogs. Along the file of turrets, the helmeted heads peered at each other. Somewhere on their left must be Red tanks. Every ten seconds, less than a thousand meters to the south, a column of mud jetted high over the trees and flew to pieces, followed by an incoming bandsaw noise.

"Let me see." Guderian snatched up the map without dropping his binoculars.

The two waist-high transmitters squealed and chattered into the wind. The flak gunner swiveled his mount nervously. They all stared ahead over the truck's armor.

The undulating mud track curved south toward the thin tree line of the river. A second narrow lane turned sharply left. General Schaal pointed toward the enemy skyline, five kilometers to the east. They could just make out crawling specks—several hundred mounted cavalry. Beyond these towered a motionless, reddish dust cloud. David glanced around the command staff. Their eyes were bleak and cruel with tension. He sat down at the file of charts.

"Curse these Russian maps!" snapped Guderian, ducking his head as a much closer .76 from Dogorobush rattled the armor with mud. "Just look at that photograph."

"It is obvious," said the *Oberst*. We have reached . . . *this* crossing. Only there are two roads, not three."

"Yes, Heinz, we should go east!" Schaal smiled crookedly.

East was into no-man's land. The seconds ticked eerily by. The forward nervous center of the entire Moscow offensive was stalled, possibly out of range, in contact with nothing at all.

The officers looked up together at a deafening crash of their own flak guns; they saw a wing tip swoop behind the treetops along the south forest. In a few seconds more, Vlasov's guns might have their range. The wind rumpled their hair.

"No, I don't like it." Guderian stared into the circle of harsh faces. His eyes fell on his aide. "And your opinion, lieutenant?"

"The left road is a new farm track; we have not reached the crossing," David said.

Across the map table, just by Guderian's shoulder, the *Oberst's* forehead had gone very red. His boot bumped David's leg. Somewhere close behind, two shells fell simultaneously.

"Nonsense, the map is recent. No farm road is so wide."

Hearing Geyer's tone, David Sunda felt the eyes of all four officers on him. *My God, the whole staff knows of our feud*, he thought.

"See for yourself." David tapped his pencil. "The farmers put ditches by their roads."

The *Oberst* did not follow the two generals' hurried glances down the lane ahead. His mouth tightening, von Geyer stared at David's face as if it belonged to the entire Red Army.

"Look, the forest—here, and here. If you are wrong, we will fall on their main defense and minefields."

"If you are wrong, and I will prove you so"—David raised his voice—"we will get lost out there in no-man's-land."

"Prove me wrong, then!" von Geyer shouted.

"That is enough, gentlemen, quite enough," General Schaal faltered.

"All right, then," David said in desperation, thinking of the molten nails and dead children and softly rapping the map table. "This is the first right bend since the mill. On the map, only one right bend shows, here—one kilometer *before* the crossing."

General Guderian turned from his arguing staff. Banging the driver's roof, he freed his tight jacket. "To the right!" he shouted over the side. "Quick—at once! Run!"

From two kilometers behind them came a snorting, then the roar of three dozen tank motors. The half-track's gliding motion resumed. Baron Sunda remained bent over the Yelnya maps without looking at the others. He was trembling with hatred, satisfaction, and dread.

Now fifteen horrible minutes began. One and then another. And David thought, This farm road is yours now, as are the pale skies through which the long-range shells are projecting and these hard Wehrmacht officers and tanks responding to your idea. All were his now, as the Russian soldiers at the Smolensk quarry and woodcutter's cabin were his, and the art of thrust and counterthrust, and hundreds of thousands already dead and dying—all now monstrously David's own.

Lifting his eyes from the maps, he could see only the clouds. Guderian and Schaal stood braced against the front armor in their flared jackets and shining cavalry boots, binoculars raised. Liebenstein and von Geyer balanced at their shoulders, gripping the overhead bar. As David glanced at him, the profiled *Oberst* had turned to stare.

"There, look! And there!" General Schaal suddenly called out, stretching his arm against the blue sky. "And there—our eighty-eights!"

As David rose, Schaal's voice was drowned. Exploding from the treetops to the west, two waves of Kesselring's fighters thundered like a drum skin above their bare heads, then were gone toward the dust cloud, feathering their square wings on the wind.

Guderian had twisted on the bulkhead, his jaw bulging. He winked at David gravely and turned back. They were going into battle.

13

THAT HAD BEEN THE COUNTERATTACK WHICH, WEEKS LATER, WOULD CLEAR THE way for the encirclement of 600,000 more Russian soldiers at Vyazma. The same night at the country estate, with Guderian away in Poland, a violent thunderstorm swept in off the steppes, drowning out the bombardment of Roslavl across the Desna by the Russian 21st and 28th artilleries.

By eleven o'clock, the soaking-wet staff officers had stopped visiting Baron Sunda in the library to check the position charts, as if they were chess situations at some men's club.

In the dark window bay, on his leather sofa next to the surgeon's, David lay twisting back and forth, even though his limbs throbbed with exhaustion.

He was no longer able to think of Hélène or that he might see his ex-fiancée tomorrow in Budapest. The cherry trees appeared in intermittent lightning flashes, followed by long growling rolls of thunder. The *Oberst*'s public defeat, instead of freeing David, seemed only to have fed his hatred—as if hatred had been a fungus already well seeded in Baron Sunda's character. The lightning crashed again violently, and he jerked on the sofa, hating the society he had always known, though with a hatred as David had never known existed; hating these gentlemen destroyers outside the library, whom he had conspired to undermine yet must continue to serve. With shame and trembling, David hated the opportunism and spectacle of this war machine and of the twenty-five massive and disorganized Red armies they faced; and he was defenseless against feeling that, through himself, there had always been something frightful about Oberlinden, his student circle, and even his parents.

His gold watch glowed in the blackness. It was already four-thirty. At six o'clock he must climb back into the car. David longed only to tear out his brain and to sleep. He was already numb to the blackened farms and to the tank shells containing charred monsters, to the madwomen and screaming children. But his hatred had grown so brutal that David heard his teeth grind during pauses in the storm. And in the flames of his falling soul he saw the torturers of civilization and of human love crushed—torn limb from limb, until every last one lay panting for God's mercy. This nightmare was so all-consuming that long after del Bianco was snoring and the storm had passed, Baron Sunda lay wide awake, loathing the evil of his life and all lives, until he wept with rage and sank into an exhausted sleep.

Instantly, dawn came. Without waking his friend, he struggled into a fresh uniform for Budapest.

Then David was carrying his case through the crowded passages. On the entrance table lay one of his wife's blue envelopes. With a further hardening of his heart, David tore it open. She had written to him in German, on Adlon Hotel notepaper.

Berlin
19 August 1941

My dear,

The very hour this letter reaches you (pray God it does) you must sit down and answer. The last of your messages to reach us was dated 26 July—almost a month! I think you must not be able to imagine what it is like each day to carry my feeling for you (and, chéri, all our memories good and bad), then to find the letter box empty! Oh, I have ways of knowing that you are not wounded. But what is happening to you out there, so far away in that huge continent? How well I remember it. It is said the Communists have been crushed as were the French and Poles. Will you be home soon then? I look at the map and at the newspapers, and one hears rumors, and I can form no impression whatever of what you must be doing. Forgive me, my dear old friend, if your Hélène sounds a little hysterical. As you see, Alaric and I are back for two days in Berlin—in part for an interview at the Prinz Albrechtstrasse, which I thought a better place than Bayreuth to discuss foreign matters. Also, one is always treated more intelligently by those in command. Even the central office is quite a charmless place, believe me, though the state police inspector, Friedlander, only asked a few questions about my nationality—and our friends in Paris. Naturally, I mentioned Johannes and Heidrun. . . .

Lieutenant Sunda stared at the sheets of onionskin in his hand. What was left of him now that could be put in a letter to this woman?

Five minutes later, Kur, his old driver from Brest, steered the Horch around a sign on a poplar trunk—NEXT STOP MOSCOW!—and they were on the road to the airfield. Putting Hélène's letter from his thoughts, David Sunda abandoned himself to that moment's joyful wave of freedom, almost like rebirth. He concentrated with all his being on the question of Justin Lothaire.

14

IN THE DAYS FOLLOWING HITLER'S FIRST SIGHT ON 4 AUGUST OF AN EASTERN battlefield—a spectacle that had caused the Führer some nausea—there was a stream of unfocused orders that tended to slow the rolling up of the Soviet defenses on the Moscow road. Instead of digging in his reservists, Stalin's favorite, Timoshenko, had been free to begin a slow advance towards Vyaszma.

Following the nasty breach of discipline between Baron Sunda and the *Oberst*, Guderian had spent the day at the Smolensk palace headquarters of the Center Army, with Hoth, von Bock, and the Chief of the General Staff, Franz Halder. At a splendid oak table, flanked by bare-breasted marble caryatids, Guderian first heard of the Führer's decision to concentrate his tank squadrons southward under Rundstedt. During those hours, among the fifteen Teutonic knights who were seated about the room, no one had smiled. Finally it was decided by the Death Preacher that Halder and Guderian should risk their careers and fly that hour to face Hitler.

In the cloudless late afternoon, as his aircraft soared westward across the forests and steppes that he had desecrated, General Guderian peered below. The plain seemed to be covered by an immense herd of brown cattle—no, the Heinkel was still low. This was the new prison camp. Guderian thought fleetingly of Zelba, where, under a heavy fog, a half million captives had tried to break out with tanks, then by cavalry charges, and finally with arms linked in chains, while Hoth's machine-gunners had reaped their lives. Was this the place from which the disgusting rumors of cannibalism were coming? Curse Erwin Rommel. He would have none of the degraded Reich Commissioners at Cyrenaica to soil his little desert triumph!

Just now the navigator had tuned in to a gloating nasal voice on Radio Berlin: ". . . the eastern continent lies, a limp virgin, in the arms of the German Mars . . ."

At Guderian's shoulder, Halder made a phlegmatic sign. The radio crackled off, silencing those words composed by the celebrated Doktor Godard. The aircraft swung and lurched violently. Guderian's voice was inaudible to their aides.

"Franz, do you think the man will listen?" he inquired of Halder. As usual, the two Clausewitzians conversed with the modesty of gods. It was the Chief of Staff who had prophesied that by this date communism would be defeated.

"History depends on it, dear friend."

"Technically speaking, it is Europe's last opportunity," Guderian continued, using his favorite adverb. "But Kiev!"

"Dreams, dreams." His neighbor smiled sadly, staring at his companion's new Oak Leaf. "The fellow will go mad to hear of mortal limits. 'Go carefully, little monk!'" Halder quoted the words once spoken to another anti-Semite, Martin Luther, before the Diet of Worms, and his eyes filled with tears.

"Are you afraid for us, Franz?"

"I faced him once before. The man's rages are like Christianity flying to pieces."

"He is only a man." Guderian smiled.

"Then face him, dear friend. Awaken him from chasing oilfields halfway to India. Only a sharp blow to the Moscow concentrations will bring down those devils in the Kremlin."

"Kluge said that we are an elephant against ants." Guderian paused to sneeze. "We would crush many, but in the end they would eat us down to the last bone."

Guderian watched the good fellow belted at his side take a handkerchief from his cuff, bury it in his eye sockets, blow his nose, and return the handkerchief to his cuff. And just then, for the first time since his awakening in the Sonnenhof at Bitburg, General Guderian experienced a solitude as heartless as this vibrating metal compartment laboring to stay above the earth.

"To the last bone? Yes." Halder glanced at him with an expression of suffering. "Tell me, what do you think of the whisperings?"

"I have one on my staff too," Guderian replied with care, thinking of his protégé, Baron Sunda. He knew that the chief of staff sympathized with the plotters. "Talk—dreams and more dreams," he said.

"Yes, perhaps there is no going back." Halder sighed with a glance toward the honest faces of their aides. "There has never been such a power. You are the only one of us left strong enough to face him."

The aircraft glided the two Wehrmacht generals into Lötzen's lakeside aerodrome as the Polish landscape was darkening.

15

FIRST GUDERIAN AND HALDER WERE DRIVEN TO STEINORT CASTLE TO SEE FIELD Marshal von Brauschitsch. It was through this fortification, that same week, that the musician Reinhard Heydrich—part Jew and son to the Hallé orchestra conductor, protégé of Jakob Stodel, and the chief of the *Einsatzgruppen* at Borisov and Babi Yar—had secretly passed on his way to Prague. In the case with his violin, the ascetic blond had carried a sheet of Reich writing paper. The signature on this document was that of another rabid German patriot, Hermann Göring. On the otherwise drab memorandum, some lines had been neatly typed. Lines of an untold strangeness, of an immortal and unequaled orginality. Words of such weight as to undo two millennia of Confucius, of Christ, of Buddha, yet as devoid of moral poetry as a spare-parts manual: ". . . measures," those most famous lines concluded, "already taken for the intended final solution to the Jewish Question."

And these words, having the power of history from Casablanca to Leningrad, now belonged to Reinhard Heydrich. At the casino at Évian on Lake Geneva, Roosevelt and Churchill had decreed that the Germans must solve their Jewish problems internally. In the coming New Year on the Wannsee, Heydrich would press further, far beyond Himmler's solution of slave labor.

In the nine months left him to live, Heydrich would build a monument to himself above Herod's as the grand inquisitor of the Jews.

On this quite recognizable summer evening, however, Guderian and Halder were unaware of the previous visitor's violin, of the memorandum, or of its words. The generals scarcely knew their host. For Steinort Castle was the headquarters of the chief diplomat, Count Joachim von Ribbentrop, flowering weed of chaos and rambler through jobs from London to Boston, then to Canada. Falsely ennobled Ribbentrop, in reality an Iago who could at once be a Socialist and a Jewish-financed anti-Semite, and who knew how to deceive entire nations, even Joseph Stalin. For an honor thus null and void, Steinort Castle itself was not splendid enough, but he must fill its halls like any nouveau-riche tycoon with servants, imported flowers, foods, and private film shows. So, flying westward from the hardened Smolensk fraternity of the Poison Dwarf and the Death Preacher, General Guderian came to this fantastic castle—now the realm of Heydrich, known as Hangman, and that unmistakable Caligula, Göring. And master over all was Hitler, the final solution to the European problem.

16

REACHING STEINORT, THE TWO GENERALS WERE USHERED INTO A TOWERING banquet hall as if they were Norse chieftains in bearskins. Von Brauschitsch received them gloomily, standing under the stone fireplace, his elegant head bowed.

"Gentlemen, I insist," he whispered. "You are forbidden to speak of Moscow."

"It has been discussed?"

"It is forbidden."

"Then I must return at once to Smolensk!" Guderian almost shouted.

"That, too, I forbid you." The field marshal smiled sadly into the tank leader's eyes.

Presently Guderian found himself, abandoned by Brauschitsch and even Halder, being driven alone through the sunset from Steinort Castle to the *Wolfschänze*. There were some pleasure boats out on Lake Mamry. How strange it was to return like this to the East Prussia of his youth. He thought of the man who had promoted him out of the ranks for his contribution to tank theory: a fatherly Hitler, with whom he had once exchanged pleasantries about their birthplaces.

In this confused state, the tank leader watched as his armed procession glided into the first cordon of minefields and electrified fences. He gave himself over to military ceremony.

At the center of the complex, a restrained young lieutenant met his car and they walked in step across a maze of forest lawns. The camouflage nets strung on wood pilings made a canopy, further darkening the sky. Guderian noticed the same monastic manner among the officers who stopped to stare at him and salute. Slightly downhill in a leafy bower was the concrete surface bunker. Moments later, Guderian stood in the underground passage through the now customary body search. He stared ahead. Deep inside the conference room there was a large architect's model of a city.

At that moment, Hitler came through the door, smiling his most fatherly smile.

17

"WELCOME, GUDERIAN."

"Thank you, my Führer."

They saluted under the caged bulb. Guderian noticed Hitler's sallow cheeks and his suspicious restraint, as of someone who expects to be snubbed. Inside the pine conference chamber were visible the sentimentally smiling faces of Jodl, Keitel, Schmundt, and a dozen other mediocre personalities. These included the humorless munitions minister, Doktor Todt, and a rosy-cheeked Bormann.

The entire chamber had turned to see the hero of the Moscow front. Guderian hesitated in the entrance, further shocked by the absence of a single civilized face to inspire him in so vast an argument. Knotting his fingers behind him, the tank leader paced slowly after Hitler to the colonnaded plaster city. Apparently this was an all-new Berlin. Guderian murmured a few compliments on the future capital of the planet, trying not to notice the blue horsefly lying dead, like Julius Caesar, on the tiny steps of the Reichstag.

"In the end, my dear general"—the man at Guderian's side interrupted himself to flick away the insect—"it is for your incomparable victories over the Bolsheviks that your Führer will build a Berlin more impressive than Paris. Never again will the instincts of our German man be dragged down by ignorant scientists, priests, and peasant races."

To Hitler's right, a bulb flashed. Through the room behind them there was an approving murmur. Replacing his spectacles, the dictator moved away to the head chair against the far wall. Guderian was left balanced over the New Berlin, his fingers still knotted behind his back. A tense silence closed over the packed room. With all his strength, and feeling like a chivalric paladin on display, the tank leader tried to remember why he had come and all that might be lost.

"Very vivid!" Hitler called down to him, between the seated rows of faces, when Guderian had summoned the picture of the armor and infantry that he had left that morning on the Smolensk sector—like a dike restraining the Communist masses. Hitler continued, "Judging from the past, would you say your men are capable of another great effort?"

Balanced alone just under the low girders, General Guderian felt his heart leap at this opening. "Yes, if they are given an object whose importance is clear to every man."

"Do you mean Moscow, general?"

Guderian bowed his assent. "Since you have broached the subject, may I give my reason?"

"Please do, Guderian." Hitler made sprays of his fingers. "I will never ignore your judgment. If, in 1937"—the man's bulging eyes passed accusingly among the attentive faces, finally resting on Doktor Todt's bald head—"if I had believed *then* your estimate of Soviet tank production as being nine hundred a month, I would not, I believe, have contemplated such a war. On the other hand, look at our stupendous victories."

Down both flanks of the long room, there were flattering grins.

Certainly, my Führer! . . . Quite so, my Führer! . . . Congratulations.

Before them, the cruelly handsome tank leader with the deep scar on his left temple stood his ground. His eyes were watering at Hitler's veiled insult.

From the moment that his brilliant technical description had died away, General Guderian felt himself swept backwards by the dreamlike confidence of the men in this room. "Incomparable victories over the Bolsheviks!" At the realization that the moment had come to argue alone against the terror of those words, the officer who had stood in the field against the *Grande Armée* and Stalin's huge armies felt his heart sink into his boots. Why was Halder not here? Guderian noticed that he had picked up a chart pointer.

Yet without knowing this himself, he had already accepted defeat—the very defeat before authority on which all the successes of his life had been based. Standing in front of Hitler's spotless map, soon he could hear his own voice as it described the suffering of great armies and the ruin of peaceful towns. His vanity experienced again the disarray of a dozen Russian armies before his tanks. At last, turning to glare fiercely down the conference table towards Hitler's distant spectacles, Guderian went on to speak of Moscow, the cranium of the Communist state—Moscow of the czars, Napoleon, and Lenin, in front of which Marshal Timoshenko was at that hour building the main defense.

His arm outstretched to hold the pointer at the junction of all the rail lines in Russia, Guderian heard a rude shout. Turning as in a dream, he was suddenly conscious of an acute exhaustion.

"My generals have no grasp of economics! No . . . grasp . . . of . . . economics!" cried the familiar red face, now approaching along the conference chamber.

"Jawohl! Jawohl, mein Führer!" voices joined in. And hearing the sublime confidence of this Anti-Christ's apostles, Guderian's vision disappeared of a fortress Kremlin that must be cracked before the brains escaped. In its place, like shimmering music, stretched the wheat lands of the Ukraine and the legendary Caucasus—and beyond these, the rich fields at Baku, with whose oil the German people would conquer America and the world. General Guderian would be at the forefront, an innocent, being delivered out of history. Already his head was engaged in the gates to immortality.

It was long after midnight when the tank leader was driven back along the lake, where German soldiers had been boating with Polish girls.

No longer did any of these things feel like a dream. Was it possible that he had scarcely fought for the Moscow plan at all? Could it be, Guderian asked himself, that the only men he had ever respected were men stronger than himself? At just that instant a hot shaft of pain shot down Guderian's chest, so excruciating that he could only sit braced upright on the lurching cushions. An unpleasant gurgling sound filled the back compartment.

Then the conqueror of France, Poland, and Smolensk fell back panting on the seat.

It was not for another thirty minutes—when the tank leader had telephoned the Chief of Staff at Steinort with the news that they must pursue the southern strategy and after kindly Halder had shouted at Guderian as if he were a traitor—that he could admit to himself that he had experienced a heart attack.

These were the breaking strains on 23 August 1941, at the summits of history, where great glaciers work upon themselves.

Such were these men, all powerful men, with no place in closely lived . farmyards—a humility that grounds the soul as mud holds the sun's heat. So that a Stalin could trust just such another mass murderer as Hitler, a Churchill shed tears over this same Stalin, and Roosevelt be seduced by a Churchill. Thus in their frailty, were two more democracies drawn into Europe's vortex of total history.

Through the months of Baron Sunda's journey home from Oaxaca, Europe had come to the last hours of its freedom. In Libya, Archibald Wavell had been stripped by Churchill of most of his command in order to equip an adventure in Greece. After four more weeks, facing Field Marshal List's army from Sedan, the last Englishmen abandoned their equipment and fled by sea to Crete as Student's dive-bombers fell shrieking and raced up. Paratroop planes crossed the lapis lazuli skies, trailing cherry blossoms—schools of lovely, poisonous jellyfish—until the airfield at Maleme was jammed with Hitler's machines. Presently, the raping of proud Greek women commenced, and on the white walls of partisan villages there was the blood of their murdered men.

At that time in North Africa, General Wavell was retreating east into Egypt ahead of Erwin Rommel's tanks, which had been first over the Meuse. Towards the shifting desert of Joseph and the prophets stretched roads of steel grids. And from Normandy to Kamchatka, Hitler and Stalin had spread, over a hundred cultures, a fresh ice of historical lies.

CARBONNE

1

TWO THOUSAND KILOMETERS OF FIRED SAND TO THE WEST OF GENERAL Rommel, in a rebel camp of the Daoura plain, nine months after the desert snows, Justin Lothaire came at last into the poverty that his father had known.

This morning he sat by an oil lamp and listened to the gentle fluting of a goatherd. Around him in the Berber tent, the newspapers, smuggled by Charlot's bookstore in Vichy Algiers, lay in precious bundles: *L'Humanité* and the *Journal de Génève*, also a pocket *Commedia* and a glass of Ahmet's mint tea. The boy's troubled eyes observed Justin's face steadily. Eli Hebron would reach them today. By tonight Justin would have been asked to go back into France.

"Justin, are you thinking of your wife?"

"Not now, little one," Justin said. "See if Lavil's Frenchman is here." So that he would not become absorbed with Luz, or with this orphan who spoke of her as of a mother, Justin rose. He pulled on his checked shirt and his sandals. Then he sat under the tent flap facing east so that he could watch the sun take the stars. Justin thought through what he would say to Eli. This must have nothing to do with his feelings about the boy.

He had lived undetected for a year now with the Arab movement, a scattering of strongholds stretched from Fez—across the old colonies of the French and Spanish, the English and the Germans to the Holy Land and Mecca and, beyond these, to the Euphrates. Justin had seen only retreats and harmed no one, though he had been struck on the thigh by the spent bullet of a *goumier* during a long flight. This had been to Justin like a sacrament of his father's death, and had made them equal. It was then that Ahmet had become attached to him.

Once again, Justin had read books, and he had grown oppressed by the lidless eye of the sun—and by the people of the Maghreb, who showed no restraint on their cruelty, or the humiliation of their women, and who were confused like horses before the new machines of war. It would have been suicide, though, to make his presence known to Lavil or to visit Grinda. Across the months they had wandered a desolation administered by *caïds* who were the agents of Vichy. Yet by tracing Hitler's works in a smuggled letter or from the newspapers or in a conversation with a village merchant, Justin had conceived the drift of events. Through Abu Grinda, he had also met a young leader, Ben Bella, who had won a Croix de Guerre fighting Germans at Sedan and yet whose name was recorded by the French in the ink reserved for Muslims.

So Justin had witnessed the disintegration of Europe's soul, as he had forseen in *Les Thébans*. Now his book too was banned, and most of France was a colony of the Nazi gauleiters. Aside from the Archbishop of Toulouse, few even in the church had taken a stand. Still, there were many shadings to Catholicism, some to the far left. A dozen newspapers had imitated *Justice*, and already there were heroes like Renouvin and Henri Fresnay and Guedon, who had a foothold in the army. But to Justin, who in Paris had felt all humanity change, these few gestures were painfully futile. With sickness in his heart, Justin had read the recent letter from Doré sent to Charlot's in Algiers. At Nice, a French Fascist called Joseph Darnand had forced the old sage and two colleagues to cancel a reading of the writer Michaud.

The power of literature had assembled for Justin, while he was hidden in the desert, the mosaic of tragedy—though for no one around him. He had followed with dread the English generals' disasters in France and Greece and against the Nazi tank flotillas now loose in the Libyan desert. At least Vichy had lost control in Syria, and Rommel could not unite with the hordes that were destroying Russia. It was promising too that this Wingate, who was as mad as a German on his white stallion, had beaten the Italians in Ethiopia; good that the bombers were unsuccessful over England and that Churchill broadcast so often. So did the exiled Pole Sikorsky speak often, and the Dutch queen from London—and the pompous French officer who gave speeches about a Free French government. In the meantime, a generation of Nazis had settled over civilization.

Through this pitiless August heat of 1941, Abdel Krim's agents had been here—with Krim still a prisoner on Reunion—and only the recent capture of an armored-car legionnaire to sharpen their tedium. As he lay awake one night, hearing the soldier's screams, the hatred of his father's blood for the French had died in Justin's veins.

Now the flies were awake. He heard shouts and the complaint of a camel, and Ahmet appeared. The boy's face was grimly indifferent. Then, down the rocky, flats, Justin recognized Eli's wings of hair coming toward them: Eli of *Justice*, Eli of the rue de Fleurus. An unrestrained laughter rose in him.

2

THE VISITOR STOOPED INSIDE THE TENT FLAP. IN THE KEROSENE LIGHT, HE examined Justin's sun-blackened temples, his creased eyes and uncut hair.

"You don't know your friend?"

The two embraced as the boy watched them. They embraced again; then
Eli vigorously wiped his cheeks and blew his nose. He fell on the rug with a
groan. Justin sat facing him and he laughed aloud to see again Eli's hairiness and
simplicity, and how he did not understand a life of goats' milk and camel fat.

"Eat something, Eli. When you've slept, my God but we will talk!"

"Do they have you speaking of God? Clearly there's no time to waste on
sleep." Eli tugged a gray packet from his boot and placed it between them.

"What's this?"

"Your wife's letter. . . . Also, the documents for an inspector of railways."

"Don't the French have de Gaulle?" Justin asked softly. "I have nothing
but a desert."

"Yourself, Marx, and I . . . are we not Semites?" Eli waved expansively.
"In Paris, your writings are passed everywhere."

"Can that be true, Eli?"

Eli spooned two bites from a tin plate. "True? It's your book which has
come true."

"Who sent you?" Justin said, frowning to hide his embarrassment. "What
do they expect?"

"Sent me!" Eli waved his arms and rocked back. "Thousands are behind
walls." He continued softly, "They say there will soon be a decree named after
the night."

"The Germans are lyrical," Justin whispered. He gathered from his
friend's sudden tenderness that the new law would be bad.

"Yes, they'll cultivate us with fear. If one German breaks a leg, a hundred
of us will disappear. It's magnificently original."

Justin gently motioned the boy to leave his tent, into which the ugliness
of Europe had entered.

"Are things moving so fast?" he said.

"Terror spreads suddenly, like ice. I've seen it paralyze the love of
mothers. Justin, the Paris gendarmerie is listing the names of Jews."

"How do you know?"

"The Party has ears. Did I ever misinform you?"

"The entire population—why?"

"Deportation. There are many more than one hundred thousand."

"Deportation. You frighten me, Eli."

"Deportation."

"To where?"

"That is the mystery."

Justin picked up the gray packet. "Where would I have more effect than
here?"

"There is one more thing." Eli was examining Justin's face. "For every act
against the Paris occupation, it's the memory of you and *Justice* that is
blamed."

"You terrify me," Justin whispered.

Three fellahin had quietly slipped into the tent. With suspicion, they watched this talkative Frenchman.

"I regret this, but we need you," Eli said, wiping sweat from his face. "The people of *L'Humanité* and also Henri Fresnay, who despises communism—and even Pivert of the International Workers' Front, whom you know from Barcelona—all of them send their greetings to Justin Lothaire. Your book has done this to you."

Eli had slumped forward with a sigh of exhaustion. Trembling with shock, Justin sat and watched the little man spoon the stew. Even Eli had come to the limit of his love for life. Justin's football companion Youssef broke their silence.

"Justin," he said quietly, "you opposed the French. Would you go to defend them now?"

Through the tent flap, Justin motioned the orphan back inside to hear his promise. He scooped a fistful of sand and slowly tossed it here and there. "Who knows why this desert must speak for Europe?" he said deliberately. "But when the head is cut from the German snake, I will come home."

Eli rocked back with his most radiant grin and kicked his boots in the air. The three Arabs smiled at his clowning. In desperation, Ahmet was staring at Justin. Unable to return this child's look, Justin hung his head to hide his tears.

"But I am only one," he added.

"It is only you whom everyone agrees on. Listen, our new idea has the name *maquis*—underbrush, a legion against uniforms, dragon's teeth," Eli went on. "It is everywhere in Europe, even in Germany. However, the very navel is in the region of the Jura by the Swiss frontier. Your tickets to Belfort are in the envelope. From the occupied town of Carbonne, *Justice* will go out once again. This time, it will be read."

"And if fascism falls back—" Justin began, when the hot sun was blocked by someone new. And now, deep in the anti-Atlas on that famous morning, was Justin not seeing Eli Hebron shake the hand of Grinda's Arab? "If ever the occupation should fall?" he continued. "Will this fire be put out?"

Eli gazed from Justin to the Berber, having already understood perfectly who their visitor was. "No, this anger will burn until the earth is set free. And so, will you return?"

"I've missed Luz more than I can bear." Justin turned soberly to the boy. "Ahmet, you must cut this hair."

"You'll see your wife again across the Swiss frontier."

"So, Frenchman," Ibn Moushmun joined in, without comment on what had been agreed. "Do you know her, this young man's wife?"

Smoking the cigar that Eli had given him, Justin could only smile as the two men spoke. He remembered a lifetime ago, when a *sale raton* had ridden with Monsieur Lavil to the Roman beach, and it had seemed urgent to him that his teacher should meet the horse breaker. That day Justin had lost his courage. Today, the link was made. And would he go back now into occupied Europe? Justin felt his face sting. But already this encampment seemed like an island in a hell of human savagery, and Luz the only paradise.

3

ONE WEEK LATER, ON 7 SEPTEMBER, A VICHY INSPECTOR OF RAILWAYS SAILED ON the steamer from Algiers.

This was a day of world war like any other. In a shuddering dive over Bryansk, the Messerschmitt ace Werner Mölders, on the way to his squadron's two thousandth killing, was showing his sixth young man of the day a last view of the sunny wheatland of mother Russia, as it revolved around a canopy spattered with his forward-blown blood. In a Madrid that was enduring a heat wave, Admiral Canaris of Nazi Intelligence (and, somehow, also of the Smolensk conspiracy), discreetly encouraged General Franco to preserve his independence from Hilter's empire of excess. At general headquarters in Tokyo, the Harvard-educated Isoruku Yamamoto had been arguing, morning after morning, for a quick and complete destruction of the American's Pacific fleet. Meanwhile, the weather in Poland was excellent, and at the picturesque new internment camp at Oswiecim—on the Krakow–Vienna railway—girls in blue skirts played Strauss waltzes to fresh shipments of teachers, priests, Gypsies, Jews, and other aspects of the Final Solution, as they patiently awaited their fifteen minutes in the delousing rooms. At that very hour, though it must be said a little behind schedule, the venerable German firm of Didier, Kori, and Topf of Erfurt was engaged in research and development for the new state market in mass crematoria.

It was a day of world war like any other. In Justin's beloved alleys, Vichy gendarmes now patrolled outside the lace shop where Jeanne Lothaire kneeled before a cardboard virgin, and he did not lie again on his roof overlooking the sea or hear the sweet voice of the nay. But there was still time to test, in the galleries of the rue Michelet, the French suit that he wore now like a *grand colon,* and later to swim with the baker's son Saadi, who knew better than Justin the human labyrinth of the casbah.

Then it was the second night and the steamer was near Marseille, its portholes ablaze to avoid being mistaken by Fascist aircraft, when Justin felt his body sicken with fear. And so began the great somnolence that is war, a deeper oblivion than even Justin had known.

4

JUSTIN FELL ASLEEP AT LAST ON THE TRAIN TO LYON. HE WOKE SITTING FACE-TO-face with a curly-haired officer in gray. Also in their compartment were two obsequious French salesmen.

Outside it was a sea-deep morning over the olive groves of Provence. Noticing the relaxed motions of his hands as he lit a cigarette, suddenly Justin was insanely happy. He was in France again. No photograph of him existed. His first front page for *Justice* was already composed. The elegant parables that he would restore to cultivation burned merrily in his heart. For this, Justin had prepared himself all his life.

"Pardon me, monsieur," he said. "What time do we reach Lyon?"

Unfortunately, the dull major from Worms spoke French equally well. Subjects available to discuss were the deep roots of the Rhone grapevine and the landscape that had brought artists here. Justin did not mention the refugees he had seen on the Marseille docks. After an excruciating half hour, the major returned to his newspaper: conquests in the East; fast Heinz strikes Kiev. Justin left the compartment. He swayed along the passage to the toilet, stunned by this fantastic new Europe that had regressed two thousand years.

By midafternoon, the skies had turned stormy. The train waited a long hour at Lyon while Justin struggled with a reckless passion to change for Paris. As he stood at the window, he had seen four black berets and two men in raincoats on the platform—militia. From now on, Justin must feign respect for the lowest functionary. He relinquished himself to this.

The *milice* did not come to Justin's compartment. The towns of the French sector seemed crowded. The country roads of Burgundy flew by. At the dinner hour they were empty except for an occasional wagon or child. After not going to Paris, Justin felt a constant urge to weep with pity for the French. He thought of his wife, how fanatically she had once proposed to him, and of their difficult time in Doré's attic. *Have you been faithful to me, Luz? What reason have I given her?* Justin thought, staring at the darkening vineyards.

The compartment lights blazed on. Seated by the blackened window, Justin fought to overcome his self-accusation. He leaned his cigarette over a match, held out by one of the two raincoats he had seen on the Lyon platform. This Frenchman had an asymmetrical face, with straggly eyebrows and bruised-looking eyes. Justin smiled and slipped the forged papers from his jacket.

As he smoked the cigarette, Justin continued to smile while his thoughts tumbled. Accusing eyes stared at him with intimacy, as if tempting Justin to expose his anger. But instead of anger, Justin was seeing all the people who had ever loved him turn to this lonely compartment with alarm.

"Darnand." The first raincoat introduced himself. He shook open Justin's papers and held it between two fingers. "You are Inspector Philippe Hériot, *Grands Chemins de Fer?*"

Absurdly, Justin also bent forward, as a man who enjoys civilized conversation . . . Darnand. Was there a connection to Doré's letter from Nice? Justin felt strengthened by the alchemy of coincidences.

"You are very sunburned, Hériot."

"I was in Oran, sir," he said, and blushed for these men who wished him to be stupid enough to die like this.

"Repairing railways?"

"Inspecting the new cylinders on our Model thirty-eights."

The snobbish gaze appraised Justin's features. "I am sure that a young man like yourself would share my dislike for democracy and filthy pig Jews."

"The Jews have no more place in our new France than so-called equality." For several moments Justin thought such words might make him vomit.

"Hériot, you seem so educated and so well exercised."

"Physical fitness is encouraged by Marshal Pétain," Justin said, his lungs bursting for a swallow of oxygen.

"As I was saying," the officer cut in sharply, "you seem a man who is wasted in your profession."

"*Merci, Monsieur. Ma petite femme dit toujours—*"

"You seem to me," the man whispered, his head now bent to Justin's ear, "the sort of fellow who might better be a Communist, a saboteur."

The documents had been thrust against his chest. Without taking them, Justin glanced toward the two black berets in the passage.

"But Monsieur Darnand!" he cried, with deep offense. "Surely you said—how can you?"

The faces surrounding Justin had altered. Darnand thrust the papers into his lap and swung to his feet. The *Vieux-Combattant's* look of intimate hunger had turned to indifference.

"Thank you for your patience." The older man stood in the compartment door. "The state can be allowed no mistakes."

Through the glass, Justin could see the officer prod his young men. He rose but his legs would not support him. Justin felt mortally exhausted by the violence of his own rage. For thirty minutes after the *vieux combattants* left the train—now, after Besançon, climbing toward the Alps through a charcoal dusk—Justin leaned against the window.

Not until several more hours had passed did he grasp that it was Justin Lothaire whom the *milice* had sought.

5

THE WALLED TOWN OF CARBONNE STANDS—AS IT HAS SINCE THE TIME OF THE Caesars, when it guarded an important pass—in the high Jura south of Pontarlier, near Mont d'Or and the Swiss frontier. A small deep lake, named in the gloomy local manner *Lac des Diables*, is bordered with cattails and boasts two row boats. There are twelve shops, including a saddler, a machine shop, and a small cheese factory. Also, there is an alley pension which in better times kept rooms for academics who came to study the paleolithic cave drawings.

From the moment that Justin doubted his friends waiting in the town ahead, he began to doubt the antiquity he had believed in since his earliest revelation at the Mahbu Public Library. Was his moral voice to be rejected and throttled at the very heart of civilization? Could there be sense in such loneliness, a desolation more alien than any desert?

Well after midnight, the bus left Justin at Carbonne and the pension opened its door. It was his first bed in two days, and when Justin woke it was ten o'clock. He went downstairs with his book and sat at one of the four tables. The patronne's croissants were fresh.

"Perhaps monsieur has come to visit our paleolithic caves."

"I will do some fishing too, if work permits."

"Ah, if you have work, then you are fortunate. Our men are traveling north."

"Life goes on," Justin said.

He waited, then he ordered a stew. Two more hours passed, and no one came in from outside. Justin Lothaire was perfectly alone. He shut his copy of Dante's *Divina Commedia* and went out into the afternoon heat. Somewhere a radio sweetly played "Parlez Moi d'Amour." Would there be Vichy state police in the area? He stooped into a saddle shop and became interested in the tack.

Justin spent an hour by the workbench, speaking of Arab horses as the old saddler sewed a pommel. How was he to keep silent, Justin wondered? As the day progressed, Leningrad was under siege . . . people were being deported. He walked back past the pension. Inside the window, the tables were empty. Justin continued out of town toward the lake. And, immediately, he saw the priest.

One arm behind his cassock, the other holding out a book, the man strolled under the trees. Justin slowed his steps. In confusion, he saw the black beard, the thick hair brushed straight back, the swollen figure. The moment for crossing to the other side had passed. Jean-Baptiste Duroc paced, as unmistakable here as outside a Les Halles basement where a prostitute had nearly died.

Justin felt himself trip and stumble. Of course he had heard the name before. Had not both Maline and Duroc spoken of Carbonne? At that moment, he and the priest came level. Justin stood looking back until Duroc had vanished through the town gate. The priest's absorption in the book seemed complete. But he must be sure. A wave of suspicion forced beads of sweat onto Justin's temples.

That night, he heard someone in the next room, someone whose breath wheezed and groaned and who talked to himself. At four o'clock Justin still lay very alert on drenched sheets, listening to the intermittent snores and whispering.

In the morning at breakfast, the wall table downstairs was occupied. A dark bony man of Justin's age, with greasy black hair and a stained jacket, was bent over a selection of Vichy newspapers. The man appeared to be Romany, a Gypsy. He stirred as Justin took the window table but showed no further interest. The patronne sponged the counter. Was Justin still sane; should he escape across the Swiss border this morning? A suspicion of himself—greater than any this town might feel—overcame him. He bought hooks and a line, folded some cheese in bread, and walked to the lake.

Doubling his jacket, Justin sat down with his soles just above the water. The worm made a circle on the lake. A row boat appeared some distance away, trailing a black, even wake. Justin had never felt so closely observed. The air was tense with the secrets of his fame. By twilight, even to wash his face was an act of meaningless absurdity. At six-thirty he went down to dinner. The radio was on: "April in Paris." The greasy hair had taken the window table. Almost with fury, Justin sat down by the wall.

"Monsieur, why do you not join me?"

"What?" Justin half turned. He knew only that he was incapable of further speech.

"You see, I bought an entire liter." The greasy hair looked at Justin with mocking eyes. "It is a cold night."

Justin sat motionless as voices droned and echoed mournfully in the dim room. Cold, had it been cold? Then Justin's throat tightened, and a vast tide of human love rolled up through his soul. They were both twisted round on their chairs.

"Yet where there is wine, it is always warm." Justin spoke thirstily the words of espionage. "And does Panurge prefer automorphic functions to Bach fugues?"

"The bishop of gold verse prefers travel in the underworld." The greasy hair showed a row of good white teeth. "Welcome to Carbonne, Philippe Hériot," he said softly.

Justin gripped his outstretched hand. "I am Hériot," he said, taking his book and jacket from the chair. "I'll get my case."

It was almost dark in the alley when Justin paid for his room and returned downstairs. In the door he skipped back.

"But what is this?" His companion had halted obediently. Screened by the window lace, they watched the town priest pass under the door lamp. The alert eyes questioned Justin.

"I met this same priest in Paris," Justin said. "It is unfortunate."

"Perhaps not. We'll see."

Fifteen minutes later, the two men were working quickly up through a steep forest over Carbonne. After a forty minute climb, they came to a moss-covered monolith. The Romany, who was named Gabriel, halted here. Out below them in the starless night, rustling like an ocean, were the great valleys of an infamous France.

Justin broke the silence. "Who will be there?"

"Some others come tomorrow," Gabriel replied, with sudden warmth. "Tonight there will be Rochet and his family, my people, Joseph, and someone who knows you; also there is a packet of letters. They have experience of printing machines. And never before this farm did I always have enough to eat."

Justin grinned but said nothing. Hearing so many names, he had felt the full range of human treachery. At that hour Justin did not care. This was to be the single great act of a life. He would not disgrace it again with mistrust. Could Eli be here already? They started down into the next valley.

After another thirty minutes, the forest floor sloped up and they were on a marshy flat. Justin saw a light. Cabbage leaves slapped his knees and tugged at the old camel-hide case that held his clothes and books. Following Gabriel, Justin went straight out toward the two-story farmhouse. He scarcely had time to draw breath. Then the low door opened and Justin felt stone under his shoes. And through the silence, across the exile of the last year, there came a conversation he could not have dreamt of.

6

THEY WERE IN A LOW-BEAMED KITCHEN, FACING A LONG TABLE LIT BY A PARAFFIN lamp. Seven or so men and women and a small girl had turned to stare at Justin in his suit. Eli was not among them. There were the excellent smells of garlic, of roast chicken, and of something else—ink. Justin's eyes rested on a shapeless, furrowed face at the far end. It was some seconds before he believed his senses.

"It's Justin Lothaire," said a guttural voice. After solemnly shaking each of their hands, Justin leaned on the table. He did not remember the man's name, but he remembered his character. "Is this possible?" Justin asked.

"Quite possible. I am Peter Tiolchak." The older man laughed softly and passed his fingers through the brush of gray hair. "Did I not promise in Barcelona that one day we would work together?"

"The Comintern must need friends after sleeping with Himmler," Justin said with compassion.

"Old Whiskers? For me, Stalin's day is over."

Just as he had years before, with Luz, Justin watched the man's wrinkled, impassive eyes and his slow smile. He felt again the colonel's realism—if he was still a colonel—and also his subtlety. Nin and Figueroa. Between them and Stalin's agent Orlov lay many shadings. First the priest from Paris, and now this! Justin knew already that nothing was to be as he had expected. At the moral temperatures in Hitler's inferno, nothing would stay pure.

"Then we are all tourists here? If you had left me fishing one more hour, I would have returned to the desert. Peter, it is incredible to see you again."

The worried faces in the shadows around Justin softened in a wave of laughter.

"*Il faut s'assurer.*" The bald Frenchman seated by the stove shrugged heavily. "There has been a search for fugitives running to the Italian Savoie."

"That is Louis Rochet," Tiolchak said. "The farm is his. He also brought the press here."

Justin smiled with pleasure at the farmer who would print the first words of a new *Justice*. He sat at the end chair. "Yes, I was questioned when we left the French sector. . . . Is there a Darnand?"

"You saw Joseph Darnand?" inquired a soft, precise tone from the darkest corner, opposite Rochet.

"Was it Darnand who tracked you in Dijon, Mandil?"

"Were it not for our people on the *Joint* . . ." The embarrassed voice fell silent.

Mandil looked about thirty, with close-cropped hair, a delicate white skin, and a face of great sensitivity. Peering round the kitchen, Justin felt the scenes that these ordinary folk had endured—fragments raining down from a corrupt enlightenment.

"But Justin, what of the town priest?" said Gabriel.

Tiolchak leaned forward. "So, Justin, you know our local priest. Does he recognize you? Still, we will have to make sure. Paul, before Justin falls asleep, let him see the stove."

"Sleep?" Justin lifted his hands. "I'm not yet ready."

As the others listened with glistening eyes, Rochet's thick-shouldered son had tugged back the big stove. Justin could make out a panel.

"Down below, Lothaire, is the short wave." Rochet began to pace, speaking with impatience for such things. "Also, a printing machine, gelatinite— many hundreds of captured passports and Luftwaffe papers to forge. My valley is very little known . . . but if visitors come, it is the Rochets who remain above. Gabriel lives in the barn. We are able to receive five hundred kilos of Swiss paper each week. We transit one hundred kilos to Fontainebleau, twice a week—never ask me how.

"Now, my friends, I wish to hear no more boasting of groups and liberation!" The flesh on Rochet's face shook with indignation. "If treachery and hunger made resisters, Lothaire, then Europe would be an army. In fact, the *grande* bourgeoisie of the cities adore the Nazis and flock to them. There is infinite deceit, but no resistance."

Propped against the stone wall, Justin shrugged. He had emptied his plate without seeing what he ate. "And you, Monsieur Rochet? The farmers of France?"

Leaving Tiolchak's side, Rochet resumed his chair with dignity. "I am the only *maquisard* here, Lothaire. I learned from others, as a prisoner-of-war in the Saar. The Germans treated me exceptionally. I hold them in great admiration. I pity them now, and I pity us. I myself will print the first page: *Justin Lothaire has returned to France, he is alive and well.*"

Everyone in the obscure kitchen, with its dangling flypaper and its onion strings, turned to Justin. He had just delivered himself into their hands. He breathed the silence—a silence of those who, because they loved life, wished to risk it. Justin's look paused on the plain face of Gabriel's wife's sister.

Tiolchak rose from the table. "Come outside, Lothaire. Afterward, Isabel will show you the attic."

By the stone hearth, the farmer's daughter blushed and covered her eyes. "Tell him about Tuesday," Joseph Mandil called after them, as Tiolchak pulled shut the farmhouse door.

7

OUTSIDE, THE NIGHT SKY WAS CLEARING. THE AIR WAS RAW IN THE NORTHERN light. As they came to the paddock fence, Justin sighed.

"How long have you been here?"

"Since before our army apocalypse—four months." Tiolchak laughed, "It was I who sent for you. We are both marooned."

"Sent for me . . . why?"

"You are not the most single-minded, but you are the most honest man that I ever met. Perhaps, the most intelligent."

"I read too many books. Who was the most single-minded?"

"Lenin. My friend, next week is critical." The colonel's musical tones murmured on. "Eli Hebron will come from Paris, and Vera from Bern. They will bring ciphers for the London *France-Libre* and for the *Joint* in Toulouse; also contacts to Fresnay and to the underground in Prague and Warsaw, via the *Journal* in Geneva. To say nothing of the network of *passeurs* between here and Perpignan. Next Tuesday, here in the Jura, there will be the first coordinated sabotage in France—a rail tunnel on the Doubs. Our information was a rare fluke."

Justin searched above their heads for the north star. Had this old friend not been sent from the east? A believer's discipline would always be stronger than his word. This Peter, whom he so liked, might be the strongest leader he had ever met. But Justin would have to know the man completely. At that thought, a terrible suspicion seized him.

"They say that sabotage is an art," he said.

"Mandil and Rochet are completely reliable."

"Yes, they are fine people—but listen, Peter. I'm not here for violence. I am not here to play with trains."

"Why then?"

Pulling his jacket round him, Justin leaned on the cold fence. He was so confused and exhausted he had begun to tremble.

"To reclaim a million minds from Hitler's hands. To tell a story deeper than history, and to tell it with such heat that torturers recognize themselves."

They were silent, hearing the musical note of water from the steep forests. A crescent moon had suddenly flown up, opalescent on the rim of the gorge.

"You know that Lorca did not survive?" Tiolchak went on. "The most gentle writers, ones you know, are being assassinated. Our Stalin has arrested many, many more. I know this. Justin, you will have to participate. Even you.

"But listen. Tiolchak was speaking now with satisfaction. "Up there, beyond that notch to the southeast, is a forest plateau crossed by every species of spy and refugee migrating between East and West. It is the Panama Canal of the underworld. Yet for some reason they have not closed it."

"Perhaps they use it too," Justin said. "And Rochet's Paris messenger?" It was over this pass that Luz would come to him.

"Rochet's two brothers were also German prisoners. The one who is alive drives trains. Single sheet newspapers can go in hay bales and be slipped into copies of *Match* and *Marie-Claire*. Important texts will be smuggled to the British embassy in Geneva to be translated and dropped along with bombs over cities to the north and east."

Justin leaned back with a laugh under the night sky of Europe. "Glorious! And deadly too. You, Peter, is this easy for you, a Leninist?"

Tiolchak was offering him a smoke. In the moonlight as they lit up, Justin was aware of a change in the imperturbable Russian. The movement of the two coals rhymed their understanding.

"Lothaire, I'm fifty-two years old," Tiolchak began. "When I was your age, I served in the Hussars of Czar Nicholas and was twice wounded at Lvov. It was exactly as today, the German haters and the German lovers. A million starving Jews. Later I spoke with Tukhachevsky and many others of the originals. They believed without the slightest doubt that man was clever enough to build a lasting world, free of any sorcery of gods and devils or the oppression of privilege. We saw before us a Russia dancing peasant dances and singing peasant songs.

"Then, not long after Barcelona, I was delivered into their hands. I spent two months in Yezhov's *float*. I do not wish you to hear of the torture before each other, of entire families, not even of their bravery. They brought me to trial three times because of my friendships. I did not betray one word. The third time was in the old club for noblemen. I saw Bukharin insulted by that cutthroat Vishinsky, who at this very hour is Old Whiskers' special aide!"

They waited against the fence in the silent French night. Tiolchak's murmuring voice had suddenly thickened with anger, and Justin knew he was weeping.

"I think often of the foreign ambassadors, all of them so effete. Yes, I was condemned too. However, there is a sealed letter I left long ago in London— Vishinsky would have fallen. So he needed me to be seen alive before English journalists. After what I heard and saw, I will not soon return. Still, when I look back across it all, when I ask myself what future I believe in, I can tell you, Justin, without doubt, that it is Socialist. Once you have experienced such a dedication to your fellow creatures . . ."

". . . It is the banishment of all selfishness," Justin concluded for him. But even that, he thought, was not enough.

Tiolchak kissed him with great affection on both cheeks. Then, handing over a packet, the colonel trudged away to the cellar where the others slept. Six hours before, Justin Lothaire had been no more than a *bicot*, lost in a village of Hitler's Europe. Had he since grown immense on the suffering of his time?

Presently, Justin followed Isabel Rochet and her lamp up a steep staircase and down a cavernous loft like a ship's hold, to a door at the end. He thought of Ahmet, alone another night in the desert.

"Do you wish to hear me sing, Philippe?"

"Now, little one? I am very, very tired."

"Then tomorrow. You see? Back here is your bed, by the chimney. The bricks are always warm. Is the actress truly coming here?"

8

THEN AT LAST JUSTIN LOTHAIRE WAS ALONE, SEATED ON HIS BED IN THE DIM ATTIC of the well-hidden farmhouse. In the occupied night he thought of the trusting faces lifted to his downstairs in the kitchen. He had dreaded this hour all his life.

And how would it be when they were hurt, or when hundreds of their villagers died over a few twisted rails? What could these annoyances mean to a machine of mass domination, possessing planes and tanks? One squadron had more power than all undergrounds put together. Were the resistance fighters on this honest farm choosing suicide? Their attempt would be crushed. The ciphers would never come, the press would be broken up. Peter did not think that, did he? The Colonel was no child, nor was Rochet—

nor the priest, Duroc. Least of all the priest. Duroc's archbishop in Lyon was the greatest Fascist of them all. Perhaps a solution would come to Justin by morning.

Biting through the neat cord, Justin tore the package and spread a full dozen envelopes on the quilt. On top were six sheets in his wife's neat hand, then one apparently unopened letter from Johannes in Berlin. There was a much older green letter from Moscow and two retaped envelopes addressed in David's bold, rhythmic hand, sent from Mexico and Potsdam. Some scholars in Algiers and Paris had written to him, and so had Duncan from New York. Last there was a plain envelope from Germany addressed to Monsieur Justin, care of the Lamberts. He tore this with quick fingers. Inside was an uneven handwriting he had never seen before, that wound up along the borders and across the letterhead. This scrawl overwhelmed him, as if he were for the first time seeing the body of the woman he loved. He rose with the letter under the low beams.

Bayreuth, 23 August 1941

My dear Justin,

Yes, it is Hélène who is writing to you. And I have made very certain that this will reach you, because I must write in French, and because Luz would be upset by my weakness. You know how she needs to think me in command of things. But after all that has happened these last months and I have heard nothing from David in almost a month—you see, there is no one else left here or in Paris I would turn to. So will you forgive me? . . ."

Justin lifted his eyes to the little drawn curtains. Don't be a fool, he thought, this extraordinary person is simply warning you of her husband's disappearance. But every nerve told him that Hélène had written to Justin as his wife, that for her the old beautiful, terrible question had been answered. The letter went on to describe a journey to Berlin from Central America and the birth of a son. There followed the tortured detail of David's departure—this could not be—to join a tank general's staff in the invasion of Russia.

Reading those lines, Justin felt his legs go weak. But the closing paragraph did not focus on Russia.

I, too, can speak now as an exile! You see, I am close to you at last. It would make little difference if I lived in England, in Vichy, or in Germany. Races, classes, gods, patriotism, the human Will? The men who use those words seem to me half crazed. Yet masses are enslaved to them! Justin, I have had time to read a dozen books I found locked in a cupboard—including your Thébans. How can there be so many books, when so few contain what is profound and redemptive? Do you know, I feel no significant meaning in what the rest of us in the world are doing? And I have heard stories which guarantee that worse is to come. Can you, with whom I am alone at last, explain what is the true and narrow path? What David has done, and what you think it correct to do? You will have a few minutes, Justin—perhaps you might send me on your thoughts. I need only to know that I have not offended you with naive and foolish anxieties. Otherwise, I wish you well, wherever you are.

You have my love,

Hélène

A few minutes, Hélène—a few minutes? Justin held the stationery to his nostrils. For this letter, she would have the rest of his life. The lingering impression, as he fell into a sleep strangely free of fear, was of how he was to be provided now with all that was needed.

Yet from his first night in that brave and lonely valley of the *maquis,* Justin's concentration was troubled by a love for his life and by a kindness toward the lives of others.

9

IN THE MORNING NO CLEAR ARGUMENT HAD COME TO HIM, NOR ON THE NEXT. THE attack was primitive and coarse, but Peter had been right. Justin would go with them.

By sunrise on Tuesday, working surely in the cold shadows of first light, Tiolchak, Rochet, and Mandil had strung their charges. They had come forty kilometers from the farm and its printing press, and from the two dozen pages of satire and contempt that had flowed once again from Justin's pen. As the morning sun fell on the splendid scenery, Justin was almost relieved. This act, the grossest bully could understand. As an observer he would get to know the other men. It would be easy.

The east forest rose steeply above the wide river course. In the hollow of pine roots, where he lay stretched next to Joseph's upturned face, Justin could just see the tunnel mouth. The dripping arch was at their level, two hundred meters along the service path. The two main lines emerged directly onto a short bridge. The skeleton of girders fell far below, crossing the three riverbeds and their grass banks.

That had been the morning. By evening they were still by the tunnel. The sun was getting low. A fisherman appeared, working along the middle stream. Justin and Mandil had talked hungrily, laughing often, of the nineteenth-century philosophers, the romantic composers, and Rousseau. At the farm, Mandil had been hypnotized by Justin's parody on Himmler's craving to be Genghis Khan. Now he was growing ugly.

"I would like us to do the next train, Justin."

"The tunnel will be enough," he said, suddenly feeling sick and unprepared.

"Then do the tunnel now!" Gabriel called to them from the rock face.

"Are the orders we have not clear?" Justin shrugged. "Look, the fisherman caught something."

"Then talk to the others. Louis may have left."

"We can't move in daylight. No one will have left."

Justin thought of the Paris boulevards as they would be at this hour. In a rush, the reality of Hélène's letter began receding from him into dream. He had only heard some minutes before that there might be killing. For this missing detail, Justin had no wisdom ready. The great writers were silent. All that day Mandil had counted the steady movement of a Wehrmacht division toward the east. Joseph's visible nervousness when they did not push the detonator on each crowded train had reassured Justin. He had quietly reminded the boy of the English message—to trap only the locomotives. Now Joseph was again pleading to seal an entire train. A mountainful of crushed and suffocated Germans.

"Suppose, as they tell us, this one is a prison train?" Justin quietly repeated. It was in this way that one took leadership of what one knew nothing about and feared.

He watched the fisherman in the river below delicately wave the wisp of fly rod. He thought of the beaten donkey he had once defended in an Algiers street market. Yes, it was the old desert riddle of God's violence. On the near side of violence there was Thoreau and Gandhi, who was liberating a continent. Yet violence was a tunnel by degrees. One either died within it or came out on the far side, like Trotsky. And beyond, even Trotsky's skull could be split by a Stalin or a Hitler. Yet the passive resistance of Joseph Mandil's people ended in the special prisons, which Justin knew of from *Justice* but would not mention. The solution was neither to travel through the tunnel of violence nor to smother evil inside. The solution was to demolish the tunnel itself and so prevent its use. The territory upon entering the tunnel belonged to man— but that beyond the tunnel? From that the soul of a generation did not come back through. And if that generation were an entire society?

Thinking over this governing metaphor, like Plato's cave, Justin had finished his last cigarette. One did not waste a good smoke on abstractions. By tomorrow, Hitler would know of this railway crossing.

"Justin? Justin?" Joseph whispered, and he was no longer the highly strung terrorist of the last hour. "It is possible I will not get through. If so, there is something you at least should be told."

"You won't be killed, Joseph," Justin said quietly, as he so often had, seated over the brazier at *Justice*. "This may come to nothing."

"Still, I am a witness. From the *Stalag* in Munich to Carbonne I could not stop to breathe. I can tell you where such prisoners are traveling."

The destination is a mystery, Eli Hebron had said to Justin in a Berber tent. Now, in this warm French dusk, waiting as at the gates of the underworld, there was a silence over the farms of the Jura that drew at their hearts. Justin concentrated between the pine trunks, on the innocent-looking tunnel arch. They had fifty minutes. As Joseph's swift speech rose and fell at his side,

Justin knelt far forward. He looked from under his slouch hat at the fisherman in the river below. Behind them, lying against the rock face, the Romany moved his feet; Gabriel was not asleep. Then as if Mandil's agonized murmur had the power to move time, forty more minutes leapt by. Still bent forward in the steep forest hollow, Joseph roughly wiped his temples on his sleeve. His voice continued hoarsely.

"Now, Justin, swear: never doubt me. If you doubt the pitiful deaths these eyes have seen, I must tear them out."

"Through the tunnel," Justin said, trembling with hatred as he repeated the words Joseph had heard spoken by a monstrous prison major named Leverbein, "there is a secret understanding to beat to death whole races—" They both heard the sharpening of the river sound. Brown smoke hung round the fallen sun. Behind Joseph, Gabriel suddenly lurched away from the tunnel detonator.

"You have not sworn to me, Justin!"

"Joseph, while I live, never will I doubt it."

Then Justin skidded down the bank to the detonator and pinned the Gypsy's arms. The empty wine flagon bounded below through the trees. "Not now, like this!" Justin panted, looking into Gabriel's frightened grin. He felt his own face burn and his knees twitch. And this was another drunkenness, an anger more terrible than Justin had known anyone could feel.

Then he was flattened on the forest mat between the pine and the detonator, looking out on a land he did not know.

10

JUSTIN HAD NOT MEMORIZED THE SABOTAGE PLAN. HE GLANCED BESIDE HIM AT Joseph's fingers, screwing the little hooked terminals. The wires ran under the forest mat to the charges buried in the tunnel. When he looked back, there in the twilight was a train. It came gliding onto the bridge—two, then three big locomotives. The driving rods rose and fell in ghostly silence. Then, unbelievably, there were three more engines above the girders. The mass of smoke separated, then rose in six plumes. Steam exploded between the wheels, swallowing the railbed. A loud *whoosh* came over the gorge. And among the white billows, Justin saw the enemy.

Five tiny figures in dark uniforms, had run ahead over the bridge, pausing to look below through the girders. *These were SS!* Justin followed their movement through the pine branches. Each detail of this scene filled him with horror.

"We will let the train go in," Justin said. His metaphor for violence had vanished now. Why had Joseph not drawn up the detonator handle?

"Look! Jesus, what is this—he will be seen!" Gabriel raised his voice.

"Can he be cutting the wires?" *Do not panic*, Justin thought.

"Only those for the bridge. Should I shoot him, Justin?"

The Romany was against the big trunk, the carbine steadied on the figure under the framework. Mandil had covered the entire service path unnoticed.

"No! Peter can see him well."

Just at that moment, the engines on the bridge had tightened against the file of red boxcars. The little spoked wheels spun and caught, then spun again with fluttering beats, as of huge lungs. The guards had time to swing up on the first flatbed as the cars were bathed in the rich sunset. Justin understood then why Joseph had cut the bridge charges. Glancing toward the tunnel, he saw a figure dangle under the track. Now there were flatcars with pairs of tanks chained onto them. They were transporting armor . . . and *prisoners*. Could the attack have gone so wrong? The leviathan was entering the mountain. Smoke boiled around the tunnel arch. Gabriel had dived across the bank to the tripod automatic. They both could see Joseph run along the prison cars. He was freeing the swing locks.

The last engine had just backed into the tunnel, pouring black smoke, and the gorge was alone with the clicking of wheels. Were the wires severed? Below him in the gully, Gabriel twisted onto his back, staring wild-eyed at Justin's face. At that exact moment, Justin pulled up the handle and threw his weight on the detonator.

Below in the river, thigh deep in the cold current, the fisherman—who was having his Tuesday off, as master cook at the Château d'As, where the Nazi commandant of Besancon took his dinners, and who had noticed no disturbance of his favorite seclusion, apart from the occasional trains and the black circles the feeding trout were making on the blue reflection of this pool—saw a fish splash where his fly had drifted.

Just then hearing a muffled thump and a sound like a rockslide, the fisherman pivoted angrily. Looking up from the water, his slender bamboo pole pointed over, he saw a gold cloud of dust above the tunnel arch. All along the bridge doors were darkening, and figures began to drop out. A flatbed wagon tilted slowly against the girders. A tiny figure tipped free and fell into the smoking sky under the span.

The fisherman let go the rod and stumbled two steps backward, fell into the cold water, and staggered up, without taking his pop eyes from the little body end-over-ending into the murk below. He thought there had been a splash. In the sudden silence, still slipping back and forth, unable to find his balance, the fisherman heard a crackling sound overhead.

A dark bareheaded man with a gun was running towards him from the east forest. *A saboteur*, the Frenchman thought, and he fell in again.

The saboteur reached the grass bank and stared soberly at the floundering fisherman as bullets whizzed past. Then he splashed through the shallows. Along the riverbed from the direction of the bridge came a slighter, hawkish boy holding an automatic gun, his jacket and trousers soaked from the fall.

And seeing so close the intense look the younger men gave each other, the fisherman's anger and shock turned to a quite different sensation. Of something larger than himself and pleasantly criminal. Something true, splendid and free—the sort of thing that he would tell his children.

Forgetting his rod, the fisherman splashed to the bank and pulled himself out. He stood looking after the two men, panting with the surge of strong feelings.

"*Vive la France!*" he suddenly shouted to them, being able to think of nothing else to say. "*Vive la—!*"

But at that instant there was a stunning blow at the base of his gray hair. The chef of the Château d'As fell forward hard on the grass, boots kicking up. The water emptied from his rubber waders.

11

AS THEY MOVED QUICKLY UP UNDER THE DARK FOREST CANOPY, THEY HEARD THE resonant *klang! klang! klang!* of the tripod gun striking the bridge and locomotives. Through the dusk, this was like the tolling from a church gone mad.

Gabriel, Tiolchak, and the Rochets would cross the Swiss border that night. Joseph was still alive after his story and the fall into a deep pool. He and Justin would throw a scent east, lose it, then double back the long way round the Jura to Carbonne. They were carrying nothing but a gun, two thick salamis, and a road map.

All that night, the fugitives moved through the French forests and up the country roads. By dawn, the weather had turned gray and moistly cold. Sometimes there were French police patrols, or German motorcycles out looking for saboteurs and escaped prisoners. Through Wednesday, the terrorists dozed inside a haystack near Roulans, listening to the plowmen complain of a huge bombing and how there would be reprisals. At sunrise on Friday—the very October morning on which the first snowflakes settled on General Guderian's positions at Smolensk—Justin and Mandil waited in the forest until white smoke blew from Rochet's chimney.

While they had been away, the climbing roses on the farmhouse had gone brown. From outside the door, Justin could hear Peter speaking a musical foreign tongue. Two seconds later, they were in the smoky kitchen. Everyone talked at once. When Gabriel had reached the farm with the others at midnight, Eli Hebron was already there. They all felt clearly today the grotesque danger that the commands from remote governments had put them in. Everyone knew that Justin had pushed the detonator. Eli embraced him.

"I'm sorry, Justin. You did not come for this."

"There should not be so many people here at once," Justin said.

A short handsome woman in overalls stepped in front of Peter. "My name is Vera." She squeezed Justin's hand once. Through the strong spectacles, pale blue eyes measured him with interest. Justin sank down at the kitchen table, holding Madame Rochet's bowl in both hands. He overcame an impulse to break down. By the river in France, he had been possessed and an old fisherman now lay dead on the grass. It was eerie to hear Joseph's voice speak again in this kitchen.

"You are sure the bombing was on Vichy radio?"

"Yes, Joseph." Rochet paused, "Also that yesterday ten young men were shot in the square of Ornans." The farmer turned from his kitchen full of foreigners. He busied himself with the stove.

Listening to them from the table, Justin hung his head and tried to gulp the thick, hot vegetable soup. Could so much have happened? Were Darnand and his uniformed gang tracking them at this very hour?

"The executions, were they by the Germans—or by *Patriots?*" inquired Paul Rochet.

Tiolchak shrugged. "There could be a demonstration."

"That will accomplish nothing!" the new woman interrupted. "Ten of the SS now owe us their lives."

"Such people are of a different species. It would be a poor exchange." This morning Gabriel was serene.

In the hushed kitchen, Justin worked to unknot a second boot.

Eli gently held his shoulders. "When you have slept, Justin, I will have news. There is to be a gathering across the border."

"So soon?" Justin barely disguised his powerful gratitude.

"Justin, someone will be waiting there for you."

Moments later, Justin freed himself from Eli and the nightmare in Rochet's kitchen. The stone pantry was lit by cracks of winter light. He looked at the drying rabbit skins in the attic stairwell. This was his first moment alone in six days. Only seconds ago, the evil of Europe had boiled up in him, pungent as vomit. In the pantry, he began methodically to tug off his clothes. Bending in the faint light, he emptied the bucket into the stone basin. He splashed the hot water on his face, only half hearing his own whispers. Then, crossing his arms, Justin splashed his ribs and flanks. *And if the salt has lost its flavor?* When he had rinsed his bloody feet, Justin felt for the towel. Then he froze. Through the ladder was the hard-mouthed, pockmarked face of the young widow, Gabriel's sister-in-law. At his glance, the woman lowered her mocking eyes. She felt for the wall, moving her shoulders, her skin very smooth. What was her name? When he had first noticed this eighteen-year-old's eyes on him in the kitchen, her crudeness had seemed alien. Now, from out of a dark tunnel, there came an excruciating pity for them both. Was there not something he could give her? And the answer came that he must give her everything. Blood rushed to his head.

In the winter light the widow's bare feet were like Melanie's, going up the watertower. Catching the woman's ankle on the ladder, Justin kissed it. He heard the soft richness of her laugh. Suddenly it did not matter about the ghosts on their flesh of other men and women, any more than did the wine from a stranger's lips on a vessel of the Eucharist.

A minute later, upstairs in the little room with the quilted bed where he had read Hélène's letter, the woman crudely threw off her things. And only then did Justin's heart begin the long journey back from a rail tunnel on the Doubs. He did not think to ask her name. Late that night, when Gabriel shook Justin awake to guide him up over the Swiss frontier, the girl was gone.

Toward midnight, the moon was still a faint crescent, but the man's leggings moved upward, mounting surely. The Romany would know of Justin's visitor, for there was a closeness between them. When he next glimpsed his watch, it was one o'clock. Abruptly Gabriel held the gun across Justin's chest. They were in a narrow meadow of waist-deep grass.

"Over there is Switzerland?"

"Take it with caution, brother. The Nazis also use the passage."

"They use all the passages. I wish to find everyone alive."

"I'll warn them, Justin."

Reaching among the trees, he looked back. He had just clearly felt his soul as it rose out of the hell that Hitler had made of his life, back toward an innocence as when a scholarship boy had first seen snow. Among the shadows that Justin had just left there was no trace of Gabriel. He turned and went into Switzerland, walking with the stride of a man who will not return.

LAUENEN

1

THEN, AFTER TEN YEARS' ABSENCE, JUSTIN LOTHAIRE WAS AGAIN ON A mountain train climbing into the Oberland, close to the great hidden glaciers. The next forty eight hours would be his own.

The little carriages twisted up through walled brown vineyards. It was dark, and the turreted roofs of Montreux's grand hotels lay steeply below in webs of mist. Across the black calm of Lake Geneva, creased by one Vichy police launch, the slopes of the Dent du Midi rose against the overcast sky. The empty compartment was in cloud. The gray light brightened steadily, and suddenly Justin was in hot sunshine, clicking over fields of new snow. He took out a cigarette. Forgetfulness was coming over him.

Hours before he had still been with the leaders of the underground. They had met first two days before in a warehouse of the *Journal de Génève*, then later at the atelier of a combat photographer killed at Basra. Outside had been an ordinary, bustling day in the *Vieille Ville*. Upstairs had been twenty-nine of the most serious faces, their names unknown. They had all stared at the blown-up photographs—of tanks in Brussels, of a squadron of Dorniers over the Acropolis, of Italian soldiers rotting in Ethiopia, and of a Wehrmacht artillery deck overlooking the domes of Kiev. In the room had been Hungarians and Jugoslavs, young Greeks, Poles, the Dutch, and the Danes—and, among the French, one who Justin guessed to be de Gaulle's agent. A reporter from Suisse-Romande radio had been present, also two self-contained English agents and a Czech Communist. It would be too late now, if one of these had been the face of an informer. After a year silenced among the desert folk, Justin had not been able to control his passion to bare his soul.

With the embarrassed anger of the still living, the twenty-nine had murmured ideas of spying and ciphers, of fugitives passed along chains and of a few modest acts of sabotage. Beside these, the Jura unit's single blown tunnel seemed decisive. The story of Justin's violence was only days old, yet because of it Justin had come to represent among Europe's partisans a powerful idea, a new kind of power, the persona of a generation in one ordinary man. With an aching heart, Justin had overcome his sense of disgrace, speaking instead of a subterranean labyrinth of transports and of their destination among the mists. Later, he had attempted the most painful words. "Here we talk many languages. We are chaos, but who could say that we don't know good from evil? Our people should know that while Hitler is among us, chaos is a trail to liberation."

The mountain train swam through fields of blazing snow. Justin was losing his struggle with forgetfulness. Why had he agreed to return to these high places where he had been free? Luz might have waited for him by the lake. Where the rails crossed the road, a sign had gone past: Saanen. *Could she be just three kilometers away?* he thought. And only then was Justin released.

2

THE TRAIN SLOWED AND STOPPED BY A STATIONHOUSE. WITH A QUICK GLANCE AT the few faces, Justin slung his rucksack over one shoulder and walked slowly up the village street. Overhead, the turreted grand hotel had its hundreds of shutters closed for the war. All this was very familiar. His wife had not been at the station. During Justin's long absence from Europe, it was only Luz that he had never doubted. A poignant loneliness stirred in him.

At the Sunda chalet, up the second mountainside, Justin found the shutters bolted. His own telegram was in the letter box, along with a yellow paper. *If you arrive today, we are at Lauenen, do you remember?* The handwriting was unmistakable. Justin's impatience sharpened. . . .*We?* A suspicion had come to him. For an instant, standing alone on the cloudless mountain road, Justin saw—no longer far from him to the east—the German army as it fired and laid waste to the towns of Russia and slaughtered her tribes. In a trance, he went quickly down the hill.

Finally the postal bus departed. It wound along a river and entered the next valley. Here towering walls of stone mounted in levels over a tiny village to seal off the valley. And above these were the glaciers.

The fresh snow had melted. His wife was not at the village *Gasthof*, its creepers trained like witches. "*Eine Dame—ein Herr?*" The waitress pointed to a mud road. Justin remembered a virgin lake high above, that he had walked to with Luz in 1936—a fine place for a trap. The woodcutters pretended not to see Justin Lothaire climb by. Then, at a cow crossing, he saw a woman's slightly pigeon-toed tracks and next to them a man's. As he slowed his walk, going downhill to the milky green lake, there were the prints of a third man. Justin had stopped. He stood listening in the silence.

By the lake hutch, equally motionless, stood a little figure in a hunting coat and knickers.

As Justin started onto the grass, the man disappeared. Justin kept level with the hutch and the same large-headed man straightened into the sun. He had muscular, stockinged legs. Now Justin was hurrying down over the grass. The austere gentleman was saying something. *"C'est toi,* Justin?"

He had taken two steps forward. Then his face grew haggard and, bowing stiffly, he held out a gloved hand. Justin seized it with an anguished shout and tugged David into his arms. They almost tumbled to the grass, Justin punching David's shoulders. Then he gently steadied this man who had been his greatest friend. They stood without words under the silent sky.

"And if we had hurt each other, what if we had hurt each other!" Justin panted. "there is war all around us!" David's face had gone white.

"Justin, Luz is here." David smiled crookedly. There were tears in his eyes. Clasping each other round the neck, they softly cursed the treachery of fate.

"Ordure . . . salaud!"

"Son of a salamander," David whispered.

"Nordic bumpkin."

"And you, desert insect?"

Again the two friends stood, almost sick with the shock of so much trust. Heads bowed, no longer touching, they continued slowly along the lakeside. It had come to them that they might never meet quite like this again.

"Luz showed me your message on Monday in Budapest. Her bags were already packed, Justin. To hear that you had returned to us! I could not believe it."

"And you, who were safe in Mexico . . ." They walked slowly, needing this to be settled before they saw Luz. From high above came the faint roar of cataracts.

"I am traveling on diplomatic papers for the General Staff, Justin. I have thirty-six free hours between Budapest and Berlin, to see a factory in Winterthur. Luz expected you here last night." David was now icily distant.

"My God, you can't go back! You're not even in uniform," Justin burst out.

"As you know, the whole family is in Germany. We have a son now."

"They sent for me in the desert . . ." Justin fell silent, for he had thought of Hélène's letter.

"The partisans—I guessed as much. I'm glad, Justin."

"You confuse me," Justin said, and tears of compassion came to his eyes.

David shrugged. "The partisans have a distinct virtue."

"I wish you could be with us," Justin said, knowing the impossibility of such a thing.

"I am well placed where I am," David said deliberately. "So few of us can get close to our *petit dictateur.* "And you?"

"Yesterday, I was with the leaders from all the underground."

"I would like to have been there." David bowed his head.

Amid the coolly beautiful scenery, the sun had grown hot. David was aware now of some last limit on the patience of this once soft-hearted poet—and

Justin, of a German officer's formal restraint. It occurred to Justin: *What if to be here might be the worst mistake of their long friendship, even of their lives?*

3

THE TWO FLEURUSIANS WERE OVERWHELMED. CIRCLING FROM THE WATERSIDE, David broke the stricken silence. "Justin, before we see Luz . . . what does it mean to you, this Armageddon we're involved in?"

"In war, we're all condemned. Last week, I myself buried some of you in a tunnel."

Sitting down against a moss-covered boulder, David murmured, "Ah, yes, I heard. On the Doubs . . . at Smolensk, I shot a Russian, an officer."

Justin felt himself perspire with the effort of self-mastery. "You and I believed in the same things. David, is there really talk in your army of Hitler's assassination?"

David rose. "Yes, but there are worse than him. The worst is his biologist, Jakob Stodel."

Wiping his brow, Justin slowly crossed the path and stared over the innocent green lake. Presently he returned, and they moved on. "This Hitler, with his evil, intricate mind, is the source. Crush that mind, David, and civilization can still emerge!"

"It does not make me proud that I now wish for that. In Berlin, when Johann took me to tea with the fellow, I still dreamt there must be words of civilized persuasion to speak to him. I'm afraid they failed to come to me." David smiled bitterly.

"What?" Justin was halted in the sunshine, gripping his temples. "Johann, Hitler, a tea party? You at a tea party with this grotesque thing?"

David shrugged, with the vague frown of someone awakening from a drugged sleep.

"David!" Justin choked, his face terrible with grief. "Have you heard of the European races? Had you only drawn a cake knife across the man's throat, half a million of your fellow creatures would not have died! Think, *think!*"

The two men stood on the steaming mud and stared at each other. Justin flinched as high above them an avalanche boomed, the glaciers at work on themselves.

Just then from close by came the sound of a flute. Justin somehow spoke. "Never mind, David. Who has ever won against Hell?"

"Justin, look," David cried out, relieved that they were saved from this painful discussion.

Fifty paces farther along the lakeside, seated with an older man on an embankment of pine roots, was Luz. As she glanced towards them, David and Justin fell into step. Luz rose with an uncertain little cry.

"Oh, David . . . and Justin! You see, Bela, he arrived on time!"

Justin walked forward with David, silenced by the ethereal quality of this woman's face. Both their own were red with the effort of protecting her from the things that had just been said.

"You see? They are debating. *Ils discutent déjà*."

"No, Luz, it was nothing," David called to her softly.

With a disturbed frown, Luz seemed to recognize Justin's intensity. Without another word, she came toward him, holding some ferns in the mountain sunshine. And as if this gentle beauty might still transport him to another world, Justin crushed her in his arms—unaware of Bela, the old Hungarian, or of David as he bent to pick up the ferns that fell from her hands.

"It seems impossible, Justin." She drew free with a nervous laugh. "Look who lives in the village. Years ago, Bela accompanied my mother on the piano."

"Often, often!" The musician laughed and squeezed Luz's hand. "The Danube will not be the same again."

"With you safe in Switzerland, Mother must come too," she said.

"A man can only stand so much political foolishness." The old man frowned, taken aback by the girl's careless tone over her mother's danger. "Could you imagine a more magnificent solitude in which to gather musical ideas? Now David, this serious young man certainly wants Luz to himself. Ah, yes, of course—I will not mention below that I saw any of you."

"Stay with us, you brought her to me." Justin had reached behind his wife's shoulders, as presently they started with David back along the lake edge. "Tonight, Luz and I will be alone."

"Yes, come with us, David!" Luz urgently gripped her arms through both of theirs; then instantly, she was pulling free. "My God, what is that?"

The actress stood behind them on the path. Justin reached into his jacket and brought out the object Luz had felt. Seeing her fear at the sight of a gun, he knew the disgrace of what they had become.

David took it from her, "You will get accustomed to this, Luz." He turned over the American revolver and handed it back.

"No, Luz, you must never do that." Justin smiled, and to make a melancholy joke of it, he dropped the cartridges into his wife's shirt pocket. Then he put the gun back in his jacket. "Keep them until France . . . only give them back if you wish to."

"Now, you must both stay very close to me." Luz came alongside, and the three friends strolled on, leaving the lake behind. To Luz, who had not heard what now lay between Justin and David, there seemed only to be the windless sun and forests and the cliffs that held the glaciers. At the bottom of this mountain track was a village inn where they would have lunch. Beside the next six hours together, nothing else could matter.

In the *Gasthof* there were a dozen Swiss soldiers. The woodcutters, who in the forests had pretended not to see the foreigners in town clothes climb past, were there too with their pipes and slouch hats. An aproned woman played polkas, and the sunburnt farmers grinned and raised their glasses to sing for this redhead who had joined them, who laughed and appeared sometimes to weep, seated under the bass fiddle between her two grave young men.

For Luz had sensed from where David came and where he would return, and she now knew where her husband must shortly take her. Therefore, they talked a great deal about Hélène . . . and, later, during the long hike along the valley, about their Paris days. Linda von Siebenberg had committed suicide, and her beautiful sister, Monica, was in a Hamburg sanatorium. Wilfred Rouve lived a cryptic existence in a London under siege, and in New York Duncan Penn had become embalmed somewhere between the divorce court and his top-floor office at Penn Industries. They had all known as a student the now-famous Doctor Johannes Godard. David Sunda and the Lothaires would return alone into this world war.

By dusk their healing conversation had turned to dread. David and Justin would have no chance to speak again as they had by the lake. And though they never doubted that they would somehow be saved during these precious hours, no one spoke now of putting off their departure. Very quickly they were on the station tracks in a night mist. Luz spoke then to the austerely dignified figure in the train window.

"David, you know that this is my choice. Take care of Leni—she must be in danger, living at Oberlinden. Give her our love."

"I promise I will, Lupic." The German officer smiled bleakly down into her eyes.

Luz had begun to walk behind her husband under the train window. On Justin's face she saw the desperate belief of someone who has neglected the most important thing.

"David, don't forget the last hope!" Justin's words were half drowned by the clattering wheels. "Finish it, finish it before one more month passes!"

Leaning far out to hear him, for five seconds Baron Sunda was mystified. Then he nodded and his voice came. "Yes, it may have to be me." Their hands gripped tightly, and at that moment David's task seemed to him the most glorious one on earth. As the train circled over the bridge, he saw Justin turn on the station platform, seeming to follow its passage, Luz like a hostage on his arm. Then the image was lost in the night.

A few minutes after the train had vanished with David—now, by the same unforeseen orders that sent him on to Zurich, promoted to Rittmeister von Sunda—Luz was on the last Montreux train. Seated opposite her was the half French intellectual with whom she had lived in the Palais-Royal and whose child she had lost. Her few things from Budapest had already been emptied into the rucksack. Now on her husband's long, hypnotist's face, Luz saw again the concentration that she had first noticed beside the old musician at the Lauenensee.

Justin stared through the blackened window. He did not see the chalk-pale face across from him as Luz pulled her lamb's-wool collar around her cheeks and struggled with tears. He was already far ahead, preparing himself to take her safely over the frontier.

4

JUSTIN COULD NOT FEEL HOW MUCH THE EMOTIONS OF THAT DAY HAD SOFTENED him until, at first light next morning, they left the lonely road above St. Croix.

The moon was still overhead as he walked with his wife steeply uphill through a windy forest. Somewhere ahead of them there was a sealed tunnel filled with men and iron. For hours Justin had been too stricken by the subterranean world into which Luz was prepared to follow him to speak. There was nothing else he had to give her.

It was during the hard five-kilometer climb in the gray dawn that Luz first felt the place that she was going. The muddy woods seemed suddenly haunted by armed gangs. In some way David's race had done this to the world Luz knew. Nothing that was happening to her conveyed anything but deepest obscurity.

"Justin," she finally called to him, "I'm so frightened."

"We must keep going." Justin waited for her to catch up.

With dull terror Luz heard this man's emotionless voice and never guessed that it was she who had frightened Justin with a doubt. At nightfall he halted them in a forest. He began to strike matches in the biting cold and Luz saw it too. In the far woods that were France, there had been a tiny flicker. They walked forward, into the moonlight. Soon a familiar shadow slapped Justin's shoulder.

Gabriel stood back, his eyes glittering uncertainly at Luz. "We have missed you, *camarade*."

"About your sister-in-law," Justin said, before Luz had caught up.

"Yes, we will be discreet. Anyhow that was in the wildness of the attack."

"Yes, that's so," Justin said. Remembering the pleasant farmhouse and the quilted bed to which he would take Luz, he caught her in his arms as she came up.

Their guide shuffled his feet and looked away. Something clicked in Justin's palm like marbles, still warm from his wife's shirt. And feeling how far from the lake at Lauenen and into this tunnel he had already brought Luz, Justin reloaded the revolver.

MAELSTROM

1

B Y NOVEMBER 1941, THAT INSATIABLE AMBITION FOR POWER, WHICH HAD
invented more crimes and subjected more of humankind to its will than
any other in history, for the first time confronted one law it could not
break—the law that determines the size of all living things. In five months,
Joseph Stalin had been forced to squander fourteen thousand aircraft, eighteen
thousand tanks, twenty-two thousand artillery pieces, and two and one half
million human beings—the equivalent of the entire German force—as well as
the captive citizenry of a thousand towns. Communications between Moscow
and Leningrad had been severed. The vast wheat harvest of the Ukraine was
overrun by troops and tanks. The Marxist state was on the verge of collapse. But
the man seated on his leather couch at Kuntsevo, his head bowed in thought, was
only negotiating the price that must be paid. Nor did Stalin doubt that it would
be paid in Russian blood. The only question was, in what quantity.

During these same days Adolf Hitler, who had never listened to his generals, ceased listening to his gods. At least that was how, at Doctor Godard's
studio on the Tiergarten, Doctor Goebbels chose to interpret their Führer's
depression to the philosopher. Just that week, when the first snows had already
fallen—and as a revitalized Stalin drove his officers into action employing a
secret army under the executioner Mekhlis—Hitler had declared communism
defeated. At last the orders were sent along the front for the final assault on
Moscow.

On the afternoon of 12 November one week after Stalin's Red Square
speech invoking the czarist liberators Nevsky and Kutuzov, Rittmeister von
Sunda was being driven into the principal bastion town of Orel.

From the moment that he resumed his uniform at the Bavarian frontier
and proceeded with two engineers, first to the Saar and then to Berlin, David
had been aware of the speed at which his fame had spread. At the tank works,
as he checked production of the new heavier models, there was no one who
was unaware of the much admired young aide on Guderian's staff. David
Sunda's aura of conviction after his argument with Justin by a mountain lake
seemed only to intensify his charisma. There would be no time, though, to

analyze the deeper passions at their reunion or to contemplate a meeting with
Hélène. As David approached his few hours in Berlin, he was consumed
instead by the sea of evil on which he must now set sail. His moral fear almost
mastered him during a fleeting interview with Adam Trott.

The night bombings had become severe. As Trott guided David along the
Spree Canal—detailing Rosenberg's precise plans, not to set free, but further
to enslave the peoples of the East—the sky had been visible through the
windows of many palaces. Concluding, Adam stopped David by three
Hohenzollern cannons.

"I must also counsel you that your popularity has caused jealousy with
our uncouth friend who is in charge here. Please beware."

"Adam," David said suddenly, "let's do it now. I will deliver the package
myself." He raised his empty hands in offering, almost beside himself at the
idea of any further delays. "This very week—tell them."

Adam said nothing to this, only glancing thoughtfully at David's profile.
Finally he turned to the largest cannon.

"Look, dear fellow, you see what we are?"

"Do you mean the coat of arms?" David bent stiffly over the scrolled
barrel, dated 1617. The foundry cartouche showed a Titan devouring a child.
"*Saturnus friss das Kind allein,*" he read the motto; "*Ich friss sie alle, gross
und klein.*"

During these next hours, as David overtook Guderian, who was now in
the Moscow sector, he could not stop repeating the terrible couplet: *Saturn
eats only children/I devour them all, large and small.* After his vow of action
to Adam Trott, it no longer seemed necessary to think of Justin's words:
Go through with it, it is the only hope. All this would surely be very quickly
at an end.

The road into Orel followed the Oka River. As always the Russian countryside undulated wearily, broken only by hedgerows or by stunted trees like folk
goblins with their bare topknots. Soon a remote thudding of artillery was audible. Rittmaster von Sunda's car had to wait in front of a growing line of trucks
while a caisson was pulled from a pit of mud. Chest deep in the mud, six
regulars were trying to lift the horse's forward body, while a tall *Obersturm–
bannführer* from the *Das Reich* division paced the flank, cursing the men savagely and oblivious of the absurd aspect of his spotless black uniform in this
desolate scene.

David turned to his driver. "How long have the roads been like this,
Kurt?" He swatted his gloves and stared away from the shrieking horse.

"Days sir—a week, all along the front. When it frosts we roll; when it thaws
we sink in. Look, now we can go. Orel's happier, sir," Kurt shouted, as they
skidded past a row of peasants in tattered sheepskins. "The muzhiks like us well
enough. The corps covered the last hundred and fifty kilos so fast that the Reds
thought the armor was their own. They encountered some partisans, though."

At the driver's last words, Baron Sunda sank back on the seat. Having so feared returning to the tedious masculine vanity of this world, filled with more men carrying guns than any stag hunt at Oberlinden—to the smells of sweat and diesel fumes, of dampness and burnt powder—David nevertheless felt himself exhilarated to be back among concrete events and far from his inappropriate thoughts about Luz. . . .

Awaking to the sight of a command truck parked in the yard of a two-story grain exchange, David clutched his courier bag and climbed down.

General Guderian had just left for his new headquarters near Tula, little more than a hundred kilometers from the capital. Had events here come so quickly to a crisis? David moved with his coffee through the crowded communications rooms. He paused repeatedly in front of the wall charts, scarcely taking note of the familiar faces who came up to welcome him. The long Wehrmacht front now looked like a tidal wave, at the very point of breaking over Moscow and on into Siberia. Could the Communist defense be going into rout? The moment at which David must act might be close at hand. He remembered Moscow as he had first seen it with Hélène—its factories and golden domes, and its constellation of lights—and he felt unsteady on his legs.

Baron Sunda's trance before the charts was broken by a pig-faced Rhinelander with spectacles. "Rittmeister? A car will take you to Tula at oh-five-thirty. You have a room at the Europa. May I arrange a motorcycle?"

"No . . . no, thank you," David repeated impatiently. "Did you say the Europa?"

Outside in the night, the temperature had fallen. The crust of ice made it harder than ever for David to carry his bag through the deep mud.

"Herr Rittmeister! Would you like a ride?"

A torch beam found his face—*a face now that of a traitor*. David stepped out to a mud-spattered tank with more than twenty infantrymen on its deck. With much shouting, the men cleared a place for him by the hot engine cover. On the turret, lit by the torch beam, were more than thirty painted red stars.

"*How was Berlin, sir? . . . We'll be in Moscow for Christmas . . . they won't evacuate the caviar, will they? . . . Why doesn't Wotan turn up the heating?*" called out unmistakably drunk voices.

Once again, in the simple faces of these German soldiers who tonight considered David their greatest friend, he experienced the mystery of this land. Even as he smiled the aloof, amused smile that he knew was expected of a staff officer, David felt a love for them as intense as the horror that he had felt the last summer, seeing these same men's naked bodies as they built a bridge on the Desna. And again the words came to his lips: *Ich friss sie alle, gross und klein.*

With a shuddering roar they all lurched forward, and the tank assumed the pleasant motion of a boat in a swell.

2

ONE OF HIS COMPANIONS ON THE TANK DECK THAT NIGHT WAS A SWARTHY Hanoverian sergeant with a thin face, bulging eyes, and a schoolteacher's manner, to whom the cruelest faces turned with admiration and love. He answered David's question about the overdue shipments of ice caulks, so long awaited by every tank group from the Baltic to the Sea of Azov.

"We're in a fine state, not to mention our winter clothing! At Bryansk the battle never happened."

"Never happened?" David shouted.

"God is my witness—I wish he were here—our thirties couldn't pop their armor! Quite a panic until we brought in the eighty-eights. So we outflanked fifty of the swine. We attacked up the hill, thirty strong. Then, halfway up, we hit frost. Hell, sir, what a comedy—all thirty of us, without caulks, spinning like ducks on ice. We had to run like thieves that time."

David's head had begun to swim. Would these faithful children with their wonderful machines be asked to throw away their lives, out of negligence? The vague blur of lofty destinies that still lingered from David's trip had left him. These men too would soon be free.

"The caulks will come soon," he shouted.

"Never mind, here's the Kit-Kat Klub! Come in and have some sport with us."

David jumped down, for some reason drawn to this decadence. The men swarmed through a vegetable garden. From the basement billowed a din of accordions and wild hooting. A stage had been set up on crates, with a backdrop of quilts lit by a red bulb. As they pushed among the tables, David caught the image of a gloomy officer, performing a tango with a flushed Russian girl. On the stage lay a huge naked woman with men at her head and legs, their trousers at their boot tops. David gazed round him into the packed shadows. The hundred or so war-stained faces were all doing the same thing: shouting, laughing, and weeping with an objectless persistence.

The hysterical roar intensified. A tiny Tartar appeared, dressed in swallowtails sewn together from felt patches. This gave him the appearance of an organ-grinder's monkey. Peering and winking, this apparition sang something, then took up a coarse little dance he had apparently learned to please his German audience. This consisted of stiff-legged prancings, followed by a pulling down and releasing of his trousers. Each time he did this, the rough types pressed round Rittmeister von Sunda howled, whistled, and stamped their feet.

David's eyes had begun to sting. Loosening his uniform collar, he picked up a glass of vodka. The little Tartar monkey had just made a flourish. Four short, very plain Russian girls with braids stumbled onto the stage.

Now the girls had crossed hands in a mock *pas de quatre*, all four in peasant dress and giggling with shame. It was immediately apparent to everyone that the girl on the far right had slimmer legs and was younger than the others. And to each German soldier in that basement, this girl's slim legs and youth appeared as miracles of sweetness and poetry, and they were in love with her—that is, they wanted, quite innocently, to make love to her. Because this was not possible, as it had been with the mound of flesh they had lined up for, the gaping faces along the walls began to whistle and scream even louder and the three ugly women, imagining themselves also passionately desired, lost their fear and began an ungainly little dance in the dense smoke. They waved their skirts, cocked their heels, and clapped out of time. To each of the men in the room, not least to Baron Sunda, at the center among the tables, each of these gestures was profoundly moving. Through the deafening noise and closely packed faces, having seen the younger girl look at him persistently, David forgot everything and felt his mouth go dry.

After several minutes of pandemonium, the Tartar monkey waved his arm and a cloud of green smoke swallowed the tiny stage. After more confusion, the girls reappeared in crude German folk dresses. For a moment the shouting subsided, then burst out even louder. The four girls had climbed down into the packed basement floor. They resumed their clumsy dance through the tables. The youngest girl pushed toward David, smiling at him and awkwardly swinging her hips. He picked up the empty glass and lifted it to his lips.

"She's chosen you!" the sergeant's voice shrieked in David's right ear. "God is my witness!"

The girl had torn free from a gray-haired gunner at the next table. Her weight pressed on David Sunda's knee. He saw her blunt face before his in the red light among the circle of wild, sweating faces. David smelled the young girl's strong odor and could feel the crude jealousy of every soldier in the room center on their table. The girl pressed her fists over his ears. Through the basement was a sudden silence, and David felt her mouth on his lips. Then the basement again thundered around them. The dull, close face was looking at him oddly—no longer romantic, with the illusion of hope, but terribly human. Dense blue smoke rose between their eyes, and for an instant David saw into the girl and felt her hatred. David struggled to maintain his voluptuous smile, but suddenly he was conscious of the partisans in the countryside around—and of Justin's words.

The girl in his lap pushed away with a triumphant, nasal curse. At once, she resumed her dance, laughing at the animal shouts and at the dozens of arms that reached out to her. David was too exhausted by the din and smoke, and the emotions of that moment, to take any notice of his table companions' belligerent irritation that he had let the girl go.

For ten more minutes, Baron Sunda sat in the suffocating room, stiffly smoking his cigar and staring at the stage. The girl did not look at him again, but across five meters of uniformed shoulders, David again felt her powerful romance. He knew the terror, guilt, and triumph of being in Russia, and the vile reality of what was taking place on the Moscow road: *Ich friss sie alle, gross und klein.* And David knew that the moment when this coarse young woman had seized his head in her hands, had somehow been the truest of his life. What salvation had she seen in him? It was only now that David felt the meaning of Justin's near-hatred by the Swiss lake. Across the arena of German uniforms, the hoots and whistles had given way to an animal shouting of obscenities which only made the delirious girls lift their peasant skirts higher.

This David did not wish to see. He slipped away from the sergeant, who kept lurching up to cheer with a cigarette between his lips, each time falling back in his chair. Outside, in the dark street, David was recognized by the two soldiers left on guard, who were possessive of the Rittmeister because he had not objected to their using the tank for a spree. David vaguely took note of the piercingly sharp air.

"Was it good sport, sir?"

"God help us," David said.

"Ha-ha, God made us!" the second soldier called softly, his laughter form-ing dense little cloud signals. He held up a pocket thermometer. "Look, it has gone from minus five celsius to minus twenty-two, in one hour."

He was only half listening. "Minus twenty-two degrees? Best keep the machine running."

"Yes, sir. Going up to the front tomorrow, sir?"

Baron Sunda stumbled in a daze along the shuttered shopfronts. In this provincial desolation, hearing the boy's unmistakable dialect—from very near Oberlinden—David was seized by the undefinable passion that had begun hours before, as he gazed at the German tidal wave. In some way he now shared in this too, by virtue of a mortal oath before Trott in Berlin. Somewhere in the night, beyond these captive housefronts, the sufferings and madness of the hundred millions of innocent human beings beaten and crushed between the jaws of war had reached an unforeseeable turning, of greatest significance to the history of the human spirit. The capital of the czars, the laboratory of world communism, was almost in their grasp! In the days ahead, the chaos of possibilities would vanish and the irreversible future of human society be revealed by men David knew—Guderian and half a dozen other architects, who held before their eyes the cards of history and of men's lives. Staggering numbers of loyal and innocent men, like these by the tank, would fling away their lives on the gamble to conquer the continent that had destroyed Napoleon.

As he was possessed, in these moments by the monstrous grandeur of the design, David's moral life—his loves and family, his friendships and personal fate—all seemed suddenly meaningless and trivial. He felt himself driven by an urgent longing, beyond honor or virtue or the fear of death, equaled only by the greatest love, to enter as close as was physically possible. To see, to hear, to share in the sensations and the very being of these immortal moments that were now so near and would surely come. Were coming already, perhaps even tomorrow.

3

NEXT MORNING, IN THE LIGHT OF DAY, AS BARON SUNDA REACHED GUDERIAN'S headquarters at Yasnaya Polyana, several centimeters of fine dry snow had fallen.

The sky was lead gray. The frozen lawn, laid out in the English style under the usual birch and poplar trees, was swarming with alert faces. A steady movement of officers streamed in and out of the adjoining building, trailing clouds of condensation. David had just removed his coat in the hallway, still dangerously off guard after his delirium in the night, when there were loud voices. Guderian had appeared on the second-story landing beside the distinguished figure of Field Marshal von Bock, the Death Preacher, commander of the entire central front. David recognized Generals Schaal, Lemelson, and von Geyer, a distant relation of David's enemy on the staff.

Though the group under the low chandelier had spent the last weeks presiding over the slaughter of thousands, their expressions were calm and tactful, and despite the field marshal's seniority, they were dominated by the tank leader's humor and vitality. Catching sight of David, Guderian showed no surprise.

"Oh yes, I served under your father," said von Bock without emotion, upon being introduced to young Sunda.

Guderian winked at him. "When will we have our new motors, then?"

"The works are on schedule. However, shipments are still being diverted to the SS," David added, after a slight hesitation at the poorness of the news, and noticing the jealousy of his temporary replacement, Loki.

But Heinz Guderian only laughed, as if his weapons' new engines were of no significance whatever and could have no bearing on the successes ahead. "You will brief me tomorrow. Meanwhile, Loki will update the positions." The two commanders, trailed by their staffs as by a pack of impatient but well-trained dogs, had reached the main hall entrance. The sandy-haired officer held David's arm in a strong grip. "Incidentally, my boy, it would seem that this is to be it."

"May I be of use?" David replied, resuming their old game of influences with as much enthusiasm as he could arouse.

"Relearn the positions thoroughly."

With a second wink, Guderian continued out between the saluting guards. Halted with his coat off in the icy doorway, David understood that he had narrowly missed being witness to a decisive gamble of the Russian campaign. He also guessed from Guderian's grin that their own strategic situation was precarious and the outcome uncertain, but that once again this man had found in himself the will to infect his tank army with that same certainty of ends that the enemy had so far been unable to resist.

Baron Sunda spent that morning in a hushed high-ceilinged pavilion which served as the operations room. Even as he was briefed over the new close-scale maps, codes began to arrive on several radio sets. A bony officer whose blond hair stood on end moved arrows on the wall. So it would be, on dozens of similar charts from Leningrad to Stalingrad—and on the huge chart that few had seen at Supreme Headquarters in Lötzen, where the Führer, with whom David had once taken tea, would be manipulating the knights and rooks. From the inflamed mind of Hitler to the equally monstrous Stalin to the distant strategies of Churchill and Roosevelt—down to the last villager or sniper, fumbling with his frozen sights in the bitter gale outside—there were several million separate experiences, visions, degrees of comprehension, hates, and passionate longings. The only sense that all these beings could have agreed upon now lay in these parchments of position, number, and direction.

As minutes passed and David became involved with the situation as it appeared on the wall, an altogether new dread stirred in him. Rising, he wandered up and down the pavilion behind the group of eager, intent faces. His head began to ache. Was he going mad? Had no one seen what he saw?

The main effort was focused to the southeast of the capital, on the Kolomna-Ryazan railway. A dozen armored infantry divisions—most of them under half strength—were massed in the Tula area. On the Russian side there were many dozens of white lines. Were these all Siberian divisions equipped with the big tanks? Recalling now Guderian's fierce confidence that dawn, David felt a terrible awe. Yet even as he stood frozen, the chart officer with the brush of hair delicately prodded the salient occupied by the 17th Division northward, almost to Kashira.

Exhausted by the officers' unrelieved excitement and by the indecision of his fate while the scales would not tip, David left the main building. He went looking for the doctor in the estate's large stables. Del Bianco's friendship remained unsatisfactory because Baron Sunda had accepted it only at the hour that he had taken a life. Still, he trusted Egi more than anyone in this conspiracy that David was bound to, but which did not act.

He found his friend wrapped in blankets on a groom's moth-eaten couch. The surgeon had not shaved, nor had he taken off his bloodstained smock.

"No, no, I was not asleep." Sitting upright, Egi attempted a welcoming grin. The man seemed to be in a state from which nothing could raise him. His face worked, momentarily seeking forgotten emotions.

"Egi, what has happened?" They had been together only a week before. "This place is freezing."

"Everyone is sick!" said the hoarse voice. "I have cut off one hundred fingers, thirty two feet, and two noses. My father sends me insulting letters. However, eternity is patient."

"I brought you a Frascati."

"Do you believe it? Del Bianco's liver will take no more." At the mention of alcohol, Egi's eyes had clouded. He swayed slightly on the couch. "Did you tell her, your wife—Elena? Did you tell her about your accident?" As he spoke the name, a look of almost tender concern transformed the doctor's haggard face.

"No, Egi," David said quietly, as he turned over a food bucket and sat down before his friend. "I couldn't tell her I was there. . . . Soon, perhaps."

"You should have told her. Otherwise, your muzhik will haunt you."

"The assault on Moscow has begun. Why not take off that filthy sheet? Come down to the chart room." The Italian violently waved his hand. "Tell me about your meeting. Tell me how she looked. How did Elena hold the boy, the little one?"

"I'll save the story of my journey until this advance is settled."

"Advance? Advance?" Del Bianco cut the air between them with an open hand. "Say, if you are so interested in this advance, in the morning I will take you somewhere very special. You are in the next room? Good, I will wake you. Now I am tired."

Shocked to have found his friend so altered, David scarcely reacted in the quiet mess when the wounded von Geyer, whom he so loathed, seemed pleased to see Baron Sunda and retold the saving of Guderian's life so that it sounded like the Wild West. David took no part in the tedious speculation concerning the evil influence that Martin Bormann, Hitler's closest aide, had over the Führer. There would be no contacting Claus or Fabian while the Moscow offensive was under way.

That afternoon, Rittmeister von Sunda wrote his reports. At six he returned to the pavilion and spread out his charts. The positions had now altered noticeably. The semicircular German front—from Kalinin in the north, to Kashira in the south, at a range from Moscow of fifty to one hundred and sixty kilometers—had forced appreciable advances. But these in no way resembled the relatively effortless rushes of earlier days. The impression on David was of some weight lifter who, having attacked a giant weight and succeeded in snatching it to his chest, now was straining to sustain the rhythm for a final lift above his head. At each instant the weight came to seem less a movable body and more like a permanent wall. By midnight, as David completed his charts and went to bed, the 5th Armored Division had reached to within sixty kilometers of Moscow.

When he awoke at six-thirty, David saw a membrane of ice crystals had coated the inside of the windowpane. Del Bianco was pummeling his shoulder and David could see that he would have a last chance to behave as a good friend.

"Two pairs of socks, *barone*. It's twenty below."

Downstairs at the warm Russian hearth, David had coffee and three slices of black bread with cherry preserve. Then recalling what was taking place, he went upstairs to the operations room. Several arrows around Moscow had drawn somewhat tighter.

4

OUTSIDE STOOD A MOTORBIKE, STREAMING PLUMES OF WHITE VAPOR. THE SURGEON was seated behind the driver. After David climbed into the sidecar, the machine roared down the long drive to the stone on the Tula road.

At the gateway, they were blocked by a returning column of infantry as it crowded down the road. From where he lay bundled in the sidecar, David peered at the stained sheepskins and fur hats. These soldiers had no guns. They were Russian prisoners.

The remains of the column—six deep, and patrolled on both flanks by SS men hugging Schmeissers—took several minutes to pass. David watched the hundreds of expressionless faces swing by, many of them Tartars, with the faces of boys and streaming noses. He strained to make out the heads that turned to stare at the gates of Yasnaya Polyana and at the waiting German motorbike. But he could only see the ravaged glitter of eyes and, against a pinkening horizon, the bobbing of hats and the flutter of hair.

As the tail end went by, David noticed one of the fur-hatted prisoners staring at him fixedly. This was a tall man with a scarred, shiny complexion and a dignified manner. The figure passed, never taking his terrible eyes off David, even turning to stare back from the column—almost as someone might who had known Baron Sunda well. The metal creaked in the cold as the motorcycle lurched onto the road behind the column, heading toward Orel.

A dead sun was soon up in the ice-blue sky. Skeletons of trees drifted past. Thirty paces ahead, the sheepskin backs swayed and kept pace, the prisoners' blunt boots stirring up snow. Sometimes the Russians far ahead passed through a drift, and the gale bore it in an opaque cloud out over the plain to the east. David's frozen world grew even smaller—unquestioned as that of a shepherd who follows sheep—until it consisted of nothing but his aching forehead and the moist warmth of the scarf against his mouth. As he watched the sidecar's spinning rubber wheel and the trampled snow that advanced beneath it, David shivered so violently that his boots kept kicking inside the nacelle. Through the thickening process of his mind it occurred to him that he might walk.

Without a sign, David pushed himself up and stumbled free of the sidecar. He exchanged glances with the startled driver and shrugged at Egi. Almost immediately, he felt better. Walking ahead of the motorcycle, David unconsciously fell into step with the tall prisoner at the end of the last rank. His thoughts turned to the current of men ahead and the vast riches of knowledge they must have—of the provinces and their tribes, from Dagestan to Finland. David noticed that he was overtaking the prisoners' trudging legs. But where was the stockade?

After marching for more than an hour, the column far ahead wheeled sharply over a frozen embankment, then down through some stunted fir trees. David pushed to the right, across a snowfield, hearing close behind the trudge of the doctor's boots. Inside his own, David's toes were in pain. Ahead, the mass of Russians was emerging into a quarry pitted with shell holes. There was a burnt-out tank, a Voroshilov, with its turret derailed and the gale moaning in the hole. Under the snow were unnatural shapes.

The column surged out toward the edge of a shallow excavation. Already a huge crowd was waiting—perhaps two thousand more prisoners, spread halfway to the line of fir trees, the mass of hats, faces, boots, and fluttering coats seemed to contract more and more tightly together, as if trying to form itself into a single body. As David and the doctor stumbled closer, the gale bore away the high-pitched shouts of the several dozen German guards. Still, David heard clearly a droning murmur come from the captive mass. He felt his scalp bristle.

At that moment David saw, standing twenty paces away, the hot-tempered *Obersturmbannführer* from the mud-choked road at Orel. He bent over the doctor's shoulder.

"I've seen that one before," he shouted.

His friend's watering eyes, glanced toward David's face. Egi's frostbitten cheeks looked painful. But that detail too was remote, like the sun that shone down without warmth on the sea of fur hats.

The long wall of prisoners was separated by fifty paces from the rim of the excavation. This appeared to have been dug with explosives. The immaculate *Obersturmbannführer*, who was strongly built but round-shouldered, paced behind a file of his guards. On the snow to one side were three gray ammunition canisters. The fellow waved a crumpled paper and then began shouting in German. The wind tore at the paper. "This punishment," the officer repeated, rising on his toes with the effort of making himself heard, "is authorized by *Reichsführer* SS Himmler . . . in retaliation for the"—his tiny words vanished, then further cloudlets spurted from his lips—"two thousand German prisoners of war at Serpukhov, on orders of Marshal Koniev . . ."

Before the officer had concluded, David felt himself step forward. He was shaking with a frozen fever, his knees had weakened. He felt his left ankle turn painfully.

"*Herr Obersturmbannführer!*" David called out, for some reason noticing the man's fine cheekbones. The ridiculous words had emerged as a shout. David saw the officer's ice-cold stare focus on him without surprise or recognition. And from the rattling fir trees, out of the desolation of ice, blown upon the merciless wind, there came to him a dread beyond words. To his left, he could hear the droning protest from the nearest wall of prisoners. David was seized by a physical terror.

Was it to be this, the moment when he would act? Or should he be saved for the one act that he had vowed to commit?

"With all respect, dear fellow." He fought to suppress the quaver in his voice. "I believe that your orders are the worst joke I have ever heard."

"Joke, Herr Rittmeister? I will demonstrate what sort of joke they are."

In his stark black uniform, the *Obersturmbannführer* shouted the phrases face-to-face with David. They were standing ten strides from the closest prisoners, who eyed them with alarm. Now the unpleasant fellow had turned away and passed through the long file of his guards. Stepping up to the nearest Russians—two young men with bony faces and short clipped black hair— he jerked his arm violently. The prisoners shuffled forward, shrugging and stamping their feet and staring at the canisters.

As the two Russians moved through the line of guards, the deep murmur from the mass behind them grew louder. The front wall of prisoners shifted forward, as a mother who holds out her arms for her children. Down the line, the agitated young SS crouched and drove them back, cursing and shouting and thrusting the short ugly barrels this way and that. Meanwhile, the *Obersturmbannführer* and a comically eager young *Sturmer* had twisted the prisoners' arms behind their backs. They pushed the two solders down on the ice by the edge of the pit. The Russians did this in a sort of trusting daze, like students who have volunteered for a demonstration.

No longer believing his senses, knowing only the sweetness of these lives, David Sunda stood with the others. He saw the kneeling boys gaze out over the pit. Abruptly, there was no movement or sound, only the slapping of trousers and the groan of the wind from the forest. David saw the two SS raise their arms and press pistol barrels to the fuzzy backs of the Russians' heads. He saw the Germans' bodies strain, their faces grimace, the way the boys drew their heads away from the hard bump of the guns. He shut his eyes. Very close to David there was a coughing crack. He had begun to pant.

The space in front of the two SS was empty. The young Sturmer nearest to him laughed nervously, and David started forward. There was no ground under his feet.

"Listen to me, sir." He gasped for breath. The *Obersturmbannführer*'s arm was thick and muscular. "I will see you put down for this."

As if nothing had just taken place, several of the nearest guards had turned curiously from the mass of glaring Russian faces. One pointed a gun halfway toward David. For a moment confused by such an irregularity, the *Obersturmbannführer* tore loose his arm and slipped.

"Who is this?" he shouted at the surgeon, whom he seemed to know.

From just behind David, Egi's voice instantly replied. "Baron David Barthold von Sunda."

"A baron!" The face sneered witheringly. "What is a baron in this world?"

Turning, the *Obersturmbannführer* paced away down the bulging front rank of prisoners. He skidded twice in quick succession, and the Russians pushed back from him in terror. "Herd down these Russian animals at once!" he shouted. "*Die Gewehre-raus!*"

Del Bianco was tugging at David's arm. "You come, you should come, David. You have seen it now. . . ."

Baron Sunda had turned back. He was staring at the tall Siberian who had seemed to watch him outside Yasnaya Polyana. David was trembling, and he struggled to breathe.

Egi renewed his pleas. "There is nothing to be done here!"

Finally, he allowed himself to be dragged away over the field of snow. The gale bore after them the muffled German shouts and the rising murmur from the enslaved mob. Then David was back in the sidecar. His twisted ankle had begun to sting. The motor roared by his shoulder and David felt his friend's hand.

"We will get very Schnappsed—very, very Schnappsed! We will talk about the good things."

Beyond the woods, the machine guns had started. The gale was from behind them now, and they raced in a reckless silence over the blinding snow. At the sight of his gloves, as they clutched the handrail, frozen tears cut David's cheeks.

When they got back to headquarters, on this second morning of the offensive, he had to tear the gloves free. Turning from his friend, unable to meet his eyes, David walked aimlessly under the file of oaks. How remarkable and terrible that he was still able to stroll with his hands behind his back. That these trees were still able to stand and their branches to rattle, and his cheeks to be stung by this winter cold. What could he have in common now with anything in the world? Hearing angry voices, David paused.

On the drive ahead stood a young soldier. Beside him a *Rittmeister* with a scarred face was dressing the boy down. "We are winning because we are efficient! If everyone delayed our generals' messages while they relieved themselves, where would the fatherland be? Where . . . would . . . the fatherland . . . *be?*"

In three paces, David stepped between them. As both men stared at him in astonishment, he found that he could not speak. Then, as if the merciless wind had blown it away, David's rage subsided.

"You are wrong, *Rittmeister*," David said. "We are winning because we have been more bullying, more aggressive, and more outrageous. We have simply stunned the enemy, as you have stunned this young man."

When the courier was safely away, David became aware that someone had been watching them. Partly hidden by a trunk, on the lawn reserved for the estate's family, stood a woman dressed in black and wrapped in a sheepskin. David did not see that the woman was squat, or what her age might be, but only that she, too, must be alone and suffering. Had she forgotten that she could no longer visit the headquarters building?

Suddenly it seemed more important to him than anything could ever have been that this woman should not fear David Sunda. Forcing a smile, he took two steps. The woman drew back: David spread his hands, then bowed. She watched him alertly but did not move.

"Madame, puis-je vous accompagner à la porte?" he said.

The woman was staring up hard into David's face. Her intelligent eyes looked toward the adjoining buildings. Then he felt her arm in his, light but firm. Under his rough leather coat, Baron Sunda's chest began to ache with gratitude.

Together they walked over the uneven crust toward the family's porch. And as he felt the fragile tug of the woman who clung to his arm, David was able to think of the thing that he had just witnessed. Were they all dead by now? And the tall familiar Siberian who had stared at David—was he in the pit too? Yet when David thought of his own screams at the *Obersturmbann-führer*—and how he had made not one centimeter's progress in his identical scene with the Oberst—terror washed over him so powerfully that he could not continue the thought. As they crossed some windblown yellow grass to the porch steps, the woman looked up into David's face without surprise at the emotions on it.

"Merci, monsieur," said a voice from deep in her throat. Hesitating while the German officer bent to kiss her hand, the woman disappeared through the door.

As he limped back to headquarters, his lapels held shut round his neck, David saw Guderian's car racing up from the gatehouse.

5

IN THE DAYS THAT FOLLOWED, BARON SUNDA DID NOT ONCE LEAVE GUDERIAN'S side. While the tank leader's southern flank continued to force advances across the snowfields toward Moscow, David almost harassed his father's friend with his obedience and his precision. His entire being had become focused on the moment to come, when they could speak in complete privacy.

By the sixth day of December, when the temperature fell to thirty degrees below zero, David sensed from Guderian's manner that the moment might come soon.

That afternoon, just to the east of Spasko, the now world-famous commander had observed tanks of his 4th Division from a dugout overlooking a shallow ghostland of cornfields. The peasants had fled that morning, leaving the harvested crop half burned. The snorting and clatter from the tanks, the reports of gunfire, and the deadly hiss of bullets were muffled by the arctic wastes—on which, here and there, bodies sat frozen hard like sculptures. The familiar smells of cordite and sulfur eddied past reassuringly, along with a brief unpleasant odor when a soldier down the line was sliced in two by a tank shell. Today, for the simple Germans surrounding David, who forgot their crimes and followed orders, the business of the battlefield was as absorbing as ever. Because it was their life's work and their last belief, the unshaven soldiers who lined the ridge and the gunners behind the bulky 88s did not tire of showing off their courage under fire, cheering direct hits, and absolving themselves at once of their fallen comrades, because this was necessary and therefore acceptable. They were handsome and hardened and went on obliviously joking and taking childlike pleasure in one another's bravado, despite their iced lips and their flimsy uniforms.

But not even this nightmare could affect David's bleak detachment. For, during their twenty minutes in the chart room, he had detected instantly a faint new undertone in Guderian's ferocious command.

At noon, a dozen of the big Siberian tanks from the far ridge had reached the slope hidden below, trailed by two thousand Moscow infantry in white winter camouflage. The 4th Division's two thrusts had meanwhile been able to turn Zhukov's flanks and close behind the Russians on the distant ridge—a mockery of the vast encirclements of last summer. At one o'clock, a heavy Soviet rocket and dive-bomber attack had ensued. Burning slivers had darted into the hill seven kilometers away, while tiny buzzing dive-bombers milled like terns against the infinite blue skies. German planes had quickly appeared and given chase toward the snow clouds in the east.

As usual being without radios, the Russians invisible below had only now realized that they were encircled. Presently the enemy tanks and infantry reappeared, streaming from the valley and up the distant slope.

Three places from David Sunda, along the dugout's plank wall, General Guderian observed all this with a jaunty grin. He crouched again under a rangefinder.

"Well, now, tell them to check ranges! Thicken that fire!" he commented to the cluster of officers. "How much armor still on the other side, *Rittmeister?*"

David did not look at his notes. "At least twenty more, sir, and twenty more coming up."

"They'll never hold that ridge. Radio!" He stamped his boots on the planks, and his officers laughed. "Repeat to Geller my order to abandon the ridge! He must attack down the slope in strict formation and reverse the Reds back toward my command post."

This was the first time in all that week that Guderian had been forced to give so much ground. But from his manner, no one but his closest staff could have detected anything amiss.

David crowded with the others along the plank wall. Tiny beneath the mountainous snow clouds, the fleeing Red infantry, running in a ragged line behind their withdrawing tanks, had just reached the distant incline and started to flounder up. Without pausing, the tanks fired erratically into the dense smoke ahead of them. Now equal numbers of German tanks and infantry had appeared as dots along the far ridge—they would be Geller's—advancing out of the smoke in wedge formation. David could feel his face sting. At what price did he hope that the tiny scrambling white figures would escape on their native soil? David's stomach heaved as, head on, the Russian and German tanks drew close. In the same instant, black smoke burst from two of the white T34s. A half second later, one of the Corps' smaller tanks was hit in the magazine and exploded. The sound carried up to the generals in the dugout as a dull, oily thud. Another of the Red tanks had stopped and was reversing in a circle through the cornstalks.

But despite their slow movement up the far slope, the retreating Russians had scented freedom and did not turn back. They converged with the attacking German tanks at a third of the distance up the slope. With only a zigzag and reversing of turrets, and without pausing to fight, the enemy tanks passed through them, pivoted, and could be seen racing up the slope in disarray. Around Guderian in the dugout there was a stunned silence.

"Look!" David pointed. Dotting the length of the far skyline were more Red tanks and an indistinct mass of infantry.

For another two hours the heavy fire kept up, while Guderian's tanks withdrew across the scarred valley floor and reappeared, reversing up the near slope. It was snowing heavily when the Russian counterattack was finally halted by concentrated artillery fire, only three thousand meters below. The exhausted Wehrmacht infantry from the distant ridge now came streaming up between the cornstalks, their faces clearly visible. The eager shouting had died away. Guderian stooped by his periscope, calling orders without looking at anyone. The confused cries that came from the little scurrying ants down the slope grew louder. Dozens more lay strewn along their retreat like tumbled scarecrows.

As the disordered mob drew nearer, one sable-haired SS officer was conspicuous. While the fleeing Germans scuttled and ducked from behind the tanks to fire, the *Sturmbannführer* walked calmly upright, waving his pistol almost indifferently this way and that to direct the fire. The men, many of them wounded, had begun jumping and rolling into the dugout all along the ridge. Following Guderian's glance, David saw the panicked white faces, babbling as men do who have been seen fleeing under fire. The cool *Sturmbannführer* stood on the dugout wall beside Guderian's periscope until the men were clear, then he climbed almost delicately down the ladder. He looked around him, his gaze pausing without surprise on General Guderian.

"Well, then . . . what happened?"

The *Sturmbannführer* smiled bitterly at Guderian's question. He flicked some mud off his sleeve. "They have learned all our tricks—"

His words were swallowed by a deafening thud. An intense heat radiated through the dugout.

Scarcely twenty meters from where they stood at the barricade, one of the reversing tanks had been hit and flamed up, the gray paint instantly darkening. Someone—the goggled commander—was wrenching at himself waist-deep in the turret. As he struggled in sight of the motionless officers in the dugout, the veins standing out on his temples, the man seemed to stare across at Guderian. From inside the smoking tank came a hiss as steel splinters whirled off the inner plates. The shoulders above the turret stopped moving. The uniform began to smoke, and the expressionless staring face blackened.

Among all the officers watching this death of a fellow German, only one had lost the capacity to feel horror at this spectacle, and this was Baron Sunda.

6

DURING THE GRIM RETURN TO THEIR HEADQUARTERS, GENERAL GUDERIAN'S command column lost its way and became blocked in a snow trench. They were forced to walk the last five hundred meters.

At dusk when he reached Yasnaya Polyana through the blizzard, Guderian conducted his superior, von Bock, to the brightly lit radios adjoining the chart room. Without asking either Baron Sunda or the other dozen officers waiting at attention to leave, he contacted General Halder at Ribbentrop's castle in Poland. The Führer was occupied watching a moving picture, *Birth of a Nation*. After ten minutes, Halder's mild voice crackled over the speakers. Hoarse with anger, Guderian at once demanded that the advance on the capital should be suspended immediately and winter positions be taken up. He spoke of the heavy casualties and worn-out equipment, the frozen gunsights and breaches, the sacrifices of his men.

Through the overheated pavilion, there was a profound silence. Not one officer stirred. They all recognized the temper that Guderian was famous for, and which had prevented his appointment to supreme command. The radios too seemed to have gone dead. As von Bock added his reluctant agreement, the Death Preacher took delicate, elklike steps backwards to the length of his telephone cord. Guderian had begun thumping his fist on the table.

"Do you understand? Impossible! Suicide!" he shouted. "And please also tell our Führer to see to the winter clothing. . . . " There was a nasal crackling over the speaker. "What? Damnation, I have told the man three times, and over three months! On top of which, that shipment spent the last twenty days in Warsaw station, while my men have lost their hands and feet!"

The voice from a romantic castle on a Polish lake replied with serene patience. How could there be discussion of a retreat to winter positions while the advance on Moscow was in full swing? As always, this godlike confidence stirred a potion of dreams in the officers frozen around David. But Guderian only snorted with disgust. With a salute to the field marshal, the tank leader took his hat, tightened his shoulder belt, and marched slowly out of the pavilion past the orderlies crowded in the door.

David overtook him on the curving hall staircase. The older man was descending slowly with one hand on the balustrade. As with all men detached enough to recognize a moment when it is at hand, David was so concentrated that he could scarcely speak.

"Heinz . . . General, I know what must be on your mind. May we speak alone?"

"Ah, my young friend. Yes, things are not going well. Come then, have you visited the great author's grave?"

After the months of subtle evasions, Guderian's assent confounded David. Could the Center Army have come within his influence? How much conviction had he to draw upon?

In the dusk outside, the bitter wind had died. A horde of snowflakes settled in perfect order. The general strode in the shadows at David's side down a straight path between the lime trunks. Neither of them spoke. As the two German officers came near Tolstoy's fenced grave and sundial, which was surrounded by pits left by exploded mines, the forest darkened. They stood peering over the railing. Guderian stirred impatiently.

"Curse this winter!" he muttered, and began to pace up and down the clearing. "Curse German will. Curse the ambition that drove us all here and now abandons us." He groaned aloud. Then Guderian went on as if he were speaking not to a traitor but to the most honorable member of the most noble family in Germany. "You are too young to know what this will mean. How easily I could have overrun them. We didn't know everything, but we knew enough for that. Ah, but one dozen stupidities have brought this winter upon us. Why, God, *why* could there not have been just two or three mistakes less?"

David shuddered at the granite reality of the words that he alone was hearing by this lonely grave.

"For centuries to come," the tank leader went on with increased agitation, as clouds of condensation rose around them, "the sages will say—if war has not erased all history—that Guderian put the power of gods in the hands of an amateur, that Europe failed to defeat such an amateur, and that, finally, the insane will of this amateur eclipsed the longest-lived and greatest of all civilizations. The sages will look back on us here, at the doors to Moscow, and they will say that Guderian held Russia in his palm, but that idiot corporal took it from him. The moment passed. The opportunity for which so many died was lost forever."

The two aristocrats stood motionless in the ghostly clearing. High above and all around them the frozen wood creaked unpityingly, as if laden now with winter in place of leaves. David could hear Guderian breathing heavily. The words of defeat, once uttered here by this remote grave so far from home, haunted the trunks and snow and made the night air unbreathable.

"I must speak openly," David said. "If it means my life."

"Tell me, my boy," Guderian answered quickly. "I have watched you suffer. This afternoon was the worst. Poor Geller."

"No! This afternoon was not the worst, and your campaign against dictatorships is not over."

David Sunda's anger was suddenly in his throat and temples, each separate word burning in his heart. In the pitch darkness he could feel Guderian's face—the kind, charming, ruthless face of a military gentleman—turn to him without surprise. "Only some days ago, I myself saw our men slaughter two thousand unarmed Russian prisoners. . . ."

As he remembered the surge of that dark mass when the *Obersturmbann-führer* had separated out the two boys to be shot, David began to shake and tears came to his eyes.

"His, our idiotic corporal's, thugs are shipping millions of our occupied peoples back and forth as slaves. I am sure that it is not just God who knows what is going on behind your lines—not to speak of the vitriol that our propagandists are spreading throughout Europe."

David saw Guderian take off his peaked hat. The man's head was bowed in the tenderly falling snow.

"Germany has become swollen with conceit," David continued, with the full force of his convicion. "Our gross excesses will bring a disgrace upon our descendants and all Europe that will never be forgotten. Your sages will look back upon this moment—December 1941—and they will say it was still not too late. A few men in our civilization could still stand against Hitler's will. Sir, let us choose the side of sanity, before it is forced down our throats. Let us go back, you and the others, Hoeppner, Mannstein, Bock, and Brauchitsch, but above all you—let us go back and surprise Hitler before we are all ruined. This is our great opportunity. Your sages will say, This man Guderian, seeing the ruin of his people, turned back and freed them from the greatest evil in their history. And all the world's democracies applauded the liberator."

David paused. The man at his side had begun rhythmically tapping the fence with his boot.

"No. They will say, Guderian abandoned the honor he had always served and took the law in his own hands."

The moon had momentarily emerged. David leaned closer. The shudder of artillery fire came to them again from the east.

"Now is the moment, sir. The army and the country would follow you. A conspiracy so close to the seat of power could not be stopped. . . ."

He faltered. Over the moonlit face of Guderian had suddenly come an expression of fatherly sanctimony, a look that in a flash reminded David of an evening with Guderian years before, at his mother's dinner table, when David had challenged his father's friend about the morality of armored warfare.

"I am no plotter, Rittmeister von Sunda. For that, you must go to Herr von Kluge. But what you have said is quite safe with me and by this same point of honor I am bound by my oath to the Führer.

Suddenly cheerful, and as if he had not just called the Führer an idiotic corporal, the tank leader straightened and began slowly walking back between the lime trees. David was forced to fall in beside him.

"And, my boy, a word of warning," Guderian went on, in his usual brisk, confident style. "It is no secret that the Führer is jealous of the Sunda family. You yourself also have many enemies, here and in the SS. I can protect you only as long as you stay close to me—though for your father's sake I will not take you this time into Hitler's presence. Or perhaps you would be better off out of the military altogether."

"I have no doubt, sir," David managed to reply, his flush of terror hidden by the darkness, "that the whole world would be better off out of the military."

7

On the day following General Guderian's conversation with Baron Sunda by the grave at Yasnaya Polyana, the Japanese emperor, Hirohito—who, confident of his Nazi ally's eventual defeat, had also made a pact with Stalin—attacked Pearl Harbor and the United States declared war on Hitler at the very moment when Germany was on the verge of overcoming Russia. From that hour, there was no significant peace left anywhere on earth.

At the very hour that Baron Sunda had marched with his family's friend back up the snow path to a Tula estate—having just miscalculated the chance to bear a package that very month to Hitler's side—Japanese naval squadrons afloat on the warm Pacific sea were warming up their aircraft and watching for the rising sun.

By 20 December, Field Marshal von Bock had resigned to von Kluge his command of the tattered Moscow Front, which each day committed more vicious crimes and endured more indescribable misery. On Christmas Day—after another visit to the dictator's well-heated headquarters far away in Poland—General Guderian followed the example, not only of the Death Preacher but also of field marshals Brauchitsch, and Rundstedt and of von Leeb on the Leningrad front. Seizing the excuse of an argument with the temperamental Kluge, Guderian resigned his command. As the small, brilliant, and ruthless army that had reenacted the conquests of Bonaparte and the Caesars started to die, the half-savage masses and giant industries of Russia and America began to stir and to concentrate themselves.

And from Tula there spread across occupied Europe, through the already once-defeated German people, the terrible premonition of second defeat: a defeat like that from which the scars had not yet healed and for which the French had been so brutally thrashed at Sedan; a defeat which would be worse than death, which would crush the soul of a people and leave them scattered, void of identity; *defeat* far worse than the guilt of the vilest victory. Now the German army lay still, as a wounded lion withdraws and waits for its destroyer to come near.

In the same month that David faced the tank leader over a Russian grave and Hitler's four principal generals resigned their commands, the first extermination camp began to operate at Chelmno, in Poland.

THE TEMPLE OF FAME

1

L ONG AGO, AT HIS TABLE IN A LIBRARY OF THE CASBAH, JUSTIN HAD BEEN free of any doubt that he would see humankind transformed. Now, under Hitler, Justin longed only to have back such an innocence.

Nor had his first love for the group of *maquisards* at Rochet's farm remained pure. For in Paris, during the seven months since the group's blowing of the Doubs railway tunnel a Maquis radio operator—though he might transmit always from a different site—survived usually for two weeks. And when the Gestapo, Abwehr, Orpo, Milice, or any other of the police caught him, he was hanged from a shade tree in the Bois de Boulogne. And it was as easy now for the Germans and their accomplices in Brussels, Amsterdam, Rome, Prague, Budapest, Bucharest, Warsaw, and Leningrad. Even close to Rochet's farm in the region of the Jura, the resisters knew neither the names nor locations of the English agents they worked with, or sometimes even the politics or nationalities of *passeurs* for whom they gambled their lives in the mountains, the pilots who fell out of the sky, or the adolescents, outcasts, and misfits who were the most eager to become heroes. With so little reality in the world outside the valley to love, and so much fear, the most intense suspicions fell on the faces that surrounded them at the farm. And even here among the French underground, Justin found he was still a North African, half an Arab—furthermore, one whose wife was a Hungarian actress, whom no one but himself understood and who did not fit in as anyone's equal.

To remain himself through the deformities of such a terror, Justin had written off his life. He had written off his work and his need to trust those he loved, and he had written off his importance. He had released himself from literature, also heaven and hell, and he had written off eternal damnation. He had rehearsed himself for torture; and he had sat, as with a mother, in the lap of his own death and so put it behind him as if it had already taken place.

Yet Justin had not ceased to be afraid. He knew now that what he would never cease to fear was evil. But from the reappearance of *Justice* in the streets of Paris, the wolves of the Third Reich and even Hitler himself would soon know that Justin Lothaire was in Europe.

As spring returned to the Jura and life went on as usual in the farms of France, Justin was deafened by evil words as they rained down from the German Führer in a constant shower. Never for an hour did the sensation leave Justin. For he knew now that the falling drops were human blood.

So Justin's mocking broadsheets were sent out from Rochet's secluded farmhouse. Each day he sensed the death agonies of a thousand children, women, and men as they underwent the efficiencies of the penal colonies. Justin knew now that this was to be his work until the final hour. Among the *maquisards* at Rochet's farm, only Luz's presence kept him sane. Justin was careful not to accuse her that the end of his deep love for the others in the group had begun with her arrival. But he was grateful for the printing sessions in the farmhouse *cave*, during the early hours when Luz was still asleep in their attic.

It was on just such a dawn in May of 1942, when Justin had climbed up with Gabriel to sit outside the kitchen window in the sun, that his first news had come of Marcel Doré.

They had been sitting between the climbing roses, side by side against the stone. Before them stretched out the narrow length of the valley, from the far end of which the sun had just edged over the mountain passes. Someone important was in the area, for recently surveillance by the German units from Lyon had been active on the roads around Carbonne. No one had left the farm in ten days.

Gabriel blinked in the hot sun, and Justin sniffed the fragrant breeze that rustled the forests above. The Gypsy continued to sew the leather jacket that he was making for Justin. Justin grinned, recalling the day dream of an Algiers student long ago, upon reading of Agamemnon, that Justin Lothaire too might one day wear the skins of animals and walk on the beach of the glorious dead.

"Even in an eternity of uniforms there can be such an hour," he murmured.

"To sit still so long? Sometimes I miss the South."

"Does a world war bore you, Gypsy?"

The lean brown face turned to him. "The others are bored. One forgets why one is here."

"Haven't they seen the idiots chase us around Paris after each issue?" Justin pointed toward the passes. "You see, Gabriel, even the sun is a *passeur*."

"Justin . . . among my family, before the police rounded them up, there were thieves. I wish to know. Have you truly no fear of betrayal?"

But at that moment Justin had seen Eli Hebron striding toward them from under the great oak, and he was able to wave aside a sick welling of terror at Gabriel's last words. Was Eli then the important person being hunted? As Justin walked forward he saw a rucksack that might hold the new English codes. With a happy laugh he turned to the Gypsy's anxious face. "We'll talk later. After all, until we are betrayed we will be here."

2

Five minutes later, all the farm had gathered along the kitchen table, except for Luz and the new sentinel sent to them by the FFI. And as Justin took the end chair, unable to stop smiling at the sight of Eli safely arrived, he heard the news of an attack in Paris by the *Groupe Manouchiane*, outside the French Treasury, not one block from his and Luz's entrance at the Palais-Royal. A bystander had been hit by a bullet fired at a Communist. The victim now lying wounded in a hospital was Marcel Doré.

Eli watched Justin rise with a groan. He tried to continue, speaking of a Gestapo raid on the abandoned office of *Justice* and how two past contributors were being deported to Poland.

"I have to go, now . . . tonight!"

"Justin, there is also good news," Eli was saying. "Jean-François d'Issipe is holding a meeting to present an important prize to you."

But Justin had forgotten feeling such pain, or such hope, and he could not listen. "No, truly I must go in at once!"

"We have no orders for you to enter Paris, Justin!" Vera was incredulous, staring up at him from behind her glasses. Across from her, Peter and Rochet were wiping from their arms and faces the heavy grease of the printing machine. The farmer glanced at Justin's face.

"Ah, yes," he agreed kindly. "That is why we stay in the provinces, Justin."

Justin's gaze was still on Vera's clean hands. With a shudder, remembering Gabriel's talk of treachery among them, Justin thought, What does this icily disciplined woman who despises Luz do with her own time here? "Doré is like a father to me," he said.

"You will put everyone in danger," Vera said. "In the Paris streets you will be recognized. When you have talked, they will shoot you."

"Still, in this world, there are individuals who must be honored," he said.

Mandil was holding the can of printer's ink. He was so upset as he gestured that liquid splashed onto the table. "Do you mean the resistance to Heydrich? Or may a prize, too, be honored?"

"Joseph, Joseph." Peter Tiolchak nodded and shook his head, gazing around the kitchen at each of them in turn as if to say, If we have such a person among us then he must be trusted. "Justin, I will be sorry if you are caught. You will be difficult to replace."

"It's Doré who cannot be replaced." Justin said.

3

THE SAME NIGHT, JUSTIN LOTHAIRE SLEPT ON A CATTLE TRAIN TO DIJON. BEFORE dawn, stretched on planks over the crush of hairy backs bound for the floors of the *abattoirs de l'est*, Justin narrowed his eyes into a moist night wind. There, unmistakably, silhouetting the locomotive stacks against the horizon, was the very faint aurora of a great city. And at the first sight of Paris—now no longer his but belonging to Hitler—Justin's heart was faint and he wished then for Luz, even though she was safer left behind at the farm with Eli.

God give me the strength, he thought. It was the first time that Justin had ever used the despised word—his mother's word, from in front of a cardboard Virgin in the Mahbu lace shop.

There was a wet mist settling in the Place Saint-Michel on the morning of 2 May 1942. Justin was back in Paris.

The shops were opening. Along the Seine, vendors were selling Daumier prints to German soldiers who had murdered the sons of France. Justin struggled not to flinch at the sight of so many uniforms. Everywhere his eyes searched tirelessly, even in the gutters, for traces of a broadsheet from the Jura. The rue de Buci thronged deafeningly as Justin's feet turned toward the office of *Justice*. He took one glance and left. The Parisians hurried along the shopfronts with the usual cynical confidence, but in their eyes Justin saw the dying coals of shame.

Marcel Doré was at a graystone hospital in the Marais. At nine o'clock, Justin crossed the river. Presently, as he wound through the narrow streets of the Jewish quarter, he paused outside a *lycée*. It must be from this door that little children had only weeks before been transported to the Vélodrome d'Hiver for their voyage to the labor camps. Presently he mixed with the flow of nurses through the hospital corridors. Justin still felt shaken by the hatred with which the well-loved furniture at *Justice* had been broken and gouged. He sensed like a miracle the presence in the hospital of a man whot could do no unkindness.

At the door, Doré's very young doctor looked with subtle gravity at the visitor. The Occupation was not on his mind.

"Philippe Hériot." Justin gave the name and felt giddy before the doctor's disappointment. After Jean Moulin, Justin was now the police's most hunted enemy.

"Oh, Maître Doré is quite well. Would monsieur like coffee?"

"Yes, certainly, thank you." As the doctor left, Justin almost cried out with relief that he had arrived in time. "A double, very strong."

Stepping inside the ward's two screens, Justin saw a tiny figure stretched under blankets on an iron bed. For some seconds the eyes stared at Justin blankly; then the patient's entire face was seized by a tremendous excitement.

Before the brilliant stab of that glance, Justin stumbled as he approached the foot of the bed. His back was to an alley window. A faint clear voice broke the hush.

"I asked my sister for this. I never conceived that even you were capable of such an apparition. No, no, I feel excellent," continued Doré. "It is true; I will outlive all doctors. The bullet was no more than the insult of a Nietzschean for a Marxist—or perhaps vice versa. You have risked everything to come here."

Hiding his tears, Justin laughed over the pale hands that were knotted on the bedspread round his brown one. His last two years, in the desert and now the Jura, seemed to ebb, the burden of his life to grow weightless. "It is my reward to hear that," he whispered.

"But look at your face, my boy! Never mind, I too had a shock. I spun round twice—my soul nearly flew out."

Justin laughed again, seated now with his legs under the old sage's bed. He continued to hear the voices outside the ward. When their laughter had fallen away, Doré went on with a near intolerance that Justin had never seen before. The tendons of his neck strained.

"I heard my soul beating at the gates of my life, Justin, and called for you. It is a beautiful thing to stand so near, to breathe eternity—and then to come back to this sleepy life. I taught you so little. What can one teach that does not have still to be learned? Now at last there is something I can tell you, which you would not have found out for yourself. I had to wait an entire lifetime."

Justin felt bony fingers release him. He looked up. The old man's face was watching with a fierce intensity.

"Go on, Marcel. I understand what you are telling me."

"I believe you," wheezed the faint voice. "It is this. I dreamt I was at the battlements of Carcassonne. There was a cold gale. I felt myself float away—beyond what is recognizably modern. I lost all need to feel that this period was in some way more concrete than all the peoples and wars that went before or are yet to come."

"Are we not all of our time?" Justin said carefully, feeling himself leave this hospital room and enter an ancient garden of intimacy, a place almost feminine.

"No . . . no more than a great work is only understood in its time." The slight body under the blanket stirred restlessly. "I saw that humanity has only just begun. I saw that you, Justin, could be loved long after these trivial struggles over ideologies are replaced by others."

"Are you saying, Marcel, that what we are living through and fighting against—even Hitler—is no diferent from past struggles or future struggles? That it is merely part of history?" Justin was far from certain, and he felt terror. "But can you not help hearing this rain that falls all around us? The tears of children, the blood of the maimed?"

"Yes!" Doré's arm jerked with conviction. "Even in the struggle for Christianity, the prophets went only up to the waist in their times. Listen, I saw that I—and now you, Justin—we are more free than is written in any religion yet invented. We have evolved beyond such primitive arguments. What you once described as ideological art—your impersonal art—is merely Platonism. When science bears us on to new oceans, this movement that worships you will seem a crude romance. The human soul will need heroes more advanced than either of us has dreamt of. That is the freedom from history that you will have, Justin. But only if you do not damage yourself during this popular hysteria."

"But Marcel, isn't that what the Germans also foresee: a Circus Maximus of science heroes and armies?"

A deep groan came from under the blankets. Behind the cloth screen, the door squeaked. "Justin, Justin, I am not talking of hordes. You forget the inner landscape. You forget the powers of a pure soul."

The young doctor anxiously approached the bed, managing not to look at either Doré or his visitor. After ninety minutes, Justin felt that they had only just begun, that civilization's questions hung in the balance.

"Could I stay a while longer?" he said.

The young doctor met Justin's stare. "I am afraid that between eleven and midday all visitors must be out of the hospital for the police check."

"You see, Marcel? I must leave you until tomorrow."

From the pillow, penetrating eyes were watching Justin. Impulsively he bent to embrace the old shoulders and head. Doré's tiny chest breathed deeply. A frail hand patted Justin's back.

"Yes, yes, I will be all right. You may gamble on it."

As he emerged into the wet street, Justin saw two cars coast up. In a trance after what Doré had said, he had to check an impulse to observe the six elegant black uniforms climb out. Had these Germans been to rallies, given Roman salutes to Hitler, and beaten women to death? Was it into these hands that he must fall? With an air of perfect indifference, Justin opened his umbrella and went past them.

4

AFTER HIS DISCUSSION WITH MARCEL DORÉ, JUSTIN FELT LIGHT-HEADED TO find himself on the streets in a spring mist. Once again a scholarship student in the city of his dreams, he feasted his eyes on the current of the Paris crowd, on the busy arcades and the generous expanses of gravel. At three o'clock, feeling crazed with happiness, he approached the half-filled tables at the Café de la Paix. If this failed, there would be two more rendezvous.

On the second pass, a priest in a black suit rose from a bench with a sunken-eyed boy. The boy took off his beret and spun it on his finger.

Hysterical laughter stirred in Justin. Not once in these four hours of intense memory had he recalled his fate—or the general gathering of the FFI, the *Forces Françaises de l'Intérieur*, which Justin had guessed to be the meaning of his prize.

"How did you recognize me?"

"As the sheep recognize the goat, Monsieur Hériot."

The priest and the talkative Jules passed through a second café into an alley reeking of cats. They pushed back a steel cover and the priest went down the ladder. As Justin followed, an acrid smell attacked his nostrils and stung his skin. These sewers belonged to Victor Hugo. Would there one day be sewers that belonged to Justin Lothaire? For another half an hour, he filed between his new friends along the incline of the great pipes. Sometimes a train rumbled behind a wall like a forgotten prisoner. Once the priest's torch flickered off while they watched two light beams and a dozen legs go by along the far bank.

"Does this remind you of Rembrandt?" Justin said.

"The Flight from Egypt," the priest agreed.

Some minutes later, the three of them stood pressed in a close space. The rear panel opened onto a courtyard gate. As they crossed wet gravel under a chestnut tree, Justin still did not know where they were. Could this be Lambert's *grand hôtel*—only five minutes' walk from the hospital where Marcel Doré lay wounded by a French policeman? Could this salon of great artists be the headquarters of the underground? A minute later, after rinsing his shoes in a laundry room, he passed into a deep sitting room that was a jumble of artworks. He halted trembling and stared around him.

In the faint light from the plant terrace were thirty people, quietly conversing. Just as long ago, it was Rosa who came forward to take motherly possession of him, her large eyes watering and her arms rowing eccentrically, followed by her reticent husband, his forehead like a Japanese monk's. Forgiving this woman the indifference that she had once shown an unknown student, Justin nodded shyly.

"Welcome, Philippe Hériot," Rosa announced. "You have become a distinguished writer and a distinguished spirit of the movement."

"Yes, I am still alive . . . " Justin apologized, yet around this room faces broke into smiles. He was being led toward the familiar hunched figure, by the terrace, of one of Paris's most famous writers. Even here, hidden at the very heart of this hive ruled by Himmler, Justin had to overcome a trace of his old bitterness toward this fellow writer.

"On our last meeting you were forced to hear me read," the writer said to Justin, with modesty.

"I could recite your words," Justin replied with a faint smile, only the two of them understanding the full meaning of the exchange. But which of us conceived then, as Hitler did, a Paris occupied by cinema centurions?" With alarm, Justin listened to the electric silence. How well must the voice of *Justice* have been heard in the streets of Paris.

He stood by the familiar podium, his head bowed, until d'Issipe finished a short, elegant speech and handed Justin the prize. This was a gold paperweight in the shape of a small book. Neither the title nor the author had been engraved on it. "The writer is too important to require a name," d'Issipe said.

Noticing a rustle of affection, Justin experienced sadness and pain, as if a precious secret were being torn from him.

Next came the reports, which ranged quickly and unsentimentally from the news that German spies had photographed everyone entering the partisan headquarters in Amsterdam, to an accusation by the British that the Maquis had ransomed SOE agents to the Milice in exchange for *maquisards*, to a heated discussion of how much local control over sabotage should be granted by the Free French in London. Justin sat for two hours in silence and watched each speaker's face in turn, weighing the personalities and impressed by the coherence the movement had taken on. Under the Front National, of which Colonel Hériot was now a doctrinal head, were the Francs Partisans, Combat, and Libération and in the Carbonne sector, the Northern Libération and the OCM. The long escape routes through Belgium, France, and Spain were linked by more than a hundred Maquis groups. To old Europe a child had been born—invisible, honest and free.

De Gaulle's agent—the same Moulin who in Geneva had been called Max—was still arguing with one of Eli Hebron's friends of Popular Front days. "As you say, we must supply the most efficient units first," Moulin observed, having risen a second time with an air of strained patience. "But frankly, in London, I must deal with a certain question. For example, whether our socialist brothers are more dedicated to consolidating their power after the war than to carrying out insurgence."

"Nonsense," retorted a handsome woman seated two chairs from Justin. "It is the rapid, might I say astonishingly rapid, promotions of Monsieur de Gaulle we must keep our eyes on. Might it not be your group, Max, which has aims after the war?"

D'Issipe raised an arm. With his free hand he rang the brass flower basin. "Philippe, tell us how you feel. Your section has survived our most spectacular success."

In the ragged corner chair, Justin did not stir. Several heads bent forward to see him. "I don't feel such doubts." He was now on his feet. "Are we bureaucrats, electing future parties? You know, in Geneva, that Max and I both heard the *chefs-partisans* of the north and from Russia and the Balkans. They speak of a federation of Europe's patrias. We heard there no ideology about factions, nor mistrust of any peace that may end the Nazi tyranny. No one spoke of their personal power!" Many in Lambert's salon were frowning or avoiding Justin's eyes. He softened his tone. "It is not our role to speak of these things. For the thousands, even millions who may still give their lives, as unknown as cats on a garbage dump, we are the only hope. For them, there is only now. Don't forget such a trust while you argue about the future!"

"Silence," someone hissed. "The police are in the street!" A mustached young man had appeared momentarily in the salon door.

Sixty seconds later, Justin had left the big house with d'Issipe, by a different exit. Below, in the great pipes, d'Issipe scuttled ahead with a surprising strength, carrying his raincoat rolled under one arm. Neither spoke until they came out on a cobbled barge mooring.

"You see, Justin?" D'Issipe laughed, as presently they crossed the Tuileries. "I put the coat on now, so that Siegfried cannot smell the shit of our sewers. I will accompany you. Are you staying with Doré's sister? That was a very stirring speech," he went on, speaking much more quickly, "I envied your inspiration."

"They did not like it a bit."

"A charismatic leader is rare these days. You frightened them, that was clear," d'Issipe said, and Justin smiled at the idea that he could scare anyone. For some seconds they were both acutely conscious of their footsteps, falling almost together. Then they went out of step.

The rue de Valois, down which Justin had first set out carrying the manuscript of *Thébans,* was deserted. They paused at the familiar doorway. In ten minutes it would be curfew.

"Do not be depressed, my friend." D'Issipe squeezed his arm. "The great days for us still lie ahead."

"Good night," Justin called after him, almost gratefully. He fumbled for the key that Doré had folded in his hand. In Justin's exhaustion, had he not welcomed d'Issipe's efforts to associate them? If only, in the hour of his fame, Luz were at his side to climb their staircase. Tonight, he felt ready at last to speak of children.

5

ON 7 MAY THE LYON EXPRESS, WITH BLACKED-OUT WINDOWS, LEFT PARIS AND coasted east. Justin's fame was turning in his head like the mysterious ingredients of an alien drug. He could not think clearly about the captured map of the Jura's SS garrisons, which he had glued into the sole of his shoe, and which must mean a return to action.

At nine-thirty the next morning, Justin jumped from the last carriage down a sunny embankment of pine needles. By noon, he was striding with the jacket over one shoulder—his fate under his soles—through Rochet's east meadow. As he approached the paddock his steps slowed.

The horses had not been let out. By the cattle trough stood a gray motorbike. Justin recalled Joseph's feelings about Luz. Even the grass under his feet knew more than he. Where was she, and why had he not left his wife in Switzerland? Very slowly, Justin walked to the farmhouse. He leaned against the vines. Through the kitchen window, he heard two voices, followed by laughter. Without waiting to clear his mind, Justin pushed open the door.

Madame Rochet did not look around from what her arms were doing in the basin. At the table sat Luz, dressed in trousers and a shirt. Her cheekbones were pink, and at her side was a very young man with a sensitive face. His gray uniform gave off a negative force that held Justin in the doorway. When the German saw him, he jumped up and came gallantly forward.

"You must be Monsieur Hériot," he said, in perfect French. "Please don't be offended. Your wife has told me all about your anthropology here in Carbonne."

"Oh, yes, good . . . how do you do?" Justin said, almost choking with the effort of sincerity. He looked from Luz's relaxed gaze to the Frenchwoman's rigid back at the stove, trying not to think of how this boy had reached the innermost gates of the underground.

"Oberleutnant von Windeler, twice decorated at the Meuse!" The German clicked his boots playfully, to reassure them that they were exempt from any obligation to feel defeated. "However, my stage name was Peter Windle. Isn't it amusing? I recently saw a movie that Luz Holti made before the war."

Justin had drawn out a chair. He sat down.

"I never knew it had been shown, Luz."

She gave a charming laugh. "It was scarcely a masterpiece."

Justin was trying to catch her mood. His wife's sudden glamour frightened him, somehow cutting him off from Rochet's familiar hearthside.

"No, no, on the contrary!" Windeler's face grinned among the hanging onions, his manner as expansive as if he were in his own kitchen. "Have some of this excellent coffee." Gesturing to Madame Rochet, the officer tilted boyishly on his chair. He looked from Luz to her husband. Madame Rochet brought Justin a full cup and turned back to the stove without their eyes meeting. Her small face was chalk white and she was blinking very quickly.

"It is such a shame," the fellow groaned, shaking his blond curls with tragic wisdom. "The unit has been stationed here for a year, and I only discover the two most interesting people on the last day. That is typical, so typical."

"Where are they sending you?" Luz pushed back her hair with a gesture that tightened the shirt on her bosom. She glanced apologetically at Justin.

"To the Eastern Front, imagine! I will be able to describe to my children how I saw the Kremlin!" Windeler added with a flourish of his hand and began to tell them of his life as a banker's son, with a residence on the Hamburg Alster.

As Justin listened to this German's confessions, he began to have difficulty remembering the life he was living. His own fame in Paris, Luz's nonchalance, and the kindhearted chatter of this effeminate monster with the overintelligent eyes and the weak chin all combined in an excruciating uncertainty, whether to be friendly or to execute this person where he was sitting. At this last thought, Justin was momentarily stricken by panic.

"Oh, I should think Hitler is probably a good thing." Von Windeler rambled on. "Some of your countrymen have made far too big a calamity out of the Occupation."

"Well, he has been a little cruel, don't you think?" Luz observed, with a sort of sisterly reproach.

"But after a bit of suffering will come great improvements," said the young officer, and he rose in a spasm of friendly didacticism. Clasping his hands behind his back, Windeler crossed the kitchen to the sunny window. They all watched him peer lovingly at his motorbike, sniff the geraniums, and turn back to them with his narrow chest thrust out. "Yes, Hitler is the most excellent civilizing influence of all time. Your own Bonaparte did not have a fraction of the Führer's command of history. He is like a master cook. And you and I, who are his ingredients, must submit to whatever temperatures and alterations he arranges for us."

Flushed with embarrassment at his own eloquence, the farm's visitor squeaked back to the table, placed one boot on his chair, and shrugged disarmingly. Beyond him, Justin glimpsed the agonized face of Rochet's wife. "But now tell me of your own work here." The German was staring at him.

"The cave drawings, the village excavations, or the Neanderthal skulls?" Justin inquired. The Gypsy Rosa's yellow cat had jumped onto the table unopposed, and was licking Windeler's cup.

" Your wife only spoke of skulls."

"Well, I have just taken some fragments to Paris," he began politely. But though Justin knew the scientific detail, he could not focus. Instead, he heard himself set forth on a sort of mad parable. "Yes, this area has revealed a significant story."

"Really?" Windeler sat down again. "I suppose I can stay on a few minutes."

"There was a tribe of Neanderthals that lived in this very valley."

"No! Really?"

"Yes, and their natural enemies—the mammoth and the giant bear—lived close by. They shared the same waterhole, past where the lake is now."

Madame Rochet had turned to them from the sink. The farmhouse was so still that Justin could hear the old clock tick in the farthest room. The lieutenant seemed sincerely impressed by what he was hearing.

"There was a harmonious balance," he continued, "until a group of saber-toothed tigers happened along. As you probably know, the saber-toothed tiger had no equal in strength and agility."

"How wonderful to tell all that from a few bones." The young German seated before Justin shook his head and looked to see if Luz was equally impressed.

"That is nothing," Justin went on, almost whispering. "What we have found here is even more interesting. You see, the battle for the waterhole was not won by the saber-toothed tigers. We found their bones scattered in large quantities. This must mean that the Neanderthals united with the mammoths and the giant bears to defeat the tigers."

"*Sapristi!* Think of the exciting investigation one has missed. I could have moved in with you here. . . . Heavens, though, look at the time. I must go!" The fellow had risen, flushed with confusion. "It has been a wonderful thing to know you. Let me give you the address of our *Schloss* on the Elbe, in case you visit Hamburg. And I will be very professional. No one will hear that Luz Holti is in Carbonne. They would leave you no peace."

Luz stood beside Justin in the kitchen door and waved until the motorbike had disappeared into the woods. Then she sat down at the table, her forehead against the inside of her wrist.

"Did you see?" Justin said softly. "He polished the machine for you."

"He polished it for himself," Luz answered, in a flat voice.

6

AS IF BY A MIRACLE, PETER'S IMPERTURBABLE FACE APPEARED THROUGH THE trapdoor in the floor. Then, one after another, eight more *maquisards* came up into the cool kitchen. Gabriel's eyes met Justin's—might any of these good people now betray the farm? This doubt was almost intolerable to Justin. And seeing the courage on their faces, Justin knew that whatever the price he would pay they must have the SS map. At that moment, he loved these people as if his heart would break.

Justin noticed Luz at the table with her eyes shut in defeat. "What happened?" he said.

"She was too slow out of bed." Tiolchak peered speculatively through the window, then into the cooking pot, and Justin understood that a conspiracy had sprung up against Luz.

"I was asleep." She sat back with a brittle gesture.

"At ten in the morning?" Vera shouted.

Pushing her husband away, Madame Rochet raked her hair. She ignored the child, Isabel, now clutched to her skirt. "What kind of a boy could that be? How did his mother bring him up that he could have Hitler for a hero? He said . . . he said . . . and then, Madame Lothaire, you said, 'Is he not a little cruel?' A little cruel, a little cruel? Why"—the woman held out her hands imploringly to the embarrassed faces—"she talked to him like that, almost as if he were a normal person."

Justin, who always had defended himself in Algiers alleyways, was starting to feel more akin to Luz, who had been brought up to be without defense.
Even though he loved Rochet's cadre of *maquisards*, Justin saw them in their
narrowness and suspicion. "Madame Rochet?" he said very softly. "Luz is a
professional actress. If this Nazi had seen your performance, by now we
would all be hanging in the square at Ornans. Isabel, my dear? Go let out the
poor horses."

Justin had resumed his place. The others gathered round, astonished to
hear that he had come from a general meeting of the resistance. After Luz had
excused herself from the kitchen, Vera took the far chair beside Peter. There
was something about these two that Justin did not trust, having begun a week
before with Vera's idea to list Carbonne's collaborators for after the war. But
in his urgency to banish even this doubt, Justin began to speak.

The news of the conference took them through lunch into the afternoon.
Soon the atmosphere in the farmhouse had eased. The Nazi officer would
never return. The army he was sent to was dying like a monster on the beaches
of Russia. Above all, Justin had seen no copy of *Justice* in the gutters of
Paris. For since the New Year, every issue had been hoarded and passed
among honest people.

Even after all this, Justin knew what still had to be done. Placing his right
shoe on the table and taking out his penknife, he began to cut the sole. "From
now on," he continued soberly, like someone who says farewell, "we must
come more into the open. We will take control of their streets with paper and
also ruin their factories. We will take their lives in their most secret garrisons."

That evening, after their long-awaited release from inaction, there was a
new spirit at the farm. For with Justin's return from Paris, everyone understood that they were going to win.

Presently, he carried his bag upstairs and across the beams to the end of
the great loft. His wife was waiting in the armchair by their window, her
Elizabethan tragedies open to her lines. As Justin came in, she rose and he
crushed her in his arms.

"Have they asked you to send me back?"

"That is up to us, Luz," he said, knowing that he must not tell her about
the map. "Today you gave a performance they will not forget. These people
have led poor and unsophisticated lives. All of us have."

"I know that, Justin. Don't I treat them kindly?"

"You talked with the well-born German as you never would to them,"
Justin explained gently.

"I run the same risk you all do."

"So far . . . though not as their sister." Groaning at the inadequacy of his
words, Justin stepped to the window. How lovely and still the meadows were.

"I have developed a taste for country life," Luz said sadly. "We could
begin a family in such a place."

"My God, Luz, don't speak of the future just now—look." Reaching in his bag, Justin touched a heavy shape. He held out the gold paperweight. It looked larger and more elegant than it had in Paris.

"You keep it," he said, and felt released both from the prize and from the burden of Luz's loyalty. She had already grasped what this was. Rising with an animal vitality that he scarcely recognized, the little piece held at arm's length, his wife turned twice.

"Ever since I was a small girl," she teased him softly, "I have wanted to be the lover of a great writer."

Outside in the paddock, Isabel Rochet was lying along the mare's slowly ambling back. In the farmhouse, the cord that connected Justin's soul to the rue Mahbu, to Melanie, and to Grinda's farm had stretched so thin that it could barely withstand one further tug.

7

WHEN THE ORNAN GESTAPO CAUGHT ROCHET'S SON PAUL, THE BODY HUNG FOR three days under a lamppost. No one came forward with his name. Through those three June days, as the group kept watch on the approaches to the valley—even when a family of Armenian *passeurs* poured blessings on them—no one said much or smiled. Madame Rochet did not look up from her pots, and her husband stopped eating. In the Paris streets, one issue of *Justice* would be missed. As they watched the pink flesh on Rochet's cheeks fall away, taking with it that good-humored passion of crops and seasons, his friends knew it was the farmer whose spirit had united them. They were gentle with one another, and they noticed how at dinner the old man cut a cross on each loaf before it could be broken. Only Paul's little sister was not told. At noon on the third day, the child's laughter carried from the paddock where the foals lived, and Madame Rochet bent over the table with her face in her hands. Then, rubbing her cheeks, she glanced around at the men's terrible faces.

"You are all my boys now," she said gruffly.

Gabriel nearly upset his chair. From the open door, the Romany watched a black squall advance over the sunny forest. "We have almost two hundred in the region. We could wipe out the black berets at Besançon tomorrow!"

Rochet spoke to them at last, sounding weary and old. "It is too soon. It would be a gesture."

Madame Rochet's face twisted at the sound of her husband's voice. With a sad glance at Rochet, then at Vera, Peter Tiolchak leaned back and put his arm around the woman's thin waist. "Madame, Madame, we are all your boys."

The air had become pungent and unstable with electricity. A few drops began, then a summer shower roared into the valley, thrashing the long grass and rumbling on the metal grain-house. As Gabriel struck matches for the oil

lamp and Vera poured their coffee, no one said anything. They were all thinking how this same rain must be falling on Paul Rochet—running down his
cheeks like tears, darkening his clothes to his body, and cleansing, cleansing.

When presently Isabel burst in, giggling and wet, it was possible to smile
again and to notice the way she teased Justin over a game of cards. They all
saw the unearthly kindness with which he smiled at the child.

The drenching rain and thunder continued all that afternoon. It was as
dark as night, and Luz came down to have company. The flood cut the mud
from the forest floors and erased the meadow. Water poured down the chimney, streaming out of the kitchen door. Then the air cleared, and a hot sun
stirred mist in the forests.

It was then that Eli Hebron came splashing in across the paddock, on his
way from Switzerland. And with him came Ivanov.

8

JUSTIN AND IVANOV SHOOK HANDS. THEY EXCHANGED CURIOUS GLANCES. THIS
was a man who had destroyed tanks with bottles of gasoline, who had lived to
organize the Krakow underground before it too was destroyed. Under his
soaked jacket and his baggy trousers, Ivanov was medium in build, with sloping shoulders. The man's face was cream white, deeply creased like a dog's
around his blue eyes. In manner he was silent, modest, and indifferent, as with
an athlete or a man whom many have followed.

"Good, I am very glad," Ivanov repeated, in a French that was the equal
of Tiolchak's. Smiling automatically at Justin, he stared at Luz, then at
Gabriel. Peter and Vera greeted him without rising. This war had brought them
too many foreigners.

"Come outside, Justin, Joseph," said Eli, his eyes taking note of the
Rochets and then counting heads. "Nikolas has very striking news."

The four men stepped into the wet evening. Crossing to the east meadow,
they moved slowly along the edge of the forest. The air was crowded with the
mutter of a thousand rivulets.

"Paul Rochet?" Eli inquired.

"He is hanging outside the church of Ornans," Justin said simply. "Rosa
will take his bed and Nikolas can sleep in the barn." Looking beyond Eli's
face, he saw that Ivanov had heard but was unaffected—as the man had been
politely indifferent to the pleasant farmhouse, to his wet clothes, and to the
personalities around him.

Stepping in front of them, Eli faced Justin and Joseph. "Heydrich is
dead."

"Heydrich!" Joseph laughed drunkenly, his slight figure almost quaking.
"Our famous Heydrich?"

"Two people I knew in Prague threw a bomb," said Ivanov.

Justin could not avoid feeling a horrible satisfaction at a blow so close to Hitler, the execution of Hitler's closest associate after Himmler. They began to walk again, sometimes stooping under oak boughs bent by the dew of a million leaves.

"The Germans first shot one hundred partisans," Eli continued, almost inaudibly. "Then—over two days—a village of two thousand, to the last child."

Halted on the wet grass, Justin was suddenly so overwhelmed by grief that he could not look even at Eli. He began to walk again, and the three men stepped along at his side.

"Tell them," Ivanov said, squeezing Eli's arm so that he winced. "Tell them about Gerstein."

"I do not ask you to believe it. I do not, cannot."

"No! Don't be afraid," Justin whispered.

Eli leaned against an oak trunk, blinking at Joseph. "The Americans refused to take twenty thousand Jewish children. The English as well."

"The story," Ivanov snapped, raising his eyebrows at Justin.

"A German, they say, has been to the Nuncio in Berlin. This German worked in a labor center that was some sort of abattoir for humans."

Justin cut in. "And the Pope . . . what did the Nuncio tell him?"

Eli gestured angrily. "It seems it is the decision—I mean officially, as policy of a European state, Justin—to erase the Jewish people."

Justin clutched the wet branch overhead. The western sky over Rochet's chimney was painted with red strokes. Swallows and bats squealed and hunted among the shadows. The oak leaves splashed his face. So *this* was the work of the colossus that towered over their heads, the drizzle of words, the drops of human blood! Until that moment, Justin had not felt the scope of Mandil's confession by the tunnel.

Eli spoke again softly. "Justin, how can this be?"

Justin Lothaire was staring fixedly away from the three waiting men. Around them, the valley's hush was so tense that even Joseph's whisper jarred upon it.

"How can this be?" Eli cried. "And what if nothing can be done? Go home, Justin—save your work!" Justin had never seen his friend so afraid, the red sun trembling on the lenses of his spectacles.

Justin could feel Ivanov's gaze on him, reaching past the calculus of crucifixion that encrusted his heart. "No, Eli, God won't crush our conscience." He hid his face, lighting a new cigarette from his last. "Was it not conscience that made God in its own image? We will believe in conscience so no man living will say we did not know of this."

"Because conscience created God?" Ivanov's laugh was natural and good-natured. "That is very good, Justin, you are a clever man."

But despite his discipline, Justin went immediately to the room that his wife had made unreal with her good taste. Luz was writing in their armchair. Kneeling as before a cardboard Virgin, Justin gathered her against him.

"You are so unhappy in this place," Luz said. "You should go and talk to Father Duroc."

"Father Duroc!" Justin reeled to his feet. "Baptiste Duroc, the priest? Luz, what have you done?"

"I go to confess. He recognized your name and seemed interested to see you again."

"Why did you not tell me . . . why?"

"He is a wise man, Justin. And he has agreed to baptize our child."

9

IT WAS NOT UNTIL DAWN THAT JUSTIN OVERCAME HIS SUFFERING AT THE IDEA OF an infant, his child, to be born into the Europe he had heard described that day. Nor could he tell the others while the farm mourned Paul Rochet. Luz would have to be sent back into Switzerland. At Lauenen, Justin had taken down the name of David's lawyers in Bern.

The arrival of Nikolas Ivanov, with word of what the German broadcasts called *Kultur* and which cherished nothing at all, left Justin stricken. What wounded him most deeply was the silence of a pope of Pacelli's intellect. With resignation now, he remembered his mother in the lace shop before an icon. All that terrible night, he was tortured in his dreams by the cries of his unborn child amid the splintering of bones. Half-formed abstractions streamed over the farmhouse where the Rochets would be awake, thinking of their son. In the morning, over the protests of Peter and Joseph, Justin went into Carbonne to see Jean-Baptiste Duroc.

Two hours later, he emerged into the shady church square. He went past the *boules* pitch and its old men on green benches. Reaching the church, he pushed open the heavy door. Inside, there were no bulletin boards or notices. Several candles burned on an iron stand.

Justin was being watched. The far altar looked small under the lofty pipes of the organ. Behind them, he saw a shadow move.

A man's voice rang down. "Welcome to the house of God."

"Is it under repair?" Justin called back.

"Not the architecture, Philistine! This instrument requires constant work. It is my hobby."

By the stone flank of the altar had appeared the thick figure and intelligent mocking eyes of the priest who long ago had sent a prostitute to be treated by Doctor Lindt. Duroc's thick sandals echoed as he came forward and embraced Justin warmly. He recognized at once Duroc's unusual freedom from rectitude or stuffiness.

"Imagine my surprise, in such times, to meet a well-educated Hungarian here. And then to hear *your* name. . . . No, no, you are a hero!"

"They have made you a bishop, Jean-Baptiste."

"Entirely for my charm in entertaining visitors."

Duroc motioned him through a passage at the side of the altar. After Justin's two years of enforced suspicion, the priest's sincerity made him giddy. That this man should know that *Justice* was somewhere near!

Duroc faced him. "So, welcome to my casbah."

They were in an oak study, arranged with clerical books and velvet cushions. Sitting down in a window that overlooked the cemetery, Justin watched the priest strike a match, light a small stove, and put on a kettle.

"It is a rare experience to entertain a literary personage. In these times one does not show surprise at finding a person here or there. But I assure you, this diocese lacks a certain worldliness." They both laughed. "Therefore I hope your stay will not be a short one."

"Thank you, Jean-Baptiste. But, as you say. . . ." Justin shrugged.

"Yes, yes, never mind." Duroc gave him a discreet little smile. "Though I hear you are going to be a father."

So there began—at first hesitantly, painfully, and then with gathering relief to find himself only thirty and still capable of passionate discussion—the first of Justin's long tea conversations with Jean-Baptiste Duroc, during hours stolen from the tense work at Rochet's farm.

"And whatever became of Maline?" Justin finally asked, with a twinge of his old guilt.

"By God's indulgence, she is well! But you should see for yourself. The girl lives here in Carbonne."

"*Here*, in Carbonne? Jean-Baptiste, I am married."

"Ah, but must one not be true to one's past?" Duroc wagged a thick finger at Justin.

In months to come, they would speak of the Peloponnesian wars, of whether Socrates had been the invention of Plato, and about the nature of Saint Augustine's inspiration. Yet whenever the conversation touched on themes that were tied to the struggle over the soul of Europe, Justin's silences were as undisguised as a lover's at the deathbed of his beloved. Without appearing to notice, Jean-Baptiste would angle surely for the safe spiritual tributaries of the eternal. And though Justin felt he had thus guaranteed the bishop's protection for Rochet's farm, he made no gesture to recruit him. He noticed too that he never encountered the priest's assistants. Over the next weeks, Justin came to depend upon the meetings. The contact made easier his coming separation from Luz.

10

NEVERTHELESS, ON A WARM NIGHT IN JULY OF 1942, WHEN JUSTIN FOUND HIMSELF toiling up into the mountain passage, he listened in pain for Luz's steps behind him. Somewhere here, in the previous week, two Chalon Communists had been flayed and their bodies burned. One had been a young woman.

The air was heavy with wet grass and pine pitch. Breathing hard, Justin listened for the trusting footsteps that stumbled behind him. The silent forest was so menacing that Justin's vision blurred. After two hours, they left the long traverse under the rock face. Ahead through the trees was a moonlit meadow of waist-high grass. His wife leaned panting against him.

"The meadow is Switzerland. We have only seconds."

"Justin, is it now?"

"Don't, Luz . . . it won't be long. I have to go back."

"I love you, Justin."

Justin felt her lips on his mouth and cheeks. Do not say it, he thought. Do not ask me to go on with you! Then he was watching Luz's back recede, surrounded by the forest temple and its invisible colonnades. Justin saw the way she walked, carrying the bag that held her few things, his manuscript, and the prize.

"Luz!" Justin called softly after her. "Luz!" He took two steps after the gliding shape in the meadow. There were tears on his cheeks. But Luz was gone.

Turning, he ran crazily back down the path, carrying above his head the automatic that he had sworn not to touch again. He did not stop until France lay far below across the dunes of glowing forest, a gorge without depth or perspective. He could not stop his inward weeping, for he had only just heard the music of paradise. Now there below lay the lights of hell. He could almost see the gangs of human evil ranged against him in the night: lords and beaters, to hunt and hamstring Justin Lothaire like a wild animal. To make of him as great a monster as they.

Only then did he think of Joseph, Peter, and Gabriel—also this night at Rochet's farm. He seemed to hear again the crackle and peal of rifles across the roofs of man's city. Had he almost gone with her? Freeing the gun's action, Justin started down quickly. And this time, it was not with the desert urchin's loose saunter, conserving divinity across sands without beginning or end. He went down with the impatient stride of a man who has seen the world change before the acts of evil men and good.

11

NOW, AS A DISARMED AND HALF-STARVED GLADIATOR MIGHT LURE AN UNTESTED comrade to face a still-murderous lion—and as, stumbling against one another they might hang back in the corner farthest from this monster, caked with the blood of multitudes—so, that season, did Churchill bring Roosevelt into the arena of Europe, that he might face the German dictator.

One October night, not far from the ruins where a *lycée* teacher and a half-caste boy had talked of the great writers, an English submarine broke the surface. Lanterns were waved and the American general Mark Clark set out for the beach in a rubber dinghy. In the moonless surf, the inflatable upended the American, who had come to propose an invasion of North Africa.

The general's arrival was one day late. It was necessary to summon a second time the Fascist French commander, Charles Mast. Before sunrise, as the still sodden emissary reembarked, the inflatable capsized several more times in the waves. There had been other misunderstandings. On 8 November, when the American divisions landed, French gunners fired upon them along the entire coast from Casablanca to Algiers.

Thus was Stalin's pleas for a second front against Hitler answered. Even at that moment, along the Donets River and the Don, General Paulus was driving Marshal Timoshenko eastward with heavy losses. The Wehrmacht would shortly engulf Stalingrad, on the Volga. When news of the nervous American activities far behind his back reached the forest bunker at Lötzen, Hitler at once stripped the French state of its powers. German units occupied the southern zone of France. The darkness of Carbonne was stretched across to the Mediterranean, the Mare Nostrum.

And with each adjustment of posture by the Nazi colossus, many hundred thousands of human beings suffered the fires of hell.

SILESIA

1

A MAN LOSING HIS COUNTRY LOSES THE EARTH ON WHICH HE WALKS. In the three months of German retreats that followed the morning of the Tula massacre and General Guderian's banishment to Berlin (Tula was now behind the Russian lines), Baron Sunda could not free himself from the scene in its every detail. And one detail from those twenty minutes by the frozen pit tormented David the most—of a pallid, pockmarked face, watching David fixedly from the crowd of condemned prisoners: Ilyushin, the doctor who had delivered Hélène of Alaric in a Trans-Siberian train compartment.

But could this *really* have been Ilyushin? Lying awake at General Schmidt's 2d Army headquarters through the winter nights of 1942, David Sunda often remembered the prisoner's accusing face. In the end, however, the memory of their savior bent over Hélène's naked suffering body assumed a beauty so vivid that he could no longer remember what that *other* face, in the doomed mass at Tula, had looked like.

Then, quite suddenly, David understood that it did not matter. What mattered was that he had now lost any hope with Guderian of a swift entry to Hitler's presence. David began to look upon his fellow officers with fear and loathing, and no longer did his hatred entirely exclude even Fabian and Claus and their monstrously long-winded plottings. Outwardly, David—now promoted Major von Sunda—was unchanged. Yet in the meantime David had seen the evidence among Guderian's intelligence reports that the *Einsatzgruppen* were gathering from the villages the flesh to feed Heydrich's immortality, on a diet each passing day of fifteen thousand living bodies.

During those same months, another German was facing a dilemma between patria and self. With his rash December declaration of war on the United States, Hitler saw his dream of a thousand-year empire publicly reduced to the possibility of annihilation in months. There was already the evidence of General Zhukov's winter offensive, against the bastion towns of Orel, Briansk, Kursk, Tshev, and Vyazma, which had allowed the Red Army to penetrate fjordlike salients seventy kilometers deep. Hitler's decision to hold the towns, which had led to the resignation of the Führer's best generals, was to be repeated at Stalingrad and Kursk.

For as an uncultivated tree may grow through the architecture of a great house, until to cut it down is more perilous than to leave it, so Hitler was seen by the German people to have inhabited the soul of Europe. That April, at the Peace-Through-Sport Palace, the Führer raised his fists high above his head and exulted to his Reichstag audience that he had mastered a destiny which had ruined another man a hundred and thirty years before. Then he asked for a new law, and it was a law to end all laws. *Your Führer must be in a position to force every German to fulfill his duties or to mete out punishment with proscribed procedures.* Would the decree empower even those coarse and swollen pashas, the provincial Gauleiters? Yet even this was granted Hitler—for had the Führer not become Germany, and Germany become Europe?

Several days after Hitler's appearance in Berlin, Himmler received an order to investigate various among the aristocrats who had most indiscreetly contemplated the Führer's overthrow. The third name on the pink Special Paper—engraved with a black eagle, resembling a mythical monster—was that of Baron von Sunda.

2

ON A PLEASANT AFTERNOON IN EARLY MARCH, DAVID HAD ARRIVED EARLY—accompanied by eight of Field Marshal Kluge's staff, including von Geyer—outside a remote log cabin in the Vyazma triangle where they were to rendezvous with General Schmidt.

Orders were coming in for a spring offensive, but David was not part of the Oberst's new bridge championships in which the prizes were various quarters in Moscow. Outside the roadhouse, someone had painted RITTER'S BIERSTUBE over the dangling Cyrillic sign. In the doorway, David shut his eyes and stood holding the Center Army maps until his mind stopped whirling through the Russian spaces. He breathed deeply the familiar, sweet smell of decaying farm animals; then he opened his eyes. The dueling scars of Wehrmacht gentlemen still surrounded him. Their arrogant tones in his mother tongue pierced straight to the pit of his stomach. The Oberst was observing him.

"Are you sick, Sunda?"

"I was enjoying the sun, Herr Oberst." If only the surgeon were still here, David thought. Turning, he circled slowly through the mud around the chattering radio truck. One pinkish cloud drifted in the west like a huge lung.

What had von Geyer said to Egi? Remember Clausewitz, *meine liebe*—war is politics by other means. Yes, Oberst, Egi had replied, and shit is food by other means.

Had his friend gone overboard only that week? In the end, alcohol had so saturated del Bianco that a single drop brought on delirium. But was it not the same with Baron Sunda's horror of what surrounded him?

What, after all, of a hundred thousand frostbite cases, the butter that had to be sawed and the hands frozen to metal? What of the starving and shooting of men, women, and children? First Guderian, then Egi—now there was just the Oberst. David had reached a state of depression in which he was conscious only of the similarities between his words and gestures and those of the degraded pack who surrounded him. He scarcely remembered now his contempt for von Geyer. His own humanity had become intolerable to himself.

Inside the roadhouse, David found the seven blond officers gathered at a table. They called to the wary Tartar for kvass, and by some miracle there actually was a bottle. No one had touched the tea with plum preserves in it. Taking a tea glass, David sat on a log bench and pretended to become absorbed in the map of Vyazma. It was interesting. On three sides of this place were Red Army positions.

But his concentration had grown so weak that David could not shut out the murmured gossip from the bridge table, which concerned the enemy's varying reactions to torture. The day before Egi's breakdown, the popular young Gottfried Engle had broken his neck, showing off his idealism before Guderian's old enemy, Field Marshall von Kluge, by throwing himself down two stories down onto a Ukranian sniper. The brave partisan had taken a shot at Kluge from the headquarters basement and then tried to run away. Later, the boy had been roasted in gasoline and hanged in the square.

Trying not to listen, David glanced up from the map as the Tartar—wearing wolf-fur boots and with the flat sun-blackened face of a Chinese—carried in blue Turkish glasses. Standing scarcely as tall as the seated Germans, the Russian did almost appear to be of an underprivileged race. But just now even the heroic looks of his countrymen seemed to David perverse and repulsive.

"The barman's question to Dietrich was this . . ." Von Geyer shuffled the card deck with a glance toward Major Sunda, who was bent over his maps. David had not yet heard Sepp Dietrich—Hitler's infamous SS general, who beat prisoners with a hippopotamus whip and who had recently made inquiries among Fabian's Smolensk staff about a rumored conspiracy—referred to by these aristocrats without disgust.

Von Geyer dealt the cards with little snaps as he went on. "Had Dietrich heard the stories of the Ivans we have at Smolensk, who are so starved they eat their comrades? Oh, yes, replied Dietrich, and I always meant to ask—did the Ivans have a tasty meal? *Hat's gut geschmeckt?*"

The bridge circle exploded in unnatural laughter. And remembering the child this fool Geyer had shot the previous week, Baron Sunda's mind whirled up and out of his head. Ignoring their further talk, *of the score now being a million Jews*, David watched his hands stuff the maps in their waterproof case.

Rising carefully to his feet, he went outside and stepped over a low fence that extended inexplicably to divide the horizons of snow. There was a bench behind the woodshed.

David brushed off the splinters of icicle and sat down with a groan. Had he yet again breathed the same air as such men—and to what end? He would go mad with their crimes long before Hitler fell. Gradually, the vacant afternoon began to penetrate the throbbing in his head.

The snowfield lay west in undulations, toward a distant line of poplars. The melting troughs between the swells reflected bands of gold. David dug the heels of his boots into the snow. And without warning, he was remembering the family chalet during spring skiing, and exactly what it had felt like to be himself, *then*. Just at that moment, David reawakened to the murmur of the Wehrmacht officers. Hearing again the conceit, each soldier geared and synchronized— each carrying, as a clock carried time, the power of the whole—David was gripped by a drunken nightmare of these men, of his class, of the highest culture, so brutal and godless that perspiration streamed down his temples.

When he opened his eyes, the sun was lower on the horizon. There was an immense sweet stillness over all things.

David leapt up. At the corner of the woodshed, he caught sight of the Tartar watching him from the log house. David's heart crashed in his ears— the road was empty! Where the four cars and two halftracks had stood were canals of muddy water. Had General Schmidt's driver not understood that the major was leaving the radio truck?

David and the Russian stared at each other. The peasant took two steps backward, then stopped. David began to turn in his tracks, staring foolishly at the unending horizon. He was thirty kilometers from the Kaluga road! Again he met the Tartar's eyes. And suddenly all the weight of horror of the ten months since his arrival with Hélène at Moscow station lifted from David's consciousness. For the first time since the shooting in the Smolensk quarry, David thought of his mother's music room, and of his child, and he knew that this life of crime was over. Tears of longing swelled in his throat.

The peasant was watching him but without fear now, his wispy beard on the handle of his shovel. David turned, still holding the maps. He started down around the low woodshed. The snowfields lay as before in bands of blinding gold. Trudging more quickly now, David headed toward the line of poplars, directly southwest toward Gomel. And as the spaces opened around him, he felt the officer's honor loosen its grip on his heart. Eight hundred kilometers ahead were the Poles and somewhere beyond, Germany and Oberlinden. Was he deserting? What if Fabian's decision was being taken at that hour?

David turned and was running back in a mad panic after his shadow on the snow. Then he stopped. On the brown line of the road, the tiny figure of the Tartar stood motionless in the absolute silence, watching David. He turned once again and started forward across the snow, unconsciously clutching the map case. *Beyond this horizon and the next are a thousand more plains of snow, and in one of these I will probably die*, David thought. Immediately ahead lay a twenty-five-kilometer German corridor flanked by Red armies, which meant two even narrower no-man's lands. The crunch of his boots on the wet, heavy snow came to his ears reassuringly. His consciousness had already begun to prepare itself.

And, in truth, David Sunda did not believe that he was going to die. He experienced a sort of mad optimism that Heaven lay close by, mixed with a Sunda's confidence in his ingenuity and his right to survive the follies of the masses. At that moment, the distance home to Oberlinden and Hélène did not seem too long or too far.

Reaching the row of poplars, David stumbled and fell into a gully. He was instantly on his feet again at the edge of another blinding horizon of snow. When he glanced back between the trees, up the long incline, the tiny figure of the Tartar still stood looking after him.

3

So, FOR A SECOND TIME, DAVID SET OUT ON THE JOURNEY HOME FROM RUSSIA, only now he was traveling as a renegade, without the mantle of an ancient honor. Between the rows of poplars through which he had just stumbled, and the German frontier, were a thousand kilometers of muddy snowfields; the Pripet Marshes; support infantry; towns and hamlets run by stupid and sadistic bureaucrats; *Einsatzgruppen,* prison camps, mass graves; dog packs and wolves; roving bands of Russian, Polish, and Jewish partisans; the Gestapo; treacherous militias and desperate men of all kinds, heavily traveled supply roads and constant low-level air reconnaissance. From that hour any being he saw could be his executioner. There would be little shelter and even less food. Never had he been so self-dependent or so free. But David's awareness of an altogether new freedom came only gradually.

And for forty-eight hours, nature too seemed content to remain unaware of David Sunda's helplessness. The mild weather held. Then on the third evening a blizzard began, and presently the temperature went back below zero. David might otherwise have frozen to death on the first night. But he took no notice of nature, experiencing only an unbroken concentration on his predicament. By the third afternoon, he had acquired sheepskin clothing, boots, and gloves from a wrecked Russian Hurricane—and, from a half-devoured corpse face down by a frozen river, the documents of a pilot named Hans Scheitler. He had stolen a pail of porridge from a cabin while the farmer's wife was chopping wood, and he had spent two terrible nights rolled in a rubber sheet among fir trees. Meanwhile, David worked out a general route that would keep him clear of the main roads, to which supply movements were confined by the spring thaw.

He had halted first near the Ugra in the swarming Smolensk corridor, north of the great battleground of Roslavl. Only death did not come to David that night, hidden in an island of stunted spruces on a limitless snow plain. The windless silence of the steppes stretched, from where he lay doubled against a trunk, past the hooded campfires of great tattered armies, the peasant hearths and the blacked-out towns—from Moscow and Leningrad, still under siege, to suffering Warsaw.

Hour by hour, David writhed and shook against the hard bark. A fierce hunger had risen in his chest. In his banishment from all order, his thoughts went on twisting, as if they too longed for a place of comfort and warmth. He thought of the candlelit Vyazma officers' mess, where the others would be standing to drink toasts to their disappeared baron, though less lovingly than they had for Engle. Now they too were animals armed with steel, who would hunt him down. An unopened letter from his wife was folded inside the dead officer's jacket. There was not enough light to read it by and no light from now on.

Rolled under the branches in his rubber sheet, Baron Sunda began to weep. Memories of the nursery at Oberlinden overflowed like a rich vapor, and David was shocked to hear the sound of his sobs. He held his breath, but there was no one to listen beyond the trees, on the snow that glowed through the branches. Or were there wolves? He had never seen one. For a Wehrmacht officer, a night patrol would be more final. Pushing his fingers inside the jacket's warm fur, David touched the handle of the automatic. The crystal of his chronometer was fogged . . . only eight-thirty? The night lay out ahead, an unknown land in which his, David Sunda's, life might meet death like a sudden pit. Earlier, a plane had gone over—twelve-thirty. Good, he must have been sleeping. But what had woken him? The faintly crackling silence stretched out significantly round David's tree.

Wolves! Instantly he heard panting very close by. Yes, there it was again. Six pairs of red eyes glared down at him through the branches. David heard their gasping breath. He would shortly be like the half-eaten corpse he had seen five kilometers back. Braced against the low branches, gripping the gun, David stared wide-eyed straight up at the stars. Slowly, he rolled his eyes to the right. The snowfield that he had trudged over was as empty as before.

"Twelve hundred versts," David's lips said, sucking the soft pine needles. "Thirty kilometers a day, forty more days and nights." Then he would start the calculation over again, like Jacob in his dream, counting the rungs on a ladder to heaven.

4

DAVID WOKE WITH THE SUN IN HIS EYES. HE FELT CONVULSIVELY FOR HIS TOES, then he pulled on the wet boots. After examining the snowfields on all sides, he freed himself from the spruces and stamped his feet. Under the thick branches, the spot where David had fought through that terrible night was a hollow of pine needles. The sight of it moved him. He was almost sorry to leave. Placing a square of chocolate on his tongue, David began to suck slowly. It was six-forty. Slipping out the topographical map from General Schmidt's Group Two position charts, he pushed the case back among the branches. Then, binding the groundsheet with his belt, he trudged outward from his island in a direction to skirt the no-man's land of the encircled Red Army at Roslavl.

David was crossing a snowfield—unbroken by a single tree, as far as he could see—but he was going home. Soon even his feet had stopped hurting. He knew that he could deceive any German temporarily, precisely because he no longer shared their honor and because he hated his life.

For two days he trudged west, an insignificant insect in the empty arena between the winter lines of two giant armies, through tank-tracked farmlands and ruined villages. Leaving the Ugra, he passed Yelnya, moving into the vast spring silence without once being forced to the ground. Sometimes David saw a patrol or heard a .76 or .105 cross high overhead. With his legs he was rebuilding his freedom—farm by rotting battlefield, by river, by forest—and somehow there were no dogs, and the thaw erased his tracks.

At midafternoon on the third day, shortly after stealing the porridge, David reached an embankment of bare elms which must be the Smolensk-Roslavl road. He heard a drone from the direction of Roslavl.

There was nowhere to hide. Stepping into the middle of the road, David waved enthusiastically at the advancing armored car. The machine slowed, then pulled up. Its three occupants stared out at David's white sheepskin and tarpaulin. The temperature was falling rapidly.

"Thank God you came along," David shouted, throwing the tarpaulin in the back seat. "Crashed by the Desna—fighter group at Minsk. Going that way?"

The young men's murderous faces automatically relaxed into boyish grins. "You're still between the lines, sir," one offered.

"Will Mogilev do?" The driver laughed, evidently pleased to have a diversion after running the Soviet .76s.

The Bavarian sergeant was making room for David. "The Desna's a good walk for a gentleman! How about a wurst? Look, Schnapps . . . ugh, but that Ivan coat makes me nervous."

"Warmer than ours!" Grinning, David took a careless bite from the wurst. Were they not even going to radio Minsk for a confirmation of Scheitler's crash? The Schnapps burned down his throat. A wonderful heat spread in his chest, and tears of gratitude came to his eyes. He pretended to fall asleep against the canvas roof. Mogilev?—Mogilev was more than two hundred kilometers straight toward Brest! He could scarcely believe his luck.

During that six-hour drive, as they were waved through numerous checkpoints, he stared out in silence. He listened to the discussions between the soldiers seated in front. How many decades ago had David been like these men, even shared with them a certain patriotic identity? Could that really only have been Tuesday? Was it only two nights since his ordeal under the trees? And if he had shot Hitler when they had been face-to-face in Berlin, would none of this catastrophe have taken place?

In the front seat the bald soldier had turned. He was asking David something.

"Did you hear? There was a plot against our Führer!"

David's heart had begun to beat violently. "It happens twice a year," he said.

"No, sir, it's true—a plot inside the officer corps! There is a mob of Himmler's people right here in Smolensk. Investigating, you know?"

"*Gott!*" recited the sergeant next to David. "*Wie schön ist's doch hienieden. Wo man hinspucht lauter Juden!*"[1]

The three soldiers exploded in uncontrollable laughter until the two Alsatians at their feet joined in, whining and baying as if at the mention of their favorite quarry. But David had scarcely understood. This was the first public mention he had heard of the running civil war between the legitimate and criminal factions in the Wehrmacht. What of Treskow, Claus, and Adam— would their infuriating caution have protected them? What of his own wife, who bore his name? David pretended to sleep.

The armored car reached Mogilev after sunset. In the moonless confusion before the town hall, David was able to slip away. Following the ghostly main street, he passed a mass hospital for those too severely wounded to travel. Below the operating theater's window, he distinguished a pile of legs. Yawning, David continued on.

Twice, before he left Mogilev, the leather-coated police halted him and David snarled, as savagely as any *Obersturmbannführer,* the password that he had overheard in the armored car. Only one compulsion had the power to soften Baron Sunda now—the image, like a painfully beautiful dream, of the woman he had wrongfully returned to Europe and placed in utmost danger, the childhood friend taken from her father's fireplace, who in all her luminous faith he must hurry to save, and who alone could forgive him.

When the last blizzard of that winter began on the following afternoon, David was in a murky forest only twenty kilometers southwest of Mogilev. The temperature had dropped sharply two hours before, freezing the wurst in his pocket. As David worked through a broad growth of brambles, he kept glancing up at the charcoal blizzard clouds that towered above the pines.

"Please, merciful Lord," he muttered, to keep his mind off the dog patrols, "why does life have to end in so forsaken a place?" By this, David meant a

1. "God! How beautiful the view!
   Where e'er you chance to spit, a Jew."

place where Hélène could know nothing of him. A frozen wind sent spasms up and down his spine. He crunched forward under the thrashing trees, stumbling deeper into the night. Then, twenty paces ahead beyond a thick trunk, he saw the base of a shed. A window came into view. It was a two-story dacha. As he crouched forward, there were tracks of men and huge dogs. Gasping with fear, David stood in the doorway with the automatic. The entrance room was bare, save for a single bamboo table. The light was failing fast.

Abruptly, David staggered, a violent pounding in his skull. What was that? A scratching, as of claws. He gaped into the dark.

A long shadow was gliding down the staircase.

David lifted the gun. He saw his arm waver and the heavy-shouldered, mangy beast come, crouching horribly, over the planks. Scarcely believing the sound, he heard a menacing rumble. The flat yellow eyes were fixed on his. David heard a sharp, dry lash against the frozen air.

The monster kicked on the floor without a sound. His stomach heaving, Baron Sunda looked down at the house's former master. Then he stepped over the dead animal. His frozen boots on the stairs mingled with the banging of shutters.

There was still some linen in one cupboard, and in the kitchen a sack of horse oats. There were even books in the one bedroom that still had all its window panes. He would butcher the wolf tonight. David threw his bundle on the stained mattress. Avoiding his terrible reflection in a cracked mirror, he went to the shelf and picked out a little book in rotted blue Morocco leather, *Poètes chinois du Tang*. He just made out the French and Cyrillics. At the sight of the neat, lovingly printed words—the thoughts of a poet dead one thousand years—it was as if David were a student again; as if this age and this terrible hour were the students of other ages and other hours. And he read:

> Easy to see the drift of the times,
> Difficult to turn a single man from his way.

5

By July 1942, elements of Guderian's old 2nd Tank Army, combined with Army Group South, had broken through rapidly towards Stalingrad, and Rostov, thence toward the oilfields at Baku. But Hauptmann von Sunda was not with them.

On 7 June, the wheat was at its tallest on the rich soil that bordered the Pripet River marshes. It was a cloudless morning at a remote collective farm near the Ukrainian village of Ratno—not far from Brest and the Polish border. Despite the presence in the area of an *Einsatzgruppe,* four gold-braided little girls in flowered dresses were washing clothes and singing by a pond on which floated wild ducks. An old woman in black was weeding nettles in the yard with the same angry movements she used in all seasons. A first windless heat had fallen over this scene like a drug. The thin squeals of the three younger children rose into the immense pure silence, distant as chimes, and at the sound a wing of swallows returning late from Jerusalem broke ranks, circled, and dived low over the water.

While the eldest girl, who was about fifteen, knelt by the pond beside her basket of washing, the others spun round until they fell, gasping, on the grass floor under the deep blue sky. The smallest child snatched a red blouse, and her white legs splashed across the stream. The two other girls streamed after her up the far slope. Then together their laughter turned to a shriek. Fleeing bare feet rumbled on the ground. They raced in a wide circle, then back down to hide behind the skirts of the eldest.

A man had suddenly appeared from the hedgerow and taken several steps on the grass. Despite the heat he wore a sheepskin and fur boots, and like a holy fool he carried a bundle over his shoulder. The woman's coarse voice as she shouted the girls' names was unalarming on this dense summer air, in which nothing very serious could possibly be wrong.

The stranger halted twenty paces from the children and tumbled back onto one elbow. With an eager cry, the younger girls streamed forward and stooped down by the soiled heap. The babushka redoubled her angry shouts and trotted after them, waving a clump of nettles. By the time she reached the rushes the children, directed by the eldest, had tugged the man back to his feet.

"Are you a soldier, sir?" the girl said in an official tone.

"Look how he stares!" squealed the youngest. "He must be a deaf-mute."

"He's handsome, Nastya—and not old," teased the third child.

"Phooh, he smells like old shoes!" cried the fourth, and they shrieked again with excitement.

"Bab'shka! Bab'shka!" piped the youngest in a mewling voice, holding out a lump of yellow cheese. "Can we keep him? Can we feed him something more?"

The procession reached the stream just opposite the old woman. The man had instantly devoured the cheese, as if with shame.

"Comrade, are you a partisan?" she called.

Something about this silenced the children. They all watched the terrible face. Slowly, indescribably, the man stared from one face to another and his eyes began to glisten in the sunshine. A faint smile appeared, spreading from his temples to his cracked lips. Then, looking up, the man stared at the house.

"Oh, he's smiling," the youngest girl said, stepping into the water.

"You see?" she whispered as he knelt. "He's drinking!"

From the Ratno road at that moment came the drone of a motor. On the grandmother's face had appeared a new concern. Two foreigners were already striding down from the farmhouse. The short wiry one pulled out a pistol.

"Grandmother, look!" cried the smallest child, and she began to cry. The three other girls stepped back from the man drinking at the river's edge, their faces ugly with fear. The old woman had begun to wave at the visitors. Bending over, she dragged angrily at the drinking man's sheepskin. Her face was ugly too.

"Think of the girls!" she shrieked at him. As the two Germans approached, she began to tap her mouth and ears. "No hear, no talk."

"This animal's a partisan," said the short and wiry German.

"What is he—a deaf-mute?" asked his companion in a melodious voice, taking off his peaked hat and trying not to sound excited. One of the children sobbed with fear, and the old woman slapped her. Since catching sight of the SS *Totenkopf* patrol, the stranger had been staring at them. This seemed to annoy the Germans. The tall one replaced his hat.

"A mute, and crazy too? Finish him."

The wiry *Sturmbannführer* held out his pistol. With the barrel, he pulled back the kneeling man's matted hair and pressed the sights to his temple. There was a tremendous stillness under the open sky. All four girls were wailing now. The condemned man's face was faintly smiling.

"The safety again!" The *Sturmbannführer* inspected his pistol.

"Not in front of the brats, dumbhead," snapped the tall one. He gripped the other's wrist.

Immediately bursting out in joyful cries, the smaller children trailed the three staggering men up the slope to an open car. As he went, the captured one stared steadily below at their sister, who was still standing by the pond.

Then the captive was trussed and rolled violently into the idling car to lie wedged behind a seat. A wake of yellow dust billowed up behind the car, and the houses, the lake, and the girls faded from sight. Closing his eyes, the stinking partisan beast was instantly asleep. For, since his devastating fever at the Mogilev dacha, he had no voice to speak with. And even had he had one, the man was in no state of mind to know whether he was a Wehrmacht deserter or a Ukrainian partisan, anti-Soviet or anti-German.

.

6

SUCH DISTINCTIONS NO LONGER HAD ANY MEANING FOR DAVID SUNDA, AND would have seemed positively comic if they had even crossed his mind. Long before Pinsk and the Orinsky Canal, where he had almost drowned, he had reached that flayed condition of purity in which good and evil become blindingly distinct, and one is freed both of the fear of death and from the instinct to avoid it. Ideas of responsibility such as civilization, class, rule, honor, ally, victory, and defeat not only did not cross David's mind, the very words were beyond his consciousness. There seemed now only to be a guttural emotion, overflowing from his heart like divine laughter, and which could be heard by those who came near him, or perhaps smelled like incense. As David had kneeled among the giggling, wheat-haired angels, he had been more innocent than they. For the children could still be frightened by what they had never seen, while he had seen everything. When the Death's-Head Commando—as such human beings were called—had held the gun to his head and the girls had wept, David had only thought, *Now they are going to kill you.* And that had seemed so ludicrous and ironic that he had smiled. Nor did he dwell on it afterward. He had learned to listen to the music.

David knew now how far he had strayed from the ugly scene with Guderian by the writer's grave, and how painful was this pilgrimage of return. The music, this divine laughter (somehow linked to Hélène, as if somehow she must know that he was hearing it), played upon and enfolded everything that happened around him and gave to it all the same grand and terrible meaning. Ilyushin, and the surging of the Siberian mob, and the spattering brains of the condemned; the embarrassed excitement of the *Obersturmbannführer* as he bent the fuzzy-headed Russian forward over the pit; the intelligent, surprised expression of the man he himself had shot at Smolensk; the incomprehensible spectacles of gray and green hordes, scientifically bursting and torturing each other's flesh—all these things were raised by the music in them, from the dark torment of David's conscience to a higher conscience, united to and controlling the souls of all men, and from which warm rays of compassion shone down.

At that moment, the captured partisan felt his shoulder butted hard and he awoke.

7

THE DEEP BLUE SKY WAS STILL ABOVE, BUT ENCIRCLED NOW BY BAROQUE ROOF ledges.

"The hairy beast is starved, Dieter. You might have given him fodder."

"It's the doctor he will be needing. Phooh, the animal reeks."

"The vet wouldn't touch it. Shoot the thing, Putz!"

The sun was blocked by an officer's metal-eagled hat, solid as a mountaintop. With distaste, a monocled eye peered down at his men's spittle on the captured man's beard and face. Clearly this was no more than a village drunk.

"There is a transport to Breslau in the station. Put him on that."

The major's angelic face disappeared forever. The roof ledges wheeled and the tires began to sing. They coasted downhill over cobbles and the prisoner braced his feet, vaguely aware that they were handing him over to die in that great plan of mass murder and shifting population Hitler had once described to him—"later they will say I was too kind."

How alone man is, David thought, and again he heard the chord of compassionate sound, enfolding all things and beside which he was nothing.

"Get on! Get down! Jump!"

The prisoner was standing on a rail siding, beside a seemingly endless line of short red freight cars. Over the tops of the elms, he glimpsed the ramparts of the fortress that he and the *Oberst* had once observed being shelled. The lovely windless afternoon was like any other.

Can this be your last sight of the earth? he thought, and without warning his heart ached with love for his life. His damaged throat tightened painfully. In the grip of a nervous obsession to continue homeward, David turned to the bespectacled Dresdener. He would write a phrase for them in German and take his chances with Himmler's agents. But what was the curious droning overhead—like human voices? As the freight door tumbled back, David saw an inner wall of soiled human backs, some of their coats torn by the latches. The crowd bulged, cursing and struggling in the sunshine. An overpowering human stench was exhaled into the afternoon. A body fell onto the tracks beside David. The guard began to curse the prisoners as if he had played no role in their condition.

"Lift him—damn! The filthy beast's heavy! Head first, then."

David swayed on the sleeper, blinking at the scene above him—Russian irregulars. He allowed himself to be hoisted by the guards like a slab of kindling, his face rising above the railbed. The mass of legs heaved towards his nose and his shoulders were jammed hard—out of the air and into hot acrid shadows. David felt his boots being pushed and jammed. Then he heard the door rumble and there was black darkness. He felt his shoulders pinioned, half crushed against wet straw. A leg tugged itself free, then pushed back down inside his arm and for an instant, just one instant, David thought that he would not be able to breathe. He began a panicked struggle against the crushing grip of ungiving men's legs. Submit, submit! a voice cried in what was still David's head. And by working onto his back, and bracing out his shoulders, he gasped in a hot, acrid, unsatisfying breath. For the first time, he heard the soft tones in the dark above him.

"Don't step on him, brothers . . . never mind, he's dead—no, no! he's moving around . . . merciful Christ it's hot . . . we'd all be better off down there . . . merciful Lenin, you mean! Hey, lads, where's Breslau? The camps, God help us . . . Belsen's full, Mazdanek's to the east." There was a sudden pounding of rifle stocks, and the voices were silent. Almost at once, the train began to roll. David heard the soft human voices call back and forth in the faint gold light.

"My country, my country . . . all Russia is going into the camps, comrades . . . they're losing, now that America's landed—yes, yes, America. Look out, don't step on him."

So on a summer afternoon, David set out on the voyage of our time. A voyage that begins when the very air in its innocence, or trunk of a tree, or warmth of a familiar room seems to part, revealing the entrance to a new dimension for which God carries no papers. A dimension of cattle trains and *Lagers* without the slightest connection to any court of justice—a torrent of abject slaves streaming into an inferno.

That very long transport, bearing David and eighteen thousand Russian and Polish irregulars, partisans, Jews, and other prisoners of all descriptions, did not reach its destination—Nysa, on the line to Dresden, near the Czech-Silesian border—until late on the following day. By then, David had twice lost consciousness as they waited in the heat of a Warsaw siding. He was sick with hunger and thirst and with the filth of the closely packed bodies. Many times, in the blasphemy of his deliriums, he had wished for death.

Finally, when they least expected it, the freight door rumbled open. At once the pressure round David lightened and he tasted air as sweet as mountain water. Hands pushed under his armpits. In the corners, three other bodies lay crumpled. He balanced for a moment, blinking at the cloudy skies and at the glittering barbed wire lined with motionless shaven heads all bathed in orange light. Below David's boots, sly blunt faces were looking up at him— the voices with whom he had shared the intimacies of the ghastly night. Beyond the host of tents he could see cornfields, a river lined with Lombardy poplars, and a gray haze of mountains with pink cumulus above them.

"There he is! Good man, good man!" "Well, here's home, brothers." The Russian voices droned back and forth.

Now German voices were shouting them down. All along the tracks went the sharp abusive shouts, as if the skull-hats needed to warn themselves along with the prisoners that there could be no use in either side succumbing to pity. And as David was dragged from the soiled carriage along with thousands of prisoners for two kilometers in both directions, through the constant dream of fugitive hordes and immense lands, he was once again aware of a face watching him from the gathering crowds.

8

DAVID'S FIRST VIEW OF THE NEISSE EXPERIMENTAL FORCED LABOR CAMP, WHERE one hundred thousand prisoners of war were triple-fenced on a perfect machine-gun traverse of a hillside, was one of utter desolation.

This was the last clear impression that he had. For in his next forty-eight hours—that is, two full days shoveling chemical powder in the factory workshop, held at gunpoint beside a two-meter bin from which he could come and go only at a jog—David grasped that at the rate he was shedding weight he would remain alive for three more weeks.

By then, there were many other things that David knew about those limitless perimeters of fork posts and electrified wire.

He had heard it whispered that there were other such camps in Hitler's eastern zone, where the two great Socialisms were grinding the masses between their jaws, but that little about this busy place was known outside. He knew that just hundreds among these mobs of half-savage faces had been on this hillside for more than two months, and that only the most ruthless would be alive in a further two. David also knew that the whitewashed perimeter building with the red cross on it contained no medicines or doctors but only Lithuanian thugs to detect those men whose bodies had no further worth. In other words, the struggle for life that continued hour upon hour in the bunkhouses, soup lines, and quarries was a faceless present, without past or future, whose sole function was to work all life out of his body with the most efficient economy. Until that hour, David had believed that his flight through the lines of hunting armies had been the worst thing a man could know. He knew now that it had been little more than a gentleman's gesture in the face of the old order. Now he would undergo the modern age.

From the instant he knew all this, it was no longer possible for David to long for earthly rest or to accept that the things to which he bore witness would in a score of days be extinguished forever, and himself with them. In that same hour David began to calculate, with an animal cunning that he had never before conceived of, when and how he would expose his family name to the SS bureaucracy.

Yet he might never have known at all if it had not been for his encounter in the camp gate.

9

WHEN HE HAD BEEN UNLOADED FROM THE TRAIN, DAVID HAD NOTICED A FACE lifted to his from among the double flanks of bare heads. "*Alles 'raus! Alles 'raus!*" roared voices overhead. Then David was sinking among the Russians and being carried down, then up, through a chest-deep chemical dip and down the corridor of sunken faces: French, Greeks, Slavs, Tartars, Hungarians, Jews, Italians—the whole of Europe was here! Above, on the right bank, as he took his feet, two elegant SS with Schmeissers were watching him. One looked familiar. He had David's features and black hair.

"*Schnell! Schnell!*" screamed the guards.

"Lift your feet, comrade!" a voice hissed in German. "Otherwise, they'll shoot you."

Almost fainting, David twisted in that sea of shoulders and glimpsed again the white pock-scarred face with the receding red hair. The man gave him a grin—simple and unassuming, even contented. David looked away and his legs carried him forward. The new prisoners marched on down the kilometer-long mud avenue in two hushed columns reeking of disinfectant. The terrible faces that lined the flanks stared back without hostility or welcome, or even the memory of emotion.

The wet tattered columns were being halted. In the unearthly silence, his country's huge red flag billowed above David, making little riffling snaps. The camp *Oberführer,* a flabby hyperthyroid Prussian of the old school, had appeared on the main porch above David's position. Loudspeakers carried a short harangue in crude Russian, on making "Christians and Workers" of them. Then the throng of men broke forward through the buildings. A deep section of the well-used stalags seemed to be empty. A hand gripped David's arm.

"Look, comrade, to the south. My mountains."

Had both of them come so close to home? David suppressed a hunger stronger than starvation to speak his own tongue. Was it possible? A social parasite, even in a place like this? Knowing even then the insanity of that reaction, he put his arm over the Silesian's shoulder and felt himself half carried after the others in search of bunks. Was he to be fed tonight? David's last image was of a tight, acrid closet of raw pine, with tiers of niches.

Much later, though this was only one minute, David was awake. A guard squatted gigantically in the sand between the bottom shelves. Ignoring the Silesian, who was holding out a cigarette—a cigarette!—the familiar face bent to grin at David. It was his lookalike from the gate. The fellow had recognized a Wehrmacht officer.

"On your feet, filthy stinking animal!"

He had one instant to cover his kidneys as the sneering face vanished. A heavy boot began violently to pound David's left flank—neck, ribs, groin, head. The young man crouched to swing his leg. Pushed against the plank wall, David could go no farther. A vast buzzing filled his ears.

David had been staring for some time at the light flex, which was wound onto a rafter, before he knew that he was conscious. Like a miracle, the Viennese had gone. A cigarette was smoking under his nose. He sucked the wet paper, shaking with hatred.

"You are a hard one," whispered a voice. "Not one sound."

"I simply forgot . . ." David mouthed the German, no longer caring. These were his first spoken words in the many weeks since Mogilev. Furthermore, David thought without shame, he would kill that guard. He blew out the smoke and groaned, trying to concentrate. Only one mistake now. . . .

"I am Otto Horvath."

"David."

"*Enchanté*, King David. *Aber hörst du* . . . Listen to me!" The man was propped with one elbow on the sand between their niches. "I was first to the east. Mostly Poles, Jews, many priests too. I saw the death of Bishop Kowalski . . . incredible. Have you not heard of him?"

"I have not heard of him." David concentrated, their darkened faces close under the shelves.

"A sad and beautiful scandal!" the Silesian whispered, his waxen face now red. "The Superior of the famous nunnery died, and the bishop succeeded her. She had exerted a strong personality." Kowalski was not able to control the nuns. The discipline, the grace of the entire order was thrown into doubt.

Kowalski was a good man. It frightened him to hear the nuns speak of lost faith and disintegration. To reunite the order, the bishop turned to the last power left to him. He took the nuns as lovers, to the last one. It is said that for a long time, before this thing became a public outrage, the order was reunited. The nuns were consumed with the fire of good works and a devotion to the Supreme Being.

"The Nazis brought him into camp." Horvath stared into David's face. "They kneeled this old man in a line of naked partisans. Two skull hats forced him on his knees and beat him with their stocks. This took two minutes, but I can swear that Kowalski did not make one sound. I was in that row of prisoners."

The stalag was silent. David Sunda lay back smoking, his gaze on the shadowy bunks. Like a drug, the Silesian's strange story had flowed into his veins. The murderous hatred for the guard escaped from his heart, and promptly David slept.

At first light the sirens howled and thousands of unshaven men flowed at a trot from the barracks, formed in snakes for their large tins of bitter porridge, and then lined up for the head count. The food had awoken a violent hunger in David. As he fell in beside the Silesian—Horvath was about thirty, shorter than himself, and ruggedly built—they passed handcarts that were being pushed by inmates.

"And those?"

"For last night's dead. Yes, there were six in with us—two above Petrov and Zinn. Our game is up, my friend!"

As their crowd wheeled into the main throng, the laborer at David's side laughed again. Seeing his own animal terror mirrored on every one of these hard prisoners' faces, David guessed the strange powers of his new friend.

"It is said that a *Reichsführer* SS came last week, along the barbed wire moats . . . he was worried about the job's effect on his guards!" His companion chuckled again with such pleasure and sadness that David could not help joining in, though the sound was crazed and tears came to his eyes.

That was David Sunda's twelfth hour. From that first sunrise on their hillside, which was silent save for the shouts of the guards and occasional *crack* of someone being shot, David felt himself fall farther and farther behind his new acquaintance. From their boyhoods—Otto's in a Silesian boom town, his own at Oberlinden—the man now shoveling two bins away from him, powdered the colour of bananas from hair to feet, had been insatiably learning what a soul needed to know and far more. It was as if there could be no catching up, and every hour David would fall farther behind, as if in this Silesian, now calling warnings to the others about their eyes, now teasing sneers from the guards, David had found the key to the mystery with which he had come face to face in a train compartment in Siberia. The mystery of how to live.

At six o'clock, when smoke from the commandant's kitchen faintly smudged the August evening, a dozen guards came like wolves through the stalags, administering beatings. Then David saw something in Otto that he would never forget. He had sat resting on his bunk, testing his rib and the bones of his hips. But with all his hunger for dignity, Baron von Sunda could not prevent the flutter of his muscles as the pounding and shouts reached the next room. Now the dim light bulb was swinging wildly. This was his twenty-fourth hour, and it was a new world.

Five seconds later, the scarred leather boots were by David's shoulder. He could see Otto, squatted between the farthest bunks, whispering to Zinn and Vassili. Signaling to them, Otto looked up with perfect composure.

A moment later, the three men were a heap of striped ticking on the sand, the skull hats lunging over them. One *Untersturmführer*—David saw the Viennese—climbed between the bunks and jumped down on the huddled bodies. "*Schweinesel Communisten . . . Scheiss! Juden! . . . Scheiss! . . . Scheiss! . . . Scheiss!*" the Viennese shrieked, rhythmically climbing up and jumping down. When he was tired, another man pounded Zinn's head on the planks with crashes like a hammer. Then the boots marched out, past the shelf on which David lay convulsed with terror.

Before he could move, Otto beckoned David with a kind face. "Listen, it is very interesting," he called softly, exactly as if Zinn and Vassili were not feeling their bodies and there were not a deep split swelling up on his own temple. That was when David learned the impossible truth of this place.

The next dawn, before the sirens, the four of them were marched to a shed by the south wire. Presently, when the throngs of men surged from the village under rain clouds to form up for labor detail, David and Otto passed in the opposite direction, pushing a handcart.

"Yes, I arranged it." Otto answered his thought "For this work they will feed us."

In his thirty-seventh hour, David could only stare at the man's temple, which had risen in a vicious lump. For it was true—his meal tin had held enough porridge to fill his stomach. Who else in the camp was aware of the mortal fact? This had come upon David too fast. It left no time to think.

At Neisse, there were some twenty handcarts. Each could carry ten of the broken bodies downhill through the south wire, across fields that were being worked by Polish peasants, to an excavation in a birch forest. There they were packed neatly on lime, layer after layer like fish. That day, after first being caned by their aging guard, Franzel, up and down the silent barracks and tents, they made the trip eight times. Twice David fainted—but the porridge stayed down. On the fourth trip, one of the corpses, a boy, awoke, and Franzel allowed them to push it back uphill. All the way the body made a piteous animal crying. David walked beside the boy's head.

Today was Sunday, and as they passed a guards' dormitory, David looked up with his hand on the whimpering boy. The Viennese was on the roof, lying in the sun with his body oiled. Panting, with tears in his eyes, David stared behind them until the house was out of sight. The reptile basking on the roof did not look over.

From that hour on, through every minute of David's new animal cunning, he was measuring how he could get in to see the fat *Oberführer*. Of one thing Baron Sunda still had no doubt. That his name could shake apart this depraved bureaucracy. It would be perilous, however, to confide such knowledge to any guard. A *Sturmführer* like the Viennese would torture it out of David and claim the credit. Franzel might be too depressed and obedient to think of that.

It was not until the handcart's last run in the evening that David reflected on the figures of the dead. Could it be that six hundred men had died on this day alone and made the trip over the fields to ferment in the pit? Had he, David Sunda, seen eighty of their starved corpses flung onto the smoking pile?

As Otto rattled the empty cart back up the track, David trailed behind. Quickly, before he could be caned, he muttered a few words about plans that he had found on a Russian at Smolensk. Franzel was terrified to hear one of the prisoner beasts speak high German. Shaking all over, he rubbed the medal on his hat. Yes, he would see the *Oberführer* SS Laufer, who was from Poznan.

So, in David's forty-eighth hour, he found himself with the guard on the same porch before which he had stood—now many lifetimes ago—soaked with disinfectant. The screen door opened. They marched together into the cool shadows.

10

THE LITTLE *OBERFÜHRER* SS WITH THE ENORMOUSLY BULGING EYES STOOD waiting beside his desk in the red sun. On the wall behind him hung a painted *Totenkopf* plaque.

"*Sturmführer*, please go outside!" he shouted.

"*Ja, Herr Oberführer.*" Franzel clicked heels and backed out behind the prisoner.

When the door had shut, the camp commandant advanced excitedly toward David, glaring into his face. The *Oberführer* was over fifty, with hair clipped in a brush and a lividly sunburnt face. Two paces from his visitor he stopped, held a loose glove to his nose, and paced back to his desk. David stood struggling to keep his sanity as this person took his chair.

"You speak good German."

"I am German."

The *Oberführer* had placed a pistol on his papers. As David took a step closer, he saw four whips on the wall like billiard cues. The nerves round his countryman's mouth must be dead; saliva glistened on his chin.

"You are certainly a traitor," the *Oberführer* continued, after a full minute of silence. "What is more, you look like a Jew. Do you know the value of your life in my camp?"

"I have seen it, *Herr Oberfürher.*"

The *Oberfürher*'s eyes reddened. Barely disguising his excitement, he leaned forward. Then, twisting sideways, he lowered his voice.

"If you are wasting my time traitor, I will tear you to pieces with my hands. If you tell me everything, *everything*, I personally as a gentleman can guarantee that you will experience my gratitude. I am told that you have seen the plans for the Red Army counteroffensive."

This person—a gentleman? Standing in the hot sun over the SS commandant's desk, David thought that he would faint. He leaned with both hands on the desk, needing to believe what he knew to be taking place here. And if the entire Abwehr were hunting for Baron Sunda?

"*Herr Oberfürher*, I did not come to talk of plans," David said. The commandant's pudgy hand jammed an automatic against David's throat.

"Stinking piece of pigshit! I give you five seconds."

"I am Baron David Barthold von Sunda. . . ." He was almost in tears, uttering that glorious name here at the very end of the world.

"Impossible—impossible!" shrieked the *Oberführer*, his lids blinking rapidly.

As the prisoner lurched backwards in the sweltering office, the veined eyes followed his features with a look of gathering consciousness. The commandant shook his cheeks violently. "No, it cannot be! It is impossible . . ."

David felt hysteria choke in his throat, where the commandant was still pointing the gun. "*Herr Oberführer* Laufer!"—a hope had seized him, of indescribable sweetness—"you must release me from this place at once. As a gentleman, you cannot possibly know all that is going on here!"

At these words, the man facing him sank back limp in his chair, the forgotten pistol in his palm. Through the window behind him David could see a tall prisoner separate from the late work detail, circle aimlessly, then fall in the mud. There was a sharp *crack*. The *Oberführer* was still gaping at him with an expression of abject shock.

"I must insist. Release me at once," David cried out.

Quite suddenly, the little *Oberführer* SS had leapt up and was coming around the desk. David took two steps back.

"Never—do you hear me?—never!" he shouted, stabbing his arm toward the rafters. "Any Jew could try to impersonate Baron Sunda—I do not accept your claim, and neither will anyone else!"

"I must insist," cried David, shaking now with horror of this person, this place, and of himself.

"Do not insist or I will shoot you here and now!" the *Oberführer* screamed. "Set you free? You—for telling such fantastic lies? No one will believe them."

"*Herr Oberführer SS,*" David shouted.

"Get out!" The commandant gripped his arm. "Get out! And if you ever so much as speak our tongue again in this camp, I will have you shot."

11

BARON SUNDA WAS SENTENCED TO REMAIN SILENT INSIDE THE NEW LABYRINTH of the forced-labor camps. They never saw Franzel again. In another week, David was mysteriously seconded with the Silesian to a kitchen commando. He no longer judged the world, and the world no longer noticed this emaciated man who was present at the grave of some four thousand destroyed lives. David left behind forever his terror of the naked corpses out of love for the men who had inhabited them, while his dull hunger to see their executioners' blood spilled before his own intensified, until it deprived him of sleep. Each day, as the deliriously violent guards reappeared, hundreds of people perished. And with every hour on this Polish hillside, what mattered more and more was to find meaning in the piles of corpses and later, in the kitchen, to intervene tirelessly for the living. If civilization's last kindness was to attend the suffering of innocent men and women, then that was a kindness he would be equal to. Somewhere on the way, David surrendered the last of what he had once been.

One day, in the late winter of 1943, when David had survived at Neisse for seven months, Otto Horvath disappeared. Without explanation, a hundred men had been rounded up before the *Oberführer*'s bungalow and then jogged to some trucks.

By now, David's sanity clung to every aspect of his companion's life, from Otto's early ambition in a coal agent's family, and later teaching both engineering and Schiller in the commercial town of Glatz, to his recruitment by the partisans of the Pripet Marshes, his capture by a Fascist French expeditionary group and interrogation by its commander—a certain Joseph Darnand. Amid the trainloads of newly arrived strangers, the loss of David Sunda's friend and guide shook his deepest being. No longer could he ignore a dark urge, which had begun for David on Guderian's staff at the time of the drunken Borisov massacre, that his own body should descend to join those in the pit. Yet one evening just twelve days later—after another five thousand nameless bodies had lined a new forest pit—Otto walked into the soup shed, dressed in new striped ticking. Throughout that day their watering eyes met again and again along the smoking soup canisters, and David knew that something still more terrible had happened to Otto, and between them.

Finally the blackout came to the hillside of Neisse camp. Searchlights like ghosts licked this way and that among the sleeping stalags. Head to head in their window bunks, David and Otto could whisper at last.

"Ah, David, King David. Otto has been in such a place."

"Where, Otto? Why did they take you off?"

" Because I am an engineer of lift gears."

"A slave camp—?"

Miklos hissed from the bunk below. They lay still and waited as the bulky Latvian Viktor, who that morning had whipped the genitals of three Communists, glided under their window.

"Worse?" David whispered.

"A factory, a *metropolis* of murder." Hearing David's stillness, Otto went on in phrases, taking deep breaths. "Near a Yid town, Oswiecim, I worked in a warehouse to regulate a new furnace. Many, many stinking bodies—children. Others up to their knees after gold fillings with hammers and chisels, searching for El Dorado."

"How can that be!"

"Wait." Otto's breath came sharply. "The day the first lift worked, my leader was *so* delighted. Oh, my David, he had been a novice in our greatest monastery. He laughed as the bodies rolled in with their faces torn. . . ."

A powerful light had fallen on their bunks. Feeling for Otto's shaven head, now like a skull, David held it against his own. "Say it."

"He said—" For some seconds Otto shook silently. "He said, Just think of yourself at the very gates to Paradise. The man said, All our boyhoods, did the Catholic priests not talk of degradation? Well then—and he hit my arm with a crop—well then, is this not degradation? No? Tell me that!"

"He is mad!" David held Otto's trembling head. "He is only a madman."

"Yes, outside the countryside was so beautiful. My God, the birds were singing."

Together they waited for Otto for a very long time.

"And you, David?" he went on then. "Why have you lied to me?"

"Lied, Otto—lied?" David felt a crumpled paper being pushed into his hand. He lay silent, waiting for the searchlight. The center-tower light flickered back and lingered delicately on their window. David recognized a formal photo from long ago: the front page of a *Beobachter.*

Wehrmacht major, Baron von Sunda: Plotter still sought by the Abwehr, after General von Tresckow ends life with hand grenade, as bomb on aircraft fails to ignite. Once again Providence has saved our Führer!

Henning von Tesckow! David's mind hurtled to a group of officers he had met in the lobby of a Smolensk hotel. What of Claus and Fabian, and what if he had stayed?

"How old is it?"

"Ten days."

"My wife, my wife—I must go tomorrow! Laufer knows my name," David admitted and felt his head seized.

"Take me with you."

"Both?" David's heart beat fast.

"You could trick them."

"You mean to die, Otto? You, who saved me?"

"No, out of Europe—America."

"America?" David panted. Otto, famous among each new transport to this *Lager,* whom everyone needed?

"All my life, I have been the slave of men with papers," the Silesian whispered harshly. "After the Germans, there will be Russians, judges, armies—men behind desks! Until you, I never saw a free man. Take me with you!"

They were both madmen now. David felt tears running over his mouth. "You will die with me," he said. The searchlight was back. He felt the clipping pried from his fingers.

"Look . . . look!" Otto hissed, and in the white light David saw Otto stuffing newspaper in his mouth. Then, after all, they were laughing, without a sound. Otto seized his neck, and they kissed passionately the bones of each other's cheeks.

Three evenings later David and Otto did escape—in the uniforms of Balzer and the Latvian, and bearing on their tattooed wrists the coordinates of hell. It had been done, as it could only be done, by lying at last in the carts among the smoking dead. Later, the dog packs sent to track the fugitives through the fields and burial forest were unable to regain the scent beyond the river where the lime had been washed away. Accordingly, *Oberführer* SS Laufer—who was almost as horrified to have let Baron Sunda escape as to have been holding him—made an entry in the camp logbook, just below one concerning the first transport of ten thousand prisoners-of-war to Birkenau. On 2 April 1943, partisans had brutally murdered two of his *capos,* stolen their uniforms, briefly escaped, and then been drowned in the Neisse, which was overflowing its banks.

WALPURGISNACHT

1

IN BERLIN IT WAS ALREADY LATE ON AN AUTUMN NIGHT IN 1943. ACROSS the blacked-out city, its citizens had been asleep for hours.

But in Doktor Godard's studio with its forty-centimeter telescope under a dome of stars, a weak desk lamp still burned. Plato lay curled in his box, sometimes woofing softly at a dream, while his master paced nervously, wearing the vermilion bathrobe in which his wife liked to find him.

At the age of thirty-one, the celebrated Doktor Godard was at his prime. Yet aside from a certain lengthening of his hair and thickening of his figure— barbers had become scarce in Berlin, and the rowing club on the Havel was too deserted to be a pleasure—the philosopher had really not changed very much since his faculty days. In the period since his still-painful breakup with David Sunda—and, more recently, having been threatened by his friend's plots against the Reich's leaders—Johannes had grown more isolated than ever and better endowed with official connections. He had even detected a certain vagueness in Hélène, when she had inquired after Justin and Duncan. Nevertheless, as he circled the studio, Johannes's step had the same springiness it once had on Paris nights, as a student setting out across Saint-Michel to rehearse Bach. Only an hour ago he had sung through from memory the entire part of Christ, accompanied by his recordings of the Saint John Passion. Now his feet on the cool wood were naked, because it was warm and because he felt sick with desire.

The summer had lingered unusually late. In the last weeks, the bombers— which now droned regularly across the Berlin sky, making flashes that inter-rupted Doktor Godard's sightings of a possible binary star in the constellation of Ursa Major—had been less easily chased away. Recently, Heidrun had not thrown her wild fancy-dress parties. The clamor of German conquest too had grown remote, as the ocean might draw back from a volcanic island before it is engulfed by a tidal wave. Johann frowned.

Had a little brown bat just flitted between the curtains, made two passes across the bookshelves, and vanished by the desk? Now by his telescope, Doktor Godard became lost in thought. This bat was the sort of morbid vision his mother was likely to have. The old woman's last letter had seemed almost deranged: more biblical quotations—this time the words of the prophet Samuel's ghost, summoned before Saul by the Witch of Endor. *The world is departed from thee, King Saul, and become thine enemy. Because thou obeyest not the voice of the Lord, he will deliver Israel into the hands of the Philistines!* For a son who had risen to the supreme heights of pure reason, it was depressing to observe his old mother sink still deeper in superstition. Strange, too, for in the last year Frau Godard had seemed so happy to direct the clinic of Wildisches-Gladbach. As always, her son would spend Christmas there—without Heidrun, of course.

Yes, he had lost contact with the war, and the war had lost contact with Johannes. Not once in the last months had the conceited fools at the Ministry of Enlightenment asked after the philosopher's progress, though he was still sent his retainer. Since Hélène had moved permanently to the family estate with Alaric and her two-year-old—the result, Johannes had jealously worked out, of one night at the Adlon Hotel during David's last cryptic stopover in Berlin—he had not enjoyed going out into the capital. How was it that his friends should leave him here in this accusing solitude, to tend civilization's most sacred fires? Very occasionally, he might still have tea at Kränzlers when Doktor Godard's powerful defender among the universities, Heidegger, came to the capital, or go to visit the house of Heidrun's conductor. Soon enough the Pax Germanica would come and Johannes's precious light—like Noah's dove—could venture forth. The only strife then would be the competition among the mandarin class to produce more exalted scholars, artists, and men of science. Doktor Godard himself had laid the plans for a Christian Renaissance with these very domes and institutes at its center. What better leitmotif could underlie the endless dumb marching and the gangs of uniforms?

But the more time Johannes spent at home, to prepare this uplifting speculation for his ministry, the more his wife was out, living extravagantly and touring the Reich's capitals to sing grand opera. Heidrun knew every restaurant, celebrity and influential drawing room in Europe, yet she never mentioned her parents in Brazil. It was this easy passion for the world outside that kept Johannes as helpless as ever before his wife.

In fact, not until this morning's overheard conversation between two neighbors had Johannes once found the courage to doubt her. Releasing the telescope, he pushed out onto the balcony. Heidrun was somewhere below.

2

IN THE MOONLIGHT, THE BRANDENBURG GATE AND THE ORNATE SKYLINE OF ROOFS lost their manmade quality and appeared mysteriously organic, like ruins in a jungle. Johannes stared toward a sound he had just heard until his head spun.

Then he saw his wife. She had moved into the light some thirty paces away. He could see the thick hair hanging over her naked shoulders, the iridescent satin gown. The woman walked slowly, arms swinging together, staring up fixedly at the night sky. Even now, at the sight of Heidrun Dolin, returning alone to the house, Johannes could not help feeling hope.

By the time her key rattled in the door he was downstairs under the bright chandelier in the entrance hall, swaying with a terror of the places where she might have been. In the blaze of lights, the singer's slanted dreaming eyes fixed on Johann's with impersonal tolerance. Instantly, his tender relief was overcome by something else, something alien.

"Why did you leave the car out?"

"You might have been asleep."

Heidrun leaned back to shut the door, and Johannes saw her red hair and hazel eyes. Her voice was like cool deep water.

"It is four o'clock—where have you been?" His cry sounded childlike in the silent hall. For a long time, his wife did not say anything. Her smile had about it something lawless, charming and obscene, cutting into the trusting sentiment Johannes needed to feel for her.

"Have you been up with your books?" she whispered, stroking his cheek.

"Where have you been?"

"Shall I take you with me then? Do you want to come too?" The woman leaned forward, and a ghost of perfume and smoke enveloped him. "Shh! It is time you came with me. I will make you . . . lose . . . your . . . senses."

"Tell me, Heidi!" He groaned, beginning to forget where he was. "Are the stories true?"

"What stories, my love?"

"The stories of—the stories, the bacchanals. In the mountains. The parties, the soldiers. . . ."

"Your embarrassment is so charming, Johannes," she said.

Hearing this woman's soft wanton laugh, devoid tonight of its usual boredom, Johann could not help laughing too. He felt himself tremble toward something vile. Heidrun's hair rustled against his cheek.

"The Venusberg of the officers? Yes, I was there. And I have danced, danced and sung for them too, those strong young warriors."

"My God, Heidrun, what have you done?" He forced his wife's shoulders against the door panels. But Heidrun's soft flesh yielded easily to his hands.

"Shall I take you with me, then? Will you come too?"

"My God, it's almost dawn." Johannes was still whispering.

"Now, on the carpet!" Heidrun said. "The servants are asleep."

As Heidrun removed her arms from the straps of her dress, the limp satin fell in folds around her waist, and perspiration streamed down Johannes's cheeks. She followed his eyes.

"Yes! You must look. Hundreds looked! And below is the well they drank at. Johannes, desire is the pulse . . . beautiful, like blood flowing. Yes, blood, rushing in the underground rivers, pressing up to escape. All the young fighters with their blood rivers beating."

"Impossible, monstrous! You with all those others!" Johannes somehow suppressed his cry. Again they were whispering like criminals.

"Yes!" Heidrun laughed, now singing her *Liebestod*. "You see, my little professor? And when you have devoured me, we will go like the Celts to gather the dew that the gods send down to purify the world."

Sly fingers moved down his shirt, but Johannes barely felt them. Hearing the coarse note in his wife's voice, he had felt the horror that lay across the world. Yet in Doktor Godard's mind something as ancient as any Celtic rite was already willing. He felt his fingers drawn down into a web of hair. Yes, the night was already gone, he was thinking. At dawn they could purify themselves. Then he was not thinking at all.

3

YET WHEN THE FIRST CHEERFUL SERVANTS' VOICES CAME FROM THE HALL, AND the body of the famous Dolin was falling asleep under her canopy of goblins and cat-headed cherubs, Doktor Godard did not feel in the least bit purified. Even to be in the same room with her was intolerable.

The moment that Heidrun began her soft snoring, he escaped upstairs through the villa, locked himself in his studio, and began to pace. It was a Monday, and the tram bells and bustle came reassuringly from the Berlin streets. But Johannes had seen the pale new sunlight on the hall carpets.

"Well, old dog," he tried to joke, "the mind that ruled the spirit that governed the mysteries of the universe has lost its luster, don't you think?" Plato observed him from the window. The sound of the voice now made famous to all Nazis by Goebbels's radio speeches only confirmed the gross excesses that his wife had boasted of in the early hours. But—still worse—Johannes was not even surprised! This very hour he must ship a few possessions to his mountains. Then he would flee Heidrun—perhaps in search of a position in Paris. Or he might be forgiven by his colleagues at Princeton.

At the second *click, click*, Johannes looked around. Could there be someone on his balcony? It was not until the glass doors were unlatched that he recognized his visitor. The sun had just risen.

"Francisco!" he cried, only just overcoming an impulse to weep. "How did you get up, why not come to the door?"

His old protégé looked elegant in a suit, though he must have climbed a drainpipe from the garden. They had not met since the institute scandal, when the boy had given his disgraced professor a Labrador puppy. Francisco did not smile as he tested the lock on the door to the hall.

"In fact, I have been twice to this house. Are you being kept prisoner here?"

"What? Did they really not let you in? No, no, come to the couch! I'll boil you some tea."

"Johann . . . Johann," Francisco said softly.

"Tell me, what are you doing in Europe?" Johannes chattered deliriously, wiping dry tea leaves off the wet spoon. "How is your work on Spinoza?"

"Four years ago I was smuggled over the Basel frontier by the Red Orchestra. Now they are all dead . . . I have come to you at last. That is my work for Spinoza."

"Which orchestra? I don't understand."

From the studio corner, Doktor Godard turned to meet the gaze of the presence now seated in the sunshine. How could his closest acolyte have been replaced by a polite stranger? What were these brutal workings of fate Johannes knew nothing of here in the philosopher's studio? "Life is confusing . . . I will have to leave Berlin," he said.

"There is no use now. You should have done that long ago."

"Why, Francisco? Were we not above the blunderings of politics?"

"Doktor, I am putting myself in your hands," the man whispered, with careful emphasis.

"Forgive me." His teacher sank exhaustedly into an armchair. "My nerves are in a bad state. Heidrun has been—"

"You are still a good fellow, Johann. Only not made for our times."

"Surely there must be innocence. . . ." Johannes hid his face. Presently he went on, quoting Goethe. "'He who forever strives upward, can he not be saved?'"

"Perhaps you could strive upward another way, Doktor. I believe you knew of a resisance group, the White Rose?"

Seeing the younger man's embarrassment for him, a bolt of hysterical anger flashed through Johannes—for this Jew and for all Jews. And in that illumination, the night over Europe was lit by a demonic light. Doktor Godard glimpsed as if it were a nightmare, in all its vileness, the terror of his life.

Just then, fortunately, Francisco smelled something and he jumped up to tilt the telescope. Caught in its lens, the sun had started burning the portrait of Goethe! This made neither of them laugh, and presently, for the first time since his fall at the institute, Doctor Godard again heard the names of his judges. Even then, two of the scholars had belonged to the secret circle opposing Heidrun's Nazi friends. Every one of them was now under interrogation. Schlemmer had lived only three houses away!

"But we do not hear these things!" Johannes cried out. Then he remembered the letters to him, embossed with a rose. What had he done with them, shredded them into the toilet? And once again Doktor Godard knew the seriousness of his case, and hatred flashed in his heart.

Francisco sat forward in the sunshine. "You must listen to me now."

Johannes slumped onto the couch next to the Argentine. His disciple began to speak. The veins rose on Francisco's temples, perspiration glistened on his cheeks. When he had finished twenty minutes later, Doktor Godard threw up his hands.

"Francisco, what are you saying? It sounds quite mad." This was all too much. Why must he listen? First Heidrun, now production techniques to murder entire races.

"I'll come back tonight. Now you should go to bed, get some sleep. We need you fresh.

Presently Doktor Godard spirited his caller downstairs and out through the kitchen door. Francisco suddenly clutched his teacher's hand and squeezed convulsively. Tears came to his eyes.

"Think, *think*, what you are in a position to do!" he whispered.

After Francisco had gone, Johann took a bath and tried to understand what had just happened. He thought about the curious contrast between the sense of military order in the streets and the hidden, decadent chaos revealed by Heidrun. He was so possessed by this train of thought that when he rose from the tub, he felt more purified that if he had bathed in all the dews in Wales.

4

"HERR DOKTOR! ARE YOU WELL, HERR DOKTOR?"

Johannes opened his eyes and saw before him the Gobi desert.

"Yes, yes, Hilda. What day is it?"

"Why, it is still Monday, " the old chambermaid protested delicately.

Could this be Monday afternoon? Had his acolyte of long ago sat here on this couch that very morning? Leaping up, Johannes examined the portrait of Goethe. A hole had been burnt through it. He began to struggle with his clothes. Without seeing anyone, light-headed in the rush of his old passion for knowledge, Johannes reached the front colonnade. Francisco would have to wait for him. Putting on his hat, he almost ran out through the gate.

He took the direction of the Reichstag. There was a small Wehrmacht parade snapping its boots along the forest curve that led from the Brandenburg Gate. The woman and the two old men ahead of him did not pause to watch. Johannes was vaguely aware of the surrender of Field Marshal Paulus's entire army and of the recent setbacks at Kursk, much the way that he knew of dying suns in remote galaxies. But what was he to do, and what was his "position"? As he went past the Adlon Hotel and approached the empty Reichstag grounds, he at once sensed the change. No longer could Doktor Godard feel nostalgia for this stage where he had once, as Heidrun's lover, known nympholeptic raptures. He halted on the grass beyond the ministry columns to stare at the officials, climbing with the voiceless efficiency of ants up and down the flight of steps. At the thought of the evil that might be in each of them, his heart thundered in his ears like the great drum of the *Dies Irae*.

As his legs moved off over the cobblestones, a huddled group clattered down the Reichstag steps toward him. Two big plainclothesmen were half carrying a little scar-faced man, who moved his legs as if he were walking. Close to where Johannes stood, a car door was flung open. The three men rushed into it with almost comic purposefulness, and the car sprang away from the curb. An ageing guard gave off a faint, intimate scent of hops.

"I recognize you, Herr Doktor. The guard rushed up slavishly to tell Johannes what had happened. "That was our Jugoslav broadcaster. Went crazy, he did. '*Ladies and gentlemen, what you are about to hear is nonsense and a pack of lies, and if you are still sane switch it off.*' Ha-ha, what a joke."

Johannes's shock at the spectacle of one-human being in the physical power of two others had just been replaced by a greater one. Had he instantly been recognized in this place? The Reichstag's entrance hall was already lit. Groups of officials, some in uniform, stood whispering here and there. At a desk behind a barrier sat a hawk-faced officer. As Johannes approached, a group of civilians he had never seen before materialized in front of him, speaking several languages—all of which Johannes understood.

"*Doktor Godard, what is your opinion of American morale?*" . . . "*What is your opinion of Japanese* Kultur?" . . . "*Did Field Marshal Göring really tell you . . . and is the colonization of Europe a success?*"

The philosopher waved his hand and smiled, so as not to hurt their feelings. Surely they were not addressing him? He had glimpsed Göring only once at the opera—yet suddenly he felt uncertain as to whether he might also have spoken to the Air Marshal at the Eagle's Nest. Johann leaned on the receptionist's table. He was trembling like a criminal. To his amazement, the fellow jumped to his feet and his right arm shot out in the Roman salute.

"Heil Hitler! You visit us at last, Herr Doktor Godard."

"Would it be—is Doktor Goebbels in?" Johann had flinched at his own insincerity. He had not seen Goebbels once since their afternoon on the tennis court with his old schoolmate, Herder.

"I am terribly sorry, Herr Doktor Godard. The Minister is on a one-day trip to Warsaw. You might care to see Reichsführer Himmler?"

But before Doktor Godard could answer, he felt a hand grip his shoulder. He struggled to recognize this familiar figure in the black uniform—the square, close-shaven jaw, the intelligent, sarcastic eyes.

"Joachim! What are you doing here?"

"You know me, always expanding my circle of friends. Thank you, *Obersturmführer*, I will accompany Doktor Godard."

As if there had never been anything else on his mind, Johannes found himself strolling back outside. He vaguely remembered that their last meeting had not been friendly. Waiting below them was a horse and carriage. Was it almost night again? He had only just left his bed.

"Well, Hansel! And how do you enjoy your notoriety?"

"I had no idea," said Johannes. "I cannot imagine what it means."

Herder released his arm and faced about. He seemed more highly strung than ever in his tight uniform of an *Oberstgruppenführer.* "What does it mean? It means that the spirit of our greatest philosopher belongs to the state. Though naturally, you are too intelligent to hold real power."

Doktor Godard was replacing his hat. At his old schoolmate's words, a sickening ray of guilt flashed through his brain.

"Come, Professor. We will take the carriage. I'm tired of machines. You don't look your old self. Thinking too much, perhaps? It's as bad as drinking alone. . . ." Joachim Herder's nasal voice chattered on as if no powers of independence were left to Doktor Godard. "Yes, Hansel, you should see my new house. Do you remember the séances where you met Heidrun—the Grail, the Tibetans? They take place now *chez moi.* Tonight, Heinrich, Adolf, and some of the originals will drop by for a childrens' party. Later we will view *Gone with the Wind.* . . . You know, the boss almost never visits now from that unamusing Wolfschänze. While we are waiting, I will show you some fascinating short reels."

Now, in starlight, the edifices of blacked-out Berlin drifted by like ruined temples. Tonight, Heidrun was to sing Isolde. Perspiration poured down Johannes's face. What had the broadcaster said? And had *he*—the philosopher Doktor Godard—ever uttered, until this hour, less than perfectly distilled truths? Johannes remembered his optimistic words, composed for the Eastern Front. What if everything—everything around him—*was* a pack of lies? His precious light would be extinguished!

The carriage was just passing the windows of Johannes's old corner apartment when suddenly Joachim heard his voice.

"Do you think I am an imposter?" Johannes challenged. "I've seen your tricks before. You've arranged all this to disgrace me and drag me deeper into Hitler's plans. What *are* his plans, Joachim?"

It was the curfew, and as they approached the Marienkirche, Johann heard an angry voice float across the empty boulevard. The carriage driver did not stir on his seat. "I have decided to leave Germany. I will take a post in France or in America." *What was this? What was he saying?* Johannes fell back against the leather bench, gasping in the fresh night air. Next to him, Herder bent forward with a scarcely disguised sneer. Holding out a handkerchief, he spoke at last. "For all the celebrated brilliance of that mind, professor, you do say stupid things. And you are far too handsome."

5

"I HAVE A SURPRISE," JOACHIM HERDER CONTINUED, IN SUPREME GOOD SPIRITS. "It's an antique globe."

But Doktor Godard was trailing him like a sleepwalker as the towering

THE BOOK OF KINGS

doors opened. The philosopher was scarcely conscious that he was entering the Hohenzollern mansion that he had so often glimpsed behind a wall during lonely promenades. As they wound up the great tongue of a staircase and moved along the ornate loggias, he drew away from every shadow as if it were alive.

"Look, Hansel, I have made this salon my study. And here is my treasure." Herder was drawing the blackout curtains. A chandelier blazed on.

"Why, that is exactly like my globe!" Johannes frowned.

"Its identical mate: 1792—!" Herder laughed shrilly and cracked his knuckles. "Only look, yours is of the Earth and of Day . . . mine is of the Heavens and of Night."

His friend's hoarse voice as he pronounced the last word had made the philosopher's knees weaken. At that moment, Joachim was rummaging in a cabinet, and he appeared not to see Doktor Godard sink onto the *fauteuil* and stare at the pink nudes and satyrs disporting overhead. When he turned, the *Oberstgruppenführer* was balancing a heavy film projector. Like a priest with a chalice or a seer with a glass ball, he set the machine on a cloisonné table.

"Here, surely, is Satan's supreme creation. With this little gadget, the most natural scene will be turned to dreams and twisted beyond all reach of conscience." Showing almost genuine feeling, Herder glanced across the room at the gentle scholar. "With *this*, one can confuse even the senses of a saint—until the simplest soul suspects the image in his mirror."

Johannes stirred, but he was powerless to rise, let alone to rush home through the curfew across half Berlin. "Five minutes at your ministry had that effect on me," he said.

"Not beaten yet?" laughed his childhood friend. "Well, there is still an hour before the master of the world is due. Have something strong to drink. What you are about to see is no Hollywood romance."

"It is reality that we're drinking against. Your little toy there is meant for escape!" Johannes called after him, as Herder crossed the huge floor. The mansion around them was perfectly still.

"Then let us escape," hissed Joachim, and the suites of rococo furniture vanished in near darkness. Spots revolved before the philosopher's eyes. A ten-meter square of unnatural light appeared. There was a colorless image, a framework against a brick wall. A boy appeared, wearing a sweater and baggy trousers. "This is a common case," observed a voice over the whining motor. "A Pole who married one of our countrywomen."

Doktor Godard caught the arms of his chair, but the face had shot downward. A vertical tether had appeared above the head. The figure flickered, expanded—now there was only the tilted face, the mouth and eyes open. The boy was sticking out his tongue. Abruptly, as Johannes rose to his feet, the picture vanished. Like a red-hot coal, the image flew into the tissue of his mind. Herder's voice came through the murky room.

"Still fighting for that precious innocence? This next one will keep you in your seat."

Now there were three new faces. Doctor Godard sank back. "Are not those Dicker and Marquardt . . . is that Friedrich Sunda?"

"Don't worry, Hansel. The baron has been saved for other dramas!" Herder laughed pleasantly, and the two kindly faces from the White Rose's circle of dissenters darkened. Their tongues came soundlessly out, their eyes rolled. . . . Gears whined and clicked. In his chair, Doktor Godard gave a whimpering cry. Above him, the faces in the flickering light had vanished, replaced by a small room. He recognized the prim schoolmaster, Himmler, seated facing an old man.

"That man is the Reichsführer's medium," Joachim called. "We have nicknamed him the Warlock of Endor. The Warlock's words to Himmler were that Providence will abandon us and our Führer will lose his powers."

Once again, Doktor Godard opened his mouth and nothing emerged. Recalling then his mother's quotations, Johannes saw history advance like the prow of a great ship.

"Oh, ha-ha! That scarcely matters. For Adolf, there can be no turning back. Look, here is his supreme experiment. Can you conceive of such a mob? Millions of Gypsies, Jews, Communists, and Russians, ignorant as lambs awaiting slaughter. There beyond that wall is Jakob Stodel's latest design in asphyxia tanks—"

Doktor Godard spoke. "My God!"

"And speaking of lambs, here is someone you will remember."

"Margaret!" Johann cried out, clasping his ears with his hands. "Joachim, can it be our Gretchen?" And his thoughts fled back to the mountains above the village of their childhood.

"Very good, Hansel—and after all this time!" Herder's form swayed above the projector beam. Margaret was a young woman wearing striped pajamas, slumped dejectedly on a bench in what appeared to be a garden. "Incurably mad, old friend. But don't worry, they were all put out of their misery years ago."

Ten paces from the whirring machine, Doktor Godard had risen, blinded with tears that did not spill. "Gretchen too?" he whispered in the utter darkness.

"Insane for love of you, little doktor. Now don't tell me that you have regrets, that you didn't know."

But Johannes had begun the eight steps to the loggia door. His fingers bumped along a wall and threw a light switch. What had been people with real lives was now a ghost of light on a salon wall. Overhead, the naiads floated over the ceiling with nipples as red as strawberries. Yet here below, like a proof, were Joachim's black uniform and Doktor Godard's hat.

Johannes's hand slipped at the sound of his own voice. "How can you grin coolly at the torments of thousands, Joachim?"

"Of millions, Doktor," Joachim corrected. "Millions of nameless human refuse with nobody to vouch for them. Still, Hansel, this may be my last film show. To be honest, I feel the day of doom is close for our absolute state. Anyhow, my supply of hatred is running out."

"Are these films real? Is Gretchen dead?"

Herder stiffened nervously and giggled. The gentle Doktor Godard had just taken three threatening steps toward him. "She was your victim, Hansel, not mine," he said savagely.

"And this monster, Hitler—he is the Second Coming of Satan himself."

"Doktor, why always sound naive?" The Nazi officer was baiting him as if he were in some circus. "There are more than a few Satans on this earth. In a few minutes you can tell him yourself. You see, there are no gods or devils really—only geniuses like you and him."

"He . . . and *I!*" Johannes's voice rang out. At the thought of Hitler, probably on his way here from the Chancellery, his limbs went weak.

"Both the Führer and yourself have a vision of the world's entire order in your powerful minds. What is the difference?"

"I wish every last human being love." Johannes paced the huge carpet. "He wishes every human being fear!"

The black-uniformed officer grinned at Doktor Godard's angry shouts.

"I will leave Berlin and Germany tonight." With a powerful new love, Johann had remembered Francisco. What did his acolyte want him to do?

"You are running away? First collect your wage from the 'monster,' the very man who shielded your innocence and left you to study all these years. You and your post-Kantian philosophy are the property of the Nazi revolution."

The officer watched Johannes from among the salon's center chairs, his lips moving faster and faster. In a world that Johannes had only loved, had a childhood friend wished for his destruction? He lurched forward. With a laugh, clutching the projector's weight, Joachim backed against a chair and fell.

For an instant the *Oberstgruppenführer* lay motionless and Johannes felt grief. Then, in the silence that followed the thud of the projector, they were wrestling. Johannes looked around them, half blinded by his first violence to anyone. The tripod legs were bolted to the floor.

Seconds later, Joachim Herder was bent backwards on the globe, bound by the projector cord. Two silver *Totenkopf* buttons popped off his uniform and clattered on the floor.

"You will see! In the end, the entire world will worship Hitler"—Herder's shouts followed him to the door—"a man as large as history! That is the law of power. . . . Think of Alexander, Caesar, Genghis, Bonaparte! His power will grow greater still!"

Johann shivered violently as he put on his hat. He could scarcely look at the terrible raving figure arched over the globe. Herder wrenched at the rubber cord.

"Running away, coward! Thinking only of saving yourself!"

"If everyone alive, even you and I, had worried for their soul's salvation, none of this would have happened," replied Johannes, and he switched off the chandelier. He went quickly down the stairs and crossed the dim hall.

The first thing that Johannes thought of as he ran among the luminous Prussian statues in Herder's garden was Heidrun. With reason now come down to earth, he must no longer ignore her depravities. The primeval galactic light fell like ice upon the lawns and bushes. There was no sign yet of Joachim's guests, or of their children. Johann musn't not stop until he was in his mountains.

But the sleeping Berlin night resembled no other that he had ever known. Doktor Godard was overcome by a wave of such rending terror that he sank to his knees beside the fountain. And taking off his hat, he ran his hand over the grass and wiped the dew across his mouth and temples.

6

IT WAS SEVEN-THIRTY BY THE TIME THE PHILOSOPHER SAW THE VILLA FROM among the oleanders. Entering through the scullery, he could hear Heidrun warming up somewhere overhead. So late an opening of the opera confirmed Hitler's presence in Berlin. The sound of her deceiving throat shook Johannes, and it released him. As long as he could hear her, he would not be interrupted.

Upstairs, Johannes searched the rooms for his acolyte. If he had returned, he couldn't get in, as Hilda had relocked the balcony door. Sweeping together his notebooks, some money, and his ministry gasoline vouchers, Johannes took one final look around his studio. Then, holding Plato under his arm, he slipped back downstairs and crossed the hall.

Fifteen minutes after his return, he stepped through the gate onto the Tiergarten. He could faintly hear Heidrun's voice as she repeated a lilting phrase, again and again, each time with a different inflection. He was perspiring heavily. Even then, having grasped the hard truth of his wife's promiscuous soul, Doktor Godard was torn. He experienced a last, excruciating pity. God, too, was still in Berlin, although weary of his flock.

Seconds later, Doktor Godard climbed into the Mercedes. Plato turned twice and curled on the passenger seat as Johannes's tired arms wheeled the machine into the hunting forest. Already he was thinking of the village and the girl, Margaret. For of all the things he had learned today, that Gretchen might be dead was the only one he could not believe. Nor must he be silenced before he could tell his mother about the truth of the words that she had sent to him through the years.

After Potsdam, Doktor Godard caught the new autobahn. Somewhere ahead lay the Alps.

Across the next eighteen hours, Johannes no longer thought about Heidrun and Francisco, or about Joachim lashed to the astronomer's globe. He did not think about these things because he did not know how to think about them. He wished only to be punished for the years he had lived in his mind, while evil consumed the world he had known. All he had to do was sit long enough in this small reliable theater of stars, dimmed headlights, and green luminous instruments—and to remember a silent lake among the cliffs, and the barn with its milk pails, where a boy had ached with impatience for Gretchen's kiss. He thought of his mother's kind eyes and ready laughter. He thought of the chapel, with its pulpit, like a cocoon, and its pastel lives of the saints. Finally, he thought of the altar itself, and of how it had been to sing the Saint John Passion—all through that long night of roadblocks, scattered lights, and convoys.

Just before seven o'clock, the starless sky turned charcoal gray. It was still so dark that Johannes left the headlights on. Past Karlsruhe, after a few more hours on the Rhine plain, he and Plato drew near the Swiss frontier. On an uphill grade beyond Ulm, they were stopped by a barrier manned by the security police. The youngest guard, who had curly brown hair, walked slowly to the car. There was not a blemish on this officer. It was as if he had never smiled.

Johannes had not eaten or slept in two days. As he offered his Ministry papers, his hand was shaking and imprecise.

"*Ja so*, Doktor Godard?" The young man glanced at Plato's thumping tail. "Where are you going, Herr Doktor?"

"I am going home—that is, to Wildisches-Gladbach."

The policeman turned and waved. The barrier was rising. It was like a miracle. It came to Johannes, then, how much he had come to rely on the eager salutes and fawning grins of this state apparatus.

In ten more kilometers the road bent sharply, and Johannes saw two peaks, buried in snow clouds. Then, looking far below, he glimpsed three climbing black cars. His mouth had gone dry. Now, at last, Johannes recognized a pear orchard and the track along its flank. The Mercedes bumped uphill into a very dark forest. Familiar barns appeared on the left, and he saw again Pastor Manlius's greenhouse. The pastor himself was just closing the door. But there was no time to stop. The roads joined by a stone trough among a tiny cluster of houses—Wildisches-Gladbach. And, as Johannes accelerated into his village, he saw two things in quick succession.

Could that be Margaret's father drunk on the *Gasthof* bench? So she *was* gone, forever! Then there were three soldiers blocking the road ahead. His mudguard hit the tallest one as Johannes wheeled the car around then, past the fountain, and into an alley that led to the chapel. He felt an impact on the back of his head. He opened the door and climbed down. The cobbles came up at him.

Now Johannes was on his hands and knees, staring at a black stain on the dirt. He could see the chapel door very clearly, and it was exactly as he had dreamt of it. Then he lay stretched on his back with Plato licking his hair. He gazed up past helmeted faces at the cloudy sky. *If only there were light.* Then the sky darkened further, as if under an immense weight.

Then it was very bright and somehow, looking up, Johannes Godard saw again the chapel's rafters and the central beam with its demons and smiling sun, its rabbits and its saints. The faces of his mother and Pastor Manlius were bent over him. His mother was stroking his hair and she was weeping. He knew that he was dying, and his heart began to soften and soften, and he submitted himself. "Mother, I am so glad I woke." There was music, and Johannes, turned his head to hear it. His neck and shoulders ached and he began to cry.

"My son—Johannes?"

The chapel lights turned Elsa Godard's gray hair to a ring of sparkling webs. Johannes smiled at his mother. He knew he would never have to be Doktor Godard ever again. "Mother . . ." he whispered, wishing to tell her about her prescient letters. He saw his mother's kind, clear eyes shut, her eyebrows draw together. Her wide lips began to tremble, and she bowed over his chest.

Among the silent farmers and woodcutters in the chapel entrance there was a commotion. They had heard of the philosopher's return. These people— each one of whom had known Johannes Godard since he was a boy—huddled against the walls as the three state policemen from the autobahn checkpoint entered the chapel. The police pushed through and the fallen man strained upward, the veins of his temples swelling as he lifted his head, bleeding freely from the gunshot wound.

"The cross," said the white-frocked priest. "He wishes for the crucifix." The curly-haired policeman stepped forward, as if to seize the fugitive before he could die. Two older men held him back.

The dying man saw none of this. He rolled slowly, straining to lift his eyes to the altar cloth. "Give me light!" wept a faint voice.

The woman bent beside the dying man gave out a terrible cry. She threw herself across him, shaking and tugging. But the body in her arms was lifeless.

So Johannes Godard died, and one of the purest lights went out of Europe.

7

STILL HITLER'S MACHINE OF DOMINATION BORE CIVILIZATION FORWARD. THE extermination chambers continued to devour human flesh. The front-line Führers, and a continental array of police with no other ethics than *Kultur*, vulgarity, and force, continued to pillage even the pillagers, to desecrate further what was already ruined, and to profane what had long since been raped. With ferocious conviction, the Europe the Fleurusians had known as students consumed its long-accumulated virtue.

"And if you still try to defend the infamies and horror perpetrated by Bonaparte, that Antichrist"—Duncan Penn, now divorced in New York, had cynically enjoyed quoting this line from the old czarist court, during the Thanksgiving week before America was itself attacked by Japan—"then you are no longer my friend."

Now two years later, as Hitler took time to shower rockets on London, an altered Duncan Penn would reflect how humble Napoleon seemed—who had abandoned Russia after only two months—beside Hitler, who would leave behind not even a democratic code. In Hitler's aftermath, Duncan knew by now, there would be superhighways, ballistic missiles, factories built by slaves, a "people's car," and patents for the rapid mass slaughter of innocents.

In the still naive summer of 1942—with even the Nazi ally to the east, Japan, wounded at the heart of her empire of water—the technology of war-fare seemed only to gain in violence and embrace the planet: faster, it seemed, than Duncan, then still in Georgia, could be trained for battle. The instruments of conflict were being purified of all moral restraints and accelerating toward the last, most ancient, honor: total annihilation. The new armies had become like fighting birds who circle ever upward, leaving the suffering earth far below and pursuing each other over higher in an ecstasy of hatred, where the air is thin, the violence limitless, and the views always magnificent.

So that June in 1942, the Japanese and Americans decided in a single day the enslavement of the Pacific—and the theater to which Duncan would be sent—launching against each other armadas of steel to resolve ownership of a spit of sand called Midway Island. Only months earlier, the emperor had sunk half of the United States fleet at Pearl Harbor on his way to a conquest of California. Recently, though sixteen bombers had flown impudently over Hirohito's palaces in Tokyo.

At dawn on 3 June, a thousand ocean miles west of Hawaii, 121 Imperial ships had emerged from fog banks with their crews on deck, chanting magic slogans and making libations of rice wine to the rising sun, trailed by aircraft-carrier wakes the width of city blocks. Already they were being circled on the horizons by enemy fliers of many races.

Squadrons of pure-blooded Shinto pilots swarmed into the glorious

Pacific skies to meet the surprise attack—Duncan had heard the naval tactics analyzed the same week on his army instructor's blackboard. By ten o'clock, most of the Japanese planes had been back on their floating airfields to be rearmed and fueled. It was for that moment that Admiral Nimitz had withheld his dive-bombers.

In five more minutes, the *Akagi*, the *Kaga*, and the *Soryu* had all received bombs though their flight decks, transforming those floating cities of racial purity into crematoria, erupting sky-high pillars of fire. In three more hours, the last of Japan's aircraft carriers subsided into the tropical sea, amid frenzied legions of sharks. Yet even after that mortal wound, throughout Hirohito's empire of islands, down mainland China to Burma and Singapore, the corrupt machine of domination gathered momentum. And for three more years, the cruelties of the thwarted Japanese race grew into a legend that rivaled Hitler's.

The Führer's ambition, too—even after the city of Stalingrad was turned into a furnace where the soldiers wounded among Paulus's broken 6th Army had bled vodka—continued to consume Hitler's own people and anything else of any value in his grasp. Months after Stalingrad, in July of 1943—as Duncan took his unit ashore on the beaches of Sicily—Hitler had been launching a million German soldiers with a thousand tanks under Kluge and Mannstein against a two-hundred-kilometer Russian line at Kursk, defended by the armies of marshals Vatutin and Rokossovsky. During the next three days, in history's largest battle, the Russians were driven back fifty kilometers, losing another two thousand tanks. But Hitler's army, caught among the minefields and rocket barrages, was like a lion by now too crippled to fight on open ground.

And again, Stalin offered to negotiate peace with his fellow dictator. In a recurring dream, he had seen the many million ghosts of his own exterminations one day lining up to cast votes against him. But Hitler's only remaining justification was in his conquered lands and his power to further enslave and pillage them.

So it was, on 6 June 1944, that five thousand ships landed fifty thousand armed Allies, Duncan among them, on the beaches of the Atlantic Wall. And two weeks later—three years after David Sunda had witnessed Guderian's assault at Brest—Marshal Zhukov unrolled a massive offensive along the entire length of Hitler's eastern lines.

In Berlin, gone now were the Wienerblut orchestras in lakeside parks, the tea cakes and potted flowers, and the glorious rallies with their Wagnerian accompaniment. The mask of the Nazi conqueror fell away and, before all eyes, the face of the Antichrist came into view. And in his power were three hundred million of the still living—among them, seven million of the earth's fifteen million Jews.

THE ABYSS

1

FOR THREE YEARS, FROM A STONE FARMHOUSE BY CARBONNE, ROCHET'S band had gone out to fire tiny arrows into the colossal German Reich. Despite the heartbreak of so many *maquisards* in the valleys around denounced and executed, Rochet's farm had not once been searched during the incessant sweeps by the Abwehr and the Orpo.

Every Sunday, the Rochets went to mass. Later, the farmer would sip one beer with his friend the mayor of Carbonne. It was from the mayor, who admired the Germans, that those at the farm knew that the French Fascist leader Joseph Darnand was back. The old men of the *boules* pitch greeted Rochet with mournful respect. No one pressed the farmer about Philippe Hériot, the young inspector of railways, who his brother had sent to take his dead son Paul's place. The town priest, too, preserved the silence of the church.

Justin continued to write, and twice a month a few thousand Parisians searched the boulevards for clandestine bulletins carrying Justin's serial, set in a mythological city of philosophers, virtuous men, and women somewhere under Hitler. Many laughed, until tears ran down their faces, at the antics of the most infamous collaborators. Its author knew that his writings were not art, for the readers of war were not the readers of peace, and later no one would understand.

While Rochet's *maquisards* became absorbed by violence, Justin grew so gentle that he dreaded ever again being called to kill even a moth. For, in the reflex with which he had pushed the detonator handle by a railway tunnel seventeen French and German men were crushed to death. Justin had continued three more years only through his oath never again to join in such an act.

Yet the forests seemed just the same. The clear stream, stooped over by willows, still ran over rusted pebbles. Gabriel sewed leather and inhabited the barn, which had a nesting eagle in the loft. The farm was aware that Isabel Rochet had reached puberty and that there were six calves and two winter foals. Outside the valley, Europe lay in ruins. The evidence was as close as the concentration camp known as Natzweiler in the Vosges, organized by SS Josef Kramer—whom the underground had traced to his present promotion as master-exterminator at a Polish camp called Auschwitz.

When sometimes Justin wondered why so very few in all Europe had risen against Hitler, he was forced to grasp a difficult idea. Moral law was only worth dying over when you possessed nothing else. Even the church was too rich. Justin had tried hard not to think about this—as he did not think about Luz's last letter from the Alps, or how Johannes had been shot to death just across the Constance frontier; or to ask himself about David, who was long missing on the Smolensk front; or wonder about Duncan Penn, who if he were alive would be in the heavy fighting on the Rapido. Above all, he tried not to think about how Hélène, alone now in Germany, or of his daughter, Sarah, whom he had never seen. In the suffocating heat of so much anger, he struggled for breath, thinking how all that he had loved was being lost.

It was then that Justin knew he must put down his pen and, beside the others, begin the most dangerous voyage back to peace.

2

THAT NIGHT IN MAY OF 1944—AS, ONE THOUSAND KILOMETERS TO THE EAST, the crematoria administered by the farm's old neighbor, Herr Kramer, were accelerated to their full capacity—Justin had for the first time invited the band, all together, down the long ladder into Rochet's cave. Overhead, the kitchen was sealed and the fire extinguished. At the designated frequency, a voice from the English Parliament crackled over the short-wave radio.

When finally Mandil switched off the receiver, the farmhouse overhead was absolutely silent. Ivanov, who spoke no English, was frowning at the brandy racks. The others had turned to Justin as if they could not believe their ears.

"Nikolas, he says Europe is to be set free."

"It's a lie," answered the Pole.

"Just say it if it's true, Justin."

"I have proof." Justin stood among them, beside the press from which fifty printings of *Justice* had gone out. "They will transmit a line of Verlaine, a second line when approaching the last forty-eight hours. Then we will rise against them. . . . It will be the moment of our greatest danger."

"The danger is already among us." Seated on the ledge behind Tiolchak, Nikolas had disassembled his automatic on a wine crate. "A year ago the Montmartre cabarets were packed. There were Frenchmen who were the worst Nazis . . . there was little underground. Now the Germans lose their grip and thousands will come to rescue us. Are we to embrace such deserters? Will this new Europe be the old Europe?"

"You will not speak in this manner of France in my husband's house!" broke in Madame Rochet, her cheeks shaking. Aside from Justin and Peter, only she was unafraid of Nikolas.

"Listen, *compagnons*, this will be the general uprising," Justin said, with a terrible premonition, for already he had felt hatred build around him. "A signal will go to the resistance *chefs*—from Oslo, to Budapest, to Athens. It will be like a change of seasons. Nikolas, your old commander in Poland, Komorowski, will even attempt to seize Warsaw."

"Only he would give away none of his arms to the ghetto rising," Mandil observed to Louis Rochet.

"And so"—Peter Tiolchak calmed them with a strange smile, smoothing his flat brush of hair—"after a lifetime, are we truly to see a revolution in Europe?"

Justin raised the flat of his hand, but the farmer spoke first. "There will be no revolutions from this farmhouse!"

"What! Can you have forgotten, Justin?" Vera walked up and down the wall of crates, grasping her temples. "The sneering collaborators in Paris, the Gauleiters to whom they crawl on their bellies? The *Klugerloss*, which gives any stupid turncoat gangster the right to shoot you on sight? What better time than now to remove these collaborators, these murderers."

"Have you forgotten the POUM, which we saw betrayed by the Comintern in Barcelona? Even Manouchiane betrayed in Paris, for whom Doré was shot?" Justin answered very softly.

Vera defied him. "And the Nazis' massacres at Lidice and Tula? The transportations?"

He managed to smile at her. "No we aren't forgetting entire towns wiped out, as at Putten and Palmiry. Or the three hundred chosen at random in Rome." Justin's voice broke, and the slowly swinging lamp bumped his hand. "But, with the planet looking on, better if there is no crime in our hearts."

"Your words, Justin" Nikolas was eating alone, seated against the barrels. "They aren't strong enough for what we have seen."

Madame Rochet took some blue papers from her blouse. "Look, Justin, Vera and I have made a list of the famous *collabos* of the *région* Carbonne—Besançon."

"Then they'll face their victims!" Justin's emotion was so great that his voice fell to a whisper. "You will give Europe what this pope, who might have walked alone on the battlefield between armies, has never even dreamt of—the ceremony of judgment! But we won't lead a revolution."

"Yes, Justin, that's it!" Mandil had stepped to his side. Then around the press, everyone began to clap. Only Nikolas did not stir, and only Justin saw, and took note.

3

FIFTEEN MINUTES LATER THEY BROKE UP. ON THE KITCHEN CLOCK, IT WAS ALMOST midnight. Justin sat down at the press and Rochet moved from the far end.

"You're tired, Justin."

"Sit beside me," Justin said, pushing the candle between them.

"Even after Paul, it's hard to understand these days ending," Rochet said.

"We've had such hours . . . yet think of peace, Louis." The Frenchman shrugged, and even in his exhaustion, Justin felt an anguished love for these old people. He bent his head.

"You will go too?" Rochet asked.

"I must go," he said.

Since the farmer had lost his son, the anger and the ambition had gone from him. Louis withdrew now into long silences, and sometimes neglected even the razor's edge of discipline that divided the few friendly farms from the many *collabos*. It had hurt Justin to see the old Rochet disappear: the sensible Rochet who could read the northern sky, the eyes of his animals, the earth and the crops. The wise Rochet, full of contempt for this war manufactured in factories and great capitals. Justin loved this man for his simplicity, almost as complete as his own. How would it be for these old people, when Justin went to his fate?

"Will you come back to us from time to time?"

"I'll come back." He rested his hand on Rochet's thick shoulder.

Instead of going straight up to the loft, at the end of which Rosa might be waiting, Justin left the house and went along the stream. Tonight the moonless Jura forests were gloomy and ominous. When the time came, would his terror be greater over his body's death or his soul's? Justin did not listen to the silence hidden behind the tearing sound of the water. As he turned back, seeing a faint light ahead, a powerful sensation came over him that something was about to happen.

Rosa was waiting by the stone basin, as on the first night. "Justin, I'm pregnant, " she said at once.

He reached in the dark and gripped her rough strong hand. The girl drew away.

"No!" she said angrily. "I'm pregnant—we cannot."

There was a rapt silence between them. "Then I will speak to Gabriel," Justin said finally.

There was an angry rustle. Before Justin could concentrate, she was gone. *I have been here too long, God—if there is a God*, he was thinking, minutes later as he lay stretched on his bed, listening to the worms in the ceiling beams. Then, as if tonight were not enough, Justin heard from the barn a groaning shout—"Oh!"—followed by utter stillness. Nikolas had woken from one of his nightmares. *Please give me the strength to finish*, he thought. This praying, too, was one of Justin's new habits. Tonight, so close to his death, he knew that sleep would not accept him.

4

AT THE END OF EACH DAY, THERE WAS NIGHT. MAN WAS INTENDED TO SLEEP through the night—or, like Abu Grinda, by a splashing fountain, to observe the night watch. Justin had not come to Carbonne to duel with the night but to be a stronger presence than any Fascist in the day, where they were only men. *Nacht und Nebel,* Hitler and Himmler had named their state terror: Night and Fog. With terror one could convince anyone of anything. With terror one could switch off someone's light. Smart fellows, the Germans, to have put *Nacht und Nebel* into men like Nikolas Ivanov.

Justin knew now that Nikolas came from a peasant village near Lublin and that he had been twice in the hands of the *Einsatzgruppen*. That was when the Nazis had put *Nacht und Nebel* into him. Nickolas did not talk about it, but was there a word for the elusive suggestion in the man's gaze? His light-gray eyes watched the farm's affectionate displays of humanity with the polite indifference of a man who hears a story repeated and chooses not to believe it.

Under the dark beams Justin rested his head on his hands, having felt a cool breeze over his chest. Had not the farm—although surrounded by a division of SS—smuggled out two hundred fugitives and a dozen pilots? There was no longer a *collabo* factory within a hundred kilometers that had not experienced thefts or wreckage. What of Justin's one hundred thousand ringingly honest words? Yet in Nikolas's eyes, nothing would purge the terror of *Nacht und Nebel* except the torture of Fascists.

Now, on this first night of summer, Justin was only half asleep.

For an hour, two vague impressions had drawn attention to themselves. The first concerned Justin's mother in the lace shop before the cardboard Virgin. Of the second, there was only a name that repeated itself, like the words of a song that has been memorized before the meaning is known. "Jakob-Stodel," went the tune, "Jakob-Stodel." Why had David Sunda mentioned this ugly name at their last meeting, by the mountain lake?

Maybe tomorrow I'll pay Father Baptiste a visit, he thought. Thinking then of his child with Rosa, which would live long after he was gone, Justin fell asleep. Outside his open window, across the forests of the Jura, and even in the alpine huts among the great glaciers of the Berner Oberland, few others slept that night.

5

THE SEA LANDINGS IN JUNE, ALONG THE STORMY BEACHES OF ERWIN ROMMEL'S
Atlantic Wall, had not been thrown back. Within days, the breach was widened
to a hundred kilometers. A large invasion army moved ashore.

In the east, Stalin had since Christmas been testing his stricken rival's
bastion defenses. Now, along a fifteen-hundred-kilometer front, from Latvia
to the Carpathians, Marshal Zhukov opened his new offensive. All across
Reichsführer Himmler's theater of torture and power, the Resistance—
a flowering weed made up of exiled governments, Comintern, partisans and
FFI—prepared for a general rising. Very quickly, huge numbers of those not
yet committed, and also many repentant collaborators, expanded the fragile
brotherhood to field strength. Trapped in a jungle of ideologies, the crippled
lion grew savage, its slightest scratch lethal with a carrion of murdered multitudes. All but too late, the sea of rescuers was flowing back.

By high summer, traveling as fast as Guderian had four years earlier, the
3rd Army under the American general, Patton was clattering along the unde-
fended roads of northern France. Now it was the Nazis who disintegrated and
scattered. Field marshals fell and were snatched back. Erwin Rommel was
wounded by a strafing aircraft, and von Kluge was summoned from Russia
to replace him. Now finally did the cultivated circle of whisperers from
David Sunda's first winter in Smolensk dispatch his companion, Claus von
Stauffenberg, to the *Wolfschänze* with a bomb—only to be caught and
become a star in another of Herder's filmed execution entertainments.
Soon after, in terror of their Führer's now limitless savagery, Kluge and
Rommel took their lives. And so it was that Heinz Guderian—whose loyalty
to the honor of the officer caste was unblemished—became Wehrmacht
Commander, while with each advance the Americans and the English fell
jealously to their usual exchanges of insults and apologies. The liberation of
Europe was under way.

In the second week of August, Justin listened in Rochet's cellar to the
voice of Bor-Komorowski as he called upon Churchill to support a nationalist
rising of twenty thousand partisans in Warsaw. Tiolchak merely shook his
head and smiled. Justin had been told by the French resistance head, Colonel
Rol, that even Paris was to be liberated. The same day, the band from the farm
began to bicycle out codes for the sabotage of the town halls, the *gen-
darmeries,* the army depots, and the communications at Belfort, Dijon, and
Besançon—and for the capture of Carbonne and Chambéry as bastion towns
of the underground.

Five days later, General Patch landed the 7th Army on the Mediterranean's
Côte d'Azur, accompanied by Algerians and by the French, under de Lattre of
Sedan. The force came quickly up the Rhône valley toward the Jura. And as

the Nazi garrisons packed their bags and fell back, the *maquisards* came out to harry them.

Yet, when at last the crippled lion lay dead, would Europe still be there . . . or was that lion Europe?

6

WITH TWO SENTINELS OUT ON THE VALLEY APPROACH ROADS, THE CARBONNE cell gathered for the last time under the floor of Rochet's kitchen.

Three of the six Alpine leaders had come. No one smiled as the faces gathered around the typesetter's lamp glanced appreciatively at each other. The more sophisticated southern *chefs* were cautious as they heard voices they had known for years on the mobile transmitter. None of the three recognized Justin Lothaire, who listened alone from the cellar's farthest corner.

"Here . . . here . . . and here, the enemy antennae are powerful!" Eli Hebron directed his nicotine-stained fingers over the Rhone sector with the authority of a field marshal.

Pellier, the schoolteacher from Dijon, shrugged reluctantly. "Our sector's beacon is the only one they employ for their aircraft—"

Peter Tiolchak interrupted him, almost whispering. "If we miss one beacon, we bungle the affair. What do you think, Philippe?"

From outside the competitive circle of shoulders, Justin spoke gently, watching Pellier. "Fascists do not exist without orders. Frederic—do you not speak German?" Across the twenty faces turned to Justin from above the stooped figures of Vera and Dorliac, who they all knew was English, someone was examining him. Behind Nikolas's lenses, his eyes had dark circles under them.

"There are six more transmitters." Even as Justin's mind spun out this plan, his heart was already hidden in a lonely cabin beyond the lake of Carbonne, where the rain would be falling. "We know the garrison's positions and its codes. One might invent a counteroffensive, false Allied positions and so forth."

Long after the noon showers, one after the other, the farm's visitors slipped off, on the southern roads or north into the Vosges. There was little time left. General Patch had approached Lyon, and there was SS movement in the passes around Carbonne.

At the kitchen door, a familiar *maquisard* blocked Justin's way. "Can you really be going to the town?"

"Yes." Justin gripped Eli's arm and squeezed it hard.

"We have only days now. What could be so important?"

"Oh, Eli, I can do nothing more here" he said, and a confession was in his eyes. "I can't bear to watch if they're hurt in all that's coming."

"They need you, Justin, even those who were unaware that they were standing by the press of *Justice.* You are the genius of their liberation."

"I'm alone among them." With impulsive tenderness, Justin squeezed Eli's neck and went out into a dusk that smelled of wet earth. The crisis now was very close. He moved quickly past the barn, splashed through the creek under the great oak, and started up the muddy gorge.

He heard the rumble of a storm, but his whole being had leapt ahead to Maline's room in the wild wood. During the past nights the powerful lust had knotted his stomach, ugly because he could find in himself no trace of guilt toward Rosa nor toward Luz, not even toward the memory of Hélène. On such a night in May—awake with things that could not in decency be thought about—Justin had risen and slipped out of the valley, past the sentinel, François, and on to the darkened town. He had walked quickly down by the lake in search of the cabin that Maline's father had left her.

As in his Paris days, when she had almost died after having Justin's child cut out of her, Maline greeted him without surprise. She had changed. This woman of the *halles,* who had sold her lean body to be soiled by all Paris, had grown out her beet-red hair. Her face had filled out like a farm woman's. Without makeup, Maline's eyes had the heavy-lidded drowsiness of a Flemish virgin. Her old nervous agitation had calmed—returning to that childishness for which Baptiste had once sent her to see a psychoanalyst in Zurich. The shopkeepers of Carbonne supported Maline, and she was happy for Justin to come and sit in her flowered chair and watch her with his desolate eyes. Once she had told him she would do anything that he asked. When Maline saw his face, she did not mention this again. In the cabin there were no sounds, apart from the snapping fire and the twitter of nesting birds. Justin would stare at the wallpaper of bathing beauties from magazines, at the stuffed boar's head, at her torn bedspread and the collapsed shoes—all smelling of sweat, garlic, and mildew. He would listen to the harmless tide of her thoughts, and these things would crush him.

Through the last four years, this woman, Maline Rouget, had lived without awareness of Justin's role in the war. Now, in Maline's hidden cabin, Justin could almost hear again, as on Mediterranean evenings, the clamor and violins of the medina. When he watched her make her curiously good soup, he would remember the first time he had seen her—with the Fleurusians at Polidor—and he would feel sick with desire. Justin knew that she wished to receive him. As he sat by the stove and watched her witch's absorption as she circled a pan on the fire, his knowledge from life inside the tunnel prevented any move toward her. Maline simmered her vegetables, talking continuously in patois, and Justin listened in a trance. Sometimes his throat tightened with compassion.

"The birds, you see the birds? Is that you, Justin? Listen to them, always singing around me. Father would not have allowed it. . . . You are the only good one, Justin. That is what I say in confession. I had one friend and he has returned. Oh, did you go away? You did not. *Pourquoi tu me regards comme ça?* This tablecloth is cracked . . . cracks, cracks everywhere. Saint Francis too, but his birds had other voices. What did I tell you, Justin?" Maline would suddenly turn, as if the cabin door had opened. Frowning into space, she would hold out imaginary bread and twist her palm into a cup. A thorny branch hung through the low window. Sometimes a finch rushed in, made a beating sound over Maline's hand, and fell out through the curtains. Maline shook her head and stared into the pan. To Justin her motions were not in the least disturbing. They filled the day with a happiness he could scarcely remember.

"Maline . . . Maline?" he said, lighting a cigarette. He waited for her to hear him. "The soup—where did you learn that?"

"Eh?" Maline looked seriously around the walls until she saw the eyeless boar's head. "Jean-Baptiste told me. He said Papa killed the boar right outside this very door." She seemed to lose her thread of thought as she continued, "Where did you shoot it, Justin?"

"I never shot anything!" Justin almost shouted.

Now, lost in these thoughts just two hours after the final conference at Rochet's farmhouse, he had come to the great boulder. Justin looked east over the forests. There below him was Carbonne. Instead of taking the steep path to the lake, Justin followed a traverse through the trees. He could see the church steeple below. It caught the sun from under the charcoal clouds. Snow on the first day of September?

Justin's boots skidded. With a bruising blow, he pitched head over heels down the leafy bank and lay panting in a hollow of tree trunks, not because of the fall but from a lash of terror that had drained his arms and legs. The trees stirred with an ominous sound. The advancing storm had crushed out the evening light and absorbed the eastern forests behind a gray wall. Justin was sobbing—Justin, who never wept. He moved his boots in the leaves.

7

TWENTY MINUTES LATER, WITHOUT THINKING TO FOLLOW THE USUAL ALLEYWAYS, he walked into the church square. It was Sunday, and a group of old men were at the *boules* pitch. They turned to watch Rochet's silent worker with the lean face cross quickly under their elms to the church.

At that moment, Justin was thinking of Jean-Baptiste's library and of their fine debates. As he twisted the iron ring, he heard behind him the clink of metal balls. Then he was enveloped by the ancient odor of tallow and sandalwood. In a pew halfway to the altar sat someone in a black shawl. Candles had been lit. His muddy boots moved through pools of colored light from the side windows. The sacristy door was open. Justin could feel that there was no one above, but he started up. At the head of the staircase, he stood blinking at the pastel calendar of saints' days.

Justin's eyes were fixed on a light penciling next to the numerals for September. The mark was no more distinct than a crushed mosquito: J. STODEL—ST. CROIX 24:00.

J. Stodel? Justin felt momentarily deranged by the familiarity of that name.

Downstairs among the benches it was much darker. The candle flames twinkled like stars. There was no sign of the black shawl. Taking four slow steps, Justin sat on the front pew. For several minutes, he stared at the painted wooden crucifix. Moved by its stillness, he felt ashamed and shut his eyes. Father in Heaven, he thought, why did you give me a life that I cannot understand? The innocent have perished without dignity. The worshipers of the State are in hordes, there is nothing which they have not desecrated. I and I alone am left, and they seek my life, to take it away . . .

On the hard pew, Justin straightened. Had there been whispering in the church?

"Lothaire! Lothaire!"

Justin got to his feet. In the darkness, very close behind him, two wild-looking young men were crouched between the pews, holding guns on Justin's stomach. More black uniforms skirted the shadows along the flanking vaults. Then an oily-skinned officer advanced, his thin neck protruding from a tight collar.

"It's Lothaire, all right!" The officer stood very close. "Dear sir, stand still. Hands out—the Bolshevik prayer, ha-ha!"

Justin held out his hands, wrists slightly separated. *Had the priest also betrayed Rochet's farm?* Without looking at them, he felt the other troopers surround his body. He gazed in the *Hauptsturmführer*'s shallow, desperate eyes. He had never seen any Nazis up close and crazed by their mission. They stood awkwardly in a circle while the officer fumbled with a slipknot.

"No, no, Lothaire, press the hands together!"

There was a crash and the troopers skipped back nervously. The wind had slammed the church door. Duroc was gone.

"Why are you smiling? This is no smiling matter. No, out that way!"

They led him through the church. The windows were vibrating, and it took three of the excited young men to open the doors. As they came out with the prisoner into the square, the frigid gale sucked up the sand in a yellow plume that coiled over the little crowd waiting by the *boules* pitch under the elms, and for a moment, as he walked at the end of the cord, the cloud swallowed the houses and townsfolk like a desert jinni.

8

ALWAYS, SINCE THE ALLEYS AT ALGIERS, A *SALE BICOT* HAD BEEN READY FOR what was happening, and he walked with great patience among the agitated Nazis. It was suddenly as dark as night.

"Is it really him?"

"That is Lothaire. Doesn't he look the part?"

"Will it be the *Lagers?*" shouted the most unpleasant of them, his blond hair whipping his face. He yanked at his barking Alsatian.

"Of course they will hang him! We could hang him here."

The prisoner made no sign. On the lips of these imbeciles the last words had no reality. From the moment Justin heard their whispers in Duroc's church, he had awaited the instant to break and run. The troopers held a more respectful distance, since the *Hauptsturmführer* had said that Justin would be hanged. The branches over their heads bent and flayed, and three SS hats went bounding toward the Auberge gate. Only one guard ran after them. How had these pathetic children not searched him for cyanide? Justin slowed his legs against the freezing wind, not letting the cord tighten in the *Hauptsturmführer*'s hand. A boy in shorts, with his hair in a brush, fell into stride with Justin down the steep alley to the prefecture. On the bright entrance steps there were salutes between the French and the Germans.

As the doors opened to a hall, Justin glimpsed four men in black berets as they stretched to get a look at him. *"Schnell,* traitor, *schnell!"* He heard the *Hauptsturmführer*'s voice, and he went up the steps. At the sight of the extra men, Justin had felt agonizing disappointment—as if he had expected a miracle. Shaken by his weakness, he stood facing a wall. Then he was led down a brick passage into a cage with bars on four sides. Justin understood that his interrogator was not yet in Carbonne. The Abwehr might be better than the state police or the French.

"There are many uniforms in this town," Justin said softly.

He recognized both his guards: Pivard the *patissier*'s assistant and the vineyard doctor, Bouceron. They would not know Justin's face. Both men stiffened on their chairs. Neither one moved. Justin's clothes were soaked, but there would be no time to catch cold. A very long silence ticked by; then a pan of thick stew was brought. Justin forced himself to eat it. Then he sat down again on the thin mattress and put up his legs.

At once, he swung them back—something in Justin had jumped up, raced around the cage and up and down the bars, rattling them. It wept and begged these two Frenchmen to set him free. The iron bed rattled softly under him. Was this hour his last? What of the children he would never see, the boy Ahmet he had left in the desert? You brought yourself to this, a voice said. You entered into violence, and now you have no soul! Justin worked a finger through a hole in his jacket lining. Conjuring a vision of all the people he had loved and might now betray, he felt the gel cyanide capsule. Eli had been right and Justin mistaken; he was not alone. To keep their secret, if it still was one, he would die. Right now he was hungry.

"Don't stare at me like that!" The primitive-looking younger *milicien* was on his feet.

"Am I too important for a smoke, brothers?" he said, with friendliness. Bouceron, with the black eyebrows that met, stepped forward. There was perspiration on the doctor's cheeks. A cigarette fell at Justin's feet, then the matches.

Justin could lie back now, for he would need his strength. A wave of drowsiness moved over him, as if he were freezing to death on a glacier. What if it was the bishop who had denounced him? Justin flinched violently on the mattress—a crash like a piano falling had come from the next room. The prefecture cat streaked from under him. The older *milicien* went out and came back.

"Planes. . . ." Pivard's flat red face stared accusingly through the cell bars at Carbonne's famous prisoner.

Justin could hear a string of bombs fall farther away, punching the earth. They must be after the German tanks, he thought. Justin stared at the ceiling and Hélène came to him, like a flood of unearthly beauty, and so real that he seemed to smell her skin. Then he saw Lavil's patio in Algiers with a small girl playing by the fountain. Then it was Luz by a lake in the Swiss Alps and David was telling Justin about Hitler's private scientist, Jakob Stodel . . . *Jakob Stodel!*

The sight of the bars of his cell crashed in on the sweetness of Justin Lothaire's daydream. As he sank back shivering on the mattress, he heard the *milicien* click a safety catch. What words had been marked on the saints' day calendar? *J. Stodel—St. Croix: 24:00?* The second of the month would be tomorrow! St. Croix was the mountain passage from Switzerland. Tomorrow night Hitler's scientist, the man who had designed the Topf ovens, was coming over these mountains. He would be on his way to Lisbon and the Brazilian jungles—and it was Jean-Baptiste who was to meet him! Now, far more urgently, Justin knew he must somehow sleep.

"On your feet! He has a nerve, sleeping late."

Justin sat up in daylight. Hard faces were gathered in his cell. Whoever had been of too high rank to be already in Carbonne had now arrived. A gaunt shaven-headed *milicien* lassoed a sash over Justin's neck and roughly drew it tight around his eyes. He felt a shock on his shoulder and stepped forward. Justin had found the strength to die. Still, knowing about Jakob Stodel, he did not wish to die quite yet.

They marched quickly through a small space; then a large number of feet were going down two flights of stairs. There were tense whispers. A door opened and they were in another small space. Justin felt a blow on his chest and he was falling backward. Then he struck something; he was sitting on a chair. This was where it would be. This was his hour.

"Good, now leave us! And so—this is Lothaire?"

There was a silence. Justin sensed that Jean-Baptiste Duroc was in the room. Cords were being tightened across his chest. He heard slow steps circle the room in front of him.

"Well, well," continued the voice. "It is the Inspector of Railways."

Hearing again the cultivated cynical voice, Justin felt his scalp bristle. Something vibrated twice. More bombs.

"You will not trick me again."

"Because you have no time left, Darnand!" Justin was struck suddenly twice on the face, and he sank backward with the chair hard against the stone floor. Half a dozen hands gripped him and lifted. A door banged, and Justin knew that Duroc had gone. Under the black sash, his eyes were wet with rage. The poison capsule of his salvation was out of reach forever. A hand gripped and yanked back Justin's hair, until his neck was stretched. Something cold and sharp stung his throat.

"Someday, when we have more time, Lothaire," said the voice of Joseph Darnand, "you must explain to me why you came back to France. Why fight us? You could never have hoped to win. You embarrass man by asking him to think of such things. It is not natural for men to bestow virtue on themselves. Only God may do so. *Bien, ça suffit!*

"You and I, Justin, we have one hour for our work. In this hour, I will hear from you all locations, names, and directives. Your Communist friends are tearing up the Rhône. We must act before they destroy all of France."

"In one hour I will be dead," Justin said, "and you will know nothing." He felt his throat ache. The breath blew again in Justin's ear.

"Listen closely, scum," it whispered. "I will smear your face with the juice of your eyes. I will tear your testicles like yolks and feed them to you in a molten spoon. I will hammer an ice pick up your nose. And only then, perhaps, will I drill holes in your spine. I saw it in Russia. All men confess."

Justin's lungs heaved in great sobbing pants. *Please, God, help me!* a voice shrieked in the terror of the blindfold. There was a pop, and glass tinkled around him. A close-shuddering boom bumped the air, then a second, and then there arrived the biggest sound that Justin had ever heard. Not a sound with place and tone at all, but an all-surrounding *hwunk!* that split and tore the earth, that ripped out its gravity, hot-pummeled and resonated this room, and cast them all spinning into the silent cosmos of the stars.

THE EAGLE

1

THERE HAD BEEN THE HUGE SOUND FOLLOWED BY A CRACKLE OF MUSKETS across the rooftops of Sidi Idriz. Justin had returned into his former self through showers of fluttering silver coins, then down through the circle of net where the great fish waited, down, down, falling unobserved into an intimate blackness where he heard a still, small voice. Then again Justin was rising in the company of the voice until he felt himself close to awakening, almost as if he were still alive. Then he was very close. A pain in his chest grew and grew. He felt his legs among heavy sharp edges, and there was the chokingly strong smell of cordite and metal. Justin moaned in querulous experiment like a newborn babe . . . he was blind! He drew his arm upward to his face. Something pulled free of his right eye and he saw a gray light. Particles floated toward his face like white dust—the sky. He was in the tunnel of violence.

Reeling to his feet under the sooty clouds, Justin raised his face to the lacerated roof eaves around the place where the prefecture had been. He was naked among the monstrously alive. Then, quite abruptly, he remembered Jakob Stodel, and for several seconds in his nakedness he thought that he must be mad if such a man could pass freely through, breathing this frozen air. Justin had earned this—*he and the biologist would be alone together in the passage.* His steel watch was broken. As he stared at its empty face, the full memory returned.

Justin crawled up the basement steps, pulling himself on the skeleton of cell bars. Above, in the alleyway, two men and a nun drew back from the blood-caked figure climbing from the bomb site. With tears of gratitude running over his face, he swayed past them up the shopfronts. He saw the stone water trough ahead and one old couple. The church square was clouded with snow. Then Justin saw Gabriel run into a garden, two houses along.

2

THEY SAW EACH OTHER AT THE SAME TIME. WITH A SCARED FACE, GABRIEL turned and walked slowly toward Justin. Joseph Mandil appeared at the head of the street, wearing a suit and carrying a briefcase. When he saw Justin, he broke into a run.

"The devil! Can it be him?"

"Deaf and frozen. Is he shot?"

"We'll have to wash him down."

"Where? The pumps are off!"

"Quick, into the trough! Stop gaping, old mother, get some sheets. This is Lothaire!"

"Lothaire is dead," said the woman's husband, taking her hand.

"Does he look dead?" Gabriel waved his Sten gun toward the auberge.

Justin allowed himself to be carried over the snow. The simple little voice was still with him, and he felt a tenderness for his two friends and these frightened old people.

"Strip him," Mandil said.

"It's freezing!" Gabriel objected, but he began to unwind the stiffened shreds of Justin's shirt. Indistinct figures were racing back and forth across the snowy square. Citizens began to gather round.

"My God, my God!" A red-haired woman crossed herself. "It is a miracle!"

"And snow in September," added an old man timidly.

With quick tenderness, their hands stripped the stinging shreds from Justin's skin. He stood barefoot on the snow; arms caught him around the knees and shoulders. Justin cried out as his body was lifted to the trough and he was choked by the blow of the water. For three counts he twisted, burning, in the trough while hands rinsed him. Then as he heaved with shock he was again in the church square with the wind cutting his flesh. Justin could hear now the crack of guns. At the sight of his wounds, several turned away.

"He's in ribbons," Mandil said.

"Quick—the sheets!"

So they wrapped him in white sheets, and the little group fell back to let them pass.

Inside the Auberge des Juras, a fire was burning and there were tables piled with fashion magazines. The well-dressed *patron* with the head of a hyena—he who for four years had made good money off German officers and would do so again if the town were retaken—officiously sent a waiter for clothes. Then he pushed the one wooden chair before the fire for the naked *maquisard* wrapped in a bloody sheet.

"Darnand?" Justin asked, as he was seated instead on the stone fireplace and Gabriel emptied bandages on to a table.

"He is on the loose . . . but look at you, a hundred wounds." Gabriel was frightened.

Joseph squatted next to them, facing the door. He looked up into their *chef*'s face with terrible passion. Justin was bent almost into the flames. "It's done, Justin, Carbonne is taken. All the roads are blocked. There is even a light tank, though with little ammunition."

"Only bandage the bad holes," Justin whispered. He did not look down at himself.

"Peter, Vera, and the others are in the town hall." Joseph took the gun from Gabriel and held out a bandage. "Eli, Louis, and some of the farmers have begun executions." He glanced toward the salon door and with the gun barrel angrily waved back a bourgeois couple in tweeds.

"And Chambéry? . . . Pontarlier? . . . Besançon?" Justin whispered. The *patron* had reentered the salon, carrying a neat pile of clothes.

"They are just beginning. When you were taken we moved the attack forward."

"Yes, I might have talked."

Mandil grinned. The *patron* stood apart, trying to hear them. "Everyone hoped that you *would* talk, Justin."

Justin gazed back at Mandil. "What time is it?" he asked.

"Nineteen-thirty."

"Good . . . good," he repeated, and a strange look came into his eyes. While Gabriel knotted the ends of the chest bandage, Justin pulled on the *patron*'s trousers and socks. He felt the white band of the Maquis being tied over his jacket sleeve.

"Listen. . . ." Justin coughed hoarsely and waited for his head to stop spinning. "An urgent matter came to me while I was in the hands of Darnand. Your success here is a great one, but remember that a few tanks can take this from you. Think of Vercors. I myself must be in the passage at midnight."

"But *chef!*" Joseph seized Justin's wrist. He and Gabriel looked at each other again. "Peter is presiding at the *mairie* in the name of the Comintern."

Behind the reception desk, waiting as if he might make a run for it, the *patron* watched the three *maquisards* argue. Now he saw the wounded man rise and move slowly toward his auberge's heavy glass doors.

Outside, Justin could see the blizzard falling densely under the porch lantern. Turning to Mandil and thus forever forfeiting his redemption, Justin accepted a revolver from his hand. As they appeared on the auberge steps, the woman who had called it a miracle hurried away with the boy who had walked beside Justin Lothaire to the prefecture. He started in the opposite direction, toward the town hall.

3

FROM THE MOMENT HE CAME OUT OF THE TROUGH, NAKED AND BLEEDING, Justin's mind had shed a clear light on everything that went on around him. All this in the streets of Carbonne was merely politics. Out in the nets of the night, he felt a monster in motion.

The three armed men walked loosely in step down a steep alley, wound to the right, and continued down, and for the first time Justin took note of the carnival mood. Even in the settling snow, every door and window was open, filled with more faces than he had dreamt could be in Carbonne.

"Tomorrow the school will be shut. No one's working."

"Look, Justin!" Joseph Mandil laughed, turning all the way round as they strode down the cobblestone street. "Isn't it like the *Paris-Commune?*"

There was a sharp pain in Justin's broken ribs, and he pressed his fist to his mouth. There was no blood. When they saw him smile, the onlookers began to call. "Lo-thaire! . . . Hey, Lothaire. . . . Bravo!" An old and a young man, in feathered hats and carrying fowling pieces, stepped from a door and fell in behind Gabriel. A few houses along, two *poilus* emerged in trench helmets: grim and angrily satisfied with themselves. "Look out, Jacques!" a woman called after them.

"Lothaire! Lothaire!" The cries echoed through the bright alleys. A girl with glistening eyes leaned from a window, holding a cluster of flowers. When the Maquis leader lifted his terribly sad face, she dropped the bouquet and he caught two buds. Holding up his revolver, he pulled the stems through the butt ring. More flowers were scattered over the snow ahead. Mandil and Gabriel slipped and skidded at Justin's side.

Then, quite suddenly, their procession came to a crossroads on a park. The town hall was lit by a Nazi floodlight. Already the dark street in front was blocked by a noisy crowd of men, most of them in berets with their collars turned up. As the mob divided for the *chefs partisans,* two shots sounded through the milling snow. There were angry shouts from a blackened alley beside the *mairie.*

Justin pushed into the alley with Joseph and Gabriel. He glimpsed, just ahead, a mound of uniformed bodies and several not in uniform. Then he saw Eli. His old friend was dragging a *milicien;* the young man's toes still twitched and his staring eyes wavered. Blood stained the snow. Above on the bright *mairie* porch was Nikolas Ivanov beside a horribly sneering *Obersturmbannführer* whom Justin had never seen. He saw Nikolas's face and felt the mob push him forward. Tortured voices called out, "Shoot the butcher! Shoot him!"

The *maquisard* forced a rifle muzzle against the German's tight lips. In the sudden stillness, they all heard the pin click. Nikolas cursed and clubbed the man twice on the temples. The officer fell on his knees, lifting his eyes to the floating snowflakes. Taking the barrel in both hands, Nickolas brought the carbine down twice. The *Obersturmbannführer* fell on his face, his knees humped up trembling. Not a sound came from the crowd of men in the alley mouth. A violent rage shook Justin and he took ten steps over to Eli. With what was beside them, he could hardly speak. Then Eli saw him.

"Justin! Justin, are you still alive?"

"And you, Elisha?" His voiced quaked. "What are you doing?"

"This is it, Justin! The revolution has begun," Eli cried shrilly.

"Leave this. Come with me. Jakob Stodel himself is right now traveling to Carbonne!"

The agitated face stared blindly into Justin's. It was almost night. "You are alive!" Eli croaked. "You are alive!"

Justin pulled free. As he climbed the floodlit *mairie* steps, his empty stomach was heaving. Joseph had to fight a way for him through the crush of shoulders to reach the confusion within. Here and there in a white-tiled hall stood town magistrates in neat suits. A group of petitioners lined one wall. Peter Tiolchak sat at ease behind a desk stacked with files. Beside him on a low stool was Vera, her spectacles missing one lens. As they pushed in, she nudged Peter. He met Justin's eyes.

"Are we to be reunited with our friends?" Tiolchak said to him softly. "Tonight, you and I are veterans together."

Justin sat down on the desk, breathing heavily. He looked around at the four staring magistrates, at the men with petitions, and then at Peter. Vera looked at the revolver in Justin's fist. He knew his swollen face was webbed with shrapnel cuts.

"You believe that we are still together in this?" Justin and Peter gazed at each other.

"This is no romantic crusade, Justin." Vera rapped the desk, her eyes colder than a man's. "It is the organ of the FTPF People's Republic."

The bearded young farmer Arnaud appeared, looking pleased with himself. "Four tanks are coming by the Chaffoise road—" He gaped at Justin.

Tiolchak had not looked up.

"Cancel this disgrace, Peter." Justin picked up his friend's cigarette and drew on it. "We have no time. Lock up the suspects and prepare to defend Carbonne."

"Stop this, Lothaire? Try to halt an earthquake."

"You, who were in the Hall of Mirrors?" Justin leaned on Vera's chair. "Remember, Peter, I ask you to remember!"

From outside the disordered town hall came the sound of shooting. The angry din intensified. The moment that she heard Justin's tone, Vera resumed her signing of forms. Before she could stop him, Justin seized a paper that she was holding out to a young magistrate. Vera clutched at it with an incomprehensible snarl. Tiolchak's furrowed cheeks were very red.

The form was a summary execution slip, signed for the Provisional Republic. The space for the accused was left blank. Over their desk in this smoky hall, the three of them were speechless. Vera rose to her feet. The farmers in the entrance fell silent and pushed forward to be near the *chefs partisans.*

"Vera, no more of these papers," Peter said very softly.

"But they are butchers of mothers and children. These Fascists are criminals a thousand times over!" Vera cried out, almost in tears with hatred as she paced the hall of faces. "Do you wish us to feed them like house cats? No, justice now—or I swear that you will see them go free! Their crimes will haunt us for ever!"

"Do you wish me to repeat myself?" Peter said gruffly, adding something in Russian. He looked wearily at Justin.

"The revolution is over," Justin said simply. "Ready yourselves to defend Carbonne."

"And you, Lothaire?" The woman leaned on the desktop. She stared at him through her broken spectacles and he saw the kindness of her exposed eye.

What if Vera proved right? But Justin was to be alone with Jakob Stodel in the tunnel of violence. "I am needed on the mountain. There is someone who must not pass through . . ."

Turning from the desk, Vera flung out her hands. "Men, arm yourselves! Barricade the north approaches!"

". . . one who is Hitler's scientist," Justin went on, as his old friend rose.

"*Compagnon, compagnon.*" Peter bent to Justin's ear, ignoring the dozen armed citizens crushed against the desk, all shouting at once. "We must fight beside the people. We can only free the captive. Geniuses of evil are symbols for writers like yourself to track down alone—in your place, in your hour."

One of the shouting men was a tall American in a raincoat. "Sir, excuse me, sir! Claflin of *Post* magazine." Peter vaguely waved the man toward Vera. "Please, sir, can you tell me where to find Lothaire? They say he is in Carbonne alive."

Feeling as though he were coiled in barbed wire, Justin rose to his feet. He was close to fainting. The American glanced toward him and drew back with distaste. Taking the gun from the desktop, Justin held out his free hand to Tiolchak. They had not shaken hands since Barcelona. The Russian took it, very firm and polite.

"I will return in the morning, in our place, in our hour."

"In our place, in our hour."

Peter smiled and ceremoniously rubbed a tear from his eye. Turning from them, Justin pushed a way through the packed corridor. Joseph and Gabriel were keeping back a crowd of angry shopkeepers who had gathered to denounce their neighbors. Two salamis were thrust into Justin's hand.

Joseph drew near. "Should I go with you?"

"Stay close to Peter. I'll be at the farm by sunrise."

When Justin emerged from the *mairie,* many citizens had gone home for dinner. Perhaps seventy men of Carbonne huddled as the snow fell, listening to Eli and Nikolas call directions for the defense of their town. There was the shriek of a German tank shell. Two of the arched streetlamps had been shot out. Vague shapes slowly swung underneath like giant marionettes in some backstage wardrobe. So this was victory. This was the promised utopia of the simple and the oppressed—the ancient grandeur of European arms and the romance of rebellion. This was the end of the rage for justice that Justin had been loyal to since his dream on the rue Mahbu. He felt like running, vanishing from this scene and from these faces.

He remembered the gun in his hand. Pushing it into his belt with Gabriel's salamis, he turned and went down the far steps. This blizzard of September had stayed on the ground and was filming over the bloodstains. Above these houses were the mountain passages, somewhere up in the night. Tiolchak had been right—Justin was alone now. Even Peter had not understood the meaning of Jakob Stodel.

4

YET NO WISDOM COULD HAVE READIED JUSTIN LOTHAIRE FOR THE LONELINESS as he left behind Carbonne's last orchard and its beehives and went up into the forests. He longed to lie down and weep. Thoughts came one after another. Concentrating on the muffled squeak of his boots, Justin began to devour the first salami.

After forty minutes by Joseph's watch—ten more than usual—Justin reached the monolith from which the *passeurs'* trail forked down to Rochet's farm. He lay under the overhang, moaning softly to ease his pain. It was ten o'clock. Justin shifted the revolver to his back, under the tweed jacket of a *collabo*. He could no longer detect the companionship of his own spirit, which had been replaced by a hunger to face Jakob Stodel.

Rising again, he reeled on into the *passage*, his feet feeling for the flat of the ridge. The snow had turned to a fine ice spray. From the dark valley below, Justin heard the *punk-punk* of tank guns and the crackle of light fire—the Sainte-Marie road. Somewhere still alive at that hour were Himmler, Göring, and Hitler. And, in a smoke of delirium, Justin saw before him the clandestine Berlin scientist Jakob Stodel—who had extinguished the lives of millions and now had hurried away, warm with anxiety for his own life. Then at last Justin felt an insane fury. He did not know that he had started running until his legs doubled and he lay groaning without grief or satisfaction. Rolled against a pine trunk, he broke the revolver. Six of the eight cartridges were unfired.

Justin got back to his feet. He was drenched in sweat and shaking with cold, but his will to this final crime had escaped the torment of his body. The frozen forest world drifted toward him. Twice, Justin missed the path, retraced his steps, and solved the visual errors. At eleven-fifteen, he looked up and saw the luminous walls of the pass. The snow had stopped. There were a few remote farm lights. All he had to do, Justin thought, was stay awake and not go mad. He did not consider retreating through the tunnel. Sometime during that day he had ceased thinking of life.

5

FOR SOME MINUTES JUSTIN HAD BEEN CROSSING OPEN FIELDS OF SNOW, THE ONLY disturbance the irregular *crunch-crunch* of his shoes. Now this was joined by a splintering sound. In the starlight, there was the glitter of ice crystals. Then, just ahead, between aisles of pine boughs, he saw the oval of the frontier meadow. Was he delirious? This was not the *passage* but an ice nursery of delicate shapes, clustered all down the narrow clearing.

Justin could see sprays like opera fans, some the size of peacock tails. Crouched on the pine needles, he reached out; there was a scraping rattle as of broken glass. The unfamiliar sound shook him. The ice vegetation waited, a point of interstellar silence at absolute zero. What if Stodel did not come? Justin stared out over the jagged reef of frozen light. The blackness under the far trees was Switzerland. Drowsiness was back, a warm luxurious weight. Again raising the revolver by its barrel, he struck himself. Anyway, he was dying. A numb agony had spread from his buttocks.

Midnight: no movement, not a sound. The mud under the pine needles was cold. He did not know that he was asleep for a long, happy, warm, empty time. He seemed to hear a meaningless crashing. Justin opened his eyes.

Someone was in the crystal meadow. Voices, as if this were a dream.

Among the pine trees, Justin half rose. His legs buckled and he clawed the rough bark, fighting out of the depths of sleep. A hot wetness came from his cheek. Just then, he saw something move.

A heavy-coated shape was kicking through the clearing. The shape came toward him. There was a crash and tinkle of glass. Justin took two steps, his breathing so quick that he must open his mouth not to groan. The figure's head was bent out of the moonlight; in one hand there was a small valise and in the other a hat. The black shape plowed with determination through the ice fans, splintering the mountain hush. Justin saw a bald man's gray fringe and spectacles.

He took another step, his head and shoulders exposed now in starlight. Justin clicked back the hammer and raised the revolver.

Abruptly the meadow and forests were silent. The *passeur* had halted in the platinum glow, knee deep in broken ice fans. Justin clearly saw a square face and domed forehead. With his free arm he steadied himself. Raising the hand with the hat, the stranger pushed up his spectacles. The broken fronds tinkled at their feet. Checking the heave of his lungs, Justin took one last step and pointed the revolver at the man's abdomen. In front of him, a cultivated face gazed alertly to the right, then to the left. Shoes stumbled another splintering step. They were very close. The gentleman looked down at Justin's hand and then up.

"*Qu'est ce que c'est?*" the man whispered. The accent was high German.

Justin did not move. The fact of the voice half choked him.

"You're the priest?" the voice incredibly rose. "Don't you know I am Dr. Stodel!—"

In the frozen silence, the explosion of the first shot split the night air. It groaned among the cliffs.

Justin stared down at the body kicking in front of him. He heard a continuous gurgling groan and pointed the revolver. There was a second lashing thud. But the thing tangled in the coat at his feet flopped more wildly. Arms flailing, it rolled back and forth, shattering ice clusters with a tinkling sound under the starlight. "My God," Justin hissed. "Lie still, lie still!" He pointed the revolver and fired; pointed and fired again, aiming for the invisible sneering face: three, four, five, six!

The scraping crashes stopped. The shapeless heap lay still, a black depression among the fronds. Justin lowered his arm. The gun pulled free from his finger and fell on the pine needles without a sound. There were urgent shouts. Justin looked up across the ice garden. He saw several legless shapes detach themselves from the far trees—a Swiss patrol.

Turning from the moonlit ice, he started back into the forest. Then Justin was running, his mind bursting with the enormity of his act. All around him there arose, amid the frozen silence of the passage, a splintering din—like the noisy clamor of several million of murdered souls, smashing among the delicate dead fans and fossil leaves of the crystal meadow.

6

MUCH LATER, IN THE VALLEY FAR BELOW, JUSTIN LOTHAIRE DREAMT A DEEP, free, powerful dream. He was in the Atlas, and from inside the citadel came the small boys' wailing of the circumcision. And then there were the two *kef*-magicians with the white pigeons fluttering, tails fanned, on their long greasy hair. "*Yu-u-u-umi-yumi-yumi!*" one magician groaned, pulling the wet brown ears from the neck of the pouch, so that Justin thought he was going to find out at last. The pigeons fluttered above and scratched lovingly on his chest. Justin felt himself shaken, and he wriggled deeper into his happiness. But the jostling came close.

"Lothaire, old fellow, wake up!"

He gazed through a summery mist at the sloped rafters. Yes, unmistakably this was his farm attic, where two women, Rosa and his wife, had slept by his side. Where Luz had conceived their child, and where Justin had had the time to write a Sophoclean parable on wars.

"You are Sunda's Englishman," he whispered. "Is it still snowing?"

"Your old favorite, Wilfred Rouve," the man laughed. He looked toward the door where Madame Rochet stood watching Justin, her face white and sunken. "I was sent because I could recognize you. You took some recognizing. Madame here tells me that you were in their hands. However, we should be quick."

"And the rising?" Justin had just then remembered. "Besançon and Chambéry. . . . what time is it?" As he shook off sleep, he felt the dream empty like blood from his dying body.

"The general rising was premature and rather amateurish," said the Englishman with enthusiasm. "The FFI may take the Alps, where there is a dribble of Germans. Here, I believe only Carbonne changed hands. This morning your comrades were under siege in the *mairie*. I should think they've been taken by now. You'd best get out."

"Justin, you should not stand up." Madame Rochet went to the bureau, and he glimpsed the bottles and bandages. "Where were you last night?" she asked him, sitting down between his knees on Luz's little wicker chair. She pressed the tinctured gauze to Justin's chest.

Dropping his eyes, Justin looked at himself for the first time. The flesh was torn away with lacerations down to the navel. On his ribs there was a bruise the color and size of a gramophone record, the exposed bone at the center tooth-white. He could hear the birds singing. It was a bright hot cloudy day. At the thought of the ice meadow, Justin felt sick, and he knew that the Justin he still remembered did not exist. "Jakob Stodel came through the frontier. I shot him."

"Good Lord, man, you don't mean Hitler's big scientist?"

Justin looked up at this visitor to the rue de Fleurus, and his face stung. The thing was already becoming deformed. "It was stupid," he said. "I should have fought beside my friends."

Rouve laughed. "What you did was historic. Carbonne was a waste."

"Rouve, Madame Rochet's husband is in the town!" Justin said.

"I am sorry, madame," said Rouve with great charm. "They should be able to hold out until the Americans come up."

Madame Rochet turned from Justin's chest. Her hard suspicion had gone. "The Americans—do you think so, monsieur?"

"Paris fell days ago. The Americans are at Lyon."

"Paris, free?" Justin whispered. He was thinking of a corner café by the Théâtre de l'Odéon and of the Luxembourg in autumn. He thought of Hélène by her fireplace, and of the trapeze garret.

"The liberation, Justin." Rouve was crouching behind Madame Rochet, watching the *chef-partisan*'s face. "I am here to take you in. It is you who Free France wishes to broadcast as the voice of the underground. In Paris you will help form a new government. The execution of Stodel will guarantee your authority. They are talking of a trial for the Nazi bosses."

"Oh, Rouve." Justin rubbed his cheek on his wrist. "The men I have fought beside for three years are still fighting in the *mairie* of Carbonne. Am I to leave them for celebrations in Paris?"

He had stepped to the window, past this friend of Rittmeister von Sunda. It would be strange company with whom to enter Jerusalem.

"Listen to him," said Madame Rochet. "It will be for us all."

"Go on, then," Justin said in English, "but I will not be their hero."

"There is no one else, Justin." Rouve concentrated, not moving a muscle. "I know the Underground; they are Comintern, innocents, opportunists, and thugs. We should go now. The SD are here with dog packs. They know who they are looking for. The Resistance has finished its job. Come to Paris."

"Will we get through the lines?" Justin said, after a long silence, and he saw the Englishman suppress a grin. Rouve did not look again at Madame Rochet. In five minutes, Justin had gathered what he would need. Rosa, who was carrying Justin's child, had gone to the cave in the forest. There was no time to wonder if he would ever see her or this place again.

Outside, by the car of an Abwehr colonel, the morning was warm and smelled of the earth. Already they were different people. As Rouve unstrapped the tonneau cover, Justin pointed overhead. "Do you see, our eagle from the barn?"

"Still so romantic? But that's no eagle, old man—it's a kite. Are you all right? Don't be a fool, Lothaire. Get down under the canvas!" Rouve called after him.

It was as if none of the last years had taken place. Justin walked slowly back through the clucking hens. As he came near Madame Rochet, Isabel stood behind her looking, confused.

"Marianne, it's over," he said. "Tell them I will soon be back." For a moment he held the woman's tensed shoulders. "Tell them that they are my family. Eli will know where to find me. Also, seal up the cellar," he said, his mind working now.

"We will listen for you on the radio, Justin. You are a fine man."

"All fine men and women," Justin said. Releasing her, and ruffling Isabel's hair, he walked stiffly across the mud yard. He did not look back.

7

IN THE CAR, THE ROAD TO CARBONNE TOOK ONLY FIVE MINUTES. JUSTIN LAY braced behind the seats and gazed up at the rippling shadows of trees. As the truth of the rebellion fell behind he felt a second wrenching grief, like that when a desperate love affair is over.

Rouve had stopped them. They were in town. Justin could hear him drawling in relaxed German to someone who laughed. They started up again.

"Well, old man, it seems the *mairie*'s been cleaned out."

All of them gone? In the dark compartment, Justin was breathing hard. He noticed the way that the car slowed as they passed the butcher's shop. He did not have the strength to ask what the Englishman could see. The car began to shake with the speed.

"Justin, tell me. Why was your show always so small? Surely the guerrilla thing could have been made more efficient. What good are heroes who always get shot?"

Behind Rouve, Justin concentrated on the poplars overhead. They flickered by regularly, like sentinels of his glory—now eighteen times a killer. And trying to imagine Paris free, without David and Johannes, without Eli or Joseph or Gabriel, his body relaxed and he was asleep.

Justin awoke many hours later. He was on a stretcher, being carried by tall soldiers with white armbands. An older man with a pencil mustache was walking beside him. As they passed under a carriage arch, Justin saw Rouve . . . Americans. He had not seen so many Americans since the great ship off the beach of Algiers.

"Jesus, is that him? Are you sure?"

"Beyond all doubt."

"Major, the brigadier would like to interview this man as soon as possible!"

"The brigadier will have to hold his horses," said the pencil mustache. "Now cut off those leather pants."

Lying among them on the stretcher at Châtillon, Justin closed his eyes and wept. And he knew that what had a greater reality for him than all else—than being an assassin, or the voice of his dead comrades, or that Hitler's power was dying and Justin might soon be left alone in the world with his books, might even possibly see Hélène—was the hope from his dream of the glorious dance of fathers and sons through the white roofs of Sidi Idriz. Of the happiness to which his life might still return.

8

IN THOSE SAME DAYS TO THE EAST, THERE STIRRED AN IMMENSE ARMY, A HORDE, a different kind of man—five hundred divisions strong—a hundred races, marching along a 1,200 kilometer desolation from Riga to Bucharest. As the better concentrated Germans began to yield front after front, five million Soviets on horseback and on foot moved after Marshal Zhukov's tank waves, westward toward the winter.

Withholding his masses from Hitler's main force in Poland, Stalin ordered Georgy Zhukov first to wheel south across the Nazi bastions in the once-sovereign states of Hungary, Romania, and Bulgaria. Thus, as if in answer to Baron Sunda's powerful impressions long ago on a Siberian railway, the toughest and most devout men on earth rode and walked out of Holy Russia as once they had driven Bonaparte's men before them, both marches in turn reenacting the onslaught of Genghis Khan. Out of a Byzantium of log cabins and European palaces, across soil turned to mud during the madness of the *Einsatzgruppen* by the blood of the eight hundred murdered villages, flowed the horde. Eating raw vegetables, sleeping on frozen ground, and feeding their horses on straw roofing, this army of tribesmen and ex-serfs reached the Russian frontier, crossed it, and entered Europe.

Presently in his conference room at the Wolfschänze—which it had been necessary to rebuild after von Stauffenberg's bomb—Hitler discovered himself to be losing all influence over the little wood blocks and flags. As the battleground drew close, the Führer redoubled his once-profitable tyranny over Guderian's frightened field marshals.

Not far away, Warsaw's second general rebellion had lasted through the rise and fall of Carbonne. During those weeks, while a quarter of a million citizens were dying to free Poland without communism, Bor-Komorowski had finally appealed to Stalin for support—as the ghetto's Jews had once pleaded with Komarovski himself. Just now, the Red Army lay encamped in a suburb across the river. While divisions of SS far more savage than any beast retook the ruined capital, the Soviets did not stir. Not long after the ensuing massacre of partisans, the Red Army in turn engulfed Warsaw. The Revolution had acquired its largest colony.

For the peoples of the West these were high-hearted times. Nor had the love of peace ever been stronger than during those weeks. But love is blind and among human affections the blindest is the love of peace.

9

WINTER CAME, AND ON THE CRIMEAN PENINSULA SEVERAL AIRCRAFT BUMPED
down at Saki airport, not far from the fortress of Sevastopol. One after the
other, three politicians wearing well-polished shoes crossed the tarmac and
climbed into waiting cars. Under a lifeless sun, the cavalcades began the
five-hour drive to the czarist spa of Yalta, where separate palaces had been
prepared. Throughout that mountainous drive, the soldiers of two entire Soviet
divisions lined the flanks, rhythmically presenting arms, to honor the statesmen of a civilization they had failed to save.

The American leader arrived at the Livadiya palace feeling as shaken as
Hitler and Himmler had been, beholding a scenery of shattered tanks, animal
carcases, and ruined towns. "I am feeling more bloodthirsty," he said
innocently to his aides, as his wheelchair was rolled through the patio of the
tuberculosis clinic.

As dusk came, all three world leaders were in Yalta. By the night of
the final banquet, power had built up so quickly that everyone knew an end-
game was upon them. Despite the doctrine of a liberated Europe, Stalin still
appeared to be denying Poland its freedom. Later that evening he insisted on
the forced return of all fifty thousand Soviet Russians, including Vlasov's
divisions and the entire Cossack army. To show their respect for their dinner
partner's colossal offensive, the American and the Englishman threw in a
firebombing of Dresden, where refugees from the Red advance were at that
moment concentrated. Churchill had earlier sent the order himself—to be
executed that very Shrove Tuesday, when the children of the city would be in
festival costume.

Now, at their candlelit banquet in a room looking onto the Black Sea, the
three statesmen came at last to the point. Appetites around the table that night
were good. At one point someone handed along his menu—which included
White and Red Salmon Shamaya, Quails, Turkey, and Partridge, Vol au Vent
of Game, and Sturgeon in Aspic—to be autographed as a relic of this summit
of power, where glaciers work upon themselves.

Among the smiling faces, Roosevelt found that he was losing the game.
"Let me reassure you, Josef, no one will ever underestimate the price your
people have paid."

"Josef, you must really try to understand!" Winston took off his spectacles, no longer feeling quite so sure of his unique influence over this Russian
they had fought beside and for whom he had done so much. "The Polish right
to democratic freedom—for which, after all, England went to war—is a matter of honor, and you must not ignore it!"

Churchill's dinner partner had turned his wolf's eyes to stare at the
Englishman's hairless, pink face. "Winston," he replied, "we understand well

this matter of honor. But for Bonaparte and now Hitler, Poland has been the gateway to Moscow. For us, Russia's control of Poland is a matter of life and death."

Before his victims could counter, Josef Stalin raised his glass. "May I propose a toast to you, Winston. I know few examples where the courage of one man has been so significant to the future history of the world."

Late the same night at the Koreis Palace, which once had belonged to the decadent Prince Yusupov, Josef Stalin met briefly to accept congratulations from Molotov and Vishinsky. Then, when he was alone in his room Stalin, who had never liked vodka, drank a half-liter of excellent French Burgundy and went to bed.

THE REFUGEE TREK

1

S INCE THE FALL OF MUSSOLINI, AND FOLLOWING THE JULY IN WHICH Claus von Stauffenberg was executed for his attempt on the Führer's life, the German people had been left alone to pay—now, at last, with their own lives—for the need to trust in the dark soul of one man.

On 2 February 1945, Heinz Guderian, chief of the German General Staff, traveled with his aides from Zossen to Berlin to see Hitler.

The military situation was not inspiring. An immense horde of Communists under Marshal Zhukov was stretched from the Oder and Neisse rivers to the Danube. Two weeks earlier, at Hohensalza, they had set foot on German soil. In the West, the combined American, French, and English armies lay along the Rhine and the northern frontier. Yet as General Guderian—now, after the fall of so many colleagues in the Smolensk conspiracy that he had refused David's plea for him to join, promoted supreme military head of the Third Reich—marched from the Chancellery past the batteries of 88s, this evening was like any other.

The snow lining the path had frozen into ridges that were the same dull white as the Berlin sky. Now the bunker's steel fire doors swung inward and they all heard, somewhere below, a familiar lecturing voice. To overcome the sudden pressure on his chest, Guderian laughed and stamped his boots. But as the chief of staff stooped underground into the overheated tunnel packed with coats, his face was heavy and unhealthy. His eyes had wrinkled sacks under them, and their expression was one of permanent strain.

Looking back now over those years in which Heinz Guderian had enjoyed the love of his soldiers—years of staggering victories and disappointments exceeding any in history—there lingered still his original doubt, from a summer's dusk at Bitburg, about the exact motives of the supreme head. And against that doubt Guderian had resisted with all the pride of a Prussian gentleman. From roughly the time of his protégés Baron Sunda's desertion at Smolensk, the struggle had grown into a sort of hypochondria. It was not without some inner conflict that he had turned over the July plotters—Guderian's fellow officers—to Heydrich's successor, Kaltenbrunner, and thence to

Roland Freissler of the People's Court. The more that Guderian had struggled to restore his belief in Hitler, the more hopelessly he became disenchanted. No matter how fiercely he hunted them down, Guderian's doubts returned.

Today, as he emerged under the strategy-room lights, the chief of staff carelessly took in Hitler's straight black hair. The dull-witted Field Marshal Keitel was to be there, three generals from the Brandenburg front, and also Hermann Göring. To Guderian there was something reassuring in Hitler's cramped arm and doughlike skin. The Führer was suffering for his people. Had not Guderian brought with him a plan to save Germany?

"No! No! *No!*" Hitler began to shout two hours later, staring around the brilliantly lit charts at each face in turn. In fact, Hitler liked and wished to trust Guderian—and he had even intended to agree with his presentation—but his anger flew out of him like wind through a gutted mansion. Stamping his foot, he clutched his left elbow with his free hand. "*No*, I say! *No!*"

Guderian made a sign that the tense chamber should be cleared. When he was alone with Göring, Hitler, and Keitel, he leaned over the pile of maps, his face glowing feverishly. "My Führer, consider General Gehlen's excellent charts of the Landsberg positions—" Guderian summoned the last of his strength. Landsberg was only a hundred kilometers to the east of Berlin.

With a frown, Hitler had been observing his chief of staff's face. "As for Gehlen," he suddenly interrupted, "I know the man is insane! You will send him to psychiatrists!"

"If you commit General Gehlen," Guderian managed to continue, his chest now aching, "you must commit me as well."

"Very well, then, Mr. General-Chief, dismiss the man!"

"With all respect, I could not do that."

But this odd fellow, dressed today in impeccable uniform, seemed to have forgotten Gehlen's insanity. They all momentarily heard voices laughing, cut off by a fierce hiss. Hitler pushed the black forelock over his ear. He gestured, as if to remind himself of something.

"Never mind, this alliance against me of Bolsheviks and ultra-capitalists will not hold together. King Frederick was saved. . . ."

Across the strategy table, buried in the Führer's, bunker, not one of the uniformed gentlemen stirred. It was almost as if the sane order of the world depended on their patient immobility; as if, through quiet meditation, the potent dream that had brought them to this moment in history could be lured back among them. But Hitler's perplexed frown suddenly softened to fatherly good spirits.

"Meanwhile, I would like you all to read Joseph's research into our great emperor's penal code. God in Heaven, and they say that *I* have been cruel? Look, my good fellows: molten iron, chains, forceps!"

After the chief of staff's audience concluded, Göring motioned him into the crowded lounge. As the marshal poured black coffee into two cups placed on a canasta table, Guderian stared past the man's powder-blue uniform at Hitler's steel bookshelves. His doubt had returned like a fever. In great rushing heaves, Göring whispered into his ear.

"Never mind, dear fellow, you did better than most. Terrible place, no windows!"

He paused, loudly sucking his coffee. Guderian could still remember the fellow back before the war, as an intelligent young airman, rather than this evil decadent.

Göring resumed in a whisper. "We have not done anything so bad. Our real problem will be Heinrich's camps. Without them—"

"Excuse me, excuse me!" the chief of staff, Guderian, cut him off suddenly and walked away across the carpeted concrete, taking small, slow steps.

The air marshal stared round him in surprise, but the group of generals gathered under the wall chart made no sign of noticing Guderian' air of ill health. What bores these old Junkers are, thought Goering, and again he filled his cup.

2

EIGHTY KILOMETERS TO THE EAST, AT FRANKFURT ON THE RIVER ODER—ACROSS the lines of two massive mechanized armies—the supreme commander of the Red Army was visiting the wounded from the battle to secure the bridgehead. The surgeon in charge was Ilyushin.

Vaslav Semyonovitch Ilyushin had not been among the Siberian prisoners at Tula, three years before, as David had imagined. That same December he had been commandeered to run a field hospital during the defense of Moscow. One year later, a fellow peasant conscript of the czar's army had had his friend appointed to be his staff surgeon. Ilyushin, however, had not changed. His pockmarked and constantly perspiring face leered more eccentrically than ever, though now he was continually drunk. Zhukov had never understood his old comrade, either his philosophy or his cynicism. But, as sometimes happens with men who have never asked questions or tasted weakness, for that very reason he admired Ilyushin tremendously. Furthermore, the surgeon seemed oblivious of his friend's rank. This impressed the good soldier most of all.

Tonight, Marshal Zhukov's suite was in the hospital's domed gallery. The chandeliers overhead flickered on and off, absurdly starting and stopping the urgent movement among the hundreds of beds. Not one was empty, and many of the wounded were doubled up, with other bodies pushed underneath their beds. The fighting had involved many factions, and it was logical that some among these throngs of men must be anti-Soviet partisans, overtaken deserters, or members of Vlasovite units fighting in German uniform. A soft-spoken, mysterious NKVD colonel in spectacles—a survivor of Stalin's purges within his own secret police—trailed the marshal's staff. There was a suffocating stench of burned flesh, disinfectant, and excrement. Now and then, some lonely soul cried out for his mother and died.

"Clearly what is needed here is a Volga of vodka." Ilyushin had emerged from his surgery to meet them. He paused for a front-line courier with snow on his fur hat.

The young Ukrainian handed the marshal an envelope with a red stripe and stared at the incomprehensible scene under the arcades. His eyes fixed on the chief surgeon's blood-splattered face and medical coat.

By contrast, the marshal radiated an exuberant satisfaction. And in his presence who would forget the disgraces and the sacrifices that the Russian peoples had endured across the last years; who could help but feel moved by the Soviet masses, or by their patriotic advance, or deny a rush of blood at the sweet revenge that awaited them, just a ten-minute flight to the west—*Berlin! Had not Moscow herself been almost in the grip of the Gauleiters?* Now, as Ilyushin's friend read the letter to the officers surrounding him, his face seemed almost to be that of revolutionary Russia, like some childish giant who marvels that anyone could have designs on him.

The supreme commander's entry had not gone unnoticed. Dozens of those who were not dead or dying had risen on their elbows to watch. Some were grinning, while others wept. Above the din, there rose the shrieks of a boy in the far colonnade whose chest sutures had torn and who was bleeding to death. From behind the nearest column, hung with dead men's coats, Zhukov and Ilyushin turned to gaze across the sea of men.

"Tell Marshal Konev"—Zhukov raised his voice, so that at the farthest end of the gallery faces turned—"tell him that the Fascists are outnumbered twenty to one! Tell him that there will be no more Red retreats. No Red retreats!" He held the dispatch in the view of all.

In reply, an explosion of shouts thundered through the galleries—though to deny retreats had been Stalin's only consistent strategy, whatever the cost might be in men's lives. Now those same men's trusted commander returned the dispatch to the courier. Tears were running down that young man's cheeks. Disdaining to rub them away, the corporal saluted violently. Zhukov had turned to his old friend, his best friend, with a strange light in his eyes.

"What does that comrade think he is doing?" the surgeon repeated.

By the litter nearest to them, the secret policeman had gripped the lapels of a soldier whose head was in bandages. The body dropped back in an awkward position. "This one is Latvian. A Lat traitor, in a stolen uniform!"

"His cranium is in fifty pieces—" Ilyushin appeared unable to continue.

The marshal recognized at once his surgeon's guttural passion: this man on whom, across revolutionary Russia's difficult thirty years, Zhukov had always counted to show only cynical amusement. He made a grab for Ilyushin's arm but it was wet and slipped free. The guards held the soldier erect, his bandaged head dangling back. The NKVD colonel turned to Ilyushin with interest.

"Return my patient to his bed," the surgeon muttered.

The marshal addressed his friend thoughtfully. "Vaslav Semyonovitch! Colonel Stratnoy, this man is a dying soldier of the motherland."

The policeman raised his almost hairless eyebrows. The group stood knee deep in the sea of wounded men. "Precisely, comrade marshal, a Russian— with all respect, a traitor."

"You Gestapo are . . . are very . . . efficient at devouring our . . . our men!"

Even in the gallery's din, the group of staff officers had all heard Ilyushin's teeth chatter with rage. At their center, Zhukov instantly regained his disciplined calm. He knew the signs very well, and he was sorry.

"Yes, comrade surgeon?" inquired Stratnoy.

"How . . . the stupid in-inefficiency of your people . . . your little father, Joseph! I have seen a m-m-million comrades die of that!"

For five more seconds, the supreme commander of Stalin's armies stared at his lifelong friend. The gifted fellow had begun to gasp, as children in fits of rage sometimes cannot breathe. Just then they were cut off in the darkness.

As the lights came back on, the police colonel was pulling the surgeon round by the shoulder. The passion contorting Ilyushin's face had strangely vanished.

"At least give him to the psychiatrists!" Zhukov said awkwardly. "He is not responsible . . . it is delirium tremens," he lied. It was the most that I could do, the marshal observed to himself, as he turned to the huge ward and raised both arms for the sea of desperately cheering soldiers.

But the sight of that long-familiar face—snarling and trembling just in front of his as if possessed by a devil—had made a lingering impression even on Georgy Zhukov. It was an hour before he could again think clearly of Berlin, waiting just over the flickering skyline with Hitler inside it. It was still another hour before he could regain his proper emotion concerning the long and bloody road through Stalingrad, Kursk, Moscow, and Leningrad, down which the Russian people had fought to gain their freedom.

Among all three armies now gathered on the Rhine, as through the immense Red Army sprawled along the Oder and the Neisse, there was one firm belief: the belief that this wild beast, which once had been the gentle race of Bach, Goethe, and Brahms and which now was fighting to the death, was the embodiment of pure evil—that once Berlin had fallen, all such tortures, gassings, razzias, and levelings of cities must end forever.

3

ALL THROUGH TWO WINTERS AND TWO SUMMERS THEY HAD RETURNED, FROM THE velvet wheat fields of Kansas and the rugged Black Hills of South Dakota; from Omaha; Mobile, Memphis, and St. Louis, Salinas and Eureka; from New York and Philadelphia: seven million American soldiers, entered the European theater.

In the U.S. 3rd Army, there was impatience at the scholarly pace of Field Marshal Montgomery's joint invasion plan. Ten days before Christmas, the 26th Infantry still lay behind the 9th Armored Division on the River Our, between Vianden and Echternach in the mountainous Luxembourg forest— that same Ardennes through which, four and a half years ago, General Guderian had led the conquest of civilized society.

Major Duncan Penn's battalion had come up, on General Middleton's orders, through the town of Reisdorf in broad daylight. Colonel Smith— a career officer from Sioux City, who suspected easterners and Ivy League graduates equally and who kept the division's football heroes well to the rear—had ordered Major Penn's much-decorated unit to relieve a forward position guarding the Sûre bridge. And so it happened that at dusk, in a thinning snow, Duncan Penn lay hidden with his sergeant Henry Virgin on pine needles above a river ravine and saw Germany for the first time.

Tonight, the Nazi realm of magic and violence was a forest wall that appeared very close across the ravine's silent down-drifting snowflakes. Cullie's voice came to them, muffled by the slope.

"Hey, Grapes! Is that yonder . . . is that Germany?"

Stretched beside Sergeant Virgin, Major Penn ignored the excitement in the battery. "Now, why do you think they left the bridge?" he said.

Sergeant Virgin lowered his binoculars. Having fought Germans across Europe in order to lie tonight on this pine ridge, they could not stop staring across into the dark forest.

During the fifteen months since Salerno, the major's hair had gone gray. He could no longer reproduce the trusting smile which, on the rue de Fleurus, he had never known how to keep off his face.

"Ain't it still," Henry said softly. "Ain't it awesome?"

"Quite peaceful. But that's it—the Rhineland." Duncan Penn pronounced the name as long ago in Paris he had heard it said by Johann and David. He had not once mentioned that time to his men, and he did not talk about it to himself. It was the one aspect of his life that he could still love. This made the subject painful, more painful than to think about war, which—like Hélène Le Trève's brother—he had learned to do so well.

"Middleton sure put us out of the action in these passes."

"I wouldn't count on it." As Major Penn listened to the sound of the river, he knew that someone else was hearing it too—killers, killers like himself.

Nearby, in the radio tent, Schneider had on the earphones. He lifted one cup.
"Anything from the general?"

"They ain't interested sir," Schneider answered, his eyes averted.

Duncan did not repeat what he thought: that today's penetration of the lines by American jeeps, driven by Nazis spreading false information, suggested a big counterstrike. He motioned Henry to hand him the new map.

"Okay, Grapes. Let's examine your piece of the river."

"Boy, you are jumpy. It's God's work, them giving you leave tomorrow. Ever seen Paris?"

"Maybe I would miss this place."

"Now don't go missing us!"

"I like it here. It's a great site."

Later, in the tent, Duncan made out Henry kneeling at his cot. There was just one person left that he cared for as much as this primitive man, though this was not his wife, who, after landing the East Coast's most eligible bachelor had betrayed him. There would be nothing now for Major Penn to go back to. Here in the ruins of Europe there was Hélène Sunda—alone now, and possibly just two hundred miles away somewhere between the ridge and the advancing Red Army.

From Pierre Le Trève he knew that, in 1940, Hélène had almost gone to New York from Mexico. Duncan would have lived for Leni then—even pregnant with David Sunda's child. He would not go to Paris tomorrow, not if she might still be somewhere ahead.

His body stretched in a sleeping bag, in this forest packed with every kind of machine of violence, Duncan thought about the present problem of sleep and dying. He thought of how his body resembled the deceased, seen in hundreds of surprisingly dust-clotted fragments at Cassino. Here, beyond this river, there must be the scarcely believable camps. Duncan believed in them; what if Smith again put him in charge of burial duty? He would have preferred to bury the ones he had torn up himself—how many had there been, a dozen? —though there could easily have been twice that number. Sweat trickled down his ribs.

Duncan drew up his bag, and there came to him the reassuring smell of himself. "Who are you praying for, Henry?"

"Laverne," he mumbled.

Laverne, Duncan thought, and the comedy of American innocence stirred sweetly in his mind. Laverne never looked at anyone except Henry and walked with God. Cadwallader Benton, the Klan dragon, had gotten Henry defrocked and drafted for marrying a mulatta—though Laverne's father had sworn that her mother was a carpetbagging Persian. It was funny how Duncan could smell the very earth and love the characters in Virgin's life, but not in his own.

"Hey, Duncan, are you awake?"

"I'm awake, Henry."

"It's been coming to me from that mountain yonder, Rhineland."

"What has?"

"Well, it spoke to me, I heard it clear. It said, This is my defiled soil." Inside their tent, the honeyed Carolina drawl rose in a soft singing. "You remember, most all God's children follow other gods? Then he warns that any nation takes on God's own punishment will be thrown on its knees? Oh, I looked at that hill in Germany, and I knew we were acting out the Lord's will to His satisfaction! We are smiting His faithless children, and we are entering that forest of Satan to bring out the helpless lamb!"

"Shut up that goddam noise!" called a voice from the next tent. For twenty seconds, in this ancient teutonic forest, Major Penn bit his tongue hard in terror at the wild laughter about to burst out of him. Somewhere in their tent, Henry's piety rambled on in a whisper.

"That's fine, Henry. That's fine." Duncan Penn lay still for a time. "Henry, I've been thinking. Why not take leave in my place? I could give you a letter to my lawyer in New York. He'll take good care of Laverne."

"You think the Krauts will attack. You want me out."

"Sorry, Henry, it's not for you. It would be worse having to come back, that's all."

"You really think your lawyer can do something?"

"Seward can do most anything. Just not for me."

"Why not?" Henry whispered. "Why not?"

"Because I never knew the right order to give him."

The following afternoon, Sergeant Virgin left the Our–Sûre front for Paris. Before the next dawn—in that same mountain sector where no activity was expected—a bombardment began in what would be Hitler's final heavy assault and the greatest battle ever fought by Americans.

Unknown to Sergeant Virgin, that night Satan had been at the Ziegerberg, one hundred miles to the east. Just one hundred miles beyond that, Hélène Sunda would remain scarcely aware of anything taking place on the Western Front.

4

AFTER BARTHOLD VON SUNDA'S DEATH AT OBERLINDEN THE WINTER BEFORE— shortly followed, as if out of yearning, by that of her adored mother-in-law— Hélène had occupied the old people's bedroom with its view over the Franken forest. She placed her dressing table where it caught the morning sun, as once it had in the little room under her father's roof.

One morning at seven o'clock, in Hélène's fourth year at the Sunda estate, she had just sat down when far away she heard a telephone ring. Flooded with not altogether pleasant emotions, the brush still sunk in her hair, Hélène waited until she heard Gustav's step approach along the corridor where the portraits of ancestors were hung. They have seen him, she thought, as she had thought a hundred times before. Today she felt sure of it; her children's position would soon be clear. Without putting down the brush, Hélène rose and took six unsteady steps toward the parlor doors.

"Good morning, madame. A call from Berlin."

"Good morning, Gustav," her voice sang tenderly. "Did they say who it was?"

"Yes, madame, a *Gruppenführer* von Friedland."

Hélène abruptly turned and walked slowly to the windows to hide the flush that had covered her body, from her knees to the roots of her hair. When she turned back, it was behind the mask of an experienced woman, which Hélène knew that she was not. In the doorway, the old gamekeeper shifted his weight from one foot to the other.

"Please tell Herr Friedland that I am not taking calls."

Gustav nodded sympathetically and then shook his head. "I'm afraid— Herr von Friedland left only the message that he will stop by tomorrow evening."

"Very well, Gustav. I shall meet you and Kristof by the stable at nine."

For twenty minutes, Hélène remained standing, as Gustav had left her, by the dresser examining her emotions. Her momentary pleasure at the thought of the attractive officer coming *here*, to David's family home, had instantly given way to panic at some unnoticed change in herself: a relaxing of her natural sentiments against evil, which had begun with the shock of burying her husband's old parents on Templar's Hill.

When she looked back over her life, as she often had through the last months of 1944, the only clear sense Hélène could find in it was that she had married a universally respected man whom her parents loved and that she had entrusted her being to him. As a result, Hélène found herself, at twenty-eight, neither in Paris nor in Mexico, but a mother of two small boys in charge of a vast agricultural estate, expected to produce food for a military empire that had occupied the European democracies, Africa, and Russia: an empire run by men who had ruined her father. All this, Hélène how knew, was how David had kept his promise to her in a Mexican garden and secured her safety. Until recently, her husband had sustained this by unspecified duties in the East. Yet even in her strange position, she had never doubted the principle of her life— with the fatalism that considers all nations and races equally unreliable, and which prefers to put its trust in fate and knowledge, and in itself. But the Nazi's forte had been censorship, and knowledge was difficult.

After the head of Oberlinden's thirty Polish *Arbeiters*, Kristof, had come with the news that France was to be liberated, and after Hélène had lost touch first with Luz and then with her sister-in-law in Budapest, she was left with no personal letters safe to write. There was only her brother-in-law Freddy, who telephoned Hélène every Wednesday from Berlin without ever taking a serious tone. These enigmatic calls only intensified her excruciating uncertainty. Equally, the idea of a free Paris had awoken in Hélène a powerful homesickness. Yet an even more powerful irony never left her—how, in the midst of her princely life at Oberlinden she felt drawn to the existence of common folk, far more vividly even than in Oaxaca.

The *Arbeiters* knew she was French, and they trusted her. And it was when she had been forced to work next to Gustav and Kristof, to keep the western fields under cultivation, that Hélène had come to have more profound feelings about the person to whom her husband had once accorded the highest respect. She felt no alarm that Justin had never replied to the most naked confession of her life. The fact that she could expose herself—perhaps even to contempt, and to such a person—now gave Hélène as much peace as anything that she had done.

Such new feelings were associated with the field along the river, which it had been her idea to sow with the new quick-growing seed.

This morning, as she pulled on her riding breeches, Hélène concentrated on the memory of their wet limbs at that midsummer's reaping—in the company of Heinrich's family of girls, Kristof and his wife, Marya, and the other Poles. There had been four boys, six old men, and a dozen women her own age, the younger ones half stripped, their skirts tucked up in the heat. Hélène thought of the earth, and of the oak with its branch stretched along the ground, which she knew from every angle, having herself plowed two big circles around it, the leather reins looped from the sorrel's sweat-darkened buttocks and around Hélène's back, her feet balancing across upturned clods, her hands aching on the rubbed wooden handles. She remembered her sensations when she had called them all to the field through the dawn mists, before Gustav or Kristof believed that the new smaller grain could be ripe. Hélène had hidden any doubts from them, thinking of the seed diagrams she had studied in her father-in-law's library. The sun had blazed down to glisten on their wet, brown skins. Hélène's limbs had been wet, too, and her shirt under her arms becoming stained.

At noon, when the old men and boys had staggered to the shade under the oak with their ham breads, cheese, and Kolsch, Hélène had let the women lead her to a grassy meadow among the pines where the river ran. She remembered how Kristof had looked at her, so that she had moved closer to Marya, and how through the work they had touched the earth, as if making love to it, even though she knew such thoughts in a young baroness would not be understood.

Still later—when they sat on the grass with their bare feet in the water, and the laughing Polish women had rolled down their dresses from their burned necks and splashed water on their white breasts—Hélène had smiled at Marya's challenging look and pulled the stinging wet material down over her breasts too. The peasant women had stared at her, shyly curious. Then Hélène had laughed gaily, and the women had laughed too and splashed water at her. Later they sang, and Hélène had lain among them with her eyes shut, unable to keep her face from smiling.

From that afternoon, so late in her life, Hélène was aware of Kristof and the dozen other men among the farms. No longer were they remote protective figures to whose masculinity she felt indifferent. Through their days' work, Hélène had been able to hide this with her customary aloofness. At night, there had been the dreams, which seemed to have impregnated her through her intense imagination—itself like some root capable of drawing truth from the Bavarian air. On such days she would work herself into a state of exhaustion, to protect the promise of her life, which she had put into words in a single unanswered letter.

It was on that same evening that Hélène had first heard her missing husband was an anti-Hitler conspirator. She awoke now from the memory, standing dressed at her window, alone in command of this silent architecture where there had been no guests in a year, and with all the eyes on Sunda lands watching to see what she would do.

5

ONE OF THE FIGURES WHO FREQUENTLY TROUBLED HER SLEEP WAS MARK Friedland, who, she had recently been told, was the liaison between Himmler and the head of the Gestapo, Heinrich Müller. When Hélène thought of him now, the man's nerveless arrogance seemed obvious. How could it not have been clear to her then? Or perhaps it had been precisely the man's subtle, mocking cruelty that had attracted her? This thought returned to torment Hélène, long after the memory of her pompous admirer had become so loathesome it made her feel physically ill.

Yet she had given her attention to him for two meals, and those two meals had allowed Mark Friedland to cross the moral gulf that lay between them. There had been whisperings—at the time of Johannes Godard's disappearance—about a revolt inside Warsaw, crushed by a rabble of Russian thugs under the guidance of the German police. Hélène had only to remember Kristof's face when she had repeated that rumor told her by frightened cousins of the Sundas' old financier, Ellic Levin, to feel sure it was true. Someone among her husband's polite, smiling countrymen must be responsible— and *Gruppenführer* Friedland had a spacious Berlin office at 8 Prinz Albrechtstrasse, the establishment of the state police.

Now, because a lonely and selfish young woman had accepted two lunches from this person, he felt free to drop in uninvited—here, to Oberlinden, the family seat where David's father and mother had loved and trusted her—while her husband, who had risked his life to oppose such people, was missing and might even be in police hands! If Hélène could have taken back those two lunches by chopping off four fingers, she felt sure she would have paid that price now. But the thing was done. It was her duty alone to undo it without endangering her children, the farmers on the Sunda lands, or the workers under her protection. And—what to Hélène seemed most important of all— not one among these loyal folk should for a moment suspect her. Therefore, even before the sound of Gustav's slow step had receded down the corridor, Hélène knew she would receive Mark Friedland in the music room, where all that passed between them would be heard clearly in the pantry.

Before speaking to Frau Gerta or going to the nursery, Hélène descended carelessly to the hall telephone, behind one of the stairway's supporting titans. Yes, there it was, in Gustav's neat, square handwriting: *G. F. von Friedland, visit at six o'clock.* She knew at least that he would be punctual. What Hélène instinctively feared most in the meeting to come was uncertainty.

Returning upstairs to the nursery door, Hélène paused with her forehead to the wall. She had heard her sons giggling inside—were her children trapped with her in a cage with a dangerous beast? Stepping through, she breathed the sweet stuffy smell of cozy bodies. As Hélène stooped over the corner bed, a tiny hand closed on her finger, and her heart contracted for this life that clung to hers. She kissed the knuckles like a string of beads. There was a rustle, and vigorous little arms choked her neck, pulling her down on the covers.

"Mama, Mama, Mama!"

"All right . . . all right, my little morsels! You may get up."

Gently freeing herself, Hélène crossed to the curtains. Below in the winter sun, Kristof's blond head was moving along the orchard wall. "Well, then!" She rested her hands on the warm, hard tops of her sons heads. "No music exercise today."

"Good-good-good-good!" Rickie squealed.

"Why, Mama, why?" inquired Albert, in a small voice.

"I have things to do, my dears. I think we may take a trip soon."

"Where? Where, Mama?" the boys cried together. Albert had climbed onto a chair to examine his mother's face with a serious gaze.

"That is a secret. But it will be a beautiful trip."

As she left the nursery, Hélène felt shaken by her feelings. In her riding boots, she paced nervously back past the crusader armor. It was not until she approached the kitchen staircase and heard the clatter and voices from below, that Hélène realized she was frightened to go down.

Her father-in-law's six black Labradors looked from their new mistress to the staircase. Then they followed her slowly down the north wing, lined with medieval portraits of her sons' male line. In this war, had not millions of good women faced the same helplessness and taken mortal decisions? Still, she felt appalled and humiliated that at last it was her turn to face a danger far worse than giving birth to Alaric, whom they called Rickie. She knew she had no right to show fear: in fact, less right than anyone else, because she had tasted the greatest happiness. Of this, for some reason, Hélène felt quite certain.

Almost drunk from her concentration, she had come to a carved door. This led over a little stone bridge to the balcony of the chapel. Impulsively, Hélène opened the door and went through. Without crossing herself she sat on the front bench, her hands in her jacket, and frowned at the little white-robed altar below.

"And so, Father, what should I do?" Her lips formed the words, speaking to him as to an old friend. "This time next year, where will my babies be? Will I have behaved as you would like? Above all, father, I beg you to protect David from any harm, especially from the harm that an unworthy wife has brought on him."

Between the chapel walls where, it seemed an age ago, Hélène had seen all the Sundas gathered in her honor to hear the Munich Boys' Choir sing Bach's B-Minor Mass, there was a vacant hush. As the minutes ticked by, her imagination gave up its intense struggle to master what was about to happen, and her place in it. A curious and not unpleasant peace settled in her mind, and she thought of the buttered croissants waiting below, and of the day's work. Suddenly she felt quite sure that from these simple things an answer would come to her.

However, there was one thing that Hélène would never know. At the precise moment at which she had imagined before her the heavy Berlin façade of 8 Prinz Albrechtstrasse, Friedrich von Sunda—charming Freddy, who had danced with Hélène in Saint-Moritz and warned an exhausted mother at Moscow Station—had been in a corner of that towering courtyard, naked and twisting violently, with his feet directly above his head, nailed to a stubby black cross made of railroad ties.

Now, Friedrich's body hung loose. The snowflakes settled on his soles, while two of Mark Friedland's Smolensk agents—once bank tellers on the Kurfürstendamm—stood whispering nearby in their smart leather coats.

6

AS THE FOREST FIRE ADVANCES, ALL NATURE BECOMES VISIBLE IN ITS DISARRAY. Creatures of every shape respond to panic with movement—bearing nothing in their hearts but the warrens and nests where they were born and where, only moments before, they had imagined themselves to be eternally secure. Acre after acre, the stream of living things gathers to a flood.

As the Nazis lost ground, they also lost Hitler's underground monastery, Ribbentrop's *Schloss*, and Heydrich's crematoria. Panic spread among the millions whose nests and burrows lay in the paths of the crazed Nazi retreat and of the avenging Communist advance. By the first snows, the trickle of carts and horses setting out from a thousand towns had thickened to a constant stream. These streams flowed together and grew into a huge gloomy Nile of homeless families, crawling west under towering clouds. From across the Nazi occupation, people of all tribes and faiths who longed for liberation mingled now with the poison trickle of camp personnel and collaborators, shifting westward toward the borders of democracy. And almost as soon as they began, the refugees began to starve, with the weak left by the wayside.

To Hitler's efficient generals, as they puzzled over the repeated checkmate of their positions, this migration only reflected the logic of their tactics. To the goggled motorcycle guards who cleared the roads for the puzzled generals, these inconvenient pilgrims were a filthy and above all disorganized rabble with no rights. But to each of the uprooted beings, struggling mile after mile into the sunset through cutting winds that blew the ice particles on the road into a luminous orange dust, and with only the memories of their ruined hearths, these officers were like devils, with inexplicable powers of life and death.

By the first weeks of January, the waves of refugees had reached westward past Dresden and Zwikau and were only three days from Bayreuth. Perhaps it was this new presence, which Kristof had heard imperfectly described over his crystal radio, that Hélène had sensed on the morning of *Gruppenführer* von Friedland's call, as it spread tremors of anxiety across the countryside.

7

ON THAT FRIDAY DUSK, THE BARONESS GAVE INSTRUCTIONS NOT TO LIGHT THE big drawing-room fire. Instead, she asked Frau Gerta to take tea with herself and the boys by the stone hearth that was kept burning in the servants' pantry.

Even when Hélène had bathed away the mud from the fields in the lion's-paw tub, brushed the hayseeds out of her hair, and put on her most austere tweed suit, the unreal daze hung over things, as if she had received a physical wound. In this pantry, she could forget the fabled ballroom above, the ghostly tapestried halls and the male ancestors. She had only to hold the elements of her world together for a few more hours.

Hélène had coiled her hair in a tight chignon, and she had a little headache. Beyond the flicker of the logs, Gerta knitted without looking up. On the rug between them, Rickie and Bertie lay among the Labradors, murmuring over a book with yellow-tinted photographs of Indian chiefs. Her sons' little shoes waved above their heads, emphasizing certain points. On her lap, Hélène's hands worked at her own knitting with the urgent precision of a spider preparing its web. Her gaze wandered—from the children's swaying feet, to the dogs, to the china cuckoo clock, to Gerta's face, down to her hands, and then back to Gerta's face. *Something beyond my control will come tonight,* Hélène was thinking, *and all these things may be taken away from me.* Her soul held on to them, silently suffering. When she looked at Gerta her throat tightened, until presently it was sore.

The large round head of her husband's old governess had an aspect piti- fully unfinished and doughlike. Her face and neck were very red and pleated, and most of her thin red hair had fallen out. As if to compensate for this hope- less and comic ugliness, Gerta had been given an expression so humble, so grateful and innocently mild, that no one beholding this old woman, who had been denied a life of her own, could feel anything but humility. And in fact Hélène had grown to love Gerta as much as anyone in her life, and more than any man.

"Gerta."

"Yes, *Mutti*?" Gerta looked up from her brown sock.

"An officer may stop at Oberlinden tonight, at six or so."

"We have much to put up with these days."

Hélène laughed a little huskily, and she felt again the soreness in her throat. "If he comes, I will see him in the music room. Put the children to bed at seven."

"You must not worry about the children. What time shall I put *you* to bed?"

"Am I such a child, Gerta?"

"Very few men could deserve a wife like you."

"Thank you, Gerta . . . if only that were true." Feeling further calmed, Hélène picked up the needles and resumed her knitting.

Through this long day, certain scenes had returned to her in a different light. In particular, she remembered two balls, given in the last month by well- bred neighbors. The gossip was that both balls had continued long after Gustav had driven Hélène home. There was even one story—she had smiled at this in disbelief—of groups of naked bodies, and of one gentleman wearing nothing but a horse tail. Was the final breakdown of all civilized society far nearer than was understood publicly?

Hélène recalled now a scene with Heidrun Godard at the opera in Bayreuth, more than a year ago. That October, Joseph Goebbels had called for a special performance of Wagner's *Ring*. Over the telephone from Berlin, Hélène had accepted an indisposed Heidrun's invitation to attend *Siegfried*. There would be a chance to see Johannes again, whom she still remembered fondly despite his rupture with her husband.

Yet the night before, without any explanation, Johannes had left Berlin to visit his mother. Hélène had found herself seated alone with Heidrun in the Führer's box. She suspected that Heidrun was a chronic liar, and she had never much liked her. In particular, Hélène felt offended by the constant aura of sexual conceit that accompanied the singer like an electric storm. Since David's national disgrace in absentia, Heidrun took a pitying sisterly tone with her and constantly reminded Hélène in little ways of what a distinguished man Doktor Godard was, how he had risen from a humble background and yet was thoroughly modern. Hélène had realized, that cool autumn afternoon, how little insulated she now was from the Fascist bourgeoisie. Nor had she been sufficiently impressed by Act One.

"Hélène, I have seen it a hundred times. But when I hear this most sublime leitmotif, I feel sure that man knew what it was to be a God!"

In their box that afternoon, Heidrun had leaned forward to expose her shoulders and red hair to the uplifted faces. And seeing this woman's animal beauty, and her expensive good taste, Hélène had despised herself for the twinge of self-pity she had felt for herself and for David. Tears came to her eyes. "Perhaps you are right, Heidrun. But I think the music is really not very good—it lacks subtlety."

The famous singer laughed indulgently, her bosom swelling above her gauze dress, her lips cherry-colored. It made Hélène feel sick to have a woman flirt with her.

"You have simply not released your primal spirituality. But you will have more chance as the new age develops. Ouf, I feel wonderful tonight!" Heidrun straightened, pulling the gauze tight so that Hélène saw her nipples. "I can feel the gods at their castle in Valhalla stretch and prepare themselves. The mastersingers will sing again. The Grail will be found. The maidens beneath the waves of the Rhine will lead us to the treasure of gold. Oh, my dear, think when science is banished from the earth, when all is once again mystery, music, and heroes!"

The curtain at the back of the box opened, and in the sudden daylight, Heidrun turned to the handsome young man who had entered their box. His face was drawn.

"Go on then Klaus, speak! This woman is my confidante."

"*Gnädige Frau-doktor* Godard?"

"I am Heidrun Dolin, what is it?" Heidrun raised her rich voice.

"Madame . . . Doktor Godard . . . a terrible thing has happened! Your husband . . . has disappeared."

Heidrun sank back in her seat without a sound. "It cannot be possible," she finally said.

"Yes, yes, it was in his village. His mother was there." Noticing curious faces turn to them among the crowd below, the young man became alarmed. Hélène gestured at him angrily. Stammering, he clicked heels and withdrew from the box.

"Poor Heidrun! Shouldn't we go now?"

It would have been cruel to suggest it was all a mistake. Hélène had known instantly that it was true. And in this beautiful woman's expression—

that of a spoilt girl who has been shockingly punished—she saw that Heidrun knew it too.

"Poor Heidrun! Come, let's go."

The singer turned then and stared at Hélène with an expression of bewildered grief.

"No, I will wait until the end."

The two women had remained seated, hand in hand, until the end. And when *Siegfried* was over and the lights came on, Hélène had found a different woman at her side—a coarse, overly made-up woman, lacking the glamour that blazed from her moments before.

In the pantry at Oberlinden, Hélène woke from these images and found her sons at her feet and Gerta's kind face examining hers. She glanced at the clock: ten minutes to six.

At once she rose. Arranging her wool as if she would soon be back, Hélène went quickly up the stairs to the music room and sat at the piano. Only a year ago, Maria Pisani had played this instrument. Who would follow Hélène Le Trève?

Finding no sense in Brahms's antlike notes, Hélène began the most intricate scales she could think of. Then, over the angry waves of harmonics she heard the deeper rumble of engines. She rose and walked to the curtains. Outside in a billow of condensation waited two automobiles with hooded lights, flanked by motorcycles. Were she and her children to be taken away in these? Hélène returned to the piano and began to play the Brahms.

8

WHEN HÉLÈNE LOOKED UP FROM THE PIANO, HER VISITOR MADE A SIGN TO GO on playing.

Hélène's cheeks reddened, and she fixed her eyes on the music. At the sight of that cold steady smile—and the uniform—a last hope had died in her. She had somehow imagined that, despite his rank, Mark Friedland's uniform would be gray. She couldn't recognize in this vain officer the eccentric ex-radical journalist whom she had briefly liked and even compared to Justin. The tea service arrived and Hélène's listener advanced silently, resting his hand under the music light. Seeing the black straight hairs on that hand, she shuddered and thought of her children, close by in the warm pantry. She nodded, and the pale fingers turned the page.

The first movement ended. Through the room there was a profound silence. Closing the music, Hélène slipped from the far end of the bench and walked easily around the instrument to meet her visitor.

"Good evening, *Gruppenführer* von Friedland. Welcome to Oberlinden." She held up her hand with a careless smile and the man bent over her. But though Hélène remembered that Mark Friedland had the effete custom of kissing his own thumb, this evening she felt his lips against her skin.

"Hélène, I am so glad to see you again," he said, with tense formality, glancing at the love seat. "I had no idea that you were an accomplished musician."

"Do you think so, *Gruppenführer?*" she said, making an effort to hide her bitterness from this man who kept a spy in the village, and a dossier on her family in Berlin. Walking to the low table, she tinkled the silver bell and then closed her hand around it.

After waiting for Hélène to be seated, Friedland sank down stiffly against the curtains. "But if you keep calling me that, I shall be forced to call you Baroness—which I know you don't like."

Hélène stared at him with a bemused smile. The consciousness of some lurking contradiction in this state policeman lounging in the shadows made his flirtatious note incomprehensible to her.

"All right then, if you like . . . Mark," Hélène conceded. "I would like to hear about Berlin, Mark," Hélène went on, "and where your trip will take you. First, though, have you brought me any news of my husband?" A faintly piteous note had escaped from Hélène as the intimate word came to her lips.

With an irritable glance around the music room, her visitor began to unbutton the top buttons of his tight jacket—and there came to Hélène the quite distinct impression of another world of people with whom Mark Friedland might behave very differently. This impression was so immediate and terrible that for an instant she had to struggle violently with her instinct as a mother to throw herself at this man's feet—to submit to him—to do anything to restore whatever human interest there had been between them. As if sensing her willingness, the policeman sat forward, drew his shoulders together, and smiled at her.

Hélène flinched, hearing claws against the door, but it was only her dogs. Feeling that instant of mystical terror fall behind, she breathed in quick breaths of anger and humiliation. As she watched the tea leaves tumble at the bottom of the policeman's cup, Hélène was trying desperately to understand her mistake. She looked up and met Friedland's gaze.

"Unfortunately, Hélène, at least in our German empire there is still very little to add to the story of your misguided husband. After the desertion at Smolensk, just a trace here or there. . . ."

At the mention by this high official of David's misguidedness, *as if he were alive*, Hélène experienced a rush of devotion.

"Despite your husband, my dear, I will tell you a secret of state."

The man had actually looked over his shoulder toward the pantry door! Hélène lowered her voice too. "Mark, you know I am discreet."

"The truth is, Baroness, that some of my superiors are attempting an arrangement . . . you know, diplomatic channels . . . naturally, without informing the supreme authority. On Wednesday, I will meet the opposite party in Zurich. Many questions must be turned over—for example, this Jewish mess. Still, you understand, I can be very persuasive." Friedland waved his hands, clattering the teacup. He had grown agitated.

Hélène gazed back at him without humor. "I have noticed it. I suspect that you know our state of affairs better than the leaders," she said, and beneath the English tea table she felt the *Gruppenführer*'s boot against her slim shoe. She did not withdraw it. They were both smoking.

"It is remarkable that you should see this." The man's grin revealed black gums that receded from his teeth. "In fact, Baroness, I have seen all the reports that they are not brave enough to show our Führer. With modern weapons, defensive positions—still, the end is very close. The Baltic ports will go last."

"But when, Mark? Can you tell?"

"Two or three more months," von Friedland confided, with some difficulty controlling an exultant laughter. The man's eyes watered, and beads of sweat lined his narrow brow.

"And we, Mark? What of us?" Hélène inquired, sinking back with the air of someone caught up in events she cannot understand. "Your people are keeping us prisoners here."

"Yes, my dear, you are in some peril. I have myself seen proposals to make an example of the Barons Von Sunda. Furthermore, you could not cross any frontier or battle lines."

Friedland sat back and stared speculatively over Hélène's head. Presently, after tapping off an ash, he turned to her with an air of luxurious possession.

"Baroness, you have guessed my feelings." he said finally.

For several seconds Hélène was unable to speak. "I think I know," she murmured finally, making a signal to him that they must not be overheard. "For that reason, I had hoped I might rely on you to help me with some problems—ideas, principles—that have been making my life extremely unhappy for months."

"Hélène!" The officer leaned forward as if someone had pushed his shoulders. His face was suddenly coarse with gratitude and willingness. "What can I do for you?"

"Tell me, Mark," Hélène said very quietly, "do you believe in God?"

"You can't be serious?" The man across from her blew smoke through his nostrils and frowned, seeing the Baroness's gentle, sincere eyes fixed on him.

"And you?" she whispered, with an almost motherly intimacy. "Are you serious?"

Over the last thirty minutes a realization had grown on Hélène. This person's physical presence in her music room at Oberlinden had gradually brought back a more detailed sensation: of her feelings three years ago in Berlin, following their two lunches. At that time, she had felt sufficiently alarmed by this man's fascination with her to confess to the young priest at the cathedral. At the memory of her absolution, she experienced a moral happiness so intense that, just for one instant, she forgot both her children's danger and all sense of where this conversation was taking them.

Across the tea table from this strangely nerveless woman, Mark von Friedland accepted Hélène's blush as the seal on his sexual conquest.

"Are you serious? I would like to know," she repeated.

"What do you mean?"

"You are not unsophisticated like your colleagues," Hélène went on, in a sympathetic tone. "Do you seriously believe in the things you are doing?"

"Naturally, naturally I believe in them! As much as you believe in God." The *Gruppenführer* smoothed back his wavy black hair with the hand holding his cigarette. "And when this incarnation of the ancient movement has been defeated, it will reappear, to be misunderstood all over again—in America, quite likely, or Arabia. Do you know in Dostoyevsky the famous chapter about the Spanish inquisitor? Ah, well, the only difference between that priest and our Führer is, of course, the stink of actual corpses. . ."

Friedland faltered, vaguely divining that this insight might not be quite suitable for such a romantic moment. He cleared his throat, but the young woman under the lamp still observed him with a quiet smile.

"You remember, in that book, the brothers—the one who believes in God and the one who does not?"

"Alyosha and Ivan?" Hélène said.

"Ivan's voice is the voice of our beliefs. Yes, he says that man's most ancient impulse is to build a world church state. He says that what the majority prefer to a God of conscience is an institution. When your pope helped out our Führer, the supreme priest chose the institution, rather than condemn the faithful to solitude with only God and their consciences. Very soon, one of our heirs will complete the church empire. Science has put the power of extermination in our hands to accomplish such a destiny. Our chief, too, once was an artist, and tried to struggle alone with his conscience and God. He saw the futility of that gamble, and now he is like a great sculptor who lays the human bricks and burns the waste, for the future world of science and mysteries requiring no God!"

Hélène's head and legs were aching. The smoke from their cigarettes drifted in the lamplight above the grand piano. It was seven-thirty. Upstairs in the nursery, Gerta would be turning out the boys' light.

9

"YOU SHOULD TRY ONE OF THESE CHOCOLATES, MARK. WITH SUCH AN INTELLECT, it is surprising that you have not been made Hitler's successor. It must all be true then," she continued quietly. "The gassings, the tortures, the doctors?"

Her visitor nodded wisely, as if acknowledging a fundamental principle of the universe. "Spiders, leopards, and Caesars—all of them poison and dismember. Some great man must make a historic sacrifice of his conscience for the social good and never weaken."

"Your model leader demands that a whole race sacrifice its conscience—in order to destroy the helpless?" Hélène heard herself begin to argue with the *Gruppenführer*.

Even then, lounging at the tea table, Friedland took this riposte to be Hélène's quite natural erotic excitement at his mastery. "Man longs to come close to himself, so he seeks pain. He longs to grow close to others—therefore he needs conquest. For every monastery you build, there will arise a slaughterhouse. Do you see how you inspire me, my dear woman?" he added.

"And I am inspired by you, Herr Friedland."

Without answering further, Friedland suddenly rose to his full height. He walked heavily to the darkened windows. "I wish I did not have to leave before nine. It would have been pleasant to remain for dinner."

"You have not yet been invited," said Hélène, smiling slightly.

Turning quickly from the window, the *Gruppenführer* sank down close to her on the love seat. Without warning, he caught Hélène's hand. With the greatest effort of her life, she overcame the reflex to seize it back out of his grip. Under the lampshade, a brutal male face stared coldly into her eyes. She saw the pores on his nose.

"You are an exceptional woman, my dear."

"Mark, do you recall the end of your inquisitor priest?"

"No." The *Gruppenführer* frowned, but this time he was listening. "Tell me."

"Well, the inquisitor tells Christ that he will execute him again. In reply—" Hélène's voice filled with emotion. "In reply, Christ kisses the inquisitor, who is shaken but does not change his ideas."

Friedland was staring into her face. Before he could reply, Hélène stretched and gently kissed the *Gruppenführer*'s forehead.

The officer sat back with a start, staring at Hélène as if the touch of her lips had reminded him of something, as if he had just found himself blasted out of some furnace room of roasting bodies into this peaceful cool room of books, trays, of his gracious companion. And as Hélène saw his face soften at her side, she could not find in herself one ounce of Christian compassion for the man. This time, she could not keep her terror from showing on her face.

Recovering, he announced, "We are wasting precious time. It is my intention to sleep with you."

Hélène's face had turned bright red, and she was once again a mother bird, beating her broken wing to draw away the predator. Her expression took on a certain wildness. Strange words came to her lips. "Well, Mark," she whispered, radiant with loathing, "I hope you are a powerful lover. I have good breasts, and my legs are even better, and very strong!"

The *Gruppenführer* rose suddenly to his feet, jolting Hélène's chair. "Yes, but for another night. Tonight I must fly to Munich by nine o'clock."

As the Baroness von Sunda held the passage door for her visitor, the six Labradors pushed around to stare at him, their eyelids lowered. Making a visible effort not to kick at the dogs, Friedland clicked his boots and bent to kiss the back of Hélène's averted head.

In the last two hours, Hélène had taken matters into her own hands. This was as bitter to her as if she had renounced her faith in God.

But for *Gruppenführer* SS von Friedland—who had personally over-seen frenzied mass butcherings in eleven Ukranian villages—the full disappointment and desolation of that moment did not strike home until he stepped out of the great house and the warm circle of the baroness's kindness and saw his goggled cyclists waiting on the snow to guide him to his next appointment.

10

THE PASSAGE OF THE POLICE HEADLAMPS OVER THE SNOW HAD BEEN OBSERVED closely from the east cottage. Quartered here was the chief of Oberlinden's *Arbeiters,* along with the two families whom he had restrained from denounc-ing the baroness when she had harbored Yids. Kristof was a monarchist, as proud and independent as a Cossack ataman, who had never before been will-ing to take orders from any woman and who recently had treated his wife badly. Tonight, he noted with satisfaction that the salon and bedroom windows remained dark.

When presently his eyes, too, had turned from the shadow on the hill and the buildings' occupants became lost in their dreams, the light of the moon crept down Oberlinden's great façade, and it began to glow above the frozen orchards and fir forests, like a second moon, anchored to the earth.

Hélène could never afterward bear to recall the state of her mind that night, nor the visions which had passed through it. The moment she was back at dinner with Gerta by the pantry fire, she had understood the danger in which she, a mother, had put her sons. All she could recall now of the violent strug-gle by her mother-in-law's piano was that she had flaunted her contempt for the national hero. Yes, and had *Gruppenführer* Friedland not confessed his authority over her family's movements and his intention to return here after Zurich? At that moment, Hélène's haughty defense of her virtue—of all virtue—appeared to her the luxury of a spoiled child.

Much later that night, she found herself sitting up in bed. Had she been trying to sleep while thinking such thoughts? Surely, Hélène Le Trève was not afraid to join the vigil of millions of terrorized souls that night. Turning on the bedside light, she stared at the photographs of herself in Paris, Mexico, and

Berlin. She examined the one with David and their friends, arm in arm and laughing under the balcony on the rue de Fleurus. In the days ahead, she must be as concentrated, modest, and austere as she remembered Justin to be.

From the moment she switched on the bedroom lights, Hélène had known she would decide to leave Oberlinden. The realization came to her as a lonely desolation—as if she were leaving forever the civilized happiness of her past.

Where is he now? she thought. I am still young. Why did he never answer my letter? For it was not until she heard that her husband might still be alive that Hélène had felt again, like a disaster, the depth of her feelings for Justin.

11

NEXT MORNING AFTER HER BREAKFAST WITH GERTA AND THE BOYS, HÉLÈNE sent word by Gustav to the chief tenants to meet her for apple juice in the trophy room. Here her husband had faced his father during the Hindenburg visit, long before the war. Hélène turned to the men grimly as Kristof led them through the door, her alarm at her own inexperience intensifying. There were also several women in green work clothes, a total of at least thirty sunburnt faces—people she had rarely seen, except during some act of kindness given or received in these difficult times. Though several farmers had sons in Russia, there had been no reaction to the news of her husband's treason. Her eyes rested on Margitta, whose delivery had come just after Albert was born, while the girl had mastitis, and whose baby Hélène had secretly nursed for several days.

All at once, she understood from their embarrassed glances that everyone was aware of the shameful scene with her terrible visitor and knew their French baroness must now leave Oberlinden. Hélène remained quite still with her boots crossed, trying to greet each person, any one now a possible informer, as they came in and smiled at her. Over all this hovered her final acceptance that Berlin's torture racks existed and that her own body was not exempt.

"Yes, yes, Baroness, go on," said the cook's old wife.

"Thank you." For some seconds, as she struggled with her suspicion of these people, Hélène did not trust her voice to say more. "Thank you, my dear friends. As you will hear officially, the Red Army—or it may be the French, the Americans, or the English—will soon be at Oberlinden. The refugees from Poland may reach us in two days. When they come, then you, Kristof, and all your people will be free to go. The rest of you keep working and hide your women, and you should be left alone. As for myself and the children . . ."

Among the old German farmers who blocked Hélène on all sides, there was a rustle and a disapproving murmur, as if their sympathies might lie with the *Gruppenführer!*

"But Baroness." Gustav tapped disapprovingly at a side whisker. "Oberlinden has not been left alone without a Sunda since Napoleon."

"I am a quite ordinary Frenchwoman, but I understand what you mean. I will ask my husband's brother to return from Berlin."

"Baroness, your place is here," said Gustav firmly. "It is not right for you to go. We will not allow you to make this decision."

"How will we plant the new grain, madame?" said Margitta's mother, shaking her handsome gray head.

"I must think of the safety of the Baron's children," Hélène began, and flushed a deep red. She could not fully fathom these people's objection to her freedom of movement. Could it be simply that they cared for her? With a final effort, Hélène banished all doubt.

"*Ja, ja*, Gustav, the children!" cried a woman's voice. "Did you think of them?"

"I shall come back very soon," Hélène offered, as she gave Gustav an imploring smile. And seeing the gamekeeper incline his head, Hélène took two steps forward and began to shake the hands of the men who stood nearest to her. For just five seconds she stared frankly into Kristof's blue eyes, trying to interpret the warning hidden in them, and at last she held his strong rough hand too.

Then the thing was done, and the workers all began noisily to discuss what the young baroness had told them: what for centuries they had been able to avoid considering, yet were now being given the responsibility to understand.

Once the decision had been taken, it was settled that Hélène's best course would be to try and reach the Baltic port of Lübeck, there to put herself and the children at the mercy of the Swedish Red Cross. She and Gustav would take the small Daimler, with enough cans of gasoline from the estate's private stores to complete the five-hundred-kilometer drive. It was during this interval of momentous confusion, with a thousand things to arrange and settle, that Hélène several times found herself sobbing helplessly. As the hour of her flight came near, her two years spent on this hillside awaiting the return of someone called Major von Sunda appeared to her a just and significant duty, even one happily performed. She felt quite capable of submitting further years to it, and even her life if need be. Yet there could be no doubt whatever that the moment had come for the Sunda heirs to go down from Oberlinden.

In this state of mind, late that night, Hélène wrote an emotional letter and left it in the one place where she knew that her husband would look: the leather box containing Arminius's buckle. Once this had been done, she felt a pleasant exhaustion and relief. It was as if she had cut out her heart and was willingly leaving it behind for him at Oberlinden.

Yet even in her last minutes, before she could be set free, there was one more calamity to be endured.

12

HÉLÈNE FIRST HEARD A RUMBLING, LATE ON SATURDAY AFTERNOON, AS SHE paused in the music room. Sails seemed to volley high overhead. In the distance, beyond that noise, she heard an eerie murmur, as of lost souls.

It was only after she had raced to the nursery, collected Albert, along with an inexplicably muddied Rickie, and reached the orchard through the gun room that she heard how, minutes before, her son had somehow been trampled on the east road, and how a bearded man had carried the terrified child home.

The refugee trek was at Oberlinden!

No one among the servants huddled in the tree shadows could tell the baroness where the smoke had first been seen. She stood with them shivering on the snow and hugged Bertie as he screamed for a toy bear he had dropped in the coal chute. Through the bare branches, high above the second-story windows, Hélène saw thirty-meter flames spring and lick beneath the snow clouds. Just then, with a sound like the wind, the weight of snow bore down the roof and the flames vanished. A tiny cheer rose from the little crowd who seconds before had been witnesses to the ruin of Oberlinden.

And so, as if through Hélène's covenant with her husband, the building was saved—not, however, before the fire had gutted the richly decorated south wing and been sucked down the corridor of family portraits, leaping from ancestor to ancestor until it reached the huge canvas of David's father.

But there was no time to search the burned halls. Fifteen minutes later, Hélène had arranged her frightened children and Gerta under a bear rug in the Daimler's back seat. Across the stableyard, a horse that had scented the smoke thundered in its stall. Don't worry, little mare, she thought enviously. You are safe to stay. Then the car, with Gustav at the wheel, rolled into the drive, just as it had done a hundred times before, and an intuition that she should be prevented from leaving grew to a harsh ache in her breast.

"Stop, Gustav, stop!" Climbing back out on the running board, she turned to face the house on the hill. Against the darkening clouds, Oberlinden looked like the only home that Hélène would ever have. Turning then with a final sensation of release, she slammed the door and smiled tenderly at the two pallid faces. "Well, my little morsels!" she sang to them. "Isn't this a fine adventure?"

By now a crowd of fifty or so had gathered in the plum orchard. When they saw the car lights disappear at the gate below, they stopped waving and turned their attention to the seemingly endless stream of refugees, moving along the east road.

"Like mice from a barn!"

"Damn Slovaks, they'll be asking to stay in the manor next!"

"Best to give them what they need for their gobbling."

Felix swung his rifle. "Look at them two *Schweinerei!* Where do they think they're going?"

Where the road emerged from the forest, two small black shapes had detached themselves from the ominously silent mass. As these shadows started up the hill, they became distinct: one quite tall, carrying his pack with a dignified grace, the other short and wiry, stumbling in the snow under an equal bundle. Both wore astrakhan hats and belted sheepskins, sprouting clumps of wool. As the shapes came nearer the orchard wall, the first figure was striding faster and faster, until his companion was left struggling far behind.

13

TEN MINUTES LATER, THE BARON'S CAR HAD ROLLED THROUGH THE VILLAGE, whose folk seemed oblivious to the fire on Templar's Hill and an immense movement of refugees five kilometers away.

All through that night, as they drove northwest from the Thuringian forest into Saxony and on toward Hanover, it seemed to Hélène as if her decision had come too late and that the criminal population had already fled—leaving her between the converging armies, alone with Gustav, Gerta and her sleeping children. In the foul weather no aircraft were flying, and few cars were on the road. The villages and towns lay under an unnatural stillness, through the blackest night that Hélène could remember. The world raced toward their faces—an ice-crusted asphalt lit by hooded headlights—and she could not help dwelling on the *Gruppenführer*'s grotesque boasts and feeling haunted by the horrors that must lie around them in the dark. The clock glowed below the windshield: two o'clock.

"I think I'll sleep, Gustav. Wake me if you get tired."

"No, no, I am too old to get tired." Gustav's face, concentrated ahead to detect bomb craters, softened in the weak green light. In the rear compartment, Gerta lay snoring like a great shapeless doll with the children asleep in her arms. Both boys were sucking their thumbs. Their mother pulled her coat around her. She fixed her eyes on the blackness ahead, a blackness like sleep. Hours without shape began to pass.

Hélène's anxiety over roadblocks vanished after their third stop. The name of Sunda seemed to awaken no more than curiosity and respect. The gleaming Nazi efficiency was breaking down.

A first dull light hung over the eastern tree line when they saw the *Münster* of old Hanover and Gustav halted behind a crossroads barn to refill the fuel tank. As Hélène took the steering wheel, she seemed to feel in its heavy tug the lives of her little family. For several kilometers, it was as if she had forgotten how to drive. A few neatly dressed civilians hurried along the sidewalks, almost as if the waist-high rubble round them were still buildings and shops. Gustav, who had seen no sights such as these for a quarter of a century, stared out with a look of the most violent disapproval. On the back-seat, the boys would not drink their thermos of soup and climbed over the luggage to chatter excitedly at what was outside the windows.

Just then the road was leaving the outskirts of town. A young soldier in a poorly fitting uniform stepped out and held up a gun. The man had wide cheekbones and almost no nose.

"A *Schmeisser*, Mama, a *Schmeisser!*" Rickie hissed in Hélène's ear. Her older boy was excited by guns.

"Should I stop, Gustav?"

"Yes, don't worry," he answered, in a strange voice.

On the empty road, Hélène pulled over to a closed yellow kiosk. There were three other soldiers. The first came around to her side, examining the Daimler with an unpleasant intimacy. The other three peered in at the children and Gerta. Something was said and they laughed. The first smiled thinly at Hélène's papers and waved his leather glove.

"Heil Hitler! You will take us!" he said. With a lunge, the man's black jacket and belt were crushed against her open window. There was a thud above Hélène's head, and the Daimler moved heavily on its springs as the others climbed on the running boards. She saw Gustav's face and her own anger vanished.

"Don't say anything." She moved the shift lever and the gears made a very loud, slowly dying rattle. The car started forward. A frozen wind blew in, scented with mud. All the side windows were blocked by black uniforms and holsters. "Charming fellows," she said, and pushed a strand of long hair out of her eyes. She clutched the wheel.

"Yes, Baroness. They are taking convicts in the army now."

The steering was now so heavy that Hélène could hold the automobile on the road only with her full strength. Were she to halt, this rough fellow might demand to do the driving. Her sons must not see her fear. The steering became lighter when she pushed the speed up to fifty kilometers. There were cars on the road, now, and occasional white trucks painted with large red crosses. The drivers were soldiers in tinted yellow goggles. These were the low countries, and the raised highway crossed flat snowfields, vanishing toward the north horizon under a towering charcoal overcast.

The machine lurched hard on a tank trail of mud. By Hélène's head, a red face appeared upside down. "Go slower"—the mouth worked against the wind—"*slower!*" But before she could slow the Daimler, there was a violent banging on the roof. Not understanding what was expected of her, Hélène pressed hard on the brake pedal.

While the car was still rolling, their four passengers jumped from the running boards and ran, huddling over their guns, down the banks of the road.

"Mama! Where are they going?"

Hélène was twisted around on the seat; the trucks behind them had stopped and soldiers were jumping down also. Then, ahead of her, suspended over the road, she saw a spot the size of a mosquito. Before her heart could beat three times, a pair of pointed wings wider than the road rushed overhead with a drilling whine. The car bounced on its springs; there were pumping blasts. For a moment all was still. Then shrieks came from the backseat and Hélène was holding the wheel, watching the four soldiers strut back to the car. Ahead of them, a truck was on fire. The first soldier's face was haughty and his cheeks twitched. He and Hélène looked at each other. She was just as he had left her. The sight of the helpless and frightened children seemed to worry him.

"Stupid woman, stupid woman!" the man suddenly shouted at her. He pointed the hole of the gun barrel at Hélène's face. "Why did you not get out of the car? Do you want to be killed, stupid woman? Do you want your children to die?"

Having relieved himself with these "stupid woman"s, the soldier turned to the horizons. Then the car swayed on its springs, and the black uniforms were back against the windows. The children, Gustav, and Gerta were all staring at Hélène as if they had just seen her in death. No longer conscious of her own fears, she forced a smile. "Go on! Go on!" she heard a voice shouting from outside.

As she steered them through the heat from the burning truck, the tires drifting slightly on the ice, Hélène felt a sudden emptying calm. The hollow pointing barrel with its sights like a bird's crest, and the soldier's abusive shouts, had left her panting and humbled. As she looked out at this landscape, she thought of Russia and knew David must be dead. A dry snow had begun to settle, gusting across the road. The Elbe ports were close, now, and beyond them the sea.

In the central square at Lüneburg, their four passengers got down beside a waiting convoy. The first soldier walked to Hélène's open window. "Heil Hitler! In Hamburg, the machine will be requisitioned," he added with satisfaction.

On the road out of town, she drew the muddy Daimler over to the curb. "Gustav, please take the wheel." But the gamekeeper was heaving with gruff, moaning sobs.

"That I should see such things in Germany! That I should be too old! I am no man. I wish to be dead. I will kill myself."

Gerta's round face appeared from the backseat, mournful and puffy-eyed. "Shut up, old man!" she said. "Can't you see the young mother needs us?"

On the front seat, Gustav began nodding. "Yes-yes, yes-yes, yes-yes!" He got out. Hélène gripped the wheel, watching her husband's oldest friend walk in little steps around the car. His head was jerking. She slid over on the seat. "Yes-yes, yes-yes!" the gamekeeper muttered, jerking his head so that the snowflakes fell from his eyebrows.

As soon as they were out of Lüneburg and on the open road, Gustav's look of worry returned. The snowfall had stopped. For quite a while now, there had been columns of transports on the road, raising long billows of snow. Then in midafternoon, they saw the giant cranes that line the Elbe. Out to the west, the overcast horizon was becoming infested with very high, slow formations. Rickie leaned into the front seat, his little head against Hélène's cheek.

"Look Mama, look—the big planes are called forts!" he boasted. "The little ones are horses!"

"My dear, sit back with Gerta. Try to rest."

The foreign bombers and their escorts hammered the north German plain with a dull, incessant drone. Moving very slowly from the west, the formations were overtaking the Daimler.

"Look! Look, Mama! They are bombing, you see?"

"Very good, Rickie. Now keep down with Albert." Far ahead of them, above the cranes and green roofs of Hamburg, she saw ladders being lowered . . . these ladders were dangling near the earth. Now they touched it. Back along the highway came the sharp, violent rumble of an electrical storm.

By the time their car turned out onto the Binnenalster, the planes had moved on. Half the city appeared to be on fire, with many thousands at that very hour roasting under the shallow foundations. As when a beehive is disturbed, there was a sort of ordered pandemonium along the streets and arcades. Crowds of dazed figures milled under the bare trees, helping one another, or huddled with their possessions, or rushed about in black helmets. Twice, near the ruined *Rathaus*, Hélène saw smoking platforms, built of rails and stacked with clothing and irregular shapes that she only slowly recognized to be bodies.

"Gerta!" she called behind her, with a strange guttural urgency. And hearing her, Gerta opened her arms like a mother bear, enfolded the children's staring faces, and crushed them almost out of sight against her shapeless bulk.

14

WHEN AT LAST THEY CAME TO THE OLD RIVER PORT OF LÜBECK, THE BOYS WERE asleep. Gustav drove the car on to Travemünde along the heavily overcast Baltic estuary, the water covered with support ships of the *Prinz Eugen,* evacuating troops from the east. The convoy floated in the night like ducks turned to the wind.

The Swedish Red Cross was a three-story sailor's home. In her fur coat, Hélène pushed past two local policemen and continued on through a hall filled with oil-stained stretchers.

She found the head surgeon, called Elvström, behind a corner bed. Possessed since Lüneburg by an overwhelming passion to live and to reach

Paris with her children, Hélène stood with perfect alertness at the foot of an unconscious sailor. She stared at the boy's blackened arm and full red lips. The arm had burst, as a sausage bursts, from the shoulder to the wrist where the arm ended. Under the lampshade the Swedish doctor's fingers worked with a hooked needle and pliers. Presently though without pausing, Dr. Elvström peered up at her. This man to whom Hélène had brought all her hopes looked old, with an unsympathetic set to his mouth. A terrible thought gripped her. *What if the stories of Swedish Red Cross neutrality were untrue?*

"Can't you see I'm busy?" Elvström shouted. After several more minutes, his hand moving more and more slowly, the Swede sighed again. He peered at her coat. "Are you a doctor, eh? Can you do stitches?"

She shook her head angrily, and the man snorted. For with all the things she had seen in her flight across Germany, too many and too pitiful to be absorbed—and after her war years, spent helpless at a country seat—Hélène wished only that she could have answered him, *Yes*. Now, as she stood there at the bed, Hélène swore that, were she and her children granted life in the days to come, she would learn these things.

"All right, come along then."

They went through the tiled passage to an office, decorated with schooner hulls. Dr. Elvström sat behind the desk and yawned deeply.

"Thank you, you are very kind," Hélène began in French, and she yawned too. Across the street, she could see her sons' faces in the car window, talking with the two Gestapo agents in leather coats. Then the boys vanished and Gustav's face appeared.

"Be quick!" The surgeon said quietly.

"Dr. Elvström, my two children and I are in danger."

The man behind the desk made an angry gesture. "First, tell me your name!"

"Oh, yes. I am Hélène von Sunda."

"Surely, you are joking! . . . I see you are not." Dr. Elvström leaned forward, examining her face. "Then you are speaking of *The* Sundas, who are in the conspiracy mess. Goebbels made another *Gewitter* broadcast just last Sunday. Tell me in that case, how recently you have spoken to a relative of yours—that is, to Friedrich Sunda?"

Freddy, of the tea-dances in Saint-Moritz, known in this Baltic town? "My brother-in-law? Perhaps two weeks ago."

"You understand the Red Cross maintains a network as regards war crimes? It's confirmed . . . the executions are continuing in Berlin. Hélène, is that your name? I can think of no way to put such a thing gently. Your brother-in-law was killed—crucified—perhaps even today."

The Frenchwoman had given a whimpering cry. Now, hiding her face with her hand, she began to plead softly in a voice filled with tears, as if to someone else in the room. Elvström thought he caught the name "Friedland."

Rising from his chair, he walked up and down past the dark windows, occasionally glancing at the woman slumped at his desk. The impulse to yawn had entirely left him. "This is all I can do for you. Just across the street there is a staff room with three beds empty, but only for tonight. In five days a medical-supply ship should arrive from Stockholm. If so, you could travel as Captain Pol's guest. . . . Here, do not despair. Take a good drink," Elvström added softly.

Five minutes later, Hélène walked slowly to the car. The two Gestapo were not in sight. Her family watched her expectantly as she explained their good luck over the Swedish ship. The children's hurt looks deepened when later Hélène excused herself from putting them to bed.

At last she could go alone into the night. She did not stop until she had stumbled out to the harbor, along the ice-encrusted breakwater, to the extremity of Europe. Then at last Hélène—mother now of the remaining Sundas—let out her breath, and deep vomiting sobs tore at her until she felt that she would drown in tears. Below her feet, the arctic swell rhythmically rose and sank, advancing in huge, slow, muscular pulses to lose its power in the calm circle of the port. As she thought of Friedrich crucified, Hélène's body experienced his torture as her own. Waves of hatred rolled up in her, as she fought to rediscover the world she loved, her hearth and her family. All these things were being taken from her methodically, as if by the design of the fool in the Reichstag. A politician! A man who, as if he sensed the disgust and embarrassment of good people, had methodically set out to track down and poison their happiness with his power to outrage.

For a long time, crouched on stone steps that were almost like a love seat, while a hooded signal light on the hulk of the *Prinz Eugen* flickered serenely, Hélène groaned with this disease of hatred. Once again she thought of Friedrich, what it meant, and how it must have been. But there was nothing in her experience to compare such suffering to, and without wiping her tears she began to cry out of pity for him. Somewhere below her shoes the Baltic swell rose, then sank down deep to suck at the foundations of the continent.

Hélène sat, alone, until she felt her legs begin to freeze, and wept for all the poor lost world of people, the dream of Europe which she had lived for and loved, all of them gone now forever.

15

THE RETIRED LÜBECK COUPLE, HERR AND FRAU RUDOLFUS, COLLECTORS OF antique harpsichords, were no less suspicious than the citizens of a thousand other European towns, poisoned by *Nacht und Nebel* and now infested with spies and informers.

By night, the baroness and her family were kept bolted in the dining room with blankets and mattresses. At first the two boys were sympathetic and well-behaved, and Gerta tried to discover what had come over their mother. But Rickie and Albert quickly became disobedient. Not until dawn on the third morning, after a big air raid on the fleet, when the Swedish boat might be almost at Travemünde, did Hélène at last fall into a deep sleep.

She awoke on the dining room floor to an urgent rapping, followed by the violent rattle of latches. Through the stained glass, Hélène could see a hall light on. She heard the sound of Gustav's protests, then of other—threatening male voices. After so many days of torment, she scarcely found the will to struggle with the blissful weight that held her down on the mattress.

Without thinking to cover her nightgown, Hélène stepped over her children to the vestibule doors. Crowded between the thickly hung coats were several harsh-looking men. She stared in defeat at a wiry person with sunken eyes and high cheekbones who had cupped the lightbulb in his hands. His companion politely pushed Gustav aside and faced Hélène. The man was about forty, with considerable gray hair on his temples and a terrible but distinguished face, seemingly cut into by the effects of great hardship—the kind of face to hang resisters by their thumbs and crucify men of principle.

"Never mind, Gustav," she said soberly, remembering the *Gruppen-führer*'s threats. She had left her name at every checkpoint across Germany. As he heard her voice, an odd gravity came over the face of the second man. He halted three steps from her and freed his hands from his coat. Something was happening in Hélène. Her eyes followed the outline of his features. The man took one step closer under the light, and for Hélène the rest of the room and the other faces all vanished, and there was only this one impossible face.

"Hélène," the man said, gently, as if he were speaking to a child.

Hélène breathed in. But tears rushed to her large eyes anyway. "David," she whispered, and the walls around her swayed. And though he was not Justin, and now there never would be Justin, Hélène raised her arms uncertainly and rested her hands against the man's sloping shoulders. She hung her head. Deep, tender sobs tightened in her breast.

"Oh, David," she moaned.

The man moved against her. She felt strong, gentle, thoughtful arms close around her.

"Hélène, my little Hélène, my beloved. Hélène . . . Hélène . . . Hélène."

16

ON THAT MORNING IN LÜBECK AFTER THE SUNDAS' REUNION—SHROVE TUESDAY, as Dresden lay waiting to be bombed to the ground—an expectant silence reigned inside the sunny lace of the Rudolfuses' narrow rooms. Gerta had moved the children out of the dining alcove so David and Hélène could be alone. She patrolled the house like a sacristan until noon, red-faced and often in tears, making threatening gestures at anyone—even the Rudolfuses—who dared break the silence. In those very unusual circumstances, she and Gustav even forgot the unpleasant first impression that the Pole called Otto had made on all of them, and they questioned him about the baron's escape from Russia. And Otto, who showed an embarrassing awe of his new friends, was only too eager to describe their arrival at Oberlinden with the refugee column. Just after noon, soft voices were heard behind the dining room glass. In a few minutes, the doors opened.

When Hélène stepped through after David into the vestibule, the children pressed against her. Her cheeks were pink, and the softness in her eyes made her look almost too young to be a mother. The man was the first to break their silence.

"Well, Rickie . . . Albert?" David said.

The two wide-eyed boys came forward, and Albert kissed his father's cheeks. With a glance toward Gerta, Rickie walked unsteadily to the stranger with the frightening eyes, who waited now on one knee. Turning sideways, the boy allowed his father to take him in his arms. No one in the little vestibule spoke or moved.

"My dear old Gerta. And Gustav—ever more dashing," David continued softly.

The gamekeeper could not restrain his emotion. Seizing the baron by the ears, he kissed him on both cheeks. Gerta's red face was hidden in her handkerchief.

"Hélène?" David turned, holding his small son clasped high on his arm. "This is Otto, without whom I would not be here. Otto, this is the finest person I have known, who is also my wife."

"Ah, yes!" cried Otto, in his loud voice. "How do you do, madame?"

Hélène smiled pleasantly, overcoming a flutter of alarm. She felt her hand grasped with unnatural force. Then she lifted her eyes to examine by light of day this man who had changed so little, yet so much. Once he had accepted the death of his parents, David would still have to hear about his brother and about Johannes. Hélène wondered where she would find the strength to tell him. But now they were discussing what should be done.

The Swedish surgeon had not spoken to Baron Sunda of the medical ship. In the end, it might be more dangerous to board one of the July plotters in broad daylight—and risk submarines in a Baltic crossing—than simply to remain where they were. Two or three weeks from now, the Western Allies would be in Lübeck.

Here, there was a basement with a furnace. As for their aged hosts—Otto laughed a complicit laugh—a large bribe could be given. The old burghers would feel flattered to assist a member of the highest nobility, and of course Otto would keep close watch over them. After ten years of terror, another three weeks couldn't matter. When she heard the plan and sensed what deception might be necessary from all of them, even with such a gentle old couple as the Rudolfuses, Hélène dropped her eyes and stared at her hands.

17

THE ONE FAMILY THAT STILL BORE THE NAME SUNDA SPENT THE FINAL MONTHS OF the war in a dark cellar at Lübeck, seated hand in hand on a broken couch before a rumbling furnace, almost as once, long ago, in the Le Trèves' garden, they had talked of the glorious moments to come. But Hélène was overwhelmed—when finally she chose the moment to tell David of Johannes and of his brother's horrible end—to see her husband not lose his self possession. At that moment it came to her that this man, whom she must trust completely, was not telling the truth.

In her sleep, Hélène dreamt of a time when their souls might have floated side by side—as naturally as two leaves, which fall from the same tree onto a current too deep and strong for leaves to influence but which, even when jostled apart, follow each other, bound by time and similarity. David and Hélène had emerged still in sight of each other yet too remote for the tensions of intimacy to draw them together. What was it then, this place where he had been? When she thought of their first soundless passion on this dining-room floor, in the intimacy of her family, Hélène felt a novel horror. Hearing the old Rudolfuses cluck piously that Europe was now *Judenrein,* she would glance at her husband's face, half expecting him to be someone else.

Somehow, they had not touched again. A gentle disagreement emerged, which to Hélène seemed evidence of how far apart now their two souls were floating. Soon David spoke of his father's Will, which he had found at Oberlinden. In spite of the loss of far more extensive holdings, the old baron had inexplicably turned over the working lands to the tenant farmers, and it was becoming clear that they would be left with little more than the noble architecture itself. Hélène found it blasphemous not to accept this as enough, after the miracle of their survival. But it emerged that, since Poland, her husband had been discussing with Otto how they might rebuild the Sunda fortune. He repeated to her the story of how a boy had renounced the virtue of family tradition. This seemed to David now the one deep, pure, underground flow that ran beneath history.

Germany was ruined and would be absorbed into Europe. Europe would be absorbed into a larger western society. He, David Sunda, was the present custodian of that underground river of devotion and honor. When she heard her husband speak with gentle intensity of such things, Hélène thought of the two leaves floating apart, out toward death, and she was overcome by the desolation and futility of such a life.

Awakening one morning in March, she felt at once the change in the sound from the streets overhead.

"Listen, *chéri*, do you hear? . . . Can it be over?"

In the cellar they were all awake now, peering at David, apprehensive as convicts or hospital patients as they faced the life outside.

"*The English*," he observed, as a man in the desert might say *water!* "I must see these English." And springing up the stairs then, Baron Sunda did see them through the lace curtains. His pallid family gathered blinking outside the door in the warm spring sun. David drank in the grins of the gaunt Tommies, faces confident, as if they were bringing parliamentary justice to the world. He listened to the rustle of boots in the absolute silence, the first free men they had seen in the seven years since leaving Mexico. In that silence, the Sundas crowded timidly with the bare-headed Germans, as if they had forgotten the meaning of freedom. All except Otto, who seemed possessed by a demon bent on finding the means, hidden and never quite dishonest, to arrange almost anything.

So it was on that same spring evening, that David's family, along with Otto, Gustav, and Gerta, sat hidden between two American tanks when a transport train rolled off the Lübeck docks and wound slowly on to the main line toward Hamburg, Hanover, Stuttgart, and the Rhine. These cities, and the legendary river of the Teutonic people, were now in free territory.

18

FOR MONTHS, ACROSS MANY THOUSAND TOWNS FROM THE PACIFIC TO NORMANDY, the war had been receding. Only this was still far from being peace, and never would be for those who had once known war, its horrors and its furnaces. In a vast diaspora, the unpunished gangs were returning, millions strong, to their ruined homes—awoken from their pagan dreams and humanized by the truth—to devote themselves to forgetfulness. Across plains and mountains awakening from the deranged sleep of *Nacht und Nebel*, men and women found themselves abruptly alone with their neighbors, their families, and their victims—and with the ruin of their memories. Everywhere, in the oblivious throngs, lovers with sealed lips saw each other for the first time.

Meanwhile, in the final encirclement of the skull palaces that once had been Berlin, the thundering flicker of guns continued night after night—and the liberators hung back, as if disbelieving the Hydra they had cornered in this shoal. So, like psychiatrists not quite confident of their own sanity, the liberating generals coaxed their immense armies near the smoking city. And as Jakob Stodel's death furnaces finally died, there was nothing to be gathered but the ashes of many millions of lives.

On 1 April, the western armies reached the line of the Elbe. Three weeks later, Marshal Zhukov's divisions closed around Berlin. In two more days, Marshal Konev's men shouted and waved to American troops across the Elbe. The same evening, Mussolini was fleeing with his mistress on the road to Lake Como—where their bodies would be riddled with bullet holes by Italian partisans and returned to hang in Milan's Piazzale Loreto. Also that night, at his quarters in the Kremlin, Stalin was performing a habitual ceremony. After being notified that Hitler was at last within his grasp, and his revenge thus complete, Stalin opened a good bottle of Georgian wine, drank it down, and went to bed. Among the cratered boulevards and the roofless façades by Berlin's Tiergarten, there was no sign of anything particularly unpleasant. Buried under the Chancellory's shaggy lawn, Hitler was once again experiencing the difficulty of hiding from himself the sense of his own insignificance. Hitler felt an overpowering urge to talk.

Yes, the spectacle was over. The nameless actors on whom his power depended were dead or had returned to their homes. But was he not still important enough to have an entire planet clamor for his death? Of this Hitler felt proud. However, he did feel unease that his world-historical performance might be distorted or diminished in some way. Now at the hour of his reckoning, he experienced a vague and fading illusion of having glimpsed his immortal image reflected on the face of the world. As for the image of himself that the world might see him now—just a man sitting down to a plate of spinach, followed by chocolate cake.

Now, like bees to a hive, his ideas were returning to him, cursing and brooding thirty feet underground, to dance their news. News that the earth, the plains and the mountains, were not with him; neither were the skies and the sea nor the hearts of men. And as the returning ideas danced their news, it was that his death would leave behind only this—an anger to burn forever in the minds of men. In the hive of Hitler's mind, there was an angry swarm of visions, as when the exit has been sealed up.

SMITH

1

O N 15 December 1944, Duncan Penn had almost come to them through the tunnel of violence: to Hélène and to David, to Justin and to Luz.

That evening, Major Penn was on the Our, one thousand meters above the German lines and no great distance from the position occupied by Jean-Marc Le Trève's regiment on the afternoon that he received General Guderian's tank assault at Sedan. Tonight, as chief of staff, Guderian was observing from the Maybach camp, south of Berlin. Hitler himself was a fifteen-minute flight to the northeast of Major Penn, at Giessen.

In full battle gear, Duncan lay alert in his bag and listened for Bach among the lonely sounds in Europe's settling snow. Henry Virgin had left for Christmas in Paris only hours before, but the soft humor of Duncan's one friend in the company seemed long since to have died. Tonight, hearing the shouts from Ceppi's all-night crap game, and a sound like sifting sand from the forest overhead, he thought of his wife.

Duncan knew now—a wisdom that had advanced slowly, almost with the swing of his legs during the long marches north from Salerno—that in Paris he had courted Eustacia-Jane Wick only through the depth of what he felt for Hélène Le Trève. It seemed incredible that he had spent his student years in Hélène's company without once having thought to put himself before David or Justin, or even Johannes. Quite possibly tonight, Duncan was the last of the four still alive—with Hélène not far ahead, and nothing to stand between them but the cornered hoodlums of the Third Reich. It no longer hurt him to imagine the American woman who had betrayed him with their child, amid a life of wealth in his penthouse on Manhattan's East River. After the blood-soaked journey of the past years, such images no longer had the power to make Duncan suffer. He would never go home.

Duncan woke with a shock of pain to his ears. Before he could move, the tent canvas crushed tight over his lungs.

The first shell had torn into the roots of the big pine at five-thirty, bringing it down on the radio tent. Fifty seconds and many pounding shocks later,

Major Penn cut his way into the frozen air and clung to a fallen branch. Legs ran in front of the burning trees. As he started toward the radio tent, scared faces lifted around him.

The low cloud mat glowed yellow with searchlights, making a corridor to the north and south. There were no planes. Duncan's limbs jerked with the flow of grief turning to hatred—pity, too, for these men who would never understand the land that they must die in. Behind them, in the sky over Reisdorf, where the war reporters would be, a giant shadow was twisting up like ocean kelp.

"Tilton, get me Colonel Smith on the line. I want witnesses."

"I've got Diekirch here, Major."

They swung their arms to keep warm as Smith's Iowa voice crackled abuse: something about the Ivy League. Tilton met his eyes, smiling a little.

"No, Colonel!" Duncan was shouting. "You can't hold them if we can't. They'll go right to Bastogne!"

"Major Penn!" The radio made a rude noise. "I want you to withdraw south with the rest of the Twenty-sixth!"

"You listen to me, Smith! You put us here—I'm going to stay. I expect another two hundred men to be sent up within the hour!" Duncan was almost insane with disappointment that it could be like this. A first pulse of drab light was relieving the weight of darkness. The radio went dead.

By ten o'clock, Major Penn's unit had dissuaded three attempts by a brigade strength of Grenadiers to cross the Our. During these clattering exchanges, down across the fields of snow to the far bank where the little gray figures had swarmed out, the men saw their major walk up and down over their outstretched legs, grinning and encouraging them by name.

After the second attempt on the river below the bridge, the tension of overcaution left the unit. An important day had begun for the world. They had stood their ground. To the north the enemy was breaking through, and parachutists had dropped into Reisdorf. Back on the ridge, Major Penn did not talk about how they must be surrounded. At exactly eleven o'clock he was on the dugout planks next to Tilton, watching through a periscope.

"Sir, what do you think they're trying to prove?"

"They're trying for a knockout here. Then they can concentrate on the Reds."

"That's crazy. Why don't they just surrender?"

"Nobody's letting them surrender. They beat us and we beat them, you know the history. Then they started another war, tortured a few million people, and sent children to slaughterhouses. Now we're winning, and nobody's going to let them surrender. It's human nature."

"That's bad. Human nature is bad."

"I hate it," Duncan said, and he meant the poison in his veins that Hélène must never see.

Across the bridge below, where the road wound from behind a steep hill, a long-legged Wehrmacht officer had stepped out backward with one arm raised; then the arm fell, the figure turned. Duncan had pivoted the field glasses along the river, and he saw a second line of figures running from the forest: the soldier thugs of Sedan, Warsaw, Leningrad, and Smolensk, the hero gangs and hired killers of Saloniki, Kiev, and Salerno. Now the hard-running mob was three-quarters of the way across the open. Duncan took the bullhorn. He could just see the dark line of the dugout down to the left.

"You men in the dugout!" Duncan's voice crackled into the gorge. "Shofner, get those men up here! Damnation, Katovsky, hit the bridge!"

As they watched, Katovsky got a direct hit but the bridge remained standing. Along the ridge, Major Penn saw faces turn toward him. A thousand yards below them, the Germans were pouring out on the near bank. He could see their long coats flapping around their knees and the personality of each stride.

"All right, men, very good! Now fall back. We'll dig in at the narrows! Fall back!"

Of the three hundred men who had slept on that ridge, face to face with the Exterminating Angel, one hundred lay perfectly still where they had been for the last six hours. By noon, the men who had not gotten rides were running back down the Sûre road alongside trucks, flak guns, ambulances, and jeeps. The two Sherman tanks reversed slowly behind, protecting the retreat from the Our bridge.

The advance, by two hundred thousand Germans, had already overrun Generals Patton and Hodges for up to fifteen kilometers without convincing opposition—except on the ally's extreme left, facing the SS Myrmidon, Sepp Dietrich. The whip-wielding Dietrich from Johannes Godard's boat ride to Goebbels's villa was now a German hero.

2

At Versailles, it was not until late that afternoon as they digested a lunch of Châteaubriand, pommes-dauphinois and Mouton-Rothschild—with some pleasurable talk of the victories ahead—that Dwight Eisenhower and Omar Bradley were informed that Hitler was embarking on a third historic breakthrough in the Ardennes passes. After some concentration, the two commanders concluded that this was a spoiling maneuver and must soon peter out. At roughly the same hour, Field Marshal Model committed his seven tank divisions—one thousand tanks, bringing his forces to twelve divisions.

At three o'clock on the Reisdorf road, it was as if the glaciers of the Bernese Oberland had come down to earth.

The road made a tight S to cross the frozen river, between granite cliffs that funneled the wind. In the roar of the gale and from the waterfall Major

Penn heard no gunfire, but he could see the stone splinters strike off the rock face. Here the angle would be wrong for mortars, and there was too much wind for flamethrowers. Planes, probably, Duncan thought; then a rear attack up the road from Reisdorf. As the Wehrmacht drove him backwards, he hardened in his resolve.

The sun was low when Tilton and two other men, Ceppi and Rickles, bricked the mines. Ceppi pointed up at the sky. More planes.

"Okay . . . okay!" Major Penn waved toward the helmet of a soldier called Gifford, on the lead tank. A small avalanche loosened by a bomb high overhead broke over the first turret. It flew past in a white plume, stinging Duncan's face with ice particles. Then twelve bombs came walking through the ravine.

An instant later, Duncan was curled against Tilton. The ice mud that he was biting, that his fingers and boots were clawing into like a blind puppy, seemed to be everywhere. "Ohgodogodogodogod!" he shrieked, hearing around him the shouts and crying of a hundred other voices. He climbed to his feet and fell on his back. Then he knelt on the sparkling crystals, lurched against a trunk, and fell on his back. He was soaking hot. His helmet was off. Duncan staggered up against the tree.

In the gully below, watching him from a snow crater, were about thirty of his men. A stupid, nasal German shouting floated to them from the road. Clustered reflections flashed and flickered among the smoke and trees.

The thirty men, out of three hundred, arrived one hour later at a stone farmhouse flanking the Reisdorf road. Everything around them was clear and taut and cold as ice. Five other men had appeared. These were the rear pickets that Duncan had put out at noon. They had a hand radio. The leader, a bony forty-year-old sergeant from Nebraska, gazed around him speechless as he went to work with the radio. At the thought of the football heroes that Colonel Smith kept at the rear, Duncan felt sick and his teeth chattered.

"Yes! Oh, lord, get me Smith on the line," Duncan panted into the box.

"Who is this?" crackled the familiar voice. It sounded strained and urgent in the moonlight.

"Penn, it's Major Penn!"

There was a very long silence.

"Major. Where are you?"

"A farmhouse, about two miles from Reisdorf. I've lost most of the men—also, we stopped three tanks at Bridge Two." He paused. "Isn't it time you sent someone to get us out of here?"

Under the vine arbor, the men looked at him. A jamming signal made the box squeal in Duncan's hand. A hysterical voice jabbered in German before Smith came back more faintly.

"Major, I would consider that the greatest honor . . . the sons of bitches have us cut off. . . . I have five men left. Last heard . . . Krauts past Ettelbruck, on their way to Bastogne."

"Fine, then—fine, fine."

"I should have listened to you. Major Penn."

"Don't say that, just don't say that!" Duncan shouted.

"Goodbye, Major."

"Goodbye then, Smith."

Across that long night, the artillery got farther and farther away. That the enemy did not know they were still here made the men feel lost, and they were hungry and tired. At midnight, when they had just discovered a cider barrel in the basement, Ceppi climbed back through the vine terraces. The Germans were coming once again.

It was then, after fifty million had died, that Major Penn understood the killing was over for him. Yet the habit was still there, like insomnia. Duncan knew now he would never tell Hélène how close to her he had traveled.

The moon and the stars were out. The Reisdorf road was plainly visible where it crossed the fields. A small column of German infantry was moving along in the moonlight, the stragglers clear of the dark forest.

Seated at the wall outside the farmhouse, Major Penn aimed at the disciplined line of helmets—like a string of pearls in the moonlight—and he squeezed the handles. The gun pounded against his palms. The tracers, quick-thrown, arched over the field like fireflies and bounded up toward the stars. But Duncan did not watch the fireflies through his tears, as he concentrated fire along the string of helmets flopping onto the road, until the action jammed.

The forests were very still. Out on the road where the column had been, it was still. A thick oily flame arched toward their position in the vineyard, lighting up the blanket of snow. The strong wind broke it up, the flames showering over the field in a thousand flickering beads. Sobbing quietly for a salvation now lost forever, the privileged scion of Long Island summers stared at a new reflection by the flamethrower—of a moon. This earthbound moon flashed and his platoon's vine rows were like witches flooded with light. A barrage started in.

Then the planes will come, Duncan thought, rolling on his back. Let it be soon. He should have taken the helmet off before his head started swelling—now it would not come off. He felt very sick.

3

MAJOR PENN DID NOT WAKE FOR MANY HOURS AFTER THE DORNIERS HAD COME and gone, killing most of the men among the vines below. It was first dawn. The sun was warm on his cheek, and Duncan could no longer hear Hélène at her piano. Cullie's bloodied face watched him kindly from under the farm window. Dying now, Major Penn felt a hand on his arm. The giant Nazi tank they called a Royal was twenty yards away, mashing methodically over the tattered fatigues of the soldiers he had loved. Now Duncan was on his knees among the blinding ice. He crawled forward to halt the falling treads. How quickly the evening had come.

And that was the last thought that came to Duncan Penn—who had hated heroes and heroics, and who was now a hero—before his skull broke. Unknown to Justin, Hélène and David, or Luz, he had almost returned to them.

This detail in the overrunning of the Reisdorf road, leading to Bastogne and to the Meuse, was part of what General Manteuffel and other military experts called mopping up. By that night, the 2nd and Panzer Lehr divisions had driven the fifty kilometers to Bastogne. On the night of the nineteenth, almost at Spa, the SS 1st division was blocked and held, just three hundred meters away from a thirty-two-million-liter oil dump. On Christmas Day, the tanks of the most violent army of conquest of all time lay stalled without fuel along the roads of Luxembourg and Belgium.

NEW WORLD

1

IN EARLY APRIL, SPRING RAINS CAME TO PARIS.

Across the Latin Quarter, waiters looked out of their windows, occasionally emerging to poke the bulge under an awning with broom handles.

Then the winds passed, and the columns of rain like falling clouds, which Justin had seen as he looked from his bed across the red gables to Montmartre, became a thundering loom that wove a veil over the chalk-white temple of Sacre Coeur. Water poured on to the window ledge, and a warm spray dampened his bedcovers. Outside, the rain beat the ground, overflowing the gutters all down Montmartre and Montparnasse, and from every grating arose a sound like subterranean torrents. Between the island's narrow street and the facing embankment, Justin could see the river, thrashed to a perfect flat surface like silver wool.

During the recent months—as the wounds of Carbonne began at last to heal—he had lain by this window of a private clinic on the Isle de la Cité. When Justin first arrived in an ambulance from the American lines, he had been too weak to resist Luz's wish to keep him alive, and to pay for this out of money which she said had been in her father's will. Later, he did not have the strength to question her. Altogether, Justin had been at the clinic six months, and he felt a great urgency to be released.

From this window he had seen the banks of the Seine crowded with American soldiers. He had heard how General de Gaulle had paced alone across the Place Notre Dame, without taking notice of the bullet fired by a sniper. In this neighborhood of rich *collabos,* there were sometimes six heads thrust out of windows to exchange the latest news of the armies.

The great numbers who had sold themselves—though not selling enough of themselves to be shot or to have their heads shaved—found it easy to forget and to join in the immense daily festivals of the streets.

But to Justin Lothaire, who had forgotten nothing, least of all his failure to remain among the dead, this masquerade of hypocrites was the hardening foundation of a new world. Hitler was still alive, and his accomplices were on the run with their lives across the planet. These at last were the days of justice.

In September, at the time that de Gaulle had met the Council of Resistance to declare the restoration of the Third Republic, Justin had been delirious. Now seven months had passed, and his hunger to find the meaning of his acts had grown to a fever. Never before had Justin gone to bed for any reason other than love or sleep. Yet after having hurried out on three occasions to see certain people, each time collapsing in a cold sweat and despair, Justin had to postpone his role.

This evening, after trying briefly to concentrate on an inaccurate list of resisters to be given the French Légion d'Honneur—which a *sale bicot* had not been offered but would have declined—Justin put the paper down. He had been approached a hundred times over the last months by journalists and politicians, bringing documents like this, wanting interviews, or hoping to win Justin's support. For a time it had relieved his solitude to remember Marcel Doré, when he had been a fallen oracle, and to reply modestly to their questions. But Justin had been struck dumb to hear, retold to him, his execution during a blizzard of Jakob Stodel.

The first time he had read the article in *Le Figaro,* Justin had experienced an almost delirious nausea. He knew now that while he had been with Stodel in the ice meadow—an SS *Einsatzgruppe* from the Smolensk front had rounded up one hundred of the children, women, and men of Carbonne and had burned them in Baptiste Duroc's church. Despite the dozens of shrapnel fragments that he could name in his body, Justin could barely locate his soul's disfigurement in the newspaper's clear reportage of commitment and of dying. It was as if Carbonne were some legendary town, now sinking in an orgy of lies and corruption among the streets of civilization.

At the dark corner of his ward, the night nurse had quietly shut the door. When she saw Justin's eyes on her bobbed blonde hair, her cap like a paper seabird, and on her tennis figure in its blue and white uniform, the girl's face darkened. She hid this with a motion of her finger to her lips.

Anneke had come from Quebec among the Red Cross personnel who followed the invasion, and she had been posted to this clinic with a pitifully wounded leader of the Jura Maquis. Anneke had no sins to remember, other than being loved by her French mother and her Dutch father and having become a nurse. The girl was very lonely in Paris, and she had been profoundly and selflessly kind. She was the one thing that Justin knew was not part of the world growing sick outside this clinic.

She advanced with professional glances round at the sleeping bishop and banker occupying the other beds. "Brr, it's cold and wet. Silly man, look. Your bed is wet from the rain."

"You might have to change it for me."

She ignored his words.

"If only I had a room to myself." He was forced to whisper.

"Lucky for me that you don't have," Anneke said, and she gazed very seriously into his face. Sitting down, she began to rock her hip against the side of the mattress. Her blue eyes fell to her watch. Then without taking her finger from Justin's wrist, she stared blindly at the undercarriage of the banker's bed.

Justin was unable to speak. How was it that someone had come to him now who was like both Melanie and Rosa, someone with whom he had fallen in love so much more easily than he had fallen in love with Hélène? How was it that a girl he scarcely knew treated Justin with greater devotion than any other human being had, and at a time when his life was strewn with corpses? With more gentleness than Justin had ever seen in himself, he watched the faint rise and fall under the blue uniform of the nurse's ribs. He knew his presence held the girl in Paris, but she had not yet accepted this.

Now Anneke looked confused. Her hand moved on his wrist, and Justin saw that she had finished counting. She glanced up at him with alarm. Then her face softened with a little laugh of intimacy and pleading. Justin smiled warningly and rested his fingers on hers.

She was as simple and natural and sweet as cool milk, and all his despair fixed on her and drank it in. She pulled her hand loose and rose.

"You see, here is your wife," she whispered, and for Justin all the mysterious sensations of that Paris dusk receded.

2

LUZ'S EVENING VISIT WITH THE CHILD HAD WOKEN THE WARD. IN THE BRIGHT light, her husband was forced to nod and wave to the bishop and the banker, both of whom pretended to admire Justin Lothaire. Also as usual, the old men were enthusiastic about this wet-haired actress in an English raincoat. Justin saw the night nurse's humility before his wife's great classical grace, and he felt wounded.

"You have impressed them, Luz."

"Don't be unpleasant. Why spoil things?"

Justin examined her face and thought, What has happened to this beautiful woman in Budapest? How did she escape with the child back to Lucerne? These expensive clothes were not from Paris. The little girl allowed Justin to lift her on to the bedsheets.

"That's right, Sarah. You are very like your papa," Luz murmured, watching him with a strained smile.

The night nurse had gone and the ward was silent. Pushing her blonde curls back against his freshly bandaged chest, the little girl peeked up into her father's melancholy eyes. So they had been since the hour at the military hospital when Justin had first seen Luz with his legitimate child of Rochet's farm. He had felt then how deeply, after himself, he might also mistrust the circle of their friends. Justin had been overwhelmed to discover such an obstacle along the return to his life. Just now, as this family of three whispered by the corner bed, observed by a bishop and a banker, he was scarcely able to follow what was said. Who was this little being who looked so deeply and with such expectation into his eyes? Finally, he glanced around and Eli Hebron was in the doorway, waiting with his hands crossed.

"Heavens, I almost forgot!" Luz flushed as she rose with Sarah's hand in hers.

"Go ahead, Luz. What is it?"

"I left behind a letter from Leni, Hélène Sunda. She and David are in Basel. They will arrive here next week."

Sunda, alive . . . and Hélène? Lying on the humid sheets, Justin felt his heart begin to race painfully. He scarcely took in the fact that Luz had waited a whole hour to tell him such a thing. He did not watch her give her hand to the two old men, then bend to kiss his friend as he stood in his water-stained jacket.

The bishop and the banker feigned sleep so not to notice this obvious *maquisard*'s uncouthness. Eli had seen, and only just escaped, the final events at Carbonne, and there were streaks of gray in his long hair. His eyes watered and his voice often went hoarse. Tonight, he was having difficulty staying seated on the window chair.

"Take off the jacket, Eli." Justin lay very still, to ease the beat of his heart.

"I will, then" Eli glanced toward the banker's back. "Justin, Luz is very happy with you."

"I did not ask for that."

"Listen, *compagnon!*" The visitor raised a finger and stared at Justin's torn ear. "If you were not also a north star to women, how could you be so to yourself?"

Justin laughed with a terrible remorse. "Oh, Eli, Eli . . . however, let me hear what you discovered. I need to hear all of it."

Through the last weak light falling over Eli's bowed head, Justin could see the branches outside sway under a streetlamp. The rains had stopped. The war would end. Paris was liberated, and a new world had begun. Having returned only imperfectly from the land of the dead, should he again endure human passions? What if instead he must finally accept the desert? Justin recalled then the Russian parable of the trained falcon, which, when it escapes and flees to its wild brothers, is attacked and torn to pieces.

"Justin. Justin, are you sick?" As Eli saw the familiar concentration return to the scarred face on the pillow, he bent forward with his elbows on the mattress.

Justin had been just then with Abu Grinda at their waterhole, bathing in the blood of watermelons. "No, continue, Eli. You saw the general's aide?"

This morning, Eli Hebron had met an adviser to General de Gaulle, the tank commander who, though brushed aside by Guderian at Sedan, had recently refused in insulting terms to meet the American president. Now De Gaulle was keeping the Allies, who had driven the Wehrmacht out of France, from sharing in the establishment of the new democracy.

"It is said that millions have died, Justin," Eli was whispering. "Perhaps fifteen million, twenty . . . possibly far more. If there are Jews left alive, they are to be given Palestine. Otherwise the frontiers will only be strengthened. The classes who rule will be the same classes. Nothing will change. It is property that is winning the war."

"And our Charles de Gaulle?" Justin asked.

"They say that Churchill tied his hands at Yalta."

"Churchill supported the FFI?"

"As a convenience," Eli said. "They think we would hand Europe over to the Comintern."

"Yet these same anti-Communists wish to drive an army of *collabo* Cossacks and anti-Communist partisans equally into the hands of Stalin's executioners?"

"Exactly so—the forces of change, betrayed by the forces of stability." Eli looked up at the perspiration on Justin's temples. "Perhaps this is too much for you?"

"So Hitler's methods will linger on . . . the scientists and the propaganda, the police, the military cartels?" Justin said, feeling the eyes of the bishop and the banker on them.

"Justin? The day after tomorrow the general will invite some of the FFI to the Élysée. Naturally the others will lose their tongues. But you, Justin, if you could find the strength to be there, and to stand your ground?"

"As I kept the appointment with Stodel? You will need God to be there."

Justin's visitor laughed triumphantly. "I would allow no one else to mention God in the underground!"

When he left the ward some minutes later, Eli paused by the sleeping dignitaries and did a little dance for them.

3

AT EIGHT O'CLOCK, AFTER THE DOCTORS' ROUND, THE NIGHT NURSE RETURNED TO put out the lights. During the afternoon, Anneke had been deeply hurt to see the work of someone called Justin Lothaire in the window of every bookshop she passed. She felt frightened now by the intelligence she saw on Justin's face as she approached the window bed.

He awoke to the girl with a flush of warmth and apology. But before Justin could speak, she turned and left the ward. Justin drew the blankets over his head to shut out the banker's light. When he heard the door again he sat up. It was the concierge.

"Monsieur Lothaire, you must come downstairs. There is an urgent communication."

"A cable from Algiers?"

"Yes. A foreign country."

Using his cane, Justin let the concierge help him down the stairwell. Anneke had disappeared. The desk telephone in the office was off the hook.

"Lothaire," he said into it.

"Is that Lothaire?" A man's distant voice.

"*Oui! Qui est-ce?*"

"Justin? Justin . . . this is David Sunda. Hélène and I are in Basel."

"Sunda, David Sunda, you? How have you done this?"

There was a laugh. "Do you mean the telephone?"

Justin was concentrated in the dim room, oblivious now to Anneke and this clinic. His life and all his dreams were swarming toward him through the Paris night.

"Should I trust my ears?" he said softly. "You are alive."

"Can you hear me?" Their connection was failing. "I will be in Paris tomorrow night."

"Then come at once! . . . No, I must see de Gaulle. We could meet after that."

"Your taste in people has not changed."

"I'll make up for it at noon. And Sunda?"

"Yes, go on."

"Have you heard from Duncan, or anything of Godard—" Again the line was interrupted. Feeling that the terribly sober voice had anticipated the question, Justin's throat tightened.

"Duncan died at Christmas in the Ardennes. Johannes was hunted down, I believe by the Berlin police, more than a year ago."

"He is dead?"

"He is dead."

In his chest, Justin felt an aching pain of forgiveness. It could not be true. They did not feel dead. But the ache intensified.

Then, in the silence over the clinic telephone, he heard that others had been lost, and that these were David's family.

"I will be glad to see you!" Justin said urgently, into the mouthpiece. The line was cut off.

"Give our love to Luz." The voice came back.

"Ours to Hélène," Justin managed to say.

A moment later, Justin sat shivering with fever behind the desk, alone in a clinic on an island of the Seine.

4

THROUGH THE NEXT DAY, WAITING FOR THE CANADIAN NURSE TO AWAKEN AND come to his side, Justin fought with the disbelief that he could ever lose such sweetness. He was so moved by the girl's innocence that he would not have known how to plead his case in the face of it.

That evening, for the first time in six months, Anneke did not report for night duty. When Justin pushed open the shutters next morning, Paris was warm and dry, and he remembered then the long struggle for justice and what he must do today. As the first sun touched his face and arms, Justin knew his strength had returned. This would be the hour of words, for one still among the living to speak for the dead. Toward dusk he could go looking for Anneke.

Two hours later, Justin Lothaire was in the Tuileries gardens, walking with his cane toward the octagon lake. The children were there, sailing their boats. He saw Eli turn to meet him, and just for a moment the gold reflection off the lake blinded Justin with a brilliance like glacier ice.

"Are you ready, Justin?"

"You will not come in, having come all this way?"

"If you are there, we will all be there!"

"You make fun of me, little brother?" Justin was smiling, yet somehow Eli had looked hurt. Scarcely speaking, they circled under the chestnut trees, along the palace wall.

"It is only that they are grand men," Eli said. "I will wait for you here."

Turning the corner of the Élysée gardens, Justin approached the Faubourg gate. He felt the earth's gravity in his legs and stomach, as if he were gaining in mass. Some military cars had just entered the courtyard between more than a dozen armed guards, loitering in two groups. At the sight of these gendarmes who had served the Nazis, a painful emotion stirred in Justin. Barely using his cane now, he turned through the open gate. Someone began to shout.

"Pierrot, stop that man!"

Five of the police had closed behind Justin. A young blond swaggered forward, then called back excitedly.

"It is Lothaire, I know him well!"

The gendarme who knew Justin well led him across the gravel drive and up the porch steps to a glassed hall. Before going in, Justin looked back. The gendarmes and army drivers were grouped at the gate, watching. In the cloakroom, Justin's skin twitched as he was searched. Then they clicked in step down a gallery of mirrors and up a huge flight of stairs. What had all this confident splendor to do with the evil still living on earth? Fate, give him the words.

Justin reached a carpeted landing and braced on his stick against the new pain from his right tibia. Groups of officials glanced toward him without interrupting their discussions.

"In there, monsieur. Through the doors."

The first object that Justin identified in the huge room, staring at him from between two bay windows, was a giant painting of the revolutionary, Bonaparte. The emperor was dressed in red robes and ermine, seated on a throne. Across the parquet floor, on sofas and gilt chairs, waited a circle of some dozen old gentlemen. A very tall, mournful officer Justin momentarily failed to recognize motioned him to the one empty chair.

For the next half hour, seated on a chair facing the officer, who was de Gaulle, Justin listened to a witty monologue from one of the other gentlemen about the Paris chief of police during the days of the general rising. His gaze shifted to a younger civilian on the officer's left, who had smiled when Justin came in. At least he could be sure where this writer had been while Justin was in the hands of Joseph Darnand.

"And so, General, from the legal standpoint, if you like," concluded the first speaker, in his effete, singsong manner, "a crime was committed. Of course we might all have liked to see things done differently. But let us not overlook the high ideals of Duty, of Law, and, my friends, of Order."

Justin had last seen this colleague at Lambert's gathering of *chefs-partisans:* Jalvin, who had written books about the Barcelona and Shanghai uprisings, though without having shed blood in either. The handsome Frenchman was in the magazines far more often than Justin. There had been just one photograph of a poet of the Maghreb, showing his torn body on a stretcher. Javlin had had many different photographs in the magazine, but only the one story, of how he had driven a tank into Paris.

For a further ninety minutes, Justin listened as six of the elegant states-men spoke. Though the issues remained vague, one objective appeared to be clear. This was to find as many lofty reasons as possible to leave Europe's bureaucracy exactly as it had been before. As the minutes passed, the mood of the conference improved and Justin began to feel pleasantly lulled. Was government not too monumental an edifice—and the nation beneath too grand in its design—to be tampered with by men as modest as those in this circle? It was some time before he became aware that the meeting was three-quarters over and Justin's views had not been required.

The general stirred heavily. "Monsieur Jalvin has an opinion, I am sure of it!"

At once, Justin's colleague was on his feet. For the next fifteen minutes Jalvin paced up and down, speaking of France's mortal hour and of the bravery of her children. This ended with a call for a new French identity, to be forged from the myths and innocence of her people. The full drama of that final cry delivered in language as majestic and full of coils as a papyrus scroll—was felt most strongly by the president, in front of whom it was delivered.

"There!" The huge officer smiled thinly, slapping his knee. "At last we have met a man!"

Justin sat tensely upright, his shirt drenched with perspiration. After all these, was it he alone who would not be allowed to speak?

"Monsieur Lothaire? I see you do not agree."

Justin had somehow risen, his face aching with fever. Above the crescent of faces, he could see the chestnut trees across the Élysée gardens. If only he could be there with Eli, away from Bonaparte's alabaster skin and his questioner's measuring gaze.

From his armchair, de Gaulle examined the face of this writer and resistance leader now standing among them with a cripple's cane. He looked at the fellow's skin and at his deep-set, indiscreet eyes and thought, *There are more and more of these dangerous young men in the world. Why do they view history with such bitterness? Above all, what do the people see in them to worship?* Without searching further for an answer, the general shifted his buttocks and turned his thoughts to a less threatening issue: Churchill's attitude to Stalin. This subject was inseparable from a second and even more pleasant subject: How best should he, de Gaulle, exploit that relationship?

"This morning," the young man was saying, "I rose from the bed where I have lain for these seven months. Yet I remember as yesterday a night when I walked more freely than I stand before you now. I was climbing in the forest of the Jura, to keep an appointment with a man whose life I would take with these hands. He was a man who had conceived of machinery to murder entire races. And, my friends, he had tested it well. So look—are these a sinner's hands?"

Justin wheeled painfully in the circle of politicians, seeing their eyes, frozen now in alarm.

"My friends, we have narrowly—far more narrowly than most—escaped becoming a province in the grip of history's most sinister tyrant. Even on this day that belongs to Monet and Cezanne, the beast is buried alive in Berlin. Yet the bureaucrats of his empire have not retreated to bunkers, nor have they been herded into courtrooms. Gentlemen, it is not enough to execute a Brassilach or to elevate a few partisans to the *Députées!* If our children are not to curse this peace, it must be a society of the steadfast. Surely our modern enlightenment can sift its ranks for the beasts who still stink of human ordure and for the gangs of polite bourgeoisie who guided them! To cry 'science' must never be to cry that there is no good or evil. And though, yes, we may speak of tolerance, there can be no tolerance without repentance!"

Justin had left the circle of chairs. Turning, he saw the ministers seated with their heads bowed and their eyes averted.

"All of us will know what I mean when I say that France, in the company of all Europe, has been made to crawl on its belly!" Justin saw Jalvin turn questioningly to the president. "Or that it is in such times that we discover our truest patriots and our most masterful leaders. I do not refer to myself, certainly I do not refer to Marshal Pétain." Justin heard someone laugh. "But the people of Europe will want to see in high office many more of those who took almost sole responsibility for her virtue. Fascism is everywhere around us . . . we need experts acquainted with its methods. Gentlemen, I do not speak of any violent dislocation of the ruling classes. For that, too, may lead to madness. Nor do I wish to see enshrined the angel of revenge. No! What I am dreaming of is to see Europe elevate her most honorable men. That, General, and gentlemen, is the very essence of civilization."

As Justin finished, he was experiencing a happiness as blinding as the reflection by the Tuileries lake. Yet before he could resume his chair, the general and his guests began to rise.

"Jalvin? I would like you to come with me!"

Already, through a din of voices, the old gentlemen were moving across the ballroom. Justin could see the two heads, of Jalvin and the president, pass together out through the doors. A crushing shame bore down on his heart. Had those at the Carbonne farmhouse given their lives for cowards such as these? There were tears in his eyes. Pushing out of the chamber, he retraced his steps down the great staircases. Unconscious of physical pain, he walked quickly, like a man who has more important appointments. In the gravel yard, the crowd of gendarmes turned with silent curiosity to see Justin Lothaire pass among them.

Eli Hebron had waited in the shade under the chestnuts. At noon, when he saw his friend moving with painful slowness along the palace wall, Eli went toward him. He caught Justin's arm.

"Tell me quickly. Your words with the great men?"

Justin tried to calm the panting of his chest. It was as if he had just been in a fight.

"I found the words, but it was already settled. The meeting was a trap."

"Yet the thing was said!" Eli whistled. "To do more than that, Justin, you require a gun."

"Eli, Eli, have you not understood? What we accomplished was for nothing. The ancien régime has retaken the whole edifice. It is not over!"

"And for *this* they required the one spirit above question to be present?" Eli shouted.

Justin laughed wildly and shook his head, but he could not speak. As the two friends—still young men—walked in silence back through the Tuileries gardens, it was as if spring had not come and the innocence that slept in the perambulators was still in danger of transportation. Justin could not bear to go, after such a cataclysm, to the Le Trève mansion. He felt too compromised even to face the Canadian nurse. There was only one source of wisdom strong enough to save such a life—Doré, who in these months had not once come to Justin's bedside.

5

THE KEY THAT JUSTIN HAD CARRIED IN THE SAHARA, EVEN UNTO THE CRYSTAL meadow, still unlocked an entrance on the rue de Valois.

As he labored around the last staircase, he saw a familiar door standing open. The old man was in the shadows, with fascination observing Justin's face, as if he had materialized out of one of Doré's own fables.

"How did you know?"

"I knew, I knew!" said a voice that Justin had lived six years, that he might hear it again in these rooms.

For some moments he could not bring himself to sit on his accustomed sofa, under the Chinese ancestors. His own body, with its two hundred stitches, its shrapnel, and its distorted bones, made a threatening presence at the mysterious heart of the Palais-Royal.

"Anna, could you prepare us some green tea?" Doré's sister had momentarily appeared in the doorway, with a pleased little nod, as if he had only just visited the week before. Seated in the armchair, the old man leaned closer to him. His amused eyes examined, with great gentleness, the savagery of the desert that Justin no longer cared to hide.

"I did not see it on the last occasion," he said. "You have become quite a presence."

"You had been shot."

"Oh, you mean that occurrence?"

Doré waved his fingers vaguely. For some seconds Justin frowned at the little wrinkled face. Then he realized that Doré had meant the war. As if tasting salvation, Justin began to laugh.

Across the low table his master nodded and smiled at him. This laughter had just confirmed Doré's impression on the landing, that Justin's sanity had endured betrayal to limits never before reached. That he was among the dead, but that he wished to live again. For both of them, this was an important moment.

"Yes, yes, the attempt was noble . . . a glory of your youth. Still, dear boy, nothing has been lost," the old man whispered, as he poured the strong emerald tea. "You'll come to understand the bitterness of life and the power that it gives you—to love, to cause no one harm. All you have done is to test dreams. The dream of utopias is only a little dream."

Doré's musical tones had begun to penetrate his protégé's clenched nerves, as water penetrates dry clay. During the rising of Carbonne, Justin had cursed a classicism that kept visionaries in their studios while Europe tore itself to pieces. Just now, this old man in the armchair was leading him toward justice—this time his own. As he heard the beauty of Doré's spirit, Justin had again begun to laugh, thirstily, as he could not remember having laughed.

"I myself prefer characters to people." Doré smiled at him, raising his short gray eyebrows. "Yes, I prefer the ocean to cities, Alexander's tutor to Alexander himself. Characters are the vessels of a deeper love and are more lasting. I know you're afraid of what you have seen. You suspect it has the power to nullify the sense of everything around you."

"Yes, a little . . . that's close." He and the old master became very still among the artifacts arranged by time. Justin cradled his right hand—the hand with which he had taken Jakob Stodel's life. Doré's murmur carried to him easily.

"Well, then, you must tell me. Construct a parable or an adventure, only tell me the truth. Break me with your horrors! Then watch closely and see if I am surprised or disturbed. . . . Now, tell me," Doré whispered, with the same glitter of fascination that Justin had seen on the landing.

The story took the rest of that Paris evening to be told, as the sun set on roofs over which Hitler had recently flown like Delacroix's *Satan*. What the power of literature had brought only to Justin, and which he had strung on a single thread neither for the press nor for Luz, not even for himself—mass spectacles undetected by the most polished imaginations and tolerable only to a devil or a saint.

As the dusk fell over the interior fountains and sent governesses gliding home, a voice like Joseph Mandil's by the Doubs tunnel droned on behind the locked doors of Doré's salon. Justin spoke in a guttural whisper, his eyes fixed on a point somewhere in front of him—the focal point of all confession. His gentle audience, who might have destroyed his pride with a single word, sat quietly waiting to pass judgment. Finally, pausing to wipe his forehead and clear his throat, Justin told of keeping a bishop's appointment with Europe's most original exterminator in a freak ice storm. Only then did he find the courage to speak of his own summons to the Élysée that very morning and of his humiliation at the hands of France's old order—politicians whom Doré would not invite to dinner.

For perhaps twenty minutes, the salon of the Palais Royal was lost in brooding reflection. A weak lamp flickered on, and Justin raised his face from his hands. He could see drops of perspiration on the crown of the old sage's head. An unequaled intelligence has suffered with me, Justin thought, and a feeling came over him of wild joy and gratitude. He felt himself continue to shrink magically out of historical nightmare. Soon, Justin would be no more than a student before his master on a quiet Paris dusk. He smiled, a smile that was somewhat insane. But then, so was the answering grin from the facing cushions.

"You humble me, Marcel."

"Humble . . . humble? It is I who am humbled," Doré observed, and he sighed deeply so that Justin would not be embarrassed.

"And their evil?" Drying his eyes, Justin raised his hand in warning. "Surely, their evil will be ours?"

"It is a very great story," the old man answered him. "But time has done no work on it. And you are the same as you were, though more so. Why look like that, my boy? I am not intimidated, simply impatient for well-distilled themes. However, tell me one thing. Why did you speak of ethical rebels and civilization to a commander of tanks?"

"They have robbed the future," Justin said, but he could not avoid smiling with tears in his eyes at Doré's play of ironies.

"No, no, no." His friend lifted his face to Justin with an indescribably delicate charm. "These are merely lawyers. You and I can search the moral design—the plot will be ours. But now tell me, will Luz join us for dinner?"

Justin was not yet saved. "Wait, Marcel. *Still,* did we not hope to leave behind this sinful elite forever?"

"No; Justin." Doré smiled with serene patience. "Your science of universal justice has postponed the ceremonies of conscience. Above all, that is the future. Do you see? Luz is the future."

And in his complete astonishment, Justin finally tasted resignation. Laughing once again with his love for this old man, he sank back on the sofa. "Luz has witnessed all of it, and still knows nothing of this world."

"Yes, she is very brave," Doré whispered, as if his protégé had just said something unworthy. "How have you earned such loyalty? My boy, lock yourselves upstairs and prepare our future generation. Only tonight you must both come for dinner. . . . Anna?" he called softly. "My dear sister, are you there?"

Justin rose obediently on his cane to go for his wife. Once again, as long ago, he was an urchin of the desert, mantled in the old man's civilized grace. Then he remembered that Luz was waiting for him—in a Napoleonic palace—with David and Hélène. Recoiling, as if by a sign, Justin's soul turned to the night nurse and her perfect sweetness.

He returned to the well-loved salon. Doré was bent over the wireless; a faraway English voice crackled into the dusk. "With the surrender of Field Marshal Kesselring and the expected capitulation of defenses within Germany, the Allied victory is virtually assured . . . general armistice within a fortnight. Meanwhile, fighting continues in the area surrounding the chancellery bunker. . . ."

Through the Palais-Royal, the silence stretched out. Justin recognized now the subtle incense of the old man's rooms. His breath came quickly. And this time Justin knew that the war was over. Doré hobbled to him from the mantel. With simple formality, he held out a glass.

"The grapes in this wine," he said, "were picked in Algeria before the war."

His head bowed, Justin took the glass from Doré's hand.

"We will drink together to the armistice. This triumph, Justin Lothaire, belongs to you."

Less than a half hour later, Justin reached the address the clinic had given him, close by Les Halles. The Canadian nurse had turned in her key at noon. Her room was already occupied.

6

HÉLÈNE HAD NEVER SEEN PARIS THE WAY IT WAS ON THE NIGHT SHE CAME HOME from Hitler's ruined cities.

As their taxi geared down for the final long climb to the Arc de Triomphe—a mask of tragedy, blazing mouth open at the summit—the two boys scrambled to the window. Lit by the mist of one million bulbs, a crowd in khaki and blue uniforms, gay costumes, and hats overflowed the Champs-Élysées and halted the few cars. On all their faces, fleeting as revelers at a bacchanal, Hélène saw the same searching and intoxication.

It had been like this for several nights, as the realization had penetrated to the remotest tenement that the cloak of *Nacht und Nebel,* which could make anyone disappear, was not only thrown back but about to be burned. A joy and a jealousy had come over the people like spring madness. And as the secret fear that had united them all, informer and victim, was rinsed into the open streets, all these many thousands had followed, wishing not to be left out, to be together in it again. So, night after night, the citizenry of Paris, having felt the first twinge of loneliness as something great and important in their lives fell behind forever, streamed through the streets in desperate, conquering celebration.

Hélène stared out over the wash of heads. This was to be the moment. These were the streets she had not dared to believe in. She and her children were here. They were saved! All around the taxi streamed the people of Paris, just as Hélène had once dreamt that they would.

In the front seat, Otto rubbed his mouth. "My God! There are many, many people in this city."

"Come, come, little dear," sang Gerta, as she bumped a screaming Albert on her thigh, "soon you will speak good French."

"They will learn English too." Baron Sunda had suddenly stirred from the window. Hearing them speak German, the driver looked nervous again. Hélène had explained that they were political refugees. She forced herself to smile brilliantly at her husband, then at Gerta. As the car swung clear of the crowd and went down the avenue d'Iéna—corners she had turned in her dreams—Hélène experienced an emotion as intense as though she were at the gates of paradise, and she instantly forgot that her husband was already thinking of America.

"I am so excited," she called softly. "I am so excited."

Without smiling, David leaned forward to stare at the Le Trève entrance. It was only as he recognized this iron gate and gravel drive that he finally understood. All this was truly about to end—a flight that had begun for him, many centuries ago, on a glaring snowfield to the south of Smolensk. Tomorrow he would wake up in a bed from which no one would drive him with whips. Where no fragments could tear him, and he would feel no hunger—above all, in a house from which David need never again flee westward. But instead of the divine joy that the thought of this moment had awoken in him at every minute of the last three years, he was experiencing terror. In the morning when he awoke, there would be another life to live. At this moment, David had no memory whatever of what that life would be like.

7

HÉLÈNE HAD JUMPED TO THE GRAVEL, AND IN THREE SPRINGS SHE WAS UP THE front steps. Hearing the bell's familiar ring she bowed her head. The locks rattled, the great door swung inward, and Sylvie was standing before her.

"Mademoiselle Hélène! It is Mademoiselle Hélène!"

Sylvie had grown her hair long and she had become matronly. But Hélène did not see this, or the peeling paint on the door. All such changes—along with the memory of the last years among a race driven mad—were incidental beside the all-inclusive change of having brought her family home to this house.

"Hello, Sylvie. . . ." Hélène's voice failed her. Beyond, in the foyer with its broad staircase, she had glimpsed a gray-haired lady and gentleman coming toward her with anxious ceremony. Releasing Sylvie, she went to them.

"Papa! Papa!" Hélène whispered, as she embraced this stranger with the bushy black eyebrows. She was crying and laughing too—with love, and with exhaustion, and at the forgotten sensation of being someone else's child.

"Hello, my little morsel," Pierre Le Trève whispered with a gruff old man's emotion, forgetting his ceremoniousness and using the word Hélène imagined she had invented for her children. Then she squeezed her mother's thick, soft body, her mother who still laughed her shrill laugh and muttered endearments in precisely the same lovable, irritating tone.

After the first mindless overflowing, a constraint fell over the group gathered on the marble floor. They had all thought of the terrible, incomprehensible scenes that each of them had lived through separately, and of how there might soon be a need to speak of these things. But no one had the courage or could find the words.

"So these are my grandsons?" Le Trève put his hands on the boys' heads, which they twisted up to stare at him. "Albert, and Rickie." Stooping quickly, he caught them both around the legs.

"Pierre, your back!" cried his wife, her face red with the effort of doing the right thing. By now, everyone was feeling so overwhelmed that when the two children rose safely in their grandfather's arms, they all burst out laughing and Gerta began to weep. "My beautiful grandsons!" Eunice Le Trève continued loudly. "And you must be the famous Gerta. And you must be Otto!"

Stricken with confusion, rapidly raising and lowering his eyebrows, Otto gave each of the old couple's hands a solemn, vigorous shake. There was a silence.

"Papa, where is Grandmère!" Hélène suddenly inquired. "Where are Jean-Marc and Gnome?"

As she led them up the stairs, Pierre Le Trève laughed and shrugged. "David, you remember grandmother's views on anyone from north of Alsace. As for Hélène's brother," Le Trève hurried on, warming to his old role as the charming patriarch, though he felt in some way troubled by his son-in law, "Jean-Marc has taken a liking to army life. He is a colonel of parachutists in Algiers."

"Ah, Papa!" Hélène groaned softly, and she paused on the landing. "What is Justin going to say?"

"Oh, you mean that nice young *pied-noir!* Did you read that he had something or other to do with the Resis—"

"Sshh, my dear!" Le Trève put his arm gently around his wife as he led them into the salon. "Now is a moment for wine and family celebration. We kept the roast waiting by the oven all afternoon. Come, *mes petits choux.* It is time that I had my grandchildren around me!"

Le Trève took a basket of chocolates from the massive mantelpiece and the two sad, exhausted little faces brightened, as if recognizing a fellow conspirator. "And by the way!" he went on, with an unmistakable humility before his pallid, aloof son-in-law. "These bundles are your mail from over the last year. In this first are some registered letters on which you might do well to cast an eye."

"If you will all excuse me, I'll take a half hour and prepare myself."

"Do you remember Hélène's room?" Madame Le Trève called as David's stiffly erect back withdrew. "You will find a new double bed in it."

"Maman!" cried Hélène. The cruelty, even now, of such a concession—come too late, and from parents who had guarded her purity like game wardens—might have upset the last of her courage, had she not already become absorbed with her father's silence concerning Gnome. Could the faithful friend of her childhood be dead?

Now, standing again by this mantelpiece where so much had happened, Hélène watched the two boys struggle shyly on the couch beside her father. With a rush of emotion, she turned to the open landing. An old Labrador had appeared in the doorway. Tongue dangling, he surveyed the assembly with experienced, cynical eyes. Feeling Hélène's attention on him, Gnome licked his lips and averted his eyes with vague discomfort. *He doesn't recognize me,* she thought. And even though Hélène would never again be the child of the house, and though such a thing was quite natural, that her old friend could have forgotten her seemed a betrayal almost more painful than any she had known.

Turning from her family, Hélène paced out onto the darkened landing. She was thinking of Justin, who would be here tomorrow. What if he had seen her letter, in which Hélène had very nearly promised herself to him? *Mon coeur.* Had she called Justin that? Yet was it not absurdly, tragically true? Feeling a stab of terror, she halted at the foot of her little staircase. Gnome's yellow head was watching her from the salon door. Hélène turned quickly and started up.

For five seconds, her pet gazed after her suspiciously. Then, quite suddenly, Gnome threw up his head and bayed hysterically until the house seemed dwarfed by his roars. He raced up and down the landing, wagging his thick tail so violently that his hind legs collapsed. Then, like a much younger dog, he galloped past Hélène, rumbled up the stairs, and scrambled through her door. Gnome had remembered their old games so perfectly that he did not even stop to say hello!

"Gnome, Gnome!" Hélène called, laughing until her breast ached.

Presently then, as if nothing could change, her old friend lay on the bath rug, panting and grinning while she bathed. Afterward, Hélène put on her prewar chiffon dress with the gauze flower on its breast. All the while she hummed to herself, feeling that a sign had just been sent to her. This very evening Hélène must overcome the monstrous and unworthy sensation that she had experienced in her husband's presence ever since their first thoughtless night in Lübeck. Fifteen minutes later, feeling younger and more reckless than she had felt in years—though she shuddered inwardly at what she must do—Hélène started back down to the cheerful entrance of the family salon. Sylvie was hurrying toward her, looking agitated.

"What is it, Sylvie?" she inquired.

"Your husband!" The maid stared with fear into Hélène's face. Beginning to cry, Sylvie pointed to the murky hall below.

Hélène ran down the staircase and came to the door of her father's library. A familiar shape was stretched very still on the window sofa.

In four more steps, Hélène knelt between Otto and her mother. David lay close at her side, his hands pushed under his back. His shirt was sodden with perspiration. Then the face that she had once thought humorous and kind rolled toward her, and Hélène saw in this man's eyes an expression she had never seen before.

"Oh, no," she whispered. "Oh, no, not now!" And by this Hélène meant, *Not with Justin tomorrow.* Then, to her shock, a second, even less virtuous thought came to her. Was she not several weeks overdue? A faint light flickered in her husband's eyes, then was extinguished as David passed out from exhaustion.

After ten more minutes, the ambulance arrived. As the hospital porters carried the stretcher into the hall, before she extinguished the study light, Hélène leaned over her father's desk. Here David had only minutes before been opening his mail. A letter lay unfolded. It was from her husband's old Geneva colleague, Bernard Piers, inviting David to work on a new League of Nations that was being planned for New York. Next to it, on the leather desk-top engraved with exotic birds, lay a sort of crude pewter-colored disc.

8

ON THE DAY THAT DAVID SUNDA RETURNED TO PARIS, THE FRAGRANT SPRING AIR in the garden of the Berlin Chancellery had for many hours shuddered under the blows of the Soviet heavy artillery. Earlier, a rocket striking the east wall had sent out a hot gale, stripping bare the great linden tree to the last leaf.

Deep beneath a cratered lawn, in the tunnel that connected the command and living quarters, an awkward press of party officials murmured admiration as the defeated dictator of the European peoples moved through, silently shaking hands.

Hitler was dressed in a uniform jacket, black trousers, and well-polished shoes. His followers' display of devotion caused this twitching and much aged being, himself composed of flesh and blood, to forget the drug-induced specter from his final nap. In Hitler's brief nightmare the sun, as it burned down on the drenched earth, had created a human cloud, carrying the popula-tion of Europe high above the Alpine peaks. From the cloud, instead of rain, there had fallen bleeding flesh. Now as he lay awake in this muffled catacomb, surrounded by persons who did not wish history to forget them, the impres-sion was not easily shaken off. For here was Hitler's most rewarding invention—a place where neither God nor any fellow being could judge him beside other men. Here, Hitler could even strip himself of the Vienna Academy's verdict on his mediocrity.

In the early morning, Goebbels had gone about with his usual loud voice, advising the nervous personnel of the *Führerbunker* to remember that a movie would one day be made of their concluding scene and to behave accordingly. Their embarrassment in the tunnel, therefore, was no more than the natural self-consciousness of amateur actors. But to Hitler it was authentic proof that he was to be a giant in paradise. Presently, joined at a lunch of vegetables by his secretaries and the cook, Hitler's exhausted imagination was moved for the last time to summon the other, waking, dream—of an empire of ten centuries, uniting the Atlantic with the Pacific and ruled by the pure-blooded German dictator.

When there was nothing left on his plate, Hitler withdrew with his new bride. After helping Eva with two pills and a glass, Adolf held her until she was unconscious. Then, reflecting on Frederick the Great, and even now too great a coward to contemplate the torments of his fellow beings— though despising their ingratitude for the gift of himself—Hitler lay on his couch, placed a pistol barrel between his teeth, and blew his brains over the leather headrest.

And when Joseph Goebbels saw his master lying dead, he too prepared to die.

So, in the one thousand, nine hundred and forty-fifth year, in the fourth month, on the thirtieth day, Adolf Hitler was dead. Twelve years and forty days since that Potsdam morning of marches and banners on which Friedrich von Sunda had watched Hitler descend into Frederick's tomb, the mediocrity who had played history's most evil role was carried upstairs by four death's-head guards. Passing outside through the second bunker door, the procession continued down the garden path. Hitler's body was carried in a blanket, legs swinging from the knees, and laid beside the woman's in a sandy depression under the smoking Berlin sky, between the Chancellery steps and the leafless linden tree. Then the adjutants and the chauffeur, Linge, Kempka, and Gunsche, splashed five cans of gasoline across the bodies. An oily flame crackled up, the unnatural heat giving the onlookers an impression that the blackening shape in the pit had attempted, one last time, to blaspheme the very power of the sun. And to the great armies, closing from all over Europe on this garden to avenge their fifty million dead, it was as if truly the Antichrist were again escaping in a puff of smoke. The little group saluted hurriedly and fled back underground.

Not far away at the Empire Bank was another creature, called Max Heilige, whom the world would soon find to be an impostor. Max Heavenly was the name typed on a bank account, containing the gold from the teeth of six million Jews—four living souls lost each minute the opera had not been brought to a halt.

Pity, pity and shame—who can sing them? A stillness of spoiled dreams closes upon the world, filled with unnatural sounds. Amid this unforgiven hush, the generals turn their brutal heroes homeward—the Australians to the arid coasts of Perth, to Sydney and Melbourne; the Americans to harsh New England, to Mississippi and California; the Chinese to the open landscapes of Sinkiang or Yangtse. The Indians march like Englishmen back to their tropics of mystic poverty—and the Englishmen, weary and unvanquished, sail through the mist to their drizzling island reverie of antiquity and pagan dews. The Soviets of one hundred tribes also go home to their frozen forest wastes, as do the French, the Japanese . . . and the Germans, uneasiest of all. All carry with them the news of a great victory. But like the cities they have ruined and the children they have slain, they are broken and lack hope or aspiration.

Still, on the very dawn after Berlin's puff of smoke, as men still slept, without warning the sun hissed up and hung, leaving no more trace than a fish that leaps. With the assurance of the mother who keeps the schedule of her affections, it floated upward and flooded the firmament with the tenderest, most healing light. Across wet valleys, beauty rose chastely to meet the saga of the day. Faint bells rang over the vineyards of Provence and the valleys of the Rhine. Now all of it was safe—the churches, the frescoes, and the drowsy farms, the country homes and the Regency clubhouses. The dolls and toys of children were safe, the deep meditation of whales and nocturnal chants of Polynesians and Amazonians, all safe. Safe, too, were couples on the grass in Central Park, or strolling the temples of Kyoto; and safe the bull ring of Barcelona, the seminaries of Paris, also the Acropolis; safe the voices of small girls who sing in Urbino, and safe the temperamental Romanian pianist, playing Schubert in Alexandria.

And the morning seemed to fill with the cries and singing of a multitude of children's voices.

PART THREE

The fathers have eaten a sour grape, and the children's teeth are set on edge.

—JEREMIAH 31:29

PLACE DES VOSGES

1

BY MIDSUMMER, ANOTHER, LESS PAINFUL WAR HAD TAKEN ITS PLACE IN THE general mind. God seemed once again to be forgiving man.

This legendary war had a conclusion. It had the living, who must be good because they had kept their lives. It had the dead, who were either evil or tragic. Above all, the stagehands and the casts of the extermination rooms—the chief torturers and the millions of informers, liars, and accomplices—had evaporated, like those medieval witches who leave only a trace of powder. Blinking sadly in their places were ordinary and pitiable fellow beings. In other words, the sprawling reality of *Nacht und Nebel* had vanished into the mass unconscious, like a slaveship with its gruesome cargo concealed beneath the surface of a placid sea, leaving to a very few the salvage of the truth. In Paris, Hélène found herself face to face once again with the failures of her former life and with an ever more pressing need to bring sense to them.

2

ON A VERY HOT NOON IN JULY OF 1945 FOLLOWING HER FIRST VISIT TO THE medical library, Hélène stopped by the Théâtre de l'Odéon to collect Luz.

As she stepped into the cool foyer, where she knew that Justin Lothaire had been that morning, Hélène saw Luz with two actors in robes and a short man with a goatee.

"Ah, yes! We have certainly heard of you." The director turned with a frank curiosity to meet the much-publicized though never-photographed French presence in the July assassination plot. He noticed the woman's blue summer dress and her skin, which was darkly sunburned and slightly moist now from the summer heat.

But Hélène only shrank from the man's interest. Through the last ten weeks of her husband's illness, and as she settled the question of their sons' new lives, Hélène had not used these first hours of freedom as she had sworn she would—in every way showing her gratitude to Providence for having granted the lives of her closest family. Instead, she was seized by a passion to be alone with the sun. Hélène spent many hours each day among the chimneys of her father's roof, lying on a towel spread over a patch of soft tar. Not until the third week did it occur to her that not once had she taken the boys to mass.

In this state of mind, Hélène was distinctly troubled by David's words to her on the day he left the hospital. Later, seated together in the garden under the willow, her husband had seemed be courting her with a philosophy of enlightened aristocracy and family discipline. When she had seen the kindness and the gravity on his face—now paler and more strained than ever—Hélène had known why so many considered David exceptional. But she found very little in her heart that could agree with him.

Hélène was awoken from this thought by the laughter of Luz's friends: artists who throughout the war had performed for the executioners of Johannes, Duncan, and Friedrich Sunda. One of them had addressed her.

"Perhaps you too have a future on the stage," he repeated.

"Thank you, but I am limited to the role of mother."

"Limited!" The director vaguely brushed Hélène's bare shoulder. "Surely the mother is the ultimate role."

In the street below, as she arranged herself in her father's one remaining coupé, Hélène averted her eyes from her friend's excited gestures. Could Luz's sudden success, riding on the Lothaire name, have awoken such careless charm in a matter of months? Hélène recalled the bitter irony that her own unforeseen effect on the opposite sex had arrived at a time of her isolation. It only alarmed her—here, in her own streets, and because of the person whom she might encounter at any moment and the letter that he might have seen—to be in a marriage that imposed so weak a discipline. Her fellow beings, who had always appeared as letters that traveled around her in the secret dignity of envelopes, seemed now as naked and familiar as postcards. It was this new rawness of life that impelled Hélène to drown herself in the sun.

Hélène steered them onto the Seine embankment and heard again that distressing name as she found herself listening to the eager gossip of her childhood friend.

"Of course they say that Justin is a great figure. And if anything, that's made him even more difficult to live with."

"Yes, Justin has strong emotions—he's certainly less controlled than David." Hélène suppressed a rush of anger, to find herself speaking the same platitudes after all that had happened to them. The worst of it was that she felt more hypnotized by Luz than ever.

"Of course, David also went through a lot!" Luz added.

"Yes, it's finally over. Yet he keeps turning down jobs—Imagine. And we are nearly ruined."

"I suppose we are too," Luz said vaguely. "But now all that awful violence is over, I have Justin to myself. . . . Even better, I'm back on the stage. I'm so happy, Leni!"

Hélène jerked the coupé to a stop in her parents' drive. They sat together in the shade of the great facade while she waited for her friend to finish.

"When I play Iphigenia"—Luz searched for the part in her hair—"I feel so intensely what it was to be a barefoot pagan princess. I'm like a little boat, loaded with milk and honey, riding between the dark sea and the light blue sky."

Shading her eyes, Hélène smiled encouragingly into Luz's pale, uncertain face. Suddenly it came to her that this woman—who was a drawing-room beauty from Budapest and knew nothing of Aegean islands—was simply acting out the ideas that excited Justin. With a sudden compassion, she took Luz's cold fingers in hers.

"What you said is beautiful."

"Leni, will David be here for lunch?" Luz asked.

"I don't think so," said Hélène, letting go the hand and sorting her keys.

3

Inside, she trailed her now restless friend through the cool rooms and out to the garden table. Sylvie was serving them cold meats half an hour later when David appeared and set down his briefcase by the little Mercury. He had never before been at home during one of Luz's visits.

"Hello, Lupic . . . you see? As good as new," he said, with a charm that Hélène had not heard since Mexico. And how was it that Justin had never accompanied Luz to see David at the hospital?

"Oh, Sunda, I'm so glad you came! Hélène said you wouldn't."

"I just stopped in for a minute." David sat down on a badly corroded chair at his wife's side. With a ghostly smile that curled down the corners of his mouth, he looked from Luz's face to Hélène's, then back to Luz. "You know, I'm on my way to meet your husband?"

"Justin?" Hélène repeated, and she stared at Luz's flushed smile. "You didn't mention this."

"And neither did Justin!"

David frowned, and there was a pause in this fragile reenacting of their old selves. "Our association is well known," he said. "Too many people have been asking us when we would speak again. We're meeting in the Place des Vosges. On my strolls from the hospital, I came to think of it as the most beautiful spot in Paris."

David went on with customary wit to describe a debate that morning with a confused minister of trade over the Le Trève oil holdings, dismembered by

Laval. It was not until her husband had left them alone once again that Hélène took note of Luz's flirtation. The mention of David's rendezvous with Justin had only intensified Hélène's earlier abstraction.

Had the gods sent her *this* to drive her mad? With all her strength, Hélène tried to concentrate on her luncheon in the cool of her father's garden. How was it no one had noticed that she had not seen Justin again? Why was something which was so urgent to Hélène, and which she deserved, being denied her? And what would her husband have to say to Justin now? The two men had followed such divergent paths, and they represented such opposed human tendencies! Hélène could conceive of no point on which they might agree. She wished she could be there to protect them at that fateful meeting, rather than under these ivy-clad walls watching Luz, who had stopped being Iphigenia and was throwing crumbs of bread to a flock of sparrows.

"Leni, look—look. Come, little birds!"

"You see how they love you?" Hélène pressed her napkin to her lips and gazed steadily at her friend. What had defeated her was the image of David, as he had bent to kiss Luz, and how correct and inevitable the two had looked together. Somewhere, among the ordeals of the last years, Hélène had lost the capacity to think about herself. Now safely back in this city, seated in the rustling noon shade, her earliest suffering returned to her. And in that flood of warm inner light, all the years of loyalty, self-denial, and generosity emerged on Hélène's face—unnoticed by her murmuring companion—in an expression as gentle, subtle, and profound as those of Doré's ancient Chinese portraits.

At the same hour, her husband was in his father-in-law's car as Otto threaded them into the Marais. David had changed from his flannel suit to one of Le Trève's old linen ones. Now he stared without sight out of the open window at the sunlit alleys. The burst of affection from Luz, the companion of Justin's famous Carbonne years, had given David just the sense of forgiving contact he needed for the meeting ahead. This would be the ultimate, unavoidable test.

In recent nights, unknown to Hélène, David had lain awake, reliving Nysa camp in France's frenzied guillotining of its collaborators, and contemplating the spectacle of a republic run by Ramadier's coalition of resisters, and even of Communists! Was Justin not compared in the press to Saint-Just? How free could such a man feel, as he faced a titled patrician who had worn a Wehrmacht insignia in Russia?

Otto had drawn up by an arch that opened under an arcade. Without a word, Baron Sunda climbed out and passed under one of the low arches into the Place des Vosges.

4

SINCE JUSTIN LOTHAIRE'S AUDIENCE AT THE ÉLYSÉE—ON THE DAY HE HAD LET THE
night nurse slip from his life without confessing a word of his feelings—he
had been in that mood which is comfortable only on damp chilly days, when
the clouds never part for the sun.

Each morning he was up at six and at work by oil lamp. He did not see
the governess arrive or his wife leave for the theater. Soon his neglected
manuscript on the Inquisition, which Luz had carried half finished into
Switzerland sixteen months before with the unborn child, would be complete.
It was not until Justin stopped attending the trials and resumed writing—thus
suppressing any last temptation to be treated as a saint or to act as a judge—
that he beheld the sea of his troubles. The glorious pool of long ago in an
Algiers library had blown into angry swells that blocked his horizons and
reflected no light. Justin knew the only way he might ever relieve this climate
of contradictions was by the most worldly conversation. And just as before,
the only person to whom he could turn for this was David.

So it was that, at the appointed hour, Justin found himself winding
through streets purged of the innocent, to meet a German nobleman who had
sipped tea with Hitler.

At a café hidden in a corner gallery of the Place des Vosges, Justin ordered
a café crème and he listened to four Algerian soldiers at the next table discuss
Frenchwomen in the guttural singsong of the Kabyle.

"The tarts swing their tails and roll their eyes."

"But if one of us asks for it?"

Justin thought, How has one *raton*, born to a casbah lace cleaner, come to
have such a life in Paris? He remembered well enough David's unequaled generosity—also how, through his descent into the Nazi inferno, Hélène may have
remained her husband's witness. As Justin smoked thoughtfully in the heat, a
sweet memory came to him of her tolerant eyes and frank laugh. But Justin's
smile, caught unawares, was contorted by a sort of jealousy. The politicians
would not heed what he said. To what hope could he now claim any right?

Just then Justin opened his eyes to see a familiar figure at the exact center of the gravel. The princely phantom of Berlin and the siege of Moscow was
a mild young gentleman dressed in cream linen, waiting in the noon sun.

5

DAVID DID NOT CATCH SIGHT OF JUSTIN LOTHAIRE UNTIL THE FASCINATING,
somewhat aged stranger with a jacket over his shoulder had almost reached
him. He was unprepared for the bleak intensity on this face—a look David had

last seen on the Eastern Front—or for the many deep scars. Then the habit of social grace came to his assistance, and Baron Sunda went to meet the world-famous writer and soul of Europe's liberation.

Their four hands gripped crosswise and remained clasped. For a full minute they stood in the sun, with no sound but the cries of children, while Justin examined his student friend's lined face and gray hair. There were tears of anger and suffering in both their gazes. As they turned, neither quite walking beside the other, the rustle of their shoes on the gravel seemed to reverberate over an abyss of historical ugliness.

"I'm glad you could come, Justin."

"It's very hot," Justin said. "Take off the jacket."

Side by side now, they approached Justin's arcade table. He recognized David's English shoes and the neatly pressed linen, but he could find no point of softness in this man. Just then, David turned to Justin with an extraordinarily kind smile.

"That first sight of you was so strange . . . though really you haven't changed."

Justin stood with his head bowed, trying to find an answer to this. The specter of his greatest friend entering Russian villages in a gray uniform would not disappear. How were they to speak among all these echoes? Justin gestured toward a chair, bitterly aware of his failure to feel as he once did. When the old waiter had gone, David knitted his fingers under his chin. Abruptly there was the most naked concentration on his face.

"It has been many years, Justin."

"We have been luckier than most," Justin agreed. The triviality of their words provoked the sensation of an excruciating futility on that cloudless afternoon. Justin thought momentarily that he might pick up his jacket and leave Baron Sunda to drink his champagne alone.

"Justin?"

David bent closer with something new in his eyes, confiding and alone. Justin knew at once this was an apology. For a moment his heart softened.

"Justin, I'm glad you got Jakob Stodel."

"We wouldn't have known him if you hadn't mentioned the name."

"When I read about it in Switzerland, I thought, did he remember our conversation by the lake?"

Justin lit a fourth cigarette. He brushed ash from the wiry hairs on his wrist, quite unable to ask if Hélène had known of Luz's wartime journey with David to the Alps. "You think I would forget the story of my two trusted friends who had tea with Hitler and Stodel?" Justin observed, and he saw David's features redden.

"My God, Justin. If I'd never returned to Europe, Stodel would be safe in Bolivia by now!"

Justin felt confused. Was it plausible for even such a friend to be identified with Justin's struggle in the underground?

"If you'd simply shot that pair during your famous opportunity, millions might not have died." Justin began to shake. "Instead, you throw away all those . . . those hideous, evil months, to serve in the destruction of Russia. And you say, that was in order to *accomplish* this very same act?"

The old intimates of the rue de Fleurus had never spoken so brutally. Justin's impulse to rise from the table was forgotten. He stared ruthlessly at the anger that had frozen his companion's polite smile.

"Lothaire, as much as I respect you—more than any other man—you go too far. No, listen!" David muttered, the wicker squeaking under him. "My own brother was involved in the assassination conspiracy. Friedrich was crucified; the rest were tortured to death. Trott was garroted. No, Justin, let me speak! My parents had already died of shame. . . . At least Hélène was able to protect our Polish workers. In the East, when we saw that Stalin would not fall, we tried to lead a coup in Guderian's staff. . . . Then this man in front of you deserted; he walked out of Russia. He lived through nine months in a Silesian death camp! My God, Justin, have you no imagination? Do you think even Hitler himself ultimately foresaw what lay ahead? History rides a swell, but who knows on what beach it is breaking?"

"You were a democracy, Hitler was a popular leader!" Justin said, and his friend smiled at him coldly.

"Neither were there enough mandarins, moralists, and Comintern to keep him out," David retorted. "Oh, heavens, Justin! Do you think it was your partisans who freed Europe? It was cynical armies not much different from Hitler's. And when you knew me, was I ever German?"

At their table, set a little apart, they were both trying to control their tone. Justin stared away toward the children playing in the sun, and his head began to spin. The man seated before him, his friend, had had access to Hitler but had invaded Russia.

"I didn't hear about your family," he said quietly.

David shrugged. "There will be a lot to forgive."

"Listen, Sunda, in a revolution nothing will be forgiven. . . ." Justin gazed away at two umbrellas from the previous night's storm, crumpled by a waste bin. The struggle to retreat from such open wounds was making him giddy. "But I'm not a revolutionary," he said. "I'm only a writer."

"You will not be without a subject."

Hélène's husband held out a tin of the little cigars that Justin had forgotten and then rested it between them. On his face was a desolation such as Justin had seen in no man.

"In the compound at Nysa, when I pulled the handcarts of the dead, I sometimes dared to think of paradise. One day, you and I and the others would sit together again at Polidor."

Tears came to Justin's eyes. After everything else that had been lost, should he now surrender even his anger? With a sudden motion, he accepted a cigar. "It can never be the same."

"We should try, nonetheless," David finally said. "You and I must drink again to the living."

"To Hélène."

"To Luz." David raised his glass with slightly military stiffness.

Justin shivered a little in the heat, tasting how bitter it might be to forgive. "What was the time when you liked yourself best?"

"When I was on my own," David said. "When to remake myself seemed a heroic enterprise. And you, Justin?"

"Before I ever doubted that some great thinker could change the world," he said.

David smiled. "Then, Justin, you will have to do better."

6

So, under a sort of truce, Justin Lothaire and David Sunda returned to their lives.

Both felt vaguely cursed to find Polidor closed. It was after two when Justin trailed David among the crowded tables of a brasserie on the rue des Écoles. He was so stricken by what was taking place that he had forgotten his face would be known here.

Caught among the wall mirrors, he stood awkwardly until the clapping stopped. After being forced to exchange a few words with a bearded American war correspondent and the book critic of *Les Temps Modernes*, Justin slipped into the corner cubicle, half facing David. Had he not earned the right to eat with whom he liked?

"I could never have believed in such a scene." David put on a pair of spectacles and smiled thoughtfully. "These glasses? Starvation affects one's sight. In fact, you will be the first to hear me speak of our Silesian winter. Eventually, I might hear a description of Stodel's end."

Justin looked into David's magnified eyes. "Then do you wish us to drink to those who are gone?"

"Only to our friends . . . to Johannes, to Duncan," David managed to say, and together they tracked the students of their lost youth to the invisible instants where they had been flung through into death.

"I don't want to drink to anyone else," Justin said quietly, and a silence stretched out between them. What of Luz, or of Hélène? They faced the crowded room, oblivious of the dishes being devoured around them.

"When I see you with these people, Justin, I feel tremendously alone."

"They scarcely know me. I am already being forgotten."

"And your books?"

"You're the one who will not be forgotten. I've no doubt that Baron Sunda has been offered a role in the new Europe."

"That's quite true—United Nations, a sort of new league. Would that be of any use?"

Justin concentrated on the street traffic outside the windows, trying with all his soul to forgive the bitterness for him of David's words. He looked at the oysters the waiter had just put in front of his friend, alive and helpless in their shells. "Do you know Aesop's fable of the clay and iron pots during a flood?" he said. "The iron pot calls to the clay pot: 'I am strong; come near and I will protect you.' The clay pot answers, 'Thank you, sir, but I am afraid of your hard sides.'"

"There are few iron pots left afloat, Justin. I am not one of them. Our finances aren't secure enough for me to accept the new job."

"Not *accept* it?" Justin had replaced his fork. "But you must!"

"No .. no!" David turned pale. "I'll come back to that. First I want to hear about Stodel. I have a stake in him."

"We both took a life. What more should be said?"

After this, Justin and David sat for a long time, eating without taste or recognition. Then, under the same truce, the conversation resumed in a vein of gossip. They spoke of their children; then about Duncan's widow, Eustacia-Jane, who was said to have a son who would inherit the vast Penn fortune. This very week, Doktor Godard's widow had enjoyed a triumphal return to Salzburg in the role of Salomé.

"Yes, I met *la Dolin* in Berlin. At the time I could not understand why Hélène disliked her."

"And now?" Justin was sober. Might that have been the summer of Hélène's letter to him?

But with a sudden glacial indifference, David began to talk of Wilfred Rouve. The Englishman had attempted suicide in Austria rather than obey his idol's order to drive the rebellious Cossack army before the revenge of Stalin's firing squads.

"The fellow was besotted with the prime minister—then to receive such an order. You remember Neuville?"

"The New York decadent? He was your friend."

"He has become a monstrously wealthy broker of works of art from ruined European families."

"And ruined artists," Justin added quietly, horrified and fascinated at what they were returning to before each other's eyes.

Every time David spoke of his wife, Justin felt himself grow more tense and withdrawn. David seemed not to notice, instead extolling Luz and her flowering of personality.

"We might make a bargain . . . you and I," Justin observed.

"Of course," David said gravely. "Are there terms?"

"At the rue de Fleurus, I was always told that I should renounce politics for the written word."

"Ah yes. And myself?"

"This United Nations, David. Give your life to that." Both men were suddenly conscious that this conversation had only just begun, but that they were at the end of their strength. The waiters were dressed to go home. David shook his head.

"No, no, I cannot afford to do it." He paused. "At any rate, not for a few years. Both Hélène's and my own family have lost everything. That must sound strange, Justin, to someone whose mother cleaned lace."

Justin smiled even then. "She always told me I should be grateful for the rich."

"Believe me, Justin," David continued, reaching for some further depth of surrender, "when your books have made you wealthy, you will see. Even to be offered that job depends on a certain social stability, an independence from material pressures. You never experienced the futility, the corruption, of the old League of Nations. Our family has preserved far higher standards of service for centuries. If I can rebuild a small fortune, my sons and their grandsons may continue to be enlightened leaders. I have been devoured by Europe and its problems. We will go to America, even to South America if necessary."

"I have no interest in being rich." Justin's face was tense. "Your sons and grandsons will earn their own way."

"Without family traditions there can be no authority, only power. No stability, no respect for love."

"David! David!" Justin half rose. "Accept the job, my friend," he said. "The humble, the gentle and true, have no one to represent them. It is your fate! Such an assembly could be a new Vatican to cut across squabbling nationalisms—even across gods."

"Or a Tower of Babel? That is the very dream I left in Mexico." David waved for the bill, and Justin quickly took out three notes. "To impose power on top of power, hoping that each greater despot will be more virtuous than the last? There is only one power that is eternal and that all men recognize; that is blood. Justin, you will have my word on this—but only when I have made enough to guarantee my family."

The brasserie's old waiters from before the war attended them, while two young men helped Justin Lothaire and his guest with their jackets. As they stepped into the afternoon warmth, the friends were met by a procession of funeral carriages. On the open hearse was an abnormally large casket with an arrangement of flowers forming the word PÈRE.

Justin paused in the somber crowd, staring at the profile of this man who had been, and still was, David Sunda. "Then the world must wait until enough money is made? There will be no end to it!"

"You see, Justin?" David turned to him from the hearse. "In this flood it is *you* who are the iron pot. Perhaps I should fear *your* hard sides."

Justin shook his head, experiencing then the resources of feeling as yet hidden between them. After all that had been lost, they were still only thirty-three and at the height of their powers. A life lay ahead.

The two men separated at the corner of Saint-Michel, having given their promise to meet again with their wives. But the moment they were alone, the passions of their reunion turned to depression. David went home to the mansion of a marshal of France with the sense that his most sacred beliefs were in some way on probation. Justin returned to Doré's attic and his manuscript, feeling that, after all the sacrifices, nothing had been solved. For both of them, the crisis and the struggle still lay ahead.

EURYDICE

1

THUS BEGAN THE MOST MORALLY EXHAUSTING WEEKS OF DAVID SUNDA'S life—more tiring even than his walk out of Russia, when he had been driven by the will to live and the certainty of death. Both passions were lost to him now.

Yet in this man, Pierre Le Trève had found the brilliant son whom he had been denied in Hélène's brother. With the efforts of his father-in-law—now publicly vindicated by the trial of his old enemy, Pierre Laval—David was received as a Frenchman. And, like other Frenchmen, he was expected to put out of his mind the rise and fall of fascism and be concerned only with profiting, as much and as quickly as possible, from the new situation. Several times a day David would sit at conferences with the financiers, diplomats, and ministers of the Faubourg, assimilating new projects and analyzing data. He was offered a contract from the publisher for whom Rouve now worked to write a memoir of his ordeal. David was shaken by the suggestion that such things could have a public interest or a price.

The conferences confirmed David's suspicion that the Le Trève holdings were as irretrievably lost as those of the Sundas. The balls he and Hélène were obliged to attend left him far less inclined to stay in Europe than he had been before the war. Most alarming of all, Baron Sunda found himself courted by an unrepentant bourgeoisie, with an obsessive dislike of partisans and revolutionaries. The very scenes David longed most to forget—the futile plot-tings, the *Lager*, and his family's disaster—were alluded to over and over as the material of myths. Despite his polite protests, he was even pestered for details of his meeting with Hitler.

So David came to understand the price, measured in his precious new freedom, of working among the hard seigneurs of contracts and profits. As the war had denied him the experience of parenthood, so had it kept hidden the realities of corporate affairs. It was under these conditions that David found himself needing to face Justin Lothaire once again, to see their disagreement set to rest.

As for Justin himself, the weeks following their meeting produced an opposite anxiety: that he might have let slip the harsh discipline of his life. He found himself with a wife who was a public sensation, personal fame in Europe, more money from his royalties than he had ever seen, and even what was called a good address. Justin scarcely understood how these alien rewards had come to one whose obscure dream had been of classical aesthetics and justice. Every fiber of his soul was tense with alarm. He felt at peace now only in the company of Eli Hebron's Algerian friends, whom Justin joined each Sunday for football in the Bois de Boulogne—where the bodies of young *maquisards* had hung from tree branches.

Yet, as if to ridicule the devotion of a night nurse, not even for a moment could he stop thinking of Hélène. Very gradually, Justin was coming to hate them both.

2

ON THE NIGHT THAT THE LOTHAIRES WENT AT LAST TO SUPPER AT THE LE TRÈVES, the three children were fed in the underground kitchen. Here there was sawdust on the floor and a strong smell of garlic, sage, and roasting meat. Frau Gerta presided at the head of the table, her nearly bald head sometimes inclining on her pleated neck, to keep matters under control. She had only just begun to learn French, and after Gustav's return to Oberlinden she was alone here. Yet she was unvaryingly dignified and forgiving. No one who knew the fate of her only child in a eugenics clinic could help but feel shame at his own riches and vanity, and this would have been unbearable without her forgiveness.

"Albert, you must finish your soup!"

"My doll! Rickie—he took it, him!" Sarah shrieked on her high chair, beginning to cry. In fact this little girl, whom Luz brought as often as she could, loved these visits to the great kitchen cellar more than anything else, and especially Gerta's kind eyes. And for all the children, who had been that afternoon to ride ponies in the Bois, there was, and needed to be, nothing else but this.

"You took it, Rickie!" cried Albert. The aged Bertrand turned from the furnace and flapped his short apron at them.

Rickie screamed. "Hide it, Gnome, hide it!"

"Fighting like cats and dogs," muttered Gerta.

"Cats and dogs! Cats and dogs!" The boys jumped down and began to chase Gnome around the chairbacks, dodging Gerta's ponderous pursuit. Sylvie entered from the pantry stairs with the heavy silver soupière.

"*Zut*, what do you think of comrade Justin?" Going to the roaring furnace, the maid felt the hazelnut stuffing in the roast. "His adventures make him deaf and dumb. I must offer the soup four times before he hears me!"

Lifting the heavy tray—without a glance at her pile of illustrated maga-zines with their photos of Luz Holti—Sylvie went back up the staircase, leaving below the squeals, Gerta's *now-nows*, and Bertrand's muttered curses as he inspected in his bowl of egg whites for a trace of yolk that might keep the soufflé from rising.

In the great house overhead, it was dark. Approaching the open garden doors, Sylvie paused to rest the tray on the back of the couch. Voices came indistinctly from the candles under the willow, then a burst of subdued laughter.

"*Comme c'est beau!*" Sylvie whispered, and she began to sniff with panic at the thought of the heartless capital, swarming with soldiers and ordinary women who had children, into which she might soon be turned out. This became a hatred for Monsieur Justin, who came like a spy out of that unkind world. As the maid bent to serve the two couples—checking the silverware and holding the roast as low as possible, with the serving spoon near each plate—she breathed the scent from the actress's hair, saw the soft skin on her breasts, and heard the wild note in her laugh. Across the dim bed of crystal Madame Hélène's eyes flickered over their faces, finally resting on the hard, unworthy profile of Monsieur Justin. As she held the plate for Baron Sunda, the maid glanced reproachfully at their guest.

The unworthy Justin's eyes were fixed on herself! For some reason, at that look, Sylvie's accusation disappeared, and she felt ignorant, ungainly, and humble. During the break in the conversation, the serving plate swayed in her hands.

3

BY THE GREEN SPLASHING POOL, THE FRIENDS—WHO FOR THE LAST HOUR HAD had their four lives before them as one life—were hearing, more than anything being said, the secret voice of memories and impressions. Justin only awoke from this dream with the arrival of the roast veal. At the sight of such a dish, being served to them in a private garden at the heart of Paris, he had felt shaken by how truly little was altered, and he had glanced up at the simple *pied-noir* woman who was holding the plate as at a sister still in bondage.

There had been just two days' warning that Justin was to see again the person whose return to Paris could hold him in exile. Luz had arrived at *Justice* from a rehearsal with news of a farewell dinner for the Sundas, inter-rupting an argument with the new editor of *Justice*—that defender of Stalin's collectivizations, the Hitler pact, and the continuing purges, d'Issipe. The actress's arrival, speaking of privileged friends about to sail from Lisbon, had made Justin's old rival smile quietly.

Yet tonight, by the great staircase, when Justin had seen again the mature, mocking wisdom of Hélène's face and had held her strong hand in his—barely noting that she was some months pregnant—the intervening war had vanished. The dark weight of evil and hatred had fallen behind, and he felt his happiness as surely as if he had been at Grinda's farm. It had been that shy and tongue-tied Justin the maid had commented on in the kitchen.

Through the weak light, Hélène had taken note of Justin's absorbed glance at Sylvie. Following his thought—unable to measure whether this profoundly modest man had ever read her treacherous words of love—she took pleasure in the kindness of his glance. For Hélène had been torn, despite her own feelings about her husband, to see the suffering to which David's reunion with Justin had reduced him.

As the maid moved intently through the shadows behind their backs, the two surviving couples could scarcely look into one another's faces. At that moment, David too was feeling bewildered by the gentle, almost saintly manner of this man who only weeks before had been able to crush his soul with guilt for a million deaths.

During the nights that had followed, a single bitter truth had forced itself on David's consciousness. Yes, they might be equal in having taken one life. But while the blood on Justin's hands belonged to Hitler's depraved biologist, the blood on the hands of Major von Sunda, he now acknowledged, might have been that of Hitler himself—before further hosts of human lives had been lost.

It had taken him more weeks to come to terms with the implications of such an admission. By that time, the plans to take his family to New York had already been made. When Hélène announced that there was to be the farewell dinner, David knew instantly that at the first opportunity he would take Justin into his confidence—but that he must express no remorse, ask no advice, and beg for no forgiveness. To do so, he knew instinctively, would attribute a divinity to Justin that his friend would forgive least of all.

Humbled by the pain that awaited him, David had welcomed Justin and Luz in the empty hallway with the most sensitive solemnity. Now, at this darkened table under the willow, feeling that he had somehow been deceived by the reticent, childlike intellectual seated across from him, David could not begin to face the thing in his heart. Instead, he had guided the dinner conversation through the most superficial pleasantries about their domestic lives and future plans. Joining in, Luz had even made Justin laugh repeatedly—with a tone almost of forgiveness.

For some time, Justin had heard almost nothing of what was being said. In Hélène's look of grateful warmth, of pleasure in him as he was tonight, Justin was detecting a certain defensiveness on her husband's behalf. He was suddenly conscious that she was indeed pregnant—had Hélène wanted another child by David? What upheaval was Justin plotting to bring into the lives of these people he loved?

Now, as the others spoke, she leaned toward him. "Justin, after all this, are you happy . . . are you well?"

"I think so, Hélène. Tonight."

"Why haven't I seen you?" she asked, once again having to read his mood. She wished he could know that this pregnancy had begun on her first night with a fugitive of war; that she and David had had no further relations whatever, and how cruel this was.

"How would that have been possible?"

"Would it not have been important? You and I are close too."

"Yes, of course," he said. And for some reason, as he spoke to the woman with whom he had been obsessed for twelve years, bitterness hardened his features.

"I had a copy of your book in Germany, with the covers torn off."

Hearing those words, at the image of *Les Thébans* with its covers torn off to hide the identity of a dangerous text, Justin wished only—as his reward for six years without seeing her—to take the face of the one being he cherished between his hands as easily as he had touched other faces. The idea seemed so insane that he bent his head. Hélène did not even need to ask whether Justin had read her letter; she must see it on his face. Another thought struck him. Since she was pregnant, was the woman perhaps asking only for a pledge of secrecy?

"Yes, I liked the central character," Hélène went on gravely. "An entire people depends on him, yet he is powerless before the forces of the unconscious. He cannot prevent himself from doing just the wrong thing."

"Yes," Justin said. "That is exactly what I was after."

"And your work now?" Hélène inquired softly, almost as if he had just rejected her.

"Bad. . . . I am not sure, so much has happened," Justin went on, feeling both of them to be as vulnerable as children.

"Don't worry, Justin. Time will bring it back to you. Think of what always comes from great struggles, whether they are won or lost."

"Maybe, for those of us who will fight to the limit," he managed to say. Perhaps they should speak now of the letter.

In the suddenly hushed garden they both heard Luz's voice, talking with great confidence—almost as if she had known these people well—of Johannes, Heidrun, and Duncan and of their incomprehensible lives. Tonight, as they were speaking at last, Justin did not wish Hélène to listen to his wife, her oldest friend. Tonight must be his final chance. As Luz went on, with Hélène silenced at his side, Justin wondered how it was that he had led this fragile Hungarian to safety out of the ruins of her world. How could it be that the love letter sent to Rochet's farm, folded tonight inside his jacket, had still not been mentioned by himself or Hélène? Perhaps *everyone* knew of that wartime indiscretion and expected Justin to put it aside.

Luz seemed to have become alert to the intricate spell that was at work among the willow branches. She paused, as if to sniff the air. "I never thought we would spend an evening like this again! Leni, why must you leave tomorrow?"

"David knows that better than I do," Hélène answered quietly.

"I would go to New York if I were David," Justin said, almost drunk on disappointment and wishing only to stand back from these people.

At his side, Hélène had lowered her hands to her lap. From the torture of asking herself if Justin had received her letter, she was suddenly certain that he had. She knew then that she must say the few words that would free her from this suffering, and seal their lives for ever.

"Justin?" she heard herself begin again, "have you decided whether you will stay?"

A confusion broke over him, so dense that Justin felt himself blinded. How could he stay, once she had left? "Since you ask," he said, "I *have* felt the urge to swim in the Mediterranean again."

Hélène laughed nervously. "I understand you so well!" She glanced at David and Luz, now absorbed with one another. "I feel the same about America, even not having been there. Perhaps it's a holy land for us, as the desert is for you." She paused, then said suddenly, "Justin, during the war, did you receive a letter from me?"

The maid was approaching through the garden, bearing the blue flame of Bertrand's soufflé flambé. With a happy smile that excluded the unworthy Justin, the maid lowered the dish between David and Luz.

But Justin was looking straight into Hélène's eyes. Her letter? What did she want him to say about her letter? In her eyes there seemed to be tears of humiliation . . . then, in the dying leap of the candle flame, something else— a hot hatred, as hot as if they had been lovers all those twelve years.

"We had no mail in the Jura, Hélène. . . . And your music? Do you still play?"

"Do I still play?" She laughed gaily, folding her napkin. "In Germany my piano came into its own. I'll play you something before I put the children to bed."

Hélène rose from the table and bent with great tenderness to kiss Luz. Then they watched her cross the garden, past the green pool with its little Mercury. After some moments, during which Justin avoided David's urgent gaze, he heard her piano again, deep in the house as long ago. The piece was unfamiliar. Experiencing only a horrible pain at the sacrifice he had just made for David, he took the plate that his friend was handing across the candle flames. Hélène had stopped playing.

At ten o'clock, David led them through the darkened rooms into the great hall. Hélène had not reappeared. As David embraced Luz and then turned to Justin, both men felt a sort of incredulity that the healing conversation which followed inevitably on the Place des Vosges had somehow not taken place.

Then the Le Trèves' door closed for the last time. With his child's head asleep against his cheek, Justin walked beside Luz down the drive and out through the iron gate. Unable to look back at the great entrance through which he had carried so many passions, he led them up the street towards the flame of the unknown soldier.

"Papa?" The tiny body stirred in his arms. "I dreamt that you left us."

"No, no, little one. What a silly thing."

Luz took his arm. "It hurts me to see you angry with him, Justin. David brought us together."

"Yes, David is a fine man. He is the most civilized man that I know."

But from the hour of that summer farewell at Hélène's, Justin's marriage became intolerable to him. David, meanwhile, was confirmed in his suspicion that during his long absence his wife had become as mindlessly religious as his mother had been before her. He wondered if he would ever again find, in the ashes, a coal to rekindle her love for him. As for Luz—usually sensitive to all things, but who at the garden table, as David and her husband had lost the struggle for their friendship while the woman Justin adored sat out of reach at his side—Luz had grasped little of the specters, sublime and grotesque that had possessed the only three friends of her life; she felt her splendid new success to be caught in old instabilities.

4

IN AUTUMN—ON A SUNDAY WHEN JUSTIN LOTHAIRE HAD FINALLY ACCEPTED an invitation to the salon of Rosa and Gregor Lambert—Eli Hebron came at last to the Palais-Royal.

Europe's first winter after the war was on its way. In Paris, the evenings darkened early and the leaves curled along the empty boulevards like snow, until soon the swinging branches overhead appeared as sharp as finger bones, and the wind fluffed women's fur coats and blew the carriage horses' tails between their legs. When the atelier bell rang unexpectedly, Justin's first thought was that Hélène was in New York. Pulling off the sweater that he wore for work, he waited at the door. Soon Eli appeared up the stairs with a broad smile and gripped him by the shoulders.

Justin stared with terrible intensity at his friend, as at something hungered for but abstract. *Les Thébans* was translated into twenty languages now, yet he had felt himself losing the love of those who once followed him.

"I want you to be ready for my news," Eli said at once, and his smile deepened.

With a sudden vivid grin, Justin put his arm around his visitor's neck. Eli was tremendously excited. "I'm ready, Eli. Come in for coffee."

They entered the kitchen, with its square sunny table. Across it, the face that adorned the cover of every magazine at every kiosk in Paris glanced up at them. Eli blushed and bowed to her. Then he took off his new jacket, as Luz cleared some scripts from the bench next to Sarah. As she was led out, the little girl stared steadily at Eli's watering clown's eyes.

"Now, Eli, you must tell me," Justin said.

"Do you remember Spain?" Eli almost whispered "How at this table I told you that Figueroa's body had been found on the beach at Málaga? . . . Justin? Justin, it is time for you to go back to Algiers."

Justin's heart was pounding. *Would the revolution come now to the desert, to Algiers, even to his own alleyways?* "Eli, you know we have been ruined by such fantasies. A teller of *kef* stories must face his poverty."

"From Saigon to Madrid to Bogotá, who do the poor have but you?"

"Can't you see me, Eli?" Justin rose angrily. "I'm a writer and a snob. I don't have the courage to face my own mother. Why should they want such a wreckage?"

"Justin, I'll tell you what you know. Everywhere, infamous elites will be overthrown, all through Africa and Latin America, and in the Orient," Eli cried softly. "But Algiers will be first!"

Once again the blood pounded in Justin's temples. It was like a sign. The coffee was cold. He emptied it on Luz's geraniums and poured more. "Eli, for six years, civilization has been in a chaos of evil. The revolution did not come. Perhaps it will never come, *should* never come."

"It came here, and in America and Russia—and now it will come in Algiers. They're asking for you, Justin."

"Eli, Eli, can it be you who speaks of Russia?"

"The one who asks most is known as Abu."

Justin reached out and held Eli's wrist. Were not these the people who had loved him? "Abu . . . Abu Grinda?"

"Abu Grinda," Eli confirmed. "Will you go?"

Turning to the gable, Justin looked down at the shop arcade and at the fountains. He could see the most famous female writer in France move behind her windows. She had not spoken one public word about the Fascist empire. He thought about Marcel Doré and of the human spirit, lying half dead in the clinics of science. Then, without warning, Justin was remembering Melanie in the watertower, her frank, mischievous eyes and the hot skin of her breasts; which splendid wealth had been Justin's before he had anything. He smelled again the yellow mimosa and heard the Mediterranean, beating as ever down the long beaches. He was shocked by the beauty of these things he had left behind, to test his convictions in a meadow of ice.

"I'll say this to you alone, Eli." He returned to the table. "Lothaire no longer has certain convictions. He's not sure of political force—nor gods, nor devils, nor love. I understand incredibly little. Tell me, Eli, who am I to lead? Why should I be followed?"

Eli met Justin's stare with a smile of apology that bared his big teeth. His long hair, parted in wings from the center, floated in the rising heat. He was like an angel.

"Only because you're the best among us." Eli shrugged, then he lowered his voice. "And if you're not certain about gods and devils . . . still, surely, you're certain of man?"

"Yes, finally the earth belongs to men. They will find new heroes."

"No, it must be you. And it's time to tell you my news. Forget your indifference, Justin. Open your ears and your heart and be amazed. Listen, and I'll tell you who will be the next bishop of Paris."

Justin felt his skin begin to creep. He nodded.

"Duroc," Eli whispered. "Baptiste Duroc, Justin!"

Justin was up and away from the table so suddenly that the bench fell with a crash. He stood in the corner between the stove and the icebox, striking matches. The fifth match lit and did not break.

For, with those two well-remembered words, Justin was being swept back through the tunnel of violence. Jean-Baptiste Duroc! Plump Duroc, who had tried to control Justin through the prostitute Maline . . . who had defended the pope over the transportations. . . . Duroc, whose saints' calendar had had another name penciled on it; who had betrayed Justin Lothaire to Joseph Darnand! Justin's torturer had only very recently been executed. What was this peace which so many had died for, that such a priest should be allowed immunity by the French government, elevated as a successor to the apostles, protected by the law? It was intolerable.

"I'm promising nothing. Let me think. Tell Abu I'll see him. But no one else." Justin looked at Eli. His face softened almost shyly. "Perhaps it's time I went home."

"Good," Eli said, his eyes watering tenderly. "Each week, there's a mail plane. They say it's very easy."

"You *are* impatient, Eli." Justin laughed, suddenly feeling himself very near the casbah and Grinda's farm. "The desert has waited a million years."

"Fly, Justin! Take the plane over the sea."

With that curious invocation, Eli Hebron left Justin alone in the Palais-Royal with his work, feeling now quite certain that his much-altered friend still belonged to the revolution.

5

MORE SO EVEN THAN DURING THE ASCENT OF HITLER, THE LAMBERT SALON was now a meeting place for influential minds from all over the world. Ho Chi Minh, Bergson, Villa-Lobos, Sinclair Lewis, Picasso, Bohr, Chaplin, and Brandt had all come here, yet it was hard to say why this should be so. The pretentious Lambert was a psychiatrist, and his motherly wife only an amateur poet given to obscenity. Nevertheless, in these low-ceilinged rooms could be heard the great philosophical and aesthetic arguments of the time. In the months that followed the disgrace of the occupation—and Hitler's escape into death—these arguments had assumed an echo of trauma. Where there had once been Europe's fatted calf, now there were only gray dialectical scraps and the smell of burning flesh. The banqueters fought over these with desperate intolerance, rupturing old friendships on the finest distinctions and, where there were no distinctions, creating them.

Among all the scraps for debate that autumn, the most distinct and the least gray was Justin Lothaire. Throughout that month, a debate concerning the celebrated poet-*chef* had been carried on in the press. Armed with the news that Doré's protégé was to make his first social appearance since the war, Rosa Lambert had invited several dozen Academicians, newspaper editors, Popular Front ministers, political thinkers, literati—and even two of the new anthropologists. All of them had accepted, aside from a minister who had not dared to support Justin at the Élysée and who now had come down with gout.

Only hours after Eli's visit, the Lothaires crossed a courtyard in the Marais. Once again an outcast of the underground climbed those worn stairs. At the first din of so many heated voices, Justin halted, as if drenched with the ice water of history. Like an immense, rippling black cape, the incubus of Duroc—tonight, somewhere out in the French capital—wrapped itself around him.

Justin glided among the candlelit tables. Two people separated from an alert group under a Gold Coast totem. One was stooped and swung her arms; the other was quick and precise—Rosa Lambert, and Jean-François d'Issipe, whom Justin had not seen since their argument at *Justice*.

"Despite yourself, you make an entrance." D'Issipe grasped Justin's arm and led him away from Luz.

"In fact, I'm glad to see you," Justin replied, vividly remembering their escape from this house. It seemed scarcely credible that this cultivated man could have called Nadezhna Stalin "'limited and naive" for her suicide following her husband's slaughter of vast numbers of their fellow peasants.

"And I'm glad to see you, Justin. Many of us here are waiting to hear what you have to say."

Justin faced d'Issipe as they stood together under a wooden spirit, its features set in a pre-missionary scowl of darkness. "Not tonight."

"But *l'argument Justin Lothaire* has been in progress for months! You must say a few words, at least!"

From across the next room, the editor of *L'Express* was watching the young North-African in the worn jacket. He noted the fellow's sober profile, now bent beside that of his equally famous antagonist. It was this person who, in a Europe silenced by guilt, carried the most convincing legend of incorruptibility. The man's face could not have been other than as it was.

"Tell us, Justin"—d'Issipe was measuring his words easily—"what is your opinion of the German war trials?"

Justin had detected d'Issipe's tremor of insincerity, and he felt faint. He smiled vaguely. "I would prefer a court that judged the science technocrats as well as their crimes."

Tightening his grip, d'Issipe drew Justin into the main salon. The way was blocked by two bald men and a handsome blonde woman.

"Lothaire was just telling me that mass states should be on trial at Nuremberg," observed d'Issipe.

"Does this include the Soviet state?"

The woman joined in. "Monsieur Lothaire, do you then accept the rumors of millions purged by the Party?"

"Does one speak of millions dying as true or untrue?" Justin murmured. Perspiration started down his temples at the withering eloquence like vanity that stirred in his heart.

He caught sight then of the chaise-longue where, long ago, a student had sat in the company of Doré and Hélène. With great clarity, Justin could hear an experienced woman, more recently under the Le Trèves' willow tree, asking with sweet determination if Justin had read her wartime letter. *What if she still wanted him to do so?*

In the smoke that surrounded him, a crescent of convex lenses glinted like the eyes of wolves. "Justin, has your view of the capitalist democracies improved?"

Justin concentrated. "Capitalism? . . . Oh, naked capitalism can be as cruel as naked communism, although capitalism sometimes wears clothes." Again, these intellectuals, whose names he probably knew well, laughed before he had finished. The thoughts of Hélène could come again later.

"What is your opinion of de Gaulle?" "Should pluralism survive in Europe?" "Is film an art form?"

Justin's eloquence took stride. "Films, can convince a man of almost anything. Even the atomic bomb has not done that."

From the neighboring rooms there was a drift to join Justin Lothaire's circle. Yet something strange had taken place. Not only was Justin unable to move away, he could not stop himself from answering in riddles out of his most ambiguous depths. As in a opium dream, he recognized a questioning face beside d'Issipe: Jalvin, once again. A bitter taste came through Justin's cigarette. *Keep still*, cried a voice inside him. But even stronger was Justin's hunger to bear witness to himself.

"The religions?" he was saying. "Yes, human love is lonely for its hosts . . . and God? I no longer think that man is virtuous enough to invent him or intelligent enough to say he does not exist."

He remained on his feet, hemmed in by politely attentive faces. Who was *he* to say these things? Even in this room no one had stood alone against such mysteries. Now, with mild simplicity, Justin Lothaire was answering them. They were choosing a king.

"What lesson do you find for the West in the Socialist experiment?"

"Is art necessary any longer, Justin?"

It was as if, across his long struggle out of the dark alleys of the mind, Justin Lothaire had lived by a perfect belief that somewhere, among the supremely enlightened, all questions were forever answered. Now he felt himself caught in the grinding of great glaciers. Something stirred in Justin's heart that was ugly and terrible. What if he, or any of these here, were wrong—and his mother, as she crawled before a cardboard Virgin, had been right? At that instant Justin understood Johannes Godard and the coming of Hitler.

Yet still he continued to answer their questions, many tinged already with the sarcasm that precedes the fall of gods.

"If you will excuse me!" Justin stared around him so wildly that the blonde poetess recoiled; then he was pulling free with surprising ease. He moved through the deafening shadows, trying to overcome the terror of his words.

Behind the coats, hung like discarded souls, his hands fished in the soapy water as he stared at his face in the mirror. Tonight, Hélène was in New York and Jean-Baptiste Duroc was alive somewhere in the Paris night. Justin knew he would not go back to be told his meaningless story in the big salon. Rosa had rooms that even Justin Lothaire could be silent in.

Later, under their roof in the Palais-Royal, seated in Justin's Chinese chair, Luz watched her husband pace.

"Everything is lost. . . . I have been through too much. I have nothing more to write to Europeans who don't listen. I must return to the desert . . . alone."

Justin's ravings rang between the walls of their marriage like the hammers of revolution. In thirty seconds it was done, and he fell silent, breathing heavily. There was nothing left. All was beyond recall.

That night, and for many nights after, Justin Lothaire dreamt of a charred, alien place, neither day nor night. He lay awake, feverish with hatred of Duroc, and enacted the ways he would claim the life this priest owed him. And as he lay awake, Luz secretly lay awake with him.

6

THEN JUSTIN WOKE ONE DAWN AND KNEW THAT TONIGHT HE WOULD SLEEP AGAIN in the rue Mahbu.

That morning, the Paris air was once again bright with suggestion. Inside the atelier door there was a letter from the Sundas, who, Luz had told him, were living on Central Park. Justin had not asked to read it, and during the two-hour flight to Marseille—while the clear blue sky outside kicked and shook them as if it were trapped beast—he was repeatedly sick. After three more hours, shuddering low over the white-capped Mediterranean, he saw a yellow beach edging out. Then there were brown roads among vineyards and a green football pitch with the ends worn gray. Five minutes later, Justin pulled himself to his feet and carried his old camel-hide suitcase down the fuselage to the door.

He seemed to be dreaming. Out across the sun-baked dirt, behind a fence, there was a crowd of robed Arabs. Spelled in blue letters on the blindingly white shed was the word ALGER. Three steps down, and Justin Lothaire felt again the firm weight of the desert under his soles. He was weak and hungry—and something far stronger. He needed to lie face down on the nearby earth, to bury his fingers in it, to feel it against his stomach and face. But a dozen journalists were waiting with their Graflexes. Justin did not smile, and he declined to talk. Then he could not talk.

As he paused among the welcoming faces at the gate, Justin saw a balding Arab in a linen suit. He freed himself and walked forward past the gendarmes. The man came toward him. Justin put down his suitcase and tried to speak.

"Welcome home, Justin. Welcome."

Justin moved his lips. "Abu . . . Abu."

"Are you well, Justin?" Abu stared at the white face with its livid scars.

"Flying is for angels," he tried to say. They were both weeping. Justin held up his hand, and the picture-taking stopped.

Beyond the customs hall they met four street performers with made up eyes. Whirling their red skirts, the young men blew together on flutes. Then, laughing wildly, they spun and danced ahead of Justin. As the procession passed out through the cool lobby, trailed by the journalists, a group of armed French officers stood watching. Abu took Justin's arm.

"The gray reptile is a colonel of parachutists from China. What is it, Justin?"

"Nothing. Memories."

He had halted unsteadily in the heat. The officer near the door—the handsome one who had stared at Justin most grimly—was without question *her* brother, Jean-Marc Le Trève! In the emotion of his return, Justin was taken by surprise at the intense nostalgia he had just felt for a boy he had never even liked. He crushed out the feeling.

Dancing, swooping low, waving their feet, and piping a frantic tune—Justin knew it, "Jamalia"—the musicians led them to a carriage standing under a eucalyptus. All four salaamed with deep bows and then fled silently on their bare feet. Justin stared after them as the horse broke into a trot.

"And my mother?" He looked at his boyhood friend's hardened features.

"She was afraid of travelling so far." Abu examined Justin. "Do not misunderstand the silence of the crowd, Justin. You have heard of the revenge taken by the French at Sétif?"

"They do not say how many died."

"Five, possibly fifteen thousand Arabs. Your return is a great hour for the Maghreb."

"Certainly for me, Abu. . . . And your sister, Melanie?" Justin went on, after a shocked silence.

"Melanie? She and Michaud live with their two children at my father's farm."

"Michaud, at Grinda's farm!" Justin's incredulous gesture shook the carriage. "What of Monsieur Lavil?"

"This is not clear. They say Vichy eliminated him."

For some minutes, as they entered the city, Justin sat, with his face hidden from his gentle friend by a fountain in the mosque. Abu had spoken of the butchery of thousands. Justin stared at the waiting carts festooned with ragged Arabs and red grapes, at two urchins fighting over a crushed cat, and at the cyclists as they wove through clouds of dust. Above the horizon of palms and heat waves was the blue-gray ribbon of the Atlas. The loyal teacher gone, with whom he had discussed the Greeks on the ruins of Tipasa; and Michaud, now with children by the first and best woman he had loved. While he had endured the passions of Carbonne, had the two deep hopes of his life been cut from under him? Justin was thunderstruck. He scarcely had the strength in his life now for such disappointments.

"Justin, everything has changed for you here."

"Don't say it. There's nowhere else I belong. All this"—Justin's arm took in the Berber tents, the dusty, shouting din of the roads, the fellahin crowded in the shade patches—"all this—as with China, Vietnam, India, Brazil—all this, *my* desert, will be free one day! Until then I will return often, but never for the Comintern. We can do better than Communists."

"You Jesuit! But it's true—we *must* do better."

For the first time, the strangeness of Justin and Abu ending up in the same movement had been acknowledged. Now their carriage was among the French galleries of the rue Michelet.

"Abu, let's eat before we enter the casbah," Justin said. "I'm not ready for boiled noodles yet."

"In the morning, you'll see our three leaders. They are very interested to meet this hero of all Europe who shares their blood."

Still, at their fish bistro, Justin could not stop thinking about the powerful sense of Hélène that he had felt at the airport—nor of the perfect hatred with which her brother had looked at him.

7

THERE CAME A MOMENT FOR JUSTIN, PRESSED AGAINST THE ALLEY WALL BY A donkey balanced under bloody sheepskins, when the copper beaters began softly to taunt him: *français, sale race!* On the cornerstone overhead, where it had always been, was a blue plaque: RUE MAHBU. The sweet pain in Justin turned to anguish.

His legs carried him up the filthy alley. Just ahead was a tiny shop. Its door was open. Justin stood holding his case. His eyes moved with the beat of his heart among the terrible furnishings of this poor little room. The lace tablecloth was lifted aside, and an old woman stood before him, plain and sad-faced. A slice of orange sunset threw his shadow across her.

"Mother . . . Mother?"

Jeanne Lothaire clasped her fingers over her lean stomach. "So, Justin . . . you have come," she replied, as her eyes traveled over him very slowly, up and down.

Lifting his arms, Justin held the stiff old body awkwardly. She did not unclasp her hands. Justin released her.

His mother drew away, her hands tugging at her sleeves. "Did that Arab meet you?"

"Abu? Yes, Maman."

"Why an Arab?"

"He is my great friend."

"In the papers you look French."

"So you've seen them?" he said. They stood together by the iron mangle. It seemed impossible that Justin had never before grasped the filth and poverty of these alleys or felt the disgrace of this life. Could she not understand that her son could free her from it, as few are set free?

"Did I see the papers?" his mother repeated as she turned from him. "I will make tea."

Staring around these sacred walls, Justin felt as if he had just betrayed them, and he hated his weakness. "Yes, mint tea. This lace, Maman, do I know it?"

"Yes, Justin. Madame Michaud has been good to me. We share our sorrows. Imagine her Michel, marrying the illegitimate sister of a half-caste!"

A sick panic shot into Justin's stomach. Had he accomplished nothing in his life? "Don't I send you enough?" He was hoarse with pain. "It's not necessary to have anything to do with the Michauds or their lace."

As Justin sat once again at their table, Jeanne Lothaire went to the recess of his books. Freeing a tile, she removed a thick envelope and held it out to him.

"Take your money, Justin! Count it. I am a decent woman. I will not live on money earned from revolution. Take it . . . take it! Justin, why didn't you send me honest money, so I could move to the French quarter? There are no French left in the casbah. I don't feel safe."

"Maman, *your* husband was Arab! *Your* son is a half-caste."

"In the magazine you looked French. One stays with one's own race."

The neighbors would all know of Justin Lothaire's return. There had just been a thundering groan of desert violins. Instantly, the sound was turned down. The envelope lay untouched on the table before him. Justin stared

gravely at the woman by the stove. He had felt the cut of his mother's prejudice. Didn't she know he was received in a Paris society so high the Michauds
would have sold their house to go with him? But it was too late. Justin had
renounced all that now, to join again the people of the sands.

"How long will you be here, Justin?"

"I can't say. I don't know," he whispered. "I want to go up to the roof."

"Don't . . . stay with me here," his mother said quickly.

After the shock of their words, they sat in silence. His mother was staring
at Justin's marked face. Already, his memory of the world beyond the lace
shop was losing its clarity. As it sailed behind its old illusion, it seemed more
fabulous and heroic. At the same time, Justin's place in it seemed less sure—
as if he were looking back from beyond the grave. The walls had darkened,
and the shop grills in the rue Mahbu began to crash down.

Presently his mother reached across the packet of money and felt his
jacket. "That is good English material."

"It was from a friend."

Justin scarcely trusted himself to remember David Sunda. In the near
darkness, his mother was staring suspiciously. She neither lighted the oil lamp
nor asked him about her grandchild—or about the war. Justin listened to the
loud tick of the clock and, from somewhere among the inner loggias, the wild
laughter of a woman's voice. Thinking of the people who depended on him,
Justin struggled with an acute, annihilating fear that was spreading from his
stomach.

"Who would have thought that God would save you?"

"There was no mystery. It was hard work."

"No, Justin, you must thank God. Come to the kitchen."

"*Pardon*, Maman. That is all weakness."

His mother struck a match and twisted the spindle on the ceramic lamp.
The old woman gazed at the flame with a gentle smile. Justin was leaning
against the iron mangle, his cigarette unlit.

"Is it strong, then, to be ungrateful? My son, we are living in paradise,"
she said.

In paradise, Justin thought deliriously. *Warsaw, the abattoirs, Carbonne
. . . paradise?*

"This dangerous race you live among. Are they paradise as well?" His
voice shook. He wanted only to rest.

"I lost my French clients because of you. How else would I survive?"

Jeanne Lothaire showed little surprise as her son swayed to his feet.
"Justin, first shut the bars," she said.

When he had crashed down the grill on the rue Mahbu, and it was locked
to the ground, Justin went through to the kitchen. There was a mat on the gray
stone and, above the Virgin's niche, a cockroach, anchored in its shadow. Too
unsettled by this homecoming to think of Baptiste Duroc or of what he was

about to bring down on his mother's life, Justin crouched on the straw. One elbow under him, he stared hard at the Virgin in the niche—no longer cardboard but porcelain. Half listening to his mother's indescribably sweet voice, addressing spirits as if they were in the lace shop, Justin thought of an assassin and his victim. As he heard again the splintering thrash of the dying man, he thought of that assassin, come to inspire the bloody rising of an entire race.

When his mother had finished thanking God for the rich, and for having granted her son redemption, Justin Lothaire once again carried a mattress up onto the roof. All around him, there arose the colored lights of the souk.

As he shook out a blanket, he heard a flapping sound. He spun and crouched, his scalp bristling; there was the silhouette of a head at the top of the ladder.

"You see, Justin? It is good fortune. A stork has moved to our chimney."

"Damn! . . . damn!" Justin whispered. Had he imagined it was the angel Gabriel? He could see a wing sway in the faint light above his mother's head.

Turning from her gaze, Justin stood, a motionless shadow looking down over the tiled rookery to the sea, shining black as tar. It was just the same, the same anger and fertile hunger. And he thought, *Well, and so here you are, and you cannot come further back than this.*

Then Justin thought of Luz and knew he could never have brought her to this place.

8

For a long time he paced the ledge, drinking in the screech of trams, the honk of mules, and the husky moan of a Cairo diva, repeating over and over *habibi-habibi*—all washed together in a murmur like some ancient spiritual surf, breaking upon the desire of the night. The hiccuping, hysterical laughter of a young woman's voice echoed in his ears among the medina roofs. In his exhaustion Justin saw again, as before Hitler, the earth—its most virulent jungles, its loneliest beaches, and its most barren peaks—populated by a new race of men, bringing a fire of enlightenment to return humankind to its place in nature. The hour had come very close.

In the night it rained, and Justin was forced to carry his damp mattress back down the ladder into the lace shop. Still, he slept deeply. When he woke on the floor under the porcelain icon, all around him was Algiers the White, spread out voluptuously in never-ending day, spilling bougainvillea, hibiscus, and jasmine, and with its unabashed youths of the beaches having no secrets to tell. Justin could hear his mother's voice.

"So you are awake at last? A boy came with a letter."

"This morning?"

"Yes, now there is a Frenchman at the corner! Justin, what are you doing here?"

The ink had run, but Justin could just read Abu's Arabic scrawl. A steady rain spattered under the bead screen.

After a beignet and coffee, eaten in his mother's accusing silence, he put on his sweater under the jacket.Would she denounce him, then? The possibility could not be dismissed. Presently, taking the umbrella and bearing with him the terror of his fate, Justin set out to overthrow the place of his greatest happiness.

He easily lost his *Sûreté* shadow at the leather dyers, where the apprentices still swam to stir the great vats. For the next two hours Justin searched the town, from its staircases to the docks. The cafés like film sets along the rue Michelet were filled with a new generation of heroes after the American occupation. Justin saw the way the young men pushed their biceps forward with their fists, and how the girls strolling the galleries stacked their breasts with handkerchiefs. But he scarcely noticed the sad passing of his own generation, beside the poverty and silent humiliation that he now saw everywhere among the race of his father. Justin kept away from the watertower, and he bypassed Melanie's cafe table in the Carré Mosqué, and even Ahmet's bicycle shop in the medina wall, where Justin might still have been working today. He did not have the courage to see his cutthroat cousin, who had once delighted in cursing and throwing wrenches. He would now be afraid of Justin Lothaire.

9

A FEW MINUTES LATER HE TURNED UP A TOWERING SHAFTLIKE PASSAGE THAT mounted under gridwork bridges. Through a heavy studded door the rain thrashed on a courtyard pool and splattered from corner drains like the four rivers of the world. Four barefooted men in raincoats and a bearded one in a *cachabia*, Messali, turned curiously at Abu's side as Justin came in. When he saw these faces—Ahmed Ben Bella's, known to him from before Carbonne— Justin forgot his unwillingness. Going up to the group, he kissed each one with a faint smile: Fehrat Abbas . . . El Mehdi Ben Barka. The fifth man he knew nothing about.

"Justin . . . Justin." They were moved, their eyes flashed. Abu led the six of them around the colonnade to the elevated cubicle of a *shaikh,* where a boy tended a teapot.

"Was anyone followed?"

"Fehrat and Ahmed," Abu answered. "The French are easily tricked."

"It will be remarked that we all vanished at the same time. That is how it will be from now on," Justin said. Around him, the strong faces exchanged looks.

For four hours, that day, the *chefs* of the Maghreb were uneasily together, speaking in different tones—though always in the sweet Arabic that at any time or place is the music of the Koran. Justin's spirit was stirred as he recognized the bitter tales of the racism and corruption of the colonials, the exploitation of cheap labor, the organized prostitution, and the torture. And of the bombing of whole villages, and of the twenty thousand fellahin who had died.

"From today," the fifth one, who was called Paolo, told Justin, "we will erect antennas for our suffering in all the great capitals: London, Paris, Rome, and Moscow."

Yet the others, who were Arab nationalists, only saw in Justin a famous veteran of the European war. He examined the pale one, whose eyes were all pupil—Ben Barka from Rabat, who Justin had known in the Atlas. Sitting next to him, and beside Ben Bella, was the long-faced well-educated Algerian with the gentle laugh called Fehrat Abbas. Seated between Justin and the splendid Messali—who had run the *Étoile Nord-Africaine* in Paris before Justin had first traveled there, and who was like some magician of Sidi Idriz—was the gaunt, nervous Paolo. This man was a Franco-Chilean in contact with Juan Perón, with the rebels of the Cuban mountains, and with the movements against the French in Vietnam and Cambodia.

"The happiness of our people?" Ben Bella broke in on Justin's thoughts. "Happiness does not cause progress. Happiness will come, but it will not be for us."

This was a new generation of the liberation, Justin reflected, better educated, surer, bringing no tidings of great joy. Fehrat Abbas and Ben Bella, with his *French* Croix de Guerre, seemed as cool and ambitious as Jesuits—Jesuits of revolution.

Much later, Abbas abruptly turned to Justin and raised his arm. "In Algeria, colonialism is weak. While we watch, the Jewish refugees are driving our people along with the English out of Palestine. In China, Mao Tse-tung is consolidating his hold. Presently, General Giap will crush the French in Indochina. The oppressed races of Africa and Latin America will soon rise. Bourguiba is ready in Tunis. Justin, we should not wait any longer."

Justin stared into his tea glass. Only this was left, in the next year and forever. Did he have the courage to devote himself to such unhappiness? Justin was conscious of the group's expectant silence. He answered quietly.

"No, our success must be made inevitable. First propaganda and the infiltration of the police . . . then pressure. Blood must be drawn last, for most of the blood will be of the innocent. Freedom does not come as a single flood. It is a tide that ebbs and flows."

Later Justin showed the way in which, at each level of the resistance, a rebel only knew—and therefore could only betray—one man above in rank and two below. He sensed that if he spoke again of mercy, it would weaken the clarity of vision these men needed to conduct a liberation: the strength of the *Fana'a,* or annihilation of the self. Therefore, Justin Lothaire did not speak to them in parables of his life—neither of human love, nor beauty, nor tolerance, nor personal cultivation. Nor did he speak of the chaos and the betrayal that follow every liberation.

After each of the *chefs* had embraced Algeria's great writer, they left the colonnades at intervals. Finally Justin and Abu were alone together, just as long ago when they had dived for American coins. Justin put his arm around his friend's neck. He felt saddened and enslaved.

"They will follow you until it is done," Abu said.

"It's strange for someone who has seen what I have seen to feel like a child."

"That is an accomplishment to which the Maghreb will lay claim"—his boyhood friend seemed to remember something—"as it will lay claim to your marriage."

They had paused opposite the flooded fountain. Abu took a French clipping from his jacket. The photograph was of two actors and an actress in classical robes. Even here, when Justin saw Luz's eyes—whose vulnerability had survived a dozen media machines and the flight from Paris to the kiosks of Algiers—he experienced a powerful need to protect her.

"Why has Luz not come to meet your mother?" Abu urged Justin. "Doesn't she understand what we are doing?"

"My mother. . . ." For some seconds Justin did not continue. "Listen, Abu, soon she will be the last *pied-noir* in the casbah."

"There is nothing to fear. As your mother, she will be respected."

"But my friend . . . oh my friend!" Then Justin was sobbing, sobs that wrenched his heart, and he was bent in Abu's arms with his face in one hand. With a shudder, he stopped himself. He rubbed his face savagely on his sleeve.

"What is it? What is it?"

"Listen, she must know nothing. Tell the others. Tell them she will denounce us."

"Even you, Justin? Denounce you?"

"Yes. She must hear nothing."

"Impossible! Do not say it!"

"I would not say it if it were not possible. Tell them."

"I'll tell them, Justin."

"We will never discuss this again. . . . You asked about Luz, Abu? I have no idea if she has ever understood."

Abu stared at his friend's twisted face as they splashed along the west colonnade. In silence they dried their feet to put on their shoes.

It was from this first gathering in the flooded mosque that Justin Lothaire accepted finally that he was no longer the same man. By the time he sailed on the Marseille steamer, four days later, he had met the *chefs* twice more—in a schoolroom and at a fish warehouse. He had given his word to return to Algiers in the spring.

THE NAMELESS

1

A FTER THE DIASPORA OF THE TORTURERS CAME THE DIASPORA OF THE WISE men. For six years, wisdom flowed down from the glaciers of the Oberland, flooding the promise of the soil and veiling the sun.

The manuals of moral economics—which the boy Lothaire had read in the Mahbu Public Library—were carried by new crusaders, more savage even than those who had gone before with books of charity and love. During Hitler's coming, Marx's prophecy had been quickly corrupted by the living Stalin. Now, in the deluge of bad memories and cold hearts, the disgraced royalties of central Europe were swallowed by the one law, while in China the long campaigns were consolidated and served to the people. In African forests, Kenyatta dreamt of black freedom; Castro, in Cuban forests, dreamt of freedom from all ethnos. While England, France, and America sickened further under the burden of colonies and interests, the new rebels lived ruthless dreams of a world of free nations.

2

As THE SUN ROSE ON BARON VON SUNDA ZU SAALE'S NEW APARTMENT HIGH IN a building called the Dakota—named after one of his boyhood tutor Georg's vanished tribes—the windows flashed with a thousand others along Central Park like a film strip of the Creation.

On West 28th Street, tough flower vendors crowded the sidewalk with green buckets. At Slug's pool hall on the Lower East Side, an open door aired the soapsudsed floors while from a radio at the back crackled the nasal, lusty voice of an unknown white country singer. On the floor of the Stock Exchange, the runners were already crowded around Mahony's window, with opening bids for an electronics giant on news of a breakthrough in television. Under an awning that crossed the entire Park Avenue sidewalk, Buster Briggs—a defeated light heavyweight now bulging in an admiral's uniform—bent tenderly over Miss Hickendorfel, a minute, mascaraed, and shriveled millionairess in a fur coat, being towed to her Cadillac by a team of six shivering Yorkshires.

Alone at that hour, by her window over the park, Hélène prepared for the hospital, folding a clean intern's smock beside her sandwich bag. Far below her, boys' teams rotated on the baseball diamond. Passing down the oak-vaulted hall, she gathered the mail from the carpet.

Among her husband's embossed invitations there were two airmail letters. With a little cry, she tore open the first. It was four months since she had written her ten-page confession to Luz—the person above all who must forgive Hélène for the state she had been brought to, by being David Sunda's wife.

But from the first words in Luz's large, irregular hand, it was as if her sickness of heart was too great a burden for even this friendship—which was also Hélène's last connection, if not with Justin, at least with what he embodied.

> Rue de Valois, Paris
> 2 March 1952

Dear Hélène,

I am sorry not to have answered your long letter much sooner. Justin had just returned from another of his Algiers trips, and you have no idea of the mood they put him in.

Truly, your letter came as a surprise. Since our days at the Villa Donatello, you have always seemed so courageous and effective and loyal. To wait for David all that time—then to keep the promise that you would learn medicine! What of the American life you have made together, and your diplomas, and David, who as always has found so many friends and a good position? I have just reread your letter from the first Christmas in New York! I prefer the letters you wrote then. You spoke of waiting in line with the refugees of a hundred countries for your papers. You admitted that you were enraptured to be in that mecca of optimists. Why deny, Leni, that your marriage could not have gone better for you both—and with the children in those good, expensive schools? I am perfectly sure this mood of yours is only temporary.

How can you possibly envy my life or call my career a success? Surely you are not ungrateful for the devotion of a Renaissance man like the one two young girls used to dream about! You have such strange ideas about Justin. As you say, for some this might seem a profound existence. But why tell me that I should try to understand the man I live with? What does it mean to you that Justin is angry and suffers for every victim of Europe's past, as if we did not have enough troubles right here? Sometimes I feel no doubt that his obsessions will affect his sanity. I thank God, Hélène, that I have the stage and so many admirers. . . .

Still rooted in the hall, Hélène crushed the letter, with its staggering rejection of her right to be unhappy and buried both hands in her hair. To what failures of judgment, and treachery to her husband, had she admitted? She had no copy of what she had written. Luz's two sheets rustled loudly in this concentrated sterility at the heart of New York.

"My God!" Hélène burst out, feeling too rebuked and frightened to go on. But the worst of it was Luz's careless mention of Justin being driven mad by some unrepentant monster that lurked in their age. Here in this mecca of optimists, it was that very torment which had possessed her own marriage! "Poor Luz . . . poor Luz," she repeated, and then a wild idea came to her. *Had her friend somehow uncovered Hélène's wartime love letter?* Was she to be cut off from her most precious link through her background to all she was closest to?

Scarcely aware of what she was doing, she began to circle through the apartment. Her thoughts returned to David's crushing silence. Had a mask fallen too from this even earlier friendship? Perhaps Hélène must go now to her one confidante in New York, Duncan Penn's gracious widow, Eustacia-Jane.

It was from Jane that she had heard of the one hundred thousand dollars each that Duncan had left—to Hélène, to David, to Johannes, and to Justin— in a handwritten will posted from Luxembourg on Christmas Day, 1944. Thus had still another mask fallen away. For they had been told that the "Iron Penn" from whom Duncan had always fled had not been his father. Unknown to his friends, and to Duncan at his death, he was the son of the family's Connecticut foreman, Lem Armitage—whom Reginald Penn had fire, and who now lived in the San Joaquin Valley in California. It was Jane, too, who had leased David and Hélène the apartment at a low rent. Yet in the woman's eagerness to have her son mix with the Sunda children, Hélène had recognized the ambition of a Nashville belle. Jane was an alcoholic, who spent her time commuting by limousine to parties in Southampton.

Hélène had no will left to open the morning's second letter, from her brother in Algiers. Jean-Marc now invariably ridiculed his sister for having brought Lothaire—that enemy of civilization—into the family circle. Only then, as if returning to sanity, did Hélène think of Leonard Rinkel: Leonard, for whom she had had nothing to forgive but his atheism. She remembered the unvarying expression of modesty on the brain surgeon's face as he entered the terminal ward and could not avoid contrasting it with the bleak self-absorption that she had recently seen more and more often in her husband.

Halted in the living room, Hélène's glimpsed a figure in the hall. Her nerves leapt. Surely all three children were away? Quickly folding Luz's letter, she thrust it into her pocket.

"Hello, my dear." David came through the arch with a glance at her troubled face.

"David? I thought you were back from New Haven at six." David was to take part in a war symposium.

" As a matter of fact, I withdrew yesterday afternoon." David seemed on the verge of confessing something—something urgent.

"Weren't you supposed to stay another day?" she inquired.

David bent over her hand. "Must I find the strength for more explanations, Leni? Very well."

"After all, I am your wife," Hélène said bravely, but she instantly heard her suspicion. "I have operations, now and at noon. Shall we meet somewhere at one-thirty?" Never once, in the last six years, had either of them suggested that they eat out together. After Luz's letter, Hélène felt her resistance to this marriage lowered.

"All right.," David stared at her. "Let's make it the Sherry Netherland. I have someone near there to see."

When his wife was gone, and having changed into a blue blazer, David stepped into Hélène's bedroom. In Hélène's mirror, he examined the bruised circles under his eyes. It seemed odd—after years during which his wife had maintained their purely formal relations—that she should soften today. Could she possibly have detected David's final decision, that he must leave?

But it was too late to stop now. He had already telephoned from Grand Central Station to confirm the meeting with Bumbil.

3

LATER THAT MORNING, IN DR. RINKEL'S SURGICAL THEATER AT NEW YORK General, his assistant's performance was without the usual concentration and commitment—though only Hélène's admirer took note of this.

During the same moments, at his office opposite the Plaza Hotel, the Brazilian banker George Bumbil was feeling far too flattered by the long-awaited sight of Baron Sunda's illustrious signature to notice in this gracious man a faint undercurrent of rude temper.

An hour later at their meeting place, David was for the second time shaken by bitter passions when Hélène was twenty minutes late. Two gushy Vassar bluestockings he scarcely remembered would not leave him alone.

"Would Mr. Sunda like a drink while he is waiting?"

"Oh, hello, Mario. I'll wait for my wife."

"Ah, you've never brought her before."

As if in answer, David's heart froze with anxiety that he might still lose the strength for what lay ahead. "Well, today I have, Mario." He had just detected the face he still loved as Hélène entered from the street.

With a nervous glance at the two attractive women, she slipped onto the adjoining cushions. "More of the New York scene? I have forgotten how to dress for these occasions."

"I haven't been to a lunch for pleasure since Paris!" David instantly regained his unassailable good manners. "How was your surgery?"

"The second patient died."

"Ah, Hélène, you're becoming hard," he whispered, he in whom death stirred no emotion.

"Was I wrong to suggest today?" she inquired. Her husband's courtesy had begun to alarm her. They were both conscious now of the socialites listening at the next table. This was David and Hélène's most insoluble argument—about her greater gift for love—which had first begun on the rue de Fleurus. In it, they became like spoiled deities forever feuding on Olympus.

"No, we had to meet." David smiled to himself. "Though your tone puts me in an awkward position. You once swore never to forgive me."

"Haven't our years since Mexico put a certain wife in an awkward position?" Hélène pleaded softly, unable now to forgive David for making himself her only talisman to the past. "Why not ask her *her* feelings? They might have some bearing."

"Why now, suddenly? You're confusing me," David said, feeling angered by her kindness. "When I supported your new independence, I had little idea—"

"David, I remember you as someone of exemplary character," Hélène broke in, and she let slip a little of her old inspired warmth. "So please help me to understand. What are you and Otto trying to do? Why did you resign from your job? And what happened in New Haven?"

They were interrupted in their corner by a frieze of waiters, bearing soup in iced silver bowls. Hélène sank back in distress at what she now felt taking place between them.

At her side—his legs buried with hers under the ample tablecloth—Baron Sunda was reflecting painfully that it had never been reasonable to cross Siberia while his wife was pregnant. Nor had it been reasonable to leave her alone for three years among Himmler's gangs while he conspired futilely at the gates to Moscow. He knew he must make peace with her today—yet again David was racked with bitterness that she so feared him. Somewhere along the way he had lost the ability to confess failure before this woman's suspicion, which David could not help but share.

"Vichyssoise . . . a strange name for cold potato soup," he began, with his most unserious charm.

"I think it is rather apt," said Hélène, her premonition growing more vivid.

"What happened in New Haven, Hélène? You see, quite likely I won't continue in this country. No, listen to me!" David said, his temper rising. "We are New Yorkers for the time being. I certainly won't expect you to move again."

"We've always endured as a pair." Hélène's clinical concentration was back, reserved and courteous. Within hearing sat the French consul's wife, whose mother was a friend of Hélène's parents. At Hélène's side, David continued in a tense murmur.

"You realize what the job at Frank, Loeb meant in reality? Do you remember that Gifford Giles knew Bernard Piers, who knows many things about me?"

"And what did they find out?" whispered Hélène, still needing to serve this marriage. She felt suddenly very close to her husband and the godless rites which had tracked him out of Russia. They would endure this now as a couple.

"The poor fellows finally realized the family history."

Hélène had almost laughed. "You mean, being a baron?"

"You think that is insignificant? Right away, Bob Loeb gave me my own office and sent in their most *arriviste* clients. With all that I know, if the board had asked my advice instead, I would already have earned back the farmlands at Oberlinden! I would be working with Bernard at the United Nations!

"As for New Haven. . . ." David waved aside his wife's sympathetic touch, as if to say the damage had already been done. "After my attempt to describe conditions at Tula, the faculty and students both started to explain what had *really* happened! One suggested that I was in sympathy with the Stalinists; another, that I was a German supremacist. A Professor Karis, who understood at least that I was an amateur, recited figures on Soviet military strength to trip me up. Finally, someone said that there had never been any serious plot against Hitler. You see, if there had been, it would have succeeded!"

Hélène's eyes were fixed on David, whom she had not heard lay bare such failures in the ten years since their afternoon on the Wannsee. Now, as if they might even return to sit again under her father's willow tree, Hélène saw her husband lift a face to her luminous with conviction.

"What does this mean, Leni?" he asked very quietly. "It means that these new masters of history do not care for difficult messages. From now on, chief executives and historians will pontificate to those who have seen hell with their own eyes!"

Again Hélène rested her slender hand on her husband's. Was she to have her reward—was this most terrible mask to fall away? How much was there still to be saved by simple acts of love!

"David," she began, "I have always believed that you were condemned to travel ahead of all but the few. Think, though, of another New York. Leonard's brother was captured in Poland, like you. Now he makes deliveries around the city hospitals. Whenever I see Jerome, he has his back turned in the corner of an elevator or is creeping down a ward. Then I thank God that we're here. I hope I never have to go back."

Raising her eyes to the luxury of this Manhattan restaurant, Hélène saw the man at her side wipe perspiration from his cheeks with a napkin.

"You must understand," he was saying. "I can't abandon Europe to sink under its guilt. Somehow, I'll put together another fortune. Have our two families not always financed their civilized values?

"When I think of Europe," David hurried on, "when I think of its grandeur, its poets and heroes . . . or in death like Venice, and now like the phoenix soon to live again, to me, the rest of the earth will always be a colonial realm."

Hélène could not look at her husband. He went on alone, his tortured eyes fixed on the Burgundy label.

"Leni, I swear you will see, as Hitler did not let you, the excellent evenings at Oberlinden—the statesmen and thinkers come from almost everywhere. If I believed I would never see it again, I think it would kill me."

Lifting his eyes, David caught his wife's gaze fixed on his hands—the left on his napkin, the right holding his pipe.

"So you see?" David continued, his tone abruptly icy. "That's why, this morning, I went to see Bumbil and accepted his offer: that is, to develop investment possibilities between the Mato Grosso and the Amazon."

Hélène was staring at her husband as if she had misheard. "Then you intend to leave me behind," she finally said, her face deep red, the muscles standing out from her temples to her neck. With a fiery look she sought to cut across his stare. "You intend to leave your children?"

"In three or four years one can make a million dollars."

"David, don't say such wild things! If it fails, you may be killed. And when would you go?"

"In two weeks."

"Two weeks," she repeated. So this was their final separation, which Hélène had trailed David around the world, accepted every sacrifice, and endured hell on earth to avoid! Mechanically she summoned the strength to resist her husband's selfish act. "Do you wish your children to grow up fatherless? Have you prepared yourself for what Justin will think of you? And what will you be afterward?" Impulsively, she seized David's hands under the tablecloth and crushed them to her lips.

Seeing Hélène's innocent mouth—belonging to the same child who by a fireplace in Paris had sworn she had as many secrets as he did—pressed to hands whose secrets must never be spoken, David was overcome by pity for them both. Freeing himself, he put down a handful of bills.

Moments later, Hélène passed ahead of him out to the crowded street. Not knowing which way to walk after so hopeless a rupture, they stood through the green light by a toy vendor. A cluster of balloons towered against the deep Atlantic sky. David bought three for the children and handed a fourth to Hélène.

She shaded her eyes to look into her husband's face, now filled with tragic apology, and the string slipped from her fingers.

For some seconds they followed the balloon together, until it was a blue dot among the skyscrapers. Then they moved off in silence along Central Park, each of them already making plans.

4

So ON AN AFTERNOON IN HIS FORTIETH YEAR, BARON SUNDA CONTINUED HIS journey back to Europe, through the Amazon rain forest.

The *Conquistador,* a listing single-screw freighter of the United Fruit Company running to Belém with nearly empty holds, carried two classes of traveler. It was not until they were two weeks out of New York—with impressions of Havana and Port-au-Prince laid like molasses over the bitter final image of Hélène beside his three children as they had waved to him desperately from the dwindling 47th Street pier—that David glimpsed the ship's second class. Facing him close by under the wheel-deck canopy sprawled Otto, asleep with a newspaper trembling over his face. On the bleached deck was stacked a tiny library: the history of Candido Rondon and several chronicles of the Jesuits, cattle breeders, and agronomists of Amazonia and of the Mato Grosso. David lay motionless, no longer aching all over from his dozen inoculations, while zephyrs of sea air seared the few speechless passengers like waves of fever. Yes, he was happy. The invisible yoke of duty that from birth had held David among the tangled traces of a ruined society seemed to have broken, leaving him to dream, alone under limitless skies, of the civilized life and the empire he would rebuild for his children.

It first came to him as singing, a melodious staccato of Portuguese, somewhere overboard and ahead, swallowed at once in the thrashing pulse of the ship's passage, as if the sound had been sucked under by the bow wave. Then the smell came again, pungent, vegetable, undeniably fecund and raw as the smell of a woman's body, the fetid, suffocating reek of jungle. David heard the voice come closer.

Turning, he saw the captain and the boyish second mate emerge from the wheelhouse in their spotless uniforms. Balanced at the top of the ladder was a gaunt young African girl clinging to a bundle, her features pulled down in a prolonged moaning. Her body jerked against a man's hand holding her ankle from below. Just as the mate grabbed for the woman, the captain caught sight of his first class passenger, watching politely from the rail. The girl stopped moaning and tore out of both men's grasp. Fixing crazed eyes on Baron Sunda, she came towards him begging for something.

"Fonzo!" the captain shouted, but the boy had already caught the embarrassing fugitive around the chest. With a desperate whimper, the woman flung her bundle over the railing close to where David stood. Giving a series of hiccuping shrieks, she appeared to faint and was easily lowered back down the ladder.

David was left just as he had been, staring at the captain with no more than an animal sensation of having been very close to someone of an alien race—far closer than he ever had been in Mexico. He seemed to hear a rumble somewhere below. The sailors and young officers had melted from the decks. Tightening his collar, the older man came forward.

"Pardon, Senhor Baron . . . the boat, the hours."

"Quite, I'm sure—very hot," David murmured, and at once he saw the captain's smile replaced by a look of virile self-satisfaction.

"You will see Aruba, just there, before sunset," the man said, and David turned away. He began to think about the ship's mahogany bar and the wet glasses of rum punch.

That was all. In the heat off the Antilles, madness had flared and order been restored. Somewhere, muffled deep in his past, Baron Sunda knew he had seen all this before. He did not think again about the scene by the wheel-house on the *Conquistador* until it was brought up by Xavier Pereira, ten days later, as they sat on the veranda of the hotel at Belém. Meanwhile, at each port, he left a handful of letters for New York, Paris, and Berlin, like markers to trace his deepening insignificance.

5

"EVEN FOR SOMEONE WHO HAS ENJOYED ADVENTURES AS DISTINGUISHED AS yours," said Pereira, gently cutting the perfumed shade with his flattened hand, "our Amazon types will surprise you. It is amazing what madness can be produced by a little poverty and isolation from *la vie mondaine!*"

"That may be so." Seated in a giant-backed wicker chair, David Sunda inclined his head.

"What? What?" The Brazilian bent toward this immovable baron and blinked behind his bifocals. Bumbil's banking partner was the director of eight Belém shipping, coffee, and beef agencies, and in their search for common social ground, Pereira had been eager to confide that in his youth he had been the first lover of the ten-year-old flower of Belém, Heidrun Dolin. Now, at fifty, the man was an active six foot six, with large restless hands and square shoulders. His forehead was raked sharply to bushy brows. This lent, to that section of Xavier's cavernous head in which the brain is usually to be found, a streamlined quality, as if it had been designed to deflect rebel bullets. On his third day, utterly given over to the noble European, Pereira had dressed in his beige shantung silks, brown tie, and cream shoes. David had already been entertained at a white château on the water by Pereira's Irish wife and fourteen children—all of whom were in convents or Jesuit schools. At this moment, David still had not decided whether this man who had deflowered Johannes Godard's future wife was a free spirit of great innocence or an evil eccentric. At least Xavier had not lectured him, as several here already had, on the unrecognized genius of Hitler.

"My boy, have you formed an opinion of our military surveys?"

"That is difficult to judge, Xavier. Perhaps I should show you my idea."

Profiled against the jungle, at the end of the hotel diving board, a breast-less blonde child was adjusting her toes. The girl's buttocks flexed and unflexed in her suit. Remembering the flower of Belém, David frowned and looked down at Pereira's shaded chart.

"Do you think the department would lease me this million hectares?"

"What? What?" Pereira coughed, then chuckled fiercely. "Mary Mother of God, what will you do with it all? That is the least accessible land in the Mato Grosso."

"Most of the accessible land becomes flooded." David settled his elbows on the wicker. "Here, there is higher ground. It is true that the southern shippers are hundreds of kilometers across the Pantanal. However, transportation will improve. A pass may be cut to the northern rivers—to the Xingu here, or here."

Across the chart, Pereira had removed his glasses. He blinked at David shortsightedly. "The Pantanal is an infernal swamp. Why not consider the Rio Araguaia, here? I, personally, might choose the Rio Paraná."

"You know, the river plan is secondary. I intend to introduce plantation rubber and breed a superior zebu herd. The humble zebu doesn't shame me."

"But this ordeal of the Xingu!"

"This is my way . . . I am somewhat peculiar," David added.

This time the huge man did not cry out, "What? What?" or seem disappointed. Did anyone doubt that the Amazon would be developed? If the river venture failed, there was still the railhead at Corumbá. But above all, Pereira had seated before him this utterly nerveless gentleman of the European wars. If an aristocrat of such pure blood had asked for a loan to rebuild Atlantis, Perreira felt that he would agree.

"Brazil needs men of distinction. I would regret to hear anyone laugh at you," Xavier observed, replacing his bifocal glasses. "I—we—will provide whatever supplies, stock, or wages that you need. The Cuiaba minister will lease you the land. Now as for labor?"

"I assume there will be sufficient in the area."

"Ah, but they are bad types. *Caboclos* and *cafuzos* . . . Negro with Indio, Indio with low Portuguese . . . especially so the gold diggers. However"—Pereira bent under the veranda umbrella to squeeze David's arm—"thank God I know a native rubber exporter who owns two hundred tappers along the remote Xingu, just here. The rubber price has been falling since before Sarajevo. Two generations of these people have not earned enough to pay their debts to the trader. They are reliably willing to work after such a solitary confinement."

Baron Sunda raised his rum mug from the survey chart, on which the fate of two hundred lives had just been settled. "When the operation has worked and you have been repaid, then I will sell."

"If the Indios have not made a work of art out of your cranium . . . Ernestino! Bring us two of my special *guaracañas*! The fruit for this drink should really be ground into powder with the tongue of a pirarucu fish, to avoid losing its unparalleled powers. Now, my dear boy, I must tell you the outcome of your shipping scandal."

The Belém tycoon's unshakable new partner had his eyes fixed on a blindingly white cloud. In the last ten minutes this cloud had billowed, extending to three times its former height.

"What scandal, Xavier?" David asked.

"But were you not a witness, on the boat? At any rate, it has been suppressed." The man behind the dark lenses chuckled—intermittent snorts that shook his wide shoulders. "Did you not see one of the Negroes from steerage throw a baby into the sea?" He pressed further. "An emotional act! There had been excesses in controlling the riot. It was perhaps a little hot, the food insufficient. . . ."

At the garden pool, the blonde child adjusted her toes for a back dive. A black river storm now towered, rumbling and snapping, above the town's cathedral spire. David Sunda sat, immobilized by unthinkable images, his eyes fixed on the diving girl as she vanished into the black water. He felt an overwhelming claustrophobia. He could not utter a single protest. What if the last redemption open to someone so burdened, as by the disgrace of his banishments to Paris, Mexico, Russia, and recently New York, was to travel forever deeper into this nightmare?

"A terrible thing! Terrible!" The banker threw up his hands sympathetically. Then he crossed himself. "Almost certainly, the baby was dead. Now there is much to discuss tomorrow, you must send us your Senhor Horvath. Is it true that you met him in a war prison?"

Seeing Baron Sunda rise to his feet, Pereira folded the Cuiabá chart and presented it to him. And as he led his guest over the rain-flecked, scalding terracotta tiles past bowing waiters, the Brazilian was like some Gobi giant made out of coffee, chocolate, and coconut.

6

THE STERN-WHEEL PACKET TAKING THEM UP THE AMAZON TOOK TWENTY DAYS TO reach the border of Mato Grosso. In the first cool of every sunrise, Baron Sunda would rework his figures on fodder and beef prices, stock boat capacity and draft, multiplied—as ten years before with General Guderian—by factors of time and space. All around him, nature thickened, and for David its fevers and stench, its childlike outbursts of hot rain, and its ferocious flying things were like salvation. Along a labyrinth of islands, whose names were Indian, there appeared ramshackle Portuguese river colonies where a German *chefe* would climb down, wearing his insect veil, to ask prices and examine the barges. As if to mock his subtle equations, the silent folk who crowded back on with their livestock were rough and direct and of every color and detail of race.

After Gurupá, the boat wheeled out of the Amazon into the Xingu—which in turn narrowed day after day, and in a week from fifteen to three kilometers, until finally there were only a few hundred meters between the river's invisible banks. Needing for some reason always to wear a linen suit among the passengers in their striped pajamas, David would pace methodically among the hammocks under the foredeck awning—laboring through a book on the Portuguese history of the conquest and pausing sometimes to watch dolphins play or follow the white belly of an alligator floating downstream, ridden by a single vulture. He noted that at each stop a further day was lost while the six-monthly priest married several mestizo brides, all wearing the same brilliant white dress; also, that as much as this monastery of heat and natural scourges seemed to invigorate Baron Sunda, it did not cease to provoke moral distortions in his only remaining confidant.

Padre Arturo had not been the only person to join the boat at Gurupá. One noon *sesta*, as David had sat meditating over his notebooks, now filled with neatly ordered notes and equations as alien to the fever heat as ice, there was a thud. Next to him on the catwalk, Otto was bent over the water.

"My friend, I hate to see you unwell. That sausage was the devil."

"Don't say that word! Prepare yourself, prepare yourself."

"I ate nothing, Otto. You mustn't think of me."

"You don't know what I am thinking! Go the other way round to the lifeboat . . . be discreet."

David gazed steadily at Otto's crazed eyes. Rising, he gripped the deckhouse rail, and for several seconds images passed through his head, of lepers and mangled animals, of buboes—and of his children, if this indestructible Pole went completely mad. Then David started slowly forward, continuing round into the threshing sound from the stern-wheel. At the gangway rail he watched the forest glide like a vague smoke through blazing reflections. Then, with infinite languor, David turned to lean on his elbows.

There was only a youngish man in a straw hat and cheap stained trousers. The new passenger sat against the deckhouse under a black umbrella, reading a paperback of French pornography that David had leafed through in Belém. The eyes under the straw brim lifted, lingered dully on Baron Sunda's face, then fell back, perhaps to the scene of the three couples locked together inside a Greek train compartment.

At the rail, David's heart leapt. A nauseating wave of heat radiated from the jungle, until he felt himself drown in perspiration. David's legs carried him back, out across the deck and up the catwalk to his chair.

"Well? Is it him?" inquired a voice that David Sunda had not heard for eight years.

"Yes, I should think that it is," he whispered finally. And at this confession, that he had just betrayed the least forgiving passion of his life—to take instant revenge, even to kill—David heard again the squeak of their handcart on a Silesian hillside as they returned the still-living boy. *The Viennese, who had sunbathed naked on the guardhouse roof, surrounded by his man-eating dogs!* Sickened by the resurrection of such reality, David held up his hands.

"For us to have him . . . him." Otto groaned. "This will be sweet, it will be incredible."

"Do you wish us to go mad and get dragged back? The man is trash," David mumbled, fighting deep scalding waves of a violence he had not felt over the murdered baby on the *Conquistador.* Otto was crouched against the railing, his hair and skin almost white. He stared ruthlessly down into David's face.

"He's to go free? You are already mad!"

"They are animals, Otto. Why let them degrade us?"

"We lived for such a moment! To you, he was the vampire."

"Because he always kicked until he saw blood!" David almost cried out. "And there were twenty thousand more of him! Are we to build our ranch on the bodies of murdered fools? I'll report him to the Israelis—they will not forget."

"I cannot bear his impudence. He pretends to be a human being."

"Forgive him, Otto! Forgive him, or he will destroy us again."

The stern-wheeler had drawn in close along the current's eastern bank. Their urgent whispers drifted to the sleeping gold diggers, suspended batlike under the awning.

"Then we will let him go," Otto croaked, after several minutes of silence, his oath almost unintelligible.

"God in heaven!" David hurried on, having just felt himself overcome by a thirst to see blood. "You and I are in charge of a million hectares of Indians, illiterate bandits, and ten thousand cattle!"

As if discovered in an embrace, they had just emerged directly over a crowded village landing. At once, a dozen sweat-soaked *cafuzo* jaguar hunters were on board, carrying revolvers, carbines, and cartridge belts. The party of English nurses had not been the first ashore. A black umbrella was moving through the crowd.

David rose involuntarily, in full view of the curious faces. Otto's bald head was just struggling down the gangplank. David could do no more than to remain standing. Was this divine justice or a flux of retribution, not to be spurned by good men? He stood there in the heat until the whistle blew. But the only answer that came to him was a sick jealousy that it was not he who had gone . . . and a horror of the man who had. Just as an obscene hope had sprung up—that the being to whom David owed his life might be left behind—the devotional grin appeared below him.

Otto heaved for breath. His brow was covered with grains of earth. As the packet thrashed into motion, he gripped the stanchion, and was carried off the dock.

Seconds later, they were again sitting side by side. As the stern-wheeler gathered way, a brief explosion of curses rang out from the armed circle on the deck. David heard the flutter of soft, greasy cards being shuffled. Like gentility amid the stench of the jungle, the perfume of tobacco came to his nostrils. What if the very worst Nazis had scattered to this jungle with him, like poison ice from the impact of an alien world? David felt the sky darken and fever pour from the river. Was this at last the end of the world?

"I think I should go see the horses." Lurching to his feet, David started down the stable deck.

At nightfall, the Xingu packet tied up at Veiros. Next morning, Captain Garção found the baron and his deputy in chairs against the wheelhouse. Had the two gentlemen seen the Swiss with the mustache disembark? David turned to Otto, who answered, yes, he might have. The captain bowed with great ceremony, thanked them, and left.

"Oh, my friend, what have you done?"

"I have helped another very old friend with his burden." Otto did not open his eyes. "You *know* he needed help."

The blunt hands of the man at his side gripped the arms of his chair, the knuckles turning white.

7

THAT SAME MORNING THE XINGU NARROWED, AND EVEN FROM THE WHEELHOUSE roof they could no longer see above the flowerless green walls. Through the aftermath of prehistoric justice—when he and Otto had sat on the deck, like peace manacled to war—a limitless doubt and desolation infested Baron Sunda's heart. How would his children and their descendants judge a life such as his?

Pereira's two foremen—João Pasquas and the gaunt, humorless Manuel Tomar—were devout Catholics. The airplane rides, to São Paulo and then to Belém, had been their first journey out of the Mato Grosso. The two men spoke little and with difficulty, and they treated the *seringueiros* roughly, who were coming on board every day now with their wives and their cylinders of raw rubber. David would notice Otto going among them with Pasquas, murmuring of camps, conquests, and great wealth. Afterward his new employees would sit for hours and stare at him with awed smiles.

The days seemed to crawl through the sweltering silence with the slowness of men who are dying of thirst. Each dawn David called Pasquas and Tomar to conferences around the radio table. Under the gentian-blue walls and the stuffed jaguar, Tomar would sit chewing his cheeks, his close-set eyes running down the inventories and schedules of river livestock markets. He would lament the ten thousand disasters and certain ruin that lay ahead. When Pasquas saw the baron's vague enjoyment of his comrade's sense of the apocalypse, he began to take the upper hand with Manuel. Appearing not to notice, David encouraged a rivalry, always leaving the slight edge to Pasquas.

Pasquas would later break their silence as he picked his teeth. "*Homem*, you think he is nuts?"

"He is rich." Tomar shrugged resignedly.

"He is some kind of prince."

"No princes exist in Brazil. Maybe in America or France."

"France? Where is France?"

"Who knows? It is said that one eats well, even princes who are nuts."

"And still the people follow them?"

During the flaming sunsets, when the air cooked and the jungle was consummated in fire, the marrying priest, giving himself up to his true vocation, would tell stories of Indian tribes who enacted orgies while they ate their victims alive, of mothers performing obscenities with their sons on jungle altars, and of feuds between hired gunmen who lived carnally with wild carnivorous pigs—fairy tales, followed by lurid descriptions of witch doctors who fed still-beating hearts to sacrificial victims before they roasted their organs on braziers. It was on just such a dusk, in the third week of their great tedium— as Padre Arturo embellished a story of bare-breasted nuns who hunted monkeys to sell their paws in formaldehyde globes—that Baron Sunda heard a sharp, vibrating rap against the paintwork.

Upright on his chair, he balanced the little shaft in his hand. A quill pen or a strip of thatching? David struggled to focus his mind. He thought of the precise sound on the bulkhead.

"My God, for heaven's sake. Incredible."

"No, no!" Seated between the hammocked gold-diggers, *garimpeiros,* Padre Arturo politely turned his stool to include the baron. "It is completely true. The good nuns deflower themselves with gourds."

Hiding the arrow, Baron Sunda walked forward onto the glaring wet bow. Exactly as at Oberlinden, when his tutor Georg had told him of the puritan wilderness, for an instant David had witnessed himself in his decadence as he must have been seen by the hunter, a perfectly innocent spirit of twigs and leaves, tightening a string.

He bent to examine the sliver stirring in his hands, the timeless instrument to take his timeless life. It was the secret of the universe.

"What is this laughter, *chefe?* What is that in your hand?"

David had made a gesture to throw the thing away, but the rush winding was tangled in his wedding ring. The arrow swung under his wrist. David caught it back. He would keep this too. "You know, sometimes I believe all this will turn out."

"Naturally!" Otto laughed, nervous of David's mood. "Otherwise, would we be here?"

At sunset, they tied up below the Cachoeira von Martius. On the following morning the stern-wheeler turned downriver with the marrying priest.

It was then that they saw the powers of their baron. For in two days the four light barges and their outboard motors had been portaged. With supplies and fuel for three more weeks, the party of more than one hundred continued into the Mato Grosso, toward the mountains. At Moreno, they turned at last up the Rio Steinen.

8

SINCE THE PREVIOUS NIGHT THE NEIGHBORING INDIAN VILLAGE HAD FELT THE embarrassment of the flotilla's approach. The sixty or more *seringueiros*—summoned by simple maps, dropped in tomato canisters out of the door of Pereira's private plane, from which Baron Sunda had first looked down on this place—were waiting with eucharistic patience when the train of barges came into sight. As the first of them glided over the lagoon that was fed by clear springs, David climbed on deck, dressed in the clothes he would wear until they rotted from his back.

"Juan! Manuel!" His agitated voice broke the towering stillness after the motors had died.

"Coming, boss!"

"Coming!"

The *seringueiros* who lined the bank separated as David jumped down. Hiding his shock at their oblivion and their physical ruin, he walked slowly beyond the square of tin huts. The forest mat was woven so tight that dead trees were supported by living ones.

"*Senhor!* . . . *Senhor!*" called new voices. "*Senhor chefe!*"

Two men were shoving through the throng of straw hats. The tall mournful one wore a police jacket and a Stetson with its brim rolled to a point. Seeing the baron's eyes on him, he pushed a gaunt *seringueiro* so that he fell to his knees. Without breaking stride, he and a swollen man in shorts emerged opposite David, holding out their hands. Trapped in the knee-deep grass, Baron Sunda felt the forest wall at his back. Sixty miles from here, across this wet contagion of snakes and insects, were the savannas.

"*Heisse Stumpf!*" said the bloated one, scattering the naked children with a swing of his rifle.

"*Coronel Prado.*" His friend's blue lips hooked behind worm-eaten molars. "*A seu serviço, chefe!*"

"*Enchanté*," said David, the shock of hearing German spoken here provoking his drawing-room manner. "However—you will excuse me—I would be pleased if you would not manhandle my men!"

"These?" A slavish, insulted look had replaced the policeman's grin.

But Baron Sunda had started back, almost running, toward the riverbank, shading his eyes and pursued by his army. The local *chefes* were forced to follow, spilling information like rotten sacks that have been split against a superior mass. "I can be of use, *Senhor chefe*—privileges at the Posto Leonardo, Indian Protection Agency, United Fruit Company—"

"Excellent to meet you, Sunda!" Stumpf bounced against David and stumbled. "Fellow Germans . . . get these animal Indios out of your way . . . raided last week by Xavantes. Sunda—is that *von?* They say—I mean, I was told, are you, *wahrscheinlich*, a prince?"

"A prince? Hardly so. . . . Manuel, Juan! Farther from the water!" David shouted at the workers unloading the boat.

His uncouth cries inspired only amazed submission. Using the carbines as crowbars, Otto and Tomar were moving among the crates.

"I tell you, liquids to make rubber trees grow three times thicker."

"And the shiny metal?"

"To capture the power of the sun and make tires!"

"The *chefe* has brought the power to make sand into gold and pigs grow without feeding!"

Now a long flat crate was being jacked open, exposing in the sun sixty four-handed saws, fitted neatly in slotted panels. At the sight of this unparalleled geometry, there was a gasp from the shouldering *seringueiros*, as if the doors had just been thrown open to the temple of a thousand Buddhas. At the center of this throng, as they sweated over the glittering blades, Otto found David's face, and it was more sinister with hatred and will then it had been even in Poland.

Pasquas was driving back the mob, which had turned childlike with so much wealth and magic. "Your wishes, *chefe?*"

"I think we will not stay here," David said softly. "There will surely be trouble."

"Many are bad . . . sick."

"Tell these good people that we will build a very great *fazenda* beyond the mountains. But that now we must cut through the forest."

"Be careful, they will do what you say. And, *chefe*, there is someone from the village of the Indios. The owner of the longhouse invites the *chefe* to sleep under his roof. *Senhor*, it is a very big village."

"Would that be wise?"

"It is best, *chefe. Senhor* Otto, Manuel, and I will take watches."

Baron Sunda climbed bareheaded onto the crate of saws. He could see the tin roofs of the *seringueiros*, with Stumpf and the policeman watching him from the clearing. None of this was as he had conceived it, but while Pasquas's nasal commands rang out, all hundred and sixty pairs of eyes were fixed firmly on his face. As the foreman came to the word *serra*, David found himself waist deep in a crowd of rubber tappers, turned together to stare with moist eyes at the reddish-green horizon. Baron Sunda remembered only then, across ten years, the crowd by a pit at Tula. Was there to be another chance? With tears streaming down his cheeks, balanced on saw blades that were fresh from the forges of Vulcan, he began to print neatly in the manifest under Item 121: Dynamite. The insect-pitted faces closest to their *chefe* pressed forward to see his fingers write. Snapping the pen shut, he pushed it back into his soggy shirt.

I came, David had written, *for Hélène, for my children, and for Oberlinden. When I have made a moderate fortune, I will go back.*

But even here in the shade of his own hat, the words made little sense. It was as if someone else had written them.

9

AT SIX O'CLOCK WHEN THE SUN ROLLED OFF THE WORLD AND THE FRANTIC rhythm of "Tuca Tuca" floated from the sheds of the poor *seringueiros* like a rapture of angels, Otto accompanied the *chefe* to meet the Bororo headman, *homem de ponta*. By David's calculation they would fail without more men.

David continued alone behind a smoke of stinging flies into the crescent of huts. Ahead of him on the path to the center longhouse waited two naked men who appeared drenched in wet blood. Otto pushed past him and, as the distance closed, one of the tribesmen began to gesture in a constant, threatening chatter. As they halted, the silent one raised his hand to Otto's shirt and plucked out a gun cartridge.

"Filthy savage! Get away!"

The gesturing Indian turned to David, and he saw the glitter of hurt in the alien eyes. A child with breast buds flirted in the cabbages, clutching David's muddy boots as he approached the longhouse door behind Otto and the tribesman.

Inside the house's sun-speckled glade waited three more Bororo with pipes. The headman was said to speak Portuguese. David squatted down. In this shadowy place an animal drowsiness was coming over him.

"You have men to work for me?"

From deep among the thirty naked phantoms the tribesman who had plucked the cartridge drifted forward. He set down a gourd of black liquid.

Otto sniffed it. "Tobacco essence?"

"Accept it." David sighed deeply, yawned, and stretched. Then he heard a voice of surpassing strangeness.

"It is said that you have been to a big war."

The grinning faces of all three men were turned to him. David's drowsiness had gone. He was suddenly soaked with fever.

"That is so. Adolf Hitler's army conquered one hundred nations," he admitted very softly. "It filled the air, the forests, and the oceans with its machines. Very large numbers became slaves or were destroyed."

"How many died, *chefe?*"

"Maybe fifty million."

"Fifty . . . fifty? This is big, very big!"

In the smoking shadows, David lifted his hot face and saw these men slap their legs and call to the others seated at the end of the longhouse. "Fifty million crushed, murdered," he repeated. In this pleasant glade, were even the *Einsatzgruppen* to be admired?

"Raiding the Xavante, we killed six. Fifty is incredible!"

"*Parabéns, homem!*" laughed the man on David's left. "And you—did you kill?"

"One," David said.

"One of the fifty in such a war?"

"What was your blow . . . how did he die?"

The headman's mysterious eyes examined David's face.

"He surprised us," David whispered at last. "I shot him down."

"But he screamed? He rolled and kicked? He messed himself—*até cagar?*"

"No. He was suddenly and completely shot."

"And fifty, killed? It is very great!"

At last having comprehended the headman's error, David became convulsed with tearful grins. He was preparing to attempt the word *million* when again his mouth filled with the sweet vapors of his boyhood. He could not suppress a deep sigh. Then he exploded into laughter—and Baron Sunda and these naked men were laughing together. How he had feared this jungle in which he was buried!

"Xamante, do you have sixty men for the cutting of my road?" David said, when the balm of laughter had settled.

"And carbines? Do you have some?"

At David's side, Otto had begun to pant. Now he groaned horribly and rolled over on the rush mats. Almost before David saw the seat of the Pole's trousers, the men exploded in laughter, pointing as if at an expected joke.

David helped Otto outside. When he was back the headmen questioned him.

"You have a mother, *chefe?*"

"Of a Venetian family of popes," he answered, in a dream. "My brother was killed by my people."

"He was a witch?"

"He was crucified," David said. "My wife's family is in Paris."

Still the tribe stalked David's soul, listening for any trace of crime or dishonor that might attract revenge.

"I was with Russians, Italians, French, and Americans—and the Jews, the Arabs, and the Lithuanians. Earlier we lived in Mexico," he answered them.

"*Chefe*, in none of your clans do we have a rival. Therefore, one carbine for each man to build your road."

"*Feito!*" David agreed. "Only you must promise that the guns will be secret."

"On your life and mine, *chefe*, we agree!"

"On your life and mine," David said, and in this smoking tunnel of animal life, the leaves and thongs and the faces of the Bororo all seemed to vibrate and glow and dance. For only as these spirits of the forest made local peace with Baron Sunda's past had he fathomed the meaning of their words: that among all David's nobility and kin—the Fleurusians, the great families, cultures and capitals—there was not one with whom he himself was not utterly at war.

THE DIASPORA

1

O N THE ENDLESS FIRST DAY, BARON SUNDA LED HIS BAND AGAINST the jungle.

Across the hours, the heat had been filled with the singing of sixty saws, pulled by two hundred and forty hands, with the whistling hack of machetes, and the whinnying of the horse teams as they dragged the logs to the river. But at sunset, when they stood back and saw their day's work, a wave of rebellion passed among the ragged workmen. All along the hundred meters of jungle barrage there was an ugly tangle of wreckage. They had advanced only fifty or sixty paces into the dense vegetation.

Still, with a contempt in exact proportion to his despair, David found the strength to walk about without surprise among the shouting groups of *seringueiros,* pointing out another day's work. When they saw their baron's untroubled gestures, a trance of the unforeseeable enveloped the men, so that they could not recall what had troubled them.

On the second day, the progress seemed only slightly more satisfying. On the third day, two hundred pairs of boots and blue shorts descended by parachute, and there was an unmistakable advance of about five hundred meters. Very soon, the path of breakage and ankle-high stumps became a thousand meters. A week passed—working more by dusk than by day, stripped to the waist, palms blistered to the third layer of skin—and now three kilometers seemed less impossible. It was the first sixty paces that the men spoke of now with wonder and affection, as David paced among them in long sleeves and boots, attracting a dozen races of ravenous insects from the farthest necks and backs to the wonders of his blood . . . until after a month his skin would begin to secrete and thicken against the bites. At the first sign in camp of their wages, a malaria of greed came over the band, and David was forced to punish gambling and drunkenness. In the tenth week, eight more men from Xamante's camp joined the *chefe*'s force, and every few days the Bororo headman would make the walk along the central track beside his daughter— the flirting child who had embarrassed David before the longhouse—to sip *guaracaña* and politely observe the change that the equations in the notebooks had made in his hunting grounds. Often, during the noon *sesta,* Xamante found the baron moaning under his hammock net, drowned in his continual nightmare of Heinz Guderian—now retired in comfort at his schloss to write his memoirs.

Meanwhile, hour by hour, the jungle, a living organism cavitied and tumored by the most dangerous of all parasites, fought back with its horrible divisions. In the trees there were giant spiders and wasps, and under the flapping leaves were found clusters of larvae that bored under the skin. Vampire bats woke the night with their flutterings and drove horses mad, and jaguars gave unearthly yowls that filled the men's sleep with the sensation of their bones grinding together. Sometimes they would be stirred by a subterranean rumble and awaken to find termites risen to devour their clothes and canvas. Yet when, as at Tula, his men began to die, still neither snake nor lethal spider nor infection struck David down. He was possessed by his fate.

Then on a sweltering Christmas Day, with seven *seringueiros* dead, Baron Sunda and his foremen—all with crawling sores and half naked in their rotted shreds of cloth—saw light beneath the canopy ahead, climbed through into the sun, and found waiting for them Padre Tomas from Cuiabá, holding up a Bible in one hand and, in the other, two stock offers from Pantanal ranches.

"For God's sake, Father," cried David, half mad with grief for all who followed him, "marry my men!"

Otto had turned to him with his fingers buried in his beard. "I will admit it to you now, King David. I never thought you could do this."

2

BARON SUNDA BUILT HIS HOUSE IN EIGHTEEN MONTHS, AND IT WAS COMPLETE at the time of the first calving of twelve hundred of the lean white interbreed of zebu and domestic cow, immune to Texas fever, which thrive in the Mato Grosso. With the timid beginnings of hope, he at last took ten rolls of photographs and sent the three best views to New York. The reply came eight weeks later, on the flying boat via Belém, and was delivered to the *chefe* before dawn over a breakfast of beef. She did not understand the point of mentioning his cousin's palazzo in Sicily, said Hélène's letter, as he had simply built a smaller, sturdier version of Oberlinden. David put down the knife and fork with which he had been eating his second filet, threw open the shutters, and stumbled across the darkened veranda. He did not turn back until he reached the circle of the *vaqueiros'* adobe houses.

It was true! Apart from the burnt sienna of the façade, he had simply reinvented in miniature that stately edifice which Fischer von Erlach had concocted in Bavaria when Bach was ten years old—one hundred years before the French revolution, almost two hundred years before Darwin displaced Adam and Eve with apes, and two hundred and fifty years before the Jews experienced the Apocalypse in crematoria built on the Rhine, and man at last split the atom. Alone in the dawn dust surrounded by adobe huts—in dread now of these sad men's obedience, amid rains like Noah's flood and droughts like the plague of Egypt—David lifted his voice, and the cry "No!" was drowned in a ringing of spurs like the sound of all the locusts in history.

Finally, Xavier Pereira flew in on his private Dakota and galloped a horse up the jungle corridor, every bit like a giant made of coffee, chocolate and coconut.

"Stupendous! Magnificent!" he called from the saddle. "You are viceroy in Mato Grosso!"

"Am I not the *peão*, the witch doctor?" replied Baron Sunda, and across his face there were as many wrinkles as the mud on a dry lake. The left side sagged—as even his brother Freddy's face never had at tea dances in Saint-Moritz.

A time came for Baron Sunda when he could employ no more destitute farmers. He soon heard that they were joining the rival *fazenda* in the next valley, where they were beaten and cheated and taught to recite Stumpf's war exploits as a *chefe* with an all-white *Einsatzgruppe* operating from Smolensk. No one, however, could fathom Sôbre Xingu's magician, with the thick belt and the invariably thoughtful manner, who allowed barefoot Indian agents, reading "Little Lulu" to tramp freely through his furnitureless salons and who took no notice of even the wealthiest Cuiabá society. If a rumor had not been circulated that he was in reality a Bourbon pretender, David might indiscreetly have been shot.

During those months, stretched between two loaded revolvers on his throne of mosquito nets, David had begun to read again. In a sense it was already too late. Day by day, he was losing his memory for distinct scenes and people. Amid the wash of many races, a page of narrow civilization had no more effect than an architect's reconstruction of a lost city, or a physics formula to conceive of upheavals among invisible nebulas. The sight of a plastic Messerschmitt in Cuiabá's general store had more reality. Still, every Sunday night, David wrote a letter to his wife—though she too had now imperceptibly diverged from the Hélène who was the mother of the Sunda heirs. Nor was this only the result of lost memory. By that time, there was Melita.

For seven years after David's first hours with Hélène beneath the harpsichord in a Lübeck collector's house, he did not touch another woman.

A day came when the *fazenda* building took root in the earth, when his twelve thousand head of new cattle were making sport, and the falls and rapids of the Rio Fuego had been cheated with manual locks. On that day—the very same on which his wife's letter had arrived, turning down for the sixth time David's invitation to travel here with their children—he and Otto sat down at the huge cowhide desk to resolve their liquidity. They had spent only

$110,000. Another $60,000 was available to put in stock—even for three Scottish seed bulls—for a *fazenda* that could support two hundred thousand head. From Pereira's excitement, David knew that at Mato Grosso prices, if the river development prospered, he could sell his share for a million dollars. In an apricot dusk, he stood on the veranda and hungrily searched his sleeping monastery land. David knew then that he could drown in hatred of Hélène.

That night at dinner, he first became aware of the gaze that the house-keeper had fixed on him every night for a year, from behind Otto's balding head. In the girl's moist eyes—which peered from her cinnamon face with the secret certainty that they had detected the treasure alluded to in fragments of the wreck of recorded history—David saw a promise of inexhaustible humor. That same night he still further forgot himself.

Melita was a child of the Nigerian underworld king of the Rio de Janeiro *favelas* and his Sino-Portuguese concubine. Wishing to spare her the life he had led, Pharo had sent his daughter to be educated by nuns. For this Melita had repaid him at sixteen by fleeing with an anthropological expedition to Cuiabá and taking a job as a maid, where Otto had found her. When Melita laughed, which she did constantly, so that neither she nor the world needed to find a reason, that pealing, throaty sound could strike the perfect pitch of any man's unconscious. Late in the Amazon moonlight of the *chefe*'s bedroom—unknown to Otto—the housekeeper tore off her uniform, which was all that now separated David from the jungle. With an appetite that guaranteed he would never fall in love with her, she succumbed to him.

At the hour in which Sôbre Xingu was complete, united by the mortar and stone of the Sundas' deepest being, David was alone—rejected by his wife and children, a thousand miles from the nearest wit or refinement, caught in a world of dust. Yet he received, with the first awakening of a horror that he had not felt since the Nysa *Lager,* the news that in the nearest Kreen Akorora village, a childlike witch had been beaten to death. The next night he came to love his hands again. For Melita this was the truth, and she did not fear it. Nor did she fear the oblivious silence that followed, in which she would sit naked at Baron Sunda's desk, murmuring songs as sweetly tender as her laughter and drawing *joujous,* tropical fairies, and headless chickens with his fountain pen, on sheets of United Nations stationery.

In the months when the gold diggers, in their loneliness, had begun to construct a road to the fresh strike on Bororo territory, Sôbre Xingu had its famous prosperity. The calving that year was characterized by a fertility which resulted in a score of deaths among heifers attempting quadruplets. As David was revising his estimates for cattle barges, the early rains redoubled their intensity, and the swamp wilderness of the Pantanal was flooded as it had never been flooded in memory. On the surrounding higher ground, entire villages were lifted from their poles and railway trestles were swept away.

In this paradise of water buffalo, millions of birds' nests floated out of trees, alligators and anacondas cruised the main streets of desert towns, and the dusks were oily black with malarial mosquitoes. Huge herds—hundreds of thousands of beef cattle—began the long drive to higher ground. On the sixth day of the flood, three horsemen arrived at Sôbre Xingu, sent by northern ranchers desiring to ship, via the Rio Fuego, herds that numbered almost three hundred thousand head.

Within a month, Pereira's offer for Baron Sunda's shares arrived by parachute, along with the first Paris newspaper ever seen at *Sobre Xingu*. Heinz Guderian had died. The commander of the Western armies was President of the United States. Algeria was in revolt against the French. That is why I have not had an answer from Justin in seven years, Baron Sunda thought, and he experienced an insane belief that they would still be friends.

By now, David was visiting the new Bororo village more often than he wrote to Hélène. The longhouse gossip, so like his tutor's at Oberlinden long ago—of vendettas, animal beds, and the portents of the seasons—gave him peace from Melita's expectation and from the *vaqueiros'* hatred of the land. There had been no further skirmishes or raids on *garimpeiro* settlements, but David could not induce Xamante to immunize his people against smallpox. There had been more deaths.

By the time David Sunda stopped suggesting to Hélène that she should travel to Brazil, six years had gone by and it was *de rigueur* for every millionaire or statesman who visited Cuiabá to call on the extraordinary Baron of Sôbre Xingu.

3

THEY WERE RECEIVED ON THE VERANDA AT A CIRCULAR GRANITE TABLE. THE wheel had come by oxcart from Cáceres, where David had first seen it propped behind a church. Though the stone's carved llamas, jaguars, and beetles were unmistakably Incan, no one could explain how it had traversed the Andes from La Paz.

The fateful morning of the *vaqueiros'* Easter procession—one hour after Otto had driven out with a Royal Ranch delegation, on the first leg of their journey back to Texas—the two Indian women reappeared around David at the stone table. A hot fragrant wind off the savanna riffled the white frock of the headman's sister as she stood behind him with her needle and eyedropper, pricking a design—coiling, like the seven seas of a medieval mapmaker— across the *chefe's* shoulders and collar. The younger woman met his gaze steadily. A year before, Xamante had made David the shockingly plausible offer of his daughter Opani. Now Opani was married to Carlito from Corumbá—the *caboclo* pilot of the *fazenda's* old biplane.

The tattoo followed upon David's argument with the child's father over the smallpox vaccinations. "If you wish to guard our bodies, then you must let us guard your spirit!" Xamante had told him, gazing with disapproval at the mere numbers inscribed on David's wrist.

To reject a second courtesy from his old friend would have threatened Sôbre Xingu and the salvation of the Sundas. Still, David had insisted upon the nocturnal designs his mistress had left behind her on United Nations stationery. For during the flood, Melita had dreamt that her father, Pharo, was calling her from a dungeon in Rio. In the biplane, flown by Carlito, she had taken with her the smoking, primordial perfume of her bed—the scent of those coops where animals bred and rebred tirelessly, with no apparent concern for the salvation of their souls. A fever of humanity—which had grown to convulsion on the Smolensk road and recurred as a delirium cutting through the rain forest—had ended in the halls of Sôbre Xingu with Baron Sunda's outright dementia, among all the races of the world.

On the night of her going, Melita had been replaced by Opani. Had David later sent Carlito, like Bathsheba's husband, to risk his life?

David confronted the question hours after the design was complete, as he helped the priest with Easter in the windowless chapel before three hundred pairs of eyes, many of them the eyes of children. At each *sesta* hour, as Carlito looped and dived above the gold-diggers' road—in a rapture to be Kit Carson in the Wild West of the skies—David was secretly with Opani, who had been born in the same year that he was in Silesia, and who was of a humbling childishness. Lost in this question, David was the last in the chapel to recognize the sound of gunfire.

He did not know his full catastrophe, nor the torment of the fresh tattoo across his shoulders, until he crossed back to the main house through the equatorial heat. Reaching the main veranda, David could not find in his binoculars the cheerful shimmer of the biplane. From the eastern jungle, there came to him a distinct crackle of guns. The Indian *vaqueiros* in their Sunday clothes, murmuring by the corral, noticed that Baron Sunda did not wait for Nemo to be saddled before he set out, like a hunted man, down the red slopes of the Serra Azul. By tonight, all the Indians would be gone from Sôbre Xingu.

Until five that afternoon, assaulted by insects and gulping steadily from two large canteens, David tracked the sound of gunfire from where the Bororo had attacked the growing tip of the gold-diggers' road. Forgetting the salvation of the Sundas, David saw floating before him the image of Carlito's trusting grin and of Opani's blood-red cousins in their feathers and claws, dancing as spirits among the leaves of Eden. Then he became lost in the motion of the horse, the torment of the tattoo, and the digging of Arminius's buckle in his stomach. As they wheeled in and out of the jungle, for kilometers down the corridor, the sound of the fight seemed to move and always to recede. Then for a while Nemo splashed deeper, to the derision of birds and monkeys, along a cool jungle river that he knew.

Ahead of Baron Sunda there was a kilometer-long opening, filled with smoke and lit by the orange sunset. The palomino's lungs whistled and groaned as he paced out into the scorched village. Then with a gurgling lurch, the animal flung lather into the air and they fell together on the cane stubble. Trying to swallow, David stood with his gun by the kicking blond mound, in the smoke of the men's long house, as the parrots screamed and a cyclone of egrets coiled over his bare head. Unable to go forward, he stared at what was under the bordering trees. The Bororo had ambushed the engineers, then crossed a skeleton bridge and vanished into the northern jungle. David could see the tire marks where Carlito had been forced down before ground-looping.

The flying machine faced him, half buried under the forest canopy. David stumbled over the dead *garimpeiros* without noticing Stumpf, stretched face down among them. Coming to the biplane, he climbed through the wings and stood in the shade of the cockpit. After first clearing the red ants from Carlito's smile—sweet even in death—David began to sob uncontrollably, his hands hanging, his shirt shoulders soaked with blood, and his face lifted to the hot rain.

4

Until twelve o'clock of their last night at Sôbre Xingu, Baron von Sunda remained at his desk. First he composed a sober message to Bernard Piers at the United Nations; then, curiously autocratic notes to finance colleagues in New York and Paris; and finally, instructions to Gustav for the reopening of Oberlinden. Later he scribbled a few lines of great simplicity, to Justin Lothaire. Only then, as he had not done since before his desertion on the Smolensk snowfield, did he write to Hélène—a letter as if to the closest of friends. These last two sheets he tore into tiny shreds. After thirty minutes, during which he tried to reassemble his exact words, he burned the shreds thoroughly over a candle.

It was as if David were awakening after a long sickness. He rose repeatedly to go to his bedroom, on the remote possibility that the widowed child might have stayed. Before first light he heard Sôbre Xingu's chapel bell toll. The painful lump in his throat had returned.

Yet David had been mistaken about the bell on his last dawn. It was not tolling for Carlito. It had been Pasquas's son, who—hearing that their *chefe* had left them a stake in the great *fazenda*—had stolen into the church and was swinging his whole weight on the cowhide rope.

THE TRIBUTE

1

THE TELEGRAM FROM THE HAGUE REACHED THE LOTHAIRES IN THEIR twenty-third year, as the marriage came to its end.

This was the autumn of 1958. Though Joseph Stalin had died in his bed, across those five years the news of his human feast had grown from thousands to hundred thousands. Soon it would come to millions. Even the purest among the cadres, those who had been Justin's splendid friends in Barcelona and Carbonne, for whom he had argued in the Élysée, now carried a guilt that it was necessary to distinguish from fascism.

In Algiers, despite Justin's Lothaire's warning, the casbah baker's son, Saadi, Jacef, had sent young women through the sacred alleys, carrying bombs made behind the Mahbu public library, to blow apart dancing French girls at the beach club where Justin and Abu had once dived for silver coins. Later, festive French mobs had strung up torn Arab boys on butcher's frames, and parachutists had landed by helicopter on the very roof where Justin had lain under the desert stars, listening to the sweet pipe of the nay. He knew now that Hélène's brother, Jean-Marc was on the staff of the torturer, General Massu. Among the original circle to whom Abu had guided Justin in a flooded mosque, only Belkacem Krim was not in a French prison.

Then there was the city of his wife. For when the *éminences grises* of the Communist occupation had broken the rising of the Budapest citizenry, the names of Peter Tiolchak and Vera Lebedevna, still alive, had surfaced in the world press. Much had been expected of the celebrated Justin Lothaire, as the husband of a famous Hungarian and the steadiest light of the liberation. Yet arraigned as key witness before a humanity sealed in a tunnel of violence, he had been as if stripped of words.

It was during those autumn weeks that one day Luz had come home with a New York magazine containing a photograph of David Sunda. The most civilized man Justin knew was on a palomino stallion, gazing over a Brazilian cattle empire built with rubber tappers—penniless halfbreeds like Justin himself—by breaking into the last sanctuary of the ancient tribes. When he saw his wife's pride in her old fiancé, Justin asked himself if they must finally separate.

In Paris the season was getting under way, despite the Arabs regularly seen dead on the sidewalk by the Café Flore, or being shot at in the Métro. Along the Faubourg, the couturiers had set their winter windows; at Hermès there was a Father Christmas made entirely of silk scarves. Across the *seizième,* the nightly balls had begun in the mansions of the merchant bankers and the nobility. The street markets, with their skinned rabbits and their old women arguing the sex of ducklings, gave off a good-natured pandemonium. But none of this was as it had been before the war.

2

WHEN THE TELEGRAM FROM THE HAGUE WAS HANDED THROUGH THE ATELIER door, Luz was already depositing Sarah at the lycée, on the way to her film studio near the Bois. Moving through their lives in public, Luz and Justin had not spoken for days.

The new telephone broke in on Justin's meditation, which he had secured at the price of many hurt followers. Justin had never owned such an instrument and he did not need this one.

"Is that Mr. Lothaire? This is Sidney Shelburne."

"I do not speak with film people," Justin told the producer gently, and he rehooked the earpiece. Opening the telegram then, he read it through. Luz's telephone was ringing as Justin read it through again, and then a third time. IT IS OUR VERY GREAT PRIVILEGE the words began.

Standing under the naked kitchen bulb, with terrible eyes, Justin gazed through this attic that he had loved and hated. The greatness of a dream, long ago in the lace shop, drew at his heart . . . as once when he had hunted the tuna with Ibn Moushmun and the great fish had risen from deep beneath the trapped shoal of its brothers. Now in Justin's soul the nets tightened and tightened—and then suddenly they hung loose, shredded and spent. He was back on a Thursday morning in Paris. The dream was gone. He could not hold it; far too much had been renounced. Justin felt very small and solitary. He could not think of anyone to tell. Pulling on a jacket, he went downstairs. The door was opened by Doré's old sister.

"Anna, is Marcel here? I have been given a prize."

"Come in. Come in, my child." Anna led him down the obscure passage with its smell of camphor and books. "Marcel will be very happy for you. But, alas, he is at his farm in Vence. He particularly likes the light at this time of year."

"Of course, I knew that!" Justin was thunderstruck. How long was it since he himself had considered the quality of light?

"Can you help me, Justin?" she went on. "I let the tuning fork fall underneath the piano. Imagine, one little note—yet so important to the rest."

Feeling more and more vulnerable, Justin crawled around under Doré's furniture, looking for the tuning fork. In the end, it was the old woman who discovered it, caught in the seam of her skirt.

A quarter of an hour later, as he crossed the Pont des Arts, he was thinking of the last Frenchwoman in the casbah delivering a tablecloth to Madame Michaud through the police-checks. Soon he would return alone to the desert. He was forty-one, and the hour had come. Justin Lothaire had renounced almost everything else. What if now he refused the world's ultimate prize?

Like a blind man, lost in such thoughts, Justin emerged on the Place Saint-Germain. He at once caught sight of familiar gray wings of hair. Inside the big corner café, faces turned to him.

"*Salut*. You look terrible," Eli said, as Justin slipped in against the window.

Once again it startled Justin, faced with the sweetness of this face, to remember Eli outside the *mairie* at Carbonne. However, that was no question for today. Eli was one person whom he could never renounce. "I thought I would find you here," he said.

"I'll order breakfast. They have a new infusion machine."

"You're enjoying life, Eli?"

"Oh, is it that bad?"

"Better already."

"Don't tell me, *compagnon*," Eli observed, "that you've stopped loving it?"

In Justin's head some pressure had just loosened. A fear that he had never overcome was the fear of great personal prestige. He could count on Eli never to be impressed. Impulsively, he placed the telegram between them.

The waiter stood before their table. Gaston's café had been spoiled by the fame of its writers. But when he saw this gloomy, scarred, and always modest *pied-noir*, he became very grave. Lifting the telegram, the waiter ran a damp cloth over the tabletop, then withdrew.

Justin grinned. "Do you think I make them love life?"

"Fool, they love you more. Don't you love them?"

"I've renounced a great deal, Eli."

"Yes, you're renouncing Luz."

The telegram Justin was also about to renounce lay unfolded between his elbows. Eli's narrow brown face glanced at him. Justin knew Eli had waited for twenty years to discover the limits of his endurance, and he was at that limit now. He must be very careful not to do or say anything rash. "Eli, *they* have renounced nothing," Justin said, breaking a cube of sugar between his fingers. "Out there are a million amoral scientists and a world army of police. There is money, monarchy, and starvation. The faces in the street are just as selfish. Sometimes I don't even fathom the motives of our closest friends—"

Eli had made a warning sign. Gripping Justin's sleeve, he leaned close. Justin raised his free hand.

"So we will be destroyed," he concluded. "There is no role for us."

"One role Lothaire has not renounced, otherwise we could be clowns together!" Eli cried happily, as if that would be the finest solution.

Justin had not laughed for many months, and it was a terrible sound.

" What's your secret?" he said.

"Freedom. I never had anything to give up. Look around you. Everything has changed!"

"It's just you, Eli, you're the best man you know," Justin said gruffly.

"Oh, no, Justin, I'd give a leg for one portion of your spirit. Only don't lose hold of the siren who has bewitched Europe."

"Luz dulls my hunger for ordinary souls," Justin said.

Eli nodded. "Perhaps. But how will you do it?"

"She can go to Hollywood. Sarah will like the beaches."

"What if she returns?"

"Who ever returns from there?"

"And then?"

"Then I will stop giving up this world. I will bring myself to bear."

3

FOR SOME MINUTES, THEY SAT AGAINST THE WINDOW IN THE RICH SILENCE OF those who—having witnessed what has never been seen before—have earned the right to say what has never been said. Justin had admitted his ultimate defeat. Yet life was still there.

He slid the telegram across the polished wood. Presently, the bones of his face aching now, he reached out and nudged the sheet a little farther. Eli stared at him, then picked the paper up and unfolded it. Justin watched his friend's eyes grow large, then moist, as they read down the lines. After he had finished, Eli very carefully folded the message and held it delicately in both hands.

"Say something, Eli. What should I do?"

"Do?" Eli repeated.

"Shall I accept it?"

"Not accept it? *Merde!*" Eli grasped Justin's wrist with great force. "Renounce everything else, but not this. Go and shout it through the streets!"

"The streets will know about it soon enough." Justin felt his face turn even paler.

"You are at the gates of Jerusalem. You will accept it," Eli said softly. "Simply remember your father. Remember what Darnand said—and Baptiste Duroc, who is now a bishop of Paris. Remember Hitler's genius of gas chambers. Above all, remember the thousands who followed you. The movement will spread around the world."

"And the collaborators, Eli? where are *they* now?"

Eli had seized Justin's lapels. "Exactly, Justin. We're not alone. Let *them* hear your voice!"

Though the two men had barely spoken aloud, the entire room was turned to them in silence.

Later, Justin dropped off a critique for d'Issipe at the École Normale. After stopping to see the large offices of the new *Justice*, he recrossed the river at the Pont des Arts and walked on toward the Louvre, taking note of its monumental walls. Were such formal powers not what David had been offered and a *sale bicot* had been forever denied? Had the toils Justin had already endured, after all, been only a preparation?

In the shock of so immense a hope, his imagination had already leapt to the rostrum in The Hague, before an auditorium filled with the most educated men on earth. The world's reporters were crowded at the rear, their pencils raised. Even in the cells of Algiers, the colonial torturers put aside their hoses and wires. Then, in a voice filtered by the forgiveness of great suffering, Justin Lothaire would speak of the past and of the future. He would speak of history, of which Hitler and Stalin had made a ruin, gutted by the fires of hatred—and he would flood that ruin with parables of light. Laughing and weeping, the unpardonable rich would stream down among the masses, and the great cities would subside.

Ten minutes later Justin was in the Palais-Royal when the fair skies gave way to a violent thunderstorm. Towering yellow branches, like nerve systems in a plastic anatomy, stuttered and boomed above the gabled roofs of Paris, stark as fissures in the foundations of the universe, allowing glimpses of everlasting fire.

4

FROM THAT EVENING, WHEN LUZ FIRST HEARD THAT HER HUSBAND WAS TO WIN the Hague Award, Justin knew she might not go to Hollywood. Never had he felt so isolated in this city of the French, and he shared in his family's excitement like a stranger.

Through the next three weeks, Justin Lothaire's picture—and something called his life story—were in the papers every day. Meanwhile he listened, over blank pages, for the words of healing that he had heard distinctly on the Pont des Arts. By the sixth draft, Justin's love for the world was exhausted. Carrying the texts to a café behind the Comédie, he read them while he drank a liter of Burgundy. His first attempt was still the best. It was far short of his eruption on the Pont des Arts, but it was the speech he would read at The Hague.

From the moment at Ypenburg airport when his family was met by a crowd of reporters, Justin could sense that he was expected to say certain things and to behave himself. He was like a famous entertainer who has been hired for a special celebration. As Justin, bearing a champagne glass, moved like a ghost from Armageddon through the rehearsals and the introductions and a royal banquet at Apeldoorn, gradually his face hardened. Among the laureates were an American writer whom Justin admired and a biologist whose discovery had immunized millions. Many languages were spoken here with great exuberance. Yet Justin was aware, as of an exterminating angel, how all the men at these receptions seemed drawn to his wife and how the actress was in control of this.

In their grand hotel with its view onto the North Sea, an hour came when Justin pulled on the morning suit he had rented in Paris. He perspired heavily during the ride to the ceremonial hall. Presently, leaving Sarah and Luz in the gilt foyer, Justin Lothaire was shown inside to a front row of plush chairs. He was conscious only of the giant festoons of flowers, and he thought of a bare shop—and of his mother, now alone and protected only by his name. He remembered Jeanne Lothaire's reply to his invitation, which had accused her son of being a revolutionary, a man of violence, and a traitor to the French race.

Then the awards began, and the air became filled with the confessions of ferocious ambition. A particle physicist rose to speak about quanta and ethics; an economist spoke about individualism and mass states; then a mathematician spoke about formulas for calculating temperature in remote stars, and a biologist about the science metropolises of the future.

There was more applause, and more climbing up and down with coattails dangling. Justin Lothaire took out a folded handkerchief and wiped his temples. Above him, the driftwood-faced official had begun to describe, in nasal French, a young man who had—single-handedly in his art as in his life—unswervingly opposed the blind forces of history.

That is me, Justin thought, rising as he heard his name. *But it is not because I oppose, it is because I foresee.* As he reached the uppermost stair and stepped onto the polished stage, he was enveloped by a fragrant silence of flowers.

"Thank you, thank you," Justin repeated. Shaking the official's hand, he felt the album and the little box placed between his fingers. As Justin turned to the waves of satisfied faces, whose great day this was, he was thinking of the black Berber tents and of Paul Rochet, hanging in the rain. He thought of the innocent dead, among whom he belonged, of Hélène's lovely voice, and of David, who had given him Stodel—and of Elijah, when he had been the last believer and had challenged the worshipers of Baal to a contest between gods. Finally, Justin remembered the two magicians in Sidi ldriz with white pigeons on their heads, chanting "Yumiyumiyumi!" as one pulled the wet furry tips from the pouch, and how a boy had never found out what it was.

"It is my great honor. . . ." Landerhaut was at his side, working his bloodless lips against the silver microphone.

"Yes." Justin stood obediently at the rostrum, struggling. " The honor is mine." At the sight of his typed words—just the same, as Justin unfolded the pages—he opened his mouth. Though he was burning alive with impatience, Justin heard a soft, musical voice begin to speak.

Later, he had only one memory of what happened, before he found himself standing between his wife and his daughter at a reception for the Dutch queen. This memory was of the pain when the anger of a lifetime was torn out—a pain as if his mother's cardboard God had forsaken him. It came as Justin concluded with his vision of the toiling billions of the earth, after their rulers had renounced the taste for personal power; when the bureaucracies awoke from their psychosis of technology; when the last *Ubermensch* had chosen to live in a brotherhood faithful to the least man, as with animals who share a waterhole. In other words, when the ruthless society of power, wealth, movie stars, and prizes was overthrown.

Applause for Justin had come through the theater like a swell. As he climbed down, his eyes ached.

More men climbed up and spoke, and there was more clapping. But Justin Lothaire sat drowning in concentration—trembling, oppressed, and embarrassed as if he had been observed in a fit of raving. At the royal press reception, emptied and adrift, he was grateful to catch sight of Luz with her admirers, beyond the mountainous buffet. As his wife came toward him carrying a box, her face was more radiant and wild than he had ever seen it.

"Justin, are you mad? You left this on the stage!"

"Papa?" His daughter lowered her eyes.

"So you were not ashamed of me, little one?" he said, unable to look at Luz in her lilac dress, holding the Hague Award. Even after the miracle of his child, Justin was a man forsaken by his father.

Presently, moving away from the piles of food, he found himself next to the wiry American with cold, withering eyes. The man examined him with a twisted smile that seemed to say, This is absurd, and conversation even more so. If we speak or do not, it is all the same to me.

"I was worried about you up there, Mr. Lothaire," he said, and they both burst out laughing.

"So was I," Justin answered in English.

"That tunnel—your garden of ice. It is a risky business to be open and generous with that sort of thing. I thought the final bit would break you."

"Doesn't it serve humanity to see how things will be?"

"Let them stumble there naturally, Mr. Lothaire."

"Do you mean unnaturally?" Justin said.

"Absolutely. In the meantime, you and I will get there—"

"Quite naturally," Justin said, and they stood in silence, watching the distinguished group gathered around Luz's dress. "If ever you come to Georgia, Mr. Lothaire, we will fish for bass."

"When you visit the Maghreb, we will ride together to the holy towns of the Atlas," Justin said, his voice almost inaudible.

And so this American writer had been the first to hear. Justin Lothaire was going back to the desert.

That evening, the most excruciating depression came over Justin that he had ever known. Later, during their flight to Paris, when he looked back over those sterile scenes—the kind that Doktor Godard would have called Olympian—it seemed clear to him that everything he had been through had been inevitable. But the most inevitable of all was that Justin's words would be forgotten.

5

BY CHRISTMAS OF 1959, THE SLOW-MOVING DIVORCE WAS WELL ON ITS WAY TO being the Paris season's foremost *histoire célèbre*. There were always photographers at the café in the rue de Valois. Lothaire's publisher—who had let four of the Hague winner's books slip quietly from sight—now had out large printings of all five. Every morning, Justin still woke up next to an Austro-Hungarian princess who clung to his life with abject despair, yet without once having seen the rue Mahbu. Each morning he thought, *Today I will renounce the last of this Paris life.*

Then during Algiers' January of barricades, when Frenchmen were killing Frenchmen in the spirit of the popular front and police spies appeared to guard their door, there came to Justin Lothaire the first perfectly classical conception of his life.

In two sleepless weeks he worked out half the plot, set in the days of the defeat at the Pyramids, by Bonaparte's army, of the proud Egyptian Mamelukes. These twenty-three smudged and wrinkled pages were the indispensable heart of Justin's fable, through which at last the dream of a lace shop would equal the works of the great writers. Then one morning his precious notes disappeared, as if by *Nacht und Nebel.*

During those minutes, the garbage truck would be in the rue de Valois.

The machine had reached the second door when the photographers saw a violent-looking man break into the street, chased by an armed detective. "*Merde alors! . . . Il est fou! . . . Arrêtes, sale race!*" With the dumb despair of a mother for her child, the fugitive jumped onto the wagon. Dropping knee-deep among chicken carcasses, tins, and horse joints, the man began to shovel frantically, while the detective and the workmen looked on in disgusted silence. Somehow, he felt the heart of his work beat very close.

Almost immediately, Justin saw a taped sheaf of notes under some coffee grounds and fruit peels. With a cry he knelt to free the crushed papers. At this moment—even knowing that Luz had thrown them out—Justin Lothaire felt no anger. Excusing himself politely to the speechless garbagemen, he climbed slowly back up his stairwell to their kitchen.

"Justin, I will be late for rehearsal."

"No, no, Lupic, just one minute more. The notes are found. I am not even angry. You see what a sign this might be? Admit to me, just once, *now,* that you have never wished to understand the person you live beside. From there we can begin again."

Luz stared at him with subtle condescension. "What do you need the notes for, Justin? If you don't want this to happen, why leave them spread over the floor?"

Justin was thunderstruck. Was this impenetrably elegant woman going to blame the near calamity on *him?* Her indifference disgraced the truce he had offered her. Releasing Luz's tense fingers, he stumbled out of the door and wound down the stairs. With Doré now living in the South, there was no one left to speak to.

Automatically heading in the company of his police shadow, toward the Place des Vosges, where he had last seen David, Justin kept thinking of how he had been unable to make a final break with Luz. For months, he had killed the nerve endings that grew between them. Yet when he looked into Luz's eerie green eyes—their sufferings invisible to each other—he could not harm her. The one narrow path to freedom had never seemed to him more firmly blocked.

6

"So even *then* he was a romantic," Baron Sunda continued to James Penn, in the schooner's chart cabin. He frowned with a sort of expectant curiosity at the sun spots on his own hands.

"In what way, sir?"

"Don't you see?" the old German went on softly. "Justin had decided that his one great mistake lay in Melanie Grinda's marriage. He must have believed even then that if he could find a way back to that earliest passion, he could reenter the soul of his people. It was during the winter of the Algiers barricades that he first contacted Melanie's much younger sister, Jeanne.

"The horse breaker had sent the girl to safety, working as a governess for a Jewish family in Clichy. Jeanne had felt no recognition when she paused at the corner kiosk on the rue des Martyrs to examine an American magazine's cover painting of Justin Lothaire. Yet only two or three days later the governess had a gentleman caller. Peering down into the courtyard, Jeanne had seen a man shorter than she had imagined, dressed in an old leather jacket. He could have been her father.

"A few years after Brazil," Baron Sunda continued, I went to see the girl in Paris. She had married the bicycle racer she had been engaged to at the time of Lothaire's visit. Jeanne Grinda was a slight, bony redhead with blue eyes—quite pretty when she smiled, and with the expressive movements of a mime. She was completely uneducated. When she talked about him it was in a manner humble and perplexed, with a trace of pity. Evidently Justin spoke to her a great deal. Most of it was about the desert—places in Algeria they both knew—the *grands colons* and the working people. It was probably one of Justin Lothaire's last great visionary speeches. But by then, along with everything else, Justin had renounced his search for an audience who could fathom him. That was it. This man, fifteen years and a century of experience her senior, hypnotized the girl: *'Il a tourné ma tête.'* Jeanne had no idea how to react to Justin Lothaire as a woman, any more than she would have to some bronze statue that cultivated folk go to see in the Jardins. So she hung on to her first impression of pity, because it was her only human impression of him.

"Then for some weeks the girl heard nothing more from her disturbing visitor. It must have been that March—in a single day—that Justin rejected the two great forces of his life."

7

WITH THE SCENE OF THE NOTES IN THE GARBAGE TRUCK, JUSTIN'S LIFE ENTERED its mortal phase.

In the year since The Hague, offers from nine universities had arrived, along with invitations from union leaders to address workers in Western Europe, the East, and in the Americas. These symptoms of the world's willingness to be led by Justin Lothaire only deepened an apprehension of tragedy that made him afraid for his reason. He stayed in Doré's attic, hypnotized by the lost world of the Mamelukes. Sometimes he took long walks trailed by two police trench coats.

That final night, Justin had had the first of many dreams, possessing no familiar spice smell or song of flutes among his blown-out alleys, but only the shouting of huge industrial crowds. In the morning he gave his bodyguard the slip and went to look for Eli Hebron on the rue Dombasle, at the offices of the *Partie Communiste*.

If one had ever been in the sewers of the Nazis, it would always feel strange to walk freely through this hall. One flight up, Justin moved along the walls of romantic posters—bloodthirsty with the pride of simple folk who have linked hands to throw off the police of the colonial rich. He could remember when it had seemed a miracle that so many could feel as he did.

After the Communists' promise to Algeria, Justin did not feel the things that were in the posters, and he did not wish to look at them.

"Justin, come in. You should meet Manuel and Götz."

"No, I will wait outside." At the desk behind Eli, the East German turned to smile.

On the sidewalk outside, the few dead leaves that the storm had blown off the trees were pressed flat. Eli knew why he had come, and Justin set the pace. Recognizing their strained silence, he felt hurt. It was as if, after The Hague, people felt Justin no longer needed them. It seemed better when they were face-to-face at a tiny wall table. There was a *capitaine d'espionnage* four places away. Eli leaned close to Justin.

"I know what you will say."

"That I would not like to describe where we just were."

"Do not take it so badly. In Algiers, the Party must support the little French colons."

"Am I not an Algerian?" Justin cried. "What interests them beside the domination of the state? Must I now dislike myself?"

"My dear, good friend." Eli was looking worried. "Beware of personality cults. Everyone trusts you."

"Do they?" Justin emptied his wineglass, watching Eli without blinking. "Eli, leave the Party."

"Justin, Justin, Justin!" Eli sank back and glanced at their neighbors. "Do you want me to give up my place in the largest and most disciplined society of world justice ever invented because you don't exactly agree? Have you become an American?"

"Passive resistance liberated India."

"The Indians freed themselves by bombarding Bombay harbor. You think we can lay new tracks while the train is rolling? Justin, Algiers will soon fall."

"The Comintern has already claimed the revolutions across two thirds of this world. Our liberation must be our own, Eli. It must have limits—otherwise I will not give my name to it. There must be no blood on the gates of a true paradise."

"And you will accomplish all this alone?" Eli smiled tenderly. "Now I *know* you have the courage of a thousand men."

"Do not forsake me, Eli," Justin said softly. His soup was tasteless. Unscrewing the shaker's cap, he shook salt into the bowl. "A thousand human beings is not nearly enough." He tried to smile. "We are three billion."

After Justin Lothaire left Eli on the rue Dombasle, the desolation of Paris was so overpowering he could not organize his thoughts. As he returned to the Palais-Royal—concentrating, to be close to the humiliated Mamelukes—he saw his wife ahead in the fog, holding an opened letter.

Without a word Justin read it as they circled side by side up the stairs. It was an offer from Hollywood, to test Luz on the screen for the leading role in a work of Russian literature.

"Please help me, Justin. What should I do?"

His wife followed him into his bare studio. From the sunny window, Justin looked at this woman's thick hair, which fell from two combs almost to her waist. He looked at her brown calves, kicking back the ruff of her skirt. She carefully tanned herself on the Seine's solarium barge. Even at this moment, Justin could not help feeling a desperate worship for this angel from an extinct Europe.

"Justin . . . should I refuse?" She faced him, with one hand on his writing chair. In Justin's chest there was a flutter of criminal laughter.

"No, you must not!" he heard himself say. "You don't turn down the finest role in literature."

"Justin, this is not like you!" Luz smiled at him crookedly, and flushed. He could see her already thinking about the famous stars—of the champagne parties and swimming pools, of jasmine blossoms crushed on vast stairways. It was as if Luz had never been with Justin during Hitler's terror or in Rochet's farmhouse. It was easy now.

"Film is this century's great art form," he lied, hearing the comfortable conviction in his voice. His wife began to pace back and forth with some agitation. Justin dropped his eyes sadly. He held his American lighter under a Gauloise—the Greeks believed that all excess was a fire.

"He is a very famous director," Luz said apologetically. Being suddenly released from her husband's moral restraints had disoriented her.

"Film, Luz?" Justin went on grimly. "It will revolutionize the human mind. All literature will be made into movies. The actors who play the great roles will become those characters forever. By the end you will have had a profound effect on millions!"

Justin concluded this grandiose flourish without irony. He smiled gently as Luz laughed her vain laugh and glanced around her with a sort of nervous fear at the poor attic with its trapeze and its Chinese chair where they had lived their lives together. From the window Justin watched the woman with relief and regret and with the indifference of a sailor who abandons a struggle to keep a fine vessel off the rocks. *Everything you are*, Justin thought, *you are through your breeding. But have you ever once asked yourself what is your right?*

On that very Sunday, with their daughter, Luz flew to America. From New York, where they stayed with Hélène, they continued to Los Angeles. One week later, the telephone began to ring at midnight in Marcel Doré's attic in the Palais-Royal. Half naked in his chair, Justin listened as a high-pitched, faraway voice that he scarcely recognized to be his wife's told him how she had signed, that very day, a million-dollar contract for the next three years.

And so—well after the crises of Suez and Hungary, as Boumedienne's eleven thousand fellahin waited just across Algeria's frontier with Tunisia; in the confident years of the vast proletarian dictatorships of Russia and China, and on the eve of Communist flowerings in Southeast Asia and the Caribbean, in the second century of American democracy—Europe's most famous actress went into final exile as a technicolor movie star. Justin Lothaire was left weeping alone with his books, under armed guard, as a cultural treasure of the French.

For in his sleep Justin had dreamt again of the desert, as he had known it, before its six years of blood and revolt. Now in the first warmth of spring, the yellow mimosa would be visible on the branches. At the waterhole among the eucalyptus, the slippery brown bodies would soon splash and roll on the sharp leaves and bathe in the blood of the watermelon. At Grinda's farm, the stallions would scent the grazing mares and kick their stalls, and the yellow dog would bark and throw himself against the twenty-meter chain. In her lace shop, his mother would be clicking her rosary and thanking God for the rich. And perhaps there would be Melanie . . . Melanie in submission, damp and brown in the watertower, on the itchy blanket, on a bed of eucalyptus. Afterward, as the leaves rustled and sheep bells tinkled amid the drone of wasps and flies, their skins would be stinging and drenched. He and she, looking into each other's eyes where there are no words, knowing the serious discovery of each other's bodies. Around them then would rise the drunken, sweet reek of garlic and tears, of sweat and crushed eucalyptus, mouse droppings and rotted wood. When it was over, the interrupted throb of crickets would lift in the satiated noon. And that was all, and all there would ever need be.

Two weeks later, Justin wrote the last words of his book. The same evening he telephoned Jeanne Grinda.

THE MEEK

1

I T WAS THIRTY YEARS SINCE BARON SUNDA HAD FIRST SET OUT FROM Oberlinden. Throughout the Fascist pandemic he had cursed his boyhood independence for having eventually dislocated him to Mexico. He accepted now that it was a League of Nations sinecure, won by personal influence, that had led him to Guderian's staff and had ended in his brother's execution and in his family's ruin.

Such thoughts were on David's mind while he waited for two weeks in a New York hotel for Bernard Piers to return from Hanoi and Saigon.

At noon, the day after the delegation's return, a motorcade of limousines blocked the traffic in United Nations Plaza. Climbing out of a yellow cab on the corner of 44th Street, Baron Sunda stared up at the giant cliffside of glass. All around the *chefe* of Sôbre Xingu rose the great buildings—far higher than any church spire ever reached for God, higher even than David had flown the Spad—reaching, one felt, to galaxies and nebulas. These crashing mineral streets which the *garimpeiros* had dreamt of like El Dorado were as exhilarating and loveless as a ride at an amusement park. David still felt on his skin the scream of birds and the honest eyes of simple folk. The truth was that, behind his mask, he was no less coarse than they.

As he entered through the lobby, David was halted by a press of delegates from various nations, all vacuously similar in gray or blue suits. This was the cure for fascism, but David knew their rich souls better than they could have guessed. A cool receptionist singled him out.

"Oh, yes. Lemuel? Please conduct the baron to Mr. Piers's suite."

The sealed metal elevator hurtled upward. They decelerated, and Lemuel held his arm across David's chest. A tiny man stepped in, manacled to a courier's bag and wearing spectacles and a black hat. For several powerful seconds, as if he were again on a Silesian hillside, David experienced the horrible jolt of the familiar sunken eyes jumping over the passengers and walls.

Then the man turned and stood with his face hidden against the elevator wall, his shoulders working. A violent and uncontrollable trembling overcame David. He took a step and was about to seize this brother of the *Lagers* passionately by the shoulders when Lemuel's arm rose between them.

Performing a short, humiliated prisoner's sidestep, the courier escaped the compartment with a half glance over his shoulder. Again David gained weight as they completed the ascent. A taste of vomit had come into his mouth. He could not go in like this to a conference that might seal his fate.

"Baron Sunda? Baron Sunda? Please follow me."

David went through the open door into an office as brilliant as if it were among glaciers.

2

"SUNDA . . . AT LONG LAST!" PIERS ADVANCED AROUND THE DESK TO MEET HIM.

"Forgive me, Bernard, I have just had a shock," David said, somewhat coldly, in the face of the undersecretary's good spirits.

As they arranged themselves, his old mentor observed Baron Sunda attentively. This hugely admired European had not contacted him since he had abandoned the law project, somewhere in Mexico. David Sunda's incomplete notes, however, had recently been of great use.

"Take off your jacket, we are very relaxed here," he said. "How do you like New York?"

"They have made progress with television."

"Isn't it awful! And this is not much like the old League, is it?"

"Let us hope not. How were your travels?"

"The Diems? Oh, there is sure to be trouble," commented the now pudgy Dutchman with a sudden air of grief. "But how is your sister, Karin?"

"Do you know she was the only member of my family to visit Brazil?" David smiled, though he still felt devastated by the meeting in the elevator.

"Ah, my friend, now I understand your address at the Plaza Hotel. Are Hélène and the children still at the Dakota?"

"Surely you knew? Our separation is an ancient story." Across the huge desk, the undersecretary's eyes had hardened thoughtfully, and David understood that already in his first minutes here he had let slip some of the invulnerable mystique accumulated across twenty years. His turmoil might bear other interpretations.

"Yes, this trip was a great success. I was absolutely everywhere!" The undersecretary began to outline his Gulf of Tonkin visit, alluding, by their first names to generalissimos, kings, and ministers in Tokyo, Phnom Penh, Peking, and finally in Vietnam. He spoke with the vague air of superiority that all ambitious people acquire, whether they have succeeded or not, and Bernard Piers seemed to have succeeded.

At the altitude of this room, forgetfulness was overtaking Baron Sunda. Their conversation seemed otherworldly, as with deep-sea divers experiencing nitrogen narcosis.

"Tell me, David, what are your thoughts about a global community?"

"Has a single country yet turned over its sovereignty?"

"Is that necessary? What about the example of the American states? The Swiss cantons?" The official's eyes had grown impersonal, as if he were reading formulas off the back of them.

"Large unions can only be held together with armies," David went on. "All wars now are civil wars. Why not a conscripted world peace army?"

"A standing United Nations army? An occupation of the world?"

"Aren't we with the UN trying to refine the science of talking to each other, with the pressure to guarantee it?" He smiled, feeling again the force of ideas. "Although I think we would be better off with a field army of educators, doctors, and agriculturalists."

"But my dear friend, bureaucracy is the way we do things!" the undersecretary objected with a laugh. "What else is there?"

"Aside from conferences? A great deal, Bernard," David said resonantly. Almost distractedly, he sensed his authority.

"Splendid, absolutely superb! You have not changed a bit, David Sunda." The undersecretary paused to clear his throat. "We've known each other for thirty years, and I have yet to meet a personality better suited to our work at the UN. You know we have a roving position open in the secretary-general's office. I would have no problem easing your nomination through."

"That is very generous," David said.

"I would be proud. Please tell me I can go ahead."

Facing a floor-to-ceiling window that seemed filled with a *garimpeiro*'s dream—a strip mine of chasms and spires—David sat very still with his fingers pressed together. As he heard the offer, which could resurrect him in the eyes of Justin and Hélène and his children, he had flushed. Never met a personality better suited to work at the UN? At that moment David's soul was tracking the utterly humbled camp victim somewhere in this building.

"Good lord, David, you are only fifty years old! Isn't this what your life has been moving toward?"

"Please, Bernard." David felt himself gripped by a hunger for the rites of true friendship. "Don't think me ungrateful. We should discuss it over some good wine. Do you know the Corniche, on Forty-second street?"

The undersecretary gestured impatiently. "All right . . . though I'd planned to take you to the delegates' dining room."

"No! The food at the Corniche is excellent." David barely mastered his voice. As the two men rose, his heart was pounding in anticipation of the elevator.

This time it was empty and there were no stops. As they went out through the broad lobby, several delegates hurried up to the undersecretary and tried to involve him in issues of state. David was introduced, and he was the altogether remarkable Baron Sunda of Hitler and the July 20th plot, the escape from

Russia, and the building of Sôbre Xingu. That is, no one knew the first thing about him.

As soon as they were seated alone, two streets away up a flight of stairs, David took a doubled envelope from his pocket.

"This is something that can't wait, Bernard."

"You have only to ask!"

"The letter is from a Soviet doctor called Ilyushin. It was sent on to me from Oberlinden."

"Vaslav Semyonovitch Ilyushin?" Piers did not look up from the paper.

"In the spring of 'forty-one," David went on carelessly, to mask a sudden vital excitement, "our first son, Rickie, was born in Siberia. This Ilyushin delivered him. I was absolutely convinced I had seen him executed at Tula. Instead imagine this—the man was one of Zhukov's surgeons! He must have seen my photograph in a captured newspaper. Later in the war, Ilyushin was arrested for speaking against Beria. They sent him to Dnepropetrovsk psychiatric prison."

"And I see your doctor is still there." The undersecretary sighed deeply, as if depressed by the thought of an obscurity so complete. "As it happens, I am also the chair of a commission investigating political detentions."

"So you could help Ilyushin?"

The Dutchman shrugged, and a look of pity and disappointment crossed his face. "We have lists of twenty thousand war heroes vanished in Stalinist camps."

"Begin with one case."

"It is utterly futile, I assure you."

"And the files?"

"They must await their hour."

"That is grotesque!" David cried.

"That's nothing," Piers continued, lowering his voice. "We have secret dossiers on thirty thousand Nazi war criminals."

"Is that possible?" David whispered. "Where? You have their addresses?"

"It has been agreed to let the past sleep."

"That's not the past, it is the future. The future doesn't sleep!" David had recognized on his old friend's face the longing to flee this cramped table. To be away from these atrocities and private crusades, back in his glass office high above Manhattan. David heard himself continue, almost as if to place a curse on this bureaucrat, "They will say that even our finest men were slaves to history. That only Hitler made history his slave."

"Yes, we *are* slaves!" Piers flushed red and turned to the waitress. "Bring us some coffee—then cognac and a Benedictine." David was aware that the offer of the UN post had fallen behind forever. Throughout their lunch, the group at the neighboring table had not once broken off a loud baseball debate about the Giants.

To Bernard Piers's surprise, the rest of their meeting was conducted with affection and charm, as if his enigmatic guest wished to reassure him of something. They parted exchanging promises to meet again soon. David Sunda only turned back once to the great glass tower that held in its protection the sealed dossiers of Europe's unpunished war criminals.

3

HE SPENT THE AFTERNOON DOWNTOWN WITH OTTO HORVATH AND HIS BANKERS, disbursing fresh Sunda assets for long- and short-term profits. Arrangements must be made to redeem the mortgages on two thousand acres of refinanced Oberlinden farmland—and there was the outstanding debt at Penn Industries for his children's education.

It was not until David was on his way back to his hotel to change for dinner that the sensation of clear wisdom at refusing the United Nations post changed to one of being cornered. His thoughts returned unhappily to the magazine article in which Hélène had first discovered hints of David's Mato Grosso household. To their children, he was still no more than a military man of the disgraced German race who had abandoned them through their childhood. It was their mother who was the one witness throughout to the complex truth of their father.

Nor had the recent stopover in Berlin, and later at Oberlinden, left him eager to take up life there. Especially not after his sister and her now-impoverished count had moved on to Templar's Hill only days after David reopened the estate.

One drizzling morning, after a six-year absence, Baron Sunda had come down the gangway from the *Cristoforo Colombo* onto a West Side pier. Waiting there in the dry shed among the shouting stevedores had been a sober, dignified, and very attractive woman of forty-eight in a beige summer dress, accompanied by two restrained young men and a girl who would not smile at her father. From the woman's first noncommittal kiss on his cheek, nothing in the world seemed significant except that this intelligent woman should become again the Hélène Le Trève whom David had known all his life. In that first hour in New York, he had heard again of Dr. Rinkel, whom he must now meet, and of the room reserved for him at a hotel.

Now, fifteen days later, an altered Baron Sunda caught a taxi outside the Plaza Hotel to go home for the first time. The doorman of the Dakota held a big umbrella for him.

"Spring showers, sir. Good to see you after all the years."

"Thank you, Frederick," David said, having guessed from the man's eagerness that Dr. Rinkel had passed often through this gate. When he thought of the woman upstairs, whose understanding his life somehow still required, he felt bewildered, humiliated and enraged.

4

HÉLÈNE HAD BEEN ABSORBED FOR SOME TIME LEAFING THROUGH THE PILE OF diagnostic notes on the piano lid, written in Dr. Rinkel's fine script. She did not look up when someone paused under the living-room arch and then withdrew.

All that day Hélène, had been distracted from her work by troubling questions about her estranged husband's interview with Bernard Piers. Now she spun around and stared at the empty arch . . . it had been *him*. But somehow Hélène turned instead to the kitchen.

The black Puerto Rican cook, Yasmeen—who had arrived shortly after Gerta's death—was humming as she rolled a piecrust on the marble countertop. Yasmeen came from a jungle village called Jiukijiu, and she was Hélène's one companion each Sunday at mass. She did not like men.

Just now, in the presence of Yasmeen's soft easy charm, Hélène felt a sudden dread that David might now have reason to stay in New York. Yet could the family bear a further separation? There was so much between husband and wife, even the war itself, that might be set to rest no other way. Poor Leonard, she thought, poor Leonard. He had shown her almost saintly understanding.

Hélène picked up a knife and began to slice a small onion. Yasmeen switched off the Spanish program.

"*Señor* Sunda here, Mother?"

"I don't know, Yasmeen . . . yes." How could she admit that not a word had passed between them?

"You want I lay the wax candles?" Yasmeen loved candles. She always lit twelve at mass, one for each member of her family.

"If you would, Yasmeen. Two of them."

I have spent the day working beside my lover, Hélène thought. This evening, I will light candles for my husband. A lover and a husband, she thought, to hurt herself with such a failure. Even worse, since Luz had come through New York the previous winter, still looking thirty years old, it was Justin Lothaire—somehow alone in Paris—of whom Hélène had been constantly aware. "You should agree to see Justin, Leni, he loves you so," her girlhood friend had told Hélène. Even after their bitter years of silence, she had almost respected Luz again. How had all this come to be?

She had not become Leonard Rinkel's mistress for a year after David had left, though Leonard had wanted this and Hélène had needed it even more. Then the painful letters from Brazil had begun subtly to alter in her the idea she had of her husband. The scenes he described were so primitive and harsh that Hélène could scarcely conceive of them. Later there would be the shock of her husband's négresse and of his Indian mistress, which seemed to confirm her darkest suspicions of the Wehrmacht officer who had returned to her out of the harsh Russian landscape of perverted camps and exterminated villages.

Leonard Rinkel had always lived on the West Side, just four blocks from the Sundas. He had gone to Fieldston, Columbia, and Harvard Medical School. After he had interned and received his license, the war was almost over, and Leonard had spent six years in Boston doing general surgery, then neurology at the Peter Bent Brigham Hospital. He had come back as a full surgeon to New York General, to be near his aging parents. Leonard was very soft, dreamily thoughtful, and envelopingly warm, and he understood women better than any man Hélène had known, though she had known only one other. He could even play along with her adequately on the violin. Hélène had fallen in love with the force of Leonard's science discipline. Then she had watched his incredibly deft, sensitive fingers in the stretched caramel gloves and had fallen in love with Leonard Rinkel's hands. She never knew if it went further than his magical hands. Yet she had very nearly agreed to divorce her children's father to marry him.

That had been three years ago, at the time her general surgeon's studies ended and when the Sunda financial statements had begun their disturbing transformations. At first, the figures had started up by thousands, then months later by several hundred thousands. Then, after a further six months, half a million dollars mysteriously appeared in the accounts. Without any explanation in her husband's strange letters from Brazil, this money had been invested. The following year it had almost doubled. For another year, half the total capital had vanished into the commodities market. When it reappeared on the green accounts sheets, the neatly typed figure was almost two million dollars. Now it had risen to over three. Hélène knew little about finance, and it only deepened her alarm to find herself unable to imagine the honorable man of her youth as he tortured these astronomical sums out of some remote jungle murk. It was as if some ancient, immense, and godless power were trying to resurrect itself.

Leonard Rinkel could have had her completely then. If only he had not been so tolerant of Baron Sunda! For instead of being politely condescending about Hélène's first and only lover, Leonard had seemed to consider her husband a cultural paradigm, and he liked to question her in detail about David's character and his activities in Smolensk and on the Amazon. Somehow, this had only strengthened Hélène's sense of being David's bondswoman and had hurt her pride.

Dr. Rinkel's failure to become her champion had made her an adulteress—she, Hélène, who had resisted every kind of temptation, even at a time when her husband might have been long dead, and who had been left alone to raise her children, first in a countryside under siege and then in a foreign metropolis. But the hospital and Leonard Rinkel's hands had become too much a part of her soul, and she had continued to betray her marriage. Feeling desperate, and frightened by the maturity of her need to be loved, she had gone unsatisfactorily to confession with the monsignor at St. Patrick's. When the news had come that David was to arrive in New York from Genoa after the long separation from his family, Hélène had clung to the legitimacy of her marriage and stopped sleeping with Leonard.

She had not been prepared, then, to see the chief surgeon of New York General Hospital weep and beg her not to leave him. The fact that Hélène might be crushing a man of deep and sincere feelings touched her profoundly. For a week she took to her bed with an acute migraine, and at her first meeting with David in six years her manner had been strained. The impression had been worsened by the children's hostility on their mother's account, which had forced Hélène to be conciliatory—followed in turn by Rickie and Joanna's quick submission to David's charm, which had made her feel bitter. And because Leonard had accustomed her to an easy equality, Hélène had forgotten how to withstand her husband's powerful personality. Yes, she thought, remembering the first of his two visits, there was a strange new element in David—volatile, a little profane, but also more delicate. He did not once look at Yasmeen. Now two of the children had begun to worship their father. . . .

"There!" Yasmeen lifted the dishcloth and wiped the tears from the señora's cheeks. "Mother, man is bad seed," she said.

They looked at each other and laughed. But her husband's disturbing presence in the building could no longer be ignored. How was she to act? The children were back at their schools. However, this meant that Hélène would be alone with David for the first time in six years.

It seemed like the day before yesterday that she and this man had walked together down a wartime Turkish railway track, carrying their week-old baby in a basket. Now Rickie was six feet tall, with his father's blue eyes and the even temper of a natural athlete. He had been elected class president at Groton and as quarterback had led the school football team to a winning season, doing both these things easily, almost with an air of embarrassment, as a person might who is conserving his energy for a greater task. In the autumn, he would enter his third year at Princeton. His strengths, however, were in memory and clarity, rather than in any passion, or even need, for books and music. As for their youngest child—conceived on the floor of a Lübeck harpsichord collector's house—Joanna already had the independence of a grown woman, though she would not leave Miss Porter's School for a year. Hélène felt moved to have a daughter who had even made Luz jealous, and she could not help spoiling the girl. Fortunately, Joanna was too sentimental to be cruel, but her mother had been disturbed by recent episodes in which the girl had been discovered going to nightclubs with thirty-year-old socialites. Hélène did not know how to react to her daughter's obsession with blues singers, or to her summer plan to accept a job modeling for *Vogue*.

Her three children were like New World flowers, grown oversized on the minerals of Europe's underground calamities. Albert was the only one she understood. With his sad, harlequin's face and twice the charm of his brother and sister, Bertie devoured literature and had given a recital of Beethoven at fourteen. He feared athletics, however, and became easily hurt in friendships. He was also depressed by contact with the commonplace lives of ordinary folk. Though he had decided to study music near home, at Juilliard, Hélène worried for him. Albert was the only one of her children who understood his mother and refused to forgive his well-known father for his years of absence.

Just now, as she sliced onions in her kitchen, Hélène remembered with anxiety how she had seen her son weep during the Bach Double Concerto. There was also an episode they never discussed when Albert had been knocked about on Broadway by three drug addicts. Hélène remembered his long struggle with himself over the following months, and how from that time he had drawn his sister into his private world, developing a violent hostility to everything American.

Hélène knew she could not have raised three more promising children. But they needed a father. In the cheerful New York kitchen, she woke from that rush of dread with a sharp pain .

"*Madre,* look what you go do!"

"Oh, no—no, Yasmeen! It is only the tip."

Taking Hélène's bleeding thumb in her mouth, Yasmeen shut her eyes and sucked it. It was as if she were practicing a dark rite. Hélène could not prevent herself from laughing. Perhaps she might never do what was expected of her but must hope for some sign. Now it occurred to her that, after a half an hour, her husband would be justified in leaving. There would be no time for drinks.

5

WHEN HER THUMB WAS BANDAGED, HÉLÈNE WENT LOOKING FOR DAVID. SHE discovered him among the bookshelves that lined the dining alcove. They had both dressed formally. With the flourish of a grande dame, Hélène masked her emotion at the sacrifice that might lie ahead for her. She received his kiss on her cheek.

"David, why not announce yourself? I had to help in the kitchen."

"It can't be easy for you to have me here. I was glad to poke about."

Her husband smiled, it seemed to Hélène, with flagrantly unjustified accusation. He moved around the bookshelves to the far end of the table, where Leonard had sat so often. Once again, she noticed the way David did not so much as glance at Yasmeen as he motioned for the tureen. Hélène had intended to serve her spinach soup—which had always been his favorite at her parents' house—herself. Now, seeing this near stranger's authority as he resumed this duty, she was somehow unable to object.

When David and Hélène were seated, the flower arrangement screened their view of each other. Yasmeen came forward, adjusted the candlesticks and carried the orchids to the buffet, and they were face-to-face.

When the housekeeper had left the room, David spoke, this time with unmistakable melancholy. "Well, we have come a long, long way to be here alone."

Hélène stiffened at this echo of the riddle surrounding her husband's invisible campaign in Russia, now compounded by the struggle for Sôbre Xingu. "The children were certainly taken with you," she said.

"I would like to have seen them off. Unfortunately, the meeting with Bernard could not be changed."

"Oh—and how was it?"

"He offered me a job with the secretary-general."

"David! What did you tell him?"

"I turned it down."

"I see. Or rather, I don't see!" she burst out. Surely this must be the sign she had been waiting for. Was she free to decide what was best for their family?

David Sunda opened his mouth, intending to explain to her the moral cul de sac in Piers's offer. Yet suddenly, confronted by the impassioned face down the long table—now that of a New York medical woman who examined her husband unforgivingly, waiting for him to reveal he knew not what—no single issue in the long struggle to satisfy his conscience seemed to David of the slightest importance. He could not afford to lose Hélène as he had lost Justin. He sensed the danger in anything he might say.

At the same moment, they were conscious of what a painful start this meeting was off to. An ancestral weariness affected them. Was there still no case for a surrender to their past?

"Would you like more soup? Is this your mother's recipe?"

"Heavens, how could you ask?" Hélène said, before she could stop herself.

Yasmeen carried the plate to her with veiled, velvety eyes and withdrew after a frightened glance at both their faces. David began again.

"Hélène, you have been wonderful with the children."

"Thank you, *chéri,*" she said softly. "What you have done in Brazil is remarkable."

"Was it?" he offered. "I am not so sure."

"Oh, yes, I am sure of it! The family line is secured."

"They are fine children," David went on, with a sudden despair at the cost, even tonight, of so much forgiveness. "If anything, they are an improvement on past generations. In 1941, I would no longer have believed that possible. Leni, do you remember poor Freddy in Moscow? Do you remember carrying Rick in the midwife's basket down the railway line?"

In this hushed room high above Central Park the entire weight of the past drew them toward this moment in their marriage, demanding that tonight at last there should be peace. Yet Hélène felt terror at her first lover's direct appeal to her sentiments. She could not bring herself to mention that she had recently found Rickie's basket in a trunk. Just one more shading of mistrust, Hélène thought, just one more doubt, and she would feel free to shut him out of their lives forever. As she glanced up then at Baron Sunda's sad staring face, he suddenly struck her as completely mad.

"Why did you refuse Bernard's offer?"

"I don't care for this city," David said coldly. He wondered if she would believe this justification.

"I like New York," she was saying. "I like what my work has given me."

"So when will I meet this Dr. Rinkel? What a curious name that is."

"Leonard is not a curious man. He isn't a curious surgeon either."

Yasmeen emerged from the kitchen with the sole, and Hélène instantly regretted having chosen another of her husband's favorite dishes. But David was too shocked by his wife's defiance to notice what was set before him. His eyes rested momentarily on the exotic face of the new housekeeper.

Catching David's glance even as she exposed her own adultery, Hélène felt as if she had been slapped. "Yes," she resumed in English. "In a way, these have been the best years of my life."

"You might have spent them at Sôbre Xingu."

"How could you possibly have wanted me there?" she retorted.

Yasmeen fussed agitatedly round the table, taking away some dishes and replacing others. Both Sundas sat in a silence so taut that each sound vibrated as if they were in a heavier, denser element. At the mention of their two invisible worlds—the scientific, brightly lit world of Hélène's hospital, by contrast with the *chefe* of Sôbre Xingu's struggle with the illiterate jungle—they had felt their utter banishment from one another's lives.

My God, what has been done to our marriage? Hélène thought.

"Do you mean you *wished* to come?" he persisted.

"I don't know, *chéri*. Leonard has taught me so much here."

"Surely, though, nothing was as good as Paris?" David whispered.

"It is a wonderful thing to forget oneself and help people, corny as that may sound."

Alone at their shadowy table, husband and wife somehow continued their dinner in a sort of delirium, so horrified by the pain they could inflict on each other that they fell back on steely politesse, like that of weapons negotiators.

"While I am here"—David gave Hélène a cold uneven smile that reminded her unpleasantly of his brother Friedrich—"while I am here, I had hoped to persuade you to give up this full-time doctoring."

"Are you serious?" she burst out.

David had been about to suggest to his wife that they might begin with a cruise among the Pacific islands. "Of course I will have to go back to Germany," he said instead. "There is still so much to arrange. Also, I must do something in Paris for your father."

The woman he still loved had folded her napkin and sunk back, staring at him. Her husband's tone seemed so boastful that Hélène could not bring herself to show gratitude, though she had meant to ask just such a favor of him.

"Will you try to see Justin?"

"I hoped to. Why?" David asked stonily.

"I wouldn't," she said lightly. "You know that Justin and Luz have separated. She has gone out to Hollywood with Sarah."

He leaned forward, his face flushed. "No! How did this come about?"

So David and Hélène moved on at the most tragic hour of their lives together to gossip of friends and relatives. This time Yasmeen returned to the kitchen with an impression that the atmosphere between mother and señor had much improved. Presently they folded their napkins. David rose a little abruptly, so that the candles swayed. Hélène stood, still holding her folded napkin. An impression had come to her, as with two passengers who have just survived a near-mortal accident, of weary and tender submission.

"Oh, David, David!" she said, in her old compassionate tone.

"What, Hélène?" Turning from the living room window, filled tonight with the lights of America, David stared piercingly at his wife.

"Nothing," she said. "Really, nothing."

Hélène sat with a science magazine on the window divan until she heard Yasmeen close the hall door on the departing baron. Her heart was beating violently with relief, and she could not concentrate on the new chemical model for the chromosomes of heredity. How could they have behaved like that, she and David?

Rising, she walked through to their room and looked at the neatly made-up double bed. Only hours before she had been asking herself if they might find themselves here together this night. As if in answer, she felt her suspicions, resentment, and jealousy fall away. She remembered, as if it were yesterday, the warm, stuffy smell of the nursery at Oberlinden with her little morsels asleep there. Hélène turned and passed down the darkened corridor. Picking up the telephone, she dialed a number only four blocks away.

"Hélène? Hélène, I have been going nuts waiting for you to call!"

"He's gone . . . he's gone."

Then, putting her hand over the mouthpiece, she began to cry.

6

DR. SUNDA HAD BEEN WITH HER CHILDREN IN MAINE, AT WILKES BAY HARBOR, for three weeks. Young Jim Penn would not join them this year; a letter had come from the Ojai Valley to say that he would stay in California and try to locate his true grandfather. For all his dead father's unhappiness over family traditions, Jim sounded quite excited to be the son of a bastard. This afternoon Hélène was with Yasmeen in the living room of the rented gray-shingle house. The maid did not like being the only nonwhite for a hundred miles, and she only came when there were guests from New York.

"Heavens, why do I so dislike these parties—even if it *is* Leonard's old med professor?"

"Why do them, den?" Yasmeen said, and stared at her. "Man is dross. Man like the devil. Glad I not man!"

Hélène laughed at this, as she always did. It was true. Since the exotic, somewhat sinister Baron Sunda's presence the previous week at the local inn—the first time she had seen her husband since the final severing of their bond—Hélène had been aware of an irreparable wound in her heart. Too much had taken place. She scarcely knew any longer where she came from or who she was. She even did her thinking in English now.

On this drowsy afternoon along the Maine coves, Hélène could never have conceived of the scene taking place behind her in the wildlife sanctuary, nor of its effect on a thousand-year bloodline. Nor could she have dreamt that this very night, as Leonard was on the road back to Boston, she would sit up in a trance and for the second time in her life write a love letter to Justin Lothaire.

Earlier this same afternoon, she had sat next to Albert at the upright piano. The sanctuary branches pressed around them against the glass. It was the summer solstice, and Rickie would be working in the back bay with the hired lobstermen. His sister Joanna would be playing tennis. At his mother's side the young man watched the modest and measured way his mother fitted her hands to the keys—as if the music were already playing somewhere and she could hear it faintly through her fingers.

"Listen to the way I build the texture with the left, then draw out the noble beat with the right."

Hélène began to play. Outside the insect screens was a narrow undulating lawn. Albert swallowed, feeling the longing and pain of the never quite graspable moment. He saw the small white and large orange butterflies dance along the flowers, and he thought of the stiff sou'wester blowing across the ten-mile bay until it was broken in this thick Indian wood.

"Very well. Now you try it."

"Don't stop, Mother, don't stop!" Albert laughed reproachfully. "You get more out of the music than anyone."

"You do have the best teachers."

"What you put in it, you can't teach."

The boy seemed to have something further to say.

"What is it, Bertie?"

"Has something happened with Dad?"

Hélène felt her face go cold. Albert had questioned her endlessly on the family past, but this was the first time that he had been concerned about the present. "To tell you the truth, Albert"—Hélène rose from the bench and stared down at her hands—"I don't really know. Your father is an extremely secretive and complicated man."

"But he wasn't always complicated, was he, Mother? I mean, you and Dad will always be together now, won't you? Nothing is going to happen—things will go on forever, as easily as they seemed last week? You and Dad were just so extraordinary."

His mother was still staring into Albert's red, pitiful face.

"Stay the same forever, *chéri?* Don't you care for Leonard?" Hélène had raised one hand to her brow, trying to smile. After the ugliness she had seen in her life, it was somehow terrible to contemplate her almost complete success in protecting this grown man, her son. What did she know about forever? "Of course it will, my dear. Now look—you've broken my concentration."

Long after Albert disappeared into the rambling house and Hélène had gone for a short sail with Leonard, her son's odd smile stayed in her thoughts. In Hélène's deepening trance she searched her own experience and never imagined that a son of hers might hide half the truth or, for that matter, have anything serious to warn her about. But life becomes serious at an early age.

7

AS HÉLÈNE LEFT FOR THE YACHT HARBOR, ALBERT WAS BACK UPSTAIRS AT JO'S pine dresser. First he put on one of her big-holed records; then, very gently, he took down the photograph of his sister in a skimpy two-piece suit. The setting was a yawl by City Island at the time of their father's return from South America. Last night, Eddie Cochran had been singing "Summertime Blues" when Albert had asked his sister why she did not go to the beer and necking parties. The fellows around the Harbor had been pestering him. Because they are just boys, she had said. Then, crying a little, Jo had told him that of the nine grown men she had been dating, there was not one who had not *screwed* her. "Am I awfully bad, Bertie?" Jo had asked presently, with their old childish gravity that had nothing to do with the world or with its laws. Bertie had said no and hugged his sister. A week ago the ugly gang word would have felt remote from him and very definite. But right now, as Albert stared at

Joanna von Sunda, the word was very close and seemed to gather like a blight on her young body.

Sniffing a little and rubbing his nose, Albert set the photograph on its edge. Jo's court was up at one o'clock. The east and west shores were connected by a mile-long plank boardwalk that wound through the swampy woods. Jo would be coming along it.

Thirty seconds later, Albert was walking down the ramp as it rose and fell, keeping to the line of nails down the center. Just as he decided that Jo must have gone by the road, Bertie saw ahead—moving above the tall ferns between the trunks—a solid white tennis dress and tied-up brown hair. He stood absolutely still on planks split by winter snows.

"Bertie? What are you waiting for?" She walked up close to him with an unsurprised smile. His sister was a little shorter than Albert, her brown face very high and classical, like Rickie's. None of her features were ordinary. With their father come and gone, she was the suddenly perishable beauty of their line.

"Bertie? What is it?"

"Last night. Jo . . . the things you said."

"Oh, Bertie, I shouldn't have. You see?"

Jo's smiling face was suddenly serious, like a woman's. Albert did not want to see her like a woman. He held the tight-stringed tip of her racket. "Don't say that, Jo. Don't say it."

"Let's not talk about it. Let's go back."

"No, wait!"

Abruptly, the knowledge was drawn very taut between them.

"Stay? I mean, come with me. I feel bad."

"You look a little weird, poor Bertie. Where?"

"The moss garden," Albert said. "There are no mosquitoes."

"Are you sure you don't want to sit down?"

Standing face-to-face with her on the split planks, Albert shook his head. As he stepped off the boardwalk and went after her under the branches, down the old Indian track, he heard the light, springy *crunch-crunch-crunch* of Jo's sneakers on the dried loam. He followed the delicate flexing of her tanned calves.

They came to the coolness under the six spruces. Here the moss grew thick over deeply sunk boulders. Albert sat back in the hollow. Jo dropped the racket and sat on the stone beside him. Leaning her head against the trunk, she shut her eyes and spread out her feet.

"It's always like Eden or something here."

Albert saw Jo's chest rise and fall. The hair was matted black at her temples and there was perspiration along her lip. Albert got to his knees and moved up against her. The trunk was rough between his hands. The leaves around them rustled.

"Jo, I love you, Jo."

"I love you too, Bertie. How's the—"

"I love you Jo. Let's get it back. Hold me."

Albert felt his sister's whole body stiffen against him. The hard, sweet-smelling roundness of hair was against his cheek. Albert looked at the sun in the spruce branches and into the sunny green sanctuary beyond. Far away, the ocean swell broke constantly over the rock shelves. It all felt unreal and faraway.

"Bertie, Bertie? Oh, what are you doing, Bertie?"

"We have to, Jo. Don't you see?"

"Bertie, Bertie," she cried. "You can't do that."

"You gave it to them, Jo. It'll be ours again."

"No one can, Bertie. Nobody, not anywhere." Jo's voice was rough.

"We aren't anybody. There'll never be anyone."

"Oh, Bertie, won't they know?"

"I love you, Jo, how I love you."

"They'll see us! They'll find us!" Her voice rough.

"No one comes here."

"Rickie does—"

"He's golfing, or at the boats. . . . Oh, Jo, you're not human, you're music. Little Jo, they're yours, ours. . . ."

"Poor Bertie, oh, my little brother Bertie, Bertie."

Jo was in the mossy hollow. The dress, pants, and sneakers lay on the moss, hard-white as fragments of a statue. Jo was soft and hot up against him. They felt, as one, a breeze along the whole of them.

They were still. The birds had resumed singing.

Albert was on the mossy stone, elbows on knees, hands doubled on forehead. His sister sat against him on her curled-up calves, hugging the thickness of his leg. Her cheek nestled in the bend of his hip; he could feel her smiling. They had been just so for a long time.

The forest began to rustle. Albert shivered.

"My lovely brother," Jo whispered. "You're cold."

"I didn't know. I didn't suspect."

Albert felt his sister's body move against him. He shut his eyes. "Bertie? Bertie?"

"Oh God, if I had known."

"Bertie? I love you Bertie. I'm back—forever."

Jo's whisper was absorbed in the twittering rustle of the woods. Beyond was the circumference of shingled summer houses and, beyond, the craggy rocks, pounded by the Atlantic swell.

"Bertie? Bertie, tell me you love me. Tell me!"

Albert von Sunda bared his teeth and swallowed.

"Oh, Bertie, no! Oh, God, oh, Christ, Bertie, tell me you love me! Quick!

Oh, please tell . . . tell me, tell me! Now! Please! Oh, God, tell me that you love me! Please, oh, please, please!"

"I didn't know." Albert ground his teeth. "I didn't suspect."

Jo pulled away and was kneeling in the hollow beside him.

"Bertie," she whispered hoarsely. "For you to do it is a sin. But Bertie, don't leave me now. That's much worse."

"I can't . . . I don't know," her brother said with a groan, bending his forehead to his knees.

Jo stared at him wild-eyed, her thick hair falling around her face. "You hate me, don't you? You hate me—hate me!"

Albert tightened his eyes and knotted his fists on his temples. He tried not to hear the sound of Jo, fallen and whimpering in the mossy hollow of this sacred place. The garden was spoiled by this naked sobbing woman, his sister, lying in the pine-needle hollow. Her, his sister's, voice—rasping like the woods, repeating it over and over.

"Hates me . . . oh, hates me . . . hates me . . . you hate me. . . ."

Albert was wishing it was over. That he—they—could be away from this dangerous place. He heard the way the whimpering woman's voice beside him was fainter and fainter, and farther away.

Then something in Albert relaxed. His fingers scraped some needles into a dusty pile. Suddenly he raised his head. He stared from under the dark spruce boughs through the dappled sun to where a rotten elm was crushed down over the Indian path.

8

RICK SUNDA HAD SPENT THE MORNING WITH THREE LOBSTERMEN IN THE WINTER shed, set in the sands by the tidal back bay. The men sat with wire brushes on the sand, in a circle around the reddish yellow mound of chain, barnacles, and mussel clusters. Like the working men, Rick never wore summer shorts. As they scraped, the men had been muttering about the weather and the lobster beds, but Rick could feel their consciousness of him.

Everyone in Wilkes Bay knew that Baron Sunda had been at the Breakers Inn. Finally Googins mentioned his father, and Rick's heart sang with pride as he muttered back a thing or two about his dad's return after six years in Brazil. He could feel the men liking his embarrassment; they were eager for his father to come permanently. Thinking of how Uncle Leonard would stay away, and his parents would be together, and of his sister Jo's tennis stroke and quick pleasant laugh—Rick saw how things would be. He could hardly keep from pushing these slow-thinking men over and throwing handfuls of sand at them. It was satisfying that, as they waited for their father, Rick had still always been the best, without question, and his sister the most beautiful. Now his father and mother would be the most accomplished and most admired—and after Princeton he, Rick, could go on being ever more exceptional and widely respected for the integrity of his family, until he became the most widely loved man in the most powerful country in the world. He already felt a restless, despotic urge to break out of these bonds, into unknowable but higher adventures, to conquer and lay low. But as usual, crouched on one knee in the sand, Rick was placid and shy and only scraped the chain harder with the wire brush.

So Rickie was thinking in midafternoon—his arms stained to the elbows with rust and shell particles, feeling exhausted and hungry with conquest—when he passed the post office, left the fields, and turned into the tangled sanctuary. After perhaps three minutes he heard voices ahead. Then, coming nearer, there was crying. *Bird lovers*, Rick thought . . . then, with the crying, *kids*. Then, coming near the moss garden, he glimpsed bare skin. Rick began to tremble with eager, guilty, conquering laughter.

Very stealthily he stepped to the fallen trunk and looked through the spruce boughs. There was a man staring at him from a boulder, a man with no clothes on. Rick reeled and stumbled back, blinking with shame at such nakedness.

"Bertie . . . what the hell?" He bent under the trunk and walked awkwardly toward the foolish figure on the stone. Bertie's face embarrassed Rick and confused him. "What the hell, Bertie?" An ugly, frightening idea had begun to dawn, and he started to shiver, his stomach heaving. Abruptly the hushed, rustling air was full of vileness and danger and revenge. Alaric felt ruin spread toward the house—toward their mother and through her to their father.

"God, Bertie! God!" Rick panted. Then with purblind hate, he hit out. His brother dove for the shade.

"He's not staying with us. Dad's not staying!"

"God! Oh, God, Bertie! Oh, God!" Alaric half stumbled, half crawled to Jo. He was gasping so violently that he could barely speak. "Jo . . . Jo . . . oh, God . . . pull on . . . pull on . . . pull on . . . never mind . . . stop . . . don't . . . don't say . . . God, don't cry . . . don't hate . . . your brother . . . he is . . . he is your brother!"

Then, shaking and crying, he wrenched Jo up by her brown shoulders. Not looking down at her, his mind growing terribly clear, Alaric Sunda thought, Now I will kill the swindling, weak musician! Oh, sensitive one. Oh, conceited womanish one!

Rick turned away and stooped into the sunshine. While Jo dressed, he lit the cigarette that Googins had given him. A cold, vile moral command was settling into him like frostbite. As he looked away into the shimmering, long-shadowed puritan evening, he thought, *I'll make him feel it. I'll punish him with it so that this will be his last perversion, so help me God!*

Fifteen minutes later, Rick had stiffly walked Jo home and his sister was in the bath. For a long time, without scrubbing his arms, Alaric Sunda sat by the piano in a wicker rocking chair and stared out to sea. The east was almost dark; he could hear the little Aeronca drone back and forth over the sanctuary, laying down insecticide. The shingled New England housefronts looked down on him vacantly.

Eventually, he heard a snapping of branches from the direction of the boardwalk. Alaric got up and went to his bathroom.

9

BY THE TIME HÉLÈNE HAD BEEN FORCED TO ASSUME A COURSE THAT SHE WOULD never have conceived possible—that is, to write to her husband about Albert's condition and beg him to return from New York to discipline their children—Baron Sunda was already standing at the rail of the *France* for its July Fourth sailing.

The plan was for Otto to settle the family affairs on Wall Street; then, in three weeks, to meet him in the Alps for the drive to Oberlinden. David would keep strictly to his glorious plan, even when its sense had been lost. And the fact was, as the liner's foghorn rattled Baron Sunda's teeth and tickled him into laughter, that his thoughts did wander a little aimlessly among memories of rich food, picturesque villas, and righteous discussion. It was as if, after the tremendous flight of the Spad, he were sinking back at last to the soil of his ancestors to become like his father. His soul was weary, and there was no heat in him.

For their first dinner at sea, Baron Sunda went with the others in his white dinner jacket to the social steward and was at once recognized as suitable for the captain's table. He scarcely took note of this, only feeling vaguely oppressed at resuming acquaintance with two old Sorbonne classmates, a New York hotel owner, and an Italian minister of state. David answered their questions with such thoughtful modesty and his answers were so simple and profound that, even while making no effort to hide his indifference, his presence suggested mystery and caused a stir.

On the liner's second morning at sea, David sat in dark glasses on a deck chair, facing over the tourist deck. Stretched out astern, the wake was broad, like an avalanche of snow being laid for his lost children, leading back to the old world.

"Hello. Is this place taken?"

The deck chair next to him squeaked. David pretended to read. He had noticed this child in the first-class swimming pool. She waited until the others got out; then she thrashed, dived, and played by herself. Her energy had seemed disturbing, even a little mad. Now she was talking to him again.

"This certainly is a dreary crowd. You are my last hope though you're not exactly encouraging."

The girl's voice had the throaty texture of Mediterraneans who have drunk wine in their infancy. Feeling certain now of her madness, David was alarmed.

"Who are you?" she said.

"Who are *you*?" David murmured, without opening his eyes.

"Abi. I was on my way to America, but I was fired."

"Where are you from?"

"A beautiful island. My family is Greek, with German and Russian blood."

"*Ça ce voit.*"

"Oh, they're all dead. To the last man."

"What? You are completely alone?"

"Yes, like one of those seagulls following the boat to America, then following it back. Idiots! I'll eat lobster to Le Havre—then *frites*, with luck."

When David looked at the girl, she rolled her head away in the summer breeze. Her freckled brown features were unrefined, her mouth subtle and kind. Anything he said to this common child would immediately belong to everyone. David thought of the UN files, and of the endless banks of experience in his head, and he began to withdraw. She was asking him who he was.

"A cattle farmer." He could have said almost anything.

"That's a basic profession," Abi agreed thoughtfully, and David saw the girl's disappointment. "My father owned fishing boats. Confess. Why are you the only one who never swims?"

Sensing her misery, he felt an unfamiliar twinge of loss.

"To tell you the truth," he said, allowing his gaze to drown in the monotonous boil of the snowfield stretched behind them, "I have a rather unusual tattoo on my back."

"Ah!" The girl laughed as if she had just been granted total knowledge. "I knew there was something special about you."

"Thank you."

"Will you show it to me?"

"Is that proper for a young lady?"

"I'm twenty-eight and you are . . . sixty?"

"Fifty-one."

"Anyway"—her voice hardened, no longer at peace—"why be embarrassed about some tattoo?"

"On the contrary." David replaced his dark glasses. "It was put there in Brazil by Indian friends. I would not want the wrong people to see it."

"An Indian tattoo?"

The girl turned on her flank to examine him, as he lay like a Teutonic knight on a crypt. What if she did have a father fixation? She was enthusiastic about him without needing to decipher the universal parable he carried in the codes of his soul. All at once David understood that for the first time in twenty years a woman not entirely unlike himself was being kind to him— someone as miserable and alone as he was.

"I like you. What's your name?"

"David Sunda."

"What's Sunda?"

"A channel in the Malay archipelago," David said.

"Ah, rootless like me." Abi fell back, seeming to require nothing more from him. "I hated the islands. I went to study archaeology in Rome. Then I was at the Vatican Museum. The classical remains are very beautiful. I educated myself there, and on the Capitoline. You see this thong? A mosaic tile from Livia's house. Yes, I plundered my education off cardinals and the jewelry of the Roman conquests. Ah, but the people I was a student to!" The pained, wild look was back on the girl's face. "They were such moral dwarfs, so mean and narrow. You understand me? I lived for a while with a drunken Irish poet in Trastevere until he killed himself. I have been trying to get to America ever since."

"He must have been a bad poet," David murmured. "Having you and killing himself."

The girl was sitting up on the deck chair, holding one knee and absorbed in some reckless vision. When she continued, her voice was almost inaudible.

"Mr. Sunda, I think we should sit together at dinner. Really, couldn't we? Look at me; you saw how completely mad I was. I'm not crazy now. Think, think if I hadn't met you! Oh, do let's. What a good idea. I'll be the best dinner partner you ever had."

"I've had some quite good ones." David Sunda shaded his eyes, unable to comprehend the idiocy and the pathos of this scene.

"I know," she said, suddenly in torment. "At least I could outdo anyone on this boat."

"All right, then."

"Do you mean it? I sneaked into first class through a gate five decks down."

"Remember, this trip is supposed to be a rest."

The girl frowned at David with a simple proud calm. "Then let me arrange the table. I'll do everything."

"No," he said. "I'll do the table."

Suddenly it seemed important that this Abi should not know about the captain's table. As definitive as it had once seemed that his father and the Fleurusians—even Hitler, Stodel, Guderian, and, just now, Hélène and his own children—should fathom every exquisite twist and turn of Baron Sunda's life and honor, it was now equally urgent that this obscure young woman should be conscious of none of it. Nothing must alter the sensation of her enthusiasm for him. He felt himself move then toward a nonentity that no Sunda in history had risked.

With the steward, David arranged for a table in the darkest corner of the second-class dining room. Then he circulated a story about his wife's niece.

"Do you remember my wonderful dinner partners?" he asked the girl that night.

"I'm boring you!" She looked ready to run away and hide somewhere in the ship.

"Boring me? I wouldn't exchange the last nine hours and ten minutes for the best day of my life."

"Oh." Abi stared at him. "But there's no other day of your life that I'll ever know—nor why you aren't like anyone else, and talk too like you do. Shall I say something now, anything? Please?"

"Go on," David said.

"Let's not let the evening end. Oh, I'll be strong. In three days I will go back to my freedom and *frites*. But while we're here, there's so little time. Let me be with you. Don't tell me to go away." Following his thought, the young woman blushed defiantly. Her eyes fell as they leaned together against a movement of the ship. They were both mad now.

"You mean," David said softly, "you still want to see the tattoo?"

Abi laughed; then she blew her nose. "You're such a beautiful man, David. Such a very beautiful man."

As for Baron Sunda, the emotion of this acceptance was as intense as the hour in which he had spoken of marriage under the Le Trèves' willow tree. Almost as tenderly as then, David began the calculate how he might explain a second tattoo.

And so, in the thirty-second year of David's exile, it was Abi who taught him about the unlocked gate by the engine-room deck.

10

LATER, ON AN OVERCAST SUMMER AFTERNOON, HE GAZED BESIDE THE YOUNG woman over a flat pale sea and saw England. In the last hour they had not been able to look at each other. David said trivial, empty things. "You only left here two weeks ago—Europe is more yours than mine. If only I had your eyes."

"My eyes are yours now," Abi said quietly.

"Ah, a set is missing."

"By tonight, I will be a blind girl," she said. "I will never again see the world when it was beautiful, through the eyes of my lover."

"Come with me, then."

"That is a cruel joke. I am just a child," she said softly, for by now she had seen David's other tattoo.

"What is a child? Just let me see you smile again."

"Be careful, Mr. Sunda, even the moon will laugh at you. I'm just another lost girl."

"I only ask this." David met the young woman's frightening stare. "Do not choose me as your destroyer. There is even more to me than you have heard. If you have time in your life, I will someday have to tell you."

"Do I have time in my life—*my* life? What will I ever have more than time? No, let me tell you. I'll be your slave, your stylish assistant. When the fire leaves me, just say 'enough' and I'll go without showing a tear. I will make every minute beautiful. If it's what you want, I'll cook your food and I'll take care of your body. In return, darling, you'll let me love your fine soul. We'll always tell the truth, won't we, and be faithful?"

As Portland Bill flickered on the English coast—with Hitler's wolf packs silenced to insignificance in the yellow waves—he and Abi bent together, and the lost girl's long hair tangled around his head.

"There are things I must do in Paris and Bavaria," he began to tell her presently. "Then you and I will have three months to trek in Tanganyika and see Kashmir. We can stay at the emperor's old villa in Kyoto. The gorges of Hakone are beautiful in the autumn, and on the way back we can visit the Yucatán."

Abi looked frightened, almost insulted. "Those are pretty stories—but you don't have to."

"I warned you there were things to be told. Make me one last promise."

"You're really serious, aren't you?"

"Promise me you will never stop being a lost girl."

The woman was staring at him solemnly. David met her look and felt himself burn without fear in the fires of hell.

"All right, I promise. I will always be a lost girl."

That night in the train compartment to Paris, David began to tell the young woman what her sex already knew in him. That the man she had picked up in first class was from an incurably civilized family, and that he had a wife with three children who were nearly her age. But no matter how bitterly he spoke of his afflictions, David felt them crush her loneliness—which dreamt of everything yet which had nothing. And because he was desperate that Abi's madness over him should not be dampened, David cherished something almost suicidal in the girl's indifference to such facts.

"Think," was all that she would say, "If you only knew. Think if you hadn't found me."

11

BARON SUNDA AND HIS PRIVATE ASSISTANT REGISTERED IN ADJOINING GARDEN rooms in a hotel not far from the Jardin de Luxembourg. Next morning the Lothaires' telephone did not answer at their Palais-Royal atelier. From a very old woman at his entry, they heard that Monsieur Justin had left that very night for eastern France.

During the following days David could not always see Abi, but during their evenings she poured out to him the poetry of each day among the bookshops and the museums. To this young woman the streets of Paris had not changed. It was fantastic to her that goatherds had once rung bells here to sell students fresh milk.

The elder Le Trèves had been forced to lease all but the mansion's uppermost floor to a nouveau-riche sugar tycoon from Toulon. David did not sit again in Hélène's ivy garden with its little fountain and its winged Mercury. There was the news that his wife had tried to call him, and David took care to disguise his whereabouts. The old couple spoke of the Algerian war, and of the Arab people, with a ruthlessness that damaged their son-in-law's memory of the extraordinary times the Fleurusians had passed here. No mention was made of Justin, the most famous and accomplished of them all.

After he had attended a dozen finance meetings, David went to see his sister Karin, and her husband, Richard, who had recently used the prestige of Oberlinden to obtain a position representing a Belgian consortium. Abi accompanied David to the George V, dressed in a tweed suit.

His sister was still as icily svelte as when they had taken baths together, and she made much of her brother's conquest of the Amazon. Otherwise, both Karin and her husband seemed embarrassed by even sentimental allusions to the past. The conversation over tea was mostly about the changing fashions, the shortage of servants, and the various tax schemes and ruses to protect their manner of life. To David, this carefully guarded way of living seemed to lack both the civilized statesmanship of Oberlinden and the gay brilliance of his sister's sleigh wedding in Budapest. Or perhaps this was the effect of seeing them through the eyes of the young woman, who sat with sober dignity and only answered when she was spoken to.

Through that long week, on their rounds of various ventures—including his old friend Robert Neuville's ill-gotten million-dollar art business; or during their evening at Maxim's, where the headwaiter, Constantin, recognized Baron Sunda, took champagne with them, and boasted of serving Hitler and his field marshals during the war; or even when they went to New Jimmy's, where one had to dance to records—David began to feel that he and

Abi were alone in their romance of Europe. Beneath the nervous excitement of reconstruction, there was lassitude, pessimism, and a dread of the Red Army that was still in Europe.

"Well, and how was all that?" David asked Abi, after the lost girl had seen for herself.

"I don't think I could stand much more. David, is that bad?"

As they lay together in Abi's double bed and watched the Quartier sunset through the open moss-garden window, David Sunda's heart sank. After the long ascent from Oaxaca, through the snows of Smolensk and the equatorial forest where the ghost of Carlito still sat in his biplane, David felt himself once again hesitating at the summits of civilization.

"No, it isn't bad," David said. "It's the new rules."

"Thank you, my great love," she whispered. Sitting up next to him, the young woman blew smoke across Baron Sunda's black-scrolled shoulders, which were like a medieval alchemist's map of the seven seas. "How does it go, David? *Our God is not out of breath, because he hath blown one tempest and swallowed a navy.* We'll have fun anyway, won't we, darling? Won't there be fine music, adventure, and lovely times?"

"I'm afraid so—it is my nature. We'll have to do without *them.*"

They went to see the new film of a Russian classic, with Luz Holti in the title role. Afterward, he risked taking Abi to Balzar's, where he had last been alone with Justin. It had unsettled him to feel his old fiancée's sensational attraction emanating from a Hollywood screen. David felt then that his last link with Luz's husband had been severed. Abi seemed humbled by the actress's looks and asked David about her.

"Luz was not too wise, Abi—not always too nice."

"How can that be? She seems so noble and passionate."

"That is the writer, not Luz," he told her. "Luz's flaw was that she had always to be the most glamorous and to demolish anyone who challenged her."

"Are you quite sure I don't seem a poor second?"

"Luz would have given you the worst time of all. Don't you think you've won?"

"Then what will you call me?"

The young woman was on her second dessert. She ate like someone who had missed many meals.

"Well," David began. Then, across the room, seeing Abi's terrible passion reflected among the clientele in a mirror, they both laughed. "I don't believe that I ever went shopping for a dress. You must be a wife."

"You have one. But I will be a wife such as no one ever saw before."

Justin had still not returned to Paris when they took the *wagons-lits* to Montreux. In the mountains, David acquired a silver sports car, though not without memories of its designer, who had been among Hitler's guests along with Doktor Godard at the Bristol tea room. Two days later they passed Lake Constance, and Abi was with Baron Sunda in Germany. The autumn air stank romantically of history, like the odor of vomit that impregnates the scene of an orgy.

They picked up Otto Horvath at Munich airport, looking quite smart in a Brooks Brothers suit and horn-rimmed glasses. From the cramped rear seat, Otto showed his enthusiasm for the boss's new assistant. As the wind roared, Abi smiled at him with genuine warmth; then she kept her eyes ahead. David drove them up the new autobahn at one hundred and sixty kilometers an hour, lost in thoughts and memories that this young woman must never conceive.

Then, at a certain warm evening hour, he turned under a familiar iron gate bearing an even more familiar coat-of-arms. There, quite suddenly, on the top of the hill against a cloudless pink sunset—smaller, whiter, and more innocent than David could ever have imagined it—was Oberlinden. As the car thundered into the stable courtyard, David recognized a bent, gray-haired figure who had emerged from the plum orchard, hurrying against the weight of his feet. Could this person now be eighty-five?

"Gustav!"

"Your excellency!" the gamekeeper croaked. "Why did you not visit us from Berlin? Also, there is a letter from the baroness!"

By the kitchen steps, David and his boyhood ally embraced. They were both powerless to speak. Without pausing to unload, David insisted that they should walk again through the halls and corridors, trailed by the grave faces of Otto and his assistant. The procession was quickly joined by a dozen more retainers as the familiar scents came to David: fresh bread, oil and cordite from the gun room, and also the aromatic fragrance of old wood, tapestries, and silk. Finally, Gustav described the fire that had burned up all the long rows of ancestor portraits. David understood then what his wife's presence had meant to all these people through the war, and he felt shame that he had not come here with Hélène.

Abi, whose unerring intuition had inhabited David utterly, understood at once. She walked in a nightmare at the rear of the party through the great halls under the extravagantly illustrated ceilings.

Outside the old baron's study, David paused to glance through Hélène's letter. In a haughty tone, the pages described an unpleasant event involving their three children and in some way seemed to blame David for his absence. Angrily crumpling the letter into his pocket, David passed into the study. The baron's briefcase was brought, and he opened it on the desk. As a dozen faces watched from the door, he took out a leather box and gently placed it back on the shelf, where it had always stood. He heard a nervous giggle from the doorway. A bald stranger roughly his own age met David's gaze.

"Who is that man?"

"That is Joachim, your excellency."

But already Baron Sunda's powerful memory bore him back—back *then*, to a story that Heidrun Dolin had once told Hélène. As the vivid impression intensified, his eyes fell to the stranger's open collar . . . yes, a violent scene in a Berlin palace, a projector cord. David turned from the sight of the purple marks under the fellow's grinning mouth.

"The man came five years ago. A friend of Herr Doktor Godard, sir. Kristof hired him to tend the new accounts."

David made a vague gesture. He could not help looking again at the face in the door. The fellow's grin faltered. There was an uncomfortable stirring.

"Please tell Kristof to have this person observed until he can be removed from the property. I will deal with the rest, Gustav."

"I understand. Your excellency, dinner has been prepared."

"Please don't call me that, my dear old friend." He smiled tenderly at the old man. "Don't you see that those days are over?"

The baron continued in a trance through the east wing with Abi and Otto. In David's abstraction, the lost girl understood that her great danger was past.

For after the discovery of this exalted Nazi in the house of his forefathers, with the marks of Johann's final despair visible on his neck, David felt more removed from the faces around him than he had been at Sôbre Xingu or even in the Bororo longhouse.

That night, when the house was finally asleep, David led Abi through his mother's music room and up the pantry stairs to his parents' bedroom in the damaged wing of Oberlinden. On the following morning at ten o'clock, he sat facing a surly Kristof in the library to go over the accounts. Finally the man put down his pen and leaned back.

"Pardon me, sir. Is the baroness in good health?"

David stared at this handsome blue-eyed Pole. Then he understood. He smiled at the man sadly. "To tell you the truth, Kristof, I have no idea," David said. At that moment, he knew he would never stay here.

After he had spoken to the federal police in Bonn, David had lunch in the pantry with Abi and Otto. Presently he went with Gustav to the gun room. Together they oiled the four Mannlichers, and he admired the unpitted bores. Only then, on this windless summer afternoon, did David walk out again with Gustav along the grassy ridge toward the great oak on Templar's Hill. There they paused and looked out to the far yellow farms where the reapers were making staggered green trails. Neither he nor Gustav spoke, nor did they pay attention to two tiny white police cars just then starting uphill from the gates. As the two friends walked, very slowly and sometimes stumbling, down across the fields, they talked of the crops, the farm animals, and of the seasons.

A week later, Otto left Oberlinden for Munich and New York. Three mornings later there were two carloads of Bayreuth tourists parked at the entrance gates as a silver sports car turned out—beginning its drive over the Alps to join the round-the-world flight at Rome. Abi had on a gray print dress and wore no stockings, and she looked this way and that out of the car and laughed often. To David Sunda, she seemed like the woman he had always dreamt of.

DORÉ MORT

1

THE RESURRECTION OF THE VON SUNDA FORTUNES MEANT THAT HÉLÈNE'S brother, Jean-Marc, could, by 1962, give up his commission in the colonial army at Algiers. But first an incident took place.

The morning in question began with a game of tennis at the country club. Jean-Marc and Colonel Lapellier's widow, Françoise, had met in the cool of six-thirty, to get in two sets before the men's doubles, and so had been forced to dispense with the Arab ball boys. Françoise was two years older than Jean-Marc. Yet even though, as she ran for his powerful strokes, her muscular thighs were covered in cellulite, Jean-Marc still found Françoise a handsome woman. This morning he played his usual reliable, forceful, uninspired game—and won, also as usual.

Having submitted to Françoise's twittering flattery on the shady terrace, Jean-Marc showered, changed into his uniform—heavily decorated with honors from Sedan and the Kabyle—put on his beret, and drove in a bulletproof car to the governmental palace. They were met on the steps by his blond adjutant, Gauguin, and a senior intelligence officer. As they drove on, Jean-Marc's handsome face, still youthfully unwrinkled after a lifetime without smiles, stared along the crowded boulevards, automatically sifting the establishments of the French from the cryptic zoo life of the Arabs. He was finally deciding that Françoise would make him a good wife. That is, she would not intrude on the charming logic of his daily habits.

As the car rolled in through the gates of the civil prison, Jean-Marc saw Berthoud advancing across the courtyard. His large mustaches stooped by the open window.

"Sir, we have El Khafi!"

"Very good, Berthoud, very good."

Jean-Marc permitted himself a faint enigmatic smile as he entered the bare offices. El Khafi was in one of the uppermost cells of the FLN resistance network, which Trinquier had spent three years trying unsuccessfully to unravel. Within hours of even a night arrest, such a man's immediate links would be out of reach. At the Protection Urbaine, the orders were to extract the information without delay. In this fashion, nearly half the men of the casbah had been interrogated. And so too—as Jean-Marc came in from the blinding desert heat after his tennis with Françoise—he knew that El Khafi would already be under the *gégènne*, the water.

El Khafi, he thought, climbing the staircase speckled with dead files. It seemed nothing more than a name.

Major General Le Trève held the only key to this room. Inside there were more dead flies, like black crumbs across the desk, their tiny legs crumpled. Jean-Marc swept them away. Even beyond Françoise, his discharge in just two more weeks, and his family's fortunes having been restored through his sister's excellent marriage, today Jean-Marc felt surprised and happy. The purity of the desert dawn and the sense of his body's reliable athleticism only added to the huge exhilaration of El Khafi's presence in his power, probably in pain. All revolutionaries were Communists. World communism hated the Lamb of God so intensely it had already devoured millions of human lives. Now it was threatening the sleepy, pleasant existence of people like himself and millions no less worthy. So on this colonial morning begun so pleasantly with a game of tennis and a shower—followed by a blow struck against the inexplicable forces of change—Jean-Marc was feeling unusually, extraordinarily satisfied.

The door's wired glass rattled, and Jean-Marc recognized Berthoud's neat blue shirt and trousers. He reached for the ringing telephone and waved the inspector in.

"Le Trève." Jean-Marc instantly recognized the heavy grating voice from Paris. "Yes, Mr. President, it is absolutely true. . . . No, not yet." Jean-Marc listened eagerly to his comrade in glory from Sedan. He made a restraining gesture to Berthoud.

"Remember, Le Trève, the people of France, of the free world, expect a quick resolution of this issue."

"Wait, sir, there may be news. Berthoud?"

"We have broken him." Berthoud was smiling crookedly.

"Yes, we have!" Le Trève confirmed. "You will be kept au courant."

Jean-Marc banged the phone back on the hook. "Quick! What has he given us?"

"Nothing, sir—pardon, everything. However he will only tell you . . . that is, personally."

The silence in the office extended for several seconds. Major General Le Trève sat frowning at Inspector Berthoud's clean, neatly pressed trousers.

"Is he, then, in a position to ask privileges?"

"Yes, general. He is nearly dead."

That was very serious. Berthoud was apologizing.

"Which center is he at?"

"He is in this building, sir."

All Jean-Marc's sense of well-being had gone, replaced by an immense weight. He was acutely aware of the weakness in his knees and legs, the same legs that had run forward so obediently from the service line. This was the one thing Jean-Marc was not braced for. In fifteen years, he had never seen a *centre de tri* or witnessed an interrogation. Others had, and sometimes they talked of it. But though Jean-Marc had felt a distinct satisfaction that it was in his power to cause any Arab rebel irresistible physical pain, he saw this only as a tactical obligation and would have considered it indecent to observe such unpleasantness himself.

Just now, however, he was being marched helter-skelter through a bright courtyard office. Stepping between bars left standing open, Berthoud trotted ahead down a sloping concrete tunnel. The smells of the hot Sahara morning passed into another odor, of dampness and sweat. At once, the clear functioning of Jean-Marc's mind was blown away by animal impressions—of the broken body close by, of the astoundingly neat, clean clothes of the man ahead—all this somehow like a scene from deep in his life, by a bridge, as a young patriot was driven back from Sedan. Had he shot a poilu who was trying to desert before Guderian's advance? But Jean-Marc was in no state now to grasp the association or to enjoy the irony that had put him in his destroyer's shoes.

He was being escorted through a basement passage lit by wire-basketed bulbs. Glancing at the procession of pale green steel doors, he heard the curse of voices. This first human sound, so close to what was here—in these very cells—was awesome and horrible. Berthoud had slowed. As they halted there was a splash; then chains rattled. Jean-Marc forced himself to step through the final door.

The room within was the size of a cramped garage. Jean-Marc had sufficient composure to lift his drawn face to the six soldiers who had slapped to attention—clean-shaven, tough, serious young men. None of the glittering eyes met his. There was a dense animal stench, mingled with cigarette smoke. In this silence, broken by a faint dripping, Jean-Marc saw the large wooden tub of water, a chair, the steel ring on the wall. Then he saw the ropes, the rubber clubs, and the tangle of colored wires on the floor. On the dusky table where it—the hunted animal—was stretched, a chain fell. Jean-Marc's body involuntarily jerked, and imagining that this would be noticed, he remembered what he was there for. The face of the lean, hairy body on the table was rolled toward him.

No one had spoken. Instinctively assuming an appearance of scholarly innocence, Major General Le Trève allowed his feet to carry him forward. The cigarette ends were soft under his boots. With his hands in his uniform pockets, Jean-Marc bent over the table. The still-luminous black eyes just below his own were fixed on Jean-Marc's face.

The man was old, and looked far more intelligent than Jean-Marc had imagined. The wrist lying across the navel was bent at an unnatural angle. The thighs and the crushed, water-drenched face were caked with blood. This blood, which belonged to the body—to whose soul, in turn, Algeria belonged—was draining steadily onto the floor. No longer able to see clearly, suddenly Jean-Marc Le Trève experienced a great intimacy with the ruined human being at his side.

Who could be the cause of such a thing? was his first clear thought. Not simply these brutal, ignorant boys? Then Jean-Marc had a novel and terrible idea. What if he himself might be in some way the cause?

This was too unthinkable to be entertained. No, he was a good fellow. Was he not responsible to the president? What had de Gaulle said about the French people, the people of the world? While these senseless ideas flickered through Major General Le Trève's brain as he bent over the dying body of El Khafi, his own body was involuntarily having a different reaction. A hard, burning disgust, pity, and love had tightened like a cramp in his stomach.

"Khafi," he said, in a polite tone suitable for addressing a naked man who is dying, "I am Le Trève. Tell me the names. You will have drink . . . medicine . . . a bed. It is a sunny day."

Le Trève was vaguely aware that he sounded humble, like someone begging forgiveness of an infinitely superior being. The fellah's dark eyes looked into his, and Jean-Marc thought he saw a flicker of incredulity and pity. The unshaven jaw moved brokenly. In the room a tense voice was suddenly shouting.

"Tell him! Tell him!"

"Lo . . . thaire . . ." The swollen mouth formed the word. "Grinda. . . ."

"What? I can't hear."

Jean-Marc had heard. But he was too stunned, as he saw the pink roots of the man's teeth—quivering like the flesh of broken lobster claws—to translate the gurgling sounds. The cramp of compassion in Jean-Marc's stomach was transforming itself into a great emptiness. The naked man stretched on the table coughed deeply. Then suddenly the coughing stopped and the body began to shake. Something gurgled up on the distorted lips and ran into the beard.

"He's dead!" Berthoud swore. "Did you hear the names?"

Jean-Marc had stepped backward. He felt Berthoud take his arm. For just one second, he had imagined his legs collapsing and himself—a much-decorated officer of the Grande Armée—lying amid the blood and broken teeth before his men. After several seconds of this he was able to regain his easy indifference.

"I am afraid not. You have ruined the poor devil's mouth." Major General Le Tréve turned with a gesture of authoritative impatience.

Avoiding the eyes of his young men, who were still uncomfortably at attention, Jean-Marc backed out of the cell. As someone who holds in the last breath in his body, he strode quickly down the corridor. With astonishing strength, he took the stairs two at a time. His boots scraped up the sloping tunnel, then out through the open bars. There was a hard knot of pain in Jean-Marc's stomach, worse than the most acute dysentery.

The sunlight waiting on the yellow dirt outside was more brilliant and sweet than he had ever seen, as were the eucalyptus, and the prison's stone ramparts, and even the rim of rusted barbed wire. Jean-Marc was seeing them all for the first time—not as the man who had played tennis that morning, or who had felt the satisfaction in protecting the sleepy, monotonous lives of millions, but as if he were the ruined human soul he had just seen die. Struggling under the weight of his sweat-drenched uniform, Major General Le Trève climbed the circular stairway, his boots avoiding a fly as it spun on the worn gray stone. Excusing himself to Berthoud, Le Trève locked himself in the commandant's toilet. Then, without any concern for his decorated uniform, the soiled papers on the floor, or the stench, he kneeled, took the ceramic toilet bowl in his two hands, and was very and not at all comfortably sick.

Half an hour later, Jean-Marc got in his car and told the driver to take him home. When he got there he did not telephone Françoise, but removed his boots and his uniform, and opened the windows. Then, stretched on his bed, Jean-Marc began to review his life in every detail, like a man at the hour of his death.

2

EL KHAFI WAS THE LAST ARAB LEADER IN THE ALGIERS REVOLT TO DIE. ONE week later, France accepted defeat in her remaining major colony.

She thus followed Britain, who had voluntarily renounced her sovereignty in India, and Germany, which had twice been forced behind its frontier by armies of destruction. So the glaciers ground and worked upon themselves. And as the vast tides withdrew, taking with them the sediments of Hitler's evil will and of Marx's materialism, that age came to an end. Europe had declined, but now in its new dialetic the world was more than ever Europe's colony. The traces of moral gold in the new universal culture led back up Mediterranean rivers to the father and mother of light—to Athens and to Jerusalem. Against this light only Communist Russia, Hitler's victim, held its new colonies and dreamt of more power.

In North Africa, a week before the disappearance of El Khafi, Justin Lothaire's childhood friend Abu Grinda had been blown to pieces by an Ultra *plastique*. At the time, Justin was aware only of his daughter Sarah's return to him from Hollywood, to attend the Paris Conservatoire—on the very day that Eli had come from the Party offices, once again looking for Justin Lothaire.

They had last encountered each other at Père Lachaise, marching at the head of half a million anticolonialists to protest the police killings at the Bastille. Today, Eli met Europe's most famous writer as he emerged alone into the rue de Valois, and they went back upstairs. Justin turned on all the lights, stunned to see this man again.

"For the last time, *compagnon,* prepare yourself for an event."

Justin sat in his Chinese chair, surrounded by the bright lights, watching Eli Hebron with that wise half-smile that Hélène had fallen in love with—and which in the minds of millions was now the photographic image of Europe's tragedy. He and Eli both had gray hair. They had grown too old to disagree.

"It will be on the radio in two hours—the French are to surrender Algérie!"

"Is this possible?"

"It's true, Justin. It is your dream."

Justin felt his heart beat with an excruciating pain. Rising, he walked past the swinging trapeze into the kitchen and took out a Rioja. He drew the cork through the seal. They stood at the scarred table and emptied their glasses. Justin could not look at Eli. He was thinking of the Michauds' lace and the desert stars and of Grinda's farm, then he thought of Barcelona and the Popular Front, of the Carbonne farmhouse under *Nacht und Nebel* and Jakob Stodel, and of the flooded mosque where he had met the leaders of the desert revolt. Then Justin thought of Luz in America and of how that morning a declaration of undying love, sent by Hélène from Maine, had come like a fantasy of some distant past.

"Freedom comes late, Eli. Yet it is such a beautiful thing, a great thing."

"How, too late? The *historiques* expect you in Algiers."

"I cannot go yet."

"Justin, remember a night at Rochet's farm? You said,'I and I alone am left.' Now you are to be given back the desert. Its people are only children. They need you."

"I and only I am *not* left." Justin grinned as once Doré had grinned at him.

"Justin, don't say it."

"Do you wish an empty heart to be admired? That should not be on your conscience."

"What shall I tell them?" Eli asked obediently.

"Tell them . . . soon. You know, Eli, Doré is sick," he added.

"The old writer? Is that all?" Eli was exuberant. "*Merde alors,* Justin, what is one old Frenchman after the fall of tyrants?"

"That's just it, Eli. He is everything."

When Eli heard Justin's tone, he became embarrassed. For another thirty minutes Eli watched expectantly, as if he hoped that his friend might be transformed before his eyes.

Once Justin had longed to live in justice—purely—as a young albatross longs to fly without landing. The other Justin would have packed his camel bag with dreams for a new world and caught the train to Marseille that night. Until he was that person again, he was unworthy. Justin had not even found the words to speak to Melanie's sister of his true life, as it never reached the newspapers. His daughter was a California beach girl who was nervous with him. His constant friends were the Mamelukes.

For some time after Eli had left, Justin remained, fiercely absorbed under the reading lights. Then Jeanne came through with her sinewy good nature. She bent to kiss his brow, and over her shoulder Justin saw Anna. In the quarter of a century since he had moved into Doré's attic, the old woman had not once climbed the worn steps.

He was already out of his chair. "Marcel?"

"Come now, Justin," Anna cried softly. "Come now!"

3

JUSTIN WAS ABLE TO REACH THE LANDING, AND TO STUMBLE DOWN THE STONE stairs, because he had always expected himself to. Despite all those whom he had seen die in hatred, every fiber in his body reared away from the enormity of what awaited him downstairs.

"Is it an attack?"

"Yes, Justin."

The crisis was close now, gripping him. Through the doorway ahead, Justin saw blankets and a bright light. There was a brass bed. Its foot was toward the window onto the inner gardens.

When Justin Lothaire had rehearsed the death of Marcel Doré, he had remembered the day that a great European sage had held up to a desert urchin with a will of iron all that in civilization was exalted and innocent and wise from across millennia of classical learning. Now, all this was dying. At the sight of those emaciated limbs in an old-fashioned nightshirt—the body twisted back at an unnatural angle—Justin thought, What had Doré's motives been? For whom had he done it and how had they both been chosen? He only knew he loved this old man. It was as if Justin had never seen death before.

Jeanne gave a sympathetic little cry. She ran forward and began to tug the body straight on the bed.

"And the doctor?"

"There were many calls. Marcel broke the telephone."

"Yes, mine is cut too. Then shout down to the journalists."

"He would never go, Justin," Anna said, and she began to cry softly.

"All right," he whispered.

Doré's head was sunk into the double pillows, and the livid foot had been tucked under the blankets. On the mottled face the bright eyes—already bruised by death—followed Justin as he eased his weight onto the edge of the bed. He and Doré stared at each other. The fingers on the bedspread moved. Justin covered the slight hand in both his. There was a faint pressure in it.

"Let us hope," Doré whispered, "that it does not take too long."

"In a week we will be talking about Dante Alighieri."

The old eyes softened on Justin's face. "Have I interrupted your work?"

Justin's throat tightened. He smiled. "There is no excuse for it," Justin whispered.

Doré's eyes closed. "You recall the *Trois Contes?*"

"If only you were a leper so I could keep you warm," Justin whispered.

"Marcel! Allow me to call for an ambulance!"

"No, little sister. The priest."

"Bishop Duroc?"

"Duroc is not to come near him!" Justin almost shouted, his face red with pain at being stronger than this old sage, whom he had never seen in doubt. Even Baptiste Duroc was without significance at this hour.

Soon they could hear Anna's voice call into the rue de Valois. Jeanne resumed sponging the wooden-looking temples and collarbones. The bedspread was of a quilted cream silk, woven with colored flowers. There were dozens of old books with manila markers. This simple room was all the paradise that a humble Justin, years ago, had ever dreamt of. Now he felt a hot, unbearable wave of love for that lost time and for the limp, helpless shape that had once been Marcel Doré.

"There and there, little father," Jeanne was chanting in a monotonous singsong. "That's all right now. All's well, go to sleep."

"*Maître,*" Justin murmured through tears of rage, with a tenderness that he had thought to be lost, "you taught us all we know."

"Of my students . . ."

"Yes, Marcel?"

Doré had gone from them and was somewhere else. They were alone with a body from which no further perspiration seemed to flow. Justin looked up, and the eyes in the sunken skull held no trace of fear.

"Such a face, my boy. Such a face."

"You understand that you are my father, Marcel."

"It is not so bad. Close to death there is lucidity. Aristotle knew that nature is more perfect than our imitations. This is my last spectacle. It is a privilege to witness it in such company."

"Marcel, you will tire yourself." Anna began to weep, but her brother fixed his eyes hungrily on the half-savage face of Justin Lothaire.

"When the time comes, you must observe attentively."

"What are you telling me? I must know."

"Remember the death of Elijah."

Justin laughed, then he looked desperately across the bed at the faces of the two women. Turning back, he searched the old man's eyes. Justin knew the parable: Elisha would receive a double portion of Elijah's spirit if he could see the prophet's soul as it rose to heaven.

"Marcel, you know I would prefer you to be Socrates," he whispered.

"You are a good boy, Justin." Doré spoke in a weak voice but without visible effort. The things he said were unflawed and perfectly formed. The struggle came to Justin through the brittle fingers. A feeling of hurry was suddenly between them.

"Marcel, I must tell you," he said, feeling himself suddenly close to an answer. "It has never been I who deserved this public eulogy, it was only you. Only you understood us." Just in front of Justin, the concentrating eyes softened in polite gratitude. They immediately hardened. The bloodless lips moved.

"It was politics they wanted. I care nothing for their fame. It is God's award that I am after."

"You will have it, Marcel!" Justin almost groaned at this sacramental oath.

"Let my brother rest, Justin!" Anna cried. "Are you trying to kill him?"

All of them in the room had suddenly felt the end edge near. The free hand on the bedspread felt for the old woman's, but Doré's eyes did not move from Justin's.

"Swear something to me—solemnly."

Justin heard the note of urgency and command. He saw the white skin drawn even tighter on the skull.

"Yes," he whispered. "Tell me."

"Renounce politics—forever. Swear it!"

By Doré's deathbed, a powerful fear shook Justin. He was suddenly conscious of this wasted body, containing the greatest mind of Europe, and of the sacramental force of a dying man—all focused mercilessly on himself. He thought of the simple folk who had followed Justin Lothaire. The room was hushed. The rose vapor from the porcelain basin was being sucked through the lampshade.

"I swear it." Justin felt a pressure inside his head. "Solemnly," he added.

"And then you must find your friend . . . Hélène. She loved you. It is necessary."

Justin swayed on his chair. Must he believe in *her* now—in Hélène Le Trève? All the old forgotten smells and sensations were around him again, strong, hot, and religious. Her letter was upstairs. The bony fingers struggled in Justin's hand.

"I swear it," he whispered.

The instant the words were out, Doré's eyes, an arm's length from him across the covers, faded and drew away. Relaxed and resigned, sinking deeper and deeper.

"Anna cried out. "Marcel . . . my brother. Marcel!"

But the dying man seemed only to rest in a shallow sleep. An hour passed, and they were all exhausted. The first horrible reality of what was taking place—like the climber's first look at a cliff below—had become remote as the descent progressed. Justin asked no more urgent questions, the dying man's sister made no more possessive accusations, and Jeanne went on with her sponging without attracting attention to her presence beside the famous old Frenchman. Deep in the apartment, the downstairs bell gave two muffled rings—the doctor or the priest. The limp, damp hand in Justin's stirred.

"Marcel . . . Marcel?"

"Ah, my dear boy. We are all still here, then. How it drags on." The deathly lips wheezed. "I am ready to go. We will miss one another, though. . . ." The weak voice returned, the eyes watching Justin. " We spent too little time."

"You were always generous."

"Not enough. But do you remember when we walked in the snow?"

"In the Tuileries. We had discovered a white whale."

"Yes, I would not have minded being Melville. Life is both too short and too long."

"You never came to the rue de Fleurus, Marcel."

"Ha-ha. . . ." The hollow, meek voice began to cough. "I missed your Doktor Godard."

"Yes, but he would have hidden in his room from so much wisdom."

Justin exchanged glances with Dr. Bernard as he entered the room. The physician's shadow covered the wall of silk ancestor portraits, as he siphoned out a half syringe of sedative. Except for Justin, Doré was completely alone in his dying now. "The world will be worthless without you." He had admitted it now—Doré's death. He saw tears in the reddened eyes.

"The world will do very, very well."

Justin stared with angry desperation at the little face on the pillow; Doré was weeping for him! Just then the body jerked against Justin's elbow. A surprised, anxious brightness appeared in his old friend's eyes.

The sunken shape under the blankets suddenly arched in a fishlike movement, emitting an inarticulate sound. The body rolled back and flattened under the restraint of eight hands. Justin licked away the tears on his lips and stared helplessly. The thing which had been Marcel Doré had turned beet red.

"Hold him still!" the doctor said. There were only the gasps and the rustling from the struggle on the bed. They watched the silver needle shorten into the wrinkled, twitching arm.

But it had already ended. It was four-twenty. Marcel Doré was dead.

"May I ask you, what were Monsieur Doré's final words?" inquired the doctor

From the moment that Doré's eyes and calm voice had left Justin alone in Europe, everything in this room seemed to him disastrous and futile. Without answering, he stumbled out through the hot passage and went down the stairs to the street door.

The reporters had gone back inside the corner bar. Wheeling the other way, Justin passed into the Place des Carrousels. At the beginning of the gravel, he stopped and turned. Twenty paces behind, his blond follower had also stopped. Justin motioned to him. The boy stood. Justin walked back.

"I wish to be alone."

"No lie, Lothaire?" The detective sneered at the contact. They were two men standing on the pavement.

"Tonight," Justin said, looking bitterly into the pale blue eyes, "you will hear that Algeria is liberated."

"It can't be true."

"Furthermore, my father is dead."

In that one instant, all conceit vanished from the boy's face. He had just lost his reason for existing. The raincoat squeaked as the fellow seized Justin's hand.

"Please accept my personal condolences, Monsieur Lothaire."

Justin turned quickly away. As he walked over the gravel under the well-pruned trees, he held on to this impression of the old man's love as if it were his last hope. Here and there, governesses sat on the park benches, the roofs of their tall prams folded down. Children in school uniforms passed him with their jackets off, swinging their books on long straps. The low sun that burned on Justin's face through the rinsed evening air was feverish. Marcel Doré—the golden age that a *bicot* had found in the Mahbu public library—was it possible that it had died forever? Hélène? Politics? Justin thought of his promises. Luz's effect on his life. Desire, the anger of the alleyways, classical literature, and the desert too—once he had been able to hold these in his head at the same time. Now all that seemed vivid was the futility of all revolution. And, vivider still, the truth of his love for Hélène, who believed in God.

Justin stopped on the bridge by the Assemblée Nationale. The sun was a distorted red globe, so low one could look straight into it. Then, with a little flutter of hope, he remembered a French proverb. *Le mort saisit le vif.* The dead possess the living.

For when the detective seized his hand, Justin Lothaire had suddenly known that his struggle was over.

4

THREE DAYS AFTER MARCEL DORÉ'S FINAL ATTACK, THE TELEGRAM REACHED THE Palais-Royal. Abu Grinda was dead.

Abu's sister packed Justin's few possessions. The planes arriving from the Maghreb were crowded with fleeing *pieds-noirs,* but they obtained seats easily on the next flight out of Paris. He had still not answered Hélène's letter. Justin was going back to the desert.

At Algiers airport, Justin and Jeanne were met by Michel Michaud. Michel was now a wiry, pleasant Frenchman in rough farm clothes and a black armband. He was stiffly formal with Justin. Madame Michaud had escaped to Monte Carlo with her laces, but Michel still talked in the style of a bourgeois colon.

"Naturally you should see your mother. Also, the president wishes you to stop by the ministry. Ah, you disapprove of the car?"

"During the war, they came for you in *tractions,*" Justin said.

Michaud started down the straight, pot-holed road into Algiers. Presently, from the backseat, Jeanne asked her brother-in-law with frank simplicity about Abu's murder, and they heard that Ibn Moushmun too had died, leaving Justin the little fishing boat—Grinda's Arab, who at the circumcision had thrown a boy into the brilliant sky. Justin gazed away to the fixed blue line of the Atlas. They were passing the waterhole under the shady eucalyptus, where long ago he had swum with Abu. Justin no longer searched for the old emotions. Too many people had died.

"How did the first days go?" he asked.

"No one knew how to run things. But the spirit was a marvel. Do you see that street sign?"

Michaud had stopped the car by the first arcade. Justin put on his spectacles and looked up. RUE JUSTIN LOTHAIRE said the blue sign. The rue Justin Lothaire was a crumbling boulevard that led toward the university between rows of motorcycle sheds.

Justin spent an hour in the lace shop. His mother had greeted them without smiling. She did not mention Justin's monthly checks, nor did she appear grateful to be alive and with the curfew at last lifted. That year—while the OAS had hunted down another three thousand Arab guerrillas—there had been no lace, and the old woman bitterly blamed this on Justin and his friends.

Presently, he left Jeanne with Michaud in the traffic jam outside the ministry. Justin had not seen the president of Algeria in the ten years since their meeting in a flooded mosque. The tall soldier had put on weight, and his eyes were very gentle and cold. They embraced with sober emotion at the entrance to his office. Bulbs flashed; then the two men went alone onto the hot balcony. Below them were the rooftops and the windows filled with flowers. Beyond was the pale green sea where Justin and Ibn Moushmun had fished for the great fish.

"Who are the men sitting outside?"

"They were *fidayin* who never had jobs. Now they are drivers of state." The Arab's gentle humor sounded very modest under the empty desert sky. "You see how we have succeeded? These are the beautiful days, the days of youth," he went on, ignoring the writer's expression of mourning—for there were many such looks. "It is the hope of us all that you will occupy a high position."

"Thank you, only not yet," Justin said quietly. "I'm here for the burial of Abu Grinda."

"Grinda's story was bad luck. They always killed three of us for one of them. Now the time for violence is past. We need leaders."

"The colons leave behind complications," Justin agreed. At the balcony rail beside the president, the world-famous Algerian was frowning as he searched the rooftops of the casbah and the docks. There were tears running down his cheeks.

Justin Lothaire remained in the office another hour, to discuss plans for the new agricultural lands that had been confiscated from the French. Later, when the president conducted him back to the foyer, a small group of officials, drivers, and guards were waiting to greet him—or just to stare. Justin smiled and waved his hand. Feeling this brash new confidence of his people, and the atmosphere of enthusiastic amateurishness, he was moved. Yet recalling the dusk of Ramadan in the great square of the mosque, and the throngs of the faithful prostrated to Mecca, Justin missed the old romance of faces that were humble before the Creation. This too was the price of justice.

Then he was once again on the road to Tipasa. On either side of the straight Oran highway, yellow hills gently rose and fell. As the sun sank on the road ahead, painting the sky of the prophets blood red, the car came to a familiar stone monolith. Soon they were rattling down two polished mud tracks that hummed with wasps. And there below the green fields were the lumber stacks, wooden houses, and corrals of Grinda's farm.

The motor died. As they climbed out into the heat, a cloud of dust blew around them. Justin took off his glasses. A yellow mongrel on a thirty-meter tether barked wildly, circled, and threw himself against the chain's length. Voices were calling, "Justin! It's Justin!" Figures came from the dark kitchen door. He walked forward, feeling the dust in his sandals.

Being able to think of nothing to say, and feeling his place among them as some massive presence of Europe's violence, Justin set down his bags and shook each hand. He embraced them shyly, old Grinda first, more grizzled than ever and smelling of horses. The four awestruck Michaud children were already the size of Justin and Melanie when they had ridden the stallions that distant sunset. They all wept and kissed Jeanne and Justin repeatedly. Justin could not keep from staring at Melanie, who had grown matronly and thick-set and, for that very reason, more mysterious than ever with the things they had done together in their youth.

She had prepared a fine mutton stew, which they ate in Grinda's cramped kitchen, seated around a kerosene lantern. As befitted the occasion they were grave, and deep emotions flew between them. In all these years, there had been so much lost and so much gained. They were all overcome and spoke in murmurs. Grinda blew his nose repeatedly; Justin saw the way Melanie soberly avoided his eyes and how she blushed whenever her husband showed excitement over the famous guest. Now that Abu was gone, Justin thought—looking out past Jeanne's bare shoulder through the kitchen door, where in the faint rose dusk the new mongrel lay curled at the end of its chain—only Melanie knew of the hours they had given each other in the eucalyptus leaves of the old watertower. It was as if that time had never been. Was he jealous of Michaud? Justin wondered.

"Justin, now you are back, you must stay!" Grinda repeated gruffly several times, so Justin knew that for the horsebreaker he was a son. Yet each time Justin noticed Melanie frown and stare into her plate. He felt wounded, and the admiration of her little sister Jeanne meant less. He was a stranger among them, and the solidarity of the liberation did not help.

As always, the supper talk was about horses, crops, and the long summer, of the insufficient rain and the price of hay. Grinda was willing, though perplexed, about joining the horse farm to a cooperative. Presently they sat in the shadows with bottles of beer from the gas refrigerator, and Justin laughed cautiously with Michaud over their memories of the French *lycée*. Michel seemed no longer to remember the cats with needles through their testicles, the beating of Justin, or even Madame Michaud's tablecloth going to the lace shop. Justin changed the subject.

"It saddens me very much to think about Lavil's death. He was my great teacher," he said.

There was an odd silence around him. What in Justin's words had embar-rassed them?

"But Justin. Lavil is not dead."

Justin was feeling a curious unreality, as if Michaud's words were trying to reverse the flow of time.

"What?" he said softly. "But the Fascists—"

"He's not dead. Jean!" Michaud called to Grinda. "Is Lavil not living?"

"He is alive! He is alive!" The horsebreaker was coming forward. "I saw him a year ago, Justin."

"When you went to Sidi Idriz, I remember!" Grinda said.

They were all crowded around the visitor's chair, having felt the force of his attention—the first familiar passion that Justin had shown them, after twenty-five years of hearing his views only in magazine interviews.

Even Melanie turned from the table with a wet rag and stared at him.

"They said at the café he lived upstairs."

"You didn't speak to him?" Justin's eyes cut into Michaud.

"It was Lavil. There is no doubt."

"Sidi Idriz." Justin got to his feet. "I will go tonight."

"In the morning!" the boys called out.

"Yes." Michaud laughed. "And you must take the car,"

Justin was humbled and embarrassed, and he sat down. "The car—may I? I don't have a license."

"A license?" Grinda shouted. "What license? You are Justin Lothaire!"

In the darkness around him, there was good-natured laughter. This time Justin could not help laughing too, just because the sentiment was not quite ethical and therefore pleasantly human.

5

IN THE MORNING IT WAS COOL, WINDLESS, AND UNNATURALLY CLEAR, AND THEY could all see the folds in the mountains.

"Later there will be storms," Grinda muttered, while Michel bent by the open door to show Justin how to drive.

To a boy riding beside Abu on oat sacks in the back of the gray truck, Sidi Idriz had been a holy white city on the summit of the world. Now the truck was a tireless heap of rust behind the stables, and to Justin, sitting at the wheel of Michaud's car, Sidi Idriz was just a village in the foothills two hours inland. The straight-climbing road was very different from the road of Justin's memory. After hearing his old teacher might be alive, a hope had stirred. Justin had warned himself against this, but his soul was hungry and fragile; hardening himself made him feel sick. So Justin abandoned himself to his dangerous hope and to the new beauty of the North African road. He enjoyed the freedom and power of the automobile, and he found that he did the driving fast and sensibly, pulling off the road for each passing truck.

Now the long black hood swung faster and faster up into the Ouarsenis Massif. The cool wind blew his hair and moaned in his ears. Berber shepherds in rags beat their flocks off the road. Camels raised their heads to sneer. Now and again flat-roofed dwellings or tents made sense of this great oblivion. Haiked women balancing bottles hurried in their bare feet after files of stoic donkeys, their robes impossibly black under the sea-blue sky. All this is Arab now, and it will never be spoiled, Justin thought. As he drove on and the naked, rising plains turned from yellow to red to black, Justin thought of Michel Lavil, from whose lips he had first heard of the Greeks, of their noble thinkers and the greatness of their souls. Into his own heart, lifted on this huge emptiness—like air under a bird's wings—there came once again the desert violins and the song of the nay. Justin was steering clumsily up a series of steep curves. Then the road lengthened across a flat yellow plain.

Facing him ahead, on the distant slopes, a flow of blindingly white lava on a hill, was Sidi Idriz.

At the beginning of the town, he noticed a bullet-pocked house with a porch and two tables. Justin braked the machine onto the dust. In the desert silence, his heart beat loudly. There was an old man with very black glasses seated rigid against the wall. As Justin walked up, a younger man emerged, wiry and very ugly. Yes, said the second one, looking at the car and Justin and then back at the car, there was a Frenchman living upstairs. Monsieur must wait.

Justin sat at the second table and a glass of tea came. Lavil could never be here. This truly was the end of all worlds. The new hope at Grinda's farm had swept away the harsh monument of twenty years' exile, leaving Justin helpless to rise again. This would be the final wrenching disillusion.

He waited a long time. Bins of rotting garbage had overflowed on the unswept porch. A dozen mangy cats were squabbling over the scraps with swarms of wasps. Below the porch, a mongoloid child played with a three-legged red cur. As Justin stared, the child scooped a handful of dirt and began to rub it on the dog's swollen rectum. The animal hopped along; the mongoloid child crawled after, rubbing and rubbing. Behind his back, Justin heard footsteps. A brutal-looking young mechanic stood over him, sweating heavily. No, this was not the man. Did Monsieur not know of the café above the town?

Justin got back in the car. His state of mind had grown still worse. Yet the second café was very clean and white, with a fine view north toward the Atlas. A bare-faced girl waited on the three tables, with the unself-conscious smile of one who always searches for someone to help. Yes, there was a Monsieur Michel who lived upstairs, said the girl, and she flushed. Justin wanted to ask about the other café, but his face had alarmed her. All of it was like a dream. Michel Lavil had died twenty years ago under the Fascists.

A bell rang far off among the buzzing crickets. Justin turned to stare along the dirt track that followed the ridge. A man was pedaling between the stone walls on a bicycle. Justin rose from the white table. He walked awkwardly forward, his legs were weak.

Coming near, the man on the rattling bicycle looked gray-haired but strongly built. Now the cyclist caught sight of a stranger, motionless between the walls. He slowed, looking at Justin. The tires whirred in the dust, the gears clicking to a stop. The two men were ten paces apart. The cyclist swung his leg and placed the bicycle against the stones. Not taking his intelligent eyes from Justin's face, he came slowly forward. They met at the end of the stones.

"Professor Lavil?"

"Who asks for him?" answered the man alertly. Frowning, he took out his pipe. His thick middle-parted hair fell forward.

"It is a long way from Tipasa," Justin said hoarsely.

The man had lowered his pipe. He shaded his brow and stared at length into the melancholy eyes of this battered face that smiled down at him. Suddenly, his gaze deepened.

"Is it you, Justin Lothaire?" he said softly.

"Are you really alive?"

Lavil seized Justin's shoulders. Squinting fiercely in the sun, he examined the powerfully aged face as a man might examine a work of art he has loved, which has passed through alien hands and finally been returned. For a full half minute on the dusty stone hilltop, even the crickets fell silent. Then both men began to laugh and Justin had to turn away his face.

"Dead? They cannot kill Lavil. Up here is Olympus. I renounce the world!" Lavil shouted, and he drew Justin, now arm-in-arm with him, down toward the holy town. The girl watched them approach. "This is my daughter. Do you remember poor Shalla . . . Her mother? Is that your automobile?"

"My brother-in-law's," Justin said.

"How did you find me? How long can you stay?" Poking Justin's chest with the stem of his pipe, Lavil seemed even more naively intense than before.

"I must go back tonight. You knew they killed Abu Grinda?"

"I know, my boy, I know," the Frenchman went on, when they were under the grape arbor. Shyly, he pushed Justin behind a large wicker table. "Your life is common knowledge. Imagine, a student of mine, immortal!"

For just an instant, the older man looked embarrassed and angry, but the student was too shocked by the realization of his wild hope to take note. He opened his mouth without speaking, smiled falteringly, and passed his shirt-sleeve over the bridge of his nose. The laughter between them was in every move they made.

"Immortality . . . the devil," he mumbled, watching Lavil pace up and down the neat red tiles.

"Thank you, my boy. Thank you for this visit to your old professor. After Marcel Doré—"

"But it is myself who needs to hear *you!*"

Seated against the cool wall, with the plain stretched out far below the white rooftops, Justin had been about to speak of his catastrophe. He smiled instead into the remote haze where the desert met the sea. What needed to be said? The example of Lavil's life was enough.

"You understand, Michel—to find you here, alive," Justin said, when the Frenchman sat down.

"I have no significance!" Lavil leaned forward with boyish gravity, elbows on knees as he had always done. "So tell me. I have a hundred—a thousand questions to ask!"

They ate roast lamb in the cool under the grapes. Then they walked slowly together to the mosque, where, long ago with Ibn Moushmun, Justin had envied the boys being circumcised. Today it did not matter—even here in the crowds of this holy town—if faces turned to Justin Lothaire as he talked of his work, of his marriage to an actress, and of Europe's *Nacht und Nebel*. He spoke freely of those friends who had been geniuses, revolutionaries, and French farmers. He did not speak of those who had been aristocrats, nor did he dare to think of Hélène, who would have come with him to this place. He told of the man whom he had killed and of the men he had helped to live, and because of Monsieur Lavil's subtle gravity Justin told it beautifully, as befitted the finest life that anyone had lived in his age. At dusk, history lay at their feet like a small thing, and the drift and turn of their voices reaped its meanings with the easy swing of scythes.

"And now, Justin? What will you create now?"

"I have come back to my people, Michel." Justin crouched forward, so excited that he rocked the bottles. "We will build a great university of all cultures, unspoiled by the bad temper and provincialism of European princes. Algérie will serve as an Athens for the next act in the development of man!"

His old teacher had listened with obedient concentration to all that Justin had told him. Now he tilted back against the arbor post and busied himself with the pipe. Justin went on soberly.

"In the old days we boasted of an ethic. At least I know now that it exists, but that almost no person is its equal."

"Justin, Justin!" Lavil rose and began to walk the *terrasse*. "There is no place for you here!" he cried. "You are a world thinker. Do you know what's happening, even in Sidi Idriz—as with your café below of the *harkis,* those Arabs who took the French side? Last week, a father down there was made to eat the testicles of a gendarme and then see his little daughters' heads crushed." Lavil turned away, both hands on the arbor, until he regained his breath. "Justin, go where you will be understood, as people understand each other. The leaders of the world—visionaries, philosophers, the educated of Paris, London, New York, and Tokyo—they will follow you! Who *here* will understand you? Don't you know where you are? Have you forgotten your revolt against crude natures? Have you forgotten the ways of the desert?"

Monsieur Lavil circled the darkening terrace, waving the coal of his pipe. Drawn up against the wall, Justin was thinking of himself with Abu, as they had bathed in the blood of the watermelon. His teacher stood before him.

"How much water does it take to irrigate the sands, eh, Justin? How much can your soul contain? Think what you have built. Consider your luck in being chosen where thousands have failed. Yes—luck! Do you want to spill that to the last drop . . . here, on these sands? No, go back to Paris and write great works that will raise men out of barbarism. Here we have only just begun. You have enemies here. Algeria, China, and Russia are deserts. Your Americas, they are deserts too. Have you forgotten the desert, Justin? You ran from it, and you were right! A desert is a desert."

Puffing on his pipe, the provincial schoolteacher gazed out over the peach rooftops and the plain far below them. Second by second, the desert grew more stark and mysterious. Lavil was feeling vertigo at the presence beside him of a student who had risen to a spiritual authority, over the billions of the world, that is given only to a few men in one century. From the absorbed profile at his side, the teacher could never have known the effect of his words.

"Don't you see? There is rain coming," Justin said, hiding the horrible disappointment in his voice. "And is there not water right here? Ah, Michel, but you have troubled me!" he cried.

Against the verdict of this one man, Justin had no defense. The passion he had fed on through the long ordeal of his exile had been as desperate as the instinct of a swallow for its nest, or of a salmon to remember every stone and twist in a river so he may return to the pool of his hatching. Justin had not felt himself near that pool, even at Grinda's farm, until he had been told that his earliest teacher was still alive. Now he had just heard from that very teacher that not only was Justin Lothaire a European here in his desert, but that for some time he had been unsuited for any return.

It was not yet seven o'clock when their visitor took leave of Monsieur Lavil and the shyly questioning girl. After the black car was swallowed below the square, the girl turned to her father.

"Why is Monsieur Lothaire so very sad, Papa?"

"Nonsense, *ma petite!*" Lavil laughed with knowing pride. "Justin is simply a very great thinker. When you are an old woman, it will still mean something that he visited our little home."

As Justin drove down for the last time through the holy town, the faces he glimpsed, skirting the walls, seemed sinister and hostile. He reflected on his old teacher's testimony—how as a student Justin had been tormented by the brutishness of ignorant folk. Now, in his absence, the liberation had become a thing of rapists and thugs and of feuds between sadists. The desert and its fellahin—his Maghreb—was passing right through the tunnel of violence.

As the car gained speed out of Sidi Idriz, he could not help glancing toward the café of the *harkis* where he had first waited for his old teacher. The blind man and the child were out of sight, but the pariah was a small mound by the road. Justin switched on the headlamps. The dog was snapping at flies.

The downpour overtook him in the dark, before he was halfway from Sidi Idriz to the coastal road. Soon the desert roads were flooded. Justin had to turn and retrace his way several times before the stone monolith emerged in the headlamps. When he reached Grinda's farm, where Jeanne was waiting up for him, it was well after midnight.

6

IN THE WORKS OF THE ENGLISH NATURALIST, WE ARE TOLD OF A SALMON.

Though he makes hard shift to get into the sea, the fish will make harder shift getting back to fresh waters to possess the pleasure he formerly found in them. And the further from the sea, the fatter and better he be. But these fishes, becoming lost in fresh waters, turn sick and lean and bony gristles grow from the jaw, which hinders their feeding. Fish so lost pine away and die.

Justin Lothaire's next six years, living without Luz in a Paris after Doré, passed more quickly than had any single month in Carbonne under Hitler, when the fate of humankind had been in the balance. Not that these comfortable years were easy for Justin. All this time he was attempting to finish his work.

To his friends and his critics, this manuscript was known as his testimony. It would exceed everything he had produced so far. In fact, Justin still spent many terrible hours each day, walking up and down his new rooms with Jeanne by the rue de Fleurus, scattering notes and perspiring over sheets of paper. It was his reluctant duty to accept a flood of invitations and to translate for the Paris stage the works of several foreign writers, whose reputations were thus assured.

During these years, Justin traveled to Oxford, Kyoto, Princeton, and Buenos Aires. He ran a seminar on tragedy in Mexico City. He was invited to visit Hanoi during its civil war, and he flew in a Russian jet attacking a Hue freight hangar with PENN INDUSTRIES painted on the roof. It was in some ways like Barcelona, Carbonne, or Algiers, but instead of Germans and French there were now Americans on the opposite side. Gradually, Justin perceived that absolute justice was most easily achieved where there were enlightened rulers and no vote. He also saw that some Platonic molding had been done in the name of Justin Lothaire, and that this revolutionary justice in which the Comintern freely cited his name was sometimes as bitter as Stalin's during the purges.

Brooding over these immense historical contradictions during his travels, Justin Lothaire gradually accepted the comedy and the nightmare of the world. It made things easier. It also cooled his romanticism, and his art suffered. Now, when Justin looked back on his past, there was just a vague, lifeless cloud, like a dream one has waited too long to write down. In the end, he put off confronting Hélène's declaration of love forever. The voices in his head were stilled. He stopped seeking out the few he admired and accepted the attention of parasites. He went out a lot now with Jean-François d'Issipe, whom he had once despised—and even Jalvin, who had moved on from writing eulogies of revolutionary martyrs to scrubbing the dirt of centuries off

European palaces. Justin had not met Eli Hebron for so long that when one day he saw his friend mentioned in an American periodical as an official of the Communist Party, he was shocked to realize that he had not even thought of Eli since the preceding Christmas. He was so miserable that he had nothing with which to compare such unhappiness.

Yet during that busy time, Justin Lothaire seemed to everyone more wise, unpreoccupied, and sympathetic than ever. It was generally remarked that he had improved, as happens when a soul becomes not a prophet but merely a critic of life. When Justin beheld himself, he could sense no limits. He neither loved nor feared anything in his existence. The only limit he had left was death.

7

JUSTIN HAD ACQUIRED THE HABIT OF NOT REREADING CHAPTERS AS HE wrote them. He told himself that his experience guaranteed the work's quality. Then, one April afternoon, when he had broken off to sip a cup of coffee at his old café by the Théâtre de l'Odéon, the warm sun and the spicy smells of bread and cheese touched something in him. Hurrying home, then, he reread the Mamelukes' final hundred pages, and in fact these were not unsatisfactory.

On that late afternoon, feeling as frail as a convalescent, Justin Lothaire— now fifty-seven years old—crossed the Place Saint-Germain, drawn back to the scenes of his student days.

But still Justin was not prepared to feel again the full, crushing loneliness of nightfall. He stopped again by the Odéon for several Pernods. Justin rarely ate in restaurants, and he had not been to the Brasserie Lipp in the thirty-five years since David Sunda had taken him there with Duncan Penn and Johannes Godard. By the time his feet carried him to the door, Justin was a little drunk. The headwaiter kept him waiting for half an hour, then he was given a cramped table upstairs. The man moved Justin's two empty chairs to the adjoining table, where a tourist family was just sitting down. The Americans had three cameras and two children.

At the other neighboring table, hidden by a pillar, the editor of *Le Figaro* sat beside its book critic. Only hours before, these two men had been present at the escape, from a crowded Neuilly courtroom, of an especially ugly murderer. For months this nihilist had entertained the world press with demands that he should be guillotined. In just a few more weeks he would be named as Alaric von Sunda.

"Isn't that Lothaire . . . there behind the column?"

The editor turned casually. "The same. The master appears melancholy. But, by God, look at those scars! He could be a thousand years old."

"The most powerful thinker in Europe, and completely alone," agreed the younger man with pleasure, tightening his tie knot.

"The end of an era." The editor nodded, as if he felt himself in some way unburdened.

Alone at his table, the modestly dressed Algerian gave the waiter his order in a slurred voice. Justin's earlier feelings of tenderness, and his disappointment at nightfall, had somehow merged with the old student feeling of being friendless in a foreign city. He held up his champagne glass and with a twisted smile drank a toast, to his friends among the dead and to the fifty other millions. Then, with growing anger, he became aware of the two staring Frenchmen whose whispering he could not quite hear.

8

LATE THE NEXT MORNING WHEN HE WOKE IN HIS BED, JUSTIN—WHO HAD NEVER in his life been drunk—knew by his aching head and from the pensive figure of Jeanne, ironing in the sunny kitchen, that the grotesque memory of a scene with two journalists in the upstairs room of Lipp was only too true; that not only had it involved him, *it had been his creation.*

The same morning, as Alaric Sunda was already on a flight to the island of Ibiza, Justin did two things. He proposed, as soon as he could divorce Luz, to marry Jeanne Grinda. Then, as she cried a little and stroked his thinning hair, Justin described a trip in the new automobile to be begun that very evening, a journey into eastern France he had intended for many years. He was going back to the Jura, back through the tunnel to what he had been.

As Justin told Melanie's sister these things, he saw a fear appear on her face. He did not mention the prefecture, or the meadow of ice fans in a pass to Switzerland where he had killed a man. It scarcely seemed possible that such scenes might still be there, or that he was free to visit them.

Justin Lothaire and Jeanne Grinda spent that night at Vitry, in separate beds, at an auberge that overlooked the Marne. So it was that, before lunch on the second windy clear day, they entered the region of the Doubs, the same through which Albert Sunda and James Penn would pass some weeks later. Almost before he was prepared, they were in Besançon. Justin coasted the machine through a shady square, with a stone clock and flags, and a *boules* pitch that opened on the left. Then the street closed in. The first blue Pontarlier sign was over a radio shop. Justin turned sharp left, and they rattled steeply up onto a short Roman bridge.

There below them, all at once, was the Doubs. The river was bottle-green.

"From now on I know every tree," Justin said, changing gears.

Jeanne looked at him and slid closer on the seat.

And that was the last thing Justin Lothaire said. For as he geared down for the long traverse up the far mountainside, his stomach tightened. His palms began to sweat. There was the long right-hand bend, with the gorge below and the crusader tower rising from the rounded hill. Then Justin was blasted with familiar sensations. The murdered millions had not yet died and *he,* Hitler, was alive, too, and Stalin. The murderous Nazi horde was spread from Leningrad to Casablanca, and Luz—along with his comrades Peter, Gabriel, and Joseph—awaited Justin just ahead in Rochet's farmhouse. Now the sky seemed to fill with German codes, and Darnand's wolf sneer was hunting Justin's life as the transports clicked toward Silesia—the very air men breathed was sickening with *Nacht und Nebel.* David was plotting outside Moscow, Doktor Godard was in Berlin with his opera singer, and Duncan had made his landing on Italian beaches. Once again in the snow-suffocated pass ahead, Hitler's scientist Stodel thrashed blood through the tinkling crystal meadow.

Just then the road leveled. On the right was a long lake bordered with rushes. Ahead, between interlocking files of elms, were the red roofs of Carbonne and, above them, the church steeple where Justin Lothaire had been betrayed.

At the wheel, Justin felt a cruel pressure forcing his head forward. His feet seemed to fly up behind him, the air to compress. An excruciating nausea knotted his stomach. As his face was forced forward and down, Justin held the steering wheel as long as the pain let him. Then he twisted it violently.

9

SO IT WAS—IN THE FIFTIETH YEAR OF THE WANING REVOLUTION, IN THE TWENTY-second year since Hitler's death—that Justin Lothaire died on a country lane in the Doubs. Jeanne Grinda, who alone had been with him at the end, suffered complete loss of memory and from that moment was as pure as a saint, save for the image of a Roman bridge.

Baron Sunda lifted his eyes from the book by the English naturalist, lying open on the schooner's chart table. *But if the salmon be stopped by weirs or flood gates, and be lost in the fresh waters, he by degrees grows lean, and pines away and dies.*

That noon, by the peaceful town of Carbonne, Justin Lothaire had returned to a flood gate he would never pass.

THE GREAT BEAR

1

THE RIVERS OF EUROPE MAY BE ENSHRINED IN THE BERNESE OBERLAND, where great glaciers work upon themselves. Yet far below in the towns of men, all is not well.

The night before he led the terrorist attack on the centers of Paris government, Alaric von Sunda had the worst nightmare of his life.

At seven that evening on the rue de Varennes, Alaric took sleeping pills, set three alarms for four o'clock, and stretched out on his upstairs bed. Then the dreams began. First, there was a recurring dream of the night he had murdered a prostitute, Dorothea Drummond. Almost immediately there followed the nightmare.

The modern terrorist sleeps a strange sleep. He dreamt of a father he loved, and who had rejected him—himself a banished German officer standing knee-deep in a malarial jungle of Brazil. All around the baron in the vast quarries and the wounded rainforest, like slaves round a pyramid, were a hundred million naked, toiling bodies of all colors. In the dream a palace burned in snow, squadrons lowered net ladders that were bombs, and a boy became lost among a trek of tattered refugees . . . followed by tangled New England woods, tennis skirts, and the bloodied bodies of a man and woman, whispering endearments on a bed of moss. Instantly, here came the nightmare of the world, a worldwide plague of locusts that were human. As he thrashed in his sodden bed, Rick heard the suffocating earth cry out for air and light. The last few innocent wild things of the forests and skies waited for their mates, as their cries were drowned in the rumble of Hitler's autobahn and the thunder of exploding suns—mass crematoria fired off by burnt-out, illiterate bureaucrats who screamed any lie to claw their rivals under.

In his canopied bed, Alaric Sunda bounced up. Panting, he clasped his hands to his temples. The mansion of sleeping terrorists was perfectly still. Rick fell back on the pillows and rolled on his side. He needed to sleep. For several more minutes the young man on the bed twisted in the venomous images from the nightmare. Now he could only remember the murder.

2

FOR FOUR YEARS, HIDDEN FROM THE SUNDAS AND LIVING A DOUBLE LIFE IN THE demimonde of Paris, Hélène's accomplished elder son had courted the trusting innocence of his fiancée, Christine Gascon, even as *L'Action* met in the Gascons' unused house. And though Rick was affected by every gesture that Christine made, he had continued to visit Dorothea Drummond at least twice a week in her penthouse that overlooked his grandfather Le Trève's old garden.

There seemed to be no male weakness, among any class, religion or race accessible to jet travel, that Dorothea did not exploit and few places of power to which she had not taken her trunk and her talent, from the palaces of the Congo to the political salons of Georgetown. Wherever there was wealth, deformity and lust, Dorothea had traveled, with her costumes, and her virgins and pederasts of every hue and shape. At the end of another evening amid Dorothea's herds of clients, Rick would plead with the prostitute to renounce this life, be his alone, and so forth. On the next day, faced with Christine Gascon's unsuspecting kindness, the disgust and loathing would be back, and he would writhe with shame at the wild things he had sworn. Then one night Dorothea had said yes, and presently Rick had heard himself called hypocrite.

In his sleep, the terrorist again crushed the soft throat against a velvet window couch. *You are killing her!* a voice had shouted. Seeing that the lights were on below in the Le Trève salon, he had crushed the throat tighter, trying not to hear the woman's thudding heels. Alaric Sunda had been born in a Russian train compartment, been carried screaming from among the legs of refugees out of the smoking architecture of old Europe, and then been raised in countries without a past. But those kicking heels were the most terrible thing in his mind.

What Rick would never know was that the call girl was accustomed to being beaten by gentlemen and was expert in the old soldier's trick of playing dead. She had actuallly been strangled in her Roman bath three hours later by a Lebanese backgammon champion, who had employed a projector cord and who would confess the following year in Palm Beach.

The terrorist sank back, and the nightmare of the world recommenced. A completely new dream came to him. He was a boy with his mother in San Francisco, and he had stolen back at night into the Natural History Museum to see the ten-foot-tall brown bear, with its murky soft fur and powerful mass. The alarms were ringing. Rising out of that deep dream, Rick sat up, shaking violently. Downstairs more bells rang. For two seconds he was conscious of a healing warmth like hope, left by whatever he had dreamt. He angrily shook this off.

It was four o'clock. By ten, everything would be decided.

3

BY A QUARTER PAST FOUR, THE TWENTY-EIGHT UNITS OF *L'ACTION* WERE crowded in the Gascons' cavernous kitchen, a bleak brotherhood of students and professors in dungarees and sweaters. In the blackened carriage yard below were five small cars. Here, upstairs, were three Japanese and two Greeks, four Chileans, three Italians and five Germans—three of them women—two Thais, a Catalan, and eight others. Some of their faces were as pure and reverent as those of young lovers. Outside the kitchen's opaque window slept a damaged society imagining itself at peace, although its war criminals were still at large, many in positions of power. The terrorist leader's stomach heaved with the image of such insanity. Then it subsided and his terrible night fell away. The truth of this day must come to a continent locked in its atrocious dreams.

"Eat as much as you are able," he said softly.

"If the organism can take it," added the gangling Scot known as Mike.

There were tensed grins, even from the Japanese. While their commander sat among them, they began to recite their tasks. Less than an hour remained. Even as the minutes flew from their lives, like gas escaping from a balloon, the group's morale stayed good, from the oldest, known as Eli, who had experienced the Civil War in Spain and had known Justin Lothaire, to the chalk-white girl pianist. Between these extremes were the Japanese, who two years earlier had machine-gunned a group of American reactor physicists at Hong Kong airport. By ten o'clock, no government on earth would be unfamiliar with the words of these forgotten children, led by the ice-cold terrorist called Rick.

It had felt like this before their Lyon bombing—the unearthly sensation of an assault on a sleeping beast that foresaw nothing and intended them no harm. On the following day, green police vans filled with convicts and com- manded by ex-Milice had appeared in the cities of France. *L'Action* had known then what it meant to be called mad, nihilist, and criminal by an unre- pentant hydra that continued to build extermination arsenals in defiance of moral law, which tangled starving races in diplomatic conspiracies, and which increasingly carried out its will in secret societies and built vast computers with databases to number its enemies. That twenty-eight puritans, with pity in their heart for the tragedy of innocent things, should be called madmen, nihilists, and criminals by corrupt statesmen—this was insufferable.

In the bright, crowded kitchen of the Gascon mansion, it was five minutes past five.

"My good friends," Rick began quietly, "just one thing is significant now—to know that each of us will go right to the finish. If anyone has the faintest doubt, he must be honest and speak." When through the kitchen all eyes had fixed on him, the leader held each of their hands in turn. He came back to Eli Hebron's side. "Eli and I will be with the minister to hear your broadcast," he said.

"At eight o'clock, precise," called Toshi, who was leading the attack on the Antennes Nationales.

It was five-twenty when the terrorist cadres moved from their cramped kitchen. The automatic weapons and ammunition from the Middle East, and the Chinese grenades, were laid neatly on the foyer bureaus, according to the car. Each group was already absorbed in itself. As the door into the courtyard rattled downstairs, there was nothing more to say.

4

THE MANSION OF THE MINISTER WHOSE BOMB TESTS HAD IRRADIATED Polynesian islands lay closest. Rick's car would be the last to leave the gloomy courtyard. When the gate had closed behind each squad, they would already have passed through Justin Lothaire's tunnel.

In the plan—far more direct than anything Baron Sunda's circle had designed in Smolensk—there were two groups for the chief of police and two for the Antennes Nationales. When they had barricaded themselves inside with their hostages, the terrorists could survive for days using the emergency generator, while the appeal to mankind was delivered. With Eli Hebron, on the island of Formentera, the escaped leader had prepared a detailed program of demands, for the destruction of arms and for the transfer to the southern hemisphere of industrial wealth. Read out by the German, Marcus, in his beautiful English, the text had not sounded like the work of madmen.

The fourth car had just gone out. Their commander stood on the wet cobblestones with Eli, Marco, and Aki, the big Japanese. Watching the priestly young faces start out—children as abandoned as himself—Alaric Sunda had felt a sharp pity, almost like love. Presently he could see the gate through the fog. It was first light.

"Five thirty-five."

"Shall we go then *camarades?*"

Rick got in beside the Scot. Their lights swung away from the empty gendarme's box and lengthened down the narrow street. As he stared ahead at the shuttered buildings and the familiar sidewalks, Rick was going through the beautiful city where the Fleurusians had been young. Then that thought too fell away—and Alaric became a thing of pure destruction, mindless, thoughtless, like one of the grenades. When he imagined the other cars in motion across a sleeping Paris, they seemed to him like messengers of light.

Mike steered past the Russian embassy. Three gendarmes, huddled in their capes under a streetlamp, turned to watch the car coast by, its tail lights making a wake in the fog.

"Not too soon," Rick said. "Go slowly."

Mike kept reaching nervously to the gearshift. One of the two cars coming up the Boulevard Saint-Germain had its lights off. The signal turned green. They rolled forward. Rick turned a ferocious stare on each of the three in the back seat.

At four minutes to six, the Scot wheeled the car into the minister's street and coasted past the studded coach gate. Three minutes and forty seconds later, the others pulled on their hoods. The car nosed out around the corner and accelerated for the gate. This time there was a gendarme farther along on the facing sidewalk.

Rick tugged his hood. "Now, now!" he shouted.

The Japanese was already running for the gate with the gun swinging across his shoulders. Then Alaric was out, walking toward the gendarme standing frozen ahead of him on the sidewalk. The young man lowered the baguette from his mouth.

"You'll be a dead hero!" Rick called to him. The gendarme began to lift both hands, then he jumped for the drainpipe. The automatic recoiled violently, with ear-pounding thuds. A cloud of rust billowed out from the drain. The gendarme slid down with his knees sticking out. Rick threw himself along the gutter. There was a deafening *thunk-thunk*. Shrapnel hissed overhead, whirring and skipping down the walls.

The big gate had fallen across the street behind the car. Aki's hand stuck out from underneath. Running hard, the hooded *chef* was into the courtyard just behind the others. There were shrieks within, and shouting in the street outside. Panting with fear and hatred, Rick jumped the five steps to the servants' quarters. He fired at the lock and kicked the door in. He was so shocked to be free of himself that his legs carried him through the neat, pleasant kitchen and plunged him up the dark pantry steps before he registered any detail.

Suddenly, an old and a young woman in nightgowns blocked his way. When they saw the terrorist's face, deformed by a tight stocking, they stumbled back and began to scream. The sight of animal terror on these soft women's faces, with pillow marks still on them, filled the terrorist with miserable fury like a parent's for a screaming child. He pushed them roughly. The women shrieked and cringed against the passage wall. The hooded man swung the heavy gun across their faces. They fell together in a white heap, without another sound. He was free of himself forever. He was alone in the palace of the sinful fathers. In a blind rage like none he could have conceived, the heir to Oberlinden crossed a study carpet that skidded under his feet and then bounced off a wall going into the bedroom.

It was three minutes after six when Alaric Sunda finally reached the sleeping quarters of the French defense minister. At that very moment at Antennes Nationales, three foyer security police had shot up the remains of Toshi's squad, his second car having been blown apart by a faulty grenade. At the mansion of the chief of police, the Germans and Italians had barricaded themselves on the top floor, but they could not get the chief himself down from the roof. Across town, in the defense minister's residence, Rick gave an inarticulate cry. He kicked open the first door and stood blinking. The canopied double bed was unslept in. The terrorist took one step back, listening.

There was a click. The hooded man crouched, expecting a door to open. Instead, he recognized the bony white gentleman, profiled in the corridor ten paces away, dressed in nothing but baggy undershorts. It was the defense minister of France, aiming a gun at him. The minister got off one stray shot. The first burst from the terrorist's gun shattered his right shoulder, spinning him half onto a nearby chaise longue.

"Damn! Damn!" The terrorist leader cursed a second, ashen young man who had appeared in pajamas.

They could not leave without the minister!

As the terrorist pulled the twitching white flesh out of the line of snipers, he heard Eli's voice shout his name. "Here!" Rick called. "I have him here!" A wide stream of blood was forming a pool on the parquet floor.

"What fools . . . what imbeciles." The old toes and knees jerked restlessly with pain. The minister's left fingers agitatedly advanced and retreated across the bony chest. But the old man's voice was measured and cold. "Get out! Vermin!" The minister choked. "Kill me, filth! *Canaille!* Get out!"

The young man began to cry. *"Non, Papa, non!"*

They could hear police horns in the city all around them. Radios crackled below. "Shut up, scum, filthy corrupt swine!" the hooded man shouted, and struck the minister.

Outside the bay windows, the fog was gone. A spring sun fell into the defense minister's residence where the wounded old man was now a hostage. Scuffing feet approached them. It was Eli Hebron, alone. His hood was off.

"It's over, everywhere." Eli waved his gun vaguely at the young man, who with a sob promptly fell on his knees and held up his clasped hands. "The others are screwed."

Hearing that voice, the naked old man suddenly started writhing on the chaise longue, tearing at his captor's sweater. He had recognized Eli Hebron. "No, no, you cannot shoot me, sir—not an old man! Please, sir, have pity!" the minister blubbered, looking shrewdly from the famous old revolutionary to the hooded man beside him and deciding that this was the leader. "Please, sir . . . I humbly beg you—pity, family, France, children!"

The hooded leader wrenched himself to his feet. The defense minister's astonishing shift to abjectness had staggered his remaining sense of why he was there.

"Look! He's gone—he's dead!" Eli shouted.

Rick Sunda spun back to the wrinkled white flesh arched in the sunshine, mouth and eyes open. And now for the second time in his life, Alaric Sunda was taken in by someone playing dead—which, in the case, was lent realism by the large amount of blood on the floor.

The terrorist crashed against the far wall between the windows. He was scarcely aware of the silent crowd waiting in the courtyard below, of the beautiful day, or of the sobbing young man in pajamas, moving over the carpet on his hands and knees. He only heard Eli pant and cough like a very old man. It was nine minutes past six.

"We are going!" he hissed. "Come on!"

"Which way?"

"The balcony! The back wall!"

The last two terrorists of the group's attack were out of the residence after a brief exchange of fire. They raced through a greenhouse on opposite sides of the trays of plants, then swung down onto a short tarred roof. Two meters across, and below, there was a stone wall set with broken glass. There was shouting and the sound of running soles.

The younger man peeled off his hood, braced, and jumped. The far grass came up and hit him with a jolt. He staggered up and turned back to the wall. The roof was empty. Then he saw two hands working on the broken glass.

"Eli . . . Eli!" he screamed. Running back, he tried to jump up the three-meter wall. "Eli! Eli—oh, God, Eli!" A muffled rattle and a thud. The hands were gone. The terrorist threw down the gun and sprinted into the alleyway, tearing at his gloves.

Moments later he came out on the boulevard, smoothing his hair, with one hand pushed carelessly in his pocket. He crossed down another alleyway.

5

IT TOOK THIRTY MINUTES ON FOOT TO REACH THE GASCON MANSION. FOUR GRAY riot trucks blared past him, in the direction of the chief of police's residence.

As soon as the gate on the rue de Varennes was shut, Rick was seized by a frenzied shivering. He stumbled through to the kitchen. The dishes from breakfast were stacked by the window. He switched on the radio. Instead of Marcus's beautiful voice, intoning the litany of wrongs against humankind, the room's silence was invaded by the bland crooning of big-band saxophones.

"Jesus . . . oh Jesus!" he panted. "My God, God, God!" Switching on every radio as he spiraled upstairs, Alaric von Sunda flung off his clothes and got into the shower. Then he bandaged his ribs, put on a clean shirt and suit, and prepared to wait. But instead of waiting, he kept flicking the television channels, getting up to circle the room, then running to the telephone. There was no one in the world to call. For a moment he even thought of his mother and sister in New York. His father was somewhere in the Adriatic.

Maybe there had never been a Hitler either—or a Stodel or a Stalin, or the extermination camps, Uncle Freddy's crucifixion, or Baron Sunda in Brazil. Perhaps not even the germ weapons or the ruin of God's paradise. Then every nerve in Rick's body knew it was all true and that Eli was dead. He returned again and again to the kitchen, to stare at the unwashed plates and coffee cups. On the last radio that Rick had left on, "Japanese Sandman" wailed to an end . . . a girl's voice. It was eight o'clock.

"The news. At six o'clock this morning an international group of terrorists executed a well-designed attack on three organs of state. All three groups suffered heavy casualties as the attack was repulsed. Security losses were very light. From the Élysée, there were immediate words of sympathy, gratitude, and congratulations to the security forces. . . ."

Rick was crashing up the three staircases to the big television in the Gascon bedroom. As the screen resolved, he could make out what looked like a drunk lying against a stone wall. As the camera moved in on the face, hands appeared to prop the head, white angel's wings of hair. *It was Eli in death.*

The screen cleared. Eli was replaced by a French Donald Duck, guzzling Israeli orange juice.

Four hours later, Rick was still seated motionless in the kitchen, staring at the dishes, in the strange ebb and flow of a nightmare unknown to ordinary men. It would be months before Europe's most hated criminal could surface in East Berlin. By this evening, Christine would be back from the family vineyards at Aix. All life was a prayer too innocent to return to after the last drops of hope. No, the railway had carried Alaric Sunda past the last outpost.

Rick was on his feet, slightly swaying. The house around was as silent as an abandoned city. An indefinable impression had come over him. It softened the spectacle of the nightmare, and of his own wrecked life trailing to its conclusion.

Had it come during his sleep like a rush of homesickness? . . . A great bear? Yes, the great stuffed brown bear of his boyhood, rearing ten feet in the San Francisco museum case: the stance massive, human, the broad animal skull wider than a human torso, with inarticulate little eyes and teeth bared like iron bars—fisherman of the fast cold river, the gladed forests, the tundras and caves—towering, menacing, mysterious. In that vision, as he held his breath in a Paris kitchen, watched only by the dishes of the terrorists' last meal, Alaric knew he had forfeited his place among men. From this moment he was alone. Ahead there could be no family, no children, no natural affection, not even the fear of death. From this moment he was on the run.

Three hours later, under his own name, Alaric von Sunda left Europe forever on a bearing for Montreal.

6

THE JET SMOKED WEST, LOSING GROUND TO THE SUN. THE FUGITIVE TERRORIST fell at once into a sleep full of drafts and trembling.

When he awoke, the forests of Maine, where Baron Sunda had failed his children, were not far away. They lost altitude as the flight followed the St. Lawrence River. At Montreal, he passed the passport check. Stuffing the suit he had worn through the French police checks into a trash bin, he boarded the flight to Fort Yukon via Fairbanks, carrying nothing but his last eleven hundred dollars.

Sometime after midnight, he was back on the ground. The night air was wintry and pine-scented. The plain faces in the terminal were hostile, though without seeming to see him. The terrorist rode into Main Street, took a cheap room at Hunter's Hotel, and sank into blank unconsciousness.

He woke at one o'clock. He paid his bill, and bought a map. At the diner next door, he ate two cheeseburgers and boysenberry pie as he read the map. Then, finding the general store, he bought two pairs of fur-lined whaleskin boots, dungarees, heavy socks, and long underwear, two oiled submarine sweaters, a primus stove, a sleeping bag, a backpack, a skinning knife, and a bolt-action 30.06 with a hundred rounds of ammunition. This came to seven hundred dollars. The clerk was cautiously amiable.

"Will I find a job in Chandalar?"

"Chandalar . . . Chandalar. You from these parts?"

"The east."

"Jed?" called the clerk. "This here feller says he come from the east. Wants to know if there's jobs at Chandalar."

An old man in a baseball cap, with a face like pipe tobacco, wound slowly forward between the shelves.

"He does, eh? Better'n a hundred fifty miles," Jed muttered.

The terrorist felt his stomach tighten with impatience. His veins iced with fear of the frank eyes and the slow, exploratory silences.

The older man saw the educated young stranger's unshaven jaw set, and thought, *Each slicker them cities sends up is harder, meaner, and sadder'n the last.*

"Talk to Deegan at Mason's lumber mill."

"Fine, thanks," Rick said. The two men were blocking his way.

"Going that way myself," Jed puffed, his eyes squinted into the pipe coal. "Better come with me."

"All right, thanks. I will, then."

There was a gravel truck nosed to the curb outside. In back were five Indians in red plaid jackets, sitting side by side against the cab.

"Say . . ." It was Jed's voice over the side.

"Rick."

"Say, Rick, there's an empty cabin you could take."

"Thanks, Jed," Rick said.

And so, as once Justin had followed a resort poster at Geneva station, that afternoon Baron Sunda's beloved first son started out into the Brooks Range—the last mountains before the ice pack—to Chandalar, which might have been in the Punjab for all Alaric had known of it before he saw it on the two-dollar map.

Chandalar was a level, squared colony of two-room cabins, huddled by a lake and already in the shade of the mountains. Jed parked the truck outside Mason's Mill. In the office, a man called Deegan told Rick to come back on Monday with a pocket full of Band-Aids. The terrorist scarcely heard. The five o'clock news over the radio was drowned by shrieks from the floor below. Mantis-like, a railway trolley was clasping the great logs as it sprang them monotonously back and forth across a stationary bandsaw.

The shack was in the copse at the end of town. In Paris, it would be five in the morning. Maybe that was why Alaric Sunda's legs shook under him as he stood in the arctic twilight and stared around the empty cabin. He did not look at the dead woodchuck teeming with maggots as he carried it through the trees and dropped it in the lake. Stripped naked in the stagnant cold, he methodically changed his caked bandage and pulled on the new long johns and socks. Then, pushing down in his sleeping bag, Rick pulled the flaps over his head. As the night deepened, he shivered and perspired on the steel bed. He listened to the monotonous swish of the trees, and the Sundas in Manhattan seemed to him like a paradise of wise angels among whom he had been ignorant and so been cast down. Or was he the wise angel, unrecognized by criminals? Alaric tried then to imagine the deaths now of all three of his father's best friends. As the minutes rolled by, like silver pinballs through the machine of his mind, he knew he was still mad. The nightmare began again, this time with Uncle Freddy upside down.

Rick woke again at nine and went out for supplies. He felt calm before these glaring snow peaks that crushed him into insignificance. But when the first man he saw waved and grinned, Rick's feet carried him on past Benoit's Supplies. In the next hour, he saw everything that there would ever be to see at Chandalar. He felt better in the little graveyard on the knoll, with its bleached crosses of 1850 fur trappers, thinking of the secret bodies buried like tree sap to turn into amber.

In the low, deep store, they were waiting for him. As Rick walked to the counter, four halfbreeds about his own age turned to stare from the card table at the rear. The fat, suspendered owner grinned. Rick smiled the same doomed smile, then hardened his face.

"Beans, kerosene, matches—be twenty-eight thirty-two, Mr. Rick. How about yesterday's Anchorage paper?"

Rick looked at the stack on the counter. During the night, the Paris attack had sunk into the unfathomable. He stared at the Anchorage headline.

"No, thanks."

"Not like them eastern papers, 'course," said Benoit loudly. "See you at church t'morrow morning?"

"Church?" Rick picked up his paper sack. "Didn't know there was one."

"Hear that, men? Well, you'll get to know our chapel, I reckon." But Rick did not hear. He went out through the insulated door.

7

THAT NIGHT, LONG AFTER TWELVE O'CLOCK, ALARIC SUNDA WAS AWOKEN BY AN ugly scream. A gale rattled the windows and flailed the trees against the corrugated tin roof. Shortly, he woke again to the wind-muffled sound of a bell. The terrorist rose and pulled on his clothes. Religion . . . God? To sing hymns, with the whole of Chandalar packed in a single room listening to his voice? There was no other way.

Rick followed the tolling, through rows of cabins under the twilit sky, to a muddy intersection. He turned instead toward Mason's Mill. If he lacked the stomach to pray with Chandalar, he would work with them. At the edge of the timber stacks, Rick jumped back. The foreman, Deegan, had just stepped out, dressed in his Sunday best, followed by two big troopers in rain capes and flat-brimmed hats. They moved aside for a fourth man—someone short and bald, wearing a black Chesterfield.

The terrorist flew back along the wooded lake path that skirted under the town. Three minutes later he was in the cabin, stuffing his things in the pack as the bell tolled on. The blow of seeing Otto Horvath's grim white Polish face—the face that Rick had hated since his first consciousness, and which must never see Alaric Sunda punished alive—was so intense that he ran out of the cabin without even a glance back at his new home.

Rick was five miles up the lake before he stopped to draw breath. If he could make it to the head and cross the wide north fork of the Chandalar River, the hunted terrorist would, by nightfall, be buried in a thousand square miles of scattered fir forests, snowfields, and valleys running with game.

For the next hour, while voices were lifted in hymns of praise at the chapel in Chandalar, the thick strong Sunda legs that had borne his father out of Russia carried Rick steadily north and then west. He ran now with a fixed, easy decision, his breath and his will both settling together into the motion of his feet. Maybe they would catch him, maybe they would not. It did not matter. Rick knew now he could run forever. An hour later, he jumped and waded across the wide stone bed of the north fork and started uphill into a scattered spruce forest.

It took a day to fly in twenty bloodhounds from Anchorage. Already on Sunday night the Chandalar Inn had all eight cabins taken by reporters from Anchorage, Seattle, and San Francisco. Before Monday noon, four chartered amphibians had settled on the lake, bringing teams from the Associated and United presses, along with correspondents from New York, Berlin, and Tokyo. There were two *Paris-Match* photographers and an NBC television crew. The townsfolk of Chandalar proclaimed it a holiday, which was not quite accurate, as a brisk trade in rooms had sprung up, centered on Benoit's store. Old Jed ran hourly tours of his cabin, where the world's most wanted man had spent two nights. There were even four hookers from Fort Yukon, attracted by the concentration of bloodthirsty men. By Monday night, more than two hundred strangers were in town, and Benoit stayed open late, with Hank Jefferson hunched over his ham radio set, tuning in the world news reports. At eleven, he had his biggest success: a bulletin from Sydney referring to the "American tycoon's son turned leader of a world terrorist conspiracy . . . the biggest man-hunt in Alaskan history . . . the desolate little town of Chandalar."

In the desolate little town of Chandalar, no one had any doubt that this was the biggest thing that had ever happened to them. After the first incred-ulity and alarm, it suddenly seemed to everyone quite fitting that it should have happened here; there had always been something about Chandalar that marked it for myth and destiny. Never had the townspeople—leaving out the majority of Indians—been more conscious of their own legendary qualities. Nor was there a dearth of remembered omens of the terrorist's coming or significant impressions of his movements among them. As these things go in small towns, they came to feel a certain possessive love, awe, and pity for the fugitive with movie-actor looks, now alone somewhere high in the Smith range. They exaggerated their generosity to him and took a grudging tone with outsiders.

"He's ours," Jed was heard to say to Mr. Horvath on Monday evening, "and we'll bring him in."

Soon, with self-consciousness and civic pride, the town had assembled thirty horses with provisions. On Tuesday, a deputized posse of one hundred and twenty armed men set off from Mason's Mill amid clouds of condensation, squeaking saddle leather, the shouts of small boys, and the barking of dogs.

8

ON THE FIRST NIGHT, THE CHILD HÉLÈNE HAD ONCE CARRIED IN A BASKET ALONG Turkish tracks slept in a gully, fifteen miles up the west wall. At dusk on the second, he camped under spruces at the edge of a trout-rippled lake. When he tugged off the sleeping bag, in the stillness at first light, Alaric Sunda saw Lake Chandalar for the last time, between the mists far down the valley bowl.

Already the mill town seemed a distant past. And far beyond Chandalar—as if Rick were on the run back through time—the misguided cities of greed were being consumed in their corruption, and this corruption was falling behind his escaping feet and dissipating in the soil. From the time he had fallen by the lake to drink, Rick hungrily remembered every place that he paused or ate or looked for a camp. He noted that when he sat very still to rest, animals would emerge close by without fear. Wings of duck and geese often arrowed overhead going north. Still he knew little, not divining that this camp had been made better by Athabaskan chiefs and was thus as famous as all the terrorists in hell. He had not yet begun to rave aloud to himself.

Now on the permafrost slopes, the fugitive saw the first brown bear. It bustled along, rolling its thick pelt. As his swinging legs drove him closer between the stone summits, a plan began to form. If Alaric could not find an outlying cabin for the winter, he would skirt the towns below. The idea of shadowing the towns attracted him. The next day he ate the last of the sausages, scarcely noticing the glimmer of a helicopter in the next valley. Shortly after, he shot a doe and carved away the steaming saddle.

Then, as Alaric Sunda stopped before dark to roast the steak over an open fire, he stared below and saw the hundred men inching upward, not ten miles away. He could almost hear the distant bay of bloodhounds. And in the crackling campfire, Alaric Sunda saw Oberlinden in flames, and his toy bear lost somewhere inside it.

For three days, through two more valleys, it was like those nightmares in which the hunter can never overtake the hunted, nor the hunted draw away. Every time he went out of sight, doubling down the treeline, the straggled horsemen headed him off. He stopped trying to hide from the helicopter cameras or from the police amphibian that circled out of range. On the fourth noon—viewed on a million television screens—they trapped the master terrorist in a ravine, blocked at the summit by the splintered green butt of a glacier. All one hundred men of Chandalar, as they worked in file up a goat track in the noon heat, saw Mr. Otto's palomino collapse under him. They saw the ant-sized figure dance and curse among the boulders high above.

"I'll get that dirty son of a bitch, sir!" shouted Trooper Shater, who was eighth in line. Before anyone could answer, Shater had plunged past an already whirring camera and on up the steep grade.

Trooper Shater was six feet three, well built, and approximately the terrorist's age. His hair was shaved all around his well-chiseled cranium and clipped flat on top. In Saigon, Shater had belonged to a tunnel-rat unit, and he was proud of it and of his matched nickel-plated automatics like General Patton's.

It is true that the fugitive did not see Shater watch him through a waterfall until Rick had emptied the rifle's magazine down the ravine. It is true that he turned then and ran along the ledge, and that there, above the treeline in this

JAMES THACKARA

land of pines, was a dead oak tree. That, as Shater jumped down to the body, grotesquely impaled in the tree, the raving beast had pulled a skinning knife. That when Shater caught the driven wrist and jammed it backwards, the terrorist kept his grip, so the blade slipped under his own fourth rib.

As Otto scrambled up, David Sunda's elder and beloved son hung sideways, coughing blood. And as he died, the blood ran into Alaric's eyes, which were fixed on the distant mountains.

"You killed him," Otto muttered, tears starting down his old cheeks. "You killed Rickie Sunda."

"What you think I oughta done," snapped Trooper Shater, with the faint smile of a man who knows the law, "shake his hand?"

It is true that two days later Otto Horvath, who had loved the dead boy as he loved everything that stemmed from his friend David, flew back with the body to New York and was met there by Hélène. Somewhere in the Mediterranean, Baron Sunda—whose schooner Otto had disembarked from in ignorance ten days earlier at Rhodes—as yet did not know that his brilliant son was now the disgrace of civilization.

THE LAGOON

1

AFTER RHODES, BARON SUNDA DRIFTED BY THE TURKISH COAST, sheltering the schooner in rocky coves to visit classical ruins. An impatience had come over everyone on board to reach the holy land. At Tel Aviv, Baron Sunda would leave the boat for Washington. In their wake lay a maze of forty-two islands.

Across open water to Cyprus, as Albert's father told the last of his story, a freshness had pervaded all things. The moon that ruled the night hung ravaged and spent above Arabia, as pale as some chrysalis shed by the maturing sun. High above the schooner's decks, the great masts balanced west, cupping, in the expanses of yellowed Dacron, persistent currents of the unseen. The windward shrouds hummed, the ones to lee tinkled in the shade like Chinese glass, and over their passage the rumble of sails and the carbonated gurgle of the wake lifted aft, then began again, as if the beach were rushing to break upon the waves. And all this enchantment was no more than the infinitesimal progress of a nameless sail on the horizon of oblivion.

2

NEXT EVENING OFF CYPRUS, WHEN THE WIND DIED COMPLETELY, DAVID SUNDA was with young Penn, in a race now with the anxiety enveloping his imagination to have the story told.

Above their heads the hatch had been opened to the sky. Gradually, as the breeze died, the chart alcove came upright, elevating the orphan and lowering the storyteller. They were entering a natural bay. A face poked in from the companionway. Mr. Otto had left New York for Alaska and could not be reached.

"You say I shouldn't stop?" the Baron went on, after the cabin panel was closed, in the scathing voice of an old man. "Then you haven't understood a thing!"

"Why not . . . why? Give me time."

David shook his head. "When I look at that healthy face!"

"What do you wish to see, the ruins of Berlin?" Jim pleaded gently. For he knew now how many people, far closer to either of them, had not received this man's confidence.

A heartless laugh convulsed the baron's face. His hand jerked up from the open charts, as a sleeping child waves away a dream from which it cannot awaken. "Now the evidence of a life is out, flung away," he muttered. "If I had foreseen that it would be so useless, so easily lost. . . ." David Sunda groaned.

"No, not useless!" Jim said. "How can you say that?"

The engine, faintly pulsing in the schooner's hull, had died. The American held out the tin of cigars. Then he struck a match.

"No, the story is astounding—a parable of conscience," Jim said, unwilling to be driven off as this German gentleman's children had been driven off. Among the reflections off the water, the baron's intricate features were priest-like.

"Of conscience?" David repeated bitterly, almost in a whisper. "You are very young, my boy. I was there, and I saw. You will only risk seeing what your good health can contain. Animals are wise to have short memories. Looking back on those few seasons, I see . . . a tidal wave."

"A tidal wave," Jim repeated, and they both heard the brief muffled roar of the chain. It slowed as the anchor settled on the sand bottom.

"A tidal wave of the maimed and incinerated," David went on, his polite musical voice gathering in a toneless rush. "This wave starts in the past—and now it is so vast we cannot lift our eyes high enough. Nothing will be sufficient to resist, not the Alps, not the Himalayas, nor the Andes. This wave derives its power from women who betrayed their lovers, from fathers who with pleasure murdered children, and from mothers who gave themselves to their husbands' butchers; from statesmen and popes who sold their people's trust. This wave is made of memory that is far more than real. Those who carry the memory, my boy, will fall hardest when the wave breaks, but it is their children and their children's children, when they hear these stories, who will feel the blow."

Perspiration trickled down the young American's spine. Were they merely in the cabin of a sailing yacht, anchored next to Cyprus? Why had Otto flown to Alaska? Jim's imagination expanded—rushing out protectively through all the hosts of the world, as if to overtake Baron Sunda's tidal wave and drag it back. "Your wave has already broken," he said. "It has used itself up. "

"Yes?" David smiled with a kind of morbid hopefulness.

"The wave was fear. Man is not evil."

"So you may say. Let us hope you're right."

"You betray good men if you give the rotten ones equality."

"That is a judgment of Solomon, James Penn. Think though—I am not the one who gives rotten people equality, it is the world."

"Only material power, sir, if you'll excuse me. I don't think there have ever been so many well-intentioned people on the face of the earth."

"Nor more power. Power to crush the human spirit."

"Power to do good."

"When good men dare be strong."

"But that, surely, is the point!" When he saw this old gentleman shaken by his passions, James Penn knew he had gambled to steal Baron Sunda's immense experience from his heirs. The tragedy's survivor had just now called his bluff, as a master ceramicist might threaten to break a supreme work in front of its future owner to test his worthiness. Jim rose to his feet under the Mediterranean dusk, which was a resonant gunmetal blue.

"Hearing you now, I feel as if perhaps I have seen into the future." David sighed a heavy, aging man's sigh. "Long ago, when your father and I were students with him on the rue de Fleurus, Justin Lothaire spoke just as you are speaking."

Young Penn stood balanced, too moved to speak.

"Sit, please. I have something to say before Abi comes down." David had taken a box from the stack of land titles. The slightly oblong pewter-gray buckle made a strong and elemental shape beside Baron Sunda's gold watch. "The traditions of honor and of family duty that I believed were the deepest of values—they mean nothing to Rickie. And his sister of the photographic studios and the nightclubs? Joanna's children will have other names. Bertie will never marry. Maybe now the tradition that the Sundas have considered the highest good must take a different form. Maybe we will be more like you. So, when I die, this buckle will pass on in your name. After our last days together, I know you will not take its meaning lightly. No, don't speak."

James Penn had opened his mouth. He breathed deeply inward, then he flushed.

"Truly, there is nothing so remarkable in this—it's only a weight of iron. The meaning is in yourself."

Yet perhaps Baron Sunda had spoken these words too late. For in Alaska it was already many minutes since the hundred men of Chandalar had gathered around the quivering body of Rickie Sunda, impaled on a dead tree high under a green wall of ice.

On the schooner, swinging now to its anchor in a lagoon on Cyprus, Abi had just entered the chart room with a tray. Taking note of David's veiled expression, she recognized the buckle in James Penn's open hand. Reddening, Abi turned from the tall American's possessed gaze.

"Foolish men," she said quietly. "Come up and see, both of you. The stars and the moon are so bright. And it's warm, the rocks are unreal, and there is phosphorus in the water. If you stay down here you will miss everything."

3

ALBERT SUNDA WAS ALREADY ON DECK WITH OLIVER AND STAVROS. AS JAMES stepped out under the stars, he smelled the sage and seaweed smell of land.

Bertie called to his father, in a voice without anger, "Have you been to this place before?"

"I came here with your mother after our marriage."

Jim could make out David taking Abi's hand.

"You must have gone swimming," she said. "Let's go in now, tonight. It's so lovely when there's phosphorus."

"That's true, boss!" Stavros called.

"All right, then, I will."

Jim had not seen Albert's father swim once since they had left Pescara.

"You're in a good mood tonight," his friend commented, as they went to the main hatch.

"Careful, Albert, or you'll cheat yourself out of a swim."

"We shall see."

Albert Sunda's words were drowned by a sudden splash and the thud of the dinghy against the ladder. Oliver's body had made a foaming bright cloud. Below the schooner's boarding lamp, the sand on the bottom lay in even ripples.

Looking toward the deckhouse, for an instant Jim saw Abi in the hatch light, then the baron's still-fit figure. Across the man's shoulders and back there was a curious shadow. The tattoo, Jim thought—the Bororo theory of heaven and earth and the treatise on attaining wisdom—tattooed across the pale European skin. And in that instant, James Penn knew that every word of the old man's confession had been true, and his veins froze with the nightmare of the world.

Leaping, he felt himself rise and then crash into the sudden, cool obscurity under the schooner's mass. The weightless night air was filled with splashes, shouts, and laughter.

So that night they swam with the father, in a lagoon midway from Greece to Jerusalem. Stavros and the two Italians jumped in too, and even Stavros's wife. The water was phosphorus-charged and burst into green flames around each stroke. As he surfaced, James saw them all swim in around each other, appearing like heavenly bodies. Then he floated on his back and looked up at the schooner's masthead lights, constant as planets. Breathing in and fanning his hands, Jim looked beyond, into the open universe. His uncontrollable, tragic laughter was still there.

"Good Lord. Damn!"

"Jim . . . Jim!"

The American could see a dark head swim towards him and he knew it was the old man. "Hey, Albert!" he called, sidestroking towards the beach.

"It's a perfect harbor," David's voice observed, not breathing hard. "They say Saint Paul stopped here on his way to Rome."

"Hallowed water."

"Exactly. All right, first to the beach!"

The four gliding shapes broke into a crawl. As Jim drove forward, he felt Bertie fall behind them, and the surprisingly long stroke of the old man. Now they thrashed ahead together. His eyes opened below water, Jim saw at his side an electric flicker of lights. Then, just as he felt himself go ahead, his fingers bumped the sand. He and David Sunda floated on their backs in the darkness, and the American thought of Justin and Abu Grinda, swimming from the sands of the desert, long before the war.

Not saying a word as they smelled the strange smell of land, they watched Abi slip up in the shallows between them. She teased Albert for being last, and he laughed. They were happy together. No one mentioned that the journey was almost done.

There was still the pleasure of the slow swim back across the lagoon. Then this too ended and—dressed now and with their wet hair combed back— they were seated on deck. Around the long table, the conversation was very pleasant, no longer being on tortured subjects. There was contentment among them, and also a quiet sadness that the journey was over, each alone looking into himself. At the table end, far now from Bertie's father, Jim Penn was quietest. For he knew that there would be no more, and that this was enough.

4

IN TEL AVIV, THEY ALL TOOK THE SAME TAXI FROM THE HARBOR TO THE AIRPORT, but each went on a separate plane. David Sunda would leave for Washington and Albert for London. Abi found a flight to Athens, and the American caught one to Paris.

James Penn sat at a window by the wing, without even glancing at the name in the newspaper headlines. The flight carried refugees from Vietnam and from Bangladesh, Japanese and German businessmen, French archaeologists, American Peace Corps volunteers, and tourists. It was a sunlit plane load of pressurized refugees, but Jim's thoughts kept turning back to the story he had heard over the last weeks. Probably he should make notes. No, soon, but not yet. The Europeans had a story—the best he had ever heard. They also had a good ocean. But there would be other stories and other oceans. He was partial to the Pacific himself. The world was growing younger.

In a hotel that he liked there was a room at eighty-five francs with a window on the garden. Jim ran a bath and called the Babylon number that Albert's father had given him. An old woman answered, which was a good sign. He left the hotel number, then he bathed. Later he walked slowly to the brasserie that he remembered from the baron's story. When he returned to the hotel, there was a message from a Mademoiselle Lothaire. It was too late to call back.

Breakfast woke Jim at seven, and he ate it by the open window. The memory of Baron Sunda's life was ripening in him. When it was almost eight, his heart began to pound in his ears. Jim asked for the number and a bell rang. There was a very soft and much younger voice.

"Sarah?"

"Yes. Is that James Penn? It's very strange that you called."

"Can we meet?" he asked.

There was a long silence. "Yes, why not."

"Where, then?"

"I'm copying Breughel in the Louvre. Can you come at noon?"

Neither of them mentioned Baron von Sunda.

That morning while Justin's daughter worked, James Penn stood staring up at number 1, rue de Fleurus. The shutters were locked.

At twelve o'clock, he crunched across the white gravel of the Parc Carrousel. Climbing the museum stairs, he passed through several quietly rustling galleries of epic shipwrecks, battles, and seductions. But when he came suddenly upon a young woman, seated at an easel, who was producing an accurate imitation of the Breughel *Crucifixion,* he pretended to mingle with the few museum-goers.

Sarah Lothaire was slight and more lean-faced than the famous movie star who was her mother. Her eyes were large, deep-set, and melancholy, like the photographs on her father's books. James Penn knew at once that this young woman was of a finer quality than anyone he had yet known. Then he recalled that Justin had never dared to speak with Albert's mother.

"There is more despair in Christ's neck."

The painter lowered her arm and examined him with gravity. Standing at her shoulder, he stared hard at the original canvas, with its cruel, satisfied crowd milling on a yellow hill under a cross.

"You mean like this. "

"Like that, exactly."

She was again absorbed. Jim watched the steady tip of her brush.

"Sarah . . ."

"Yes?"

"I'm sorry about your father. It seems impossible to accept."

"His people are everywhere in this city," she answered softly, radiantly. "You must look carefully for them."

The young woman turned back to her work on the easel. For five minutes, Jim stood before the Breughel. Knowing that they were both thinking of Justin Lothaire, his soul flew to Algiers and to a lace shop. Finally he saw Sarah put down her brush. She rubbed her hands on a rag. Turning from this sudden activity, Jim walked to the leather couch at the center of the room—not to run away but to slow down his feelings. There was an American newspaper on the bench: ALASKAN MANHUNT ENDS. Jim heard a firm step approach.

"You're leaving your work?"

"With the original beside it, does that matter?"

"But if you've been very close to it?"

"To this one . . . yes." Sarah reflected. She had fallen in familiarly with his step. "Though I'm not really a painter. Not really a musician either, despite the *conservatoire*."

The daughter of a genius, without any talent? Jim experienced a slight disappointment. Instantly, he despised himself. "Well, probably I am not a biographer, or a senator either. Probably I couldn't even be a banker. What I am is a bastard's orphan," he said honestly.

They had stopped at the balustrade under the headless female Victory. Opening out below was a sunny atelier of emperors. Sarah had turned. They faced each other for the first time.

"Nevertheless, you're curious," she observed. "What is it, James?"

The piercing dark eyes that had cherished Justin Lothaire looked into Jim's. Then the young woman saw what it was and she reddened with a faint anger, lifting her face a little in defiance. No longer were they conscious of what they were hearing, of what was around them, nor of where they were. The young woman's face began to soften.

"May I carry your satchel?"

"All right, then . . . thanks."

Their faces came close. James took a grip on the old bookbag. "Sarah, could you tell me?"

"Yes?"

"With such a father, can anyone have moved you?"

For an instant, the powerful melancholy was back in this woman's eyes. "There is no one who does not move me."

"Are you in love?"

"I was in love with a professor, a *normalien*."

"And now?"

"I do not need to be in love to be moved."

Jim smiled and stared down over the balustrade.

Sarah tilted her head slightly, tightening her mouth. The smile was back in her eyes. "I know a *relais* on the island," she said. "It's good, and very cheap. Will you come with me then?"

And hearing these words James Penn knew that, soon now, he could begin to decipher Baron Sunda's life.

EPILOGUE

YET HOW WOULD A CONNECTICUT BASTARD'S ORPHAN SING THE FIFTY million dead? How could the thing be staged, when the actors had all been shot? For the living do not understudy the dead. How is the death of masses greater than the death of a single child? What is one child beside a million children, and what are fifty million dead beside the billions who have yet to die?

The dead know, and they are calling to you. So go down and listen carefully. Do not neglect to take notes. Go down wherever you are, the merely living, and you will hear. And even now, in the small and the great cemeteries of Paris, Dresden and Smolensk, and in the graveyards of Yokohama, of Manchester, and of Mainz, you will hear. From under the Gothic or Byzantine crucifix, or the wooden strip—from the bare white crosses of the unknown soldiers, like hands reaching up from the mud—they are whispering. Yes, unburied in jungle deltas of the Irrawaddy, dissolved in the lime pits of Maidenek and Birchenau, or charcoaled in the fireballs of August, their protest rises. Even in neat New England churchyards where it is forever Sunday at this hour—in the garden of perpetual youth of the fifty murdered millions—there waits an unanswerable silence. Now be alone and listen and you will hear. Far from the drug of the noise of the modern age, the imagination gropes timidly to the bones and the long hair of those not older but much younger than ourselves. In our imaginings we will dress these bones—some long, thin, and supple, others thick and sturdy—each buried with the calibrated trinkets or scraps of steel that tore them. Fifty million skulls, enough to bury the greatest square of the greatest city on earth, and in each the infinitely significant memory of a life, all now hidden underfoot, fleshless, tongueless, hollow-loined and hollow-skulled, unable to testify aboveground to what all men need to know.

Therefore, of this silence it is said that the dead have seen a sin so great they have renounced their curse rather than bring down the columns of creation. Yet they protest in whispers. So go, wherever you are—the merely living—and you will hear. And this is what the dead will say: *You will do it again. The lesson has not been learned.*

For the living, it is a long way from the fever forests, where the villages of the Bororo stand amid the scattered wreckage of recorded history, to the linked peaks called the Eiger, the Jungfrau, and the Mönch. Here, high among clouds like heaven's Sargasso Sea, where the air is as hard as frozen steel and the light blinds and scalds, the great glaciers spread out in a pure and terrible silence. And they are like an astronomer's mirror, which sleeps in the day but which at night becomes a telescope in the barrel of the universe to focus the secret of infinity. Looking down from these lifeless promontories, the tender green valley is like a paradise of innocence.

Yet all is not well in the villages of men. A new generation of climbers now comes to the Oberland. They come in larger numbers than before. They smile less, and they do not pause to nod humbly and to gaze upon the great beauty of all things. This new generation climbs very quickly and very high, and they go without guides, and very many die. Their great impatience drives them out of the cities and into the fever jungles of the New World, into the very villages of the Bororo, to the whaling hamlets of Alaska, and the monasteries of the Himalayas, or to look for life on other planets. But this great impatience too will end, as all things end which become known. On the high ice plateaus of the Oberland, nothing will have changed. For it is a long way from the Oberland to the fever jungles of the Amazon, and every inch of that way is legend.